ALASKA

Praise for
Alaska

"*Alaska* takes the reader on a journey through one of the bleakest, richest, most foreboding, and highly inviting territories in our Republic, if not the world. . . . The characters that Michener creates are bigger than life. . . . Colorful, informative, and historically accurate."
—*Los Angeles Times Book Review*

"This writer is a journalist and popular historian who functions as do storytellers and oral historians, blending fact, fiction, and myth. . . . [Michener] weaves all of these elements into a narrative to inform the reader of the poetry that approaches truth in an imagined human and national history."
—*The Christian Science Monitor*

"An outstanding achievement . . . Tells the story in gripping detail of how two unlikely Americans . . . brought the first justice to Alaska. . . . Michener creates excitement."
—*St. Louis Post-Dispatch*

"A remarkable sense of historical sweep that carries the reader along . . . You feel you *know* the place he has been writing about."
—*The Plain Dealer*

ALASKA

A NOVEL

JAMES A. MICHENER

DIAL PRESS TRADE PAPERBACKS

NEW YORK

2014 Dial Press Trade Paperback Edition

Published in the United States by Dial Press Trade Paperbacks, an imprint of Random House, a division of Random House LLC, a Penguin Random House Company, New York.

DIAL PRESS and the HOUSE colophon are registered trademarks of Random House LLC.

Originally published in hardcover in the United States by Random House, an imprint and division of Random House LLC, in 1988.

LIBRARY OF CONGRESS CATALOGING-IN-PUBLICATION DATA
Michener, James A. (James Albert).
Alaska.
1. Alaska—History—Fiction. I. Title.
PS3525:I19A79 1988 813.54 87-43232
ISBN 978-0-375-76142-3
eBook ISBN 978-0-8041-5142-9

Printed in the United States of America on acid-free paper

www.dialpress.com

11 13 15 14 12

Book design and illustrations by Carole Lowenstein

INTRODUCTION

Steve Berry

I grew up in the 1960s, a time when the extent of reading material for kids was, to say the least, limited. R. L. Stine, J. K. Rowling, Suzanne Collins, and so many others had yet to come along. In fact, what we now know as the young adult genre had yet to be invented. Back then, at least for me, it was Hardy Boys and Nancy Drew. A limited selection, but what gems those tales were—each loaded with action, adventure, secrets, and conspiracies. Wondrous stories to fuel young imaginations. I devoured them.

Then one day when I was sixteen years old, a friend handed me a dog-eared paperback copy of *Hawaii* by James Michener. Its thousand pages immediately intimidated me, as did the small print. I'd never seen so much information packed into one book. The opening sentence alone contained thirty-six words—monstrous in comparison to the prose of Franklin W. Dixon.

But what a sentence: *Millions upon millions of years ago, when the continents were already formed and the principal features of the earth had been decided, there existed, then as now, one aspect of the world that dwarfed all others.*

I kept reading.

What unfolded was a saga spanning many centuries that described how a tiny group of islands in the Pacific Ocean were formed by nature and then settled by man. The epic involved Polynesians, Chinese, Japanese, Europeans, and Americans. Its massive chapters, hundreds of pages long, featured one expansive episode after another—each intertwined—forming a chronicle that defined both the land and its culture. I read it cover to cover. Then I found more books by this guy Michener and read every one. Eventually, I started collecting them, and now, more than forty years later, I own a first edition of each, save one—*Tales of the South Pacific*. That book is hard to find. Only a few thousand were printed and, if by some miracle one of those 1947 first editions can be found, the price is through the roof. I keep every one of my Michener books prominently displayed, wrapped in plastic. I see them every day. They are a source of pride and comfort. Today, I write modern-day thrillers in which history plays a central role. Without question, the seed for that technique was planted the day I discovered *Hawaii*.

James Michener led an incredible life. Born in 1907, he was orphaned but was soon adopted by a woman named Mabel Michener, who was already raising two other children. Some of his biographers have hypothesized that he was actually Mabel's natural son, the adoption story used to protect both of their reputations. No one knows the truth, and as an adult Michener refused to comment on the subject.

By the time he turned ten, the family had moved to Bucks County, Pennsylvania. They were poor, barely able to put food on the table. His classmates, and even a teacher or two, tormented Michener about the secondhand clothes and toeless sneakers he wore every day. Later in life he recounted that taunting with a sly smile and a twinkle in his eye. He would say that those early years instilled in him an appreciation for life that he never forgot. They taught him about living simply and not attaching too much value to material things. And though he eventually earned hundreds of millions of dollars from writing, he always feared ending up poor.

Before he'd even reached twenty years of age, Michener had traveled across the country in boxcars, by thumbing rides, or simply by walking. He worked in carnival shows and other odd jobs, and he visited all but three states. Of that time, he wrote in his 1991 autobiography, *The World Is My Home,* "Those were years of wonder and enchantment. Some of the best years I would know. I kept meeting American citizens of all levels who took me into their cars, their confidence and often their homes." He would also say that those wandering years spurred inside him an insatiable curiosity about people, cultures, and faraway lands.

In 1925 he entered Swarthmore College, a prestigious Quaker institution, on a four-year scholarship, graduating with highest honors. He attended graduate school in Scotland, then returned home and taught at a school in Bucks County. He eventually ended up in New York City, editing textbooks at Macmillan Publishing.

World War II changed everything. At age forty Michener enlisted in the navy, where he discovered the enchanting South Pacific. He earned the rank of lieutenant commander and was made a naval historian, assigned to investigate cultural problems on the various islands. A near-fatal crash landing in French New Caledonia altered the course of his life. He wrote in his autobiography, "As the stars came out and I could see the low mountains I had escaped, I swore: 'I'm going to live the rest of my life as if I were a great man.' And despite the terrible braggadocio of those words, I understood precisely what I meant."

That brush with death also made him realize what every soldier was experiencing during the war, and that one day, when the danger had passed, people might want to recall those things. So each night he began writing down observations, recording comments, describing people and places. Fifty years later, in 1991, he said:

> Sitting there in the darkness, illuminated only by the flickering lamplight, I visualized the aviation scenes in which I had participated, the landing beaches I'd seen, the remote outposts, the exquisite islands with bending palms, and especially the valiant people I'd known: the French planters, the Australian coast watchers, the Navy nurses, the Tonkinese laborers, the ordinary sailors and soldiers who were doing the work, and the primitive natives to whose jungle fastnesses I had traveled.

All of that became *Tales of the South Pacific.*

The story of how that first manuscript made it to print is typical Michener—an unexpected combination of skill, determination, and luck. Using a pseudonym, he submitted the work to Macmillan, the publisher he'd worked for before enlisting. He omitted his name because he knew the company had a strict policy against publishing anything by an employee. Once the war was over he definitely intended to return to work there, but at the time of the submission he was technically a naval officer and not an employee. So the company bought the book, which was published in 1947. One year later *Tales of the South Pacific* won the Pulitzer Prize for fiction.

Michener changed publishers in 1949, moving to Random House, where he stayed for the rest of his life. More books followed—*The Fires of Spring, Return to Paradise, The Bridges at Toko-ri,* and *Sayonara.* Also in 1949 he moved to Honolulu and soon began work on his most ambitious project to date. Four years of research and three years of writing were needed to produce *Hawaii.* Its epic scope, length, and breadth proved to be the stamp of Michener's trademark style, one he would master over the next forty years. Legend has it that he finished *Hawaii* on March 18, 1959, the day Congress voted to accept the islands as the fiftieth state.

In 1962 Michener ran for Congress as a liberal Democrat but lost. Then, in 1968, he worked as secretary of the Pennsylvania Constitutional Convention. Outer space was a lifelong interest, and he served on NASA's advisory council, an experience that led to his novel *Space.*

Honors were something Michener shied away from, but in 1977 Gerald Ford bestowed upon him the Presidential Medal of Freedom, the nation's highest civilian award. Eventually, he wrote nearly fifty books, including five on Japanese art. His work has been translated into multiple languages, and there are more than 75 million copies of his books in print. These latest editions, being rereleased with new covers, will only add to that already staggering inventory.

A myth associated with Michener speaks of his cadre of researchers, used to gather the enormous amount of historical detail included in each of his epics. The reality was quite different. Most of the work was accomplished with the help of only three secretaries. He was a disciplined writer, establishing a routine early in his career and maintaining it his entire life. An early riser, he would go straight to work, where he wrote using a manual typewriter. He then had a light breakfast, maybe a meeting or two, and went back to work until around one P.M. Evenings were a time to be by himself. In the final year of his life, at age ninety, he still kept to his daily routine, except he spent three days a week at a renal treatment center, undergoing kidney dialysis.

The treatment proved painful in a multitude of ways, perhaps the most difficult being that it prevented him from straying far from home. The man who'd visited nearly every country could no longer travel. He told an interviewer at the time, "I sit in the TV room and see shows on the big ships I used to travel or areas that I used to wander, and a tear comes to my eye. It's not easy."

And that explains his death—he simply decided there would be no more dialysis. Instead, he welcomed the end.

Michener died on October 16, 1997.

I recall the day vividly. A segment on the evening news reported that he was gone. A sadness came over me, as if I'd lost a close friend—which, in a sense, I had.

In preparation for writing this introduction, I reviewed many articles written just after Michener passed. Most came from folks who'd had some personal contact with him through the years—an experience that had clearly stuck in their memory. All of them recounted what happened as if they had been in the presence of a king or head of state. It seemed a privilege to have spent just a little time with James Michener.

And that legacy lives on.

Though he was known to be fanatically frugal, he gave away more than $100 million. Recipients of his generosity included libraries, museums, and universities. He donated $30 million to the University of Texas for the establishment of a creative writing program. Several million more went to the creation of the James A. Michener Art Museum in Pennsylvania. One wing of that building was named for his third wife, Mari Sabusawa Michener, who died before him, in 1994.

He never really liked talking about himself, and he could frustrate interviewers. "Famous is a word I never use," he would say. "I'm well known. I've written thirty or forty books. I've done a great deal. I let it go at that." He was extremely generous with his autograph, so much so that he once noted, "The most valuable books are those that aren't signed."

Of my own collection, only one bears his signature.

To the frequently asked question, "Which book are you most proud of?" he would just smile and say, "The one I'm working on next."

By no means was he perfect. He could be a difficult man to know. He wasn't the type to start conversations with strangers, and he detested small talk. He had few close friends, and those who counted themselves in that number knew to tread lightly. He could be abrupt, even rude, and quite aloof. After his death we learned that he utilized collaborators on some of the big books, a fact he refused to acknowledge in life. He was married three times and at one point maintained a mistress. He was a multimillionaire, yet he would constantly fret about not having enough money to pay his bills. And though he was an orphan himself and a co-founder of an adoption agency, in the 1950s he gave up his claim to an adopted child when he divorced his second wife.

All of which shows that he was human.

But still, what a remarkable man.

Michener possessed an incomparable ability to simultaneously enthrall, entertain, and inform. Nobody else could write a two-hundred-word sentence with such grace and style. And he chose his subjects with great care: the South Pacific (*Tales of the South Pacific, Return to Paradise*), Judaism (*The Source*), South Africa (*The Covenant*), the West Indies (*Caribbean*), the American West (*Centennial*), the Chesapeake Bay (*Chesapeake*), *Texas, Alaska,* Spain (*Iberia*), *Mexico, Poland,* the Far East.

Like millions of other readers, I loved them all.

I never met James Michener. I would have loved to tell him how he sparked the imagination of a sixteen-year-old boy, which led first to a lifelong love of reading, then to a career as a writer. When, in 1990, I decided to write my first novel, it was Michener who influenced me most. By the end of that decade, though, changes had firmly begun to take hold. Today you won't encounter many two-hundred-word sentences or millennia-long sagas involving hundreds of characters. Instead, in the twenty-first century, story, prose, and purpose are expected to be tight. In the Internet age—with video games, twenty-four-hour news, streaming movies, you name it—there is just little time for thousand-page epics. Toward the end of his life Michener gave an interview in which he doubted he would have ever been published if he'd first started in that environment.

Thank goodness he came along when he did.

Now his stories can live forever.

ACKNOWLEDGMENTS

In recent books I have named all who helped in my research, and this was appreciated. I intended doing so again, but this time, because so many provided information, the list became endless and could not be included. However, certain scholars, sometimes of world renown, went beyond the normal bounds of courtesy, and read portions of the manuscript or helped in other important ways and suggested clarifications. They must be thanked.

Dr. David Stone, University of Alaska, on terranes.
Dr. David Hopkins, University of Alaska, on Beringia.
Dr. Jean Aigner, University of Alaska, on early peoples.
Professor Frank Roth, Sheldon Jackson College, on Healy and Jackson.
Dee McKenna, Nome Library, on the gold rush in that city.
Dr. Timothy Joiner, foremost expert on salmon, on that fish.
Joe Horiskey, premier Denali guide, on mountaineering.
Jonathan Waterman, Denali Park official, on that mountain.
Elva Scott, Eagle, on life at minus-fifty-two.
David Finley, Wainwright, on education north of the Circle.

My research could not even have been started without assistance from the intrepid aviators of Alaska who flew me into all corners of their state: Ken Ward to abandoned salmon canneries; Layton Bennett to the site of the sinking of the Canadian steamer; Tom Rupert to a remote part of the Yukon River; Bob Reeve, long ago to the Aleutians; and especially the helicopter men who flew me into spots that would otherwise have been inaccessible: Officers Tom Walters and Pete Spence of the United States Coast Guard to Three Saints Bay; Randy Crosby and Price Brower of the Nome Rescue Service to the remote and desolate Will Rogers memorial.

To the many others whose unstinting help and sound advice were of such value, please accept my gratitude, especially my word-processing wizard, Kim Johnson-Bogart.

Lastly, and most particularly, to my hosts Mike and Mary Ann Kaelke at Sheldon Jackson College, Sitka, my warmest thanks for allowing my wife and me to occupy their log cabin for three seasons.

FACT AND FICTION

Though it is based on fact, this novel uses fictional events, places and characters. The following paragraphs endeavor to clarify which is which.

I. Terranes. The various geological concepts in this chapter have been developed and verified in recent decades but are still being refined. Specific histories of the various Alaskan terranes have not yet been fully identified, but the great basics, like the existence, genesis, movement and collision of plates, are generally accepted. There could be no other explanation of the Aleutian Islands and their violent behavior.

II. Beringia. Few geological theories are more solidly accepted than this, especially since it will probably return to existence within the next twenty-five thousand years. The movements of animals from Asia into North America is generally accepted, but the existence and functioning of the ice-free corridor into the rest of North America is more debatable. That the mastodons arrived well before the mammoths seems irrefutable.

III. Arrival of Humans. The earliest physical evidence of the existence of human beings in any part of Alaska seems to lie on a small island off the Aleutians and is dated no earlier than 12,000 B.P.E. But other problematic finds of much earlier date in Canada, California, Mexico and South America cause many scholars to postulate human arrivals in Alaska as early as 40,000 and 30,000 B.P.E. Regardless of the earliest date, it seems certain that the order of arrival was the Athapascans first, much later the Eskimos and finally the Aleuts, who were probably an offshoot of the Eskimos. The Tlingits were pretty clearly an offshoot of the Athapascans.

IV. Russians, Englishmen, Americans. Tsar Peter the Great, Vitus Bering, Georg Steller and Aleksei Chirikov are historical characters whose actions were pretty much as described. Though Captain James Cook and his junior officers William Bligh and George Vancouver did visit Alaska and the Aleutians at this time, they are shown here in a fictional setting, and quotations from their logbooks are imaginary. The American ship *Evening Star*, Noah Pym, and all its crew are fictional, as is the island of Lapak. The experimental shooting of eight Aleuts occurred.

V. Russian Orthodoxy and Shamanism. The religious facts are historical, the religious characters are all fictional. Data regarding the settlement of Kodiak Island are historical. Aleksandr Baranov is a historical personage of great importance.

VI. The Settlement of Sitka. Kot-le-an is a real Tlingit leader; Raven-heart is fictional. Prince Dmitri Maksutov, Baron Edouard de Stoeckl and General Jefferson C. Davis, USA, are historical figures presented faithfully. Father Vasili Voronov and his family are fictional, but a heroic Orthodox priest from the area was called back to St. Petersburg to become Metropolitan of All the Russias.

VII. The Period of Chaos. Captain Michael Healy and Dr. Sheldon Jackson are historical. The *Bear* was a real ship as described. Captain Emil Schransky and his *Erebus* are fictional. The legal difficulties of Healy and Jackson were real.

VIII. The Gold Rush. Soapy Smith of Skagway and Samuel Steele of the North West Mounted Police are historical characters as depicted, as are George Carmack and Robert Henderson, the discoverers of the Yukon gold field. All the others are fictional. The two routes to the gold fields—Yukon River and Chilkoot Pass—are faithfully presented.

IX. Nome.   All characters are fictional. The Dawson-Nome bicycle adventure is based on a real trip.

X. Salmon.   All characters are fictional, but details of the salmon industry as it operated in the early 1900s are based on historical accounts. The Ross & Raglan role in Alaskan shipping, merchandising and the canning industry is fictional and is not based on any historic company. Pleiades Lake and River are fictional, as is the cannery situated on Taku Inlet, which is real.

XI. Matanuska Valley.   All American characters are fictional, but the locations and their settling and development are historic. Data regarding the Japanese invasion of the Aleutians are historic. Details of the 1971 land claims settlement are as stated.

XII. Rim of Fire.   All characters are fictional, especially the Japanese and Russian experts on Alaskan prospects. The young woman schoolteacher and the two lawyers working the North Slope are totally invented and relate to no real persons. The Japanese team of mountaineers is fictional but the climb is real. The floating ice island, T-3, is historic and functioned as stated; T-7 is fictional. The data about tsunamis originating in Alaska are accurate, and although the one that closes the novel is fictional, it could become quite real at any time. The details of Eskimo life at Desolation Point, an imaginary village, are based on reality. The Iditarod Race occurs each year, and the Jones Act of 1920 still sends cruise ships to Vancouver rather than Seattle.

CONTENTS

Jean Paul Tremblay

ALASKA

I

THE CLASHING TERRANES

ABOUT A BILLION YEARS AGO, LONG BEFORE THE CONTINENTS had separated to define the ancient oceans, or their own outlines had been determined, a small protuberance jutted out from the northwest corner of what would later become North America. It showed no lofty mountains or stern shorelines, but it was firmly rooted in solid rock and would remain permanently attached to primordial North America.

Its position, fixed though it was in relation to the larger landmass, did not long remain at what seemed the northwest corner, because, as we know from studies which flowered in the middle years of this century, the surface features of the earth rest on massive subterranean plates which move restlessly about, sometimes taking this position or that and often colliding with one another. In these ancient times the future North America wandered and revolved at a lively rate; sometimes the protuberance lay to the east, or to the north or, more dramatically, the far south. During one long spell it served as the temporary North Pole of the entire earth. But later it stood near the equator and then had a tropical climate.

It was, in effect, a fixed attachment to a wildly vagrant landmass, but it bore continuing relation to other would-be continents like Europe or, more significantly, to the Asia with which it would intimately be associated. However, if one had followed the errant behavior of this small jutting of rocky land attached to the larger body, one could never have predicted its present position.

The destiny of this persistent fragment would be to form the root-stock of the future Alaska, but during this early formative period and for long thereafter, it remained only that: the ancestral nucleus to which the later and more important parts of Alaska would be joined.

During one of the endless twists and turns, about half a billion years ago, the nucleus rested temporarily about where Alaska does today, that is, not far from the North Pole, and it would be instructive to visualize it as it then was. The land, in a period of subsidence after eons of violent uprising, lay not far above the surface of the surrounding seas, which had even yet not separated themselves into the oceans we know. No vast mountains broke the low profile, and since trees and ferns had not yet developed, Alaska, which amounted only to a minor promontory, was unwooded. In winter, even at these high latitudes, a phenomenon which would always characterize northern Alaska pertained: it did not receive much snow. The surrounding seas, often frozen, brought in so little precipitation that the great blizzards which swept other parts of the then world did not eventuate, and what little snow did fall was driven here and there by howling winds which swept the earth clear in many parts or left it lightly drifted in others.

Then as now, the winter night was protracted. For six months the sun appeared low in the sky, if it appeared at all, while the blazing heat of summer came in a season of equal length when the sun set only briefly. The range of temperature, under a sky which contained less relative moisture than now, was incredible: from 120° Fahrenheit in summer to the same number of degrees below zero in winter. As a consequence, such plants as tried to grow—and there were none that resembled anything with which we are now familiar—had to accommodate to these wild fluctuations: prehistoric mosses, low shrubs with deep roots, little superstructure and almost no leaves, and ferns which had adapted to the cold clung to the thin earth, their roots often thrusting their way down through crevices in rock.

No animals that we would recognize as such roamed this area, for the great dinosaurs were still far in the future, while the mastodons and mammoths which would at one time dominate these parts would not begin even their preliminary genesis for many millennia. But recognizable life had started, and in the southern half of the little promontory tentative forms moved in from the sea to experiment on land.

In these remote and formless days little Alaska hung in suspense, uncertain as to where its mother continent would wander next, or what its climate would be, or what its destiny. It was a potential, nothing more. It could become a multitude of different things; it could switch its attachment to any of three different continents; and when it enlarged upon its ancestral nucleus it would be able to construct miraculous possibilities.

It would lift up great mountains, the highest in North America. It would accumulate vast glaciers, none superior in the world. It would house, for some generations before the arrival of man, animals of the most majestic quality. And when it finally played host to wandering human beings coming in from Asia or elsewhere, it would provide residence for some of the most exciting people this earth has known: the Athapascans, the Tlingits and much later the Eskimos and Aleuts.

But the immediate task is to understand how this trivial ancestral nucleus could aggregate to itself the many additional segments of rocky land which would ultimately unite to comprise the Alaska we know. Like a spider waiting to grab any passing fly, the nucleus remained passive but did accept any passing terranes—those unified agglomerations of rock considerable in size and adventurous in motion—that wandered within reach. Where did these disparate terranes originate? How could blocks so massive move about? If they did move, what carried them north toward Alaska? And how did they behave when they bumped into the ancestral nucleus and its outriders?

The explanation is a narrative of almost delicate intricacy, so wonderfully do the various terranes move about, but it is also one of cataclysmic violence when the terranes finally collide with something fixed. This part of Alaska's history is one of the most instructive offered by earth.

The visible features of the earth, including its oceans, rest on some six or eight major identifiable subterranean plates—Asia is one, obviously; Australia another—plus a score of smaller plates, each clearly defined, and upon their slow, almost imperceptible movement depends where and how the continents and the oceans shall sit in relation each to the other.

At what speed might a plate move? The present distance from California to Tokyo is 5,149 miles. If the North American plate were to move relentlessly toward Japan at the infinitesimal rate of one-half inch per year, San Francisco would bump into Tokyo in only six hundred and fifty million years. If the plate movement were a foot a year, the transit could be made in about twenty-seven million years, which is not long in geologic time.

So the movement of a terrane from anywhere in Asia, the Pacific Ocean or North America to the growing shoreline of Alaska presented no insuperable difficulties. Given enough time and enough movement of the respective plates, anything could happen . . . and did.

In one of the far wastes of the South Pacific Ocean a long-vanished island-studded landmass of some magnitude arose, now given the name Wrangellia, and had it stayed put, it might have produced another assembly of islands like the Tahiti group or the Samoan. Instead, for reasons not known, it fragmented, and its two halves moved with a part of the Pacific Plate in a northerly direction, with the eastern half ending up along the Snake River in Idaho and the western as a part of the Alaskan peninsula. We can make this statement with certainty because scientists have compared the structure of the two segments in minute detail, and one layer after another of the terrane which landed in Idaho matches perfectly the one which wandered to Alaska. The layers of rock were laid down at the same time, in the same sequence and with the same relative thickness and magnetic orientation. The fit is absolute, and is verified by many matching strata.

Through the millennia similar wandering terranes seem to have attached themselves to the Alaskan nucleus. Frequently some enormous slab of rocky earth—sometimes as big as Kentucky—would creep relentlessly north from somewhere and bang into what was already there. There would be a rending of the edges of the two terranes, a sudden uprising of mountains, a revolution in the existing landscape, and Alaska would be enlarged by a significant percentage.

Sometimes two smaller terranes would collide far distant from Alaska; they would merge and for eons would form an island somewhere in the Pacific, and then their plate would imperceptibly move them toward Alaska, and one day they would touch Alaska, so gently that even the birds inhabiting the island would not know that contact had been made, but the onetime island would keep remorselessly encroaching, grinding down opposition, overwhelming the existing shoreline of Alaska or being overwhelmed by it, and no casual observer would be able to detect where or how the join of this new land to the old had been accomplished.

Now, obviously, after eight or ten such terranes had pushed against the ancestral nucleus, none of its original structure still touched the ocean, for it had been surrounded on all exposed sides by the incoming lands. A great peninsula, one of the largest on earth, was in the process of being formed, an immense proboscis reaching out toward Asia, which was also in the process of its formation. About seventy million years ago this nascent peninsula began to assume a shape vaguely like present-day Alaska, but shortly thereafter it acquired a peculiarity with which we today would not be familiar.

A land bridge seemed to rise from the seas connecting Alaska to Asia, or the other way around, and it was so broad and permanent that it provided a continuous land connection between the continents. But at this time little advantage accrued to the change, for there were few animals and of course no humans at all on earth to profit from the bridge which had been so mysteriously exposed, but a few adventurous dinosaurs do seem to have used it for crossing from Asia.

In time the land bridge disappeared, overrun by the seas, and then Asia and Alaska were separated, with the latter still free to accept such wandering terranes as might come her way and thus to double or treble her size.

We are now prepared to look at the specific formulation of the Alaskan land forms. When the northern half of the final outline was more or less set, but still awaiting the arrival of the final terranes, the Pacific Plate seems to have crashed into the continental plate on which the original Alaska rested, and the force was so great and persistent that a grand chain of mountains, to be known later as the Brooks Range, rose in an east-west direction. In the bleak and snowless area, north of the range, well beyond the Arctic Circle, would appear a multitude of small lakes, so many that they would never be counted.

The range itself, originally very high and mysteriously composed of slabs of limestone stacked one atop the other, would be eroded by wind, freezing, breakage and the action of summer rain, until the tallest peaks would stand at only six to eight thousand feet, the stumps of mountains that were once twice as high. But they would always be a noble range, the essence of the real Alaska.

South of them, spacious valleys spread out, garnering sunlight summer and winter, bitterly cold at times, delightful for much of the year. Here snow did fall, animals prospered, and all was readied for the appearance of man, and held that way eons before he finally appeared.

At a much later period a new collection of terranes from widely varied sources started moving in to complete the major outline of Alaska, and they arrived with such titanic force that an entire new mountain range was thrown up, about three hundred miles south of the older Brooks Range and parallel to it. This was the Alaska Range, a majestic row of rugged peaks which, because they are so much younger than the Brooks, have not yet been eroded down to stumps. Young, soaring, vivid in form, tremendous in reach, these peaks stab the frosty air to heights of twelve and thirteen, nineteen and twenty thousand feet. Denali, the glory of Alaska, soars to more than twenty thousand and is one of the most compelling mountains in the Americas.

Old Brooks and young Alaska, these two ranges form the twin backbones of the region and give Alaska a wilderness of mighty peaks, some of which have yet to feel the foot of man. Sometimes, when seen from the air, Alaska seems nothing but peaks, thousands of them, many not even named, and in such varied snow-covered profusion that Alaska could well be called the land of mountains.

And each one was formed by some segment of the Pacific Plate bulldozing its way into the North American Plate, submerging along the edge, and causing such tremendous commotion and movement of forces that the great mountains erupted as a consequence. When one looks at the glorious mountains of Alaska he sees proof of the power of the Pacific Plate as it noses its way north and east, and if today he visits Yakutat, he can observe the plate pushing into Alaska at the steady rate of two inches a year. As we shall see later, this produces large earthquakes in the area, and nearby Mount St. Elias, 18,008 feet, grows taller year by year.

But there is another region in Alaska which shows the operations of the great Pacific Plate at even more instructive advantage. West of what finally became mainland Alaska there was originally only water, and turbulent water it was, for here an arctic sea, the Bering, met an ocean, the Pacific, and dark waves signaled their meeting, a haunt of seal and walrus, of sea birds that skimmed the surface of the water seeking fish, and of one of the most delightful creatures nature provides, the sleek sea otter whose round bewhiskered face looks almost exactly like that of some roguish old man. In these waters, too, swam the fish that would ultimately make Alaska famous, the salmon, whose life story will prove compelling.

Here plates collided to produce a magnificent chain of islands, the Aleutians, and two of nature's most dramatic manifestations: earthquakes and volcanoes. In any century, considering the entire surface of the earth, of all the earthquakes that occur, three or four out of the ten most powerful will occur along the Aleutians or close to them, and some of the most destructive are those which take place deep within the bosom of the ocean, for then landslides of gigantic dimension displace millions of tons of submarine earth. This powerful disruption creates immense underwater waves which manifest themselves as tidal waves, more properly tsunamis, which course through the entire Pacific Ocean at speeds that can surpass five hundred miles an hour.

So a submarine earthquake in the Aleutians poses a potential danger to the Hawaiian Islands, because six or seven hours after it occurs in Alaska, its resulting tsunami can strike Hawaii with devastating power. Silently, never causing a surface wave much over three feet high, the tsunami transmits its power with vast radiating force, and if it encounters no obstruction on its way, it runs on and on until it finally dissipates. But if it does bump into an island, the waves that have been no more than three feet high come on quietly but relentlessly until they cover the land to a depth of five or six feet. This flooding, of itself, does little damage, but when these accumulated waters rush back off the land to regain the sea, the destruction and loss of life can be tremendous.

The earthquakes produced along the Aleutian chain are endless, thousands in a century, but most of them, fortunately, are only minor, and although many submarine ones produce tsunamis, only rarely are they of such magnitude as to threaten Hawaii, but, as we shall see, they do often produce local tidal waves of great destructive power.

The same tectonic forces which create situations conducive to earthquake activity produce volcanoes, and thus the Aleutians become one of the world's most active volcanic centers, with some forty volcanoes stringing along the chain. It is a rare island that does not have its crater, and some craters appear not in connection with established islands, but as lonely spots in the middle of the sea. Some stand on the verge of becoming islands, smoking above the surface for a hundred years, subsiding for half a century, then peeking their sulfurous heads above the waves to throw flames in the night.

Because of the profusion of volcanic activity along the Aleutians—a bubbling cauldron, really—Alaska holds an honored place, perhaps the preeminent place in the Rim of Fire, that unbroken chain of volcanoes which circles the Pacific Ocean wherever the Pacific Plate comes into violent contact with other plates.

Starting at Tierra del Fuego at the southern tip of South America, the volcanoes come up the western side of the continent (Cotopaxi, Lascar, Misti), then along Mexico (Popocatépetl, Ixtaccihuatl, Orizaba, Paracutín) and into the Pacific states (Lassen, Hood, St. Helens, Rainier), and then the Aleutians, where they are so ordinary that their names, often commemorating Russian sailors, are not widely known.

The Rim of Fire continues dramatically along the east coast of Asia, with many volcanoes in Kamchatka, Mount Fuji and others in Japan, a stunning array in Indonesia and on to New Zealand with its beautiful Ruapehu and Tongariro.

And, as if to prove the capacity of this area to breed violent activity, in the middle of the Pacific Ocean rise the two magnificent Hawaiian volcanoes Mauna Loa and Mauna Kea. Considering the platform from which they rise, far beneath the surface of the ocean, they are among the tallest mountains on earth and certainly the highest volcanoes.

But none of the many along the rim are more compactly arranged and fascinating to study than those dozens that cluster along the Aleutian chain; indeed, these islands could well be preserved as a universal park to demonstrate to the world the majesty of the volcano and the power of plate action.

What is the future of Alaska, geologically speaking? For interesting reasons which will be developed, we can expect that at some distant time—perhaps twenty thousand years from now—Alaska will once again be joined to Asia by the historic land bridge, while land communication to the rest of the United States may be cut.

And since the great plates of the earth never rest, we can anticipate the arrival at Alaska of additional terranes, but these may not lurch onto the scene for several million years, if then. One future event will cause comment, if people are living then who remember history.

The city of Los Angeles is now some twenty-four hundred miles south of central Alaska, and since it is moving slowly northward as the San Andreas fault slides irresistibly along, the city is destined eventually to become part of Alaska. If the movement is two inches a year, which it often is, we can expect Los Angeles to arrive off Anchorage in about seventy-six million years, which was about the time that was required for some of the other terranes from the south to move into position against the ancestral nucleus.

So Alaska must be viewed as having two characteristics: great beauty but also implacable hostility. Its intricate mosaic of disparate terranes has produced lofty mountains, unequaled volcanoes and glaciers. But in the early days the land was not hospitable to settlers. Animals and human beings who came to this promontory had to adjust to profound cold, great distances and meager food supplies, which meant that the men and women who survived would always be a somewhat special breed: adventurous, heroic, willing to contest the great winds, the endless nights, the freezing winters, the cruel and never-ending search for food. They would be people who lived close to the unrelenting land both because they had to and because they reveled in the challenge.

Alaska would always call forth the best in a small handful of daring men and women, but those who did not relish the contest or who refused to obey the harsh rules which governed it would find the bitterly cold land repellent and would flee it if they could retreat before it killed them.

The number of settlers was never very large, for in the icy tundra of the north slope only a few thousand at a time would challenge the rigors; in the grand valleys between the mountain ranges not many would adjust to the radical alternations of climate; and even in the easier enclaves and islands to the south people would not cluster when with far less effort they could enjoy the more inviting climate of California.

But because Alaska lay at the crossroads joining North America and Asia, it would always be important; and since it dominated these crossroads, it would enjoy a significance which only the brightest intellects of the region would appreciate. There would always be a few Russians who understood the unique value of Alaska, a few Americans who appreciated its enormous importance, and upon these knowing ones would depend the history of this strange, compelling land.

THE ICE CASTLE

A T VARIOUS TIMES IN THE ANCIENT PAST, FOR A COMPLEX SET of reasons which have yet to be untangled, ice began to collect at the poles in vast quantities, growing ever thicker and more extensive, until it created immense ice sheets which encroached on surrounding continents. Snow fell at such a rate that it could not melt as it would have done under ordinary circumstances. Instead, it piled to unprecedented heights, and the pressure from that on top was so considerable that the snow at the bottom was turned into ice, and as snow continued to fall, ice continued to form, until it stood in certain places more than a mile and a half thick. The weight was so oppressive and inescapable that certain parts of the earth's surface, heavily encumbered, began to sink perceptibly, so that land which once stood well above the surface of the oceans was now depressed to sea level or below.

If in any given region this enormous accumulation of ice rested on a flat plateau, a huge and quietly spreading ice cap resulted, but since the surface of the earth, because of the violent way in which it had been formed, was irregular, with mountains and valleys predominating, the ice which found itself on a slope, as most of it did, began slowly to move, under the force of gravity, to lower elevations, and as it did, its weight was so great that it dragged along with it a mass of rubble composed of sand, gravel, rocks and, occasionally, boulders of gigantic size. This lateral transport of material occurred wherever the ice field was in motion, but when a snowfield accumulated on some high plateau and began to send glaciers down valleys which might have steep gradients, the consequences could be dramatic, for then the ice formed a moving glacier which routed out the bottom of the valley and scored the sides with streaks so pronounced that they would still be visible eons later.

These glaciers could not run forever; as they probed into lower and warmer land their ends began to melt, forming massive rivers which carried ice and silt and boulders to the sea. Such glacial rivers were a milky white, colored by the flecks of rock they carried, and as they dropped their stony burden, land was formed from the detritus of the melting ice field.

If the valley down which the glacier came ended at the shoreline, the towering face of ice would come right to the edge of the ocean, where in due time fragments of the glacier, sometimes as big as cathedrals, sometimes bigger, would break away with resounding cracks that would reverberate through the air for many miles as the resulting iceberg crashed into the ocean, where it would ride as an independent entity for months and even decades. Then it became a thing of majestic beauty, with sunlight glistening on its towering spires, with waves playing about its feet, and with primitive birds saluting it as they sped by.

In time, of course, the great icebergs would melt, adding their water to the ocean, and clouds passing overhead would lift this water, carry it inland, and deposit it as fresh snow upon the ever-growing ice field that fed the glaciers.

Normally, if such a word can be applied to any natural function which by its character must vary, an equilibrium between the formation of snow and its removal as it melted into water was maintained, so that the ice fields did not invade terrains which traditionally were not ice-covered, but during what have been called the ice ages, this equilibrium was disturbed, with ice forming much faster than it could be dissipated by melting, and for centuries learned men have been fascinated by the mystery of what caused this imbalance.

Seven or eight potential factors have been suggested to explain ice ages: the inclination of the earth's axis toward the sun, for if any portion of the earth was removed even slightly from the heat of the sun, ice would result; the wandering of the earth's poles, for they are not fixed and have been located in some periods close to the present equator; the elliptical path of the earth around the sun, which deviates so substantially that the earth's distance from the sun varies greatly during the course of a year; changes within the center of the sun itself causing the value of whatever heat is disseminated to vary; chemical changes in the atmosphere; physical changes in the oceans; and other inventive and enticing possibilities.

The time span of these variables can be as short as a calendar year or as long as fifty to a hundred thousand years, so to devise a theory which explains how they interact to produce an ice age is obviously complex and has not yet been solved. To take an easy example, if four different factors in an intricate problem operate in cycles of 13, 17, 23 and 37 years respectively, and if all have to coincide to produce the desired result, you might have to wait 188,071 years ($13 \times 17 \times 23 \times 37$) before everything fell together. But if you can get fairly satisfactory results when only the first two factors coincide, you could confidently expect that result in 221 years (13×17).

There is now an attractive theory that in relatively recent times, periods of extensive glaciation over Europe and North America have occurred in obedience to three unexplained cycles of about one hundred thousand years, forty-one thousand and twenty-two thousand. At these intervals, for reasons not fully understood, the ice begins to accumulate and expand, covering areas which for thousands of years have been clear of ice fields and glaciers. The causes are natural and may in time be understood; in fact, science-fiction writers dream that they may even become manageable, so that future ice ages need not extend so far south into Europe and North America as they have in the past.

Strangely, although a permanent ice cap came in time to cover the South Pole, which was a continent, none developed at the North, which was a sea. The glaciers which covered North America stemmed from caps in Canada; those that submerged Europe, from the Scandinavian countries; and those which struck Russia, from sites near the Barents Sea. And because the movement of ice in North America was mainly to the south, Alaska would never lie under a massive ice sheet; Wisconsin and Massachusetts would, and so would a dozen other states, but not Alaska. It would become known as a cold and barren land covered with ice and snow, but it would never know in all its millennia as much ice as a more habitable state like Connecticut had once known—or Massachusetts and New York.

The world has known many ice ages, two of which lasted an appalling number of millennia when much of Europe and North America lay crushed beneath monstrous thicknesses of ice. Then winds howled across endless wastes and freezing night seemed perpetual. When the sun did appear, it was unproductive, glistening down upon dead icy surfaces. All visible living things perished: grasses and trees, worms and insects, fish and animals. Desolation ruled, and during these vast periods of frozen waste it must have seemed as if warmth and life could never return.

But each protracted ice age was followed by joyous intervals of equal length when the ice mysteriously retreated to release from its frozen prison an earth bursting with energy and the capacity to restore life in all its manifestations. Grasses flourished to feed the animals that hurried back. Trees grew, some bearing fruits. Fields, nourished with minerals long unused, bore lavish crops, and birds sang. The future Wisconsins and Austrias exploded into life as the sun brought back warmth and well-being. The world had returned to abundant life.

These first two great ice ages began to evolve so very long ago, say about seven hundred million years, that they need not concern us, but some two million years ago when the historical record was about to begin, a series of much briefer ice ages arrived, and their dates, extents and characteristics have been so well defined that they have been given distinctive names: Nebraskan, Kansan, Illinoian, Wisconsin—in Europe: Gunz, Mindel, Riss, Würm—with the last segment in each group subdivided into three parts, making six in all. The names can be ignored; they will not be referred to again, but two significant facts cannot be ignored: the last of these six recent ice ages ended only fourteen thousand years ago, with glacial remnants existing as late as seven thousand years ago, so that the men and women then living in North America experienced one of the ice ages. And the normal extension and retraction of the polar ice cap indicates that about twenty thousand years from now we may anticipate another icy incursion to areas as far south as New York, Iowa and spots in between. But of course, if history is any predictor, Alaska at that time will be ice-free and a relatively attractive place in which the residents of our Northern states can seek refuge.

· · ·

Even though Alaska did escape being submerged by these vast weights of frozen water, it was attacked by isolated glaciers which formed in its own mountains, and some were of substantial size. In the northern areas during one of the lesser ice ages, an icy finger covered the Brooks Range, carving and readjusting those mountains and building beautiful valleys. Much later, glaciers of some size came into the Alaska Range to the south, and even today huge ice fields with their probing glaciers exist in the extreme southern regions, where constant precipitation brought in by Pacific winds keeps the fields covered with snow, which packs down to form ice just as it did when the first Alaskan ice fields formed.

But most of Alaska escaped the glaciers. North of the Brooks Range, there were none. In the vast middle section, between the mountain ranges, there were none, and in isolated parts of the region to the south, glaciers did not appear. At maximum, not more than thirty percent of the region was ice-covered.

However, the later ice ages did create in Alaska a result more dramatic than that which happened anywhere else in America, and for a reason which becomes evident once it is pointed out. If an ice sheet more than a mile thick is going to cover much of North America, the water it imprisons will have to come from somewhere, and it cannot come mysteriously from outer space. It cannot *arrive* on the surface of the earth; it can come only from water already here, which means that it must be stolen from the oceans. And that is what happened: dry winds whipping across the oceans lifted huge quantities of water that fell as cold rain over the high latitudes and as snow toward the poles. As it was compressed into ice it began to expand outward, covering hitherto barren sites, and causing more and more of the incoming moisture to fall as snow. This in turn fed the existing glaciers and created new ones.

In the recent period with which we are concerned, this theft of water continued for thousands of years, until the snowfields were immensely aggrandized and the oceans seriously depleted. In fact, when the deficiency was at its worst, only some twenty thousand years ago, the level of the world's oceans—all of them—was more than three hundred feet lower than it is now. All the American states that faced the Atlantic Ocean had shorelines that extended miles farther eastward than they now do; much of the Gulf of Mexico was dry; Florida was not a peninsula nor was Cape Cod a cape. Caribbean Islands coalesced into a few huge islands, and the shoreline of Canada could not be seen at all, for it was smothered in ice.

This sharp droppage in the level of the oceans meant that land areas which had previously been separated were now joined by necks of land which the subsiding waters revealed. Australia was attached to Antarctica by such exposed land, Ceylon to India, Cyprus to western Asia, and England to Europe. But the most spectacular join was that of Alaska to Siberia, for it united two continents, allowing animals and people to pass from one to the other. It was also the only one which acquired its own name, scientists having christened it Beringia, the lost land of the Bering Sea.

It was, perhaps, unfortunate that the phrase *land bridge* was invented by geographers to designate this phenomenon of revealed land connections, because the imagery connected with the word *bridge* is misleading. The Alaskan-Siberian connection was no bridge in the ordinary sense, a narrow structure across which one could travel; it was an exposed sea floor some sixty miles east to west, but a full six hundred south to north. At its widest, it covered about the distance from Atlanta to New York (in Europe, Paris to Copenhagen). It was four times wider than most of Central America from ocean to ocean, and if a man stood in the middle, he would hardly think of himself on a bridge; he would be on a substantial part of a continent. But it was an inviting passageway, and with its functioning the story of populated Alaska can begin. It starts with the earliest immigrants.

About three hundred eighty-five thousand years ago, when the oceans and continents were in place as we know them today, the land bridge from Asia was open, and a huge, ponderous animal, looking much like an oversized elephant but with enormous protruding tusks, slowly made his way eastward, followed by four females and their young. He was by no means the first of his breed to lumber across the bridge, but he was among the more interesting, for his life experience symbolized the majestic adventure in which the animals of his period were engaged.

He was a mastodon, and we shall call him by that name, for he was a progenitor of those noble massive beasts who ranged Alaska. Obviously, a million years before, he had stemmed from the same source that produced the elephant, but in Africa, in Europe and later in central Asia he had developed those characteristics which differentiated him from his cousin the elephant. His tusks were larger, his front shoulders lower, his legs more powerful, and his body was covered with hair that was more visible. But he behaved in much the same way, foraged for the same kinds of food, and lived to about the same age.

When he crossed the bridge—less than seventy miles from Asia to Alaska—Mastodon was forty years old and could expect to survive into his late seventies, supposing that he escaped the ferocious wild cats who relished mastodon meat. His four females were much younger than he, and as was common in the animal kingdom, they could anticipate a somewhat longer life.

As the nine mastodons entered Alaska they faced four radically different types of terrain, varying somewhat from the land they had left behind in Asia. At the farthest north, facing the Arctic Ocean, lay a thin strip of arctic desert, a bleak and terrifying land of shifting sands on which little that was edible grew. During the dozen winter weeks when no sun appeared, it was covered by thin snow that did not pile up into high drifts but was whipped by intense winds across the barren landscape until it came to rest in low drifts behind some ridge or rock.

Since none of his breed could survive long in this desert, Mastodon intuitively shied away from the far north, and this left him three other areas to explore that were more rewarding. Just south of the desert and blending into it in various ways stretched another relatively narrow strip, a tundra, perpetually frozen twelve to twenty-four inches below the surface but rich in rooted plant life when the topsoil was dry enough to permit growth. Here succulent lichens abounded and mosses rich in nutrients and even an occasional low shrub with branches stout enough to provide leaves for grazing. No real trees grew here, of course, for summers were too short to permit flowering or adequate branch development, and this meant that whereas Mastodon and his family could eat well on the tundra during the long summers when nearly perpetual daylight spurred plant growth, they had to be careful to escape it when winter approached.

That left two rich areas between the northern and southern glaciers, and the first of these was a splendid, hospitable region, the great Alaskan steppe, an area of rich grass growing high most years and yielding some food even in poor years. Large trees did not customarily grow on the steppe, but in a few secluded spots that were protected from searing winds, clusters of low shrubs gained a foot-hold, especially the dwarf willow whose leaves Mastodon loved to crop. When he was especially hungry he liked to rip off the bark of the willow with his strong tusks, and sometimes he would stand for hours amidst a group of willows, browsing and eating a sliver of bark and striving to find among the low branches a bit of shade to protect himself from the intense heat of summer.

The fourth area he had at his disposal was larger than any of the previous three, for in these years Alaska had a predominantly benign climate which both allowed and encouraged the growth of trees in regions that had previously been denuded and would be again when temperatures lowered. Now poplar, birch, pine and larch flourished, with woodland animals like the spotted skunk sharing the forests with Mastodon, who relished the trees because he could stand up-right and nibble at their copious leaves. After feeding, he could use the sturdy trunks of the pine or larch as convenient poles against which to scrape his back.

So between the largesse of the new woodland and the more con-trolled but assured richness of the steppe, Mastodon and his family could eat well, and since it was spring when they entered Alaska, he naturally headed for a region like the one he had known well in Sibe-ria, the tundra, where he was certain that low shrubs and grasses waited. But now he faced an interesting problem, for the sun's heat that had enabled these plants to grow also melted the top eight or ten inches of the permafrost, turning the softening soil into a kind of sticky mush. Obviously, there was nowhere for the moisture to es-cape; the earth below was frozen solid and would remain so for countless years. As summer approached, thousands of shallow lakes thawed, and the mush thickened until at times Mastodon sank in al-most to his knees.

Now he slipped and sloshed his way through the watery tundra, fighting off the myriad of mosquitoes that hatched at this time to torment any moving thing. Sometimes, when he lifted one of his huge legs out of the swampy mess in which it had slowly sunk, the sound of the leg breaking free from the suction echoed for long dis-tances.

Mastodon and his group grazed on the tundra during most of that first summer, but as the waning heat of the sun signaled the ap-proach of winter, he began drifting gradually south toward the wait-ing steppe where there would be reassuring grass poking through the thin snow. During the early days of autumn, when he was at the dividing line between tundra and steppe, it was almost as if the shrub willows that now appeared low on the horizon were calling him to a safer winter home, but the effect of the waning sun was the more important impulse, so that by the time the first snows appeared in the area between the great glaciers, he and his family had moved into the forested area which assured an ample food supply.

His first half-year in Alaska had been a spectacular success, but of course he was not aware that he had made the transition from Asia to North America; all he had done was follow an improved food supply. Indeed, he had not left Asia, for those solid sheets of ice to the east had made Alaska in those years a part of the larger continent.

As the first winter progressed, Mastodon became aware that he and the other mastodons were by no means alone in their favorable habitat, for a most varied menagerie had preceded them in their exit from the Asian mainland, and one cold morning when he stood alone in soft snow, cropping twig-ends from a convenient willow, he heard a rustle that disturbed him. Prudently, he withdrew lest some enemy leap upon him from a hiding place high in the trees, and he was not a moment too soon, for as he turned away from the willow, he saw emerging from the protection of a nearby copse his most fearsome enemy.

It was a kind of tiger, with powerful claws and a pair of frightful upper teeth almost three feet long and incredibly sharp. Mastodon knew that though this saber-tooth could not drive those fearsome teeth through the heavy skin of his protected rear or sides, it could, if it obtained a secure foothold on his back, sink them into the softer skin at the base of his neck. He had only a moment to defend himself from this hungry enemy, and with an agility that was surprising for an animal so big, he pivoted on his left front foot, swung his massive body in a half-circle, and faced the charging saber-tooth.

Mastodon had his long tusks, of course, but he could not lunge forward and expect to impale his adversary on them; they were not intended for that purpose. But his tiny brain did send signals which set the tusks in wide sweeping motions, and as the cat sprang, hoping to evade them, the right tusk, swinging with tremendous force, caught the rear legs of the saber-tooth, and although the blow did not send the cat spinning or in any way immobilize it, it did divert the attack and it did cause a bruise which infuriated the saber-tooth without disarming him.

So the cat stumbled among the trees, then regained control, and circled swiftly so that it could attack from the rear, hoping with a giant leap to land upon Mastodon's back, from where the vulnerable neck could be punctured. The cat was much quicker than the mastodon, and after a series of feints which tired the larger animal as he tried to counter them, the saber-tooth did land with a mighty bound, not on the flat of the back where it wanted to be, but half on the back, half on the side. It struggled for a moment to climb to a secure position, but in that time Mastodon, with a remarkable instinct for self-preservation, scraped under a set of low branches, and had the cat not wisely jumped free, it would have been crushed, which was what Mastodon intended.

Repelled twice, the great cat, some nine times larger than the tiger we know today, growled furiously, lurked among the trees, and gathered strength for a final attack. This time, with a leap more powerful than before, it came at Mastodon from the side, but the huge animal was prepared, and pivoting again on his left front foot, he swung his tusks in a wide arc that caught the saber-tooth in midair and sent it sprawling back among the trees, one of its legs painfully damaged.

That was enough for the saber-tooth. Growling and protesting, it slunk away, having learned that if it wanted to feast on mastodon, it must hunt in pairs, or even threes or fours, because one wily mastodon was capable of protecting itself.

Alaska at this time contained many lions, huge and much hairier than the kind that would come later. These possessed no handsome manes or wavy tails, and the males lacked the regal quality that would someday be such a distinguishing characteristic; they were what nature intended them to be: great cats with remarkable hunting abilities. Like the saber-tooth, they had learned never to attack a mastodon singly, but a hungry pride of six or seven could badger him to death, so Mastodon never intruded upon areas where a number of lions might be hiding. Rocky tors covered with trees, deep vales from whose sides groups of lions might attack, these he avoided, and sometimes as he plowed noisily along, bending young and scattered trees to his will, he would see a group of lions in the distance feeding upon some animal they had run to earth, and he would change direction lest he attract their attention.

The water animal with which Mastodon occasionally came into contact was the massive beaver, which had followed him out of Asia. Of giant size and with teeth that could fell a large tree, these beavers spent their working hours building dams, which Mastodon often saw from a distance, but when work was done the great beasts, their heavy fur glistening in the cold sunlight, liked to play at rowdy games, and their agility differed so markedly from the ponderous movements of Mastodon that he was amazed at their antics. He never had occasion to live in close contact with the underwater beavers, but he noticed them with perplexity when they gamboled after work.

Mastodon had his major contacts with the numerous steppe bison, the huge progenitors of the buffalo. These shaggy beasts, heads low and powerful horns parallel to the ground, grazed in many of the areas he liked to roam, and sometimes so many bison collected in one meadow that the land seemed covered with them. They would all be grazing, heads pointed in the same direction, when a saber-tooth would begin stalking a laggard. Then, at some signal Mastodon could not detect, the hundreds of giant bison would start running away from the terrible fangs of the cat, and the steppe would thunder with their passage.

Occasionally he encountered camels. Tall, awkward beasts who cropped the tops of trees, they seemed to fit in nowhere, moving slowly about, kicking ferociously at enemies, and surrendering quickly whenever a saber-tooth managed a foothold on their backs. At rare times Mastodon and a pair of camels would feed in the same area, but the two animals, so vastly different, ignored each other, and it might be months before Mastodon saw another camel. They were mysterious creatures and he was content to leave them alone.

In this placid, ponderous way, Mastodon lived out his uneventful life. If he defended himself against saber-tooths, and avoided falling into bogs from which he could not scramble free, and fled from the great fires set by lightning, he had little to fear. Food was plentiful. He was still young enough to attract and hold females. And the seasons were not too hot and moist in summer or cold and dry in winter. He had a good life and he stumbled his gigantic way through it with dignity and gentleness. Other animals like wolves and saber-tooths sought sometimes to kill him for food, but he hungered only for enough grass and tender leaves, of which he consumed about six hundred pounds a day. He was of all Alaska's inhabitants in these early years the most congenial.

. . . .

A curious physical condition limited the movement of animals in Alaska, for Beringia's land bridge could exist only when the polar ice caps were so extensive that they imprisoned vast quantities of water which had previously sustained the oceans. Indeed, the prime requisite for the existence of the bridge was that the ice sheets be immense.

However, when they were, they crept across western Canada, and although they never reached Alaska in an unbroken mass, they did send forth probing glaciers, and in time these frozen fingers reached right down to the Pacific shoreline, forming a set of icy barriers which proved impassable to animals and men. Alaska was then easy to enter from Asia, impossible to leave for the interior of North America. Functionally, Alaska became a part of Asia, and so it would remain during vast periods.

At no time that we are aware of could any animal or man cross the bridge and proceed directly to the interior of North America; but since we know that eventual passage did occur, for mastodons, bison and sheep did move from Asia into mainland North America, as did men, we must conclude that such movement came only after an extended waiting period in Alaska's ice castle.

Proof of this can be found in varied data. Certain animals that came into Alaska remained there, while their brothers and sisters wandered on to the rest of North America during some interval when the barriers were removed. But the two strains became so totally separated when the barriers closed that over the thousands of years that they remained apart they each developed unique characteristics.

The movement of animals across the bridge was by no means always in one direction, for although it is true that the more spectacular beasts—mastodon, saber-tooth, rhinoceros—came out of Asia to enrich the new world, other animals like the camel originated in America and carried their wonderful capacities into Asia. And the intercontinental exchange which had the most remarkable consequences also moved westward across the bridge and into Asia.

One morning as Mastodon browsed among cottonwood trees near the edge of a swamp in central Alaska, he saw approaching from the south a line of animals much smaller than he had ever seen before. Like him, they walked on four feet; but unlike him, they had no tusks, no heavy covering of hair, no massive head or ponderous feet. They were sleek creatures, swift of movement, alert of eye, and he watched with ordinary animal interest and inspection as they approached. Not a single gesture, not one movement gave him any indication that they might be dangerous, so he allowed them to come near, stop, stare at him, and pass on.

They were horses, the new world's beautiful gift to the old, and they were on their wandering way into Asia, from where their descendants, thousands of years later, would fan out miraculously to all parts of Europe. How exquisite they were that morning as they passed Mastodon, pressing their way into the heartland of Alaska, where they would find a halting place on their long pilgrimage.

Nowhere else could the subtle relationships of nature be so intimately observed. Ice high, oceans low. Bridge open, passageway closed. The ponderous mastodon lumbering toward North America, the delicate horse moving toward Asia. Mastodon lurching toward inescapable extinction. The horse galloping to an enlarged life in France and Arabia. Alaska, its extremities girt in ice, served as a way station for all the travelers, regardless of the direction in which they headed. Its broad valleys free of ice and its invigorating climate provided a hospitable resting place. It really was an ice castle, and life within its frozen walls could be pleasant though demanding.

How sad it is to realize that most of these imposing animals we have been watching—as they lingered in Alaska during the last ice age and its intervals of friendly climate—passed into extinction, usually before the appearance of man. The great mastodons vanished, the fierce saber-tooth cats disappeared in mists that enclosed the bogs at whose edges they hunted. The rhinoceros flourished for a while, but then waddled slowly into oblivion. The lions could find no permanent niche in North America, and even the camel failed to flourish in the land of its origin. How much more enchanting North America would be if we had retained these great beasts to enliven the landscape, but it was not fated to be. They rested in Alaska for a while, then marched unknowingly to their doom.

Some of the immigrants did adjust, and their continued presence has made our land a livelier place: the beaver, the caribou, the stately moose, the bison and the sheep. But there was another splendid animal who crossed the bridge from Asia, and it survived long enough to coexist with man. It had a fighting chance to escape extinction, and the manner in which it fought that battle is an epic of the animal kingdom.

The woolly mammoth came out of Asia much later than the mastodon and somewhat later than the animals of which we have been speaking. It arrived at a time of sharp transition when a relatively mild interval was ending and a harsher one beginning, but it adjusted so easily to its new environment that it thrived and multiplied, becoming one of the most successful examples of immigration and the archetypal Alaskan animal of this distant period.

Its remote ancestors had lived in tropical Africa, elephants of enormous size with long tusks and huge ears which they flapped constantly, using them as fans to keep their body temperature down. In Africa they browsed on low trees and pulled grass with their prehensile trunks. Admirably constructed for life in a tropical setting, they were magnificent beasts.

When such elephants moved slowly north they gradually converted themselves into creatures almost ideally suited to life in the high arctic zones. For example, their huge ears diminished in size to about one-twelfth of what they had been in the tropics, for now the animals did not require "fanning" to enable them to live in great heat; they needed minimum exposure to the arctic winds that drained away their heat.

They also rid themselves of the smooth skin which had helped them keep cool in Africa, developing instead a thick covering of hair whose individual strands could be as long as forty inches; when they had been in the colder climates for several thousand years, they were so covered with this hair that they looked like unkempt walking blankets.

But not even that was enough to protect them from the icy blasts of winter Alaska—and remember that during the time we are now considering, the incursion of ice was at its maximum—so the mammoth, already covered with thick, protective hair, developed an invisible undergrowth of thick wool which augmented the hair so effectively that the mammoth could withstand incredibly low temperatures.

Internally also the mammoth changed. Its stomach adjusted to the different food supply of Beringia, the low, tough grasses, wonderfully nutritious when compared to the huge loose leafage of the African trees. Its bones grew smaller, so that the average mammoth, markedly smaller than the elephant, would expose less of its body to the cold. Its forequarters became much heavier than its hind and more elevated, so that it began to show a profile less like an elephant and more like a hyena: high in front, tapering off at the back.

In some ways the most dramatic change, but not the most functional, was what happened to its tusks. In Africa they had grown out of its upper jaw in roughly parallel form, curved downward, then moved straight ahead. They were formidable weapons and were so used when males contested for the right to keep females in their group. They were also useful in bending branches lower for browsing.

In arctic lands the tusks of the mammoth underwent spectacular change. For one thing, they became much larger than those of the African elephant, for in some cases they measured more than twelve feet. But what made them distinctive was that after starting straight forward and down, like the elephant's, they suddenly swept outward, far from the body, and down in a handsome sweep. Had they continued in this direction, they would have been enormous and powerful weapons for attack or defense, but just as this seemed to be their purpose, they arbitrarily swung back toward the central axis, until at last their tips met and sometimes actually crossed, far in front of the mammoth's face.

In this bizarre condition they served no constructive purpose; indeed, they hampered feeding in summer, but in winter they did have a minimal utility, for they could be used to sweep away snowdrifts so that mosses and lichens hiding below could be exposed for eating. Other animals, the bison for example, achieved the same result by merely pushing their big heads into the snow and swinging them from side to side.

Protected against the bitter cold of winter, adjusted to the plentiful forage of summer, the mammoth proliferated and dominated the landscape long after the much larger mastodon had vanished. Like all other animals of the early period, the mastodon had been subject to attack by the ferocious saber-tooth, but with the gradual extinction of that killer, the mammoth's only enemies were the lions and wolves that tried to steal young calves. Of course, when a mammoth grew old and feeble, packs of wolves could successfully chivvy it to death, but that was of no consequence, for if death had not come in that form, it would have in some other.

Mammoths lived to fifty or sixty years, with an occasional tough customer surviving into its seventies, and to a marked degree it was the animal's nature of death that has accounted for its fame. On numerous occasions in Siberia, Alaska and Canada—so numerous that statistical studies can be made—mammoths of both sexes and all ages stumbled into boggy pits where they perished, or were overcome by sudden floods bearing gravel, or died at the banks of rivers into which their carcasses fell.

If these accidental deaths occurred in spring or summer, predators, especially ravens, quickly disposed of the cadavers, leaving behind only stripped bones and perhaps long strings of hair, which soon vanished. Accumulations of such bones and tusks have been found at various places and have proved helpful in reconstructing what we know about the mammoth.

But if the accidental death took place in late autumn or early winter, there was always the possibility that the body of the dead animal would be quickly covered with a heavy layer of sticky mud that would freeze when hard winter came. Thus the corpse would be preserved in what amounted to a deep-freeze, with decay impossible. Most often, one has to suppose, spring and summer would bring a thaw; the protective mud would lose its ice crystals; and the dead body would decompose. Disintegration of the corpse would proceed as always, except that the freezing would have postponed it for a season.

However, on rare occasions, which could become quite numerous over a time span of a hundred thousand years, that first immediate freezing would for some reason or other become permanent, and now the dead body would be preserved intact for a thousand years, or thirty thousand, or fifty. And then, on some day far distant when humans ranged the valleys of central Alaska, some inquisitive man would see emerging from a thawing bank an object that was neither bone nor preserved wood, and when he dug into the bank he would find himself facing the total remains of a woolly mammoth that had perished in that bank thousands of years ago.

When the accumulation of viscous mud was carefully cleaned away, a remarkable object would be revealed, something unique in the world: a whole mammoth, long hair in place, great tusks twisting forward and meeting at the tips, stomach contents in the condition they were when it last grazed, massive teeth in such perfect condition that its age at death could be accurately calculated within five or six years. It was not, of course, a standing animal, plump and clean within a case of blue ice; it was flat, plastered with mud, disgracefully dirty, with leg joints beginning to come apart, but it was a complete mammoth, and it revealed to its discoverers a volume of information.

This next point is important. We know about the great dinosaurs who preceded the mammoth by millions of years because their bones have over the millennia been invaded by mineral deposits which have preserved the most intimate structure of the bone. What we have are not real bones, but petrified ones, like petrified wood, in which not an atom of the original material remains. Until a recent find in far northern Alaska, no human being had ever seen the bone of a dinosaur, but everyone could see in museums the magically preserved petrifications of those bones, photographs in stone of bones long since vanished.

But with the mammoths preserved by freezing in Siberia and Alaska, we have the actual bones, the hair, the heart, the stomach, and a treasury of knowledge that is incomparable. The first of these icy finds seems to have occurred by accident in Siberia sometime in the 1700s, and others have followed at regular intervals thereafter. A remarkably complete mammoth was uncovered near Fairbanks in Alaska not long ago, and we can anticipate others before the end of the century.

Why has it been the mammoth who has been found in this complete form? Other animals have occasionally been uncovered, but not many and rarely in the excellent condition of the best mammoths. One reason was the substantial numbers of the breed. Another was that the mammoth tended to live in those peculiar areas in which preservation by freezing mud was possible. Also, its bones and tusks were of a size to be noted; many birds must have perished in these areas in these times, but because they had no heavy bones, their skeletons did not survive to keep their skin and feathers in position. Most important, this particular group of mammoths died during a time of glaciation when instant freezing was not only possible but likely.

At any rate, the woolly mammoth served a unique function, one of inestimable value to human beings; by freezing quickly when it died, it lived on to instruct us as to what life was like in Alaska when the ice castle functioned as a refuge for great animals.

On a day in late winter, twenty-nine thousand years ago, Matriarch, a mammoth grandmother, forty-four years old and beginning to show her age, led the little herd of six for which she was responsible down a softly rolling meadow to the banks of a great river later to be known as the Yukon. Lifting her trunk high to sniff the warming air and signaling the others to follow, she entered a grove of willow shrubs that lined the river, and when the others had taken their places beside her, she indicated that they might begin feeding on the sprouting tips of willow branches. They did so with a great deal of noise and movement, for they were glad to escape the meager rations they had been forced to subsist on during the recent winter, and as they gorged, Matriarch gave grunts of encouragement.

She had in her herd two daughters, each of whom had two offspring, heifer and bull to the elder, bull and heifer to the younger. Severe discipline on these six was enforced by Matriarch, for the mammoths had learned that the survival of their species did not depend very much on the great males with their tremendous showy tusks; the males appeared only in midsummer for the mating period; the rest of the year they were nowhere to be seen, so they took no responsibility for rearing and educating the young.

In obedience to the instincts of her race, and to the specific impulses which stemmed from her being female, she devoted her entire life to her herd, especially to the young. She weighed, at this time, about three thousand pounds, and to keep alive she required each day some hundred and sixty pounds of grass, lichen, moss and twigs, and when she lacked this ample supply of food she experienced pangs of biting hunger, for what she ate contained only minimum nourishment and passed completely through her body in less than twelve hours; she did not gorge and then ruminate like other animals, chewing her cud until every shred of value was extracted from it. No, she crammed herself with vast amounts of low-quality food and quickly rid herself of its remains. Eating had to be her main preoccupation.

Nevertheless, if in her constant foraging she caught even a hint that her four grandchildren were not getting their share, she would forgo her own feeding and see to it that they ate first. And she would do the same for young mammoths who were not of her own family but under her care for the moment while their own mothers and grandmothers foraged elsewhere. Even though her stomach contracted in emptiness and pain—with warning signals shouting "Eat or perish!"—she would first attend to her young, and only when they had been provided with grass and twigs would she browse the birch tips and harvest the good grasses with her noble trunk.

This characteristic, which separated her from the other mammoth grandmothers, had developed because of her monomaniacal affection for her children. Years ago, before her youngest daughter had borne her first offspring, a once-prepotent older bull joined her herd during the mating season, and for some inexplicable reason, when the mating was completed, he remained with the herd when normally he should have left to join the other bulls who foraged by themselves until the next mating season came around.

Although Matriarch had made no objection when this old bull first appeared on the scene to care for her daughters—three at that time—she grew restless when he stayed beyond his welcome period, and by various ways, such as nudging him away from the better grass, she indicated that he must leave the females and their children. When he refused to comply, she grew actively angry, but she could do nothing more than show her feelings, because he weighed half again as much as she, his tusks were enormous, and he was so much taller that he simply overwhelmed her in both size and aggressiveness. So she had to be content with making noises and venting her displeasure by rapidly thrashing her trunk about.

But one day as she was eying this old fellow, she saw him roughly shove aside a young mother who was instructing her yearling daughter, and this would have been acceptable, for bulls traditionally commandeered the better feeding grounds, but on this occasion it looked to Matriarch as if the bull had also abused the yearling, and this she could not tolerate. With a high, piercing scream she lunged right at the intruder, disregarding his superior size and fighting ability—for he could not have bred Matriarch's daughters håd he not been able to fend off other less able bulls who had also wished to do so—and she was so intent on protecting her young, that she drove the much bigger animal back several paces.

But he, with his greater strength and immense crossing tusks, quickly asserted his authority, and in a punishing counterattack, slashed at her with such great force that he broke her right tusk at about the halfway mark. For the rest of her life she would be an aging mammoth cow with a tusk and a half. Unbalanced, awkward-looking when compared to her sisters, she moved across the steppe with the short, jagged tusk, and the loss of its balancing weight caused her to compensate by tilting her massive head slightly to the right, as if she were peeking with her squinty little eyes at something that others could not see.

She had never been a lovely creature or even a graceful one. She did not have the impressive lines of her elephant forebears, for she was a kind of lumbering triangle, apex at the top of her high-domed head, base along the ground where her feet hit, a vertical coming down in front of her face and trunk, and most distinctive, a long, sloping, ugly drop from high forequarters to a dwarfed rear end. And then, as if to make her appearance almost formless, her entire body was covered with long and sometimes matted hair. If she was a walking triangle, she was also an ambulating shaggy rug, and even the dignity that could have come from her big, graceful tusks was lost because of the broken right one.

True, she lacked grace, but her passionate love for any younger mammoth who fell under her protection endowed her with a nobility of manner, and this huge and awkward creature lent honor to the concept of animal motherhood.

She had at her disposal in these years when the ice age was at its maximum a somewhat more hospitable terrain on which to feed her family than the harsher one the mastodons had known. It was still a four-part terrain: arctic desert at the north, perpetually frozen tundra, steppe rich with grasses, strip with enough trees to be called a woodland or even a forest. However, it was the steppe that had grown in size, until its mixture of edible grasses and nutritious willow shrubs provided ample forage for the mammoths who roamed it.

Indeed, the expanded area proved so hospitable to these huge, lumbering creatures that later scientists who would try to reconstruct what life in Alaska was like twenty-eight thousand years before would give the terrain the descriptive name "the Mammoth Steppe," and no better could be devised, for this was the great, brooding steppe, trapped within the ice castle, which enabled the slope-backed mammoths to exist in large numbers. In these centuries it looked as if the mammoths, along with the caribou and antelope, would always be the major occupiers of the steppe named after them.

Matriarch moved about the steppe as if it had been created for her use alone. It was hers, but she conceded that for a few weeks each summer she required the assistance of the great bulls who otherwise kept to themselves on their own feeding grounds. But after the birth of the young she knew that the survival of the mammoths depended upon her, so it was she who chose the feeding grounds and gave the signal when her family must abandon grounds about to be depleted in a search for others more rich in foodstuffs.

A small herd of mammoths like the one she commanded might wander, in the course of a year, over more than four hundred miles, so she came to know large parts of the steppe, and in the pilgrimages she supervised she became familiar with two perplexities, which she never solved but to which she did accommodate. The richer parts of this steppe provided a variety of edible trees whose ancestors the vanished mastodons might have known—larch, low willow, birch, alder—but recently, in a few choice spots protected from gales and where water was available, a new kind of tree had made its tentative appearance, beautiful to see but poisonous to eat. It was especially tempting because it never lost its leaves, long needlelike affairs, but even in winter when the mammoths had little to eat they avoided it, because if they did eat the attractive needles they fell sick and sometimes died.

It was the largest of the trees, a spruce, and its distinctive aroma both attracted and repelled the mammoths. Matriarch was bewildered by the spruce, for although she dared not eat its needles, she noticed that the porcupines who shared these forests with her devoured the poisonous leaves with relish, and she often wondered why. What she did not notice was that while it was true that the porcupines did eat the needles, they climbed high in the trees before doing so. The spruce, just as clever in protecting itself as the animals that surrounded it, had devised a sagacious defensive strategy. In its copious lower branches, which a voracious mammoth could have destroyed in a morning, the spruce concentrated a volatile oil which rendered its leaves unpalatable. This meant that the high upper branches, which the mammoths could not reach even with their long trunks, remained palatable.

In the few places where the spruce trees did thrive, they figured in the second riddle. From time to time during the long summers when the air was heavy and the grasses and low shrubs tinder-dry, a flash would appear in the heavens followed by a tremendous crashing sound, as if a thousand trees had fallen in one instant, and often thereafter fire would start in the grass, mysteriously, for no reason at all. Or some very tall spruce would be riven, as if a giant tusk had ripped it, and from its bark a wisp of smoke would issue, and then a little flame, and before long the entire forest would be ablaze and all the grassy steppe would erupt into flame.

At such moments, and Matriarch had survived six such fires, the mammoths had learned to head for the nearest river and submerge themselves to their eye-level, keeping their trunks above the water for air. For this reason lead animals, like Matriarch with her brood, tried always to know where the nearest water stood, and when fire exploded across their steppe they retreated to this refuge, for they had learned that if the fire ever completely surrounded them, escape would be improbable. Over the centuries a few daring bulls had broken through the fatal rim, and it was their experience which had taught the mammoths their strategy for survival.

Late one summer, when the land was especially dry, and darts of light and crashing sounds filled the air, Matriarch saw that fire had already started near a large stand of spruce trees, and she knew that before long the trees would burst forth in tremendous gusts of flame, trapping all living things, so with speed and force she herded her charges back to where she knew a river waited, but the fire spread so swiftly that it engulfed the trees before she could rush clear of them. Overhead she heard the oils in the trees explode, sending sparks down into the dry needles below. Soon both the crowns of the trees and the needled carpet below were aflame, and the mammoths faced death.

In this extremity, with acrid smoke tormenting her, Matriarch had to decide whether to lead her herd back out from among the trees or straight ahead toward the waiting river, and it could not be claimed that she reasoned: If I do turn back, the grass fire will soon entrap us. But she did make the right decision. Bellowing so that all could hear, she headed right for a wall of flame, broke through and found a clear path to the river, where her companions plunged into the saving water while the forest fire raged around them.

But now came the perplexing part, because Matriarch had learned that terrifying though the fire had been, she must not abandon this ravaged area, for fire was one of the best friends the mammoths had and she must now teach her young how to capitalize upon it. As soon as the actual flames abated—and they would consume several hundred square miles before they died completely—she led her charges back to the spot at which they had nearly lost their lives, and there she taught them how to use their tusks in stripping lengths of bark from the burned spruce trees. Now, purified by the fire which had driven off noxious oils, the spruce was not only edible but a positive delicacy, and the hungry mammoths gorged upon it. The bark had been toasted specifically for them.

When the fire was totally dead in all parts, Matriarch kept her herd close to the burned-over areas, for the mammoths had learned that rather quickly after such a conflagration, the roots of tenacious plants whose visible growth had been burned off sped the production of new shoots, thousands of them, and these were the finest food the mammoths ever found. What was even more important, ashes from the great fires fertilized the ground, making it more nutritious and more friable, so that young trees would grow with a vigor they would otherwise not have known. One of the best things that could happen to the Mammoth Steppe, with its mixture of trees and grass, was to have a periodic fire of great dimension, for in its aftermath, grasses, shrubs, trees and animals prospered.

It was puzzling that something as dangerous as fire, which Matriarch had barely escaped many times, should be the agency whereby she and her successors would grow strong. She did not try to solve this riddle; she protected herself from the dangers and luxuriated in the rewards.

In these years some mammoths elected to return to the Asia they had known in their early years, but Matriarch had no inclination to join them. The Alaska which she now knew so well was a congenial place which she had made her own. To leave would be unthinkable.

But in her fiftieth year changes began to occur which sent tremors, vague intimations, to her minute brain, and instinct warned her that these changes were not only irreversible, but also a caution that the time might be approaching when she would feel driven to wander off, leaving her family behind, as she sought some quiet place in which to die. She had, of course, no sense of death, no comprehension that life ended, no premonition that she must one day abandon her family and the steppes on which she found such ease. But mammoths did die, and in doing so they followed an ancient ritual which commanded them to move apart, as if by this symbolism they turned over to their successors the familiar steppe, and its rivers, and its willow trees.

What had happened to signal this new awareness? Like other mammoths, Matriarch had been supplied at birth with a complex dental system which would provide her, over the long span of her life, with twelve enormous flat composite teeth in each jaw. These twenty-four monstrous teeth did not appear in a mammoth's mouth all at one time, but this posed no difficulty; each tooth was so large that even one pair was adequate for chewing. At times as many as three pairs of these huge things might exist, and then chewing capacity was immense. But it did not remain this way for long, because as the years passed, each tooth moved irresistibly forward in the jaw, until it actually fell from the mouth, and when only the last two matching teeth remained in position, the mammoth sensed its days were numbered, because when the last pair began to disintegrate, continued life on the steppe would be impossible.

Matriarch now had four big matching pairs, but since she could feel them moving forward, she was aware that her time was limited.

When the mating season began, bulls from far distances started to arrive, but the old bull who had broken Matriarch's right tusk was still so powerful a fighter that he succeeded, as in past years, to defend his claim on her daughters. He had not, of course, returned to this family year after year, but on various occasions he had come back, more to a familiar area than to a particular group of females.

This year his courtship of Matriarch's daughters was a perfunctory affair, but his effect upon the older child of the younger daughter, a sturdy young bull but not yet mature enough, to strike out on his own, was remarkable, for the young fellow, watching the robust performance of the old bull, felt vague stirrings. One morning, when the old bull was attending to a young female not of Matriarch's family, this young bull unexpectedly, and without any premeditation, made a lunge for her, whereupon the old bull fell into a tantrum and chastised the young upstart unmercifully, butting and slamming him with those extremely long horns that crossed at the tips.

Matriarch, seeing this and not entirely aware of what had occasioned the outburst, dashed once again at the old bull, but this time he repelled her easily, knocking her aside so that he could continue his courtship of the strange heifer. In time he left the herd, his duty done, and disappeared as always into the low hills footing the glacier. He would be seen no more for ten months, but he left behind not only six pregnant cows but also a very perplexed young bull, who within the year should be doing his own courting. However, long before this could take place, the young bull wandered into a stand of aspen trees near the great river, where one of the last saber-tooth cats to survive in Alaska waited in the crotch of a larch tree, and when the bull came within reach, the cat leaped down upon him, sinking those dreadful scimitar teeth deep into his neck.

The bull had no chance to defend himself; this first strike was mortal, but in his death agony he did release one powerful bellow that echoed across the steppe. Matriarch heard it, and although she knew the young bull to be of an age when he should be leaving the family, he was still under her care, and without hesitating, she galloped as fast as her awkward hair-covered body would permit, speeding directly toward the saber-tooth, who was crouching over its dead prey.

When she spotted it she knew instinctively that it was the most dangerous enemy on this steppe, and she knew it had the power to kill her, but her fury was so great that any thought of caution was submerged. One of the young mammoths for whom she was responsible had been attacked, and she knew but one response: to destroy the attacker if possible, and if not, to give her life in an attempt. So with a trumpeting cry of rage she rushed in her clumsy way at the saber-tooth, who easily evaded her. But to its surprise she wheeled about with such frenzied determination that it had to leave the corpse on which it was about to feed, and as it did so it found itself backed against the trunk of a sturdy larch. Matriarch, seeing the cat in this position, threw her entire weight forward, endeavoring to pin it with her tusks or otherwise impede it.

Now the broken right tusk, big and blunt, proved an asset rather than a liability, for with it she did not merely puncture the saber-tooth, she crushed it against the tree, and as she felt her heavy tusk dig into its rib cage, she bore ahead, unmindful of what the fierce cat might do to her.

The stump had injured the saber-tooth, but despite its broken left ribs it retained control and darted away lest she strike again. But before the cat could muster its resources for a counterattack, she used her unbroken left tusk to batter it into the dust at the foot of the tree. Then, with a speed it could not anticipate or avoid, she raised her immense foot and stomped upon its chest.

Again and again, trumpeting the while, she beat down upon the mighty cat, collapsing its other ribs and even breaking off one of the long, splendid saber-teeth. Seeing blood spurting from one of its wounds, she became wild with fury, her shrieks increasing when she saw the inert body of her grandson, the young bull, lying in the grass.

Continuing in her mad stomping, she crushed the saber-tooth, and when her rage was assuaged she remained, whimpering, between the two dead bodies.

As in the case of her own destiny, she was not completely aware of what death was, but the entire elephant clan and its derivatives were perplexed by death, especially when it struck down a fellow creature with whom the mourner had been associated. The young bull was dead, of that there could be no doubt, and in some vague way she realized that his wonderful potential was lost. He would not come courting in the summer ahead; he would fight no aging bulls to establish his authority; and he would sire no successors with the aid of Matriarch's daughters and granddaughters. A chain was broken, and for more than a day she stood guard over his body, as if she hoped to bring it back to life. But at the close of the second day she left the bodies, unaware that in all that time she had not once looked at the saber-tooth. It was her grandson who mattered, and he was dead.

Because his death occurred in late summer, with decomposition setting in immediately and with ravens and predators attacking the corpse, it was not fated that his body be frozen in mud for the edification of scientists scores of thousands of years later, but there was another death that occurred during the last days of autumn which had quite different consequences.

The old bull that had broken Matriarch's tusk, and had been a prime factor in the death of the young bull, strode away from the affair looking as if he had the strength to survive for many mating seasons to come. But the demands of this one had been heavy. He had run with more cows than usual and had been called upon to defend them against four or five lusty younger bulls who felt that their time to assume control had come. For an entire summer he had lusted and fought and eaten little, and now in late autumn his vital resources began to flag.

It began with dizziness as he climbed a bank leading up from the great river. He had made such treks repeatedly, but this time he faltered and almost fell against the muddy bank that impeded his progress. Then he lost the first of his remaining four teeth, and he was aware that two of the others were weakening. Even more serious was his indifference to the approaching winter, for normally he would have begun to eat extravagantly in order to build his reserves of fat against the cold days when snow fell. To ignore this imperative call of

"Feed thyself, for blizzards are at hand!" was to endanger his life, but that is what he did.

On the day of the first snowfall, a whipping wind blowing in from Asia and icicles of snow falling parallel to the earth, Matriarch and her five family members saw the old bull far in the distance, at what would later be known as the Birch Tree Site, his head lowered, his massive tusks resting on the ground, but they ignored him. Nor were they concerned about his safety; that was his problem and they knew he had many options from which to choose.

But when they saw him again, some days later, not moving toward a refuge or to a feeding ground, just standing there immobile, Matriarch, always the caring mother, started to move toward him to see if he was able to fend for himself. However, when he saw her intruding upon his satisfactory loneliness, he withdrew to protect it, not hurriedly, as he might have done in the old days, but laboriously, making sounds of protest at her presence. She did not force herself upon him, for she knew that old bulls like him preferred to be left alone, and she last saw him heading back toward the river.

Two days later, when thick snow was falling and Matriarch started edging her family toward the alder thickets in which they customarily took shelter during the long winters, her youngest granddaughter, an inquisitive animal, was off by herself exploring the banks of the river when she saw that the same bull who had spent much of the summer with them had fallen into a muddy crevice and was thrashing about, unable to extricate himself. Trumpeting a call for help, she alerted the others, and before long Matriarch, her daughters and her grandchildren were streaming toward the site of the accident.

When they arrived, the position of the old bull was so hopeless, mired as he was in sticky mud, that Matriarch and her assistants were powerless to aid him. And as both the snow and the cold increased, they had to watch helplessly as the tired mammoth struggled vainly, trumpeting for aid and succumbing finally to the irresistible pull of the mud and the freezing cold. Before nightfall he was tightly frozen into his muddy grave, only the top of his bulbous head showing, and by morning that too was buried under snow. There he would remain, miraculously upright for the next twenty-eight thousand years, the spiritual guardian of the Birch Tree Site.

• • •

Matriarch, obedient to impulses that had always animated the mammoth breed, remained by his grave for two days, but then, still puzzled by the fact of death, she forgot him completely, rejoined her family, and led them to one of the best spots in central Alaska for passing a long winter. It was an enclave at the western end of the valley which was fed by two streams, a small one that froze quickly and a much larger one that carried free water most of the winter. Here, protected from even the worst winds, she and her daughters and grandchildren remained motionless much of the time, conserving body warmth and slowing digestion of such food as they could find.

Now once more her broken tusk proved useful, for its rough, blunt end was effective in ripping the bark from birch trees whose leaves had long vanished, and it was also helpful in brushing away snow to reveal the grasses and herbs hiding below. She was not aware that she was trapped in a vast ice castle, for she had no desire to move either eastward into what would one day be Canada or southward to California. Her icy prison was enormous in size and she felt in no way penned in, but when the frozen ground began to thaw and the willows sent forth tentative shoots, she did become aware—how she could not have explained—that some great change had overtaken the refuge areas which she had for so many years dominated. Perhaps it was her acute sense of smell, or sounds never heard before, but regardless of how the message reached her, she knew that life on the Mammoth Steppe had been altered, and not for the better.

Her awareness intensified when she lost one of her remaining teeth, and then one evening as she wandered westward with her family, she came upon a sight that confused her weak eyes. On the banks of the river she had been following stood a structure like none she had ever seen before. It was like a bird's nest on the ground, but hugely bigger. From it came animals who walked on only two legs; they were like water birds that prowled the shore, but much larger, and now one of them, seeing the mammoths, began to make noises. Others poured from the immense nest, and she could see that her presence was causing great excitement, for they made unfamiliar sounds.

Then some of the creatures, much smaller than herself or even the youngest of her grandchildren, began running toward her, and the speed with which they moved alerted her to the fact that she and her herd were about to face some kind of new danger. Instinctively she began to edge away, then to move rapidly, and finally to trumpet wildly as she started running.

But very quickly she found that she was not free to move as she wished, for no matter where she tried to go with her charges, one of the creatures appeared in the shadows to prevent her from escaping. And when day dawned, confusion intensified, for wherever Matriarch sought to take her family, these beings kept pace, persistently, like wolves tracking a wounded caribou. They would not stop, and when that first night fell they added to the terror by causing a fire to spring from the tundra, and this created panic among the mammoths, for they expected the dried grass of the previous summer to burst into uncontrollable flame, but this did not happen. Matriarch, looking at her children in perplexity, was not able to form the idea: They have fire but it is not fire, but she felt the bewilderment that such an idea would have evoked.

On the next day the strange new things continued to pursue Matriarch and her mammoths, and when the animals were exhausted, the newcomers finally isolated Matriarch's youngest granddaughter. Once the young animal was cut off, the pursuers closed in upon her, carrying in their front legs, the ones they did not use for walking, branches of trees with stones attached, and with these they began to beat the encircled mammoth and stab at her and torment her until she bellowed for help.

Matriarch, who had outrun her children, heard the cry and doubled back, but when she tried to aid her granddaughter, some of these creatures detached themselves from the larger group and beat her about the head with their branches until she had to withdraw. But now the cries of her granddaughter became so pitiful that Matriarch trembled with rage, and with a mighty bellow, dashed right through the attackers, and without stopping, lumbered to where the threatened mammoth was striving to defend herself. With a great roar, Matriarch flung herself upon the creatures, lashing at them with her broken tusk and driving them back.

Triumphant, she was about to lead her frightened granddaughter to safety when one of the strange beings shouted the sound "Varnak!" and another, a little taller than the others and heavier, leaped toward the threatened mammoth, allowed himself to fall beneath her dangerous feet, and with an upward stab of whatever he was carrying, drove a sharp weapon deep into her bowels.

Matriarch saw that her granddaughter was not fatally wounded, but as the mammoths thundered off, seeking respite from their tormentors, it was obvious that the young one was not going to be able to keep up. So the herd slowed, and Matriarch assisted her granddaughter, and in this way the huge beasts made their escape.

But to their dismay, the little figures on two legs kept pace, coming closer and closer, and on the third day, at an unguarded moment when Matriarch was directing the others to safety, the creatures surrounded the wounded granddaughter. Intending to crush these intruders once and for all, Matriarch started back to defend her grandchild, but as she strove to reach the attackers and punish them with her broken tusk, as she had done with the saber-tooth, one of them, armed only with a long piece of wood and a short one with fire at one end, stepped boldly out from among the trees and drove her back. The long piece of wood she could resist even though it had sharp stones on the end, but the fire, thrust right into her face, she could not. Try as she might, she could not avoid that burning ember. Impotently she had to stand back, smoke and fire in her eyes, as her granddaughter was slain.

With loud shouts, much like the triumphant howling of wolves when they finally brought down their wounded prey, the creatures danced and leaped about the fallen mammoth and began to cut her up.

From a distance that night, Matriarch and her remaining children saw once again the fire that mysteriously flamed without engulfing the steppe, and in this confusing, tragic way the mammoths who had for so long been safe within their ice castle encountered man.

III

PEOPLE OF
THE NORTH

S OME TWENTY-NINE THOUSAND YEARS B.P.E.—BEFORE THE Present Era, which means before the reference year A.D. 1950, when carbon dating became established as a reliable system for dating prehistoric events—in that eastern projection of Asia which would later be known as Siberia, famine was rampant, and it struck nowhere with more ferocity than in a mud hut that faced the sunrise. There, in one big room excavated a few feet below the level of the surrounding earth, a family of five faced the coming winter with only a small store of food and little hope of finding more.

Their house provided no comfort except a slight protection from the howling winds of winter, which blew almost constantly through the half of the structure which rose aboveground and was formed of loosely woven branches plastered with mud. This hovel was no more than a cave-hut, but it did provide one essential: in the middle of the floor there was a place for fire, and here half-wet logs gave off the smoke which lent flavor to what they ate and endless irritation to their eyes.

The five people huddling in this miserable abode as autumn ended were headed by a resolute man named Varnak, one of the ablest hunters in the village of Nurik, who had as wife the woman Tevuk, twenty-four years old and the mother of two sons who would soon be able to join their father in his chase for animals whose meat would feed the family. But this year animals had grown so scarce that in some cave-huts the younger people were beginning to whisper: "Perhaps there will be food only for the young ones, and it will be time for the old ones to go."

Varnak and Tevuk would hear none of this, for although they had a very old woman to care for, she was so precious to them that they would starve themselves rather than deprive her. She was known as the Ancient One, Varnak's mother, and he was determined to help her live out her life because she was the wisest person in the village, the only one who could remind the young of their heroic heritage. "Others say 'Let the old ones die,'" he whispered to his wife one night, "but I have no mind to do so."

"Nor I," Tevuk replied, and since she had no mother or aunts of her own, she knew that what her husband was saying applied only to his own mother, but she was prepared to stand by this resolute old woman for as long as life remained. This would be difficult, for the Ancient One was not easy to placate and the burden of tending her would fall almost solely on Tevuk, but the bond of debt between the two women was great and indissoluble.

When Varnak had been a young man, searching about for a wife, he fastened his attention upon a young woman of rare attractiveness, one who was courted by various men, but his mother, a woman who had lost her husband early in a hunting accident while chasing the woolly mammoth, saw clearly that her son would come to harm if he tied himself to that woman, and she launched a campaign to make him appreciate how much better his life would be if he allied himself with Tevuk, a somewhat older woman of common sense and unusual capacity for work.

Varnak, captivated by the younger, had resisted his mother's counsel and was about to take the seductive one, when the Ancient One barred the exit from their hut and would not allow her son to leave for three days until she was assured that some other man had captured the enchantress: "She weaves a spell, Varnak. I saw her gathering moss and searching for antlers to pulverize. I'm protecting you from her."

He was disconsolate at losing the wonderful one, and it was some time before he was prepared to listen to his mother, but when his anger subsided he was able to look at Tevuk with clear eyes and he saw that his mother was right. Tevuk was going to be as helpful when an old woman of forty as she was now: "She's the kind who grows stronger with the seasons, Varnak. Like me." And Varnak had discovered this to be true.

Now, in this difficult time when there was almost no food in the cave-hut, Varnak became doubly appreciative of his two good women, for his wife searched the land for the merest scrap for their two sons, while his mother gathered not only her grandsons but also the other children of the village to take their minds off hunger by telling them of the heroic traditions of their tribe: "In the long ago our people lived in the south where there were many trees and animals of all kinds to eat. Do you know what south means?"

"No." And in freezing darkness as winter clamped down she told them: "It's warm, my grandmother told me. And it has no endless winter."

"Why did those people come to this land?"

This was a problem which had always perplexed the Ancient One, and she dealt with it according to her vague understandings: "There are strong people and weak. My son Varnak is very strong, you know that. And so is Toorak, the man who killed the great bison. But when our people lived in the south, they were not strong, and others drove us out of those good lands. And when we moved north to lands not so good, they drove us out of there, too. One summer we came here, and it was beautiful, and everyone danced, my grandmother said. But then what happened?"

She asked this of a girl eleven seasons old, who said: "Then winter came," and the old one said: "Yes, winter came."

She was surprisingly correct in her summary of the clan's history, and of mankind's. Human life had originated in hot, steaming climates where it was easy to survive, but as soon as sufficient people were assembled to make competition for living space inevitable—say after a million years—the abler groups started to edge northward toward the more temperate zone, and in this more equable climate they began to invent those agencies of control, such as seasonal agriculture and the husbandry of animals, which would make superior forms of civilization possible.

And then once more, in the time of the Ancient One's great-great-great-grandmother, or even further back, competition for favorable sites recurred, but now it was the less able who were forced to move on, leaving the most fit to hold on to the temperate zones. This meant that in the Northern Hemisphere the subarctic areas began to be filled with people who had been evicted from the more congenial climates. Always the pressure came from the warmer lands to the south, and always it ended with people along the edges being forced to live on cold and arid lands which could barely support them.

But there was another interpretation of this movement to the north, and the Ancient One related it proudly to her children: "There were brave men and women who loved cold lands and the hunt for mammoths and caribou. They liked the endless days of summer and were not afraid of winter nights like this." Looking at each of her listeners, she tried to instill in them a pride in their ancestors: "My son is a brave man like that and so is Toorak, who killed the bison, and so must you be when you grow up and go out to fight the mammoths."

The old woman was right about many of the men who came north. They thrilled to their contests with whale and walrus. They were eager to do battle with the white polar bear and the woolly mammoth. They fought the seal for his fur so that they might survive the arctic winters, and they mastered the secrets of ice and snow and sudden blizzards. They devised ways of combating the ferocious mosquitoes that attacked in sun-darkening hordes each spring, and they taught their sons how to track animals for fur and food so that life could continue after they were dead. "These are the true people of the north," the old woman said, and she might have added that a hardier breed never existed on this earth.

"I want you to be like them," she concluded, and one of the girls began to whimper: "I'm hungry," and the Ancient One took from the sealskin tunic she wore in winter a piece of dried seal blubber and apportioned it among the children, retaining none for herself.

One day at the turning of the seasons, when there was practically no daylight in the village, the old woman almost lost courage, for one of the children who had gathered in the dark hut to hear her tales asked: "Why don't we go back to the south, where there's food?" and in honesty she had to reply: "The old people often asked that question, and sometimes they pretended to themselves and said: 'Yes, next year we will go back,' but they never meant it. We cannot go back. You cannot go back. You are now people of the north."

She never considered her life in the north a penalty, nor would she allow her son or her grandchildren to think of it in that way, but as the hellish days of winter closed down—when days lengthened but cold increased and ice grew thicker—she would wait till the children were asleep, and then whisper to her hungry son and his wife: "Another winter like this and we will all die," for even now they existed by chewing sealskin, which provided them little energy.

"Where will we go?" her son asked, and she said: "My father spent four days chasing a mammoth once. It led him east across the barren lands, and over there he saw fields of green."

"Why not go south?" Tevuk asked, and the old woman told her daughter-in-law: "The south never had a place for us. I'm finished with the south."

So in those tantalizing days of early spring when winter refused to stop tormenting these people at the western end of the land bridge, the fine hunter Varnak, seeing his family slowly dying of hunger, began asking about the land to the east, and he came upon a very old man who told him: "One morning when I was young and with nothing better to do, I wandered eastward, and when night came with the sun still high in the heavens, for it was summer, I felt no need to return home, so on and on I went for two more days, and on the third day I saw something which excited me."

"What?" Varnak asked, and the old man said, eyes aglimmer as if the incident had occurred three days ago: "The body of a dead mammoth." He allowed Varnak time to fathom the significance of this revelation, and when nothing was said, he explained: "If a mammoth saw reason to cross that bleak land, men would have a reason too," to which Varnak said: "Yes, but you said the mammoth died," and the man laughed: "True, but there was a reason for him to try. And you have just as good a reason. For if you remain here, you will starve."

"If I go, will you go with me?" and the man said: "I am too old. But you . . ." And that day Varnak informed the four members of his family: "When summer comes we shall go where the sun rises."

The route he would take had been available for the past two thousand years, and although some had used the bridge, they had not found it inviting. Across its six-hundred-mile width north to south harsh winds blew so constantly that no trees or even low shrubs had been able to establish themselves, while grasses and mosses were so sparse that big animals could not find forage. In winter the cold was so forbidding that even hares and rats stayed underground, and few men ventured upon the bridge, even in summer. Settled life upon it was unthinkable.

But it was by no means unpassable, since from west to east, the direction in which Varnak's people would be traveling if they attempted the crossing, the distance would be no more than sixty miles. Varnak, of course, did not know this; it could have been eight hundred miles, but all that he had heard of attempts to cross it led him to believe that it was shorter. "We'll leave when day and night are even," he informed his mother, and she approved of the plan so heartily that she spread the news throughout the village.

When it was known that Varnak was going to try to find food to the east, there was excited discussion in the cave-huts and several of the men concluded that they would be wise to accompany him. So as spring progressed, four or five families began to weigh seriously the possibility of emigrating, and in the end three came to Varnak with the firm promise: "We'll go too."

On that day in March which Varnak had selected, the one when day and night were equal in all parts of the earth, Varnak, Tevuk, their two sons and the Ancient One prepared to set forth, accompanied by three other hunters, their wives and their eight children.

When the nineteen gathered at the eastern edge of their village, they were formidable in appearance, since the men wore such massive pieces of fur clothing that they looked like hulking animals. They carried long pikes as if going to war, and their rumpled black hair drooped low above their eyes. Their skin was a dark yellow and their eyes a sparkling black, so that when they stared this way and that, as they often did, they seemed as predacious as eagles.

The five women had different styles of dress, featuring decorated skins with seashells along the hems, but their faces were surprisingly alike. Each was heavily tattooed with vertical blue stripes, some covering the chin, others running the length of the face beside the ears, which were pierced for rings carved from white ivory. When they moved, even the old woman, they did so with determined steps, and as the four sleds on which each family's goods would be carried were brought into position, it was these women who grasped the reins and prepared to do the hauling.

The ten children were like a collection of colorful flowers, for the clothes they wore were varied in design and color. Some wore short tunics with stripes of white and blue, others long robes and heavy boots, but all wore in their hair some ornament, some flashing bit of shell or ivory.

Any item of clothing was precious, for men had risked their lives to harvest the hides and women had toiled tanning them and preparing sinews for sewing. A pair of men's trousers stitched so carefully that they kept out cold and water would be expected to last most of an adult lifetime, and only a few men on this peninsula would ever own two such garments.

Most important, however, were the boots, some of which reached to the knee; each group of families had to have some woman skilled in making boots from heavy hides, or the male members of that group would freeze their feet when they hunted on ice. And this was another reason why Varnak wanted to keep his mother alive: she was the ablest maker of boots the village had known in two generations, for although her fingers were no longer nimble, they were strong and could still pull reindeer sinews through the thickest seal hide.

The men of this expedition were not tall. Varnak, the biggest, stood only five feet six, with the others noticeably shorter. None of the women was much over five feet, and the Ancient One was sharply under that mark. The children were small, the three babies tiny except for their big round heads, but when dressed in heavy clothing the young ones were balls of fur with insatiable appetites.

On small sleds with runners of antler and bone, the travelers dragged behind them the pitiful supply of artifacts their people had collected during ten thousand years of life in the arctic: ultraprecious bone needles, skins not yet sewn into clothing, shallow bowls carved from heavy wood or bone, long-handled cooking spoons of ivory; no furniture of any kind, but sleeping pads for everyone and fur blankets for each family.

But they did not leave Asia with only these meager physical possessions; in their heads they carried an extraordinary understanding of the north. Men and women alike knew hundreds of rules for surviving an arctic winter, scores of useful hints about finding food in summer. They knew the nature of wind and the movement of those stars which guided them in the long winter night. They had various tricks for protecting themselves from the mosquitoes, which would otherwise have driven them mad, and above all, they knew the traits of animals, and how to track them, kill them, and use even their hoofs when the slaughter was completed.

The Ancient One and the four young wives knew fifty different ways of utilizing a slain mammoth whenever their menfolk were lucky enough to bring one down, and at a killing the Ancient One was first at the carcass, screaming at the men to cut the body this way and that so as to ensure that she received the bones she needed for making more needles.

On their four sleds and in their minds they carried one other precious commodity without which no group of people can long survive: on the sled, tucked away in protected places, they brought with them bits of iridescent shell, or pieces of precious ivory carved in curious ways, or smoothed pebbles of attractive dimension. Such trinkets were in some ways more valuable than any other part of the cargo, because some of the memorabilia spoke of the spirits who supervised the life of humans, some referred to the lucky management of animals, assuring that food would be at hand when needed, some to the placation of great storms so that hunters would not be lost in blizzards, and certain pebbles and shells were treasured merely for their uncommon beauty. For example, the Ancient One kept in her secret hiding place the first bone needle she had ever used. It was not so long now as it once had been, and its original whiteness had aged to a soft gold, but its supreme utility through generations had invested it with such beauty that her heart expanded with the great joy of life whenever she saw it among her few possessions.

These Chukchis who walked to Alaska twenty-nine thousand years ago were a complete people. Their foreheads may have been low, their hairline close to their eyes, and their movements sometimes apelike, but people exactly like them in southern Europe were already creating immortal art on the ceilings and walls of their caves, composing chants for the fire at night, and creating stories that represented their life experience. If Varnak's people brought with them no physical furniture, they did bring a mental equipment which fitted them for the tasks they were about to face. If they brought no written language, they did bring into the arctic desert and steppe an understanding of the land, a respect for the animals that shared it with them, and an intimate appreciation of the wonders that occurred in any passing year. In later eons other men and women of comparable courage and ability would venture into their unfamiliar lands with a mental equipment no more competent than what these Asian stragglers carried in their dark heads.

Because emigrations like theirs would produce such tremendous consequences in world history—the opening up of two entire continents to the human race—certain limitations must be noted. Varnak and his companions were never conscious of leaving one continent to enter another; they could not have been aware that such landmasses existed, and had they been, they would have seen that in their day Alaska was far more a part of Asia than of North America. Nor would they have been interested in knowing that they were crossing a bridge, for the difficult land they were traversing certainly did not resemble one. And finally, they were impelled by no strong sense of emigration; their complete journey would cover only sixty miles, and as Varnak reminded them on the morning they left: "If things are no better there, we can always return next summer."

But despite these limitations, had there been a muse of history recording this fateful day, she might have looked down from her Olympus and exulted: "How majestic! Nineteen little people bundled in furs moving onto the doorstep of two empty continents."

By the end of their first day, it was apparent to all the travelers except the very young that this journey was going to be extremely difficult, for in the course of that entire day they saw not a single living thing except low grasses which were permanently bent by the ceaseless wind. No birds flew; no animals watched the untidy procession; no streams flowed, with small fish huddled along their banks. Compared to the relatively rich land they had known before the hunger time struck, this was bleak and forbidding, and when they pitched their sleds against the wind that night, the runners worn from having no snow to glide upon, they could not avoid realizing what a perilous trip they were attempting.

The second day was no worse but the impact was, because the travelers could not know that they had at the most only five days of this before they reached the slightly improved terrain of Alaska; they were wandering into the unknown, and so it remained for the next two days. In all that time they came upon nothing they could eat, and the meager stores they had been able to bring with them were nearly depleted.

"Tomorrow," Varnak said, as they huddled in the bare lee of their sleds on the third night, "we shall eat none of our stores. Because I feel certain that on the next day we shall come to better land."

"If the land is to be better," one of the men asked, "why not trust that we shall find food there?" and Varnak reasoned: "If the food is there, we shall have to be strong enough to run it down, and fight it when we overtake it, and dare much. And to do all that, we must have food in our bellies."

So on the fourth day no one ate anything, and mothers held their hungry children and tried to comfort them. In the warmth of the growing spring they all survived that trying day, and on the late after-noon of the fifth day, after Varnak and another had run ahead, draw-ing upon their courage and the spare fat from other days, they returned with the exciting news that yes, in another day's march there was better land. And that night, before the sun went down, Varnak distributed the last of the food. Everyone ate slowly, chewing until teeth met on almost nothingness, then savoring each morsel as it van-ished down the throat. During the next days they must find animals, or perish.

In midafternoon of the sixth day, a river appeared, with reassur-ing shrubs along its banks, and on the spur of the moment Varnak announced: "We camp here," for he knew that if they could not find something to eat in such a favorable location, they had no hope. So the sleds were brought into position and over them the hunters raised a kind of low tent, informing the women and children that this was to be their home for the present. And to firm their decision to wander no farther until they found food, they started a small fire to keep away the insistent mosquitoes.

In the early evening of this day the youngest of the grown men spotted a family of mammoths feeding along the riverbanks: a matri-arch with a broken right tusk, two younger females and three much younger animals. They remained motionless, well to the east, and even when Varnak and five other Chukchis ran out to watch, the animals merely stood and stared, then turned back to their grazing.

In the growing darkness Varnak assumed control: "Tonight we must surround the beasts, one man in each direction. When dawn breaks we shall be in position to cut one of the younger animals off from the rest. That one we will run to earth." The others agreed, and Varnak, as the most experienced, said: "I will run to the east, to head off the mammoths if they try to return to some homeland pastur-age," but he did not move in a direct line, for that would have carried him too close to the animals. Instead, he plunged into the river, swam across, and went well inland before heading east. As he ran he kept the six huge beasts in sight, and with an expense of effort that might have exhausted a lesser man fortified with ample food, this starving little hunter, running breathlessly in the moonlight, gained the com-manding position he sought. Swimming back across the river, he took his stance beside some trees, and now if the mammoths sought to flee eastward, they would have to run over him.

As night ended, the four Chukchis were in position, each man with two weapons, a stout club and a long spear tipped at the end and along the sides with sharp bits of flint. To kill one of the mammoths, they knew that each man must sink his spear close to some vital spot and then beat the wounded animal to death as it staggered about. From long experience, they knew that the initial chase, the culminating fight and the tracking of the wounded animal to its death might take three days, but they were prepared, because they either completed their task or starved.

It was a mild March day when they closed in upon the mammoths, and Varnak warned them: "Do not try to spear the old matriarch. She'll be too wise. We'll try for one of the younger ones."

Just as the sun appeared, the mammoths sighted them, and began to move eastward, as Varnak had anticipated, but they did not get far, because when they approached him, he daringly ran at them, brandishing his club in one hand, his spear in the other, and this so confused the old matriarch that she turned back, seeking to lead her troop westward, but now two other Chukchi men dashed at her, until, in despair, she headed due north, ignoring spears and clubs and taking her companions with her.

The mammoths had broken free, but all that day as they ran in one direction or another, the determined hunters kept on their trail, and by nightfall it was apparent to both animals and men that the latter could keep in contact, no matter how cleverly the former dodged and ran.

At night Varnak directed his men to light another fire to keep away the mosquitoes, and he suspected correctly that this would command the attention of the exhausted mammoths, who would remain in the vicinity, and at sunrise on the next day they were still visible, but the camp where the Chukchi women and children waited was far in the distance.

All that second day the tiring mammoths tried to escape, but Varnak anticipated every move they attempted. No matter where they turned, he was waiting with that dreadful spear and club, and toward the end of the day he would have succeeded in isolating a young female had not the old matriarch anticipated *his* move and rushed at him with her broken tusk. Forgetting his target, he leaped aside just as the fearful tusk ripped by him, and with the old matriarch safely out of the way, he moved in, brandished his spear, and drove the young mammoth to where the other men waited.

Deftly, in accordance with plans perfected centuries before, the hunters surrounded the isolated animal and began to torment her so adroitly that she could not protect herself. But she could trumpet, and when her screams of terror reached the old matriarch, the latter doubled back, driving directly at the menacing hunters and scattering them as if they were leaves fallen from an aspen tree.

At this moment it looked as if the wise old mammoth had defeated the men, but Varnak could not allow this to happen. Knowing that his life and that of his entire group depended on what he did next, he dove headfirst, throwing himself directly under the feet of the young mammoth. He knew that one step of one powerful foot would crush him, but he had no alternative, and with a terrible upward thrust of his spear he jabbed deep into her entrails and rolled clear of her. He did not kill her, nor did he even wound her fatally, but he did damage her so seriously that she began to stagger, and by the time he rose from the ground, the other hunters were screaming with joy and starting to chase their prey. Unable to retrieve his spear, which dangled from the belly of the mammoth, he nevertheless ran after her, brandishing his club and shouting with the others.

Night fell and once again the Chukchis built a fire, hoping that the mammoths would remain within range, and the great beasts were so fatigued that they were unable to move far. At dawn the chase resumed, and guided by a trail of blood, and encouraged by the fact that it grew wider as the long day progressed, the Chukchis kept running, and finally Varnak said: "We're getting close. Each man to his duty." And when they saw the massive beasts huddling within a stand of birch trees, he grabbed the spear of the youngest Chukchi and led his men toward the kill.

It now became his duty to neutralize the matriarch, who was stomping the earth and trumpeting her determination to fight to the end. Bracing himself, he walked precariously toward her, he alone against this great beast, and for just a moment she hesitated while the other men crashed their clubs and spears against the exposed body of the wounded mammoth.

When the old grandmother saw this, she lowered her head and drove right at Varnak. He was in mortal danger and knew it, but he also knew that once he allowed that fierce old creature to rampage among his men, she could destroy them all and rescue her young charge. This must not be allowed to happen, so Varnak, showing a courage few men could have exhibited, leaped in front of the charging mammoth and jabbed at her with his spear. Confused, she fell back, giving the other men breathing space in which to finish off their prey.

When the wounded mammoth stumbled to her knees, blood streaming from many wounds, the three Chukchis leaped upon her with their spears and clubs and beat her to death. When she expired, they acted in obedience to procedures observed through thousands of years: they slit open her innards, sought for the stomach loaded with partly digested greens, and hungrily consumed both the solids and the liquids, for their ancestors had learned that this material contained life-giving nutrients which human beings required. Then, their vigor restored after the days of starvation, they butchered the mammoth, producing cuts of meat big enough to sustain their families into the summer.

Varnak played no role in the actual killing; he had given the mammoth the first wound and had driven off the old matriarch when the latter might have disrupted the hunt. Now, exhausted, deprived of food for so many days, and depleted of what little strength he had by the arduous chase, he leaned against a low tree, panting like a spent dog, too tired to partake of the meat already steaming on the new fire. But he did go to the immense carcass, make a cup with his hands, and drink of the blood he had provided his people.

When the hunters finished slaughtering the mammoth, they made a traditional decision. Instead of trying to haul the mass of meat, bone and hide back to where their families waited, they decided to make their camp at a nearby stand of birch trees, so the two younger men were sent back to fetch the women, the children and the sleds.

The shift was made with ease, for the women were so starved for food that when they heard of the kill, they wanted to run off immediately, but when the men explained that the entire camp was to be moved, the taking down of the tentlike covering and the packing of the four sleds were completed quickly, and later that day when the women and children saw the slain mammoth, they shouted with joy and, abandoning their sleds, rushed for the fire where portions of the meat were roasting.

A group of hunters like Varnak's could expect to kill only one mammoth a year, but if they were unusually lucky or had at their head some hunter with exceptional skill, they might conceivably kill two. And since the taking of a mammoth was such a rare event, certain rituals for handling the carcass had evolved through the centuries. The Ancient One, as guardian of the tribe's spiritual safety, stood beside the severed head of the beast and apostrophized it:

"O Noble Mammoth who shares the tundra with us, who rules the steppe and runs the river, we thank thee for the gift of thy body. We apologize for having taken thy life, and we pray that thou hast left behind many children who will come to us in the future. Out of respect for thee, we make this prayer."

As she spoke she dipped her right fingers in the blood of the mammoth, then placed them on the lips of all the women and children until their lips were red. For the four hunters on whom the continued existence of her people depended, she stroked with her bloodied fingers the forehead of the dead animal and then the foreheads of the men, beseeching the beast to impart to these worthy men a deeper understanding of her kind so that they might more effectively chase other mammoths in the future. Only when these sacred rites had been performed did she feel free to rummage among the entrails, seeking the strong gut that would be converted into sinewy thread for sewing.

Her son, meanwhile, was trimming away the meat from the right scapula, and when that stout shoulder blade was exposed, its bone white like ivory, he began working upon it with a stone burin that flecked away bits of the bone, until he held in his hands a sturdy scraper with sharp cutting edges which could be used in butchering the meat of the mammoth prior to storing it in cool places. His work with the burin was significant for two unrelated reasons: it produced a cutting tool which was useful now, and which, nearly thirty thousand years later, would be dug up by archaeologists to prove that human beings had once lived at the Birch Tree Site in the dawn of New World history.

Each of the nine adults had some special responsibility regarding the dead mammoth: one collected the bones to serve as ceiling ribs for whatever kind of house they would later build, another washed the valuable hide and began tanning it with a mixture of urine and the acid distilled from tree bark. Hair from the legs would be woven into a material suitable for caps, and the gristle which connected hoof to leg was saved to make a kind of mucilage. The Ancient One continued probing each piece of meat, intent on salvaging thin, strong bones for the making of needles, and one man sharpened stouter bones to be inserted at the tips of his spears.

Lacking any organized agriculture or the capacity to grow and hoard vegetables, the Chukchis were forced to depend upon their hunting skills, which were tremendous, and basic to everything else was the pursuit of the mammoth, a major source of food. So they studied its habits, placated its spirit to make it congenial, devised ways to trick it, and hunted it relentlessly. As they cut this one apart, they studied every aspect of its anatomy, trying to predict how it would have behaved in different circumstances, and when it had been absorbed into the tribe as a kind of deity, the four men agreed: "The surest way to kill a mammoth is the way Varnak did. Fall under it and jab upward with a sharp spear."

Fortified by this conclusion, they took their sons aside and taught them how to hold a spear in both hands, fall to the ground face upward, and jab at the belly of a thundering mammoth, trusting the Great Spirits to provide protection from the hammering feet. When they had instructed the boys, showing them how to fall and yet maintain control of their spears, Varnak winked at one of the other hunters, and this time when the oldest boy ran forward and threw himself on the ground face upward, this hunter, dressed in mammoth skin, suddenly leaped in the air, uttered a fantastic scream, and stamped his feet inches from the boy's head. The young fellow was so terrified by this unexpected explosion that he let the spear fall from his hands and covered his face.

"You are dead!" the hunter shouted at the cowering boy, but Varnak uttered the more serious condemnation of his cowardice: "You let the mammoth escape. We shall starve."

So the spear was handed back to the frightened boy, and twenty times he threw himself upon the ground, face up, as Varnak and the others thundered down upon him, stamping their feet close to his head, and reminding him each time as the charade ended: "That time you had a chance to stab the mammoth. If it was a bull, he might have killed you, but your spear would have been in his belly, and we who were left would have had a chance to trail him and bring him down."

They kept at it until the boy felt that when he encountered a real mammoth, there was a good chance he might succeed in wounding it so sorely that the others would have a later chance to complete the kill, and when they stopped their practice, Varnak congratulated him: "I think you will know how," and the boy smiled.

But then the men turned their attention to the second oldest boy, a lad of nine, and when they handed him a spear and told him to throw himself under the body of the charging mammoth, he fainted.

At their new campsite near the birch trees, the Chukchis unloaded their meager goods and prepared to set up their crude shelters, and since they were in a position to start afresh, they could have developed some improved style of living quarters, but they did not. They failed to invent an igloo made of ice, or a yurt made of skins, or aboveground huts made of stone and branches, or any of the other satisfactory types of dwelling. Instead, they reverted to the kind of hovel they had known in Asia: a muddy cave belowground, with a kind of dome above made of matted branches and skins plastered with mud. As before, the excavation had no chimney for the discharge of smoke, no window for the admission of light, no hinged door to keep away the small animals that wandered by. But each cave did constitute a home, and in it women cooked and sewed and reared their young.

The expected life span in these years was about thirty-one years, and from the constant chewing of meat and gristle, teeth tended to wear out before the rest of the body, so that death was hastened by literal starvation. Women often had three children who lived, three others who died at or shortly after birth. A family rarely remained in one place long, for animals would become wary or depleted, so that the humans must move on in search of other prey. Life was difficult and pleasures were few, but there was at this time no war between tribes or groups of tribes, mainly because units lived so far apart that there need be no squabbling over territorial rights.

Ancestors had patiently learned from a hundred thousand years of trial and error certain rules for survival in the north, and these were rigorously observed. The Ancient One repeated them endlessly to her brood: "Meat that has turned green must not be eaten. When winter starts and there is not enough food, sleep most of each day. Never throw away any piece of fur, no matter how greasy it has become. Mammoth, bison, beaver, reindeer, fox, hare and mice, hunt them in that order, but never ignore the mice, for it is they that will keep you alive in the starving time."

Long and cruel experience had also taught one fundamental lesson: "When you seek a mate, go always, without exception, to some distant tribe, for if you take one within your own set of huts, fearful things result." In obedience to this harsh rule, she had herself once supervised the killing of a sister and a brother who had married. She would grant them no mercy, even though they were the children of her own brother. "It must be done," she had cried to members of her family, "and before any child is born. For if we allow such a one to come among us, *they* will punish us."

She never specified who *they* were, but she was convinced that they existed and exercised great powers. They established the seasons, they brought the mammoth near, they watched over pregnant women, and for such services they deserved respect. They lived, she believed, beyond the horizon, wherever it chanced to be, and sometimes in duress she would look to the farthest edge of sky, bowing to the unseen ones who alone had the power to make conditions better.

There were among these Chukchis certain moments of transcendent joy, as when the men brought down a really huge mammoth or when a woman trapped in a difficult pregnancy finally produced a strong male child. On wintry nights when food was scarce and comfort almost unattainable, special joy came to them, for then in the northern heavens the mysterious ones hung out great curtains of fire, filling the sky with myriad colors of dancing forms and vast spears of light flashing from one horizon to the next in a dazzling display of power and majesty.

Then men and women would leave the frozen mud of their mean caves to stand in the starry night, their faces to the heavens as those others beyond the horizon moved the lights about, hung the colors, and sent great shafts thundering clear across the firmament. There would be silence, and the children who were summoned to see this miracle would remember it all the days of their lives.

A man like Varnak might expect to see such a heavenly parade twenty times in his life. With luck he might help to bring down the same number of mammoths, no more. And as he neared the age of thirty, which he was doing now, he could anticipate the swift diminution of his powers and their ultimate disappearance. So he was not surprised one autumn morning when Tevuk said: "Your mother cannot rise."

When he ran to where she lay on the ground beneath the birch trees, he saw that she was mortally stricken, and he bent down to give her such comfort as he could, but she required none. In her last moments she wanted to look at the sky she had loved and to discharge her responsibilities to the people she had helped guide and protect for so long. "When winter comes," she whispered to her son, "remind the children to sleep a lot."

Varnak buried her in the birch grove, and ten days later her grave was covered by the year's first snow. Winds whipped it across the steppe, and as it drifted about the cave-huts, Varnak wondered: Maybe we should winter in the place we left, and he went so far as to consult with other adults, but their counsel was unanimous: "Better stay where we are," and with this resolve these eighteen new Alaskans, with enough dried mammoth meat to keep them alive through the worst of the winter, buried themselves in their huts to seek protection from the coming storms.

Varnak and his villagers were not the first to cross from Asia into Alaska. Others seem to have preceded them at different spots by thousands of years, moving gradually and arbitrarily eastward in their constant quest for food. Some made the journey out of curiosity, liked what they found, and stayed. Some fought with parents or neighbors and wandered off with no set purpose. Others passively joined a group and never had the energy to return. Some chased animals so fast and so far that after the kill they remained where they were, and some were allured by the attractiveness of a girl on the other side of the river whose parents were making the journey. But none, so far as we can deduce, ever crossed over with the conscious intention of settling a new land or exploring a new continent.

And when they did reach Alaska, the same patterns prevailed. They never knowingly set out to occupy the interior of North America; the distances and impediments were so great that no single group of human beings could have lived long enough to complete the passage. Of course, had the route south been ice-free when Varnak and his people made their crossing, and had they been driven by some monomaniacal impulse, they could conceivably have wandered down to Wyoming during their lifetime, but as we have seen, the corridor was rarely open at the same time as the bridge. So had Varnak been intent on reaching the interior of North America—assuming that he could have generated such a purpose, which he could not—he might have had to wait thousands of years before the pathway was released from the ice, and this would mean that a hundred generations of his line would live and die before his descendants could migrate toward Wyoming.

Of a hundred Chukchis who wandered from Siberia into Alaska in Varnak's time, perhaps a third returned home after discovering that Asia was in general more hospitable than Alaska. Of the two-thirds who remained, all were imprisoned within the enchanting ice castle, as were their descendants. They became Alaskan; in time they remembered nothing but this beautiful land; they forgot Asia and were able to learn nothing about North America. Varnak and his seventeen never went back, nor did their descendants. They became Alaskans.

By what name should they be known? When their ancestors first ventured into the north they had been called contemptuously Those Who Fled the South, as if the residents knew that had the newcomers been stronger, they would have escaped eviction from those favorable climes. During one period when they could not find acceptable sites for their camps, they were known as the Wanderers, and when they finally came upon a safe place to live at the edge of Asia, they took its name and became Chukchis. An appropriate name would have been Siberian, but now that they had unwittingly committed themselves to Alaska, they acquired the generic name of Indians, later to be differentiated as Athapascans.

As such they would prosper across the middle section of Alaska and positively thrive in Canada. One sturdy branch would inhabit the beautiful islands forming southern Alaska, and improbable as it would have seemed to Varnak, some of his descendants thousands of years later would wander southward into Arizona, where they would become the Navajo Indians. Scholars would find the language of these Navajos as close to Athapascan as Portuguese was to Spanish, and this could not have happened by chance. There had to have been a relationship between the two groups.

These wandering Athapascans were in no way related to the much later Eskimos, nor must they be visualized as moving consciously onward in some mighty fanlike emigration, carrying their civilization with them to unpopulated lands. They were not English Pilgrims crossing the Atlantic in a purposeful exodus, with provisional laws adopted on shipboard before landing among the waiting Indians. It is quite probable that the Athapascans spread throughout America with never a sense of having left home.

That is, Varnak and his wife, for example, as older people, would be inclined to remain where they were among the birch trees, but some years later one of their sons and his wife might see that it would be advantageous for them to build their cave-hut somewhat farther to the east where more mammoths were available, and off they would go. But they might also maintain contact with their parents back at the original birch-tree site, and in time *their* children would decide to move on to more inviting locations, but they too would retain affiliation with their parents, and perhaps even with old Varnak and Tevuk at the birch trees. In this quiet way people can populate an entire continent by moving only a few thousand yards in each generation, if they are allowed twenty-nine thousand years in which to do it. They can move from Siberia to Arizona without ever leaving home.

Better hunting, an addiction to adventure, a dissatisfaction with oppressive old ways, motives like these were the timeless urges which encouraged men and women to spread out even in peaceful times, and it was in obedience to them that these early men and women began to settle the Americas, both North and South, without being aware that they were doing so.

In the process, Alaska would become of crucial importance to areas like Minnesota, Pennsylvania, California and Texas, for it would provide the route for the peoples who would populate those diverse areas. Descendants of Varnak and Tevuk, inheritors of the courage which had characterized the Ancient One, would erect noble cultures in lands that would rarely know ice or have any memory of Asia, and it would be these settlers and the different groups who would follow them in later millennia who would constitute Alaska's main gift to America.

Fourteen thousand years B.P.E., when the land route was temporarily submerged because of melting at the polar ice cap, one of the world's most congenial people lived in crowded areas at the extreme eastern tip of Siberia. They were Eskimos, those squat, dark Asian hunters who wore their hair cut square across their eyebrows. They were a hardy breed, for their livelihood depended upon their venturing out upon the Arctic Ocean and its attendant waters to hunt the great whales, the tusked walruses and the elusive seals. No other men in all the world lived more dangerously in a more inhospitable climate than these Eskimos, and none labored more strenuously in these years than a bandy-legged, sturdy little fellow named Oogruk, who was experiencing all kinds of difficulties.

He had taken as his wife, three years earlier, the daughter of the most important man in his seaside village of Pelek, and at the time he had been bewildered as to why a young woman of such attractiveness should be interested in him, for he had practically nothing to offer. He had no kayak of his own for hunting seals, nor any share in one of the larger umiaks in which men sailed forth in groups to track down whales that glided past the headland like floating mountaintops. He owned no property, had only one set of sealskins to protect him from the frozen seas, and what was particularly disqualifying, he had no parents to help him make his way in the harsh world of the Eskimo. To top it all, he was cross-eyed, and in that special way which could be infuriating. If you looked into his left eye, thinking that this was the one he was using, he would shift focus, and you would be looking at nothing, for his left eye would have wandered. And if you then hurried back to his right eye, he shifted that one, and once more you were staring at nothing. It was not easy to talk with Oogruk.

The mystery of why the headman's pretty daughter Nukleet was willing to marry such a fellow was solved rather soon after the wedding feast, for Oogruk discovered that his bride was pregnant, and at the boats it was whispered that the father was a husky young harpooner named Shaktoolik who already had two wives and three other children. Oogruk was in no position to protest the deception, or to protest anything else for that matter, so he bit his tongue, admitted to himself that he was lucky to have a girl as pretty as Nukleet on any terms, and vowed to be one of the best hands in the various arctic boats owned by his father-in-law.

Nukleet's father did not want Oogruk as part of his crew, for the hunting of whales was a perilous occupation and each of the six men in the heavy boat had to be an expert. Four rowed, one steered, one managed the harpoon, and these positions had long been spoken for in the headman's umiak. He led the way. Shaktoolik held the harpoon. And four stout fellows with nerves of granite manned the oars. In many expeditions against whales, these men had proved their merit, and Nukleet's father was not about to break up his combination simply to make a place for his lightly regarded son-in-law.

But he was willing to provide Oogruk with his own kayak, not one of the best but a sturdy craft which was guaranteed not to sink—"

light as a spring breeze through aspen, watertight as a seal's fur"—
regardless of how the waves assaulted it. This kayak did not respond
quickly to paddle strokes, but it was many times better than Oogruk
could ever have owned by himself and he was grateful; his parents,
killed when a whale overturned their small boat, had left him nothing.

In midsummer, when great sea animals were on the move,
Oogruk's father-in-law, aided by Shaktoolik, launched his umiak
from the pebbled shore fronting the village of Pelek. But before they
departed on what they knew might be a perilous excursion, they indicated with shrugs that Oogruk was free to use the kayak on the
chance that he might creep up on some dozing seal and add both a
needed fur and meat to the village larder. Standing alone on the
shore, with the rude kayak waiting some distance to the east, he
looked through squinting eyes as the abler men of the village set
forth with prayers and shouts to try to intercept a whale.

When they were gone, their heads six dots on the horizon, he
sighed at his hard luck in missing the hunt, looked back at his hut to
see if Nukleet was watching, and sighed again to see that she was not.
Walking dejectedly to his waiting kayak, he studied its awkward
lines, and muttered: "In that one you couldn't overtake a wounded
seal." It was large, three times as long as a man, and covered completely by watertight sealskin to keep it afloat in the stormiest seas. It
contained only one opening, just big enough to accommodate a
man's hips; the sealskin was secured snugly at the top around the
hunter's waist and sewn to the kayak by lengths of whale tendons
that were pliable when dry, an impermeable bond when wet.

After Oogruk eased himself into the opening, he pulled the upper
part of the sealskin about his waist and tied it carefully, so that no
water could seep through even if the kayak turned upside down. If
that happened, all Oogruk would have to do would be to work his
paddle furiously and the kayak would right itself. Of course, if a lone
man lashed into the opening was foolhardy enough to tackle a mature walrus, the beast's tusks might puncture the covering, throw the
man into the sea, and drown him, for Eskimos could not swim; besides, the weight of his bulky clothing, if it became waterlogged,
would drag him down.

When the whale-hunting umiak vanished in the distance, Oogruk
tested his aspen paddle and started out for the seas east of Pelek. He
had little confidence that he would find any seals and even less that he

would know how to handle a big one if he did. He was merely scouting, and if he happened to sight a whale surfacing in the distance, or a walrus lazing along, he would mark the beast's heading and inform the others when they returned, for if Eskimos knew for certain that a whale or a really big walrus was in a given area, they could track it down.

He saw no seals, and this did not entirely disappoint him, for he was not yet sure of himself as a hunter, and he wanted first to familiarize himself with the tricks of this particular kayak before he took it among a herd of seals. He contented himself with paddling toward that distant land on the other side of the sea which he had sometimes seen on clear days. No one from Pelek had ever sailed to the opposite shore, but everyone knew it existed, for they had seen its low hills gleaming in the afternoon sun.

He was well out from shore, some miles south of where the umiak must be by now, when he saw off to his right a sight which paralyzed him. It was the full length of a black whale riding the surface of the water, its huge tail carelessly propelling it forward. It was enormous, much bigger than any Oogruk had ever seen on the beach when the men butchered their catch. Of course, he was not an expert judge, for the hunters of Pelek had caught only three whales in the last seven years. But this one was huge, no one could deny that, and it was imperative that Oogruk alert his companions to the whale's presence, for he alone against this great beast was powerless. Six of the best men in Siberia would be required to subdue it.

But how could he notify his father-in-law? Having no other choice, he decided to stay with the whale as it lazed its way north, trusting that its course must sooner or later intersect the umiak's.

This was a delicate maneuver, for if the whale felt threatened by a strange object in its vicinity, it could with three or four flips of its mighty tail swim over and collapse the kayak or bite it in two, killing both the man and his frail canoe. So all that long afternoon Oogruk, alone in his boat, trailed the whale, seeking to remain invisible, cheering when the whale spouted, showing that it was still there. Twice the great beast sounded, then disappeared, and now Oogruk sweated, for his prey might surface at any spot, might even come up under the kayak accidentally, or be lost forever in one strenuous underwater plunge. But the whale had to breathe, and after a prolonged absence, the huge dark creature resurfaced, spouted high in the air, and continued its lazy way north.

About an hour before the sun swept low to the north in its reluctance to set, Oogruk calculated that if the men in the umiak had continued in their proposed direction, they must now be well to the northeast of where the whale was heading, and if so, they would miss it completely. So he decided that he must cut across the whale's path, paddle furiously, and hope to overtake the six hunters.

But now he had to determine which method of getting to the east of the whale promised the greatest likelihood of success, for he must not only avoid inciting an attack, which would destroy both him and the kayak, but he must also move in such a way as to conserve maximum time and distance. Remembering that whales, according to tradition, could see poorly and hear acutely, he decided to speed ahead, making as little noise as possible, and cut directly across the whale's path, doing so as far in front as his paddling would allow.

This was a dangerous maneuver, but he had far more than his own safety to consider. From his earliest days he had been taught that the supreme responsibility of a boy or man was to bring a whale to the beach so that his village could feast upon it, and use the huge bones for building and the precious baleen for the scores of uses to which its suppleness and strength could be put. To catch a whale was an occasion which might happen only once in a lifetime, and he was in position to do just that, for if he led the hunters to the whale, and they killed it, the honors would be shared with him for his steadfastness in trailing the great beast across the open seas.

In this moment of vital decision, when he was about to throw himself across the very face of the whale, he was sustained by a curious fact, for his doomed father who had left him so little did provide him with a talisman of extraordinary power and beauty. It was a small circular disk, white and with a diameter of about two narrow fingers. It had been made of ivory from one of the few walruses his father had ever killed, and it had been carved with fine runic figures depicting the ice-filled ocean and the creatures that lived within it, sharing it with the Eskimos.

Oogruk had watched his father carve the disk and smooth the edges so that it would fit properly, and since both realized from the beginning that when finished, this disk was to be something special, it was in no way foolish when his father predicted: "Oogruk, this will be a lucky one." Accepting this without question, the boy of nine had not winced when his father took a sharp knife made of whalebone, pierced his lower lip, and stuffed the incision with grass. As it healed and the opening grew wider, with larger plugs of wood inserted each month, his lower lip would form a narrow band of skin surrounding and defining a circular hole.

Halfway through this process, the hole became infected, as so often happened in these cases, and Oogruk lay on the mud floor stricken with fever. For three bad days and nights, while his mind wandered, his mother applied herbs to his lip and packed warm rocks against his feet. Then the fever subsided, and when he was again able to take notice, the boy saw with satisfaction that the hole had mended to just about the required size.

On a day he would never forget, Oogruk was taken to a sinister hut at the edge of the village and ceremoniously led inside one of the filthiest, most jumbled places he had ever seen. The skeleton of a man dangled from one mud wall, the skull of a seal from another. Dirty pouches sewn from sealskin lay about the floor beside a collection of stinking skins on which the occupant slept. He was the shaman of Pelek village, the holy man who uttered the prayers that controlled the oceans and conversed with the spirits who brought whales to the headland. When he loomed out of the shadows to confront Oogruk, he was formidable—tall, gaunt, with sunken eyes and missing teeth, his hair extremely long and matted with a filth that had not been removed in a dozen years. Uttering incomprehensible sounds, he took the ivory disk, looked at its elegance with obvious astonishment that a man as poor as Oogruk's father should possess such a treasure, then pulled down the boy's lower lip and with befouled fingers pressed the disk into the hole. The hardened scar tissue adjusted painfully to pinch the disk firmly in the position it would occupy for as long as Oogruk lived.

The insertion had been painful; it had to be if the disk was to stay in place, but when the beautiful object was properly seated, all could see, and some with envy, that the cross-eyed boy Oogruk who had so little was henceforth going to possess one treasure: the finest labret on the eastern shore of Siberia.

Now, as he sped his kayak across the path of the oncoming whale, he sucked in his lower lip, taking courage from the reassuring presence of the magical labret. When his tongue felt the ivory, carved on both faces, he could trace the talismanic whale carved there, and he was convinced that its companionship would assure him good fortune, and he was right, for as he sped past, so close that the whale could have made one thrust of its gigantic tail and leaped ahead to crush both kayak and man, the lazy beast kept its head underwater, not deigning to bother with whatever small thing was moving through the seas so close to it.

But when the kayak had safely passed, the whale lifted its huge head, spouted great volumes of water, and casually opened its mouth as if yawning, and Oogruk, looking back toward the sound of the spouting, saw how enormous the mouth was that he had escaped, and its size appalled him. As a young man he had through the years participated in the butchering of four whales, and two of them had been large, but none had a head or a mouth as big as this. For almost a minute the cavernous mouth remained open, a black cavelike recess that could have crushed an entire kayak, and then almost drowsily it closed, a desultory spout of water came forth, and the massive whale sank once more below the surface of the water, still headed toward where Oogruk suspected his companions in their umiak would be waiting. Clicking his lucky labret against his teeth, he hurried ahead.

He was now to the east of the whale, heading north, and he was so far at sea that the headlands of home were no longer visible, nor was the opposite shore. He was alone on the vast northern sea, with nothing to sustain him but his lucky labret and the possibility that he might help his people catch that trailing whale.

Since it was midsummer, he had no fear of a descending darkness in which the whale might be lost, for as he paddled he could from time to time see over his left shoulder the plodding creature, and in the silvery light of endless summer he remained reassured that the great beast was traveling north with him, but whenever he did see the whale, he saw again that monstrous mouth, that black cavern which bespoke the other world about which the shaman sometimes warned when he was in one of his trances. To travel north in the whispering grayness of an arctic midnight while a dark whale kept pace in the deep billows of the sea was an experience which tested the courage of a man, and Oogruk, even though he was determined to comport himself well, might have turned back had not the presence of his labret reassured him.

At dawn the whale was still heading north, and before the sun was much above the horizon where it had lingered through the night, Oogruk thought he saw off to the northeast something that could be an umiak, and he quit monitoring the whale and started paddling frantically toward the supposed boat. He was correct in his guess, for at one point both he and the umiak rode the crest of waves, enabling him to see the six men rowing and they to see him. Waving his paddle, he gave the sign which indicated that a whale had been sighted, and with pointing directions he indicated its course.

With surprising speed, the umiak cut westward, intending to intercept the leviathan and ignoring Oogruk completely, for it was the whale that was important, not the messenger. Oogruk understood, and with his own strokes he set his frail kayak on a course which would overtake the umiak just as it reached the whale, and now a three-part drama unfolded, with the men in the larger boat panting with excitement, the whale moving majestically ahead, oblivious of the danger about to assault it, and lone Oogruk paddling furiously, uncertain as to what his role in the forthcoming fray was going to be. And all about, in all directions, lay the gently heaving arctic sea, devoid of spring icebergs, devoid of birds, devoid of headlands and gulfs and bays. There in the vast loneliness of the north, these creatures of the north prepared for battle.

When the umiak first came in sight of the whale the men could not appreciate the size of this monster; they saw its head at times, its tail at other times, but they never saw the complete length of the beast, so they were able to convince themselves that this was just one more ordinary whale. However, when they drew closer, the whale, still unaware of their presence, suddenly breached; that is, for reasons unknown it arched itself completely clear of the water, exposing its entire body. Then, exercising tremendous power, it turned on its side as if wishing to scratch its back, and thundered back into the sea with a gigantic splash. Now the six Eskimos realized they were facing a master whale that, if it could be taken, would feed their village for many months.

Oogruk's father-in-law needed to give only a few orders. The inflated seal bladders, which would impede the whale's progress if they managed to harpoon it, were made ready. Each of the four rowers brought close to hand the spears they would use when they closed upon the whale, and in the prow of the umiak tall and handsome Shaktoolik stood erect, wedged his knees against the gunwales of the boat, his strong hands grasping the harpoon which he would thrust into the vitals of the whale. Far behind trailed Oogruk.

The harpoon which Shaktoolik tended so carefully was a powerful affair, its long shaft tipped with sharpened flint followed immediately by hooklike barbs carved from walrus ivory. But even this lethal weapon would prove ineffective if thrown, like a spear, with an overhand motion, for the force thus generated would be insufficient to penetrate the whale's thick, blubber-protected skin; the miracle of the Eskimo system was not the harpoon but the harpoon throwing-stick, which ingeniously imparted three or four times the penetrating power to the barbed shaft.

A throwing-stick was a carefully shaped, thin length of wood about two and a half feet long, so devised as to increase considerably the length of a man's arm. The rear end, which contained a kind of slot in which the haft of the harpoon rested, snuggled in the crooked elbow of the thrower. The length of the stick ran along the man's arm, extending well beyond his fingertips, and it was against this wood that the harpoon rested. Toward the front end there was a finger rest enabling the man to retain control over both the harpoon and the stick, and close nearby a smoothed place at which the thumb could steady the long harpoon as the man prepared to throw. Steadying himself, the harpooner drew his right arm bearing the stick as far back as possible, checking to ensure that the butt end was secure in its slot. Then, with a wide sweep of his right arm, parallel to the surface of the sea and not up and down as one might expect, he snapped his arm swiftly forward, released his hold on the nestled harpoon at the precise moment, and, thanks to the doubled length this gave his arm, released the flint-tipped harpoon at the whale with such force that it could drive through the thickest skin. In this intricate method the man slung the harpoon much as little David, twelve thousand years later, would sling his rock against big Goliath. It sometimes required years of practice before accuracy was obtained, but once the various tricks were synchronized, this slingshot harpoon became a deadly weapon.

It seems unbelievable that primitive man could have invented such a curious, complicated instrument, but hunters on various continents did: the *atlatl* it would be named after the example the Europeans encountered in Mexico, but all versions were similar. Somehow, men with no knowledge of engineering or dynamics deduced that their harpoons would be trebly effective if they were loaded into their atlatls and slung forward instead of being thrown. How awesome the intellectual force of this intricate discovery, but in assessing it, one must remember that for a hundred thousand years men spent most of their waking hours trying to kill animals for food; they had no occupation more important, so perhaps it is not remarkable that after twenty or thirty thousand years of experimentation they discovered that the best way to deliver a harpoon was with a sideways slingshot motion, almost like an awkward child throwing a ball.

On this day the Eskimo leader had calculated perfectly his approach to the target, and from a position a little to the right and close behind the lumbering beast, he planned to flash ahead on an angle which would enable Shaktoolik to strike at a vital spot just behind the right ear and thus provide the two paddlers on the left-hand side an opportunity to unleash their spears also, with the headman remaining available in the stern to plunge his spear somewhat behind the others. Using this maneuver, the four Eskimos on the left-hand side of the umiak would have a chance to wound this enormous creature, perhaps not mortally but certainly deeply enough to render it vulnerable to their subsequent attacks and ultimate victory. A battle of profound strategy was under way.

But as the umiak bore down, the whale became aware of its danger, and with an automatic response which astounded the men, wheeled on its midsection and swung its huge tail viciously. The leader, anticipating the destruction of his umiak if the tail struck, heeled his craft over, but this left the man in front, Shaktoolik with his harpoon, exposed, and as the tail swept past, one fluke struck Shaktoolik in the head and shoulders, sweeping him into the sea. Then, in what could only have been an accidental blow, the mighty tail smashed down, crushing the harpooner, driving him unconscious deep below the surface of the sea, where he perished. The whale had won the first encounter.

As soon as the headman grasped the altered situation, he acted instinctively. Drawing away from the whale, he looked about the sea for Oogruk, and when he saw the kayak just where it should have been, he moved the umiak in that direction and cried: "Aboard!"

Oogruk was eager to join the fight, but he also knew that the craft in which he rode was the property of his father-in-law: "The kayak?"

"Leave it," the headman said without hesitation. Any boat was valuable, and this one was his, but the capture of the whale was of paramount importance, so the kayak was turned adrift as Oogruk climbed into the umiak.

It had long been understood in this crew that if either Shaktoolik or the headman was killed or lost, the principal rower, the one fore and left, would assume that vacant role, and this he did, leaving his own post empty. At first Oogruk assumed that he would move into that seat, but his father-in-law, knowing his limited skill, quickly reshuffled the men, leaving vacant the left rear seat, where Oogruk would sit under his direct supervision. There he could do the least harm, and in this new configuration, with almost no thought to the dead Shaktoolik, the Eskimos resumed their chase of the whale.

The leviathan, now aware that it was under attack, adopted various stratagems to protect itself, but since it was an air-breathing animal and not a fish, it had to surface from time to time, and when it did, these pestiferous little creatures in their boat tormented it. And they kept doing so, regardless of the fact that they were having no success, because they knew that if they could keep the whale reacting to their intrusions, they could in time wear it down and develop that critical moment when, tired from fleeing and exhausted by this constant sounding and spouting, it would leave itself vulnerable.

All that first day the uneven fight was waged, with the men fully aware that one sweep of that stupendous tail, one crushing of those vast jaws, would doom them. But they had no alternative; Eskimos captured their food from the ocean or they starved, and abandoning the fight never occurred to them. So when the sun moved toward the northern horizon, indicating that night, such as it was, had come, the men in the umiak continued their pursuit, and all through the silvery dusk which persisted in majestic beauty until it turned into a silvery dawn, the six little Eskimos chased the one great whale.

Toward noon of the second day the headman judged that the whale was tiring and that the time had come to attempt a master thrust, so once more he brought his umiak to a position slightly behind the whale, and again moved forcefully ahead so that his new harpooner would have a clear shot, as would he and the two left-hand rowers. As the run started, he kicked Oogruk in the back, growling "Have your lance ready," showing his contempt as his inept son-in-law fumbled around to find the unfamiliar weapon.

By the time the attack was launched, Oogruk had still not located his lance, and for the very good reason that the former occupant of the left rear seat had taken his with him when he moved forward and had not replaced it. Nevertheless, when the attack was made and the great whale slid past the right side of the umiak, the man ahead of Oogruk and his father-in-law behind stabbed skillfully, doing real damage, but Oogruk did not, and the headman, seeing this dereliction, began to berate him as the whale moved on, bleeding from its right side.

"Idiot! Had you stabbed it too, it would have faltered!" and as the day proceeded, the headman returned to this supposition so repeatedly that all in the umiak came to believe that Oogruk's inability to use his lance properly had been the sole cause of this second failure. Finally the censure became so strong that the cross-eyed fellow had to defend himself: "I had no lance. I was given none." And when the others inspected the umiak they had to know that this was true, but they were so eager to blame another for their own error that they continued to grumble: "If Oogruk had used his lance properly, we would have taken that whale."

During the second mystical night, with the whale occasionally visible as it raised its gigantic tail above the waves, the headman distributed fragments of food and allowed his men to take small drinks of water, and when all understood how meager the remainder of the ration was, they knew that on the coming day they must make their supreme effort. So early in the morning the headman brought the umiak once more into the position he favored—slightly behind, slightly to the east—and with great skill he positioned the forward harpooner right where he could do the most damage, but as the man delivered his blow, the point of the harpoon struck bone and was diverted. The man seated ahead of Oogruk again struck a good blow, a deep one but not fatal, and now came Oogruk's turn. As he rose, he felt his father-in-law kicking him, so he reached out with his borrowed spear, located it perfectly, and with all his strength bore down, driving the spear deep into the whale.

But he was inexperienced, and in this moment of triumph he forgot to brace his knees and feet against the side of the umiak, and even more important, he did not let go his spear, and he was dragged into the water.

As he splashed into the icy sea, caught between the umiak and the passing whale, he heard his father-in-law curse and saw him thrust his spear properly into the whale, protecting himself from falling as he deftly pulled the spear free, the way a man should, so as to plunge it deeper on his next try.

Aboard the umiak there was commotion as some cried: "After the whale! It's wounded!" while others: "Catch Oogruk! He's still alive!" and the headman, after brief hesitation, decided that since the whale could not escape and Oogruk could not swim, he had better attend to the latter. When Oogruk was hauled aboard, salt water dripping from his lucky labret, his father-in-law snarled: "You've cost us the whale . . . twice."

This was true only in part, because the whale was less seriously damaged than the men had at first supposed, and with its remaining strength it moved ahead so fast that by the close of that third day it was obvious to the Eskimos that they had lost it. In their despair at having been so near the capture of a champion whale, they again focused on Oogruk, berating him for their defeat, citing his failure to lance the whale and his falling overboard, and a legend was born there in the sullen umiak that they would surely have taken that whale had they not stopped to rescue Oogruk: "Yes, clumsy fellow that he is, he fell right out of the umiak, and when we stopped to save him, our whale escaped."

As he listened to the accusations, he bit on his labret and thought: They forget it was me who brought them the whale. And when his father-in-law, in a spell of truly ridiculous reasoning, began to scold him for having lost the kayak, Oogruk concluded that the world had gone mad: He ordered me to leave it. I asked twice, and he ordered me twice.

It was in these ugly moments, as bitter as a man could know, when the members of his community have turned against him and have for irrational reasons vilified him, blaming him for their own deficiencies, that Oogruk realized it was useless to try to defend himself against such irresponsible charges. But his silence did not win him respite, for now the men in the umiak faced another problem: How were they to make it back home in a trip that might require three days when they had no food and little water? In their extremity they renewed their attacks on Oogruk, and one crew member even suggested throwing him overboard to appease the spirits whom he had offended. From the rear of the umiak the leader said grimly: "No more of that," but he continued to voice his unfavorable opinion of the hapless one.

And then, to the east, the men saw for the first time the headlands of the country that lay on the opposite side, and in the late afternoon sunlight it looked inviting and a place worthy of attention. It was constructed, they saw, not of mountains like the ones they had known far to the west on their side of the sea, but of rolling hills, treeless but nevertheless attractive. They had no way of knowing whether the place was inhabited or not, and they had no assurance that there they would find food, but they did believe that there it would have water, and all agreed that the headman should turn the umiak toward the shore and begin seeking a safe spot at which to land.

It was with the gravest apprehension that the men neared the shore, for they could not anticipate what might happen if this otherwise appealing place contained people, and as they breasted a small headland protecting a bay, they saw with quaking hearts that within its shelter it did have a small village. Before the headman could stop the forward motion of the umiak, seven swift one-man kayaks sped from shore and surrounded the larger boat. The strangers were armed, and they might have discharged their spears had not Oogruk's father-in-law raised his empty hands high over his head and then dropped them to his mouth in a gesture of drinking.

The strangers understood, came close to the umiak and with their eyes searched it for weapons, and when they saw that Oogruk and another man were gathering the whaling lances and holding them aside in one bundle, they allowed the umiak to follow them ashore, where an elderly man, obviously their shaman, bade them a generous welcome.

They remained three days at Shishmaref, as the site would later be known, eating food much like what they had at home and learning words that were close to their own. They could not converse easily with these people of the eastern shore of the Bering Sea, but they could make themselves understood. The villagers, obviously Eskimos, said that their ancestors had lived in this bay for many generations, and it was clear from the bones used in building their houses that they lived on just about the same sea animals as did the people of Pelek. They were friendly, and when Oogruk and his fellow boatmen departed, farewells of real emotion were shared.

This visit to the east enabled the men of the west to survive the trip home, and on this long journey the old antagonism against Oogruk solidified, so that by the time they landed at Pelek the official judgment had become: "Shaktoolik and Oogruk both fell overboard. Evil demons caused us to lose the good man and save the bad."

Ashore they circulated this dogma so persuasively that those waiting in the huts accepted it, and Oogruk was ostracized, but now an enemy more powerful than anyone in the umiak rose against him, for the shaman, that mixture of saint, priest, necromancer and thief, began to circulate the theory that Oogruk, because of the insolent way he had crossed in front of the whale, had also been the specific cause of Shaktoolik's death, for that harpooner was known to be highly skilled and more than able to protect himself from normal dangers. It was obvious that some evil force had exercised an adverse spell against him, and the logical perpetrator had to be Oogruk.

And then the shaman, shaking his long and matted locks, betrayed the animus that motivated him in this attack: he whispered to various listeners that it was not proper for a pitiful man like Oogruk to possess a labret with magical powers, with a whale carved on one face, a walrus on the other, and he began to initiate those devious maneuvers which had worked to his advantage in similar situations in the past. His immediate goal, announced to no one, not even the spirits, was to gain possession of that labret.

He noisily bemoaned the death of the harpooner Shaktoolik, weeping in public over the loss of such a noble young man, and he tried to enlist the help of both Oogruk's father-in-law and Nukleet, the pretty daughter married to Oogruk. But there he ran into difficulties, because to everyone's surprise including her father's, Nukleet did not turn against her feckless husband; she defended him. And as she began to point out the various unfairnesses in the attacks upon him, she gradually convinced her father that Oogruk had in some ways been the hero of the expedition, not the villain.

Why did she do this? She knew that their daughter was not properly Oogruk's and that her father and most others had been distressed when she married the cross-eyed fellow, but as the years passed, four of them now, she had seen on numerous occasions that her husband was a man of great character. He was honest. He worked to his ability. He cherished their daughter, tending her as if she were his own, and always he had shared his meager possessions with her when young men of far greater favor treated their wives with contempt.

In these four years she had especially compared Oogruk's behavior with that of Shaktoolik, the real father of her child, and the more she had seen of that handsome man's behavior the more she had grown to respect her ungainly husband. Shaktoolik had been arrogant, he had abused his two wives, he had ignored his children, and had displayed his inherent meanness in a score of malicious ways. He stole other men's lances and laughed about it. He took their women and dared them to resist. Brave he was, all men agreed to that, but in all other human responses he had been an ugly man, and she admitted it if others did not. So when the shaman made a great fuss about Shaktoolik's death, she watched, and listened, and deduced what webs that evil man was weaving.

Characteristically, for although she now believed that Oogruk was good, she could still not admit that he was intelligent, she took her fears to her father and not to her husband: "The shaman wants to drive Oogruk from Pelek."

"Why would he do that?"

"He wants something that Oogruk has."

"What could that be? The fool has nothing."

"He has me."

With remarkable instinct Nukleet had uncovered the shaman's other reason for getting rid of Oogruk. He did covet the beautiful labret, but that was merely to enhance his powers as a shaman; that would increase his public power. For himself, as a man living apart in a hovel on the edge of the village, he wanted Nukleet, and her daughter, and her favorable relationship to the headman. He recognized her as one of those women, not many in number according to him, who brought grace to whatever she did. Four years ago he had been perplexed as to why she would marry Oogruk instead of becoming Shaktoolik's third wife, but now he realized that she had done this through the force of her remarkable character and determination: She wanted to be first in line, not third. He convinced himself that if she now had an opportunity to become his woman, attendant to the most powerful man in the community, she would leap to the chance.

In a hundred ways this bizarre man deluded himself. Because the arctic world was a dangerous place where the successful capture of a walrus might mean the difference between life or death, the Eskimos had to placate the spirit of the walrus, and who could ensure this but the shaman? It was he who could turn the heavy blizzards away in winter, and bring rains to ease the droughts in summer. Only he could guarantee that a childless woman would become pregnant or that her child would be a son. With conviction he identified those Eskimos who were possessed by devils, and at a great price he exorcised the devils just before the clan rose up to punish the bewildered carrier of evil. In two extreme circumstances he had known that the clan's only hope of survival lay in appeasing the spirits and without qualm had identified the offending member who must be banished.

No one in Pelek would have thought of challenging this despot, for all knew that strange forces ruled the world and that the shaman alone knew how to master them, or at least propitiate them so they did minimum damage. In this way he served several useful purposes, for when an Eskimo died the shaman properly guided the spirit to its resting place through intricate rituals, reaffirming for the clan that malevolent forces would not roam the shore and drive away the seals and walruses. He was especially helpful when hunters went forth in their umiaks, for they found reassurance in his incantations for protection against malignant spirits that could bring disaster to the already dangerous hunt. In the depths of the coldest winters, when it seemed as if all life had disappeared from earth, the clan found renewed hope as he placated the spirits to prevail upon the frozen seas and bring the warm breezes of spring again to Pelek. No community could survive without a powerful shaman, so that even those who suffered at his hands conceded that their shaman's ministrations were essential. The most that anyone would say was: "I wish he was a kinder man."

The shaman of Pelek had begun to acquire his mastery of others in a quiet, almost accidental way. As a boy he had sensed that he was different, for he could look into the future when others could not. He was also sensitive to the presence of good and evil forces. But above all, he discovered early that the world is a mysterious place, that the great whales come and go according to rules which no man by himself can unravel, and that death strikes arbitrarily. He was concerned with these mysteries, as were all men, but unlike other men, he proposed to conquer them.

He did so by collecting lucky and powerful objects with which to excite his intuitions; that was why he longed for Oogruk's potent labret. He made himself a pouch of beaver skin, shiny fur outside, choice stones and bits of meaningful bone inside. He taught himself to whistle like a bird. He developed his powers of observation so that he saw conditions and relationships which others did not. And when he was satisfied that he had the capacity to be a shaman, and a good one, he mastered the art of speaking in different voices and even throwing his voice from place to place so that those who consulted him in their fears or anguish could hear the spirits addressing their problems.

He served his community well. Indeed, he seemed to have only one weakness, an insatiable craving for power and ever more power, and the young woman Nukleet was the first in the community to discover this terrible infirmity and identify it. She had started worrying about her good husband's helplessness before this forceful shaman, and quickly she had transferred that concern to herself. Now, perceiving the real danger, she asked her father to walk with her beside the sea, which was beginning to fill with ice: "Can't you see, Father? It's not Oogruk or me. It's your power he's really after."

The headman, a considerable force in any Eskimo community, ridiculed his daughter's fears: "Shamans look after the spirits. Headmen look after the hunt."

"If the separation is allowed to continue."

"He would be no good in an umiak and hopeless in a kayak."

"But if he controlled those who went in the umiak?"

She made no headway with her father, who was preoccupied with trying to bring in enough food before the winter closed in, and in the next weeks she saw little of him, for he and his men were out upon the great sea where the ice was forming, and to her relief and his, he succeeded in bringing home many fat seals and one small walrus. The shaman blessed the catch and explained to the people that the hunts had been successful because this time Oogruk had been left at home.

It was a difficult winter. Without a whale on the beach the little village of Pelek lacked many necessities, and when the long night settled in, the sea froze solid along the shore and nearly so to a far distance out. Since Pelek perched on the extreme eastern tip of the Chukchi peninsula, it lay some distance south of the Arctic Circle, which meant that even in midwinter the sun shone briefly, a cold, reluctant orb which gave little warmth. Then, as if frightened by venturing so far north, after two meager hours it disappeared and twenty-two hours of freezing darkness returned.

The effect of this cold on the sea was spectacular, for not only did the sea freeze, it also heaved and fractured and disrupted itself so that enormous blocks of ice, taller than the tallest spruce to the south, rose eerily from the surface, standing about like structures thrown by some malevolent giant. The effect was staggering, a jagged, broken surface along which one could travel by sled for only a short distance before being forced to detour the monstrous towers of ice.

But interspersed among the great blocks were spacious areas where the frozen sea remained flat, and to such places men and women came with fishing lines, and with stout poles treasured from generation to generation they pounded on the ice until they broke their way to water, and down these holes they dropped their lines with the ivory hooks with which they caught their winter food. It was arduous work to dig the holes and a bitterly cold assignment to sit there hour after hour waiting for a fish to strike, but the people of Pelek had to endure it or go hungry.

In the long hours of darkness the Eskimos, like the prudent Siberians before them, slept much in order to conserve energy, but occasionally groups of men would venture far out on the ice to where free water stood, and there they endeavored to catch a seal or two, for the rich blubber was needed to supplement the deficient diet. When such a catch was made, the men responsible butchered the seal immediately, gorging on the liver, but the slabs of meat and blubber they carried home across the ice, shouting news of their success as they approached Pelek. Then their wives and children ran to the shore and far out onto the ice to help drag home the welcome meat, and for two unbroken days the people of Pelek feasted.

But mostly in these difficult winters the Eskimos of Pelek stayed close to their huts, periodically knocking away the snow that threatened to engulf them, and huddled by their meager fires. No Eskimos in this part of the north lived in igloos; those imaginative and sometimes beautiful ice houses with their splendid domes would come later and only in regions thousands of miles to the east. These Eskimos of fourteen thousand years ago lived in excavated huts with superstructures of wood and whalebone and sealskin, much like those which the Siberians of Varnak's day, fifteen thousand years earlier, had known.

In the dark winter, fears and superstitions flourished, and it was in this enforced and nervous idleness that the shaman could best work his spells. If a pregnant woman had a difficult delivery, he knew who was at fault and he was not loath to identify the evildoer. He had not the power of life and death—that was reserved for a community consensus—but he could influence the decision. Alone in his small hut at the edge of Pelek, and inland from the sea which he tried to avoid, he sat among his pebbles and his charms, his bits of bone and precious ivories, his aspen twigs which had happened to grow in premonitory forms, and cast his spells.

This winter he directed his spells against Oogruk first, and he did this for solid reasons: Oogruk with his gentle ways and crossed eyes is the kind of man who becomes a shaman. And that lucky labret might spur him, too. Better to force him from the village. The tactic was sensible, because there was little chance that when Oogruk fled, his desirable wife would go with him. She would stay behind, that was certain. And when the shaman had collected to himself whatever powers Nukleet had, her father would then be vulnerable to him.

These men and women of Pelek, twelve thousand years before the birth of Christ, eleven thousand years before the sophistication of Athens, thoroughly understood the drives which motivated men and women. They appreciated their relationship to the land, to the sea and to the animals which occupied both. And none comprehended these forces better than the shaman, unless it was this unusual young woman Nukleet, with whom he was obsessed.

"Oogruk," she whispered in their dark hut, "I think he'll make it impossible for us to live in this village another year."

"He hates me. He turns all men against me."

"No, the one he really hates is that one over there," and she pointed to where her father slept. And she assured her husband that whereas he, Oogruk, was first on the shaman's list, while she was second, they were both no more than expendable targets by which the medicine man planned to attain his real goal.

"What's that?"

"The destruction of my father. The possession of his power."

When Oogruk, tutored by his wife, began to unravel this ugly web, he saw that she was right, and a quiet fury began to build within him. But when he tried to devise some way to defend himself and Nukleet during the shaman's first assaults, and then to protect his father-in-law against the sorcerer's major attack, he found himself helpless. The shaman was essential to the village, and anything that damaged him endangered the entire community. So Oogruk remained paralyzed.

His initial fury was transmuted into a kind of dull ache, an uneasiness which never left his mind, and it produced a curious reaction. The cross-eyed fellow began to sequester in the snow surrounding his father-in-law's hut bits of whalebone, and spars of wood washed up by the sea during the previous summer. He acquired sealskins and lengths of sinew from the bodies of dead animals, and as he furtively collected these items a plan evolved. He visualized that congenial group of huts on the eastern edge of the sea, where he and his fellow hunters had been revived when they were without food, and he thought repeatedly: It would be better over there.

When he had surreptitiously assembled enough stray elements to consider seriously what might be done with them, he had to take

Nukleet and her father into his confidence, and when he did, he revealed a revolutionary concept: "Why not build a kayak with three openings? Men paddling front and back. Nukleet and the child in the middle?"

His father quickly rejected such nonsense: "Kayaks have one opening. If you want three, you build yourself an open umiak."

But Oogruk, slow-witted as he seemed to be, saw that necessity was more important than convention: "In high seas an umiak can be swamped and everyone drowns. But a kayak, properly lashed down, can be rolled over and refloated. Then everyone lives." When his father-in-law continued to insist upon an umiak, Oogruk said with startling force: "Only a kayak can save us," and the older man salvaged his pride by shifting the discussion: "Where would we go if we had such a kayak?"

"Over there," Oogruk replied without hesitating, and in that pregnant moment, with his left forefinger pointing eastward across the frozen sea, he committed himself and his family to the idea of leaving this village forever.

So Oogruk began to build a kayak, and when word of this reached the shaman's ears, that hairy fellow crouched among his magic pieces, his tattered garments rank from perpetual use and filth, and began to cast spells, asking penetrating questions throughout the community: "Why is the kayak being built? What evil thing does cross-eyed Oogruk have in mind?"

The headman, hearing this insinuation, answered it boldly: "My stupid son-in-law lost my good kayak when he chased the whale last summer. I'm making him replace it." And by this lie the headman committed himself. He too was prepared to leave Pelek forever and test his fortunes in the world across the sea, even though he realized that over there he would no longer be a headman. The quiet glory of leading his people in decisions would be surrendered. Other men would stand in the stern of the umiak when the whale was pursued, and better men, younger and stronger, would fight the walrus and apportion the meat when the kill was made. More than either his daughter or her husband, the headman appreciated how much he was surrendering if this flight was made, but he also knew that he was powerless once the shaman turned his face against him.

When the necromancer learned that the new kayak, whose ribs now lay exposed in the snow, was going to have three openings, he deduced that all of the persons against whom he was plotting were preparing to escape his dominance, and in the last days of winter before the great sea melted to make the use of umiaks and kayaks feasible again, he decided that he must take action against the would-be fugitives, and now he stepped forth boldly to establish his authority.

"There has never been a kayak with three openings. The spirits frown on such contaminations. And why is it being attempted? The headman is preparing to sneak out of Pelek, and if he takes his hunting skills elsewhere, we shall starve." When he uttered these words, all knew that he was threatening to sentence the headman to a cruel existence: he must remain in the village to guide the hunting, but in shame he must also surrender his leadership to the shaman. In the hunt he would be a free man, in all else a suspected prisoner.

It was a diabolical punishment made possible only by the unquestioned faith these Eskimos had in their shaman, and the only recourse either the headman or his children could envisage was flight. So construction of the kayak was hastened, and when in late spring the snows melted and the sea began to show signs of breaking free of its icy blanket, Oogruk and the headman worked strenuously to complete their craft, while Nukleet, who had in a sense initiated the strategy of flight, gathered those necessary things which she and her daughter would carry at their feet during the sea crossing. When she realized how pitifully small the cargo would have to be, and how much she must abandon, she felt sorrow but no lack of determination.

Had she been inclined to waver, or be in any way dissatisfied with her husband, she would have had, in these middle days of spring, ample excuse for quitting the conspiracy, because the shaman began to implement his plan for getting rid of Oogruk and rendering her father impotent. One day when the ice was fairly gone from the sea and flowers were beginning to show, he arrived at the headman's hut accompanied by three young men who carried in their arms a worn kayak with only one opening, and in a harsh voice, his head thrown back as if he were talking to spirits, he cried: "Oogruk, whose evil ways allowed the great whale to escape, who brings additional disfavor to Pelek, it is the judgment of the spirits who guide us and of the men of this village that you leave us."

Neighbors who had gathered from the surrounding huts gasped when they heard this harsh pronouncement, and even the headman, who had led these people in so many ways and with such proven skill, was afraid to speak. But in the fearful silence that followed, Nukleet moved to stand beside her husband, and with her free left hand brought her four-year-old daughter along with her, and with this simple gesture she let it be known that if Oogruk was expelled, she would go with him.

The shaman had intended that Oogruk leave immediately, but this unexpected development frustrated that plan, and in some confusion the visitors withdrew, carrying their kayak with them. But this temporary setback did not cause the shaman to relinquish his scheme for restructuring his village and finding himself a wife, so that night young men who were never identified crept up to the headman's house in the darkness and destroyed much of the new three-man kayak.

Nukleet, out early to gather firewood, was the first to find the vandalism, and when she saw what the shaman had caused to be done she did not panic. Aware that others might be spying upon her, since the hut she occupied was apparently doomed by the spirits that guarded the village, she continued on her way to the beach to see what driftwood the sea might have thrown up after the winter freeze, and when she had an armful she returned home. There she wakened her men, warning them to make no public lamentation when they saw what had happened to their kayak.

Quietly Oogruk and her father went out to inspect the damage, and it was the former who decided that the broken ribs could be replaced and the ripped skin repaired. In three days the two men had the kayak serviceable, but this time they moved it halfway inside their hut, with Oogruk sleeping upright in the hole that remained outside, his head resting on his arms folded over the rim of the hatch.

The Eskimos of this period, and of subsequent eras too, were a peaceful lot, and they did not engage in murder, so that although the shaman had declared war against these two men, he was not free to kill them or to have them killed. That would not be tolerated. But he was, as shaman, entitled to warn his people against persons who might bring disaster upon their village, and this he did with fervor and effectiveness.

He pointed out that Oogruk's malevolence was proved by the fact that he was cross-eyed, and when he ranted: "How otherwise would the spirits make a man's eyes to cross?" he amused his listeners by crossing his own eyes for a moment and making his already ugly face quite hideous. In these tirades he carefully spoke no words against the headman; on the contrary, he praised him rather effusively for his able guidance of the hunting umiak, thus hoping to drive a wedge between the two men, and he might have succeeded had he not made one crucial error.

Driven by his increasing desire to gain Nukleet for himself, he came upon her one evening as she was gathering the first flowers of the year, and he was so taken by her dark beauty and the lyrical way she moved along the field, stopping here and there to study the spring growth, that he was impelled, against his better judgment, to run after her awkwardly and try to embrace her. When growing up, she had known several young men of considerable attractiveness, and for some months she had been a wife to Shaktoolik, the handsome one, so she knew what men were supposed to be, and not even by stretching her imagination could she conceive of the repulsive shaman as a partner. More seriously, she had discovered in Oogruk the kind of companion that women treasured, once they overlooked the obvious deficiencies. He was gentle yet brave, kind to others yet resolute when his mind was made up. In his defiance of the shaman he had shown courage and in his building of the new kayak skill, and in her more mature age, twenty-one, she knew how lucky she was to have found him.

So the greasy shaman with his matted hair and smelly rags had little to make him desirable except his acknowledged relationship with the spirits and the ability to make them work in his behalf. And when he grabbed at her now, she discovered that she was at last prepared to defy even those powers: "Go back, you filthy one." She pushed him away, vigorously, and then in the disgust of the moment she did a most unwise thing: she laughed at him, and this he could not tolerate. As he staggered back he swore that he would destroy this woman and all her companions, even her blameless daughter. The village of Pelek would know these malevolent ones no more.

Back in his isolated hut where he communed with the forces that ran the universe, he writhed in anger, devising one plot after another to punish this woman who had scorned him. He contemplated poisons and knives and sinkings at sea, but in the end his wilder passions subsided, and he decided that on the morrow, when the sun was up, he would summon the villagers and pronounce total anathema upon the headman, his daughter, her husband and their child. And in doing so, he would recite a calendar of the evil things they had done to bring discredit upon the village and incur the enmity of the spirits. He would make his accusations so violent that in the end his listeners might in frenzy decide to ignore the Eskimo aversion to killing and slay these four to save themselves from the retribution of the spirits.

But when, in the early dawn, he started to assemble the villagers and lead them to the headman's hut, where the denunciations would be made, he found most of them already gathered at the shore. When he elbowed his way among them, he saw that they were staring out to sea, where, on the horizon too far away to be apprehended by even the swiftest umiak, three figures nestling in the three protected holes of a new type of kayak were on their way to that unknown world on the far side.

Because the great sea was choppy, with a few vagrant icebergs still drifting southward, these daring emigrants in their fragile kayak were going to need three full days to make the crossing from Asia to North America, but in this bright dawn all things seemed possible, and they moved toward the east with a lightness of heart that would have seemed impossible to anyone not associated with the sea. When the headlands of Asia disappeared and nothingness lay ahead, they pushed on, with the sun streaming upon their faces. Alone on the great sea, uncertain as to what the next days might hold, they caught their breath as their kayak raced down into the trough of some powerful wave, then gasped with delight as it rose to the next oncoming crest. They were one with the seals sporting in the spray, they were cousins to the tusked walruses making their way north to mate. When a whale spouted in the distance and then sounded, flukes high in the air, the headman shouted: "Stay out there. We'll come back for you later."

Their precipitate departure from Pelek had produced two moments of such gravity that they summarized a life. Nukleet had returned from her encounter with the shaman white with shock, and when her father asked what had happened, she merely said: "We must leave in the darkness." Oogruk had cried: "We can't," and she had replied simply: "We must." She said no more, gave no explanation of how she had rebuffed and ridiculed the shaman, nor did she confess that she had brought such danger upon their hut that further occupancy was impossible.

The men, realizing that some forbidden line had been crossed, had asked only: "Must it be tonight?" and she had started to nod, but had stopped, for she realized that she must give them the strongest possible reply, one that would allow no counterargument: "We leave as soon as the village is asleep, or we die!"

The second moment of significant decision had come when the unwilling emigrants crept to the beach, father and son carrying the kayak silently, mother and daughter bringing with them the household goods. After the men had placed the craft in the water and had helped Nukleet into the center opening, where she would hold her daughter during their escape, the headman stepped naturally to the rear seat, the one from which the kayak would be commanded, supposing that he would lead the expedition. But before he could take that place, Oogruk stepped in front of him, saying quietly: "I will steer," and his father-in-law had surrendered the command.

Now, far from shore and safe from the retaliations of the shaman, the four Eskimos in their frail kayak settled into the routines that would govern them for the next three days. Oogruk at the rear, set a slow, steady pace, two hundred strokes on the right side, a grunted cry "Shift!" and two hundred on the left. In the front seat, the headman applied his powerful muscles strenuously, as if their progress depended upon him alone; it was primarily he who pulled the canoe forward. And Nukleet, in the middle position, passed drinking water to her men fore and aft and gave them bits of seal blubber to chew upon as they paddled.

The little girl, always aware of the burden she placed upon her mother, sometimes tried to ride upon the rim of the hatch, but always Nukleet drew her back, with the warning: "If you were up there and we turned over, how could we save you?" and heavy though the child grew, Nukleet kept her on her lap.

Travel did not stop at night, for in the silvery darkness it was important that forward motion be maintained, and both Oogruk and his father-in-law knew this, so when the sun finally went down in these first days of summer, they settled into a slow, steady stroke which kept the prow of the boat headed east. But no one could paddle incessantly, and when the sun rose, the men took turns dozing, first the headman, then Oogruk, and when they did, each was careful to slip his precious paddle inside the opening, jammed against his leg, from where he could retrieve it quickly.

Nukleet did not sleep during the first two days; she encouraged her daughter to do so, and when the child's drowsy head nestled against hers, she felt more like a mother than ever before, because on this great restless sea she, Nukleet, was all that protected her daughter from death. But she had two other sensations almost equally strong. Throughout the daring trip she kept her left foot against the sealskin that contained the water, assuring herself that it was there, and her right against the spare paddle which might become so necessary if one of the men should in an accident lose his. She imagined herself reaching down, retrieving the paddle, and handing it along to either her husband or her father, and there in the vast wilderness of the sea, she felt certain that if such an accident did occur, it would be her father and not Oogruk who would lose his paddle.

But on the morning of the third day she simply could not stay awake, and once when she dozed and realized that she had left her daughter unprotected, she cried: "Father, you must hold the child for a while!" but as she started to pass the girl forward, Oogruk intervened: "Bring her this way," and as Nukleet fell toward sleep she thought, with tears in her eyes: She is not his daughter but she does fill his heart.

On the afternoon of that third day the eastern lands became visible, and this inspired the men to paddle more strongly, but night fell before they could reach the shore, and as the stars came out, seeming more brilliant because they shone not only with their own light but also with hope, the four silent immigrants moved purposefully ahead, with Nukleet again holding her child close, still keeping her feet against the reassuring water and extra paddle.

It was some while after midnight that the stars disappeared and a wind began to rise, and suddenly, with the swift change of weather that region so often provided, a storm was upon them, and in the darkness the kayak began to pitch and twist as it swept down vast chasms in the sea and rose to heights that terrified. Now the two men had to paddle furiously to keep their frail craft from capsizing, and just when they felt they could no longer bear the burning pain in their arms, Oogruk would cry "Shift!" above the howling wind and they would, in perfect rhythm change sides and maintain the forward motion.

Nukleet, feeling the kayak slip and slide, clutched her child more tightly, but the little girl did not cry or show fear; though she was terrified by the darkness and the violence of the sea, the only sign she gave of her concern was the increased pressure with which she grasped her mother's arm.

And then, as a giant wave came at them from the darkness, the headman shouted "Over!" and the kayak was tumbled about, dipping far down on its left side and sinking totally under the great wave.

It had been agreed a thousand years earlier that when a kayak turned over, the man paddling it would, with a powerful sweep of his paddle and a vigorous twisting of his body, try to keep the craft turning in the direction in which it capsized; so now, submerged in dark, icy water, the two men obeyed these ancient instructions, straining against their paddles and throwing their weight to encourage the kayak to keep rolling. Nukleet automatically did the same, for she had been so indoctrinated since birth, and even the child knew that salvation lay only in keeping the kayak rolling, so as she clung ever more tightly to her mother, she, too, helped maintain the roll.

When the kayak was at the bottom of its submersion, with its passengers upside down in the stygian waters, the miracle of its construction manifested itself, for the exquisitely fitted sealskin kept water out and air in, and in this favorable condition the light little craft continued its roll, battled the terrific power of the storm, and righted itself. When the travelers brushed the water from their eyes and saw in the east the first signals of a new day, they saw also that they were nearing land, and as the waves subsided and calm returned to the sea, the men paddled quietly ahead while Nukleet clung to her daughter, whom she had protected from the depths.

They landed before noon, unaware of whether the village they had once visited lay to the north or south but satisfied that within reason it could be found. As the two men hauled the kayak ashore, Nukleet stopped them for a moment, reached into its innards, and pulled forth the spare paddle. Standing between the men, with the paddle erect in the bright morning air, she said: "It was not needed. You knew what to do." And she embraced them both, first her father, out of deep respect for all he had done in the old land and would do in the new, and then her gallant husband, because of the love she bore him.

In this way these dark round-faced Eskimos came to Alaska.

Twelve thousand years ago—and now the chronology becomes somewhat more reliable because archaeologists have uncovered datable artifacts: stone outlines of houses and even long-hidden remains of villages—a group of Eskimos who were different from others of that remarkable race existed at various locations near the Alaskan end of the land bridge. The cause of their difference has not been ascertained, for they spoke the same language as the other Eskimos; they had managed the same adaptation to life in the coldest climates; and they were in some respects even more skilled in living productively off the creatures that roamed the earth and swam in the nearby seas.

They were somewhat smaller than the other Eskimos and darker of skin, as if they had originated in some different part of Siberia or even farther west in central Asia, but they had stayed in lands close to the western end of the land bridge long enough to acquire the basic characteristics of the Eskimos who lived there. However, when they crossed over to Alaska they dwelled apart and aroused the suspicion and even the enmity of their neighbors.

Such antagonism between groups was not unusual, for when Varnak's original group had reached Alaska they became known as Athapascans, and as we shall see, they and their descendants populated most of Alaska. Therefore, when Oogruk's Eskimos arrived to preempt the shoreline, they were greeted with hostility by the long-settled Athapascans who monopolized the choicer areas between the glaciers, and it became the rule that Eskimos clung to the seafronts, where they could maintain their ancient marine ways of life, while the Athapascans clustered in the more favorable lands, where they existed as hunters. Decades would pass without one group trespassing on the lands of the other, but when they did collide, there was apt to be trouble, contention and even death, with the sturdier Athapascans usually victorious. After all, they had occupied these lands for thousands of years before the Eskimos arrived.

It was not the traditional worldwide antagonism of mountain men versus seacoast men, but it was close to that, and if Oogruk's people found it difficult to defend themselves against the more aggressive Athapascans, this third wave of smaller, gentler newcomers seemed unable to protect themselves against anyone. So when it became doubtful that they could retain their foothold in one of the better areas of Alaska, the two hundred or so members of their clan began to question their future.

Unfortunately, at just this moment in their declining fortunes their revered sage, an old man of thirty-seven, fell so ill that he was unable to guide them, and things fell into drift, with important decisions either delayed or ignored. For example, the group had in its enforced wanderings settled temporarily in the desirable area south on the peninsula which had formed the westernmost tip of Alaska in those thousands of years when rising oceans had obliterated the land bridge. Now, of course, with the bridge exposed, there was no ocean within three hundred miles of the region, but instead, there was a natural resource even more copious and varied in its richness, and upon this largesse the group subsisted.

For reasons which have never been explained and perhaps never will be, in this period around twelve thousand years before the present, the wildlife of Alaska, and elsewhere across the earth, proliferated at a rate hitherto unknown. Not only were the species of animals extraordinarily rich in variety, but the numbers of the animals were almost excessive, and what was most inexplicable, they were invariably much, much bigger than their later descendants. Beavers were immense. Bison were like shaggy monuments. Moose towered in the air, with antlers bigger than some trees, and the shaggy musk ox was staggering in size. It was a time when great animals defined the age and when men were fortunate to live among them, for to bring down even one of these beasts meant that meat was ensured for many months to come.

Predominant as in the time of Varnak the Hunter were the mammoths, largest of the animals and still by far the most majestic. In the fifteen thousand years since Varnak had tracked Matriarch without succeeding in killing her, the mammoths had increased both in size and number, so that the area occupied by this group of Eskimos had so many of the huge creatures that any boy growing up along the eastern end of this land bridge had to become familiar with them. He would not see them every day, or even every month, but he would know that they, along with the huge bears and the crafty lions, were out there.

Such a boy was Azazruk, seventeen years old, tall for his age and Asian in every item of his appearance. His hair was a deeper black, his skin a browner yellow, his eyes more sharply narrow, his arms longer than those of his companions. That his ancestors had originated among the Mongols of Asia, there could be no doubt. He was the son of the old man who was dying, and it had been his father's hope that the boy would mature into the leadership he had exercised, but year by year it had become apparent that this was not to be, and while the father never berated his son for this deficiency, he could not hide his disappointment.

In fact, with the most hopeful intentions, the old man failed to identify any area in which his son could contribute to the clan. He could not hunt; he was unskilled at flicking sharp arrow points from cores of flint; and he showed no aptitude in leading men into battle against their oppressors. He did have a strong voice when he wanted to use it, so that leadership during discussions might have been possible, but he preferred to speak so softly that sometimes he seemed almost feminine. Yet he was a good young man, and both his father and the community at large knew it. The important question was: How would he exercise this goodness if a crisis demanded that he do so?

His father, a wise man, had seen that very few men who lived a normal life escaped the great testing moments. Born leaders, like himself, encountered them constantly, and in tracking animals or building huts or deciding where to lead the clan next, their decisions were held up to judgment by their peers. That was the burden of leadership which justified the privileges. But he had also observed that the average man, the one not remotely qualified for leadership, also faced these moments when all hung in the balance. Then a man had to act swiftly, without time for meticulous consideration or a careful calculation of possibilities. The mammoth pursued in a hunt turned unexpectedly, and someone had to confront it. The kayak upset in river turbulence, and when the paddler tried to right it in the ordinary way by increasing the speed of its toppling, a rock intervened, and then what? A man who did his best to avoid any unpleasantness was suddenly faced by a bully. Nor were women exempt from this requirement of instant judgment: A baby started from the womb in an upside-down condition, and what did the older women do? A growing girl refused to menstruate, and how should that be handled?

Since life within the ice castle of Alaska presented human beings with constant challenges, Azazruk by the age of seventeen should have developed clearly defined characteristics, but he had not, and his dying father could not guess what his son's future would be.

On a day in late spring when by ill chance Athapascans from the areas to the north made a sortie against the clan, the old man lay dying. His son was with him and not with the warriors who were rather futilely trying to protect their holdings, and as death neared, the father whispered: "Azazruk, you must lead our people to a safe home," and before the boy could respond or even let his father know that he had heard this command, death resolved the old man's apprehensions.

It was not a big fight that day, merely a continuation of the pressure the Athapascans exerted on all Eskimos regardless of where they settled, but when it coincided with the death of their longtime leader, it did confuse the clan, and the bewildered men sat before their huts in the spring evening wondering what to do. No one, and especially not those who had fought, looked to Azazruk for guidance or even suggestions. So he was left alone. Facing the mystery of death, and pondering his father's last words, he left the village and wandered away until he came to a stream which flowed down from the glacier to the east.

There as he tried to unravel the thoughts which tumbled through his head, he chanced to look down at the stream, and he saw that it was almost white because it carried myriad bits of stone flaked from rocks at the face of the glacier, and for some time he marveled at this whiteness, wondering if it represented some kind of omen. As he pondered this possibility, he saw protruding from the black mud that formed the bank of the river a curious object, golden in color and shining, and when he stooped to rescue it from the mud he saw that it was a small piece of ivory about the size of two fingers. Possibly it had broken off from some mammoth tusk or been brought inland from a walrus hunt ages ago, but what made it remarkable, even in those first moments when Azazruk held it in his hand, was that either by chance or the work of some long-dead artist, the ivory represented a living thing, perhaps a man, perhaps an animal. It had no head, but there was a torso, a joining of legs and one clearly defined hand or paw.

Turning the object this way and that in the fading light, Azazruk was astounded by the reality of this piece: it was ivory, of that he was certain, but it was also something living, and to possess such a thing created in the young man a sense of awe, of challenge and purpose. He could not believe that the finding of this lively little creature on the precise day of his father's death, when his clan was in confusion, could be an accident. He realized that the person whom the great spirits had led to this omen was destined for some significant task, and in this moment of discovery he decided to keep his find a secret. The figure was small enough to be hidden within the twist of deerskin he wore, and there it would remain until the spirits who had sent it revealed their intentions.

Then, just as he was about to leave the stream whose turbulent waters were still as white as the milk of a musk ox, he was halted by a choir of voices, and he knew the sounds emanated from the spirits who had sent him the ivory figurine and who watched over the fortunes of his clan. The voices announced in a beautiful whispering harmony which only he could have heard: "You are to be the shaman." And they sang no more.

A message like this, which might have produced tumults of joy in the heart of any ordinary Eskimo, since it would mean authority and constant intercourse with the spirits who controlled life, caused Azazruk only consternation. From his earliest days his sagacious father had found himself opposed to the various shamans who had been associated with his clan; he respected their unique powers and acknowledged the fact that he and his people had to rely upon their guidance in spiritual matters, but he resented their constant intrusion upon his day-to-day prerogatives. He had warned his son: "Stay clear of the shamans. Obey their instructions in all matters concerning the spirits, but otherwise ignore them." The old man was especially disgusted by the slovenly habits of the shamans and the filthy skins and matted hair in which they performed their mysteries and rendered their judgments: "A man doesn't have to stink in order to be wise." And the boy had had numerous opportunities to witness the justice of his father's strictures.

Once when Azazruk was ten, a scrawny Eskimo from the north had attached himself to the clan, proclaiming arrogantly that he was a shaman and offering to take the place of a wise man who had died. The deceased shaman had been somewhat better than average, so the inadequacy of the upstart miracle worker became quickly evident. He brought no mammoths or bears to the hunting areas, no male babies to the birthing beds. The general spirit of the village was neither improved nor mended, and Azazruk's father had used the unfortunate example of this inadequate man to condemn all shamans: "My mother taught me they were essential, and I still believe it. How could we live with spirits who might attack us if we did not have their protection? But I do wish the shamans could live in the spruce forest and protect us from there."

But now as Azazruk stood with the ivory figure hidden against his belly and heard the tumbling brook beside him, he began to suspect that his newfound treasure had been sent by the spirits to ratify their decision that he, Azazruk, was destined to be the shaman his people needed. He shivered at the implication and tried to dismiss it because of the heavy responsibility such a position entailed; he even contemplated throwing the unwelcome emissary back into the stream, but when he took the ivory from his waist and started to do so, the little creature seemed to be smiling at him, face or no face. And the unseen smile was so warm and congenial that Azazruk, tormented though he was by his father's death and these strange happenings, had to chuckle and then to laugh and finally to leap in the air in a kind of manic joy. He acknowledged then that he had been called, or perhaps commanded, to serve as shaman to his clan, and in this moment of spiritual acceptance of his obligation, the spirits showed their approval by causing a miracle to happen.

From the aspen trees lining the magical stream came a lonely rogue mammoth, not of exceptional size but huge in the evening shadows, and when it saw Azazruk it did not halt or shy away; instead it came forward, oblivious of the fact that it was inviting peril. When it reached a spot not four body lengths away, it stopped, looked at Azazruk, and remained rooted in place, its monstrous feet sinking slightly into the soft soil, and there it stayed, cropping aspen and willow leaves as if the Eskimo did not exist.

Slowly Azazruk withdrew, a step at a time, until he was well clear of the trees and the stream. Then, in a kind of mystical trance, he walked solemnly back to his village, where women were preparing his father for burial, and when various men, impressed by his grave mien, came to attention, he announced in sober tones: "I have brought you a mammoth," and the hunt was on. Four days later when, because of his ardent assurances to the men, they fought the great beast and killed it, the village realized that at the moment of his father's death that good man's spirit had passed into the body of his son, who predicted that the rogue mammoth would run east for two days after the first stabbings and come back the last two, seeking familiar haunts in which to die. Indeed, the creature returned to within a short walk of where Azazruk had found him, so that when he died his hulking carcass lay almost in the spot where it would be consumed. "Azazruk has power over animals," the men and women said as they butchered the mammoth and feasted on the rich meat.

And he seemed to have just that, for two weeks later when one of the village men was attacked by a pair of lionesses and badly clawed about the neck, everyone assumed that the man must die, for it was known that lions had so much poison in their claws that death was never escaped. However, this time Azazruk had run out, driven away the lionesses, and proceeded immediately to poultice the bleeding wound with leaves growing low in the forest and with moss, and the villagers were astounded to see the stricken man soon walking about and twisting his neck as if nothing had happened.

When Azazruk assumed spiritual leadership he made two innovations—which consolidated his control and made him more acceptable to his people than any other shaman within memory. He refused, utterly and with visible moral force, to accept any responsibility for military, governmental or foraging duties; he pointed out repeatedly that they were the prerogative of the leader, a daring, tested man of twenty-two and one for whom Azazruk had great respect. This man was brave, had a wide knowledge of animal habits, and asked no one to do what he himself was not prepared to do first. Under his leadership the clan could expect to protect itself at least as well as before, perhaps even better.

Second, Azazruk established practices that had never been tried before among his people. He saw no necessity for a shaman to live apart from others, and certainly no need to be filthy or unkempt. He continued to occupy his father's hut—a place half underground, half wood and stone above—and there he cared for his caribou trousers, his sealskin cloak. He made himself available to people with problems, and he especially attended to children in order to get them started in proper directions. Specifically, he assigned them tasks: girls were expected to be able to handle the skins of animals and the bones of mammoths and reindeer; boys were required to learn about hunting and the construction of implements used in the chase. He wanted the tribe to have a skilled flintknapper, another who knew about the handling of fire, another clever in the tracking of animals.

Azazruk believed that most of his power derived from the fact that he understood animals, for whenever he moved about the vast lands between the glaciers he was attentive to the beasts that shared this paradise with him. Size was of no concern to him. He knew where the little wolverines hid, and how the badgers stalked their prey. He understood the behavior of the small foxes and the devices of the rats and tiny creatures that burrowed under the soil. Sometimes, when he himself hunted or helped others to do so, he felt momentarily like a wolf stalking a herd, but his major delight was always those larger creatures: the mammoth, the great moose, the musk ox, the tremendous bison and the powerful lion.

If man had a certain majesty because of his superior wit and cleverness of hand, these animals so much larger than he had their own majesty, and it derived from the fact that in this area of bitter winter cold they had found ways to protect themselves and to survive till spring warmed the air and melted the snows. They were as wise in their own ways as any shaman, and by studying them, Azazruk hoped he could perhaps detect their secrets and profit from them.

But when his study of the animals was concluded, and he had mixed their wisdom in with what he was learning about human beings, there remained another world of the spirit which neither he nor the animals could penetrate or inhabit. What caused the great winds to roar out of Asia? Why was it always colder to the north than to the south? Who fed the glaciers, when anyone could see that almost daily they died when their snouts reached dry land or the sea? Who called yellow flowers to birth in the spring and red ones in the fall? And why were babies born at almost the same time that old men died?

He spent the first seven years of his leadership in wrestling with these questions, and in that time he devised certain rules. The shiny pebbles he had collected, the oddments his mother had treasured, the sticks and bones which had omen-power were of profound assistance when he wished to summon the spirits and converse with them. From such dialogue he learned much, but always in the back of his mind there remained that vision of the piece of golden ivory shaped like an animal or a man, like a smiling man perhaps, even though it had no head. And he began to see his world as an amusing place where ridiculous things happened and where a man or woman could obey all the rules and avoid all the perils but still fall into some absurd situation at which their neighbors and the spirits themselves had to laugh, and not furtively either but with great guffaws. The world was tragic, and fine men and strong animals died arbitrarily, but it was also so preposterous that sometimes the crests of mountains seemed to bend together in laughter.

In Azazruk's ninth year as shaman the laughter ceased. Illness brought in from the sea struck the village, and after the bodies were buried, the Athapascans invaded from the east. Mammoths left the area, the bison followed, bringing hunger, and one day when all things seemed to conspire against the clan, Azazruk summoned the village elders, more than half of them older than he, and said bluntly: "The spirits send warnings. It's time to move."

"Where?" the leader of the hunters asked, and before Azazruk could offer a suggestion, the men advanced the negative answers.

"We can't go toward the home of the Great Star. The people who hunt the whale are there."

"And we can't go to where the sun rises. The people of the trees are there."

"The Land of Broken Bays would be reasonable, but those people are fierce. They will drive us back."

And so the logical options were discarded. It seemed that this unfortunate group, so small that it commanded no power, was wanted nowhere, but then a timid man, one who could scarcely be called a leader, suggested: "We could go back to where we first came from," and during a long silence the men considered this retreat, but to them the land their ancestors had left two thousand years before was not a viable memory; there were tribal recollections of a decisive trip from the west, but no one remembered any longer what that ancient homeland had been like or what strong reasons had compelled the old ones to leave. "We came from over there," an old woman said, waving her hand vaguely toward Asia, "but who knows?"

No one did, and that first broaching of the subject came to naught, but some days later Azazruk saw a girl cutting a friend's hair with a clamshell, and he asked: "Where did you find that shell?" and the girls told him that in their family there was a tradition that several such shells had been brought to the village in times past by strange-looking men who spoke their language, but in a curious way.

"Where did they come from?"

The girls did not know, but next day they brought their parents to the shaman's hut, and these older people said that they had not known the shell-bearers: "They came before our time. But our grand-mother told us they had come from that direction," and both agreed from their different memories that the strangers had come from the southwest. They had not been like those in the village, but they had been likable visitors and they had danced. Everyone whose parents had heard the ancient stories agreed that the shell-bearers had danced.

It was this accidental intelligence, born of no sensible reasoning, which launched Azazruk in his contemplation of going to the place from which the shells had come. After much thought he concluded that since movement into no other area was practical and since continuation where his people were seemed destined to produce increasingly bad results, their only hope lay in lands that were unknown but which supposedly were habitable.

But he could not recommend such a perilous journey without ratification from the spirits, so for three long days he remained practically motionless in his hut, his fetishes spread before him, and in the darkness, when hunger had induced a kind of stupor, they spoke to him. Voices came from afar, sometimes in tongues he did not understand, at other times as clear as the bellowing of a moose on a frosty morning: "Azazruk, your people starve. Enemies insult them on all sides. You are too powerless to fight. You must flee."

This he had already accepted, and he considered it strange that the spirits should repeat the obvious, but upon reflection he withdrew that harsh judgment: They are moving step by step, like a man testing new ice. And after a while the spirits reached the core of what they wished to say: "It would be better, Azazruk, if you went toward the Great Star to the edge of the frozen land and hunted the whale and walrus in the old way. So if you are brave and have many bold men, go there."

Beating his hands against his forehead, he shouted: "But our leader has no fighting men in sufficient number," and the spirits said: "We know."

In total frustration Azazruk wondered why the spirits would recommend he go to the north when they knew it was so hazardous, but what they said next drove him to a frenzy: "In the north you would build umiaks and go forth to hunt the great whale. You would chase the walrus and perish if he caught you. You would hunt the seal, and fish through the ice, and live as your people had always lived. In the north you would do all these things."

The words were so insane that Azazruk started to choke. Air caught in his throat, and he fell forward among his fetishes in a faint. He remained thus for a long while, and in his frenzied dreams he realized that in giving these impossible orders, the spirits were reminding him of who he was, of what his life had been for generations untold, telling him that even though he and his clan had lived inland for two thousand years, they were still people of the frozen seas which lesser men would not dare to challenge. He was an Eskimo, a man of wondrous tradition, and not even the passage of generations could erase that supreme fact.

When he revived, cleansed of fear by the insistent messages of the spirits, they spoke calmly: "To the southwest there must be islands, or how could the strangers have brought shells?"

"I do not understand," he cried, and they said: "Islands mean seas, and seas mean shells. A man can find his heritage in many different forms." And they said no more.

On the morning of the fourth day Azazruk appeared before the worried people who had spent the previous night outside his hut, listening to the strange sounds coming from within. Tall, gaunt, clean, sunken-eyed and afire with an illumination he had not known before, he announced: "The spirits have spoken. We shall go there," and he pointed toward the southwest.

But back in his hut, where his people could not see him, his resolve faltered, and he was overcome by terror at what might happen on such a journey, over distances to strange lands that might or might not exist. Then he saw that the little ivory figure was laughing at him, ridiculing his fears and sharing with him in its timeless way the wisdom it had acquired when part of the tusk of a great walrus and when lying for seventeen thousand years in the muck of a glacial stream while a universe of dead fish and stricken mammoths and careless men drifted past: "It will be joyous, Azazruk. You will see seven thousand sunsets, seven thousand sunrises."

"Will I find a refuge for my people?"

"Does that matter?"

And as he tucked the little figure back in its pouch he could hear the laughter, the chuckling of the wind coming over a hill, the exhilaration of a whale breaching after a long submarine chase, the gaiety of a young fox chasing birds aimlessly, the wonderful, hallowed sound of a universe that does not care whether a man finds refuge or not so long as he enjoys the irreverent pleasure of the search.

The nineteen years during which Azazruk led his wandering people back and forth in southeastern Alaska were among the most glorious this part of the world would ever know. The animal kingdom was at its apex, providing an endless supply of noble beasts well suited to the stupendous land. The mountains were higher then, the surging glaciers more powerful, the wild-running rivers more tumultuous. It was an energetic land whose every feature struck notes of wonder, from the winters so cold that prudent animals went underground, to summers in which a multitude of flowers filled the plains.

It was a land in those years of enormous dimension; no one man could travel from one end to the other or traverse the multitude of glacial rivers and soaring peaks. From almost any spot a traveler could see snow-capped mountains, and when he slept at night he could hear powerful lions and huge wolves not far away. Of special interest were the brown bears, as tall as trees when they stood erect, which they liked to do, as if boasting of their height. In later years they would be known as grizzlies, and of all the animals that came close to camps where travelers halted, they were the most perplexing. If food was available, they could be as gentle as the sheep which inhabited the lower hills, but if they were disappointed or enraged by unexpected behavior, they could tear a man apart with one swipe of their tremendous claws.

In these days the bears were immense, sixteen and seventeen feet tall, and in the uninitiated they produced terror, but to Azazruk, as one who had learned to consult with animals, they were big, awkward, unpredictable friends. He did not seek them out, but he spoke with them when they appeared at the edges of his people's camps, and when he came upon them he would sit calmly upon a rock and ask them how the berries were among the birch trees and what the mighty bison were up to. The great bears, always big enough to bite him in two, would listen attentively, and sometimes come close enough almost to nudge him, and smelling that he was unafraid, never harmed him.

That was not the case with one young hunter, who, seeing a bear with the shaman and not knowing that a special relationship existed between the two, had attacked it. The bear, bewildered by this sudden change, fended off the hunter, but when the man attacked a second time, it swung its right paw, almost decapitating the young assailant, and lumbered off. This time the shaman's ministration with leaves and moss proved futile; the man was dead before words could be exchanged, and the camp saw that great bear no more.

Why did it take nineteen years for this ordinary group of Eskimos to locate their new home? For one thing, they did not speed to some established target; they drifted along, sampling this place and that. For another, rivers were sometimes in flood for two or three summers at a time and mountains intruded. But principally the fault was the shaman's, for whenever he came upon a likely spot, he wanted to believe that this was it, and he tended to remain with his choice until adversity became so great that survival dictated a further move.

Always the people allowed him to decide, for they were aware that in shifting so radically to new terrains, they must have the unqualified support of the spirits. Once in the later years when they were well established on the shores of a huge lake teeming with fish, they wanted to remain, and even when the spirits warned the shaman that it was time for his people to move, they spent two years dawdling along the shores of the lake, but when they reached the western extremity where a lively river left to seek the sea, they obediently packed their few belongings and moved on.

During the next year, the seventeenth of their pilgrimage, they were faced by problems far more crucial than usual, for even the most casual exploration proved that they were entering not merely upon new land but onto a peninsula bordered on both its narrowing shores by ocean. But the spirits encouraged them to test the peninsula, and when they again found themselves in close contact with the sea, after an absence of two thousand years, powerful changes began to take place, as if racial memories long subdued were surging back to the surface.

Responding to the salt air and the splashing of waves, these wanderers who had never eaten shellfish or caught fish in the sea found themselves enthusiastically doing both. Artisans began building little boats not much different from the kayaks their ancestors had known, and those craft which did not take well to waves were quickly abandoned, while others which seemed adapted to the sea were improved. In a score of little ways, many of them of apparent insignificance, these onetime Eskimos were becoming sea people again.

Azazruk, as fearful as any about forging ahead into a world so different, was encouraged to continue by the unwavering support of his fetishes, for when he spread them in his skin hut beside the ocean, they spoke only approvingly of this venture, and the most ardent encouragement came from the little ivory figure. "I think," Azazruk said to it one night as the waves of a rising sea thundered outside, "that you wanted to bring us to the sea. Did you once live here?" And above the storm he could hear the little figurine laughing, and on later days, when the seas were calm, he was sure that he heard chuckles from that pouch.

The clan spent that year pushing ever westward, exploring their peninsula as if just around the next hill they would find the refuge they sought, but sometimes in the distance they could see smoke from unidentified fires and this meant they were not yet safe. In this uncertain state of mind, they reached the western end of the peninsula, and now they were confronted by a question, the answer to which would determine their history for the next twelve thousand years: should they try to maintain a foothold on the peninsula or should they plunge ahead onto the unknown islands?

Rarely does a people have an opportunity to make within a limited period a decision of such gravity; choices are made, of course, but they tend to creep up on a society over a much longer period of time or even to be made by refusing to choose. Such a moment would occur eons later when black people in central Africa had to decide whether to move south out of the tropics to cooler lands fronting the southern oceans, or when a group of Pilgrims in England had to decide if life was likely to be better on the opposite side of the Atlantic.

For Azazruk's clan their moment came when they elected, after painful deliberation, to quit the peninsula and try their fortunes on that chain of islands stringing out to the west. This was a daring decision, and of the two hundred who had left their relatively secure settlement eighteen years before, fewer than half had survived to enter the islands, but many had been born along the way. In a way this was fortunate, because it meant that the majority of those who would execute the decision would be younger and more prepared to adjust to the unknown.

It was a sturdy group that followed the shaman across the narrow sea onto that first island, and they would require both physical stamina and moral courage to exist in these forbidding terrains. In the chain there were more than a dozen major islands they might have chosen and more than a hundred lesser ones, some little more than specks. They were dramatic islands, many with high mountains, others with great volcanoes covered with snow much of the year, and Azazruk's people looked in awe as they moved along the chain. They explored the big one later to be known as Unimak, then crossed the sea to Akutan and Unalaska and Umnak. Then they tried Seguam and Atka and twisted Adak, until one morning as they probed westward they saw on the horizon a forbidding island protected by a barrier of five tall mountains rising from the sea to guard its eastern approaches. Azazruk, repelled by this inhospitable shore, cried to his rowers in the first boat: "On to the next one!" but as the convoy

passed the headland to the north, he saw opening before him a splendid wide bay from whose central plain rose a towering volcano of
perfect outline and surpassing snow-capped beauty that had been
sleeping peacefully for the past ten thousand years.

"This is to be your home," the spirits whispered, adding a reassuring promise: "Here you will live dangerously yet know great joy."
With this surety Azazruk headed toward the shore, but halted when
the spirits said: "Beyond the headland there is a better," and when he
explored further he came upon a deep bay rimmed by mountains and
protected on the northwest, from where storms came, by a chain of
islands curved like a protecting hand. Along the eastern side of this
bay he found an estuary, a kind of fjord flanked by cliffs, and when
he reached its head he cried: "This is what the spirits promised us!"
and here his wandering clan established their home.

The travelers had not been on Lapak even one full season before,
on a much smaller island to the north, a tiny volcano, which reached
not a hundred feet above the sea, exploded in a dazzling display of
fiery fumes, as if it were an angry whale spouting not water but flame.
The newcomers could not hear the sparks hissing as they fell back
into the sea, nor know that on the far shore, beneath clouds of steam,
a river of lava, apparently endless in supply, was pouring into the sea,
but they did witness the continued display, which the spirits assured
Azazruk they had organized as a welcome to his new home. And
because the young volcano sputtered whenever it was about to explode, the newcomers named it Qugang, the Whistler.

Lapak had a broken, rectangular shape, twenty-one miles east to
west at its widest, eleven north-south in its two extended arms. Eleven
mountains, some reaching more than two thousand feet high, rimmed
the outer circumference, but the shoreline of the two bays was habitable and in certain places even inviting. No tree had ever stood on the
island, but a lush green grass grew everywhere, and low shrubs appeared wherever they found a valley offering protection from the
wind. The salient aspect, apart from the two volcanoes and the protecting mountains, was the abundance of inlets, for this was, as the
spirits had foretold, an island totally committed to the sea, and any
man who elected to live on it knew that he must make his living from
that sea and spend his life in obedience to its waves, its storms and its
abundance.

Azazruk, surveying his new domain, noted with assurance the

several small rivers that threaded inland: "These will bring us food. On this island our people can live in peace."

Prior to the arrival of Azazruk's people the island had never known inhabitants, although occasionally some storm-driven hunter in his solitary kayak or group of men in their umiak had been tossed on the island, and one morning some children playing in a valley that opened onto the sea came upon three skeletons of men who had died in dreadful isolation. But no group had ever tried to settle here, and it was generally supposed that no woman had ever set foot on Lapak before Azazruk's people came.

However, one day a group of men who had gone fishing in one of the rivers that came down from the flanks of the central volcano was overtaken by nightfall and sought refuge in a cave high on a mound overlooking the area of the Bering Sea subtended by the chain of islands, and when morning came they saw to their astonishment that their cave was occupied by a woman unbelievably old, and they ran to their shaman with cries of "Miracle! An old woman hiding in a cave."

Azazruk followed the men to the cave and asked them to wait outside while he investigated this strange development, and when he was well within the cave, he found himself facing the withered, leathery features of an ancient woman whose mummified body had been propped upright, so that she seemed to be alive and almost eager to share with him the adventures she had experienced in the past millennia.

He remained with her for a long time, trying to visualize how she had reached this island, what her life had been like and whose loving hands had placed her in this protected and reverential position. She seemed so eager to speak to him that he bent forward as if to hear her, and in a low voice he spoke comforting words to himself, as if she were uttering them: "Azazruk, you have brought your people to their home. You will travel no more."

When he returned to his hut by the shore and took out his stones and bones for guidance, he heard her reassuring voice directing his decisions, and much of the good that his people enjoyed on Lapak Island came from her sage advice.

With no trees and little space suitable for such agriculture as had been developed at this time, how did the immigrants expect to live?

From the largesse of the sea, and it was astonishing how the oceans had anticipated the needs of these daring people and supplied them in abundance. Were they hungry? Every bay and inlet on the island teemed with whelks and shellfish and slugs and seaweed of the most nutritious kind. Did one hunger for something more substantial? With a string made of seal gut and a hook carved from whalebone, one could fish in the bays and be almost certain of catching something, and if a man found a pole among the flotsam, he could perch himself upon a protruding rock and fish in the sea itself. Did one require timbers for building a hut? Wait till the next storm, and onto the shore right before one's land would come an immense pile of driftwood.

And for one who dared to leave the land and venture upon the ocean itself, there was a richness no man could exhaust. All he needed was the skill to build himself a one-seated kayak and the courage to trust his life in this frail thing that even the smallest wave could crush against a rock. With his kayak a man could go two miles from shore and catch beautiful salmon, long and sleek. At ten miles he would find halibut and cod, and if he preferred, as most did, the heartier meat of the large sea animals, he could hunt for seals, or venture out into the body of the ocean and test his courage against titanic whales and powerful walruses.

It was easier to spot a whale than one might suppose, for the islands of the chain were so disposed that only certain passages were available to creatures of this size, and Lapak rested between two of them. Whales cruised so close to the headlands that they were regularly visible, but their hunting became an uncertain matter. The brave men of the island would chase a whale for three days and wound it grievously, but fail to bring it to shore. With tears in their eyes they would watch the leviathan swim away, although they knew it to be so stricken that it must die at sea and drift ashore at some distant spot to feed a group of strangers who had played no part in its capture. But then some morning a woman rising early in Lapak to gather kelp along the shore would see not far off an object floating on the sea, and it would be of such tremendous size that it could only be a whale, and for a moment she would think it a live wanderer that had ventured close inland, but after a while when it did not move, a surge of overpowering excitement would possess her and she would run screaming to her men: "A whale! A whale!" and they would rush to their kayaks and speed out to the dead giant and attach inflated sealskins to its carcass to keep it afloat as they nosed it slowly toward their shore. And when they butchered it, with women beating on drums, they would see the fatal wounds inflicted by some other tribe and even find harpoon heads behind the whale's ear. They would give thanks to the unknown brave men who had fought this whale so that Lapak could eat.

It was some time before Azazruk's people discovered the real wealth of their island, but one morning as the shaman huddled in the middle of the island's first six-man umiak, built by a powerful hunter named Shugnak, the boat strayed among the chain of little islands leading to the small volcano. Since these rocky protrusions were dangerous, Azazruk warned Shugnak: "Not too close to those rocks," but the hunter, younger and more daring than the shaman, had seen something moving in the masses of matted kelp that surrounded the rocks, so he pressed on, and as the umiak entered the tangled seaweeds, Azazruk chanced to see a swimming creature whose appearance so startled him that he cried aloud, and when others asked why, he could only point at this miracle in the waves.

Thus the men of Lapak made their acquaintance with the fabled sea otter, a creature much like a small seal, for it was built similarly and swam in much the same way. This first one was about five feet long, beautifully tapered and obviously at ease in the icy waters. But what had made Azazruk gasp, and others too when they saw the creature, was its face, because it resembled precisely the face of a be-whiskered old man, one who had enjoyed life and aged gracefully. There was the wrinkled brow, the bloodshot eye, the nose, the smiling lips and, strangest of all, the wispy, untended mustache. From its appearance, exaggerated in the telling, would be born the legend of the mermaid, and in fact, this face was so like a man's that later hunters would sometimes be startled by the watery vision and refrain momentarily from killing the otter lest an involuntary murder take place.

In the first moments of meeting this amazing creature, Azazruk knew intuitively that it was special, but what happened next convinced him and Shugnak at the stern of the umiak that they had come upon a rare sea animal: trailing along behind the first otter came a mother, floating easily on her back like a relaxed bather taking the sun in a quiet pool, while on her stomach protruding above the waves perched a baby otter, taking its ease too and idly surveying the world. Azazruk was enchanted by this maternal scene, for he loved babies and revered the mysteries of motherhood, even though he had no wife or children of his own, and as the loving pair drifted past he called to the rowers: "What a cradle! Look at them!"

But the hunters were staring at something even more extraordinary, for trailing behind the first two otters came an older fellow, also floating on his back, and what he was doing was unbelievable. Perched securely on his ample belly lay a large rock, and as it rested there, held in place by his belly muscles, he used his two front paws as hands, and with them he slammed down upon the rock clams and other similar sea creatures, knocking them repeatedly until their shells broke so that he could pick out their meat and stuff it into his smiling mouth.

"Is that a rock on his belly?" Azazruk cried, and those in the prow of the umiak shouted back that it was, and at this instant Shugnak, who was always tempted to throw his lance at anything that moved, swung his paddle so dexterously that the rear of the umiak moved close to the basking otter. With a skillful launching of his sharp lance, Shugnak pinned the unsuspecting clam-eater and dragged him to the boat.

Secretly he skinned the otter, throwing the flesh to his women for a stew, and after the skin had cured for some months, he appeared with it draped about his shoulders. All marveled at its softness, its shimmering beauty and unequaled thickness. Trade in sea-otter skins had begun, and so had the rivalry between Azazruk the benevolent shaman and Shugnak the master hunter.

The latter saw from the beginning that the fur of the sea otter was going to be treasured by men, and even though trade to far places was still thousands of years in the future, each adult on Lapak wanted an otter skin, or two or three. They could have all the seal-skins they wanted, and they made admirable clothing, but it was the sea otter that the islanders craved, and Shugnak was the man who could provide them.

He quickly saw that to chase these otters in a six-man umiak was wasteful, and drawing upon tribal memories, he directed his men to build approximations of the ancient kayaks, and when these proved seaworthy, he taught his sailors how to hunt with him in groups. Silently they would prowl the sea until they came upon a family of otters, with some fat fellow cracking clams. On some lucky days his men would bring home as many as six, and the time came when the islanders discarded the flesh and kept only the pelts. Then the massacre of the otters became appalling.

Azazruk had to intervene. "It is wrong to kill the otters," he said, but Shugnak, a good man and in things other than hunting a gentle one, resisted: "We need the pelts." It was obvious that no one really *needed* the pelts, for seals were plentiful and the otter meat was found to be tough, but those who already had otter-skin garments reveled in them while those who lacked them kept urging Shugnak to bring them skins.

The hunter's view was simplicity itself: "The otters are out there and they do no one any good, just swimming about and cracking clamshells on their bellies." But Azazruk had a deeper understanding: "The animals of land and sea are brought to earth by the great spirits so that man can live." And he became so obsessed with this concept that one morning he climbed to the cave of the mummified old woman, where he sat for a long time in her presence as if consulting with her.

"Am I foolish in thinking that the sea otters are my brothers?" he asked, but only the reverberation of his voice responded.

"Could it be that Shugnak is right to hunt them as he does?" Again there was silence.

"Suppose we are both right, Azazruk to love the animals, Shugnak to kill them?" He paused, then asked a question which would perplex subsequent philosophers: "How can two things so different both be right?"

Then, like all men and women throughout history who would consult oracles, he found the answer within himself. Projecting his own voice toward the mummy, he heard her speak back with warm assurance: "Azazruk must love and Shugnak must kill, and you are both right."

She said no more, but there in the silent cave Azazruk fashioned the phrase that would sing in his islanders' minds: We live off the animals, but we also live with them. And as he elaborated his perception of what the spirits intended, many listened, but most still yearned for their otter skins, and these began a whispering campaign against their shaman, alleging that he did not want the otters to be killed because they looked like human beings, whereas everyone knew they were only big fish covered with fur of great worth.

The island community split down the middle, with some supporting their shaman, others backing their hunter, and in thousands of these early communities in Asia and Alaska there were similar fractures, the dreamers versus the pragmatists, the shamans responsible for the spiritual well-being of their people versus the great hunters responsible for feeding them, and throughout all ensuing eons this unavoidable struggle would continue, for on this issue men of good will could divide.

On Lapak Island the conflict came to a focus one summer morning as Shugnak was preparing to take his one-man kayak out to catch sea otters and the shaman halted him at the shore: "We do not need any more dead otters. Let the creatures live." He was an ascetic, with a mystical quality which set him apart from other men. He was a quiet man, but on the infrequent times when he did speak, others had to listen.

Shugnak was entirely different: stocky, broad of shoulder and heavy of hand, but it was the savage look of his face that marked him as a great hunter. It was reddish rather than the yellow or dark brown of the typical islander and distinguished by three powerful lines parallel to his eyes. The first was a huge length of whalebone stuck through the septum of his nose and protruding past each nostril. The second was a fierce, bristly jet-black mustache. And the third, most impressive of all, was a pair of rather small labrets set in the two corners of his mouth and connected across his chin by three links of a chain intricately carved from walrus ivory. He was dressed in skins from sea lions he had caught, and when he stood erect, his powerful arms broadening his torso, he was formidable.

On this morning he did not propose to have the shaman interrupt his hunt, and when Azazruk tried to do so, he gently put him aside. Azazruk realized that Shugnak could knock him down with only a push, but his responsibility for the welfare of animals could not be surrendered, and he moved back to obstruct Shugnak's passage. This time the hunter grew impatient, and without intending any irreverence, for he liked the shaman so long as the latter tended his own affairs, he shoved Azazruk so sharply that he fell, whereupon Shugnak strode to his kayak, paddled angrily to sea, and continued his hunting.

A tenseness fell over the island, and when Shugnak returned, Azazruk was waiting for him, and for several days the two men argued. The shaman pleaded against what he feared might be the extermination of the sea otters, while Shugnak countered with hardheaded realism that since the creatures had obviously been brought to these waters to be used, he intended using them.

Azazruk, for the first time in his long years of leadership, lost his composure and inveighed rather ridiculously against all hunters and their prowling kayaks, and he became so offensive that the people started to turn away from him. And he realized that he had made himself so foolish in their eyes, had so alienated them, that he had no recourse but to relinquish his leadership. So one morning before the others were awake he gathered his fetishes, left his hut by the sea, and walked mournfully to the headwaters of a distant bay, where he built himself a mud-walled hut. Like a thousand shamans before him, he was learning that the spiritual adviser of a people had best remain aloof from their political and economic quarrels.

He was an old man now, nearly fifty, and although his people still gave him credit for having led them to this island, they no longer wanted him meddling in their affairs; they wanted a more sensible leader like Shugnak, who could, if he put his mind to it, learn to consult with spirits and placate them.

In his sequestered hut Azazruk would end his days in exile. From the shores of the bay he could collect enough shellfish and slugs and seaweed to survive, and after some days big-hearted Shugnak provided him with a kayak, and although he had not paddled much before, he now became reasonably skillful. Often he would venture far from shore, always to the north toward those waters which had perpetually lured his people, and there, deep in the waves, he would talk with the seals and converse with the great whales as they drifted by. Occasionally he might see a group of walruses plowing northward, and he would call to them, and sometimes in the warm days of summer he would spend the entire night—only a few hours long—under the pale stars, at one with the vast ocean, at peace with the sea.

But the times he treasured were those in which he found himself in the kelp close to some family of sea otters and he could see the mother floating on her back with her baby on her bosom, the pup's wide eyes gleaming at the new world it was discovering, or greet the happy old man with whiskers as he floated past with a rock on his belly and two clams in his fat paws.

Of all the animals Azazruk had known, and his friends were legion, from the towering mammoth to the crafty lion, he prized most highly these sea otters, for they were creatures of distinction, and as his years drew to a close he conceived the idea—for which he had no reasonable justification—that it was the sea otter who best represented the spirits that had guided him through his honorable and productive life: It was they who called me when we lived on those arid steppes to the east. It was they who came at night to remind me of the ocean where I and my people belonged. And one morning when he returned from a night voyage on that maternal ocean and sat among his fetishes and took them from their pouches so they could breath and talk to him, he realized with joyous surprise that the headless ivory piece he had cherished had never been a man, but a sea otter lazing along on its back, and in that moment he discovered the oneness of the world, the unity of spirit among mammoth, whale, bird and man, and his soul exulted in this knowledge.

They did not find him until some days later. Two pregnant women made the long journey to his hut to enlist his aid in ensuring healthy babies, and when they stood near his door and called him without receiving an answer, they supposed that he was once more out on the ocean, but then one of them spotted his empty kayak well up on the shore, and she deduced that he must still be within his hut. When the women entered they found him seated on the earth, his body fallen forward over his collection of fetishes.

The chain of islands to which Azazruk led his clan would later be known as the Aleutians and their residents as Aleuts (Ahl-ay-oots) and a stranger, more complex collection of people would rarely exist on this earth. Isolated, they developed a unique way of life. Men and women of the sea, they derived their entire subsistence from it. Each group self-contained on its own island, they felt no necessity in these early days to invent war. Secure within the world governed by their benevolent spirits, they achieved a satisfactory life. Tragedy they knew, for at times starvation threatened, and most families lost fathers and husbands and sons when sudden storms swept the great seas upon which they depended. They had no trees, nor any of the alluring animals they had known on the mainland, and no contact with either the Eskimos of the north or Athapascans of the center, but they did live in close contact with the spirit of the sea, the mystery of the little volcano that sputtered off their shore and the vivid life of whales, walruses, seals and sea otters.

Later experts, looking at the inviting way in which the chain of islands reached out for Asia, constituting almost a land bridge of its own, would conclude that a particular tribe of Mongolians from Asia must have walked across this supposed bridge to the far western group of islands, populating each of the more easterly ones in turn.

It did not happen that way. The Aleutians were settled east to west by Eskimos like Azazruk and his people, who, if they had turned north when they crossed the real land bridge, would have become indistinguishable from the Eskimos of the Arctic Ocean. Having turned south, they became Aleuts.

Azazruk, who would be revered in island legend as the Great Shaman, left two heritages of importance. For his trips on the ocean in the closing years of his life he devised an Aleut hat which would become perhaps the most distinctive head covering in the world. It was carved of wood, although baleen from a whale could also be used, and it came straight up in the back to a fairly high level. There it sloped downward in a broad sweep forward, stretching gracefully in front of the eyes and at a beautifully dropping angle, so that the sailor's eyes had a long visor to shade them from the glare of the sun. In this form alone the hat would have been distinctive, for it provided a lovely artistic form, but from the point where the erect back joined the long slope forward, Azazruk had fastened five or six graceful arching feathers or stems of dead flowers or bits of decorated baleen, so positioned that they arched forward above the visor. This wooden hat was a work of art, perfect in every proportion.

When a group of six or seven Aleuts, each in his own kayak, each with his Azazruk hat, visors sloping forward, feathers atilt, swept across the ocean, they were memorable; and in later days when European artists traveling with explorers sketched them, the hats became a symbol of the arctic.

The shaman's other contribution was more lasting. When children born on Lapak had pestered him to tell the exciting legends about the other land from which the clan had come, he always referred to it and its glaciers and fascinating collection of animals as the Great Land, for it had been great, and to leave it had been a sad defeat. In time those words came to represent the lost heritage. The Great Land lay back to the east, beyond the chain of islands, and it was a noble memory.

The Aleutian word for Great Land was Alaxsxaq, and when Europeans reached the Aleutian Islands, their first stopping point in this portion of the arctic, and asked the people what name the lands hereabout had, they replied "Alaxsxaq," and in the European tongues this became Alaska.

IV

THE EXPLORERS

O N NEW YEAR'S DAY OF 1723 A GIANT UKRAINIAN COSSACK
stationed in the remote town of Yakutsk, most easterly of the
Siberian posts, became so outraged by the gross tyrannies of the governor that he cut the man's throat. Immediately arrested by six junior
officials, for no three could have handled him, he was beaten, manacled, and tied to an exposed pillar on the parade grounds facing the
Lena River. There, after nineteen lashes from the knout on his bare
back, he heard his sentence:

> "Trofim Zhdanko, cossack in the service of Tsar Peter, may
> heaven preserve his illustrious life, you are to be conveyed in
> shackles to St. Petersburg and hanged."

At seven the next morning, hours before the sun would rise in that far
northern latitude, a troop of sixteen soldiers set out for the Russian
capital, forty-one hundred miles to the west, and after three hundred
and twenty days of the most difficult travel across the trackless
wastelands of Siberia and central Russia, they reached what passed
for civilization at Vologda, where swift messengers galloped ahead to
inform the tsar of what had happened to his governor in Yakutsk.
Six days later the troop delivered their still-shackled prisoner to a
dank prison, where, as he was thrown into a lightless dungeon, the

guard informed him: "We know all about you, Prisoner Zhdanko. On Friday morning you hang."

But at half after ten the next night a man even taller and more formidable than the cossack left an imposing house along the Neva River and hastened to a waiting carriage drawn by two horses. He was bundled in furs but wore no hat, his thick head of hair blowing in the frosty November wind. As soon as he was settled, four men on horseback, heavily armed, took positions before and after his carriage, for he was Peter Romanoff, Tsar of all the Russias, and destined to be remembered in history as The Great.

"To the prison by the docks," he said, and as the coachman drove down one frozen alleyway after another, the tsar leaned forward and shouted: "Aren't you glad it isn't spring? These streets would be hubdeep in mud."

"If it was spring, Sire," the man shouted back with an obvious touch of familiarity, "we wouldn't be using these alleys."

"Don't call them alleys," the tsar snapped. "They'll be rock-paved next year."

When the carriage reached the prison, which Peter had prudently placed close to the docks where he knew that sailors from all the shipping nations of Europe would be brawling, he leaped out of his carriage before his guard could form, strode to the tightly barred portal, and banged on it clamorously. It was some moments before the sleepy watchman inside could muster himself and come complainingly to the tiny wicket, set in the center of the heavy gate, to ask: "What noise at this hour?"

Peter, showing no displeasure at being stopped by such a functionary, said amiably: "Tsar Peter."

The watchman, invisible behind his wicket, betraying no surprise at this remarkable answer, for he had long known of the tsar's propensity for surprise visits, replied briskly: "Open immediately, Sire!" and Peter heard the gates creaking as the watchman pushed them apart. When they were sufficiently ajar for the carriage to enter, the coachman indicated that Peter should jump in behind him and enter the prison courtyard in state, but the giant ruler was already striding forward and calling for the chief jailer.

The noise had awakened the prisoners long before their custodian was roused, and when they saw who it was that was visiting at this late hour, they began to bombard him with petitions: "Sire, I am here unjustly!" "Sire, look to your rascal in Tobolsk. He stole my lands."

"Tsar Peter, justice!" Ignoring the criminals who did the shouting, but noting their complaints against any specific agent of his government, he proceeded directly to the heavy oaken door guarding the main entrance to the building, where he banged impatiently on the iron knocker, but he had done this only once when the watchman from the gate shuffled up, calling in a loud voice: "Mitrofan! It's the tsar!" Then Peter heard vigorous activity taking place behind the massive doors constructed of wood he had imported from England.

In less than a minute, Jailer Mitrofan had his door opened and his head bowed low: "Sire, I am eager to obey your orders."

"You better be," the emperor said, clapping his appointee on the shoulder. "I want you to fetch the cossack Trofim Zhdanko."

"Fetch him where, Sire?"

"To that red room across the way from yours," and assuming that his order would be promptly carried out, he marched unguided to the room on which he himself had done the carpentering a few years before. It was not large, for in those first days of his new city Peter had visualized it as being used in exactly the way he now proposed, and it contained only a table and three chairs, for he had supposed that here prisoners would be brought for interrogation: one chair behind the table for the official, one at the side of the table for the clerk taking down the answers, and that one over there for the prisoner, who would sit with light from the window glaring in his face. At night, if such interrogations had to be conducted, the light would come from a whale-oil lamp on the wall behind the official's head. And to give it the solemnity its intended purpose required, Peter had painted the room a sullen red.

While waiting for the prisoner to be produced, Peter rearranged the furniture, for he did not wish to stress the fact that Zhdanko was a prisoner. Without calling for help, he moved the narrow table to the center, set one chair on one side and the other two facing it from the opposite side. Still awaiting the arrival of the jailer, he paced back and forth, as if his energy were so great that it could not be controlled, and as he heard footsteps coming down the stone corridor, he tried to recall the fractious cossack he had once sentenced to prison. He remembered him as a huge mustachioed Ukrainian, tall like himself, who after his release from jail had been dispatched to the city of Yakutsk, where he was to serve as military constable enforcing the orders of the civilian governor. He had been a worthy soldier up to the moment he fell into serious difficulty, and in memory of those better days the tsar now mumbled: "Good fortune they didn't hang him out there."

The latch rattled, the door opened, and there stood Trofim Zhdanko, six feet two, broad-shouldered, black-haired, fierce drooping mustache, huge beard which bristled forward when the owner jutted out his chin to argue a point. On the march to the interrogation room, surrounded by guards, the jailer had warned him who his nocturnal visitor was, so as soon as they entered, the big cossack, still manacled, bowed low and said softly, with no theatrical humility but with sincere respect: "Sire, you do me honor."

For just a moment Tsar Peter, who hated beards and had sought to prohibit them in his empire, stared at his hirsute visitor, then smiled: "Jailer Mitrofan, you may remove the shackles."

"But, Sire, this man is a murderer!"

"The shackles!" Peter roared, and when they jangled to the stone floor he added gently: "Now, Mitrofan, take the guards with you as you go." When one of the guards showed hesitancy at leaving the tsar alone with this notorious criminal, Peter chuckled and moved closer to the cossack, punching him in the arm: "I've always known how to handle this one," and the others withdrew.

When they were gone, Peter indicated that the cossack should take one of the two chairs while he, Peter, took the one on the other side. Having done so, he placed his elbows near the middle of the table and said: "Zhdanko, I need your help."

"You've always had it, Sire."

"But this time I don't want you to murder my governor."

"He was a bad one, Sire. Stole as much from you as he did from me."

"I know. Reports on his misbehavior were tardy in reaching me. Didn't get here till a month ago."

Zhdanko winced, then confided: "If a man is innocent, that trip from Yakutsk to St. Petersburg in shackles is no Easter outing."

Peter laughed: "If anyone could handle it, you could." Then he grew serious: "I stationed you in Siberia because I suspected that one day I would need you there." He smiled at the big man, then said: "The time has come."

Zhdanko placed both hands on the table, far apart, looked directly into the eyes of the tsar, and asked: "What?"

Peter said nothing. Rocking back and forth as if perplexed by some subject too weighty for easy explanation, he kept staring at the cossack, and finally asked the first of his significant questions: "Can I still trust you?"

"You know the answer," Zhdanko said with no show of humility or equivocation.

"Can you keep important secrets?"

"I've never been entrusted with any. But . . . yes, I suppose."

"Don't you know?"

"I've never been tested." Realizing that this might sound impudent, he added firmly: "Yes, if you warned me to keep my mouth shut. Yes."

"Swear you'll keep your mouth shut?"

"I swear."

Peter, nodding his satisfaction with this promise, rose from his chair, strode to the door, opened it, and shouted down the hall: "Fetch us some beer. German beer." And when Jailer Mitrofan entered with a pitcher of the dark stuff and two beakers, he found the cossack and the tsar seated side by side in the middle of the room like two friends, the table behind them.

When the first deep drafts had been drunk, with Zhdanko saying: "Haven't had that in the past year," Peter opened the conversation whose subject would dominate much of his life in the next months and all of Zhdanko's: "I am much worried about Siberia, Trofim." This was his first use of the prisoner's given name, and both were aware of the significance.

"Those Siberian dogs are difficult to train," the cossack said, "but they're puppies compared to the Chukchis out on the peninsula."

The tsar leaned forward: "It's the Chukchis I'm interested in. Tell me."

"I've met up with them twice. Lost twice. But I'm sure they can be handled if you go at them properly."

"Who are they?" Clearly, the tsar was temporizing. He was not concerned about the fighting qualities of these Chukchis perched on the far end of his empire. Every group his soldiers and administrators had encountered on their irresistible march to the east had been difficult at first, tractable when reliable government and resolute force were applied, and he was sure the Chukchis would prove the same.

"As I told you in my first report, they're closer to the Chinese, I mean in appearance, habits, than to you Russians or us Ukrainians."

"But not allied to the Chinese, I hope?"

"No Chinese has ever seen them. And not too many Russians, either. Your governor"—there was a slight hesitation—"the one who died, he was deadly afraid of the Chukchis."

"But you went among them?"

At this point Zhdanko had an invitation to play the hero, but he refrained: "Twice, Sire, but not by choice."

"Tell me about it. If you reported it, I've forgotten the details."

"I didn't report it, because I didn't come off too well." And there in the quiet room, toward midnight, he told the tsar about his two attempts to sail north from his headquarters in Yakutsk on the left bank of the great Lena River, largest in the east, and of his failure the first time because of opposition from the hostile Siberian tribes that infested the area.

"I'd like to know about the Lena."

"Majestic river, Sire. Have you ever heard about the Mouths of the Lena? Maybe fifty little rivers all running into the Great North Ocean. A wilderness of water. I got lost there."

Very gently Peter asked: "But you certainly never met any Chukchis on the Lena or at its fifty mouths, as you call them." He hesitated, then said: "Everything I've heard puts the Chukchis much farther east."

Zhdanko took the bait: "Oh yes! They're out on the peninsula. Where the land ends. Where Russia ends."

"How do you know that?"

The cossack leaned back and reached behind him for his beer, then, turning to face Peter, he made a confession: "I've told no one, Sire. Most of the men involved are dead. Your officials in Yakutsk, like that damned governor, never cared, as if what I'd discovered had no value. I doubt if your other officials here in St. Petersburg would have cared, either. You're the first Russian who gave a damn, and I know exactly why you're here tonight."

Peter showed no displeasure at this intemperate outbreak, this blanket castigation of his officials. Smiling, he said with the greatest conciliation: "Tell me, Zhdanko, why am I here?"

"Because you think I know something important about those eastern lands."

Peter smiled and said: "Yes, I've suspected for some time that when you made that river journey north from Yakutsk, and of that part I was informed, you did much more than sail down the Lena River to its many mouths, as you reported."

"Where do you think I went?" Zhdanko asked, as if he too were playing a game.

"I think you went out into the northern ocean and sailed east to the Kolyma River."

"That I did. And I found that it also enters the ocean by many mouths."

"I was told that by others who had seen the mouths," the tsar said in a manner which indicated that he might be bored.

"But not by anyone who approached from the sea," Trofim said sharply, and Peter laughed.

"It was on a second trip, about which I did not bother to inform your despicable governor . . ."

"You took care of him. Let his soul rest."

"It was on this trip that I encountered the Chukchis."

This was a revelation so significant, so pertinent to the hammering questions being asked in learned circles in Paris, Amsterdam and London, let alone Moscow, that Peter's hands began to tremble. He had heard from the greatest geographers in the world, men who dreamed about little else, two versions of what happened at the northeast corner of his empire, there at those capes shrouded in mist and frozen for more than half the year in great cakes of ice. Some in Paris had argued with him: "Eminent Sire, at the Arctic Circle and just below, your Russia has an unbroken land connection with North America, so that the hope of finding a sea passage from Norway to Japan around the eastern end of Siberia is fruitless. In the far north, Asia and North America become one body of land."

But others in Amsterdam and London had tried to persuade him differently: "Sire, mark our words, when you find navigators brave enough to sail from Arkhangelsk past Novaya Zemlya and on to the mouths of the Lena . . ." He had not interrupted them, for he did not care to reveal that this had already been accomplished. "You will find that they could, if they wished, keep right on sailing from the Lena to the Kolyma and around the easternmost cape and straight down to Japan. Russia and North America are not joined. A sea intrudes between them, and although it is probably frozen most of the year, it is still a sea, and as such, it will have to be open during the summer."

In the years since his epochal travels in Europe and his work as a shipbuilder in Holland, Peter had accumulated all the shreds of information he could glean from supposititious accounts, rumors, hard evidence and the canny speculation of geographers and philosophers, and he had in this year of 1723 concluded that there was an ocean passage open most of the year between his most eastern possessions and North America. Having accepted this as proved, he was now interested in other aspects of the problem, and to solve them he needed to know more about the Chukchis and the forbidding land they occupied.

"Tell me about your second trip, Zhdanko. The one where you met the Chukchis."

"This time, when I reached the mouths of the Kolyma, I said to myself: 'What lies beyond?' and I sailed in good weather for many days, relying upon the skilled Siberian boatman who captained my ship, a man who seemed to have no fear. Neither of us understood the stars, so we don't know how far we went, but in all that time the sun never set, so we had to be well north of the Circle, that I know."

"And what did you find?"

"A cape, and then a sharp turn south, and when we tried to land we found those damned Chukchis."

"And what happened?"

"They turned us back, twice. Pitched battles. And if we had tried to force our way ashore, I'm sure we'd have been killed."

"Could you talk with them?"

"No, but they were willing to trade with us, and they knew the value of what they had."

"Did you ask them questions? I mean with signs?"

"Yes. And they told us that the sea continued south forever, but that there were islands just beyond in the mists."

"Did you sail to those islands?"

"No," and when the tsar's grave disappointment showed, the cossack reminded him: "Sire, we were far from home . . . in a small boat, and we could not guess where the land lay. To tell you the truth, we were afraid."

Tsar Peter, who realized that as emperor of a vast domain he was obligated to know what the situation was in all its parts, made no reply to this honest admission of fear and failure, but after a long swig of beer he said: "I wonder what I might have done."

"Who knows?" Zhdanko shrugged, and Peter was glad that he had not cried effusively: "Oh, Sire, I'm sure you would have plowed on!" because Peter was not at all sure. Once, in crossing from Holland to England, he had been caught in a furious Channel storm and he knew what fear could do to a man in a small boat.

But then he clapped his hands, rose, and began walking about the room. "Listen, Zhdanko, I already know all this about Russia and North America not touching. And I want to do something about it, but in the future, not now," and the interrogation seemed to be ending there, with the tsar going back to his unfinished palace and the cossack to his hanging, so Zhdanko, fighting for his life, boldly reached out and grabbed Peter's right sleeve, being careful not to touch his person, and said: "In the trading, Sire, I obtained two things which might be of interest to you."

"What?"

"Frankly, Sire, I want to trade them to you, for my freedom."

"I came here tonight to give you your freedom. You were to leave this place and take quarters in the palace near mine."

Zhdanko stood up, and the two big men stared at each other across the narrow space which separated them, and then a big smile broke across the cossack's face: "In that case, Sire, I shall give you my secrets freely and with thanks." And he stooped to kiss the hem of Peter's fur-lined robe.

"Where are these secret things?" Peter asked, and Zhdanko said: "I had them spirited out of Siberia and hidden with a woman I knew in the old days."

"Is it worth my while to go to her tonight?"

"It is," and with this simple declaration Trofim Zhdanko left his shackles lying on the prison floor, accepted the fur cloak the tsar ordered the jailer to give him, and, side by side with Peter, passed through the oak door and climbed into the waiting carriage while the four armed horsemen formed up to protect them.

They left the river docks, where Zhdanko could see the gaunt timbers of many ships under construction, but before reaching the area leading to the rude palace they veered inland away from the river, and in the two-o'clock darkness searched for a mean alley, where they stopped at a hovel protected by a door without hinges. The drowsy occupant, when finally wakened, informed Zhdanko: "She left here last year. You'll find her three alleys down, house with a green door."

There they learned that the woman Maria still protected the valuable package the prisoner Zhdanko had sent her from Yakutsk. She showed neither surprise nor pleasure in seeing her friend Trofim again, and for the very good reason that when she saw the soldiers she supposed that this very tall man with Zhdanko was an official of some kind who was going to arrest the cossack for having stolen whatever was in the package.

"Here," she muttered, shoving a greasy bundle into Peter's hands. Then, to Zhdanko, she said: "I'm sorry, Trofim. I hope they don't hang you."

Eagerly the tsar ripped open the package, to find that it contained two pelts, each about five feet long, of the softest, finest, strongest fur he had ever seen. It was a dark brown that scintillated in the weak light and much longer in each hair than the furs with which he was familiar, though dealers brought him only the best. It had come from the treasured sea otter inhabiting the icy waters east of the Chukchi lands, and these two pelts were the first of their kind to reach the western world. In his first moments of examining these remarkable furs, Peter appreciated their worth, and he could visualize, even then, the immense importance they would enjoy in the capitals of Europe if they could be supplied in assured quantities.

"These are excellent," Peter said. "Tell this woman who I am and give her rubles for having saved them for me."

The captain of the guard told Maria as he handed her the coins: "This is your tsar. He thanks you," and she fell to her knees and kissed his boot.

Her gesture did not close this unusual night, for while she was still genuflecting, Peter shouted to one of his guards: "Fetch it," and before the man returned, the tsar had forced a startled Zhdanko onto the hut's only chair. When the guard produced a long, dull and murderous-looking razor, Peter cried: "No man, not even you, Zhdanko, stays in my palace with a beard," and with considerable force he proceeded to hack off the cossack's beard, taking with it a substantial helping of skin.

Trofim could not protest, for as a citizen he knew that the law forbade him to wear a beard, and as a cossack he must not flinch when the unsharpened razor pulled hair out by the roots or cut into his face. Stolidly he sat there until the barbering was completed, then he rose, wiped the blood from his newly revealed face, and said: "Sire, keep hold of the empire. You'll never make a barber," and Peter tossed the razor to a guard, who allowed it to fall to the floor lest it cut him. Placing an arm about his astonished cossack, the tsar led him to their carriage.

Peter the Great was in no degree diverted from his main interest in far eastern Siberia by the fact that a new and wonderful kind of fur

appeared to be available there. Of course, he had his tailor, a Frenchman named DesArbes, adapt the furs to three of his ceremonial
robes, but then forgot about them, for his perpetual concern was with
the actuality of Russia—where it was and how it related to its
neighbors—and in safeguarding it for the future. And now, when occasional rushes of blood to the head warned him that even he with all
his strength was mortal, he began to focus on three or four major
projects which had to be given direction or consolidation. Russia still
had no reliable seaport, and certainly no warm-water one. Relations
with all-powerful Turkey were not good. The internal government of
Russia was sometimes a disaster, especially in those districts far from
St. Petersburg where a letter of instruction might take eight months
for delivery and two years for a response to reach the capital if the
recipient was desultory in conforming and replying. The road system
was deplorable in all parts save a fairly reliable route between the two
major cities, and in the far east, nobody in power ever seemed to
know what was going on.

So, important though furs were, and much of Russia's wealth
came from the brave men who trapped in the Siberian wilderness, the
providential discovery that the waters off the Chukchi lands would
provide a fur as resplendent as that of the sea otter was no cause for
immediate action. Peter the Great had learned, more from his experiences in Europe than from what he saw in Russia, that in the far east
his nation faced two potential dangers: China and whatever European nation ultimately controlled the west coast of North America.
He already knew that Spain, through her ancillary agent Mexico, had
a strong foothold on the part of America facing the Pacific Ocean
and that her power extended unchallenged all the way down to Cape
Horn. By his constant study of maps then available, and they were
becoming more complete each year, Peter saw that if Spain attempted
to project her power northward, as she probably would, she must
ultimately come into conflict with Russian interests. He was therefore
much concerned about Spanish behavior.

But with that intuition which so often assists great men, especially those responsible for the governance of homelands, he anticipated that other nations more powerful today than Spain might also
extend their power to the Pacific coast of North America, and he saw
that if either France or England, each with a foothold on the Atlantic, were to do so, he might one day be faced with pressure from such

a country applying it in Europe on his western borders and in America on his eastern.

Peter loved ships, had sailed in them and believed that had his life developed differently, he might have made a fine sea captain. As a consequence, he was fascinated by the capacity of ships to move freely over the waters of the world. He was close to completing his grand design of making Russia a sea power in Europe, and his empire had derived so much advantage from this new posture that he was considering building a fleet in Siberia if conditions warranted. But first he had to know what those conditions were.

Accordingly, he spent much time planning a vast enterprise which would place a Russian ship of stout construction in the seas off Siberia with a commission to explore the area, not for any specific item of information but for the kind of general knowledge on which the leader of an empire could rely when making prudent decisions. Concerning the vital question of whether his Siberia touched North America, his mind was made up: it did not. But he did have considerable mercantile interests in the area. He already conducted profitable trade with China overland, but he wanted to know whether he could do better by sea. And he was most eager to trade with Japan on any terms, for the few goods which reached Europe from that mysterious land were of such high quality that they excited him as they did others. Above all, he wanted to know what Spain, England and France were doing in this important ocean and be able to estimate what they were capable of doing. Eighty years later the American president Thomas Jefferson, a man much like Peter, would want to know the same things about his newly acquired western possessions along the Pacific.

When his ideas were in a yeasty froth with no firm structure—often the precedent to man's most constructive thinking—he sent for this cossack he had come to trust, this rough, unlettered man who seemed to know more about Siberia than most of the more learned officials he had sent there to govern, and after preliminary sparring to satisfy himself as to Zhdanko's energy and continued interest, he reached a favorable conclusion: "Trofim, you're twenty-two, great age to be. A man's approaching his apex then. By God, I wish I were twenty-two again." Motioning Zhdanko to join him on a bench, he continued: "I have in mind to send you back to Yakutsk. Beyond, maybe. Perhaps all the way to Kamchatka."

"Place me under a better governor this time, Sire."

"You'd not be under a governor."

"Sire, what could I do on my own? I can't read or write."

"You'd not be on your own."

The cossack rose, walked about, and said: "I don't understand," and Peter said: "You'd be on a ship. Under the command of the best sailor we could find." Before Trofim could show his astonishment, Peter became all excitement, waving his hands about and talking louder each minute: "You'd go to Tobolsk and pick up some carpenters, to Yeniseysk and get some men knowledgeable about tar, then on to Yakutsk, where you already know everyone and can advise what men to take to Okhotsk, where you will build your ship. A big one. I'll give you the plans."

"Sire!" Zhdanko interrupted. "I cannot read."

"You shall learn, starting this day, and as you learn you will tell no one why you are learning." Now Peter rose and stalked about the room with his arm linked in Trofim's. "I want you to take a job at the docks. Where we're building ships . . ."

"I don't know much about timber."

"You're not expected to bother about timber. You're to listen, to judge, to compare, to serve as my eyes and ears."

"For what?"

"To advise me as to who the best man is down there. Who really knows ships. Who can handle men. Above all, Zhdanko, who is as brave as you proved to be."

The cossack said nothing; he did not try with false modesty to deny that he had been brave, because it had been his daring feats in the Ukraine at age fifteen which had brought him to the tsar's attention. But Peter could only guess at what acts of courage had allowed this man who knew nothing of the sea to venture down the Lena River and along the coast to the land of the Chukchis and to protect himself along the way.

Finally, as they paced together, Peter said: "I wish I were to be the captain of that ship, with you the officer in command of troops. We would sail from the coast of Kamchatka, wherever it is, to all of America."

During the time that Trofim spent working in the shipyard at day and learning to read at night, he discovered that most of the constructive work being achieved in St. Petersburg, and a massive amount was under way, was being done not by Russians, but by able men from other European nations. His tutor Soderlein was from Heidelberg in Germany, as were two of the medical doctors at the court. Instruction in mathematics was in the hands of brilliant men from Paris. Books were being written on a variety of subjects by professors imported from Amsterdam and London. Astronomy, in which Peter took great interest, was in the hands of fine men from Lille and Bordeaux. And wherever practical solutions to problems were required, Trofim found Englishmen and Scotsmen, especially the latter, in charge. They drew the plans for the ships, installed the winding stairs in palaces, taught the peasants how to care for animals, and watched the money. One day as Peter and Trofim discussed the still shadowy expedition to the east, the tsar said: "When you seek ideas, go to the French and the Germans. But when you want action, hire yourself an Englishman or a Scotsman."

When Zhdanko delivered letters to the Academy in Moscow he found it populated by Frenchmen and Germans, and the porter who led him about the newly furnished halls whispered: "The tsar has hired the brightest men in Europe. They're all here."

"Doing what?" Trofim asked as he clutched his parcel.

"Thinking."

In the second month of this training, Zhdanko learned one other fact about his tsar: the Europeans, especially the French and Germans, might do the thinking, but Peter and a group of Russians much like him did the governing. They supplied the money and said where the army would go and what ships would be built, and it was they who ran Russia, make no mistake about that. And this perplexed him, for if he was to help select the sailor who was to command the vast expedition that Peter had in mind, he felt obligated to identify some Russian capable of directing a task of such magnitude. But the more he studied the men along the waterfront and listened to reports about them, the more clearly he saw that none of the Russians was remotely capable of the task, and he was loath to tell Peter, but one day when asked how his thinking was going, he had to speak out: "I hear of two Germans, one Swede and one Dane who might do. But the Germans with their mighty ways would be unable to control Russians like me, and the Swede fought against us three times in the Baltic wars before joining our side."

"We sank all his ships," Peter laughed, "so if he wanted to continue being a sailor, he had to join us. Are you speaking of Lundberg?"

"Yes, a very good man. I'll trust him if you choose him."

"And who was the Dane?" Peter asked.

"Captain-of-the-Second-Rank Vitus Bering. His men speak well of him."

"I, too," the tsar said, and the matter was discussed no further.

But when alone Peter spent careful hours reviewing what he knew about Bering: Met him that day twenty years ago when our training fleet stopped in Holland. Our admirals were so hungry for anyone with experience at sea that without examination they commissioned him sublieutenant. And they chose well, for he rose fast, Captain-of-the-Fourth-Rank, the Third and Second. He fought manfully in our war against Sweden.

Eight years younger than Peter, Bering had retired with honor at the beginning of 1724, taking up residence in the stately Finnish seaport of Vyborg, where he expected to live out the remainder of his life as a gardener and watcher of naval ships as they passed up the Gulf of Finland to St. Petersburg. In the late summer of that same year, he had been summoned to Russia to meet with the tsar: "Vitus Bering, I should never have allowed you to retire. You're needed for an exercise of the greatest importance."

"Your Majesty, I'm forty-four years old. I tend gardens, not ships."

"Nonsense. If I weren't needed here, I'd go on the journey myself."

"But you're a special man, Your Majesty," and when Bering said this, a round little fellow with pudgy cheeks, a twisted mouth and hair drooping close to his eyes, he spoke the truth, for Peter was a good fifteen inches taller and possessed of a commanding presence which Bering lacked. He was a stolid, capable Dane, a bulldog type of man, who had attained a position of eminence by his rugged determination rather than because of any quality of dramatic leadership. He was what the English mariners liked to call a sea dog, and such men, when they fastened their teeth onto a project, could be devastating.

"In your own way," Peter said, "and in a way vital to this project, you too are special, Captain Bering."

"And what is your project?" It was typical of Bering that from the start he allocated the project to the tsar. It was Peter's idea, whatever it was, and Bering was honored to be his agent.

Zhdanko did not hear what Peter said to Bering in reply to that question, but later he left a memorandum of some importance in which he said that Peter had spoken to Bering much as he had spoken to him, Zhdanko: "He said he wanted to know more about Kamchatka, and where the Chukchi lands ended, and what European nations held what settlements on the west coast of America." There was, Zhdanko felt sure, no discussion as to whether Russian territory was joined by land to North America: "That was taken for granted by both men."

For some weeks Zhdanko watched the fat little Dane moving about the shipyards, and then he disappeared. "He's been called to Moscow to meet with some Academy men stationed there," a workman told Zhdanko. "Those fellows from France and Germany who know everything but can't tie their own cravats. He'll be in trouble if he listens to them."

Two days before Christmas, a holiday that Zhdanko relished, Captain Bering was back in St. Petersburg and was summoned to a meeting with the tsar which Zhdanko was invited to attend. As the cossack entered the business room of the palace he blurted out: "Sire, you've been working too hard. You don't look well."

Ignoring the observation, Peter showed the men where to sit, and when a certain solemnity clothed the room, he said: "Vitus Bering, I've had you promoted to Captain-of-the-First-Rank because I want you to undertake the major mission of which we spoke last summer." Bering started to expostulate that he was unworthy of such preferment, but Peter, who had been continuously ill since leaping impulsively into the icy waters of the Bay of Finland to rescue a drowning sailor and who was now apprehensive lest death cut short his grand designs, brushed aside the formality: "Yes, you are to cross overland to the eastern limits of our empire, build yourself ships in that spot, then conduct the explorations we spoke of."

"Exalted Majesty, I shall consider this your expedition, sailing under your command."

"Good," Peter said. "I'll be sending with you our ablest men, and as your aide, this cossack who knows those areas, Trofim Zhdanko, who carries with him my personal approval. He's a tested man."

At this the tsar rose to stand with his cossack, and when fat little Bering took his position between the two giants, it was like a hill standing between two mountain peaks.

A month later, before he had an opportunity to spell out the details of the exploration, Tsar Peter, called properly the Great, was dead at the premature age of fifty-three. The governance of Russia fell into the hands of his widow, Catherine the First, an extraordinary woman who had been born into a Lithuanian peasant family, was orphaned young, and married at age eighteen to a Swedish dragoon who deserted her after a honeymoon of eight summer days. Mistress of various well-placed men, she fell into the hands of a powerful Russian politician who introduced her to Peter, who, after she had borne him three children, married her gladly. She had been a stalwart wife, and now, with her husband dead, she desired only to execute the orders he had left unfinished. On 5 February 1725 she handed Bering the temporary commission he would hold during the expedition, Fleet Captain, and his orders.

The latter were a muddled set of three paragraphs which had been drafted by Peter himself shortly before his death, and although the instructions about crossing all of Russia and building ships were clear, what to do with those ships, once built, was most unclear. The admirals interpreted the orders to mean that Bering was to determine whether eastern Asia was joined to North America; other men like Trofim Zhdanko, who had spoken to Peter in person, believed that he had intended a reconnoiter of the coast of America, with a possibility of claiming that unoccupied land for Russia. Both interpreters agreed that Bering was to try to find European settlements in the area and to intercept European vessels for interrogation. No major explorer, and Vitus Bering was that, had ever set forth on a grand voyage with such imprecise orders from his patrons who were paying the bills. Before he died Peter had certainly known what he intended; his survivors did not.

The distance from St. Petersburg to the east coast of Kamchatka, where the ships were to be built, was an appalling five thousand nine hundred miles, or, considering the unavoidable detours, more than six thousand. Roads were perilous or nonexistent. Rivers had to be used but there were no boats to do so. Workmen were to be picked up en route from remote little towns where no skilled hands were available. Large stretches of empty land which had never before been traversed by a group of travelers had to be negotiated. And what was to prove most irritating of all, there was no way whereby officials in St. Petersburg could forewarn their officials in far-distant Siberia that this gang of men was about to descend upon them with requirements that simply could not be filled locally. At the end of the second week Zhdanko reported to Bering: "This isn't an expedition. It's madness." And this was said during the good part of the trip.

Twenty-six of Bering's best men, driving twenty-five wagonloads of needed materials, set out ahead of him, and he followed shortly thereafter with six companions, including his aide Trofim Zhdanko, with whom he established the firmest and most productive relations. During the troika ride to Solikamsk, an insignificant village marking the start of the bleak lands, the two men had an opportunity to learn each other's foibles, and since this trip was going to require years, not months, it was important that this happen.

Vitus Bering, his aide discovered, was a man of sturdy principles. He respected a job well done, was willing to praise his men who performed well, and demanded the same kind of effort from himself. He was not a bookish man, which reassured Zhdanko, to whom the alphabet had been a problem, but he did place major reliance upon maps, which he studied assiduously. He was not overly religious but he did pray. He was not a glutton but he liked clean food and hearty drink. Best of all, he was a leader who respected men, and because he was perpetually aware that he was a Dane giving orders to Russians, he tried never to be arrogant, but he also let it be known that he was in command. He had, however, one weakness which disturbed the cossack, whose method of controlling his subordinates had been so different: at any critical moment Bering, like all the Russian officers in command, was expected to convene his subordinates and consult with them regarding the situation that faced them. When they had formed their recommendations they then had to submit them in writing, so that he would not have to assume the entire blame if things went wrong. What disturbed Zhdanko, Bering actually listened to the prejudices of his assistants and often acted upon them. "I'd ask their opinions," Zhdanko growled, "then burn the paper they signed," but apart from this deficiency, the big cossack respected his captain and vowed to serve him well.

For his part, Bering saw in Zhdanko a man of resolute courage who, at that time of crisis in Yakutsk, had been willing to risk his life by murdering his superior when that man's irrational behavior threatened Russia's position in Siberia. As Tsar Peter had revealed when informing Bering about Trofim: "The man he killed deserved it. Zhdanko did my work for me." Bering asked: "Then why did you bring him to the capital in chains?" and Peter had explained: "He needed cooling down." Then he laughed and added: "And I had always planned to use him later in some fine project. Yours."

Bering recognized that this cossack had enormous strength, both physical and moral, and he found a special reason to like him, for as he said to himself: He did sail down the Lena River. He did test those northern seas. He saw further that his aide had a gargantuan appetite, a quick anger, an equally quick forgiveness, and a tendency always to choose the more difficult way of doing things if that way produced a challenge. He decided early in their trip that he would not look to Zhdanko for advice but he would certainly rely on him for assistance in troubled times. At Solikamsk he had an opportunity to put his theories regarding the cossack to the test.

Solikamsk was one of those minute stations at which travelers halted only for greasy food for themselves and very expensive oats for their horses. It contained only sixteen rude huts and a surly innkeeper named Pavlutsky, who began to complain as soon as Bering's men and wagons descended upon him: "There's never been so many. How can I be expected . . . ?"

Bering started to explain that the new empress herself had ordered this enterprise, whereupon Pavlutsky whined: "She may have told you but she didn't tell me," and in this protest he was correct. The poor man, accustomed to a solitary post rider now and then heading from Vologda to Tobolsk, was overwhelmed by this unexpected influx: "There's nothing I can be expected to do."

"Yes there is," Zhdanko said. "You can sit right here and keep your mouth shut," and with this he lifted the innkeeper and plopped him on a stool. Threatening to break the man's head if he uttered one word, the huge cossack then began ordering his own men and Pavlutsky's to break out what food there was, all of it, for the men and such forage as could be provided for the horses. When the way station itself could produce only a portion of what was needed, he ordered his men to search the nearby huts and fetch not only food but women to cook the meal and men to feed the horses.

Within half an hour Zhdanko had mobilized nearly everyone in Solikamsk, and the hours from sunset to midnight were frenzied with the running about of the villagers as they attended to the wants of the travelers. At one in the morning, when his two casks of ale were emptied, Pavlutsky, a much-humbled man, came to Bering, pleading: "Who is to pay for all this?" and Bering pointed to Zhdanko, who placed his arm about the innkeeper's shoulder and assured him: "The tsarina. I'll give you a paper which the tsarina will honor," and in the light of a flickering oil lamp in a cruet, he wrote out: "Fleet Captain Vitus Bering ate 33 meals and 47 horses. Pay to supplier Ivan Pavlutsky of Solikamsk." When he delivered this to the bewildered host, he said: "I know she'll pay," and he hoped this would be the case.

From Solikamsk they traveled by troika over frozen fields to the important stopping place of Tobolsk, but east of there the snows were so formidable that they had to idle away almost nine weeks, during which Zhdanko ranged the countryside to requisition additional soldiers, overriding the protests of their local commanders. Bering, on his part, ordered a monk and the commissar of a small village to join too, so that when the troop marched north out of Tobolsk they numbered sixty-seven men and forty-seven wagons.

When they left this relatively comfortable town they had been on the road exactly one hundred days and had covered the respectable distance of nearly fourteen hundred miles in the dead of winter, but now the well-tended post roads began to vanish and they had to travel down rivers, across barren wastes and in the shadows of forbidding hills. The treasured troika with its warm furs gave way to carts, and then to horseback, and finally to booted feet trudging through snowdrifts.

In the early summer of 1725 they covered only two hundred and twenty miles—Tobolsk, Surgut, Narim—but finally they came upon a river system which allowed them to raft speedily. One day they reached the brooding frontier fortress of Marakovska Post, where Bering said prayers to the notable missionary Metropolitan Philophei, who had only a few years before converted the people in these parts from heathenism to Christianity. "It is a noble work," the Dane said to his aide, "to bring human souls into the knowledge of Jesus Christ," but Zhdanko had other problems: "How are we going to get our men and all this baggage over the mountains to the Yenisei River?"

By the most diligent effort they accomplished this, and for a few weeks thereafter had easy going, for ahead lay a chain of rivers down which they could boat to the little town of Ilimsk on that greater river whose distant upper reaches Zhdanko had once explored, the Lena. But now another crushing winter was upon them and they had to abandon any further attempts to forge eastward. In miserable huts and with barely adequate food they survived the dismal winter of 1725–26, adding to their roster thirty blacksmiths and carpenters. They were now ninety-seven in all, and if they ever reached the Pacific with at least some of the building materials they were carrying, an unlikely possibility, they would be prepared to build ships.

Not one of them, except Bering of course, had ever even seen a real ship, let alone built one, Zhdanko having sailed in improvisations, but as a carpenter named Ilya said when impressed into service: "If a man can build a boat for the Lena, he can build a ship for whatever that ocean out there is called."

Vitus Bering was a man rarely distressed by conditions he could not control, and now, locked into this miserable, snowbound prison, he showed Zhdanko and his officers what a stubborn man he could be. Prevented from moving north or east, he said: "Let's see what's south," and when he inquired, he was told that in the important town of Irkutsk, more than three hundred miles away, the present voivode was a man who had formerly served in Yakutsk, the town to which they were heading, and the one in which Zhdanko had murdered the commander. When Bering inquired of his aide: "What kind of man was this Izmailov?" Trofim replied enthusiastically: "I know him well! One of the best!" and with no other information, the two men set forth on this arduous journey to acquire whatever additional facts about Siberia the voivode might have.

It was a fruitless trip south, for as soon as Zhdanko met the voivode he realized that this man was not the Izmailov he had known. Indeed, the present governor had never stuck his nose into the lands east of Irkutsk and would be of no help for the impending travels into those areas. But the governor was an energetic fellow who wanted to be helpful: "I was sent here three years ago from St. Petersburg, Grigory Voronov, at your service," and when he learned that Zhdanko had once explored as far east as the Siberian village of Okhotsk, he interrogated him strenuously about conditions on the eastern marches of his command. But he was equally interested in what discoveries Bering might make: "I envy you the chance to sail in those arctic seas."

When the three men had talked for about an hour, Voronov summoned a servant: "Inform Miss Marina that the gentlemen would appreciate tea and a tray of sweets," and shortly into the room came a big-boned, handsome girl of sixteen, with flashing eyes, broad shoulders and a way of moving which proclaimed: "I'm in charge now."

"Who are these men, Father?"

"Explorers for the tsarina." Then, turning to Bering, he said: "Concerning the fur trade, I have good news and bad. Down at Kyakhta on the Mongolian border, Chinese merchants are buying our furs at phenomenal prices. On your travels, pick up all you can."

"Is it safe to visit the border?" Bering asked, for he had been told that Russian-Chinese relations were strained, and it was Marina who responded in a voice trembling with excitement: "I've been twice. Such strange men! One part Russian, one part Mongolian, best part Chinese. And the excitement of the marketplace!"

The voivode's bad news concerned the overland route leading to Yakutsk: "Agents tell me it's still the worst journey in Siberia. Only the bravest attempt it."

"I made it three times," Zhdanko said quietly, adding quickly with a smile: "That's a damned cold trip, I can tell you."

"I'd love to make a trip like that," Marina cried, and when the visitors left to prepare for their journey north, Bering said: "That young lady seems willing to go anywhere."

So back to Ilimsk, Vitus Bering and his company trudged, more than three hundred miles of tortuous terrain, and there they waited on the banks of the still-frozen Lena River, but when spring finally thawed the valleys and streams, they rafted nine hundred miles to the eastern stronghold of Yakutsk, where Trofim showed Bering with great excitement that portion of the mighty Lena he had twice navigated, and when the Danish sea captain saw that massive body of water so close, in a sense, to the Arctic Ocean, he gained a new respect for his energetic aide. "I long to sail that river," Bering said with deep emotion, "but my orders are to the east," and Zhdanko said with almost equal feeling: "But if our journey prospers, may we not see the Lena from the other end?" and Bering replied: "I would like to see those hundred mouths you spoke of."

It required the entire summer of 1726 and into the fall to move the eight hundred miles from Yakutsk to Okhotsk, that bleak and lonely harbor on the huge sea of that name, for now the full meaning of the fearful word *Siberia* became clear. Vast wastelands without a sign of habitation stretched to the horizon. Hills and mountains intervened, with turbulent streams to ford. Wolves followed any body of men, waiting for an accident that would provide them with a defenseless target. Untimely snows swept out of the north, alternating with blasts of unexpected heat from the south. No man could plan a day's journey and expect to complete it on schedule, and to look ahead for a week or a month was folly.

When, on the lonely uplands of this forlorn area, one did meet a traveler coming from the opposite direction, he was apt to be one of two kinds: a man who spoke no known language and from whom no information could be got, or a cutthroat who had escaped from some terrible prison compound not visible from the trail. This was the Siberia which terrified wrongdoers or antiroyalists in western Russia, for a sentence to these unrelieved monotonies usually meant death. And in these years the very worst part of the entire stretch was the region which Fleet Captain Bering now had to negotiate, and at the end of autumn, when not even half his goods had reached the eastern depot, it began to look as if he would never become a true fleet captain because he seemed destined never to have a fleet.

The trips back and forth between the two towns that year were so awesome that when porters bearing heavy loads staggered into Okhotsk, they sometimes fell in a heap, for they were totally exhausted. Bering had to make the arduous journey on horseback, since wagons and sleds could not cross the mountains and muddy flats and even cargo sleds became snowbound. At first Zhdanko remained at the western end guarding the supplies, and then, in a burst of energy, he made two round-trip journeys.

When, worn to thinness, he dragged in the last of the timbers he supposed that he would be awarded with a rest, for he believed that he could not complete another journey, but just as the snows of early winter began, Bering learned that one small party of his men was still stranded in the badlands, and without his having to ask his constable to go rescue them, Zhdanko volunteered: "I'll fetch them," and with a few men like himself he went back over those snow-covered trails to bring in the vital supplies, and it was providential that he did, because it was this group of sleds that carried many of the tools the shipbuilders would need.

Bering and his men were more than five thousand miles from St. Petersburg, counting their detours and doubling back, and they were beginning their third winter on the road, but it was only now that their worst difficulties began, for without proper materials or experience, they were supposed to build two ships. And it was decided that this could be most expeditiously done not here in settled Okhotsk but far across the sea on the still-primitive peninsula of Kamchatka.

That dubious decision having been made, they now had to face the next step, a perplexing one: any hastily built temporary ship sailing from Okhotsk would land on the *western* shore of the peninsula, but departure for the exploration would have to be made from the *eastern.* So, on which shore should the ships be built? When, as was his custom, Bering consulted with his subordinates, two clear opinions quickly emerged. All who were European or European-trained recommended that he land on the western shore, cross over the high mountains of the peninsula, and build on the eastern: "For then you will have clear sailing to your target." But the Russians—especially Trofim Zhdanko, who knew northern waters—argued that the only sensible thing would be to build the ships on the western shore, the near one, and then use them to sail around the southern tip of Kamchatka and head north to the serious business.

Zhdanko's recommendation made maximum sense—for it would enable Bering to avoid that man-killing haul of building equipment across the backbone of Kamchatka where mountains soared to fifteen thousand feet—but it had one serious weakness: no one at that time knew how far south the peninsula ran, and if Bering followed his aide's advice, he might spend a fruitless year trying to breast the southern cape, wherever it was. Actually, it was about one hundred and forty miles from where the ships could be built, and it could have been breasted in five or six easy sailing days, but no map of that period was based on hard evidence, and those who guessed placed the cape hundreds of miles to the south.

Against Zhdanko's vigorous protests, Bering decided to land on the western shore at a lonely, wind-swept spot called Bolsheretsk, a settlement of fourteen mean huts, and there, as summer waned, this indomitable Dane, now forty-seven years old, launched an operation which stunned his men and staggered the imagination of those seafaring men and explorers who heard of it later. He decided that he could not afford to waste a fourth winter in idleness, so he ordered all the gear, including the timbers to be used for building the ships, to be transported by dogsled across the entire peninsula and over mountains that would be covered with snow. He did this so that he could build on the eastern shore and thus be ready to sail directly north when winter ended. Zhdanko, seeing the first of the heavily burdened men start out, shuddered when he visualized what lay ahead, and when, as planned, he brought up the rear with some of the most valuable equipment, he gritted his teeth and told his men: "They have a hellish blizzard in the mountains ahead. Called the *purga,* and when it rages, each man to dig his own hole!"

He and his cadre were on the highest hills in February when the temperature dropped to minus-fifty, and despite the fact that winds usually did not blow at that temperature, a dreaded *purga* roared down from northern Asia, whipping snow and sleet ahead of it like bullets. Although Zhdanko had never before been caught in such a storm, he had heard of them, and shouted to his men: "Dig!" and with fury they scooped out ten and fifteen and twenty feet of snow on the lee side of some huge rocks, and into these holes they crept while snow piled over the openings.

Zhdanko had to go down eighteen feet before he hit a solid base, and at that depth he feared he would be so totally covered as to be lost, so that as the storm raged, he constantly pushed himself up through the falling snow and sleet, and when dawn broke and the storm abated, he was able to break clear and begin to search for his companions. When they dug out of their burrows two of the men began urging that they return to their starting point, and others would have supported them had not Zhdanko, with that fierce pride which motivated so much that he did, lashed out with his right fist and knocked one of the men backward into the snow. Seeing him fall, he leaped like a mountain cat upon the man and started bludgeoning him about the head with his powerful hands, and it was obvious that he was going to kill the defenseless man, but one of the others who had said nothing quietly interceded: "Trofim, no!" and the big man fell back, ashamed of himself, not for having rebuked the man but for having done so to such an excess.

Chastened, he reached down, helped the man to his feet, and said jocularly: "You've worked hard enough today. Bring up the rear." Then he added: "But don't try to run back. You'll not make it."

That journey across the peninsula in dead of winter was one of the most hellish in the history of exploration, but Bering held his men together, and when they reached the eastern shore, he immediately put them to clearing away snowdrifts so that they could start building. It was a forlorn spot that had been chosen for this improvised shipyard, but never in his adventurous life did Vitus Bering show to greater advantage. He seemed to build the ship himself, appearing at every danger spot whenever needed. He spent eighteen hours a day in the long spring twilights, and whenever an aspect of the plans drawn up in St. Petersburg seemed incomprehensible, he deciphered them or made up his own rules on the spot. And his gift for improvisation was incredible.

Tar for caulking the ships had been lost somewhere en route, and it was no use blaming any individual. Somewhere in the six thousand miles from the capital—perhaps on one of the handmade boats plying some unnamed river, or in the dreadful stretch east of Yakutsk, or during the two great blizzards in the Kamchatka mountain passes—the tar had been lost, and the *St. Gabriel,* as they decided to call their ship, could not go to sea, for if left uncaulked, the open seams in her sides would admit enough water to sink her in twenty minutes.

For the better part of a day Bering studied this problem, then gave a simple order: "Cut down those larch trees," and when a huge pile had been assembled, he had the trees cut into lengths and from their bark he distilled a kind of sticky substance which, when mixed with a heavy grass, made a passable caulking, and the shipbuilding proceeded.

However, it was with another invention that he gained popularity with his men. Telling them: "No man should sail a ship that has no spirits for a cold night," he directed them to collect various grasses, roots and herbs, and when he had an ample supply he set up a fermentation process which, after many false starts, finally produced a strong beverage that he designated brandy, and of which his enthusiastic men laid in a copious amount. More immediately practical, he set other men to boiling seawater to obtain extra supplies of salt, and he directed Zhdanko to catch all the fish possible so that an oil could be made to take the place of butter. Larger fish were cured to serve instead of meat, which was not available, and he directed men to weave strong grasses together to make substitute ropes to be used in an emergency. In ninety-eight days—4 April through 10 July—this energetic man built himself a seagoing ship in which to make one of the world's premier voyages of exploration, and after only four days' rest, he sailed forth. Then came one of the mysteries of the sea: the daring man who had braved so much, who had already spent three and a half years in this quest, sailed north for only thirty-three days, saw another winter approaching, turned about, and scurried back to his Kamchatka base, arriving there after a total cruise of only fifty-one days out and back, despite the fact that the *St. Gabriel* carried a year's provisions and medical supplies for forty men.

Once again on land, with heavy snows about to descend, the men huddled in improvised huts and passed the winter of 1728–29 accomplishing nothing. Bering did interrogate a group of Chukchis, who told him that in clear weather they had often seen a mysterious shore across the sea, but for Bering the weather remained so foul that he did not see this land.

When spring brought good weather, he launched the *St. Gabriel* again, sailed boldly east for three days, became disheartened, and sailed back to Okhotsk. This time, ironically, he did go south, as Trofim Zhdanko had suggested two years ago, and he did easily round the southern tip of Kamchatka. Had he followed that easy route the first time, he would have had months of cruising time in the North Pacific and would also have avoided that fearful crossing of the peninsula during the blizzards.

It was time to go home, and since he now knew the good parts and bad of the Siberian road-and-river system, he made it to St. Petersburg in a rapid seven months and four days. He had been absent on his heroic travels for more than five years but had been at sea on his explorations slightly over three months, and about half that was spent on return trips.

But since the instructions handed him had been vague, it cannot be said that his voyage was a failure. He did not, of course, confirm Peter's conviction that Asia and North America were not joined, nor did he sail far enough to encounter Spanish or English settlements. He did, however, excite both Russian and European interest in the North Pacific and he had taken the first tentative steps in making this bleak area a part of the Russian Empire.

Vitus Bering, the stubborn Dane, had been back in the capital less than two months when, despite the criticism and rebuke ringing in his ears because of his failure to sail either west to join the Kolyma River or east to prove that Asia was not joined to North America, he had the temerity to propose to the Russian government that he lead a second expedition to Kamchatka, and that instead of using about a hundred men, as he did the first time, he would now do it on a scale that would ultimately require more than three thousand. With his recommendation he submitted a careful budget in which he proved that he could accomplish this for ten thousand rubles.

The grandeur of his behavior in this negotiation was that he blandly refused to admit that he had failed the first time, and when critics assailed him for his supposed deficiencies he smiled at them indulgently, and pointed out: "But I did everything the tsar ordered me to do," and if they said: "You didn't find any Europeans," he replied: "There weren't any," and he maintained pressure on the government to send him back.

But the sum of ten thousand rubles was not to be spent lightly, and as Bering himself admitted, the expedition he now had in mind could run to as much as twelve thousand, so the government officials began a careful reexamination of his qualifications, and after interviewing his senior assistants, they came to the cossack Trofim Zhdanko, who had seen nothing wrong with Bering's conduct of the first expedition and who, having no family or pressing business in western Russia, was prepared to go east again.

"Bering is a fine commander," he assured the experts. "I was in charge of troops and can tell you that he kept his men working and happy, and that isn't easy. Yes, I'd be proud to work with him again."

"But what about the fact that he didn't go far enough north to prove that the two continents don't touch?" they asked, and he surprised them with his answer: "Tsar Peter himself once told me . . ."

Their jaws dropped: "You mean, the tsar consulted with you . . . ?"

"He did. Came to see me the night I was about to be hanged."

The interrogators ended the meeting at this point to ascertain whether Tsar Peter had actually gone to a waterfront prison to conduct a midnight talk with a cossack prisoner named Trofim Zhdanko, and when Jailer Mitrofan verified that indeed the tsar had come on just such a mission, they hurried back to question Zhdanko further.

"Peter the Great, may his honored soul rest in peace," Zhdanko began solemnly, "was already thinking about the expedition in 1723, and what we discussed he must have told Bering later. He already knew that Russia did not touch America, but he was very eager to know more about America."

"Why?"

"Because he was the tsar. Because it was proper for him to know."

The learned men hammered at the cossack for the better part of a morning, and all they learned was that Vitus Bering had failed in no commission that the tsar had given him, except the finding of Europeans, and that Zhdanko was eager to sail with him again.

"But he's fifty years old," one scientist said, to which Trofim replied: "And able to do the work of a man twenty."

"Tell me," the head of the committee asked abruptly, "would you trust Vitus Bering with ten thousand rubles?" and Zhdanko replied truthfully: "I trusted him with my life, and I'll do it again."

That interrogation, and others like it, took place in 1730, when

Trofim was twenty-eight, and in the years that followed, an energetic debate developed as to whether such an expedition should be made entirely by sea, which would be both quicker and cheaper, or by land-and-sea, which would enable the St. Petersburg government to learn more about Siberia on the way. No decision was reached for two years, and it was not until 1733, when Bering was fifty-three, that he was able to leave St. Petersburg on the overland route.

Once more he and Zhdanko were immobilized for two dreary winters by the snows of central Russia, and once again he was held in Okhotsk, and then his real troubles began, because bookkeepers back in St. Petersburg submitted a devastating report to the Russian treasury: "This Vitus Bering, who assured us that his expedition would cost ten thousand rubles or twelve at most, has already spent more than three hundred thousand before leaving Yakutsk. Nor has he placed his foot aboard his two ships. How could he? They haven't been built yet." And the nervous accountants added a shrewd prediction: "So a foolish experiment budgeted at ten thousand may ultimately cost two million."

In a kind of dull and futile rage the authorities cut Bering's pay in half and refused him the promotion to admiral that he sought. He made no complaint, and when he fell a full four years behind schedule, he merely tightened his belt, strove to maintain the spirits of his men, and went ahead with the building of his ships. In 1740, seven years after leaving the capital, he finally launched the *St. Peter,* from which he would command, and the *St. Paul,* which his able young assistant Alexei Chirikov would captain, and on 4 September of that year he led the two ships forth for their great exploration of the northern waters and the lands that bordered them.

They sailed bravely across the Sea of Okhotsk, rounded the southern tip of Kamchatka, and put in at the recently established seaport town of Petropavlovsk, which would become so crucially important in the next century and a half. It lay at the head of a remarkable bay, protected on all sides and facing south away from storms. Long arms of land safeguarded ships at anchor and comfortable houses for officers and bunks for crew lined the shore. No civilians lived here yet, but it was a splendid maritime installation and in time would be an important place. Here Bering and Zhdanko settled down for their eighth winter, 1734 through 1741.

Among the men stationed in the houses hugging the shore was a thirty-two-year-old German naturalist of unusual ability, Georg

Steller, who had been brought along with astronomers, interpreters and other scientists to lend the expedition intellectual dignity, and he better than any of the others was prepared to do just this. Avid for learning, he had attended four German universities—Wittenberg, Leipzig, Jena, Halle—leaving with a determination to extend human knowledge, so during the land part of the trip he had studied whatever materials were available on the geography, astronomy and natural life of Russia all the way from the Baltic Sea to the Pacific Ocean, and at the end of this tedious journey and its protracted delays, he was hungry to get to sea, to visit unknown islands and set foot on the unexplored shores of North America. In his unflagging enthusiasm he told Zhdanko: "With luck, I will be able to find a hundred new animals and trees and flowers and grasses."

"I thought all grass was alike."

"Oh no!" and the German enthusiast, using broken Russian, explained to Zhdanko some two dozen varieties of grass, where they flourished, how animals used them, and the great good that could be accomplished if men cultivated them intelligently.

Eager to turn the conversation away from a subject in which he had little interest, Zhdanko pointed out: "Sometimes you speak of birds and fishes as if they were animals."

"Well, Trofim, they are!" And here came another lecture that lasted the better part of a morning. At one point the other man interrupted: "To me a bird is a bird and a cow is an animal," at which Steller applauded, crying almost joyously: "And so it should be, Trofim! And to you an eagle is a bird. And a halibut is a fish. But a scientist sees that all such creatures, including man, are animals."

Zhdanko, drawing himself erect, thundered: "I am not a fish. I am a man."

Steller, reacting as if the huge man were a bright child in a beginner's class, leaned forward and asked gently: "Well then, Scholar Trofim, what would you call a chicken? In some ways it looks like a bird, but it runs on the ground."

"If it has feathers, it's a bird."

"But it also has blood. It reproduces sexually. So, to the scientist it is an animal."

"What new animals do you propose finding?"

"That's a silly question, Trofim. How do I know what I'll find until I find it?" He laughed at himself, then added: "But I have heard of a remarkable beast, the sea otter."

"I once had two sea-otter pelts."

Steller was eager to learn all that he could about this legendary animal, so Trofim related all he remembered about his two otter pelts and how he had given them to the tsar of blessed memory and how splendid the fur had looked on Peter's robes. Steller leaned back, studied the cossack, and said admiringly: "Trofim, you should be a scientist. You noticed everything. That's quite wonderful, really." And then he became a teacher of children again: "Now, what would you call a sea otter. He swims like a fish, that you know. But he is clearly not a fish, that you also know."

"If he swims, he's a fish."

"But if I pitched you overboard right now, you'd swim too. Would that make you a fish?"

"I can't swim, so I'm still a man."

The two ships remained tied up in Petropavlovsk harbor, delayed by frustrating accidents. To use the summer to advantage they should have sailed before the middle of April; they planned to depart the first of May, but at the end of that month workmen were still making repairs and alterations. Also, word was received that the expedition's supply of ship's biscuit, on which sailors lived, had become completely spoiled, so that sailing really should be delayed for one more winter. Since they had to wait for adequate provisions, they convened an emergency meeting in which a plan of action was proposed and ratified by the senior staff.

And now science, which the German Steller praised so highly, intervened to hamper the whole adventure. Some learned man, a century earlier or more, had acquired through rumor the idea that a vast land lay between Asia and North America. It had been discovered, legend said, by the indomitable Portuguese navigator Dom João da Gama in 1589 and was reputed to contain great riches. It had been named Terra da Gama, and since the nation which first laid hold on it would stand to gain enormously, the Russians hoped that Bering would find the island, map it, allow Steller to explore it for ores, and hide the facts from other nations.

Since the ships would not be able to leave harbor before June, and since the sailing season would be short, it was obvious that a majority of the good days would have to be spent in searching for Terra da Gama, with only a few reserved for the search for America, but nevertheless, on 4 May 1741 the wise men of this expedition, and there were many, agreed that their first duty was to find Terra da Gama, and to this decision they signed their names: Comandeur Vitus Bering, Captain Alexei Chirikov, Astronomer Louis De Lisle de la Croyère and seven others. Tragically belated, on 4 June 1741 they began their futile search for land that did not exist, named after a legendary Portuguese who had never sailed anywhere, for the substantial reason that he, too, never existed.

After having satisfied themselves that there was no Terra da Gama and could never have been, the ships headed eastward, but had the ill fortune to become separated during a blow, and despite the fact that each captain behaved properly during a frantic two-day search, the ships never saw each other again. Chirikov's *St. Paul* had not sunk; it sailed on ahead and Bering's *St. Peter* was not able to catch up. After thrashing about futilely, Bering resumed his sail to the east, and in this tandem formation the Russian ships approached North America.

Should Fleet Captain Bering, to use the title to which he had been temporarily promoted at the start of this unfortunate expedition, be blamed for the parting of his two ships? No. Before sailing, he had laid out the most minute instructions for maintaining contact, and he, at least, followed his rules. As in so many instances during his long probing of the eastern seas, he was plagued by bad luck; storms pushed the ships apart and heavy fogs made their reunion impossible. Misfortune, not malfeasance, was to blame, and the fact that both ships did proceed to the shores of North America proved that his orders were clear and obeyed.

And then, on 6 July, Bering's luck changed, and at half after twelve in the afternoon a light drizzle ended and out of the clearing mists rose a congregation of the grandest snow-covered mountains in America. They perched on what would be the corner of the future boundary between Alaska and Canada and they soared in white splendor sixteen and eighteen and nineteen thousand feet into the blue skies, with a score of lower peaks clustered about. It was a magnificent sight, a justification for the entire voyage, and it excited the Russians with a promise of what might come to pass if they ever attained sovereignty over this majestic land. It was an awesome moment when the mountain Bering named St. Elias, more than eighteen thousand feet high, soared into view. Europeans had discovered Alaska.

But the seas that guard this northern wonderland rarely permit prolonged investigation, and a few hours later the log of the *St. Peter* read: "Passing clouds, air thick, impossible to get a bearing because the shore is hidden by heavy clouds." And early next day it read: "Heavy clouds, rain," and later the familiar entry for any ship attempting to navigate in these waters: "Heavy clouds, rain."

On the third day, when exploration of the newfound land might have been expected to begin, the log read: "Wind, fog, rain. Though the land is not far away, yet because of heavy fog and rain we could not see it." So Bering, who discovered Alaska for Europe, never set foot upon the continent; however, four days after sighting Mount St. Elias he did come upon a long, skinny island which he also named St. Elias because it was the saint for this day. Later Russians would rename it Kayak Island because of its shape.

And now one of the unbelievable debacles of the Bering expeditions occurred. Bering, concerned primarily with the safety of his ship and getting back to Petropavlovsk, decided to inspect the island only casually, but Adjunct Steller, perhaps the most luminous intellect on either voyage, protested almost to the point of insubordination that his life for the past decade had been dedicated exclusively to this supreme moment when he would step upon a new land, and he made such a childish commotion that Bering grudgingly allowed him a brief visit ashore. But as he left the ship a trumpeter sounded a sardonic flourish as if some great man were departing, and the sailors jeered in derision. Steller took with him as his only helper Trofim Zhdanko, whom he had convinced of the importance of science. Upon landing, the two men initiated a frenzy of running about, grabbing rocks, staring at trees, and listening for birds. They tried to study everything at once, for they realized that the *St. Peter* might have to put out to sea at any moment, and they had spent only seven or eight hours collecting when a signal from the ship alerted Zhdanko to the fact that it was about to sail.

"Herr Doktor Steller! You must hurry."

"I've just begun."

"The ship is signaling."

"Let it signal."

"Herr Doktor, frantic signals."

"I'm frantic." And he had cause to be, for he had studied in Germany long years in preparation for an opportunity like this, and he had traipsed for eight years across Russia to get to Kamchatka, and lately he had been at sea for weeks, and finally he had landed on the American continent, or one of its islands less than three miles off-shore, and he was being allowed less than a day to carry out his work. It was infuriating, inconsiderate and insane, and he told Zhdanko so, but the cossack, an officer of the ship in a manner of speaking, had learned to obey orders, and Fleet Captain Bering was signaling that the longboat must return immediately and fetch Steller with it.

Actually, what Bering said to those about him was: "Signal him to come aboard at once or we sail without him." He had his ship to consider, and although he could easily have given the German scientist two or even three days ashore, he was a nervous Dane and he kept always in mind the agreement reached prior to sailing: "Regardless of what happens, the *St. Peter* and the *St. Paul* will return to Petropavlovsk on or before the last day of September 1741."

"Adjunct Steller," Zhdanko said sternly as he moved close to the sweating scientist whose arms were laden with samples of this and that, "I'm going to the longboat, and you're going with me," and he began to drag and push the protesting German off the island. That night, the following remarks were entered in the log:

> The yawl returned with water, and the crew reported having come across a fireplace, human tracks, and a fox on the run. Adjunct Steller brought various grasses.

Later, as Bering was preparing to sail for home, he sent Zhdanko and a few crew members back to St. Elias Island on a mission which symbolized his personal interest in doing a good job for his Russian masters, but this time he did not allow Steller to go, for he had learned of the German's refusal to quit his collecting at the termination of the first trip:

> The men who returned on the small yawl announced the finding of an underground hut, something like a cellar, but no people. In this hut they discovered dried fish, bows and arrows. The Captain Commander ordered Trofim Zhdanko to take to that hut a number of government things: 13 yards of green material, 2 knives, Chinese tobacco and pipes.

In this quiet and generous way began the lucrative trade that Russia would soon be conducting with the natives of Alaska. Georg Steller's summary of his day was more acerbic: "I spent ten years of preparation to perform a task of some importance and was allowed ten hours to complete it."

But if Bering did not appreciate what Steller had accomplished during the time allotted him, history does, for in those brief hours ashore he perceived the significance of North America, the character of its western ramparts and their potential importance to Russia. His work that day constitutes one of the finest applications of human intelligence within restricted confines.

Vitus Bering was not the first Russian to see Alaska, for when his ship, the *St. Peter,* lost contact with the *St. Paul,* the captain of the latter, Alexei Chirikov, spent nearly three full days searching for his missing partner, and then entered in his log:

> At the fifth hour in the morning we gave up looking for the *St. Peter* and with the assent of all the officers of the *St. Paul* we went on our way.

In shipshape fashion the younger captain proceeded with his exploration, and on 15 July 1741, a day earlier than Bering had sighted the cluster of great mountains, Chirikov sighted land some five hundred miles to the southeast. Coasting northward, he passed close to the beautiful island which would later be occupied by Russians, Baranof, and the exquisite bay which would house their capital, Sitka. In doing so, they saw a snow-covered volcano of near-perfection, to be named by a later explorer of far greater reputation Mount Edgecumbe, but they did not tarry to investigate one of the choice areas of the region.

However, a short distance to the north Captain Chirikov did dispatch a longboat to another island, under the direction of Fleet Master Dementiev, who had ten armed men to assist him. The boat ducked in among a nest of small islands and was never heard from again. After six anxious days of being immobilized by bad weather, Captain Chirikov put three technical men in a second small boat— Bosun Savelev, Carpenter Polkovnikov, Caulker Gorin—and sent them to find the first crew. At the last minute Sailor Fadiev cried: "I want to go along," and he was allowed to do so.

This boat also vanished, and now the men of the *St. Paul* had to make fearful decisions. With no small boat of any kind by which food or water could be brought aboard, and only forty-five casks of water left, they faced disaster:

> At the first hour of the afternoon the officers reached the following decision, which they put in writing: go straight to the harbor of Petropavlovsk in eastern Kamchatka. Ordered the crew to catch rain water and commanded that it be rationed out.

Thus the great expedition proposed by Vitus Bering staggered to an inconclusive ending. No officer had set foot on Alaska proper; the scientific excursions had been aborted; no useful charting was done; and fifteen men had already been lost. The adventure which Bering had said could be completed for ten thousand rubles would ultimately consume the two million predicted by the accountants, and all that would have been proved which was not already known was that Alaska existed and Terra da Gama did not.

Now came the worst. When Bering's ship, the *St. Peter,* headed west from its encounter with the great mountains, it followed more or less the lovely curve of the Aleutian Islands, but the ship was now so sluggish that it could make only sixteen or seventeen miles a day against the wind. From time to time the lookouts sighted one of the islands, and several of the grand volcanoes that dotted the chain were also visible, soaring perfectly into the sky and covered at their peaks with snow.

The sailors found little comfort in this beauty, for scurvy of the most virulent kind attacked them. Without fresh food and with inadequate water to accompany what biscuits they did have, their legs began to swell and their eyes to glaze over. They suffered violent pangs of hunger and unsteadiness in gait. Each day their plight worsened, until the entries in the log became monotonous and mournful:

> Frightful storm and great waves . . . all day waves from both sides washed over the deck . . . terrific storm . . . 21 men on sick list . . . by the will of God, Alexei Kiselev died of scurvy . . . 29 men on the sick list . . .

During the last days when ordinary activity was possible, the *St. Peter* hove to off the shore of Lapak Island, the one to which the Great Shaman Azazruk had led his emigrants twelve thousand years earlier, and here they encountered islanders who provided them with water and seal meat which helped sustain them during the month of September.

Since most of the junior officers were now incapacitated by scurvy, the yawl which went ashore was captained by Trofim Zhdanko, who requested that Adjunct Georg Steller assist him, and this was a fortunate choice, because the German had been ashore only a few minutes when he began scampering about and grabbing grasses. "This is no time for such nonsense!" Zhdanko protested, but Steller waved a handful of grass in his face, shouting with glee: "Trofim! This is an antiscorbutic! It can save all our men who are ill!" And off he went, enlisting three Aleutian children in his search for the acid-tasting grasses which he knew would combat the dreadful scurvy. Had he been given time, he might even have saved those members of the crew on whom death had already fastened his gaze.

But the man on whom this brief visit was to have the most lasting influence was Trofim Zhdanko, for when late in the day he came upon a hut dug deep into the ground in the old style but faced with stones carefully placed and covered with a solid roof made of whalebone and stout driftwood beams, he wanted to know more about the man who had built so carefully, and when finally the frightened fellow came tentatively forward, black hair down in his eyes, a big walrus bone stuck through his septum, Zhdanko handed him some of the goods Captain Bering had given him to appease the natives: "Here, this Chinese tobacco, this hand mirror. Look at yourself. Aren't you handsome with that big bone in your face? This fine cloth for your wife, and I'm sure you have one, with that handsome face. And this ax, this pipe and this tobacco."

The Aleut who received this largesse, which Captain Bering had wanted to get rid of before returning to Siberia, realized that he was being offered gifts; the miraculous mirror alone proved that, so in the custom of his people he knew that he must give this huge stranger, two heads taller than himself, something in return. But when he looked at the munificence of what Zhdanko had given, especially the ax made of metal, he wondered what possibly he could give that would not seem niggardly. And then he remembered.

Beckoning Zhdanko to follow him, they went to an underground storage area, from which the Aleut produced two walrus tusks, two sealskins and, from the dark rear, the pelt of a sea otter longer and more handsome than either of those Trofim had given the tsar. It was a full seven feet long and as soft and gentle as a handful of blossoms. It was magnificent, and Zhdanko allowed the Aleut to know he thought so.

"Have you many out there?" he asked, pointing to the sea, and the man showed his understanding by waving his arms in the air to represent plenty. And he indicated that his kayak resting on the shore was the best on this island for catching them.

Steller, meanwhile, had succeeded in collecting a large armful of weeds, some of which he was already chewing vigorously, and when the boatswain signaled that the longboat was leaving, he summoned Zhdanko and offered him a handful of the life-saving grass whose ascorbic acid would counteract the onslaughts of scurvy. When he saw the sea-otter skin he reminded Trofim of their conversation, and it was evident that he hoped that Trofim would give the skin to him to augment his meager collection. But the cossack would have none of that. Turning away, he said: "Wonderful island. I wonder what it's called?"

Now the German showed how clever he was. Handing Zhdanko his armful of grass, he faced the Aleut, and using wonderfully orchestrated movements of hands and lips, he asked what name his people gave this island, and after a while the man said: "Lapak," at which Steller bent down, touched the ground, and then rose to embrace with his arms the entire island. "Lapak?" he asked, and the islander nodded.

As Steller turned to view the island, he saw off its northern shore a splendid small cone of rock emerging from the sea, and by gestures he asked if it was a volcano, and the Aleut nodded yes. "Does it explode? Fire? Lava flowing into the sea? Hissing?" Steller asked all these questions, and received answers. He was pleased that he had discovered an active volcano and tried to ascertain its name, but this was a concept one or two degrees too difficult for the language these men had invented in half an hour, and he did not learn that in the twelve thousand years since Azazruk had first seen the nascent volcano, then less than one hundred feet above the surface of the sea, it had erupted hundreds of times, alternately rising high in the air or falling almost beneath the waves. Now it was of intermediate height, about three thousand feet, and tipped with a light cover of snow. Its name in Aleut was Qugang, the Whistler, and as Trofim Zhdanko studied it, there in the near distance rising so handsomely from the waves, he told Steller: "I'd like to come back here," and the German replied as he gathered up his grasses: "So would I."

• • •

The elixir that Steller brewed proved an almost perfect cure for scurvy, since it supplied all the nutrients missing in the belly-filling but blood-depleting diet of biscuit and salt-pork fat. But now one of the recurring ironies of the sea took place, for the very men whose lives could have been saved by imbibing the horrid-tasting stuff refused to try it. Steller drank it and so did Trofim, convinced at last that the German scientist knew what he was doing, and so did three junior officers, who saved their lives thereby. The others continued to refuse, and in this they were supported by Captain Bering himself, who growled: "Take away that mess. Do you want to kill me?" And when Steller railed against this folly of rejecting the life-saving substance, some men whispered: "No damned German can make me drink grass."

By mid-October, long after the *St. Peter* was supposed to be safe in Petropavlovsk, the men wallowing about in the storm-stricken ship were dying from the dreadful effects of scurvy, and entries in the log were piteous:

Terrific gale blowing. Today I became ill with scurvy but do not count myself among the sick.

I have such pains in my feet and hands that I can with difficulty stand my watch, 32 on the sick list.

By the will of God died the Yakutsk soldier Karp Peshenoi, and we lowered him into the sea.

Ivan Petrov, the naval carpenter, died.

The drummer boy Osip Chenstov, of the Siberian garrison, died.

10 o'clock died the trumpeter Mikhail Totopstov. Grenadier Ivan Nebaranov died.

On 5 November 1741, when the *St. Peter* hove to off one of the most miserable islands in the northern seas, far past the end of the Aleutians, Captain Bering, himself stricken with a severe case of scurvy, assembled his officers to consider objectively their tragic condition, and to open the meeting, Zhdanko read the report prepared by the doctor, who was too ill to participate: "We have few men to handle this ship. Twelve are already dead. Thirty-four are so weak they may soon die. The total number of men strong enough to handle ropes, ten, and of them, seven can move about only with difficulty. We have no fresh food and very little water."

Faced with such blunt facts, Bering had no option but to recommend that his ship, the one in which he had dreamed of accomplishing so much, be beached on this forlorn spot, there to build a refuge where the sickest seamen might have a chance to survive the bitter winter that was descending upon them. This was done, but of the first four men sent ashore, three died in the rescue boat—the cannoneer Dergachev, the sailor Emilianov, the Siberian soldier Popkov— and the fourth man, the sailor Trakanov, died just as he was being handed ashore.

Then came that blizzard of sorrowful entries: Stepanov died, so did Ovtsin, Antipin, Esselberg, and then the pitiful notation:

On account of sickness I had to stop keeping a regular journal and am just making notes like this.

On 1 December 1741, during the blackest single day of the journey, Captain Bering sought out his aide, and with a burst of energy that was remarkable in one so old and so ill, he moved about the camp, encouraging everyone and assuring them that this winter would pass as had the other difficult ones they had shared. He refused to admit that this situation was far worse than difficult, and when Zhdanko tried to tell him how perilous things were, the old man stopped, stared at his assistant, and said: "I would not expect a healthy Russian to talk like that."

Zhdanko, realizing that his captain's mind was wandering, gently led him to his bed, but he could not make the old lion lie down. Bering continued to move about, giving orders for the management of the camp. Finally he staggered, reached for things that were not there, and fell into Zhdanko's arms.

Unconscious, he was placed in the bed from which he would never rise. On the second day he slept, but on the third he asked for full details on what was being done aboard ship, and then he again lapsed into unconsciousness, which Zhdanko said was God's mercy because of the extreme pain the old fighter was experiencing. On 7 December, a bitter cold day, he wanted to be taken out to the ship, but this Zhdanko refused to do. In lucid moments, Bering discussed intelligently the work still to be done before the expedition could be considered a success, and he judged that the expedient thing to do would be to dig in for the winter, break the *St. Peter* apart, build from its timbers a tight small boat called a hooker, sail to Petropavlovsk when the weather was good, and there build a new ship with better strength in its timbers and return to explore seriously those inviting lands close to that great nest of mountains coming down to the sea.

Zhdanko encouraged him in all this dreaming, and on that night of 7 December he slept beside this extraordinary Dane whom he had grown to respect and love. At about four in the morning Bering wakened with a host of new plans, which, he told Zhdanko, he felt sure the authorities in St. Petersburg would approve; when he tried to explain them in detail he lapsed into Danish, but there were none of his Danes still living to understand.

"Go back to sleep, Little Captain," Zhdanko said, and shortly before five o'clock on that storm-swept island the old man died.

But now the survivors took hold of themselves, as Bering had hoped they would, and despite blizzards and inadequate food, the gallant forty-six surveyed the island, reported on its possibilities, and did exactly what Bering had planned: from the wreckage of the ship *St. Peter* they constructed the hooker *St. Peter,* thirty-six feet long, twelve feet wide, five feet three inches deep. In this frail and crowded craft all forty-six sailed the three hundred and sixty miles to Petropavlovsk, where they landed on 27 August 1742, an appalling nine years, one hundred and sixty-three days after the departure from St. Petersburg on 18 March 1733.

When they landed they learned that their companion ship, the *St. Paul,* had had its troubles, too. Of her seventy-six officers and men who sailed in June, only fifty-four returned in October, four months later. They heard with sorrow of how the two boats with fifteen knowledgeable seamen had vanished near a beautiful island, and they understood what had been involved when a local officer reported: "On the journey back to Petropavlovsk they were smitten with scurvy and many died."

The harshest judgment on Vitus Bering was that he had been unlucky. All events seemed to conspire against him; his ships leaked; the stores that he anticipated did not arrive on time, or were lost, or were stolen. Many other captains conducted voyages of much greater extent both in miles and time than his from Kamchatka to Alaska and back without being struck by such a virulent outbreak of scurvy, but he was so adversely marked by fate that on this relatively brief cruise he lost thirty-six in one ship, twenty-two in another. And he died without ever having encountered the Europeans he sought.

And yet this doughty, stumpy Dane left a heritage of honor and a tradition of seamanship which inspired the navy of a great nation. He had sailed the northern seas with a vigor that excited the men who accompanied him, and in all the logs of his ships there is no entry which speaks of ill feeling against the captain or disturbances among the men under his command.

In the seas he wandered so ineffectively, two memorials remind us of his valor. The icy water that lies between the Pacific and Arctic oceans carries his name, the Bering Sea, and it seems to borrow its character from him. It is dour; it freezes hard; it is difficult to navigate when the ice crowds down; and it punishes those who miscalculate its power. But it also teems with a rich animal life and rewards good hunters and fishermen enormously. It is a sea deserving to be named after someone rugged like Bering, and in this narrative we shall meet it repeatedly, always with respect. At the close of the following century thousands will swarm to its shores and some will find in its magical sands the golden wealth of Croesus.

The Russians also named after him that forlorn island on which he died, and a more wretched memorial no good sailor was ever given. But there will always be critics to claim that he was not a good sailor and they will cry: "No first-rate seaman ever attempted so much, managed it so poorly, and accomplished so little." History does not find it comfortable to adjudicate such debate.

The exploration of Alaska was conducted by two contrasting kinds of men: either purposeful explorers of established reputation like Vitus Bering and the other historic figures we shall be meeting briefly, or tough, nameless commercial adventurers who often achieved more constructive results than the professionals who preceded them. In the early development this second wave of men in motion was made up of rascals, thieves, murderers and ordinary toughs who had been born in Siberia or served there, and their guiding motto as they began to probe the Aleutian Islands was brief and accurate: "The tsar is far away in St. Petersburg and God is so high in heaven He can't see us. But here we are on the island, so let's do whatever's necessary."

Trofim Zhdanko, miraculously alive after his winter of near-starvation on Bering Island, became through an odd combination of circumstances one of these commercial adventurers. Having made his way to Russia's eastern terminus at the seaport of Okhotsk, from which he supposed he would be sent home, he gradually realized, during a six-month waiting period, that he had no desire to go back: I'm forty-one. My tsar's dead, so what's in St. Petersburg? And my family's dead, so what's in Ukraine? The more he examined his limited prospects the more he was attracted to remaining in the east, and he started asking what his chances were of landing a government job of some kind, but he had made only a few inquiries when he learned a basic fact about Russian life: "When there's a good job in any of the alien provinces like Siberia, it's always some official born in homeland Russia who gets it. Others need not apply."

The best government job he could hope for as a Ukrainian in Okhotsk was as a laborer on the new harbor that was being built to accommodate trade with Japan, China and the Aleutians, if such trade ever developed, which seemed unlikely, since the ports of the first two nations were closed to Russian ships while the Aleutians contained no harbors. Despondent, and perplexed as to what ugly things might happen to him if he did return to St. Petersburg, now that new officials were in power, he was lazing in the sun one June morning in 1743, when a man, obviously a Siberian, with dark skin, Mongolian features and no neck, accosted him: "The name's Poznikov, gentleman merchant. You look like a strong one."

"I've met men who could best me."

"Have you ever sailed?"

"I've been to the other shore," and when he pointed toward America the merchant gasped, took him by the arm, and spun him around for closer examination.

"You were with Bering?"

"Buried him. A great man."

"You must come with me. You must meet my wife."

The merchant led him to a well-appointed house overlooking the harbor, and there Zhdanko met Madame Poznikova, an imperious woman obviously not Siberian. "Why do you bring this workman to see me?" she asked her husband rather sternly, and he said with obvious meekness: "He's not a workman, dearest, he's a sailor."

"Where has he sailed?" she demanded.

"To America . . . with Bering."

When this name was spoken, she moved closer to Trofim and, as her husband did in the street, swung him around to inspect him more closely, turning his big head this way and that as if she had perhaps seen him before. Then, shrugging, she asked with just a touch of scorn: "You? You were with Bering?"

"Twice. I was his aide."

"And you saw the islands out there?"

"I was ashore, twice, and as you know, we spent one whole winter there."

"I didn't know," she said, taking command of the conversation and asking Trofim to sit while she fetched a drink made from the cranberries which abounded in these parts. Before resuming her interrogation, she cleared her throat: "Now tell me, Cossack. Were there really furs on those islands?"

"Wherever we went."

"But I was told by the first ship that returned, Captain Chirikov's, that they saw no furs."

"They didn't land, we did."

Abruptly, she rose and stalked about the room, then sat down beside her husband, and with her hand on his knee as if seeking either his counsel or his silence, she asked very slowly: "Cossack, would you be willing to go back to the islands? For my husband, that is? To bring us furs?"

Zhdanko breathed deeply, endeavoring to suppress the excitement he felt at being offered an escape from a dead life in western Russia: "Well, if it could be done . . ."

"What do you mean?" she said sharply. "You've already done it." She waved her hand, brushing aside any questions: "Crews, ships, that's what Okhotsk is for." Suddenly she was standing before him: "Would you go?" and he saw no purpose in delaying his enthusiastic acceptance: "Yes!"

During subsequent discussions of how such an expedition could be organized, it was she who laid down the principles: "You'll sail to the new harbor at Petropavlovsk, a thousand easy miles in a stout Okhotsk ship belonging to the government. There you'll be only six or seven hundred miles from the first island, so you'll build your own ship and sail forth in early spring. Fish and hunt all summer, come back in autumn, and when you reach here Poznikov will take your furs to Irkutsk . . ."

"Why so far?" Zhdanko asked, and she snapped: "It's the capital of Siberia. All good things in this part of Siberia come from Irkutsk." Then, with a show of modesty: "I come from Irkutsk. My father was voivode there." And as she uttered this word, she and Trofim pointed at each other and broke into laughter.

When Poznikov asked: "What's so funny?" she choked, took Trofim by the wrist, and shook it vigorously: "He *was* with Bering! I saw him with Bering!" and she drew back to study him: "How many years ago could that have been?" and Trofim said: "Seventeen. You brought us tea and your father told us of the fur trading in Mongolia." After a moment's pause, he asked: "Did you ever return to that trading post on the border?"

"I did," she said. "That's where I met him," and she pointed to her stolid husband, showing no affection but great respect. Then she clapped her hands: "Ivan, I hire this cossack here and now. He's to be our captain."

Ivan Poznikov was in his fifties, hardened by the cruel winters of Siberia and even more by the harsh practices he had been forced to employ in his dealings with Chukchis, Kalmucks and Chinese. He was a big man, not so tall as Zhdanko but broader in the shoulders and just as powerful in the arms; his hands were immense, and on several occasions when facing ultimate danger his long fingers had clamped around an adversary's neck and remained there, tightening until the man fell limp in his hands and died. In trading he was equally brutal, but because through the years of their unequal marriage his wife had hammered at him, he allowed her to run their family and its business.

When Trofim met the Poznikovs that first morning he had wondered how this dynamic woman, daughter of a voivode sent out from the capital, had consented to marry a mere Siberian tradesman, but in the following weeks when he saw how this pair dominated the eastern fur trade he remembered the interest she had shown in it as a girl in Irkutsk. Apparently she had seen Poznikov as her main chance to learn the mysteries of eastern Siberia, so she had stifled her social ambitions, accepted him as her husband, and expanded his business sixfold. It was she who supervised the trading, making most of the major decisions, for as Poznikov confided: "I do better when I listen to her."

One day while the two men were working on plans for establishing a chain of trading posts in the Aleutians, Poznikov made a casual remark which indicated that perhaps the Madame, as both men called her, had done the proposing which resulted in their marriage: "We were on the Mongolian border, and I was astonished at how thoroughly she knew fur prices, and I said: 'You're wonderful!' and to my surprise, she said right back: 'You're wonderful, Poznikov. Together we would make a powerful team.'" Neither man commented further.

When it became clear that it was going to require much longer to arrange the first trip to the Aleutians than planned, it was Madame Poznikova who suggested: "Time's come for us to get our furs to Kyakhta on the Mongolian border," and she proposed that Zhdanko hire six armed guards to escort them through the first five hundred miles of forbidding bandit country between Okhotsk and the Lena. But when details were completed, Trofim learned that he would be protecting not only the merchant and his wife but also their sixteen-year-old son, a brash, ill-mannered young man who bore the highly inappropriate name of Innokenti.

During their first hours together Trofim learned that the son was arrogant, opinionated, brutal in his treatment of inferiors, and miserably spoiled by his mother. Innokenti knew the answer to everything and volunteered to make all decisions. Because he was a large lad, his firm opinions carried more weight than they might have otherwise, and he took especial delight in telling Zhdanko, whom he considered little better than a serf, what to do. Since the distance to Yakutsk was about eight hundred miles, it was obvious that the journey with the pelts was not going to be a pleasant one.

To ease the tension as they plodded through the wastelands of Siberia, Trofim devised a nonsense rhyme like the ones his mother had sung in the Ukraine:

"Irkutsk to Ilimsk to Yakutsk to Okhotsk!
No one can handle such difficult names.
Okhotsk to Yakutsk to Ilimsk to Irkutsk!
When you're a cossack they're easy as games."

"That's a stupid song," Innokenti said. "Stop it!" But the six guards were so attracted by the difficult names and broken rhythms that soon the entire column except the boy chanted "Okhotsk to Yakutsk to Irkutsk," and the tedious miles became more bearable.

When they were more than halfway to Yakutsk, Trofim was so pleased with the progress they were making and with the congeniality of the two older Poznikovs that one night as they camped on the barren side of a Siberian mountain, he beckoned the big merchant with the drooping mustaches and no neck, and in the moonlight whispered: "I brought with me a special fur. I think it's valuable. Will you sell it for me when you get yours to Mongolia?"

"Glad to. Where is it?" and from his voluminous blouse Trofim produced the remarkable pelt he had acquired on Lapak Island. As soon as Poznikov felt its extraordinary quality, and even before taking it to a light, he said: "This must be sea otter."

"It is," Trofim said, and the merchant whistled: "I didn't know they grew so big!" and Trofim said: "The seas out there are full of them."

In the next moments Zhdanko learned why the bull-necked Siberian had been so successful even before he acquired his capable wife, for Poznikov adjusted the flickering light so that it illuminated the fur without revealing its presence to the six guards, who might be spying. Then, he lifted one tip after another, satisfying himself as to its quality by rubbing it between his fingers, tugging at it gently at first, to be sure it had not been glued onto the pelt, and when Zhdanko was not looking, giving it a tremendous yank. Satisfied that the fur was real, even though of a type with which he was not familiar, he pressed it against his face, then blew upon it to separate the hairs so that he might see the subtle variation of color along the length. Then suddenly, in a gesture which startled Trofim, he pressed both hands heavily upon the fur and pulled the hairs roughly apart so that the animal skin was revealed for him to judge of its health, and when all this was done, he stood up, walked away from the lamp so that no watcher but Zhdanko could see him, and holding his right hand high above his head, he allowed the full length of this gorgeous pelt to reveal itself.

When he returned to the light, he masked the fur, sat down beside Trofim, pressed the pelt into his hands, and whispered: "Madame must see this," and when he and Trofim slipped quietly into her tent, he told her: "We've found a treasure," and he indicated that Trofim was to show her and Innokenti the pelt. As soon as she saw it she tried to assess its value with a set of tricks totally different from the ones her husband had used. Standing erect and adopting the poses of a princess, this imposing thirty-four-year-old woman draped the pelt about her shoulders, took a few steps, wheeled, took some more steps, and bowed before her son as if he had invited her to dance.

Only then did she give her opinion: "This is a fine fur, worth a fortune," and when Trofim asked hesitantly: "How much?" she offered a figure in rubles that amounted to more than seven hundred dollars. He gasped and said: "There are hundreds out there," and she restudied the pelt, hefted it in her hands, then held it against her face: "Maybe nine hundred."

It was unfortunate that Innokenti had heard this, for he could not keep from boasting to one of the Siberian guards the next morning: "We have a new kind of pelt. Worth more than a thousand rubles," and as the days passed, this man told the other guards: "In those bales they never open they have hundreds of pelts worth fifteen hundred rubles each," and the Siberians began to hatch a plot.

As the little caravan entered a canyon girt by low hills, one of the Siberians whistled, whereupon all six turned on the Poznikovs and their personal protector, Zhdanko. Knowing that he was the one they must dispose of first, the three biggest guards fell upon Trofim with clubs and knives, expecting to kill him instantly, but with an instinct gained from many such encounters, he anticipated their thrusts, and calling upon his extreme strength, he held them off.

And to the amazement of the guards who had attacked the three Poznikovs, expecting an easy victory, the family turned out to be Siberian tigers, or worse. Madame Poznikova started screaming and beating about her with a walking stick, which she wielded with fury and direction. Her son did not run for cover, like an ordinary frightened sixteen-year-old; grabbing at one of the men, he caught him by an arm and swung him into a tree, and when the rogue stumbled, Innokenti jumped upon him and with his fists beat him senseless. But it was Poznikov himself who proved the most valorous, for after manhandling his own assailant, choking him with his huge hands, he sprang to help Zhdanko, who was still fending off his three attackers.

One of the men had a long, sharp knife pointed at Trofim's throat, and Poznikov, fighting off the other two, leaped on him but could not wrest the weapon from him, and the desperate man now plunged the knife deep into the merchant's belly, pulling it upward and to one side, leaving it there to complete its work. Poznikov, realizing from the terrible course of the knife through his vitals that he was mortally wounded, screamed in some old Siberian tongue to his wife, and she stopped flailing about with her stick and dashed to his side.

When she saw what had happened, assessing it, like him, as certain death, she grabbed at the handle of the long knife, ripped it from her husband's belly, and looked frantically about. Seeing the man that her son had fought off, she leaped on him as he lay on the ground

and plunged the knife into his throat. Pausing only to jerk it out sideways, she turned toward the man whom her husband had downed,
and with a wild yell she bent over him, stabbing him three times
about the heart.

The four other guards, watching with horror what this frenzied
woman was doing, started to flee, leaving the supposed cache of otter
pelts behind, but Innokenti tripped one of them, pinned him when he
fell, and shouted for his mother to give him the knife, which she did,
and he stabbed the man many times.

Three Siberian scoundrels and Merchant Poznikov lay dead in
the canyon, and after Trofim and Innokenti had buried the latter
under a pile of stones, Madame in solemn words spoke the truth
about the fight: "Innokenti was very brave, and I'm proud of him.
And I knew what to do when I grasped the knife. But we would all
have been dead if Zhdanko had not held off those first three . . . so
long . . . so valiantly." She nodded before him and told her son to do
the same, in respect for his behavior as a true cossack, but the boy
refused to do so, for he was lamenting the death of his father.

Maintaining watch against the three runaway guards lest they attempt to return with allies to capture the caravan, the travelers held
counsel as to what they had best do to protect themselves and their
precious cargo, and since they were well over halfway to the Lena
River they agreed that it would be wise to push ahead through the
remaining two hundred miles, and in the morning, after paying tearful farewell to the grave of Ivan Poznikov, merchant-warrior, they set
forth across some of the loneliest terrain in the world: those barren
upland reaches of central Siberia, when days were a forlorn emptiness
with nothing visible to the horizon and nights a wind-howling terror.

It was in this testing land that Trofim came to appreciate the extraordinary family of which he had become a part. Ivan Poznikov
had been fearless in life, courageous in death. His widow Marina was
a remarkable woman, the equal of any man in judicious trading, an
astonishing performer when turned loose with a long knife. Watching her adjust to the loss of her husband and the rigors of the march,
he understood why Ivan had been willing to place in her hands the
management of his business. Now, in the most dangerous parts of
their journey, she offered to stand guard while her men slept. She ate
as frugally as they. She tramped the difficult miles without complaint,
helped tend the horses, and smiled when Trofim paid her a compliment: "You're a cossack in dresses."

Her son Innokenti was a problem, for although he had behaved astonishingly well during the attack on their caravan, fighting like a man thrice his age, he remained an unpleasant youth, and his killing of a man made him even more arrogant than before. He had a visceral dislike of Trofim, a distaste for his mother's leadership, and an inclination to do all those irritating things which caused elders to distrust him. Able he was, likable he would never be. And Trofim heard him complain: "Three robbers dead, and the cossack didn't kill one of them. A woman and a boy saved the caravan."

Madame Poznikova would have none of this: "We know who protected us that night . . . who held off three . . . miraculously, I think." And it was Zhdanko who guided them across these hazardous wastes. He selected the places to halt and then volunteered to stand the night watches. He kept an eye out for bears, went first into the streams that had to be forded, and in every way performed like a true cossack. But despite this constant exhibition of leadership, Innokenti refused to accept him as anything but a serf; he did, however, obey Trofim during the march, intending to be rid of him when it ended.

In this disciplined way, the three travelers completed their fourteen perilous days on the lonely trails and came to that hill from which, exhausted but still prepared to forge ahead, they looked down upon a most beautiful sight, the wide, flowing Lena River. Here they rested, and Zhdanko, gazing at the river, said: "When you sell the furs, you'll have rubles instead of pelts. And then we'll have to worry about getting them safely back to Okhotsk," but Madame said sternly: "This time we'll hire honest guards."

In Yakutsk she faced a different problem: finding honest merchants to barge her bales up the Lena River to the big markets on the Mongolian border; but calling upon old acquaintances of her husband's, she concluded a promising deal. Before dispatching them, she took the merchants aside and revealed the special pelt she was sending to market: "Sea otter. Nothing else like it in the world. And I can provide an assured supply." The men studied the exceptional fur and asked why her husband had not come with one so valuable, and she said: "He came and was killed by our guards," and she added: "Help me to find six I can trust not to kill me on the way home."

After they had provided reliable men from their own ranks, they said: "Bring us all the sea otter you can catch. Chinese merchants will fight over such fur." Smiling thinly, she offered them a guarantee:

"You'll see me often in Yakutsk," and on the trip home she discussed with Trofim and her son how the Aleutian Islands could be exploited.

When they were back in Okhotsk, a town building itself into a city, she was in her house only one day before she summoned Trofim, to whom she said frankly: "Cossack, you're a tremendous man. You have both courage and brains. You must stay with me, for I need your help to control the fur islands."

"I have no mind to marry," he said.

"Who said marry? I need you in my business."

"I'm a seaman. We're no good at business."

"I'll make you good." Then she added pleadingly: "Poznikov, rest the good man's soul, he'd been a merchant for years. Accomplished nothing, until I put iron in his backbone."

"My job is in the islands."

"Cossack, you and I, we could own those islands and all the furs they contain." She moved to face him directly: "But neither of us can do it alone." Her voice rising to an irritated shriek, she cried: "Cossack, I need you."

But he knew what his destiny was: "I shall go to the islands. And bring you furs. And you shall sell them," and from this simple resolve he would not retreat. However, when she said in ill-disguised disgust: "If you must go, take Innokenti with you. Teach him wisdom and control, for he has neither," he assented: "I don't want him. He's already ruined, I'm afraid, but I'll take him," and she grasped his arm: "To hell with wisdom and control. Teach him to be a reliable man, like his father, like you; otherwise, I am sore afraid he'll never be one."

Any serious shipbuilder looking at the pitiful craft in which Trofim Zhdanko and the eighteen-year-old Innokenti Poznikov proposed to sail with eleven others from Petropavlovsk across the Bering Sea to Attu Island, westernmost of the Aleutians, would have been appalled. Green timbers had been used for the main structure of the boat, but not for the sides, which were of sealskin, some heavy enough to withstand real shocks, some so thin they could be punctured by any shard of ice that struck them. Since nails were almost nonexistent in Kamchatka, the few that were obtainable were used to bind main pieces of wood; for the other areas thongs of walrus and whale had to suffice, which made one practiced sailor groan: "That thing wasn't built, it was sewed."

The finished product was little more than a sealskin umiak somewhat strengthened and big enough to hold thirteen fur traders and their gear, particularly their guns. Indeed, there were so many firearms aboard as to make the boat resemble a floating arsenal, and their owners were eager to use them. But the chances that such a flimsy vessel would ever reach the Aleutians seemed improbable, and that it could get back loaded with bales of pelts, even more so. But Zhdanko was eager to test his luck, and on a spring day in 1745 he sailed forth to capture Alaska for the Russian Empire and riches for his motley crew.

They were a brutal lot, prepared to take risks and determined to win their fortunes in the fur trade. Forerunners of Russia's expansion to the east, they would set the pattern for Russia's behavior in the settlement of Alaska.

What kind of men were these? They were divided into three clearcut groups: true Russians from the rather small tsardom in northwest Europe centering on two great cities, St. Petersburg and Moscow; adventurous men from all the other parts of the empire, especially Siberians from the east; and a curious group called by the difficult name *promyshlenniki,* which was comprised of petty criminals from anywhere who had been sentenced by the court to a choice between death or forced servitude in the Aleutians. Taken as a mass, they were usually all called Russians.

These ugly men were blessed with gentle winds that kept their improvised sail full, and after twenty rather easy days requiring little paddling, Zhdanko said: "Tomorrow, maybe. Or next day." They were heartened by the large number of seals they were seeing, and early one morning as Innokenti peered eastward he spotted, bobbing on the waves, their first sea otter.

"Trofim!" he called, for he continued to treat the cossack like a serf. "Is that one?"

There was little space in the unroofed boat for movement, but Trofim edged his way forward, stared into the morning light, and said: "I see nothing." This irritated Innokenti, who shouted impatiently: "There, there! Floating on its back."

And now when Trofim looked he saw one of nature's strangest yet most pleasing sights: a female sea otter swimming along on her back with a baby nestled securely on her belly, both looking at ease and enjoying the shifting clouds in the sky. Trofim could not yet be sure they were sea otters, but he knew they were not seals, so he moved to the back, took the tiller, and steered toward the floating pair.

Unaware of what a boat was or a man, the mother otter continued her lazy swim as the hunters drew near, and even when Innokenti
raised his gun and took aim, she attempted no evasive action. There
was a loud bang, she felt a crushing pain through her chest and sank
immediately to the far depths of the Bering Sea, dead and of use to
no one. Her baby, left afloat, was clubbed by a heavy paddle, and then
it too sank to the bottom. Of all the sea otters that would in the years
ahead be killed by careless hunters firing prematurely, seven out of
ten would sink to the bottom before being caught for their fur. With
Innokenti's first gun blast, the extermination was under way.

Having lost what Trofim and the others certified as a true sea
otter, the young fellow was not in a happy mood when later that
morning one of the men shouted "Land!" and the boy took no pleasure in watching as the lone island of Attu emerged from the mists
that enshrouded it.

They had made landfall at the northwest corner of the island,
and for an entire day they coasted along its northern face, encounter-
ing nothing but forbidding cliffs and the lifeless stare of what appeared to be barren fields, no tree or even a shrub. They did pass the
mouth of one bay, but its flanks were so precipitous that any attempt
at landing would have been foolhardy, and that night Innokenti prepared for bed with the whining observation: "Attu's a rock."

However, next morning, after breasting a low headland at the
eastern tip of the island, they saw facing them a wide bay with inviting sandy shores and spacious meadows. Gingerly they made a landing, and supposing the island to be uninhabited, started inland. They
had progressed only a short distance when they discovered the miracle of Attu. Wherever they moved they were faced with a treasure of
bright flowers in the most profuse variety: daisies, red flamers, lu-
pines in many colors, lady slippers, thistles, and two which astonished them: purple iris and gray-green orchids.

"This is a garden!" Trofim cried, but Innokenti had turned away,
and suddenly wailed: "Look!" and from the opposite end of the
meadow, coming toward them, was a procession of native men wearing the distinctive hats of their island, long visor in front, straight
back, and flowers or feathers stemming from the crown. They had
never before seen a white man, nor had any of the invaders except
Zhdanko seen islanders, so mutual curiosity ran high.

"They're friendly," Zhdanko assured his men, "until something
proves different," but it was difficult to convince them of this, be-

cause each islander had sticking horizontally through his nose a long bone and in his lower lip one or two labrets, which imparted such a fierce appearance that Innokenti shouted: "Fire at them."

Trofim, countermanding the order, moved forward, holding in his extended hands a collection of beads, and when the islanders saw their glittering beauty they whispered among themselves, and finally one came toward Zhdanko, offering him a piece of carved ivory. In this way the serious exploitation of the Aleutian Islands began.

The first contacts were congenial. The islanders were an orderly group: smallish men with dark Oriental-looking faces who could have come out of northern Siberia a year ago, they went barefoot, wore sealskin clothing, and tattooed their faces. Their language bore no resemblance to any that the men from the boat had ever heard, but their wide smiles showed their welcome.

But when Zhdanko and his crew made their way to one of the huts in which the islanders lived two things happened: the Attu men obviously did not want the strangers to approach their women and children; and when the Siberians forced their way inside one, they were repelled by the darkness of the underground cave in which they found themselves, by its confusion and by the awful smell of fish and rotting seal fat. In that moment the tension began, for one of Zhdanko's men growled scornfully: "They're not human!" and this became the consensus.

Nevertheless, in several of the thirty-odd huts the newcomers did find small piles of sealskin, though with whom the islanders could be trading no one could guess, and in two huts they found well-tanned pelts of the sea otter. Their long quest—starting in Okhotsk and ending with their daring venture across the Bering Sea in their improbable boat—seemed assured of success.

It was not difficult for Zhdanko, who was an ingenious man, to explain to the men of Attu that if they brought him sealskins, he in turn would trade them for things they wanted from the boat; and that was preliminary to informing them that what the strangers really wanted were pelts of the sea otter. But that was a different matter, because through the centuries the islanders had learned that the sea otter was the rarest creature in their ocean and that to catch him was not easy. But the traders finally convinced the islanders that the latter must go forth in their kayaks and bring back furs, especially those of the otter.

The name of the young paddler who now took it upon himself to instruct Innokenti in island rites was Ilchuk, some five years older and a skilled hunter who had been instrumental in bringing to shore the only whale that Attu had captured in ten years; its baleen had been used by Ilchuk's sisters in the creation of numerous useful articles and a pair of baskets that were not only practical containers but also works of art.

When Trofim saw these baskets and other things made from whalebone and ivory, he began to alter his opinion of the Attu islanders; and when he and Innokenti were finally invited into Ilchuk's hut, he saw that they did not all live like animals. The hut was orderly and arranged much as a house in Siberia would be, except that it was mostly underground, and when the winds of winter began to blow, Trofim understood why the houses were kept so low; had they been any higher, the gales would have blown them away.

Now, in the dark winter, tensions between the two groups flared, because the newcomers, hungry for furs, wanted the island men to continue hunting regardless of weather, while the Attu men, well acquainted with the power of winter storms, knew that they must stay ashore till spring. The one who applied the greatest pressure was Innokenti, nineteen years old now and increasingly brutal in his relations with others. Always aware that it was his family that had built the fur trade, he found it impossible to accept an intruder like Zhdanko, so he placed himself in charge of the growing bales and of the operations which promised to bring in more. Trofim, a quarter of a century older than this callow youth, surrendered control of fur hunting but resolved to retain command of all else.

As soon as there was any cessation of storm, and sometimes two or three days in a row would be relatively calm, Innokenti ordered Ilchuk and his men to venture forth, and if they showed reluctance to do so, he raged until it became clear to the Attu men that they had somehow, by steps they could not now recall, become slaves of the strangers. This feeling was intensified when two of Innokenti's men appropriated young women of the settlement, with such pleasing results that a third man plucked off one of Ilchuk's sisters.

There was resentment, but on Attu relations between adult men and women were customarily easy, so that the tempers which might have flared elsewhere did not erupt here, but what did matter was Innokenti's unwavering insistence that the men go out to sea when all their instincts and long experience warned them to stay ashore. This radical alteration of their life systems they opposed, and when, on a clear day, Innokenti demanded that Ilchuk and four of his men go out, there was a momentary flare-up, which ended quickly when Innokenti produced his gun and ordered the men with gestures: "You go or I shoot."

Grudgingly they went, pointing to the sky as if to say "We warned you!" and before they were out of sight of land, a great wind blew in from Asia, bringing sheets of freezing rain that came parallel to the sea, destroying two of the kayaks and drowning their occupants. When Ilchuk led the surviving boats back to shore he began to rage at Innokenti, who stood quietly for several minutes, but when the other Attu men joined the recriminations, surrounding him on three sides, he lost his composure, raised his gun, and shot one of the protesters. Ilchuk, seeing the man fall and realizing that he was fatally wounded, started to leap at Innokenti, but he was seized by two of the Siberians, who threw him to the ground, then kicked him about the head.

Trofim, hearing the gunfire, ran from where he had been working on a driftwood house, and by virtue of his size and authority, brought order to what would otherwise have degenerated into a riot which might have caused the deaths of all the invaders. It was the last time he would exert his authority over the men, for when he shouted: "Who did this?" Innokenti stepped brazenly forward: "I did. They were attacking me," and when the others supported this claim, thrusting their chins forward belligerently, Zhdanko realized that leadership of the expedition had passed to Innokenti. Almost lamely he said: "Warfare has begun. Each man to protect himself," but it was the younger man who gave specific orders: "Bring our boat closer to our huts. And each man to sleep with us, not with his native woman."

The man who had taken as his bed-partner Ilchuk's sister ignored this last instruction, and two mornings later, when the winter fog lifted, his body was found on the beach stabbed in many places.

Now the warfare became hateful, sullen, a thing of dark shadows and sudden retributions. With only twelve men left, including himself, Trofim tried to regain control by making peace with the more numerous islanders, and he might have succeeded had not an evil affair frustrated him. When Ilchuk, a wise islander who lamented the sad deterioration, came with two fellow fishermen to arrange with Trofim a kind of truce, Innokenti, who was watching nearby with four of his followers, allowed them to come close, then flashed a signal, whereupon the Russians leveled their guns and killed all three members of the peace team. Next day, when one of the island girls charged Innokenti with having murdered her brother in the ambush, he proved her correct by murdering her, too.

Vainly Trofim tried to halt the killings, and in quick succession six more islanders were slain, after which it was meekly accepted that a new order had come to Attu. When spring made orderly hunting of sea otters practical, Innokenti and his group had life on the island so rigorously organized that kayaks went out regularly, and came back with the furs the traders craved. It would be difficult to explain just how these eleven—five Siberians, three Russian petty criminals, two from other parts of the empire and the boy Innokenti—maintained control over the population of an entire island, but they did. Murder was a prime persuader—eight, two dozen, then thirty, all executed coldly and at such times and places as to create the most intimidating effect, till everyone on Attu knew that if fishermen-hunters were tardy in doing what the strangers wanted, someone was going to be shot, usually the delinquent fisherman and sometimes several of his friends.

Even more difficult to explain was how Trofim Zhdanko allowed all this to happen, but in the affairs of men under pressure, decisions are made as a consequence of events far beyond their control; chance determines, not planned thought, and each bloody incident on Attu strengthened Innokenti's hand and weakened Trofim's. Of all these episodes of killing, he participated in none, for as a cossack trained in killing at the tsar's command, he had learned that murder was justified only if it quickly brought a workable peace. On Attu, Innokenti's aimless slaughter brought no peace, only more furs, so by midsummer Trofim realized that the situation had degenerated so badly that the only sensible strategy was to leave the island with what furs had been accumulated and head for Petropavlovsk.

When he proposed this, many of the crew were so eager to leave Attu that he regained a modicum of leadership, but once more chance intruded to deny him that position, for when in mid-July 1746 he organized the men secretly for an escape, an island woman detected the strategy of flight and informed her men, who made plans to murder all the strangers before they reached their boat.

When the bales were aboard and the twelve survivors about to push off, the islanders tried to rush them, but Innokenti had anticipated this, and as the shouting men and women surged toward the boat, he ordered his men to fire straight into the middle of the crush and then to reload and fire again. They did, with terrible effectiveness.

As this first group of invaders from Russia to spend a winter in the Aleutians finally retreated to the safety of the Bering Sea they had slain, since the day of their first landing, sixty-three Aleuts.

Their sail home was a tale of horrors, for in their frail boat, with no deck and only a modest sail attached to a flimsy mast, they headed into adverse winds blowing out of Asia and had to confront in turn a broken spar, a near-swamping, rotten food, a raving sailor close to insanity and closer to death at the hands of Innokenti if he did not stop his rantings, and interminable storms which threatened for days to capsize them. Trofim, as the only one aboard experienced in navigation, was given control of the pitiful boat, keeping it afloat more by courage than by skill; and when survival seemed impossible and some counseled "Throw the bales overboard to lighten ship," he might have done so had not Innokenti, with iron resolve, cried: "Don't touch them! Better dead trying to make port with our furs than alive without them." When the storm abated, the boat limped home with bales intact, and the Aleutian fur trade was under way.

As Trofim and Innokenti climbed ashore at Petropavlovsk they found a surprise awaiting them, for in their absence Madame Poznikova had moved her headquarters to this excellent new harbor and built on a prominent rise along the shore a spacious two-story house with a lookout on the top floor. When Trofim asked: "Why so big a house?" she said bluntly: "Because we three are going to live here." He gasped, but she pressed on: "You're getting to be an old man, Cossack, and I'm not getting younger." He was forty-four that year, she thirty-seven, and while he did not feel old, he was aware, from his experience in losing the leadership of his men on Attu Island, that he was no longer the tireless young Ukrainian for whom the world was an endless adventure.

Asking for time to consider what she was suggesting, he roamed the waterfront, looked at the small boats resting there, and visualized the islands to which they would in time be sailing, and two facts remained rooted: Madame Poznikova is a remarkable woman. And I long for the islands and the lands to the east. He would be honored to have a woman like Madame for a wife and pleased to work with her in the fur trade, but before committing himself, certain things would have to be agreed upon, so he walked back to the new house, called her to the front room, where he sat rigidly like a nervous businessman asking a banker for a loan, and said: "Madame, I admired your husband and respect what you and he accomplished. I would be honored to associate with you in the fur trade. But I will not ever again sail to the Aleutians without a proper ship."

Astonished by this extraordinary response to her proposal that they marry, she burst into laughter, and cried robustly: "Cossack, come see!" And she led him down the main street of Petropavlovsk to a formal shipyard which had not been there when he sailed out two years before. "Look!" she said with pride. "That's the ship I've been building for you," and when he saw how sturdy it was, he said: "Perfect for the Aleutian trade."

After the wedding she forced her son Innokenti to take the name Zhdanko and to call Trofim *father,* which he refused to do: "He's not my father, that damned serf," and he bristled even if someone called him the cossack's stepson. His mother, embarrassed by such behavior, summoned the two to stand before her: "From this day on we're all Zhdankos, a powerful new life for everyone. You two will conquer the islands one by one. Then on to America." When Trofim protested that this might prove to be more difficult than supposed, she cried: "We're destined to move east, always east. My father left St. Petersburg for Irkutsk. I left there for Kamchatka. The furs, the money are waiting for us out there." And in this way the Ukrainian cossack Trofim Zhdanko acquired a ship he wanted, a wife he admired and a son he abhorred.

When, thanks to the example set by Madame Zhdanko, the court at St. Petersburg discovered what a bonanza they could reap in the Aleutian fur trade, companies of adventurous men were encouraged to test their fortunes in the islands. These informal groups were composed mainly of cossacks, especially those trained in the harsh disciplines of Siberia, and a more cruel group of invaders never descended upon a primitive people. Accustomed to dispensing harsh discipline among the unlettered tribes of eastern Russia, they devised new barbarisms for dealing with the gentle, simple-minded Aleuts. The brutal precedents set by Innokenti Zhdanko during the first encounter on Attu Island became the norm as the cossacks pressed eastward, and more outrages were invented as the marauders approached the larger islands in the middle of the chain.

Of course, when the first group after Trofim and Innokenti came in their flimsy sealskin boat to Attu and tried to land, the enraged natives, remembering what had happened before, stormed down to the beach and slaughtered seven traders, an event which enshrined in Russian folklore the belief that the Aleuts were savages who could be tamed only by gun and knout. But when the second expedition sailed on to Kiska, the next sizable island in the chain, it encountered natives who knew nothing of white men, and here the cossacks initiated a reign of terror which produced many furs and more dead Aleuts.

On sprawling Amchitka, next in line, the islanders were quickly subdued by the relentless invaders. The natives had to remain mute when these men stole their women. They had to sail forth in all weathers to hunt for sea otters. Of the otters killed in the new and wasteful ways introduced by the Russians, far more than half sank useless to the bottom of the Bering Sea, but since those brought to shore fetched increasingly high prices when caravaned down to the Mongolian border, the pressure to continue hunting mounted, and with it the barbarities.

In 1761, Madame Zhdanko, eager to see the establishment of Russian control over the Aleutians and Alaska before she died, replaced Trofim's aging ship with a new one built with real nails, and in it she dispatched Innokenti, a mature man of thirty-four and ruthless in his ability to bring home maximum cargoes. To protect her investment in the ship, she suggested that Trofim captain it, even though he was fifty-nine: "You look like a man of thirty, Cossack, and this ship is valuable. Keep it off the rocks." The plea was not an idle one, for like the slain otters, of a hundred vessels built by the Russians in these parts, a good half sank because of faulty construction, and the half that remained afloat were apt to be commanded by such inadequate captains that a large number crashed on rocks and reefs.

In the decade ahead, the Zhdankos, father and stepson, leapfrogged many smaller islands in order to land directly on Lapak, the attractive one guarded by the volcano about which Trofim had spoken repeatedly when recounting his adventures with Captain Bering. When the boat hove to off the northern coast and Trofim saw the unforgettable land which he and Georg Steller had explored back in 1741, he reminded his crew of how generously he had been treated and issued stern orders: "No molesting of islanders this time," and as a result of this humane caution, the first weeks ashore saw none of the atrocities that had befouled the other islands. Trofim, searching for the native who had given him the otter skins, learned that he was dead, but one of the fur traders who had acquired a few words of Aleut on a previous mission informed Trofim that the man's son, one Ingalik, had inherited the old man's two kayaks and his leadership of the island clan. Hoping to make friends with the young man and thus avoid what had happened on the other islands, Trofim sought him out, and learned to his dismay that word of Russian behavior had now penetrated all the islands and that the people of Lapak were terrified as to what they might expect.

Trofim tried to placate the young man, and things might have got off to a good start had there not been among the traders a very rough cossack with shaved head and big red mustaches named Zagoskin who was so obsessed by otter pelts that he insisted the men of Lapak go out immediately to the hunting grounds. Young Ingalik tried to explain that there was little chance of locating any animals now, but Zagoskin would not listen. So at his command a pair of traders lined six kayaks on the shore, and their owners, not yet identified, were ordered to get into them and go out to hunt sea otters. When no one responded to this stupid order, Zagoskin grabbed an ax and raged among the kayaks, destroying their delicate membranes and crushing the frail driftwood frames on which they depended.

This destruction was so insane that various islanders, unable to comprehend such folly, began to mutter and move toward the frenzied cossack, who continued slashing. But Innokenti could not allow even the least sign of rebellion, so after ordering the Lapak men by sign language to retreat and seeing they were not going to obey, he stopped trying to dissuade them. Instead, he lifted his gun and ordered the rest of his men to do the same, and at a signal from his left hand, they fired.

Eight Aleuts died in that first volley and three more in a second, by which time Zagoskin, like a wild man, was prancing over their dead bodies and hacking at them with his ax. An awful hush fell over the beach, and then women began to wail, high-pitched, terrible wailing that filled the air and brought Trofim to the scene of carnage. Having come late, he could not apportion the blame for this tragedy, but he was certain that his son and Zagoskin had been primarily responsible, but who had done what he could not decipher. He was revolted, but before long, he would have to endure two more acts so vile that the once-honorable Zhdanko name would be darkly stained.

The first occurred only two months after the initial slaughter on the beach. Under evil encouragement from Zagoskin, Innokenti intensified his normal proclivity for atrocious actions, and in the weeks following the first batch of killings, there were several other isolated incidents in which either Zagoskin or Innokenti murdered Aleuts who were tardy in obeying them.

Both of these ugly men enjoyed participating in the exciting hunt for otters, and they ordered islanders to build them a two-seat kayak in which they could together engage in the chase. Zagoskin, because his arms were stronger, paddled in the rear, Innokenti in front. In the fourteen thousand years since Oogruk had navigated his kayak in pursuit of the great whale, the men of the north had developed an improved paddle, one with a blade at each end, so that the paddler did not have to reverse the position of his hands when he wanted to change the side from which he paddled. And both Zagoskin and Innokenti became expert in using these two-ended paddles.

Their kayak was not really needed in the hunt, and they realized that sometimes it seemed to do more harm than good, but the chase was so exhilarating that they insisted on participating. A hunt went like this. Some keen-eyed Aleut would detect what appeared to be an otter out toward Qugang, the whistling volcano, and signaling, he would speed directly to that spot while other craft would swing wide and take up positions forming a circle around where the otter was presumed to be. Then silence, no blade moving, and before long the otter, not being a fish, would have to come up for air. Then all would swarm down upon it; it would dive; and quickly the boats would form another circle, in the center of which the otter would surface. When this was repeated six or eight times, with the poor otter always forced to come up for breath in the midst of the tormenting kayaks, it would approach exhaustion, until, finally, it would surface almost dead. Then a club over the head, a swift grab before it sank, and the prized animal was lashed to one of the kayaks, its head smashed in, its fur undamaged.

Zagoskin and Innokenti had their greatest fun when the circle enclosed a mother otter floating on her back with her baby on her belly, the creatures moving along as if on a summer's outing. Then Innokenti, in the front, forced the mother to dive. But the infant could not stay under water as long as its mother, so as soon as the latter felt her child struggling for air, she returned to the surface, even though she knew that this meant danger for herself. Once more afloat, she became the target for the circling canoes, which, driven by Innokenti's wild cries, closed in upon her again. Again she dived, again her child struggled for air, and again she rose amid the threatening kayaks.

"We have her!" Innokenti would shout, and with a burst of speed he and Zagoskin would virtually leap at the anguished mother, clubbing at her till the babe fell from her protective grasp. When the pursuers saw the little one afloat, Zagoskin would club it, reach out with a net, and pull it into the kayak. The mother, now bereft of her child, would begin swimming madly from one boat to another, searching for it, and as she approached each one, lamenting like a human mother, she suffered the blows that came from the gloating men and swam on to the next, pleading all the while in a high-pitched wail for the return of her child.

Finally, so weakened and so bewildered by her fruitless search that she dared not dive, she remained on the surface, her almost human face turned to her tormentors as she sought her baby, and thus she remained till someone like Innokenti bashed her over the head, knocked her senseless, pulled her into his kayak, and cut her throat.

One day as they returned to shore, after two such killings, some of the Aleut fishermen protested against the slaughter of the baby otter and its mother, pointing out to Innokenti in their sign language that if he and Zagoskin continued doing this, the supply of otters in the seas surrounding Lapak Island was bound to be depleted. "And in that case," the protesters reasoned, "we will have to go too far to sea to find the otters you seek."

Innokenti, showing his displeasure with such an interruption, brushed aside their objections, but Trofim, when he heard about the argument, sided with the Aleuts: "Don't you see what killing the mothers and babies will mean before long? No otters for us to use in trade or for them to use as always."

This warning coming from his own stepfather infuriated Innokenti, who replied insolently: "It's time they learned, that we all learned. Their job from here on is to kill sea otters. Nothing else. I want bales of those pelts, not a few handfuls." And ignoring Zhdanko's counsel, he and Zagoskin initiated the harsh routine of sending the Aleut men out every day to hunt the otter and of disciplining them by means of blows and deprivation of food if they were not successful.

In the meantime the two leaders continued to sail forth, and with the forced assistance from others, to chase mother otters with their babes, and one afternoon when the sun was clouded Innokenti saw such a pair and shouted to the attendant Aleuts: "Over here!" The chase ended as always, with the baby slain and the mother otter swimming almost into the arms of an Aleut, pleading piteously. This Aleut, a fine hunter, mindful of his relationship to all things living, refused to kill needlessly when neither food nor fur was really needed, and ignored Innokenti's shrieks of "Kill her!" The Aleut allowed the mother to escape and looked in disgust as Zagoskin beat the water with his paddle in frustration.

When they reached shore, Innokenti rushed up to the man who had refused to kill the otter, berating him for his disobedience, and the man was so outraged that he threw down his paddle, indicating in terms that could not be misunderstood that he would no longer hunt otters, male or female, with the white men, and that from this day on neither he nor his friends would kill mothers and babes. Innokenti, enraged by this defiance of his authority, grabbed the islander by the arm, swung him around, and struck him so solidly with his fist that the man fell to the ground. The other islanders began to mutter among themselves, and soon there were signs of such general defiance that Zagoskin, frightened, fell back, and the Aleuts, judging mistakenly that they had made their point, now swarmed at Innokenti to persuade him to stop abusing them.

His reaction was radically different from what they expected, for Innokenti, calling for all his men to assist him, ran to fetch his and Zagoskin's guns, and when the Russians in tight assembly marched on the startled Aleuts, the latter retreated, having learned what guns were capable of. But Innokenti did not intend this show of power to end with a mere display, and when the islanders were cowed, he uttered that dreadful phrase which was so often resorted to in these years when civilized Europeans were meeting uncivilized natives: "It's time we taught them a lesson."

Utilizing three of the willing Russian traders, he had them choose at random twelve Aleut hunters, who were lined up one behind the other, with the man who had started the protest in front. When each Aleut was prodded forward, so that he stood tightly wedged against the man in front, Innokenti cried: "We'll show them what a good

Russian musket can do," and he loaded his gun heavily, moved close to the head of the file, and took careful aim right at the heart of that first troublemaker.

At this moment Trofim Zhdanko came on the scene and saw the hideous thing that was about to happen: "Son! What in God's name are you doing?"

His unfortunate use of the word *son* so infuriated Innokenti that with the butt of his gun he struck Trofim in the face. Then, with icy rage he fired, and eight Aleuts, one after the other, dropped dead while the ninth fainted, for the bullet had ended against his ribs. The final three stood transfixed.

Innokenti had taught the Aleuts a lesson, and it was as a result of this that he was able to establish on Lapak Island, once so pleasant a place to live if one loved the sea and was unaware that in other parts of the world trees existed, a dictatorship so complete that every man on the island, Russian or Aleut, had to work at his command and the women to serve at his pleasure. Lapak Island became one of the more ghastly places on this earth, and the honorable old cossack, Trofim Zhdanko, huddled alone in his hut, steeped in shame and powerless to oppose the evil his stepson had created.

As the eighteenth century drew toward a close, the governments of many nations learned of the riches available in the northern waters, and also of the vast territories waiting there to be discovered, explored, and claimed. The Spaniards, moving north from California, would send out a fleet of daring explorers, Alessandro Malaspina and Juan de la Bodega among them, and they would contribute significant discoveries, but since their government did not follow with settlements, they accomplished nothing lasting except the naming of certain headlands along the coast.

The French would dispatch a gallant man with a glowing title— Jean François de Galaup, Comte de La Pérouse—to see what he could find, and he left a record of daring adventure but little hard knowledge of the island-studded seas among whose reefs future navigators would have to move.

In 1778 the English sent to these waters a slim, nervous man of ordinary parentage who, by virtue of his maritime brilliance, resolute courage and general common sense, would make himself into the world's foremost navigator of that day and one of the top two or three of all time: James Cook. On two flawless voyages to the South Pacific he had in a sense cleaned up the map of the ocean, locating islands where they belonged, defining the shorelines of two continents, Australia and Antarctica, informing the world of the glories of Tahiti and finding in the process a cure for scurvy.

Before Cook, a British warship could leave England with four hundred sailors and expect one hundred and eighty to be dead by the time the voyage was over, and sometimes the toll reached the appalling figure of two hundred and eighty. Cook, unwilling to captain a ship that was little more than a floating coffin, decided in his quiet, efficient way, to change this, and he did so by instituting a few sensible rules, as he explained to his crew at the beginning of their memorable third voyage: "We have found that scurvy can be controlled if you will keep your quarters clean. If you wear dry clothes whenever you can. If you follow our rule of one watch on, two off so that you get plenty of rest. And if you will each day consume your portion of wort and rob."

When sailors asked what they were, Cook allowed his officers to explain: "Wort is a brew of malt, vinegar, sauerkraut, such fresh vegetables as we can procure, and other things. It smells bad, but if you drink it properly, you will not catch the scurvy."

"Rob," said another officer, "is an inspissated mixture of lime, orange and lemon juice."

"What's *inspissated*?" someone always asked, and the officer would reply: "Captain Cook uses the word all the time," and someone would persist: "But what's it mean?" and the officer would growl: "It means 'You drink it.' If you do, you'll never get scurvy."

The officers were correct. Any sailor who consumed his wort and rob was miraculously immune from the gray killer of the seas; in wort about half the ingredients were by themselves ineffective, especially the malt, but the sauerkraut, and particularly its fermented juice, worked miracles, and of course, although the lime and orange juice were of small account, lemon juice was a specific. The inspissation, in which Cook put so much store, had no effect whatever; it was merely a process which thickened the lemon juice and made it easier to transport and administer.

By his stubborn insistence that scurvy could be cured, this quiet man and devoted leader saved thousands of lives and enabled Britain to build the world's most powerful fleet. Now, in the years when England was fighting her American colonies in places like Massachusetts, Pennsylvania and Virginia, the British government had sent this great explorer forth once more to end speculation about the North Pacific, and he, having solved the various riddles of the South Pacific, eagerly accepted the challenge to confirm once and for all whether Asia did join with North America, whether there was a Northwest Passage across the top of the world, whether the Arctic Ocean was free of ice—because a learned scientist had proved that unless ice was somehow moored to land, it could not form in an open sea—and particularly, what the coastline of the newfound Alaska was. If he could solve these nagging questions, Great Britain would be in position to claim all of North America from Quebec and Massachusetts in the east to California and the future Oregon in the west.

On his famous Third Exploration, which would cover parts of four years, 1776–79, Cook would not only discover the Hawaiian Islands but also become the first European to explore properly the jagged coastline of Alaska. He would chart and name Mount Edgecumbe, that splendid volcano at Sitka; he would explore where the future Anchorage would locate; he would cruise the Aleutian Islands and position them properly in relation to the mainland; and he would run far north to where the frozen Arctic Ocean confronted him with a wall of ice eighteen feet high along its face, the ice that the earlier expert had proved could not exist.

It was a marvelous journey, a success in every respect, for although he did not find the fabled Northwest Passage which navigators had been seeking for almost three hundred years since Columbus discovered America, he did demonstrate that the supposed passage did not enter the Pacific in ice-free waters. In moving to the north to prove this point, Cook had to penetrate the wall erected by the Aleutians, and he did so by heading for the passage just east of Lapak Island. When he cleared the headland and looked west he saw rising from the Bering Sea the volcano Qugang, the Whistler, which now stood one thousand one hundred feet above the surface of the sea.

Cook, after surveying the construction of Lapak, was the first to deduce from its semicircular form that it had once been a volcano of immense dimension whose center had exploded and whose northern rim had vanished in erosion, but he was more impressed by the copious and inviting harbor, where he sent ashore a foraging party to procure such provisions as the islanders could provide. The two young officers in charge were men destined in later years to make resounding names for themselves. The senior was Shipmaster William Bligh; his assistant, George Vancouver. The first watched carefully everything that happened on the island, taking careful note of the two Russians who seemed to be in command, Zagoskin and Innokenti, whom he did not like at all and whose insolent manner he said he would correct in short time if the two served under him. Vancouver, a born navigator of unusual abilities, noted the position of the island, its harbor capacity, its capacity for provisioning large ships, and its probable climate insofar as that could be judged from a brief visit. It was obvious that Cook had picked his staff with care, for these two were among the ablest men sailing the Pacific that year.

The visit lasted less than half a day, for by midafternoon Cook felt that he must push the *Resolution* northward, but he took with him only a fraction of the information he could have had, and the fault was his. Amazingly, in view of his meticulous foresight in planning his cruises, on this one into northern oceans where it was known that the Russians had penetrated, he brought with him no one who could speak Russian, nor any dictionary of that language; authorities in London still refused to believe that Russia already had a sizable foothold in western North America and had every intention of enlarging it. However, Cook was able to make this entry:

> We came upon a promising chain of treeless islands whose occupants came to greet us in two-man canoes wearing the most enchanting hats with long visors and decorations. I encouraged artist Webber to make several depictions of both the men and their hats, and he complied.
>
> The chain of islands contained one called Lapak if we understood what its Russian occupants were saying. We mapped the whole and charted a fine harbor on the north coast, guarded by a beautiful dead volcano 1,100 feet high six miles due north. It was named something like Lewgong, but when I asked a second time for the name they whistled at me, signifying what, I do not know. Perhaps it is their sacred volcano.

George Vancouver in the last hour of his stay ashore met up with the Russian named Trofim Zhdanko, and in this grizzled warrior he recognized a man much different from the two brash younger men whom both he and Bligh had disliked. Desperately he longed to share ideas with this wise old man, and the Russian just as eagerly wanted to ask these strangers how they had managed to get such a fine ship, how they had navigated it from Europe, and what they judged the future of these islands to be. Alas, the two could not converse except in the most fragmentary sign language.

When shots were fired from the *Resolution*, warning Bligh and Vancouver that sailing time was at hand, the old cossack did hand each of the officers who had been so congenial a sea-otter pelt, but unfortunately, he had, in his generosity, given them two of the best, and Innokenti, seeing this, unceremoniously grabbed the pelts from the hands of the English officers and substituted two of inferior quality. Vancouver, always a gentleman, saluted and thanked both father and son for their generosity, but Bligh glared at Innokenti as if he wanted to smash his insolent face. However, when the two men regained their ship, Bligh penned in his logbook a revealing entry:

> On this Island of Lapak I met a most disagreeable Russian named, if I caught what he said, something like Innocent. He repelled me from the moment I saw him, and the longer I suffered his unwelcome attentions the deeper grew my loathing, for he seemed the worst type of Russian.

> But when I observed the compliant manner in which the natives obeyed him and the enviable peace and order prevailing on his island, it was clear to me that someone in authority governed this place firmly, and that is always to be desired. I suspect that prior to our arrival, there may have been disturbances here, but prompt action on the part of someone quelled them, and if the credit goes to this Innocent, I withdraw my strictures against him, for order in any society is of maximum value, even if sternly achieved.

In this casual manner, and with such bland acceptances of what the Russian terror had achieved, the great English navigator James Cook crossed lanes with the Russian navigator Vitus Bering: each landed briefly at Lapak; each remained about the same amount of time; each sent ashore a subordinate who would gain fame on his own account—Cook sending two, Bligh and Vancouver; Bering only one, Georg Steller—and each sailed on, the Russian in 1741, the Englishman thirty-seven years later in 1778.

How different the two men were: Bering the bumbling, unlucky leader, Cook the impeccable captain with only one detectable flaw and that showing itself only at the end; Bering, who sailed under the most rigorous orders from his tsar or tsarina, Cook, who once he left sight of England sailed under his own orders; Bering the hesitant explorer who scurried back at the first sign of adversity, his tasks uncompleted, Cook the nonpareil who invariably went the extra mile, the extra continent; Bering, who advanced the art of navigation in no particular, Cook, who altered the definitions of the words *ocean* and *mapmaking;* Bering, who had grudging support from his government and no international acclaim whatever, Cook, who lacked for nothing in England and who heard the cheers of an entire world ringing in his ears for more than a decade; Bering often with no uniform and then a miserable one that fitted poorly, Cook with his prim hand-tailored officer's garb topped by an expensive cockaded mariner's hat. How differently the two men behaved and how different their careers and contributions.

When Cook sailed on his second of three great journeys, England and France were at war, and the fighting at sea was vigorous, but both warring nations agreed that James Cook in his *Resolution* be allowed free passage anywhere he chose to sail, for it was acknowledged that he was doing the work of civilization in general and would not fire upon an enemy French warship even if he met up with one. During his third voyage, the one to Alaska, England was at war with her American colonies and, by extension, with France also, but once more the three warring nations agreed among themselves to let James Cook sail where he would, for by his perfection of the cure for scurvy, which Georg Steller had pioneered, and his promotion of this treatment through the fleet, he saved far more lives than would have been gained in a victorious battle. This second safe-passage arrangement was masterminded in part by Benjamin Franklin, the practical-minded American ambassador to France, who knew an international benefactor when he saw one, and Cook was that.

It was said earlier that as a navigator Cook had only one failing. He was apt, when tired, to be short-tempered, so that when, in February 1779, he found himself in Kealakekua Bay on the Big Island of Hawaii surrounded by mildly hostile natives who could have been placated with gifts, he lost his patience and fired a gun into a threatening crowd, in which a Hawaiian of some importance had already been killed. In a flash the infuriated watchers fell upon Cook, clubbed him from behind, and held his head under water when he fell into the surf.

Vitus Bering and James Cook, two of the grandest names in Alaskan history, had mournful ends, the first dying of scurvy on a bleak, treeless, wind-swept island at the age of sixty-one, his life and his work incomplete. The second, having conquered scurvy and the farthest oceans, died at fifty-one because of his own impetuousness on a beautiful tropical island far to the south. The oceans of the world were made more available by the explorations of such men.

But there was in these years another kind of explorer, the commercial adventurer, and in 1780 such a one wandered almost accidentally into Lapak Bay in a small, incredibly tough little ship called the *Evening Star,* a two-masted, square-rigged whaling brig out of Boston. It was captained by a small, wiry man as resolute morally as his ship was physically. He was Noah Pym, forty-one years old and already a veteran of the dreadful gales at Cape Horn, the trading marts at Canton, the lovely coastline of Hawaii, and all the vast empty spaces of the Pacific where whales might hide, for if his ship was not big, it was valiant, and in it Pym was ready to challenge any storm or any group of hostile natives gathered on a beach.

Unlike Bering and Cook, Pym never left port with support from his government or cheering notice from his fellow citizens. The most he could expect would be a one-line notice in the Boston newspaper: "On this day the *Evening Star,* Noah Pym with crew of twenty-one, sailed for South Seas, intended stay six years." And as for the great nations agreeing among themselves to give this tough little fellow free passage, they were far more likely to sink him on sight in the supposition that he was sailing for the enemy. Indeed, he had in his time fought off the warships of both France and England, but this was a misnomer, for what he really did was maintain a sharp lookout and run like a frightened demon at the first sight of a sail that might prove threatening.

Zagoskin and Innokenti were out in their two-man kayak chasing sea otters when the *Evening Star* hove into sight off the south shore of Lapak Island, and they were astounded when a voice from the aft deck called out in good Russian: "Ho there! We need water and stores."

"Who are you?" Innokenti called, establishing that he was in charge.

"Whaler *Evening Star,* Boston, Noah Pym commanding."

Innokenti, surprised that a ship from that far distance should have found Lapak Island, shouted back: "Good harbor on the north shore south of the volcano!" and with Zagoskin paddling strongly from the rear seat, he led the way.

When the ship anchored between the shore and the volcano, Innokenti and Zagoskin climbed aboard and satisfied themselves in two minutes that whereas the *Evening Star* did carry one gun fore, it was not a warship. Neither man had ever seen a whaler before, but under the tutelage of the sailor who had called to them in Russian, they quickly learned what the procedures were, and just as quickly saw that Captain Noah Pym out of Boston was, though small, a leathery individual with whom it would not be profitable to quarrel accidentally.

They learned that this amazing little brig which had traveled so far—Cape Horn, China, a try at Japan, Hawaii—had in its crew sailors who could speak most of the languages of the Pacific, so that wherever the ship anchored, someone could conduct business with the natives. Only one man spoke Russian, Seaman Atkins, but he loved to talk, and for two rewarding days he, Innokenti and Captain Pym traded information on the Pacific.

Pym, once the ice was broken, enjoyed the swift interchange: "Six men in Boston own the *Evening Star* and they award me a full share for serving as their captain."

"Do you also receive pay?" Innokenti asked.

"Small but regular. My real pay comes from my captain's share of the whale oil we deliver and the sale of goods we bring home from China."

"Do the sailors share?"

"Like me, small pay, big rewards if we catch whales." Pym pointed to a sturdy young fellow, a New Englander almost as hefty as Zagoskin and with the same kind of scowl: "That's Kane, our harpooner. Very skilled. Gets double if he succeeds."

"Why have you come into our waters?" Innokenti asked, and Harpooner Kane frowned at the word *our,* but Captain Pym answered courteously: "Whales. They must be up there," and he pointed toward the arctic.

Zagoskin broke in rudely: "We see them coming past here sometimes," and he would have said more had not Innokenti signaled that this was privileged information. The baldheaded Russian was obviously irritated by this tacit reprimand, and both Pym and Atkins caught the warning, but neither commented.

On the third day the men of the *Evening Star* met Trofim Zhdanko, now in his late seventies and still unbearded out of his respect for the memory of Tsar Peter, and they liked him from the start, in contrast to their rejection of the two younger men. The old fellow, at last in the company of someone who could speak Russian, poured out his recollections of Captain Bering, that hard winter on Bering Island, and the remarkable accomplishments of the German scientist Georg Steller: "He went to four universities and knew everything. He saved my life because he made this brew of weeds and things that cured scurvy."

"Now what might that be?" Pym asked. He had the habit of staring hard at anyone with whom he was speaking on important subjects, his small eyes closing almost to beads, his close-cropped head of brown hair bent forward.

"Scurvy is what kills sailors."

"I know that," Pym said impatiently. "But what was in the brew this Steller made?" Trofim did not know exactly: "Weeds and kelp, that I remember. First time I tasted it I spit it out, but Steller told me, right over there it was, behind that group of rocks, he said: 'You may not want it but your blood does,' and later on, when we spent that dreadful winter on Bering Island, I looked forward to the little amount of brew he allowed me each day. It tasted far better than honey, for I could feel it rushing into my blood to keep me alive."

"Do you still drink it?"

"No. Seal meat, especially blubber and guts, they're just as good. You eat seal you never have scurvy."

"What will happen up here?" Pym asked. "I mean Spain, England, France, maybe even China? Don't they all have an interest in this area?" And he pointed eastward to the unknown area which the Great Shaman Azazruk had once called Alaxsxaq, the Great Land.

"It's already Russian," Trofim said without hesitation. "I was with Captain Bering when he discovered it for the tsar."

On the evening before departure Captain Pym broached with Zhdanko the navigational problem which had brought him to Lapak, and it was premonitory that he did not reveal his questions to either of the two Russian leaders, for he already distrusted them: "Zhdanko, what do you know of the oceans north of here?"

Since it was obvious that Pym was toying with the idea of sailing north, a difficult adventure, as Zhdanko had learned from his own explorations beyond the Arctic Circle, the cossack felt he must warn the American: "Very dangerous. Ice comes crashing down in winter."

"But there must be whales up there."

"There are. They swim past here all the time. Going, coming."

"Has any small ship . . . like ours . . . sailed north?"

Since Zhdanko did not know where Captain Cook had sailed after leaving Lapak Island, he could honestly warn Pym: "No. It would be too dangerous."

Despite this advice, Pym was determined to probe the arctic seas before other whalers would dare to venture into those icy waters, and he remained firm in his desire to explore them, but he did not share with Zhdanko his plans, for he did not want the other Russians to know them.

Next morning, Pym allowed himself an uncharacteristic gesture: he embraced the old cossack, for he saw in his noble bearing and generosity in sharing his knowledge of the oceans a man in the true tradition of seafarer, and he felt renewed for having been in contact with him. Summoning Atkins, he said: "Ask the old fellow why he lives alone in this little hut?" and when the question was put, Zhdanko shrugged, pointed to where his stepson and Zagoskin were whispering, and said with resignation and repugnance: "Those two."

After Pym, with no knowledge or charts to guide him, sailed his *Evening Star* north from Lapak, he entered a world into which no other American had ventured or would soon do so. Yankee ships had penetrated the rest of the major oceans, following quietly in the more spectacular wake of Captain Cook's ships. But the constant search for whales, whose oil for lamps, ambergris for perfumery and baleen for the stays in women's corsets would produce fortunes for shipowners and their captains, made exploration of untapped seas obligatory. To go north of the Aleutians was daring, but if whales existed in the area, the risk was worth it, and Noah Pym was a man to take that risk.

He lived a hard life. He was a devoted father, but he was away on his voyages for years at a time, so that when he returned home he scarcely knew his three daughters. But the results were so profitable to all concerned in his expeditions that both his owners and his crew urged him to sail yet again, and he did much sooner than he would have on his own account. He kept a cadre of reliable hands with him—John Atkins, who spoke both Chinese and Russian; Tom Kane, the expert harpooner without whom the ship would have been powerless when a whale was sighted; and Miles Corey, the Irish first mate, who was a better navigator than Pym himself—and even in bad weather he slept easily knowing that these men and others like them were in charge. He suspected that Corey was a crypto-Catholic, but if so, he created no problems aboard ship.

With the Aleutians left far behind, the *Evening Star* entered upon those dangerous waters which seemed so congenial in early spring, so fearful in October and November, when ice could form overnight, or come crashing down of an afternoon, already formed into great icebergs farther north and now cruising free on their own.

Noah Pym, in search of whales instead of knowledge, captured one whale south of that narrow strait where the continents seemed to meet, and having heard in Hawaii the rumor that Bering and Cook in their larger ships had proceeded farther north without incident, he decided to do the same. In the Arctic Ocean, Harpooner Kane struck a large whale, and when Pym laid his ship close to the dying beast, landing boards were laid to its carcass so that sailors could cut it up, searching for baleen and ambergris and throwing great slabs of blubber on the deck for reduction to oil in the smoking pots.

While the brig lay idle as the oil was rendered, Corey, in a voice that betrayed no panic, warned the captain: "Should the ice start to move down upon us, we must be prepared to run." Pym listened, but since he had no experience in such waters, he did not appreciate how swiftly the ice could strike. "We must both watch it closely," he said, but when the harpooner stabbed a second whale with a splendid shot, work on salvaging it became so exciting, with promise of full casks for the long sail home, that Pym forgot about the impending ice, and for several triumphant days attended only to the bringing aboard of baleen and blubber.

Then, like some giant menace looming out of a fevered dream, the ice in the arctic began to move south, not slowly like a wanderer, but in vast floes that made giant leaps in the course of a morning and stupendous ones overnight. When the floes appeared, almost out of nowhere, the free waters around them began to freeze, and it required only a few minutes for Captain Pym to realize that he must turn south immediately or run the risk of being pinned down for the entire winter. But when he started to give the order to hoist all sails, First Mate Corey said in a voice that still showed no emotion: "Too late. Head for the coastline."

The advice was sound, the only one that would enable the *Eve-*

ning Star to avoid being crushed by the oncoming ice, and with an adroitness that far abler navigators than they might not have been able to exercise, these two New England men used every breath of wind to shepherd their little whaler with its thrice-precious cargo toward the northern coastline of Alaska, and there at a spot almost seventy-one degrees north, later to be christened Desolation Point, they stumbled by sheer luck into an opening which led to a substantial bay, at whose southern end they found a snug harbor surrounded by low protecting hills. Here, shielded from pounding ice, they would spend the nine-month winter of 1780–81, and often during that interminable imprisonment the sailors would not curse Pym for his tardiness in leaving the arctic but praise him for having found "the only spot on this Godforsaken shore where the ice can't crush us to kindling."

They had barely started constructing a refuge ashore when Seaman Atkins, the one who spoke Russian, cried: "Enemy approaching over the ice!" and with expressions of fear that could not be masked, the twenty other crewmen looked up from their work to see coming at them across the frozen bay a contingent of some two dozen short, dark-faced men swathed in heavy furs.

"Prepare for action!" Captain Pym said in low voice, but Atkins, who had a good view of the oncoming men, cried: "They aren't armed!" and in the next tense moments the newcomers reached the Americans, stared in amazement at their white faces, and smiled.

In the days that followed, the Americans learned that these men lived a short distance to the north in a village of thirteen subterranean huts containing fifty-seven people, and to the vast relief of the whalers, they found that the villagers were peacefully inclined. They were Eskimos, lineal descendants of those adventurers who had followed Oogruk from Asia fourteen thousand years earlier. Six hundred and sixty generations separated them from Oogruk, and in the course of time they had acquired the skills which enabled them to survive and even prosper north of the Arctic Circle, which lay nearly three hundred miles to the south.

The Americans were at first repelled by the meagerness of the lives these Eskimos lived and by the tight meanness of their underground huts roofed by whalebone covered with sealskin, but they quickly came to appreciate the clever ways in which the chunky little people adjusted to their inhospitable environment, and were dumfounded by the courage and ability the men exhibited in venturing forth upon the frozen ocean and wresting from it their livelihood. The sailors were further impressed when half a dozen men from the village helped them build a long hut from available items like whalebone, driftwood and animal skins. When it was completed, large enough to house all twenty-two Americans, the men had reasonably comfortable protection against the cold, which could drop to fifty degrees below zero. The sailors were awed when they saw how much these short men, rarely over five feet two, could shoulder when helping to carry the *Star*'s supplies ashore, and when all was in place the Americans settled down for the kind of winter they had known in New England—four months of snow and cold—and they were astounded when Atkins learned from sign language that they could expect to remain frozen in for nine months or perhaps ten. "Good God!" one sailor moaned. "We don't get out till next July?" and Atkins replied: "That's what he seems to be saying, and he should know."

The first indication of how ably these Eskimos utilized the frozen ocean came when one of the powerful younger men, Sopilak by name, if Atkins understood correctly, returned from a hunt with the news that a monstrous polar bear had been spotted on the ice some miles offshore. In a trice the Eskimos made themselves ready for a long chase, but they lingered until their women provided Captain Pym, whom they recognized as leader, Seaman Atkins, whom they had immediately liked, and husky Harpooner Kane with proper clothing to protect them from the ice and snow and wind. Dressed in the bulky furs of Eskimos, the three Americans started across the barren ice, whose jumbled forms made movement difficult. Such travel bore no relationship to ice travel in New England, where a pond froze in winter, or a placid river; this was primeval ice, born in the deeps of a salty ocean, thrown sky-high by sudden pressures, fractured by forces coming at it from all sides, a tortured, madly sculptured ice appearing in jagged shapes and interminably long swells that seemed to rise up from the depths. It was like nothing they had seen before or imagined: it was the ice of the arctic, explosive, crackling at night as it moved and twisted, violent in its capacity to destroy, and above all, constantly menacing in the gray haze, stretching forever.

It was upon this ice that the men of Desolation Point set forth to hunt their polar bear, but after a full day's search they found nothing, and night fell so quickly in these early days of October that the men warned the seamen that they would probably have to spend the night far out on the ice, with no assurance that they would ever find the bear. But just before darkness, Sopilak came plodding back on his snowshoes: "Not far ahead!" and the hunters moved closer to their prey. But it was a canny bear, and before any of them had a chance to see it, the first of its breed any American would encounter in these waters, night fell and the hunters fanned out in a wide circle so as to be able to follow the bear should it elect to flee in the darkness.

Atkins, who stayed close to Sopilak and who seemed to be learning Eskimo words by the score, moved about to caution his mates: "They warn us. The bear is dangerous. All white. Comes at you like a ghost. Do not run. No chance to escape. Stand and fight and shout for the others."

"Sounds dangerous," Kane said, and Atkins replied: "I think they were trying to tell me they expect to lose a man or two when tracking a polar bear."

"Them, not me," Kane said, and Atkins proposed that in the coming fight, the three Americans stay together: "We have guns. We'd better be prepared to use them."

The Americans and most of the Eskimos slept uneasily that night, but Sopilak did not sleep at all, for he had hunted polar bears before, with his father, and had been present when a great white beast, taller than two men when it reared on its hind legs, had crushed a hunter from Desolation with one smashing blow from its paw. It had driven the man right down against the ice and then torn at him with all four of its sets of claws. The man and all his clothing had been left in shreds, and that bear had not been taken.

There had been other hunts, some of them led by Sopilak himself, in which the monstrous beasts, more beautiful than a dream of white blizzards, had been tracked for days and brought to heel by wisdom and courage. Toward dawn Sopilak instructed Atkins: "Tell your men to watch me," and though the seaman tried to explain to the Eskimo that the Americans had guns, which would give them a sizable advantage if the fight did materialize, no matter how often in the darkness Atkins raised his arms and went "Bang-bang!" Sopilak did not understand. He saw only that they had no clubs or spears, and he feared for their safety.

When a pale, silvery cold light broke, a scout far to the north signaled that he had the polar bear in sight, and none of the three Americans who experienced the next moments would ever forget them, for when they rounded a huge block of ice thrown high above the surface of the frozen sea on which they moved, they saw ahead of them one of the world's majestic creatures, as grand an animal as the mastodons and mammoths that had once crossed over to Alaska near this point. It was huge, so completely white that it blended with the snow, and agile with a lumbering grace that caused the human heart to hesitate, so overpowering was the sense of beauty and awkward energy the bear exhibited as it began to move away. A supreme example of animal majesty, it seemed to be at one with the ice sheet and with the frozen sky. A light snow that began to fall as day brightened enhanced the dreamlike quality of the hunt as Sopilak's men began their chase.

The polar bear, unique among its genus in color, size and speed, could easily outrun any one man, and it also had the capacity to dive headlong into those strange openings in the ice where water flowed free, swim vigorously to the other side, clamber with amazing ease onto the new ice, and scamper off to other frozen areas where the men could not pursue, since they could not cross the open water. But it could not outrun half a dozen pestering men, especially when with spears and clubs and wild shouting they prevented it from attaining open water. So the long day's fight was about equal: the men could harass it and keep it from open water; it could outrun them and swim short distances to new positions. But in the end their persistence and anticipation of its moves enabled them to stay close and to drive it so that it winded itself, and in this manner the fight continued.

But as day began to wane, and it was brief at this autumn latitude, the men realized that they must soon come to grips with the bear or run the risk of losing it in the long night. So two Eskimos, Sopilak and another, became much more daring, and in a pair of coordinated thrusts they ran at the bear, confused it, and with Sopilak's spear damaged its left hind leg, and when they saw that it was wounded, two other men dashed in from behind, evaded the deadly swipe of its forepaws when it turned, and struck again, in the same leg.

The bear was now seriously wounded, and knew it, so it retreated until its back was against a large block of ice which protected it in that quarter, and now the men had to attack from positions where it could spot them from the moment they began to approach, and in this posture it was formidable, a towering white giant, red-bloodied in one leg but the possessor of claws that could rip out a man's guts.

In this moment of equal battle, when the Eskimo who first charged knew that he stood a strong likelihood of being disemboweled, none of Sopilak's hunters volunteered to make the possibly sacrificial run, so the master hunter knew that it devolved upon him. He succeeded in striking the bear's undamaged right leg, but in endeavoring to escape, he fell under the bear's full glare, and a mighty swing of the right paw sent him sprawling flat upon the ice and exposed to the bear's revenge.

In this extremity, two Eskimos darted bravely out to incapacitate the bear, regardless of what happened to Sopilak, but they were so tardy that the bear had time to leap at its fallen enemy and would have crushed him and torn him apart had not Captain Pym and Harpooner Kane discharged their rifles at this moment to stagger the great white monster. With two bullets in it, an experience never known before, the bear stopped and gasped, whereupon Atkins fired his gun, and this bullet lodged in the bear's head, causing it to lose control and to fall powerless across the prone body of the master hunter.

There the marvelous bear died, this creature of the frozen seas, this magnificent giant whose fur was often whiter than the snow upon which it moved, and when the seven Eskimos saw that it was truly dead they did something that amazed the three Americans: they began to dance, solemnly and with tears streaming down their faces, and the man holding wounded Sopilak erect so that he too could participate began to chant a song that reached back five thousand years, and there as darkness fell the men of Desolation wept and danced in honor of the great white creature they had killed. Seaman Atkins, watching this performance, appreciated its meaning instantly, and in response to some ancient force that his ancestors in Europe had revered, he dropped the gun which had been instrumental in killing the bear and joined the dancers, and Sopilak took his hand and welcomed him to the circle, and picking up the rhythm, Atkins joined the chant, for he too honored the splendid white bear, that creature of the north that had been so majestic in life, so brave in death.

Sopilak had a fifteen-year-old sister named Kiinak, and in the days following the kill of the polar bear she worked with her mother and the other women of Desolation in butchering and tending to the valuable bones, sinews and magnificent white skin. As she did so, she became aware that the young seaman from the *Evening Star* was placing himself near her, watching her. With the Eskimo words which he was acquiring so rapidly, he had been able to explain to Sopilak and his mother that he, Atkins, as one of the cooks aboard the American vessel, wanted to learn how the Eskimos handled the meat of the bear, the walrus and the seal that they caught in winter, and this explanation was accepted.

But the Eskimo men who had participated in the famous hunt of this bear also knew that it was only the bravery of Atkins and his leader, Noah Pym, that had saved the life of Sopilak, and since they had told the story of those culminating moments, the heroism of the young man was known throughout the village, and his attendance upon the butchering and Kiinak was accepted and even encouraged. Several times Sopilak told the villagers: "The young one saved my life," and whenever he said this, Kiinak smiled.

She was a vivacious girl, just under five feet tall, broad-shouldered, broad-faced, with a smile that charmed all upon whom it fell. But her outstanding characteristic was a heavy head of very black hair, which she kept cut so low that it obscured her eyebrows and shook from side to side when she laughed, which she did many times each day, for she loved the great nonsense of the world: the pomposity of her brother when he killed a walrus or captured a seal, the posturing of some young woman trying to attract the attention of her brother, or even the whimpering behavior of a child who was trying to enforce his will upon his mother. When she talked, she had the habit of using her left hand in a wide, careless sweep to brush the hair out of her eyes, and at such times she seemed quite gamin, and the older women of the village knew very well that this girl Kiinak was going to give the young men of the village much to think about as the time came for her to select a husband.

There was one other charming aspect, which John Atkins noticed the first time he saw her in the hut she shared with Sopilak and his young wife: Kiinak was not, like many Eskimo women, heavily tattooed about the face, but she did have two parallel slim blue lines coming down from her lower lip to the edge of her chin, and they gave her rather large, square face a touch of delicacy, for when she smiled the lines seemed to participate, thus making her warm smile even more generous.

When the butchering of the bear was completed on the spot where it had been slain, and the hundreds of pounds of rich meat

lugged ashore for treatment in various ways, Atkins had no utilitar-
ian reason for lingering about Sopilak's hut, but he did, and it was
not long before the gossipy women of Desolation began predicting
that something of interest was going to happen one of these days.
And now came an amusing contradiction, the kind that confused
many societies: the older women were romantics who reveled in
watching how young girls attracted and bewildered young men, and
they spent many hours speculating on who was going to go to bed
with whom and what kind of scandal this might produce; but they
were also rigorous moralists and protectors of village continuity.

Through long centuries they had learned that Eskimo society
functioned best when girls postponed having babies until they had
fastened themselves to some reassuring man who would provide for
their children. Widespread flirtation and even bedding down with
this attractive young fellow or that was permitted and even
encouraged—for example, if two aunts had an ungainly niece who
looked as if she might never catch a man; but if that niece had a child
without first having found a husband, these same aunts would excori-
ate her and even banish her from their hut. As one wise old woman
said while watching the courtship of Seaman Atkins and Sopilak's
sister: "It's always better when things go orderly."

The romantic half of their concern was quickly resolved, for although Atkins had returned to his long hut half a mile away when
the butchering ended, he remained there only two days, after which
he came plodding back to Desolation on snowshoes, longing to see
his Eskimo lass. He arrived at noon, bringing with him four ship's
biscuits as a present to Sopilak, his young wife, Sopilak's old mother
and Kiinak. Tasting the strange food outside their hut so as to enjoy
the final few hours of faint haze before winter clamped a perpetual
frozen darkness over all, they asked Atkins: "Is this what you told us
about? Is this what white people eat?" and when he nodded, they
said, not contemptuously: "Seal blubber is much better. Fat to keep
you warm in winter," and Atkins laughed: "We'll soon find out. Our
biscuits are almost gone."

And within the next week the Eskimos were starting to provide
the marooned sailors with seal meat, which they learned to enjoy,
and with seal blubber, the part of the animal that enabled the Eskimos to live in the arctic, which the white men could not force themselves to eat. And one afternoon, as John Atkins helped bring the
meat to the ship, accompanied by Sopilak, who had caught the seal,

he returned to the Point and lived thereafter in Sopilak's hut, sharing a sealskin bed with laughing Kiinak.

When the last days of November brought total darkness to the ice-bound ship, the twenty-one Americans living in the long hut—Atkins no longer being with them—settled into a routine which enabled them to withstand the terrible isolation. Most important, each day at what they judged to be high noon, Captain Pym attended by First Mate Corey marched to the rude ship's clock and ceremoniously wound it so that they could ensure having what they called Green-wich Time, which made it possible to calculate where they were in relation to London. The principle was simple, as Captain Pym always explained to each new sailor coming aboard his ship: "If the clock shows it's five in the afternoon at the Prime Meridian in London, and our shot of the sun shows it's high noon here, obviously we're five hours west of London. Since each hour represents fifteen degrees of longitude, we know for certain that we're at seventy-five degrees west, which puts us in the Atlantic some miles east of Norfolk, Virginia." Within a few years, wandering sea captains like Pym would have one of the new chronometers being perfected by English clockmaking geniuses, and with it they would be able to ascertain their longitude precisely; for the present, using the rough clocks available, they could only approximate. Latitude, of course, had been determinable with amazing accuracy for the last three thousand years: in daylight, shoot the noonday sun; at night, shoot the North Star. "159 degrees West Longitude," Pym would chart each day as he completed winding, "70 degrees, thirty-three minutes North Latitude." No other explorer had been so far north in these waters.

From the inadequate tables which mariners like Captain Pym carried with them, he calculated that at this latitude north the sun would quit the heavens sometime near the fifteenth of November and not reappear as even a sliver until sometime in late January. Harpooner Kane, hearing him speak of this, asked in a kind of stupor: "You mean, no light at all for seventy days?" and Pym nodded.

But on the midday of November the sun was still faintly visible for a few minutes, low in the sky, and Pym heard Kane tell the others: "Tomorrow it'll be gone," but on the sixteenth it still lingered. How-ever, two days later the merest edge of the sun appeared for two min-utes, then disappeared, and the sailors battened down their minds and their emotions, going into the kind of hibernation which many of the other arctic animals followed.

They were surprised, however, by the discovery that even at this great distance north, a kind of magical glow did appear each midday, illuminating their frozen world for a few precious minutes, not with actual daylight but with something more precious: a wonderful silvery aura which reminded them that the loss of their sun was not going to be perpetual. Of course, when this ambient glow vanished, the ensuing twenty-two hours of pitch-black seemed more oppressive and the penetrating cold more devastating. But when things seemed at their worst, the aurora borealis appeared, flooding the night sky with colors the New England men had never imagined, and Seaman Atkins, on his casual returns to the long hut, informed them: "The Eskimos say that the People Up There are holding festivity, chasing bears across the sky. Those are the lights of the hunters." But when the temperature dropped to what Captain Pym estimated as colder than seventy-below, for even oil froze solid, the men ignored the lights and huddled by their driftwood fire.

A prudent captain, Pym insisted that his men rise from their beds at what would have been dawn if there had been a sun, and he wanted them to eat such food as they could assemble at stated meal hours. He asked Mr. Corey to maintain a watch around the clock, especially in the direction of Desolation Point, warning: "Many ships in the Pacific have been taken by natives who appeared friendly." He assigned tasks to keep his men occupied, and week by week he devised ways to make the long hut more habitable, and each afternoon, two hours after lunch, he and Corey and Kane hiked across the ice to check upon the status of the *Evening Star.* Each day they inspected the planking to see if ice pressures had broken the stout body of the ship, and they saw with relief that the sides were so properly sloped that the crushing ice found nothing solid to push against. When it did move in with such tremendous force that it would have destroyed any ship not carefully built, it found only the curved flanks of the *Evening Star,* and when it pressed against them it lifted the ship gently aloft, until the keel stood some two feet above the surface of where the unfrozen water would have been. The ship had been lifted right into the air, and there it stayed as if it were some magic vessel in a dark gray dream.

"She's still firm," Captain Pym reported each afternoon as the inspectors returned.

But the solemn moment came at what would have been sunset, local time, when in the blackness of perpetual night Noah Pym gathered his sailors and by a whale-oil light conducted evening services:

"Oh, God! We thank Thee that our ship is safe through one more day. We thank Thee for the minutes of near-light at midday. We thank Thee for the food that reaches us from Thy sea. And we ask Thee to watch over our wives and children and mothers and fathers back in Boston. We are in Thy hands, and in the dark night we place our bodies and our immortal souls in Thy care."

After such a prayer, delivered with surprising variation as he invited God's attention to their daily problems, he asked each of his sailors in turn, those who could read, to take the Bible which accompanied him on all his trips, and read some personally chosen selection, and rarely did the soaring words of this Book resound with more meaning than there in the long hut beside the Arctic Ocean as the sailors read the familiar verses they had learned as boys in distant New England. One night, when it was Tom Kane's turn to read, this normally violent man chose from Acts a selection of verses that seemed to speak directly to their marooning and their encounter with the Eskimos:

"'But not long after there arose against it a tempestuous wind . . . And when the ship was caught, and could not bear up into the wind, we let her drive. And running under a certain island . . . we had much work to come by the boat . . . But when the fourteenth night was come, as we were driven up and down . . . about midnight the shipmen deemed that they drew near to some country . . . Then fearing lest we should have fallen upon rocks, they cast four anchors out of the stern and wished for the day . . .

"'And when it was day, they knew not the land: but they discovered a certain creek with a shore, into which they were minded, if it were possible, to thrust in the ship . . . And falling into a place where two seas met, they ran the ship aground . . . And so it came to pass, that they escaped all safe to land.

"'And when they were escaped . . . the barbarous people shewed us no little kindness: for they kindled a fire, and received us every one, because of the present rain, and because of the cold.'"

His constant remembering that he was still an officer of a church back in Boston and that he was, in a very real sense, responsible for the moral welfare of his sailors, often placed Captain Pym in difficult situations, as when he put his whaler into some island port and his men ran wild with the tempting girls with flowers in their hair who came at them skimming over the water on boards. Not being unnecessarily prudish, he looked aside while his men reveled, then reminded them of their perpetual duties when he had them back at sea attending his evening prayers. He also knew that they would raise hell when they hit ports like the one serving Canton, and he told himself: Stay clear. Let the Chinese bash heads.

But his magnanimity ended where marriage or its local equivalent was concerned, and when he saw how deeply Seaman Atkins was involved with Sopilak's sister, he realized that he could not ignore the moral problems which could result, and one morning in December when no hunting for seals was under way, he walked on self-made snowshoes to Desolation Point, where he sought the hut occupied by Sopilak, and once inside, he asked to meet with Atkins and the girl with whom he was living, but three others concerned in these matters insisted upon attending also: Sopilak, his mother and his young wife, Nikaluk. Seated in a circle on the floor, Captain Pym started his discussion of the timeless problems involving men and women.

"Atkins, God does not look with favor at young men who live with young women in an unmarried state—to the eventual detriment of those young women when the ship sails and they are left behind."

Now developed a bizarre situation in which young Atkins, as the interpreter in the group, was required to repeat in Eskimo the castigation his captain had delivered, but the relations which had always existed between Noah Pym, one of the notable captains out of New England, with his men were such that Atkins felt obligated to translate honestly, and when he did, Sopilak's mother broke in vehemently: "Yes, it is all right to make"—and here she used a gesture which could not be mistaken—"but to leave a baby behind and no man to feed it, that is no good."

For the better part of two hours these six people on the edge of the mighty ocean, whose frozen blocks cracked and snarled as they spoke, discussed a problem which had confused men and women since words were invented and families came into being for the nurturing and rearing of new generations. The contradictions were timeless; the obligations had not altered in fifty thousand years; and the solutions were as obvious now as they had been when Oogruk sought refuge in these parts fourteen thousand years ago after family problems on the far shore.

The climax of the discussion conducted in such an awkward manner and with so many participants came when it was revealed that John Atkins from a little town outside Boston, a good Protestant and unmarried, was profoundly in love with the Eskimo girl Kiinak and she in turn was so lost in love for him that come midsummer she was going to have his child.

Interpreting of this last intelligence was not required, for when Kiinak pointed to her growing belly, her mother leaped from the ground, dashed to the door, and began shouting into the darkness: "The bad one is going to have a baby and she has no man. Woe, woe, what is happening in the world?" Her cries attracted three other gossips her age, and now Sopilak's hut was filled with recrimination and noise and attacks against both the girl and her lover, and when the riot was sorted out, Captain Pym learned to his confusion that whereas it was completely wrong for Atkins to have got this fine young woman, fifteen years old, with child, it had been quite all right for them to have conducted all the steps leading up to that unfortunate development.

It was at the height of this complicated moral chaos that Pym first became conscious of the fact that Sopilak's wife was indulgently smiling at his confusion, as if to say: "You and I are above this nonsense," and he found himself blushing and awkwardly aware that they had formed a kind of partnership. Nikaluk was tall for an Eskimo, thinner than usual, and with an oval face unmarked as yet by tattoos. Her hair was jet-black and trimmed straight across her eyebrows, but she lacked the impishness of younger Kiinak, who had now moved close to Atkins as if to protect him from the condemnatory women who were shouting at him.

The impasse was settled when Atkins suddenly rose to announce in Eskimo that he wanted to marry Kiinak and that she had told him she wished to marry him. Now the four older women danced with glee, and embraced Atkins and told him what a fine man he was, with Captain Pym all the while standing aghast at this unexpected result his visit to Desolation Point had produced. But Nikaluk, still smiling condescendingly from the rear, made no attempt to quiet the confusion or give Pym any sign of reproof for the disturbance he and Atkins had created.

As the turbulent morning drew to a close, Pym told the crowd that he believed Atkins should return to the long hut with him and talk things over, and although the older women feared that this might be a device for preventing the promised marriage, they had to agree with Sopilak, who was the leader of their village, that it should be allowed, so after holding hands ardently with his young love, Seaman Atkins solemnly bound on the skis that Sopilak had made for him and followed his captain back to the long hut.

There Pym gathered the crew, informed them of what had transpired in the village, and awaited their amazed responses, but just as Harpooner Kane was about to make a suggestion, Pym interrupted: "Mr. Corey, I believe we have missed winding the clock," and after the two men gravely attended to this ritual, Pym restated their position at the edge of the Arctic Ocean: "159 degrees West Longitude . . ."

In the public meeting to discuss the possibility that John Atkins might have to marry his Eskimo girl, the first alternative voiced was eminently practical: "If she's pregnant, find some Eskimo to marry her. Give him an ax. They'll do anything for an ax," and before Captain Pym could oppose such an immoral proposal, several other sailors pointed out how impossible it would be for a civilized man from Boston, and a good Christian, to take back with him a savage who had never heard of Jesus, and this sentiment was about to prevail when a surprise comment altered the whole course of the debate. Big Tom Kane growled: "I know this girl and she'll make a damned sight better wife than that bitch I left in Boston."

Several sailors whose minds were undecided happened to be looking at Captain Pym when these harsh words were spoken, and they saw him blanch, gasp, and then say sternly: "Mr. Kane, we do not invite such comments in this ship."

"We're not aboard ship now. We're free to speak our minds."

Very quietly Captain Pym said: "Mr. Corey, will you accompany me and Harpooner Kane in our inspection of the *Evening Star*? And you will come with us, Seaman Atkins."

Across the ice the four men went, and once aboard their ship

Captain Pym began the daily examination as if nothing untoward had happened. They saw that the ice, still pressing in from the ocean, had as before struck the sloping sides of the ship and lifted her higher in the air rather than crushing her against the shore; the sides were tight; the caulking held; and when the thaw came she would sink back into the sea, ready for the trip to Hawaii.

But when the inspection was completed, Pym said almost sadly: "Mr. Kane, I was sore grieved by your intemperate outburst," and before the big man could apologize, the captain added: "We know of your tribulations in Boston and sympathize with you. But what shall we do about Atkins?"

Corey interrupted: "What Tompkin said is true. She is a savage."

Pym corrected him: "In her own way she's as civilized as you or me. The way her brother catches bears and seals and walruses is as able as the way you and I catch whales."

Corey, not silenced by this apt comparison, addressed his next remarks to Atkins: "You could never take her to Boston. In Boston a dark savage like her would never be accepted." And Atkins astonished the three men by saying rather innocently, as if he were in no way annoyed by this intrusion into his affairs: "We wouldn't go to Boston. We'd leave ship in Hawaii. I liked what I saw there." Before the men could respond, he nodded deferentially to the captain: "Granting your permission, sir."

There in the dark hold of the whaler, with the casks of valuable oil on all sides, Captain Pym considered this surprising development. Almost as if an act of God had descended upon his ship, he could in one sweep salvage his Christian conscience, help to save the soul of an Eskimo girl, and get rid of the consequences by putting the young couple ashore in Hawaii. On only few occasions in a navigator's life would he encounter an opportunity to do so many sensible things at one time and discharge the responsibilities of all concerned.

"You have my permission," he said as ice pressed upon his ship and the timbers creaked.

Back in the long hut, he informed the crew that he would, as a captain legally entitled to do so, perform the wedding of his Seaman Atkins to the Eskimo lady, but he also pointed out that for the marriage to be acceptable, it would have to be conducted aboard his ship, for he was not entitled to act in that capacity elsewhere. And he then skied to the village to deliver the same message, and when he made it clear to the intended bride, who now spoke a bit of English, that a celebration was to be held to which the entire village would be invited, she ran through the huts, shouting: "Everybody come!" and when she returned to where Captain Pym waited she kissed him warmly, as Atkins had taught her to do. Astounded by her boldness, Pym blushed furiously, and then he saw young Nikaluk smiling once again.

That wedding aboard the creaking *Evening Star* was one of the gentlest affairs in the long history of the white man's contact with the Eskimo. The Boston sailors decorated the ship with whatever bits of ornament they could construct, and that was not much: a scrimshaw here and there, a doll of stuffed sealskin, a striking block of ice carved with hammer and chisel by a carpenter, showing a polar bear rearing on its hind legs. When the Eskimos caught on to the idea of decorating the empty ship, they were far more inventive than the sailors, for they brought across the ice ivory carvings, things made of entire walrus tusks and the most wonderful items woven and constructed from baleen, until Captain Pym, comparing what they had done with what the Americans had accomplished, asked First Mate Corey: "Now who is civilized?" and the dubious Irishman answered cogently: "Taken together, what they've brought wouldn't signify in Boston."

The service that Captain Pym conducted was a solemn affair, outlined in pages printed at the rear of his Bible, and it was made doubly relevant by a passage which he arbitrarily quoted from Proverbs:

> "'There be three things which are too wonderful for me, yea, four which I know not: the way of an eagle in the air; the way of a serpent upon a rock; the way of a ship in the midst of the sea; and the way of a man with a maid.'

> "During this voyage we have seen eagles in the air and serpents on land. The way our ship escaped ice in the sea was truly mysterious, and which of us can understand the passion which has impelled our man John Atkins to take as his bride this lovely maid Kiinak?"

The ceremony made a profound impression on the Eskimos, for although they understood nothing of its religious significance, they could see that Pym took it with such high seriousness that this must be a true marriage. At its conclusion the older women attending Kiinak began to chant ritual words reserved for such occasions, and for a few precious moments there in the darkness of the *Evening Star* the two cultures met in a harmony that would not often be repeated in years to come, and never exceeded.

But of all the persons participating in this occasion and in the limited feast which followed, only pregnant Kiinak detected a collateral event which was going to have even greater significance, for as she watched the women during the feasting she observed her sister-in-law, and she whispered to her new husband: "Look at Nikaluk! She's in love with your captain."

And as the long, dark winter drew to a close, and the sun returned to the heavens, no more than a silvery shadow at first, peeking its head above the horizon for a few minutes, shivering and running away, Nikaluk was powerless to hide the abiding affection she felt for this strange man, so different from her husband, the notable hunter Sopilak. She was loyal to her husband and reverenced his skill in leading the villagers and keeping them provided with food, but she also recognized in Captain Pym a man of deep emotion and responsibility, one in touch with the spirits who ruled the earth and the seas. She observed how his men respected him and how it was he who made decisions and said the important words. More even than her admiration for his qualities was the fact that she thrilled to his presence, as if she knew that he was bringing to this lonely village at the edge of the icebound ocean a message from another world, one which she could not begin to visualize but which she knew intuitively must have aspects of great power and goodness. She had known two men from this world, Atkins, who had loved her husband's sister, and Captain Pym, who controlled the ship, and they were in their way as fine as her husband.

But there was also the fact that she was captivated by the idea of Pym, by the possibility that she might lie with him as Atkins had done so easily with Kiinak and with such joyous results. Driven by these impulses, she began to frequent the places where Pym would be, and she became the object of gossip in the village, and even the sailors in the long hut knew that their married captain, the one who took the Bible so seriously and had three daughters in Boston, had caused an Eskimo woman to fall in love with him, and she with a husband of her own.

Pym, an austere man who took life seriously, thrashed about in a blizzard of moral confusion: sometimes he refused to acknowledge that Nikaluk was in love with him; later, when he did confess to himself that complications threatened, he assumed no responsibility for them. In either case, he made not the slightest gesture toward Nika-luk, not even so much as giving her a glance, for he was absorbed in what he deemed a much more weighty problem. "When," he asked his officers at New Year's, "can we expect the ice to melt?" and one of them who had read books written by Europeans about Greenland gave it as his judgment that the ice would not start to melt till May, but when Atkins asked among his wife's people, they gave an appall-ing date which translated into early July, and when Pym himself con-sulted with Sopilak, he was satisfied that this later date was probably correct.

Only then did despair settle upon the men of the *Evening Star,* for in autumn when the ice trapped them they had accepted their impris-onment, expecting it to last till the end of March, when spring thawed New England ponds. And at the onset of winter they were almost eager to see if they had the fortitude to withstand its historic blasts and were proud when they did. But now to greet a new year and to realize that summer would be more than six months distant was in-tolerable, and frictions developed.

Some wanted to shift their quarters to the ship, but the Eskimos warned vigorously against this: "When ice melts, strange things hap-pen. Maybe worst time." So Captain Pym ordered them to remain ashore, and each day his inspections were more careful. He was con-siderate in dealing with men who gave trouble, assuring them that while he understood their anxieties, he could not tolerate even the slightest show of insubordination.

He was pleased, therefore, when the Eskimos organized hunting trips far out on the ice, which still showed no signs of melting, for then his more adventurous men could accompany them to share the dangers. He himself went once to where a long lane of open water had lured sea lions north, and he had shared in the dangerous task of killing two and then lugging them home over the ice. "If we keep busy," he told the men and himself, "the day will come when we'll break free."

As the day Captain Pym calculated to be the twenty-fourth of January approached, he encouraged his crew by telling them that the sun, still hiding beneath the horizon, would soon be returning to the Northern Hemisphere, and at a speed that would make the noonday twilight grow longer and brighter. And he explained to those sailors who knew no astronomy: "Yes, the sun is heading north, and it will keep coming till it stands directly over the Arctic Circle. Then day-light will last twenty-four hours."

"Tell it to hurry up," one of the sailors said, and Pym replied: "As with all things ordained by God, like the planting of corn and the return of geese, the sun must follow the schedule He gave it." But then he added a curious bit of information: "The ancient Druids, who did not know God, expressed their joy at the sun's responsible behavior with prayer and song, and since the Eskimos are also prim-itive people, I suppose we can expect the same."

But he was not prepared for the things that happened at Desola-tion Point, for when on the twenty-third of January the sun threw unmistakable signals that on the next noon it would show its face, the villagers went wild, and children cried: "The sun is coming back!" Drums were produced and tambours made of sealskin fastened to rims of driftwood, but what seemed to be the focus of attention and delight was a huge blanket woven years ago from precious fur spin-dled into thread and woven into a stout cloth. It was colored with dyes gathered along the shore in summer and from the exudations of sealskin and walrus.

That afternoon Sopilak and two other men in ceremonial garb came solemnly on their skis to the long hut to announce that on the morrow, at high noon when the sun would reappear, the sailors were invited to its celebration, and gravely they bowed as Captain Pym had done when conducting the wedding in his ship. First Mate Corey, speaking for the crew, promised they would be there, but when the Eskimos had gone he said, not spitefully but with a certain cynicism: "Let's see what these savages are up to," and half an hour before noon on the twenty-fourth he and Captain Pym led their entire com-plement of sailors over the frozen snow to Desolation Point.

In the silvery darkness they joined a solemn crowd, a group of people who had lived for many months without sunlight, and there was muffled excitement as the Eskimos looked to the east where the sun had regularly reappeared in years past, a hesitant disk bringing rejuvenation to the world. When the first delicate rays flickered briefly and a gray light suffused the sky, men began to whisper and then cry out in uncontrolled joy as shoots of flame came forth, heralding the true dawn. Watchers from the dark huts smiled, and even the sailors felt a surge of joy when it became apparent that the sun really was going to appear, for they had resented this strange dark winter even more than the Eskimos, and as the villagers gazed in awe when the sun itself peeked over the edge of the world to see how the frozen areas had sustained themselves during its absence, a woman began to chant, and one of Pym's sailors shouted: "Jesus Christ! I thought it would never come back!"

Then, in the brief moments of that glorious day when hope was restored and men were assured that the world would move as it always had, at least for one more year, people began to cheer and sing and embrace, with the sailors jigging in heavy boots with old women in parkas who had not expected ever to dance again with a young man. And there were tears.

But now things happened that the sailors could not have imagined and which, perhaps, had never before happened at Desolation Point, unpremeditated acts which captured the essence of this glorious moment when life began anew. Along the beach, where great blocks of ice protruded like the backdrop to some drama enacted by the gods of the north, a group of girls, eight or nine years old, danced, and their little feet clad in huge fur-lined moccasins moved so gracefully as their bodies smothered in furs bent in unusual directions that the sailors fell silent, thinking of their daughters or little sisters whom they had not seen for years.

On and on the dancing of the little girls continued, elfin spirits paying respect to the frozen sea, feet clomping handsomely in the snow as they performed steps which had graced this day and this seashore for ten thousand years. It was a moment in time that would be frozen in the memory of all the Americans who saw it, and two big sailors, overcome by the sudden beauty of the spectacle, remained in the background but in their own clumsy way aped the movements of the little girls, and old women clapped, remembering those years long ago when they had greeted the returning sun with similar dancing.

But no one watching these little girls reacted in the way Captain Pym did, for as he followed their unaffected steps and saw the joy with which they smiled at the sun, he thought of his own three daughters and unprecedented judgments came to his lips: "My daughters never showed such joy in their lives. In our home there was little dancing." Tears came to his eyes, a symbol of his confusion, and he kept staring at the dance; he could not join it as his sailors did, but he understood its significance.

While the sun was still visible on its brief stop to say hello, excitement grew among the huts, where Eskimo men busied themselves with something that Captain Pym could not see, and after a few moments all the Eskimos cheered as Sopilak and his fellow hunters, mature men all, brought forth the big blanket which Pym had seen earlier but whose purpose he had been unable to guess. Laughter and excitement attended its passage to the spot where the girls had been dancing, but still none of the Americans could fathom why a mere blanket should be causing such a flurry. But then it was unfolded, and Pym saw that it had been made in the form of a circle with a rim strengthened to provide handholds, which most of the men in the village now grabbed. At signals from Sopilak, they simultaneously pulled outward, causing the blanket to form the surface of a huge drum, which was instantly relaxed and as quickly drawn tight again. Under Sopilak's skilled timing, the blanket pulsed like a living membrane, now loose, now taut.

When the men indicated their confidence that they could operate the blanket, Sopilak paused, turned to the crowd, and pointed to a rather pretty girl of fifteen or sixteen with braided hair, a large labret in her lower lip and prominent tattoos across her face. Obviously proud to have been chosen, she jumped forward, flexed her knees, and allowed two men to toss her in the air and onto the waiting blanket, which had been drawn tight to receive her. As watching women cheered, the girl waved to assure them that she would not dishonor them, and Sopilak's men began to make the blanket pulse, lifting the girl higher and higher, but as she had promised the women, she deftly maintained her balance, remaining erect on her feet.

Then, suddenly, the men tightened the blanket furiously, all pulling outward at once, whereupon the girl was tossed high in the air, perhaps a dozen feet, and there she seemed to hang for a moment before falling back to the blanket, upon which she landed still upright on her feet. The villagers applauded and some sailors shouted, but the girl, surprised at how high she had been thrown that first time and knowing that much more was to follow, bit upon the upper edge of her labret and prepared for the next flight.

This time she soared aloft to a considerable height, but still she maintained her footing; however, on the final toss she went so high that gravity and a spinning motion acted upon her heavily padded body and she came down in a heap, collapsing with laughter as the men helped her descend from the blanket.

Kiinak, clutching her husband's hand, told him: "None went higher than me, but that was last year," and he, always aware of her pregnancy, said: "That was last year." However, after two more saucy girls went flying up toward the sky, Sopilak relinquished his place on the blanket and came to stand before his sister, saying: "To make the baby strong," and gravely she took his hand and accompanied him to the blanket.

"Wait!" Atkins shouted, terrified at the prospect of his gravid wife's flying through the air and landing on the taut blanket with a thump, but Kiinak held up her right hand, indicating that he must stop where he was. Agitated as never before, he watched as she was lifted onto the blanket and her brother resumed his place in the circle of men holding it.

Gently, as if dealing with a baby already born, they started the rhythm of the blanket, chanting as they did, and then at a nod from Sopilak they imparted just the right gentle lift, and the pregnant girl rose slightly into the air and was expertly caught as she descended, suffering no shock whatever from her brief flight. When she rejoined her husband, she whispered: "To make the baby brave."

A very old woman, one who had soared to the sky when young, was similarly honored, but the lift was too modest for her tastes. "Higher!" she shouted, and Sopilak warned her: "You asked us to," and his men applied just enough pressure to send the old one well into the air, where miraculously she controlled her feet so that she landed upright. The sailors cheered.

And now it was the villagers who did so, because gravely Sopilak stepped before his wife and invited her to leap upon the blanket, which she did without assistance. For some years, when she was sixteen to nineteen, Nikaluk had been champion of the village, flying with a grace and to a height which no other girl could match, for it was not the men alone who determined how high a girl on the blanket would rise; the use of her half-bent knees and the thrust of her legs helped too, and Nikaluk was bolder than most, as if she hungered for the higher air.

The rhythm started. The blanket pulsed. The excitement intensified as Nikaluk prepared for her first leap, and the sailors leaned forward, for they had been told by Atkins: "The champion. None higher." However, both Nikaluk and the men working the blanket knew that on her first three or four tries she was not going to rise very high, because both she and they had to test strengths and calculate just when to snap the blanket with maximum power, timing it with the bending of her knees.

So the first four tosses were experimental, but even so the rare grace of this lithe young woman was apparent, and the sailors stopped talking to watch the elegant manner in which she handled arms, legs, torso and head during her ascension, and upon no observer did her lovely motion have a greater effect than upon Captain Pym, who stared at her floating in air as if he had never before seen her.

Then, with no warning, she shot skyward at a speed and to a height which left him astounded: "Oh! Goodness!" More than twenty feet above his head she hung motionless, every part of her body in delicate alignment, as if she were a renowned dancer in a Paris ballet, a creature of extreme beauty and grace. And now slowly, then gathering speed, she started downward in a posture that looked as if she would have to land awkwardly, but at the last moment she established control and landed on her feet in the middle of the blanket, smiling to no one and preparing herself and her knees for the next flight, which she knew would carry her even higher.

Coordinating with unspoken signals from her husband, she flexed her knees, took a deep breath, and soared into the air like a bird seeking new altitudes, and as she sped aloft, Captain Pym noticed a strange aspect of her flight: Those big fur boots she wears, her heavy clothing, they seem to make her more graceful, not less, and her control doubly impressive. She was a wonderful flying young woman, and there were not on the entire earth at that moment more than a dozen women, regardless of race, who could have equaled her performance and none who could excel. High in the air, with the sun about to bid her farewell, she hung at the apex of her art and she knew it.

On the last upward thrust of the blanket, she went higher than ever before in her life, and this was not because her husband pulled the blanket especially strongly but rather because she synchronized her whole body in one supreme effort, and she did this solely because she wanted to enchant Captain Pym, whom she knew to be staring at her, mouth agape. She succeeded in making a lovely arc through the sky against the quickly settling sun, and as she returned to earth like a tired bird, she smiled for the first time that morning and looked boldly at her captain in a gesture of triumph. She had been aloft where no woman of that village had ever been before; she had been one with the newly born sun and the great ice field whose days were limited, now that her earth was moving into warmth. And when she was lifted from the blanket she experienced such a surge of victory that she went not to her husband but to Noah Pym, taking him by the hand and leading him away.

The celebration of the sun lasted twenty-four hours, and three events in the course of that celebration became part of the tradition of the village of Desolation Point, some treasured, some better forgotten. The young woman Nikaluk went with the Boston captain Noah Pym to a hut where they made love throughout the night. The rough sailor Harry Tompkin from a seafront village near Boston crept down into the bowels of the *Evening Star* to tap a keg of Jamaica rum which had been stowed aboard for medicinal and other emergencies. With the dark, delicious fluid he and two of his mates got drunk, but what was more significant in the history of Alaska, in their generosity and general mood of celebration, they shared their alcohol with Sopilak, who was staggered physically and emotionally by its stupendous effect. And when the sun came up for a second dawning, certifying that its return was legitimate, the old women of Desolation gave Captain Pym a present which in time would strangle him in a remorse that would never dissipate.

The lovemaking was a beautiful experience, a splendid Eskimo woman, pride of her village, striving to understand what the coming of this ship to her shore signified, sought to hold on to such meaning as she could discern. She knew that Noah Pym was the finest man she would encounter in this brief life, and since she had for three months longed to be with him, she had deemed it proper to make her desires known at the celebration of the sun when she performed her ultimate act of reverence, the faultless leap to heights never attained before.

Her boldness in leading him to the twilight hut was not surprising in this Eskimo village, for although the older women disciplined the younger, forcing them to marry in an orderly way so that their babies could be protected and reared in security, no one assumed that marriage ended the desires of people, and it was not unusual for a young wife or husband to behave as Nikaluk had done; no stigma attached to it and life went on after such an affair pretty much as it did before, with no one the worse because of it.

But since sailors like those from the *Evening Star* went home from Eskimo land averring that "this here husband offered our captain his wife, as hospitality, you might say," the legend grew that the proffering of a wife to a traveler was Eskimo custom. It was not. About the same amount of affection between traveler and local wife developed at Desolation Point as in a rural community outside Madrid or one close to Paris, or London, or New York. Nikaluk the Eskimo sky-dancer from Desolation had sisters all over the world, and many of the good things that happened in the world did so because of the desire of these strong-minded women to know of the world before the world left them or they it.

But Sopilak's disastrous introduction to rum was not a universal experience. White men had distilled this drink, so exhilarating, so liberating, for many decades and they had introduced it to people all over the world, and Spaniards or Italians or Germans or American colonists could imbibe it moderately, celebrate immoderately, and be little affected next morning. But others, the men of Ireland and Russia, for example, or the Indians of Illinois, or the Tahitians whom Captain Cook respected so highly when they were not drunk, and especially the Eskimos, Aleuts and Athapascans of Alaska, could not accept alcohol one day and leave it the next. And when they drank, it did terrible things to them. On the morning that Sopilak, the great hunter, accepted the liquor from the unwitting Harry Tompkin, the long decline of Desolation Point began.

When Sopilak swished that first taste of rum about his mouth he considered it too biting and too strong, but after he swallowed it and felt its effect all the way down to the depths of his stomach, he wanted another sample, and with its warmth began that indescribable swirl of dreams and visions and illusions of endless power. It was a magical drink, that he realized in those earliest moments, and he craved more and then more. As spring returned he became the prototype of those myriad Alaskans who in later days became addicted to alcohol, prowling the beaches and waiting for the arrival of the next whaler out of Boston. They had learned that such ships brought rum, and no finer gift in the world existed than that.

It was a filthy business the good Christians of Boston were engaged in, Captain Pym's brother and uncle among them: fabrics to hungry buyers in the West Indies, slaves to Virginia, rum out to the natives of Hawaii and Alaska, and whale oil back to Boston. Unquestionably wealth was created, but the slaves, the whales and the Eskimos of Desolation Point were destroyed.

The present that the old women of the village gave Captain Pym was delivered on the second morning after he had with a remorse never experienced before left the hut of love and taken Nikaluk to her own, where he found her husband lying in a drunken stupor on the ground. In that awful moment he saw two old women pointing at him and Sopilak, and he could deduce that they were praising him for having used sorcery on the fallen man so that he could enjoy his wife. They were criticizing neither Pym nor Sopilak; in a sense they were congratulating the former for a rather neat trick.

Then other women appeared bearing in their arms a garment on which they had been working for some time, and after they had raised Sopilak to his feet and slapped his face a couple of times, he took the garment from them, smiled sheepishly at the men who had gathered, and held out his arms to Captain Pym. John Atkins, who approved of all that was happening, translated:

> "Honored Great Captain whose guns saved my life when we
> fought the bear, and who helped Tayuk and Oglowook to kill
> him when I could not, our village offers you this gift. Your
> men have been good to us. We honor you."

Bowing, he allowed the garment to fall free, and the sailors who were still celebrating fell silent as they saw the noble cloak which their captain was receiving. It was pure white, heavy, long: the fur of the polar bear taken on that early hunt.

Everyone insisted that he put it on, and he stood embarrassed and ashamed as Sopilak and Nikaluk draped the glorious cape about his undeserving shoulders. He wore it all the way back to the long hut and even during the inspection of the ship, but that night as the time approached for evening worship he laid it aside, and when the men looked to him for prayer, he turned ashen-faced to his first mate and said: "Mr. Corey, will you offer prayer? I am unworthy."

Pym's surrender of evening prayer to others had a constructive aftermath, for when the trying days of late April arrived, with permanent daylight but no indication that the frozen sea would ever relinquish its stranglehold on the *Evening Star,* the sailors grew at first restless and then downright belligerent. Fistfights erupted for no reason, and even when they were halted by Corey's quick attention, a general surliness prevailed.

When it looked as if real trouble might erupt, one of the ship's quietest men came to Captain Pym, saying shyly: "Captain, sir, I've found proof in the Bible that God knows our plight and has promised rescue." When Pym showed astonishment that the Lord should be concerned about this lost little ship and its sinful captain, the sailor asked: "I was wondering if I might read Scripture tonight?" and Pym had to say: "That's no longer my province. You must ask Mr. Corey," and when the young man did, Corey gave quick assent, for if anything promised to ease tensions, he would try it.

So after evening meal, with the light as bright as it had been at midday, this frail young man, his voice throbbing with emotion, read from an obscure passage in the often overlooked book of Zechariah:

"'Behold, the day of the Lord cometh, and thy spoil shall be divided in the midst of thee.

"'And it shall come to pass in that day, that the light shall not be clear, nor dark:

"'But it shall be one day which shall be known to the Lord, not day, nor night: but it shall come to pass, that at evening time it shall be light.

"'And the Lord shall be king over all the earth: in that day shall there be one Lord, and his name one.'"

Closing the Bible reverently, the sailor leaned forward to offer a brief emendation: "Clearly, men, this prophecy pertains to us. When we sell our whale oil, the shares will be divided. When the ice melts, and it surely will, we shall be set free. Already we have continuous day, as the Lord ordained. And at evening time there is light, and the Lord our God does reign as king over all the earth. Since He has promised to save us, there is no need for bitterness now."

Several sailors, grateful for what seemed like divine intervention, clapped hands as he finished, but Captain Pym, suspecting that he had outlawed himself from such dispensation, shivered and stared at his knuckles, but his remorse did not prevent him from spending hours and then days and finally nights with Nikaluk, so that when the ice did finally begin to melt, with the *Evening Star* slowly resuming her position as a ship floating in water, Nikaluk started asking the inevitable questions, using the patois which the sailors and their women had developed over the nine months of the marooning: "Captain Pym, s'pose Atkins take Kiinak with him. Why not you?"

He told her frankly: "You know I have a wife, children. You have a husband. Impossible."

Without rancor, but with a realistic assessment of the situation, she said: "Sopilak? He what you call drunk all time." And she began insisting that Pym take her with him. She had no concept of either Hawaii, where Atkins was going, or Boston, where the others were headed, but she was confident and with good reason that she would fit in and find for herself and Noah an acceptable life, but for two conclusive reasons he found it impossible to consider taking her to Boston: I already have a family, and even if I didn't, I could never show her there. No one would understand.

He was nowhere near brave enough to share that second reason with her, especially since Atkins had had no hesitancy in marrying Kiinak, Boston or no, so he postponed telling her definitely that he would be leaving her behind when the ship sailed. Yet he could not break himself away from her, for he was ensnared in the great passion of his life, the one that awakened a man to what love and women and a life's destiny involved. She had already placed an imprint on his life that would never be erased, neither by time nor regret, and in a perverse way he found intense pleasure in strengthening the experience. He was in love with Nikaluk, and when he was away from her he could visualize her flying in the air, her heavy boots prepared for a sudden landing, her arms and hair outflung in a vision of wonder that few men ever had of their women. She was of the sky, and the ice, and the endless nights, and the quiet harmony of this village beside the Arctic Ocean. "Oh, Nikaluk!" he sometimes cried aloud when he was alone. "What will happen to us?"

He did not, like many American men who were in those days exploring the world and new societies, engage in sentimental reflection about the poor island girl left behind, as if she were going to cry her heart out while he went on to better things, unaware that she was going to handle the situation rather easily in her island paradise while he would be tormented about island memories when he returned to Philadelphia or Charleston. No, Pym saw Nikaluk as a human being equal to himself in all ways except the possibility of her living in Christian Boston. Corey had been right; she was, in so many respects that mattered, a savage.

But he continued to wear the polar-bear cloak and to luxuriate in its richness and the memories it held of those great days hunting on the ice. The long coat became his symbol as he moved about the *Eve-*

ning Star preparing her for sea. One morning Atkins brought his wife aboard, and when Captain Pym saw her, smiling and eager for adventure, his breath caught and he wished he were that young seaman bringing Nikaluk, so much more mature and lovely than Kiinak, aboard for the long voyage to the closing of his life.

The sun shone. The sea relaxed. The ice retreated, baffled for another summer but sullenly hoarding its strength for a swift return in autumn, and sails were set. All the people of Desolation came down through the mud to watch the departure, and it might have been a gala morning except that with the raising of the gangplank, this final severance from the shore that had treated the visitors so hospitably with seal blubber and dancing and loving women, Nikaluk ran from her husband, approached the departing ship, and wailed: "Captain Pym!" Her husband ran after her, not to rebuke but to comfort, but he had that morning drunk the last of Harry Tompkin's rum, and before he could catch his wife he fell in the mud and lay there as the ship withdrew.

Land had scarcely been lost on the journey south to Lapak Island, where the whaler would replenish as best it could for the long run to Hawaii, when Captain Pym, on the bridge, suddenly called out: "Mr. Corey, this polar bear is strangling me!" and with frantic hands he tore at the beautiful cloak, throwing it from him and kicking it into a corner when it fell.

When Harpooner Kane heard of the incident he went to the captain, saying: "I, too, helped kill the bear. Can I have the cloak?" and Pym said hurriedly and with a sense of overpowering guilt: "You are entitled to wear it, Mr. Kane. You have not covered it with shame." And during the long, cold trip to Lapak Island, Noah Pym continued to refrain from reading the evening prayers, for he was indeed strangled: the bear, and Sopilak fallen in the mud, and Nikaluk flying magnificently in the air were all fragments of his agony, especially his memory of those little girls, so untouched by the coming of the *Evening Star*, dancing on the frozen beach to rejoice in the return of their sun.

The enforced stop at Lapak Island was brief and terrible. When the little brig entered the familiar water between the volcano and the island and saw the Aleuts in their kayaks and elegant hats, Harpooner Kane cried: "Home port!" but they had barely anchored when the sight of Kane in that rich white cloak excited the two reprobates, Innokenti and baldheaded Zagoskin, to start whispering among their men: "That ship out there must be crammed with furs," and after two days of adroit spying, prolonged by dilatory action in delivering provisions to the ship, the talk became: "Properly led, sixteen determined men could take that ship." When this was secretly discussed among seven ringleaders, Innokenti reminded his fellows of something he had spotted when the *Evening Star* stopped at Lapak on its way north: "Captain Cook had soldiers aboard his ship. This one has none." And now the plotting began.

No one had yet made a specific proposal of piracy, but Innokenti, remembering how Captain Pym had relished talking with Trofim Zhdanko, encouraged the New Englander to spend time in the old cossack's hut, and this necessitated the presence of the interpreter, Seaman Atkins, who took his wife along. The sessions were protracted, and Trofim had an opportunity to see what an excellent wife the young American had acquired in the Eskimo girl Kiinak, and he became especially concerned about her pregnancy: "How wonderful that one of the first Americans in these waters found himself an Eskimo girl that he wanted to marry . . . before a priest . . . like decent human beings." He returned several times to this theme, finally betraying his deeper concern: "How much better these islands would have been if men like my son had taken Aleut wives." He smiled at the young couple and said: "You're beginning a new race. May God bless you."

With Trofim was a boy named Kyril, son of a Russian brigand and an Aleut woman whom he had raped and later killed. The Russian had sailed off to an eastern island in the Aleutians, abandoning his son, who began to frequent Zhdanko's hut, where he helped the old man. Trofim was especially eager that Kyril see how easy and normal it was for a man like Atkins to marry an Eskimo woman like Kiinak: "Let this be a lesson. Good lives come from good beginnings."

"Are you married?" Captain Pym asked, and the old man said proudly: "Most powerful woman in Siberia. She'd make a grand tsarina," and he asked Pym: "Have you a family?" and the captain flushed a deep red, giving no answer, but Trofim needed none; what the trouble was he could not guess, but that there was trouble he knew.

While these wandering conversations were under way in the hut, Innokenti and Zagoskin, defeated men in their advancing years who had accomplished nothing but destruction, were huddled with their fellow conspirators, coordinating their attack on the *Evening Star:* "Tomorrow when the captain and the young couple go to talk with the old fool, you and you, keep them inside. Then Zagoskin and I, with you three, board the ship as if bringing them supplies. He goes below with one helper. I stay on deck with two. And all of you speed out in your kayaks. At this signal," and he shouted in Russian, "we take the ship."

"And if they fight?" one of them asked.

"We kill as many as we have to."

"The others?"

"Like the ones in the hut? We deal with them later. But get the ship, because then we can do almost anything." It had been secretly agreed between Innokenti and Zagoskin that after capturing the ship, all survivors would be taken to nearby Adak and murdered, the blame being placed upon the Aleuts there.

The plot was uncomplicated and brutal, with an excellent chance for success, except that on the target day Captain Pym did not visit Trofim and Kyril; he stayed aboard ship and this meant that Atkins and his wife stayed too, but the conspirators were so sure of success that the plan went forward. At one in the afternoon the two leaders came to the *Evening Star,* accompanied by three traders, as agreed. They brought with them a substantial supply of stores, and as they began to deliver them, other men with more goods set out from shore.

Noah Pym, learned in the lore of ships' being taken by land-based natives, was below when the second contingent started to come aboard, and instinctively he rushed toward the door of his cabin, crying: "Mr. Corey, what goes on?"

He was met by Zagoskin, who gave a loud bellow signaling that the fight had begun, and then clubbed Pym over the head, cracking his skull and knocking him to the deck. From that fallen position the dazed man raised himself on one elbow and tried to defend himself, but with a heavy boot Zagoskin kicked him in the face, whereupon Zagoskin's Siberian helper beat the little New Englander to death. He died trying to save his ship, which in his last moments he supposed he had lost. He uttered no final words, entertained no last thoughts. He was not even allowed time for prayer, which had been absent from his lips for so long.

Young Atkins and his wife, hearing the commotion in the captain's cabin, ran to his assistance, just in time to be clubbed to death by Zagoskin and his helper, who were then free to rush topside to help Innokenti clear the decks, but when they reached there they found far more confusion than they had anticipated, for First Mate Corey, an iron-tough Irishman, assumed that Pym was dead and that the salvation of the ship depended on him. Armed with pistol and sword, he killed two attackers and forced their leader Innokenti to stay back. But now, seeing huge Zagoskin coming at him, he shouted: "Help! Help!" threw down his empty pistol and grabbed a belaying pin, determined to kill as many Russian pirates as possible before surrendering the ship.

At this moment a huge man in a long white cloak rushed on deck, wielding a long harpoon in each hand. It was Kane, shouting: "Pym's dead. Kill them all!" And without stopping to take careful aim, he threw one of his lethal spears at the approaching Zagoskin. It sped through the air like a slim bolt of lightning, struck the Russian just above the heart and pinned him like a helpless seal to the mast.

Not satisfied that the harpoon had killed the man, Kane leaped at him as he stood speared and with his other harpoon stabbed him twice, once through the neck, once through the face. Then, failing to jerk the first harpoon loose, he abandoned it, grabbed the club with which Zagoskin had killed Atkins and his wife, and rampaged about the deck, striking with fury any Russians he encountered.

Joining with Corey, who was defending himself with only a belaying pin, Kane pointed to Innokenti and shouted to all the Americans within earshot: "He's the bastard! Kill him!" and with that he launched his other harpoon at the instigator of the attack. He missed, and when Corey lunged at him, Innokenti deftly sidestepped and gained a moment to survey the deck where plans had gone so terribly wrong. He saw the dead Russians, his partner Zagoskin skewered against the mast, and both Kane and that damned Irishman summoning their men, so in one bloodstained second he made his decision. With a wild dive over the side he abandoned his cohorts and ignored the fact that he couldn't swim. With the superhuman power that men can often muster in the face of mounting disaster, this amazing scoundrel flopped about in the sea like a stricken fish, reached an empty kayak, upset it sideways, thrust his legs into one of the hatches, righted it, and with long skilled strokes fled toward shore. Corey, seeing him about to escape punishment, grabbed a pistol from a sailor and tried to shoot him, but missed.

After the Boston men had tossed overboard the corpses of Zagoskin and his fellow pirates, Corey said in controlled voice, as if nothing of importance had happened: "Up anchor, prepare sails. Mr. Kane, you are promoted to First Mate. Report to me on the condition of the crew."

The last sight the Russian fur traders had of this doughty little ship—which had explored the seas, chased whales, and survived being pinned down in an arctic winter—was a file of men standing at attention along the port gunwales while the new captain read solemnly from a Bible, and a big man in a long white cloak lifted three bodies, one by one—Captain Pym, Seaman Atkins, the pregnant Eskimo girl Kiinak—and pitched them into the Bering Sea.

But that was not all, for when the ceremony ended, the new captain ordered the ship's ineffectual gun unlimbered, pointed ashore, and fired. A cannonball of no great weight ricocheted across the rocky land of Lapak Island, coming to harmless rest close to the hut occupied by Trofim Zhdanko, who had watched the events of this day with shame and horror.

This attempted piracy occurred in the spring of 1781, and combined with the near-loss of the *Evening Star* in the ice pack off Desolation Point, it deterred other American whalers from adventuring into the Chukchi Sea and Arctic Ocean for half a century, but by 1843 the floodgates would be opened, and a few years later nearly three hundred whalers would brave these northern seas.

After the *Evening Star,* first of that gallant breed, escaped to the south and a memorial stone was erected to indicate where Zagoskin's pierced and mutilated body had drifted ashore, it seemed as if the fur traders were willing to dismiss the affair of the *Evening Star* as nothing more than a good risk which had gone astray. "We came this close to taking that ship," Innokenti said to the men who closed ranks around him. "That damned harpooner." He ignored Zhdanko when the old man asked: "Why did you have to kill that fellow and his wife?" for his son felt that this could happen in any lively action. As for the killing of the captain, who had been so congenial during his two visits, that was also one of the accidents of war.

When his stepfather asked: "But was it war?" Innokenti snapped: "We are at war with anyone who thinks to take this new land from us," and when Zhdanko asked further what made him sure that

Americans would want an island like Lapak, with no trees and a diminishing supply of seals and sea otters, he said: "Yes, this island is
used up. The natives are no good. But there are others better than
this farther east." And it was this indication that his son planned to
continue eastward with his slaughter, his piracy and his wanton killing that decided the old man.

On a fine overcast day with no rain or wind, perfect for hunting
otters, Zhdanko surprised Innokenti by saying: "Fine day. We've
been enemies too long. With Zagoskin gone, let's see if we can catch
some more furs," and when they went to the kayak in which Zagoskin
had sat in the stern so that Innokenti could club the otters forward,
the old man said: "I'll paddle here," and his son shouted to some
idlers on the beach: "Come help us form the circle," but only two
others responded.

Trofim led the way, far from shore and into the shadow of
Qugang, assuring Innokenti: "I've seen otters out here," and they
came at last to a spot from which the actions of the three kayaks
could not easily be followed by the men on the beach. Here they did
find otters, and as Innokenti started the abbreviated circle in pursuit
of a female with a babe on her belly, the mother proved surprisingly
agile, dodging this way and that, aided of course by the fact that the
circle did not contain enough boats.

Innokenti, infuriated by his stepfather's tardy response in adjusting to the otter's tactics, cursed at him and at the other paddlers,
threatening the latter with beatings when he got them ashore: "Form
up! Come at her faster when I chase her your way!"

A few minutes later, when the hunters were grievously misposi-
tioned, thanks to Trofim's ineptness, Innokenti turned to berate him
again, when the old man, from his rear position, gave the kayak such
a violent lurch that the front spun completely around, tossing Innokenti into the sea.

He did not panic. Cursing Trofim again, he did as before when he
dove off the *Evening Star*, flailing his arms and thrashing out violently to grab the leading hole of the kayak, and he would surely have
saved himself a second time, except that when he reached up,
Zhdanko moved swiftly away, looked down at his son, and struck
him full in the face with the blunt side of his paddle. Then, as if he
were hunting a helpless mother otter who had to surface, he waited
for Innokenti's head to rise above the surface, whereupon he moved
swiftly to that spot and almost crushed his skull with a second blow.

Biding his time, he paddled gently, waiting for the bloody head to appear, and when it did he calmly pushed it back under, keeping it there for many minutes. Only then did he wave his paddle furiously and start shouting: "Help! Innokenti has fallen."

Many days after the body came ashore, so waterlogged and decomposed that no one could say what had happened during the otter hunt, the boy Kyril came to Trofim's hut, and after prolonged silences during which the old cossack thought: He's the same age as Innokenti was when I met him, but how different, the young fellow said hesitantly: "I saw what happened when we chased those otters."

Trofim made no response, and after a while the young man said: "No one else saw but me. I was in front position."

Tears came to the old man's eyes, not of regret but in response to the great contradictions of life. The young hunter did not notice them, for he was assailed by his own bewilderments—this old man whom he loved had killed his own son—but he did gain composure to say: "He fell from the kayak because he turned too fast. Only he could be blamed. I saw it. I told the others."

Again there was silence, during which each knew the other to be engaged in a deliberate lie, but to absolve their mutual guilt, Kyril added: "He was a bad one, Old Father. To kill that girl who had treated us so gently. To kill so many islanders. He deserved to die, and if he hadn't drowned himself the way he did, I would have killed him." He hesitated and the silence grew ominous: "I don't know how, but I would have slain that one, Old Father."

Zhdanko weighed most cautiously what he wanted to say next, because each separate word must convey its exact meaning, and he wasted perhaps half an hour staring at the volcano and speaking of inconsequential things, then in a low voice: "Kyril, it is time again for me to take our pelts to Petropavlovsk. Madame Zhdanko will be waiting there with bales she's been collecting, too, and she'll have a ship to take me to Okhotsk and I'll have to go overland through the bad country to the Lena River." Subtly he changed pronouns: "Then we'll pole the barge toward Irkutsk. Now that's a fine town, believe me. And we'll go on to Mongolia and trade our pelts to the Chinese buyers, but you'll have to be careful with them or they'll steal your back teeth."

He rocked back and forth in the cold sunlight, then asked: "Would you like that?" and the lad cried: "Oh, yes!"

"It could take three years, you know. And with the leaky ship we have we might not even reach Kamchatka, but it'll be worth the try. And when we sail back to Lapak we'll quit this miserable place and move east to Kodiak, which they tell me is rich in fur."

Kyril considered this for a moment, then asked: "But if you want to go to Kodiak, why don't we go now?" and Trofim explained: "Because I must inform Madame Zhdanko that her son is dead. She's a most worthy woman and should hear this only from me."

"Did she know . . . about Innokenti?"

"I think mothers always know."

"Then how could she go on loving him?" and Trofim said: "That's the mystery of mothers."

And this old man of seventy-nine, who should have been long retired, sat dreaming of turbulent seas, and robbers in a storm-swept Siberian pass, and the arm-wrenching torture of poling a barge up the Lena River, and the excitement of haggling with Chinese over the value of an otter pelt, and he was impatient to wrestle once more with the old challenges and test his strength against the new in Kodiak.

For he knew that an explorer should dedicate his life to probing eastward, always eastward toward the sunrise: as a lad from a trivial Ukrainian village north of Lvov he had traveled east to serve Tsar Peter in Moscow, then across Siberia to meet Madame Poznikova, and on to the Aleutians, where he had known those honorable captains—Bering, Cook, Pym—and even to the coastline of America, where he had aided the great Georg Steller. And always there had been the noble challenge of the next day, the next island, the next stormy sea.

"I have no son," Trofim said quietly, "and you have no father. Shall we load our leaky ship and take our furs to Irkutsk?"

V

THE DUEL

I N THAT MEMORABLE YEAR 1789, WHEN FRANCE LAUNCHED THE
revolution which would bring its people freedom from excessive
tyranny, and the former American Colonies ratified their revolution
by initiating a new form of government under a remarkable constitution ensuring freedom, a group of vicious Russian fur traders committed a great atrocity against the Aleuts on Lapak Island.

Two small boats appeared in the harbor, commanded by ruthless
bearded traders who put into ruthless execution a cruel order: "All
males above the age of two, off to the boats." When women came
solemn-faced to the shore to ask: "Why?" they said: "We need them
on Kodiak Island to hunt otter," and when they asked: "For how
long?" they said: "Who knows?" And when the two boats sailed that
same afternoon, husbands and wives felt a panic which warned them:
"We shall never again see each other."

When the lamentations ended, the women faced the hideous necessity of reorganizing their lives in ways never before contemplated.
The islanders lived from the sea, but now there were none who knew
how to hunt seals, or catch big fish, or go after the great whales that
spouted past the island on their way north. Along the beach stood
kayaks and harpoons and long clubs for knocking seals in the head,
but no one remained who was practiced in using them.

The situation was not only perilous but also extremely frustrating, for the Aleutian Islands marked the line where the vast Pacific Ocean collided with the Bering Sea, and enormous upthrusting currents brought ocean edibles constantly to the surface: plankton thrived, so shrimp could grow fat, and when they did, salmon could feed upon them, and when the salmon were plentiful, seals and walruses and whales could feed well. Nature threw an abundance of seafood to the surface at the Aleutians, but only brave and daring men could harvest it, and now there were no men. When storm winds swept out of Asia, they seemed to be crying: "Where are the hunters of Lapak?"

In executing this barbarous policy the Russians had to be aware that they were operating against their own long-term interests, for they needed the Aleuts to do their hunting and fishing for them, but if they removed and ultimately killed off all adult males, the population could not be replenished, for male two-year-olds would not have time to mature to an age at which they could father other children. However, they were spurred to this insane behavior because they still believed that the Aleuts were less than human, and the mechanics of their grisly plan did seem workable, for with men absent, the supply of food would diminish rapidly.

But there was one characteristic of Lapak and the other Aleutian islands which the Russians overlooked: people lived longer here than elsewhere in the world, and it was not too unusual for men or women to reach into their nineties. Reliance on a balanced diet focusing on seafood rather than meat had something to do with it, but so did clean air from the sea, an orderly life, hard work and a sturdy inheritance from ancestors who had crossed from Asia. At any rate, there was on Lapak in 1789 a great-grandmother of ninety-one who had a granddaughter of forty who had a lively daughter of fourteen, and this strong old woman decided not to die easily.

The great-grandmother was called by her family and friends Old One; her granddaughter was Innuwuk. The fourteen-year-old girl bore the lovely name of Cidaq, which meant *young animal that runs free,* and no more appropriate designation could have been awarded her, for to see this child was to see movement and vitality and grace. She was not tall, nor was she plump as some Aleut girls were at her age, but she did have the big round head which indicated an Asian heritage, the intriguing Mongolian fold to her eyes, the elegantly tinctured skin. In the left-hand corner of her lower lip she wore one delicate labret carved from an old walrus tusk, but what made her distinctive was her long, silky black hair, which reached almost to her knees and which she kept cut straight across her forehead, right down to her eyebrows, giving herself the appearance of wearing a helmet, and customarily she scowled from under it.

But often, for she loved the vitality of life, her round face would break into a smile as big as a rising sun: her eyes would squint almost shut, her white teeth would flash, and she would throw her head back to utter sounds of joy. Like most Aleut and Eskimo women, when she spoke she kept her lips close together, so that she seemed to mumble or perpetually whisper, but when she laughed with her head back she was Cidaq, the little deer, the young leaping salmon, the little whale skimming through the seas in the wake of its mother. She, too, was an adorable little animal, and she belonged to the land which sustained her.

Now she was about to starve. With all the richness that the two seas provided when they met, she and her people were about to starve. But one afternoon when Old One, who still moved about with ease, was looking at the pathway between Lapak Island and the volcano, she saw a whale gliding past, not moving rapidly but lazing along, sounding now and then, revealing its enormous length by the occasional flipping of its tail or a sporadic turn on its side. And she thought: One whale like that would feed us for a long time. And she decided to do something about it.

Exploring the beach with the aid of a driftwood cane that she had carved, she chose six of the best two-hatch kayaks and asked the help of Innuwuk and Cidaq in separating them. Then she moved among the women asking who knew how to operate a kayak, but she found none. A few had broken taboos by riding in them and some had even tried to paddle them, but none had studied the intricate principles of using them in hunting otter or seals, and it would have been unthinkable for them to go after a whale with their husbands. But they did know what the ocean was and were not afraid of it.

However, when Old One started to put a team together—six boats with twelve paddlers—she ran into opposition. "What are we doing this for?" one cautious woman asked, and when she snapped: "To kill whales," this woman and others began whimpering: "You know that women cannot go near whales, or touch the kayak that goes after them, or even let our shadow fall across one that is going after whales."

Old One considered these objections for several days and, in consultation with her granddaughter Innuwuk, conceded that if things were normal, the troubled women could consult the shaman, and he would certainly advise them that the spirits would curse the island hideously if women trespassed on the path that whales took past the island, and that to touch a kayak about to be used in a hunt would be to ensure the escape of the whale and even, perhaps, the death of the men pursuing him. The evidence of ten thousand years was against the threatened women of Lapak Island.

But at the close of the third day of this speculation Old One stood firm, with the precept her grandmother had taught her long before the appearance of any Russians: "Can do? Must do!" which meant that if a desirable thing could be done, you were obligated to try. When she proposed this operating principle to Innuwuk, the latter said with obvious apprehension: "But everyone knows that women and whales have never . . ." In disgust the old woman turned to Cidaq, who stood silent for a moment, reflecting on the gravity of what she was about to say. When she spoke she did so with a firmness and a willingness to break old patterns which would characterize the remainder of her life: "If there are no men, we'll have to break their taboos. I'm sure we can capture a whale," and Old One, encouraged by this eager response, said: "After all, men do certain things to catch a whale. It isn't all mystery. We could do the same things." And the two agreed that it was nonsense to believe that spirits would want an island of women to starve to death because there were no men at hand to pursue whales in the traditional way.

Assembling the other women, Old One harangued them, with Innuwuk and Cidaq at her side: "We can't just sit here and starve. Berries we have and shellfish from the lagoons and maybe a salmon or two in the fall. We catch birds, but it's not enough. We need seals and maybe a walrus if one comes along, and we must have a whale." She invited her granddaughter to ventilate her fears, and this Innuwuk did, most ably: "The spirits have always warned women to stay clear of whales. I believe they still want it that way." This brought loud assent from those locked in tradition, but then little Cidaq stepped forward, tossed her long hair from one hip to the other, and said: "If we must do it, we can do it. And the spirits will understand." When the younger women nodded hesitantly, she turned to her mother, held out her hands, and pleaded: "Help us," and with a nudge from Old One, this perplexed woman submerged her fears and joined those who said that taboo or not, they would speed out to sea in the shadow of the volcano and try to catch a whale.

From that moment, life on Lapak changed dramatically. Old One never relinquished her determination to feed her island, and she convinced even some recalcitrants that the spirits would alter the old rules and side with them if they were working to save their lives: "Think how it is when a pregnant woman is giving birth and baby starts out backward. Obviously the spirits intended that baby to die, but Siichak and I . . . we've done it many times . . . we turn the child around and thump on the belly and it comes out right, and the spirits smile, for we have corrected their work for them."

When some still held back, the old woman grew angry and demanded that Siichak, the midwife, come and stand with her, and when this insecure woman did, Old One cried, grabbing her granddaughter's hand: "Siichak! Did I not call you when this one was pregnant with Cidaq here? And did we not reverse the spirits, and bring forth this child properly?" And the midwife had to confess that Cidaq would have been born dead if she and the old woman had not intervened. After that the program to catch a whale went more smoothly.

Old One decided early in the process that she herself was too old to manage a harpoon, and when she looked about for someone who could, she concluded there was only one real candidate strong enough, her own granddaughter: "Girl, can you be trusted to do your best? You have the arms. Have you the will?"

"I'll try," Innuwuk mumbled with no enthusiasm, and Old One thought: She wants to fail. She's afraid of the spirits.

Now the six crews began to practice in the calm space between Lapak and the volcano, with various women recalling bits of the procedure. One knew how to tip the harpoon with flint, another how to make and inflate the sealskin bladders that would float behind the harpoon after it had been stuck in the whale, so that a visible trail would always be available. And still others recalled what their vanished husbands had said about this fight or that. They failed to recover all the knowledge they needed, but they accumulated enough to make a try.

But, as Old One had foreseen, her granddaughter failed miserably in her attempt to master the throwing-stick: "I can't hold the stick and the harpoon at the same time, and when I try, I can't make the harpoon fly the way it should."

"Try again!" the old woman pleaded, but it was no use. Since boy babies were instructed in the use of this intricate weapon from the age of one, it was absurd to think that an unpracticed woman could master it in a few weeks. So in the end the women agreed that when the whale came, they would paddle their canoes so close to it that Innuwuk could reach out and push her harpoon into the huge gray-black body. A sillier strategy had rarely been devised.

In late August a nine-year-old girl who kept watch came shouting: "Whale!" and there in the passageway between the islands swam this monstrous creature, forty tons at least, and the prospect of untrained women going forth in frail canoes to give it battle was so unnerving that one crew member simply ran away. But this left five kayaks, and Old One could remember when her husband and one other craft managed to puncture a whale and harry it to its death.

So the five teams went solemnly to the beach, no one showing eagerness for this battle, and it had been agreed that Cidaq, a strong girl at fourteen, should sit in the rear of Innuwuk's kayak and guide her mother close enough to the whale for the harpoon to be driven home, but when they approached the beast and the women saw how tremendous it was and how pitifully small they were, all lost heart, even Cidaq, and not one craft came within stabbing distance of the whale as it moved sedately past.

"We were like tiny fish," Cidaq confessed later as she spoke with her disappointed great-grandmother. "I wanted to paddle closer but my arms refused." Burying her face in her hands, she shuddered, then looked up from beneath her bangs and said: "You can't imagine how big it was. Or how small we were." And the old woman said: "Yes, I can. And I can also imagine all of us dying here . . . eyes sunken . . . cheeks gone . . . and no one to bury us."

The plan to catch a whale for Lapak was salvaged in a curious way. When the ten women scuttled back home without having come close to the whale, they were so ashamed of themselves that one young woman, who had been married only a short while before the men were taken away, said: "Norutuk would have laughed at me," and in the silence that followed, each woman visualized the manner in which her husband would have teased her: "Imagine a bunch of women going after a whale!" and they longed to hear that teasing. But then the young wife added: "But after he teased me, I think Norutuk would say: 'Now go and do it right.'" And more even than Old One's determination, this voice of reassurance from the absent men they had loved put fire into the hearts of these women, and they resolved to catch their whale.

Heartened by this resolve, Old One resumed with terrible concentration training her teams, and hammered at them that next time they must go right into the face of the whale, no matter how big, and bring it back. And on the fifth day of their training she appeared with a three-hatch kayak, and she told her women: "When the whales come, I ride here with my own paddle, Cidaq rides in back to steer, and Innuwuk sits up here with her harpoon, and we have taken a pledge that we will go into the jaws of that whale if we have to, but we shall lodge our harpoon in that whale." However, even as she spoke, she doubted that Innuwuk would have the courage to do it.

Then came one of those revelations which enable the human race to progress, for as Innuwuk slept she dreamed with horror of the moment when she would be sitting in her kayak, reaching out with her harpoon to stab the great whale, and she woke bathed in sweat and terror, for she knew she could not do that thing. But as she lay in the darkness, trembling, she suddenly had a vision, a kind of synthesis of brain and imagination and kinesthetic control of her muscles, and in a blinding flash she understood how a harpoon-thrower worked. Again and again she drew back her right arm, feeling an imaginary stick and harpoon in place, and as she threw her arm forward she felt all parts of this marvelous machine harmonizing—shoulder, arm, wrist, fingers, stick, harpoon, flinted point—and she leaped from her bed, ran out to the shore, grabbed harpoon and stick, and with great swinging movements of her arm, flung the harpoon far and true. After the sixth proof that she had mastered the mysteries, she ran shouting to the others: "I can do it!"

And in the dawn when they saw with what accuracy she could throw her harpoon, and from what a distance, they knew that next time a whale swam into their sea they would have a strong chance of landing it.

The six crews were ashore when the little girl watching the straits came shouting: "A whale!" and then, as if she realized the terror her information would cause in some, she added: "A little whale!" and the women ran to their kayaks.

They were very small, these women who presumed to attack leviathan, none over five feet one, and with Old One, who had masterminded the assault, at less than four-eleven and ninety-one pounds, one for each year of her adventurous life. Cidaq, watching her climb in with her driftwood paddle, knew that the frail old woman could contribute nothing to the speed, but everything to the courage of the other five crews. As for herself, Cidaq was determined to take her craft right up against the whale: "Mother, be ready! This time we won't fail!" And trailing behind Old One, the other teams went forth to do battle.

The little scout had been correct, for this whale weighed only nineteen tons, a great deal smaller than the first giant, so that when the women saw it coming toward them, many thought: This one, maybe! and they moved ahead with a courage they had not known they had. From the rear of their canoe, Cidaq paddled with undeviating direction, assisted by counsel from Old One in the middle, who kept dipping her paddle from side to side, and both called to Innuwuk perched in the prow: "Steady! You've proved you can do it." And finally, with a slingshot thrust that was exceedingly powerful for an untrained woman, the harpoon was lodged, and from another kayak a safeguard was stabbed home, and the bladders streamed out, and for two days of grandeur and terror and hope the six groups, driven by Old One's indomitable zeal, trailed their stricken whale, and in due course towed it slowly, triumphantly back through the Bering Sea to the salvation of their island.

In 1790, after the women had proved they could survive for an entire year, a small, hull-wrecked ship, the *Tsar Ivan*, put into Lapak to take on fresh water. It had been dispatched from Petropavlovsk by that indestructible entrepreneur Madame Zhdanko, who had crammed into it a horrible collection of dregs from Russia's jails who had heard the sentence popular with judges in those days: "To the gallows or the Aleutians." They had chosen the latter, permanent exile with no hope of reprieve, but with every intention of murdering island officials if they got the chance.

When the *Tsar Ivan* hove to, its crew, not realizing that the island had been abandoned by the Russian government, found the marooned women in a state of perplexity. They hoped that the ship was going to carry them to their husbands, but knowing the Russians, they feared new abuses, and as soon as the sailors spoke, they knew it would be the latter: "No woman gets on this ship!" and there was stolid grief as the women realized that they really had been left here to die.

There was among the criminals a multiple murderer named Yermak Rudenko, thirty-one years old, big, burly, bearded, and a scoundrel almost impossible to discipline. Knowing that he had nothing more to lose, he swaggered about exuding so clearly the threat "Don't touch me!" that officials let him alone. He had been ashore only a short time when shrewd Old One spotted him, and sidling up with Russian words she had acquired, she began speaking to him about this and that, but always mentioning her great-granddaughter Cidaq, and she started this man's thinking along such lines by arranging one day when the other men were loading water that Rudenko and Cidaq were left alone in the old woman's hut, and later that afternoon made her proposal: "Why not take Cidaq with you to Kodiak?"

He was startled by the idea, but as the old woman pointed out: "She speaks Russian. She's a wonderful child. And believe it or not, she's already helped kill her whale." This last claim was so preposterous that Rudenko began asking about the supposed killing of a whale by a girl not much more than fifteen, and the women confirmed that it was true, and to prove it they showed him and the other Russians how the skeleton was being used in imaginative ways.

When Innuwuk learned what her grandmother was proposing, the sale of Cidaq to this rude sailor, she protested bitterly, but the old woman was adamant: "Better she live in hell than never to live at all," and she allowed no counterargument: "I want this child to know life. I don't care what kind of life," and when Rudenko showed interest in what Old One was proposing, she took Cidaq aside: "I dragged you into the world by one foot. I slapped life into your lungs. I have loved you endlessly, more than my own children, for you are a treasure. You are the white bird coming from the north. You are the seal diving to escape. You are the otter defending her young. You are the child of these oceans. You are the hope, the love, the joy." Her voice rose almost to an impassioned chant: "Cidaq, I cannot see you perish on this forlorn island. I cannot see you, who were made for love, go down to lifeless leather like the mummies in the caves up there."

When the terms of sale were agreed upon, with the women of Lapak receiving a few trinkets and some lengths of gaudy fabric, Old One and Innuwuk dressed Cidaq in her best furs, warned her to be on the watch for evil spirits, and led her to the shore where the three-hatch kayak awaited. "We'll take you out to the ship," Old One said as Cidaq carefully stowed the small bundle that contained her meager belongings. However, at the last moment a woman for whom the family had had little respect ran up with a labret handsomely carved and suited for the spot at the corner of the girl's mouth: "I carved it from the bone of the whale you and I caught," and before Cidaq stepped into the rear hatch of the kayak, she removed the gold-colored walrus labret she had been wearing and gave it to the surprised woman, inserting in its place the new white one from her whale.

It was now time for Old One to take her place in the middle, but before she did she created a great stir along the beach, for she had asked another old woman to bring to the departure objects whose unexpected appearance tugged at the heart of every woman in the crowd. Bowing gravely, Old One took from her accomplice three of the famous visored hats of Lapak, those made and worn by the hunters of that island, and handing one to each of the other two members of her family, she donned the third, an elegant affair of gray and blue with plumes of silvery baleen and sea-lion whiskers, and thus attired she directed Cidaq to head for the *Tsar Ivan,* but when the women ashore saw the splendid hats on the waves once more, they cried "Ah me!" and "Woe, woe!" and tears fell like mist for a scene that they would never again see: the men of Lapak going forth in their gala hats.

At the gangway to the ship Old One took Cidaq by the hands, ignoring the leering insults shouted by sailors along the gunwales. "It's not a proper thing we're doing, Girl," she said, gripping Cidaq's fingers tightly. "And the spirits may frown. But it's better than dying alone on this island. In days ahead, Cidaq, never forget. Whatever happens, it's better than what you left."

The *Tsar Ivan* had scarcely left the shadow of the volcano when Old One's pragmatic philosophy was put to the test, for Rudenko, who now owned her, dragged Cidaq below, ripped off her sea-otter garments and began the series of brutal acts which left her dazed and humiliated. What was worse, when he was finished with her, he passed her back and forth among his brutish friends, who abused her in ugly ways, keeping her stowed in the fetid hold of the ship and feeding her only intermittently after forcing her to submit to their indecencies. Since Rudenko acknowledged no responsibility for her well-being, her treatment degenerated so savagely that several times during the fifty-two-day passage to Kodiak she suspected that before the voyage ended, she might be tossed overboard as a nearly lifeless object of no further use.

It was as dark an experience as a young girl could have, for among the seven or eight men who slept with her, there was not one who developed any affection for her or any feeling that he should protect her from the others. They all treated her as inhuman, a thing of scorn. But she knew that on Lapak she had been a child of value, the leader of girls her age and the peer of the boys, and that the awful indignities she was suffering were the price she had to pay to escape from a situation that was even worse. Remembering her great-grandmother's words, she never once considered ending the abuse by throwing herself overboard, even when her tribulations became almost unbearable. Not at all! If this passage to Kodiak was her only chance for survival, she could endure it, but she did take careful note of the men who humiliated her and kicked her when they finished with her, and she vowed that when their boat landed at Kodiak, if it ever did, she would have certain scores to settle, and sometimes there in the darkness a sea-swept smile would take possession of her entire face, and with her tongue she would touch the new labret: If I helped kill that whale, I can handle Rudenko. And she devised so many heartening possibilities for revenge that the creaking of the ship and the hideous behavior of its passengers ceased to distress her.

The journey did end. Contrary to expectations, the rickety *Tsar Ivan* limped in to Kodiak Island, and when its stores had been unloaded to the cheers of the starving Russians stationed there, Cidaq was allowed to gather her pitifully small bundle and step into the barge that would ferry her into the turbulent life of this island colony. But even though she was now free, she could not leave this dreadful ship and its equally dreadful passengers without saying farewell, so when the barge pulled away she looked up to where the men who had misused her were laughing at her from the gunwales, and cried in Russian: "I hope you drown! I hope the great whale drags you to the ocean depths!" And despite her fury she flashed that grim smile which seemed to warn: "Watch out, Masters! We shall surely meet again."

Her first glimpse of Kodiak Island told Cidaq that it was both similar to Lapak and much different. Like her home island it was barren, indented with bays and rimmed by mountains, but there the resemblance ended, for it contained no volcano; but it did offer something she had never seen before. In certain meadows there were alders, low-growing shrublike trees, and the manner in which their leaves and branches moved back and forth puzzled her. In a few protected spots clumps of cottonwoods with peeling white bark collected, and at the far end of the village in which she would be living rose a single majestic spruce whose towering height and dazzling green-blue color amazed her.

"What is that?" she asked a woman hauling fish from a boat.

"A tree."

"And what's a tree?"

"There it is," and Cidaq remained gazing upward at the spruce.

Three Saints Bay was a small collection of rude huts hugging the shore of a bay shaped like an upside-down capital L, but it provided safe anchorage for boats engaged in the fur trade, because it was further protected by a large island a quarter-mile offshore; but it had little hinterland for development, since it was pinched in at the foot of tall mountains.

It was two days before Cidaq, existing as she could from hut to hut, learned the major difference between Lapak and Kodiak: the people of her new home were divided into four distinct groups. There were the Aleuts like herself who had been imported here by the Russians; they were small in size, in numbers and in importance. Then there were the natives who had always inhabited the island, Koniags they were called, big, difficult, quick to anger and outnumbering the Aleuts twenty or more to one. One Aleut who had known Cidaq on Lapak told her: "The Russians brought us in because they couldn't control the Koniags." Next up the ladder came the fur traders, wild and horrible men stationed here for life unless they could contrive some excuse late in their lives to accompany a shipment of furs back to Petropavlovsk. And finally there were the few true Russians, usually sons of privileged families, who served here for a few years before they stole enough to retire to estates near St. Petersburg. They were the elite, and the three other castes behaved as they directed, and occasionally warships put into Three Saints to enforce the discipline they dictated.

What Cidaq lacked the experience to understand at this early date was that her Aleuts were slaves; there was no other word for it, because over them their Russian masters exercised absolute power from which there was no escape, for if an Aleut tried to run away, hostile Koniags might kill him. With no women on hand to share their misery, and no children coming along to replace them, the Aleut men slaving on Kodiak were exactly like the Aleut women in isolation on Lapak: both were condemned to live brief lives, die, and speed the extermination of their race.

The fur traders were not much better off, for they were serfs, tied to the land without chance of betterment or the possibility of ever establishing a proper home back in the Russia from which they were exiled. Their only hope was to catch some native woman, or to steal one from her husband, and with her have children known as Creoles who might in time gain Russian citizenship. But for the most part, they were the property of the company, and until they died were to toil endlessly to enhance the riches of the empire.

These cruel traditions were in no way exceptional, for all Russia was governed in this manner, and the superior officials who reached Kodiak saw nothing wrong in this pattern of endless serfdom, for that was how their family estates had been run in the homeland and that is how they expected things Russian to continue perpetually.

Life on Kodiak was hell, for as Cidaq was discovering, there was insufficient food, no medicine, no needles for sewing and no sealskins to be sewed. To her surprise, she saw that the Russians had adjusted to their surroundings on Kodiak far less intelligently than her Aleuts had done on Lapak. She existed outside official channels by hiding with one impoverished family after another and, close to starvation, watching as the strange life on Kodiak unfolded. She was spying, for example, one morning when Russian officials, supported by a pitiful ragtag of soldiers, rounded up most of the new fur traders who had shared the *Tsar Ivan* with her and forced them at bayonet point into a fleet of small boats which, with much commotion and cursing, was about to set forth on what an Aleut whispered to her was going to be the "world's worst sea trip," the seven hundred and eighty miles to the two remote Seal Islands, later to be known as the Pribilofs, where fur seals abounded in numbers that were unbelievable.

"Will they come back?" she asked, and the man whispered: "They never come back." And then she gasped, for at the rear of the line filing into the boats she spotted three of the men who had abused her, and she was tempted to call out to them in derision, but she did not, for at a short distance behind them, his hands in manacles, came Yermak Rudenko, hair awry as if he had been fighting, clothes torn, eyes flashing fire. He had apparently been warned of what life was going to be like on the Seal Islands, a sentence from which there would be no reprieve, and he was still refusing to comply.

"March tidy!" Cidaq heard the soldiers growl in Russian as they prodded at him, and for just a flashing second she thought: Aren't they glad he's in chains! And she amused herself by wondering what Rudenko would do to these skinny, undernourished men if his hands were unbound. But then she remembered him as the animal he had been and smiled to think that he was about to endure some of the punishment he had visited upon her.

A whistle blew. Rudenko and the other stragglers were shoved aboard, and the file of eleven small boats sailed forth on a voyage that would have been a test for one large, well-built one. Cidaq, watching the boats disappear, found herself alternately hoping that they would sink to give her revenge and praying that they would survive because of the poor Aleuts who were also being taken to lifelong imprisonment on the Seal Islands.

She had no such ambivalence about her own position, for each day she survived caused her to give more thanks that she had escaped the lonely terror of Lapak Island. Kodiak was vital; its people might be caught up in storms of hatred and frustrated vengeance, and its managers might be distraught over the decline in sea otters and the necessity to sail so far for seals, but there was energy in the air and the excitement of building a new world. She loved Kodiak, and even though she lived far more precariously than she ever had on Lapak, she constantly reminded herself that she was living.

And because she was now fifteen, with an intense interest in everything about her, she saw that things were not going well for the Russians, who faced open warfare with the Koniags and rebellion from natives on other islands to the east. Scores of men from Moscow and Kiev who had considered themselves superior in every way to the primitive islanders now died at the hands of those who showed that they had mastered night ambush and daytime surprise attack.

But what saddened Cidaq was the obvious deterioration of the Aleuts, who were being strangled by malnutrition, disease and abuse; their death rate was shocking, and the Russians did not seem to care. On all sides she saw signs that her people faced inexorable extermination.

For a brief while she lived with an Aleut man and a native woman—not married, for there was no Aleut community to arrange or give benediction to marriages—who strove to maintain a decent life. He obeyed the rules of The Company, going out day after day in search of otters, and he hunted with superior skills, conducting himself properly and living on what meager food The Company provided. He complained to no one lest he be sentenced to the Seal Islands, and his woman was equally obedient.

But then disaster of the most arbitrary and cruel dimension struck. The man was taken from his job of otter hunting and sent without warning to exile in the Seal Islands. One of the worst traders from the *Tsar Ivan* raged into the hut one night looking for Cidaq, and not finding her, beat the woman about the head, hauled her off to where four of his companions were roistering, and all abused her through three nights, strangling her at the end of their celebration. After two weeks of hiding alone in the hut, Cidaq was captured by the same five fur traders and raped repeatedly. They might eventually have slain her, too, at the conclusion of their sport had not an extraordinary man arrived quietly in Three Saints with a fiery determination to halt the slow death of his people.

He had appeared mysteriously one morning, a gaunt figure emerging from the forested area to the north as if he were a creature accustomed to woods and high mountains, and had the Russians seen him coming, they would surely have turned him back, for he was too old to be of service to them and too wasted to be of much use to anyone else. He was in his sixties, unkempt, wild-eyed, and brought with him only an outrageous collection of odds and ends at whose utility no Russian could have guessed: a pouch of agatelike stones polished by long residence in some riverbed, another pouch of bones; seven sticks of various lengths; six or seven bits of ivory, half from long-dead mammoths, half from walruses slain in the north; and a fairly large sealskin which covered a squarish bundle that gave him his unusual powers. It contained the well-preserved mummy of a woman who had died thousands of years ago and been buried in a cave on Lapak Island.

Slipping quietly into the northern edge of the village, he headed by instinct for the tall spruce whose spacious roots had been partly exposed by erosion. There he laid aside his precious bundle and started to dig among the roots like an animal burrowing. When he had produced a sizable excavation, he erected around and above it a kind of hut, and when it was finished he took residence inside, installing his bundle in a place of honor. For three days he did nothing, then quietly he began circulating among the Aleuts, informing them with funereal gravity: "I have come to save you!"

He was the shaman Lunasaq, with experience on various islands where he had never accomplished much or attained real stature, for he had preferred living apart, communing with the spirits that govern mankind and the forests, the mountains and the whales, and helping where needed. He had never married, felt uncomfortable with the noises made by children, and did his best to avoid contact with the Russian masters, whose odd behavior bewildered him. He could not, for example, conceive how anyone in power could separate men from women, as the Russians had done in stealing all the men from Lapak Island and leaving the women behind to die. "How," he asked, "can they expect to produce new workers for their boats?" Nor could he comprehend how they could kill all the otters in the sea, when by restraint they could ensure all they required, year after year to the end of time. Above all, he could not understand the crime of older men debauching the very young girls whom they must later marry if either the men or the girls were to survive in any meaningful existence.

In fact, he had seen so many things evil in the conduct of Russians on the various islands they occupied that he knew of no sensible thing to do but come to Kodiak, where The Company headquartered, to see if he could not bring some kind of relief to his people, for it grieved him to think that he must soon be leaving them in the sad conditions under which they now suffered. Like Thomas Aquinas, Muhammad and Saint Augustine, he felt driven to leave his world a little better than it was when he inherited it, and as he settled down amid the roots of the great tree that protected him, he realized that compared to the might of the Russian invaders with their boats and guns, he was almost powerless, except for one asset which he had and they did not. In his sealskin bundle he had the old woman, thirteen thousand years old and more formidable each year she existed. With her help he would save the Aleuts from their oppressors.

Quietly, like the stormless southern wind that sometimes blew in from the restless Pacific, he began to move among the little Aleut men who served so obediently the dictates of the Russians, always reminding them that he brought messages from the spirits: "They're still the ones who rule the world, Russians or no, and you must listen to them, for they will guide you through these ugly days just as they guided your ancestors when storms tormented them." He let it be known that among the tree roots at his hut he had the magical instruments which enabled him to communicate with those ever-present spirits, and he was reassured when men in twos and threes came to consult with him. Always he delivered the same message: "The spirits know you must obey the Russians, no matter what insane orders they give, but they also want you to protect yourselves. Save bits of food for those days when none is issued. Eat some seaweed every day, for strength lies there. Allow the baby seals and baby otters to escape. You'll know how that can be done without the Russians' seeing. And abide by the old rules, for they are best."

He helped when illness struck, placing the sick man on a proper mat and surrounding his head with shells so that the sea could talk with him, enclosing his feet with his sacred stones so that he might remain stable. And on those occasions when faced with problems for which he could find no answers, he produced the mummy, this withered creature whose sunken eyes in her blackened face stared out to give reassurance and counsel: "She says that you will have to go to the Seal Islands, no escaping. But there you will find a trusted friend who will support you through life." He never lied to the men sentenced to the islands, or assured them that they would find wives and have children, for he knew that this was impossible, but he did tell them that friendships of the kind that sustain life were possible, and that men of good sense sought them out, regardless of the terror in which they otherwise lived: "You will find a friend, Anasuk, and a kind of work that only you can do. And the years will pass."

Now when boats set out for the Seal Islands he appeared openly on shore to bid the Aleuts farewell, and during the latter part of the year 1790 the Russian officials became accustomed to this spectral figure, wondering occasionally where he had come from and who exactly he was. They never suspected that he was restoring a tiny shred of decency and integrity to their establishment, for from what they could see of their own people—Russian officials and trader-serfs alike—everything was going pretty much to hell.

In due course the shaman Lunasaq heard of one of the saddest cases of Aleut despair, the girl Cidaq, who was being passed from one criminal to another despite Company rules forbidding this, and one day while her current trader-serf was absent unloading a kayak filled with furs, he presented himself at the hut in which she was temporarily living, and when he saw her bedraggled hair, her wan face and the labret almost slipping from her lip, so emaciated had she become, he grasped her hands and pulled her toward him: "Child! The good spirits have not abandoned you. They have sent me to help you." And he insisted she accompany him immediately, and leave the moral squalor in which she had been living. Defying Company rules and the possibility that her Russian trader might beat him to death to recover his woman, he led her to his hut among the roots, and once they were inside, he uncovered his most precious treasure, the mummy.

Placing Cidaq before the wizened old face, he chanted: "Girl, this old one knew far more terror than you ever have. Volcanoes in the night, floods, the raging of the wind, death, the endless trials that assail us all. And she fought on." He continued in this way for some minutes, not aware that little Cidaq was trying hard not to laugh at him. Finally she put out both hands, one to touch his, the other to touch gently the lips of the mummy.

"Shaman, I don't need her help. Look at this labret. Whalebone. I helped kill this whale. The day will come when I'll kill every one of the Russians who have abused me. I am like you, old man, I am fighting every day."

And then, in the dark hut, the connection of Cidaq and the mummy began, because the long-dead old woman from Lapak spoke to the young girl from her island. Yes, the mummy *spoke*. Through decades of practice Lunasaq had perfected his gift for ventriloquism until he could not only throw his voice a considerable distance but also make it resemble the speech of different characters. He could be a child appealing for help, or an angry spirit admonishing an evildoer, or, especially, the mummy with her vast accumulation of knowledge.

In the first of their many discussions these three spoke of Russian tyrants and sea otters and men sentenced to the Seal Islands, and particularly of the revenge that Cidaq was planning to visit on her oppressors: "I can wait. Four of them, including the worst, are in the Seal Islands already. We'll never see them again. But three remain here in Kodiak."

"What will you do to them?" the mummy asked, and Cidaq replied: "I am willing to risk death, but punish them I will."

"How?" the ancient one wanted to know, and Cidaq said: "I could cut them when they're asleep," but the mummy said: "Cut one, and they cut you. Forever."

"Did you face such problems?" Cidaq asked, and the old one said: "Everyone does."

"Did you get your revenge?"

"Yes. I outlived them. I laughed at their graves. And here I still am. But they? Long gone. Long gone."

The hut was so filled with the sound of the mummy chuckling at her memories of retribution that no one hearing it could be aware of the skill with which Lunasaq used his voice to create the sound of laughter, nor when he had suddenly stopped being the mummy and spoke sternly in his own voice: "I would remind you that Cidaq's problem is not vengeance but the continuation of her people. Her problem is to find a husband, to have babies."

"Seals have babies. Whales have babies. Anybody can have babies."

"Did you?" Cidaq asked, and the ancient one replied: "Four. And it made no difference whatever."

Again Lunasaq broke in: "But you were living secure with your own people," and the mummy said: "No one is ever secure. Two of my children died of starvation." And the shaman asked: "How did they die and you survive?" and the old one explained: "Old people can withstand shocks. They look past them. Young people take them too seriously. They let themselves be killed." She then spoke rather brusquely to the shaman: "You deal with this child too harshly. Let her have her revenge. You'll both be astonished at the form it will take."

"It will come?"

"Yes. Just as the Russians will soon be coming to this hut to thrash us all. But Lunasaq, my helper, has taken care of that, and your big help will come in ways you cannot guess. Three ways, coming from many directions. But right now, hide me."

The mummy was barely secreted when two trader-serfs broke into the hut and began thrashing the shaman so brutally that Cidaq supposed he would die. But immediately the beating started, a group of five Aleuts with clubs rushed into the little hovel, and in the confined space struck the attackers heavily about their heads, and they did such a thorough job that the roughest one stumbled out of the hut with his head smashed and fell dead, while the other man ran screaming, with two Aleuts flailing at him from behind.

Miraculously, the other Aleuts spirited away the corpse and disposed of it in a gully beneath a pile of rocks. The trader who survived his beating tried to incriminate "Some Aleuts who attacked me with clubs," but his reputation and that of the dead man were so wretched that The Company was not unhappy to have the latter off their rolls, and a few days later they shipped the survivor off to a lifetime of duty with the seals. After watching with grim satisfaction as he was taken away, Cidaq returned to the shaman's hut, where, surprisingly, the mummy showed little interest in the incident: "Of no consequence. Those two are no loss and you're no better off. What is important is that the three ways I promised you are about to come to pass. Prepare. Your life is changing. The world is changing."

The shaman now made the mummy speak in a voice which created the illusion that she was retreating from the hut, but Cidaq pleaded with her to stay, and when she did linger, it was the shaman who interrogated her first: "Will the ways be helpful to me, too?"

"What is helpful?" the old one snapped, almost impatiently. "Is Cidaq helped because one oppressor was slain and the other exiled? Only if she does something herself to profit from it."

Through the years the mummy had acquired a personality of her own, and with it she often voiced opinions contrary to the shaman's. It was as if a willful student had broken loose from the tutelage of her teacher, so that occasionally, on significant topics, the shaman and his obstinate mummy actually conducted a debate.

"But will not the new ways be harmful?" the shaman asked, and again she answered with a snappish question: "What is harmful of itself? Unless we allow it to be?"

"Can I use the new ways? To help my people?" Lunasaq asked, and there was no reply, for the old one knew that the answer rested only with the shaman himself. But when Cidaq asked almost the same question, the mummy sighed and remained silent as if in deep recollection, then sighed again. Finally she spoke: "In all the years, and I have savored many thousand, the ones I remember are the ones that brought me challenges—a husband I never appreciated until I saw the way he handled adversity . . . the two sons who refused to learn hunting but who became master builders of kayaks . . . the winter when all lay sick and only one other old woman and I had to catch the fish . . . that awful year when the volcano at Lapak exploded right out of the ocean, covering our island with ash two elbows deep, and my husband and I took survivors four days out to sea so we could breathe . . . and the peaceful nights when I laid plans for a better life."

She stopped, and seemed to aim her voice directly at Cidaq, and then to shift it toward the shaman, the one who had ensured her continued existence through this present span of years: "Three men are coming to Kodiak. They bring the world and all the world's meaning. And you are to receive them, each of you in your own way."

Then, with a much softer voice, she spoke only to Cidaq: "Did it feel good when you saw that Russian slain?"

"No," Cidaq said. "It felt as if it were over. As if something had ended."

"And you didn't gloat?"

"No, it was just over. Something evil was ended, and I had little to do with it."

"You're ready for those who are coming." Then she asked her shaman: "How did you feel when he was slain?" and Lunasaq replied honestly: "For him, I was sorry that he had lived so poor a life. For me, I was glad, for I have so much more work to do here at Kodiak."

"I am glad for you both. You're ready. But nobody has asked me how I feel. The three are coming to me too, with their problems."

"How do you feel?" the shaman asked, for the mummy's well-being fortified his own, and she said: "I told you the good years were those when something brought challenges. It is long overdue for something exciting to happen on this forsaken island." And on that reassuring note she retired to prepare for the next confrontation in her thirteen thousand years.

The first of the three arrivals was a man who was returning illegally. Nobody on Kodiak Island had expected to see him again, and he appeared on a mission which astounded those with whom he came in contact. He was Yermak Rudenko, the huge, hairy trader who had bought Cidaq, and he had escaped from the Seal Islands a man determined to do anything rather than go back. When The Company officials found out that he had stowed away on a boat returning with a shipment of pelts, they arrested him, and he stood in the rude office at the head of the harbor and asked with mock contrition: "Do you know what it's like up there? Before, no one ever lived on the islands but seals. Now a handful of Aleuts, a few Russians. One ship every year. Little to eat. No one to talk to."

"That's why we sent you there," interrupted a young officer who had never known hardship. "You proved incorrigible here, and you'll go back on the next boat, because that's your station now and forever."

Rudenko blanched, and all the fury he had displayed when dominating the *Tsar Ivan* and the traders on Kodiak vanished. To face the awful loneliness of the Pribilofs for the rest of his life was more than he could bear, and he began to plead with the officials who controlled his destiny: "Nothing but rain. Never a tree. In winter, ice binds all things, and when the sun returns, nothing but seals crowding the island. A boy of six could kill the quota in a week. Then nothing."

From his huge body with its large muscles and heavy shoulders the fight seemed to drain and certainly the arrogance seemed to vanish. If the judgment was to be that he must get on a small boat and sail back to that bleak land, he knew that he would jump off en route or kill himself after he landed; to waste the years of his life in such barren futility was more than he could absorb: "Don't send me back!"

The officials were obdurate: "We sent you there because we could do nothing with you here. There's no place for you in Kodiak."

In despair, a man flailing about for any escape, he uttered a plea which, though irrelevant, would engage Kodiak for the remainder of his violent life: "My wife is here! You can't separate a believing Russian and his wife!"

The news astounded his listeners, who turned to one another, asking: "Has anyone seen this man's wife?" and "Why weren't we told of this?" The upshot was that the officer in temporary charge of Company affairs said: "Take him away and let us look into this."

The investigation was put in charge of a junior naval officer, Ensign Fedor Belov, who initiated inquiries while Rudenko was kept in chains, and as a result of tedious interrogations the young officer learned that the prisoner Rudenko had indeed purchased an Aleut girl on the island of Lapak and that although he had treated her poorly, he could be considered in some respects her husband. When Belov informed his superiors of this, they became actively concerned, for as the temporary head pointed out: "We've been ordered by the tsarina to help Russians establish families in these islands, and she said specifically that if native girls converted to Christianity, marriage with them was to be encouraged." And since the tsarina in question was Catherine the Great, Autocrat of Autocrats, whose probing fingers went everywhere, it was advisable that any ukase issued by her be enforced.

So Ensign Belov was sent back to work, and now the subject of his investigation was Rudenko's supposed wife. Did she exist? Was she a Christian? Could the marriage be solemnized by Kodiak's solitary Orthodox priest who was drunk most of the time? He tackled the last problem first, and when he found Father Pëtr, a broken-down clergyman of sixty-seven who had made repeated fruitless appeals for return to Russia, he found the old man ready to comply with any request made by The Company, to which he must look for his meals and lodging: "Yes, yes! Our adored tsarina, whom God preserve, has instructed us, and our revered bishop in Irkutsk, whom God preserve, worthy man . . ." Mention of the bishop's name diverted his thoughts to the seventh appeal he was drafting to that worthy, praying for relief from his arduous duties on Kodiak. Now he lost this thread also, and with a blank stare coming from his heavily bearded white face, he asked humbly: "What is it you want me to do, young man?"

"Do you recall the trader Yermak Rudenko?"

"No."

"Big man, very difficult."

"Yes, yes."

"He bought a girl on Lapak Island. Aleut, of course."

"Sailors will do that."

"He's been on the Seal Islands for almost a year."

"Yes, yes, a bad one."

"Would you marry this Rudenko to his Aleut girl?"

"Of course. The tsarina told us to—yes, she did."

"But only if the girl became a Christian. Would you baptize her?"

"Yes, that's what I was sent here for, to baptize. To bring heathens into the love of Jesus Christ."

"Have you baptized any?"

"A few, they're a stiff-necked lot."

"But you would baptize and marry this one?"

"Yes, that's what the tsarina ordered. I saw the order, sent out by our bishop in Irkutsk."

It was apparent to Ensign Belov that this old fellow knew little of what he was doing or ought to be doing. He'd been in the islands several years, had baptized few, married even fewer, and learned none of the languages. He represented the Russian civilizing effort at its worst, and it was into the wide gap left by his lack of missionary zeal that shamans like Lunasaq had been able to slip.

"I'll forward your request to the bishop at Irkutsk," Belov promised. "And will you prepare to solemnize this marriage?"

"Thank you, thank you for sending the letter."

"I asked about the marriage."

"You know what the tsarina said, may heaven protect Her Royal Highness."

So Ensign Belov reported to the officials that Rudenko did have a wife of sorts and that Father Pëtr was prepared to baptize and marry her, as the tsarina had instructed. When the officials asked if Belov had seen the young woman and did he deem her worthy to become in effect a Russian citizen, he answered: "Not yet, but I believe she's here in Three Saints and I'll pursue the matter diligently."

Making further inquiries, he learned that her name was Cidaq and that she was living, if that word could be so used, in a hut whose former owner had been killed in some way; the details were cloudy. To his surprise, she turned out to be a modest young woman, perhaps fifteen or sixteen, not pregnant, exceptionally clean for an Aleut and possessed of an adequate Russian vocabulary. Realizing that she was terrified by his presence but unaware that this was because she feared being implicated in the murder of the trader, a matter which had been quickly dropped, he strove to put her at ease: "I bring good news, very good news."

She took a deep breath, for she could not imagine what it might be. "A great honor is to be bestowed upon you." He leaned forward when he said this, and she leaned to hear: "Your husband wants to marry you legally. Russian church. Priest. Baptism." He paused, then said with great pomposity: "Full Russian citizenship." Holding his position, he smiled at her, and was relieved to see the huge smile that broke across her face. Grabbing her by the hands and suffused by his own joy, he cried: "Didn't I tell you? Great news!"

"My husband?" she finally asked.

"Yes. Yermak Rudenko. He's come back from the Seal Islands."

And here began the deception which would enable her to gain her revenge on Rudenko, for with the cunning of a knowing little animal, Cidaq masked any physical or verbal response which might betray her repugnance at the thought she might be rejoined to Rudenko, and in the pause she began to contrive a score of ways by which to pay back this horrible man. But realizing that she must know more before she could take the next step, she feigned delight at hearing about him: "Where is my husband? How soon can I see him?"

"Not so fast! He's here in Three Saints." Then the young officer said gravely, as if bringing ultimate dispensation: "And The Company says that if you marry him properly, he can stay here."

"Wonderful!" she cried, but then he added the caveat which would enable her to complicate things: "Of course, you have to convert to Christianity before the church wedding can take place."

Showing mock horror, she asked: "Otherwise they'd send him back?"

"Might even shoot him."

"You mean, he came back without permission?"

"Yes. He was burning to be with you again."

"Christian? Marriage? Is that all that's needed?"

"Yes, and Father Pëtr says he's ready to supervise your conversion and marriage."

Her round face radiant with feigned gratitude, Cidaq smiled at Ensign Belov, thanked him for his heartwarming news, and asked like a young woman deeply in love: "And when can I see Master Yermak?"

"Right now."

Three Saints Bay had no jail, which was not surprising, since it had little else that an organized society required, but there was in Company offices a room with no windows and a double door, both parts of which could be kept locked, and when the bolts were shot, the young officer led Cidaq into the dark room where her supposed husband sat in shackles. "Yermak!" she cried with a joy which pleased but did not surprise the prisoner, for although he realized that he was taking a gamble in relying upon her to achieve his freedom, he was arrogant enough to believe that she would be blinded by this dazzling opportunity to become the lawful wife of a Russian and would forgive him all he had done to her in the past.

"Yermak!" she cried again, like a dutiful wife. Breaking away from Ensign Belov and running to her persecutor, she took his manacled hands, kissed them, and then, pushing her smiling face into his beard, she kissed him again. Belov, witnessing this emotional reunion of a Russian fur trader and the island girl who adored him, sniffled and went off to inform the authorities that the marriage should proceed.

As soon as Cidaq was free of Rudenko and Belov, she hurried to the shaman's hut: "Lunasaq! I must speak with your mummy!" and when the sealskin pouch was opened, Cidaq revealed with laughter the surprising opportunity that had chanced her way: "If I marry him, he stays here, and if I don't, back he goes to his seals."

"Remarkable!" the mummy said. "Have you seen him?"

"Yes. Manacled. Guarded by a soldier with a gun."

"And what did you feel when you saw him?"

"I saw him with my hands about his neck, strangled."

"And what shall you do about this?"

In the time since she first saw Rudenko's hateful face she had perfected her devious strategy: "I'll make everyone believe I'm happy. I'll let them think I'm going to marry him. I'll talk with him about our life here in Three Saints . . ."

"And you'll relish every minute?" the ancient one asked.

"Yes, and at the last moment I'll say 'No' and watch as he's dragged back to his forever prison among the seals."

The mummy, who had been a practical woman in life, which explained her long persistence thereafter, asked, "But what reason will you give . . . for changing your mind?"

In response, Cidaq uttered words which would create the most intricate complications: "I'll say I'm unable to surrender my old religion and become a Christian."

At this frivolous statement Lunasaq gasped, for now religion, the essence of his life, was involved, and he foresaw the danger in playing such a game. The withered mummy was left to one side in her sealskin pouch, and Lunasaq, the endangered shaman, took sole control: "Did you say you were thinking of turning Christian?"

"No, they said it. I'd have to join their church before I could marry Rudenko."

"Surely, you'd not think of that?"

Continuing to play games, she said half humorously: "Well, if he were a decent Russian . . . like young Belov, for instance . . ."

Gravely the shaman placed Cidaq on a stool and took a position facing her; then, as if he were summarizing his entire life, he began speaking: "Young woman, have you not seen the Russian Christianity? Has it done anything for our people? Has it brought us the happiness they promised? Or the warm house? Or the food? Do they love us as their Book says they should? Do they respect us? Or allow us entrance to their places? Have they given us any new freedoms, or preserved the ones we built for ourselves? Is there anything . . . any one thing you can think of . . . any good thing their god has given us? And is there any good thing which we already had which they have not taken away?"

From her sack the mummy groaned at this accurate summation

of Christian rule under the Russians, and fortified by this encouragement the shaman continued, his unkempt locks shaking whenever he
made a persuasive point: "Did we not in the old days on our islands
know happiness with our spirits? Did they not keep food swimming
past our islands, protect us in our kayaks, bring our babies safely to
birth, bring back the sun each spring, ensure a harmony in our life,
and enable us to maintain good villages where children played in the
sun and old men died in peace?"

He became so agitated by this vision of the lost Aleutian paradise
that his voice rose to a plaintive wail: "Cidaq! Cidaq! You've survived
great tribulation. The spirits have saved you for some noble mission.
Do not at this time of crisis even think of embracing their ignoble
ways. Cidaq, stay with your people. Help them to regain their dignity.
Help them to pick their way honestly through these testing times.
Help me to help our people."

He was trembling when he finished, for his spirits, those forces
which animated the winds and activated the sun, had vouchsafed him
a glimpse of the future, and he saw the rapid and painful demise of
his people if they abandoned the old ways. He saw the drunkenness
increasing until men lay senseless; he saw strange illnesses slaying his
dark Aleuts but never the white Russians; he saw vibrant young
women like Cidaq debauched and discarded; but most of all, he saw
the remorseless decline and eventual disappearance of all that had
made life on Attu and Kiska and Lapak and Unalaska resplendent,
saw it all dragged in the dust until even the spirits who had supervised that life would be gone.

A universe, an entire universe which had known its episodes of
grandeur, as when two men alone on the vast sea, protected only by
a sealskin kayak with sides that even a determined fish could puncture, went up against leviathan—they two hundred and fifty pounds
in all, he forty tons—to fight him to the death. This universe and all
it comprised was in danger of being extinguished, and he felt that he
alone was responsible for its salvation. "Cidaq," he whispered, pleading and anguish almost stifling his voice, "do not scorn the tested old
ways which have protected you in favor of bad new ones which promise a good life and deliver only death."

His words had a powerful effect on Cidaq, and she sat in a kind
of trance as he produced from his bundles those revered symbols
which had guided her life so far: the bones, the pieces of wood, the
polished pebbles, the ivory harvested so painfully from the sea. Dis-

tributing them about her in the designs to which she was accustomed, he began chanting, using words and phrases which she did not understand but which were so potent that into the room came the spirits that governed life, and they spoke to her as in the days of her childhood: "Cidaq, do not desert us! Cidaq, the others promise a good life but never produce it, not for our people. Cidaq, cling to the ways that enabled your great-grandmother to live so long and so bravely. Cidaq, do not transfer your allegiance to strange new gods that have only boasting and no power. Cidaq! Cidaq!" Her name reverberated from all corners of the hut until she feared she might faint, but then from the mummy sack came comforting words: "First things first, Cidaq. Smile at Rudenko. Give him reason to hope. Then send him back to exile with the seals. After that we must grapple with the things that perplex our shaman, for they perplex me, too."

The round-faced girl with the sunburst smile shook her head vigorously from side to side as if to clear it for the tasks ahead, then promised her shaman: "I'll not allow them to make me a Christian, not a real Christian, that is," and she left the hut, smiling once more and trying to imagine how Rudenko was going to look at the last moment when she refused to marry him and he realized that she had tricked him into going back to the seals.

The mummy had predicted that three men would arrive at Kodiak with disturbing or hopeful messages, and Rudenko had been the first, with news that was all bad; but now a second was approaching, with creative ideas, and he came not a moment too soon.

By 1790, Russian colonization of her American territories had stumbled to the lowest level achieved by any European nation in bringing its civilization to newly discovered lands. Spain, Portugal, France and England all performed better, and it would not be until Belgium behaved so atrociously along the Congo that any nation would come close to the malperformance of Russians in the Aleutians. They destroyed the reasonable systems by which the islanders had governed themselves. They depleted food supplies, so that people starved. They nearly exterminated the sea otter, so that a wealth which might have expanded forever almost vanished. And worst of all, they crushed old beliefs without substituting viable replacements. Drunken old priests like Father Pëtr at Three Saints converted less than ten Aleuts to Christianity in nineteen years, and even to these willing souls they brought no spiritual reassurance or worldly improvements. Conditions were so bad that an impartial observer would have been justified in concluding: "Everything the Russians have touched, they've debased." But now reform was coming, from Irkutsk.

During that winter of 1726 when Vitus Bering and his aide Trofim Zhdanko were snowbound on their way to Kamchatka, they made a voluntary detour to the regional capital at Irkutsk, not far from the Mongolian border, and there they consulted with the voivode, Grigory Voronov, whose able and forceful daughter Marina impressed them so favorably. This Marina married the Siberian fur trader Ivan Poznikov and later, after he was slain by brigands on the way to Yakutsk, the cossack Zhdanko. She had said, during her introduction to Zhdanko: "All good things in Siberia come from Irkutsk," and this was still true.

During the intervening years the town had blossomed, becoming not only the administrative and commercial focus of eastern Russia but also the center from which radiated those imaginative ideas which enrich society, and no agency was more energetic than the Orthodox Church, whose local bishop was determined to inject religious vigor into Kodiak, the most eastern and backward of his administrative areas.

When Bering and Zhdanko met Marina Voronova they were not aware that she had a younger brother named Ignaci, who had remained behind in Moscow when his father moved east to assume his governorship. This Ignaci had a son Luka, who in 1766 had a son Vasili, who, from his earliest days, showed an inclination toward holy orders. As quickly as possible after finishing his preliminary studies, this Vasili sought entrance to the seminary in Irkutsk and in 1790, at the age of twenty-four, he qualified himself for ordination. But now a vigorous debate occupied the Voronov family and Great-Aunt Marina Zhdanko from Petropavlovsk, eighty-one years old, had come all the way to Irkutsk to make her strong opinions known, which she did to the irritation of many.

The problem confronting the family was a curious one. In the Russian Orthodox Church, priests at the time of ordination were required to make a difficult choice, one which determined the future course and limits of their lives. A young man, his heart aflame with zeal, could elect to become either a black priest or a white, and this designation included priestly costumes proclaiming the decision. A white priest was one who elected to serve the public as head of some local church or as a missionary or as a lowly assistant in God's work. Significantly, he was not only allowed to marry but encouraged to do so, and when he did establish his family in the community he became inextricably affiliated with it. A white priest was a man of the people, and much of the good work of the church stemmed from his and his family's efforts. Luka Voronov, Vasili's father, had been a white priest serving the Irkutsk countryside, which meant that his son, growing up in this tradition, had been indoctrinated as to its merits.

But other young priests, fired with either ecclesiastic ambition or an honest desire to see their church well administered, chose to become black priests, knowing that this would prevent them from ever marrying but knowing also that to their care would be handed the governance of their church. Any boy aspiring to become a metropolitan in Russia or even in a major province like Irkutsk, must choose the black, take a vow of chastity, and adhere to these decisions through life, or he would find himself rigorously excluded from any significant position in the hierarchy. It was an ironclad rule, one admitting no exceptions: "Church leaders come only from the black."

Young Vasili was strongly inclined to follow in his father's footsteps, for no priest in the Irkutsk area was more highly regarded than Luka Voronov, not even the bishop himself, who was, of course, a black. And with considerable encouragement from his father, Vasili would have followed his father's example had not Great-Aunt Marina voiced firm opinions to the contrary: "Child! It would be horrible to cut yourself off from eventual leadership of our church. Don't even think of electing the white. You were destined from birth to be a leader, maybe even the supreme leader."

Her nephew Luka, the young priest's father, reacted rather vigorously to this advice, which he felt visionary: "My dear Aunt Marina, you know and Vasili knows that leadership in our church does not seek out priests from Siberia."

"Now wait! Just wait! Because you forsook the high moral road, Luka, and turned your back on preferment, which I never understood, there's no reason why your gifted son should do the same. Look at him! Has he not been ordained by God Himself to be a man of leadership?"

When the family turned to stare at Vasili, dignified in his seminary robes, blond, tall, straight, handsome in appearance and reverent in manner, they saw in him a young man eligible for distinguished service in their church. He was, as his great-aunt properly observed, a man destined for greatness. But his father saw something else nobler than the possibility of preferment: he saw a young man born to serve, perhaps in the humblest position the church provided, perhaps as a metropolitan, but serving always the noble responsibilities of his religion, as he, Luka, had striven to serve. The young seminarian had that touch of grace which ennobles men, regardless of where chance assigns them; he had a calling, a demand from outside as sharp as a sergeant's insolent cry on a cold morning. He was called to do the Lord's work and was eager to do it wherever assigned.

So he was about to announce his preference for the white when Great-Aunt Marina astounded her family: "Knowing the importance of this meeting, I took it upon myself to consult with the bishop, and I asked him to be waiting outside just about now, to give us guidance. Luka, see if his carriage has arrived." And shortly the bishop himself appeared, bowing to the great lady whose ample funds had so often enabled him to complete work the church had started, especially in the islands.

"Madame Zhdanko, as I told you the other day, you grace Irkutsk," and she said without embarrassment: "As did my father before me." Then, belatedly: "And as Luka has, in his own way."

She did not propose to waste the bishop's time in persiflage: "Vasili thinks that if he is to serve the Lord, he must elect the white."

"At his age I chose the black."

"And were you able to perform the Lord's work just as capably?"

"Maintaining a healthy church is perhaps the Lord's most urgent desire."

Marina did not gloat, but she did want more than platitudes: "Bishop, tell me truthfully, if this young man takes the black, would you consider him for a post in the Aleutians?"

Members of the family gasped at the impertinence of this inquiry into church politics, but the old woman knew she had few years remaining, and in the islands which her late husband had loved, there was work left uncompleted. The bishop was not surprised at the old lady's frontal approach, for her past beneficences entitled her to some meddling, especially since a member of her own family was concerned. Asking for more tea, he balanced his cup, munched on a sweet, and said: "Madame Zhdanko, I am, as you well know, profoundly worried about the posture of our church in the islands. The tsarina has placed on my shoulders responsibility for seeing that the

Holy Word is disseminated there and that the savages are brought
into the family of Christ."

Staring at each family member in turn, he sipped from his cup,
put it down, and said with what amounted almost to sorrow: "And I
have failed. I've sent one priest after another out there, good men in
their time, but old men, too, who have banked the fires of ambition
and zeal. They waste their lives and the church's funds. They drink,
argue with Company officers, ignore their true charges, the islanders,
and bring no souls to Jesus Christ."

"You make my summary for me," the fighting old woman cried
with that intensity which had never diminished since it was ignited
while she was a girl here in Irkutsk. "We need real men in the islands.
That is, if we're to build a civilization there. I mean, if we're to hold
that new empire and not surrender it like cravens to the English or
the Spanish, let alone those damned Americans whose ships are beginning to sneak into what ought to be our waters." She was obviously prepared to sail to the islands right now, as either governor,
admiral, general or head of the local church.

"I've considered the suggestion you made the other day, Madame
Zhdanko, and yes, if this fine young man elects the black, he will do
so with my blessing. He has a great future in this church. And he can
start at no better place than the Aleutians, where he can launch a
whole new civilization. Do well there, young man, and your opportunity for serving the church is unlimited." Then, with a bow to Marina,
he added a practical note: "What I need to head the church in Kodiak
is not some young fellow who will marry a local girl and subside into
gentle drunkenness like his predecessors, but someone who will
marry the church and build a strong new edifice."

Encouraged by such words, Vasili Voronov, the most promising
young man ever to have graduated from the Irkutsk seminary, chose
the black, took vows of celibacy, and committed himself to the service of the Lord and the resurrection of His disreputable Orthodox
Church in the Aleutians.

Marina Zhdanko, although over eighty, possessed such demonic energy that when she finished instructing her grandnephew Vasili as to
how he was to conduct his religious life, she turned with great vigor
to the straightening out of her own affairs. Since she was already in
Irkutsk, where The Company of which she was a leading member

kept its headquarters, she felt she ought to initiate certain changes in management, and the male members of the board were surprised when she stalked into their office with the firm announcement: "I want to send a real manager to organize our Aleutian holdings."

"We have a manager," the men assured her, but she snapped: "I want a man who will work, not whine," and when they asked: "Have you someone in mind?" she replied enthusiastically: "I certainly have."

There was at this time in Irkutsk an unusual businessman, one Aleksandr Baranov, in his early forties and the veteran of rugged Siberian mercantile wars. Marina had seen him occasionally, picking his way about the streets, head bowed as if contemplating some master move, and she had been intrigued by the stories men told about him: "He's low-born, no family background at all. Has a wife that no one ever sees, because when he first came to Siberia she promised: 'I'll join you soon,' but she never did. He's served everywhere, honest as the sunrise but always wiped out by some disaster not of his making."

"But he is honest?" she asked, and everyone agreed: "None more so."

"What's this I've heard about a glass factory?" she asked, and a most improbable story unfolded: "I was with him when it happened. We were drinking beer when a maid, a real peasant, dropped a beer stein and broke it. Now, glass, as you well know, costs money in a frontier like Irkutsk, so the barman began to knock the poor girl about for having broken such a costly item. Pavel and me, we berated the man for his brutality, but Baranov sat there with fragments in his hands, and after a while he said: 'We ought to make our glass here in Irkutsk. Not haul it all the way from Moscow.' And do you know what he did?"

"I can't imagine," Marina said, and another man explained: "He wrote to Germany for a book on glassmaking, then learned German from a merchant so he could decipher his book, and with no practical experience, never saw one piece of glass blown, he opened a glass factory."

"Did it fail, like his other dreams?"

"Not at all! He made fine glass. You drank from his work at dinner."

"What happened?"

"Imports from big factories farther west began to stream in, much cheaper prices." When Marina asked if this competition drove Baranov out of business, the men vied with one another to answer her question: "Not Baranov! He looked at the imported glass and said: 'This is better than I make,' and he closed down his shop to serve as agent for the other people."

"I'd like to meet a man with such good sense," Marina said, and when Baranov was brought before her, she saw a short, unkempt, pudgy man, bald as an iceberg, hands clasped over his belly as if preparing to bow before some approaching superior, but with sharp, dancing eyes that betrayed his eagerness to explore any proposition that might be laid before him.

"Do you know the fur trade?" she asked, and for half an hour he described recent developments in the Aleutians, Irkutsk and China, with a recommendation as to how Aleutian furs could with improved routing be speeded to St. Petersburg.

Her next question—"Are you earning much as a salesman in the glass business?"—provided him with an opportunity for an oration on how the Aleutians could be developed by someone with imagination and a little assured capital.

Before the hour ended she was satisfied that he was the man to represent both Russia and The Company in the Aleutians: "Hold yourself in readiness, Mr. Baranov, while I do some investigating," and when he was gone she returned to her directors with a succinct recommendation: "The man we need in the islands is Aleksandr Baranov." When the men protested that he had failed in everything, she reminded them: "But you all said he was honest. I'm saying he has imagination . . . and force of character . . . and common sense."

"Then why has he failed?" they asked, and she said: "Because he did not have an old hand like me setting policy and bright young men like you providing him with funds."

No better summary of Russia's needs in her American adventure than this had so far been voiced, either in Irkutsk or St. Petersburg, and the directors recognized it, but one cautious man protested: "Baranov may be too old."

"I'm twice as old," Marina snorted, "and I'd sail out to Kodiak tomorrow if I had to."

"You might as well bring him in," the men said grudgingly, and after a few minutes of Marina's expert questioning, Baranov revealed himself as a man who had a clear view of future possibilities, and she complimented him on his astuteness: "Thank you, Mr. Baranov. You seem to have three attributes we seek. A surplus of energy, boundless enthusiasm and a vision of what Russia might accomplish in her islands."

"I hope so," he said modestly, bowing slightly.

The directors, aware that Marina was rushing them into decisions they might not wish to make, were so resentful of her intrusion that they started to demonstrate the flaws in her nominee: "Mr. Baranov, we're sure you understand that The Company has two obligations. It must make money for us directors here in Irkutsk. And it must represent the wishes of the tsarina in St. Petersburg." When Baranov nodded enthusiastically, one of the directors pointed out acidly: "But you've never turned a steady profit on anything you've attempted." Without embarrassment, the chubby merchant smiled and said: "Always I've made a good start, then run out of money. This time I'd have the same good ideas and your job would be to see that I had the funds."

"But could you keep the tsarina happy?" they asked, and with a tradesman's simplicity he answered: "Make money and you keep everybody happy."

"Well said!" Marina cried. "That could be the motto of our company." But now the directors raised an even more subtle objection: "If you did become, as Madame Zhdanko seems to be recommending, our representative in the Aleutians, you would be Aleksandr Baranov merchant, and for protection you would be forced to rely upon some naval officer of noble lineage." No one spoke, and then, from an older man: "And as you know, there can be on the face of this earth nothing more contemptuous than a Russian naval officer looking down his nose at a merchant."

Another director agreed, then all leaned forward as he asked: "Mr. Baranov, do you think you could handle a naval officer?"

With the simple grace that characterized this unusual man, he replied: "I've never been vain. I've always been eager to concede the other man any rights to which he considers himself entitled. But I've never been diverted from the task which requires to be done." Looking from one man to the other, he added: "I am only a merchant, and nobility is far beyond my reach. But I have something the noble officers will never have."

"And what is that?"

In the quiet of this office in Irkutsk, Baranov the indefatigable dreamer gave his answer: "I know that Imperial Russia must use the

Aleutian Islands as stepping stones to a great Russian occupation of North America. I know that the supply of sea-otter pelts is already dwindling and that other sources of wealth must be found."

"Such as what?" one of the directors asked, and without a moment's hesitation this amusing little fellow with the trigger-quick brain revealed his compulsive vision: "Trade."

"With whom?" someone asked, and he replied: "With everyone. With the Hudson's Bay Company at Nootka Sound, with the Spaniards in California, with Hawaii. And across the ocean to Japan and China. And with the American ships that begin to invade our waters."

"You seem hungry to embrace the entire Pacific," a director said, and he replied: "Not me, Russia. I see a constant movement of our empire to all corners."

His vision was so grand, so all-encompassing that on the morrow the directors, frightened by its implications, brought in an officer who represented the tsarina and the more responsible elements in her government: "Mr. Baranov, these men tell me that you have soaring visions."

"The future of Russia demands them."

"But have you any comprehension of Russian policy? No? Well, let me explain, and I shall use no shadowy meanings or oblique references. Our policy is to defend ourselves at all costs from dangers in Europe. That means we must do nothing to alert or offend anyone in the Pacific. If you become our man in the Aleutians, you must not offend Britain in North America, or Spain in California, or the United States or Japan or China or even Hawaii. Because the fate of Russia will not be determined in these waters. It will be determined only in Europe. Do you understand?"

What Baranov understood was that the temporary concerns of Russia might be in Europe but that her long-term interests lay in the Pacific, and a powerful foothold in North America would, in the future, be of the greatest significance. But he also knew that as a mere merchant, he had no power base or standing from which to put his grand designs into operations, so he dissembled: "I understand my orders. If I'm sent, I'm to tend the islands and touch nothing else."

Now he was to receive his first lesson in imperial diplomacy, for the officer looked about the room, lowered his voice, and said quietly: "Now wait, Mr. Baranov. No one said that, not at all. If you're sent to Kodiak, you're to probe outward in all directions. A fort here if the natives will allow it. Trade with Hawaii if practical. Exploration deep into California when the Spaniards aren't looking. And above all, secure us a foothold on North America."

In the silence that followed, Baranov did not say triumphantly: "That's what I was saying." Instead, he nodded to the official, then to each of the directors, and said: "Excellency, you're a wise man, a prudent man. You show me horizons I had not seen before," and the tsarina's officer smiled bleakly, like a winter sun in northern Siberia.

Few imaginative men in history were given diplomatic assignments more precisely tailored to fit their peculiar talents than this one handed to Aleksandr Baranov. As a lowly merchant with no social standing, he was to compete on equal terms with haughty naval officers from the nobility. In a dying fur market he was to earn a profit. In an ocean where he must not make any overt moves he was to extend Russian power in all directions. And burdened with a wife who was never with him, he was to civilize and educate the wild islands of the northern seas. Nodding to those who were about to send him on this impossible mission, he said with quiet dignity: "I'll do my best."

Next day he learned that he would have help, for at a luncheon arranged by Madame Zhdanko he met with the Bishop of Irkutsk, who said ominously: "The tsarina is aware that the international reputation of Russia depends upon how successful we are in establishing a Christian church among the natives, and, frankly, we've not accomplished much. If the tsarina ever learns how remiss we've been, control of Russian America will be ripped away from The Company and you'll never see a pelt again." He glared at Baranov as if he were responsible for past error, and thundered: "We expect you to mend these matters."

"I can't do it alone," this practical man replied. "And certainly can't do it with the kind of priests you've been sending to eastern Siberia."

The bishop surrendered to these blunt truths: "To correct my church's past deficiencies I shall be sending with you a priest of true devotion and unlimited promise, Madame Zhdanko's nephew, young fellow named Vasili Voronov." At this, Marina rang a bell, and a servant brought into the room the young man who had already garbed himself in the black robes of a priest whose life was to be dedicated to the welfare of his church, and for the first time these two conspirators, the aspiring young cleric determined to save souls in the islands and the energetic businessman afire with a desire to enlarge Russia's power, met. Neither man, at that moment, appreciated how important in his life the other was to be, but each knew that a partnership had been established whose purpose was to Christianize, civilize, explore, make money, and extend the might of Russia deep into North America.

Father Vasili Voronov, who left Irkutsk months before Baranov could arrange his affairs, had not been in Kodiak a full day in 1791 before he identified the man with whom he would wrestle for the spiritual leadership of Russian America. He was walking about, exploring his parish, when he saw coming toward him a tall, gangling Aleut man of untidy appearance and haunted eye who appeared to be roaming aimlessly, with no apparent affiliation with The Company, and from his disheveled looks, with not even a home. He was the kind of person Vasili would normally meet only when visiting him in some pastoral capacity, like the distribution of alms or the extension of sympathy over a death, but this old man had such a penetrating gaze, and was obviously so interested in the new priest, that Vasili felt compelled to know more about him.

Nodding austerely, a gesture that was not returned, he hurried back to Company officials and asked: "Could that strange-looking Aleut be a shaman?" and the Russian said: "We think so," but Vasili uncovered no substantial proof until he queried Ensign Belov: "Yes, he's a known shaman. Lives in a dugout among the roots of the big spruce."

Satisfied that he was on the track of the devil, Vasili asked to see the acting manager, who listened respectfully as the young priest warned about "the presence of Anti-Christ in our midst," and agreed that Voronov should "keep a sharp eye on that one." But the priest's attention was soon directed to his major task, for a Company official informed him: "You arrive at a propitious moment. A young Aleut wants to join the church, so you have your first conversion waiting."

"I'll see him at once," Vasili said, and the official made a correction: "It's a girl," and when the young priest inquired into the matter, he discovered that this was a conversion with strings attached, for when he met with Cidaq to discuss what conversion meant, he found her strangely ambivalent. Obviously she was interested in becoming a Christian, for this would mean that she could enter the favored world of the Russians, but she lacked the emotional intensity of a real convert, and this dualism was disturbing. And even after three long discussions, with her looking soulfully into his eyes as if in search of enlightenment, he failed to discover that she was playing games with him, and had he learned that she was interested in Christianity only as a weapon with which to castigate her would-be husband, he would have been outraged.

But fortified by his innocence, Father Vasili forged ahead with his instruction, and the beauties of Christianity were so real to him that Cidaq, despite her original scorn, began to listen. She was especially impressed with his stories of how Jesus had loved little children, for this had been one of the attributes of her Aleuts which she sorely missed, and twice when the priest elaborated on this she found tears coming into her eyes, a fact which Vasili noted.

Unaware that in fencing theologically with Father Vasili, she was confronting a far more dangerous adversary than either Ensign Belov or old Father Pëtr, she found herself increasingly seduced by the Christian testimony on redemption, for this was completely alien to the teachings of the shaman and the mummy; for them there was good and evil, reward and punishment, and no vagueness in the dichotomies, and to learn that there was another view of life in which a human being could sin, repent, and gain redemption, with the sin being totally erased, was new and perplexing. After asking a few preliminary questions which revealed her honest interest, and which provided Vasili with an opportunity for an enthusiastic elaboration of this cardinal principle, she unwittingly asked the question that would entangle her in the real and very beautiful mysteries of Christianity: "Do you mean that a man who has done really awful things can be redeemed?"

"Yes!" he replied with great excitement. "It's exactly that man that Jesus came here to save."

"Did he come to the Aleutians too?"

"He came everywhere. He came especially to save you."

"But this man . . ." She hesitated, dropped her question, and sat for some moments staring out the window toward the spruce tree. Then she said in a low voice: "He is a real man, this one. He did terrible things to me, and now he wants to marry me."

Vasili jumped back as if he had been struck, for he had supposed that Cidaq was thirteen or fourteen, and in the society he had known at Irkutsk, girls that age did not marry. "How old are you?" he asked in a state of shock, and when she said "Sixteen," he stared at her as if seeing her for the first time.

But her last statement had contained so many surprising revelations that he had to sort them out. "You're sixteen?" Yes. "And a man wants to marry you?" Yes. "And he's been a terrible man?" Yes. "What did he do to people?"

In a low, controlled voice she said: "He did them to me," and Vasili gasped, for up to this moment he had seen her as a child of some maturity who was perplexed by the arrival in her primitive community of the advanced concepts of Christianity; to discover that she was of marriageable age and bewildered by problems relating to that was confusing. Had he known that she was grappling in her own unsophisticated way with the most profound moral and philosophical problems—nothing less than the nature of good and evil—he would have been astounded.

Keeping the discussion on the only level he comprehended, he asked: "What could he have done to you?" and his continuing innocence made him so attractive to Cidaq, that in her sympathy for him she realized that she was already much older and better informed than he.

"He was ugly" was all she thought him capable of understanding at this time, but Vasili pressed on, unaware that he was about to detonate a bomb that would shatter him far more gravely than it would her: "In what way did he harm you? Did he steal? Did he lie?"

A half-smile sneaked across her face as she stared into the eyes of this earnest young man who was trying to bring her into his religion, and she recognized his goodness of spirit and his desire to help, but she felt it was time he understood aspects of life that apparently he did not know. In quiet, unemotional words she told him of the depopulation of Lapak and the intended death of the women remaining there, and by the daze that came over his face she saw that he could not believe his people capable of such brutality, and for a while she lost him as he contemplated Russia.

But when she resumed her narrative she brought him back with a force that sickened: "So I was sold to this man on the *Tsar Ivan,* and he kept me in the hold of the ship, without much food, and when he was through with me he passed me along to his friends and there was no day or night." Now Vasili closed his eyes and tried to close his ears, but she continued with her account of her life in Kodiak: "So this evil man was shipped off to the Seal Islands and I was free of him, but others like him caught me here in Three Saints, and I might have been killed, but the shaman brought help and we killed the worst of the men who abused me."

Once more the details cascaded so rapidly that Vasili could not absorb them: "What do you mean by *abused*?" and she replied: "Everything."

"When you say killed, you don't mean you *murdered* someone!"

"Not exactly." He sighed, then gasped anew when she added: "The shaman fetched five Aleuts with clubs and they beat the man to death and we hid his body under rocks."

He leaned back, clasped his hands, and stared at this child, and when the physical horror at her account had passed, the psychological shock remained: "Twice you said that you went to the shaman. You mean that strange old man who lives among the tree roots?"

"He's the keeper of our spirits," Cidaq said. "He and the spirits saved my life."

This was too much: "Cidaq, his spirits do not control the world. The Lord God does, and until you and your people acknowledge this, you cannot be saved."

"But Lunasaq saved me, and he was able to do it only because the mummy warned us that the men were coming to kill us."

"The mummy?"

"Yes. She lives in a sealskin sack and is very old. Thousands of years, she said."

"Said?" he asked incredulously, and she replied: "Yes, she talks to us about many things."

"Who are *us*?"

"Lunasaq and me."

"It's a deception, child. Don't you know that wizards can throw their voices? Make anything talk, even old mummies? The Lord has brought me here to end the reign of wizards and shamans, to bring you into the salvation of Jesus Christ." He stopped, resumed his position near her, and stared once more into her dark eyes: "They tell me you wish to join His regiments." The metaphor missed her, and she asked: "What?" and he translated: "They said you wanted to become a Christian."

"I do."

"Why?"

"Because they said I couldn't marry Rudenko, that's the evil man I told you about, unless I did."

Again the statements were incomprehensible, but patient questioning elicited the truth: "You're converting only to get married?" Yes. "Why would you marry a man who had treated you this way?" and because she was an honest young woman, devoid of duplicity when she was not playing games, she told him: "I discussed this with the shaman and the ancient one, and they approved when I told them that I would fool you Russians and make believe that I was becoming a Christian so that I could marry Rudenko."

Vasili was completely lost, unable to believe that she could have devised such a strategy, and confused as to why: "But what did you hope to gain by such trickery?"

Again she had to be honest: "When that evil man's heart was joyed with the thought of escaping the Seal Islands, I wanted to look at him and all the Russians and say in a loud voice: 'It was all a sham. I did it to torment you. I will never marry you. Now back to the seals . . . for the rest of your life.'"

In that ugly moment of complete revelation, Vasili no longer saw her as a delightful, innocent child of thirteen. He heard her low voice as a wanton cry from some ancient past when horrible spirits roamed the earth and devastated souls. He was shattered to learn that such hardness of heart could exist in a young girl like Cidaq, and he felt his own secure world trembling.

Of the horrors she had endured in the hold of the *Tsar Ivan* he had no conception, and the slaying which had rescued her from a continuation ashore he was able to dismiss as one of those fractures of the peace to be expected among sailors, but her proposed use of Christianity to exact revenge was abhorrent, and the discovery that her shaman had encouraged her in this perversion strengthened his resolve to eliminate shamanism from Kodiak. From here on, it would be a battle to the death.

But first he must attend to the spiritual needs of this child, and the purity of his own soul, which had been nourished and kept untarnished by the simple country faith of his father and mother, enabled him to regard Cidaq for what she was: half-child, half-woman, brave, honest and surprisingly uncontaminated by what had happened to her. She was, like him, a pure spirit, but unlike him, she was in mortal danger because of her traffic with a shaman.

Putting aside other tasks, he directed his considerable spiritual energy to the salvation of her soul, and with extended prayer, and exhortation, and the telling of noble Bible stories, he showed her the ideal nature of Christianity, and having discovered that she was moved by Christ's relation to children, he stressed that aspect, and now, having learned that she had been forced into sin, he emphasized especially the theory of redemption. Christ was no longer one who could redeem the hypothetical sinner Rudenko; He could now redeem Cidaq.

After five unbroken days of this incessant pressure, Cidaq said, with no conviction but only to please the young priest: "I feel called to Jesus Christ," and he interpreted this as a true conversion, shouting to the members of his little world: "Cidaq is saved!" He told the Company managers, the sailors, the uncomprehending Aleuts that the child Cidaq was saved, at which the trader who had escaped murder at her hands growled: "That one's no child!"

On Sunday after service in his rustic church at the end of the world, Father Vasili informed his tiny congregation that Cidaq had elected to march under the banner of Christ, and that she would, in conformance to the law of the empire, take an honest Russian name: "Henceforth she will no longer be called by her ugly pagan name, Cidaq, but by her beautiful Christian name, Sofia Kuchovskaya. *Sofia* means *the wise, good one* and *Kuchovskaya* is the name of a fine Christian woman in Irkutsk." Kissing his convert on each cheek, he proclaimed: "You are no longer Cidaq. You are Sofia Kuchovskaya, and now your life begins."

With the perplexing simplicity that characterizes many devout believers, Father Vasili became fixed upon a course of theological action which seemed to him completely rational, indeed, inescapable: Sofia has become a Christian, and with her love and faith she can redeem the prodigal son Rudenko. Together they can find a new life that will bring honor to Russia and dignity to Kodiak.

Eager to believe that Rudenko was no more than a repetition of the Biblical prodigal son who had perhaps drunk too much or wasted his patronage in what was euphemistically termed *riotous living,* and incapable of believing that any man could be inherently evil, the young priest saw that his next task was to convert him as he had Sofia, and since he had never met the criminal, he asked Ensign Belov to take him to the darkened room where Rudenko still lingered.

"Be careful of this one," the young officer warned. "He killed three men in Siberia."

"It's just such men that Jesus seeks," Vasili said, and when he sat with Rudenko, still in manacles and assigned to the next ship returning to the Pribilofs, he found the murderer still convinced that the girl he had purchased on Lapak was going to prove the agency for his rescue from the Seal Islands. Assessing Father Vasili correctly as one of those benign priests who could be convinced of anything, he saw that it was important for him to win the man's good graces, and he presented himself as submerged in contrition: "Yes, the girl you now call Sofia is my wife. I did buy her, but I developed a sincere affection for her. She's a good girl."

"What about that sinful behavior in the hold of the ship?"

"You know how sailors are, Father. I couldn't stop them."

"And the same kind of behavior here at Three Saints Bay?"

"I suppose you know that one of them was killed by the Aleuts? He's the one that did it all. Me? My father and mother were followers of Jesus. Me too. I love Sofia and am not surprised she's joined our church, and I hope that you'll make us man and wife." He made this final plea with tears filling his eyes.

Vasili was so affected by the prisoner's apparent transformation that the only matter which remained to be clarified concerned the murders in Siberia, and Rudenko was eager to explain: "I was wronged. Two other fellows did it. The judge was prejudiced. I've always been an honest man, never stole a kopeck. I wasn't supposed to be sent to the Aleutians, it was a mistake." Now, speaking of his deep love for his wife, he became even more unctuous: "My whole aim is to start a new life in Kodiak with the girl you call Sofia. Tell her I still love her."

He delivered these sentiments with such a display of religious conviction that Vasili had to suppress a smile, and even though the priest knew that Rudenko had committed the murders, he was disposed to accept the man's longing to begin a better life. Everything Vasili had been taught about the wishes of God and His Son Jesus made him want to believe that repentance was possible, and next day when he returned to talk with the onetime criminal, he asked that the manacles be struck from his wrists so they could talk as man to man, and at the end of the dialogue he was convinced that illumination had entered Rudenko's life.

Yearning to save what the prophet Amos called "a firebrand plucked out of the burning," Vasili reported to Sofia: "God's wishes will be served if you marry him and initiate a true Christian home."

In saying this, he was viewing her not as an isolated human individual with her own aspirations but as a kind of mechanical agent for good, and he would have been astonished had someone pointed this out. It was no tortured chain of theological reasoning which produced this impersonal conclusion, but rather the teachings his parents had hammered into him: "Even the lowliest sinner can be reclaimed." "God is forever eager to forgive." "It's a woman's job to bring her man to salvation." "Woman must be man's beacon in the dark night."

So when Vasili spread his plan before Sofia, he told her: "You are Rudenko's beacon in the dark night," and she asked: "Now what does that mean?" and he explained: "God, who now has you in His care, loves every man and woman on this earth. We are His children and He longs to see each of us saved. I grant your husband has had a troubled past, but he's reformed and wants to start a new life obedient to Christ. To do so, he must have your help."

"I never want to help that one. Let him go back to his seals."

"Sofia! He's a voice crying in the night for help."

"I was crying in the night, real tears, and he gave me no help."

"God wants you to fulfill your promise . . . marry him . . . save him . . . bring him into eternal light."

"He left me in eternal darkness. No."

The proposal was so repugnant, so contrary to common sense that she allowed Vasili no time to develop it. Leaving him abruptly, she marched openly to Lunasaq's hut, unaware that in joining the Christian church she had obligated herself to forswear all others, and especially shamanism. When she came to what had been the source of her spiritual instruction, she cried: "Bring out the mummy! I want to talk with a woman who knows about these things."

And when the mummy appeared, Cidaq blurted out: "They've made me change my name to Sofia Kuchovskaya so I can be a good Russian."

The mummy laughed: "You could never be a Sofia. You are forever Cidaq."

"And they say I must go ahead and marry Rudenko . . . to save him . . . because their God wills it."

The mummy sucked in her breath so sharply that she whistled: "Suppose you do ruin your life to save his, what will that accomplish?" and Cidaq explained: "It's called salvation, his, not mine."

The shaman was bold and unrelenting in his rejection of all the priest stood for: "Always the interests of the Russians come first. Sacrifice the Aleut girl to make the Russian man happy. What kind of god gives such advice?" And as he ranted on, he revealed his motives to Cidaq, who thought to herself: He's afraid of the priest, knows that the new religion is powerful, but even so, a shaman may know what's best for Aleuts, so she listened respectfully as Lunasaq concluded his diatribe: "They crush us step by step, these Russians. The Company makes slaves of us, they bring in their priests to assure that everything is the way their spirits intended. And each day, Cidaq, we fall lower."

Now came an example of how the shaman's utilization of the mummy had endowed the ancient relic with a character and mind of its own, for when Lunasaq pretended to be the old woman, he became one, drawing upon his long familiarity with how women thought and expressed themselves: "On the islands women served their men, making their clothes, collecting the fish and the berries, chanting when the men went out to fight whales. But I never felt that we were lesser, only different and with different capacities. What man on what island could bear a child? But this new faith, it's quite horrible, to sacrifice a girl like you to a brute like Rudenko in order to make him feel better." She surprised Cidaq by laughing: "Once we had a man like your Rudenko. Bullied everyone. Beat his wife and children. Once when he didn't do his share he caused the death of a good fisherman."

"What did you do about it?" the shaman asked, and the old woman replied: "There was a woman in our village who caught the most fish and sewed the best sealskin pants. One morning she told us: 'When the kayaks return tonight, you three join me when I go out to unload his fish, and while he is still in the canoe, watch me.'"

"What happened?" Cidaq asked, and she said: "He came in. We waded out to get his fish. And at this woman's signal, she and I pulled him from his kayak and the two others joined us as we held him under the waves." She reported this without gloating: "Sometimes that's the only way." And Cidaq asked: "The other fishermen must have seen you. What did they do?"

"They looked the other way. They knew we were doing their work for them."

"And what should I do?" Cidaq asked, and the old woman replied in heavy words: "These are troubled times, child." Then, realizing that this was an inadequate answer, she added: "Some evening when the kayaks come home through the mists, you'll discover whatever it is that must be done."

"Should I let them marry me to that one?" and in posing this question she saw nothing wrong in seeking moral advice from the shaman and his mummy, because she still felt herself a member of their world. She would look to her new priest for guidance in ethereal matters, to her old shaman for instruction in practical affairs.

The shaman, seeing an opportunity to reinforce his control over her, leaped at her question: "No! Cidaq, they're using you for their purposes. This is corruption, the destruction of the Aleuts." Fighting to preserve the Aleut universe of sea and storm and walruses and salmon leaping up the stream, he cried: "It is not Rudenko who should be drowned at dusk, but the priest who gives such advice. He's here to destroy us." But the mummy had other counsel: "Wait. See what happens. In my long years I've found that many problems are solved by waiting. Will the baby be a boy or a girl? Wait nine moons and you'll see." And Cidaq, as she left the hut, knew that the shaman spoke only of this year, this body of contradictions, whereas the mummy spoke of all the summers and winters there were to be, and their joint counsel made more sense to her than Father Vasili's.

Sofia's brazen return to the shaman's hut, and to a religion she was supposed to have forsworn, alerted Father Vasili to the fact that the struggle for the soul of this young woman was far from decided. She had been baptized and was technically a Christian, but her faith was so wavering that he must take dramatic steps to complete her conversion. Inviting her to the driftwood building he called his church, he sat her on a chair he had made, and began: "Sofia, I know the pull of the old ways. When Jesus Christ took His new faith to the Jews and the Romans . . ." She understood not a word he was saying. "It is not I who has brought the true religion to Kodiak, it is God Himself, who has said: 'It's time those good Aleuts were saved.' I didn't come here. God sent me. And He did not send me to the island. He sent me to you. God longs to take you, Sofia Kuchovskaya, to His bosom. And even if you don't want to listen to what I say, you cannot escape listening to what He says."

"How can He tell me to marry a man like Rudenko?"

"Because you are both His children. He loves you equally. And He wants you to serve as His daughter to save His son Yermak." For

more than an hour he pleaded with her to embrace Christianity completely, to forswear shamanism, to throw herself onto the mercy of
God and the benevolence of His Son Jesus, and he was shocked when
she finally halted the persuasion by throwing at him the arguments
she had heard in the hut: "Your god cares nothing for the woman,
me, only for the man, Rudenko."

He jumped back as if he had been struck, for in the harsh rejection of this island girl he was hearing one of the permanent complaints against the Russian Orthodox faith and other versions of
Christianity: that it was a man's religion established to safeguard and
prolong the interests only of men, and he realized that he had instructed this capable young woman in no more than half the basics
of his faith. Humbled, he took her two hands and confessed: "I've
left out the beauty of my religion. I'm ashamed." Fumbling for a
clear way to express the aspect of his faith that he had overlooked, he
mumbled: "God especially loves women, for it is they who keep life
moving forward."

This new concept, beautifully developed by the ardent young
priest, had a powerful effect upon Sofia, who remained fixed to her
chair in a kind of trance as Vasili collected from his altar area those
revered symbols which summarized his religion: a depiction of the
crucifixion, a lovely Madonna and Child carved by a peasant in
Irkutsk, a red-and-gold icon showing a female saint, and an ivory
cross. Distributing them before her in almost the exact pattern that
Lunasaq had used when displaying his icons, he began pleading with
her, using words and phrases best calculated to summarize the exquisite significance of Christianity: "Sofia, God offered us salvation
through the Virgin Mary. She protects you and all other women. The
most glorious saints are women who saw visions and helped others.
Through such women God speaks, and they beg you not to reject the
salvation they represent. Abandon the evil old ways and embrace the
new ways of God and Jesus Christ. Sofia, their voices call you!" and
from all corners of the rude chapel her name seemed to reverberate
until she feared she might faint, but then came the compelling words:
"As God has sent me to Kodiak to save your soul, so you have been
brought here to save Rudenko's. Your duty is clear. You are the chosen instrument of God's grace. Just as He could not save the world
without the help of Mary, so He cannot save Rudenko without your
help."

When Sofia heard these radiant words she realized that her new

Christianity had been made whole. Hitherto it had concerned only men and their well-being, but these new definitions proved that there was a place for her too, and in these transcendent moments of revelation came a wholly new vision of what a human life could be. Jesus became real, the Son of Mary through the benevolence of God, and through Mary's intercession women could attain what had for so long been denied them. The women saints were real; the cross was tangible driftwood that had come to whatever island it was that these women saints occupied; but above all the other mysteries and the precious symbols of the new religion rose the wondrous message of redemption and forgiveness and love. Father Vasili had brought to Kodiak a new vision of the universe, and Sofia Kuchovskaya at last recognized and understood it. "I give my life to Jesus," she said with soft simplicity, and this time she meant it. Her conversion was completed.

Because she was a young woman of integrity, when she left the chapel she went directly to the shaman's hut, where she waited until Lunasaq brought forth his mummy: "I've seen a vision of the new gods. I'm reborn this day as Sofia Kuchovskaya, and I've come to thank you with tears in my eyes for the love and assistance you shared with me before I found the light."

A kind of wailing filled the hut, emanating both from Lunasaq, who realized that he was losing one of the major battles of his life, and from the mummy, who had known for many seasons that the changes taking place in her islands boded no good: "Cidaq, you're like a young walrus tumbling on dangerous ice. Beware!" This accidental reminder that her name signified a young animal that ran free brought to mind the immense loss she was facing, and she whispered: "I shall tumble, no doubt. And I shall miss your comforting. But new winds are blowing across the ice, and I must listen."

"Cidaq! Cidaq!" the mummy cried, and this mournful intonation was the last time this child of the islands would hear that precious name, for now she knelt before the shaman, thanking him for his guidance, and before the mummy, whose sensible support had been so important to her in times of crisis: "I feel as if you were my grandmother's grandmother. I shall miss you."

Eager to retain contact with this worthy child, the shaman caused his mummy to say with no show of anxiety: "Oh, but you can still come talk with me."

Then came the wrenching moment: "No, I cannot, for I am now

a new person. I am Sofia." With that, she bowed once more to these ancestral forces in her life, and with tears in her eyes she left them, apparently forever. When the hut was bereft of her presence, the old shaman and the ancient one remained silent for some minutes, then from the sack came a scream of mortal anguish, as if the end of a life as well as the end of an idea had come: "Cidaq! Cidaq!" But the once-owner of that name would no longer hear.

It was a wedding which none who attended would ever forget. Huge black-scowling Yermak Rudenko appeared almost pale from his long incarceration, beetle-browed, hunched over, embittered by his previous treatment but relieved at having escaped a return to the Seal Islands; he resembled in no way a bridegroom, for he looked much as he had in his previous incarnation, a skulking murderer of defenseless travelers. Sofia Kuchovskaya presented a striking contrast. Young, exuberant, lacking even the slightest sign of her former mistreatment at the hands of her intended, her hair marvelously long at her back, neatly trimmed almost to her eyelashes in front, and with that big smile in place, she looked to be exactly what she was: a young bride somewhat bewildered by what was occurring and not at all certain that she was in control.

The guests were all Russian or Creole; not one Aleut had been invited, since this day was held by the officials to be one when a native girl was being allowed entrance to Russian society. For her the evil old days of paganism were dead; the bright new days of Orthodox faith were beginning, and it was assumed that she would be grateful for the improvement in her status.

Even Rudenko enjoyed the metamorphosis. He was no longer just another brutal convict sentenced to the Aleutians or a runaway from the Seal Islands; he was now the agency for performing a major mission for the tsarina, the bringing of an Aleut pagan soul into Christianity. He bathed in his newfound respectability and behaved like a real Russian settler.

Father Vasili was engulfed in emotion, for Sofia was the first Aleut woman he had converted and the first Aleut of either sex whose entrance into Christianity could be taken seriously. But to him Sofia was much more than a symbol of the change that would sweep the islands; she was an admirable human being, triumphant over disasters that might have deranged a lesser person, and gifted with a keen sense of what was happening to her people. In saving this young woman, Vasili said to himself as he approached the canopy under which he would stand as he read the wedding service, Russia's getting one of the best. And in his black robes he married them.

There were singing and dancing by the Russian sailors and speeches by officials, who congratulated Sofia Rudenko on her entry to their society and her husband Yermak upon his release from custody. But on the third day these celebrations were marred by the sudden intrusion of the disheveled old shaman, who left his hut, came onto Company property, and in a wild shaky voice berated Father Vasili for having conducted such an infamous wedding.

"Go back, old fool!" a guard warned, to no effect, for the old fellow persisted in his disturbing accusations until Rudenko, irritated by this interruption of festivities at which he was the central figure, rushed at the shaman, bellowing: "Out of here!" and when the old man pointed a long finger at the bridegroom, crying in Russian: "Murderer! Debaucher of women! Pig!" Rudenko became so angered that he began clubbing at him with his fists, and he struck him so often and so hard that Lunasaq staggered, tried to steady himself by holding on to his assailant, then took two sharp knocks to the head and fell into the dust.

Now Sofia intervened. Pulling her husband away, she knelt beside her old counselor and gently slapped his face until he regained consciousness. Then, ignoring her wedding guests, she started to lead him to his hut, but to her surprise Father Vasili interceded, placed his own arms about his enemy's trembling body, and led him to safety. Sofia, watching the two men disappear, knew that she should be with them and began to run after them, but Rudenko, infuriated by what had happened and his wife's participation, grabbed her by the arm, spun her around, and struck her so heavily in the face that now she lay in the dust. He might have kicked her, too, had not Ensign Belov intervened, lifted Sofia to her feet, and brushed away the dust. The dark blood dripping from her chin, where Rudenko's fist had cut the flesh enclosing her ivory labret, he could not wash away.

Yermak Rudenko was not disciplined for beating his wife or thrashing the shaman, because most Russians considered Aleuts less than human and proper objects for brutal punishment. In lawless Kodiak, Russian opinion was that all native wives, Aleut or Creole, profited from a justified beating now and then, while the castigation of the shaman was seen as a service to the Russian community. But when Father Vasili heard of what Rudenko had done while he was helping the shaman to his hut, and saw during prayer services the extent of Sofia's cuts, he did not go to console her, but he did accost Yermak: "I've seen what you did to Sofia. This must never happen again."

"Mind your business, Black Robes."

"It is my business. Humanity is my business." The frail priest looked ridiculous, speaking thus to the huge trader, and both men knew it, so with a big paw, not a fist, Rudenko pushed Vasili away, and the priest's feet became so entangled that he fell. Others saw the accident, for that was how it should be defined, since Rudenko did not strike the priest, and they interpreted it as yet another thrashing their bullyboy had administered to an interfering priest, and when they saw that Vasili was afraid to take counteraction, they began to denigrate him, until it became general opinion that "we were better off with drunk old Father Pëtr, who knew enough to stay clear of our affairs."

Some days later, when Sofia appeared at prayer with her left eye bruised, Father Vasili knew he could no longer avoid taking action, and when service ended he approached the bully, and said in a voice loud enough for others to hear: "If you ever abuse your wife again, I shall have you punished."

The listeners laughed, for it was obvious that the priest had neither the personal strength to punish Rudenko nor the authority to demand that some official do so, and this pusillanimity indicated the low estate to which The Company had fallen.

But this situation was about to change, a third visitor was about to reach Kodiak, and his arrival would make a vast difference. On a day in late June 1791 a sailor, looking down the bay on whose shores Three Saints stood, spotted a small sailboat that looked as if it had been slapped together from bits of wood and sealskin. Unfit for ocean travel or even the crossing of a lake, it was struggling to make landfall before it disintegrated, and the sailor wondered if he should first hurry to the shore to try to save it or run for help.

Choosing the latter option, he dashed toward town, shouting: "Boat arriving! Men aboard!" Assuring himself that he had been heard, he ran back to the shore and tried to haul the boat onto the rocky beach, but the near-dead sailors, beards salted white, were unable to help. When he tried to do the job alone he recoiled in horror, for in the bottom of the boat lay the corpse of a baldheaded man too old for such adventure.

The first islander to reach the stricken craft was Father Vasili, who shouted to those coming behind: "Hurry! These fellows are near death!" And as others arrived he started to administer rites to the body in the bottom of the boat, but as he did so the man groaned, opened his eyes, and cried with delight: "Father Vasili!"

The priest jumped back, looked more closely, and gasped: "Aleksandr Baranov! What a way to report for duty!"

When the exhausted men were lifted ashore and given hot drinks, it was Baranov, miraculously revived, who surprised both his shipmates and those who had rescued him—brushing off his muddied clothes, pressing down his few strands of hair, and taking command of the impromptu meeting at the edge of the bay. His report was brief, its items recognized by all who sailed in Russian ships:

"I am Aleksandr Baranov, merchant of Irkutsk and chief manager of all Company affairs in Russian America. I sailed from Okhotsk in August last year and should have reached here in November. But you can guess what happened. Our ship was leaky, our captain was a drunkard, and our navigator put us onto rocks seven hundred miles off course, losing our ship in the process.

"We spent a dismal winter on an island with no people, no food, no tools and no maps. We survived principally because this fine fellow, Kyril Zhdanko, son of our lady director in Petropavlovsk, had island experience and courage. He built this boat, sailed it to Kodiak, and now receives promotion as my assistant.

"If Father Vasili, a friend of mine from Irkutsk, will lead us to his church, we will offer thanks to God for our salvation."

But when the procession reached the pitiful shack that served the priest as his church, Baranov voiced loudly a decision which informed the islanders that a new man with strong ideas was now in charge: "I will not give thanks in that pigsty. Not fit for the presence of God, or the work of a priest, or the attendance of a chief manager," and under the open skies beside the bay he bowed his bald head, folded his arms over his sagging belly, and gave awed thanks to the various miracles that had saved him from drunken captains, stupid navigators and a winter's starvation. At the conclusion of the prayer, which not the priest but he gave, he reached for Kyril Zhdanko's arm and said: "It was a near thing, son," and before that day ended he issued what sounded like contradictory instructions. To Zhdanko he said: "Begin planning immediately to move our capital to a more likely spot," but to Father Vasili: "We'll start building you a real church tomorrow."

Zhdanko, who knew that he would be doing most of the work, protested: "But if we're leaving this place, why not wait to build our new church at the other spot?"

"Because I have no commission more important than giving our church proper support. I want conversions. I want children learning Bible stories. And I certainly want a decent church, because it represents the soul of Russia."

But when Zhdanko discussed this preposterous decision in greater detail, he found that what Baranov really wanted was some building, any building, that carried on top the comforting onion dome of a Russian church: "Sir, I don't believe we have anywhere on Kodiak a man who can build an onion dome."

"Yes, you do!"

"Who?"

"Me. If I could learn to make glass, I can learn to make a dome." And on the third full day of his residence in Three Saints this energetic little man identified a building which, if its top were knocked off, would support an onion dome which he, Baranov, would build. Assembling woodmen to provide him with timbers and sawyers to cut curved planks, he scratched Kodiak for nails and commandeered the few crude hammers, and soon he had rising in the cool air beside the cottonwood trees a fine onion dome, which he wanted to paint blue, but since Kodiak had only brown, he settled for that.

At the dedication he revealed his strategy: "I want every board to be numbered, in sequence, because when we move to our new location, we'll take our dome with us, for I do believe we've built a good one."

The incident of the dome convinced the people of Kodiak that this dynamic little man, so like a gnome, so unlike a manager of frontier posts, was determined to make Russian America a vital center of trade and government, and his broad interest probed into all aspects of life in the settlement. For example, when the attractive young girl

Sofia appeared with a black eye, he summoned Father Vasili: "What happened to that child?"

"Her husband beats her."

"Husband! She looks an infant. Who is he?"

"A fur trader."

"I should have known. Have him brought here," and when the hulking brute shambled in, Baranov shouted: "Stand at attention, you dog!" And when it became possible to conduct a reasonable disciplinary interview, the new manager snapped: "Why do you think you can smash your little wife about?"

"She . . ."

Moving very close to him, the little fellow bellowed: "She what?" and before Rudenko could respond, Baranov shouted: "Fetch me Zhdanko!" and when that no-nonsense Creole appeared, adopted son of the powerful Madame Zhdanko and future governor of the Aleutians, Baranov gave him one simple command: "If this swine ever beats his wife again, shoot him." Turning with scorn to Rudenko, he said: "I'm told you like to kick priests about, too. Kyril, if he ever touches or in any way threatens Father Vasili, shoot him."

So a kind of rough order was established at dissolute Three Saints, a kind of peace descended upon the Rudenko household, and under encouragement from Baranov the new religion flourished while the former receded ever deeper into the shadows. Chief Manager Baranov attended mostly to the task of moving Three Saints to a more favorable spot at the other end of Kodiak, but he had completed only the provisional planning when Rudenko, chastened by the threats of death that Baranov had made, came crawling in to curry favor: "Sir, have you ever hunted the great bear of Kodiak?"

When Baranov replied that he had not even heard of such a bear, Rudenko fell over himself to offer expert guidance into the beautiful wooded area well to the north of Three Saints where mountains rose out of the sea to the majestic height of nearly forty-five hundred snow-capped feet. A party of six was arranged, and during its expedition Rudenko showed himself to such advantage, tending to all matters and working diligently, that Baranov concluded he must have seen the fur trader at a temporary disadvantage in that first meeting, so on the third night out he told Yermak: "When you behave yourself, you can be an admirable man," and Rudenko replied: "Under your new rules I always behave."

When they detected signs that one of the monstrous Kodiak bears was in a region of rolling foothills and spruce trees, Rudenko assumed command, sending four skilled helpers in various directions until they had circled the still unseen beast. Then, with everyone moving toward the center of the area thus subtended, they approached what Rudenko assured Baranov in whispered instructions was going to be a massive one: "Stay behind me, Chief Manager. These bears can be terrifying." With his left arm he pushed Baranov to the rear, and it was fortunate that he did, because at this moment a hunter on the opposite side of the ring made an unplanned noise, alerting the bear, which started running right at Rudenko.

When it loomed out from a cluster of trees, stopped, and reared upward to scout what lay ahead, Baranov gasped, for it was immense, a towering animal with awesome claws. Instinctively, Baranov sought a tree behind which to hide, but the nearest one was too far away for him to reach before the bear swiped at him with a raking paw. The few steps the manager did succeed in taking saved his life, for the terrible claws penetrated only the back of his parka, ripping it with a sickening noise. However, because Baranov was so slow and the bear so swift, another swing of that mighty paw would surely kill the man, but here Rudenko boldly thrust himself between man and bear, brought his rifle up, and pumped a bullet upward through the animal's throat and into its brain. The bear staggered sideways, struggled for nearly half a minute to maintain its footing, and finally collapsed in the snow. When a shaken Baranov and Rudenko measured the dead beast, they found that erect, it would have stood eleven terrifying feet, and Baranov asked: "How can they grow so large?" and Rudenko explained: "Kodiak's an island. More berries than you ever saw. Lots of grass too, and nothing to bother the bears. So they eat and grow and eat and grow."

Baranov ordered that after the beast was butchered, with edible parts being sent back to Three Saints, the skin be salvaged and mounted for his office, and it was this towering stuffed bear, looming down from his corner, that subsequently saved Rudenko's life, for after he gained the good graces of the new manager, he wrongly believed that this restored his right to thrash his wife, who, as an Aleut, merited no regard. In a sickening scene he accused her of some trivial fault, and when in her customary style she not only denied his charges but mocked him with her silence, he became enraged and beat her about the face.

When boys ran to the shaman's hut to inform him of what Rudenko had done, he asked only one question: "You said she was bleeding?" and they replied: "Yes, all over her mouth," and then he knew that he must intervene, for if the Russian managers had visible proof of such misbehavior and refused to take action, he must. So he bade the mummy farewell and marched forth to what he suspected might be his last undertaking as a shaman, but one he could not avoid.

Thin, unkempt, bent slightly forward, an old man burning with a determination to preserve his one true religion and fight evil influences that were paralyzing his people, he walked boldly to Rudenko's hut, crying as he approached: "Rudenko, the spirits place a curse upon you! Never again will you see your wife! Never again will you abuse her!"

Inside the hut Rudenko was sharing with two companions a kind of beer fermented from cranberries, young spruce needles and seaweed, and the noise outside became an irritation, especially when Rudenko heard words which threatened him. Going to the improvised driftwood door, he was disgusted to see the wretched figure of the shaman: "Begone! Let honest men drink in peace!"

"Rudenko, you are cursed! Evil of great dimension will fall upon you!"

"Stop your caterwauling or I'll thrash you."

"Rudenko, never again will you abuse your wife. Never again . . ."

From the doorway Rudenko leaped upon the shaman, and as he did so, his two cronies tumbled out, eager to beat the old man, even kill him, but it was Rudenko's intention merely to scare the shaman and drive him back to his hut. "Don't hit him!" Rudenko shouted, but he was too late, for his friends dealt such heavy blows at the old man that he reeled back, fought to control his feet, and stumbled off toward his hut, where he collapsed among its roots.

Father Vasili quickly heard what had happened, and although he had opposed all that the wizard did, he knew that Christian charity required him to help this man who had endeavored to hold his community together prior to the arrival of Jesus. Hurrying to the hut, he entered for the first time the shaman's dark world.

He was appalled by the gloom, the dank earthen floor, the bundles piled here and there, but he was more aghast at the condition of the old man, for he lay in a heap, hair disheveled, blood speckling his gaunt face. Cradling the shaman's head in his arms, he whispered: "Old man! Listen to me. You'll be all right."

For a long time there was no response, and Vasili feared that his adversary was dead, but gradually the fierce old battler recovered the energy which had kept him struggling against great odds for the past years of Russian occupation and the onslaughts of Christianity. When he finally opened his eyes and saw who his savior was, he closed them again and lapsed into a lifeless stupor.

Father Vasili stayed with him most of that afternoon. Toward dusk he called for children to fetch Sofia Rudenko, and when she stood in the doorway of the hut, anguished by what she saw, he said simply: "He's been hurt. He needs attention," and with a fearful glance about the filthy, disorganized place, he asked in wonderment: "Sofia, how could you have thought there was illumination here?" Without waiting for an answer, he left her, unaware that he had been present as the old religion of shamanism was perishing in its struggle with Christianity.

Unfortunately, the children who were sent to summon Sofia were nearby when Rudenko returned home, bellowing: "Where's my wife?" and they told him: "She went to the shaman's," and this infuriated him so that he shouted for his two drinking companions: "Let's finish that old fool right now!" and the three stormed out to the hut among the roots, found Sofia there tending the shaman, and Rudenko struck her across the face before tossing her out. Then they dragged the old man to his feet, and as he toppled forward, Rudenko met him with a mighty smash to the face, knocking him to the floor. As he fell the men kicked him to death, and in this brutal manner the Russian Christians terminated their debate with a pagan religion they were fated to displace.

The shaman's murder provoked confusion for Kodiak's two administrators. Father Vasili, hearing of the death, hurried to the hut, where he assumed control, as if it were an adjunct to his church, which in a way it had been. Feeling no sense of personal triumph in the defeat of his rival, he lit a candle beside the corpse, stared, nauseated, at the blood which stained the earth, and felt tears of compassion welling in his eyes as sailors finally carried the dead body away. But after he had knelt to pray for the departed soul of his misguided but valiant opponent, he rose with renewed determination to end this plague of shamanism. With the zeal that young men experience when they know they are doing right, he began to gather the ridiculous assembly of twigs and bits of carved wood and scraps of polished ivory and the stones with which the shaman had presumed to converse with spirits, and piling all this junk into a heap where the body had lain, he scattered inflammable spruce needles over it and with his candle set it afire.

As the pile began to blaze, people ran up, shouting: "Father Vasili! Get out . . . quickly!" But as he started to leave he saw in a darkened corner a sack made of sealskin, and when he opened it he found that it contained a dark, leathery substance, and half-choking from the noxious fumes of the burning symbols, he muttered: "This must be the mummy Sofia spoke about," and when he pulled the bag apart he found himself facing this stubborn old woman of thirteen thousand years.

With a shudder at the heresy she represented, he was about to pitch her into the fire when Sofia dashed into the hut, saw what was happening, and, too late, she screamed: "No! No!" Then she watched with horror as flames consumed the old woman whose spirit had refused to die.

"What have you done?" she cried, and when the priest left the hut she followed him into the night air, shouting at him, but she was soon silenced by her outraged husband. With a savage slap he struck her across the face, and she fell to the ground. For a long moment she lay there, staring at the flaming hut, and then she surrendered to the great confusions of her life. "She's fainted," Father Vasili cried, and two Aleuts picked her up.

At this moment Chief Manager Baranov arrived at the scene, and when he learned of the shaman's murder he was aghast, for he appreciated the complications that might arise. Like all Russians, he held shamans in contempt, but he also recognized that they were a constructive agency in keeping Aleuts under control. "Who did this thing?" he asked, and then he saw Sofia Rudenko, held upright by the two men, her face a mass of bruises.

"Rudenko," Kyril Zhdanko replied. "He did both. Killed the shaman. Beat his wife," and without being instructed to do so, he set off to apprehend the criminal, who had now committed his fourth murder.

When the bearded hunter was hauled into the temporary office of the chief manager for punishment, Baranov took one look at him and remembered his earlier threat to shoot Rudenko if he ever again beat his wife, and now, since that offense had been compounded by murder, he had double reason to act. But as he faced Rudenko, he saw in the corner behind the wretch the huge stuffed figure of the Kodiak bear, and he remembered that he was alive only because of this renegade's bravery. With disgust he handed down his verdict: "Rudenko, you're a disgrace to Russia and mankind. You have no right to live, except one. You saved my life when that one attacked, so I cannot shoot you as I threatened. Instead, your marriage to Sofia Kuchovskaya is annulled, for it should never have occurred in the first place, and you will be taken back to the Seal Islands, the only place I can think of that God might want you to live."

Refusing to listen to Rudenko's impassioned promises of reform, he told Zhdanko: "Guard him till the next boat sails north," and with a glance of repugnance toward Rudenko, he left to console Sofia with news that her infamous marriage to Rudenko was dissolved.

But he had not taken into account the priest, Father Vasili, whose devout parents he had known in Irkutsk and whom he respected for his piety. When he told Vasili: "The marriage between Sofia Kuchovskaya and the brute Yermak Rudenko is dissolved, you should never have married them in the first place," Vasili replied firmly, relying first on the Gospel According to Mark: "'What therefore God hath joined together, let not man put asunder,'" and then on an equally powerful injunction from the Irkutsk countryside: "Thunder and lightning shall not separate a man and his wife, even though God Himself sends the thunder."

"I didn't mean that I was annulling the marriage," Baranov apologized. "I meant that since you performed the ceremony, you would do so."

But Baranov underestimated the zeal with which this young priest adhered to the teachings of his Bible: "A vow is a solemn engagement undertaken in the sight of the Lord. There is no way I could annul it."

"You mean, this fine child . . . her husband banished to the Seal Islands . . . as a Christian she has to live alone . . . the rest of her life?"

In his reply, Father Vasili revealed the harshness of his Christianity, for when the practical problems of a human life, in this case the welfare of the innocent child Sofia Kuchovskaya, conflicted with the teaching of the Bible, it was the child who had to sacrifice: "I concede that Sofia has known great sorrow in her life, the tribulations of Job, and now we place yet one more upon her. Well, God nominates some of us to bear His yoke so that others can appreciate His ultimate grace. That is Sofia's assignment."

"But to waste her life . . . ?"

The priest was adamant: "That's the cross she must bear," and he would not deviate from this harsh judgment.

At this juncture it must have seemed to the people of Kodiak—Russian and Aleut alike—that in the great confrontation between the two religions, Father Vasili had triumphed. He had bested the shaman, who was dead, removed the pernicious influence of that provocative mummy, whose ashes were banished to a proper grave, and had won for himself a church with an onion dome, symbol of the best in Russian religion. But anyone who offered that hasty judgment would be ignoring the power of the Aleutian Islands to strike back.

Scientifically, the disaster could be easily explained, but to the Aleuts it was obviously the revenge that Lunasaq and the destroyed mummy exacted on Father Vasili.

A vigorous earthquake eighteen miles below the surface of the Pacific Ocean caused a massive submarine cliff three miles below the surface to collapse. The crumbling cliff spewed downward nearly a cubic mile of mud and rock, and this dislocation created a monstrous tsunami which sped eastward as a gigantic lateral surge of water moving deep within the ocean, never creating a visible wave of more than two feet at the surface but rushing with fearsome power toward Kodiak at a speed of four hundred and sixty miles an hour.

When it reached the mouth of Three Saints Bay it did not come as one engulfing tidal wave; its forerunners entered quietly, but the following waves kept coming and coming, and their speed was so great and the pressure so persistent that the water rose rather quietly ten feet, then twenty, and finally fifty-seven. For nine dreadful minutes it hung there, after which it rushed out of the bay with such gurgling force that it sucked all things along with it.

Father Vasili, scrambling over the rocks to save the precious icons of his newly domed church, had reached only a small hill when he saw a sight so infuriating that it made him question the justice of the God he served. The turbulent waters were not touching the lone spruce which had served as the shaman's temple, but they were tearing the Christian church from its foundations, tumbling it this way and that until it smashed to splinters on a cluster of rocks.

The loss of life at Three Saints, pinched in as it was along the bay, would have been tremendous had not young Kyril Zhdanko responded to the first sign of the incoming surge: "Terrible danger! I saw this once on Lapak!" and he released the prisoner Yermak Rudenko to help rush people to higher ground. The powerful convict responded by dragging first the dazed Father Vasili and then Chief Manager Baranov up the side of a steep hill. Perching them like children on a rock that looked as if it might remain above the surging waters, he had gone back down the hill a third time to rescue others when a towering wave swept in, turned all things upside down, and sucked him to his death.

The great tidal wave of 1792 solved problems for one Russian at Three Saints but raised perplexing difficulties for another. Chief Manager Baranov had decided during his first hours at this spot that the location had not been well chosen and that an anchorage to the north would be more advantageous. The site he chose seven months before the wave demonstrated his mind-set, for spiritually and emotionally Three Saints had looked backward toward Russia and its affiliations with the past, while the town of Kodiak would look eastward toward the future and the looming challenges of North America. Three Saints carried an umbilical cord to old Siberia, Kodiak to new Alaska.

As he and Zhdanko labored over their plans for the new capital, he asked Kyril: "Are you the natural son of Madame Zhdanko, of Petropavlovsk?"

"Adopted."

"Was your father the trader they tell about?"

"My birth father must have been some Russian serving on Lapak Island. My true father, Zhdanko."

"What happened to him?"

"He was eighty-three. We came home from trading furs. Walked from Yakutsk to Okhotsk . . ."

"I've done that."

"He was tired, almost worn out, that I could see. When we reached Petropavlovsk, I said: 'Father, let's rest,' but he had always longed to see Kodiak. Wanted to control the peltries here. So we set forth when he was eighty-five."

"What happened?"

"On the way he died. We bound him with rocks from the ballast and pitched him into the Bering Sea. Not far from the volcano that guards Lapak Island. As a boy I used to sit with him and watch its glow in the twilight."

Baranov stopped in his planning, knocked on wood, and said fervently: "By the grace of God, I'd like to see eighty-five. The building you and I could do!"

The second man whose life was sharply modified by the tidal wave was Father Vasili, for on the mournful day when the sixteen victims of the flood were buried, he mumbled when required to pray for the departed soul of Yermak Rudenko, for he could not in decency, when so many present knew the truth, embroider that brutal man's life with platitudes. And even had he been able to exalt charity over reality, he would have been deterred when he looked across the grave to where Sofia Kuchovskaya stood impassively staring at the rumpled soil which would cover her accursed husband.

In that accidental glance the young priest saw in vivid flashes the history of this valiant girl: her abandonment on Lapak, her hideous escape in the hold of a ship, the beatings and abuses, her fealty to an old religion, her embracing of the new. She was, he thought, a young woman of crystal character who had allowed nothing to sully her and who had represented the best of an old society that was dying to make way for a new. He saw her firm jaw, the dark knowing eyes, the controlled little body, and finally, as the grave was closed, the irrepressible smile, not in triumph over evil but in pleasure at the ending of an episode. He could almost hear her sigh as she looked about as if to ask: "Now what?"

On the day after the funeral Baranov summoned Father Vasili to the ruins of his office to hand him a surprising commission: "I consider myself responsible for every human being in these islands, Russian, Creole, Aleut, Koniag, makes no difference to me."

"I feel the same way, Chief Manager."

"But I intend doing something about it. How many children did the tidal wave leave without parents?"

"Fourteen, fifteen at least."

"Start an orphanage for them. This afternoon."

"But I have no funds. The bishop promised . . ."

"With you, Vasili, the bishop promises and never delivers. With me, it's The Company. 'You'll have everything you need, Baranov,' but the money never arrives."

"Then how can I . . . ?"

"I will pay. The honor of Russia demands it, and if the gentlemen

who run The Company are not considerate of Russia's honor, the
merchant who runs Kodiak is." And forthwith he provided the money
for the orphanage out of his own meager salary.

"But who's to run it?" he asked the priest, and after some reflection, Vasili remembered how Sofia, during her conversion, had been
so deeply moved by his tales of Christ's care for children, and he said:
"Sofia Rudenko would be ideal."

"She's not more than fifteen, just a child, really."

"She's seventeen."

"I can't believe it," but when she was sent for, and Baranov asked
bluntly: "Child, how old are you?" she said: "Seventeen," and he
asked: "Do you think you could run an orphanage?" and she asked:
"What's that?" When it was explained, she said: "Father Vasili told
me that Jesus said 'Suffer little children to come unto me.' Children
are my joy," and the Kodiak orphanage was established with
Baranov's funds and Sofia's love.

Baranov, determined to see anything he launched succeed, told
Vasili: "Get her started properly," and the young priest maintained
supervision, teaching her the rudiments of her new job and instructing the orphans in their new religion. As he worked close to Sofia he
was encouraged by the enthusiastic manner in which she became
mother to the infants, older sister to the girls and boys. She was so
influential with the youngsters that an older Aleut told Baranov: "If
she was a man, she'd be our new shaman," but Sofia knew this was
not accurate, for a real-life shaman had slipped into the remnants of
Three Saints in an effort to keep the Aleuts away from Christianity,
but his magic now seemed shabby, and compared with the spiritual
miracles that Sofia at her orphanage and Father Vasili in his improvised church were accomplishing, he achieved nothing and left.

As Sofia worked at the orphanage, Vasili had repeated opportunities to observe how she was maturing as she entered her new life, and
in multiple ways he was drawn to her. She was serious, yet always
ready to burst into her warm smile. She was industrious, but available
for rough-and-tumble play with her children, and above all, she made
people of whatever age or racial background happy in her presence.
And in the way that happens with certain fortunate women, as she
approached her twenties she grew more lovely, more complete. A full
inch taller now, her face less rounded, the whalebone labret slightly
less conspicuous, she was what one visiting sea captain called: "That
adorable lass," and one evening as Father Vasili left the lively warmth

of the orphanage and walked under the stars to the bleak building serving as his church, he looked up at the shaman's spruce and cried aloud: "I was never meant to be a black. I've been in love with her since the day I stepped on this island."

He interpreted it properly as an inevitable development and in no manner as shocking as it would have been had he served in the Roman Catholic clergy, where celibacy was an act of faith and dedication; in the Orthodox branch, as he had observed in the case of his own father, far more than half the priests were whites who had married with the encouragement of their bishops, who, even though they were black and celibate, preached: "Marriage is the normal condition of man." To switch from black to white involved a change only in direction, not faith.

But even such a limited switch was not easy to accomplish, so on the day that Three Saints shut down, with all Company work moving to Kodiak, Vasili went to talk with Baranov, who was packing the one small box which held the few possessions he had been able to accumulate in the colony.

"Chief Manager, I seek a boon."

"Granted. No manager ever had a better clergyman."

"I want you to write to my bishop in Irkutsk."

"He won't give you a kopeck. You'll have to make do."

"I want him to release me from my vows."

"My God! Are you leaving the church? Your parents . . ."

"No! No! I want to cease being a black. I seek to be a white."

Baranov sat heavily upon his box and stared at the young cleric, and after a very long silence, he said in a voice so low that Vasili could scarcely hear: "I've been watching you, Vasili, and I know your problem. I know because I too have fallen in love with an island woman. And I shall take her as my wife."

Shocked by such a confession, the young man became once more a monitory priest: "Aleksandr Andreevich, that's a terrible thing to say. You have a wife in Russia."

"True, and she says she may join me one of these days, but she's been saying that for twenty-three years."

"Aleksandr Andreevich, if you commit bigamy, I shall have to report you to St. Petersburg."

"I'm not going to marry her, Father Vasili, just take her for my wife till my real wife comes." Then he added in a low voice: "Which will be never, and I cannot live alone."

Vasili, who had come to consult about *his* problem, found himself engulfed in Baranov's: "She's a wonderful woman, Vasili. Speaks Russian, has dutiful parents, is neat in the house and can sew. She promises she'll take the Russian name Anna and attend our church regularly." Looking up from his box, his round face beaming, he asked: "Have I your blessing?"

There was no way this young priest could sanction such cavalier treatment of the marriage vow, but on the other hand, to untangle his own affairs he had to have Baranov's letter to the bishop, so he temporized: "Will you write to my bishop?" and by this digression he let it be known that he would not publicly castigate Baranov if the latter took a common-law wife: "After all, Chief Manager, I'm not leaving the church. I just want to switch from black to white."

"In order to marry Sofia?"

"Yes."

"I'll write. If I was younger, I'd take her myself." But then he broke into such irreverent laughter that Vasili blushed, thinking that Baranov was making fun of him. He was, but not in the way Vasili feared. "Remember what you said when I wanted Sofia's marriage to Rudenko annulled?" And now he gave a good imitation of the serious young priest: "'A vow is a solemn engagement undertaken in the sight of the Lord. There is no way I could annul it.' Well, my young friend, you're certainly eager to annul your own vows."

Vasili blushed again, so deeply that Baranov snapped his fingers at having made a discovery: "You haven't asked her yet, have you?" and Vasili had to confess that he had not. "Come along!" the energetic manager cried. "We do it now."

And on his stout little legs he ran to the orphanage, where he summoned its startled mistress. Facing her, with Vasili's hand in his, he said: "Since I think of myself as your father, I must inform you that this young fellow has asked for your hand in marriage." Sofia did not blush, or at least if she did, it was not visible through her golden skin, but she did bow, keeping her head down until she heard her priest saying softly: "I labored to save your soul, Sofia, but equally to save you. Will you marry me?"

She now knew enough to understand the meaning of his black robes, which she reached out to take between her fingers: "What of this?" and he said: "I have thrown it off as you threw off your sealskin dress when you became a Christian," and, with a smile that swept her face, she said: "I would be proud."

Since two or three years sometimes elapsed between the arrival and departure of a ship at Kodiak, there could be no quick response to Vasili's application to change from black to white, and even if permission had been obtained, it might be another three years before a priest arrived to conduct a wedding, so Baranov made a practical proposal: "If I'm going to live with Anna as my wife, you should do the same with Sofia . . . that is, until a priest can come to straighten things out."

"I couldn't do that." But then Baranov cited the ruling theology of the distant Aleutians: "The tsarina's in St. Petersburg, and God's high in the heavens, but we're here on Kodiak, so let's do what's necessary."

In this bizarre manner the two leaders of Russian America, old manager, young priest, took their island wives. Cidaq Sofia Kuchovskaya Rudenko Voronova would become the mother of that later Voronov who would illuminate Russian America and bring into fruition Baranov's dreams. The gifted Anna Baranova would serve as the chief manager's mistress for years and give birth to two excellent children, one of whom would become the wife of a later Russian governor. Upon word of the death of the real Madame Baranova, never seen in Siberia or the islands, Anna would become Baranov's legal wife, whom he presented to all as "the daughter of the former king of Kinai." Visitors found no difficulty in accepting this legend, because she was indeed queenly.

In the protracted battle between shamanism and Christianity, the latter won, but it was a murderous victory, for when Vitus Bering's men first stepped ashore on the Aleutians in 1741, the islands contained eighteen thousand, five hundred healthy men and women who had adapted masterfully to their treeless but sea-rich environment. When the Russians departed, the total population was less than twelve hundred. Ninety-four percent had been starved, drowned, forced into slavery, murdered, or otherwise disposed of in the Bering Sea. And even those few who survived, like Cidaq, did so only by merging themselves into the victorious civilization.

VI

LOST WORLDS

WITHIN THE SHADOW OF THE LOVELY VOLCANO THAT guarded Sitka Sound, the Great Toion lay dying. He had for thirty years dominated the multitude of mountainous islands which comprised his domain and had brought order among the headstrong, sometime mutinous Tlingit Indians, who were reluctant to follow the lead of anyone. They were a powerful lot, these Tlingits, resembling in no way the more placid Eskimos of the far north or the gentle Aleuts of the island chain. They loved warfare, enslaved their enemies when possible, and were afraid of no man, so that after the Great Toion died, relinquishing the power he had accumulated so craftily, the Tlingits knew that there might be a period of confusion, warfare and sudden death before the next toion proclaimed and established himself.

When the big slave known as Raven-heart became aware that his master was dying, panic captured him, for he realized that the very strengths which had made him the prime slave of the toion—his bravery in war, his alertness in defending his master—would condemn him to death, for when a toion died, it was the custom among the Tlingits to kill almost at that instant three of his finest slaves so that they could attend him properly in the world beyond the mountains. And since Raven-heart was by any judgment supreme among the toion's slaves, he would be awarded the honor of being the first to have the back of his neck stretched across the ceremonial log, while a smaller log, held by four men, was pressed down upon the front of his neck until life was crushed out—strangling him without marring his body for use in the next world.

The big fellow had never before been afraid. His history was one of constant struggle against odds, and in the mainland valley which his clan occupied he had been a principal defender against enemies who tried to invade from the higher lands to the east. He became known as a champion, the one on whom the valley Tlingits depended for their protection and their freedom, and even when the more powerful Tlingits from Sitka Island, led by the Great Toion, invaded in their canoes, sweeping all before them, when they came up against Raven-heart and his nine companions, they were halted, and it required two dozen of the invaders four bruising days to overcome Raven-heart's men. Three of his companions died in the battle, and he would have been among the dead except that the toion himself commanded: "Save that one!" and he was entangled in vines cleverly thrown about him, immobilized, and hauled before the victorious chief, who asked: "Your name?"

"Seet-yeil-teix," he replied in a surly manner, using three Tlingit words that meant *spruce-raven-heart,* and when the toion heard that his conspicuous captive was a Raven he smiled, for he himself was an Eagle, and although this implied natural competition against the Ravens, he had to acknowledge that a warrior, if he was a good Raven, could be exceptionally clever and formidable.

"How did you win your name?" he asked, and his captive replied: "I was trying to jump from this rock to that, fell into the stream. Wet and angry, tried again. Fell again. This time very angry, tried again. Just then a raven tried to pull loose something from a spruce limb. Slipped backward, tried again. And my father shouted: 'You're the raven.'"

"The third time, did you make the jump?"

"No. And the raven failed too. When I was bigger I jumped, and my name remained."

Because of his unusual persistence, he had been valuable to his tribe when unusual tasks confronted them, and he succeeded so often that he acquired a daring approach to everything, whether in battling other clans in actual warfare, or in building a house, or in decorating it with the proper totems when it was completed. It was this daring which had led to his capture, for when the Great Toion's army moved against Raven-heart's clan, the latter led the defensive sorties and raced so far ahead of his supporters that he was easily surrounded.

Now, as the toion gasped away his final moments, making death for Raven-heart inevitable, the captive made his boldest move. Slipping away from the wood-and-wattle big house in which the toion had lived since gaining ascendancy, Raven-heart moved carefully among the six tall totem poles that marked the place and edged toward the heavily forested area to the south. Cautiously he endeavored to slip into the deeper part of the forest, but was prevented by the noisy arrival of sixteen mourners coming from that direction. Jumping nimbly behind a large spruce, he heard them pass, lamenting the approaching death of their leader, but when they were gone, he leaped onto the path they had been following and dashed headlong into the saving comfort of the tall trees and the shady glens they protected. Once safe among the spruce, he began to run with an almost demonic fury, for his strategy required that he be removed as far as possible when the old man died.

He reasoned: If they can't find me at that moment, they can't kill me then. Of course, if they catch me later, they will kill me for having run away. But I have one good chance. If I can find an American ship and get aboard, I can tell them I was busy bartering, and they'll have to believe that. This strategy was not irresponsible or ill-founded, because he was one of the Tlingits who had learned enough rudimentary English to conduct trade negotiations with the Americans, whose ships stopped in Sitka Sound with considerable frequency.

So as he ran, he began calling silently upon those ships he remembered servicing with deer meat and fresh water when the Americans had come for peltries: *White-Dove,* come flying. *J.B. Kenton,* help me. *Evening Star,* shine to guide me.

But now the bad weather for which Sitka was famous descended like a feathery blanket, gray, thick and hanging but a few feet above the earth and the surface of the bay. It quickly became impenetrable, and any chance Raven-heart might have had of saving his life by attaching himself to some trader vanished, and for three agonizing days he hid among the spruce trees along the edge of the bay, waiting for the fog to lift.

On the evening of the third day, when he was hurting from hunger, he heard a muffled sound which electrified him. It seemed to be the firing of a cannon such as mariners used to create echoes from which they could deduce their approximate distance from the looming peril of rocky shores, but it was not repeated as would have been the case had this been such a probing shot. On the other hand, the cannon fire might have been so effective that only one shot was required, and with this hope to feed on he fell asleep in the lee of a fallen spruce.

In the early dawn he was awakened by the raucous voice of a raven, and no better signal from the other world could have been devised, because all Tlingits, from the beginning, had been divided into two moieties, the Eagle Clan and the Raven, and every human being on earth belonged to one or the other. Raven-heart was of course a Raven, which meant that he must defend that moiety in games between the two clans and in contests of a more serious kind, such as the providing of totem poles for the village commons or the bringing in of fish. As a Raven, he must marry only an Eagle, a provision established thousands of years earlier to protect the cleanliness of the race, but the child of a Raven man and a woman Eagle was an Eagle, and as such, was dedicated to the furtherance of that clan.

There was a belief among the Tlingits, and he subscribed to it, that although Eagles were apt to be more powerful, Ravens were by far the wisest, the wittiest and the cleverest in utilizing nature or in winning advantages over adversaries without recourse to fighting. It was known that mankind received water, fire and animals to feed upon through the cleverness of the First Raven, who outsmarted the primordial protectors of those boons to mankind. "All the good things were kept apart," his mother's brother had told him, "and we lived in darkness, cold and hunger until the First Raven, seeing our sorrow, tricked the others into letting us share these good things."

Now, when the raven cawed in the early dawn, he knew it was a signal that some rescue ship lay in the bay, and he ran to the water's edge expecting to see the vessel which might have fired the cannon the night before, if that was indeed the sound he had heard. But when he stared into the fog he saw nothing, and in his disappointment he could feel the crushing log upon his throat. Disconsolate and starving, he leaned against a spruce and glared at the invisible bay, still shrouded in gray, and in his extremity, very close to death, he again pleaded silently with the American ships to show themselves: *Nathanael Parker,* help me. *Jared Harper,* come close to save my life.

Silence, then the sound of iron against wood, and the arrival of a vagrant breeze which moved the fog a little; then, mysteriously, as if some powerful hand were drawing aside a curtain, the revelation of a shiplike form, followed by its quick submersion in the shifting mist. But the ship was there! And in desperation, ignoring the danger he placed himself in by revealing his position to searchers who might be trailing him, he ran to the shore and knee-deep into the water, crying in English: "Ship! Ship! Skins!"

If anything could lure the Americans, assuming they were Americans, to shore, it would be the promise of otter skins, but there was no response. Edging deeper into the water, in which he could not swim, he cried again: "Good Americans! Otter skins!" Again there was no response, but now a stronger gust of wind swept aside the fog, and there, not two hundred yards away, miraculously safe amid the dozen tree-studded islands that protected Sitka Sound, lay the Boston trader *Evening Star,* with which he had traded in the past.

"Captain Corey!" he shouted, dashing into the waves and flailing his arms, and making such a commotion that someone on the brig had to see him. An officer put a glass upon him and called to the bridge: "Native signaling, sir!" and a boat was lowered and four sailors rowed it hesitantly shoreward. When Raven-heart, overjoyed at being saved, waded forward to meet it, he found himself facing two rifles pointed right at his chest and heard the stern command: "Stand, or we fire!" Captain Miles Corey of the trader *Evening Star,* fifty-three years old and Pacific-hardened, having known too many commanders who had lost their ships, did not take any risks, anywhere, at any time. Before leaving the *Evening Star* in the skiff, the sailors had been warned: "It's one Indian. But there could be fifty lurking in those trees."

"Stand, or we fire!" the men repeated, and as Raven-heart froze, waist-deep in water, one of the four shouted: "My God, it's Raven-heart," and he reached out his paddle so that the Tlingit with whom he had traded before could make his way into the boat.

It was a gala reception that Captain Corey and First Mate Kane arranged for their old friend, and they listened attentively as he explained the predicament which had sent him alone into the forest. "You mean," Captain Corey asked, "that you'd have been killed? Just because the old man died?"

In his broken English, Raven-heart pleaded with them: "You say me on ship four days, eh? You say fog too much, eh? Four days."

"Why is four days so important?" Kane asked, and Raven-heart turned to explain. The two men were of about the same size, each a

muscular, fearless brawler, and for that reason Kane, the former harpooner, was attracted to the Tlingit, who explained: "I suppose to be
killed three days ago. Suppose run away, catched, killed now. But if I
on ship, trading with you . . ." By lifting his hands as if relieving them
of bonds, he indicated that with such an excuse he might be spared.

The omnipresent Sitka fog had once more descended upon the
Evening Star, this time so heavily that even the tips of the two masts
were invisible from the deck, so Corey and Kane assured the endangered slave: "We'll probably be in this soup two more days. You're
safe." And to celebrate they broke out a bottle of good Jamaican
rum, and there, in Sitka Sound, protected by the volcano and the
circle of unseen mountains, they reveled. When Raven-heart felt the
fine dark liquid exciting his throat, he relaxed and told the Americans
of the many pelts he had helped assemble for them, and they were so
pleased by this intelligence that they in turn showed him the goods
that they had brought from Boston to enrich his Tlingits.

"These are the casks of rum," Captain Corey said, indicating the
eighteen barrels stowed in safety belowdecks, "and what do you suppose these are?" Raven-heart, with a copper ring through the septum
of his nose, studied the dozen squared-off rectangular wooden cases,
and said: "Me not know," whereupon Corey ordered a sailor to draw
the nails—"And save them"—from one of the lids, and there, nestled
in oil-soaked rags, lay nine beautiful rifles, and below them, in similar
ranks of nine, twenty-seven others. These twelve boxes, packed in
orderly manner by the gunsmiths of Boston, contained four hundred
and thirty-two first-class long-barreled rifles, and the kegs stowed behind had enough powder to last two years, along with supplies of
lead for bullets and molds in which to make them.

Raven-heart, satisfied that no one could order him killed if he
brought such power to his captors, smiled, grasped Captain Corey's
hands, and thanked him profusely for the tremendous boon the Bos-
tonians were bringing the Tlingits: rum and guns.

A minor offshoot from the powerful Athapascans who populated interior Alaska, northern Canada and much of the western United
States, the Tlingits were a collection of about twelve thousand unique
Indians who had moved far south into what would later be Canada
and then fishhooked back north into Alaska, with their own language and customs. Divided into various clans, they occupied the

southern littoral of Alaska and especially the big offshore islands, their principal location being the excellent land surrounding Sitka Sound on the island of that name.

The people of the dead toion had chosen for their center a conspicuous promontory in the sound, one which rose to a small hill that dominated everything. It was an excellent site, surrounded by at least a dozen rude mountains that formed a protective semicircle to the east, with the majestic cone of the volcano standing as beacon to the west. But as the Russian Baranov had learned when he first saw the sound some years before, one of its most attractive features was the horde of islands, some no bigger than a tea table, others of considerable size, which speckled the surface of the water, breaking up surging storm waves that would otherwise have roared in from the Pacific.

When the fog finally lifted, Captain Corey gingerly threaded his *Evening Star* through the islands, bringing her some hundred yards from the foot of the hill, and fired a cannon to inform the Indians that he was prepared to trade with them for pelts, but when the time came for such trade, the Americans found themselves in a predicament. Ever since the ambushing of Captain Cook in the Hawaiian Islands, captains and crews had remained on their trading ships and invited natives to come aboard with their goods, while sailors armed with rifles maintained watch. However, at Sitka the Tlingits were preoccupied with burying their Great Toion, so the Americans launched a longboat, and with Raven-heart perched in the prow, they ignored custom and rowed ashore.

At first, the grieving Tlingits waved them away, but when those in charge of the ceremony saw the slave Raven-heart standing amongst the visitors, they announced that they had spent the last five days seeking him as one of the three slaves to be slain so as to provide the toion with servants in the next world. When Captain Corey and First Mate Kane realized that the Tlingits were determined to take Raven-heart from them and put him to death, they indicated that they would not allow this, but since they had only four sailors in the boat, and they without arms, they knew that the Tlingits could overpower them if they tried to make a serious protest. So with a sense of sinking shame at abandoning a good man who had placed his life in their care, they made no further objection when some of the elders seized Raven-heart and started hauling him to the ceremonial log.

But now an important man in Tlingit history stepped forward, the bold young chieftain Kot-le-an, a tall, sinewy fellow in his early thirties, dressed in shirt and trousers made from choice pelts and draped in a decorated white tunic of deerskin. About his neck he wore a chain made of shells and on his head the distinctive hat of the Tlingits, a kind of inverted funnel from the top of which streamed six ornate feathers. Like Raven-heart, he had a slim copper ring in his nose, but his brown-red features were made distinctive because of his drooping black mustache and neatly trimmed goatee. In height, slimness and mien he was visibly differentiated from the other Indians, and in voice, determination and willingness to act he displayed a moral force which made him the acknowledged military leader and principal aide to the toion.

The six Americans had not encountered Kot-le-an on previous trips to Sitka, for he had been absent on punitive forays against troublesome neighbors, but even had he been present they would probably not have met with him, because he felt that trade was beneath him. He was a warrior, and it was in this capacity that he now stepped forward to prevent the execution of Raven-heart. In words that the Americans did not understand and which were not interpreted for them, since Raven-heart had previously provided that service, the young chieftain voiced a decision that would soon prove to have been prophetic: "One of these days we shall have to protect our land from either the Americans like these here today or Baranov's Russians gathering strength in Kodiak. As your leader in battle, I shall need men like Raven-heart, so I cannot let you take him."

"But the Great Toion also needs him," several of the old men cried. "It would be indecent to send . . . ."

Kot-le-an, a man who loathed oratory or extended debate, responded by nodding to the elders, then ignoring them and grasping Raven-heart by the hand, pulling him free of both the Americans and the funeral managers: "This one I must have for when the battles begin," and in this abrupt manner the life of the big Tlingit was saved.

The Americans then watched with horror as two male slaves, young men in their teens, were dragged down the hill to the seashore, where their heads were held under water until they strangled. Unmarred, their corpses were then hauled back up the hill and placed ceremoniously beside the dead body of the Great Toion, whereupon four of the stoutest Tlingits grabbed the slave who had been selected to replace Raven-heart, stretched him across the sacrificial block of wood, and placed across his neck a slim driftwood log, pressing it down until all twitching in the body ceased. Sadly, as if mourning the loss of a friend, they placed this third body across the toion's feet, and signaled to the watching Indians that the burial of their chief could proceed.

After the funeral ceremony was concluded, trading for the pelts collected by the Tlingits proceeded, and ten of the eighteen barrels of rum were exchanged, under the mediation of Raven-heart, for seal pelts. No sea otters, the fur that China, Russia and California wanted, were in evidence, and it looked as if the *Evening Star* would have to sail without trading the guns, which the Tlingits really sought. However, just as Captain Corey was about to give the signal "Haul anchor!" Raven-heart and Kot-le-an drew up to the ship in a small wooden rowboat recently built in imitation of those used by American ships, and when the two men were aboard the *Evening Star,* Raven-heart showed the young chief who had saved his life the dozen boxes containing the guns, telling him in Tlingit: "There they are. The guns you need."

Kot-le-an, spotting immediately the box whose top had been removed earlier to show Raven-heart the guns, pulled the loose boards aside and saw the handsome dark-blue barrels and the polished brown stocks. Even had the guns had no practical purpose, they would have been beautiful, but as rifles capable of protecting the Tlingits from would-be invaders, they became objects of immense importance.

"I want them all," Kot-le-an said, but when this was interpreted, Captain Corey demurred: "We trade only for sea otter."

When this was translated, Kot-le-an found it impossible to control his rage. Stamping the deck with his moccasined feet, he shouted: "Tell him that we have enough men to take the guns!" but before Raven-heart could speak, Corey grabbed Kot-le-an by the arm, swung him about to indicate the four cannon on the port side pointing directly at the houses atop the hill, and then to the four on the starboard, which could be pivoted around. "And tell him," he snarled, "that we have one aft and one forrard, ten in all."

Translation was not necessary, for Kot-le-an knew what cannon were. One year ago an English ship, having fallen into dispute with Tlingits on the mainland, had lost a sailor in a brawl, and in retaliation had bombarded the offending village until only one house remained standing, and Kot-le-an knew that American whalers were even quicker to exact vengeance. Capitulating to Captain Corey's superior strength, he instructed Raven-heart: "Tell him in five days, many otter pelts."

When Corey saluted this information, as if Kot-le-an were the ambassador of a sovereign power, the Tlingits withdrew, and as they departed First Mate Kane assured them: "We'll wait five days." Within the hour the Americans saw numerous small boats set forth from Sitka Sound to visit outlying settlements, and during the next days they watched them returning much deeper in the water than they had been when departing.

"We'll be getting some otter pelts," Corey assured his men, but even as he prepared to leave ship he ordered Kane: "While Kot-le-an can see, train half our cannon on the hill, half on the shore where he'll be, and have the men stand ready." Kot-le-an, watching these preparations, was satisfied that no surprise attack from his side was going to succeed, but he also knew that the Americans, having come so far from Boston, could not return with an empty hold. They needed furs as badly as he needed guns, and from this pragmatic base the barter proceeded.

When Corey stepped ashore and saw the enormous number of pelts assembled under duress, he realized that whereas the sea otter might be extinct in the Aleutians, the Pribilofs and Kodiak, it was still swimming vigorously in these southern waters, and at the end of two hours of close inspection, he saw that he could with great profit to his ship dispose of his entire dozen cases of guns. So the deal was struck: "Tell Kot-le-an I will give him all the guns. You saw them, four hundred and thirty-two. But I want all these pelts and this many more." Pulling aside nearly a third of the pelts, he indicated that this was the requirement, then stood back, allowing Kot-le-an time to digest this new demand.

As a warrior, the young chief did not relish bartering, he was more used to command, but his apprehensions about the future were so strong that he knew he must have those guns the *Evening Star* carried, so with a gesture which astonished Corey, in a low voice he issued orders to his men, who moved aside a beached boat to disclose a hidden cache of otter pelts half again as large as the additional demand being made by Corey. Showing his contempt, he started kicking the skins toward the pile already belonging to Corey, and when he had thus moved some dozen pelts he growled to Raven-heart: "Tell him he can have them all."

When the precious cargo was safely stowed upon the *Evening*

Star, with a value many times the cost of the guns, Kot-le-an and Corey stood facing each other, and in a formality which the Tlingit had learned from English captains, he held out his right hand, and Corey took it. But the American was so surprised at the gesture and so pleased with the results of this barter that on the spur of the moment he told Raven-heart: "Tell Kot-le-an that because he gave us extra fur, we shall give him extra lead and powder," and he ordered his sailors to bring forth a substantial chunk of lead and nearly half a barrel of powder.

With warm feelings on both sides, the deal was concluded, and two days after the *Evening Star* sailed from Sitka with a fortune in otter skins to be traded in Canton for twice what Corey had calculated, the prudence of Kot-le-an in making this lopsided deal was confirmed. A small armada of Russian ships and Aleut kayaks came into the bay, passed insolently beneath the hill where the local Tlingits kept their headquarters, and threaded its way eight miles to the north, where, in a spot which seemed to be completely surrounded by protecting mountains, they proceeded to unload the material required for the building of a major fort.

The armada, headed by Chief Administrator Aleksandr Baranov, was not a trivial one, for it brought one hundred Russian men, some wives and nine hundred Aleuts to Sitka with the avowed purpose of establishing here the capital of Russian America, from which the mainland north of California could be developed as a major Russian holding. On 8 July 1799, Baranov led his people ashore, and his aide Kyril Zhdanko planted a Russian flag in the loamy soil beside a gently flowing river. Then Baranov asked Father Vasili Voronov, who had come with him to serve as spiritual mentor of the new capital, to offer thanks to God that although the long trip across the open ocean from Kodiak had experienced grave difficulties—scores of Aleuts dying from poisoned fish, hundreds perishing at sea—the Russians themselves had completed it safely, and that was what mattered. Prayers said, the chubby little master of Russian imperialism stood uncovered, wiped his bald head, and proclaimed: "As the old century draws to a close and a bright new one, full of promise, is about to begin, let us apply all our energies to the building of a noble capital city for the greatness that is to be Russian America."

With that, in a loud voice he christened the fort-that-was-to-be "Redoubt St. Michael," and Sitka's Golden Age was under way.

When Kot-le-an and his aide Raven-heart saw the Russian armada creep past their hill at the southern portion of the bay, their first impulse was to muster all the Tlingit troops and engage in whatever activities might prove necessary to repel the invaders and prevent them from landing, whatever their intentions. But when Kot-le-an took the first steps to put this plan into effect, a curious relationship, which would govern the rest of Raven-heart's life, came into operation. "Tell me what to do," he said to Kot-le-an, and by this statement he meant that whatever order was issued at any time, he was prepared to execute it regardless of danger to himself, because, as he said, "I am already dead. The log is across my throat. I breathe only at your pleasure."

"So be it," the young chieftain said. "What you must do first is scout out their positions and strength."

So Raven-heart, keeping to the woods, crept up the eight miles to Redoubt St. Michael and set up an observation post, from which he took careful note of the Russian potential: Three ships, not strong like *Evening Star* but many, many more men than the Americans. About a thousand men, but only one in ten are Russian. The others, what can they be? He studied the non-Russians with care, reasoning that they could not be Tlingits or from any clan associated with the Tlingits: They're shorter, darker. They wear bones through their noses and some of them have that strange sloping hat. He noticed two favorable aspects: They know how to make boats and none of our people can handle paddles the way they do. He decided that in a fight on the water, these little men would be formidable, and that with eight or nine hundred such fighters in support of the three big ships, the Russians would give a strong account of themselves.

They're Koniags, he concluded, and rumor had swept through the islands in recent years that these men of Kodiak were able warriors, to be avoided if possible, but before he reported this to Kot-le-an he wanted to assure himself as to the facts, so one night when the moon was gone, he crept close to where the outlines of the fort had been dug and waited in the darkness till one of the workmen wandered out.

With a leap and a big hand about the man's face, he dragged the man back into the trees, where he gagged him with a handful of spruce needles and bound him with sinew thongs. Sitting on him till daylight, he then hefted him across his shoulders like a bundle of pelts and marched back to Sitka Hill with him. There, others who were familiar with the languages of the Bering Sea identified the workman as an Aleut, and when they interrogated him they learned that he had been born on Lapak Island and had been taken as a slave to Kodiak. He revealed further that all the non-Russians at the redoubt were Aleuts. When asked: "Are your people happy to be working here?" he replied: "It's better than the Seal Islands."

Satisfied by further scouting that the cadre really was Aleut, Kot-le-an and Raven-heart decided that an attack in total force stood a good chance of driving off the Russians, for, as Kot-le-an pointed out, "If the others were all from Kodiak, it might be difficult, but we know that in battle we can overpower Aleuts." And an attack would have been mounted except that, to Kot-le-an's astonishment, the new toion, without adequate discussions among the warriors of his tribe, not only arranged a peace treaty with the Russians but actually sold them a portion of land at and around the growing fort.

Enraged by this supine surrender to what he properly perceived as a mortal threat to Tlingit aspirations, Kot-le-an assembled all who were disgruntled with this invitation to Russian interference in ancient ways, and harangued them:

"Once the Russians fix their fort on this bay, we Tlingits are doomed. I know them from what others say. They will never let go, and before we know it, they will demand this hill and this portion of the bay. They'll want the island there and the volcano and our hot baths and the shore beyond. All the otters will belong to them, not us, and for every American ship that comes here now to trade with us and bring us the things we need, six of theirs will come, and not for trade. With guns they'll steal everything we have.

"I am not happy with what I see as our fate if we let them stay unchallenged. Our totems will crumble. Our canoes will be driven from the bay. We will no longer be masters of our lands, for the Russians will smother us everywhere and in everything we want to do. I feel the terrible hand of the Russians pressing down upon us like the log that presses upon the throat of a condemned slave.

"I hear our children speaking not our language but theirs and I can smell the coming of their shaman among us and our souls will be lost to wander forever in the forests and the moaning will never end. I see these islands changed, and the seas lifeless, and the skies angry. I see the imposition of strange orders, new enforcements, totally different ways of life. And above all, I see the death of Tlingits, the death of all we have fought for through the years."

His words were so powerful, and so predictive of the future which many of his listeners were beginning to fear, that he might have enlisted hundreds in his drive to eliminate the Russians and their Aleut allies had not the leader of the Russians, this little man Baranov, anticipated such a ground swell. On a day in August, as summer was beginning to fade, this clever Russian, always attentive to the safety of his flanks, got in his biggest ship and had his sailors bring him down the bay to the Tlingit settlement, and as he approached the landing, where sailors carried him ashore through the waves, the sun came out in full radiance, so that he climbed the hill the first time on a day as beautiful as this part of Alaska provided.

It's an omen, he said to himself, as if he could foresee that he would spend the glory years of his life atop this fortuitous hill, and when he reached the lofty summit, with the new toion coming forth to greet him, he stopped, looked in all directions, and saw as if in a revelation the incredible majesty of this spot.

To the west swept the Pacific Ocean, visible beyond the hundred islands, the highway back to Kodiak, out to the far Aleutians and on to Kamchatka and the ramparts of Russia. To the south rose a squadron of mountains, marching backward in file to the end of the horizon, green then blue then misty gray, then almost white in the far distance. To the east, crowded close in, stood the glory of Sitka, the mountains that dipped their toes in the sea, big and powerful but also gentle in their green finery. They were mountains of infinite variety, of changing color, of surprising height to be so close to the sea. And to the north, where he was already building, he saw that splendid sound, island-dotted, ringed with its own mountains, some as sharp as needles carved from whalebone, others big and comfortable and rounded.

He was so enchanted by the rich variety of this scene from the hill that he was tempted to cry out at its wonder, but his Russian merchant's canniness warned him not to reveal how struck he was lest his Tlingit hosts fathom his interest in their paradise. Dropping his head and keeping his arms folded across his belly, as was his custom, he merely said: "Great and Powerful Toion, in appreciation for your many kindnesses in helping us to establish our little fort on your bay, I bring you a few humble gifts." And motioning to the sailors who accompanied him, he had them unroll bundles which contained beads, brass, cloth and bottles. After these had been distributed he asked his men for the *pièce de résistance*—and he called it by just those words in French—and they produced a somewhat rusty, out-of-date musket, which he handed gravely to the toion, asking one of the sailors to provide powder and ball plus an exhibition of how the old gun should be fired.

When the sailor had everything in order, he showed the toion how to handle the gun, apply his forefinger to the trigger, and discharge the ball. There was a flash of fire as the excess powder burned away, a feeble blast from the end of the gun, and a slight rustle of leaves as the ball bounced its way harmlessly through the treetops below the hill. The toion, who had never before fired a gun, was excited, but Kot-le-an and Raven-heart, who had nearly five hundred first-class new rifles hidden away, smiled indulgently.

However, it was canny Baranov who seemed to triumph, for in response to these impressive gifts, offered with such voluntary good will, he was given the loan of fifteen Tlingits, who would move to the fort and supervise the Aleuts in catching and drying the multitude of salmon which had begun streaming into the small river to the north of the fort. Kot-le-an, infuriated by this easy capitulation of his toion to the blandishments of the strangers, did gain one advantage: he insinuated into this group of temporary workers his man Raven-heart, so that when Baranov returned to the fort with the salmon experts, he took also a spy with unusual powers of observation and deduction.

At the fort, Raven-heart performed like the other Tlingits, standing knee-deep at the mouth of the river with a wicker scoop, which he dipped among the multitude of fat thirteen-inch salmon as they returned to their natal stream to spawn and give rise to the new generation. They left the salt water like myrmidons, each fish in file behind another, fifty or sixty files across, so that at any one spot at the river mouth for these relatively few days, thousands of fish passed, driven only by their urge to return to the fresh water where they had been born years ago, and there to lay the eggs which would renew their species.

A blind man with a torn net could catch salmon at this spot, and when Raven-heart and his mates had thrown several thousand ashore, they showed the Russians how to spot females rich with roe and how to eviscerate the fish and prepare them for drying in the sun. Baranov, watching the stacking up of food in piles of unbelievable size, told his Russians: "This winter nobody starves."

In the evenings, when work was done and the Tlingits were left to themselves, Raven-heart utilized his time in memorizing details of the growing fort. He saw that the promontory was divided into two halves: one inland, consisting of a blockhouse that could be furiously defended from fixed gun emplacements and portholes through which rifles could be fired; the other half, a collection of small buildings outside the main blockhouse and not heavily defended. These sheds and barns, he concluded, were to be sacrificed in case of an attack, with all defenders withdrawing inside the fortress, which had to the rear, away from the seafront, a huge square yard with walls two feet thick. Invading and taking that fortress was not going to be easy.

But the more he studied the redoubt the more clearly he saw that a determined assault, which took first the outlying buildings without destroying them and then laid siege to the blockhouse, could succeed if some way were found to break into that huge enclosed yard at the rear, for then the attackers could nibble away at the central redoubt while enjoying protection from the very buildings provided by the Russians, and in time the latter would have to surrender. Redoubt St. Michael could be captured, provided the attackers were led by a man like Kot-le-an and staffed by determined aides like Raven-heart.

When the salmon season ended, in late September, the Tlingits were sent back to their hill, with the understanding that they would not be needed next year, since the Russians and Aleuts were now proficient in the business of catching and preserving the valuable fish. Fourteen of the Tlingits left the redoubt merely with memories of a reasonably pleasant stay, but Raven-heart departed with complete plans for capturing this fort, and as soon as he rejoined Kot-le-an, the two men drew up diagrams of the Russian installation and procedures for destroying it.

During the remainder of 1799 the impetuous young men were prevented from putting their scheme into operation by the hesitancy of their toion, who was awed by Russian power, and by the thought-ful leadership of Aleksandr Baranov, who anticipated and frustrated any Tlingit moves. Whenever it looked as if the Indians on their hill might be getting restive, he threw them off balance by offering them trades of surprising generosity, and once when several hundred of them threatened actual rebellion, he boldly marched among them, advising them to come to their senses. "He's a brave one," the Tlingits said, and in this manner Kot-le-an and Raven-heart were neutralized by Baranov's clever moves, even though they continued to regard him as their chief enemy.

In the summer of 1800, at the end of the first full year since the Russian arrival at Redoubt St. Michael, when Raven-heart's spying warned him that the fortress had been completed in good style and ahead of schedule, Baranov, to the surprise of all, loaded one of his ships with pelts from Sitka waters, hoisted sail, and set out for Ko-diak, where his wife, Anna, and his son, Antipatr, waited in the big log house which served as the capitol of Russian America. He had gone to Kodiak expecting to load there with supplies forwarded from main-land Russia, but when he landed he heard the pitiful news: "No ship has reached us in the past four years. We're starving." So his attention was diverted from his outpost at Sitka and directed to the problem which would assail him all his life in Alaska: How can I increase the power of this colony if I'm ignored and neglected by the homeland?

With Baranov tied down in Kodiak, no help from that quarter could be forwarded to the new establishment at Sitka, and in the summer of 1801, Kot-le-an and Raven-heart suspected that the Rus-sians would be so weakened that they would not be able to defend themselves. But just as the Tlingits were preparing their attack, the Boston trader *Evening Star* put into the sound on a return trip from Canton, and whereas on all previous visits it had anchored near the hill to conduct trading with the Tlingits, this time it sailed right past, as if acknowledging that now it was the Russian fort that was impor-tant. Seething with anger, Kot-le-an suffered the indignity of having to get into a boat and trail along behind the trader as if hungry for its favors, and then wait in the sound until the Americans had com-pleted details with the Russians. "I have been made a stranger in my own land," the young chieftain fumed to Raven-heart, who took ad-vantage of the enforced idleness to coach his leader in the steps that would be required when the attack on the redoubt took place. That it would occur, neither man doubted.

But it did not happen in 1801 because supplies from the *Evening Star* strengthened the four hundred and fifty Russians who now operated the place, making an assault at this time inadvisable. However, on its way out of the bay, the *Evening Star* did stop at the Tlingit stronghold, where Captain Corey and First Mate Kane proved their basic friendship for the Indians by showing them a corner of the hold in which they had hidden from Russian eyes the trade goods that the Tlingits really sought, casks of rum and flat boxes filled with additional rifles made originally in England and shipped to China.

"We saved the best for last," Corey assured the Indians, and as before, Raven-heart scrambled among the small settlements scattered about the littoral, collecting the still-surprising harvest of sea-otter pelts. When the barter was concluded, Corey and Kane met with Kot-le-an on the hill, and as they shared a bottle of rum, the Americans drinking little but pouring generously for the Tlingits, Corey observed: "Wouldn't it make sense to join these two settlements? Russians and Tlingits working together?"

"In Boston," Kot-le-an asked with surprising acuity, "do you and your Tlingits work together?"

"No. That wouldn't be possible."

"Here, too, it is not possible," and Corey, remembering the large number of guns he had sold these warlike Tlingits, looked at his first mate and with a gesture so slight that only Kane could see it, shrugged his right shoulder as if to say: "What happens is their business, not ours," and that afternoon he made final calculations on his cargo of whale oil and otter skins, weighed anchor, and headed for Boston, which he had not seen in six years.

When he was gone, Kot-le-an told Raven-heart: "We'll wait. If you want to build your house at the southern salmon stream, do it now," and this invitation, thrown off so casually, marked a turning point in the slave's life, for it released him, by implication, from servitude. Because if a Tlingit was free to build his own house, it meant he was also free to take himself a wife to help occupy that house, and for some time now Raven-heart had been eying with increasing excitement a Tlingit girl who bore the lovely name of Kakeena, a name of lost meaning belonging to her great-grandmother. She had not only the bland, open face which bespoke spiritual ease but also a nobility of bearing which warned the world: "I shall do many things in my own way." The daughter of a skilled fisherman, she was sixteen, and for some lucky reason had escaped both tattooing and the inserting of labrets into her lower lip. She was, in these early years of the new century, the self-confident yet modest type of young woman who, in these times of change, might be expected to marry with some Russian in exile, forming with him a bridge between past and present, between Tlingit and Russian.

But even as a child she had sensed that this was not going to be possible, for she was fiercely devoted to the Tlingit way of life, and she saw that the spiritual distance between the Tlingit village and the Russian fort was so great that it could not be honorably bridged unless the Tlingit woman surrendered her identity, and this she knew she would refuse to do. In recent months her parents had begun to wonder: "What will become of our daughter?" as if they were responsible for her salvation and not she. They were pleased when several young Tlingit and Russian men displayed their lively interest in her, and during the latest visit of the *Evening Star* they had been aware that First Mate Kane had tried several times to get her into his bed, but she had rebuffed both him and the local lads for the good reason that she had, when she was only fourteen, identified the slave Raven-heart as the finest young man in the region. In subsequent years she had witnessed his sturdy courage, his loyalty to Kot-le-an, his ability in trading with the Americans and, above all, his comely manner, for she saw in his face the same kind of stately calm she had seen in her own when allowed to borrow one of the magical mirrors provided by Captain Corey.

So in this quiet summer of 1801, Raven-heart had three tasks, to the completion of which he could apply his entire energy: win Kakeena as his wife, build them a house on the banks of the salmon stream beneath the big spruce trees, and carve himself a totem pole like the ones that had graced his home village to the south in the days before his capture and servitude.

The various tribes of Tlingits were so different in nature that they scarcely seemed like members of the same family. The Tlingits at Yakutat to the north were almost savage, so intent were they on warfare, raiding and the killing of prisoners. Those like Kot-le-an on the hill above Sitka Sound were warlike enough to defend their terrain but also gentle enough to appreciate the rewards of peace, if it could be obtained on their principles. Those to the south, where Raven-heart had lived, existed along the borders of the Haida people, a distinct branch of Athapascans with their own language, and from them had acquired the gracious habit of carving for each village and prominent home a totem pole of red cedar, tall, stately, colorful and a re-cord of events important to that village or that home. Kot-le-an's people rarely carved totems, and the Yakutats burned them when overrunning a village, but Raven-heart, living as he must in alien land, would not feel easy in any house which was not protected by its totem.

So with the vigor which characterized him, he launched all three of his assignments simultaneously. Asking Kot-le-an to accompany him, he marched to the fisherman's hut where Kakeena lived and solemnly asked her father: "May I have the honor of taking your daughter to wife?" and before the father could respond, Kot-le-an assured him: "This one can be trusted."

"But he's a slave," the fisherman protested, to which Kot-le-an replied: "No more. Honor erases that," and the marriage was ar-ranged.

That afternoon, on the banks of the salmon stream a mile east of the hill in the heart of a noble stand of spruce trees, Raven-heart and Kakeena began felling the logs which would form their home, and in the early evening, when the outlines of their house had been staked out, they hauled ashore the cedar log from which he would carve his totem. Next day, with the help of Kot-le-an himself and three of his assistants, the log was lifted onto the supports which would hold it free of the ground while Raven-heart carved, a task which would oc-cupy his spare time for nearly a year.

As he worked on the log, carving only the side that would be exposed in front, he incorporated a personal selection of those precious images which summarized the spiritual history of his peo-ple: the birds, the fish, the great bears, the boats that plied the waters, the spirits that directed life. But he did not do so haphazardly; in obedience to the same principles that had guided Praxiteles and Michaelangelo in fashioning their sculptures, he followed highly tra-ditional patterns for relating forms and color so masterfully that the totem, as it gradually emerged, would be no mere illustrated pole standing before a house, but a forceful, sophisticated work of art, magnificent in its final appearance. He and Kakeena were pleased with it when it was finally ready for erecting into place, and they were honored when the toion, Kot-le-an and the shaman came south to honor and bless it as it rose in the air, a signal that in the house below lived a Tlingit family that took life seriously.

Married, with a house three-quarters built and a bright totem in place, Raven-heart was at work in June of 1802 when Kot-le-an and two of his men ran east to the salmon stream with exhilarating news: "The Russians were never weaker. Now's the time to destroy them." So Raven-heart was dispatched to complete his spying, and from a thicket east of Redoubt St. Michael he determined various significant facts: the dangerous adversary Baranov was not in residence; his trusted assistant Kyril Zhdanko was gone too; with so many of the Aleuts returned to Kodiak, the total complement at the fort seemed to be about fifty Russians and only two hundred Aleuts, a number which could be defeated; and whereas the number of small, unprotected buildings along the shore had increased, the big fort itself and its attendant palisaded square had not been strengthened.

Reporting to Kot-le-an and his aides, Raven-heart said: "Same as the plans we drew up before. Strike by boat from the bay, by land from the forest. Take the small buildings in the first blow, dig in, and then overwhelm the redoubt."

"The first part easy?" Kot-le-an asked, and Raven-heart nodded. "But the second part?" Kot-le-an asked, and his spy gave an honest answer: "Very difficult."

When the force of Tlingit boats left the southern part of the sound at eleven o'clock at night in late June, the sun had barely set, and as the quiet flotilla moved north, coordinating its movement with that of the warriors infiltrating through the forest, the fort was outlined in the silver glow of a midsummer Alaskan night in which darkness would never come. Silently the two forces converged, and at four in the morning, coincident with the return of the sun, they fell upon the Russian encampment, occupied immediately all the unprotected buildings, and swept into the palisaded yard, and then, following tactics which the spy Raven-heart had developed two years before, attacked the spots he had seen to be weakest, broke through, set the Russian buildings afire, and cut the throats of the defenders as they fled to escape the flames. Russians and Aleuts alike perished, and only those fortunate enough to be absent on fishing or fur-hunting parties escaped.

When the carnage was completed, Kot-le-an, its instigator, stood among the dead bodies and cried: "Let this be a warning to the Russians! They cannot come and steal Tlingit land!" After burning the Russian ships and boats, the victorious Tlingits marched in triumph back to their hilltop home, conquerors of Sitka Sound, protectors of Tlingit rights.

• • •

Although astonished by the ease with which he had eliminated the Russians, Kot-le-an did not even briefly suppose that a determined man like Baranov would allow such a humiliation to go unchallenged. What response the Russians would make and when, he could not anticipate, but certain that it must come, he initiated unusual precautions. Striding out to where Raven-heart and his wife were still at work on their new home, he announced bluntly: "This is the best site on the island. Our fort must be here." Raven-heart, who had spent considerable energy in building as much of the house as was finished and in carving his totem, started to protest this invasion, but was stopped by Kakeena, who stepped forward with a boldness that surprised him: "Kot-le-an, we shall have no rest till we drive the Russians from our land. Take our house." And when Tlingits arrived to convert their home into a military headquarters, she worked with them. Later, it was she who suggested that the whole area be enclosed in a high, thick, spear-studded palisade, and on the construction of this she also helped.

The completed fort—a collection of strong small buildings protected by a palisade—stood close to the salmon stream on the east and not far from the sound on the south. To the east it was guarded by a dense forest whose older trees fell in crisscross positions when they died, forming an impenetrable thicket. When all was done, Kotle-an told his people: "We cannot defend this hill. Russian ships could lie in the sound and bombard us with their cannon, but down on the point where we have our new fort, they'll not be able to get close enough to harm us."

"When do we move there?" some women asked, but the toion replied: "Not before the Russians come . . . if they ever do," and Raven-heart, hearing this almost boastful statement, thought: Kot-le-an's right. A man like Baranov will return. He'll have to.

So the dream of Raven-heart and Kakeena was lost in the plans of war. The house was built, but it served as a military headquarters, and the totem was in place, but it stood before a Tlingit version of the Russian redoubt and not before a home.

"Can we hold it against the Russians?" Kakeena asked, and her husband equivocated: "We built it strong. You can see that."

"But can the Russians fight their way in? The way you did against them?"

"One of these days we'll see," he replied, and a kind of nervous, passive waiting began. Then in September 1804, Russian ships crowded with fighting men began appearing in Sitka Sound, first the *Neva,* come all the way from St. Petersburg, then the *Jermak,* the *Katharina* and the *Alexander.* Three hundred and fifty two-man kayaks also reported at the end of a fearful crossing of the gulf that separated Sitka from Kodiak. Toward the end of the month the sound was dominated by a hundred and fifty Russians and more than eight hundred Aleuts, all well-armed and eager to avenge the destruction of Redoubt St. Michael two years before. Since it was assumed by the Russians that they would have to storm the hill the Tlingits had occupied in the past, on the night of 28 September, Baranov brought his ships close to the foot of the hill, with every intention of investing it under gunfire in the morning.

But when dawn broke next morning and the Russians began marching up the hill behind Baranov, a brave man prepared for battle, they found to their surprise an unoccupied fort; all the Tlingits had fled to their big new fortress a mile to the east, where the totem stood protecting the main gate, whose supporting walls were twenty inches thick. Announcing that he had won a victory, Baranov assigned troops to man the abandoned fort and hauled up seven cannon, which were emplaced so as to command all approaches. "I don't know where the Tlingits are," he told his men, "but they will never again occupy this hill," and he would enforce that decision for the remainder of his life.

The Tlingits, safe in their new fortress and satisfied that they could hold it against any Russian pressure, laughed when they heard how Baranov had attacked an empty fort, but their attitude became more grave when spies reported: "They're beginning to load extra men on the four warships anchored at the foot of the hill." This news did not frighten Kot-le-an, but it did make him wonder how much damage the guns on those four warships could do, so he dispatched Raven-heart to parley with Baranov and settle the terms under which the two groups could share this handsome bay and the riches it commanded.

With one young warrior at his side, and with a white flag atop a tall pole, Raven-heart strode down the path leading through the forest, expecting to spread before the Russians the terms which Kot-le-an would be proposing, and he was shocked when he reached the fort to be dismissed abruptly with the scornful words: "Our commander does not deal with underlings. If your chief wishes to converse with us, let him appear in person."

Humiliated and enraged, Raven-heart stormed back to Kot-le-an, informing him that there was no purpose in further negotiation, but during Raven-heart's absence, the young chief had become more convinced that peaceful sharing was better than open warfare, so in the morning Raven-heart, accompanied by a special emissary, returned to the hill, this time by water and in a ceremonial canoe. As Raven-heart brought the canoe to a landing place, the emissary began to chant a flowery message of peace:

> "Mighty Russians, we of the Mighty Tlingit seek your friendship. You took our land for your redoubt, we took back your redoubt for our land. We stand even, toe to toe, hand to hand, so let us abide in peace."

With that, the emissary threw himself from the canoe, lay in water up to his nostrils, and looked pleadingly at the Russian sentries, who whistled for officers to come. Down the steps leading from the hill marched two young men who when they saw the floating emissary began laughing. When they saw that Raven-heart was back again, they spat out the same contemptuous message: "If your chief has a message, let him come in person," and they were about to withdraw when Raven-heart unfolded before them one of the largest, silkiest sea-otter skins this area had ever produced. In English he cried: "This is our present to the Great Baranov!" and the gift was so compelling that the officers led him up the stone steps to the fort, where Baranov accepted the pelt graciously, giving him in return a complete suit of woolen clothing.

In Tlingit the former slave, now a man of considerable dignity, said: "Great Baranov, we seek peace," at which the Russian spelled out his demands: "You must leave two hostages with me. You must confirm our ownership of this hill and such surrounding territory as I shall designate for our headquarters. And you must remain peacefully in this area and trade with us."

After asking for two repetitions of the demands, Raven-heart asked: "You want all this land?" Baranov nodded. "And you want us to live obedient to your commands?" Again the Russian nodded, whereupon Raven-heart drew himself up to his considerable height and said: "I speak for our chieftain Kot-le-an and for our toion. We shall never accept such terms."

Baranov did not flinch. Looking inquisitively toward Captain Lisiansky of the *Neva,* who nodded, he said almost casually: "Tell Kotle-an that our attack will begin at dawn tomorrow." And by the time Raven-heart reached his canoe, where the emissary waited, the two Tlingits saw that Russian soldiers and hundreds of Aleut fighting men had started streaming toward the four ships and the kayaks.

On 1 October 1804 the four warships were ready to sail the short distance to the Tlingit fort and start bombarding it, but an infuriating calm settled over the sound, and the big ship *Neva,* on which the Russians must depend, could not be moved. However, the *Neva* was commanded by Captain Urey Lisiansky, a determined and resourceful fighter, and he resolved the impasse by lining up more than a hundred kayaks, which, by means of ropes attached to their sterns, pulled the heavy ship slowly into position. Kot-le-an, watching this herculean effort, whispered to Raven-heart: "They mean to fight," and stern preparations were ordered.

The efficiency of Captain Lisiansky was somewhat diluted by the fact that Baranov, fifty-seven years old and overweight, fancied himself a military genius with the right to lead into battle a force consisting of about one-half the effectives. Dubbed by his men the Commodore, he believed that his experience in Siberian brawls and minor island skirmishes qualified him as a tactician, and he shouted orders like a battle-tested veteran. However, buffoon though he seemed to some, his gallantry and lust for vengeance on the Tlingits who had destroyed his redoubt so inspired his men that they were prepared to follow him anywhere.

But before leading his men forward in the actual assault, Baranov, remembering battle stories he had read, believed he was honorbound to offer his enemy one last chance to surrender, so he sent forward three Russians under a white flag. When they neared the Tlingit fort, the one in command cried in loud voice: "You know our demands. Give us land. Hostages. And stay here peacefully to trade."

From inside the fort came laughter and then a volley which rattled high in the trees over the negotiators' heads. These men, afraid that the next shots might be directed at them, scampered back to the *Neva,* where they told Baranov how they had been received. He did not rant, but to those about him he said: "Now we take their fort," and as agreed beforehand, Captain Lisiansky dispatched four small boats, heavily armed, to destroy all the Tlingit canoes left on the beach. The battle had begun.

Now Baranov, clad in a suit of wood-and-leather armor, sword held high, waded ashore at the head of his men, determined to assault the walls and demand surrender. Supported by three small portable cannon, he stopped to listen for sounds of Tlingits inside the fort, heard none, and cried: "They've abandoned it, just like they did the hill," and with a bold, peasant heroism he led his men right up to the walls.

But as soon as they came well within musket range, the walls erupted with fire from hundreds of good Boston rifles, and the effect upon the invaders was disastrous, for the unexpected volley struck many full in the face.

When the Russians retreated in disorder, the Tlingits broke from their central gate guarded by the totem pole and descended upon the disorganized men, killing and wounding without having to dodge any counterfire. And had not Captain Lisiansky sped to Baranov's relief, a general slaughter would have occurred. The first round, clearly won by the Tlingits, had been a disastrous defeat for Commodore Baranov.

Back aboard the *Neva*, he revealed to his officers a major wound in his left arm, and after he was put to bed under a doctor's care, Lisiansky summed up the fracas: "Three of my men dead, fourteen Russians wounded and countless Aleuts, who fled like rabbits at the first gunfire. But we gained one victory. Baranov is wounded just seriously enough to keep him from marching forth again. Now let's organize this siege and blow that fort apart."

But before the cannonading could begin, there was an ugly portent that this battle was to be a no-surrender affair like the earlier assault on Redoubt St. Michael, where all Russians present were slaughtered, for onto the beach almost in range of their enemy's pistol fire came six Tlingit warriors bearing spears aloft, on whose tips was impaled the body of one of the dead Russians. At a whistle from their leader, the Tlingits jabbed their six spears sharply upward, driving the points so far through the body of the corpse that the metal tips shone red with blood. Then, at another signal, they threw their spears forward, allowing the body to splash into the bay.

Minutes later the cannonading began, and when word reached the deck that a fourth Russian had died from his wounds, the fire intensified. For two days the bombardment continued, and a sortie in strength under Lisiansky ranged the area before the fort, killing any Tlingits they encountered, but in doing so, they saw that the great wooden fence constructed by Kot-le-an and Raven-heart had sufficient thickness to repel even the biggest cannonballs.

"We won't win by trying to knock down the fence," Lisiansky told his men, and after this was reported to Baranov he consulted with his captain, the elevation of the guns was raised, and cannonballs of destructive size and frequency began raining down into the fort's interior.

Lisiansky, watching them land with rarely a miss, assured Baranov: "They won't be able to tolerate this for long," and grimly the fat little merchant smiled.

During the first days of the siege there had been great jubilation inside the fort, for then the Tlingit defenders gained three significant victories: their palisaded walls had proved to be impervious to Russian fire, they had repulsed the first land attack with heavy loss to the enemy, and without suffering any retaliation they had successfully taunted the Russians at the seashore, spearing the corpse and tossing the body into the waves. "We can hold them off!" Kot-le-an cried in those moments of initial victory.

But when the cannonading began in earnest, with the Russians firing over the walls, the tides of war shifted dramatically. There were, inside the stockade, some fifteen separate buildings clustered about the house that Raven-heart and Kakeena had started, and with hellish luck the Russian cannonballs began striking these wooden buildings, smashing them apart and killing or badly wounding the occupants. Children shrieked as the destruction continued, and there was a terrible moment when three shots in a row struck the Raven-heart house, scattering embers and starting a fire which quickly consumed the entire building. Raven-heart, watching the raging flames, had a premonition that he was seeing the demise of all things the Tlingits cherished, for this house had been a symbol of his release from slavery and his acceptance into the strongest of the Tlingit tribes.

However, knowing he must not allow either Kakeena or Kot-le-an to see his apprehension, he passed among the fort's defenders with words of encouragement: "They'll stop. They'll see they can't conquer us and they'll go away." But as he uttered such words during the third day of the bombardment he was interrupted by a scream from Kakeena, and supposing that she had been hit by one of the cannonballs, he ran toward where he had last seen her, but when he reached her he found her standing, mouth agape and looking toward the sky. Unable to speak, she pointed heavenward, and then he saw what had caused her outcry: a shot from the *Neva* had struck his totem halfway up and had shattered it, knocking away the carefully carved top with the raven and leaving a jagged stump, still tall but forever decapitated. Remembering the legends of his people and their spirits which he had carefully carved in the pole, he was distraught, but still he did not allow himself to show his distress at the loss of yet another aspect of the life he loved and had hoped to defend. And the bombardment continued.

As daylight waned on the sixth day, Kot-le-an came to Raven-heart with a message the latter had not expected to hear: "Trusted friend, take the white flag and go to them."

"Asking for what?"

"Peace."

"On what terms?"

"Any they propose."

For some minutes, while Kot-le-an gathered a team of six to accompany his messenger, Raven-heart stood in the middle of the wreckage and felt the ground swaying under him. A dream was coming to an end, a world was being lost, and he had been selected to be the man to do the surrendering, but before putting into effect the signal of submission, his entire body revolted—eyes refused to see, feet to move, and mind to accept the horrid duty—and he cried to no one: "I cannot!"

It was Kakeena, not Kot-le-an, who persuaded him: "You must. Look," and she pointed to the destroyed houses, the row of corpses not yet buried, the universal signs of loss. "You must go," she whispered.

Astonished that it was his resolute wife who was uttering these words of defeat, he turned to stare at her, and saw that she was grimly smiling: "This time we've lost. Save what we can. Next time, when they've grown careless, we'll crush them." And when he moved toward the gate through which he would lead his messengers of surrender, she walked beside him to the beach, where he called in English to the Russians, who halted their bombardment when they saw his white flag: "Baranov, you win. We talk."

Through a brass trumpet came a reply in Russian: "Go to bed. No more bombardment. In the morning we will come."

At these words, which meant that the siege was over and that Tlingit hopes of recovering Sitka were doomed, Kakeena began a high-pitched wail which Russian listeners interpreted as a lament for lost hopes; they would have been astounded could they have understood her words: "Ai me, the waves have left our shore and only rocks remain. But like the rocks we will endure and in the years to come we shall return like the waves and smother the Russians." And as the enemy sailors listened in the falling darkness, they heard one Tlingit voice after another join in the supposed lament until the shore was filled with what they construed as grief but which was, under Kakeena's leadership, a commitment to revenge.

When Raven-heart and his contingent returned to the fort, they were greeted by silence. The cannonading had stopped, but so had purposeful movement by the Tlingits. Standing in confused groups, they discussed what to do next, and as Raven-heart went from one gathering to the next, he found only consternation and lack of any plan as to what action they must take after the surrender, but toward midnight Kot-le-an and the toion assumed command, and their directives were short and brutal: "We shall cut across the mountains and leave this island forever." And as those fateful words were whispered through the fort, their awful meaning became clear, for to cross Sitka Island at any point was a monstrous undertaking, considering the jagged mountains and the lack of trails. But the Tlingits had decided to flee, and in the four hours after midnight there was in this destroyed fort a hurricane of activity.

Only Raven-heart and Kakeena had actually lived on this beautiful point between the salmon creek and the bay, so only they had mementos which they wished to take with them—for him, a fragment of the totem; for her, a shattered wooden plate—but all who prepared to flee carried recollections of their majestic hill overlooking the bay, and all were heavy-hearted.

As dawn approached, two groups of refugees had special and heartbreaking tasks: appointed men roamed through the fort killing all the dogs, especially those who had attached themselves to specific families, for to take them on the journey ahead would prove impossible, and there were moments of grief as some animal that had bounded with love at the sound of a child's voice was slain, but this sadness was soon forgotten, because a comparable team of women led by Kakeena was passing through the assembling crowd, killing all the Tlingit babies.

Early on the morning of 7 October, as the mists lifted and the bright autumn sun appeared, sailors from the *Neva* and the three other ships lined up on the beach behind Commodore Baranov and started their triumphal march to accept the surrender of the Tlingits, but as they approached the fort they saw no people, heard no sounds, and with uncertainty they drew closer, whereupon a cackle of ravens took to the air, and one superstitious sailor muttered: "They feed on the dead," and when Baranov peered past the sagging gates, knocked awry by some cannon shot, he saw the desolation, the litter of dead dogs and the tiny human corpses. It was a moment of dreadful victory, accentuated by the sudden appearance from a shattered house of two old women too ancient to travel who were guarding a six-year-old boy with a crippled leg.

"Where have they gone?" Baranov demanded of the women, who pointed to the north. "Across those mountains?" the interpreter asked, and they said "Yes."

As they spoke, Kot-le-an, Raven-heart and the toion who had lost his kingdom were leading their people across rough land covered by immense spruce trees, each trunk as tall and straight as a line drawn in sand. The going was so difficult that only a few miles would be covered that day and it would be painful weeks before they reached the northern limits of Sitka Island. When they did, they would have to halt for the building of canoes to ferry them across Peril Strait, after which they would have to find some kind of refuge on inhospitable Chichagof Island, a place infinitely more brutal and unyielding than Sitka Sound.

But they persisted, and finally reached the northern edge of the island, and when they saw, across the strait, the mountains of their new home, some wept, for they knew they were making a miserable exchange. But Raven-heart, having been dispossessed before in his turbulent life, told Kakeena: "I think we can make a home over there," and as he spoke, a fish jumped in Peril Strait and he told his wife: "Good sign."

• • •

Now came the fifteen amazingly productive years, 1804 through 1818, which confirmed the reputation of Aleksandr Baranov as the father and chief inspirator of Russia's fragile empire in North America. Fifty-seven years old when his burst of energy began, he displayed the enthusiasm of a boy going after his first deer, the wisdom of a Pericles building a new city, the patience of an island Job.

As a builder he was indefatigable, for as soon as the last fragment of the Tlingit fort was burned, including all parts of the totem pole, he hurried his people back to start work on the hilltop, where he built himself a modest cottage from which he could survey the sound, the volcano and the surrounding mountains. During his lifetime that cottage would be rebuilt into a more imposing house of many rooms, and after his death, into a grandiose mansion three stories high and crammed with rooms of all sorts, including a theater. And even though he would never see or occupy it, it would always be known as Baranov's Castle, and from it Russian America would be governed.

At the foot of the hill he outlined a generous area including a large lake, and this he enclosed within a high wooden palisade; it would be the Russian town. But now a curious problem arose, for Baranov called his settlement New Archangel, while ship captains of all nations, and the Tlingits and Aleuts who shared the site, continued to call it Sitka, the name by which it would ultimately be known. So the fine town would have two names used interchangeably, but only one important rule: "No Tlingits allowed inside the palisade."

But even as he proclaimed that law, Baranov made plans for the day when the Indians would return to help him build a greater New Archangel, and when a huge area adjoining the palisade was cleared, he explained to the townspeople: "That's to be kept for the Tlingits when they start to come back. They're sensible people. They'll see we need them. They'll see they can live better sharing this spot with us than hiding out in the wilderness, wherever they are now."

That crucial decision made—"Russians inside the walls, Tlingits outside"—Baranov turned his energies to the construction of a major town, and with the help of Kyril Zhdanko in a time so short it startled the workmen doing the building, he had a huge barracks for his soldiers; a school which, as in the case of the orphanage in Kodiak, he paid for out of his own meager salary; a library; a meeting hall for social affairs, with a treasured corner in which a piano imported from St. Petersburg was housed for the dances he sponsored and a stage for the one-act plays he encouraged his men and their wives to perform; plus a dozen other necessary buildings like sheds for the overhaul of ships putting in to New Archangel and shops in which their instruments of navigation and their cannon could be overhauled.

When these day-to-day essentials had been ensured, he turned to Father Vasili: "With this safe start behind us, Father, we'll now build you a church," and with a zeal twice what he had shown before, he plunged into the construction of St. Michael's Cathedral, which he liked to call "our cathedral." Converted from an abandoned ship, it was a wooden affair, taller than any of the previous buildings, and when its lower stories were well finished, Baranov himself supervised the erection of a modified onion dome, and on the day of solemn dedication, with a choir chanting in Russian, he could truthfully tell the parishioners: "With our fine cathedral in place, New Archangel becomes Russian forever and the center of our hopes."

Some weeks after the dedication he received a confirmation of his dreams, which gave him profound joy, for an aide came rushing up the hill, shouting: "Excellency! Look!" and when he ran to the parapet surrounding his cottage, he saw a score of Indians looking tentatively toward the palisade in the hope of permission to build houses in the space Baranov had set aside for them.

If the Russians on guard were perplexed by the arrival of these former enemies, Baranov was not; he had been expecting them, and now he shouted as he hurried down the hill: "Bring food! Those old blankets! A hammer and nails!" And with gifts spilling out of his fat arms, he went to the Tlingits, forcing the goods upon them, and when an old man who spoke Russian said: "We come back, better here," Baranov had to fight back the tears.

However, this moment of exaltation was soon lost as he began to experience the frustrations which would cloud the remaining years of his life, and he himself caused the unpleasantness, because the more important he made New Archangel, the more frequently the Russian government sent naval ships to support the island, and this meant inevitably that Russian naval officers would be appearing in blue-and-braid to inspect "what the merchant Baranov was doing out there." And as he had been warned in that famous meeting in Irkutsk so many years ago, when he was being interrogated as to his ability to manage The Company's properties, "there's nothing on earth more insolent than a Russian naval officer."

The one that Tsar Alexander I selected in 1810 to prowl the

Pacific in the warship *Muscovy* and torment local officials in Kodiak and New Archangel, especially the latter, was a prime dandy. Lieutenant Vladimir Ermelov, a brash twenty-five, was almost a caricature of the young Russian nobleman perpetually ready for a duel if his honor was in any way impugned: tall, thin, mustachioed, hawklike in countenance, severe in deportment, he considered enlisted men, servants, most women and all merchants as not only beneath contempt but also beneath civil courtesy. Brave in battle, a fairly good naval officer, and always prepared to defend his behavior with either sword or pistol, he was a terror on any ship he commanded and a dazzling white-uniformed cynosure wherever he came ashore.

Lieutenant Ermelov, scion of a noble family that had provided Russian rulers with some of their most pigheaded and ineffective counselors, was married to the granddaughter of a real grand duke, which gave her an unchallenged patent of nobility, and when she traveled aboard ship with her husband, both she and he believed that she served as personal representative of the tsar. Alone, Ermelov was formidable; when supported by his arrogant wife, he was, as a junior officer told Father Vasili without being reprimanded, "damned near insufferable."

When Ermelov sailed out of St. Petersburg in command of the *Muscovy,* he had known almost nothing about Aleksandr Baranov toiling away in the farthest east of the Russian possessions, but during this long voyage, which would take him around the world, he anchored in many ports, and in conversation with Russian or English or American captains who had stopped at either Kodiak or Sitka, he began to hear strange tales about this unusual man who had stumbled by accident, it seemed, into a position of some importance in the Aleutians, "those damned, fog-ridden fur islands, or was it Kodiak, which isn't much better," and the more he heard, the more perplexed he was that the imperial government had placed such a man in charge of one of its increasingly important areas.

Madame Ermelova, who had been called Princess before her marriage to Vladimir and who was still authorized to use that title, was especially irritated by what she kept hearing about "this damned fellow Baranov," so that by the time the *Muscovy* left Hawaii in 1811, they were crammed with tales about "that crazy Russian up in New Archangel, as they're calling it now," and the Ermelovs were pretty well fed up with the man they both considered an interloper, Ermelov for political reasons, his wife for social: "Vladimir, I know a dozen fine young men in St. Petersburg worthy of a position as governor, and it's damned irritating to think that a clown like this Baranov has outdistanced them." Her irritation manifested itself in her first letter home from New Archangel; it was addressed to her mother, the Princess Scherkanskaya, daughter of the grand duke and a person attuned to social niceties:

Chère Maman,

We have arrived in Amerika and I can summarize our entire experience by telling you briefly what happened when we went ashore. From the sea we recognized where we were by seeing the splendid volcano which resembles so much the engravings we have on Fujee-yamma in Japan, and soon after progressing past this entry point, we saw the little mount on which our eastern capital stands. It is a promising site, and if the buildings surmounting it were of appropriate construction and ornamentation, it might in time prove to be an acceptable capital, but alas, although the area consists of nothing but mountains, there is no stone for building, so what happens? The low, rambling buildings without any sign that an architect or an artist was involved in their planning consist of untempered wood poorly put together and left unpainted. You would laugh at what they call their cathedral, a gross, unplanned, ugly pile of wood topped by an amusing construction which passes for a kind of onion dome, which can be so handsome when done well, so pitiful when the various pieces don't quite match.

But this "cathedral" is a work of art compared to what the natives proudly call their castle atop the hill. Again unpainted, unplanned, and in a very real sense still unbuilt, it is a collection of barns, no less, one added to the other in haphazard style and allowing no possibility of later improvement. A team of our finest St. Petersburg architects could not salvage this place and I'm quite certain it will grow worse as time passes and new additions are added at random.

However, I must confess that on a clear day, and they do come occasionally but mostly it's rain, rain, rain, the country surrounding the hill can look supremely beautiful, like the best of the lake scenes we saw in Italy, for in every direction mountains of surprising height come right down to the water, forming a kind of rocky, tree-covered cocoon in which New

Archangel rests. And with that volcano standing guard, you have a setting worthy of a master planner.

Instead, we have Aleksandr Baranov, a miserable merchant striving ridiculously to be a gentleman, and I shall tell you only one thing about this foolish and incapable man. When Volya and I were presented to him, and we had not seen him before, he came forward, bowing low as was proper, a fat little fellow with a round little belly and a costume sewn by some provincial tailor, because no two parts fitted. When he came closer I gasped, and Volya whispered to me, almost loud enough to be heard: "My God, is that a wig?"

It was and it wasn't. It was certainly made of hair, but from what animal I would not care to guess, for it resembled no hair that I had ever seen before and I'm quite sure it wasn't human, unless it came from the beheaded member of some savage tribe. And obviously it was intended to serve as a wig, for it did rest upon his head, which I found later to be quite bald. But it was not that kind of wig which gentlemen and public officials in Europe can wear with such distinction, like Uncle Vanya's, for example. No, this was a kind of carpet, with a sickly color, no proper texture and absolutely no shape. It was a most sorry affair.

But now comes the unbelievable part. To keep it on his head, Monsieur Baranov used two strings of the kind you see French peasant women use to keep their bonnets on while milking their cows, and these strings he brought under his chin, where they were tied in a bowknot big enough to have served as his cravat. Later, when this fat little fellow with his absurd wig stood beside my dear Volya, receiving the sorriest lot of guests in all of Russia, not a gentleman among them, the comparison was preposterous and I almost cried from shame for the dignity of Russia. There he stood in his nightcap wig, and beside him stood Volya, erect, proper and never more worthy in his white uniform with the gold epaulets Uncle Vanya gave him.

We cannot leave New Archangel too speedily for me, and if the above is not enough, I now find that this tedious Baranov has a native wife whom he preposterously calls the Princess of Kenai, wherever that is, but when I protested about this disgrace to Russian dignity, my informant reminded me that the local priest, a man named Voronov, also has a native wife.

What in the world is happening to Mother Russia that she is so careless with her children?

With fondest thoughts, ever your loving daughter,
Natasha

The *Muscovy* remained at New Archangel for nine tedious months, and week by week Lieutenant Ermelov and his princess became more openly contemptuous of Baranov, ridiculing him before his own men as a low merchant and castigating whatever moves he made to improve his capital. "The man's an impossible dolt," the princess observed loudly at one party, and in his frequent reports to St. Petersburg her husband wrote disparagingly on Baranov's intelligence, managerial ability and understanding of Russia's position in the world. More seriously, in three different letters Ermelov initiated those ugly questions concerning Baranov's use of government funds which would haunt him in subsequent years:

> When one considers the funds which our government has had to pour into New Archangel and then looks at the little which has been accomplished, one has to question whether this grubbing little merchant has not sequestered a fair share of them for his own selfish purposes.

These attacks on himself Baranov could accept, since he had been forewarned to expect them from any naval officer who was also of the nobility, but when the Ermelovs began to vent their bile on Father Vasili, accusing him of improprieties that were plainly ridiculous, Baranov had to intercede: "Esteemed Princess, I really must protest. There is no finer clergyman in eastern Russia than Vasili Voronov, and in that comparison I include His Reverence, the Bishop of Irkutsk, whose piety is famous throughout Siberia."

"Pious? Yes," she granted. "But isn't it offensive to have the leading church figure in an area as big as this with a wife who was a short time ago a savage? It's undignified."

Under normal circumstances Baranov, never wishing to excite the animosity of the Ermelovs, would have allowed this condemnation to pass unchallenged, but in recent years he had become an intense defender of Sofia Voronova, whom he saw as the epitome of the responsible Aleut woman whose marriage to a Russian invader would form the basis of the new mixed race, Russian-Aleut, which would populate and in time govern Russia's American empire. As if eager to prove the correctness of Baranov's predictions, Sofia had already given birth to a fine boy child, Arkady, but the underlying reason for Baranov's predilection for this smiling, lovely woman lay in the fact that once more he himself was without a spouse. For reasons he could not fathom, his native wife, Anna, was behaving exactly like his Russian wife: she was refusing to leave comfortable Kodiak to live with him in what she considered a less desirable residence, New Archangel. Deprived of two wives, he brought his two half-native children to Sitka, where he acted as both father and mother, and resigned himself to the fact that he was one of those men unable to hold on to a wife.

But in this loneliness he found increasing pleasure in watching the marital progress of the Voronovs, and the more he observed the gentle, loving manner in which these two people discovered fulfillment in each other, the more he saw in them the emotional satisfaction denied him in his own marriage. Vasili Voronov was proving to be an almost ideal clergyman for a place like New Archangel. Courageous in battling frontier situations, loyal in supporting the lay governor, and dedicated to the law of Jesus Christ on earth, he moved about his enormous parish like the first disciples, and wherever he touched or paused to give comfort, he produced an almost tangible Christianity. If the early fur traders brought disgrace to the concept of Russian imperialism, Father Vasili erased that stain by bringing love and understanding.

In this work he was supported by his Aleut wife, who continued to organize and tend nurseries and orphanages and who formed a glowing bridge between her pagan fellow Aleuts and her husband's Russian Christianity. She was, Baranov thought, an ideal pastor's wife, and in his support of her efforts he became a kind of father to her, so he was not disposed to allow Princess Ermelova to denigrate her.

"I beg your pardon, Princess," he said, after listening to the latest diatribe, "but I have found Madame Voronova, whom you call a savage, to be a true Christian; indeed, a jewel in our North American crown."

The princess, not accustomed to rebuttal from anyone, looked down her patrician nose at this ridiculous baldheaded man—Baranov wore his wig only on ceremonial occasions—and said haughtily, as if dismissing some peasant: "Monsieur Baranov, here in New Archangel, I see hundreds of Aleuts and they are all savages, the priest's wife among them."

Fully aware of the dangerous course he was pursuing, Baranov thrust his fat little chin out and said: "I see in those same Aleuts the future of Russian America, and none is more promising than the priest's wife."

Startled by this rude refutation, the princess snapped: "Mark my words, you'll see that one slide back into the gutter. If she poses as a Christian, it's only to deceive men like you who are so easily fooled," and when she next saw her husband, she stormed: "Baranov spoke harshly when I reprimanded him for defending that pathetic Aleut woman attached to the priest. I want you to inform St. Petersburg that this Voronov is making a spectacle of himself with that little savage."

Vladimir Ermelov had, in the wisdom that married men acquire so painfully, learned never to oppose his strong-willed wife, especially since she maintained close contacts with the tsar's family. But this time he did quietly ignore her fulminations against Sofia Voronova because in his dispatches home he simply had to report glowingly on the conduct of her husband, and it was these first assessments which were to pave the way for the extraordinary events which emerged later in the life of Father Vasili:

> The worse Baranov appears, and I have reported only his most glaring defects and malperformances, the better does his priest Vasili Voronov stand out as an exceptional churchman. In the perfection of his approach and accomplishment he is almost saintly and I commend him to Your Excellency's attention, not only because of his religious perfection but also because he represents Russia so ably. He has only one drawback that I have been able to detect: he is married to an Aleut lady of markedly dark complexion, but if he were to be promoted to a superior post, I suppose he could be released from her.

Now, when the princess railed against both Baranov and Sofia Voronova, Lieutenant Ermelov loudly agreed with her regarding the man but remained silent when Sofia was the target, and in this persistent way he continued to undermine Baranov's leadership of the colony, for as he told his wife and anyone else who wished to listen: "Just as you cannot operate a naval ship with peasants, so you can't run a colony with merchants. In this world gentlemen are at a premium."

As the *Muscovy* was preparing to quit New Archangel for the return trip to Russia, documents arrived confirming Ermelov's basic attitudes, for one set of papers brought severe rebukes to Baranov for his supposed laxity in minding The Company's funds and his tardiness in bringing order to his vast domain stretching from Attu Island in the west to Canada in the east, while another set informed Lieutenant Vladimir Ermelov that the tsar had authorized his promotion to lieutenant captain.

Baranov, mortified by the harshness of the criticism, sought counsel with Father Vasili, to whom he poured out the misery of his position: "I had hoped that the next ship would bring me the funds to do the work required and perhaps a notice that I had at last been recognized with a title of some kind—nothing big, you know, just this or that of the third class, but with a ribbon testifying to the fact that I was now a member of the lesser nobility . . ."

Here he broke down, a sorely disappointed man in his sixties, and for some moments he fought against tears. "There, there, Aleksandr Andreevich," the priest whispered, "God sees the worthy work you do. He sees your charity to children, the love with which you bring Aleuts into the bosom of His church."

Baranov sniffed, wiped his eyes, and asked: "Then why can't the government see it?" and Voronov gave the answer which had resounded through the centuries: "Preferment is not dispensed in rational portions," and after a thoughtful digestion of this truth, Baranov laughed, wiped his nose, and said: "True, Vasili. You're six times a better Christian than the Bishop of Irkutsk, but who recognizes it?"

Then, self-pity laid aside, he took the priest's hands and said with great solemnity: "Vasili, I'm an old man and very tired. This endless work eats at a man's soul. Twenty years ago I begged St. Petersburg to send a replacement, but none has come. That ship down there, it brings condemnation of my work but no money to help me do better and no younger man to take my place." Now, dealing with real disappointments and not with transitory wounds to his vanity, he could no longer control himself, and tears of the most burning kind welled from his eyes. At the end of a long, distorted life he was a failure and a worn-out one to boot, so he sat before his priest, shoulders shaking, head bowed: "Vasili, pray for me. I am lost at the end of the world. I know not what to do."

But an even greater humiliation awaited. When Ermelov received notice of his own promotion, his wife initiated a gala celebration which would include all the ships in the bay, the multiple rooms atop the rock, and even the Aleut workmen inside the walls and the Tlingits outside; and the princess arranged it so that naval funds would pay for the ship festivities, while the celebrations ashore would be charged against Baranov's depleted treasury. When the chief administrator learned of this duplicity he was outraged: "I *have* no treasury. I *have* no money." But as the entertainments began and Baranov witnessed the jollity of the sailors and the Indians, he found himself caught up in the celebration, and at its height, when Lieutenant Captain Ermelov, straight and severe as an ash-tree harpoon, stepped forward to receive from Father Vasili the oath of allegiance, Baranov cheered with unfeigned generosity, even though both he and the priest knew that he was many times more effective as a commercial-political manager than Ermelov was as a naval geopolitician.

A lesser man than Baranov might have been immobilized by the incredible position in which he now found himself: not only to be accused of stealing Company funds when The Company refused to send him any funds, but to be accused of diverting this Company money to his personal use at the very time when he was spending his own funds on work The Company should be doing, like caring for widows and orphans! It was insane, but he refused to let it disorient him, taking refuge in a comforting saying and an even more comforting visit south. The saying explained and forgave everything: "That's Russia!" and the excursion soothed away mortal wounds.

Seventeen miles south of New Archangel, lost in a wilderness of islands and surrounded by mountains that rose from the sea, lay one of nature's miracles: a spring, rank with the smell of sulfur, which bubbled forth in a copious steaming flow that could be mixed with a trickle of icy water from a nearby stream, making it bearable to soak in. For a thousand years or longer the Tlingits had treasured this spring, hollowing out spruce trunks to serve as pipes to feed water from the spring and nearby stream into a stone-lined hole dug in the earth. Ingeniously, the Tlingits had fixed the cold-water pipe with a swivel so that it could be swung aside when the hot water was properly tempered.

It was a congenial place, hidden among trees, protected by mountains, but so situated that one could luxuriate in the tub and gaze out upon the Pacific Ocean. One of the constant regrets voiced by Kotle-an and Raven-heart in their distant exile was: "I wish we could go back to the hot bath," and one of the first things the Russians did when they captured the hill was to sail south and build at the sulfur spring a proper housed-in bath with two real pipes to bring in the two kinds of water. In time they had a spa equal to any in the homeland, and as soon as Baranov had the area pacified he began his visits to the baths. Was Ermelov behaving outrageously? Off Baranov scuttled to the hot baths. Was his replacement seven years overdue? Down he went to the sulfur treatment, and as he lay back in the tub, working the two pipes with his toes, and the hot water steamed him to a rose-petal pink, he forgot the irritations which others wreaked upon him, and in his repose he visualized the great things yet to be done.

So on the happy day when the *Muscovy* finally sailed from New Archangel to carry Lieutenant Captain Ermelov back to Russia, Baranov stood on the shore, waving farewell with the obedient enthusiasm of an underling, but as soon as the ship was out of sight he called for an assistant: "Let's go to the baths. I want to cleanse myself of that odious man," and deep within the therapeutic waters he formulated those remarkable steps which would make his tenure in the east so productive and so remarkable to later historians.

When he sailed back to New Archangel after his visit to the baths, his shiny round head was bursting with new ideas, and he was pleased to see that yet another foreign ship had anchored during his absence. As he drew close enough for the letters on the bow to become readable he smiled—*Evening Star* · BOSTON—and he supposed that Captain Corey was bringing in his hold much-wanted cargo, like food and nails, and just as much that was not, like rum and guns.

Relieved to see an easygoing American ship replace the stiff and disagreeable *Muscovy,* Baranov greeted Captain Corey and First Mate Kane warmly, inviting them to his home on the hill and learning from them the details of Napoleon's latest triumphs in Europe. With the generosity which marked all his dealing and which accounted for discrepancies in his accounts, if there were such, he told the Americans and Father Vasili as they dined together: "Now I understand! Russia's been so frightened of Napoleon, the tsar hasn't had the time to bother about us out here. Or send us the money he promised."

But as this first evening wore on, difficult questions existing between America and Russia began to surface, and Baranov said with considerable frankness: "Captain Corey, this town is most delighted to see you back in these waters, but we trust you'll not be trading rum and guns to the Tlingits."

Corey answered with a shrug, as if to say: "Governor, we Americans trade as we can," and Baranov, interpreting the shrug correctly, warned in an amicable way: "Captain, I have orders to halt your trade in rum and guns. Such trade destroys our natives, makes them useless for any worthy purpose."

Very firmly Corey replied: "But our nation insists upon its right to trade anywhere on the high seas and with any goods we wish."

"But this is not the high seas, Captain. This is Russian territory, just the way Okhotsk would be, or Petropavlovsk."

"I think not," Corey said without raising his voice. "Where we sit tonight, yes. Sitka Sound is Russian." Like most foreigners, he spoke only of Sitka Sound, never of New Archangel, and this added to Baranov's irritation. "But the waters hereabout, they're open sea and I shall treat them as such."

Very evenly Baranov replied: "And my orders are to prevent you from doing so."

Miles Corey was a small, grimly determined man who had spent his life contesting the seas and their harbors, and Russian threats did not alarm him any more than had the threats of Tahitians or Fijians: "We honor without question your preeminence here in Sitka, but you have none in what we deem international waters."

"So you intend to peddle your rum and guns to our natives?" Baranov asked, and Corey said with firm politeness: "We do."

It was curious, and a fact long to be debated by historians and moralists, that in these years the two Anglo-Saxon nations which presumed to follow the higher dictates of religion and public behavior, England and America, should feel themselves entitled by some moral justification which others could not discern to trade as they wished with what they called "the backward nations of the world." In defense of this inalienable right, England felt herself justified in forcing opium upon the Chinese; while America insisted upon the right to trade rum and guns with natives everywhere, even, it must be admitted, to her own warlike Indians in the West.

So when Aleksandr Baranov, this doughty little merchant, proposed to halt such trade in his territory, men like Captain Corey and First Mate Kane stated firmly that the rights of free men entitled them to trade with natives under Russian rule as they wished and without fear of retaliation from Russian arms. "It's simple, Governor

Baranov," Corey explained. "We sail north, well away from Sitka, and trade our goods for pelts, and no one's the worse off."

"Except the natives, who remain drunk all the time, and we Russians, who have to spend vast sums to protect ourselves from those who now have guns," and he pointed to the palisade which had to be maintained at such heavy cost.

The problem was not resolved that time. The superior American morality prevailed, and the *Evening Star* laid plans to sail north to dispose of its goods for the dwindling supply of sea-otter pelts. However, on the last night ashore, a conversation occurred which had a profound effect upon development in this part of the world, for while Captain Corey talked with the Voronovs about Tlingit and Aleut history, Baranov and onetime-harpooner Tom Kane sat off to one side, looking down upon the silvery gray beauty of the harbor, and the Russian said, "Mr. Kane, New Archangel will never be the first-class city I plan until we have our own shipbuilding yard. Tell me, how difficult is it to build a ship?"

"I've never built one."

"But you've sailed in them."

"Sailing and building, two different challenges."

"But could a man like you, who knows ships so well, do you think you could build a ship?"

"If I had the proper books, yes, I suppose I could."

"Can you read German?"

"I was fifteen before I could read English."

"But you did teach yourself?"

"I did."

"So did I," Baranov said. "I wanted to start a glass factory, got a book from Germany and taught myself to read that language."

"Was the factory any good?"

"Satisfactory. Look," and he produced a German text on shipbuilding, an elaboration of the one Vitus Bering had used a century earlier.

Kane, hefting the volume and inspecting a few drawings, handed it back: "A glass factory can work if it's merely satisfactory. A ship can't." So he dismissed Baranov's implied invitation but he could not dismiss the man's penetrating vision of what Sitka might become, and when he asked about this, he knocked the top off a volcano from which erupted a lava flow of ideas.

"I want to build ships here, a score of them. And plant a colony in

California, where the Spaniards accomplish nothing. I think we ought to trade with China. And with a captain like you in his own ship, Hawaii would be wide open for trade and maybe even settlement." Reaching out and taking Kane by the arm, he asked: "What did you think of Hawaii?" And there at the edge of the Pacific, Kane was lured into disclosing his admiration, indeed his longing, for those heavenly isles.

"Somebody ought to take over those islands," he said enthusiastically. "If Russia doesn't, England or America will."

Now Baranov became more pressing: "Mr. Kane, a man your age . . . How old are you? Past fifty? You ought to be captain of your own ship."

Kane smiled bitterly: "Our first captain, fine man named Pym, promised to promote me along the line to captain one day. But he got himself killed at Lapak Island. So I stayed on with Captain Corey, thinking he'd promote me the same way. Never happened. So then I thought maybe one of these days the old fellow would die and I'd take over. But you can see for yourself, he's past sixty, strong as ever, and he told me the other day he'd decided never to die. So I work on." He stopped, laughed, and admitted: "He's a good captain and I'm not unhappy."

So the *Evening Star* traded a few goods with Baranov's people, weighed anchor, and sailed on to the next island north, where they sought out Kot-le-an and Raven-heart, providing them with many guns and their followers with casks of rum. But when the time came to sail north toward Yakutat, where other Tlingits longed for guns with which to attack Kot-le-an's people, because Tlingits enjoyed nothing more than a good battle now and then—among themselves if no Russians were at hand—First Mate Kane stayed behind with Raven-heart, and when Corey sent a boat to fetch him, Kane said: "Tell him I'm staying here," and the ex-harpooner spoke so forcefully that no one cared to challenge him.

"What shall we do with your things?" the sailors asked, and Kane said: "There are no things. I brought them with me." And two days later he and Raven-heart were in a canoe paddling down to Sitka, where Kane informed Baranov that he had come south to start a shipyard, while Raven-heart used this opportunity to scout out the Russian defenses against the night when his Tlingits would attack once more.

• • •

When Tom Kane of Boston, using a German shipbuilding manual whose words he never learned to read but whose drawings he followed, completed building four ships, *Sitka, Otkrietie, Chirikov* and *Lapak,* his employer, Baranov, was ready to make his long-planned moves in the Pacific. Commissioning a group of bright young men and giving them two ships, he sent them off to occupy a fine site north of San Francisco, and the Spaniards were so inattentive to this invasion of their territory that they allowed the Russians to gain a substantial foothold.

So a remarkable situation developed in this part of the world. Before cities like Chicago or Denver were even thought of, and while San Francisco had no more than a few score of residents and the future Los Angeles none, Sitka was a thriving town of nearly a thousand, with its own library, school, shipyard, hospital, navigation center, civil government and navy. In addition, it controlled a solid foothold in California, and under Baranov's prudent leadership, seemed destined to command the entire west coast of the Pacific down to San Francisco and probably beyond.

From that solid beginning, Baranov decided to reach into the central Pacific, for after Kane had finished with his shipbuilding, he was given command of the *Lapak,* with orders to establish good relations with King Kamehameha in Honolulu. Since Kane and the king already knew each other favorably, the wooing of Hawaii proceeded so rapidly that other nations began to fear they might have to take steps to thwart it, but Baranov's astute guidance strengthened the friendship between Hawaii and Sitka and for a spell of years it looked as if the golden islands were destined to fall under Russian control.

But now hammer blows began to strike Baranov. Close to exhaustion, he pleaded with St. Petersburg for three boons: money to complete building his beloved capital at New Archangel, a replacement to serve as chief administrator and, at the end of one of the most productive public services in Russia, some small shred of recognition—a medal, a ribbon, a title no matter how mean—that would lift him out of the category of despised merchant and enable him to believe, no matter how briefly, that he had won by his energy and imagination a patent of minor nobility.

The money never came. But the distant government, acknowledging at last that Baranov was an old man, did appoint a replacement who would assume responsibility for the government, an able fellow named Ivan Koch who had compiled a good record as commander at Okhotsk. Baranov, delighted by the prospect of having free time to work at the things which really interested him and knowing Koch to be a good man, sent a letter of warm congratulations, which Koch never received, for while at Petropavlovsk on his way to his new duties he died with tragic suddenness.

Once more Baranov besieged St. Petersburg with appeals for a successor, and this time a much younger man with good credentials was shipped out to New Archangel aboard the *Neva,* a reliable ship familiar with the eastern Pacific. From the lookout room in his house Baranov watched with delight as the *Neva* approached the bay, then with horror as it ran into a storm off Edgecumbe volcano and sank within reach of land, taking to their death most of her complement, including the new governor.

It was a savage disappointment, worsened by the return of the notorious *Muscovy* under the command of Baranov's avowed enemy Vladimir Ermelov, who, since his wife the princess did not accompany him this time, arrived in a foul mood. Among his secret papers was one which instructed him to probe the rumors which he himself had circulated during his previous visit:

> *You are to inquire as judiciously and secretly as possible into the financial deportment of Chief Administrator Baranov, who has been reported to us as having sequestered for his own use funds belonging to The Company. If in the process of your investigation you find him guilty of defalcations, you are hereby empowered to arrest and incarcerate him prior to his return to St. Petersburg for trial. In his absence you will serve as Chief Administrator.*

But now the complexity of government in Russia manifested itself, for in the same mail pouch, directed not to Ermelov but to Baranov, was a letter which brought him great satisfaction. It came from a different branch of government, obviously, for it said:

> *Know Ye All, We do confer upon said Aleksandr Andreevich the rank in the Civil Service of Collegiate Councilor, with social standing equal in rank to a Colonel in the Infantry, a Lieutenant Captain in the Navy, an Abbot in the Church, and entitled to be addressed by all as Your Excellency.*

Alexander I

The duty and privilege of announcing to the world that Chief Administrator Baranov was now His Excellency Collegiate Councilor Aleksandr Andreevich Baranov fell by tradition to the senior officer present, who happened to be Lieutenant Captain Vladimir Ermelov, commanding officer of His Majesty's warship *Muscovy*, and on a bright morning which would bring bile to the throat of that young nobleman, he had to preside on the hill when Baranov, his incredible wig tied under his chin, stepped forward to receive the great honor which the tsar had bestowed upon him. With taut lips and in a whisper so low that few could hear, Ermelov read in grudging terms those words which lifted Baranov into the nobility. It was then incumbent upon Ermelov to place about Baranov's neck the ribbon from which was suspended the shimmering medal he would henceforth be entitled to wear, and then came the worst moment of all, for by custom Ermelov was now required to kiss the recipient on both cheeks. He planted the first one with obvious repugnance, and as he made preparations to award the second, he grumbled in a voice suddenly so loud that all could hear: "For the love of Jesus Christ, take off that wig."

Two weeks later, when Ermelov was well on his way into the garbled books of the New Archangel office of The Company, he was required to discharge an even more disagreeable obligation, for one of his young officers, scion of one of Russia's noblest families, came to him with a request which stunned him:

> *"Respected Lieutenant Captain Ermelov, with your permission, sir, I want to marry a local girl of impeccable reputation, and in obedience to custom, I beg you to represent me when I make my petition to the girl's father. Will you do me the honor, sir?"*

Ermelov, aware of his responsibility to protect the noble families of Russia and to prevent hasty marriages which would damage them, sparred for time with the ardent young man. Holding himself very erect and looking his most severe, he asked: "Surely you're mindful of the exalted position your family occupies in Russia?"

"I am."

"And you know that you must not stain its impeccable reputation by an improper marriage?"

"Of course, my parents would be appalled if I behaved poorly."

"So wouldn't circles at the court deem it imprudent if you were to marry some chit of a child here in New Archangel? Some Creole, no doubt?"

"I'd never do that. This young lady is the daughter of a princess. She's lovely and will glow in even the highest court circles."

"A princess? I thought my wife was the only princess in New Archangel, and she's no longer here." He coughed. "Who is this paragon?"

"Baranov's daughter Irina."

The cough turned into a choking sound, and then into a sputter: "Do you believe that nonsense about Baronov's wife being the daughter of some stupid king somewhere?"

"Yes, Excellency, I do. Baranov showed me a paper signed by the tsar himself, legitimizing his second marriage, and another confirming his new wife in her title as the Princess of Kenai."

"Why haven't I heard about such a ukase?" Ermelov stormed, and the young suitor explained: "It arrived after you returned to Russia," and when he borrowed the precious papers to show Ermelov, the reluctant officer had to honor them. So on a solemn summer day, with the sun reflecting from the many mountaintops, Lieutenant Captain Ermelov, in his best dress uniform, accompanied his aide to the hill, where they were met by His Excellency Baranov wearing over his ears his wig and upon his chest his medal. "Your Excellency," Ermelov began, the words sticking in his throat, "my distinguished aide, a young man of excellent family well regarded by the tsar, seeks permission to marry your daughter Irina, lineal descendant of the kings of Kenai."

Baranov, bowing before the man who was now of rank no higher than his own but of a more ancient lineage and therefore entitled to respect, replied in a low voice: "You do our humble house great honor. Permission granted," and the three men repaired to a balcony, from which they could look west to the volcano where the *Neva* had foundered, north toward the site where Redoubt St. Michael had stood before Kot-le-an and Raven-heart destroyed it, and then to the mountains where Raven-heart was plotting his revenge.

With his daughter married into the nobility and his own patent of nobility firmly about his neck—he wore it on all occasions, even when drinking beer at the close of day—Baranov should have been at the golden apex of his life, a man respected in New Archangel, valued at The Company offices in Irkutsk, and esteemed in St. Petersburg for his sagacity in handling problems in the Pacific, but as the months passed, it became obvious that Lieutenant Captain Ermelov was probing Company records to prove that the old man was a thief, and as the scandal grew, Baranov withered.

He was seventy now, resident in the islands for an unbroken twenty-six trying years, and his health had never been good since the day of his arrival, when he lay almost dead at the bottom of that improvised boat in Three Saints Bay. Four or five times subsequently he had been near to expiring, but he had struggled on, subduing adversities which would have collapsed a lesser man. He had brought order among the trader-hunters, utilized creatively the Aleuts, and conquered the warlike Tlingits. On a mountainous island at the edge of North America he had constructed a capital worthy of a vast territory, and above all, he had defended widows and cared for orphans, spending his own money in doing so. To end his life accused of petty thievery was almost more than he could tolerate and twice he contemplated suicide, but he was prevented from indulging in such negative actions by the unwavering loyalty of three trusted friends: Father Vasili and his wife, and his aide Kyril Zhdanko, who in these latter days stepped forth as his protector and the man who could be relied on to see that his grand designs moved forward.

As the rumored accusations of thievery intensified, he appeared infrequently in public and when he did he moved furtively, as if he realized that people in the settlement were speculating as to when he would be thrown into irons and bundled aboard the *Muscovy* for return to Russia in disgrace. Lieutenant Captain Ermelov did nothing to defuse these rumors; indeed, he encouraged them, waiting for the day when he could inform the man who would come out from St. Petersburg to replace Baranov: "I think we have a case against him. We'll be leaving for Russia promptly."

During this time, an American ship put in to Sitka Sound, where it traded openly with rum and guns, now that Baranov no longer had the energy to combat this evil traffic. Then the ship sailed north to the remote settlement in which Kot-le-an and his aide Raven-heart continued to collect rifles against the day when they could once more attack the Russians. But now when they learned from the Americans that their old foe Baranov was being shipped back to Russia in disgrace, they decided they had one last score to settle with the old man, and as soon as the ship departed, these two who had fought Baranov so assiduously climbed into a canoe and started paddling south to meet for the last time with their adversary.

They were spotted from a distance as they came into the island-studded sound, and as they glided resolutely through the myriad islands, word flashed through the capital that Tlingits in war dress were approaching the hill, and everyone who could rushed down to the waterfront, where with great dignity the two warriors were approaching the landing. When they were close enough for their identity to be established, a wild cry surged through the settlement: "Kot-le-an is back! Here comes Raven-heart!" And Baranov himself came down the eighty steps that separated his house from the shore, ignoring those who fell back to whisper about him and going directly to where the canoe was being pulled ashore.

As soon as Raven-heart stepped on dry land he halted, raised his right hand, and launched into a ten-minute oration delivered in a deep, thundering voice. The highlights of his message were memorable:

> "Chief Warrior Baranov, builder of forts, burner of forts, your two enemies who destroyed your fort to the north, who lost our fort down here, greet you. In all our battles, you were toion. You fought well. You behaved with generosity when you won. You have given our people who live beyond the palisade a good life. Manager Baranov, we salute you."

With this, the two warriors, still big and powerful, moved forward to embrace their old enemy, and after warmly welcoming them, Baranov suggested: "Let us climb the hill together," and there on the porch of his hilltop house these three good men who were losing so much surveyed the noble theater in which they had played out their tragedy. "Up there's the fort we drove you out of," said Raven-heart, explaining how he had scouted the defenses while smoking salmon. "And down there's the fort you Tlingits thought could not be taken," Baranov said, and Kot-le-an surprised them both by saying: "My heart broke when your cannon shattered our totem, because then I knew we had lost."

They shared the saddest reversals an older man can know, the loss of dreams, and that evening dusk fell with a heavy sadness, but it was relieved somewhat when Baranov left them for a moment to fetch a most surprising gift.

Retiring to his room, he tied on his wig as ceremony required, placed about his neck the medal proclaiming his nobility, and lifted from a wooden trunk a bulky article in which he took considerable pride. It was the wood-and-leather suit of armor which he had worn when marching against the Tlingit fort. Holding it forth in both arms, he approached Kot-le-an and said: "Bold Chieftain," but then his voice broke. For some moments he stood in the growing dark, striving to control his tears, and as his shoulders trembled his wig bobbed up and down, so that he was about as ridiculous as any make-believe commodore could be. Finally he controlled himself, but he dared not trust his voice, so in silence and with a kind of love for these men who had proved so valiant he handed them his armor, even though he had good reason to believe that at some future date, after he was gone, they would come storming back to try once more to destroy the Russians.

In disgrace and threatened with prison when he reached St. Petersburg—except that Father Vasili Voronov had volunteered to travel at his own expense to the capital to defend his friend from the insane charges lodged against him—Baranov left Sitka Sound a prisoner aboard a Russian warship, which wandered across the Pacific to Hawaii, whose wondrous islands he had almost brought into the Russian Empire, and then down to the unlikely port of Batavia in Java. Here, in one of the hottest, most feverish outposts of the Pacific, he was kept penned up aboard ship, until his frail body collapsed in final surrender.

He died on 16 April 1819 near the strait which separates Java from Sumatra, and almost immediately the sailors weighted him with iron, tied his beloved medal about his neck, and tossed him into the ocean.

Three men of noble bearing had wrestled with the Pacific Ocean and all had perished in their attempt. In 1741, Vitus Bering died of scurvy on a forlorn island in the sea named after him. In 1779, James Cook was slain on a remote beach in Hawaii. And in 1819, Aleksandr Baranov died of exhaustion and fever near Sunda Strait. They had loved the great ocean, had conquered it in part, had been destroyed by it, and had been consigned in death to the vast, consoling sea.

Baranov was not a great man and sometimes, as in his enslavement of the Aleuts, not even a good man. But he was a man of honor, and in the Alaska he molded his memory would always be revered.

• • •

In 1829, ten years after the death of Baranov, the old warship *Muscovy* put in to Sitka Sound, bringing as passenger from St. Petersburg a bright-eyed young university graduate who was returning to his home island after a course of study in which he had distinguished himself. This was in the time when his father's friend, Kyril Zhdanko, served as the interim chief administrator, a notable appointment in that he was the first Creole to occupy that powerful position.

The returning young man was Arkady Voronov, himself a Creole as the son of the Russian priest and the Aleut convert Sofia Kuchovskaya. Twenty-eight years old, he came with an appointment as assistant manager of trade affairs and with a passionate attachment to a young woman he had met during a visit to Moscow. So, after greeting his parents with the affection that had always marked his relationship to them, he paid his respects to Chief Administrator Zhdanko and then repaired to his room in the priest's quarters next to St. Michael's Cathedral, the little wooden church with the big onion dome and the pretentious name. There, as soon as his bags were stowed, he wrote to his beloved back in Moscow:

> *My darling Praskovia,*
> *The voyage was simpler than the others had predicted. Five easy months, with a halt at the Cape and another in Hawaii, where I had expected to find many friends from Baranov's day. Alas, they are now our enemies because of errors made by others, and I'm afraid we've lost our chance to make those islands part of our empire.*
> *Sitka Sound is as beautiful as I remembered it, and I long for the day when you stand here beside me enjoying its majesty of islands and mountains and lovely volcano. Please, please convince your parents that it is safe to make the trip, which really isn't so long, and then to live here in what's becoming a major city.*
> *I have given your silhouette in its ivory frame the place of honor on my table, the first item to be unpacked, and I am now hastening to the offices of The Company to acquire data on New Archangel so that your parents can be reassured that it is a real city and not merely an outpost in the wilderness. I shall resume this letter before I go to bed.*

When young Voronov left the cathedral and climbed the hill to the castle, where Zhdanko waited to instruct him as to his duties, he saw all about him the signs of a bustling town, not a city as he had described it to Praskovia, but a prosperous settlement which no longer depended solely on furs for its wealth. In one direction he saw the tall windmill that operated a grist mill; in another, the smoking fires where fat from various sea animals was being rendered for soap. There was a walk for spinning rope, a smithy for forging varieties of gear, a boilermaker who made his own rivets, a foundry for casting bronze, and all sorts of carpenters, sailmakers and glaziers.

What surprised him was one small shop for making and mending watches, and another for the repair of compasses and other nautical instruments. And for the general population, there was one tailor, three dressmakers, two doctors and three priests. There was also a school, a hospital, a place for public dining, an orphanage run by his mother, a library.

Stopping at a corner where the main road intersected with one perpendicular to the bay, he asked a man carrying boards: "Is this place always so busy?" and the man replied: "You ought to see it when an American ship puts in to trade."

From Zhdanko himself he learned the facts about his new post: "I'm proud to have at my right hand the son of two people who have been so important to me. Your father and mother, Arkady, are special, and I hope you remember that. But you asked for the facts. Total population inside the palisade, nine hundred and eighty-three. That's three hundred and thirty-two Russians with the right to return to the homeland, and a hundred and thirty-six of their wives and children. Then we have a hundred and thirty-five Creoles who do not have the right of return. We have forty-two children in the orphanage, a horrible number, but we do have accidents and parents do run off. To round out, we have inside the walls three hundred and thirty-eight Aleuts helping us with our hunt for sea otters and seals. Total, nine hundred eighty-three."

"And do the Tlingits still live outside the palisade?" Arkady asked, and Zhdanko replied grimly: "They better." Then he summarized the Russian experience with this brave, intractable people: "The Tlingits are different. You never pacify a group of Tlingits. They love their land and they're always ready to fight for it."

"So you think the walls are still necessary?"

"Positively. We never know when those people out there are going to try once more to drive us off this island. Observe our cannon up there," and when Arkady looked up at the hill he saw that three of its guns were aimed down at the bay to fend off any ships which might intrude unexpectedly, but nine were directed at the Tlingit village outside the walls.

What reassured him even more than the guns was the energy with which Russians, Creoles and Aleuts attacked the problems of daily living. A few educated Creoles like himself or trusted ones like Zhdanko supervised Company affairs, and Russian clerical types like Mr. Malakov kept accounts, but most were out in the sun conducting the businesses that one would expect to find in a thriving seaport. The average Creole did manual labor and most Aleuts went out regularly in their kayaks.

He did not find time to finish his letter that first evening, for Chief Administrator Zhdanko and his Creole wife invited him to the hill, where sixteen Russian men, each convinced that he could govern the colony better than the Creole, and their wives had joined to welcome young Voronov to his new post, and he was awed by the handsome new building which had replaced the house he had sometimes visited when Baranov occupied it. The place was now quite grand, with several stories, imported furniture and an even better view of Sitka Sound because obstructing trees had been removed. "Everyone calls it Baranov's Castle," Zhdanko explained, "because we feel that his spirit still resides here."

It was a gala evening, with a husband-and-wife team playing four-hand music on the two pianos and a set of surprisingly good baritone solos by Chief Clerk Malakov. He sang first a selection of arias from Mozart, then a rousing medley of Russian folksongs in which the guests joined, and finally, a most moving rendition of "Stenka Razin" whose grand, flowing notes reminded his listeners of distant Russia.

Next night, after a day of inspecting the palisade and seeing the intricate gateway through which a limited number of Tlingits were allowed entry to trade, Arkady did find time to complete his letter:

I have now seen New Archangel inside and out, and I beg you, Praskovia, to gain permission from your parents to sail here on the next ship, for this is a complete little city. We have a good hospital, doctors trained in Moscow, and even a man who fixes teeth. The houses are made of wood it's true, but each year the city grows, and both the chief administrator and I expect it to have two thousand citizens before very long. Of course, it has that now if you count the Tlingits who live outside the walls.

And I must tell you one thing more, which I confide with great pride. My father and mother occupy a place of considerable honor in this part of Russia. He is known far and wide, through all the islands, for his piety, and he is loved by the natives because he has taken the trouble to learn their language and help them in their way of life before he ever importunes them to become Christians. If there is a saint walking this earth today, it is my father. Indeed, they call him a living saint.

And Mother is his equal. She is, as I told your parents most explicitly, an Aleut born, but she is now, I do believe, a better Christian than my father. Goodness radiates from her face and sanctity from her soul.

I was, as you may remember, awed by the notable traditions of your Kostilevsky family and said many times that you had a right to be proud of your heritage, but I feel the same about my father and mother, for they are establishing the new line of nobility for Russian America.

One terribly important fact, Praskovia. When you leave Moscow to come here, you must not think of yourself as going into exile at the ends of the earth. People leave here all the time to return to the mainland. Irkutsk is a splendid city where my family served in both government and the church. Hawaii is gorgeous with its wealth of flowers. And some travelers go back to Europe by way of America, which takes a long time if you round the Horn but which is, I am told, rewarding.

And if, as Baranov taught Zhdanko to do, we establish significant holdings on the North American continent, you and I could well be important factors in the new Russia. My heart beats with excitement at the possibility.

All my love,
Arkady

Through a bizarre twist, it was this letter which precipitated the final wrenching crisis in the Voronov family, because when Praskovia's parents received it, they were so struck by that forceful paragraph in which Arkady spoke of his father's accomplishments in Kodiak and Sitka that Kostilevsky senior showed the passage to church authorities in Moscow, who copied the paragraph, adding the one about Father Vasili's wife, Sofia, for circulation among the authorities in St. Petersburg. There Lieutenant Captain Vladimir Ermelov was asked his opinion of the priest Voronov in New Archangel, and Ermelov replied enthusiastically: "One of the finest," and he instructed the church fathers as to who else now resident in Moscow had knowledge of the eastern lands, and all who were consulted testified that Vasili Voronov, white priest from the noteworthy family of Voronov in Irkutsk, was about as strong a churchman as the Orthodox Church had produced in a long time. In the discussion thus launched, Arkady's fortunate use of words was often repeated: "They call him a living saint."

Improbable as it seemed at the time and unlikely as it seems now, the leaders of the church, spurred on by Tsar Nicholas I, who sought to revive the spiritual force of Russian Orthodoxy, decided that what St. Petersburg needed was a forceful, devout man from the frontier uncontaminated by churchly politics and renowned for his sanctity. For a host of intricate reasons they focused their attention on Father Vasili Voronov, wonderworker in the islands, and the more they investigated his credentials the more satisfied they were that he was the solution to their problems. But no sooner had they announced their decision to the tsar, who applauded it, than a knotty problem arose.

"It's understood, of course," the present metropolitan pointed out, "if Father Vasili accepts our invitation to come to St. Petersburg as my successor, he will have to surrender his white robes and transfer to black."

"No difficulty, Holiness. You'll remember that when he took orders in Irkutsk, he did so as a black."

"Why was it he changed? To marry?"

"Yes, when he had assumed his first office, on that big island they call Kodiak . . ."

"Now I remember. You told me about this last week, didn't you?"

"On a busy day, Holiness. He fell in love with an Aleut woman, you'll remember."

"Yes." He reflected on this for some moments, striving to recall his own youth and to imagine distant frontiers about which he knew nothing: "Aren't Aleuts . . . well, they're pagan, aren't they?"

"This woman was, but she's proved to be a most unusual type. More Christian than the Christians, they say. Charity among the children."

"That's always a reassuring sign," he said, but then, as the long-time spiritual guardian of his church, he jabbed his thumb down on the real problem: "If she's as saintly as you say, and her husband must renounce his white robes and take on the black, will there not be an outcry against him and us if he leaves her at her advanced age? How old is she?"

No one knew exactly, but a priest who had visited New Archangel offered a guess: "We know her husband is sixty-three. She's probably in her mid-fifties. I saw her several times and she seemed to be about that age." He stopped, but before anyone else could speak, he volunteered: "A fine-looking woman, you know. On the short side but no savage, not at all."

The metropolitan, wanting to keep the discussion on the main theme, asked: "Would Voronov divorce her in order to reassume the black?" and an elderly churchman said: "To lead Christ's church, a man might do anything."

The metropolitan looked harshly at the man and said: "You may not believe it, Hilarion, but there were many things I would not have done to attain these robes." Then, to the others: "Well, would he take the black?"

"I think so," said a cleric who had served in Irkutsk. "Service in the Lord's cause would be enticing. And the opportunity to accomplish good is not to be lightly bypassed, either."

"If you mean power, say so," the metropolitan snapped, and the cleric replied sharply: "Very well, I do mean power."

"Does this Voronov seek power?" the old man asked, and one of his younger helpers said firmly: "He has neither sought nor avoided it. The man's a real saint, I assure you."

"Goodness, goodness," the metropolitan muttered. "In one family on a remote island I never heard of, we have a male saint and a female saint. Remarkable." But when others started to assure him that this was the case, he looked at his advisers and asked the most difficult question of all: "If we lure him to St. Petersburg with our dazzling prize, will she let him go?" and the priest who had seen her at work said: "She would understand if he were called to glory. He broke his vows to marry her. She would, I'm sure, advise him to do the same if he now seeks to marry the church."

With that assurance, the powers in St. Petersburg reached the extraordinary decision, applauded by the tsar, to bring into the highest office of the Orthodox Church the saintly priest from the parish farthest from the capital, Father Vasili Voronov of St. Michael's Cathedral in New Archangel. But the metropolitan, eager to know that a successor had been selected but not eager to have the man appear in St. Petersburg too soon, suggested: "Let us appoint him Bishop of Irkutsk this year and Metropolitan next year, when I shall be too old to continue in the office." And even those energetic churchmen who wanted a new leader now had to agree that promoting Father Vasili by easy steps was the preferred route, and even though the tsar wanted a new man quickly, he too capitulated to this strategy, but to protect himself, announced publicly that early next year the grand old man of the Orthodox Church would be retiring.

In this strange and devious way, Vasili Voronov received secret notice that if he resumed the black, which he had abandoned thirty-six years before, he would be appointed Bishop of Irkutsk, the town from which his family had come, with every likelihood of further preferment later on. The naval officer who delivered this exciting information added, as he had been directed by the tsar himself: "But of course this would necessitate a divorce. And if your wife, as a member of a people Russia is endeavoring to win over to Christianity, objected . . ." He shrugged his shoulders.

When Father Vasili studied the confidential papers which verified this extraordinary proposal he had two reactions, which he could voice only to himself: I am not worthy, but if the church in its wisdom calls me, how could I refuse? and then immediately: But what would Sofia's role be in this? And without even discussing the profound problem with his son, he left his cathedral and walked from one corner of the palisaded area to the most distant, back and forth past the warehouses he had helped build, then past the stores that Kyril Zhdanko had helped start, out to where the Tlingits gathered on the other side of the palisade, and back to the church which would never have come into being without his hard work and that of his wife. And when her name or her image came up, he realized the cruel choice that was being offered him.

For three days he was unable to broach the subject with her, and he refrained for a good reason: he felt sure that if she knew of his chances in Irkutsk and later perhaps in the capital, she would encourage him to change robes and accept the opportunity, even though it would mean leaving her behind. And he did not wish in decency to place her in a position in which she must do the choosing. He alone would decide what was right, and he would then place his thinking before her and encourage her to oppose it if she felt she must.

Satisfied that neither of them would act selfishly or in haste, he spent a fourth day largely in prayer, which he uttered with that simplicity which had always characterized him:

"Heavenly Father, from the time I was a child I knew that I wanted to live my life in Thy service. Humbly I have striven to do so, and as a young man I took my vows without even considering any alternative. But inside three years I was altering those vows in order to marry a native girl.

"As Thou knowest, so well, she brought me a new vision of what Thy church and its mission can be. She has been the saint and I the servitor, and I could do nothing to injure her. But now I am called to a higher service in Thy church, but to accept it, I must once again revise my vows and commit a grave wrong against my wife.

"What am I to do?"

That night was the fifth in which he carried this extraordinary problem to his bed, and as before, he tossed fitfully, unable to close his eyes, but toward dawn he fell into a deep, replenishing sleep from which he did not break till nearly ten. His wife, aware that he had been under some kind of pressure brought by the most recent ship from Russia, allowed him to sleep on, and when he woke she stood waiting with a tall glass of tea and the comforting words: "Vasili, you've been worried about some perplexing problem, but I see in your face that God has solved it during your sleep."

Accepting the tea gently from her hands, he swung his feet onto the floor, took a long, thoughtful drink, and said: "Sofia, the tsar and the church want me to move to Irkutsk as bishop, and from there in due course perhaps to head the church from St. Petersburg." Without hesitation, for he was speaking from a vast reserve of faith, he started to say: "And this would mean . . ." But she ended the sentence for him: "It would mean that you would have to take the black robes again."

"It would," he said, "and after consulting God, I've decided . . ."

"Vasili, you started life in the black robes. Would this be so great a change that you should be sleepless?"

"But it would mean . . ."

The two lovers, each of whom had molded his or her life to the other's, crossing bridges that lesser persons might have been afraid even to test, let alone leap upon, looked across the brief space which separated them, she a little Aleut woman less than five feet tall, dark of skin and with a whalebone labret in her lip, he a tall Russian in a nightshirt, white-haired and bearded and troubled. For a painful moment neither knew what to say, but then she took the tea glass from his hands and placed her hands in his, and with the strange and lovely pronunciation of Russian words which her Aleut upbringing and the presence of the labret produced, she said: "Vasili, with Arkady here to protect me, and perhaps soon with a wife to help, I have no fear, no claim. Do as God directs," and he said: "Last night, after the midnight bell from the castle, I knew that I must go to Irkutsk." He uttered the words softly, then pressed her hands and added: "And may God forgive me for the wrong I commit against you."

Once the decision was made, neither of the Voronovs reviewed it, and neither subjected it to harsh reconsideration or recrimination. Before noon that eventful day they asked their son to accompany them to the castle, where they sought a meeting with Zhdanko, and when the four were settled in porch chairs overlooking the bay and the mountains, Father Vasili said unemotionally: "I have been selected Bishop of Irkutsk. This means that I must return to the black robes I wore as a young man. And that means that my marriage to Sofia Kuchovskaya must be dissolved." Allowing time for this dramatic news to take effect, he reached out for the hands of Zhdanko and Arkady, saying as he did so: "I must leave the care of this wonderful woman to you two men." And during the next half-hour he did not speak again.

The others discussed a chain of obvious topics: Who would replace him at the cathedral? Where would Sofia live? What would be the responsibility of both Zhdanko and Arkady? And for that matter: What was Zhdanko going to do when his provisional term as chief administrator ended? And even: Is the palisade strong enough to withstand an attack by the Tlingits, an ever-constant threat? By these practical steps, which reminded everyone that life in New Archangel must go on, even if the spiritual head of the community was moved to a higher obligation, the three participants chose among the various options available to them, and they did so in highly sensible ways, as if acknowledging that Father Vasili was no longer a part of their lives. But when they were finished, with the course of Sofia's future life determined within reason, Father Vasili broke down, covered his face with his hands, and wept. He was leaving a paradise which he had helped create and whose spiritual values he had both defined and protected. He had helped build a world, and was now surrendering it.

He was a white-haired old man, somewhat stooped, somewhat slowed in his movements. He spoke with greater caution and was prone to reflect on his defeats rather than his triumphs. He had seen much of the world's folly, and although he had been forgiving, he did wish that he'd had more time to combat those aspects of life which were wrong. He was, to put it simply, closer to God than he had ever been before, and he believed that he was prepared because he had learned to do God's work in whatever position he finally found himself.

The ship which had brought the news of his elevation to bishop required eleven days to finish its duties in Sitka Sound, and during the latter stages of the stay Father Vasili completed all details relevant to his departure. But on the last day, when everyone knew that the ship would be sailing at eight the next morning, he had to face the fact that within a few hours he must say farewell to his wife forever, and this became increasingly painful as the sun set and the long hours of night loomed. Sitting with Sofia in the main room of the modest house next to the cathedral, he began by saying: "I can't remember when I first saw you. I know it was at Three Saints and I know it involved the old shaman in some way." He hesitated, then chuckled as he recalled his long duel with that frenzied man: "All that really mattered between us, I can see now, was that my parents had introduced me to God and Jesus and his had not had an opportunity to do so." She nodded: "He was an obstinate one. I hope I can defend my beliefs as valiantly as he did his."

They spoke of the tragic manner in which so many Aleuts had perished during the Russian occupation, and he said truthfully: "Months go by, Sofia, without my ever thinking of you as an Aleut," and she said quickly: "I think of it every day. I mourn the world we lost, and sometimes at night I see the forsaken women on Lapak, too old and weak to venture out for their last whale. My heart breaks."

Then they spoke of the good days they had known, the birth of Arkady and the dedication of the cathedral, and this set Vasili to laughing: "It seems I'm to have a real cathedral, maybe even a scintillating one, but whatever form it takes, it can never be a more dedicated House of God than the one you and I built here in New Archangel."

At the mention of this place, they thought of Baranov and of how it was his will power which had built the thriving little town. "He thought of it as the Paris of the East," Vasili said, and the darkened room grew silent. A saintly man was deserting his even more saintly wife, leaving her for the rest of their lives for no reason with which she was associated, and there was no more to say.

When Praskovia Kostilevskaya, daughter of the notable Kostilevsky family in Moscow, arrived in New Archangel, men working along the waterfront stopped to stare at her, for a young woman of her striking elegance and beauty was rarely seen in this frontier town. She was much taller than either the Aleut women or the average Creole, and her skin was markedly whiter, for she was one of those Russians with a strong admixture of German blood, in her case Saxon, which accounted for her blue eyes and lovely flaxen hair. She had a warm smile but also an unmistakable patrician manner, as if she knew how to be congenial toward superiors and haughty toward inferiors, but the general impression she created was one of competence and self-assurance.

When it became known that she was the young woman who had come this great distance to marry Arkady Voronov, cynics said: "He's a Creole and he'll never be able to hold a woman like that."

To give her time to comply with religious law, her marriage to Arkady had to be delayed for three weeks, and during that time she began to have doubts about New Archangel, for the weather was typical of this part of Alaska. The warm Japanese current which swept clear across the North Pacific came so close to shore that it produced heavy moist clouds which clung to the mountains, completely obscuring them for days at a time. After the nineteenth rainy day in a row Praskovia lost patience, and wrote to her family, using, as cultivated Russian women did, a host of French words to describe her emotions:

Chères Maman et Soeur,
I have now been on this rain-soaked island for nineteen
days and have seen nothing but mist, fog, low clouds and the

most gloomy aspect of nature a human being has ever witnessed. Everyone here assures me that when the sun reappears I shall be seeing a glorious congregation of mountains encircling us, with a beautiful volcano off to the west.

Now, I am willing to believe that not all the people here are prevaricators, so I suppose the mountains do exist, but I find that one must take that on faith, for the visitor rarely sees them. One dear lady, hoping to raise my flagging spirits, assured me yesterday: "Rarely does an entire month go by without the clouds lifting for at least a day," and with that hope I shall go to bed tonight, praying that tomorrow may be that one day in thirty.

Arkady is even more delightful to be with than we thought in Moscow, and I am divinely happy. We have purchased a small wooden house near the castle, and with imagination and ingenuity we shall transform it into our hidden palace, because on the outside it will not be much.

I'm not sure whether the exciting news about Arkady's father has circulated in Moscow, but he has been ordained as Bishop of Irkutsk, with every likelihood of becoming, before the year is out, Metropolitan of All the Russias. So you shall be seeing the father in your city while I entertain the son out here in mine.

And now the best news of all. Arkady has been appointed second-in-command to supervise the transfer of power from the temporary chief administrator to the permanent one, and when that's been done, to continue as second-in-command until such time as he becomes chief. For the time being, his mother lives with us, a wonderful Aleut woman under five feet tall and with a kind of ivory earring fixed in a hole at the edge of her lower lip. She smiles like an angel and will allow me to do no work, for she tells me in good Russian: "When you're young enjoy your husband, for the years pass too quickly." In a later letter I'll tell you what happened to her marriage, but maybe you can figure it out for yourselves.

When the tantamount widow Sofia Voronova heard her prospective daughter-in-law complaining about Sitka's weather—she preferred the Tlingit name for her town—she feared that the high-born young woman might prove an unsuitable wife for her son, and she watched carefully as Praskovia made her way about the colony. She knows what she's doing, Sofia said to herself, and when she saw Praskovia go outside the gate to talk with Tlingit market women, she thought: And she's not afraid. But intuitively this elderly Aleut who had witnessed so many dramatic turns in human life feared that any young woman as pretty as Praskovia, and from a city, must lead her husband a difficult life, and she awaited the forthcoming wedding with trepidation.

But then, as if this bright child from the social circles of Moscow had anticipated Sofia's fears, she came to visit her two days before the wedding to say: "Mother Voronova, I know I must seem strange to you, and I'm not going to try to change your mind. But I also know this. Arkady could not be the fine man he is unless someone had taken charge of him and taught him manners and how to treat a wife. I'm sure it was you, and I thank you."

Then, to Sofia's astonishment, for Russian women in Sitka had never been so bold, Praskovia asked: "What do you call that thing you wear in your lip?" Sofia, appreciating this openness, replied: "A labret," and her visitor said pertly: "All right, now you must tell me what a labret is."

Sofia did, but Praskovia was still not satisfied: "I suspect that one must be very special. Could you . . . ?" She let her question hang, and for a very long moment Sofia looked at her, wondering: If I told her, would she understand? And in the end she concluded that it did not matter whether this young stranger understood or not; she was going to be Arkady's wife, and the more she knew of his heritage the better. So in a quiet voice she began to tell of life on Lapak Island, and of the death sentence on her people, and of how she and her mother and her great-grandmother had killed the whale: "A woman in the village made this from the bone of the whale we killed, and gave it to me as I left the island." Seeing that Praskovia was transfixed by the story, she added: "Of all the women on Lapak, I was the only one who escaped, and I shall wear this labret till I die out of my love for my people!"

Praskovia sat silently for a long time, kept her hands over her face, and finally rose and left without uttering a word, but on the following day she came back, laughing in a bright youthful manner, to tell Sofia: "In Russia the bride wears something her mother wore at her wedding. I wish I could wear that labret of yours for just one day," and the two women embraced, each assured that there would never be trouble between them.

Now when the citizens of New Archangel used the phrase *the Voronovs* they meant the young administrator and his attractive wife, and the older possessors of that name were largely forgotten. Nor was Baranov mentioned very often, and when Kyril Zhdanko was replaced by a permanent chief administrator from Russia, a man with a minor title, he too faded from conversation. A new generation had come in to run what amounted to a new town, and when the American shipbuilder Tom Kane died, the last of the old breed was gone, the arrival of a steam-propelled ship from San Francisco signaling the new day at sea.

Arkady Voronov had been in his position as general manager of Company affairs for only a brief period when his capacity for leadership was tested, because from the islands to the north the Tlingits under a new toion decided that the time was ripe for a renewed attempt to retake Castle Hill, throw down the palisade, and return the settlement to its original Indian owners. With careful planning, the accumulation of many weapons and the stealth for which they were famous, they began infiltrating southward at such a steady rate that soon they had a sizable army in the valleys east of the settlement.

With the heroic Kot-le-an dead, they were led by the tested old warrior Raven-heart, who was ardently supported by his implacable wife, Kakeena, and their twenty-year-old son who, because of the spectacular way they had developed, was known as Big-ears. Together the three would form a powerful fighting unit, with Kakeena urging her men forward and providing food and hiding places when they were either recuperating from wounds or plotting their next assaults.

Raven-heart decided to position his best men near the palisade gate through which the Tlingit women would enter with their goods for market. At the exact moment, he, Big-ears and six others would force their way through the gate and break it off its hinges, allowing a hundred or so warriors to flood the palisade. What happened after that would depend upon the degree of success attained by the first wave, but all were prepared to accept large losses at first in order to subdue the Russians.

At six in the morning the men hiding among the spruce trees

north of Castle Hill heard the sound of the morning bugles, and at eight they watched as two Russian soldiers directed a half-dozen Aleut workmen to throw open the wicker gate. One Tlingit woman entered bearing clams. Another came with seaweed. And as the third moved forward with her fish, Raven-heart, his son and their bold companions dashed into the compound, killing one Russian soldier and forcing the other to flee. Within minutes the battle for New Archangel had begun, with the Tlingits enjoying what appeared initially to be a victory.

But Arkady Voronov, commanding from the hill, was the kind of young man who was not afraid to make instant decisions, and at the moment he saw the gate collapse he knew he must wipe out that threat, so without considering the consequence to his own people or the enemy, he shouted to his cannoneers: "Fire!" and two iron balls of tremendous power ripped into the mass of people struggling at the gate, killing fifteen attacking Tlingits and seven Creoles—five men, two women—who had come there to barter with the pacified Tlingits.

When Raven-heart saw some of his best men crushed by the cannonballs, he was first enraged, then sobered by the realization that those nine great cannon on the castle walls were going to be used, and he shouted to his men: "Take cover!"

For three hours the Tlingits remained inside the walls, wrecking whatever they could reach when outside the range of the cannon and defending themselves by taking positions in houses and doorways. It was brutal warfare, which could have continued till nightfall had not Voronov decided upon drastic measures. Dodging from one cover to another, he told his men: "Engage them. Don't let them escape through the gate. But when you hear the bugle, run back like hell, because I'm going to fire those cannon."

With that, he ran up the hill to the castle walls, where he trained six of his cannon on the heart of the fighting, that spot near the gate where Russians and Tlingits tangled in one indecipherable mass. "Bugler!" he cried, and in the next instant the Russians fled the spot, all except one young fellow who tripped, tumbling down among the Tlingits. For a split second Voronov considered holding his fire to allow the fallen lad a chance to get away, but then he saw the milling Tlingits: "Fire!" and six ricocheting balls swept through the confused mass of Tlingits, killing or maiming two out of three.

Raven-heart, alerted by the bugle call, escaped the fusillade, but as he made for the wall, seeking to follow his son with a giant leap, Voronov directed his cannoneers to fire again, and a huge ball struck the Tlingit leader full in the back, crushing his bones and throwing him against the fence that he had been about to climb. Pinned there by his own flesh and bones and tattered clothes, he hung limp for a moment, after which rifle fire from the windows of a nearby house cut him down.

Thus ended the attack of 1836 and with it the last hopes of the Tlingits . . . during this generation. Of Raven-heart's four hundred and sixty-seven men, fully a third had been slaughtered inside the compound, and he had died with them. The green hills, spruce-covered and lovely in either snow or sun, would know his breed of Tlingit no more.

Kakeena, a widow now, would take her son to a new refuge on an island more distant than Chichagof, and there he would remember this day and plot the manner in which he would lead his expedition for revenge, because no Tlingit like Kot-le-an or Raven-heart could ever accept defeat . . . and Big-ears, brooding on his island, would be such a Tlingit.

Sofia Voronova, the young commander's mother, watched the battle from the castle, and at first she was proud of the manly way in which her son was conducting himself, but when, with victory assured, the big guns continued firing at houses well outside the walls, "to give the Tlingits a lesson," she saw that peaceful Indians who had elected to live side by side with the Russians were being slain.

"Stop it!" she cried, rushing at the gunners. And her cry was so different from what her son and Praskovia were shouting in this moment of victory, that they were astonished. Turning away from the final salvos of the bombardment, they looked at her in amazement, and saw that she was staring at them as if she had never seen them before. In that moment a wall as high as Denali rose between them.

As soon as the cannons were silent, she turned away from her son, going down the steps to work among the wounded, inside the palisade and without, ministering to those who had lost an arm or a friend or a child, and as she did so she found that she was identifying not with the Russian victors but with the shattered Tlingits, as if she knew that the latter deserved her help while the former did not.

When the Tlingits convinced her that they had been as surprised by Raven-heart's attack as the Russians, she felt a surge of sorrow for these confused people who had surrendered a life of great freedom in order to live in a settled community next door to what her husband had called "Christian civilization," only to find themselves trapped in a war not of their own making but in which they suffered most. Recalling her own childhood when similar injustices happened, she concluded that it was the kind of thing that was bound to occur when patterns of life were in collision, and she moved back and forth between Tlingits outside the gate and Russians inside, assuring each that life could proceed as it had in the past and that guilt rested on no one.

She convinced few—her son telling her that the Russians might have to expel the Tlingits altogether; the people outside the gate rebuffing her with a threat to leave New Archangel and join up with the rebels in a new assault. Unwilling to accept such disillusionment and remembering how on Kodiak she had been instrumental in bringing Aleuts and Russians together, she persisted in her efforts to bind these two strong-minded groups into one workable whole, and gradually it was her view of the future that prevailed.

"Tell them out there," her son said one morning, "that we want them to stay. Tell them that when the gate opens tomorrow they'll be free to bring in their goods as usual."

"You need them, don't you?" she asked, and he said: "Yes, and they need us," and that evening she went to the still-apprehensive Tlingits: "The gate will be opened tomorrow. You must bring your food and fish as before."

"Can we trust them?" asked a man who had lost a son in the fighting, and she replied: "You must."

Reassured, they clustered about her, and in a friendly manner started to question her. One asked: "Were you an Aleut before the Russians came to your island?" and she laughed to brighten the evening: "I still am."

"But in those days you were not of their church?" and she said that she wasn't.

"But you are with them now, aren't you?" an inquisitive woman asked, and when Sofia said that she had been married to the tall man with the beard who had preached in the cathedral, several wanted to know: "Is your new religion . . . ?" They did not know how to finish their question, until a man blurted out: "Is there a god, like they say?"

She remained with them a long time that night, telling them of the beauty she had found in Christianity, of its gentle message where children were involved, of the benign role played by the Blessed Virgin and of the promise that God made regarding life eternal. She spoke with such simple conviction that for the first time, in their hours of distress, certain of the Tlingits perceived a religion that was gentler and more worthy than the one they had been following. It was a persuasive description of Christianity that she offered, for despite the fact that this religion had treated her poorly at the close of her life, taking her husband from her, it had still been the glory of those middle years which seemed to count more than the others.

But if she helped the confused Tlingits find a balance between old and new, she could not do the same for herself. At night, in the darkness of her room, she experienced a profound longing to be with the people of her childhood. At times her mind wandered, and she believed that she was once more on Lapak Island, or in the kayak with her mother and great-grandmother chasing the whale, and her yearning for the old days became so persistent that one morning she passed through the gate to speak with two Tlingit men she had come to know during the aftermath of the battle.

"Could you take me to the hot baths?" she asked, pointing south toward that congenial spot where she and her husband and Baranov and Zhdanko had so often gone for relaxation and restoration.

"The Russians will take you," the men protested, afraid that any unusual act on their part might be interpreted as a renewal of hostilities, but she brushed aside their fears: "No, I want to go with my own people," and with those words she made the last important decision of her life. She was not Russian; she was not of their society; she was what she had always been, an Aleut girl of enormous courage, an Indian like the Tlingits, cousin to their leaders Kot-le-an and Raven-heart. If she journeyed to the springs which the Indians had been using for a thousand years, she wanted to go in the company of these gallant Tlingits of the coastal islands.

But to protect these men who would take her south, she instructed several women: "When we're gone, go to the gate, ask for Voronov, and tell him: 'Your mother has gone to the hot springs. She's all right and will be back by nightfall. If not, in the morning.'" And off she set for one of the finest parts of the Sitka region.

Picking their way through the myriad islands, keeping the great volcano well to the west, they wove in and out of narrow channels, with the mountains guarding them on the east and the placid Pacific smiling at them from beyond the little islands. It was a voyage as wonderful this day as it had been when she had first gone with her husband and Baranov, and she caught herself thinking: I wish it would never end. And then the more painful wish: When we get there, I'd like to see Vasili and Baranov and Zhdanko waiting. And with such thoughts she lowered her head, ignoring the rim of mountains that welcomed her to the ancient springs.

When the two Tlingits deposited her on the shore, she told them: "I'll not stay long," then she added hopefully: "I'm very tired, you know, and maybe the springs will help."

Slowly she climbed the easy hill to where the hot sulfuric waters bubbled from the earth, and when she entered the low wooden structure erected by the tireless Baranov, she threw off her clothes and eagerly immersed herself in the soothing water, which at first she found almost too hot to manage, but as she became accustomed to the heat, she luxuriated in its comfort.

After she had lain thus for some time, the waters reaching up to her chin and bringing their therapeutic smell as close as it could possibly come, she lapsed into a kind of dream world in which she heard a ghostly voice whispering her real name: "Cidaq!"

Amazed, she opened her eyes and looked about, but there was no one else in the bath, so she dozed again, and once more from the arched ceiling came the shadowy voice: "Cidaq!"

Now she wakened, splashed her face with water, and chuckled, remembering the day when her husband and Baranov had taken her to the hut beneath the big tree at Three Saints to convince her that the clever shaman Lunasaq had been able, by ventriloquism, to make his mummy talk. "It was a trick, Sofia," chubby Baranov had explained. "I can't do it very well. No practice. But look at my lips," and he had astonished her by keeping them almost closed while words poured out, seeming to come from a root which he kept tapping with a stick.

How they had laughed that day, the two men careful not to deride her for having believed in spirits, she exulting in the joy she felt in the brotherhood of her new faith. Now she laughed again at the thought of how she had been deceived. But then, with the hot water reaching almost to her lips, she drifted again, and desirous of communing once more with the old woman of Lapak, she spoke in a kind of hypnotic daze, talking alternately for herself and the mummy: "Have you heard that they took my husband from me?"

"Young Voronov?"

"He's not so young anymore." Then proudly she added: "Metro-politan of All the Russias, that's something."

"And now he's gone. And Lunasaq is gone. But you had a good life on Kodiak and Sitka, didn't you?" The mummy used the old names for these locations, not the new Russian ones.

"Yes, but at first, when I thought of losing you and Lunasaq, I could not be happy."

"Does it really matter? Don't you suppose that he and I were mournful too, having lost you for a while?"

"I am not unhappy in my new religion."

"Who said you were?"

"You just said you were mournful to have lost me."

"As a friend. What do I care how you pray? What really counts, in the very old days and in all the days to come . . ." The dome became filled with the ancient one's voice: "To live on this earth as a bride lives with her husband. To know the whales as brothers. To find joy in the frolics of a mother sea otter and her babe. To find refuge from the storm and a place to enjoy the sunshine. And to treat children with respect and love, for with the passing years they become us."

"I've tried to do those things," Cidaq said, and the old woman agreed: "You did try, little girl, the way I tried and your great-grandmother. And now you're very tired from so much trying, aren't you?"

"I am," Cidaq confessed, and the old one asked gently: "Does it really matter?" and she was gone.

In the silence that followed, Cidaq lay back, allowing the water to grow increasingly hot and sulfurous, and as she stared upward, she thought: Her religion is of the earth, the sea, the storms, and it's nec-essary to a good life. Voronov's religion was of the heavens and the stars and the northern lights, and it's necessary too.

Images from her two lives filled the walls of the bath: the great tsunami knocking down Vasili's church but allowing the shaman's lone spruce to stand; shadows on Vasili's crucifix at dusk; that first whale that terrified the women sliding past, enormous even now; the cluster of children she had cared for after the tsunami; Baranov with his wig drifting to one side; the joy with which Praskovia Kostilev-skaya from a noble family in Moscow stepped ashore to marry Arkady in distant New Archangel; and dominating everything else, the stately white volcano lifting its perfect cone into the sunset.

She knew she had been blessed to have been privileged to share these two worlds equally, and although she had lost both, for she had rejected the Russian way, she did retain the best of each, and for that she was grateful. The heat increased; the images became a kaleidoscope of the years from 1775 to 1837; and the voice sounded no more, for her final question had summarized it all: Does it really matter?

It does matter! Cidaq concluded. It matters enormously. But you mustn't take it too seriously.

After waiting on the beach for more than two hours, one of the Tlingit boatmen said: "I wonder if something's happened to the old woman?" and he insisted that his partner accompany him up the hill so that an honest story could be told if things had gone wrong. When they reached the bath they found Sofia floating free upon the surface of the water, facedown, and the cautious one began to wail: "I knew we'd get into trouble." They wrapped her in her clothes, carried her down the hill and perched her in the center of the canoe, then started paddling home.

When they neared the landing at the foot of the castle they began waving their paddles, and people on the shore saw only the two men fore and aft and their priest's former wife sitting upright in the middle seat, but as the canoe neared the shore they realized that she was dead, and men began running toward the castle, shouting: "Voronov!"

In the years following the death of Sofia Voronova, the thriving town of New Archangel discovered, as had so many settlements in the past, that its destiny was being decided by events which occurred in locations far distant and over which it had no control. In 1848 gold was discovered in California; in 1853 war broke out in the Crimea between Turkey, France and England on one side, Russia on the other; and in 1861 a much bigger civil war erupted in the United States between North and South.

Gold in California excited people in all parts of the world, sent a jumble of them crowding into San Francisco, and altered alliances throughout the eastern Pacific. A totally unexpected development occurred in New Archangel, where the chief administrator sent his assistant on a scouting trip to Hawaii and California to ascertain what the influx of Americans to the west might mean to Russia's interests. Placing their children in the care of two Aleut nurses, Arkady invited his wife to accompany him, and under palm trees in the familiar town of Honolulu they heard for the first time a rumor which astonished them. An English sea captain, fresh from a trip to Singapore, Australia and Tahiti, asked casually, as if all Russians knew of the matter: "I say, what will men like you elect to do if the deal goes through?"

"What deal?" Voronov asked, his interest piqued by any suggestion that trade involving Great Britain and Russian might eventuate.

"I mean, if Russia goes ahead and sells your Alaska to the Yankees?"

Arkady gasped, leaned back, and looked with consternation at his wife: "But we have heard nothing about such a sale."

"We heard talk of it more than once when we put into port," the Englishman said, and Voronov asked pertinently: "By English interests?" and the captain said: "Nothing substantial, you understand, but those discussing it were from various nations."

"But were there any Russians?" Voronov persisted, and the man replied without equivocation: "Indeed there were. Usually they were the ones who broached the subject."

Voronov leaned back and said quietly: "I don't intend to boast, but for some years I've been second-in-command in New Archangel. My father was a leading force in the islands before he was promoted, and I can assure you from all of us that we have no intention of disposing of what is becoming a jewel in the Russian crown."

"I'm told it's a splendid place, Sitka Sound," the Englishman said quickly.

In Honolulu no more was said about the possible sale of Russia's American holdings, and after arranging for the continued shipment of Hawaiian fruit and beef to New Archangel, the Voronovs moved on to San Francisco, where on the third night at anchor in that glorious bay behind the headlands, a Russian ship captain had his men row him over to Arkady's ship, and within minutes of their greeting he was asking for details about the possible sale of Alaska to the United States.

"Nothing to it," Voronov assured the worried man, but then he corrected himself: "At least not in Alaska, and I think we'd be the first to know."

So the matter was dropped, and next day Voronov went ashore to inspect the burgeoning city for himself, and as he sat sweltering in a waterfront saloon where sailors gathered, he heard one of the bartenders saying: "What a place like this needs is someone to haul ice down from those mountains out there."

"None forms that could be used," a veteran of the high country explained. "Snow falls, but it don't form ice."

"Well, it ought to," the sweating bartender said. Then he added the words which led to Voronov's enhanced reputation in the Russian colony: "Somebody ought to bring ice down here from up north," and that night, back on his ship, Arkady told his wife: "I heard the strangest idea this afternoon."

"That we're really going to sell Alaska?"

"No, that's dead. But this man in the bar, it was very hot, we were sweltering, he said: 'Someone ought to bring ice down here.'"

Praskovia, fanning herself with a palm frond brought from Honolulu, studied her husband for a moment, then cried enthusiastically: "Arkady! It could be done. We have the ships, and God knows we have the ice."

When they returned to New Archangel in early October they hurried to the rather large lake inside the palisade, and after asking a score of questions learned that ice formed in late November, very thick, and lasted until well into March. "Properly protected," he asked the men advising him, "how long into the summer would it stay frozen?"

"Look up there," and on the mountains surrounding the sound, in nests protected from the sun, and even in gullies where the drifts had packed down, he saw ample supplies of snow which had lasted through a warm summer. "Properly packed so air don't hit it, and kept in a barn so the sun don't strike, we keep ice around here through July."

"Could you do that on a ship?"

"Better. Easier to keep it from the wind and sun."

He spent three tingling days discussing his mad project with all the knowing men he could locate, and on the fourth he instructed the captain of a ship heading for San Francisco: "Tell them that on the fifteenth of December, this year, I'll be sending down a shipload of the best ice they ever saw. Arrange for a buyer."

The cold came early that year, and when the ice was thick on the big lake he and some clever Aleut workmen devised a system for cutting out perfect rectangles of ice, edges square, four feet long, two feet wide and eight inches thick. What these men did was build a horse-drawn gouger, not a cutter, with the left-hand drag merely a marker to keep the rows straight, the right-hand a sharp metal point which scored the ice in a long unbroken line. That done, the gouger was reversed, with the marker now retracing the line already cut while the metal point scored a parallel line two feet distant from the first. Then, moving the gouger to a position so that it could cut across the two scored lines, the outline of the rectangle was completed.

This done, pairs of men with huge trunks of spruce moved along the rectangles, dropping the trunks heavily upon them and breaking them loose into handsome blue-green blocks of ice, which were speedily hauled to the harbor and stacked into the waiting ship. When a hold was filled, with no way open for air to reach the closely packed blocks, heavy matting was tucked over the ice and topped with spruce branches, which formed pockets that would trap what air did seep through the decking. For no more than thirty-two dollars a ton, perfect New Archangel ice could be delivered in San Francisco.

Three weeks ahead of schedule, Voronov's first cargo of ice made its way south, where it sold for an amazing seventy-five dollars a ton. Arkady had launched a trade which, during the frozen months at least, promised to be more lucrative than peltries. And with the bonanza thus provided, the energetic young assistant administrator launched the building program which would make New Archangel the leading town by far in the North Pacific. He strengthened the palisade, improved his father's cathedral, made shore improvements to aid vessels, and erected a snowstorm of new buildings: stores, an astronomical observatory, a new library, a Lutheran church with an organ, and on the top floor of the castle, much enlarged, a theater for the presentation of plays or the exhibition of singing and orchestral talent by companies from ships putting into the harbor.

By the time all this was completed, New Archangel had accumulated a population of nearly two thousand, not counting the nine hundred Tlingits who still clustered outside the gates, and as Voronov observed at a castle dinner for the local notables: "Any talk of selling this place to anyone would be preposterous."

But in 1856 the Crimean War imposed such a burden on the Russian economy, and such a grievous threat to her security in Europe, that serious discussions were held at the highest levels of government regarding the practicality of ridding the empire of her far eastern holdings, and whereas from New Archangel, Arkady Voronov was able to submit the most cogent reasons why places as promising as Kodiak and New Archangel should be retained, in St. Petersburg, Baranov's old nemesis Vladimir Ermelov, now an admiral with a lofty if unearned reputation, smothered Arkady's reasoning with sharp and pertinent official documents:

> Even if our present position in the Crimea were not so perilous, and even if conditions in North America were more stable and predictable, it would be advisable for His Imperial Majesty to rid himself of the incubus our eastern territories impose. The entire territory called in the popular vernacular *Alaska* should be sold if possible, given away if necessary. Four basic facts dictate this as the only practical solution.
>
> First, Alaska is impossibly distant from the real Russia, months from Okhotsk, many dangerous weeks from Petropavlovsk. Communication by land is impossible, even from one part of Alaska to the next, and by ship dangerous, costly and time-consuming. To send a messenger from St. Petersburg to a place like New Archangel and wait for his return with a reply can take more than a year, and there is no possibility of speeding the process.
>
> Second, with the demise of the sea-otter trade, for the animal is practically extinct, there is no feasible way to make money in Alaska. It has no natural resources except trees, and Finland near at hand has much better. It contains no metal reserves, no present trade, no skilled natives to make anything for future trade. It will always be a deficit possession and money will be saved by getting rid of it.
>
> Third, conditions in North America are chaotic. The future of both the Canadian territories and the United States is precarious, and one can expect Mexico to launch a war of some kind to win back the territories stolen from her. For us to remain in Alaska is to invite certain trouble from various quarters.
>
> Fourth, and I have saved this most important reason till last. Even though the United States shows signs of breaking apart, its citizens also show many signs of wanting to take under their control all of North America, from the North Pole to Panama, and if we retain holdings in that area which they have marked out for themselves, we must sooner or later find

ourselves in conflict with that rising power. The United States
doesn't realize it now, but its more forward-looking citizens
already long for Alaska, and in the years ahead that desire
will augment.

My most fervent advice is that Russia rid herself of this
doomed holding now.

It is possible that a copy of this report, by clandestine means, found
its way into the hands of President James Buchanan, former Secretary of State, with a warm regard for Russia which he acquired while
serving as ambassador to that country in 1831. At any rate, by the
time the Crimean War drew toward a close, many Americans in high
places were aware that Russia was at least contemplating the sale of
Alaska to the United States.

And now one of the more curious developments of world history
evolved, almost by accident. On those hilly battlefields in the Crimea,
soldiers of many European nations combined to fight against Russia,
who stood them off alone. Again and again, outnumbered and out-
generaled, she lost on the battlefield, but in the courts of world opinion she had one stalwart supporter and friend: the United States. At
every critical point, America, for reasons never explained, sided with
Russia, and let it be known that she was doing so. She strove to prevent an even larger coalition from forming against the tsar. She sent
many letters affirming her moral support, and she did nothing to
embarrass Russia about the potential sale of Alaska. Of all the nations involved in the Crimean War, even peripherally, the two who
formed the warmest alliance were Russia and the United States.

So it was natural, when that war ended, that those in Russia who
wanted to divest themselves of what they deemed an incubus should
look with favor toward the United States, and in the period of serious discussion no one in Russia spoke harsh words against the United
States as a possible buyer, and had times been normal, it is quite
probable that President Buchanan would have completed the sale
sometime between 1857, when his incumbency began, and 1861,
when it ended in the Civil War.

That dreadful war, so comprehensive in terrain and devastating in
loss of life and disruption of commerce, made any foreign adventure
like the purchase of an unknown part of the world impossible. The
war dragged on; money became unavailable for anything else; and for

two desperate years it looked as if the Union would be shattered, leaving no one in authority to talk purchase with Russia.

But now the second half of the curious development occurred, for when the fate of the Union seemed most precarious, with European nations eager to pounce on the remains, Russia sent her fleet into American waters, with the implied promise that she would help defend the North against any incursions by European powers, particularly Britain and France. One Russian flotilla steamed into New York harbor, another into San Francisco, and there they waited, saying nothing, making no boasts, just riding at anchor and waiting. Those ships were to the North in 1863 what the American letters of reassurance had been to the Russians in 1856, not tangible military assistance but perhaps something equally important: the knowledge in dark days that one does not stand alone.

When the war ended in the spring of 1865, the two nations which had supported each other in such times of crisis were prepared to effect the sale that had been discussed over so many years, and it was significant that each nation supposed it was doing the other a favor. The United States thought that Russia had to sell and was seeking a buyer; Russia was under the impression that everyone in Washington was hungry to grab hold of Alaska. How misinformed the two friends were!

During both the Crimean and the Civil wars, Arkady Voronov, a mature man now, and his gracious wife, Praskovia, continued to live and work in New Archangel as if the future of their part of Russia were engraved in marble. They refurbished the castle and began living in one of the new wings; they increased trade with nations of central and western Pacific, like Hawaii and China; and they improved almost every aspect of colonial life.

It was Praskovia's idea to send promising Creole boys to St. Petersburg for their education, and already some were returning as doctors, teachers or minor administrators. Inspired by the performance of her saintly father-in-law, she had led the way in imploring monasteries across Russia to contribute the treasure of icons, statues and brocades that now graced the cathedral, making it one of the richest artistically east of Moscow.

As if wishing to double the attractiveness of Alaska, St. Petersburg dispatched a dashing young prince to govern it, Prince Dmitri Maksutov, whose title reached back to the days when Tatars from central Asia invaded Russia, giving its people the Asian cast which differentiated them from other Europeans. He was a handsome, able man who had, during his services to the tsar, married an attractive woman whose father taught mathematics at the Naval Academy. After bearing three children, this gracious lady had died prematurely, so that when the prince arrived in Alaska he brought with him a charming young wife named Maria, who, as the daughter of the governor general of Irkutsk, was familiar with Alaskan affairs. She proved to be an ideal princess for this frontier post, a gracious woman interested in everything, and she headed a court in which the locals were honored to participate.

During the first day in their new home Prince Dmitri confided his plans to Maria: "We'll be here ten or fifteen years. Make this place a capital in every sense. Then back to St. Petersburg for an additional title and a major promotion." The couple had been in residence only briefly when they realized that to attain their ambition, they must rely on some trusted local aide, and it did not take them long to identify the one person qualified to give such assistance.

"This man Voronov," the prince told his wife. "Exceptional."

"Isn't he a Creole?"

"Yes, but his father was chosen by Tsar Nicholas himself to serve as Metropolitan."

"His mother? Wasn't she a native?"

"A saint, they say. You must ask about her," and when the princess did, she learned from everyone she asked that Sofia Voronova had indeed been a saint, and she became Arkady's most ardent supporter. It was she who invited the Voronovs to the Maksutov quarters, and then entertained Praskovia so that their husbands could conduct a serious discussion.

It took place at a table bearing a collection of maps, and from the prince's opening remarks, it was clear that he was determined to translate those lines of the map into a reality they had never before had: "Voronov, I am almost physically distressed whenever I hear the phrase you used in your last dispatches."

"What, Excellency?" Voronov asked with a disarming simplicity, for as the older man and one with an unsullied reputation he was not awed by the new commander.

" 'Russia's island empire in the east.' "

"I apologize. I don't seem to understand your objections."

"Island, island! If St. Petersburg thinks of us as a collection of islands, they'll think small. But Alaska"—he waved his hand toward the unknown mainland—"is a vast land, as grand maybe as all Siberia." He slammed his hand down on one of the maps and said: "Voronov, I want you to explore that land, to alert St. Petersburg as to what we really have."

"Excellency," Voronov said, moving the prince's hand from the map, "I've already been just where you pointed," and he indicated the forbidding land on which the future capital of Juneau would one day stand. "It's just like the land here at New Archangel. A cramped foreshore, then nothing but mountains deep into what must be Canada."

Impatiently, Maksutov pointed to where the castle stood: "We built a fairly good place here. Why not the same over there?" and with his slim forefinger Voronov indicated the difference: "Excellency, the land behind our town is beautiful wooded terrain. The land over there is one vast field of ice, forever frozen, forever throwing glaciers down into the sea."

For a moment there in the comfort of the castle, Prince Maksutov experienced the stern reality of the land he had been sent to govern, because in various English and German books he had seen engravings which demonstrated what an obliterating force a glacier could be, but he had never suspected that monstrous examples existed less than a hundred miles from where he now sat. But he was not deterred by this knowledge; he had progressed in government not because he was a prince but rather because he was a stubborn man, and now, surrendering his concept of building a new town on the mainland, he moved his hand boldly to the north to where some enthusiastic Russian cartographer—using fragments of information provided on scraps of paper sent to St. Petersburg by ship captains, fur traders and missionaries—had sketched what he conceived to be the course of the great, mysterious Yukon River. The prince and Voronov studied this awesome stretch of nearly a hundred miles of shoreline where the Yukon degenerated into a tangle of would-be mouths, some of them finishing as dead ends. From either the river side or the sea, it would be impossible for an uninstructed traveler to identify the proper route, and to send any man, no matter how clever or brave, into that ugly snarl of river, channel and swamp was to condemn him to at least a year of thrashing about, but Maksutov was obdurate.

"Voronov, I want you to go far up the Yukon. Make sketches. Talk with our people, if you can find them. Tell us what we have."

Arkady had inherited from his Orthodox ancestors both courage and a sense of commitment to whatever tasks his occupation required, and he now told his superior: "I understand that you need to know what goes on up here," and with a sweep of his hand he indicated on the map a huge frozen area. "But I wonder if the approach should be through the mouth of the Yukon? Or better said, the mouths of the Yukon?"

"How else?" Maksutov asked, and Voronov evaded the question: "Look, Your Excellency, at what happens if I do penetrate that tangle at the mouth . . . and who knows if I could identify the proper entrance?" While the prince watched attentively, Voronov traced that immense sweep to the south that the Yukon takes at the beginning of its course inland. "A man could waste a year picking his way through that morass."

"He could," Maksutov agreed, but then he punched his right fist into his left palm, making a sound like a rifle shot: "Damn it all, Voronov, I know that priests have gone up the Yukon to a mission outpost called . . ." He could not remember the name of the place but he did recall hearing that some priest currently reporting to his superiors at the cathedral had made exactly the kind of journey he was proposing to Voronov, and an Aleut messenger was dispatched to find the man.

While they waited, Voronov assured the prince: "I want to go. I want to see the Yukon. But I prefer to do it from an orderly approach," and Maksutov said: "I'd not have it any other way."

Now the priest, a bedraggled, incredibly thin fellow with an unkempt beard, watery eyes and of an uncertain age—he could have been forty-seven or sixty-seven—appeared before the two administrators and fell immediately into profuse apologies, but for what, the two managers could not ascertain. Cutting through the verbiage, the prince asked rather sternly: "Name?" and the trembling man replied: "Father Fyodor Afanasi."

"Is it true you've been up the Yukon River?"

"Nine years."

"How old are you?"

"Thirty-six," and this simple statement told his inquisitors much of what they needed to know about the great river: it made young men old.

Dropping his voice to a more congenial level, the prince asked: "Then you know the area well?" and the priest replied: "I walked hundreds of miles."

"Now look, you didn't walk up and down the Yukon. It's a river."

"And most of the year it's frozen."

"Most of the year?" the new chief administrator asked, and Father Fyodor nodded: "September to maybe July."

"How far up the river did you go?"

"Five hundred miles. To Nulato. That's as far as Russian troops have penetrated." He hesitated, then added the unpleasant news: "It's only the beginning of our territory, you know. Nulato's only a short way up the Yukon, really."

Voronov whistled in amazement, then asked: "How would I get to Nulato?" and both he and the prince were astonished by what happened next, for the priest—after asking meekly "May I?"—shuffled through the maps until he found one covering much of the eastern Pacific: "Your best approach, sail from New Archangel down to San Francisco . . ."

This was so preposterous that both listeners protested: "But we want to head north to the Yukon, up this way," and on the map they indicated that Sitka Sound lay well to the southeast of the Yukon, whereupon Father Fyodor said: "Of course, but there are no ships going that way. So down you go to San Francisco, about twenty-eight days, then across the ocean to Petropavlovsk."

"We don't want to go to Siberia," the prince shouted. "To the Yukon."

"But that's the only way to reach the Yukon. About one month in transit."

Voronov, who was jotting the elapsed time on a slip of paper, noted that he had now been at sea about two months and was still an ocean and a continent away from his target.

The priest droned on: "From Petropavlovsk you will cross over to this little storm-swept harbor of St. Michael, maybe ten days."

"But that's nowhere near the Yukon," Voronov protested, and the priest, wincing, said: "I know. I once got laid up there for two months."

"Why?"

"Big ships can't enter the Yukon. You must wait at St. Michael for a skin boat to take you across the bay and into the Yukon." Tracing this dangerous route on the map, he added: "Boats capsize trying to make this crossing."

Rather dry in the mouth, Voronov asked: "But now at the end of three months we're in the river?"

"You are. And with any kind of luck and two months of hard rowing and poling, you may get to Nulato before the Yukon freezes."

"What month are we in?" Voronov asked, and the priest said: "Everything must be scheduled according to the Yukon. It's ice-free only briefly. So if you leave New Archangel in late March, you should get to St. Michael in late June, just right for the thaw. That would put you in Nulato safely before the freeze."

"You mean I'm to stay in Nulato all winter? Till the ice goes out again?"

"Yes." When Voronov totted up the time it would take him to get from New Archangel to Nulato and then back, he and Prince Maksutov realized that he would have to be gone at least a year and a half, and just to go from one Alaskan base to another. Both men were appalled.

But then Father Fyodor dangled a slight ray of hope: "I once followed a much different route," and Voronov cried: "I'd like to hear it!" and back to his maps went the priest.

"Same first part. San Francisco, Petropavlovsk, St. Michael. But now, instead of heading south in a riverboat to the Yukon, you head north to this little place Unalakleet."

On the map this was a dead end, leading to no river, no thoroughfare, and a good sixty miles from the Yukon, which at that point would be heading almost due north, but Father Fyodor relieved their apprehensions by assuring them: "There is a trail across the mountains, some parts very high, and it intersects the Yukon about here."

"How would I negotiate the trail?" Voronov asked, and the priest said: "You'd walk."

"And when I reached the Yukon?"

"You'd be in a party, of course. Have to be, or the Indians might kill you."

"Are they like the Tlingits?" Voronov asked.

"Worse," and with a long finger he pointed to various Russian installations where Eskimos or Athapascans had either murdered everyone or burned the place: "Most often they did both. Here at St. Michael, many dead. At Nulato, where you want to go, three burnings, same number of murders. Toward the mouth of the Yukon, this little place, two burnings, six murders."

Voronov cleared his throat and asked: "From St. Michael to

Nulato by your overland route, how many days?" The priest tried to recall his own experiences, for he had made the journey in both directions, then guessed: "I left St. Michael once on July first, an excellent time except for mosquitoes, and reached Nulato on August fourth." Voronov groaned, but then the priest added: "Now, if you were willing to trust a dogsled, you wouldn't have to remain in Nulato for nine months. You could hire a sled, Indians have them and love to travel, and come right down the middle of the frozen Yukon and across the pass to Unalakleet and over to St. Michael."

At this point Prince Maksutov, increasingly horrified by the difficulties involved in exploring his domain, cut a Gordian knot: "Arkady, suppose I diverted one of our ships direct to Petropavlovsk, bypassing San Francisco? Commandeer a smaller ship there for the run across to this Unalakleet? Over the mountains on the dogsled, a short, swift visit of inspection at Nulato, and right back down the frozen Yukon, with the ship waiting for you off the mouths of the Yukon? What would that take?"

Jotting down new figures, and giving himself the benefit of the briefest delay at each junction point, Voronov announced with some pleasure: "Supposing not one day's delay, about one hundred and fifty days. With normal disappointments, two hundred days."

But Father Fyodor blasted such plans: "Of course, when you reached the sea it would be frozen too, just like the river."

"Till when?" Voronov asked, and the priest replied: "Same schedule. Solid ice till about July . . . maybe the middle of June," and the two administrators groaned.

But Prince Maksutov, more determined than ever to have a report on his dominions, told Voronov: "We'll handle it however the ice allows. Pack your bags." Arkady saluted, turned to leave, but stopped abruptly to offer a sensible suggestion: "Father Fyodor, you know the area. Would you come along to show me the way?" and the priest replied enthusiastically: "I would love to see my people again. I lived among them nine years, you know," and he smiled at the prince as if the Yukon he knew were some Isle of Capri, a vacationland basking in the sun.

So the trip was scheduled, and Prince Maksutov, fulfilling every promise he had made, diverted a rather smart ship to Petropavlovsk. On it he sent a letter to the commandant there, requesting that Voronov be forwarded speedily across the Bering Sea to St. Michael, but when the time came for departure, Maksutov and Voronov were presented with a problem no one had anticipated: Praskovia Voronova announced that she would be accompanying her husband to Nulato. This occasioned much turmoil, for although Arkady was delighted with the prospect of having his intelligent and energetic wife along, Prince Maksutov put his foot down: "The Yukon is no place for a lady!"

And there matters stood, until the impasse was resolved by strong advice from an unexpected quarter. Father Fyodor, hearing of the argument, announced in what was for him a bold voice: "A woman on the Yukon? Splendid! The men would be delighted and so would I."

"Why, in God's name?" Maksutov shouted, and the priest replied: "Precisely! It's in His name I make the suggestion. Our Athapascan women should be allowed to see how a Christian woman lives." Then, blushing, he added: "How she looks," and it was agreed that Praskovia would join the expedition.

New Archangel–Petropavlovsk–St. Michael–Unalakleet, it was a journey to two continents, half a dozen cultures. The travelers passed great glaciers, a score of volcanoes, whales and walruses, terns and puffins, until they reached a bleak and barren shore where Father Fyodor spent three hectic days trying to find a team of natives to serve as porters while they crossed the high country leading to the Yukon. As the Voronovs traversed this barren but exciting land marked by low mountains, they learned how overwhelmingly vast inland Alaska was and how ferocious its mosquitoes, for at times they settled upon the travelers like a flock of sea gulls descending upon a dying fish.

"What do you do about these dreadful things?" Praskovia asked in despair, and the priest said: "Nothing. In six weeks they go away. If this were September, you wouldn't be bothered at all."

After they had been on the trail some days, one of the Indians who spoke Russian said: "Tomorrow, maybe, the Yukon," and the Voronovs rose early for their first glimpse of this great river whose name so fascinated geographers and others who speculated on the nature of the earth. "It's a magical word," Arkady told the priest as they breakfasted on smoked salmon, but Father Fyodor corrected him: "It's a brutal word. It's a river that never allows you to travel it easily."

But Voronov could not be discouraged by the reports of another man, so after breakfast he and Praskovia rushed ahead, and at the conclusion of a hard climb, reached a point from which they could look down into the broad valley that opened up below them. Since the mists which obscured it from time to time had cleared, Arkady and Praskovia could see clearly this great and powerful river, twice as wide as they had expected, much lighter in color because of the monstrous load of sand and silt it brought down from distant mountains.

"It's so big!" Arkady cried to Father Fyodor as the priest puffed up to the vantage point, but when the latter saw his old friend, his nemesis, he said matter-of-factly: "In spate I've seen it reach from that hill to this one. And in late spring when the ice breaks up, chunks as big as a house come sailing right down the middle, and heaven help whatever they strike."

The Voronovs remained on the hill till the rest of their party had passed, speculating on what the river must look like a thousand miles farther up, where the Canadians, those mysterious people the Russians never saw, had their footholds. They were enchanted by the Yukon, awed by its turbulent power and mesmerized by its incessant flow, this messenger from frozen lands, this symbol of Alaska.

"Come along," Father Fyodor said. "You'll see enough of it before we leave," and this frank assessment was proved accurate when the party descended to the level of the river and started up its right bank, for their way was constantly impeded by many small rivulets that wandered down from the north to join the great stream; to cross these required wading, and since one seemed to appear each half-hour, the Voronovs had wet feet most of that first day, but at dusk they approached the small but important settlement of Kaltag, where dogs began barking as children screamed: "Father Fyodor! He comes back!"

In the explosive moments that followed, the Voronovs gained a completely different impression of what life in central Alaska could be, for they were surrounded by a new kind of native, the taller, sturdier Athapascans whose ancestors had reached Alaska long before either the Eskimo or the Aleut and who served as progenitors to the Tlingits. Like the latter, they were a warlike lot, but when they saw that their onetime priest, Father Fyodor, was back, they swarmed about him with cries and presents and manifold expressions of their love. For two exciting days the travelers remained in the village, with the Voronovs getting an idea of what it was like to be a missionary on the frontier.

During this time Arkady had an opportunity to witness the wisdom of Father Fyodor's strange statement when Prince Maksutov objected to Praskovia's joining the expedition: "Our Athapascan women should be allowed to see how a Christian woman lives," for the Kaltag women trailed along with Praskovia wherever she went, marveling at her appearance and joining with her when she laughed. Those who spoke Russian asked innumerable questions, wanting to know specifically: "Is your bright hair real?" and "Why is it so different from ours?" and from the direct manner in which she answered even their most personal questions, they knew that she respected them and was meeting them as equals, and this friendliness encouraged them to ask more questions.

Arkady, watching her performance, said to himself: She likes this village and this river! and he loved her even more than before because of her willingness to see and accept Alaska as it was. When he mentioned this to her after one of her sessions with the women, she cried: "I do love this strange land. I think I now understand Alaska."

On the morning of the third day, when they were about to depart, Praskovia, with her practiced woman's eye, noticed that one Athapascan, no longer a girl but not yet a woman, was taking a special interest in the priest, bringing him the best bits of food and protecting him from the importunities of the children. Praskovia began studying the young woman, noticing her handsome carriage, the subtle coloring of her skin, the attractive way she wore her hair in braids, and she thought: That one was meant to be the mother of children, the custodian of a house.

So when the time came to leave the village, she went to Father Fyodor and said: "That girl, the smiling one, she'd make a fine wife," and the priest blushed, looked to where Praskovia pointed, and said, as if he had never seen the woman before: "Yes. Yes, it's about time she was finding herself a husband," and he nodded to Praskovia as if thanking her for her sensible suggestion.

The journey up the Yukon to Nulato required three days, and they were days the Voronovs would never forget, for as they progressed northward the river broadened out until it reached a mile and a half from bank to bank, a massive stretch of water pressing always toward the distant ocean, which now lay nearly five hundred miles away, counting all the twists and turns. On the bosom of the river, which seemed to move past the boat with rugged determination, the Voronovs felt themselves to be entering the heartland of a great continent, a feeling totally different from any they had previously experienced in their gentler part of Alaska where islands and stretches of open sea predominated.

"Look at those empty fields!" Praskovia cried, pointing to the land that reached down to the river's edge and seemed to stretch off to infinity.

"A field," her husband said reflectively, "makes you think of orderliness, as if someone had fenced in an area and tended it. The land up here goes on forever." It did, and across much of it no human being had ever moved, and as they contemplated its awesome immensity the Voronovs began to comprehend the terrain they governed. For long stretches there would be no trees, no hills, no animals moving, not even any snow, just the boundless emptiness, so lonely and forbidding that Praskovia whispered: "I'll wager there aren't even any mosquitoes out there," and Arkady asked: "You want us to let you off? Test your theory?" and she cried: "No! No!"

Yet in a perverse way it was the brutal nothingness of this trip up the Yukon that enchanted the Voronovs. "This isn't a garden along the Neva," Arkady said, anticipating the sentiments of those thousands of men from all corners of the world who would soon be crowding into the empty spaces of Alaska. They would deplore the loneliness, the difficulties of travel and the dreadful experience of fifty-five degrees below zero, but they would also revel in the fact that they had been able to withstand and conquer this gigantic, forbidding land, and fifty years later, as their lives drew to conclusion, they would cherish above all their other accomplishments the fact that "I traveled the Yukon."

Toward the close of their third day on the river the Voronovs saw around a bend a sight which caused them to cheer: the tight little fort of Nulato, its two wooden towers defying the world, a Russian flag flying from a central pole. As they drew close and men ashore began firing salutes from rusty guns and an ancient cannon, Arkady felt a surge of emotion: "This is the last outpost of empire. My God, I'm glad we came."

The garrison, some twenty Russian traders and soldiers, were as delighted to see their old friend Father Fyodor as the people at Kaltag had been and ran to the shore to embrace him, but when they did so, they stared in amazement to find that a woman, and a pretty one at that, had come so far up the Yukon, and when Praskovia tried to debark, four men reached for her, lifted her high in the air, and with shouts and imitated bugle calls carried her into the fort, while her husband trailed behind, informing the garrison commander of his official position in the government and his interest in their fort.

It was a rough, frontier stronghold perched well back from the right bank of the Yukon, but so located as to command far reaches of the river in all directions. Built in the classic form of four lengths of long buildings joined to enclose a rather spacious central square, it was dominated by the two stalwart towers and protected by a double-strength palisade which surrounded the entire structure. Having been overrun three times in the past, with considerable loss of Russian lives, it was not going to be an easy target in the future, for during daylight hours one soldier manned each tower; two at night.

After samovars bubbled with hot tea, and toasts were drunk, and garrison members reported on their experiences with the surrounding Athapascans, a fierce lot according to them, the commanding officer, an energetic clean-shaven young lieutenant named Greko, signaled one of his men, who blushed, stepped forward, bowed to the Voronovs, and said: "Gracious visitors, this humble fort at the edge of the world is honored by your presence. As a token of our respect, Lieutenant Greko and his men have prepared a special treat." At this point he broke into uncontrollable laughter, which left the visitors bewildered, but now Greko took over.

"It was that rascal's idea, not mine," he said, pointing to the young fellow, whom he now punched in the arm: "Go ahead, Pekarsky, tell them what you and those others did," and Pekarsky, after holding his hand over his mouth to stop his laughter, straightened up, bit his lower lip, and announced in a butler's manner: "Come this way, *monsieur et madame*," but the French, proving too much to handle under the circumstances, threw him into such convulsions that Lieutenant Greko had to intervene.

"The men have paid you a great honor, Excellency. I'm proud of them," and he led the way out of the meeting and into the square, where soldiers, still hungry for a glimpse of the beautiful woman from Moscow, stared and nudged one another as she passed, her golden hair glowing in the darkness. They went to a low building outside of which lay stacked a huge pile of logs, which had been cut far upstream and floated here. *"Voilà!"* the young officer cried, and when he pulled open the door the Voronovs found themselves entering a typical thick-walled Russian bath, with an outer room in which to undress, a very small middle area nearly filled with logs, and an inner room lined with low benches facing a collection of red-hot rocks heated by wood piled on from below. There were also six buckets of water to be thrown on the rocks to provide clouds of steam, so that within minutes of starting a bath, one would be engulfed in a cleansing, relaxing vapor.

"We could not maintain a fort here without this," Greko said, and he bowed to his distinguished guests and departed.

The promise of a good steam bath was so inviting that the two Voronovs almost raced to see who would reach it first, and when Praskovia won, for she had no high boots to unlace, she cried: "Heaven at the end of an arctic trip!" and her husband replied with that accuracy which can be so infuriating: "We're a hundred and twenty-one miles south of the Circle. I checked," but as the steam rose about them she replied: "It's arctic to me. I could feel the river preparing to freeze," and without warning she burst into tears.

"Darling?"

"It's been so wonderful, Arkady. There we were, all those years at Sitka Sound with our beautiful volcano thinking we were in Alaska. I'm so glad you brought me." She wept for some moments, then took her husband's hand: "When we were on the river I had the feeling that we were heading into eternity. But then I saw the soldiers come running down to embrace Father Fyodor, and I realized that people lived here and that eternity was somewhere far beyond." Her tears stopped, and she said: "Quite far beyond, I think."

She had been correct about the coming of winter, for after they had explored this part of the Yukon, going some twenty miles farther on to where a large river debouched from the north, and after they had met with members of various Athapascan tribes coming to the fort to trade, Arkady announced one morning: "I think we're ready to head downstream," and he supposed that because they would be drifting with the current rather than poling against it, the five-hundred-mile trip could be made speedily, but Lieutenant Greko corrected him.

"You'd be right if this were the beginning of summer. Easy ride. Pleasant, really. But this is autumn."

"If we started right away?"

"Fine. River's open here and it remains open for some time. But at the mouth it freezes early. The cold winds coming in from Asia hit there first." Allowing time for these facts to register, he then said: "Excellency, if you and Madame were to leave here now, you might very well be frozen in halfway down, and there you'd be, eight months in an arctic winter with no possible chance of escape."

Arkady called for his wife to join him so that she could hear the lieutenant's warning, and long before Greko finished, she blurted out: "We'll stay till the river freezes. Then return the way we came," and Greko, hoping to forestall any reconsiderations, jumped at the suggestion: "Good! You'll be most welcome here and we'll have time to find you a first-class dog team for the return."

So the Voronovs, he the son of the Metropolitan of All the Russias, she the daughter of a socially prominent family in Moscow, dug in for the opening days of a real Alaskan winter, and they watched with fascination as the thermometer began its steady and sometimes precipitous descent. One morning Praskovia wakened her husband with a rough shake: "The Yukon's freezing!" and they spent that whole day watching as ice formed along the shores, then broke away, then formed again, then vanished. That day it would not freeze.

But three days later, in mid-October when the thermometer suddenly plunged to three degrees above zero, the mighty river surrendered and ice began to rush across from shore to shore as if it operated under directions of its own, and two days later the Yukon was frozen.

Then came the exacting days of testing to see how thick the ice was, and Lieutenant Greko explained that no matter how cold it became, the bottom of the Yukon never froze: "The current below and the protection of the snow on top prevent the cold from taking command. In mid-January it'll still be flowing down there."

When various teams of dogs were brought in, Praskovia found delight in making their acquaintance: big gray-brown malamutes, white Eskimo dogs, mongrels with powerful bodies and inexhaustible energy, and others the Russians called huskies. They were dogs unlike any she had known in Russia, and although some snarled when she approached, others recognized her as a friend and showed their appreciation for her attention. But none became pets, nor did she try to make them so; these were noble animals bred for a particular purpose, and without them life in the arctic would have been difficult.

She found that she was loving the experience of extreme cold, but one night when the mercury thermometer dropped to minus-forty-two and quit, she was stunned by the force of weather at such temperatures, the way icy air sped down into the lungs, almost freezing them, and the curious manner in which a face could be fairly comfortable one minute and frozen the next. When she realized that the thermometer could not register below the low forties, she asked Greko what the actual temperature was, and he consulted his spirit thermometer and said: "Minus-fifty-three," and when she asked: "Why don't I feel it to be that cold?" he said: "No wind. No humidity. Just this heavy, heavy cold weighting everything down."

It did not weigh her down. Every day she ran and leaped outside the fort, and not until she had exhausted herself, and felt the cold threaten her very bones, did she hurry inside. "If I stayed out there," she asked Greko, "how long before I'd freeze?" and he called to a soldier, who showed her his wrecked ears and a big white scarlike place on his right cheek.

"How long did that take?" Greko asked, and the man said: "Twenty minutes, about as cold as this."

"Is your face permanently damaged?" she asked, and the man answered: "The ears are gone, the face will be all right, maybe a brown spot later on."

That night, in the heart of Alaska that few Russians would ever know, she had the most exciting experience of all, for over the fort at Nulato, where twenty-two Russians huddled against the bitter cold, the northern lights began their heaven-encompassing dance. The Voronovs joined Lieutenant Greko in the center of the frozen square, inside the protection of the wooden barracks and the double palisade, and there they watched the great ebb and flow of the colored lights as they pranced across the midnight-darkened sky. "How cold is it now?" Praskovia asked, and Greko said: "Maybe sixty-below," but the Voronovs only huddled deeper within their furs, for they did not want to move inside while this fantastic performance filled the heavens.

Later, as they drank tea and precious brandy with Greko, Praskovia said: "We've seen Alaska. Without your help we might never have known it existed," and he said: "There's three times as much that none of us has seen," and he agreed that on the day after tomorrow they could safely begin their journey back toward Sitka Sound.

There was an abrupt change in plans on the return journey, but it had only happy consequences. When they reached the village of Kaltag, where they would have to leave the frozen river in order to take the hill route to Unalakleet, Father Fyodor informed them, with embarrassment: "I'll be staying here. They need a priest." Arkady, although distressed at the prospect of continuing what was a dangerous journey without Father Fyodor's help, had witnessed the admirable manner in which this scarecrow of a man fitted into Yukon life, and he had to consent.

"Will you explain to the religious authorities at the capital?" the priest asked, and Arkady said: "I can see this village needs you," and was about to express his appreciation for the help he had given the party, when Praskovia marched up, holding by the hand the attractive Indian girl she had noticed on the earlier visit. Going to the priest, she said: "You proved yourself to be a dear, good man, Father. But you'd be twice as effective with a wife," and she placed the young woman's hand in his.

When it was understood by everyone, even the children, that Father Fyodor was taking a wife and staying in their village, the young bride said firmly: "It would be wrong to make the Russian couple cross the mountains by themselves!" And with the help of her father she arranged for a team of dogsled men to carry the Voronovs and the priest and his bride across snow and ice to where the Voronovs would wait for the thaw and a ship that would take them back to New Archangel.

As their ship pulled into Sitka Sound the Voronovs saw running down from the castle, in a manner quite undignified for a noble chief administrator, the agitated figure of Prince Maksutov, who shouted, as soon as he saw the Voronovs: "Go over to that English ship!" and as they veered course to pull alongside the merchant steamer, they saw Maksutov jumping into a small boat, which two sailors rowed to the English vessel.

When the Voronovs climbed aboard the visiting ship, they waited at the railing for Maksutov to join them, and when he did they saw that he was ashen-faced. "I want you to hear the news they've brought!" and he hurried them toward the captain's quarters, where they were met by a plump, jovial Scotsman who introduced himself: "Captain MacRae, Glasgow."

In a fevered rush Prince Maksutov presented his two guests, then blurted out: "Tell them what you told me," and Captain MacRae said: "It's such a bizarre story I'd like to have young Henderson along. He heard it first and checked it out after I'd heard it from a different source." So while Henderson was sent for, the Voronovs waited, quite in the dark as to what had been happening during their long absence. Probably England and Russia at war again, Arkady said to himself, but when Henderson appeared to stand beside his captain, the two Britons delivered quite a different story.

"It seems," Captain MacRae began, "and we have it on unimpeachable authority both from the Americans in San Francisco and our consul there, that Russia has sold Alaska—land, company, buildings, ships, everything—to the Americans."

"Sold?" Voronov gasped. Long ago he and Praskovia had heard rumors of a possible sale, but that was when Russia had her back to the wall in the Crimea and needed money. To sell now would be insane. He and his wife had just seen the grandeur and promise of Alaska, and could not imagine losing such a treasure. His agile mind leaped from one possibility to the next. In the end he asked an almost insulting question: "Prince Maksutov, how do we know that these two men are not saying this to put us to some disadvantage? I mean, if there's war between our nations?" As soon as he saw the prince blanch he realized how intemperate his question had been, and he turned to the two British officers and apologized.

"Not at all!" MacRae said, his round face beaming. "This gentleman is quite right. All we've brought you, as I warned you before, Prince, is a San Francisco rumor. A very solid one, as I said, but only a rumor until you receive official confirmation from your own people." He invited the Russians to stay, then ordered a steward to bring drinks for everyone, and as the Voronovs sat in stunned silence, MacRae said almost jovially: "Henderson here gave a damned good account of himself in the Crimea. Said you chaps were mighty handy with your heavy guns."

For some time they talked about the affair at Balaklava as if it had been a cricket match played in the distant past with no rancor left behind, but when that gracious interlude ended, Voronov addressed Henderson: "Please, sir, would you share with my wife and me exactly what happened?" and the young officer told of having been in a San Francisco waterfront saloon of the better type, with officers from another British ship and a French, when an American businessman asked: "Any of you Johnnies headed for Sitka? I suppose you know it belongs to America now?" Henderson said that since his ship was heading for Alaska, he asked to know more, and a general discussion evolved into which several Americans were brought, and two of them had knowledge of the sale.

Henderson had then run back to his ship to alert Captain Mac-Rae, who did not believe the yarn but who did hurry to the British consul, who said that although he had no solid knowledge of the transaction, he had been forewarned in the pouch from Washington that the sale had been confirmed by the American political leaders and that the price agreed upon had been $7,200,000.

"Good God," Voronov gasped. "How many rubles is that?"

"A little better than two to one, maybe eleven, twelve million rubles."

"Good God," Voronov repeated. "The Yukon River alone is worth that much."

"Have you been to the Yukon?" MacRae asked, and Praskovia replied: "Far up. It's a treasure, and I refuse to believe it's been sold."

MacRae, feeling sympathy for the difficult problems facing these Russians so far from home, invited them to join him for tiffin, during which he did his best to relax their tensions, but when he asked them what they might do if the rumors proved true, he received two sharply different answers. Prince Maksutov said with diplomatic propriety: "I'm an official of the government. I'd stay here to effect an orderly transfer, salute as our flag came down, then sail home."

"You wouldn't protest the action?"

"Six times in the past three years I've advised St. Petersburg to hold on to Alaska. If a contrary decision's been made, as you suggest, I'll have no more to say."

"But you wouldn't continue to live here in Sitka Sound?"

"Under the Americans? Unthinkable." Realizing the pejorative nature of that comment to a representative of a third power, he added: "Nor under anybody else, including you British." MacRae, appreciating the reason for the correction, said: "I'd feel the same way."

But now Praskovia broke in: "Leave this lovely place? Never!"

"You'd surrender your Russian citizenship?"

Arkady, hoping to forestall an answer his wife might later regret, interrupted: "How can we predict what the rules will be? If America has bought Alaska, she might want to kick us all out, so your question is premature."

"Not at all!" strong-willed Praskovia snapped. "America needs people. So much empty space. So many of their men killed in the war. They'll be begging us to stay." Looking at each of her listeners in turn, she added: "And the Voronovs will be staying. We've made this our home." After she launched this challenge, the fire went out of her, and she looked only at Prince Maksutov: "You did a terrible thing, sir, when you sent us to Fort Nulato. You allowed us to see Alaska. And we fell in love with it. Here we shall stay to speed its development, and I won't give a damn who owns it."

"Bravo!" MacRae cried. "I'll toast you both on later trips." Trying her best to smile at this levity, she failed miserably, dropped her face into her hands, and wept.

The transfer of Alaska from Russia to the United States formed one of those unbelievable incidents of history, because by 1867, Russia was nervously eager to get rid of it, while the United States, still recovering from the Civil War and immersed in the impending impeachment of President Johnson, refused to accept it on any terms.

At this impasse an extraordinary man monopolized center stage. He was not a Russian, a fact which would become important more than a century later, but a *soi-disant* baron of dubious background, half Austrian, half Italian, and a charmer who was picked up in 1841 for temporary duty representing Russia in the United States and who lingered there till 1868. In that time Edouard de Stoeckl, parading himself as a nobleman, although no one could say for sure how or when or even if he had earned his title, became such an ardent friend of America that he married an American heiress and took upon himself the task of acting as marriage broker between Russia, which he called his homeland, and the United States, his adopted residence.

He faced a most difficult task, for when the United States showed hesitancy about accepting Alaska, support for the sale withered in Russia, and later when Russia wanted to sell, half a dozen of the most influential American politicians led by Secretary of State William Seward of New York looked far into the future and saw the desirability of acquiring Alaska to serve as America's arctic bastion, yet the hardheaded businessmen in the Senate, the House and the general public opposed the purchase with all the scorn they could summon. "Seward's Icebox" and "Seward's Folly" were two of the gentler jibes. Some critics accused Seward of being in the pay of the Russians; others accused De Stoeckl of buying votes in the House.

One sharp satirist claimed that Alaska contained nothing but polar bears and Eskimos, and many protested that America should not accept this useless, frozen domain even if Russia wanted to give it away.

Many pointed out that Alaska had no wealth of any kind, not even reindeer, which proliferated in other northern areas, and experts affirmed that an arctic area like this could not possibly have any minerals or other deposits of value. On and on went the abuse of this unknown and somewhat terrifying land, and the castigations would have been comical had they not influenced American thinking and behavior and condemned Alaska to decades of neglect.

But an ingenious man like Baron de Stoeckl was not easily diverted from his main target, and with Seward's unflinching support and admirable statesmanship, the sale squeaked by with a favorable margin of one vote. By such a narrow margin did the United States come close to losing one of her potentially valuable acquisitions, but of course, had one viewed Alaska from the vantage point of frozen Fort Nulato in 1867, with the thermometer at minus-fifty-seven and about to be attacked by hostile Athapascans, the purchase at more than $7,000,000 would have seemed a poor bargain.

Now the comedy intensified, became burlesque, for although the U.S. Senate had bought the place, the U.S. House refused to appropriate the money to pay for it, and for many tense months the sale hung in the balance. When a favorable vote was finally taken, it was almost negated by the discovery that Baron de Stoeckl had disposed of $125,000 in cash for which he refused to give an accounting. Widely suspected of having bribed congressmen to vote for land that was obviously worthless, the baron waited until the sale was completed, then quietly slipped out of the country, his life's ambition having been achieved.

One congressman with a keen sense of history, economics and geopolitics said of the whole affair: "If we were so eager to show Russia our appreciation for the help she gave us during the Civil War, why didn't we give her the seven million and tell her to keep her damned colony? It'll never be of any use to us."

So the sale was completed and the scene of the comedy moved to San Francisco, where a fiery Northern general named Jefferson C. Davis—no relative of the president of the Confederacy—was informed that Alaska was now American property and that he, Davis, was in command of the icebergs, the polar bears and the Indians. A short-tempered man who during the Civil War had gunned down a

Northern general to whom he had taken a dislike—the other general died and Davis was forgiven on the grounds that he, Davis, did have a short temper—he had spent the postwar years chasing Indians on the Plains, and accepted his job in Alaska under the impression that his duty there would be to continue chasing Indians.

On 18 September 1867 the steamer *John L. Stevens* sailed from San Francisco bearing the two hundred and fifty soldiers who were to govern Alaska for the ensuing decades. One who left that day wrote a dismal account:

> As we marched in battle gear to our waiting ship, no maidens stood on the corners to throw roses at us and no enthusiastic crowds gathered to cheer us on our way. The public was so disgusted with our purchase of Alaska that they showed only contempt as we passed. One man shouted directly at me: "Give it back to Russia!"

> When the *Stevens* reached Sitka a holy mess developed. The Russians follow a calendar which is eleven days behind ours, so everything was confused. Also, in Alaska they keep the Moscow day, which is one ahead of ours. You figure that out. At any rate, when we arrived the Russian commander said: "You're here early. This is still Russia and no foreign troops can land till the American commissioners arrive," and we poor soldiers have had to stay in our stinking ship's quarters ten days looking at a volcano off our port side, which I can see as I write. I don't like volcanoes and I certainly don't like Alaska.

Finally, the ship bearing the American commissioners came into the sound, and now the troops were permitted, belatedly, to land; they were a grumbling unhappy lot, but soon they were engaged in the formality of transfer, which to everyone's surprise took place that very afternoon.

It was not a well-managed affair. Prince Maksutov, who could have handled it beautifully, was prevented from doing so by the presence of a stuffy minor official sent from Russia to represent the tsar, while Arkady Voronov, who knew more about the Russian holdings than anyone else, was not allowed to participate at all. There was, however, a certain formality that pleased the few people who climbed the eighty steps to Baranov's Castle, where the Russian flag streamed from a ninety-foot pole made from a Sitka spruce. There were cannon salutes from the bay and a proper ceremony for the lowering of one flag and the raising of another, but a painfully silly mishap marred the ritual, as explained by Praskovia Voronova in a letter home:

> Although we had already signified our intention of becoming American citizens, Arkady, as you would expect, wanted the farewell Russian performance carried out with proper dignity, as would befit the honor of a great empire. He rehearsed our Russian soldiers with great care in the lowering of our flag and I helped mend torn uniforms and supervised the polishing of shoes. I must say that our troops looked pipe-clay neat when Arkady and I were finished.
>
> Alas, it came to naught. For when one of our most reliable men pulled the halyards to lower our glorious flag, a sudden gust of wind whipped it about the flagpole, fastening it so tightly that nothing could be done to dislodge it. The poor man with the rope looked woefully at Arkady, who indicated with his hands that he should give it a good tug. He obeyed, but succeeded only in ripping off the bunting which decorated the flag and tightening the flag even more securely to the pole. It was obvious that no amount of pulling was going to loosen that flag, and I almost broke into cheers, thinking it to be an omen that the sale would not take effect.
>
> At this point Arkady left me, swearing under his breath, and I heard him tell two of his men: "Get that damned thing down. Now!" They had no idea of how this could be done, and I am humiliated to confess that it was an American sailor who called out: "Rig up a bosun's chair!" I couldn't see how this was done, but pretty soon a man was clambering up the pole like a monkey on a rope, and he broke our flag loose, tearing it further in his haste.
>
> Freed at last, it fell ignominiously earthward, where it landed on the heads of our men, who failed to catch it in their hands, and then it became mixed up in their bayonets. I was mortified. Arkady continued to swear, something he rarely does, Prince Maksutov looked straight ahead as if there were no flag and no pole, and his pretty wife fainted.

I wept. Arkady and I are determined to remain here in Sitka, as it is now to be called, and to be the best citizens we can be of our new nation. He is staying because his mother and father had such close associations with these islands, and I shall stay because I have grown to love Alaska and its enormous potential, and when you come to visit us next year I believe you will see a city twice this size and twice as prosperous, for they assure us that when America assumes control, it will pour millions of dollars in here to make this a major possession.

It was not premature for Praskovia and the other Russians who were selecting American citizenship to announce their choice, because in the days before the transfer, Prince Maksutov had assembled the heads of families and explained in glowing terms the Russian-American treaty which would govern such matters. Standing in his crisp white officer's uniform and smiling warmly, he was obviously proud of the work his committee had done: "Both countries deserve commendation for the excellent rules they've agreed to. Great statesmanship, really." When a young teacher from the local college, one Maxim Luzhin, asked for details, Maksutov patiently explained: "I helped draft the regulations, so I can assure you that you'll be fully protected, however you choose."

"For example?" Luzhin pressed, and the prince said: "If you want to go back to Russia, you can do so anytime within three years. We'll provide free transportation to your home district. If you elect to remain here and become Americans, your new government promises you full citizenship automatically, no restraints because you're Russian, and complete freedom of religion." Smiling at people who trusted him, he told them honestly: "Not often in life do you get two choices, each one excellent. Choose as you wish. You can't go wrong."

So when the Voronovs participated in the transfer ceremonies they did so as American citizens, but their transition into their new homeland was a rude one, for no sooner had the American flag risen to the top of the pole on that first day than General Davis issued a startling order: "All Russians on the hill to vacate their quarters before sunset!" and a major directed his soldiers to occupy the buildings.

Arkady went to the major, and in a quiet, respectful voice, explained: "My wife and I have elected American citizenship. Our home is up there," and he pointed to their quarters atop the castle.

"You're Russian, aren't you?" the major growled. "Out by sunset. I'm taking those rooms."

When Voronov, burning with indignation, informed his wife of the order, she laughed: "The prince and princess have been tossed out of their quarters, too. General Davis wants their rooms."

"I can't believe it."

"Look at the servants," and Arkady saw the Maksutov possessions being toted down the hill.

The Voronovs moved their goods into a small cottage near the cathedral, where they watched as their Russian friends made agonizing choices. Those who had enjoyed their life in Sitka longed to remain, willing like the Voronovs to trust their fate to American generosity, but friends in Russia applied such strong pressure for them to return home that most decided to sail on whatever steamer arrived to carry them to Petropavlovsk.

"What will happen to them when they get to Russia?" Praskovia asked, and Arkady replied: "I wouldn't like to guess." But now distraught neighbors, unable to decide for themselves, came to the Voronov cottage, asking Arkady what to do, and usually he advised: "Go home." And if a husband and wife differed in their choice, he invariably counseled a return to Russia: "There you know what your neighbors are going to do."

This repeated recommendation that people who harbored doubts should go back to Russia had a surprising effect on him, for although he had started with a firm resolve to stay in Alaska, his constant projection of himself into the minds and conditions of others revealed how insecure in his choice he was. One evening as he and Praskovia walked home from a meeting with the Maksutovs, who were reconciled to returning home and perhaps even eager to do so, Arkady said without warning: "Praska, are we doing the right thing?" and she temporized, wishing to know the full range of his doubts: "What do you mean, Arkady?" and he revealed his uncertainty: "It's a fearful decision, really. The rest of our lives. We don't know Russia anymore, we've been away so long. And we don't know America, because we can't predict how they'll behave ten years from now . . . or even now, for that matter. This General Davis? I wonder if he has any concept of what Alaska is. I wonder if he's very bright."

"I'm certainly not impressed with his first decisions," Praskovia said, "but he may get better." She encouraged her husband to spread out all his fears, and as he ventilated them she saw that they were nothing more than the sensible alternatives that any people their age should consider when making a decision of such gravity: "Go on, what's your greatest fear?" and he said gravely: "That it's the last big choice we'll ever make. Not for me, really. I was never attached to Russia, you know. I'm from the islands. But you . . ." and he looked at her with the great love which had always been the mark of Voronov men. His great-grandfather and his grandfather, both in Irkutsk, had enjoyed the good fortune of loving their wives. His father, Vasili, had found in the islands a love with his Aleut bride that few men know, and he had been the same. From the first moment he saw Praskovia during his student days in the capital he had loved only her, and now he feared that he might be behaving as his father had done when he surrendered Sofia Kuchovskaya in order to accept soaring promotion in the church. He was thinking of himself and not of his wife, and very quietly he said: "I'm an island man. I'm forcing you into a cruel choice."

She did not laugh, or even smile at his ingenuousness, but she did take him by the arm and lead him toward the cathedral, where they entered together to find rude chairs in the back among the shadows, and there she informed him as to her vision of the future: "Arkady, you're sixty-six. I'm fifty-eight. How many years are we gambling on this thing? Not many. An error, if we make one, won't be the wastage of an entire life." Before he could respond, she said with great force: "At Nulato, watching the Yukon sweep past, feeling the immense cold, getting to know those sled dogs and seeing how Father Fyodor was greeted in the villages . . ." She smiled and squeezed his hand: "I made my choice then, whether Alaska remained Russian or not. This is my home. I want to be here to witness the conclusion of our great adventure." Before he could speak, she concluded: "Arkady, I do believe that if you elected to go home to Russia, I might stay here by myself." Then she added in a confidential whisper: "Truth is, but don't tell the prince, I actually prefer their American name Sitka to the Russian name New Archangel."

After that revealing moment, Arkady stopped advising anyone what to do, nor did he volunteer any information as to what Praskovia and he would do when the first ship sailed, the one that would take Prince Maksutov and his wife away. Instead, the Voronovs bought a somewhat larger house that was being vacated by a family heading home, and in it they began accumulating those comfortable odds and ends that would mean so much to them when Sitka became a totally American city. "It's to be a wonderful new life," Praskovia said, but Arkady, who was witnessing each day the inability of the Americans to govern their new possession, had additional reasons for apprehension.

As Christmas approached in that fateful year 1867, the Maksutovs held a farewell dinner party to thank those trusted friends who had worked so hard for Russia but who now elected to become American citizens. "I cannot challenge your decisions," he said gently, "but I pray you will serve your new homeland honorably." He explained that although he must remain two more weeks to complete the transfer, his wife would be sailing on the morrow. And then nature pulled a cruel trick. During these weeks of departure Sitka's normal fog and gloom had established a mood proper for farewell, but on the final day the mists lifted, revealing Sitka in its refulgent grandeur: there stood the noble volcano, the rim of snow-clad mountains, the myriad green islands, the green onion dome of the Orthodox cathedral, the trim neatness of the most congenial port in Russian America.

"Oh, Praska!" the princess cried as she embraced her friend. "We're throwing away the most beautiful town in the Russian Empire," and it was in bitterness that she made her departure.

Two weeks later the Voronovs formed an honor guard for Prince Maksutov as he marched in dignity down the hill to where a small boat waited to ferry him to his waiting ship: "I leave Alaska in the hands of you Voronovs. You know it better than anyone else." From atop the hill, General Davis, now ruling from Baranov's Castle, ordered a salute to be fired, and as the echoes reverberated through the mountains and valleys of Sitka, the Russian Empire in Alaska came to an end.

The United States assumed responsibility for Alaska on 18 October 1867, and by early January 1868 it was apparent to the Voronovs and the Luzhins that no sensible form of government—indeed, none at all, sensible or ridiculous—was going to be installed. General Davis and his soldiers were supposed to be in charge, but only a part of the blame could be placed on them.

The fault lay with the American Congress, which, remembering the irresponsible oratory opposing the purchase of Alaska, had claimed that the area was worthless and populated by no one meriting serious attention. So, incredible as it would seem to later historians, America refused to give Alaska any form of government. It refused even to give it a proper name: in 1867 it was called the Military District of Alaska; in 1868, the Department of Alaska; in 1877, the Customs District of Alaska; and in 1884, simply the District of Alaska. From the first day of ownership it should have been designated the Territory of Alaska, but that would have presupposed eventual statehood, and orators opposing the suggestion ranted: "That icebox will never have enough population to warrant statehood," so the area was initially denied the step-by-step learning experience of first being an unorganized territory with judges and sheriffs, then an organized one with its own legislature and emerging government, and finally a full-fledged state.

Why were normal rights denied the area? Because businessmen, saloonkeepers, trappers, miners and fishermen demanded a free hand in garnering the riches of Alaska and feared that any form of local self-government might pass laws restricting them. And especially because Alaska was then and would remain America's blind spot. No matter what happened here—what riches were uncovered, what triumphs achieved—the American people and their government would not believe. For generations this treasure would be left to float adrift in icy seas, like an abandoned ship whose planking slowly rotted.

By mid-January, Arkady Voronov began to fear that a kind of creeping paralysis had engulfed Sitka and the rest of Alaska, but he did not appreciate the depth of the confusion until he talked with the young teacher Maxim Luzhin: "Arkady, you can't imagine the situation! An enthusiastic businessman from California came north on the ship that brought the troops. He wants to move here and open some kind of trading business. But he can't buy land for a home and office because there is no land law. And he can't start his business because there is no business law. If he settles here, he can't leave his property to his children, for there is no office to legalize wills or enforce them."

When the two Russians looked into other impediments, they were told: "You can't call upon the sheriff to protect your rights, because there is no sheriff, no jail and no court to appeal to for redress, for there is no court, which is understandable, because there is no real judge."

Together the two men climbed the hill to inform General Davis of the concern the Russians had for their safety amid such chaos, and when they met him at ease in his quarters, they were struck by how handsome and military he looked. Tall, lean, carefully erect, with a heavy black beard, a voluminous mustache and a romantic wealth of dark hair which covered much of his forehead, he looked a born ruler of men, but when he spoke the illusion was shattered: "I'd like to enforce the law, but there is no law. And I can't make guesses about it because no one knows what Congress will do." When they asked what form the new government would probably take, he said: "Legally, I think we're a Customs District, so I guess when a customs officer arrives, he'll be in charge."

Despite the perspicacity of their questioning, they could elicit no substantial explanations from the general, and they left the meeting both confused and disheartened, so they were not surprised when, upon the arrival of a passenger ship, well over half the local Russians decided to leave Alaska and head back to Siberia. When General Davis saw the huge number departing, he tried ineffectively to entice them to remain, but they'd had enough of American vacillations and would not listen.

Voronov and Luzhin, better able than Davis to estimate the high quality of those who were fleeing Sitka, consoled each other and their wives with the hopeful thought: "Those of us who are staying will have extra work to do . . . and extra opportunities to do it," and each of the four was determined to be the best possible American citizen.

The rest of the Russian story is quickly and sadly told. After the first contingent of émigrés fled, the undisciplined American troops, with no clear mission to occupy them or any stern leader to keep them under control, began to run wild, and Voronov, like the other Russians who had stayed behind, became appalled at what was happening.

Aleut women who had worked as servants of Russian families transferred their duties to the barracks where the soldiers were billeted, and before the week was out three cases of the ugliest kind of rape were reported. When nothing was done to discipline the men, they went outside the palisade and raped two Tlingit women, whose husbands promptly killed a soldier in retaliation, but he was not one of the rapists.

This particular case was resolved by paying the aggrieved husbands twenty-five American dollars each and sending the mother of the dead soldier a medal and the news that her son had died bravely in action against the enemy.

But now the violence extended to Russian families, who began locking and barring their doors, and two of the men complained bitterly to General Davis, but nothing happened. However, Voronov assured his wife: "This madness will stop."

It didn't. When a gang of drunken soldiers staggered down to a nearby village and assaulted three women, the Tlingits retaliated with a series of hammering counterblows, which General Davis interpreted as a dangerous insurrection against American rule. Dispatching a gunboat to the offending village, he ordered the place to be chastised; it was totally destroyed, with heavy loss of Tlingit life.

This resulted in the rupture of contact between the occupation force and the Tlingits, which meant that little fresh food made its way into the town. Tempers ran high, and one afternoon as Praskovia returned from a visit with distraught Russian neighbors she saw something which sent her screaming for her husband.

When the Voronovs and the Luzhins reached the front door of their cathedral they saw that in the sanctuary, at the iconostasis and throughout the main body of the cathedral everything breakable had been smashed, paint was smeared over the walls, and the pulpit was destroyed. The cathedral was a wreck; it would take thousands of rubles to restore it, and even at that cost the icons hallowed by time could not be replaced. When General Davis was informed of the sacrilege, he shrugged his shoulders and absolved his men of any blame: "No doubt some angry Tlingits sneaked in when we weren't looking."

That night those Russians with administrative or mercantile experience met at the Voronovs' to discuss what could be done to protect their rights and perhaps their lives, and the consensus was that since General Davis would not assume responsibility for his troops, the only practical thing to do was to appeal to the captain of the first foreign ship putting into Sitka, and Arkady volunteered for the assignment.

It was a French ship and the captain was a man well versed in maritime tradition. After listening to Voronov's recitation of complaints, he fumed: "No self-respecting general allows his troops to rape," and he marched directly to the castle and made a formal protest. Davis was outraged at this interference, and his assistant, who took note of Voronov's name in the Frenchman's recitation, warned the Frenchman that if there was any further intervention from him, "the cannon up here will know what to do."

That night, perhaps by accident, perhaps by design, three soldiers went to Voronov's house while he was known to be absent at a protest meeting, and tried to rape Praskovia, who fought them off vigorously and ran from the house screaming for help. Before she could make good her escape, one of the men grabbed her, dragged her back into the house, and started stripping off her clothes.

Neighbors alerted Voronov, who came running home in time to find his wife practically naked in their bedroom, fighting and scratching and gouging at the three men, who were laughing maniacally. When they saw that three big Russians were crowding in behind the enraged husband, they beat a planned retreat through a back window, smashing it and as much kitchen-ware as they could.

The other Russians wanted to chase the soldiers, but Voronov would not allow this. Instead, he gathered his wife's clothes, helped her dress, and then hurriedly packed everything that could be crammed into three bags. In the dark of night he led Praskovia, the Luzhins and their children down to the shore, where he signaled the French ship, in vain. Throwing off his shoes and jacket, he entered the cold water and swam out, shouting as he approached the ship: "Captain Rulon, we seek asylum!"

In the darkness the Voronovs and Luzhins fled Sitka.

VII

GIANTS IN CHAOS

AMERICAN MALADMINISTRATION HAD A DEVASTATING EFFECT on Sitka, for its lovely port, which had been the site of more than two hundred visits a year by ships of all nations, saw arrivals drop to nineteen stragglers with little to offer in trade and less money with which to purchase local goods.

The population of the town, once among the finest in North America, dropped from more than two thousand to less than three hundred, and with its skilled work force gone to Russia, Sitka saw its Custom House receipts decline from more than $100,000 a year in the heyday of Russian control to $21,000 under the Americans and then to a shocking $449.28.

And year by year, the leaders of the Tlingits, watching this debacle, grew bolder, moving out of the fastnesses to which they had retreated under Russian pressure, edging always closer to where the protective palisade had once stood but stood no more. Sitka was in terrible trouble.

But the lack of government had an even more destructive impact on the other parts of Alaska, as a chain of incidents will demonstrate.

• • •

When the consortium of landbound wealthy New Bedford owners learned that their Captain Schransky wanted to christen their new brig the *Erebus,* they complained that this name, which bespoke underworld and hell, was improper for a whaler owned by God-fearing Christians. He told them sharply: "It could bear no name more appropriate, for it will be sailing into the white hell of the arctic ice and snow," but when he wanted to paint the ship a solid, funereal black, they demurred: "Our forefathers sometimes gave their lives defending New England ships against pirates, and we will not have one of our ships sailing under that fearful color."

When Captain Emil Schransky, six feet four inches tall, with Nordic white hair and heavy beard, insisted that black was the color he wanted—"If it's to be a hell ship, which it has to be to make money in these waters, let it have a proper hell color"—a compromise was reached: it was painted a blue so dark and snarling that from a distance it appeared black, and it was under this fearful color that the *Erebus* sailed south for dreaded Cape Horn, whose passage would throw her into the broad Pacific. There she would chase the bowhead whale into the Bering Sea, with yearlong expeditions against the fur seals of the Pribilof Islands and the walrus of the Chukchi Sea. Oil taken from the whales would be delivered to Hawaii; sealskins and walrus tusks would be sold in China, and in between such commercial forays the *Erebus* would prowl the Pacific, seeking any cargo of opportunity. The ominous dark ship commanded by the formidable captain with the white hair and beard never engaged in outright piracy, but Schransky would be prepared to do so should a likely opportunity safe from detection present itself.

He was forty-five years old when he assumed command of the *Erebus,* a huge man in every way. Born in Germany of Prussian-Russian parentage, he had been thrown out of his turbulent home at the age of eleven and had promptly shipped aboard a world-trader out of Hamburg. Educated in the cruel academy before the mast, he had been at the age of fourteen a bare-knuckle brawler, willing to take on and sometimes seeking out cabin boys four and five years older than himself. He was a gouger, a knee-er, an arm-wrencher and a terror who, after he reached his full height at twenty-two, rarely had to use his fists. He was not averse to doing so, but he was just as pleased to lean heavily upon some minor troublemaker and slowly muscle him away from the scene of trouble, saving his punishing fists for real enemies whom he felt he must destroy before they destroyed him.

Enraged, he could become a terrible foe, two hundred and forty-eight pounds of incarnate fury, all windmill arms and kicking feet and great white beard snapping in the breeze as he came roaring at whoever had in some way infuriated him. At such moments he struck for the kill, and although he had not yet actually slain an American sailor with his fists, two who had shipped with him, one from Maine, one from Maryland, had never recovered from the terrible beatings he gave them. The Maine man died five months later in Lahaina; the Marylander lived along the Santiago waterfront, his brains addled and his left arm useless. Others, less severely punished, recovered, with arms slightly atwist from the breakings or teeth missing in front.

He was a massive man with massive powers and massive enthusiasms, but it was his driving compulsions that made him something more than just another German-Russian sailor with gargantuan appetites. Any ship he stepped upon as captain was his ship, and the financial owners were not welcome aboard; it would be unthinkable for any of them to accompany him on a voyage, or even part of one. He sailed to make money, and he possessed an uncanny faculty for smelling out where it was going to be found. (He had once made a small fortune in sandalwood which other captains had bypassed.) And he despised all governing bodies, all restraints and rules. He kept his ships away from their home ports for four and five years because by doing so he could avoid interference from the owners, and as soon as he rounded the Horn, for he avoided the Cape of Good Hope, calling it "the route home for milksops," he seemed to breathe more easily, taking deep drafts of the salt air of the Pacific, which he sometimes referred to as "the Ocean of Freedom," for he was able to negotiate from Chile to China without surveillance from local policing agencies.

But it was when he penetrated the Aleutians and broke out into the Bering Sea that he began to operate with that abandon which characterized his captaincy. Prior to 1867, when Alaska and its surrounding seas passed into American control, he had been a scourge of the Russian masters of the Bering, for he had scorned their attempts to keep him away from the Pribilofs, where he would sweep in unexpectedly to harvest a whole shipload of forbidden sealskins. He also liked to rampage along the Siberian coast north of Petropavlovsk, trading with natives whom the Russians themselves were afraid to approach, or come storming down the western coast of Alaska in chase of bowhead whales, which he seemed able to catch when even the local Eskimos could not. He sometimes spent an entire year in and out of the Bering Sea, harvesting its riches and keeping them semi-frozen until he decided to make port at Lahaina or Canton.

He kept honest books, and frequently sent huge amounts of money home to his New Bedford owners by way of some returning ship against which he had been competing for years, and when the time came for him to head back for New England, ship captains came to him, begging him to transport their profits, for he was known to be trustworthy. "He's his own law," a Boston captain said with great force, remembering his own contests with Schransky, "and he's destruction to his enemies, but there's nobody I'd trust with my cargo or my cash sooner than Captain Emil."

The Russians before 1867 and the American authorities thereafter did not hold Schransky in this high regard; to them he was a predator, a scoffer at rules, a thief in the night, a pirate where seals were concerned, and the scourge of the Bering. He seemed ordained by some evil power to prowl the arctic, for he had a sixth sense of when he must flee these unforgiving waters before ice grabbed his vessel, immobilizing it for eight or nine months, and whereas incautious captains were sometimes trapped for the winter, he never was. No better description of him was ever given than the admiring one offered by an Eskimo at Desolation Point as he watched the *Erebus* slip out of that northern anchorage just before the arrival of the ice pack: "Cap'n Schransky, he's a polar bear in a black coat. The ice whispers to him 'I'm comin',' and out he goes."

In this harsh world he might have been considered an ideal captain, except for three ugly flaws which estranged him from other rough-and-ready types. He was known as a niggardly captain who kept his crew on meager rations while afloat and then encouraged them to gorge themselves at their own expense when they hit some Hawaiian port. However, his sailors put up with his penury because when the time came to split profits with his crew he was generous.

His second flaw was that he was contemptuous of the great sea animals on which his prosperity depended. He hunted them callously, sometimes wounding and losing through drowning two whales or walruses for every one he hauled up to his ship. If a mate protested this arrogant waste of animal life, he growled: "The seas are endless. There'll never be a lack of whales or anything else," and during the long hunting season of 1873 he put this philosophy in practice in several gruesome ways.

When the *Erebus* sailed through the protective arc of the Aleutians, always a magnificent moment, it was in the Bering Sea only two days when one of the men sighted a pod of nine magnificent bowhead whales, great slow-moving creatures making their way north to the colder seas they loved. In the old days, some hundred thousand of these noble animals had threaded through the northern seas; now there were less than ten thousand, and Captain Schransky's abusive manner of hunting them helped explain why.

"On the starboard beam!" he shouted to the mate at the wheel, and when the *Erebus* swung around to head off the whales, some of them forty feet long and weighing forty tons, the boats were launched and three teams of rowers and harpooners started in pursuit of the placid beasts, who were unaware of the dangers into which they were heading.

The hunters of the *Erebus* had two enormous advantages. The long harpoons they used had in their sharply pointed heads toggles which fitted snugly against the shaft as the harpoon stabbed into the flank of the whale, then sprang open to form a T inside the whale's body so long and strong that the whale could never dislodge it; and to the other end of the harpoon were fastened big inflated seal bladders which prevented the stricken whale from either diving or swimming rapidly ahead. Once a whale had four or five *Erebus* harpoons in it, with trailing bladders, it was doomed.

But if it managed to swim too far from the ship, Captain Schransky let it go; he did not pursue endlessly: "It's gone! Get that next one!" So in this attack on the nine whales of the pod, his men killed three, but only one of them was captured for its oil and baleen; the other two wandered off to perish at a distance. However, that one proved a bonanza, for it rendered many casks of oil and, even better, immensely long strips of baleen, the bonelike substance that enabled the whale to filter out the plankton from the huge amounts of seawater it passed through its gaping mouth.

"Get all the baleen!" Schransky shouted as his men worked the whale, for he knew that in the fashion shops of Paris and London this whalebone, as it was called, was essential. He could afford to let the two stricken whales escape, for this one catch would bring him more than seven thousand dollars.

His hunting of the walrus was equally brutal: three huge beasts shot with rifles, only two and sometimes one retrieved for their ivory. But it was his treatment of the fur-bearing seal that was most ruthless. Evading American patrols with the same clever tricks that had fooled the Russians, he slipped into the Pribilof Islands, that remarkable pair to which most of the world's seals came to have their young. Watching for an opportunity, he landed swiftly on Saint Paul, the northernmost island, where his men armed with clubs rampaged among the defenseless seals, beating them over the head and crushing their skulls. It was not difficult work, because perhaps six hundred thousand seals clustered on this island, a slightly lesser number on southerly Saint George, so the killing could continue as long as the men's arms could wield their bloodied clubs.

In the time of the Russians, when perhaps two million seals had come to the Pribilofs, they appreciated the fact that they had an almost inexhaustible treasury here and policed the harvest so that the immense herd was sure to be replenished, but when avaricious men like Schransky were not restrained, the seals on the Pribilofs were threatened with extinction.

However, the real slaughter, the one that all the maritime nations of the world opposed and strove to abolish, was pelagic sealing, the kind that Schransky particularly enjoyed and from which he profited enormously. Pelagic hunting, derived from the Greek word *pelagos* meaning sea, as in *archipelago*, consisted of chasing down the seals, most of them gravid females, when they were in the open sea totally defenseless, slaughtering them with ease, and ripping from their wombs the partly formed young whose skins had a special appeal in China. It was an operation that sickened many sailors forced to engage in it, but it was remunerative, and if a captain had no conscience and a ship fast enough to elude Russian or British or American patrol boats, a tidy sum could be made from pelagic campaigns.

Captain Schransky was known as "the King of the Pelagic Sealers," and this year he was determined to sail into Canton with his holds full of choice pelts, so he kept two lookouts forward to spot, if possible, the areas in which the oncoming seals might show, and when one of the men shouted "Seals, five on the port bow!" he sped the *Erebus* toward that spot, and when the boats were launched, the men rowed in among the defenseless seals and started stabbing and beating them to death. Since seals could not stay submerged indefinitely, and since a boat with four strong rowers could overtake them when they had to surface for air, the slaughter was concentrated and endless.

Especially vulnerable were the pregnant females; their mortality was above ninety percent in any area that the boats reached, and in time the Bering Sea was reddened with their blood. But again, a shocking eighty percent of all seals killed were not retrieved; they sank fruitlessly to the bottom of the sea as the *Erebus* signaled for its boats to return so that it could proceed on its way to China and the riches that awaited it there.

Captain Schransky's third flaw was the most serious, for its evil consequences would survive long after he departed these waters. Abstemious himself and allowing no drunkenness aboard his ship, he early discovered the enormous profits that could be made by filling his hold in New Bedford with casks of rum and molasses and pushing them on natives who had little or no experience with alcohol. The consequences in the lands bordering the Bering were disastrous; natives developed such a craving for rum or the hoochinoo rotgut they distilled from the molasses—named after the local tribe that first made the stuff and quickly abbreviated to *hooch*—that sometimes entire villages were wiped out because men, women and children destroyed themselves with incessant drinking.

It seemed that everyone in the arctic with good sense was opposed to this traffic: the Russians had outlawed it early and policed their shores vigorously; missionaries preached against it; and New England moralists deplored the sinful transactions in which these crews were involved. But captains like Schransky found the great wealth to be derived from the trade irresistible, so gradually, village by village, in both Siberia and Alaska, the natives were corrupted.

With the change of national ownership in 1867, the tough Russian captains who had maintained some kind of order in the Bering Sea turned over the responsibility to poorly trained American seamen in the Treasury's revenue cutter service, whose cumbersome ships, the *Rush* and *Corwin,* proved incapable of disciplining the *Erebus.* So for nearly eight years, 1867–75, Captain Schransky enjoyed unchallenged mastery of the northern waters, slaughtering seals as he wished and purveying hooch wherever he anchored. He had become dictator of the oceans, obedient only to his own law.

This year, 1875, he was only forty-eight, and it was while laying to off Cape Krigugon on the Chukotsk Peninsula in Siberia that he summarized the future as he perceived it: Three more returns to New Bedford, that could take maybe eighteen years. I'll be sixty-six. One grand final sweep . . . all the seals in the Pribilofs . . . all the rum our ship can hold. Then buy a home by the sea . . . maybe New Bedford,

maybe near Hamburg. In his speculations it never occurred to him
that a man might be coming into these waters almost as tall as he,
almost as brave, almost as good a fighter and, because of his exceptional personal history, many times more determined.

If in the whaling season of 1875, Captain Schransky had chanced to
put in to the little settlement at Desolation Point on the Alaskan side
of the Chukchi Sea, he would probably have prevented a murder, but
since the summer was waning fast, he required none of the goods
that Desolation could provide. Also, his inner compass–thermometer–
ship's-wheel warned him that the freeze was going to strike rather
sooner than it had in previous years when he had stopped there. So,
keeping well out into the Chukchi, he hurried south.

As he disappeared, taking with him the last group of white men
the region would see for nearly a year, the vengeful Eskimo Agulaak
understandably felt that perhaps the time for retaliation had come,
and he began to lay plans for the undoing of the missionary Father
Fyodor, the Orthodox priest who had come north from the Yukon to
open a mission here in 1868.

The priest was appreciated by the Desolation Eskimos, for he was
a generous, understanding soul who lived in the Eskimo manner,
using a timber-roofed underground dwelling until he and his wife
and their young son had collected enough driftwood to build themselves a proper cabin; *proper* meaning a lean-to, with a stout wall
facing the frozen sea and the great blasts of cold air coming out of
Siberia, a crude fireplace with an improvised chimney, and a whole
southern wall more or less open to the elements but protected in part
by three caribou hides that served as flaps to be pushed aside, one
after the other, when one wanted to enter.

The cabin was warm, well insulated with packets of moss stuffed
in cracks, and a lively center for the informal meetings which occupied so much of Eskimo life. Here the young people of the village
gathered for their informal courtships, and along its warm walls sat
the older Eskimos, listening as one of their members told of heroic
adventures in the olden days. It was a satisfying life, and when Father
Fyodor's wife produced another child, a girl this time, the little cabin
echoed with singing, for the priest and his wife had made themselves
a central part of the community.

If the priest, forty-seven years old and one who never looked at another man's wife, had become the target of the would-be murderer Agulaak, what evil force had begun to prowl the Point, bringing Agulaak under its malevolent spell? It would have been fruitless to argue with the tormented Eskimo that no force was assailing him, for evidence to the contrary was overwhelming. On each of his last two walrus hunts, far out on the ice, he'd had a beast under his magic control, only to lose him at the critical moment: Something spoke to the walrus, warning him that I was there. I didn't hear the voice but I know it was whispering. Last spring, when the caribou came down from the northeast, as they so often did when making their rounds of the north, he had trailed the herd as always, had selected his spot where the bigger animals must pass, and had watched in despair as one after another of the sleek beasts came almost within range of his spears, then veered away. On a later hunt, when he took the rifle that he had acquired from the *Erebus* two years before when it came to trade, almost the same thing happened: the caribou appeared on the horizon in great quantity, came right down the slough they always followed, then swung away when someone or something warned them that Agulaak was waiting.

From a series of unprecedented defeats like this, it was easy for him to deduce that someone at Desolation Point was casting a spell upon him, and since the area had at this time no shaman whose incantations would solve the mystery, Agulaak was left to stew in his own twisted imaginings, and the more he brooded about the magic that had been directed against him, the more clear it became to him that this intruder, Father Fyodor, must be the man responsible.

He was, first of all, a Russian, which of itself awarded him unusual powers. Then he was a priest, which involved incantations, the burning of incense and behavior of the most suspicious kind. Most condemnatory was the fact that the man had an Athapascan wife, for it looked to Agulaak as if the priest had married her for the specific purpose of insinuating her into the Eskimo community at Desolation for its ultimate destruction. As a boy he had heard endless tales of how the Athapascans connived to cast spells upon Eskimos, and these recent events involving himself proved that some malefic force was operating in the village and on the hunting grounds.

At this point, when he had convinced himself that it was Father Fyodor's Indian wife, who had taken the Biblical name Esther, who was working against him, a curious transferral of guilt took place, for as a self-respecting Inupiat Eskimo trained in the rigors of hunting and warfare, he could not in decency direct his ire against a woman, regardless of how malevolent her spells, but he certainly could strike out at the misguided man who had brought her into the community. So his anger now focused on the priest, and the more he pondered the wrongs done him by this white man, the more embittered he became.

Agulaak decided that since Father Fyodor had to be the activating cause of everything bad that had befallen him, he must be destroyed. And once he had reached this verdict, he never looked back: his only problem was when and how.

He was a canny fellow, rather superior in his hunting skills when evil forces were not working against him, and while he did not try to contrive anything clever which would deceive the other villagers as to who had done the killing, for it was essential that everyone know that he, Agulaak, had cleansed the village of its evil agency, it was imperative that he find a time and a situation appropriate for the deed and one in which the priest's unquestioned powers would be at a disadvantage or perhaps totally neutralized. This required artful plotting.

Agulaak's twisted mind suggested a variety of actions which he dismissed, and then a maneuver which seemed positively brilliant when he weighed it. What he did was get his gun, load it heavily, march to the hut in which the mission church met on Wednesday evenings, and wait until Father Fyodor appeared with six parishioners at the close of service. Moving to within eight feet of his enemy, he suddenly produced his gun, took careful aim, and in the presence of six witnesses, shot the priest through the chest. Death was immediate, as Agulaak saw, for he remained at the murder site grinning vacuously at the witnesses.

And now the absurdity of Alaska in these lawless years manifested itself, for there was no governmental agency in the entire district that had authority to move into Desolation Point, apprehend the murderer, and carry him off to trial in an established court before a legally impaneled jury. The people living in or near Desolation did not feel qualified even to arrest Agulaak, let alone try him, and as for placing him in jail to prevent further outrage, there was none within almost a thousand miles. So this madman was allowed to roam free, and citizens took precautions to prevent his attacking them while they prayed that with the coming of spring thaw next year, some

American ship might put in to Desolation with an officer aboard to exercise the rudiments of governmental authority.

This inability to handle an ordinary civic problem placed an unusually heavy burden on Father Fyodor's widow, for she was now an Athapascan intruder in the midst of an Inupiat Eskimo community, with two children, a boy, Dmitri, of nine and a girl, Lena, of two. A devout Russian Orthodox Christian, she continued to offer her hut for informal religious services, but in doing so, she intensified Agulaak's suspicions and animosity. Neighbors warned her of threats the madman was making against her as he wandered aimlessly about the village, but there was nothing she could do to protect herself against him.

Her son, however, had access to his dead father's Russian rifle, and he was old enough to appreciate the danger Agulaak presented, so one wintry day when there was a wisp of gray dawn for about an hour at noon, and he saw Agulaak approaching his mother's hut, Dmitri suddenly jumped in front of him, gun pointed at his chest, and cried: "Agulaak! If you ever come one step closer to my mother, I'll shoot!"

The demented fellow, convinced that the dead spirit of the priest had come back to earth in the person of his son, was terrified of the lad, drew back from the Russian gun, and fled.

He was seen thereafter wandering about the edges of the village and sleeping sometimes in the wind-shadow of this hut or that. On the occasions when he spoke with villagers, he warned them about the ghost of Father Fyodor who had returned to seek vengeance, but he seemed unable to comprehend that if this were true, it would be himself, Agulaak, who would be in danger. He had never really understood that he had murdered the priest, but he continued to be terrified of little Dmitri, who rarely appeared in public without his gun.

In such sad, broken ways the remote villages of Alaska stumbled on without a government.

Like some dark raven scavenging the northern seas, looking for the latest disaster upon which to feed, the *Erebus* coasted along the shore of Siberia, seeking some Chukchi village whose citizens it could defraud of their pelts trapped during the last winter, but the Siberians had become accustomed to Captain Schransky's harsh ways and remained indoors, hiding their furry riches until his sinister ship departed, with him standing, white-crowned and bareheaded, peering for an advantage.

Disappointed in this portion of his expedition, he coasted north to that cape which brought Asia closest to America, and there he headed east for the big, well-populated St. Lawrence Island, whose northern three villages had provided him with good pelts in the past. But he approached the towns with mixed feelings, because in recent years men of the villages had become aware of the value of their furs and demanded high prices in barter goods like cloth for their wives and saws and hammers for themselves.

Determined to put a stop to this sophisticated trading, Captain Schransky had decided long before sighting St. Lawrence that this time he would use less expensive tactics, so when he anchored off Kookoolik, principal settlement on the northern rim, he took ashore not the customary items of hardware and cloth, but a keg of rum, and with it he taught the people of St. Lawrence how barters were going to be conducted in the future.

Dispensing the rum liberally, he ingratiated himself with the natives, until there was nightly dancing and singing, then men and women lying inert till dawn. Swift affairs developed between the sailors and the village maidens while the girls' customary suitors lay drunk in corners. However, the salient outcome of the induced debauchery was that the islanders, always hungry for the alcohol, brought forth their carefully hoarded stores of sealskins and ivory tusks, which they traded for abominably low prices as calculated in rum.

At the end of three weeks, when Schransky had pretty well denuded Kookoolik of its treasures, he brought ashore two barrels of dark West Indian molasses, but after tasting the bittersweet fluid the islanders said that they did not care for it and wanted rum instead. Now Schransky initiated them into a new pleasure that would guarantee the destruction of their village: he taught two of the older men how to transform molasses into rum, and when the first heady distillate appeared, the islanders were lost.

In the season when they should have been at sea catching seals and storing both the pelts and the meat, they were reveling on the beach, and in the more arduous months when they should have been tracking the walrus for its ivory tusks and again for the meat which, when dried, would sustain them through the coming winter, they were drunk and happy and heedless of the passing season. There had never been so much unmindful happiness in Kookoolik as there was that long summer when they learned how to drink rum and then make more from the treasured kegs of molasses. Of course, when the *Erebus* sailed, all the valuables of the village went with it, and one old woman who did not like the taste of rum was already asking, vainly: "When are you men going to go out and catch the food we'll need for winter?" No one paid any attention to the problem she raised or to its solution.

When the *Erebus* moved along to the village of Sevak at the eastern end of the island, the sailors came upon a people who loved to dance, so when they were introduced to rum and the fascinating secret of how to manufacture it, the village echoed with the sound of Eskimos singing old songs as they engaged in one of the world's most curious dance forms: men and women stood with their feet solidly planted on the floor, as if set in frozen lava, while their knees, middle, torso, arms and head twisted rhythmically in contortions that no ordinary human would imagine. If to the rest of the world the word *dance* meant *to leap or skip about in an artistic manner,* to these Eskimos it meant something quite the opposite: *keep your feet firm but move your body artistically.*

At first the sailors found the Sevak dancing monotonous, but after they had watched it for several nights, some of the more adventurous took to the floor, listened to the beat of the chanting, and stood with their feet firmly planted while they contorted their bodies in ways never tried before as some old women of lively spirit danced beside them. Toward dawn this glorious summer, the dancers fell drunk while walruses and whales passed the island unmolested.

A feature of all the celebrations on St. Lawrence that surreal summer was the tall austere figure of Captain Schransky standing off to one side as he watched the debauchery, taking a perverse delight in following the steps of the islanders' degradation: now that girl is going off with Adams; now that old woman is beginning to stagger; now the man with the missing teeth is about to collapse. Like an uninvolved Norse god, he watched the frolicking of his earthlings and found sardonic amusement in their destruction of themselves.

At the third village, Chibukak at the extreme western end of the island, he used a minimum of rum to acquire a maximum of pelts, for in the waters off this point seal and walrus were easiest to capture, and the villagers had accumulated a substantial store of furs that they would normally have traded with adventurous ships setting out from Siberia, but since Russians had been forbidden over the past century from taking alcohol to any part of Alaska, they could not bring to Chibukak the exciting goods that Captain Schransky offered.

Here the devastation was even more tragic than at the first two villages, for the riches of the sea were so abundant that prudent fishermen could lay in a rich store of food with a few weeks' work in late July and August, but this year the precious days were spent in revelry and song and concupiscence. Here no sage older woman warned the men of the dangerous track they were following, for the women, too, stayed drunk from one festivity to the next, and when the *Erebus* finally sailed, the grinning people of Chibukak lined the shore to bid their good friends farewell, as pelts of seals and walruses accompanied the ship southward.

When the dark *Erebus* was about to leave St. Lawrence, Captain Schransky spotted on the southern coast the tiny village of Powooiliak, and he judged that because of its isolation, it might never have been visited by Siberian traders. If so, it would probably have an accumulated store of ivory, and he was about to put in to investigate when a sudden shift in the weather warned him that ice was not far off, so he surrendered the ivory of Powooiliak and headed south toward the southern limits of the Bering Sea.

There, on a day in early autumn, he found himself drifting in the midst of a large movement of seals that had left the Pribilofs and were heading for the warmer waters in which they would winter, and although he knew that taking seals under such circumstances was forbidden, the temptation to fill his hold to the limit with pelts for trade in Canton was too great to resist, and he ordered his men to attack the seals, who in midocean were especially vulnerable. This was not true pelagic sealing, for it was occurring in autumn when the females were not pregnant, but it was outlawed by all nations bordering on the seal routes; however, since it was unlikely that any patrol ships would be in these waters at this time, the cruel harvest continued.

There was, however, by accident and not design, a slow, inadequate ship, the revenue cutter *Rush,* limping home from a mishap which had deterred it in the Pribilofs, and when its captain saw the *Erebus* slaughtering the seals, he fired a warning shot to alert the trespasser of his presence, but even as he did so he realized that beyond warning the poacher, there was not much he could do. When the *Rush* came slowly up to the sealing area, the *Erebus* insolently eased off at about the same speed, and for most of one morning the charade continued.

Finally, with all sails spread, the *Erebus* put on a burst of speed, maneuvered insultingly close to the impotent *Rush*, and hurried toward China with its riches. It was the dominator of these seas and it would comport itself as Captain Schransky determined, not some pusillanimous captain of an American patrol boat.

During the last days of spring 1877 the Tlingit Indians, who clustered outside the palisade protecting Sitka, kept close watch upon happenings in the capital, and saw with amazement that the steamer *California* had anchored in the sound for the purpose of removing the entire army garrison, whose troops boarded the ship on the fourteenth of June and left Alaska forever on the morning of the fifteenth.

"Who will take their place?" one Tlingit watcher asked his companions, but no one knew, and it was as a result of this confusion that three thoughtful Tlingits, who would have been termed warriors in the old days, sequestered a canoe where the Americans in command, whoever they might be, could not observe it, and on a silvery night, when the sun disappeared only for a few hours, left Sitka, paddled due north to that maze of enchanting narrows which led to Peril Strait, and from there into noble Chatham Strait, which bisected this part of Alaska. At the northern tip of Admiralty Island, which lay to the east, they turned south through the lovely passage on which the future capital of Juneau would one day sit, and then, with a left turn toward Canada, they entered one of the choice small waterways of the region, Taku Inlet, from whose left bank, hidden amidst glaciers, debouched a beautiful mountain stream, Pleiades River, and there at the mouth of the river stood a cabin erected many years ago. It was to the redoubtable occupant of this rude dwelling that they had come seeking counsel.

"Halloo, Big-ears!" they shouted as they approached the cabin, for they knew from experience that he was prone to shoot at intruders. "Ivan Big-ears, we come from Sitka!" And when the calls were repeated, a tall, big-boned Tlingit in his sixties, with white hair and erect posture, came to the cabin door, stared toward the riverbank, and saw men he had known forty years earlier when they fought the Russians in repeated battles that the Tlingits usually lost.

Striding down to the bank, he greeted his onetime companions, then asked them bluntly: "What brings you here?" and his nostrils widened when he heard their reply: "The Americans in Sitka. They grow weaker every day. The time's at hand, Big-ears . . ."

"Come! Let us talk," and as they told him of the chaos in which the American occupation foundered, he listened grim-lipped, and by the time their mournful litany was finished, his mind was made up: "It's time to strike," but one of the messengers warned: "I've thought so, too. We can surely defeat the fools who hold the hill now, but I'm worried about the rush of new soldiers who might be brought in," and Big-ears had a sage response: "Not a big battle with war cries. Slow pressure, day by day, until their spirit is broken and we regain our ancient rights."

Like a Kot-le-an of a later day, he spoke as a wise man of his tribe, one who had spent his life brooding upon the unjust way in which his people had lost their glorious land at Sitka, and this report of degenerating American control inflamed his ardor but did not confuse his generalship: "A big battle would produce big news, and ships filled with soldiers would speed up from the south, but each day more pressure, more advantage to us, and there will be no alarms."

He was fortified in this strategy by an act of folly committed by the incompetent Treasury official who had assumed command at Sitka. A Tlingit living in a village on Douglas Island came hurrying up Taku Inlet in his canoe, with distressing news: "Trouble in our village. Four white miners tried to abuse our women. We fought them. Now the warship is coming from Sitka to punish us, because they claim we attacked them." The word in Tlingit for *warship* carried no implications of size: the approaching vessel could be either a huge man-of-war or a corvette, but the impression created was one of military power, and Ivan Big-ears, who had been forced to take a Russian first name in 1861 when he knew the tsar's power to be already fading, wanted to see for himself what American power was in the waning days of its control, so he and his visitors set forth in two canoes, moving quietly along the shore so as not to be seen by the approaching warship.

Accompanied by the messenger from the village about to be attacked, they slipped out of Taku Inlet, hid in the mouth of the strait that led to the settlement, and were concealed there when a small

American ship steamed into the quiet waters, located the wrong village, and began shelling it so ineffectively that at the first salvo, which missed completely, the occupants fled to the surrounding forest, from where they watched as the fourth salvo finally struck their empty shacks, battering them to pieces. Triumphantly the ship patrolled the shoreline for about an hour, with no soldier brave enough to go ashore to assess the damage, and then, with a final salvo that merely ricocheted among the trees, it retired to report another American victory.

When it was safely gone, Big-ears and his companions, including the messenger from the village that should have been the target, paddled across the strait to the wreckage and explained to the bewildered villagers as they came out of the forest: "They fired on the wrong place," and from that settlement as well as the other, Big-ears enlisted Tlingit warriors, who agreed that the time had come to move against the incompetents who occupied Sitka, and in succeeding weeks men from the Taku Inlet area began quietly infiltrating the capital.

Had Arkady Voronov still been in residence at Sitka, he would have known of the increased Tlingit pressure within a week, but the Americans now in charge of the place drifted amiably on, unaware that they were surrounded by an enemy that grew stronger each passing month.

Now came the darkest period of the American occupancy of Alaska. The presence of the army, inadequate though it had been and preposterous as its commander, General Davis, had seemed to the citizens who were ruled by him, had nevertheless provided a semblance of government, and of a hundred typical acts it performed in the post-1867 period, some ninety were either constructive or neutral, and now to have even this inadequate symbol of government removed was to invite disaster.

First the outward signs of control disappeared from the streets of Sitka. Police, even the few who were present, exercised no authority. Port facilities deteriorated so badly that the few ships which did put in left quickly, with vows never to return to such poorly administered facilities, which meant that customs revenues declined month by month. Smuggling became endemic, and rum, whiskey and molasses flowed unimpeded into the settlements. Miners and fishermen did as they wished, evaded such laws as there were, and decimated the supplies that used to flourish near Sitka. Foreign ships trespassed on seal rookeries that were supposed to be protected, and threatened to exterminate walruses, whales and the frolicsome sea otters who had begun to make a comeback.

But the most ominous development surfaced when Tlingits like Ivan Big-ears started drifting in from outlying districts, joining up with local dissidents and indulging in pressure behavior that terrified the white citizens. There were no murders, no burnings, simply the reappearance of Tlingits into areas from which they had been expelled by Baranov. And to the average white man unfamiliar with the old days, the sudden appearance of a tall, powerful Indian like Ivan Big-ears could be both terrifying and a premonition that dreadful things were about to happen.

What the Tlingits wanted was well represented by Big-ears. "We must be free," he told his fellow conspirators, "to live where we wish according to our ancient ways, to have the new government respect our tribal laws and customs." Since there was no resident authority to which he could make these reasonable demands, he was forced to further them by insinuating his people into the daily life of Sitka, and when he did this, the locals felt that they must resist.

There was a family from Oregon living in Sitka at this time, the Caldwells—husband, wife, son Tom aged seventeen, daughter Betts aged fifteen—and they had come north through Seattle with the understanding that Mr. Caldwell could open a lawyer's office in the capital, and he came well prepared for such service to the frontier community. He brought with him three crates of lawbooks, especially those dealing with territories and new states, both of which he assumed Alaska would become in the near future. He was most disappointed to learn that law and courts were not major concerns of the little capital, and as for an office from which to practice, there was no legal way by which he could acquire land on which to build one, nor were there any spare buildings that one could buy with assurance of obtaining a title.

"What can I do?" he asked in growing frustration, and a man who had been living in Sitka since the Russian days said: "I think your wife might be able to get a job teaching at the new school," and in disgust Mr. Caldwell said: "If there's a job open, I'll take it," but then his problem became: "But where will I find a place to live?" and the same adviser told him: "There's a big house down the street. Used to be lived in by a Russian family. Great people, went back to Siberia."

Mr. Caldwell said: "I don't think we want to buy a big house," and the man said: "Good, because it ain't for sale. But a very nice Aleut woman married to a Tlingit fisherman runs it, and she takes in boarders."

So in one day the Caldwells received the good news that they could rent rooms at the old Russian house, as it was still called, and the bad news that whereas there was a teaching job at the informal school, only a woman would be considered. As a result, Mrs. Caldwell became a teacher in a school that had no visible means of support, for it had no tax base, there being no agency to assess taxes, whereas her husband, with the ingenuity of a man who had wanted to leave settled Oregon for the adventure of the Alaskan frontier, devised five or six imaginative ways to earn a little money other than by being a lawyer. He did paperwork for citizens who had to communicate with offices back in the States. He served as agent for the few ships that steamed into port. He helped at the coaling station where those same ships acquired fuel for their trips north. And he was not above work-ing as either a day laborer or a handyman. Neither he nor his wife had a steady salary, but with what they did earn, plus some money picked up by their son, who was just as adaptable as his father, the Caldwells survived, and when the father received small commissions from miners and fishermen, they came close to prospering.

But always Caldwell listened to rumors and actual reports as to when Sitka was going to have a court system, and Alaska a formal system of government in which a lawyer could make a decent living: "When that time comes, Nora, there's not going to be anyone in Alaska who'll know more than I will about the ins and outs of com-merce and customs and the importation of goods and the manage-ment of mining and fishing. Surely, things will have to be straightened out, and then the Carl Caldwells come into their own."

Of course, during the dismal years of 1877 and '78, his hopes of action from Washington were disappointed, and instead of order coming to Alaska, grievous disorder came. Caldwell first became aware of impending danger when his wife came home from school one afternoon with perplexing news: "One of our children who plays with Aleuts said that a famous Tlingit warrior who fought the Rus-sians many times . . ."

"What about him?"

"He's come back to Sitka."

"What does that signify?"

"I asked one of the other teachers, and all she said was that her brother had seen him at the edge of town. Name Ivan Big-ears, a famous warrior . . . like the child said."

"Never heard the name," Mr. Caldwell said, but during the next days when he made quiet inquiries he learned that Ivan Big-ears, if it was indeed he, had fought against the Russians and had fled to voluntary exile somewhere to the east. "If he's come back," one older white man said, "it can only mean trouble. I was here when he battled the Russians. Never won but also never accepted defeat."

Caldwell asked what this Big-ears looked like, and another man said with obvious fear in his voice: "I think I saw him the other day. Tall, robust man in his sixties. White hair. Dark even for a Tlingit."

About this time Caldwell noticed that the Aleut-Tlingit couple who ran the Russian house in which the four Caldwells stayed became aloof, unwilling to talk with their boarders, and when Carl tried to discover why the change had occurred, he discovered, through the kind of detective work that lawyers enjoy doing, that the owners of the house were entertaining secret guests at night, and when the three older Caldwells established a watch, the son saw four Tlingits slipping into the back of the house. "Was one of them tall, older, white hair?" Carl asked in a whisper, and his son said: "Yes. He's in there now."

Carl swore the boy to secrecy: "Important things may be involved. Speak to no one." But he himself stayed up all night, keeping watch on the rear door, and toward dawn he was rewarded by a clear glimpse of a tall, handsome Tlingit who must have been Ivan Big-ears.

In subsequent weeks the four Caldwells, for now the daughter had joined the detective work, accumulated fairly solid evidence that the Aleut-Tlingit community was engaged in some kind of conspiracy which involved Ivan Big-ears and at least several scores of Indians from other settlements across the water. And once this distressing theory was formulated, this clever family amassed a disturbing amount of substantiating data—more secret meetings in the back of the house, Tlingit men who could not be identified as locals lurking along the edges of the town, a gun stolen here and there, a subtle arrogance among the natives which had not existed before. Carl Caldwell said: "With the army gone and no agency to replace it, the Tlingits have grown bold. Something bad is bound to happen."

His wife said: "If the rumors I hear are true, enough Tlingits have filtered in to wipe us out."

Tom said: "The men at the dock told me more guns had been stolen," and Betts reported that Tlingit children had begun to push white children off the footpaths.

Caldwell exploded: "Dammit, if we can see trouble brewing, why can't the officials?"

But who were the officials? When it was agreed that Caldwell must go to them and present his suspicions about a possible uprising of the Indians, it became obvious that there was really no one in authority with whom he could conduct a meaningful conversation. The little customs boat which had shelled the wrong village near Taku Inlet still lay at anchor in the harbor, but its captain, having made a fool of himself at that bombardment, showed no disposition to do so again in response to the crazy suspicions of a man who had been in town less than a year.

So when Caldwell broached the subject, the captain stopped him with a rambling discourse: "Were you here when General Davis was in command? No? Well, folks hereabout thought poorly of him, but when he left here he was assigned to the Oregon-California boundary where the Modoc Indians was actin' up. Real bad Indian named Captain Jack come out under a white flag and shot the American general, man named Canby. Davis was appointed to replace him, and with great courage captured Captain Jack and saw him hanged. At the end of the Modoc affair, he gained a commendation and spent his remainin' time in service chasin' Indians, who he despised. A real hero."

Caldwell had not come to talk about a general he had never known, but when he tried to bring the conversation to a serious discussion of the impending crisis whose outlines he saw so clearly, he accomplished nothing and left the customs boat in despair. "They didn't even listen," he told his wife, and that night when Ivan Big-ears and five of his lieutenants crowded into the Russian house, Caldwell managed to overhear their agitated conversation, but since it was conducted in Tlingit, he understood nothing except the spirit of the words, but the animosity in the voices could not be masked.

However, at several points in the Indian debate about timing and tactics, men did use individual English words or phrases, and from them Caldwell obtained such confirmation as he needed: "*ammunition, ship in harbor, early morning, three men running* and other words pertaining to military action, and toward dawn, when he had heard enough, he convened his own meeting to discuss the steps that would have to be taken: "If the United States can't protect us, and if there isn't any government here to take action, the only practical thing we can do is throw ourselves on the mercy of the Canadians," and this strategy his three listeners agreed to. But how to reach the Canadians with a plea for help?

Tom had kept a map of the approaches to Alaska which the steamship company bringing them to Sitka had provided, and from its imperfect data he calculated that the distance to Prince Rupert Island and the seaport of that name would be about two hundred and eighty miles: "Three men in a good canoe could get there in four days, if they're good men."

"Would you be one of them?" Caldwell senior asked, and Tom said: "You bet."

The question then became: "Nora, if Tom and I have to go south to fetch aid, can you and Betts protect yourselves till we get back?" Before she could reply, he pointed toward the back of the house: "With them scheming on the other side?"

"We'd go to the church," she said calmly, "find safety with the other women and their men," and when she looked at her daughter, Betts nodded.

Tom's suggestion that to paddle nearly one hundred miles, the first half through open seas, would require at least three men was so sensible that his father had to agree: "We must find a third man before we can set out," and in the next days as he scanned the community, peering into white faces to calculate who might have courage, he settled upon a choice between two men who impressed him with their general bearing. One was an older fellow named Tompkins, who like Caldwell worked at various jobs; the other, a much younger man named Alcott, whom Carl had seen along the waterfront when he worked the ships.

His inclination was to approach Tompkins first, and this was a good hunch, because when he did, Tompkins surprised him by saying immediately: "Of course there's bound to be trouble," but he shied off when Carl suggested begging for help in Canada: "Too far. They'd never help Americans, anyway. They want Alaska for theirself," and it looked as if the Caldwells would not be able to enlist his help.

However, that very afternoon a group of Indians who had come into town from the north began acting in a rowdy manner in the center of Sitka, and so terrified newcomer whites that a general panic ensued, but the quick disciplining of the rambunctious Tlingits by other Indians associated with Big-ears quieted the affair, so that the general uprising which many now feared did not occur. That was enough for Tompkins, who came to report his decision: "We've got to get to Canada for help." In the meantime, however, Caldwell had approached Alcott at the waterfront, and this bright young fellow had accumulated his own strong evidence: "Things got to blow to hell pretty soon. Canada? Hadn't thought of it, but there's no help around here," and he insisted upon joining the expedition, making four.

It was not a canoe in the sense that a frail birchbark affair in Pennsylvania would be called by that name; the one that Tompkins provided was a sturdy, spruce-ribbed, solidly built craft which had every chance of surviving in the ocean part of the journey. It could, in calmer water, provide space for eight paddles and ample room for four, regardless of the waves, and when the men met to inspect the craft, it was young Tom who voiced their judgment: "We can get to Canada in it," and the adventure was under way.

The white men used as much craftiness in slipping out of Sitka as Ivan Big-ears had used when slipping in. Waiting for one of those gray, misty dawns when all things in Sitka, even the brooding mountains, seemed clothed in silvery garments which made them invisible, they took off undetected by the Tlingits, sped out of Sitka Sound, ducked in and out through the protecting islands for the first leg of the journey, then headed south for the first perilous reach of open ocean, where they found the waves frighteningly big but not overwhelming. It was a heroic trip, with muscles strained and stomachs taut, but in time they reached that wilderness of islands which provided an inside passage nearly to Prince Rupert. There was a final dash across unprotected ocean, but at last the weary messengers paddled into the safety of the Canadian harbor.

In one of the fortunate accidents which help determine history, equal in results to times with careful planning, when the four men from Sitka reached Prince Rupert they found in its harbor the Canadian warship *Osprey,* a vessel of no great size stationed there to protect Hudson's Bay Company outposts on the coast, and because Prince Rupert was at the western edge of Canada, its officials were in the habit of making up their own minds without seeking approval from some distant capital: "You say the Indians are about to overrun

Sitka? Why doesn't your own government take steps? You say there is no government? Unbelievable."

So the first task of the Sitka men was to convince the Canadians that things were as bad in Alaska as they said, but Carl Caldwell was a persuasive man, and within an hour he satisfied the men of the *Osprey* that without their help, real tragedy threatened in Sitka, and by nightfall the little Canadian warship was steaming north to protect American interests.

Was Sitka in the closing days of February 1879 in the perilous situation that the Caldwell party reported? Probably not. Responsible Tlingit leaders like Ivan Big-ears had no plans to murder the white population in their beds; what they sought was fair ownership of the land, assured supplies of food and hardware and cloth, some kind of sensible control of salmon fishing, and a just participation in the law-making procedure. They were willing to do battle with whatever military force might oppose them, and men like Big-ears were prepared to die in defense of their beliefs, but in these delicate days when the *Osprey* hurried north to put down a bloody revolution, the attacking Tlingits had no plans for one. Indeed, any kind of responsible government in Sitka would have been able to parley with the Tlingits, resolve their concerns amicably, and avoid serious trouble, but of course there was no government.

The *Osprey* steamed into Sitka Sound on 1 March 1879, and its bold show of power, with guns at the ready and uniformed troops marching ashore, quieted even the remote possibility of Tlingit revolt. No lives were lost. The Caldwell women did not have to seek sanctuary in the old Russian church. And the Tlingits who had been meeting in the rear of their house gradually dissipated, with outside warriors like Ivan Big-Ears returning sadly to their isolated homes, aware that justice would be denied them for decades to come.

In this manner the legend was born that a Canadian warship had saved Alaska for the United States when no American agency was brave enough to assume responsibility. Caldwell, in a surge of emotion aboard the *Osprey,* helped launch the myth: "It's been a dark day in American history. Even this General Davis they laugh at wouldn't have allowed this shameful thing to happen." In April, when an American warship finally arrived, the Canadians courteously retired, taking with them the gratitude of the community.

Later, an able, quiet-spoken Commander Beardslee reached Sitka in the *Jamestown,* whose afterdeck became the capital of Alaska, with Beardslee issuing orders regarding things about which he knew little. Fortunately, he had the advice of Lawyer Caldwell, and many of the good rules the latter had sought were promulgated by Beardslee, who installed Caldwell as a kind of judge in an informal court.

It was not a good system of government and both men knew it, but it was the only one available, so for two years these well-intentioned men more or less ran Alaska, but neither believed such a system could prevail. "It's a disgrace," Beardslee growled one day when something had gone wrong, and Judge Caldwell agreed. But they did not take themselves too seriously, because at this time Sitka contained only one hundred and sixty whites and Creoles, plus about a hundred Indians, and all of Alaska had only thirty-three thousand people, counting everybody.

The implacable course of history and the nature of the human beings who enable it to evolve make it impossible for a condition like that of Alaska in the post-1867 period to continue. Either revolution churns the chaos, as the uprising of the Tlingits nearly did, or some alien power steps in, as Canada might have done, or some giant like Abraham Lincoln or Otto von Bismarck steps forward to take command and reshape things sensibly. Alaska in these crucial times was blessed in having two giants of dissimilar character come to its shores and assume responsibility; between them they brought a semblance of government to an abandoned region.

The first of these men was an irascible dark-browed mariner with the good Irish name Michael Healy, who had a foul vocabulary, an insatiable craving for strong drink and an inherited willingness to use his fists. A hulking six feet two with a temper he could not control, he was hardly the kind of man one would expect to evolve into a respected leader, but that's what happened in the frozen seas of the north. Born in Georgia, he hated the cold, but of all the American seafarers of his time, he better than any other mastered the arctic seas and tamed the wild coasts of Siberia and Alaska.

He had been a junior officer during that humiliating experience in 1876 when the inadequate revenue cutter *Rush* tried to discipline the semipiratical *Erebus* for illegal sealing, and he would never forget the oath he took as he watched the insolent white-haired captain of that ship glide away with an insulting grin. "I'll get that bastard," Healy swore, and the rest of what he vowed to do with the German when he caught him would be unprintable. He was so infuriated that an American vessel, a warship really, had been demeaned that he retired to his quarters, sneaked out his smuggled liquor, and got drunk. Late at night, when he sobered a bit, he promised the tame parrot he kept with him on his cruises: "By the saints, we'll get that cocksure bastard. Somewhere when the ice is thick and he can't run from us . . ." and his dark right fist punched at air.

On duty in the little revenue cutters, Lieutenant Healy, Commander Healy and, finally, Captain Healy gained increasing praise from his superiors and repeated humiliation from the *Erebus,* but he did not lose these near-battles through incompetent seamanship or any lack of courage, but only because he sailed an inferior ship. Once while in charge of the *Corwin,* the better of the two revenue cutters, he caught the *Erebus* engaged in illegal sealing at the Pribilofs: "We have him, men! Hard to!" But almost as if aided by divine winds, the big indigo ship unfurled its square sails and ran right away from the cutter. Pursuit was impossible, and the government ship had to limp off to other duties as Captain Schransky, standing on the bridge of his sleek vessel, laughed once more at Healy's frustration.

If the profane and hard-drinking Irishman failed repeatedly in his attempts to discipline the dark rogue ship, what did he accomplish on his tours of duty through the northern oceans? To find the answer, one must accompany him on one trip made in the late 1870s. In early spring, in command of the *Corwin,* he sailed out of San Francisco with a full crew and considerable implied powers, for he was the major American representative in Alaska and the surrounding waters. Putting in to Sitka on the way north, he listened to local complaints and summoned to his afterdeck scoundrelly men accused of selling hooch to Indians; these he fined, making careful duplicate copies of receipts showing his handling of the money involved.

From there, following the reverse of the historical course which had brought Aleksandr Baranov to immortality at Sitka, he crossed an arm of the Pacific that carried him to Kodiak, where a deputation of old-time Aleuts and newcomer Americans awaited his decision on a fishing-rights controversy which had embittered the two groups. Moving ashore this time, but taking a ship's scribe with him, he listened patiently as the contesting parties made their presentations, then surprised everyone by announcing: "Let's think about this carefully," and he invited the entire party back onto the ship, where a feast from the *Corwin*'s supplies was provided. There was no public drinking, of course, since a major responsibility of the *Corwin* or any other cutter was to end the illegal sale of alcohol to natives, but he did slip into his cabin for a healthy nip from the bottles he carried hidden there. At the conclusion of the feast he took the leaders of the two factions, some seven men, to the railings of the cutter and said: "You Aleuts have ancient rights which must be respected. But you newcomers have rights too. Would it not be sensible if you shared the ocean in this way?" And when he handed down a verdict worthy of a judge, the combatants accepted it, for on Kodiak as elsewhere in these waters it was understood that "the word of Cap'n Mike is as good as we'll ever get."

From Kodiak he sailed westward to the Aleutians proper, putting in at Unalaska, where he learned from six daring shipwrecked sailors, who had made it through great hardship to that haven, that twenty of their mates were still marooned on the north coast of the big Unimak Island to the east. Diverting his cruise to that bleak island, he rescued the men, sailed back to Unalaska, and paid with government funds for the forwarding of all twenty-six sailors to Kodiak, where they would transship to San Francisco.

From Unalaska he sailed across the Bering Sea—for he always chose this in preference to the Pacific Ocean, since that sea was in a certain sense his body of water—to one of his favorite towns, Petropavlovsk, at the southern end of the Kamchatka Peninsula. In this beautiful land-protected harbor he met with old friends, learned from them what had been happening along the Siberian coast and where tribal wars were brewing. Since Russian officials looked upon him as an arm of their marine police, the last nights ashore were riotous and drunken affairs, with Mike Healy being lugged back aboard the *Corwin* in time for a dawn departure to the north.

His next stop, at Cape Navarin, far distant from Petropavlovsk, had great significance this year and would have even more for the years ahead. Heaving to off the forbidding coast, he fired a salute which brought ten or fifteen canoes speeding out to the *Corwin,* where normally there would have been only a sullen silence. But Healy had raised the American flag, and now men and women who had some years before rescued sailors from an American shipwreck clambered up the sides of the *Corwin* to greet these new Americans. When all were aboard, Healy lined them up as if they were dignitaries representing an alien potentate, then fired another salute and had his bugler blow assembly. In broken Russian, which only a few of the Siberians who spoke only Chukchi would have understood had it been perfect, Healy said with the visible emotion that possessed him at times of solemn significance:

> "The Great Ruler in Washington always knows when some-
> one of good spirit aids an American who is in danger. You
> and you and you went out into the sea to rescue our sailors
> from the doomed ship *Altoona*, and you kept them in your
> yurts for more than a year. You delivered them in good health
> to the rescue ship sent by the Russians, and the Great Ruler in
> Washington has told me to come here and thank you."

He then asked that members of the visiting party line up before him so that each could receive a gift of considerable value—a saw, a set of tools, enough cloth for three dresses, a parka, a set of kitchen pots, a ceremonial hat with feathers for the chief. On and on the gifts appeared, each one personally chosen by Captain Healy, each one delivered personally by his hands. When the presentations were over, he mumbled to his first mate: "Next time an American ship gets wrecked along this coast, the sailors will have no fear."

But the lasting outcome of this good-will visit came by accident, for the Siberians were so gratified by this gesture of appreciation that they insisted upon taking Captain Healy back onshore with them, and while there, his restless imagination forced him to ask: "How can you live so well on land that is so poor?" and he poked his forefinger into the fat that covered these healthy people, and they explained: "Reindeer," and they showed him how, at the edge of their village, they maintained pens made of wooden timbers, inside which clustered herds of reindeer, nine owned by one family, thirty to a group of families, perhaps sixty in a community-owned group.

"What do they eat?" and they pointed to a far hill where a shepherd boy tended a herd of free-roaming reindeer that grazed on the tundra moss, and he sent runners, one to replace the shepherd, one to bring him back to the village, and when the boy arrived Healy gave him the belt off his own trousers and said that the Great Ruler in Washington wanted him to have it for his brave behavior three years ago.

• • •

From Cape Navarin he proceeded up the Siberian coast past St. Lawrence Island and the Diomedes and into the Chukchi Sea, where he stopped at a lonely village whose residents had once traded with him, and they too had troubles which they placed before him, and in his dark-browed way he listened to words he did not begin to comprehend, but finally a sailor who knew some Russian found a Siberian who knew a little, and they pieced together what the problem was and what a reasonable solution would be. Delivering this judgment, he resolved the matter for the time being at least, and one of his men said to him when they were back aboard the *Corwin:* "The Russians at Petropavlovsk would be afraid to come up here and listen to a problem like that," and he said with some truth: "But this is my ocean. These are my people."

He ran from Siberia across the Chukchi Sea to an anchorage he knew well, Desolation Point, where he learned with dismay and personal sorrow that a fine missionary, Father Fyodor, had been murdered by a demented man who still roamed loose after all this time because there was no jail in which to incarcerate him. When he was caught and brought before Healy on the *Corwin,* only a few questions sufficed to show that the poor fellow was incompetent, so he was locked in the brig, which all the cutters had. Healy then went ashore to visit with Mrs. Afanasi and her two children, and he heard how Dmitri with his Russian gun had protected his mother against the crazy man, and Healy said: "I have aboard ship a medal for a brave lad like you," and when the ship was about to sail southward to its other duties, Dmitri was rowed out and Captain Healy rummaged through his pile of gifts and came up with a medal he had bought along the waterfront in San Francisco. It showed an eagle, and as he pinned it on the boy's tunic he said in his deep, solemn voice: "This belongs to a real hero."

His next stop on this particular trip was at forlorn Point Hope, where winds from the north were incessant and where his lookout spotted a group of white men huddling among sand dunes, and when small boats were sent to investigate, they discovered something so terrible that when Captain Healy, back aboard the *Corwin,* was told of it, his face turned almost black as he thundered: "I want no record of this. No entry in the log. We did not stop here," but then impulsively he jumped down into the longboat, sped ashore and gathered the marooned men, treating them gently as if they were his children, and brought them to safety aboard his ship. Then he fled to the sanctuary of his cabin, where his first mate found him caressing his parrot and mumbling: "Who knows? Who knows?"

"We know damned well who knows," the mate said in great anger. "They're cannibals. They ate the flesh of their own companions, and from what I can piece together, they probably killed some before they died naturally."

"Who knows?" Healy mumbled, whereupon the mate grew bitter: "I know, that's who knows. Henderson knows. And so does Stallings. They're goddamned cannibals and we won't have them aboard this ship."

Almost pathetically, Mike Healy looked up at his righteous mate and asked: "Who knows what you and I would do? Who goddamned bloody knows?" And during the remainder of the trip, till the marooned sailors could be handed over to other authorities, they ate apart, ostracized by the other men, but Captain Healy sat with them to talk of how they had lost their whaler in the ice pack, and he listened attentively as they told of how the timbers strained and cracked and tore apart as the relentless ice continued its crushing advance. Before the next stop he summoned the first mate and said: "I want to make an entry in the log. 'At Point Hope we rescued six sailors marooned when their whaler *Cassiopeia* out of New Bedford was lost in the ice.'"

"Is that all? No dates? No disposition?"

"That's all," Healy roared, and when the entry was made he signed it.

He next put in at Cape Prince of Wales, a place which was to be of great importance to him in later years and of a determining influence now, for when he was rowed ashore he found a sizable group of Eskimos starving because the catch of seals and whales had been disastrous, and no other food was available. It was here, for the first time, that he said to his officers after they had fed the emaciated natives: "How ridiculous? Over there in Cape Navarin the Eskimos— they must be the same people, you go back far enough—they had rolls of fat, with no more food from the land than these people over here. What's the difference? They have reindeer . . ." It was then that his great idea was born: "Why not bring a hundred, a thousand reindeer over here? Our Eskimos would live like kings."

From Cape Prince of Wales he drifted down to the mouth of the Yukon River, where he dispatched two ship's boats to go upriver thirty miles, dispensing medicines and news, and when he heard about life along the great river he said: "I'd like to go up it about a thousand miles."

He was now back in the Bering Sea, and with a long sweep toward the west he came to the north coast of big St. Lawrence Island, and when he anchored off the easternmost settlement of Sevak he expected to be greeted by many canoes, for the *Corwin* was known to these natives, but in the entire village there was no sign of life. He was in the prow of the first boat ashore, and what he found at first perplexed him and then aroused a bitterness beyond expression, for every single person in Sevak was dead.

As they walked about the village, trying to find out what had happened, one of the sailors pointed out that there were no seal bones lying about, no walrus or whale: "They had nothing to eat, sir. They died of starvation. But why . . . ?"

The mystery was not solved at Sevak, or even at big Kookoolik, where many natives had lived; all there, too, were dead, and again there were no seal or walrus bones, but there were clear signs of kegs in which rum had been delivered and molasses distilled. But it was not until the *Corwin* reached Chibukak that the solution was found, for there a pair of natives from the village of Powooiliak on the southern coast, the one that Captain Schransky had wanted to visit but could not because of the storm, had come to prospect among the ruins, and they said: "Much rum. Much molasses. All July, August dancing, lovemaking along the shore. No men in umiaks chasing whales. At end they come to us, begging food. We have none to share. They all die."

"Who did this?" Healy fairly bellowed, standing amid desiccated corpses.

"Big dark ship, captain very big, white hair. He taught them molasses, took all their ivory."

Healy did not ask his men to bury the corpses; there were too many. The major part of an island population had been wiped out, and the man responsible appeared to be outside the law, an empire to himself, bounded by the North Pole and Tahiti, by Lahaina in Hawaii and Canton in China. Now his apprehension became more obligatory than ever, for he was the defiler of a society.

But Healy in the *Corwin* was no match for Schransky in the *Erebus,* and when toward the finish of this year's tour of his domain, Healy saw the *Erebus* off to the west still shooting seals in midocean, he ignored the difference between their two ships and bore down upon him as if he would ram the poacher, but Schransky easily avoided him, moved off to the west, and told his first mate: "The *Erebus* will never be disciplined by a goddamned nigger."

Captain Michael Healy, Lord Protector of the Arctic Seas, was an American Negro. As a young man striving to make his way in the customs hierarchy, he had learned to wear a hat that covered his dark forehead and a large mustache that obscured the blackness about his mouth, so that many people knew him for some time before they realized he was a black man.

His father, Michael Morris Healy, was a tough-minded Irish plantation owner in Georgia who took as his wife a marvelous slave woman named Elisa. Together they had ten children of such extraordinary grace and promise that Healy said: "It would be a crime to have children like ours grow up to be slaves," which would have been the legal situation had they grown to adulthood in Georgia. Therefore, with tremendous personal effort Healy and his wife accomplished the impossible: they spirited their ten children out of Georgia, enrolled them in cooperating Quaker and Catholic schools in the North, and watched them develop into what was probably the outstanding group of black siblings in American history.

Four of the boys made historic names for themselves: one became a leading bishop of the Catholic church; another became a respected doctor of canon law; Patrick, the third son, early showed the unusual academic talents that carried him to the presidency of Georgetown University, and he was for some twenty years, in the latter part of the nineteenth century, one of America's leading and most respected educators; and the fourth son, Mike, ran away from school, went to sea, and became in time one of the most honored captains in the Treasury's revenue cutter service.

Three of the girls became nuns, one ending her career as Mother Superior in a major convent. It is interesting to speculate on where these extraordinary black children acquired their unusual talents, which were recognized by so many white people in so many diverse areas of performance. Certainly, from the courageous behavior of their father they could have inherited the strong character they manifested, but there seems little in this Irishman's background which would account for their intellectual preeminence, and one can speculate that perhaps this sprang from the remarkable slave girl Elisa. At any rate, they formed in these years one of the most distinguished groups of brothers and sisters in America, matched perhaps by a comparable group from the Adams family of Massachusetts, but one must remember that the Adams children enjoyed every advantage from childhood on and suffered from no fear of being stigmatized as slaves. The contribution the ten Healys made to America was incomparable, but none of the other children attained the headline prominence of Mike.

His feats in the northern seas became legendary, and newspapers reveled in writing about his heroics. Did a group of careless whalers tarry too long off Desolation Point and become icebound, with starvation threatening? Mike Healy in one of his frail cutters would speed through ice floes that would have crushed an ordinary ship six times over and miraculously find open tracks leading him to the stranded sailors. Did tragedy strike in some remote village on the Siberian coast? Mike Healy dauntlessly arrived on the scene to save the Russians. Did a whaler sink during a storm in the Bering Sea? Who rescued the castaways six months later but Mike Healy, who chanced to stop at their unpopulated Aleutian island on a hunch. And whomever he rescued, no matter in what lost corner of the arctic, that person could be relied upon to sing his praises when returning to civilization.

His popularity extended across the nation, and one Canadian in a small western town when asked who the President of the United States was, said without hesitation: "Mike Healy. He runs everything."

But knowledgeable maritime people were not fooled by the adulation he received from the unwitting public; they were aware that frustration gnawed at him because he proved powerless to drive Emil Schransky from the seas which Healy had taken under his protection. Whenever men who knew the oceans gathered, they marveled at the impunity with which the German captain acted in the seal islands, the way he operated at will in the pelagic-sealing areas, and his flagrant abuse of alcohol and rum and molasses in devastating native villages. Not even the disaster on St. Lawrence Island, which by now was well known among seamen, deterred Schransky from repeating his performance elsewhere, and then running to Hawaii or China with his corrupt bounty. He was a thorn in Mike Healy's side, and the excuse was always given by Mike's apologists: "If only he had a ship as good as Schransky's, the duel would be even. As it is, he has no chance." And because of this imbalance, the image of the huge captain with the white mass of hair and beard continued to haunt the former slave from Georgia.

But help was forthcoming, through a route so intricate that no one could have planned it. Dundee, on the east coast of Scotland, was not a major shipbuilding city by any means, but in 1873 a shipyard there, with a reputation for constructing unusual crafts to specification, received an order to build a ship stout enough to withstand the ice fields off Labrador and Greenland, and as a result, in 1874 a stubby, rugged vessel was launched which would, when it finally sank eighty-nine violent years later, be remembered as one of the great small ships of history. It was christened the *Bear,* 198 feet 6 inches stem to stern, 29 feet 9 inches beam, 18 feet 8 inches draft, 1,700 tons displacement. Its construction was an eclectic marvel: hull of Baltic oak, ribs of a heavier Scottish oak, decks of Burma teakwood, prow and sides sheathed with Australian ironwood, bottom of American yellow pine, iron fittings cast in Sweden and the navigation instruments assembled from seven different European and North American maritime nations.

The *Bear* was a three-master rigged as a barkentine—big square sails on the foremast, deft little fore-and-aft sails on the main and mizzen masts—but what made it look like the awkward little powerhouse it proved to be was a full-fledged steam engine forward of the mainmast served by a huge, squat smokestack at midships. When it was delivered to its future owners for work in the North American ice field, its builders promised: "Square sails will give you drive, fore-and-afts maneuvering quickness, and the engine the ability to plow through ice. But the real secret? Look at that prow!" It was treble thick, fortified by oak and ironwood, and capable, said the proud marine architects who devised it, "of breaking its way through any ice it faces."

At that moment, at the beginning of the *Bear*'s life at sea, it was thought that the ship would serve some routine purpose, but later, when it was dragooned into a rescue operation, it achieved fame on front pages across the world: the American arctic explorer Adolphus Greely had gone bravely into the northern waters of the Atlantic, lost his ship in a crushing ice pack and nineteen of his men in the ensuing attempt to walk back to civilization. All rescue efforts by normal ships having failed, the *Bear* was purchased by the American government for the huge price of a hundred thousand dollars and hurried to the supposed scene of the disaster.

Now an entirely different kind of ship was in the arctic, and its double-stout construction enabled it to break its way through ice fields that no other could have penetrated and, to great acclaim, to rescue Greely and six other survivors. In the aftermath, while the world was applauding this extraordinary ship, someone had the clever idea of transferring it to the revenue cutter service in Alaska, where it would be most useful.

Around the Horn it went in November 1885, arriving in San Francisco after only eighty-seven days at sea. By chance, when the *Bear* docked, Captain Mike Healy was available for a new command, and without much forethought he was given this well-regarded ship which already had a reputation as exalted as his own. It was a remarkable wedding of man and machine, for when he moved his gear into the captain's quarters and arranged a perch for his parrot and a hiding place for his booze, he said: "This is home," but it was only when he saw that amazing prow with its fantastic thickness of ironwood that he dared reissue his earlier oath: "Now we drive that bastard from the seas."

In 1886, Healy took his new command north, all the way to icebound Barrow at the tip of the continent, where he muscled his way through floes that no ordinary vessel would even have attempted, and luck was already sailing with him, for he rescued three groups of sailors whose ships had been crushed by the ice. When he delivered them back to San Francisco they spent half their praise on Healy, half on the *Bear,* and thus the legend of the ship was augmented: "It can go anywhere. It'll save a thousand lives up there. And with Healy in command, the seas will be safe."

In going to and from Barrow, the *Bear* passed in sight of St. Lawrence Island, and the memory of those three dead villages tormented Mike Healy's soul, and it infuriated him to think that the *Erebus* was still prowling these waters and breaking all laws with impunity. Time and again he would cast anchor off some village on the Alaskan coastline, only to find that the *Erebus* had already been there with its cargo of rum and molasses for which it had obtained two or three years' supply of ivory and pelts.

Powerless to punish the marauder or even catch him, he had to sail disconsolately back to San Francisco and report that "the brig

Erebus, Captain Schransky, out of New Bedford, has been selling rum to the natives and engaging in pelagic sealing and poaching the rookeries, but an attentive patrol failed to apprehend him." Even with his more powerful ship, the Negro Healy could not catch the Nordic Schransky.

But when a giant engages in valiant battle, and Mike Healy was a giant, he is often joined by another eager to lend support, and together the two, who might have been strangers six months earlier, achieve miracles. Such a second giant was approaching Alaska from the hilly region around Deadhorse, Montana, on a wintry afternoon in February.

Sheldon Jackson was that amazing man. Even though he had been warned in the last settlement that a blizzard might be brewing, he was traveling alone. Forty-three years old, he had a complete beard and heavy mustache to make his little face look more dignified, a matter which concerned him deeply, for he wished always to impress strangers favorably despite his diminutive stature. His exact height would always be a matter of debate, for his detractors, a numerous band, claimed that he was under five feet, which was preposterous; he referred to himself as five four, which was equally absurd; because he favored built-up shoes, he looked to be about five two. But whatever his height, he often looked a dwarf among men markedly taller than he.

Now he plowed ahead through the snow that was beginning to drift, but he had no worry about his ability to make his destination before dark. God wants me to get there, he assured himself, and this was more than enough to fuel his energy, for he was a missionary of the Presbyterian church, absolutely convinced that God intended him for some great work and increasingly suspicious that it might be outside America that he would perform his miracles of conversion. Therefore, when he came to the top of a small hill from which he had been certain, as he climbed it, that he would see the town of Deadhorse, population 381, and found before him no town lights, but only another hill, and this one larger than the last, he merely adjusted his heavy pack, squared his frail shoulders, and said aloud: "Well, God, You must have it hiding on the other side of this one," and down into the light but swirling snow he marched, stopping now and then to clear his steel-rimmed glasses.

The dip was quite deep, but he interpreted this as a protection God had placed around this town, and his enthusiasm flagged not one bit as he reached the bottom and started the upward climb, for it was inconceivable to him that Deadhorse would not lie just beyond the ridge. On his way to the top the snow increased noticeably, but this gave him little concern, for he thought: It's good that I'm almost there, because this storm could get bad, and upward he struggled, as secure in his faith as he had been when doing his missionary work in the mountains of Colorado or the flatlands of Arizona.

As he neared the top of the hill he was hit by a blast of snow borne by a strong wind that came howling over the crest, and for just a moment his little feet lost their hold and he slipped backward, but he quickly caught himself, struggled to the top, and saw below him, as he had known he would, the flickering lights of Deadhorse.

But now a more serious problem arose, for instead of a town of 381, there stood before him a village of eight houses, well scattered. He had been grossly deceived by the Presbyterians at his last stop, but since they were Presbyterians, he could not think ill of them: Perhaps they never made the trip here themselves.

He had in his pocket the name of the man to whom he was being sent, Otto Trumbauer: Sounds more like a Lutheran than a Presbyterian. But when he stopped at the first house and asked for the Trumbauers, he was told: "You must be that missionary fellow they said was comin'. Trumbauer's expectin' you. He's two houses along," and when he knocked on the Trumbauer door, it was flung open with a hearty cry: "Reverend, we've been holdin' supper for you," and he was pulled into the warm room.

Mrs. Trumbauer, a hefty woman in her forties, said as she closed the door: "You got here just in time. Take off that pack and your coat." A son in his twenties and a thin young woman who was apparently his wife helped Jackson get rid of his heavy garments and found a place for him at the waiting table.

At supper he learned the bad news, for the elder Trumbauer said: "There has to be some mistake. We got only eight families here, two of them are Catholic, two are atheist, and of the other four, only three of us have any interest in starting a Presbyterian church."

Jackson heard the dismal report with only a slight wince: "Jesus didn't start out with twelve disciples. The church marches forward with what soldiers it has, and you two men look like stout ones." He insisted that the two other Presbyterian families be invited in that very night, so that the first meeting of the Deadhorse Presbyterian Church was held while a small blizzard piled snow outside.

The adult men, on whom the labor of building even a small church would fall, were not eager to commit themselves to such a task, but Jackson was adamant; he had been sent to Deadhorse to start a Presbyterian church and he was determined to do so: "I do believe I've organized more than sixty congregations and helped build at least thirty-six church buildings west of the Mississippi, and my commission now is all the Northern states starting west from Iowa. Your fine town is in an ideal spot for a church which will bind this whole area together."

In succeeding weeks the two male Trumbauers were astonished by the physical and moral energy of this little man who had come on foot over the mountains to live with them during the building of their church. He worked like the strongest man present, and on Sundays he preached inspired sermons that ran for more than an hour, even though his entire congregation consisted of only three families. However, this changed when he visited the two atheist families and was informed that they were agnostic rather than atheist. "Join with us on Sunday," he pleaded. "You don't have to believe, just hear the message." Then, in what was supposed to be humor, he added in his awkward way: "We won't take up a collection," and he was so sincere in his invitation that one of the families did stop by the Trumbauer house to hear the next Sunday's sermon. It dealt with missionary work, and during the communal dinner that followed he revealed the sources of his surprising energy: "In my freshman year at Union College back east I heard a call: 'Sheldon, there are people overseas who do not know the Word of God. Go to them, take them My Holy Word.'"

"You didn't go overseas. You said you worked in Arizona and Colorado."

"When I graduated from Princeton Theological, I went before an examining board for the foreign missions, and their doctors said: 'You're too frail and weak for service in foreign countries,' so they sent me to Colorado and Wyoming and Utah, where I helped build church after church, and now I'm in one of the most demanding regions of all, Montana and Idaho."

"What do you mean," a young man asked, "when you say 'I heard a call'?" and Jackson replied with startling vigor: "Sometimes to some people you're standing alone in a room or you've been praying, and Jesus Christ himself comes into that room and says in a voice so plain it sounds like a bell: 'Sheldon, I want you for my work,' and ever after your feet are headed in that direction and you are powerless to turn aside." No one spoke, so he ended: "That voice called me to Deadhorse where Jesus Christ wanted one of His churches to be built, and with your help, not mine, it will be built."

He was being too modest, for his contribution to the small log building was tremendous; he worked nine and ten hours a day at the most difficult jobs of construction, and sometimes the women laughed when they saw him coming down the road carrying one end of a log while some huge young fellow struggled with the other end. He was good with a hammer if he could have the help of one of the homemade ladders, but always on Sunday he was prepared for his sermon, and had the ones he delivered at Deadhorse been collected in a small booklet, they would have provided a logical exposition of the philosophy that underlay the missionary effort.

But what staggered the three local families was that in addition to his day's labor and his Sunday sermons, the little man spent most of his nights after supper writing voluminous copy for a popular religious journal he had started in Denver and for which he still felt responsible. As the work on the log church neared completion, the Trumbauers and their Presbyterian friends recognized Jackson as a true man of God, a Christian without a flaw, and they were pleased to have known him. Mrs. Trumbauer said, as the time approached for his departure for some town in Idaho that needed a church: "I've never had a man in the house, not even my own father or Otto's, who caused me less trouble. Sheldon Jackson is a saint." And then she added: "Hadn't we better tell him? It might break his heart to find out later."

The families held private discussions in another home and concluded that if one balanced the honorable with the practical, the best course would be to finish the church, have a big dedication ceremony, and then tell him, and that was the plan that was followed.

When the time approached for committing this church to the service of Jesus Christ, Jackson went humbly to the nonreligious families and pleaded with them to help in the dedication: "It's for the good of the whole community, not just a few Presbyterians," and then, stifling his pride and his convictions, for he waged unceasing war against Catholics and Mormons, he went to the Catholic families and invited them also to the celebration, using much the same arguments: "I will be dedicating a church. You will be helping the community to take a step forward." He was so persuasive that on the Thursday, a day of the week that he specifically chose so that the agnostics and the Catholics would feel free to participate, which they did, he preached a sermon that was a marvel of friendliness and devotion. All his customary exhortation was muted, and to listen to him, the Presbyterian church had not an enemy in the world nor was there any other Christian denomination with which it was at odds. Most earnestly he wanted this church to be a force for good in a community which he was sure would be a growing one.

And at the feasting he moved from family to family, all eight of them, assuring them that with the opening of this church, a new day was dawning in Deadhorse, and he was so convinced by his own rhetoric that when he saw tears in the eyes of the Presbyterian women, he assumed that they were the joyous tears of Christian triumph.

They were not, but it had been agreed by the three families that they would wait till Jackson was packed for his move into Idaho before telling him the painful news, but one night when he was busy in the Trumbauer dining room finishing a report for his Denver publication—it dealt with the triumph of Jesus Christ's message in the town of Deadhorse, Montana, a settlement he refused to call a village—Otto Trumbauer coughed and said: "Reverend Jackson," and when the little fellow looked up he saw the entire Trumbauer family ranged before him. Obviously, something of moment had agitated these good people, but what it was he could never have guessed.

"Reverend Jackson, we've tried every way on earth to avoid this, but there's no way out. Us and the Lamberts, we're movin' back to Iowa. Our families have farms for us to work there, and we can earn a livin', somethin' we can't do here."

Jackson dropped his pencil, looked up, wiped his glasses meticulously, and asked for confirmation of the astounding news: "Iowa? You're leaving here?"

"We got to. No future for our children here. Nor for us."

For the first time since he was trapped in the growing blizzard, Sheldon Jackson allowed his shoulders to sag, but then he tensed them for the Lord's work: "Why, if you knew you were leaving . . . ?"

"Did we stay to help build the church?" Mr. Trumbauer finished the question, but he was not allowed to give the answer; his wife did: "We discussed that, all the families, and we decided that you were a true man of God sent to us on a special mission." She burst into tears, and it was up to her husband to add: "We agreed that we would build the church and leave it as a beacon in the wilderness."

Jackson squared his shoulders, rose, and grasped in turn the hands of all the Trumbauers: "You were right in your decision! God always directs us in the right path! I started six, maybe eight churches in the Colorado mountains that never took hold, but there they stand, as you say, beacons in the mountains to remind those who will come later that Christians once labored here." But then his indomitable optimism manifested itself: "But this town will never become a wilderness! I see expansion, families moving here from the Dakotas, and when they arrive, there'll be your church waiting for them, for no collection of houses is ever a town without a church at its center."

He left Deadhorse in a state of positive euphoria, a little man with a big pack, eyeglasses that collected mist and dust, and a conviction rooted in rock that the work he was doing was ordained by God and supervised by His Son Jesus Christ, but the judgment which Mrs. Trumbauer voiced as he departed—"Reverend Jackson, you're a saint without a flaw"—was far from true, for he had another side to his nature which had not had an opportunity to reveal itself during his constructive visit to Deadhorse.

On the snowy day that Sheldon Jackson left Deadhorse, Montana, to push westward, an informal gathering of the board which governed Presbyterian missions convened during a retreat in a rural setting overlooking the Hudson River in New York. A tall, worried clergyman, who obviously wanted to be fair, started the afternoon's discussion with an announcement which brought discomfort to all who heard it: "As your chairman it's my duty to be scrupulously just in what I say, but I must advise you that our dear and respected friend Sheldon Jackson has done it again. We don't know where he is or what he's up to. After we took him out of Colorado, where he, as you know, was pursuing his own ways, he obeyed our orders for a while, taking proper steps to develop the area we assigned him."

"Which was?" a minister asked.

"The Northern states and territories west of the Mississippi, but not including Dakota, the state of Oregon or the territory of Washington."

"That's a vast area, even for Jackson. Where's he supposed to be?"

"We directed him to work in Montana. Where he actually is, who can guess."

"Isn't it about time," an impatient clergyman in his sixties asked, "that we discipline this young man?"

"He's not so young, you know. Must be in his forties."

"Old enough to behave himself."

"That he will never do," the chairman said as he produced a single sheet of notes. "But before we take any action regarding this little hurricane, I want to bring before you eight aspects of his behavior, for he is consistent, and the first three refer to the finest attributes any missionary could exhibit. *First,* he is a born missionary. From his earliest days at Union College he had a specific calling to Christ, and whereas he is not loath to challenge the veracity of your calling or mine, he never doubts the authenticity of his. He is therefore by his definition a better missionary than you or I, and he is not afraid to point this out. *Second,* he has, from early childhood, been a committed Presbyterian. He believes without question that ours is the world's superior religion, and the doubts that assail the rest of us from time to time, the great debates about the nature of God and the paths to salvation never touch him. The two Johns, Knox and Calvin in that order, settled it for him!"

The clergymen discussed this second point for some time, and one man spoke for several: "To have a faith as solid as that . . . maybe I envy him," but another minister from New York cautioned: "You may have used the wrong word, Charles. Not as *solid* as that, as *simple.* He knows what he's for and what he's against."

"For example?" Charles asked, and the speaker ticked off his response: "He's for Jesus Christ and against Catholics, Mormons and Democrats." Charles did not laugh: "I wish I knew even ten things for sure . . . no questions, no doubts. Jackson knows ten thousand." And the second speaker said: "And he's convinced that you and I don't know even three."

The chairman continued: "Out of this rock-solid conviction comes the third attribute you've all noticed, his remarkable gift for persuading others to listen to him attentively. Small, contentious, single-minded, you'd expect him to turn people away, but it's just the opposite. He attracts them the way honey attracts flies, and they'll listen to him discuss the basic principles of religion and particularly the work of missionaries."

At this point the discussion stopped, and the clergymen reflected on the positive attributes of their difficult colleague; all granted him his piety, dedication and surprising ability to cooperate with the other Protestant denominations, but most had felt the lash of his venomous tongue, and after a pause, which included the nodding of heads in agreement with what had been said so far, the analysis continued:

"*Fourth,* and this fault had better be admitted up front, for it accounts for many of the problems we've had with Jackson and will have in the future. For a devout Christian, which he certainly is, and a man who has devoted his life to missionary work, he displays a singular skill in going for the jugular of anyone whom he considers an enemy. This accounts for the fact that if you take a hundred of his acquaintances in either Colorado, Washington or the church in general, you find fifty of them revering him as a saint, fifty reviling him as a serpent."

This called for a show of hands among those present, and the score was saint three, serpent fourteen, with many of the latter eager to relate how Jackson had battled with them over points not worth the effort. But these same men nodded in agreement when one sagacious elder pointed out the fundamental fact about Jackson's place among the Presbyterians: "He is our front-line general in the fight against darkness. He's the one, above all others, who ensures that our efforts in the field equal those of the Baptists and Methodists. Like him or not, he is our man."

"I was coming to that," said the chairman, who had been repeatedly savaged by Jackson, "for he does have his virtues. *Fifth,* early in life, for reasons not easy to explain, he developed a conviction that if he wanted something, he should go right to the top. Have you ever visited Washington with him when he wants something important? He slams his way into someone's office—congressman, senator, cabinet ministers, the President himself. He told me once after having lectured a senator: 'These are good men, but they need guidance,' and he's ready to offer it anytime, anywhere, on any subject. I've often wondered why a man so small, so insignificant, can bully a senator six feet tall, but he does."

Several men testified to Jackson's extraordinary power in Washington, and one said: "He's made himself the voice of morality, especially Presbyterian morality, and that counts for something."

The chairman now came to one of the fundamental talents of Sheldon Jackson: "*Sixth,* his power stems from his capacity to con-

vince large numbers of women church members to support whatever
program he's fostering at the moment. They'll write letters to Washington and, most important, contribute large sums of money for his
various projects, like that extraordinary church newspaper he still
publishes in Denver, although he hasn't been there for years. He depends upon these women, beseeches them for funds, and thus places
himself somewhat beyond our control."

A choleric minister who had often been the subject of Jackson's
vituperative attacks said: "I watched him address a group of women
in Maine whom he'd never seen before, and he was using the approaches that he'd found productive in Western states like Colorado
and Iowa. He warned them about the dangers posed by the Catholic
church, but they'd heard enough of that in Massachusetts and Maine.
He saw he wasn't getting anywhere, so he switched to a hard-hitting
exposé of the Mormon church in Utah, but most of them had never
heard of the Mormon church, so that fell flat. Obviously agitated—I
could see he was perspiring—he suddenly launched into a heartrend-
ing account of guess what? Out of the blue, with no preparation
whatever, he gave them a tearful account of how Eskimo girls in
Alaska were being seduced at the age of thirteen by rascally goldminers, and his pictures were so vivid and lamentable that even I had
tears in my eyes. Now, he's never been to Alaska, knows nothing
about it, but he convinced those good Presbyterian women that unless they contributed heavily to the mission work he was planning for
Alaska . . ."

"Who said we're sending him to Alaska?" an irate clergyman
shouted, and the informant said: "He did. That is, he didn't actually
say we were sending him. He said he was going."

Surveying the group almost belligerently, the chairman asked:
"Did anyone here mention Alaska to him?" and one clergyman said:
"The last place on earth we'd want him meddling. That's Oregon territory. Tell him to mind his own business," and several members
mumbled: "Amen."

So the chairman returned to his bill of indictment, but before he
could speak to the next point he was interrupted by chuckling coming from the group's oldest member. "Did I say anything improper?"
the chairman asked, and the man said: "Heavens, no! I was just recalling that I was on the committee that interviewed Jackson years
ago when he wanted to be one of our overseas missionaries. I read
him our verdict: 'You're too frail for the hard work of an overseas

post.'" When the gross inaccuracy of this prediction struck the meeting, everyone joined in the laughter.

"*Seventh*," resumed the chair, "he's displayed an insatiable appetite for publicity. From the first he's appreciated the power that can come to a man, particularly a clergyman, if he's seen by the press to be an agent for good. He saw early that this would protect him from bodies like ours who might not want to support his more outrageous plans. And he was never willing to leave good publicity to chance; as you know, he started or had others start some four or five religious newspapers or journals in which his good works are extolled and in whose columns it is always he who accomplishes things and not the hardworking missionaries who work in silence. Since he acquired that honorary degree from that little college in Indiana, and I have reason to believe he initiated it, he always refers to himself in his journals as Dr. Sheldon Jackson, and nine-tenths of the people who work with him are convinced that he really earned a doctorate in divinity."

The board members discussed the little man's remarkable ability at promoting himself, and there were notes of envy as they recalled one illustrated article after another which spoke of his heroic efforts, but then the meeting closed with an almost irrelevant comment, *Item Eight*: "Jackson has always been an ardent Republican who believes that when the United States government is in such hands, God smiles upon our nation, and that when Democrats come into power, the forces of evil are set loose. This outspoken devotion aids Presbyterianism when the Republicans are in control of the nation, as they have been for so long, but it could damage us if the Democrats ever took over."

In the discussion that followed, it was agreed that since the Democrats were not likely to assume national power in the foreseeable future, the Presbyterians might as well run the risk of allowing Jackson to continue as their spokesman in Washington, but all were firm about the resolution which the board passed at the end of their meeting:

Resolved: that the Reverend Sheldon Jackson be complimented on his new missionary successes in Dakota, but that he be admonished to keep this Board informed of any future movements before he makes them. He is specifically directed not to move into Oregon or Alaska, since those areas are the domain of the Oregon church.

But even before these stern directions could be handed to a secretary for transmission to Jackson, a messenger arrived at the retreat with a communication from distraught church leaders in Oregon:

> The Reverend Sheldon Jackson appeared in our midst without warning and proceeded to infuriate everyone. After creating a great disturbance, he left us for Seattle and Alaska. When we warned him that the latter was Oregon's responsibility, he told us bluntly that he read his commission to include everything from the Mississippi River to the Pacific Ocean and that it was time someone attended to Alaska. We informed him that our church already had missionaries in place in Wrangell, but he retorted: "I mean a real missionary," and he sailed north.

In this abrupt and unauthorized manner Jackson carried the Word of God and the salvation of Jesus Christ to darkest Alaska, and it was a curious fact that for the first seven definitive years of his mission he received not a penny of aid from the Presbyterian church, which was outraged by his insolent behavior. He paid the huge expenses of the Alaskan experiment, one of the most successful in American missionary efforts, solely from the funds turned over to him by adoring women whom he visited each winter on hortatory expeditions. At a time when he was accomplishing miracles in the frozen north, he spent half of each year back in various states imploring women's groups for help, or in Washington hectoring Congress for better laws and more money for Alaska.

He became the close personal friend of almost everyone in government who was destined for spectacular promotion, especially those who were Republican or Presbyterian, which was how he attached himself early to the coattails of Senator Benjamin Harrison of Indiana, who was both, and who, when he became President, would look to Jackson for counsel as to what should be done in Alaska. At a mere five feet two, with the stubby legs of a child, this Presbyterian minister had transformed himself into a giant.

When Dr. Jackson arrived in Alaska, illegally his opponents said, he put his tremendous ingenuity to work, and achieved two brilliant successes: he persuaded his friends in Congress to grant him the resounding title of General Agent for Education for Alaska, which carried no salary and for the early years no government funds, but which did empower him to have impressive calling cards made which he used to bully anyone opposing his plans; and he hectored the Treasury Department into assigning him free passage aboard any of its revenue cutters that were sailing to any point that he wished to visit in the execution of his duties. With these assurances in his pocket and with the continued financial support of the women's clubs back home, he was prepared to set forth on his life's work: the humanization and education of Alaska.

In these beginning years Jackson led a frenetic life. During the spring and summer months he jumped aboard any available cutter to explore the arctic seas, engage in battle against alcohol, arrest malefactors, help dispense law, visit Siberia, plan the development of Alaska, and with his own money provide many of the services which the government should have funded. Then, for the six months of fall and winter, he would be back in Washington or New York or Boston, lobbying and lecturing on the future of Alaska. During one typical twelve-month period he traveled 37,624 miles, and a fellow clergyman guessed that in that time he had given not less than two hundred lectures on behalf of Alaskan education: "Sheldon's ready to launch into a lecture if he can find an audience of six."

But whenever he was on the verge of achieving some improvement, he found himself frustrated by the fact that the United States still refused to provide Alaska with any kind of government or adequate tax base, and in his frustration he would roar back to Washington, breathing fire, to bombard Congress. It was there, with his traditional foresight, that he formed his close acquaintanceship with the promising senator from Indiana, Benjamin Harrison, grandson of the ninth President. The senator listened to his pleas for a law that would enable Alaska to govern itself, became convinced by Jackson's moral force, and in 1883 began to work in the Senate for such a law. In 1884, spurred vigorously by Jackson, Senator Harrison finally maneuvered through Congress an Organic Act, giving Alaska a civil government of sorts, with one judge, one district attorney, one clerk of court, one marshal—four deputies to bring law and order to an area of more than five hundred thousand square miles. It was pathetically inadequate, but a step in the right direction.

Jackson, of course, had hoped for self-governing territorial status, but Congress would not concede this, for it would have implied that sooner or later the territory would become a state, as all the other emerging sections of the United States were doing, and that, ranted the lawmakers, was preposterous: "That icebox will never have enough people to become a state." "Self-government? Hell, the entire area has only nineteen hundred people, I mean white people of course." "If the Army don't govern it, the Navy should."

But not even Jackson appreciated the almost fatal inadequacy of the bill he and Harrison had helped pass; he learned, however, when he returned that spring to Sitka, for he had not been in his summer home two hours before he was visited by an irate Carl Caldwell, the former lawyer from Oregon and now a leading citizen of Alaska: "What did you allow Congress to do, Dr. Jackson?"

"We didn't allow it. Harrison and I forced it."

"But the Oregon bit? That nullified everything."

"Now wait," Jackson said defensively. "Congress refused to give us territorial status. Best we could get was that we should be governed by the same local laws as Oregon."

At this, Caldwell leaped from his chair: "If it was the laws of Oregon, it would be all right. What you gave us are the ancient laws of the territory of Oregon. It became a state in 1859. You're taking us back to the way Oregon was in 1858," and when he spelled out the monstrous limitations this placed on Alaska, Jackson sat with mouth agape: "We can't have jury trials in Alaska because Oregon territorial law said that to be eligible, jury members must be taxpayers."

"Sensible rule," Jackson said. "Provides responsible men for jury duty."

"But we have no taxes in Alaska; therefore, no juries." When Jackson gasped, he continued: "Many of the best laws in Oregon Territory related to counties, but we can't have any of those laws because we have no counties."

"That's ridiculous," the missionary who fathered the law grumbled, but Caldwell was far from finished with his critique: "No one can buy land here, because Oregon's law made no provision for a land law. Worse, for the same reason, the great Homestead Act which has settled the West can't be used here to give settlers free land. But what really strangles us is that we can have no local legislature because Oregon in those days didn't have one." On and on he went, sometimes showing Jackson chapter and line of the antiquated law, so that by the time he was finished, Jackson realized that with his help Congress had returned Alaska to a straitjacket; he saw that he would have to fight most of his battles all over again, and he began that night to flood Congress with new letters of advice and his women supporters with new appeals for funds, because when he engaged in battle, there was no truce, no surrender.

But it was not until the new officers authorized by the Organic Act of 1884 arrived in Sitka to take control of Alaska that he realized the jeopardy he was in, because President Chester Arthur, under almost unendurable pressures from office seekers, had appointed some of the most despicable rascals available at the time, and from the moment they arrived in Sitka they determined to get rid of the troublesome little missionary about whom miners, fishermen and rumrunners complained.

Ringleader of Jackson's enemies was the district attorney, a notorious drunk. His marshal was little better, but it was the federal judge, a man of enormous power, who was the real disaster. Ward McAllister, Jr., was the incompetent nephew of the man with the same name who served as social dictator of New York. All had received their appointments to good-paying jobs through the political pull of their friends and without regard to their competency, which was nil.

They had not assumed their offices long when, with the connivance of the district attorney and Judge McAllister, they issued in secret an indictment for the arrest of Jackson, then waited till a maximum number of local citizens were at the dock to see the departure of a steamer on which Jackson was to sail. At the last possible moment Deputy Marshal Sullivan went aboard with handcuffs to arrest the little missionary and haul him off to jail.

In the next weeks Jackson suffered indignities he could not have imagined, but in the end he was rescued by a most improbable source of justice. President Arthur, responsible for these infamous appointments, left office, and almost immediately after the Democratic reformer Grover Cleveland assumed the presidency, he canceled the Arthur appointments, replacing them with more standard politicians, who served Alaska well. One of the first things the new team did was quash the indictment of Sheldon Jackson, who nevertheless continued to believe that the nation was served best when Republicans were in power.

It was about this time that Jackson participated in one of the most farseeing acts of Alaskan history, one that was rarely if ever duplicated in other newly settled frontiers. Communicating with the leaders of other American churches, he proposed a mutually enforced division of Alaska into a dozen or so religious spheres of influence, each the preserve of one denomination into which proselytizing missionaries from other sects would not intrude. What he proposed was a grand religious truce, and primarily because his reputation as a man of integrity was so widely recognized, leaders of the other groups adopted his suggestion.

As he explained it to the people of Sitka: "Because the Presbyterians were first on the scene, we get Sitka. But since this is the easiest part, we're also taking the most difficult, Barrow in the extreme north." Modestly he added: "It'll be the northernmost mission in the world." When he spelled out other terms of the agreement, he sounded like some follower of Jesus in the Book of Acts apportioning the missionary responsibilities of the infant Christian church: "Our good friends the Baptists are taking Kodiak Island and lands nearby. The Aleutian Islands, where much work needs to be done, to the Methodists. The Episcopal church picks up the work already done decades ago by their cousin church, the Anglicans of Canada, along the upper Yukon. The Congregationalists have volunteered to accept a most difficult area, Cape Prince of Wales. And a fine church you may not know, the German Moravians of Pennsylvania, are going to take God's Word along the Kuskokwim River."

In a later wave of ecumenical enthusiasm, other churches volunteered to become part of this grand arrangement: the Quakers of Philadelphia, always in the forefront where such work was to be done, received Kotzebue and a mining area near Juneau; Swedish Evangelists got Unalakleet; and the Roman Catholics received the vast areas about the mouth of the Yukon which had once been served by the Russian Orthodox missionaries. It was an extraordinary example of ecumenism at its best, and much of the credit went to Jackson.

But verbal agreements, noble though they may be, and actual implementation are two vastly different things, and years passed before any of the major American churches implemented their promises. There were no Baptist missions, no Methodist, not even a Quaker. In despair, for he saw the natives of Alaska perishing because the Word of God was denied them, Jackson implored the major churches to get moving, but with no results. He went to Philadelphia to visit with the Quakers, whom he was sure he could persuade to move north, but he accomplished nothing, so in a kind of moral despair he spent a steaming hot night in August 1883 in the Quaker city drafting a letter to the Moravian church centered in nearby Bethlehem. He implored them to continue in Alaska the noble work they had begun with the Eskimos of Labrador, and once more he received for his labors nothing but silence.

But his letter must have had some effect on the stalwart Germans of Bethlehem, for during Jackson's visit to the United States in the following winter he received without any preliminary encouragement an invitation to visit Bethlehem and present his vision of Alaska's needs to the Moravians. Hastily boarding a train in Philadelphia, he journeyed north to the quaint and lovely old German city, where he delivered one of his most inspired orations, telling the audience: "The Moravian church has always been in the forefront where missionary work is involved. It's your tradition, your soul. Now God's call reaches you one more time: 'The Eskimos of Alaska are languishing for My Holy Word.' Dare you say no?"

The solemn burghers who supervised the church agreed that night that they would send an exploratory mission to the Kuskokwim River by the end of 1885, and when the five young, devout farmers—three men, two wives—saw that great twin of the Yukon and the hunger among the people for medicine, education and Christianity, which they interpreted as the reason why white men prospered, the young missionaries wrote back to Bethlehem: "We are needed," and one of the finest groups of religious workers ever to reach Alaska followed in due course, and the logjam of indifference was broken. Quickly the Quakers took up their appointed areas, then the Baptists and the Methodists, and soon Alaska was dotted with those missions, often stuck away on remote sites, which would in time account for the civilizing of the Great Land.

One day when Jackson was at work in Sitka, the new cutter *Bear* hove into the sound, and before it could be anchored, Jackson had made the decision which would determine so much Alaskan history: That's the kind of ship I'd like to sail in. By midday he had presented his authorization for passage to the first mate, who looked down his nose at the strange little man offering it and said: "Captain'll have to clear this," and for the first time the missionary was led into the quarters of Captain Mike Healy, who had begun to drink heavily the moment the *Bear* reached Sitka, and who now sat with his parrot on his shoulder.

Irritated by this unwarranted intrusion, he let loose a chain of his most violent oaths, glared at Jackson, and ended: "Now what in hell do you want?"

Had the little missionary quailed before this onslaught, the possibility of any relationship between the two men might have died there, but Jackson was a truly fearless man, and drawing himself up to his most impressive posture, he shouted in his strongest oratorical voice: "Captain Healy! I am a man of the cloth, and I do not allow such profanation of God's name in my presence. And I have also come to Alaska to stamp out the alcohol trade, and you, sir, are drunk."

Startled by the little gamecock, Healy began to say "You're right, Reverend . . ." when his parrot came forth with a few choice curses of its own, whereupon Healy cuffed him so that his feathers seemed to fly as he fled to the safety of his perch: "Shut up, you!" He then turned his attention to his visitor: "What does your paper say?"

"It's from the Treasury Department and it says that I'm to have free passage aboard your ship as long as I am in pursuit of my duties."

"And what are your duties?"

"The bringing of God's Word to the Eskimos. The education of the children of Alaska. And the stamping out of the liquor traffic."

To Jackson's amazement, Mike Healy, whose life had been saved by education, rose unsteadily, reached for his hand, and pledged a support which would last for twenty years: "I'm for everything you're for, Reverend. Education saves souls, and strong liquor is the curse of the Alaskan native."

"You seem to be well cursed yourself, Captain."

"In my private life. As captain of this ship, one of my major duties, stamp out the trafficking in hooch."

"And what is hooch?"

"Rotgut, booze, John Barleycorn. It kills Eskimos. It wipes out entire villages." He fell back in his chair, reached for a glass which Jackson had not seen before, and finished his drink. Then he looked up with a roguish smile and said: "Bring your gear aboard. We sail for Kodiak and Siberia at four." And thus the partnership between these two unlikely men was initiated.

Healy was six feet two, five years younger and twenty years more powerful; Jackson was exactly a foot shorter, so that the top of his head came to Healy's windpipe. Healy was a believing Roman Catholic, with brothers and sisters occupying important roles in that religion; Jackson was a devout Presbyterian who, like John Knox before him, railed against Catholics. Healy was a Georgia Negro who legally should have been a slave; Jackson was the product of that social and religious ferment which had swept the rural area of upper New York State—Elizabeth Cady Stanton, Lucretia Mott and Joseph Smith, to whom the secrets of Mormonism were revealed, sprang from the same source—and he believed that Negroes, Indians and Eskimos were humans who deserved God's love but not social equality with white men. Healy was a man devoted to a profane vocabulary and booze; Jackson was a man of rectitude who felt it his duty to lecture miscreants and save them from their folly. Their differences were tremendous, and they were never hesitant about displaying them.

But they had three beliefs in common, and it overrode all these differences: they both believed that Alaska could be governed if one found men of good will to make the effort; they were prepared to volunteer for that duty; and both sought justice for the natives.

Their first cruise together sealed their friendship, because whatever difficulty they ran into, they seemed to perceive instantly its moral overtones, and to a startling degree, each approved of what the other recommended. Now it was no longer Captain Healy of some grubby revenue cutter dispensing rude justice along the shores of the seas; it was the noble ship *Bear* steaming into harbor, its engine puffing smoke, with a distinguished ship's captain aboard, supported by a self-appointed doctor of divinity. They formed a majestic pair, two giants moving into an area that had been pestered by midgets, and after the first visit of this *Bear* to a new village, the authority of Healy and Jackson was established.

On this first trip together they straightened things out at Kodiak, provided stores to the Russian garrison at Petropavlovsk, delivered and enforced a set of judgments along the Siberian coast, and wound up at Cape Navarin, whose settlers streamed out in canoes once they learned that Captain Healy was back, for they remembered the gifts with which he had been so generous on his last trip. It was here that Healy took Jackson ashore to inspect the reindeer herds upon which these Siberians lived so bountifully, but the missionary did not at first appreciate the significance of the visit, for he had not yet seen Alaskan Eskimos starving for lack of winter food.

"Reindeer!" Healy cried. "You load the *Bear* with them, a good wind offshore, and two days later you land them in Alaska."

"Would that be possible?"

"We could do it right now if we had the authority, and the money to pay these people for their surplus." The two Americans became so excited by the prospect of utilizing Siberian experience to save Alaskan lives that they assembled the herders of Cape Navarin, and Healy harangued them about the possibility of a trans-Bering trade in reindeer, and when he told them what they would receive in return, they became so enthusiastic that Healy told Jackson: "When you get to Washington, see if funds are available."

"But are the reindeer that necessary?"

"You'll see."

And when they crossed the Chukchi Sea and landed at a chain of settlements—Barrow, Desolation, Point Hope, Cape Wales—and Jackson saw the devastation that an uncertain food supply wreaked at these points, he reached a firm conclusion: "Captain Healy, you and I must do two things to save the Eskimos. Bring them a mission which has a school attached, and bring them reindeer."

On the way home the *Bear* diverted for a stop at St. Lawrence Island, where Healy showed his missionary friend the ruination wrought by the rum and molasses from the *Erebus*. Jackson was appalled when he saw the skeletons still lying about, and that night as the sturdy *Bear* plowed southward he sought out Healy as he conned the ship on its way through the Bering Sea: "Captain, if you were the man who discovered the death of those villages, and if you knew the reason, how can you possibly go on drinking?"

"I'm not perfect," Healy said. "And if you were perfect, you wouldn't have so many good people mad at you . . . I mean, disgusted with you."

"Drunkards, miners with no conscience, the riffraff of Sitka—I welcome their enmity, Captain."

"But I'm talking about the good people. Oh, I learned a lot about you in Seattle before I met you."

"I was put on earth by God to do His will, and I must do it my own way."

"I was put on earth by who knows? I was put here to sail a ship, and I do it my way."

So these two imperfect men, each of whom would have enemies as long as he worked in Alaska, sailed southward with visions of what they hoped to accomplish: to Christianize the Eskimos, to bring order to the oceans, to transfer deer from Siberia to Alaska, to educate, to educate. On this last ideal they both agreed, as the dramatic events of their second trip together would prove.

They were only a few days out when Jackson, under the cold northern stars of October, asked: "Captain, you never mentioned the *Erebus* before we reached St. Lawrence, but it eats at your soul, doesn't it?"

"It does."

"Would you care to tell me about it?" and in a flood of profanity Healy told of his endless struggle with this renegade ship, of the cruel way it flouted the laws that were supposed to protect not only Eskimos but walruses and seals: "He lurks out there in the spring, against the laws of all nations, and he waits for helpless female seals, pregnant, swimming north to give birth, and he guns them down with rifles and rips out the baby seals to sell the soft skins to China."

"He should be destroyed," Jackson said, and Healy told him: "With this ship under me, I could destroy him," and he retreated to his cabin, where he got drunk.

In the latter days of the trip Jackson remained on deck a good deal, a small man decked out in sealskin garments obtained in Siberia. When sailors asked him what he was doing, he gave evasive answers, for he was on a kind of fool's chase: he wanted to spot the *Erebus*, a ship he had never seen but which he already hated, and late one afternoon he did spy a black ship, or so it seemed, far to the west, and he ran to inform Captain Healy.

"It's the bastard," Healy cried. "Look, you can see his white hair in the glass," and there, commanding his outlaw ship, stood Emil Schransky, who had spotted the *Bear* long before the *Bear* had spotted him. He had heard that Captain Healy had a new cutter but he did not believe the tales told of it, and especially he scorned the man in charge of it: "No damned nigger can outsail me!"

But at the moment when in the past he had unfurled his great black sails to play cat-and-mouse with the slow cutters that Healy had been using, he realized that he was facing a much different kind of ship. He saw the smokestack belching a black cloud, the oversize square sails opening to embrace the wind and, most frightening, that formidable prow double-sheathed in oak and ironwood.

Too late he shouted: "Prepare to run!" for even as his sailors insolently broke out the last bank of canvas they saw to their consternation that the *Bear* had outsmarted them, had turned on a sixpence to head directly at them.

"He's trying to ram us!" Schransky cried in unhidden fear, and he was right, for Mike Healy, this despised black captain, was about to smash his terrible prow right into the midships of the *Erebus*.

"Hard aport!" Schransky bellowed to his steersman, and the man tried to turn the dark ship parallel to the course of the *Bear* so that the latter would glide harmlessly past, as in former duels.

But this time Healy possessed his old wiles plus a powerful new ship in which to perform them, and standing amidships with his parrot screeching on his shoulder, he gave precise orders to his helmsman, who whipped the *Bear* about to send her crashing thunderously into the splintering timbers of the *Erebus*. Grinding on, propelled by the engine, the prow locked tight in the vital innards of its great dark enemy.

Quietly Mike Healy, the loser in so many previous encounters, gave commands which he had rehearsed: "Gunners, stand ready to rake their decks! Sailors, board!" And an astonished Schransky, rendered impotent by this combination of a superior ship captained by a superior mariner, had to stand mute in a posture of surrender as Healy's victorious men swarmed aboard.

As Healy left the *Bear* to stride onto the *Erebus,* he saluted its captain, as the rules of the sea required, and then, with his revolver at the ready, he smiled coldly at Schransky and sent his men rampaging through the bowels of the captured ship. His many previous humiliations were handsomely avenged, and both he and Schransky knew it.

His officers found the kegs loaded with rum and molasses; others came upon the holds filled with sealskins. "All overboard!" Healy commanded, and Schransky's men had to watch in sullen silence as the heads of the kegs were bashed in and the contents poured into the scuppers. Up came the illegal sealskins, worth a fortune in Canton, and into the dark Bering Sea they went.

It was only at this point that Sheldon Jackson felt free to leave the *Bear* and step onto the *Erebus,* and when Captain Schransky saw him in his preposterous sealskin uniform he thundered: "And who in hell is he?" and Healy replied: "The man who brought us here, the one who spotted you first."

"Throw him overboard too," Schransky growled, but now Healy delivered his ultimatum: "Look at my ship, Schransky. Study that prow which cut right through you, that engine. There's a new day in Alaska, Schransky. If I ever see you in the Bering Sea again, I'm going to overtake you and ram you and send you to the bottom, with all hands."

As he stood there in the growing darkness, preparing to give the orders that would retract the *Bear* from the gaping hole in the *Erebus,* he was two inches shorter than the German, many shades darker, but he spoke with an authority that had come late in his life and after many defeats, but at long last he was in command of the Bering Sea, and he was determined to remain so. When he returned to his own ship he left Jackson behind on the *Erebus,* and there were many things about which the little missionary wanted to lecture the big blond captain, especially those destroyed villages on St. Lawrence Island, and he opened his mouth to start his preaching, but when he looked up at that mammoth head so much higher and tougher than his own, he judged that silence was advisable, so without speaking he stepped gingerly across the shattered timbers and returned to his quarters.

It was Jackson's second trip with Healy that changed missions from mud-roofed hovels into true churches and schools, for when the rugged *Bear* steamed out of Sitka Sound, its smokestack belching sparks, every available corner of the deck was crammed with lumber, and ready-made doors and roof beams. Behind it trailed an old schooner piled with additional timber.

This year the *Bear* did not stop at easy ports like Kodiak and Dutch Harbor; instead, it plowed ahead through heavy Bering Sea storms to a first stop at Cape Prince of Wales, where two Congregational missionaries had for two years tried to survive in a hovel half underground. When the *Bear* dropped anchor on the Fourth of July, these surprised young men saw three ship's boats setting out from the mother ship, laden with lumber and sailors, and when the latter climbed ashore and unloaded their cargo, they did not merely deposit it there for the missionaries to use; they turned to and began that afternoon building them a church and a school.

That evening, as if to celebrate the holiday, the trailing schooner pulled in with the bulk of the timber, and the next morning Captain Healy himself joined the work crew, while Dr. Jackson scurried about, helping to dig the foundation trenches for the walls. Every man aboard the *Bear* except the cook worked on this mission church, and at the end of eight days they turned over to the astounded missionaries a center from which they could begin to Christianize this area.

When the *Bear* moved on to Point Hope, one of the loneliest villages in the world, the sailors who went ashore to work on the mission building were introduced to the Alaskan mosquito: it came in three versions, one more ferocious than the next, each strain thriving about three weeks in late spring and early summer. They took turns, as if to say: "We'll send in the little ones to make people nervous, then the medium size, and three weeks later the giants." They were fierce enemies, able to penetrate any opening in the clothes and bite deeply, until they sent some men almost crazy.

"What do you do when these things hit?" a sailor asked the lone missionary, and he said: "You give thanks they last only about nine weeks," and the sailor whined: "I want to go back to Cape Wales and civilization."

On the second day at anchor, Healy and Jackson joined the workers ashore, and again a solid church was built, despite the mosquitoes, but the strongest wood was saved for the next anchorage, farthest Barrow, where the world ends and the Arctic Ocean piles its ice nine months of the year and the sun vanishes completely for three months and more or less for five. Here the sailors met a missionary who was striving to implement Jackson's vision of civilization advancing through the Word of God to the most remote corners of the world.

Through Captain Healy's energetic intervention, space was secured in a government building to serve as temporary school-mission until his sailors could erect a regular structure, one strong enough to withstand the rigors of Barrow, where in this year not one house rose more than three or four feet above the ground. So Healy and his men worked with special care to make this Presbyterian mission a building that would withstand the pressures of the arctic for decades. After eleven days they turned over to the young missionary a rural masterpiece, a church that would illuminate the little village to which whaling vessels came in June, and where they perished in ice if they lingered too long in October.

Not long after leaving Barrow, and firing a parting salute to the new church which loomed like a beautiful volcano above the shacks of the village, the *Bear* swung into shore and anchored off the little wind-swept village of Desolation Point, where the residents clustered on the shore to greet the captain who in the past had meant so much to the security and prosperity of their settlement.

Healy waved to them all, but not seeing a certain individual, he called out: "Where's Dmitri?" and a villager said: "He's Father Dmitri now. Here he comes," and from up the shore came an umiak containing a young man and one passenger, a woman. When it came closer, Healy saw that the man was the same young man who as a boy some years ago had protected his mother from the madman Agulaak. He was twenty-three now, a self-ordained missionary who had assumed in Desolation the leadership position once filled by his murdered father.

When Jackson met him, the young man explained that he supposed he was responsible to the Russian Orthodox Church to which his father belonged, and now began one of the uglier demonstrations of Jackson's behavior in remote areas. When he went ashore with Dmitri and his mother he said bluntly: "We've brought you a real church. The sailors will start building it tomorrow, but it's to be a Presbyterian church, so you really must become a Presbyterian missionary."

"We're Russian," the widow of the martyred Father Fyodor said, but Jackson overrode this: "You're American, and there's no place in our society for a Russian church." When he learned that Dmitri, who was revered as Father Dmitri by everyone in Desolation, was teaching the children in the village the Cyrillic alphabet, he said to the crew of the *Bear:* "The wrong religion in the wrong language," and forthwith he launched an unabashed campaign to persuade—and when this failed, to force—Dmitri to convert to Presbyterianism: "After all, you must remember, Dmitri, that we Presbyterians were given responsibility for the northern reaches of Alaska."

When Dmitri refused apostasy, in which he was supported by his mother even though she had herself been born of Athapascan parents who now favored Methodism, Jackson became unpleasant, threatening him with the loss of the church and school the sailors had begun to build: "We didn't bring all that lumber here to build a church for Russians. It's an American church and it's to have an American missionary."

The likelihood that his obstinacy might cost his village the bright new buildings it so badly needed caused Dmitri so much grief that he consulted with his mother, who surprised him by taking from the little store of treasures she kept wrapped in a cloth behind a log pole in their underground hut the medal that Captain Healy had given her son so many years ago: "He gave it to you because you had been brave. You should still be brave and not allow the little one to make you surrender your father's religion."

At her insistence, Dmitri waited till Reverend Jackson was busy with floor plans for the school, which he was prepared to build despite his threat not to do so, for he was convinced that Dmitri would eventually appreciate the tremendous advantage of turning Presbyterian, both for himself and for the village. Then, making sure that Jackson did not see him, Dmitri jumped into the small umiak he had used when the *Bear* first anchored, and before long he was aboard the ship. Asking for permission to speak with the captain, he was ushered into Healy's quarters, where he was startled both by the parrot and the fact that the captain was close to being drunk. But when Healy, a good Catholic, learned what his trusted friend, the little missionary, was up to—the conversion of a good Russian Catholic into a Presbyterian—he sobered in a hurry, jumped down into Dmitri's umiak, and ordered the young priest, or would-be priest, to take him ashore.

Once there, he hurried to where the school was being built, grabbed Jackson by the sealskin under his chin, and demanded: "Sheldon, what in hell are you doing to this boy?"

There was a confused attempt at explanation, a charge of kidnapping by Mrs. Afanasi, who came running up, and a great embarrassment on the part of Dmitri, who had not wanted the incident to develop in this manner.

The debate between Jackson and Healy continued for two stressful days, with the missionary arguing that since he had provided the lumber for the buildings, he had a right to say what kind of structure they should go into, and the captain arguing with equal force that since it arrived on the ship which he commanded, he had the privilege of saying how it should be used. Unfortunately, he had an imprecise understanding of the Russian Orthodox priesthood, and when on the second day he learned that Dmitri was planning to marry a local Eskimo girl who was at best a pagan, he became completely confused. His brothers who had high positions in what he called the real Catholic church did not run around getting married, nor did his sisters who were nuns. There has to be something terribly wrong, he said to himself, in a church which allows its priests to marry.

Nevertheless, he felt obligated to defend any Catholic church, and he did so with vigor, but he had never before argued religion with a moral cyclone like Sheldon Jackson, and when the church and school were finished, they were consecrated as Presbyterian structures, with Father Dmitri taking passage on the *Bear* to Seattle, where he would, through the help of local Presbyterians, be converted into Reverend Afanasi, the first Inupiat Eskimo to bear that august title.

But during the trip south to Kodiak, Captain Healy argued with the young man so persuasively, defending Catholicism as the one universal church, that he almost prevailed upon Dmitri to leave the *Bear* in Kodiak, return by some other ship to Desolation, and operate the new buildings as Catholic structures. But then the matter of Dmitri's wedding came up, and Healy, who was now quite drunk, stopped trying to understand what was happening. Jackson, who had anticipated this moment, stepped in, took charge, isolated Dmitri from the captain, and kept him on board the *Bear,* which carried him to Seattle and the ministrations of the good Presbyterians in that city.

In this manner, Desolation Point became a fountainhead of Presbyterianism in the north.

During one of Sheldon Jackson's later cruises, the *Bear* was at sea for more than six months, and the missionary became aware that two of the junior officers were showing signs of irritation about having to serve so long away from home port and with a black captain. He overheard one of the young fellows complaining as they finished work on the school at Cape Prince of Wales: "Have you noticed that Reverend Jackson, who's supposed to distribute money and materials impartially, always favors any school run by Presbyterians? Damn little for Baptists or Methodists, but it's only natural, him being a Presbyterian and so vehement about it."

After the *Bear* touched at Desolation Point, the other officer said: "I'd like to see an accounting of Jackson's funds. He gave three times as much money to the young minister here, and when I asked him about that, he said: 'This is my church,' but what that meant he didn't explain and I didn't ask."

The officers openly voiced their displeasure with Captain Healy when the *Bear* made a long detour to Cape Navarin for the ridiculous purpose of picking up Siberian reindeer for transplanting to Alaska to feed Eskimos who might otherwise starve. When one man asked: "Why are we doing this?" the captain replied: "To enable good people to stay alive," and the other said: "If God wanted reindeer to feed Alaskan Eskimos, He'd have put some on our side of the Bering," and Healy replied without rancor: "Dr. Jackson might argue that we're doing work that God overlooked."

But the young men had cause for complaint, because when the
Bear returned to those very natives to whom it had so generously
given gifts in appreciation of their assistance in rescuing American
seamen, and the ones who had promised they would sell reindeer to
help Alaskan Eskimos, the herders grew massively protective of their
animals and would not part with a single one. The officers watched
with growing bitterness as Healy sailed the *Bear* more than a thousand miles along the coastline of Siberia, pleading in vain for the
stubborn Asians to sell him reindeer, and the young men also noted
that Jackson was just as ineffective in trying to buy animals. At the
conclusion of this wasteful excursion, one of the officers wrote to his
father:

> This trip has been a shameful waste of government time and
> money. I begin to suspect that Jackson and Healy are plotting
> to sell their reindeer, if they ever get any, for private gain. The
> U.S. Gov't. could well investigate this scandal.

Despite the fevered efforts of the two would-be humanitarians, they
were able to purchase no reindeer at Cape Navarin, but farther north
at Cape Dezhnev, where the Siberian coastline turned sharply eastward toward America, they came upon a village which allowed them
to buy nineteen of their precious herd, but the same officer wrote:

> With persuasion so ardent that it was unbecoming in the rep-
> resentatives of a Great Democracy, they finally purchased
> nineteen animals, but at a cost per beast that was unconscio-
> nable. This whole affair smells.

On the choppy trip across the Chukchi Sea three of the reindeer died,
but sixteen did survive to become the foundation of a herd in the
Aleutians, with more to follow in later years.

The court-martial in which Captain Healy would soon find himself
enmeshed was partly his own fault, because once he had delivered the
reindeer, he should have headed back to his home port of San Francisco to allow his sea-weary crew shore leave. But he was so enam-
ored of the Bering Sea that he decided to make one last, quick scout
north—Jackson would ultimately make thirty-two different trips to
the land of the Chukchis—and it was on this sortie that he spotted an
American whaler, the *Adam Foster,* engaged in pelagic sealing. Run-

ning forward at full sail-and-steam, he drew alongside the offender and ordered his men to board, and when some thirty energetically obeyed, he and Jackson followed suit, leaping adroitly onto the captured ship.

However, the sealers, who stood to make a great deal of money if they could get their illegal catch to either Hawaii or China, put up a surprising defense, during which Healy suffered a wound to his left shoulder and a bleeding slash along his cheek. Infuriated by this act of what he deemed warfare, he urged his men to subdue the attackers, and when they did he calmed his temper and ordered three reprisals: "All rum and molasses into the scuppers. All pelts into the Bering. These six ringleaders and those three who assaulted me, trice them up!"

Jackson did not know what this horrendous word meant, but the young officers did, and as it was uttered, one moved to Jackson's side and whispered: "Oh, this should not be done! They're Americans." He made this protest because, erroneously, he believed that in a crisis the clergyman would have to side with him against Captain Healy and his drunken, profane behavior, but in this supposition, as he was about to find out, he was wrong. Jackson was not his man; he was Healy's.

So, much to the officers' horror, the nine sailors were triced up, that is, their hands were handcuffed behind their backs and ropes were passed through the cuffs and over a yardarm. Crewmen from the *Bear* then pulled on the loose ends of the ropes, and the miscreants were hauled just far enough aloft so their toes could barely reach the deck, and there in fierce agony they remained dangling for seven minutes, after which they were dropped, some of them senseless, to the deck.

Standing over them, Healy said: "You'll not take arms against a ship of the United States government," and one of the officers whispered to Jackson: "But they didn't take arms," and the missionary, who believed that crime deserved punishment, defended Healy: "The punished men were selling rum and killing pregnant seals."

Back aboard the *Bear,* two relevant things happened: Mike Healy, agitated by the pain from his wounds and the excitement of boarding a ship in midocean, got drunk, and one of the officers sought out Sheldon Jackson for an impassioned discussion of the afternoon's events: "No captain has the right to storm aboard another ship and trice up nine of its sailors."

"Captain Healy serves under orders to do just that. Stop unlawful sealing. Punish men and ships that sell alcohol to natives."

"But certainly not to trice men up by their wrists behind their backs. Reverend Jackson, that's inhuman!"

"It's the law of the sea. Always has been. An alternative to hanging. You ought to be glad he didn't keelhaul them."

The officer, appalled that a clergyman should defend such behavior, was goaded into saying something which, had he been a more sensitive young man, he would have regretted later: "You don't sound much like a Christian, defending a man like Healy."

Jackson rose from where he was seated on the edge of his bunk, pulled himself to his full height, looked up into the young man's eyes, and said: "Michael Healy in the Bering Sea reminds me of St. Peter on the Lake of Galilee. I'm sure Sailor Peter was a rough-and-tumble man, but he was Christ's chosen apostle on whom he founded his first church. The church in Alaska depends upon the good works of Captain Healy."

This comparison was so odious that the officer cried: "How can you say that about a man who blasphemes and gets drunk all the time?" and when Jackson snapped in reply: "I dare say Peter used rough language aboard his ship, too," the young man stormed from the cabin.

Late that night, when Healy was more or less recovered from his bout with the bottle, Jackson went to the captain's quarters, allowed the parrot to rest on his left shoulder, and said: "Michael, I'm afraid you and I have constructed permanent enemies in your young officers. They can't understand why you don't behave like a storybook sea captain, and they certainly think I ought to be like every minister they knew back home."

"They're young, Sheldon. Never had to captain a ship. Never chased the *Erebus* back and forth across the Bering Sea."

"They think I ought to condemn you because of your blasphemy and your drinking."

"I think you should, too. But on the other hand, I think you forgot you were a minister of the Lord when you made young Father Dmitri turn Presbyterian in order to keep the church we gave him." To halt such lugubrious thoughts, Healy snapped his fingers: "They want us to be gods, but we're only men."

The two reprobates talked long into the cold night, speculating now and then on what the young officers might be plotting.

• • •

They soon found out, for when the *Bear* doubled back to Kodiak with three prisoners taken at the Pribilofs, the officers dispatched a telegram to the headquarters of the revenue cutter service in San Francisco, lodging serious charges against their commanding officer:

> Michael Healy, captain of the revenue cutter *Bear* has been consistently drunk on duty to the impairment of his responsibilities, has repeatedly used vulgar and abusive language against his officers and men, and has behaved with extreme cruelty to nine American sailors from the whaler *Adam Foster*. As officers under his command, we request that he be court-martialed.

By the time the *Bear* returned to its duty station off the coast of Siberia, the *Adam Foster* had docked in San Francisco, giving the local newspaper people a horrendous account of its run-in with the *Bear* and of Captain Healy's unwarranted tricing up of nine American sailors.

However, in the scandal that developed in the California papers, a force much more powerful than the captain of the *Adam Foster* entered the guerilla warfare against Mike Healy. Mrs. Danforth Weigle, president of the San Francisco Woman's Christian Temperance Union, had been searching for some time to find a foolproof case against some ship's captain who abused his men while under the influence of John Barleycorn, and when she read the lurid accounts of Mike Healy's behavior, she and her entire membership lodged formal complaints against him, demanding that he be summoned home, court-martialed, and dismissed from the service. Now all the envious people who had felt that this Negro mariner was growing bigger than his britches united to call for his trial and dismissal.

Bowing to the public clamor and especially to the pressures brought by the W.C.T.U., Healy's superiors had no alternative but to wire him at Kodiak to return immediately to San Francisco to defend himself in a general court-martial against charges of drunkenness, gross and improper behavior toward subordinates and, in the case of nine American sailors, the use of cruel punishment long outmoded in the navies of civilized nations.

He had left Kodiak long before the telegram arrived and spent the summer in the far reaches of the northern seas. During his sail south at the end of the season he learned of the statements made against him, and discussed them with Reverend Jackson: "They mean to do me in, Sheldon. The captain of the *Adam Foster* bringing charges! I should have had him hanged from his own yardarm."

It was Jackson who foresaw the real danger in the threatened court-martial: "The women, Michael. They'll prove the most powerful of your enemies. I've always found the women to be the final arbiters."

"Can I count upon you for support?"

"To the end, but I am worried."

"You'll come to San Francisco? Testify for me?"

"You're the best captain there's ever been in the Bering Sea, Russian or American."

"James Cook was up here, you know."

"I didn't include the English."

So it was agreed that Healy and Jackson would make a united stand against the considerable forces arrayed against the former, but Jackson's promised testimony did not come to pass, because when the *Bear* put into Sitka to disembark him, the doughty little clergyman faced a kind of court-martial of his own, for a special investigator with plenipotentiary powers had been dispatched from Washington to check upon the numerous charges of malfeasance lodged against him. Although he was not thrown into jail this time, it was obvious that he would not be able to go to San Francisco to testify in defense of his friend, for he had to save his own neck.

The court-martial of Michael Healy was a solemn, miserable affair. Five senior officers from the nation's armed services sat in judgment of a popular hero gone sour, and the very newspapers which had inflated his reputation as the savior of the north now seemed to revel in his debasement as a tyrant, a brute, a foul-mouthed rascal and a drunk, but this was understandable, because in the opening days of the trial the evidence against him was devastating. Clean-looking young sailors from the *Adam Foster* testified, one after another, that whereas they had done nothing wrong, "merely tried to protect our ship, as you gentlemen would do, he comes aboard, abuses us, and trices us up." They explained in harrowing detail what *trice up* meant, and one man showed the court scars that resulted from the seven-minute ordeal when handcuffs had cut into his wrists. The marks were vivid.

The nails were hammered into Healy's coffin by Mrs. Danforth Weigle, of the W.C.T.U., who had long visualized this trial as the triumph of her organization's fight against alcohol on American ships. A fine-looking woman, with a low, cultured voice and not a crusading harridan at all, she made an impressive witness, for her testimony was brief and to the point: "American sailors have for too long been victimized by drunken brutes who have tyrannized their men once they sailed from port and left the protection of courts ashore. No case more savage than that of Captain Michael Healy has come to our attention, and we demand that he be sent to jail for his crimes and dropped from the service of the United States."

She asked that members of her committee who specialized in legal aspects of the problem be allowed to testify, and these ladies completed the devastating case against the black officer. When the prosecution closed, most observers in the stuffy courtroom supposed that Healy's fate was sealed, and stories resembling obituaries appeared in the papers, lamenting this deplorable conclusion to a career which had had its moments of nobility, as when the *Bear,* on various rescue missions, saved many sailors whose ships were trapped in ice.

But traditions of the sea run deep, and when the prosecution rested, a parade of the ordinary seamen whose lives Mike Healy had saved from shipwreck came forward to testify in his behalf. Junior officers who had served under him were eager to tell of how his indomitable will had saved the *Bear* when crushing in the ice pack seemed inevitable. A representative of the Russian Empire told the court of how, when he was stationed in Petropavlovsk, his officers looked to Mike Healy and the *Bear* as their right arm along the Siberian coast, and there was a moment of terrible drama when a survivor of a shipwreck at Point Hope took the stand:

"We lost our ship when the ice come in sudden in October. We was nine men made it ashore. The rest went down."

"Did you get any ship's supplies ashore with you?"

"Some."

"How long were you marooned?"

"Till June next year."

"How did you survive?"

"We built lean-tos against the wind. Driftwood."

"I mean eat? What did you eat?"

"We shot two caribou. We rationed careful. We ate bacon rind, anything." Here he paused, looked away from the court, and sought the eyes of his salvation, Mike Healy. "Then he come with the *Bear.*"

"Go on. What then?"

In a very low voice, which did not reach to the back of the room, he said: "He knew from lookin' that in April and May when there were no caribou, no stores, we'd been forced to eat the bodies of them as died."

The last words were lost in whisper, and the court asked the sailor to repeat, but a man in the front row of the audience said clearly: "They were cannibals," and the room fell into confusion. When order was restored, the sailor said: "Captain Healy knowed what we'd done . . . been forced to do, that is . . . and he took us under his wing like we was his children. No sermons, no lectures. I remember exactly what he said: 'We are all men of the sea. We plow a fearful furrow.'"

The room was silent as the sailor stepped down, and at that juncture it was clear that the five-man court was not at all as certain of Healy's guilt as it had been the day before, but he would still have been found guilty of at least certain charges had there not been a commotion at the rear of the court, with the marshal shouting: "You can't go in there!" and a gruff voice responding: "We're goin' in!" and into the proceedings came a six-foot-four mariner with a huge head of snowy white hair and beard, followed by two junior officers and an ordinary seaman.

"Who are you, barging in like this?" the president of the court demanded, and the intruder said: "Cap'n Emil Schransky, *Erebus,* out of New Bedford," and he said that since maritime matters were under judgment here, he demanded a right to testify.

"Would your testimony be pertinent?" the presiding officer asked, and he replied: "It would."

He was allowed to come forward, and without even looking at his old enemy, he began in a restrained voice: "If there is any San Francisco newspaperman present, he'll be able to verify that for better'n ten years me and Mike Healy, the man on trial, fought each other up and down the Bering Sea. He was for the Eskimo, I didn't give a damn. He was against pelagic sealin', it was my gold mine. He fought anyone who brought rum or molasses to the Eskimos, I didn't. Year after year I outwitted him because I always had the best ship. Then he got the *Bear* with its steam engine and defeated me. Almost sunk me. Threatened to shoot me if I ever invaded his sea again. I said to myself: Schransky, you had the best ship and did what you pleased. Now he has the best ship and he'll do what he pleases."

"But what did you do?"

"I said: 'Let him run the Bering as he likes. The Pacific is a big place.' I left."

"Why did you come here today?"

"Because me and my men read what you were doin' to Mike Healy. What the people from the *Adam Foster* whined about. The *Adam Foster*! What a pitiful ship. What a ship to bring charges against anybody. My men wouldn't waste time spittin' at the *Adam Foster,*" and his three associates nodded.

"And these good women ravin' about his drinkin'. What did he do when he finally captured the *Erebus*? Dumped all our rum and molasses down the scuppers. Ask the *Adam Foster* what he did when he captured them. I'll bet they'll say first thing he did was dump their rum. Healy was fierce against alcohol for Eskimos."

He concluded his testimony with a surprising statement: "I fought Healy for a decade, and always I had the best ship. But he fought me like a tiger, because he represents the best traditions of the sea. Even a master ship like the *Bear* is no good unless it has a master like Healy. That damned nigger with his parrot drove me from the arctic seas, and no lesser man could've done it. And if we went to sea again, we'd still fight, and the man with the best ship would win." From the witness stand he saluted his longtime enemy and retired to the back of the room followed by his men.

The judges filed out, returned after the briefest possible consultation, and rendered their verdict: "The citizens who lodged charges against Captain Michael Healy did not do so frivolously. His actions must have seemed deplorable to them. But the sea is governed by noble traditions accumulated through centuries and from the experience of many nations. Unless they are enforced by captains like Michael Healy, no ship can sail safely. This court finds him Not Guilty on all charges." The audience, divided sixty percent for conviction, forty for acquittal, groaned and cheered while Emil Schransky rose from his seat, uttered a wild yell, and saluted Healy once more.

When order was restored, the court continued with its verdict: "But since not even the ablest captain can be allowed free rein for intemperate behavior at sea or for abusive language directed against his subordinates, this court must take into account that on three past occasions Captain Healy has received severe reprimands for drunkenness and misconduct, 1872, 1888, 1890. We recommend that he be deprived of command for a period of two years."

But his turbulent life continued. In 1900, on his first trip after regaining his command, he escaped a most serious court-martial pertaining to his abuse of a woman passenger only when his protectors had him declared temporarily insane, and in 1903, at the conclusion of his final command, he was again reprimanded for "unofficerlike and indecent language in the presence of his officers and crew." Unrepentant, he moved ashore, and died a year later.

In Sitka the government's case against Sheldon Jackson rehashed old charges against him, but with new and more effective citizens making them. As the population of Alaska grew, the numbers of miners, businessmen and saloonkeepers increased proportionately, and these groups had always been violently anti-Jackson, but since their speakers were now more literate, they painted him in dark and dictatorial colors: "He wants to tell everyone how to behave, but he himself is an unchristian, ungodly tyrant." He had also acquired a new body of enemies, the members of the Russian Orthodox Church, who felt that if the little missionary wanted to declare war against their church and their language, which he obviously did, they would take up arms against him. Most telling was a voice not heard before, and therefore extra persuasive: "If Reverend Jackson spends six months a year attending to personal business in Washington, and six months cruising with his drunken crony on the *Bear,* how much time per year has he left to mind his duties in Alaska?"

At the conclusion of this round of testimony, things looked gloomy for Jackson, but the investigator was no fool, and before issuing his conclusions he sought a secret meeting with Carl Caldwell, now a full-fledged judge in the Alaskan court, who confided: "Everything his enemies say about Jackson is true. But his enemies say the same thing about me, and if you set up your office here, they'd lodge the same charges against you. Nobody can be neutral where Jackson is concerned. He often irritates me, and I'm sure he'd irritate you. But you must have deduced from the character of his enemies that he's one of the best forces in Alaska. He represents the future."

Paralleling the court-martial in San Francisco, the government man in Sitka began by conceding that the charges against Jackson had been brought in good faith, and he said so; there were many reasons why men of serious mind could dislike this obstreperous little man, but like Mike Healy, he was necessary for the well-being of his society. So the verdict had to be: "All charges dropped with prejudice," which meant, as Caldwell explained: "They can't be revived again."

But of course that applied only to Alaska, because when Jackson returned to Washington, members of his own church conspired against him, bringing charges of misapplication of funds, disobedience to orders and arrogance in the conduct of his missionary efforts. But his defenders pointed out that while others sat in offices pondering the niceties of formal administration, he had been on the firing line, sleeves rolled up and winning souls to God. His loyal women, seeking to remind the public of his astonishing accomplishments, published a small pamphlet summarizing his work:

> In unflagging dedication to God's work from Colorado to Arizona to Montana to Alaska, with yearly returns to Washington to instruct Congress, he traveled more than a million miles using every known form of transportation, including his own feet. He organized from scratch more than seventy congregations, for whom he personally built more than forty church buildings. He often gave four or five speeches in one day for a total that ran into many thousands, and church organizations launched by him collected for missionary and other religious work a proved total of $20,364,475, for in the work of the Lord he was tireless. We shall not soon again see his like.

But perhaps the most revealing portrait of this contentious little man, who continued all his days to make friends and enemies in equal proportion, can be found in his battle with the Post Office Department, of which he was a paid official. It was his belief that since the Great Land was now American, its villages should carry respectable American names, and since he had the right to choose the names, he saw no reason why they should not honor the Presbyterians who had helped civilize the new territory. Accordingly, he dumped fine old Eskimo and Tlingit names and replaced them with ones like Young, Hill, Rankin, Gould, Willard and especially Norcross and Voorhees, good Presbyterians all, the last two being relatives of his whom he wished to honor. One of his most interesting switches was getting rid of Chilkoot, attached to a beautiful village west of Skagway; for it he substituted *Haines,* the name of the chairwoman of the Presbyterian Women's Committee, who had never seen Alaska but who had contributed generously to Jackson's support. His principal change, however, was to drop the historic old Tlingit name of Howkan in favor of his own, Jackson.

This caused a furor, for the residents did not want to lose their historic designation. Jackson, however, was adamant, and pestered Washington to ignore local complaints and retain the new name, which honored him. But when the Democrats assumed national leadership under Grover Cleveland, the Post Office Department restored the name but spelled it Howcan, at which Jackson, with a burst of spleen which proved he had no shame or sense of the ridiculous, deluged Washington with requests that Howcan be changed back to its proper name, Jackson. He accomplished nothing, but when the Republicans rewon the presidency, he sent a sharp letter to John Wanamaker, the new and Presbyterian postmaster general:

> With the Republicans again in power we expect to receive just consideration. . . . During Cleveland's administration the Democrats had it changed back to Howkan, out of opposition to myself. With our Republican victory, it became Jackson again. Now I hear there is a local movement to make it Howkan once more. Please notify the clerk in charge of these proposals that you wish it left Jackson, and greatly oblige.

But his foes prevailed, and changed the name back to a misspelled Howcan.

The two American giants in Alaska, Michael Healy and Sheldon Jackson, were in some ways reminiscent of the two earlier giants Vitus Bering and Aleksandr Baranov. In each instance the first of the pair was an imposing sea captain who exerted his will and his command over the northern oceans, while the second member was insignificant or even comic in appearance but gargantuan in determination to forge ahead despite opposition. Each of the pairs left an indelible imprint on Alaska, especially the second and less imposing members, but the greater similarity seems to be that each of these four explorers and dreamers was a badly flawed man. They were not resplendent conquerors like Alexander the Great or continent builders like Charlemagne. They were ordinary men who drank too much or were foolishly vain or who started things they did not finish or who were objects of ridicule to their colleagues. All four were subjected to official harassment or legal investigations or the censure of court-martial, and each ended his life in a kind of disgrace.

Alaska did not produce supermen, but in its formative periods it was served by men of character and determination, and it is a fortunate land which knows such public servants.

VIII

GOLD

THE CATACLYSMIC INCIDENTS WHICH PRODUCED THE SCENIC grandeurs of Alaska began at least a hundred and twenty million years ago, but the events which gave rise to the most dramatic development in Alaskan history started much earlier.

About eighteen billion years ago, insofar as science can determine from signals left behind, an explosion of indescribable magnitude took place, and what had previously been a void became occupied by gigantic clouds of cosmic dust. Different men with different insights or mind-sets have described this beginning of the beginning in different ways, but regardless of its cause, the event seems to have set our universe spinning; all that happened thereafter stemmed from its complexity and overpowering force.

We cannot reasonably guess what happened to the major portion of the dust thus set in movement, but about nine billion years ago a minor portion—staggering in size though only a fraction—began to coalesce into what would ultimately become the galaxy of which we are a part. In this galaxy some two hundred billion stars would form, the one we see rising each morning as our sun being one of the smaller. We must not take too much pride in our galaxy, wonderful as it is, because it is merely one of more than a billion; quite often the others are greater in dimension and larger in their starry populations.

About six billion years ago an immense agglomeration of cosmic dust within our galaxy began assuming the shape of a huge swirl much like the ones we will see in the heavens this night if we have a good telescope, for all the processes here mentioned are still being repeated in other parts of the universe. Out of this swirling mass of cosmic particles a star began to evolve and with it the nine or ten accompanying planets which together would make up our solar system. Our sun, therefore, is probably about six billion years old, with some of the planets slightly younger.

Now our figures become more precise. About four and a half billion years ago cosmic dust somehow related to what was happening in the sun began to agglomerate into what would ultimately become our earth. For the first billion years of its existence the earth seems to have been a turbulent cauldron in which violent physical and chemical alterations were taking place.

Composed at first mainly of hydrogen and helium, the interior of the earth accumulated such heat and pressure that nuclear reactions occurred, and out of them began to take form the more than one hundred distinct elements upon which the earth would be constructed. Iron, one of the principal elements, being heavier than most, concentrated in the central core, where in a part molten, part solid form it would exert the unifying force which held the earth together, determine much of its movement, establish the magnetic poles, and lend stability to the whole. Mixed with generous amounts of nickel, this central core of iron helped in manifold ways to keep the earth functioning.

At the center, in a heat inconceivable, under pressures never known on the surface and driven by nuclear reactions, the semiliquid components of the earth were sorted out, forming all the basic elements which would later comprise the earth as we know it. Essential substances as diverse as lead, sulfur, nitrogen and arsenic emerged, each with its peculiar atomic weight, each with its preassigned and unique position among its neighbors.

One of these elements, Number 79 in line with an atomic weight of 196.9, which made it conspicuously heavy, was a bright metal with an alluring appearance and a curious set of propensities. Gold, far from copious in its distribution throughout the mass of the earth, had a specific gravity nineteen times that of water, so that if any one of the major oceans had been comprised of gold rather than water, its sheer weight could have collapsed the system.

A major characteristic of gold was its reluctance to react with other elements, staying stubbornly to itself. In this respect it differed strikingly from the element carbon, which formed relationships with almost any substance with which it came into contact. Carbon formed more than four hundred thousand different compounds, gold almost none. Also, carbon metamorphosed itself into an almost endless chain of useful or valuable products: petroleum, carbon black, anthracite, graphite and limestone. A notable characteristic of carbon was its capacity to restructure itself late in the life of earth, when altered conditions produced altered forms. Thus diamonds, one of the spectacular manifestations of carbon, did not come into being until relatively late, when a unique combination of elementary material, heat and pressure transformed carbon into something quite dazzling.

Gold, on the contrary, began as gold, and remained gold, despite the hammering of heat, and atomic reactions, and the ever-present invitation of other metals to join them in exotic new combinations. Gold tended to associate with the heavier elements related to iron, but it also showed a slight affinity for sulfur. It combined occasionally with the exotic mineral tellurium, but refused to do so with oxygen, the way so many other minerals did. There would be no gold oxide. Gold did not rust.

Because of its insularity, gold was known as a noble metal, an adjective applied also to those rare gases which refused to combine with other gases. The word did not refer to lineage, or attractive appearance, or value; a metal or a gas was *noble* if it stood by itself, had great persistence and a reluctance to deform itself in union with another element. According to such definitions, gold was certainly a noble metal.

It seems to have moved upward from its originating cauldron by following fissures in rocky formations, depositing itself here and there in arbitrary and diverse patterns. At times, like any other liquid under pressure, it found some convenient crevice and spread laterally, coming to rest at various levels, never in great concentrations like lead or sulfur, but in areas so widely scattered that no logical reason could explain their placement.

When man succeeded in exploring most of the surface of the earth, he would find deposits of gold in places as varied as Australia, California, South Africa and on the banks of a trivial snowbound stream on the Canada-Alaska border, close to the Arctic Circle.

Gold could be found in two dramatically different circumstances. Like other metallic elements, copper and lead for example, it might rest well below the surface of the earth in concentrations laid down millions of years earlier. This gold would be mined, as metals have been mined for some four thousand years, and there would be no great difference between the mining of gold and the mining of the other metals. A deep shaft would be sunk; walls would be shored up by timbers; and at promising levels laterals would be sent out to explore veins.

What would be found in such a below-the-surface gold mine? Not concentrations of the noble metal, waiting to be dug out and brought to the surface. What was common was a quartz rock containing flecks of gold so minute that the unpracticed eye could scarcely recognize them. A find of tremendous value would be a hunk of quartz whose cross section showed traces of gold no larger than pinpoints— not pinheads—and so widely dispersed that the uninstructed would have to look twice to see them.

Such rock, broken loose from its underground hiding places and brought to the surface, would be crushed and sluiced with water, and now the weight of gold became important, for invariably it would sink to the bottom, where it would be trapped in riffles while the apparently heavier but lighter quartz rock was carried off by the water. To mine gold in this way required courage to delve into the earth, dynamite to break the quartz loose, and a constant flow of water to sluice the crushed mixture.

The second way of finding gold was the more exciting. Through millions of years as the upper crust of the earth shifted and rose and fell, veins of rock containing minute traces of gold were exposed to the elements, allowing abrasion to take place. Freezing winters fractured the quartz; incessantly dripping water broke down the rock; gravel at the bottom of swift-moving streams acted like sandpaper on wood; and volcanic displacement brought to the surface new deposits to be abraded.

As the suddenly released flecks of gold found their freedom, their fate was determined by their weight. They moved for a while with the motion of whatever stream was carrying them, then irresistibly they fell to the bottom, and as they came to rest, certain hydrodynamic forces dictated where they would accumulate. If a stream was tumbling headlong down an incline, they would seem to be almost internally driven to seek some quiet nook in which to escape the turbulence.

If a quiet creek was meandering over fairly level land, its cargo of gold would fall into some outer curve where the relative speed of the water slowed. But all the flecks came to rest somewhere.

The finding of this surface gold was known as *placer* mining—the word rhymed with *gasser*—and the mark of the placer miner was a man with a beard holding a tin basin beside a creek, panning a load of gravel to see if it showed colors, flecks of gold, then building a crude sluice of some kind to bring lots of water to wash away lots and lots of gravel. To find gold locked in quartz, a man had to dig deep into the earth; to find placer gold in its easier locations, one sometimes had to dig only two feet and lift up not tons of rocks but only a covering of gravel or sand.

Through centuries of gold seeking, men had devised a dozen rules of thumb to guide them in locating where placer gold was hiding, and men who had been on the various gold fields became uncanny in their ability to find the noble mineral. If you brought onto a new field a gang of men practiced in the fields of Australia, California and South Africa, they would find the gold, while amateurs from Idaho, London and Chicago would not.

Three practical rules seemed to prevail. The first knowledgeable men on a new field preempted the good spots; those who arrived late found little or nothing. However, the second rule kept the hopes of the general public alive; just often enough some lucky prospector who knew nothing about gold stumbled upon colors, scouted about, and by sheer chance staked himself a bonanza. This did not happen often, but it did happen.

The third rule was not widely understood, but it accounted for some of the great finds. In seeking placer gold, one followed stream beds, because moving water was the only possible agency by which placers could be deposited. But since the gold had been laid down over millions of years, and since a stream could wander notoriously during even one man's brief lifetime, what the prospector should investigate was not necessarily the little stream as it existed today but the mighty one that might have existed a thousand years ago, or a hundred thousand, or even a million. Perhaps, along the Yukon River and its tributaries in 1896, the place to look for gold was not along the banks of the Klondike, that magical stream with the magical name, but on ridges hundreds of feet high where some river of significance had laid down its gold three hundred thousand years earlier.

• • • •

In the summer of 1896 a broken-down American prospector with an unfavorable reputation because of his propensity for lying, George Washington Carmack, happened to strike up an acquaintance with a dour, proper Scotsman born in Canada. Robert Henderson could have laid claim to the title *gentleman* had he preferred, for he favored strict personal behavior and austere business rectitude. Had he no weaknesses? He was an inveterate snob.

The two formed a solid but unlikely partnership, because although each was willing to work hard and undergo privation when seeking gold, there was one difference which superseded all others. Carmack was a squaw man, legally married to an Indian woman whose two shiftless brothers, Shookum Jim and Tagish Charley, occasionally helped him in his prospecting. Henderson did not countenance this; he was honor-bound to share information and potential profits with Carmack, even though Lying George, as he was called, did have an Indian wife, but he could not tolerate the two brothers-in-law. Therefore, when Henderson announced that he had made a find on a small tributary to the Thron-diuck River, which debouched into the Yukon, Carmack and his two Indians went over the hills to help him develop his find and share in the profits. But Henderson made things so unpleasant for the Indians, refusing insolently to sell them tobacco, that Carmack decided to reject his share of the claim and strike out on his own.

The three men, leaving Henderson to his modest find, climbed over the hills to the west and started their own prospecting on Rabbit Creek, an insignificant tributary to the Thron-diuck. There, on the afternoon of 17 August 1896, they sluiced the gravel from their pan and found settled on the bottom gold flakes and nuggets worth four dollars. Since a pan which showed gold worth ten cents was known as an exciting find, Carmack and his brothers-in-law realized that they had struck a bonanza. Hasty additional trials maintained the exhilarating average of four dollars a pan.

In the wild excitement, Carmack remembered that he had two obligations to discharge, one moral, one legal. Morally he must inform his partner Henderson of the find, but he was so irritated by the latter's treatment of the two Indians that he remained on his side of the mountain, leaving Henderson unaware of the stupendous discovery and unable to share in it.

Carmack's legal obligation could not be avoided. When a miner found gold he was required to do two things: file a proper claim with the government and immediately inform other miners as to where his find was and its probable richness, so that they could stake their claims. Carmack, leaving the Indians to guard his rights, sped down the Yukon to the old mining town of Fortymile on the left bank of the river, and there he staked his title to what would thereafter be known as the *Discovery Claim*, five hundred feet running along the bank of Rabbit Creek and across it on both flanks to the crest of the first rise.

His legal obligations discharged, he then proceeded to the saloon, where he announced at the top of his voice: "The biggest strike of all!"

He also laid claim to three other five-hundred-foot sites: *Number One Above, Number One Below* and *Number Two Below.* Carmack, as the principal claimant, was entitled to *Discovery* and *One Below,* the other two were for Shookum Jim and Tagish Charley. Henderson's interest was not protected.

The habitues in the little settlement, accustomed to Carmack's lying ways, refused to believe that he had found anything. However, when he produced the empty rifle cartridge in which he kept his largest nuggets and dumped it onto the assayer's scales, the men's eyes widened. As prospectors long in the field—and meager scatterings of gold had been known in this region for a dozen years—they were familiar with the qualities of gold peculiar to each site along the Yukon. This came from none of the established mines. It was new gold; its quality was supreme; and the size of the nuggets suggested that it came from a major find, not from the weak tail of some small placer.

The great gold rush was on! Before nightfall, hungry prospectors from Fortymile were speeding upriver to stake their claims above and below Carmack's *Discovery.* When fresh hordes streamed in they rejected the traditional names of these trivial streams. The Throndiuck, a name of maximum difficulty which no one could pronounce, was quickly changed to the Klondike. Carmack's little Rabbit Creek was given the traditional gold-field name Bonanza, while an even smaller contributor—which would prove richer than any of the others—was appropriately called Eldorado. It was these enchanting names that would flash around the world.

Almost every facet of this fabulous stampede, perhaps the largest in history, had its ironic aspect, none more striking than the one which launched the field. Said a Canadian in a letter home to his wife:

> *We Canadians are resentful of the fact that our fellow countryman Robert Henderson, of Nova Scotia, New Zealand and Australia, has been so badly treated in these gold fields. We are certain that he made the first find and that the disreputable American, the squaw man George Carmack, and his Indian helpers defrauded him of his rightful claim to half their find.*
>
> *However, I must confide to you alone, and do not speak of this to anyone, but I think that maybe Henderson deserved what he got. I heard him say long before the find was made that "I do not (ugly words) propose to let any (ugly words) Indian (ugly words) share in my finds of gold."*
>
> *We have reason to believe that Carmack's strike is so wonderfully rich that Henderson's refusal to work with Indians has lost him more than two million dollars.*

A second irony of the great discovery on the Klondike was that although it occurred in mid-August 1896 and was widely known along the Yukon, verifiable word of its amazing richness did not reach the Outside until 15 July 1897. How could information of such a bonanza, to borrow the name of the creek where it happened, be so long concealed?

The Yukon River, 1,993 miles long with much of its course close to the arctic, freezes early, some parts in September, and thaws late, some segments not until June or occasionally July. So for those months, August 1896 till July of the next year, Carmack and his fellow millionaires were frozen in with their secret. But now a determined little Yukon River boat, the sternwheeler *Alice,* of meager draft, forced a passage through the June ice and puffed into Dawson City, the boomtown, which incoming miners from the region had hastily constructed at the mouth of the Klondike.

When the crew learned of the tremendous strike and saw the boxes and bundles of gold the lucky prospectors intended taking to the Outside, they quickly unloaded the life-saving fruit and vegetables they had brought to the near-starving community and turned their little craft around in hours, loaded it with the new millionaires, and headed downstream to where ocean liners would be waiting near the mouth of the Yukon. As the *Alice* pulled out of Dawson another sternwheeler arrived, so that all the miners who wished to return to the States found passage.

After a journey of nearly fourteen hundred miles, the two little boats reached the Bering Sea, where they turned north to deposit their historic cargo of men and gold at the entrepôt of St. Michael. There, after several days of vast dinners consisting of fresh fruit, vegetables and delicious canned foods, heavy in vitamins to fight off the incipient scurvy from which so many suffered, the argonauts with their gold were lightered out to either the *Excelsior,* bound for San Francisco, or the more famous *Portland,* for Seattle.

As the two steamers approached mainland United States, few passengers could anticipate the storm of publicity they were about to cause, for they assumed that news of their staggering finds must have percolated to the outer world. Word had been forwarded to Canadian officials, who dismissed it as just one more exaggerated report from the Yukon: "We know there's gold up there. Always has been. But never in such amounts." Also, a daring dog-team driver had made a heroic trip up the Yukon and across the forbidding Chilkoot Pass to alert American officials stationed in that area, but since these men could not believe the extent of the find, word was not sent south. And a Chicago newspaper received an account from one of its reporters, but since they did not trust him, they printed almost nothing.

The *Portland* achieved immortality by accident, for although she left Alaska first and made the long journey home in less than a month, and although her course was shorter than the *Excelsior*'s, she did not arrive in Seattle until two days after the latter had already docked in San Francisco. There was, of course, some excitement along the California waterfront, but its newspapers failed to appreciate the magnitude of what had happened at the Klondike.

William Randolph Hearst's fledgling *Examiner,* always eager for spectacular stories, almost ignored the arrival of the gold, and only cursory stories were circulated nationally by rival San Francisco papers, the *Call* and the *Chronicle.*

However, by the time the laggard *Portland* pulled into Schwabacher's Wharf in Seattle on the morning of 17 July, the citizens of that city had already been informed by San Francisco that adventurous men with great hoards of gold were coming home. An imaginative reporter, one Beriah Brown, who deserves to be remembered, had shown ingenuity by going out at dusk in a little boat to intercept the incoming ship and had through the night interviewed its passengers. Preparing his story for that day's papers, he pondered how most effectively to report this striking story, and he must have considered phrases like "a huge amount of gold" and "much gold" and "a treasure trove of gold." Discarding them all, he hit upon one of the memorable phrases of American journalism:

> At 3 o'clock this morning the Steamer *Portland* from St. Michael for Seattle, passed up the Sound with more than a ton of solid gold aboard.

Those words, "a ton of gold," sped across a nation hungry for the metal and seriously in need of it. In banks, in small business houses, in homes where killing mortgages had to be paid off, and in the hearts of men yearning for a more accommodating money system, the words "a ton of gold" became an enchantment, a lure that could not be resisted.

How did men react to this thundering bugle call? In a small Idaho town one John Klope, unmarried and embittered by reverses, heard the summons and cried: "At last! Gold for all!"

And in a cramped, rickety house in a mean quarter of Chicago, a man whose optimistic father had named him after a President of the United States, Buchanan Venn, was forty years old and disgusted by how sadly his life had deteriorated. Half afraid to voice the revolutionary thoughts which assailed him, he whispered to himself: "Dear God! Perhaps!"

In the northern corner of Idaho's panhandle, not far from the Canadian border, lay the little town of Moose Hide. It was visited by no railroad, for the trans-Canada line ran to the north through Winnipeg and Calgary, while the nearest American road, from Chicago to Seattle, ran to a junction some miles to the south at Bonners Ferry.

News came late to Moose Hide, and good news sometimes not at all, so on the eighteenth day of July 1897, its citizens did not learn from their newspaper, for they had none, of the arrival in Seattle the day previous of a ton of gold. John Klope, a taciturn young man of twenty-seven, remained ignorant of an event which would in due course mean much to him.

Klope was the son of an Idaho farmer who had in the race of life kept just a few yards ahead of both the sheriff and president of the small bank in Coeur d'Alene to whom he had mortgaged his farm some years before. In order to help pay off this loan, son John had had to quit school at thirteen to work at any jobs available, but since these were years when the supply of gold in the United States was severely limited and the circulation of paper money even more so, the Klopes had a difficult time paying off their mortgage. But because they stinted themselves on the luxuries of life and many of the necessities, they succeeded. The farm was now theirs, but it represented not a bountiful life, only the victory of Slavic stubbornness.

Incredible as it might seem to others who took pride in their ancestry, John Klope did not know for sure where his ancestors had originated, or what their name had been in the old country. In school his mates had called him "that Polack," but from something his father said one evening, he judged that he was not Polish; however, the alternative was not spelled out, and he concluded, correctly, that the original Klopes had lived in a territory near the Carpathian Mountains which had changed hands many times. He was satisfied with that status, which was good, because his father could not have clarified the ancestry had he wished, and his mother knew even less about hers.

He was John Klope, not a Pole, not a Scandinavian and not a German—merely an American and happy to be one, like many of his neighbors. In the Klope family one never heard the lament "I wish I'd'a stayed in the old country," because if vague fragments of memory did adhere to that cliché, they were not pleasant.

Klope did not resent the fact that because of poverty he had been denied an education, for he would have had little success in any subjects then being taught, but he did most furiously object to the stranglehold which banks and the money system imposed upon the lives of hardworking families like his, and had he chanced to live in some large city, Chicago or St. Louis, he might well have become radicalized. Sometimes in the evening when the young men of Moose Hide lounged on the street corner after supper, John would listen to those brighter than he explain the difficulties under which the local farmers suffered, and he would say nothing, but later, when the discussion had changed to girls, he would suddenly blurt out: "The man who has the gold sets the rules."

In 1893, when terrible panic gripped the nation and when the freight trains of the Great Northern chugging in to Bonners Ferry carried little cargo, Klope's preoccupation with gold seemed less arbitrary, for now neighbors who had not paid off their mortgages began to feel the icy sting of the nation's inadequate money system. Farm after farm was foreclosed, and many young people with whom he had associated when he still attended school had to move away to the slums of cities like Chicago and San Francisco.

This painful removal of people had an effect upon Klope that even he did not understand at the time. During his school years he had been vaguely aware of a small, lively farm girl named Elsie Luderstrom; he had never approached her and certainly he had never walked her home, but he knew that she was kindly inclined toward him and he felt that when they both grew older he might very well want to speak with Elsie. Before he could do so, her family farm was taken back by the bank and she was whisked away in the silence of the night, as it were, to Omaha.

He never saw her again, but with her departure went his chance for a normal life of awkward courtship at nineteen, marriage at twenty-two, children at twenty-four, and the inheritance of either his father's farm or hers in his thirties. Without his knowing it, Elsie Luderstrom had held the key to his life, and the key had been lost.

"Banks is what did them in," he growled one night as the young men met, and from that solemn judgment, not entirely correct but still relevant, he began to focus upon the need for a man to control his own sources of wealth. A farm was not enough; what seemed at the moment to be a good job on the Great Northern was not enough; and even one's own responsible character was inadequate, for there were no better men in America than Klope's father and Elsie's. They had struggled; they had saved; they had been frugal; and they had been overtaken by this nationwide panic. If there was in all America one young man to whom the call of Klondike gold would seem imperative, it was John Klope.

On the afternoon of 20 July 1897 he heard about the strike. A business traveler from Seattle to Chicago had changed trains in Spokane and come up to Bonners Ferry and made the customary joke: "Where's the ferry?" and old-timers had explained for the fiftieth time: "It used to cross the Kootenai," and later the jokester would refer to it as "the Hootenanny which runs through Bonners Ferry." Many local people would have been just as happy if such travelers stayed home, but this one brought sensational news, for he carried with him newspapers from Seattle, and when people in the rooming house read the headlines and asked if they could have one of the papers, he said: "Keep it. I'm sure the Chicago papers will have the story."

By afternoon of 20 July word had filtered up to Moose Hide, and it so excited John Klope that he dashed in to Bonners Ferry and asked to see the man who had brought the news. When he found him, he asked: "They said you had two papers. Could I see one?"

"Here, with my compliments." Then he laughed: "If you go to the gold fields, good luck."

On the way home Klope stopped three times to read the article about the ton of gold, and he became so excited that by the time he reached his farm he was prepared to leave immediately for the Klondike. There was nothing to stop him. He was not really needed to run the farm; his mother and father between them could have managed a place four times the size of their few acres. He was, if the truth were known, a drain on their resources and he knew it. He was not even peripherally involved with any young woman, so his departure would not prevent the formation of a useful marriage. He had no real friends, and even the young fellows on the corner had begun to think of him as "that queer older man." He was not only prepared to join the stampede to the Yukon, he was almost impelled to do so.

At that time, had Klope been a student of geography, he would have seen that he was already about as close to the Klondike gold fields as he would be if he moved to one of the other starting points like Seattle in Washington or Edmonton in Alberta. In a straight line he was only one thousand three hundred and seventy miles from the Klondike, not much farther than to Chicago, but had he tried to negotiate that distance, he would have found himself entangled in some of the most forbidding terrain in North America. Wisely, he decided, even before he reached home, to approach the Klondike by way of Seattle.

When he sat with his parents at supper and showed them the newspaper, he did not wait for them to digest the amazing story: "I'm heading there tomorrow." It was indicative of the Klope family that his father replied simply: "I could let you have a hundred and fifty," and John said: "Added to what I have, it'll be enough." Mrs. Klope did not speak, but she felt it high time her son got out of the house and took steps of his own.

John never looked back. He was not able to depart, as he had first said, on the next day, but early on the day after that his father drove him to Bonners Ferry, where they learned that a train would soon be heading south to Spokane and on to Seattle. After an awkward fare-well, John said: "You better head home, Pop. I'll be all right." And off went the elder Klope, in no way unhappy that his son was making this move.

When Klope reached Seattle he found the city in turmoil, for the en-tire population seemed to be concentrated in the area around Schwa-bacher's Wharf, from which steamers were leaving for Alaska, and rarely since the days when nondescript craft plied the Mediterranean had any port seen such an amazing variety of seagoing vessels. There were ocean liners the equal of many crossing the Atlantic, but there were also river tugs hastily fitted out for the relatively quiet Inside Passage to Juneau and Skagway. There were sternwheelers intended for use along the Mississippi and big, rickety sidewheelers which had been used as excursion boats on the placid waters near Seattle.

Regardless of what the individual ship looked like, all its space was taken by the time Klope reached the waterfront seeking passage to anywhere in Alaska. In two frustrating days, he found not a single berth available, and since each new train from the east brought fresh hordes like himself, the problem worsened. In his despair at being so close to gold but forestalled from grabbing for it, he asked at the store of the principal outfitters, Ross & Raglan, where he was purchasing his necessities: "How can a man find passage to the Klondike?" and they told him: "We have one ship, the *Alacrity,* but she's booked solid through March of next year." The clerk, seeing his disappointment and knowing him as a man who spent money freely in buying his gear, said: "If you go to the far end of the docks, I believe there's an old Russian ship being refitted. I forget the name, but anybody out there will show you where she's berthed."

"And you think she won't be sold out?" Klope asked, and the clerk said: "I doubt it."

When he found the Russian ship, the *Romanov* of Sitka, he un-derstood why her tickets had not been at a premium, for she was one of the most extraordinary ships presuming to make the run. Hastily built as a Russian sidewheeler for use in the protected waters of southeast Alaska, she had been purchased by Boston seafarers when Russia abandoned the area in 1867 and after long service in the seal-ing trade had been brought to Seattle, where she had for some years plied the quieter waters of the bays and inlets. Later she had been fitted with an additional boiler that burned coal and a spasmodic propeller that operated in conjunction with the two sidewheels. It thus had two completely different systems for propulsion and three instruments for shoving itself through the sea: two wooden sidewheels and a slightly bent metal propeller.

This ancient ship, leaking at many points but never enough to cause sinking, proposed to make the three-thousand-mile journey through rough open and often turbulent seas to St. Michael, the ocean port where passengers and cargo would transfer to smaller steamers for passage up the Yukon. The fare would be one hundred and five dollars for the proposed three-week run, and by the time of departure, every usable spot on the ship would be taken. During a gold rush such a statement did not carry its customary meaning; it did not mean that all berths were occupied; it meant that even sleeping room on the deck and in the cargo areas below was filled. A ship which in its most favorable days of 1860 could have carried perhaps fifty passengers would now set forth with one hundred and ninety-three.

An irony of the situation was that none of these American passengers spoke of themselves as "heading for Alaska." It was always "We're off for the Klondike!" Alaska was an unknown entity, not yet acknowledged as being part of the United States, and as for the Yukon, that great river which they would have to travel if they sailed in the *Romanov,* few had ever heard of it, and those who had, supposed it to be Canadian. John Klope, a typical passenger, was stumbling into an area about which he knew nothing.

He sailed from Seattle on 27 July 1897, expecting to reach St. Michael in three weeks, which would have been ample time for one of the big steamers, and from there to move promptly into the Yukon on a smaller boat, landing in the Klondike not later than early September. It was indicative of his attitude toward life that during this sea passage he made friends with no one. He was not an unapproachable man, and if some stranger had taken pains to make his acquaintance, he would have responded, but it was not his nature to strike up conversations, share secrets, or form partnerships. He was John Klope, no known ancestry, no special attributes, just a tall, somewhat thin, stoop-shouldered man, clean-shaven, neat in his ways, and content to remain aloof.

The *Romanov* plowed the seas with which she was familiar at a somewhat slower speed than announced; in fact, she seemed to crawl along, as if her diverse means of propulsion counteracted one another. A well-run modern steamer should have made the three-thousand-mile run in nineteen days, and several did, but the *Romanov* limped along at a speed which would require at least a month. One passenger familiar with ships spread the report: "We're making no more than ninety miles a day. If we hit bad weather, we could take five weeks."

When she finally wheezed into St. Michael on 25 August 1897, three days ahead of prediction, Klope and the other passengers began to learn the realities of Alaskan travel, because there was no harbor waiting and certainly no wharf. The *Romanov*, like all other vessels arriving here, had to anchor about a mile offshore and wait till cumbersome barges worked their way out to unload passengers, luggage and freight. And when these barges finally did reach land, they usually stopped some yards from the shore, so that passengers had to wade to safety; women were sometimes carried on the backs of men who acted as informal stevedores.

Ashore, the people of the *Romanov* encountered a predicament which beset even the newcomers from better ships: there were no riverboats available for the long journey up the Yukon, and it seemed likely that none would arrive on their downward journey in time to make another trip up before the freezing of the river.

"Impossible!" some of the *Romanov* passengers stormed, but when they talked with officials they learned that the mournful situation was true: "The Yukon is no ordinary river. It flows north of the Arctic Circle, you know. And it freezes at different times at different places."

"But not in September!"

"Especially in September, in some places. And if it freezes anywhere, it halts all traffic . . . obviously."

"When does it thaw in spring?"

"May, if we're lucky. More likely June. Last year, early July."

"My God, it's only open . . . what? Three months?"

"Three and a half, if we're lucky."

"How often are you lucky?"

"Not very often."

Now an icy blast seemed to play upon the horde of gold seekers stranded at St. Michael. The weather was still comfortably warm, but threatening ice seemed to be moving closer, and when Klope heard that the *Romanov* was heading straight back to Seattle lest it be trapped in arctic ice drifting down into the Bering Sea, he asked:

"You mean, the whole sea out there freezes?" and the locals said: "Sure does. If a captain ain't spry, he can get trapped maybe in September and certain in October."

"What's he do?"

"Well, if he's lucky, he stays pinned there for nine months, right offshore where we can see him. If he's unlucky, ice keeps coming at him, crushes his ship and turns it into kindling, like over there." And when, along the bleak, treeless shore, Klope saw the remnants of various large ships which had been destroyed by the impersonal, pounding ice, he became obsessed with a determination to get out of St. Michael and up the Yukon before the ice trapped him too, but he found not a single riverboat available for the trip; three departed while he searched, but since each was crammed with men standing along the rails, not another passenger could be accommodated.

When it looked as if the *Romanov* people would be stranded in St. Michael, a town of less than two hundred, mostly Eskimo, Klope heard of a certain Captain Grimm, a boatowner familiar with the Yukon, who had a disabled craft which he was willing to put into the water if a boatload of passengers would pay in advance so that he might in turn pay for boiler repairs which his old sternwheeler simply had to have before it could move a foot.

At first Klope was doubtful about such a transaction, for he suspected that the name Grimm depicted the captain's character: He's probably just another banker wearing a different suit, but when no alternative appeared, he was forced to consider Grimm's offer. As usual, he found it difficult to discuss anything with anybody, but fortunately, there were other would-be passengers willing to assume that chore, and an outgoing young man from California with mining experience moved through the small community asking pertinent questions, then reporting to the stranded gold seekers: "Everybody says Grimm has a good reputation. And he really does need money. His boat can't sail unless it has a working boiler."

With this provisional information, the passengers encouraged the miner, whom everyone called California, to pursue his investigations, and this time he returned with exciting assurances: "They say Grimm's about the best captain sailing the Yukon. Knows every twist and turn. And they say that when you're on the Yukon, the twists and especially the turns become important."

No vote was taken, but by general acclaim the castaways agreed to provide Captain Grimm with the funds he needed, and Klope was assigned to see that the money was spent only on repairs. He helped the three skilled Eskimos employed by Grimm, and in sixteen days they completed a job of extensive overhaul. On 13 September the river steamer *Jos. Parker,* Captain Grimm, pulled out of St. Michael with sixty-three fully paid passengers when it would ordinarily have carried thirty-two. Baggage and stores were so plentiful that temporary wooden sides had to be erected around the foredeck, and atop this cargo half the men would sleep.

From St. Michael to the mouth of the Yukon was seventy miles over the open Bering Sea, and night fell and the next dawn arrived before the little craft reached the amazing delta of the Yukon, where Klope learned that no real mouth of the great river existed; there were some forty mouths emptying into the sea over a distance of almost a hundred miles. "The trick," said Captain Grimm as he maneuvered his boat, "is to find the right one," and the passengers stood amazed as he picked his way through this tangle of swampland and tributaries and dead-end channels. At last he came upon the one channel in these parts that would enable him to move upstream toward the gold fields.

The Yukon had several peculiarities. It rose far to the south in mountains less than thirty miles from access to the Inside Passage, but instead of joining the sea there, it chose to travel one thousand nine hundred and seventy-nine miles before entering the icy waters of the Bering Sea. It started north like all the other great rivers of the arctic—Ob, Yenisei, Lena and Kolyma in Siberia, and Mackenzie, greatest of all, in Canada—but unlike them, it did not empty into the Arctic Ocean or its subsidiaries, for after crossing the Arctic Circle at Fort Yukon, it seemed to grow afraid of the frozen north. Turning sharply westward, it fled the arctic and wandered sometimes almost aimlessly toward the Bering Sea.

A major peculiarity was that for much of its distance it was a braided river—that is, it broke into many strands which meandered here and there, so that at some points there was not one Yukon but twenty, or even thirty—and only a good ship captain or an Indian long familiar with the river could pick his way in and out. The chance that a stranger could navigate the Yukon when it became braided was minimal.

It was this formidable river that Captain Grimm in his *Jos. Parker* proposed to battle, always against the current, for thirteen hundred and fifty-five increasingly cold miles. Since the *Parker* could make about eighty miles a day, if it could take aboard enough cords of wood along the way, the trip should require some seventeen days, but when the little boat reached Nulato, where the Russians had prospered, they ran into a peculiar difficulty which warned the passengers that their journey was sure to be prolonged.

As the *Parker* drew to shore where the old palisade had stood, Captain Grimm saw to his satisfaction that some nineteen cords of neatly cut wood, 4×4×8, awaited him, enough, as he told passengers nearby, "to get us to Chicago if the Yukon ran that way . . . which one of these days it might . . . if it took it into its head."

But when he tried to purchase the needed fuel, he was informed that most of the piles had been preempted for riverboats belonging to the Alaska Commercial Company of Seattle, while the rest had been spoken for by boats of Ross & Raglan of the same city.

"Can't I get even one cord? To carry us to the next depot?"

"All bespoken."

"Can I hire someone to cut wood for us?"

"All engaged."

When it became obvious that the only way the passengers aboard the *Jos. Parker* were going to reach Dawson before the river froze would be for them to cut their own wood, parties were arranged and men fanned out across the barren countryside to find what trees they could, and after a four-day delay, the boat continued upstream, but at the next depot it was the same story, and this time when Klope left the boat with his ax he grumbled: "I didn't think I'd have to chop my way to the Klondike."

But chop he did as the projected quick trip to the gold fields was agonizingly prolonged. As September waned, the man called California raised the question: "At this rate, can we possibly reach Dawson before the river freezes?" But when he and a man known as Montana broached the subject with Captain Grimm, the latter gave his reassuring smile and said: "That's my job."

The attention of the worried passengers was distracted by the fact that they were about to enter the notorious Yukon Flats, a desolate and almost frightening area one hundred and eighty miles long in which the Yukon became hopelessly braided, as if some headstrong girl had purposely tangled her hair. Since the area was seventy miles wide, reaching out from both banks, it covered more than twelve thousand six hundred square miles and was about six times the area of Connecticut.

On first acquaintance it had not one redeeming feature: few trees, no surrounding mountains, no swift-moving streams, no villages clinging to the banks, merely an endless expanse of swampland, the overpowering Yukon Flats. John Klope, as a farmer who knew good land when he saw it, was appalled. But those familiar with the Flats developed an affection for them; here birds thrived in numbers unimaginable, and hunters from North Dakota to Mexico City were indebted to the summer breeding grounds thus provided for game birds which could have flourished nowhere else. Geese and ducks abounded. Wild animals of the most valuable kind proliferated: martin and mink and ermine and lynx and fox and muskrat and others whose names Klope would not have recognized. Larger game lived here, too: moose with enormous horns, caribou in winter, bears along the edges, savage mosquitoes by the billion.

But the pride of the Flats was the innumerable lakes, some little larger than a table, others as big as normal counties. At one spot the Yukon itself broadened into a lake of tremendous size, and occasionally fifty or sixty lakes would be linked together by minute streams, forming a chain of jewels resplendent in the cold sunlight.

How many lakes were there in the Flats? An explorer who had traveled the two major rivers which joined the Yukon here—Chandalar to the west, Porcupine coming in after a very long ramble through Canada—estimated that the area as a whole must contain at least thirty thousand independent clearly defined lakes: "What amazed me most, as I reflect upon it, was the excessive number of oxbows, those almost circular streams cut off from any main body of water, no entry, no exit, proof that in times past a meander had been eliminated when a flood altered the course of some little stream."

Riverboat captains had a less enthusiastic opinion of the Flats, for as Captain Grimm explained: "If you choose wrong at one of the braids, you can travel for a day before you find yourself at a dead end. Then you waste another retracing your way back to the main channel, supposing you can find it."

On 1 October 1897, Captain Grimm apparently lost his way in one of these landlocked braids, for after stumbling about during most of a long, cold morning, he confessed to his passengers: "We seem to be lost," and they knew that they were still fifty miles short of Fort Yukon, which they had to reach in order to obtain the next load of wood. Some men grumbled, and when Grimm decided to stay where he was and spend the night against the shore rather than retrace his course, two men came close to threatening him, but others provided sager counsel and no threats were voiced. During the argument Klope took neither side, for although he desperately wanted to reach the gold fields, he suspected that Captain Grimm knew what he was doing.

It was extremely cold that night, and in the morning the passengers were wakened by Montana, who was shouting about what was happening in their cul-de-sac: "Look at those fingers of ice!" And when Klope reached the railing, he could see delicate probes reaching out from shore as the colder water there began to freeze.

Few travelers had ever had an opportunity to watch a great river actually freeze, and although the braid in which the *Parker* was trapped was not part of the main current, the process was the same. While the middle of the river remained free, with no indication that it was about to freeze, thin ice did form at a few spots where the water touched land, but for the moment these isolated incidents indicated little, for they were not extensive nor did they reach far enough into the river to constitute any menace. No man could have walked upon the fragile ice thus formed.

But as Klope watched, a miracle occurred, for without warning of any kind, no cracking or popping, an entire stretch along the shore suddenly congealed, and it would remain so until June.

Now the watchers grew apprehensive, and at a spot well ahead of the *Parker,* that is, up near the closed end of the braid, they saw a second miracle, this one of greater import, for as the icy fingers coming out from land grew more sturdy, they suddenly leaped outward from each shore, joining in the middle of the braid as if forming a congratulatory handclasp, and in that instant, that part of the Yukon was frozen. The process was mysterious, quick and beautiful.

By afternoon, with the temperature far below zero, ice began to move out from the waterline of the *Parker,* and Klope stood with California as its fingers groped for those reaching out from shore, but night fell before they could witness completion of the jointure.

By next morning, 3 October, most of the Flats were frozen shut and even the mighty river was sending out preliminary fingers. By nightfall this section of the Yukon would be closed to navigation.

"That's why I ran in here," Grimm explained. "I didn't tell you at the time, because you wouldn't have believed the river could freeze so swiftly. If we'd tried to finish the run to Fort Yukon, we'd have been locked in the big ice and most likely been crushed when it moved."

"How long will we be trapped here?" California asked, and Grimm said: "Till June."

"Oh my God!" Montana cried, and Grimm said: "We're only one of many. Take heart. I've chosen one of the safest spots on this river. Less wind. No fear of creeping ice."

In a good winter the *Parker* might have provided a comfortable eight-month refuge for perhaps thirty men; any hope of keeping sixty-three content was impossible, and before that day was out some men were demanding refunds of their money. With his beard jutting out, his feet firmly placed, his eyes atwinkle, Olaf Grimm lined out the simple truth: "I undertook to get you to Dawson. I didn't promise when. Now, all men will scour the area to find what trees there are and bring us some wood, because if you don't we'll freeze to death, and I'll do my share of the chopping."

He explained where the privies would be built, "and any man not using them will be shot." He asked for volunteers to hunt for moose and caribou, "and you must go out right now to catch what you can before the heavy snows."

As this resolute man spoke he conveyed the impression that he had faced such situations before and intended to see that his passengers survived this one. He was conciliatory; he sympathized with men who were sorely disappointed; but he allowed no excuses, gave no exemptions from the work that he knew had to be done. When California complained, with reason: "If you knew we were going to freeze in, why did you leave St. Michael?" he said truthfully: "Because you people wanted to come. And we'd have made it on schedule if we'd been able to buy our wood on the way."

That winter eleven river craft were imprisoned in ice. None handled the situation better than the *Jos. Parker,* and when one of the passengers returned to the boat with news that he had killed a moose, he accepted the praise due him, then asked: "Ever since I've been aboard this damned ship I've wondered why it was called the *Jos. Parker.* Comin' back just now, I understood. The name-board ain't big enough for a full first name."

"That's right," Grimm said, thankful for any diversion. "Named after the father of the man who built it. Josiah Parker. Nice trim name, I always thought."

On 4 October, John Klope, still burning to get to the gold fields, spoke with Captain Grimm: "Living like this has got to get worse and worse," and Grimm said: "Yes."

"Could I walk to Fort Yukon?"

"Fifty miles. Rough sledding. Take you maybe three, four days."

"But it is just ahead, on the river?"

"Sure is." The veteran hesitated, for he would not want it said later that he had encouraged men who had started up the river under his care to leave their boat at the beginning of an arctic winter. At other ships other captains were facing the same moral problem; from one ship a lone man with dogs would set out for a journey of twelve hundred and fifty miles and make it. From another, a man who liked to paint watercolors would go three hundred yards and freeze to death.

Captain Grimm said, very carefully: "You and I, Klope, could make it. I've watched you. You're disciplined. But I wouldn't want to try it with some of those others. And don't you. Stay here and live." It was a masterful statement, a warning not to leave the safety of the *Parker* but at the same time a challenge, and Klope, ignoring the former, embraced the latter.

When it was learned that he was going to trek overland to Fort Yukon, eleven other men volunteered, and in some cases demanded, to go along, and suddenly he found himself the leader of an expedition. The idea terrified him, because although he had no fear about succeeding on his own, he doubted that he could hold a disparate group of men together if they ran into trouble, nor did he want to. Cleverly, he handed the management of the expedition over to loud-spoken California, who enjoyed giving directions, and justifying Klope's decision, California proved to be resourceful and a good leader, although to Klope's taste, a trifle domineering.

Well bundled, the twelve who wanted to get to Fort Yukon bade farewell to the ice-locked *Jos. Parker* early on the morning of 5 October, expecting to cover no less than thirteen miles a day, which would put them safely in Fort Yukon on the late afternoon of the eighth, and since darkness did not come till about five-thirty, they assumed they would have ample light. What they did not anticipate was the extreme roughness of the route they had chosen.

The Yukon did not freeze flat and smooth like the lakes some of them had known in the States; because it froze in arbitrary ways at sharply varying times, its surface was uneven, crumbled at times, and broken by irregular upthrust blocks. California, distraught by the impediments thrown up by the Yukon, shouted: "What in hell happened to this river?" and Montana explained what was obvious to an out-doorsman: "It freezes here but not there. Free water floods in, covers the frozen ice and freezes. Then more free water comes in below, everything buckles." He assured California that a level route could be found through the ice chunks, but the latter had had enough. Kick-ing at the blocks, he growled: "Let's get away from this damned river."

But when he led his team away, he soon faced the myriad lakes and the frozen swamps between. This tundra was dotted with large, round tufts of matted grass called by everyone in Alaska nigger-heads. To cross such country, one had to lift one's legs high to step from low ground to high, and then take longer strides than usual to reach the next niggerhead. It was painful going.

By alternating between the jagged ice of the river and the uneven surface of the frozen swamp, the informal expedition moved at a painful pace that would cover not thirteen miles a day as planned, but no more than eight. The trip would thus require not four days but six, and since the men had geared themselves to an easy four-day dash over the kind of snowy roads they had known in states like the Dakotas and Montana, they were disheartened.

Fortunately, the cold was not yet excessive, and no wind blew, so that even the weakest of the men did not suffer, and when night came they were not so exhausted that they were unable to care for them-selves, but they were thoroughly tired.

It had been planned that they would sleep with snow piled about them like a blanket, for this would deflect the wind and allow each man to hoard his body heat. They ate sparingly, for they had brought along only enough food for the projected four days, but as California said: "Short rations won't hurt anyone. And we'll soon be there."

The first night's rest was brief, for the men found it difficult to sleep in their snow beds, and while no one suffered from a lack of clothing, no one was properly clothed, either, for such exposure. As soon as dawn began to show, about six-thirty, the men were eager to resume their march, and with a day's practice behind them, they han-dled the difficult terrains more adeptly. But if California led them onto the river, they wanted to wander among the lakes, and if he ac-ceded to that suggestion, they rather quickly asked for the river. At dawn some had predicted: "Yesterday was learning. Today we'll do fifteen miles," but they covered barely half that distance.

Klope slept soundly that second night. He had seen that when neither he nor Montana set the pace, the file would lag, so he stayed in front most of the time, yielding only when Montana saw that he was tiring. The two men never spoke of what they were doing or of their growing suspicion that some of them were not going to make it to Fort Yukon.

On the night of the fourth frustrating day, when three of the men became almost too weak to lift their legs high enough to negotiate the niggerheads, it was apparent to Klope that emergency measures must be taken, and he consulted with both California and Montana. The latter said: "We got to put someone at the rear. Else we're gonna lose somebody back there."

"They can see our trail," California said, but Montana would not accept this easy answer: "Trouble is, in this weather the man at the end says: 'I'll lie down for just a minute,' and you never see him again. Frozen solid."

Klope volunteered to walk last, and it was fortunate that he did, because the men detected as being weakest began to lag dangerously, and he spent a trying day urging them to keep moving forward. Twice the major file forged so far ahead that he had to shout at the top of his voice to make them slow down until his three flagging charges could catch up. By nightfall two others had fallen behind, and when California, whose courage and determination helped keep the men together, consulted with his two assistants, Klope reported: "I'm not sure I can make them keep up for another day," and to make things worse, that night the temperature fell precipitously.

Shortly after midnight California shook those still sleeping in the protection of the snow: "Better start moving, men," and in the shadowy light of a waning moon they started what they would later remember as the worst night and day of their lives.

That sixth day they elected to stay with the river, picking their way slowly past protruding blocks, and at times John Klope, bringing up the rear, thought that the silent figures ahead of him looked like ants moving across a white blanket, but such poetic comparisons were banished when one of the laggards simply fell in a heap, unable to respond to Klope's commands that he rise.

When helpers hurried back, they found to their horror that the man had not fainted; he had died. Yes, on the Yukon River some miles below the safety of the Fort, a bank clerk from Arkansas had died of exhaustion, and after his body had been placed under a blan-

ket of snow, a subdued and sometimes terrified group of eleven resumed its slow march forward.

Klope was not unduly distressed by the death. He was aware that
men died in arbitrary ways; on a neighboring farm a man he knew
well had been strangled when the reins of a rearing horse caught
around his neck, and once during a visit to Bonners Ferry he had
heard men shouting at the railroad station, where a workman had
been crushed between two boxcars. So he could absorb the shock of
death. But when the party halted at noon for rations, he heard something that did frighten him tremendously. California, seeking to dis-
pel the gloom attendant upon the death, was giving encouragement:
"It was fifty miles in all, and I calculate we've covered forty-two,"
when a man from Ohio said: "I heard Captain Grimm say: 'It's only
fifty or sixty miles to Fort Yukon.'"

The possible addition of ten miles to what was already a hellish
journey terrified Klope, for as rear man he had witnessed better than
anyone else the utter exhaustion of the weakest members. When California and three other strong men moved apart to discuss the situation, Klope was impressed by the forthright manner in which the
leader conducted himself: "I want the four of us to pledge that we
will not forge on ahead and forget the others. We'll stay with these
men and get them to Fort Yukon."

"But what if the time comes when one of us has to rush ahead,"
Montana asked, "to bring help?"

"You three can draw straws. I'll stay."

"Could it have been sixty miles?" Klope asked, and California
snapped: "No."

That afternoon the temperature dropped to ten degrees below,
but mercifully no wind accompanied the fall; however, another man
walking not far ahead of Klope collapsed and died, not instantly like
the first, but in terrible, rasping pain over a period of forty minutes.

Klope buried him, and then the real horror of this forlorn journey began, because the Yukon became excessively humpy while the
swamps were barricaded by niggerheads that were barely negotiable.
At half past four what arctic daylight there was would begin to fade,
and the men would face the punishment of a long, bitterly cold night
without adequate protection.

Klope did not lose courage; he could never do that so long as the
lure of gold pulled him forward, but as he estimated the waning
strength of the laggards, he realized with deepening concern that as

many as three could perish during the coming hours, and he called for the other strong marchers to join him. "What shall we do?" he asked, and California replied: "Keep moving ahead. All night. Otherwise we could all die."

"And if those over there . . . ?" California studied Klope's forlorn group sitting numbly in the snow, either unaware of or indifferent to the fact that their lives were under discussion, then said: "Keep them going as long as possible. If they die, don't stop to bury them." And he returned to the lead, where he spurred the marchers on.

It was almost dusk on that terrible day when one of the weakest men espied an amazing sight, which he called to Klope's attention: "Dog team!" And there to the north, picking his way carefully through the frozen swamps of the Yukon Flats and obviously headed toward Fort Yukon, came a man running behind a sled drawn by seven large, powerful dogs. He was dressed in Eskimo garb, his exposed face surrounded by the fur-lined hood of a parka, his body so swathed in heavy garments that he looked almost round. He had not yet seen the struggling men, and there was a chance that he might speed by without stopping, so with a wild shout Klope started running northeast in hopes of intercepting him.

The other men, hearing the shouts, turned and saw the speeding dogsled, and without a moment's hesitation California began running too, and because he started from a better angle, it was he whom the sled-driver finally saw. Commanding his huskies to halt, he came forward to meet these strangers, and a moment's glance at the weary file whose men had taken rest in the snow satisfied the man that he had come upon a party of cheechakos in peril.

He was Sarqaq, half Eskimo, half Athapascan Indian, and he ran a dogsled out of Fort Yukon. He spoke little English but understood many words, and when he asked California: "Fort Yukon?" he comprehended the answer.

"How far?" California asked, and he said, holding up one finger: "Tomorrow." But then California asked: "Your tomorrow or our tomorrow?" and Sarqaq did not understand. Klope solved the problem by putting his hand on one of the dogs, a handsome white-faced animal fifth in line from the lead, and with his fingers imitated the four swiftly moving legs of a dog. Then, using his own feet, he plodded slowly forward: "Dog one day? Man how many?"

Sarqaq, whose brown face was as round as if it had been drawn with a compass, laughed, showing white teeth: "I now. You tomorrow."

Klope was in no way a religious man, but he sighed: "Thank God." He and California and the others in strong condition could certainly survive till tomorrow night; the weakest could perhaps be taken to warm beds by the dogsled. Taking the driver by the arm, he pointed to the resting men: "Two, three. Maybe die," and with sign language he indicated men dying from lack of will.

Sarqaq understood immediately, and without even a minute's hesitation knew what he must do. Furiously he started throwing off his sled the piles of fur and caribou meat he was delivering to Fort Yukon, and when it became apparent that he was unloading cargo to provide space to transport the threatened men, Klope said: "I go get," but Sarqaq stopped him: "I go," and with curt commands he swung his dogs about, sped to the line of men, who uttered feeble cheers, and asked: "Who go?" holding up three fingers taken from the mitten which protected them from freezing. The men waited for Klope to identify the three worst cases, and when he had done so, these men, barely aware of what was happening, were loaded aboard the sled.

Then came a moment of the most painful indecision, for the seven men left behind could not anticipate what might happen. Were these three alone to be saved? Was Fort Yukon really only one day away? Could they survive any more nights in this dreadful cold?

Sarqaq, anticipating their fears, smiled like a rising moon and said to Klope: "Watch meat. Wolves." And to the men from the *Parker* he said: "Cut meat. Chew it. Wrap in furs. I come back. Many sleds." And off through the darkening night he sped.

It was about four in the morning when one of the travelers, who was moving about to keep himself alive, heard from the east the sound of dogs. Listening for confirmation lest he deceive his companions, he heard the unmistakable sound of men cheering on their teams, and he began shouting: "They're here! They've come back!"

From wherever they had been sleeping and in whatever postures, the survivors leaped to their feet and peered into the moonlit night. Slowly, like the vision in a narcotic dream, dogsleds began to appear upon the Yukon, with the figures of men running behind, and as they became reality the freezing men began to scream and shout "Hurrah!" and weep.

• • •

In 1897, Fort Yukon was no longer a fort, but when erected half a century earlier, it had been a rather formidable place, and a drawing made by the intrepid English explorer Frederick Whymper, in 1867, still showed the imposing four blockhouses, inside whose square nestled several homes, and two enormous barns for the storage of furs being bought and merchandise being sold by the Hudson's Bay Company, whose daring traders had established this most remote of their outposts.

In 1869, Fort Yukon provided an outstanding example of why Canada and the United States were such good and sensible neighbors: that was the year when young Otis Peacock and his army team proved that the Canadian Hudson's Bay Store was far inside American territory. Instead of raising a ruckus, American and Canadians had diplomatically moved the store—twice, because after the first move, it was still trespassing on American soil.

For some years Fort Yukon had been a thriving little settlement of about a hundred and ninety people who earned a modest living by collecting furs from Indians and by servicing the occasional riverboat like the *Jos. Parker* when one stopped by, but with the discovery of Klondike gold, the town had flourished and was now crowded.

When the Eskimo Sarqaq, as he was called despite his part-Athapascan blood, and the other sled drivers delivered the ten white men to the Fort, a curious situation developed. California, the man who more than any other had been responsible for keeping the travelers moving forward, suddenly lost his nerve, and when a third man died at the Fort, he took the blame upon himself. For three days he sat in a stupor, overwhelmed by the tragedy in which he had participated. Klope and others told him: "You kept us going," but he could not accept this; he felt compelled to take responsibility for the deaths of his three companions and the near-deaths of the others.

Klope was not being honest when he said that it had been California who had saved the expedition. Both he and Montana knew that they, too, had held the team together and that many more would have died had not Klope refused to let them do so. But he sought no accolade for having done what he considered his duty; instead, he sought out his rescuer, Sarqaq, and spent hours with the Eskimo's ten dogs.

Sarqaq was known as an Eskimo because that was an easier identification than half Eskimo, half Athapascan; besides, he looked like a prototypical Eskimo, with stocky build, round face and pronounced Oriental features. He was an amiable man, much given to grinning, which made his face shine like a full moon, and he enjoyed having Klope take an interest in his dogs.

He maintained ten, even though he preferred to use only seven on his sled; the extra three would be fed into the team as present members aged or grew refractory. For example, he had not much use for the dog that Klope had liked in those first moments of their meeting in the Flats, number five in line. By some instinct, Klope had identified the one dog that was not a pure husky, as if he had spotted some variation in character.

"Not husky," Sarqaq said. "Maybe half-half." A white man who had once owned the dog had given it the name of Breed, indicating a mixed heritage, and when Klope heard that the dog was mixed, he supposed that this accounted for the difference he had noted.

Breed looked like a husky; he had the white mask, the extremely dark hair edging his eartips, the heavy coat and the powerful front legs. His eyes were framed in white and he also had a thin white stripe down the middle of his forehead. His body was a brownish gray and his whole attitude one of alertness. His weakness was that he did not fit in with the other dogs, and if he did not mend his ways and quickly, Sarqaq would have to replace him, because one difficult dog could ruin a team.

As Klope spent these October days with the dogs, he slowly acquired an understanding of these remarkable animals, so unlike the ones he had known in Idaho. The most important beast in a team was the lead dog, and Sarqaq's was almost unbelievable in its intelligence and its love of mushing at the head of six other dogs almost as capable. It was the lead dog who disciplined the others, who threw its total weight into the straps, who kept the sled always moving forward and who designated the track. It was responsive to Sarqaq's commands and even anticipated them, and although it could not be said that it loved its master, for it stayed aloof from humans, it obviously did love the job of leading the team and protecting the heavy sled they drew.

Dog number two in line was known as the swing, and it was its responsibility to transfer the leader's decisions to the dogs behind. Often when the lead dog died or became too old for continued service, the swing took over; in the case of Sarqaq's team, this would not occur, because although his swing was admirably suited to that job, it would not make a good leader; it was too amenable to suggestion.

Of an importance almost equal to the lead dog was the last in line, the wheel dog, for it was its task to see that the moves of the other dogs did not imperil either the safety or the progress of the sled. A knowing wheel could be worth the whole remainder of the team if it saw to it that their considerable efforts were properly applied to the moving sled, and Sarqaq had about the best wheel in the business.

That accounted for the three principal dogs; the others were lumped together as the team, and sometimes it seemed as if they did the hard work. Each dog had a name, but since these names were in some native dialect, Klope did not master any but Breed's. He was not an impressive dog when the sled was in motion, and when on three occasions Sarqaq allowed Klope to accompany him on short trips into the countryside, John saw that Breed lacked that strange mixture of respect for discipline and determination to pull regardless of sled weight which characterized the outstanding dogs. Breed was something else, a fierce animal yet one that seemed to crave human companionship, and in John Klope he found a man who had a similar need for animal friendship. A man to whom human associations did not come easily or warmly was developing a powerful affection for this dog.

He was therefore dismayed when, after a poor performance by Breed which caused the lines to tangle, Sarqaq said in disgust: "No good dog. Maybe shoot."

"Wait!" Klope pleaded, but that night when they were back at the Fort, another dogsled man who spoke fairly good English explained: "Husky, malamute same. Good only for hauling sled. No good for that, get rid of them."

"But would you shoot one of your own dogs?"

"No good, maybe better shoot. Dog's whole life, to be in traces, pulling. Lose that job, maybe dog want to be shot."

"Wouldn't you keep it . . . as a pet?"

The driver, an Athapascan, laughed and called to two other drivers: "He asks husky sled dog a pet?" And the men roared with delight at this further proof that Outsiders never understood the arctic.

In the days that followed, Klope spent more time with Breed, and with each passing experience he saw in him an animal capable of enormous affection and willing to share all experiences with this man who had taken an interest in him. Now when Klope came to where the dogs were tied overnight—for had they been allowed to run wild, they all might have disappeared—Breed strained at his link chain to reach him, and when Klope moved close the dog leaped upon him, and pawed him and tried to lick his bearded face. But such behavior intensified Sarqaq's belief that Breed had no place in an orderly string of working dogs.

It became unthinkable to Klope that such an animal should be destroyed merely because it did not serve obediently the whims of some man, and several times he tried to broach the matter with Sarqaq, who dismissed the subject almost scornfully.

As the survivors from the *Jos. Parker* recovered from their ordeal on the Yukon Flats and their courage returned, some started to think of trying to move south to their destination, but the managers at Fort Yukon dissuaded them: "That's more'n three hundred miles. And it'll be bitter cold now. You fellers lost three men comin' only fifty miles, in what we call good weather."

"But if we wait till this damned river thaws, all the good claims will be taken."

"We wait every year," the Fort Yukon men said. "And besides, young feller, all the good claims was taken two years ago. You got plenty time to claim on nothin' land, so stay here where there's a hot stove and somethin' to eat."

Such advice became more relevant when a dogsled driven by two Indians straggled in from the south with a horror story: "Starvation in Dawson. People ordered to leave by the Mounted Police. They reached Circle City, pitiful condition. Frozen toes had to be cut off. Fingers gone. One man lost a leg."

This portrait of conditions in the south so discouraged the *Parker* men that any thought of trying to reach the Klondike before the thaw made boat passage possible was discarded. That is, it was discarded by everyone except John Klope, who was still tormented by his gnawing mania to get to where the gold lay hiding. Each new hardship made him more determined to ignore difficulties, so that when the fugitives from Circle asked the authorities at the Fort whether a rescue mission of any kind could be mounted to get food to those trapped there and in Dawson, he said without hesitation: "I'll go," and the Indians laughed. They had meant: "Is there any local dogsled man who will attempt it?" They said that the trip north had exhausted both them and their dogs; they had no intention of volunteering.

Two days after the request circulated, Sarqaq came to Klope: "You say you go?"

"Yes."

"You, me, maybe?" When Klope jumped at the invitation, the Eskimo asked: "You pay?" and now Klope had to think. Carefully he explained that he had already paid the money intended for his fare to the captain of the *Jos. Parker,* and with signs he indicated that if he, Klope, wanted to stay in Fort Yukon till the river thawed, the *Parker* would be obliged to carry him to Dawson for no extra payment.

The explanation was painfully drawn out, but finally Sarqaq understood that Klope would not pay, and there the matter rested for two days. But on the third day, just as gold-hungry Klope was about to volunteer a limited fee for the trip, Sarqaq returned with his own proposition: the two men would load their sled with all the food that Fort Yukon could spare; they would hurry it to Dawson; and there they would sell it for a profit. There seemed to be no risk in such a venture: Sarqaq was certain his dogs could make the trip; he knew that he could and he suspected that Klope was the kind of white man who had just as much endurance as any Eskimo; and both men trusted that if they could get the food to Dawson, they would be sure to find customers who would pay for it.

All was set, except for one detail: Klope would have to buy the food from the commissary at Fort Yukon, and he would have to pay cash, relying upon the successful termination of the rescue mission for repayment. He considered this for several days, for unlike Sarqaq he could visualize many reasons why such a daring venture might fail, but in the end he was so determined to reach the gold fields before the rest of that year's crowd that he agreed to put up the money. On 20 November 1897 it was known throughout Fort Yukon that Sarqaq and the American were going to attempt the dash to Dawson, three hundred and twenty miles to the south over trails that were frozen deep and covered with snow, along a river that was filled with block ice. If they made twenty-five miles a day, they felt they could cover the distance, with rests for the dogs, in eighteen days, which would put them on the Klondike well before Christmas.

On the day before departure two things happened which heightened the tension of the men. Klope went to California, whom he admired, and said: "You want to come along? You were the best man on the other trip." But the man who had proved so valiant on the venture from the *Jos. Parker* had not yet regained his courage, or, more kindly, he had spent it all on that disastrous expedition when only his will power had prevented it from ending in total horror. Now he could do no more than shudder when Klope suggested a repetition. Drawing in his shoulders as if to prevent Klope from getting at his vitals, he shook his head. He had seen the Yukon in autumn and he could not imagine it in winter.

When Klope warned, "The gold fields will be all taken," he looked up in amazement, asking: "Gold fields?" When the Yukon thawed he intended catching a boat downstream for St. Michael and Seattle; under no circumstance would he go upstream toward Dawson, either in the spring when the river opened or now when it was frozen tight, and only when Klope saw the terror with which the invitation was rejected did he acknowledge to himself the dangerous trip he was about to undertake.

Sarqaq heard a more frightening story. The two drivers who had reached Fort Yukon with news of starvation in Dawson related what had happened when a boat tried to rush supplies to that beleaguered town: "Boat got lots of wood for burnin', extra food. Good captain, good Indian pilot through the channels. Everything good. If reach Dawson, save many people."

"What happened?" Sarqaq asked, and the informant said: "Him, me, we reach Circle one day before boat. No food there, no medicine. One hell of a time, I tell you." At this point he looked to his fellow driver for confirmation, and the man nodded.

"Next day many cheers. Boat come in. But captain say: 'This food for Dawson. People starving in Dawson.' But people in Circle say: 'People starving here, too. We take your food.' Big words, maybe big fight. Men with guns. Captain say: 'Okay, damn you, take food and let others starve.' And men run all over boat, take all food. Boat stay there empty. Pretty soon, boat fast in ice. Never go to Dawson because captain say: 'What the hell?'"

Then the first driver made his point: "Sarqaq, s'pose you and dog team, food go to Circle, same men stop you. Same men take everything. No food can go past Circle, damn sure."

The three drivers talked for some time, discussing routes which could be traversed without the men of Circle becoming aware that a dog team was in the vicinity, and on the night prior to departure Sarqaq informed Klope of his strategy: "Not bad men, hungry men.

We go . . ." and with his hands he indicated the town of Circle on the left bank of the river while a dog team headed far to the east on the right bank.

California and Montana were up early to help finish last-minute preparations, and by the time dawn arrived, almost the entire Fort was present and making predictions: "They'll never make it" and "No white man can go that far in winter" and "If anyone can make it, Sarqaq can." Klope, growing impatient at any delay, was about to stride off when an old woman, daughter of some early Canadian miner and an Athapascan squaw, came pottering out to stop him yet again. She brought with her an object which she obviously considered precious, a crock made of clay, inside which lay something wrapped in a damp cloth. A widow now, she served as cook for one of the merchant dormitories, and as she handed Klope her treasure she said, with the wisdom of decades in the north: "It can never be a house without this. God would not allow."

Klope thought the gift must be a Bible, but why have it in a damp crock? "What is it?" he asked, and proudly, with fingers gnarled from much labor, she loosened the cloth, and when Klope peered inside the crock all he could see was a loose round ball of what looked like the dough from which his mother had baked German cookies.

"What is it?" he repeated, and the old woman said: "Sourdough. Keep warm. Keep with you. It will make life . . ." She hesitated, for she could not think of one word that could describe the difference between having a good strain of sourdough and none.

Her family of sourdough dated back to 1847, when the Hudson's Bay people built the fort in which her grandmother had worked as cook. The dough had reached the Yukon after a perilous trip from eastern Canada, where its ancestry had come after a similar trip from Vermont, where the strain had already been kept alive for forty years, dating back to 1809. It was a gift of antiquity and civilization and love which the old woman was turning over to Klope, and it was a responsibility too. In crocks like this, under damp cloths like this, the women of Vermont and Quebec and Fort Yukon had kept the strain of yeast viable, and now she was turning the job over to a new caretaker.

Weighing the crock in both hands, Klope said: "I can't carry this all the way to Dawson," but she warned him: "Gold comes, goes." With a sweep of her hand she indicated all the men of Fort Yukon:

"They look, they look. S'pose they find? Gamble it away. Pretty women." Pressing the crock into Klope's hands, she said: "But good sourdough . . . it goes on forever." In the world she had been able to observe from the lonely fort on the Yukon, gold had accomplished very little, but a family with a reliable crock of sourdough was on its way to happiness.

This crock was obviously too heavy to lug all the way to Dawson City, but Sarqaq, immensely reverent where a strain of proved leaven was concerned, solved the problem. Calling for one of the little glass jars in which California farmers were now packing their cooked vegetables, he transferred the sourdough, and showed Klope how to carry it close to his body so the precious yeast did not freeze.

With the old woman's blessing and cheers from the men, the two daring travelers set forth, and as they pulled out of the Fort they presented sharply contrasting appearances. Klope was tall and thin, dressed in an American's version of what an arctic explorer should wear, which was about the same as what an American farmer in Idaho should wear: heavy clothes, heavy leather boots, heavy cap with very heavy earflaps. It was good clothing, appropriate for a day's hard work in cold weather, and he presented an impressive figure when he stepped behind the sled. An observer would have said: "He's not one to fool with." But how the clothing would serve for eighteen days when it could not be taken off at night, one could not guess.

Sarqaq, a short butterball of a man, wore clothing which his people had developed over thousands of years of arctic living. No item was heavy; all seemed to be composed of many layers of the thinnest and lightest skin possible. His boots were made of caribou leather, tanned to perfection, and lined not only with caribou but with the almost weightless fur of baby seal. His trousers were miracles of lightness and durability, stiff when he put them on, supple as he began to move. He wore five shirts and jackets, each seemingly thinner than the preceding one, and his hood was a marvel, a capacious cavern in which his head could hide from snow and sleet, and from whose edges he would gain both protection and warmth, for it was trimmed with wolverine hair that had the mysterious quality of not allowing ice to form along its tips.

The Eskimo's arctic costume had one further advantage, not a minor one: it was completely watertight, and would, if its wearer were suddenly pitched into some ocean wave or river, keep him dry for up to an hour. It was formidable gear, in which a man could work all day and sleep all night with the maximum comfort available in the arctic. One would suppose that with this advantage in clothing and with a superior knowledge of dogsleds and river trails that Sarqaq would outdistance Klope in everything, but that was not to be, for the big man knew how to husband his strength and how to pull "courage from the gut," as he phrased it.

An Eskimo with seven good dogs could harness them in either of two ways: some excellent drivers liked to have three pairs, each pair yoked side-by-side, with a lead dog in front, his chain locked into the chain which ran down the center and attached to the sled. If a man had seven or nine superbly trained dogs long accustomed to this hitch, that was the way to do it, but there was an element of show in such a harnessing.

Tough-minded men who liked to move a maximum weight of cargo hitched their seven dogs in tandem, one directly behind the other, with each dog's harness tying directly into that of his follower. Such a hitch had the advantage of allowing the three key dogs—lead, swing, wheel—to perform at maximum and to utilize whatever skills they had mastered. Sarqaq, who had done much hauling in the areas bordering on the Yukon Flats, preferred the tandem hitch and used it to perfection.

Regardless of which harnessing the driver adopted, his dogs pulled the same kind of sled. If the trip was for show, or for the conveying of young women or a well-to-do couple, the sled looked like an ordinary sleigh familiar in either Russia or the United States: a commodious and well-upholstered place for two persons to sit, a handrail for the driver in the rear to use when he caught a ride, and long after-runners for him to stand on when doing so. But when, as in Sarqaq's missions, the sled had to carry the maximum freight, it was a low sturdy vehicle with no frills, wide, heavy runners and no sides, the freight being kept in place by numerous rawhide thongs.

Either of these marvelous machines—for they constituted two of the world's most effective users of energy—required special conditions: in most snow where a trail had not already been established, the man in charge of the sled had to go in front, on snowshoes, to break a path; the dogs by themselves could not do this, for they would waste their energy fighting snow which might be so deep that it covered their nostrils. When a man drove a dogsled he worked.

Of course, if a driver was lucky enough to be traveling along a river whose ice had been frozen to a glassy smoothness, which happened occasionally even on the Yukon, he might ride for several hours, because the dogs loved such a gallop when only slight friction retarded their sled. But generally, in a typical day's travel of twenty-five miles, the man would run at least twenty, gliding over the snow on his big webbed shoes.

Since each dog weighed about sixty pounds of concentrated muscle and could haul about one hundred pounds over terrain that was not excessively rough, Sarqaq's seven dogs ought to haul a total weight of seven hundred pounds, but since the sled itself, severely trimmed, weighed ninety pounds, the effective weight of foodstuffs for starving Dawson could be a little over six hundred pounds, less the weight of dog and human food carried.

During the first hour out of Fort Yukon, Sarqaq established the patterns to be observed: "Always that way," indicating southeast. "Start before daylight, stop after light goes," or twelve hours at least a day. "Try for twenty-five miles a day, with stops, rest," this indicated by fingers and gestures. "Five days, stop one day, dogs sleep," because no dog could work as hard as a man nor as long. "You, me walk. Maybe good time, ride," but mostly they would do what Klope had called as a boy the dogtrot. "Eat? You, me that," and Sarqaq indicated the dried food on the sled, including pemmican made of caribou, moose and bear. "Dog eat?" And there came the major problem.

Sarqaq's dogs worked extremely hard and were constantly hungry, but tradition said that they must be fed only at night. It seemed to Klope that a quarter of the sled's load was dog-salmon dried the previous summer; a pound and a half of this nutritious food heavy in oil would keep a big dog alive and able to work and, when mixed with just a little dried oats or meal, the salmon gave the dogs more energy than they required.

In the cold, salmon did not turn rancid and dogs never tired of it, gulping down great chunks even though it contained sharp tiny bones which might have killed less sturdy breeds. To carry so much cargo merely to feed the dogs was in one sense extravagant but in another not, for without dogs, there could be no safe human traffic over the vast expanse of the arctic.

To supplement the dried salmon, on which the dogs would be quite content to feed permanently, Sarqaq was always on the alert for animal tracks, because if he could kill a caribou or a moose, or perhaps a bear wandering from its hibernation, the dogs could be fed for two or three days with a healthy change of diet and no depletion of the dried salmon. In fact, Klope deduced after several days of travel that since Sarqaq had brought along insufficient salmon for the proposed eighteen days, he was gambling on supplementing the fish with a caribou now and then. Accordingly, each of the men kept an eye cocked for signs of game, and Sarqaq was quite willing to halt progress for an entire day while he tracked some animal, for he knew that whenever he caught one, he improved the chances for bringing this long and daring venture to a successful conclusion.

When either he or Klope departed on such a hunting excursion, two rules were in effect: the hunter would take with him the extra dogs to help drag home the kill, and after the man had been absent for three hours, the other man would light a smudge fire to indicate where the sled was waiting, for otherwise the hunter might have no clue as to where either he or the sled was.

It was strange, almost to the point of being unbelievable, but in this windless, almost treeless north, a fire giving off smoke would send a signal high into the air, almost half a mile straight up, with never a waver in the column. The smoke just hung there motionless until it gradually dispersed. A traveler could often tell where people were living, beyond the rise of a hill, by the column of steam which hung suspended over their outdoor privy; such a signal could be seen for miles.

It was during a foray for meat that Klope made the hesitant suggestion which modified this trip, for as he was about to set off in search of a moose whose tracks were visible along the river, he asked if this time he could take as his drag-dog not the extra animals, but Breed, who lay in harness like the six other members of the team.

"Maybe good," the Eskimo said, and Klope went off with only Breed, leaving the extras behind.

It was a day Klope would never forget, gray-blue sky, hazy sun low on the horizon, snow bright but not enough to cause snow blindness, a probability of snaring a moose, and the joy of the dog at heel. Breed loved the chase, but he was well enough trained to respond when Klope gave even the softest signal. Breed was in the hunt too, and he wanted to bring down the moose upon which he and the team could feed. It became a rare partnership, even on that first day, and toward dusk, which came at an appallingly early hour, they approached their moose. Now Breed remained at Klope's side as they both edged into position, and when the gun fired, he leaped like the discharge of a cannon to trap the moose by a leg lest it stagger on merely wounded.

Now the problem became how to drag this heavy carcass back to the sled, and where was the sled? Scouting the horizon before total darkness fell, Klope located the pillar of smoke, hitched Breed to the one-dog harness, and looped the free end about the moose's neck. It was problematic whether the dog could pull so heavy a load—some four hundred pounds—but with help from an initial push by Klope, the fallen animal began to edge forward, and through special effort which Breed knew was required, the dead animal began to slide across the snow.

Klope, watching in admiration, muttered to himself: "He knows he's bringing home something important," and that did seem to be the case, for the dog stepped high, ears alert, dark eyes peering from side to side, harness taut, handsome silver-brown body straining forward. It was such a triumphant return that as darkness fell, with Klope spotting the sled, he fired into the night an exultant shot which reverberated in the frozen air.

Soon there came sounds of excitement in the camp, the barking of other dogs, the welcoming cry of Sarqaq; then the butchering of the meat, the tossing of offal to the hungry dogs and the warm good of coming home at end of day. But in the morning there came the ugly moment when Klope saw that Sarqaq had harnessed his team without including Breed, who was thus demoted to serving merely as a spare.

Shoving the dog forward, Klope said: "Here's Breed," but Sarqaq growled: "No damn good," and Breed was dropped from the team.

Klope, realizing that he knew little about operating a dog team, said nothing, but he was sorely disappointed, and so, apparently, was Breed, who showed his displeasure at not being harnessed with his six mates. And since the spares were kept together in a small harness of their own to prevent straying, Breed could not even walk with Klope, and it would have been difficult to decide which was the more disappointed.

During the first leg out of Fort Yukon, Sarqaq kept to the river, picking his way across the rumpled ice, and one cloudless afternoon he came upon a long stretch of glaze ice as smooth as a mirror, and since this was the first time that Klope had experienced such ice, the Eskimo encouraged the white man to ride on the rear runners, and for about an hour, with Sarqaq lagging far behind, Klope and the seven huskies skimmed over the ice through the windless beauty of an arctic day. It was a thrill Klope could never have imagined, this timeless, placeless, noiseless movement through a world of white. When the ride ended, with the dogs showing no tiredness but lying happily on the ice, Klope wanted for one brief moment to shout, but shouting was not his style. "Good dogs," he said, rummaging in the cargo for bits of salmon to throw them.

But when the Yukon took a slight curve to the southwest, forming in effect a detour from straight-line passage, Sarqaq left the river and kept to the east. This deviation was practical only because the dreaded Yukon Flats tapered out at this point, providing the dogs with relatively flat land; it was made imperative because Circle and its hungry men lay in wait just ahead, and if Sarqaq and Klope tried to rush their cargo of food through that snare, they were going to lose everything. So well back from the river they ran, not pausing to hunt for game and missing one day of rest they should have allowed the dogs.

When they returned to the Yukon south of Circle, the temperature began to drop so precipitously that Sarqaq feared they might not be able to move ahead, and he began to look about for accumulations of snow in which the dogs could burrow if the cold became unbearable.

It did. It went down to thirty-below, where Sarqaq's thermometer ceased to register, then down to forty-two, then to forty-seven. Had a heavy wind also been raging, men and dogs would probably have frozen. As it was, the cold was almost clement; if you stayed out in it with face exposed, you ran the risk of losing a nose or an ear, but if you protected yourself and your dogs, survival was surprisingly easy. As Klope moved through the extreme cold he kept hugging his left elbow close to his side, for this enabled him to feel the jar of sourdough against his skin, and he developed the conceit that he was like one of the gods he had read about in fifth grade, the custodian of a sacred fire, and the idea gave him pleasure: The leaven may not be any good when we get it there, but it won't be frozen.

Survival for the dogs consisted of burying themselves like rabbits in the snow till only their black noses were visible; you could find them by watching for their frozen breath hanging in the silent, motionless air. For men it was much the same; at fifty-one-below they used their sled as a wall, piled snow about them as an added windbreak, and found as much comfort as they could.

As they lay immobilized, Sarqaq chastised himself for having been so stupid as to come back onto the river: "Colder here," and with his mittened hands he made the sign of wind blowing, but as Klope pointed out: "No wind. None at all," and the Eskimo agreed: "No wind, but cold follows river," and he showed with his mittens how the bitter cold moved up and down the Yukon as if propelled by some strong wind.

"How could that be?" Klope asked, and the Eskimo replied, in effect: "You tell me. But it is colder, isn't it?" And it was.

When daylight came on the eighth day of their trip, Klope noticed that Sarqaq had his mittens off and was carving some small object. "What are you doing?" he asked, and the Eskimo said: "For you." It was a pair of sun goggles to prevent snow blindness, for if a white man with his lack of pigmentation, but any man really, remained surrounded by snow when the sun shone, his eyes would fight against the glare so strenuously that he would go temporarily blind, or, if the cold was sufficiently intense, permanently so. To prevent this, the Eskimos had long ago learned to wear protectors carved from ivory, bone or wood, or even cut from caribou hide if nothing better was available; the guard covered the eye completely but provided a very narrow slit, less than a quarter of an inch vertically and not more than an inch horizontally, through which the traveler could see where he was going. Often the goggle was painted black to reduce glare to a minimum, and as Sarqaq delivered this valuable survival tool to his companion he warned: "Sun strong, no more hunt," for even with such a shade, continued exposure to the arctic sun as it beat against snow could be perilous.

When the intense cold relaxed, one of the worst Sarqaq had known, the men resumed their southern push, and the Eskimo received a lesson which startled him. That he had a high regard for Klope had been proved by his willingness to share this trip with him, but this did not prevent his holding all white men in gentle deprecation. "They can't work the way we do," he told his Eskimo and Athapascan fellow drivers. "They can't move over the tundra like us. And they cry at cold weather." Since all native people accepted such evaluations as an act of faith, the sled-drivers nodded.

But now, in the later stages of the run when the white man should have been exhausted, Klope was showing surprising strength, and during one day's run of twenty-seven miles he led most of the way, spent no time riding, and at the end of day was in much stronger condition than Sarqaq. The Eskimo, noticing this, supposed that it was because of something he, Sarqaq, had eaten, but since the two men had shared the same rough food, this theory didn't make much sense. And when on the third successive day Klope ran and worked somewhat better than the Eskimo, the latter said admiringly: "You white man work good." It was high praise.

They were on the river, fortunately, when they came upon those remarkably fine cliffs which hemmed it in at the old-time mining settlement that some hopeful prospector had christened Belle Isle and which later realists would call by the more appropriate name of Eagle. It was a noble spot, rimmed in by mountains which occasionally formed cliffs delineating the river. There was an island, which in summer, Klope conceded, might be pretty enough to warrant the *Belle,* but what he liked especially about Belle Isle was its sense of being a little universe of its own, and when he saw in rapid succession a moose, a pair of red foxes and a line of caribou, he supposed that the animals felt the same way.

The spot was memorable also because it was here, or close to it, that American territory along the Yukon ended and Canadian began. Beyond Eagle, John Klope would pass for the first time into foreign country, but he had no one to discuss this with because to Sarqaq, there were no boundaries from the North Pole to the South, it was all land which had to be dealt with in the same way. When the temperature dropped to minus-sixty-six, you dug in; when it rose to a comfortable minus-ten, you made as many miles a day as you could.

When they were about forty miles out of Dawson they were once more overtaken by severe cold, this time accompanied by a stout wind blowing up the Yukon from the north, and were forced to hunker down in an area of snow and scrub trees. Placing their sled against the direction from which the wind came, they cut trees to provide additional shelter and allowed the dogs to burrow into the drifts for what heat could be accumulated there.

When better weather prevailed, Sarqaq suggested they both hunt for moose or caribou to take into the starving town, and after making arrangements as to how each would return to the river in order to regain the sled, they set forth, Sarqaq with two of the spare dogs, Klope with the help of Breed and a one-dog harness with which to bring back meat if any was taken.

It was a bitterly cold, lonesome hunt, with both dog and man suffering from the extreme weather, and so forbidding was the cold that no animals were on the move. Klope shot nothing and returned to the Yukon, that great river locked in ice, in bad temper. Sarqaq was not there, and since darkness came each December day sooner than on the day before, it was obvious that unless he was found, and quickly, night would fall and the two men would face some eighteen hours apart.

The first thing Klope did was build a smudge fire, but the force of the wind soon dispersed what should have been the signal pillar; however, he added more wood in hopes that if Sarqaq smelled smoke, he would be able to trace it to its source. Registering carefully in his mind every turn he made, he moved out in widening circles, shouting for his companion but receiving no reply, and he was about to retrace his steps when Breed, with hearing more acute than his, began to whine and look to the north. There, after a demanding tramp, they found Sarqaq and his two dogs beside a dead moose whose unexpected death throes had wrecked the Eskimo's left ankle.

Stoically, Sarqaq had waited, certain that if any companion he had ever traveled with could find him, it would be this stalwart American. When Klope knelt over him he said: "Kill moose. Run to knife. Head come around, horn smash ankle."

Klope said: "I'll help you to the sled," but Sarqaq was too much a man of the tundra to allow that: "We go, wolf eat moose. You get sled, I guard." And he refused to leave the kill.

So Klope returned to the river, harnessed the dogs, and drove the sled to where Sarqaq waited. In the lowering darkness they butchered the moose, attended to Sarqaq's ankle, erected a protection against the bitter night wind, and settled in till dawn.

In brutal cold they made their plans. Sarqaq, hobbling about in tremendous pain, gave the impression of a man who had suffered a slight bump: "We harness all dogs, even Breed." When this was done with makeshift hitches, he insisted that all good cuts from the dead moose be stowed on the sled, which became possible because the dogs had finished the initial stores of dried salmon. Then he and Klope released the dogs, allowing them to gorge themselves on the offal and the scraps.

Now came an amazing decision. Klope had supposed that Sarqaq would ride atop the loaded sled and that the extra dogs would provide hauling power to carry both him and the moose, but the Eskimo, always mindful of his dogs and the purpose of this trip, refused to ride. With the aid of a stick and one hand on the sled, he proposed to walk the remaining miles to Dawson City.

He started valiantly, maintaining a pace that astonished Klope, but as Sarqaq pointed out: "S'pose me alone? No help? Me walk all same."

Drawing upon the inherited strength that had brought his ancestors across the Bering Sea and then enabled them to survive in the world's most inclement surroundings, Sarqaq maintained his pace for about an hour, but when they were safely back on the Yukon, he relaxed his terrifying determination and fainted.

Halting the dogs, Klope struggled to get him onto the top of the sled, tied him there, shouted to the dogs "Hi!" and off they went.

They spent the two final nights on the river, cold and frightened as to what might happen to Sarqaq's leg, but next morning they had traveled only a short distance when they caught sight of Dawson, that turbulent city where thousands of men pinched themselves in between mountain and river. Klope stopped the dogs, leaned forward on the handles of the sled, and bowed his head from exhaustion. He had completed one of the world's most demanding trips: nearly four hundred miles by train to Seattle, three thousand miles by sea to St. Michael, seventy miles along the Bering Sea to the Yukon, nearly fourteen hundred miles up that stubborn river to Dawson. He had earned the right to find his place in that city and try his luck on its gold fields.

When they burst into Dawson, with desperate men firing off guns to welcome them, Klope acted vigorously: he sold the cargo of food, including the moose meat, for a small fortune; he persuaded Sarqaq to give him Breed, which the Eskimo did because he knew that this misbegotten dog, so useless in the traces, had saved his life; and he rushed out to the Klondike, to learn that every inch of both the Bonanza and Eldorado shorelines had long since been staked. When laughing men, secure on their own claims, told him that there might be free sites about four miles away, where there was no gold, he stormed back into town prepared to fight anyone bare-knuckle for a claim.

Men who had been on the fields for a couple of years had learned to stay clear of newcomers who were semiwild with disappointment like Klope, and since this particular specimen had that big Eskimo dog that bared its teeth, they gave him extra room. It was probable, the more experienced men thought, that this one would wind up with a bullet through his chest before long.

They did not know that John Klope was quite a different type of person; he did not propose to die in some blazing shoot-out in a Yukon alley. He was angry not at the men who had filed on all the promising sites, but at himself for having arrived so late. He did not stop to reflect that from the time he had heard of the Klondike, on 20 July 1897, to this sixteenth of December in the same year, he had wasted scarcely a day. The layover in Seattle had been minimal; the stop in St. Michael needed to rebuild the *Jos. Parker* had been inescapable; while the stay at Fort Yukon had been necessary for him to complete arrangements with Sarqaq. Even so, he cursed his luck.

Now his problem was: Where do I find a place to sleep? and there was no easy solution, for most of the town was housed in tents whose temperatures at night could drop to minus-forty. Rarely had so many men lived in such misery, and he could find no one to take him in, even though he had saved lives by bringing in the cargo of food.

The main thoroughfare of Dawson—the entire place had been empty swampland only a year and a half before—was a gaudy stretch called Front Street, with saloons galore, a theater, a dentist, a photographer and forty other kinds of establishments for the separation of miners from their gold. No spot along Front Street was hospitable to Klope and his dog, but there was another street parallel to Front, nothing more than a line of dives, called Paradise Alley, and here in ramshackle cribs lived the women who had come to service the miners.

Some had climbed the Chilkoot Pass, others had been brought up the Yukon on the *Jos. Parker* by their pimps, and some came as actresses, seamstresses or would-be cooks. Failing to find the employment they had hoped for, they wound up on Paradise Alley in whatever kind of pitiful housing they or their pimps could find.

In one of the more commodious cribs lived a large, noisy, blowzy Belgian woman in her early thirties. She was one of eleven professional prostitutes who had been conscripted as a gang in the port of Antwerp, brought across the ocean and across the United States to work the gold fields. They had been imported, the locals claimed, by an enterprising German businessman who knew what a gold rush needed, and they were some of the best workmen, to use an odd term, in the Klondike.

The lead woman in the biggest crib was known widely and favorably as the Belgian Mare, and when Klope complained openly about being unable to file a claim or find a place to sleep, an American in a bar told him: "I spent four nights at the Belgian Mare's. She rents an extra bed."

So down Paradise Alley, Klope picked his way to the Mare's crib, and she did have an extra bed and she was in the habit of renting it out. Of course, there were only flimsy walls separating the rooms, so that anyone renting the bedroom almost had to participate in the Mare's lively and repeated profession, but Klope, always a loner, was able to blot out the reality of the Mare's occupation.

He was, however, grateful to her for her generosity, and especially for her good will, because although she spoke no English, she did go out of her way to make him comfortable, as she did with all men. It was when he took her out to breakfast one morning—sourdough flapjacks and moose-meat patties—that he met the man whose claim he would ultimately inherit. He was Sam Craddick, a disgruntled miner from California, one whose father had struck it moderately rich in the Gold Rush of 1849, the real one they spelled in capital letters. Craddick had expected to find lodes of gold similar to those in California, and the idea of washing tons of sand to find flecks of placer gold disgusted him.

"Have you a claim?" Klope asked, and the man said: "When I reached here last summer, all the good sites were taken. I met the Mare same way you did."

"So you staked no claim?"

"Hell yes, I staked one. But not down on the streams where the gold is. High up on a hill overlooking Eldorado."

"Why would you stake up there?"

And while the Mare wolfed her flapjacks, for she was a prodigious eater, Craddick used the slab-sided breakfast table on two trestles to explain mining theory to Klope: "Today, yes, you find gold along the streams down here. And that's where you'll always find it, time out of mind, if it ain't in a lode like in California."

"You think the mother lode lies under the hills?"

"I do not. I don't think there's a mother lode in the whole of Canada, or Alaska either."

"Then why did you claim on a hill?"

The miner said: "Today's gold, yes, it's found down here in the running stream you see. But yesterday's gold, and maybe the bigger lot—where was the stream that captured it?"

"You mean, there could've been another river?"

"That's what the experts say."

"But wouldn't it be lower? Not higher?"

"Ten years ago it would be lower. But let's say a million years ago? Who in hell knows where it could've been?"

Klope asked: "You mean it could've been much higher than today's river?"

"You ever see pictures of the Grand Canyon?"

"Everybody has."

"Remember how that little river cut that deep canyon? Maybe it was something like that." Craddick stared at Klope, then asked abruptly: "You want to buy my claim? The whole damned thing?"

"Why would you sell?"

"Because I'm fed up. This is hell country compared to California."

Klope thought: He's saying just what that fellow from California said. Maybe the Klondike is too tough for these men. Out loud he asked: "How big a claim?"

Craddick, aware that he had on his line a buyer on whom he might unload his mine, said honestly: "Standard size. Five hundred yards parallel to the stream. Usual distance east and west."

Klope interrupted the Belgian woman eating her pancakes: "Is he a good fellow, yes?"

The woman laughed, embraced Craddick, and cried: "Damn good man." She called for other men in the tent restaurant to testify, and when with the help of hand signals she explained the question, the men confirmed her opinion: "He is honest and he does hold a legitimate claim on the hills above Eldorado."

But when the Mare started out to defend the reputation of a man whom she knew to be reliable, it was difficult to stop her, and now she left the restaurant, stood in the middle of the frozen street, and with her right fingers to her lips uttered a piercing whistle. From a store midway down the street a young man in the red and blue uniform of the North West Mounted Police appeared. When he saw, as he suspected he would, the robust figure of the Belgian Mare, he walked sedately down to see what was the matter this time.

He was a fine-looking officer, twenty-eight years old, clean-shaven, and with the frank, open manner that betrayed his origin in some small Canadian town far to the east. He was Sergeant Will Kirby, taller than the average member of his distinguished force but no heavier. Since his job had required him to learn French, he conversed easily with the Belgian woman, who told him that the American Klope was demanding references from Craddick, whom she knew to be a trustworthy man.

When Kirby called the men out from the saloon, for he had been taught by his superiors to avoid both saloons and brothels, he recognized the miner at once: "Sam Craddick is a good man. I've known him more than a year."

Klope asked: "If he was here a year ago, why didn't he get one of the good claims?" and Kirby said: "Even then it was too late."

In no way did the officer suspect Craddick of trying to pull an illegal trick, for he was a decent man, but Kirby did think it best if he knew what was going on: "Is he trying to sell you a claim?"

"Yes."

"Where is this claim?" he asked Craddick, and when the latter said: "On the hill at Eldorado," Kirby said with guarded enthusiasm: "That's a serious site. Good things have been happening around there."

He did not want to know how much the seller was asking, but when the figure, fifty dollars, slipped out, he whistled and told Klope: "If you don't take it, I will." With that, he saluted the Mare and moved on.

Klope had the money and a burning desire to own a gold mine of any sort, so he said that he would buy, cash in hand, if the miner would show him the claim and sign a transfer of sale at the Canadian government's office.

Eager to dispose of what had been nothing but an irritation, the miner said: "You know, you're getting a cabin, not finished altogether. That goes with the sale."

"Let's go see it. Now."

So Klope paid for the Mare's breakfast, untied Breed, and set out with the miner to walk the thirteen miles to Eldorado, and when they reached there, Klope found that everything the man had said was true. He had a claim. It was atop a hill. He had started to dig deep into the frozen earth. And he had already built about three-fourths of a one-room cabin. It was, the man said, the best damn buy on the Yukon: "I don't think there's a flake of gold down there, but it's a real claim in a real gold field."

It was now late in the afternoon of the twenty-second, and neither man wished to take that long hike back to Dawson, so the miner suggested: "Why don't we stay here?" and they made rude beds in the half-finished cabin. As the man was about to go to sleep, he suddenly cried: "Damn near forgot!" and when Klope inquired, he explained: "You got to start your mix at night if you want flapjacks in the morning," and when he left his bed to rummage among his stacked goods for some flour, Klope asked: "Do you put some sourdough starter in the flour?" and the man replied: "No other way."

Now Klope rose to make a hesitant proposal: "I brought some sourdough all the way from Fort Yukon, and I was wondering if it was still any good."

"Try it someday and see."

"Could we try it now?"

Craddick studied this, then gave a judicious answer: "Mine's run out. I borried some from Ned down the line. I know this is good. If we just try yours and it ain't, we got ourselves no breakfast."

Klope considered this, then made his own proposal: "Why don't we try both?" and the miner said: "Now, that makes sense."

In the morning he was up before Klope, whom he awakened with good news: "Pardner, you got yourself some real live sourdough!" and he explained how a substantial pinch of old dough rich in proliferating spores of yeast, when mixed in with ordinary flour, a little sugar and water and allowed to ferment overnight in a protected place, would generate the finest cooking yeast in the world and produce a new dough that produced delicious flapjacks.

"Looks to me like your dough did three times as good a job as Ned's," and when Klope studied the two pans of rising dough, he agreed.

The first pancakes made from his leaven were, he proclaimed forcefully, the best he had ever tried: chewy, tasty, excellent when flooded with the almost frozen syrup from a big can. "They'd be even better with butter," the miner said, but even he had to admit that just as they were, they were pretty good.

"You got yourself a good strain," he said. "It'll work well up here as you dig your shaft."

After breakfast he instructed Klope in the intricacies of this type of mining: "What we do, every man on this hill, is light a fire every night, from September when the ground freezes hard to May when it begins to thaw. The fire softens the ground, maybe eight inches. Come morning, you dig out that eight inches and pile it over here. Next night and every night, you build yourself another fire. Next morning and every morning, you dig out the eight inches of thawed earth till you have yourself a shaft thirty feet deep."

"What do you do with the earth?" Klope asked, and Craddick pointed to a score of earthen piles, frozen solid: "Come summer, you sluice all that earth and maybe you find gold."

The miner shouted down the hill to a man working on a lower level: "Can we see your dump?" and the man shouted back: "Come ahead, but hold that dog."

So Klope, Craddick and Breed climbed down to the lower level, halfway to the rich creek below, and studied the large pile of frozen muck. The owner said: "Cain't tell as how there's much color in there, but Charlie, three claims down, says he believes he'll sluice forty, fifty thousand dollars outen his pile of mud."

"How does he protect it when he's down below working?" Klope asked, and both miners laughed: "There's millions lying around these diggings this wintry day. And it better stay right where it is, because if any man touches a thimbleful of my frozen muck, there's fifty men will shoot him dead."

On their way up the hill they passed a grizzled man in his sixties who had a larger-than-average pile of frozen earth beside his cabin. "Louie," Craddick said, "I hear you found real gold," and the man said: "Hasty assay said maybe twenty thousand dollars."

"Could I see what real gold looks like?" Klope asked, and the old man kicked at his pile until he broke loose a frozen fragment, and when he and the California man looked at it their faces broke into glorious smiles, for they were seeing a rich deposit. But when Klope looked he saw nothing and his face showed his disappointment.

"Sonny," the man said, "it don't come in minted gold pieces like the bank has. It's them teeny-weeny flecks. My god, this is a rich deposit!" And now when Klope moved the chunk of earth in the sunlight, he saw the flecks, golden and pure and extremely small. So this is what he had come to find, these minute particles of magic?

Back at his own mine, Craddick took Klope down the square opening he had so laboriously cut through the frozen soil, and for the first time in his life Klope heard the word *permafrost*: "Our curse and our blessing. We have to work like hell to dig it loose. But it's so permanent, here forever, that we don't have to timber our hole the way my pappy did in California. We dig a hole, it remains same size till doomsday or an earthquake. And when you do reach bedrock . . ."

"What's that?"

"Where the ancient river collected its gold . . . if there ever was a river, or gold." He sighed over lost dreams, and added: "When you reach bedrock, you just build more fires and melt sideways rather than down, and the permafrost holds everything together . . . even the roof of your cave."

They were about seven feet down when the miner said this, and when Klope looked up he asked: "How do I get my thawed earth up to the pile?" and from bitter memory the man laughed sardonically: "You load it in this bucket which I'm givin' you and you climb out of the shaft, takin' this rope with you, and you haul it up and dump it, and then you climb down with the bucket and do it all over again." He stopped and chuckled: "That is, unless you can teach that dog of yours to haul up the bucket and dump it."

"Is that how all those men . . . ?" and the miner nodded: "That's how they all did it. The men like me who found nothin'. The lucky ones who took out half a million."

The two men walked back to Dawson, with Breed in tow, and next morning they appeared at the Canadian registry office, where they met Sergeant Kirby filing a report. "I bought the claim," Klope said, and Kirby replied: "You won't regret it." And minutes later Klope had in his possession the valuable paper which stated that a transfer had been made and that he now owned "Eldorado Crest, Claim #87 in Line, formerly in the legal possession of Sam Craddick of California, now belonging to John Klope of Moose Hide, Idaho, this 24th day of December 1897, $50.00 U.S.A."

As night fell and a group of sentimental miners toured the frozen streets singing Christmas carols, Klope felt that he knew the rock-bottom fact about gold mining on the Klondike: Luck, I was lucky to get here alive. I was lucky to meet Sarqaq before it was too late. I was lucky to find a helpful woman like the Mare. And I was damned lucky to buy as good a lease as I did. I know the chances of finding gold in that hole are a thousand-to-one against, but no wiseacre back in Idaho will ever be able to laugh at John Klope: "That fool farmer! Went all the way to the Yukon and never found hisself a mine."

On the last day of July 1897 a tall elderly gentleman, garbed in the uniform of a Confederate general, complete with a big Robert E. Lee kind of hat and a pair of cavalryman's boots, was lounging in the offices of Ross & Raglan, one of Seattle's principal shipping firms. Idly inspecting the hordes of would-be gold seekers from all parts of the globe who cluttered Schwabacher's Wharf, his inquisitive eye fastened upon a family obviously from somewhere to the east, and even more obviously ill at ease. "They're running away from something," he muttered to himself. "They're nervous, but they do look decent."

The man appeared to be in his forties, a wispy sort of fellow unsure of himself, as if he were waiting to hear directions from his employer. A clerk perhaps, the watcher thought. The wife was in her twenties, an undistinguished sort of woman, and their son, who seemed standard in every way, was probably thirteen or fourteen.

The man watching started to chuckle as the three argued among themselves as to whether they should all enter the shipping office or only one, with the wife making the decision. Placing her hand in the middle of her husband's back, she shoved him toward the open door and turned to watch him enter.

The onetime Confederate studied the husband as he tentatively approached the counter, then heard him say to the shipping clerk: "I've got to get to the Klondike."

"Everyone does," the clerk said, "but our big ships are sold out, every inch of space through the October sailings, when ice closes down all the major ports."

"What am I to do?" the man asked in a kind of desperation, and the clerk said: "I might find you space on a converted tugboat, Seven hundred dollars, and grab it, because tomorrow it'll cost eight."

When the man winced, the clerk showed a twinge of sympathy and said: "Between you and me, pardner, the price is too high. Our big ships are the rich man's route. Take one of our little R&R boats to Skagway and climb over the Chilcoot Pass. Save yourself a bundle."

Since the man was now confronted with conflicting decisions, he told the clerk: "I better discuss this with my wife," but as he was about to leave the office he felt his arm being grabbed by someone he did not know, and looked up to see the smiling face of a Confederate officer, who asked: "Are you by any chance seriously considering entering the gold fields in one of their leaky saucepans?"

Startled both by the general's appearance and by his question, the man nodded, whereupon the stranger said: "I shall offer you invaluable advice, and trust me, it's worth more gold than you'll ever find along the Klondike." He introduced himself as the Klondike Kernel and produced three clippings from Seattle newspapers attesting to the fact that this honored veteran of a North Carolina regiment, who had fought with both Lee and Stonewall Jackson, had prospected in the Yukon from 1893 through the height of the discoveries in 1896,

and had come south on the *Portland* "with a gunnysack of gold bars
so heavy two members of the ship's crew had to help him drag it to a
waiting cab, which rushed him and the gold to the assayer's office."
The papers said that the Klondike Kernel, as he was favorably known
among his fellow tycoons, refused to give his real name "lest avaricious relatives descend upon me like a flock of vultures," but his gracious ways attested to his good breeding in North Carolina.

He wanted to talk. Having been immured in lonely cabins for so
long and having wasted so many years in fruitless search before striking it rich on Bonanza *Forty-three Below*, he was now eager to share
his knowledge and counsel with others: "Did I hear you say you had
three in your party?" and when the nervous fellow said: "I didn't say,"
the Kernel explained: "I saw you talking with your wife and son.
Fine-looking pair." Then with an all-embracing smile he added: "I'd
better meet them so you'll all understand the situation."

When they stood together in the street the man said: "We're from
St. Louis," and the Kernel said effusively, with a low bow: "Ma'am,
you are mighty young to have a boy that age."

"He's a fine boy," she said.

"Dear friends," the Kernel assured them, "I have nothing to sell.
I seek to steer you to no store where I receive a commission. I'm a
man who scratched his way from one end of the Yukon to the other.
I loved every minute of it, and seek only to share my experiences so
that good people like you don't make the same mistakes."

"Why did you leave?" the man asked defensively.

"Have you ever seen the Yukon in winter?"

"If you have all this money, why don't you go back home?"

"Have you ever seen North Carolina in summer?"

He said he could save them both money and heartache if they
would but listen, and he was so persuasive, so congenial in the way he
seemed to be trying to protect them, that they accepted his invitation
to lunch. The wife assumed he would take them to some fancy restaurant, and she was eager to go, for she had not eaten well on the
journey west; prices on trains were too costly.

"I take my lunch at a little saloon down the way. Excellent food
for twenty cents." Stopping in the middle of the wharf, he said: "I live
as if I was a poor veteran of the war in a small town in Carolina in
the year 1869, which was a very poor year indeed. I still cannot believe that my gold is in the bank. I'm sure I'll waken and find this all
to have been a dream."

That lunch lasted four hours, and repeatedly the Kernel assured his guests that they were doing him a favor: "I like to talk, always did, kept my men moving forward in the darkest days of the war."

"Were you a general?" the man asked, unable to resist the charm of this amiable man.

"Never higher than a sergeant. But I was the one who led the men."

Starting in the second hour he instructed his guests as to just what they would find on the gold fields. Asking the waiter, whom he tipped five cents, for a pencil and paper, he drew with remarkable skill a detailed map of the path from the ship's anchorage at Skagway, across the mountains and down the twists and turns of the Yukon: "Understand two things, my dear friends. In Alaska the ship does not land you. There are no docks to land at. It anchors way out here at the edge of a great sand flat. You have to work like animals to move your goods ashore before the tide engulfs them.

"Then you carry them, piece by piece, nine miles inland over roads that are merely trails. Then you come to this very steep mountain, not even horses can climb it, and in deep snow you lug every single pound of your goods up and over that mountain." He shocked them with the angle of the climb: "Thirty-five degrees. Inhuman."

The boy studied the drawing and said: "Any steeper, a man couldn't climb that in snow," and the Kernel said: "Even the way it is, many can't."

Then, when his listeners seemed properly awed, he asked: "And how much weight are you going to have to transport over that mountain? I mean each of you. You, Mrs. . . . I didn't catch the name." When she offered no response, he accepted the rebuff: "How many pounds of gear do you think your frail little arms are going to have to carry up that mountain and over?" Somberly he stared at each of the travelers, then said slowly: "One ton. You will each have to carry one ton over the mountains. You, ma'am, will have to lift up one ton and carry it up an angle like this in the snow."

Leaving his guests open-mouthed, he got up and started moving about the saloon, asking politely if this man or that would lend him his gear for a moment, and within a few minutes he had accumulated a small pile, with the owners standing in a circle watching his performance. Lashing many of the borrowed articles together, he said: "I'd judge this to be about fifty pounds, wouldn't you?" and men who were expert at that sort of thing agreed that yes, that was about fifty.

"The reason we use fifty is that's about the best a man can do heading up that mountain. So if you've got to haul a ton across—"

"Why so much?" a watcher asked, and the Kernel turned to face him: "Son, at the top of the mountain there's a Mounted Police station, and they will not let you enter their country unless you bring with you a ton of supplies."

"Why not?"

"They don't want you starving to death in Dawson City. I went six days without food in Dawson, and some went longer. We buried them."

He now turned to the boy: "Young feller, can you divide fifty pounds into one ton?"

"How much is a ton?"

The Kernel stared at the boy's mother: "Ma'am, don't you teach your son anything?"

She was not awed by this bearded stranger, for she recognized him as a man with a compulsion to talk, to share his experiences, so when he asked loudly, to impress the watchers: "Ma'am, I'll bet you don't know how much a ton is," she laughed and said: "It's a lot, that I do know."

"Young feller, it's two thousand pounds. Now, at fifty pounds a load, how many trips up that mountain will you have to make to hoist your tons of goods across?"

"Forty."

"You pass. Grade of C." And with that he hoisted the load of goods, borrowed a strap, and tied it to the wife's back: "Now, young woman, I want you to walk out that door, down to the corner and back," and he shoved her on her way.

When she returned she was not smiling. For the first time since leaving home she had some understanding of the adventure on which they had embarked: "It's heavy. I don't think I could climb a mountain with it."

"How about you, son?" and he strapped the burden onto the boy's back and sent him down to the corner. When he returned he, too, was subdued and willing to learn.

"I'm not going to send you, Mr. . . . What did you say the name was? Because if you can't handle fifty pounds straight up the face of that mountain, you have no right to leave Seattle."

He spent the third hour sharing with them the secrets of survival: "You must take with you two essentials besides the food. A good whipsaw for cutting the logs you'll need to build your boat at Lake Bennett, and be sure to buy the best, because whipsawing logs is the worst job in the world." When the wife asked what it consisted of, he asked for more paper, tipped the waiter another nickel, and proceeded to draw an excellent sketch in perspective of a log whose bark had been removed. It was perched over a pit, with one man down in the pit holding on to one end of an eleven-foot saw, while above him, on a low platform, stood his partner holding on to the other end: "Up and down you go, the man on top swearing that the man below is not pushing the heavy saw back up, the one on the bottom cursing because the man on top isn't pulling his weight." He turned to the couple: "I hope the minister who married you tied a tight knot, because it's going to be tested when you whipsaw the boards for your boat."

"What was the other essential?" the wife asked, and he said: "A coal shovel. Because when you climb that mountain forty times, which you'll have to do, there's another route parallel to it, much steeper, so when you get to the top and stow your goods—"

"Who watches them?" she asked, and he said: "Nobody. You make a little pile at the top and mark it as yours. A stick, a flag, stones, anything. That's yours, and as long as you work on that mountain your goods are safe, even though you're at the bottom and they're alone at the top."

"There must be thieves."

"Occasionally. Very occasionally."

"What do you do about them?"

"In my day we shot them. Fifteen, sixteen miners in a cabin. Man in charge says: 'This here fellow, name of Whiskey Joe, he stole Ben Carter's cache, Ben almost died. What's your verdict?' And we'd all say: 'Shoot the son-of-a-bitch, stealing a man's cache' and two minutes later the thief was shot dead." One of the men who had gathered near the table to listen said: "He's telling the truth."

"You ever shoot a thief?" the boy asked, and the Kernel said: "No, but I voted to have it done and helped bury the body after. Son, if you ever stole anything wherever it is you came from, don't do it in the Yukon or you're going to be shot dead."

"What is the shovel for?" the wife asked, and he nodded slightly, his beard brushing the table: "Thank you, ma'am. Sometimes I wander. Buy the lightest-weight shovel you can find. Carry it up to the top every time. Because after you stow your goods at your cache . . . Now, you understand, there may be a thousand other caches up there alongside yours. It'll look like a Persian market on a busy day, and when the snow comes, it'll all be covered in white six feet deep."

"So that's why you need the shovel."

"It is not. When snow hits, people just push and shove and kick and scrape, and pretty soon their goods are uncovered, as good as new if they've been properly packed. The shovel, ma'am, is for coming down. You walk about fifty yards from where your goods are, and before you lies a very steep hill, you couldn't possibly climb it coming up. And you couldn't walk it going down. So what you do, you sit on your shovel, handle out forward between your legs, and you give a push with one hand, and zooooey! You get the damnedest ride down the face of that mountain."

"Could two ride one shovel?" the boy asked, and the Kernel said: "If you were both skillful," and he sent one of the watchers to fetch a shovel, and since there were sixteen or eighteen establishments nearby specializing in the outfitting of would-be miners, a broad shovel was soon produced.

"Too heavy, much too heavy. But the size is right. Ma'am, you sit in front, knees drawn up if you can. Son, you fit this board under your mother's seat and let it stick out a little in back. You sit on it," and when they were perched precariously on the shovel, he gave them an imaginary shove and cried: "Zooooey, down we go!"

When the shovel had been returned, he said: "Two other things are advisable. A good square. Very light, weighs almost nothing, but you'll need it when you build your boat. And at least three good books apiece. Tear the covers off to cut down weight, but get books of substance for the long days of waiting. There's much to be said for a long book."

With the skill that he had manifested before, he drew a sketch of the boat they must build on the shores of Lake Bennett, and the wife complimented him: "You draw very well."

"General Lee said I should've gone into the Engineers, but I had no schooling."

"You speak so well. You use bigger words than I do," and he said: "In the Yukon you read a lot. You might walk forty miles to trade books, and the man you're heading to visit is overjoyed to see you. One man had a dictionary, traded it to me for a novel by Charles Reade. A dictionary can be very exciting when the night is six months long."

"How long is that boat you're drawing?" the man asked, and the

Kernel penciled in the dimensions of a boat he had once used, 23'
long 5' 6" in the beam: "It's got to carry three tons and three people.
I do declare, ma'am, you're a slight woman to have a son as big and
sturdy as this one."

In the fourth hour he reached the core of his advice. Pushing
back his chair, he asked: "Would you good people care for a little
food as we approach the real problem?" and he ordered four more
twenty-cent meals. The food was copious and good, but when the
waiter asked: "Drinks?" the Kernel said: "Never touch it," and the
waiter said: "For the twenty-cent meal you're supposed to buy drinks
too," and the Kernel said: "Give four beers to those men over there
and four more—that'll cover lunch—to those over there."

He then turned solemnly to his guests, and in carefully chosen
words, spread their options before them: "Now, from what I've said,
two things ought to be obvious, the first realistic, the second cruel."

"Yes?" the wife said, leaning forward. He liked this tough-minded
little woman and addressed his two explanations to her: "First, if you
sail to Alaska now, no matter where you go, St. Michael or Dyea,
there is no way you can get to the gold fields this year. The lower
Yukon will be frozen, so that way's blocked. And if you did succeed
in getting over the Chilkoot Pass before the heavy snows, which I
doubt, you'll find Lake Bennett and the others frozen up, so somewhere, at great expense of time and health and patience, you'll have
to hole up for the winter." He paused to let this harsh truth sink in.

"Is that the realistic thing or the cruel one?" she asked, and he
said: "That's realistic. Now, the cruel fact you must already have figured out for yourselves. When you do reach the gold fields next
spring, which is the earliest you can get there, you'll find that every
likely spot for digging gold has been staked out. I got there four days
after the big strike in 1896, and I had to settle for *91 Below* on Hunker Creek. Turned out to be the poorest creek of the bunch. I don't
know what the numbers will be next year. Maybe *291 Below, 310
Above*, if there's that much land available. And even if there is, it
won't be land with any promise."

"Then we're too late?" the man asked, his face ashen.

"Yes."

"But you just said you started with a poor claim," the wife said,
boring in. "And you came out with a fortune. The papers said so."

"I started with a bad one on Hunker Creek. Wound up with that
good one on Bonanza."

"How did you do it?"

The Kernel patted her on the cheek: "So complicated, that trade, I'd be ashamed to tell you."

"Did you steal it?"

"The other man thought so." He shook his head, partly in embarrassment, partly in disbelief that he had been able to conclude such a swap.

"Then our chances aren't good?" she asked, and he said: "They are not, and any honest man who came south on the *Portland* with me will tell you the same, if he has any interest in your well-being."

"Then why do the newspapers . . . ?"

"Seattle wants to keep this alive. To keep the stores open. The shipping companies. The bars like this one." Then he added a sagacious observation: "And it's people like you, streaming in, who help keep the rush alive."

"Is it all a lie?" she asked, and now the Kernel rocked back and forth before his plate of savory stew. He wanted to explain an intricate fact, and he wished attention to be paid: "Oh no! It's not a lie. It's just that the facts are different from what they say."

"How do you mean?" she asked, and he explained: "You'll not get any gold up there. Believe me, if you took a hundred men like me who knew the fields like a book, men of enormous experience . . . Only two or three of us out of a hundred found any gold to speak of."

"But they came off the *Portland* in dozens, I saw the photographs."

"They didn't photograph the hundreds who stayed behind, the old men in the tiny cabins, the young men freezing at the bend of the creek."

Rapping the table with her spoon, she demanded: "Tell us what you're trying to say."

He bowed: "Ma'am, you deserve a straightforward answer. You'll find no land worth claiming at the diggings, but smart people like you, if you have courage and even a little nest egg, you can find the real gold mine in Dawson City."

"You mean a store? A hotel?"

"I mean opportunity unlimited. Men like me will be out there digging for gold. You and your husband can be waiting in Dawson to take it away from them. This may sound ugly, ma'am . . . Damn it all, what's your name?"

"Missy. My mother named me Melissa, and this is Buck, and this is Tom."

"Pleased to meet you good folks. I don't mean to be harsh or mean-spirited. But Dawson is a tough place, except that the Canadian police do try to enforce some kind of limits. That gives bright people like you and Buck a fighting chance to earn a real fortune."

"What would we need?" Missy asked, for since listening to the Kernel she had begun to surrender hope of finding gold in the customary way.

"Money," the Kernel said. "Here in Seattle and in Dawson the rule's the same. If you have ten dollars, you're infinitely better off than if you have only nine."

"But if you don't have ten?" she persisted, and he ignored her, digging into his plate for more of the good stew. Finally he looked up: "Can't you see the situation? Don't go to Alaska now. Wait till April, when the snows stop and the ice begins to thaw. And the boat fares drop."

"And what do we do while we wait?"

"Work. Get jobs, all of you. Save every penny. So that when you do leave for the Yukon, you arrive with enough money to make a splash. If you're clever, and I think you are, you can double your money and then double it many times again."

"How?" Missy insisted, and he said: "Once you reach Dawson, you'll see a hundred ways," and later, when she saw one of the photographs of the famous gold town she saw that one of its characteristics was the blizzard of carefully painted banners hanging from the false-fronted stores which provided some kind of service:

DOUGHNUTS AND HOT COFFEE 20¢

GOLD ASSAYS IMMEDIATE

LAUNDRY MENDING FREE

DR. LEE, TEETH PULLED

As Missy studied the photographs, Buck did some figuring: "If we don't sail north till April . . . that's eight or nine months to wait. What should I do? What should any of us do . . . to earn money?"

"Aha!" the Kernel said without hesitation. "You find the best-paying job you can . . . anything," but Buck, remembering a year without employment of any kind, could not visualize getting work so easily, and it was here that the North Carolinian proved most helpful.

"Tom?" he asked. "What can you do?"

"Deliver papers. I was good at that."

"No, no! It doesn't pay enough," and he was about to dismiss that possibility when the boy said with the enthusiasm that the Seattle waterfront engendered: "I don't mean one door to the next. I mean this whole wharf area . . . going out to meet the ships coming in. Lots of new possibilities."

"And what can you do?" the Kernel asked Buck, but Tom broke in: "Pop can manage furniture accounts better than anybody."

"What experience?"

"Hardware. Big furniture."

"You're the man they need," the miner cried, rising from his chair and dragging Buck three blocks toward the center of the city, with Missy and Tom following.

He took them to Ross & Raglan, the store that had outfitted him years before when he first went into the arctic and which now was crowded with goods required by gold seekers. Calling for Mr. Ross, the Kernel reminded that industrious Scotsman of who he was and displayed the newspaper clippings to prove his identity: "I want you to hire this man, Mr. Ross. He knows goods. He can bring some order into this place."

So many of Ross & Raglan's clerks were leaving for Alaska that the merchant was eager to find a responsible replacement, and after a series of inquiries as to Buck's capabilities, he asked: "Can I write to your former employer for a reference?" and Buck said: "No. We left St. Louis after a misunderstanding. But you can see that the three of us are responsible."

"Are you married to this lady?"

"He certainly is," the North Carolinian said, and the enthusiasm of this miner who the papers said had brought nearly sixty thousand dollars on the *Portland* was so infectious that against his better judgment, Mr. Ross employed Buck on the spot.

The Kernel then took Tom to the offices of the *Post-Intelligencer* and insisted that the paper hire this intelligent lad to organize the distribution of the journal in areas that had been served only sporadically before: "I mean the waterfront, the new bars, the ships coming in."

Again, the excitement of the gold rush was so pervasive that the managers of the paper listened to a proposal that would have been dismissed as outrageous a year before. Tom got a job, on trial, and now the restless miner turned his attention to Missy.

It was not yet completely dark as he hurried the Venns along one of the major streets until he came to a fashionable restaurant, where he left Buck and Tom at the front door while he took Missy to the back. There, forcing his way into the kitchen, he asked to see the manager, and since in these frantic days Seattle was accustomed to bizarre behavior, the manager listened when the Klondike Kernel introduced himself, showed his credentials, and said: "My young friend here is a master waitress, widely regarded in St. Louis. She's on her way to the gold fields and needs a job till April."

"Can you do hard work?" the manager asked, and when Missy said "Yes," he said, almost with a sigh: "You can start right now."

"I can start in an hour," she said, and he said: "Don't disappoint me."

In slightly over an hour, the North Carolina miner had landed three good jobs for his new friends, and when, back at the bar, they asked why he had done this, he said: "I wish I was thirty. Starting up the Chilkoot again, rafting down the Yukon in a thing I built myself. I want to see you do it right." But as they rose to leave, he terrified them by placing his hands on the table, staring at each in turn, and saying: "I like you three. People of character, and I'm going to help you all the way. But you have got to tell me who you are and why you're here."

"What do you mean?" Buck stuttered, and the Kernel patted him reassuringly on the arm: "When you came into that shipping office you were scared to death. Looked at me twice to see if I was a policeman or a detective. What have you stolen? What crime? What are you running away from?" Before the man could respond he turned to Missy: "You! You're the salt of the earth, I can see that. But you can't possibly be the mother of this boy, can you? How old are you?"

"Twenty-two."

"And you're not married to this one, are you?" When she began to remonstrate, he said: "How do I know? You don't look married. You don't treat him as if he was your husband." When she asked what this meant, he said: "You treat him too nice."

Now it was Tom's turn: "And you, young fellow? Have they kidnapped you? Get you out of a reform school?" When Tom started to speak, the Kernel put his hand on his arm: "Not now. Think it over. Decide if you can trust me. Half the people coming through here have secrets they'd rather not reveal." He then looked seriously at each of the three: "But if I am to help you any further, wherever you're from, and it certainly isn't St. Louis, you must tell me the truth."

Badly shaken by the Kernel's final salvos, they convened at midnight, following Missy's stint at the restaurant, and leaped into an agitated discussion of their plight, with Missy saying: "He was uncanny. Twice I remember him looking at me funny when I said something that wasn't exactly true."

"But how did he know we weren't from St. Louis?" young Tom asked, and then Buck raised the real question, the one that each of the other two had wanted to ask but had been afraid to: "Suppose he is a detective? Suppose the Chicago police telegraphed him with our descriptions?"

The tiny rented room fell silent as the three fugitives contemplated this frightening possibility, and with the sounds of life crashing down about their ears, they went to bed and tried to sleep.

If the Kernel was a detective, he behaved in contradictory ways, for in the days that followed he did everything possible to help them start successfully in their new jobs, and after their working hours he reviewed item by item the things they must buy for their great adventure in the gold fields: "Six thousand pounds and each ounce must mean something." He arranged for Ross & Raglan to give Buck, as an employee, a discount on the purchases he made there and located a grocery that was eager to get rid of large supplies of dried goods before the New Year: "Buy them, Buck. They'll keep." But it was Buck himself who compiled the famous list that so many newcomers used as their buying guide. It itemized the hundred or so necessities a prudent gold seeker ought to purchase before he left Seattle. At the top the card said: "You will find every piece of this equipment at Ross & Raglan," and then he demonstrated his growing ingenuity by adding at the bottom a helpful reminder:

> Ross & Raglan, always mindful of their customers' welfare, most urgently recommend that each prospector take with him a small kit containing medicaments sure to be needed.

Borax	Essence ginger	Laudanum
Iodine	Chlorate potash	Chloroform

Quinine	Toothache drops	Acetanilid
Iodoform	Spirits of nitre	Witch hazel
Paregoric	Belladonna plasters	Carbolic salve

Such a kit can be purchased for less than ten dollars at Andersen's Drug Store, which is connected in no way with Ross & Raglan. Andersen's also recommends that men take along Monsell's salts for hemorrhages, in quantities according to each man's susceptibility to attack.

The disclaimer that R&R had no financial interest in Andersen's Drug Store and received no return on this free advertising was only partially true, because Buck did collect a small commission on each medical kit he helped sell.

But whenever they met up with the Klondike Kernel they were aware that he was watching them with far more than casual interest, and they grew nervous when he invited them to take meals with him. "You're my Seattle family," he said, and when Missy asked: "Haven't you any in North Carolina?" he parried: "That place seems to grow ever more distant." Then, instead of goading them to reveal their secrets, he confided his: "When I left this harbor years ago for Alaska, I had one ambition. To show those bastards back in Carolina. And all the time I grubbed along the Klondike, I consoled myself with the thought that with my increasing hoard of gold, I'd show them back home."

"What changed it?" Missy asked, and he said: "North Carolina don't seem so important now," but quickly he amended the statement: "Fact is, there's no one there who would remotely understand what the Klondike meant."

The three felt honored, in a way, that he had shared his thoughts with them, but this did nothing to alleviate their suspicions about him, for as Buck warned repeatedly when they were alone: "He could still be their detective."

Because each of them worked diligently, their savings grew, and this gave the two adults a happy feeling of security, but it was Tom who was enjoying himself most, for as he became familiar with the waterfront, meeting the dazzling steamships which came up from San Francisco or the old ones limping down from St. Michael, he began to sense what a magical city Seattle was. It dominated the extreme northwestern corner of the nation, with great trains arriving daily from various parts of the country; it also dominated trade with

Alaska, which had no other outlet. It was a city built on a captivating waterfront, with lakes and islands and stretches of water reaching to the horizon north, south and west. It was girt with massive mountains both east and west, and what surprised Tom, as it did Buck and Missy, the city did not lie on the ocean, as they had always supposed; it lay some eighty miles inland along waterways that served both Canada and the United States.

"I like this city!" Tom often cried when he saw it from the deck of some incoming ship to whose passengers he had sold copies of the *Post-Intelligencer,* or when he met a decrepit scow, barely afloat, which had limped down from Skagway and Juneau bringing three men who arrived with gold and sixty-three with nothing.

He knew the operation of the Seattle waterfront as intimately as a boy could in the limited time he had worked it, and one night he went running to the restaurant where Missy worked: "Wonderful news! The *Alacrity,* that little steamer owned by Ross & Raglan, they need a head stewardess for the Skagway run and they told me you can have the job."

"When?"

"They sail tomorrow at four in the afternoon."

"How much pay?"

"They said tips were plentiful . . . really generous."

She told Tom to wait till she could leave work, then accompanied him to where the *Alacrity* was docked, preparing for her return run to Skagway. As they neared the trim little vessel, Tom said: "A new ship like this, it makes the run to Skagway in six days, even with two stops."

Nervously, but with pride, he took Missy to see the captain, who was in his nightshirt: "Captain Reed, this is the one I told you about."

"You a hard worker?"

"He told you I was, didn't he?"

"I mean really work. Get this crew in the dining room straightened out?"

"I can, but what's the pay?"

"The tips are very generous."

"But from you? For getting things in order?"

Captain Reed considered this, then parried: "I suppose you'll jump ship the minute we hit Skagway."

"You know that my son will be here in Seattle."

"He said he was your brother."

"So, how much pay?"

"Two dollars a day. Your bunk. Your meals. And the tips have been very generous."

"Three dollars and I'll take it."

"I said two and I said you'd be treated generously. Take it or leave it."

"I'll take it."

"Be here at oh-seven-hundred."

"He said you sail at four in the afternoon."

"But we feed people at oh-eight-hundred. Be here."

Now Missy faced three obligations: she must inform her present employer that she was leaving the restaurant, she must tell Buck that she would be on the *Alacrity* during the coming months, and she must in decency explain matters to the Kernel, who had been so helpful. Grappling with the easiest first, she asked Tom to walk back to the restaurant with her and wait outside while she talked with the owner. He understood: "In Seattle everything happens. Good luck in the gold fields."

"I'm not going there at once," she tried to explain, but he said, not unpleasantly: "When you go, you go." To her astonishment he gave her an extra five dollars: "We can use you when you come back broke."

Explaining to Buck presented no problems at first, for he appreciated the fact that she would be earning substantially more than at the restaurant and that she would also be learning how prospectors reached the gold fields, but when she added that now they must level with the Kernel, he cried in real anxiety: "Why? Why?" and she said: "To clear things," and he said: "But suppose he really is a detective?" and she said: "There is no way that good man can be evil," and Tom supported her.

So at about one in the morning of the day she would make her first tour to the north, the three of them walked soberly to the saloon where the Kernel was sitting at his usual table, and Buck said: "They want to talk," and the Kernel rose, bowed politely, and said: "Why have you decided so late at night?" and Missy said: "I start work on an R&R ship tomorrow, and we owe you an explanation. You've been like a father to us."

"I've tried to be," and to his astonishment it was Tom who broke the ice, saying, "It was during the starving time in Chicago. My grandmother, my father and me, we had no food at all, no jobs of any kind . . . nothing."

"It was the Panic of '93," Missy explained, and Buck, who was still ashamed of those days when he failed the family, remained silent, so Tom continued: "Missy was in charge of charity for our church, and that's how we got to know her." He looked at her with love, there in the smoky saloon, and she said: "The minister came to me and said: 'Missy, there's one of our families, the Venns, we haven't seen for three weeks. They may be starving in silence.' And they were."

Painfully the recollections of that terrible time returned, and in reluctant pieces the three told how she, Missy Peckham, had made contact with the Venns, how a few dollars of church money a week had kept them alive, and of how their courage kept them afloat, but Tom said something else: "It was Missy who did it. I know that whenever the church money ran out, she gave us her own, and that's when we all fell in love with her."

On this extraordinary clue, the Kernel raised his two forefingers, pointing one at Buck, who had not yet spoken, one at Missy. "You also? You fell in love?"

"He had a wife," Missy said, and before she could describe the situation, Tom broke in: "A terrible woman. My mother, and a really terrible woman."

"Now, that's a harsh thing for a boy to say," the Kernel said reprovingly, and Missy said: "But she was. She tricked Buck into marrying her because . . ."

"Do you really need to tell me so much?" the Kernel asked, for he realized that he was getting more answers than he had sought, but Missy said: "Yes. You asked, and you're the only friend we have in the world."

At last Buck felt free to speak: "We thought you were a detective. Sent out from Chicago to trap us."

"What did the pair of you do?" and again he pointed at each at the same time. "Murder her?"

"No," Missy said, "but we might have. After Tom was born she abandoned him, ran away with two or three different traveling salesmen, a woman of great vanity."

Again Tom broke in: "She left me for eleven years, then when my father—he's not my real father but lots better than that—and Missy and I were a good family, she came back to Chicago and wanted to claim me as her child."

"It was unfortunate," Missy said. "When she brought two lawyers around to make us give up the boy, Tom told them all to go to hell.

Very wrong, because when the judge heard that a son had told his mother to go to hell, he became furious and said he would not only take Tom away from us, he would have Buck put in jail for adultery."

"That was when we decided to flee to Alaska," Buck said quietly. "The judge handed down a court order, and we ignored it."

The Kernel leaned back, ordered drinks for everyone and sandwiches too; then, pointing to the crowded bar, he said: "Half the men in there are probably under some kind of court order, and if they wanted to dig up my record in Dawson, I'd be under one too."

They spent the next two hours unraveling the tangled story of Chicago, one in which the three fugitives had been treated so very badly, and at one point the Kernel said: "You know, Buck, I guessed some of this that first day when I saw you talking in the street with your family. You looked like a man who'd been defeated . . . carrying a terrible burden. And you, Missy, you looked like a bossy woman who had to provide backbone for three."

"Not for me," Tom said, but the Kernel looked at him indulgently and said: "Yes, many a boy younger than you goes out to find a job when he has no father or the father he does have can't find one," and Missy said sharply: "Maybe you did, sir, in your day, but that wasn't 1893," and very sternly she added: "There were no jobs, and with the skimpiest church funds I tried to keep eleven families alive." Placing her hand in Buck's, she said: "We know. For us the gold fields will hold no terrors."

At five in the morning, when the first rounds of breakfast coffee were being served, the Kernel gave the Venns some solid advice: "What with Missy's new job and Buck's, you'll be making good wages. Save them in a bank, not a stocking somewhere that can be rifled by thieves or wasted when you think you need something. Go to the Klondike with money in your pockets, for then you can set your own speed."

At six, as he and Missy stood in the middle of the street while Buck and the boy climbed to their quarters to fetch her bag, she asked: "Why have you been so kind to us?" and he remained silent, for there were too many answers—his loneliness, his inclination always to back the underdog—but finally he selected one: "You're the kind of people that Alaska was invented for. Down on your luck, struggling back." Then he offered a strange one: "And because you back your man so strong."

"And you?" Missy asked. "What drove you, years ago?" and again he had a score to choose from: lost battles, little country villages reduced to ashes, mortgages in peril, but he voiced one that truly pertained: "You and I are cousins, Missy. Marry him," but she said: "We've done so much already, kidnapping and disobeying court orders, we don't need bigamy too."

"But isn't the other one divorced . . . and remarried?" and she said gloomily: "She don't bother with things like that."

At seven the three men walked her down to the *Alacrity,* where they kissed her goodbye as she boarded for her maiden voyage. "You're my family," the Kernel said. "Behave yourselves."

So through a chain of happy accidents the Venns found themselves locked in with the fortunes of the merchant shippers Ross & Raglan. Buck's excellent work for the firm assured his promotion and the offer of continued employment should he wish to stay in Seattle and forgo the gold rush. Missy was so able aboard the *Alacrity* that she too was promoted to jobs of greater responsibility.

Even young Tom had been drawn into the Ross & Raglan orbit, for as he enlarged his operations along the waterfront he had, as his service for the captain of the *Alacrity* proved, been of use to the smaller ships controlled by the firm. One morning as he delivered papers to Ross & Raglan's dockside office, the manager, Mr. Grimes, called from his desk: "Young man?" And when Tom, a husky, well-mannered boy big for his age, reported to him, Grimes said: "We could use a young fellow like you."

"Doing what?"

"Running messages to the ships. Tracking down freight. Many things."

"I like working down here."

"I noticed that. You'd be suited for what I have in mind," so Tom signed on with Ross & Raglan, but he also retained his lucrative newspaper route, starting at four o'clock each morning, finishing well before the ship office opened.

The Venns were now prospering so reassuringly that considerations for the future had to surface, and during the next layover of Missy's ship, the family held long discussions, in which Tom was the spokesman for staying in Seattle: "We have good jobs. We've saving money. And Mr. Grimes said I could have free mornings if I wanted to go back to school."

When the Kernel heard that Tom was talking of skipping the gold fields and staying in Seattle, he thundered: "Son! What is the matter with you? The great adventure of the century, and you want to miss it?"

"But you've warned us a dozen times we'll find no gold."

"Gold? Who's talking about gold? Four of the best men I ever knew in Dawson found no gold. I'd rely on those men any day of my life, and I'll wager they're just about as happy now as I am," and Missy added: "I see it on the Skagway run. Men who come out of the gold fields seem to carry a secret. 'We did it. We were there.'"

So it was agreed that come the middle of March they would take their savings out of the bank, catch a Ross & Raglan steamer to Skagway, go over the low ground to Dyea, and start up the Chilkoot. When they informed the Klondike Kernel of this decision he said: "My heart explodes with happiness for you. You'll never regret it," and a few days later he was gone. No one knew where he went, or even by what means he left Seattle. Missy was surprised, and said so frankly, that he had not bid them farewell or given Tom a going-away present, but a month later she received a registered letter from St. Louis, sent in care of Buck at the store. It contained two one-hundred-dollar bills, the first she had ever seen, a beautiful green on the face, resplendent gold on the back. Each had a brief note pinned to it, and one read: "This is for you." The other said:

> When you reach Dawson City, look out for a lady in the cribs on Paradise Alley called the Belgian Mare. Give her this and tell her the Klondike Kernel sent it.

On 15 March 1898 the Venns regretfully terminated their various jobs with Ross & Raglan, assembled their carefully chosen gear, and booked passage on the next trip of the *Alacrity* to Skagway. The fare, with a place to sleep and full meals, was thirty-four dollars for each adult, twenty-four for Tom, but when Buck went to pay for the tickets, Mr. Grimes said: "Total bill fifty dollars, courtesy of Malcolm Ross, who hopes you'll all come back to work for him."

Buck, who had never been on a ship before, stood transfixed at the railing as Missy explained which parts of the land were American and which Canadian. For him, this inland passage, with mountains to the east, large islands to the west and vast glaciers snouting their way into the ocean, was both a delight and a wild promise of greater scenes to come. He was sobered by the magnitude of the adventure they had undertaken and determined to succeed in it. As he contemplated the dreaded Chilkoot, the ominous rapids in the Yukon, he found himself thinking less and less of the gold that the Kernel had warned would not exist.

Tom deplored leaving Seattle, and as the *Alacrity* moved away from Schwabacher's Wharf with a steam-driven speed that really was alacritous, he felt tears coming to his eyes: This is a great city, I'd like to live in Seattle. I hope we find a million dollars in gold and bring it back here. As he stared at the receding profile of the town he had grown to love, he could identify almost every watery inlet along the broken shore, every hill that he had climbed with his papers. He could feel the vitality of this fine port hidden deep behind the protective mountains, and he loved even the strange sound of the name: *Seattle!* I'll be back!

On the evening of 23 March, prior to arrival off the Alaskan port of Skagway—navigable water ended about a mile from the town, which was approached over a wide sandy beach—Buck held a long family meeting to discuss a strategy for getting through the concentration of thieves without losing savings and property.

"It can be done," Missy said. "I've been to Skagway many times. Crooks everywhere, but if you stay clear, nothing happens."

"I have the money sewed in my clothes," Buck assured them. "Talk to no one. Hire the horses and let's hurry across to Dyea."

These precautions proved unnecessary, for at supper that night the captain of the *Alacrity* announced: "Because there's a big buildup of people coming out of Dyea, we'll move the ship over there three days from now. Anyone wishing to disembark at Dyea is invited to stay aboard."

So transiting the hellhole of Skagway was avoided, and during the two days the ship stood off that infamous port, Buck stayed in their cabin, guarding his family's funds and keeping his eye on their luggage stored on deck. But Tom wanted to see the notorious place, and to Buck's surprise, Missy said she was eager to chat with two women she had come to know while working the Skagway run, so on the second day she led Tom to the gangway, descended to the flats, and paid a sturdy man twenty-five cents to carry her through the low waves and deposit her ashore. Tom, refusing such aid, sloshed along behind her, watching everything: how lighters drawing only a few inches came out to unload the ship, how horses drawing carriages came far onto the sands, and how the little coastal town loomed up from below its crest of mountains.

Ashore, Tom found Skagway to be an intriguing place, for Missy kept warning him against practically every person they saw: "He's not a minister. He's Charley Bowers. He talks sweet and steals every cent you have." Later she said: "He's not a real policeman. He's Slim Jim Foster, shoot you dead if you bump into him." And according to her, the institutions in Skagway were as bogus as the people: "See that bank; it really isn't one. They accept your funds and you never see them again." Nor was the post office really a post office; letters dropped in its slot were never heard of again.

"Why doesn't someone report such stuff to the sheriff?" Tom asked, and she explained: "There is a sheriff, sure. Right over there. But he's not really one, either. Uses anything you say as an excuse for stealing you blind."

"What is real?" Tom asked, and she replied without hesitation: "The saloons," and when Tom studied the main streets, rough and unpaved, he saw at least three dozen whiskey joints.

Missy, however, was not awed by the boomtown, and with what Tom considered great courage she led him to a false-fronted building serving as the 317 Oyster Bar, with parlor attached. Marching boldly in, she said: "My name is Missy Peckham. I'd like to see Soapy, if he's in," and she indicated the back room where the notorious boss of Skagway held court.

A waiter stopped shucking oysters and disappeared, returning in a moment with a slim, fine-looking bearded man dressed in a business suit which would have passed muster in Denver, from whose worn-out gold fields he had come only a year before. He was about thirty-five years old, reassuring in appearance, and old-world polite in greeting Miss Peckham, in whose care he had once sailed.

"Tom," she said as the man gravely bowed, "this is Jefferson Randolph Smith, an important gentleman in this town."

"You were so attentive to me aboard the *Alacrity*," the famous gambler said, "could I invite you and Master Tom to an oyster stew?" She said: "We'd be honored, Mr. Smith, but Tom here wants to see the start of your White Pass."

"He'll see that in due course, I'm sure."

"No, we're entering by way of Dyea."

At mention of this rival town, a hated competitor for the Klondike traffic, Soapy stiffened: "Surely you're not going by that miserable route? Son, you climb that Chilkoot Pass once, you'd be exhausted for a week, and you'll have to climb it forty times! Do, please, for your own sake, Miss Peckham, take the easy route. Unload your baggage here at Skagway and let my people help you get organized."

"Tom wanted to see White Pass. He wants to see everything."

At this rebuff, Smith bowed graciously: "My good and trusted friend, if your young man wants to see the start of our commodious trail, the only practical way to enter the Klondike, you and he shall go in comfort. You were very kind to me aboard your ship, and I can do no less when you're in my city." He summoned from the back room a man named Ed Burns, who whistled for a henchman named Blacktooth Otto: "Get out the horses and take these two for a ride."

"Where to?"

"The start of White Pass."

"They goin' over?"

"Shut up and get goin'," and soon Blacktooth appeared with three rather good horses.

In January 1897, Skagway had consisted of a few scattered houses; by July of that year, it was becoming an exploding tent city; and now, in March of 1898, it was a real Alaskan boomtown, with streets sometimes knee-deep in mud or ankle-deep in dust and with stumps two feet high in the middle; with timbered houses unpainted and often without windows; and with the inevitable false-front stores emblazoned with carefully and sometimes ornately lettered canvas signs proclaiming a score of different services. In these days the name of the town, derived from Indian words meaning *Home of the North Wind,* was most often spelled *Skaguay,* but the variation in name did little to erase the monotony of the ugly place.

Blacktooth Otto was a big stupid man who talked more than his employer might have liked, for as they rode toward a rocky canyon which led toward the pass over the mountains leading into Canada, he first said what he had been directed to say: "You look, huh? This much better than Chilkoot, huh? You come Skagway you got no trouble." But then he shifted to subjects which really fascinated him: "Last week, five men shot in White Pass. Next corner, you look, huh?" And when Tom, riding ahead in the excitement of his first day ashore in Alaska, followed the trail around a nest of boulders, he saw dangling over the passage the swaying body of a hanged man.

"What did he do?" he asked, his voice close to shaking as he leaned away to avoid striking the corpse with his shoulder.

"Sheriff and those arrested him."

Tom thought it strange that a legal arrest should have ended in a hanging along a trail, but Blacktooth Otto next revealed that "the sheriff and those" had also been responsible for the five shootings, but Missy whispered the words which unlocked the mystery: "Soapy Smith," and as they rode deeper into the canyon their guide spoke of other incidents which could be attributed only to the nefarious Soapy.

Tom started to say "Why doesn't somebody . . . ?" but Missy indicated that he should keep his mouth shut, and the boy dropped that question, asking Blacktooth: "Why did the sheriff and those feel they had to shoot them?" and he explained: "Mr. Smith looks after everything. Good man, huh?"

Now the attention of the travelers was diverted from Mr. Smith's curious system of government to a horror much more immediate, because as they entered the first stages of the White Pass trail, which they had to concede was much lower than what the snowy Chilkoot seemed to be in the famous photographs they had seen, the bodies of horses, apparently worked to death among the boulders that strewed the pathway, began to appear, first one with a foreleg broken and a bullet between the eyes, then an emaciated beast that had fallen and found itself unable to rise, and had simply died where it fell.

Tom was sickened by the sight of these once noble animals come to such disastrous ends, but then, at the next corner, they saw a defile which was literally crammed with the fallen bodies of dead horses. He counted seven, their legs at wry angles, their necks draped grotesquely over rocks, and finally they came upon four that had perished one atop the other, and he became sick.

Now a different horror surfaced: a short distance beyond, Blacktooth halted his tour: "More better we go back." Two men, partners since leaving Oregon, had come to the end of their expedition and to the end of their horses, for two of their three grotesquely loaded animals had fallen, and each man was kicking and cursing the beast for which he was responsible, and as the men slowly began to realize that these animals would never again rise, they started screaming at them, as if the horses were at fault and not the lack of oats and the poorly stowed burdens and the rocky trail. It was a scene of madness, which revealed the horrors of the trail, and as one of the men whipped out a revolver to shoot one of the fallen horses, his partner, remembering what they had paid for the beasts and still hoping to salvage their services somehow, tried to protest: "Not my horse, damn you!"

whereupon his partner turned his gun away from the fallen horses and shot his companion right through the head.

"We go back, huh?" Otto said, not in fear and not much worried by the incident. Tom and Melissa followed obediently, and for the rest of their journey the boy would have no complaint about the tribulations of the Chilkoot, for he had seen the alternative.

When they returned to the *Alacrity* that evening they faced still another change of plan, for the captain revealed that Soapy Smith had come aboard the ship with a warning that if it dared sail to Dyea to unload passengers heading over the Chilkoot, when it was supposed to land them at Skagway, where the Smith hoodlums could get a shot at them, he, Soapy, would direct his sheriff to prevent the ship from ever landing at Skagway again, and any crew members already ashore would be arrested and held in jail till Lynn Canal froze over. In furtherance of his ultimatum, Soapy posted his armed guard along the shore with orders to nab all sailors on shore leave.

Since it was obvious that Soapy held the commanding cards, the captain had acquiesced, announcing to the passengers who were still aboard: "You must disembark here. Mr. Smith will arrange for the transfer of your baggage to the shore and then over the hill to Dyea," and when some of the men, unaware of Soapy's reputation, began to demur, the amiable dictator smiled, pardoned himself for intruding in this abrupt way, and explained: "It's a matter of law and order."

So next morning the Venns had to supervise the unloading of their three tons of gear and its laborious delivery across the sandy flats to the chaotic shore, where vast mounds of goods lay stacked just far enough inland to escape the tide. When they had their gear assembled, quite a distance from town and some nine miles from the sister port of Dyea, Buck told Missy and Tom: "We're in real trouble tonight. An officer on ship warned us that if Soapy Smith's men can't trick you in town, they'll rob you here on the beach or along the trail."

Afraid to leave their goods unguarded on the beach, Buck decided to form a mutual protection arrangement with other stranded travelers, and had started to approach a stranger with such a proposal when he caught Missy's frantic signals to desist. Hurrying back to Missy and Tom, he learned that this was one of Smith's men sent to make just that kind of deal. "If you'd gone along," Missy said, "he'd have steered us to some place where he could have knocked us down and stolen everything of value."

So the Venns remained on the beach that night, guarding their goods and staying clear of the town where they would have been in greater danger. They were more fortunate than two brave miners with experience on the California gold fields, for when they slam-banged their way into town, willing to challenge anyone to molest them, two of Soapy's henchmen calmly shot each through the heart and left the bodies prone and bleeding in the dusty roadway, where they were ignored by passersby in the morning.

How could such blatant murder have been allowed? How could a boomtown clearly a part of the United States exist without law of any kind other than the smoking end of a revolver? Even the railroad boomtowns of Wyoming, the cattle towns of Kansas, the gold towns of California, the fledgling oil towns of the Southwest had not paraded their lawlessness with such flagrant disregard for organized society; some attempt was always made to preserve orderly government, and an honest sheriff or a powerful clergyman could usually be found to lead the community to a more respectable existence.

Alaska was different because its heritage was different. In the Russian days the Slavic forebears of Soapy Smith said: "St. Petersburg is far away and God is up in heaven." When the Americans finally assumed power, there was that incredible thirty-year period when the new owners made no attempt to govern, when there were no codified laws or courts to enforce them. No people in the organized states and, least of all, the members of Congress, could visualize the raw anarchy in which Alaska, this latest and potentially most important addition to the Union, was allowed to rot like a melon at the end of a very long vine. Soapy Smith, this tinhorn Colorado gambler whose crimes at Skagway were far worse than the Venns knew about, was the specific creature of the American system of governing its colonies. If he and his henchmen were a hideous blot on the United States, the culprit was not Smith but the American Congress.

In the morning the Venns, with their goods and their money fortuitously intact, sought to hire two of Smith's draymen to haul their gear the nine miles across the low hills to Dyea, and this transaction could also have produced danger and the possibility of losing everything had not Blacktooth Otto, prowling the beach to see what he might promote, spotted Missy and Tom and recognized them as

Soapy's friends. Running to town, he burst into the 317 Oyster Bar with the news: "Mr. Smith, that lady, that boy, yesterday. They're on the beach."

Commanding Blacktooth and another henchman to fetch horses and a dray, Smith walked slowly down to the beach, greeting citizens as he went and studying with careful eye the various improvements that had appeared in the growing town since his last inspection. He liked what he saw, but he liked even more that vast accumulation of goods on the flats. If four hundred and fifty stampeders had landed in recent days, and if each had brought a ton of goods, the amassed pile of wealth on the shore was almost incalculable, and Soapy intended siphoning off his fair share, say thirty percent of everything.

When he found the Venns he was exceptionally courteous to Missy, whom he admired, and fairly courteous to Buck. He offered them both whatever assistance they needed, and said: "I do hope you'll be taking our White Pass and not that dreadful affair at Chilkoot." Buck, almost trembling with apprehension over being so close to Smith and bewildered by the man's graciousness, said firmly but without the least hint of aggression: "We've decided to try the Chilkoot."

"You're making a bad mistake, my friend." Then Tom blurted out: "We saw those dead horses in your canyon," and Soapy replied, with just the slightest touch of irritation: "Horses are not meant for our canyon. Men have no trouble."

He asked if they would care to take breakfast with him, prior to their march to Dyea, but Missy replied, as if she were still a stewardess on the *Alacrity:* "You were far too kind yesterday," and he bade them goodbye with a flourishing kiss of Missy's hand and a stern admonition to Blacktooth: "Take special care of these good people."

They arrived at Dyea, a town much smaller than Skagway but free from the attentions of Soapy Smith and his gang, before noon on 1 April 1898, and there took stock of their situation. "We can thank God," Buck said, "that we escaped Soapy Smith. Only five hundred and fifty miles to go, and most of it a soft ride down the Yukon."

But they were not wholly free of Soapy Smith, because his man, Blacktooth Otto, lingered as they talked, and when they finished, he surprised them: "I'm supposed to haul you on to Finnegan's Point." This was a spot five miles farther up the trail, and since one had to cross and recross the little river running down the middle of the footpath, the assistance would be invaluable.

"We'll go," Missy said immediately, and when Buck questioned her wisdom, she said wisely: "Anything to get the gear closer to the pass."

But after they crossed the corduroy bridge that carried them into Finnegan's, a problem arose which had perplexed every newcomer: there was no hotel, no orderly place to store goods, and no police protection. "Are we supposed just to dump our goods here?" Buck asked, and Blacktooth said: "Everyone else does."

"Who guards them?"

"Nobody."

"Don't thieves steal them?"

"They better not!" Blacktooth was unable to imagine his boss, Soapy Smith, as a thief, and he supposed that what happened on the trail out of Skagway was always the fault of some careless traveler. Saluting the Venns, he and his partner left the family on the trail, their little mountain of goods piled beside them.

"I'm not going to leave all this here without a guard," Buck vowed as he began to pitch their canvas tent, but a man who had made many trips along this difficult roadway advised against such action: "Believe me, pardner, go back to Dyea and get a good night's sleep in a hotel while you have the chance," and on his own he ran ahead and whistled for Blacktooth to turn around and carry these good people back to Dyea.

The Venns now faced a dilemma: a good bed and a hot meal versus the protection of their cache, and Buck made the decision: "Sooner or later we'll have to be in one place, our goods in another," and their adviser said: "That's talking sense, pardner. Look at all those other caches. That's how we do it."

As they rode in comfort back to the hotel they could not avoid staring into the faces of gold seekers coming up the trail, and after a few such encounters, Missy could differentiate between them: "This group coming next, they're on their first trip to Finnegan's. Bright eyes, looking this way and that, oohing and aahing over the snow-covered mountains. But look at these next three! They've been back and forth a dozen times. How can I tell? They look only at the ground to find the best place to step."

Before depositing the Venns at the Ballard Hotel, Blacktooth Otto confided to Tom: "You shoulda been in Skagway last night. Two men shot dead on the main street."

"What did they do wrong?"

"It was dark. You couldn't see."

Buck was up before dawn, goading his companions to hurry on to their cache, where a team of smiling Indians awaited them: "We carry goods, Sheep Camp, five cents a pound." With horror, Buck calculated the bill would be three hundred dollars for a distance of only eight miles, and from Sheep Camp to the summit would cost twice as much.

"We'll carry it," Buck said, and the Indians predicted: "You be sorry!"

Because this was not yet the sharp incline, Buck proposed that he try to carry sixty pounds, Tom forty and Missy thirty, and in that disposition they started out. Eight miles on level ground with no pack would have been a smart task, but over this rocky trail with its insistent upward grade it became a torment. Nevertheless, because they were eager and in good shape, they made two round trips that day. At sunset Buck was back at his figuring: "One hundred and thirty pounds a trip between us. I don't think we can make more than two trips a day. To move three tons . . ." His face grew ashen: "That's more than three weeks. Hotel bills and all, maybe we better get some Indians," and when Missy set herself to the task, she found another team, husky young men, who would portage the lot to Sheep Camp for one hundred dollars. After that day's toil, Buck voiced no objection.

Five days later, when they were safe at the Scales, with their gear beside them waiting to be weighed, elevations became more important than distances. It was less than a mile to the summit, but when the Venns stared at that incredible ladder of twelve hundred steps carved out of ice, Tom consulted his map and informed the others: "When we get there . . . three thousand seven hundred feet high," and Buck shuddered: "We've got to carry three tons to that height?"

Missy, the practical one, ignoring this talk of the terrifying climb, said: "You know, a man could land naked at Dyea beach and outfit himself up here at seven cents on the dollar . . . or maybe for nothing," and she pointed to a vast accumulation of stuff that had been discarded: "A man or woman staring at those steps can decide in a hurry that they don't really need a folding table or a sewing machine," and forthwith she began to identify those things she was sure they could do without.

That night the Venns saw, in all its ugliness, a demonstration of why the leaving of unguarded treasure on the trail was possible, for there was a commotion outside and cries of "We caught him!" and then a deep voice shouting "We got him red-handed!"

Even those already asleep piled out of the grubby tent hotels—there were eleven such places, one worse than the other—to witness the drumhead trial of a vagrant named Dawkins who had committed the one unforgivable crime along the trail. Murder in hot blood was acceptable if there was even a shadowy justification; desertion of a wife was not uncommon; and the lesser wrongdoings of a frontier society were tolerated, but on the arctic frontier, where to tamper with a man's cache might mean his death, theft was unforgivable.

Trappers would leave a month's supply of food in some cabin so far removed that you might think no one could ever reach it, but during an unexpected storm some forlorn man would stagger in exhausted, find the can of matches, the carefully cut branches, the pine needles and the food, and he would be saved. He could consume the entire month's supply of food if necessary, but he must replace it. He must cut new branches, ensure that there were matches ready, and leave everything in place for the next emergency. Even if he had to double back fifty miles to replenish the cache, he was honor-bound to do so, and because many a trapper or prospector owed his life to this tradition, it was sacred. In a lawless land this was the supreme law: never violate a cache.

Well, Dawkins had seen stacked at the edge of the Scales an extra parka that would nicely replace his worn and poorly lined affair. The parka had been neatly tied in a bundle and partly hidden in a growing pile of goods, so that no one could possibly believe it had been abandoned, but he had taken it. He had been seen and chased and caught, and now the sourdoughs in the crowd, the old-time Alaskan adventurers as opposed to the newcomer cheechakos, convened a miners' court, a fearsome affair that had become necessary because the government provided no control.

While a lantern was held close to the face of the accused, the men who had caught him stealing told their story, which Dawkins could not refute. "Shoot him!" a grizzled sourdough cried, and several took up the cry, but a Presbyterian minister, on his way to the gold fields to try to bring a little morality to a corrupted land, protested: "Men, a sentence like that would be excessive. Show compassion."

"He showed none. Steal a cache, you murder a man."

"Give me a gun," snarled another man. "I'll shoot him."

The minister pleaded so earnestly that even some of the sourdoughs reconsidered, and a veteran stood before the clergyman, inches from his face, and offered a compromise: "We'll give him thirty lashes."

"Thank God," the minister said, not guessing what the rest of the sentence was to be.

"But you must apply them. Or we shoot."

Now Dawkins broke his silence, for he knew the sourdoughs meant business: "Please, Reverend."

So Dawkins was stripped, his hands were tied to a stake—which took the place of a tree, for there were none amid the snows—and a rawhide rope with a wooden handle and a big knot tied at the end was handed to the clergyman, while two sourdoughs said: "We'll count."

Ashen-faced, the minister accepted the improvised cat-o'-nine-tails, but recoiled: "I can't."

"Lash him," a sourdough shouted, "or I shoot."

"Please!" Dawkins pleaded, and the trembling minister, biting his lip and closing his eyes at the crucial moment, swung the rawhide and brought the heavy knot across the man's back. Dawkins made no sound, and the watchers shouted "Stronger!" But on the sixth lash, when the culprit's back was bleeding, the minister could see only the form of Jesus Christ being lashed by Roman soldiers on the way to Calvary, and he fell prostrate in the snow, his shoulders heaving as sobs wracked his body.

An old prospector, whose life had been saved by a cache north of the circle, snatched the rawhide, and as the solemn voices counted seven . . . eight . . . nineteen . . . twenty the punishment continued, but before the twenty-first blow fell, Missy Peckham threw herself upon the old man's right arm and the beating stopped. Dawkins, who had fainted, was cut down, dressed in his own parka, and revived with snow. When he could walk he was headed down the hill to Dyea and told: "Get going." He was seen no more.

The Venns slept late next day, for it was Sunday, but at about eight Buck began to build nine bundles of gear, with the admonition: "Today we start up the steps. Endless daylight, so we'll try for three trips." Then he made a most sensible decision: "Forget what anybody else is trying to carry. For us, lighter loads. Me, fifty pounds, Tom thirty-five, Missy twenty-five." At this news Tom did some more calculating: "Oh! For three tons that's going to be fifty-five trips."

"Fifty-five it'll have to be," Buck said, but as he was about to heave Missy's onto her shoulders, men came into camp shouting: "Avalanche! They're all dead!"

It was not a warning. It was fact. From the southern face of a mountain more than two thousand feet above the Chilkoot, a vast accumulation of snow and ice had come crashing down, burying a portion of the trail to a depth of twenty or thirty feet.

"How many trapped?" Buck shouted as he threw aside Missy's bundle and grabbed for one of the shovels.

"Mebbe a hundred," and the messenger went shouting up and down the camp as volunteers grabbed whatever they could and rushed toward the avalanche, which was much bigger than the frightened crier had said and had engulfed even more people.

They did not all die. Cheechakos who had been on the trail only a few days, men and women alike, clawed at the snow and ice to make extraordinary rescues. Many had shovels, which were ably used, but one thoughtful man from Colorado, learned in the ways of avalanches, had brought a pole, which he used to probe through the snow till he struck something hard. Then others dug like moles where he indicated, often finding only rock but occasionally bringing to the surface someone still alive. This man and his pole saved more than a dozen.

In all, some sixty gold seekers perished that Sunday morning, but not even a disaster of such magnitude could diminish the passion with which the survivors hungered for gold or slow the incessant traffic up the mountain. Hordes from below had been set in motion, and it seemed that nothing could halt them, not even crushing death. Half an hour after the cascades of snow had obliterated the path to the top, gold-savage men had tramped out a new path, looked sideways at the site of the tragedy, and plodded on.

Because the Venns had spent half a day helping with rescue work, it was late afternoon when they eased their way into the line of prospectors climbing the stairs, and once they claimed a place in that struggling chain, there was no way to rest or turn back; they were on a steep, upward pathway to hell. If a man simply had to urinate, he could step aside and do so with no one noticing, but when he struggled to reenter the chain, he might try vainly for more than an hour. On Chilkoot, no one helped anybody.

The three Venns, clinging tenaciously to their places, approached the last sixty vertical steps as dusk fell, and for one fearful moment

Missy wavered and looked as if she might have to surrender her place in the line, but, gasping for breath and nearly fainting with exhaustion, she clawed her way to the summit, looked back at the swarming humans mechanically following her, and thought: My God! To do that fifty-four more times!

In that act of climbing to the top of a mountain, where goods lay stacked in hundreds of different piles, some of them fifteen feet high, the Venns and the other stampeders entered an entirely new world. Arbitrary and chaotic it was, but it was also a world where reason and law prevailed. For this lofty point represented the boundary between American Alaska and the Yukon Territory of Canada. It was a line drawn in the snow with no legal authority to justify it; actually, the American boundary should have been quite a few miles to the east, but this high pass became the permanent boundary between the two nations because some remarkably stout-hearted men said it was.

They were a contingent of the North West Mounted Police, sent out to an undefined border to establish an undefined law. Few men in North America ever served their nation or their people better than these, for when they took one look at the preposterous situation that the Americans had allowed to develop, they said simply, but with great force: "The law is going to be what we say it is." And this law, eminently reasonable and just, was forthwith adopted, enforced, and accepted.

Indeed, many Americans struggling up the Chilkoot Pass from the moral swamp of Skagway were gratified to find at the crest of the mountain a body of resolute men who said: "This is the boundary. These are the laws. And you will obey both." Like wayward children who have been running wild without supervision but know inwardly that reasonable discipline is better, the cheechakos climbing over the pass embraced the law of the Mounties.

The rules as they evolved on the spot were practical: "You cannot enter unless you bring in supplies for one year, particularly food. You must pay Canadian customs on every item you do bring in. You cannot sail down the first rough lakes and then the Yukon unless you build yourself a stable boat capable of carrying yourself and your gear. And each boat must be numbered so that we can track its successful passage to Dawson." They justified this last demand by citing a sobering thought: "When people went down the lakes in just anything and without proper numbering, scores drowned."

In obedience to these rules, late on Sunday, 3 April 1898, the

Venns placed their first load of goods under the protection of the Mounties, and for the first time since leaving Seattle they felt safe in doing so. But the next days in early April were shattering, for Buck's easy supposition that they could make three round trips a day was totally impractical. The ice stairs were so steep and the weights so punishing that two trips proved the maximum, and on some days the wait to get into line was so protracted that only one trip could be made, and one night Missy groaned as she crept into her sleeping bag: "Oh God! We'll be at this all of April."

But they strove diligently, up that icy stairway watching always for the next avalanche, taking not a single step in an upright position, always bent parallel to the earth from the waist up, legs failing, lungs collapsing, sodden eyes fixed to the ground but always vaguely aware of the man ahead, whose back was also parallel to the ground, for he too carried fifty pounds up those stairs of ice.

It was a human effort not matched in America by any of those star-led pioneers who had settled the continent. None had known a worse task than these thirty thousand who climbed the Chilkoot when the late storms of winter were still raging.

On one trip, when Missy and Tom reached the top, they found their earlier deposits under fifteen feet of sudden blizzard and could not even estimate where their vital treasures lay. In their desperation they were assisted by a handsome young sergeant of the Mounted Police, a clean-shaven, blue-eyed man from Manitoba in central Canada named Will Kirby, twenty-eight and determined to make a name for himself in the North West force. He loved the outdoors and had been both a trapper and a voyageur, one who canoed down remote rivers to explore trade possibilities.

When he saw Missy and Tom poking through the April snows, searching for their buried cache, he came to their aid: "I don't want to see you fretting over a little snow like this. Last January it was seventy feet high up here."

"That's impossible," Missy snapped, not eager to be patronized after her exhausting climb, but he produced a photograph of himself and two other Mounties standing then right where they were today, and no sign of habitation was visible: "It can snow up here. Now, what kind of cache had you been building?"

Mollified by the photograph, although she suspected it was a fake, Missy indicated about where the Venn goods lay and described what they looked like, and as the three shoveled and kicked snow and probed, Sergeant Kirby told them: "There was a man last January, during the fierce storm, he did a clever thing," and when he described what this inventive man had done, both Missy and Tom recognized immediately that it could work again. So when they found their cache, with Kirby's help, they hastened down the mountain and told Buck what they had heard. And he cried: "It'll work!"

He would require several props: a securely fixed rock at the top of Chilkoot, and there were many of them; two sleds, which could easily be made from scattered bits of timber; a very long rope; and five additional men, the heavier the better. Buck saw quickly that he had available all the ingredients except the very long rope, but he had seen among the household goods discarded along the trail from Sheep Camp to the Scales several skeins of heavy rope, so he left Missy and Tom at their depot and scrambled back down along the trail he had so recently climbed. He did not find the rope he had remembered but he found some of more recent vintage abandoned among the trunks, the furniture and the excessive household goods.

Grabbing the rope, he hurried back to the Scales, where he studied the laboring men about him, settling ultimately upon four likely candidates. Sergeant Kirby had recommended six in all, but Buck believed he could work more effectively with four others besides himself. Assembling them outside his tent, he divulged the plan: "If we climb to the very top of the Chilkoot, fasten a self-made block-and-tackle to a rock that can't be budged, and build us two sleds capable of carrying us five men, see what we'd have?" And slowly the four listeners began to visualize what the Canadian Mountie had divulged to Missy and Tom: "Hey, if we five got on one of the sleds and let ourselves slide down the mountain, the other sled packed with our gear would have to go up!"

It worked. They climbed to the top of the pass and found, with Kirby's help, an appropriate rock, to which they attached their crude block with the rope tackle passed through the pulley. When the sleds were attached, top one empty, bottom loaded with gear, the five men climbed to the top carrying very light loads, which they quickly deposited at their respective depots on the Canadian side. They then ran to the waiting sled, onto which they placed themselves so that they could push with their hands, and when the sled was eased to the top of the steep incline, Buck gave the signal and the fifth man, in back, started pushing the sled until it gained momentum. With a final shove which sent it downhill, he jumped aboard, and the men had the extraordinary satisfaction of feeling themselves sliding down the mountain while the other sled, loaded with the heavy baggage, crawled up the hill as if pulled by invisible hands.

The experiment was more successful than even Sergeant Kirby had predicted. Said he when Missy and Tom next reached the top of the mountain: "It takes an American to build a machine," and he was pleased as he saw how the men had perfected the operation. These particular Americans were going to negotiate the Chilkoot Pass the easy way.

In the meantime Missy and Tom were making their trips with what might almost be described as joy, for they carried to the top loads that were much diminished but which invariably contained a shovel, and when they unloaded their burdens at the Venn cache and saluted Sergeant Kirby, they moved away from Chilkoot proper, going instead to the very steep slope covered by many feet of snow. Here Missy placed a board on the shovel, pointed the handle downhill, then sat as far forward as possible. Tom, placing himself behind her and resting part on the shovel, part on the extended board, grasped her by the waist and down they sped like children on a painted sleigh.

The ride became so exciting, so refreshing with the cold wind blowing in their faces, that they found themselves actually hurrying up the last few icy steps of the Chilkoot so they could run over to the precipitous drop and hurl themselves downward on their magical shovel. Tom, holding tight to Missy, who half steered the shovel with her heels, felt that this was the most joyous thing he had ever done, exhilarating beyond words, but once when Kirby saw them speed off he became worried, and when they next climbed the pass he took them aside: "I saw you steering with your heels, Mrs. Venn. I wouldn't do that, because at that speed, if your heel caught on anything, even a small piece of ice, your leg would bend back and it might even tear off. Surely it would snap." So after that the rides were a little more circumspect, with both Missy and Tom preventing the shovel from descending too fast.

One evening, when Buck's sled and Missy's shovel reached the Scales at the same time, one of the men on the sled told Missy: "We like the way your husband takes charge of things. You must be proud of him." And when she talked with Tom during their hikes up the mountain, she said: "Have you noticed, Tom, how much stronger your father seems to be? Other men show respect for him. He makes decisions and sticks to them." And Tom replied: "It's as if he was waiting all those years for this to happen," and Missy, in a burst of affection for this maturing boy, grasped his hand and added: "Same thing's happening with you, Tom. By the time we get to the gold fields, you'll be a man."

Sergeant Kirby, watching this energetic team move its goods so adeptly, told his fellow Mounties one night: "We've seen some pretty horrible Americans come up that slope. But have you noticed those three Venns? They make up for a lot of the others."

One of the Canadians asked: "Why do you look after them so much?" and he said: "I have a boy at home, about half their boy's age. I'd be happy if he grew up as responsible." He reflected on this for some moments, then added: "And I have a lot of respect for a man like Venn who keeps things moving. Who maintains order," and one of the older Mounties asked: "You also have quite a bit of respect for Mrs. Venn, don't you?" And there the conversation ended.

The Chilkoot Pass had its photographers, too, men of daring and endurance who lugged huge cameras and heavy glass plates to the most remote locations so as to take three-minute exposures of tiny figures set against vast snowfields. One such bold experimenter was a twenty-one-year-old man born in Sweden but reared in Wisconsin, where at the age of fifteen he had opened a full-time professional photography studio. Mesmerized by the magnitude of the Klondike gold rush, he was one of those prudent men who perceived that his fortune was to be made not washing sand in some mountain stream but in making pictures of the men who were.

He seemed to be present everywhere, his industry combining with good luck to put him in the right place at the right time. For example, on that fatal Sunday when the avalanche struck, he was not far away, and three of his shots show Buck Venn and son Tom, among hundreds of others, digging for bodies. But one of his most memorable pictures, taken on that same day, shows Missy Peckham looking small, determined and appealing against the snow. She stands erect, in heavy boots, a jaunty Russian peasant's cap on her head. Her skirt is extremely full, falling in neat folds to her boot tops and gathered at her waist in a circle so tiny it seemed to divide her into two different halves. Her blouse, not unusually heavy despite the snow, fits very tight across the middle but is voluminous at the shoulders and topped by the neatest possible little collar. Six bright buttons adorn the front, but even such features are obscured by the determination that glows from her face. It is not a pretty face, in the advertiser's sense, but it is so marvelously controlled that it is almost heroic. The young woman who stares from this photograph intended getting to the gold fields.

On the day that the five-man team hoisted the last of its supplies into Canada, and the duties had been paid, the men parted, each following his own vision of how best to reach the gold fields. As the Venns prepared to take their cargo downhill in nine or ten easy sledloads, Sergeant Kirby took them aside for a curious message: "When a man dies on the slopes, if he's alone, I have the job of looking after his belongings, and if he carried an address, we send his money and his papers home. His goods we sell . . . whatever we can get for them. An old man died up here the other day. Must have been sixty."

"What's the problem?" Buck asked, and Kirby said: "He didn't leave much but he did have this very good sail. He may have been connected with ships, because the sewing on the canvas is special."

"I don't follow."

"Mr. Venn, hasn't anybody told you? It's a long way to Lake Lindeman. When you get there it'll be frozen, and when you finish with it, there's a far distance to Lake Bennett, where you must build your boat for the river trip to Dawson. But if you mount a sail on your sled, what with the strong winds around here, you'll skim all the way to the lake." He added: "I'll sell you the sail for two dollars, and I advise you to take it." When Buck handed over the two dollars, Kirby asked for a signed and dated receipt: "We like to keep things strictly legal, seeing two different nations are involved."

Descending the Canadian side of Chilkoot Pass was almost a pleasure; leaving Tom at the top to help with loading the sled, Buck took Missy down to the bottom of the steep incline to assemble the goods as he brought them down, and he traveled so fast that he often became airborne when vaulting over some bump in the snow. Missy, watching him come around the corner as he approached the rapidly building store of goods, cautioned him: "Sergeant Kirby warned me not to stick my legs out at the speed Tom and I were going. You're coming down twice that fast. Be careful."

Once the goods were down off the mountain, the nine miles to Lake Lindeman consisted of a gentle, easily negotiated slope, and now the dead man's sail became invaluable, for Buck built a small wooden box into which the bottom end of the mast could be stepped, and guyed with ropes to keep the top erect. With a yardarm in place, he could expose a huge amount of sail, and thus impelled, could almost sail over the packed snow.

Again the three Venns were separated: Tom guarding the cache at the foot of the mountain, Missy at the delivery point, and Buck either sailing happily downhill with a load of gear or trudging back with the empty sled.

On the last sail downhill from the top of Chilkoot Pass, Buck brought Tom with him, and when the careening sled pulled up where Missy waited, the boy saw that their goods were now stashed beside the first lake, a beautiful body of water whose shores contained a blizzard of white tents housing an informal town of thousands, with snowy roads and two improvised hotels which served hot meals. Gazing in awe at this improbable sight, Tom cried: "The whole world seems to be white."

The Venns were now at the spot where the Yukon River was supposed to begin and where Soapy Smith's route from Skagway joined. The repeated cargo trips down Lake Lindeman, about six and a half miles each way, were a dreamlike adventure, for the surface was frozen smooth, allowing the sled to skim along. The surrounding hills were deep in snow, the air was crisp, and there was a constant wind blowing away from the Chilkoot and directly toward where the travelers wished to go. "This is the best journey we'll have," Buck predicted as they moved through this world of winter beauty, modified by a strong hint of coming summer in the air.

On his third trip down Lindeman, Buck allowed his sled to slide rather far to the right, which threw him onto an unexpected rough patch in the ice. Wind, or the inflow of water from some unseen stream debouching from the mountains, had caused blocks of ice to erupt, marring the smooth surface. He tried kicking his sled away from them, and sprained his right foot. It was not serious, but he wished to avoid such a problem on his remaining trips, so when he dragged his sled back to the western end of the lake he asked Tom to see if he could find some kind of pole which could be used to maneuver among the ice blocks, and the boy found one about nine feet long and stout enough to protect the sled. On subsequent trips, the wind continued to push Buck toward the right bank, but with the pole he was able to shove the sled away from the blocks.

On his last trip he packed the sled with the remaining eight hundred pounds of gear and perched Tom on top. Lying back, guiding the sled by tugging on the lines holding the sail, they glided speedily down toward Lake Bennett—where they would build their boat for the Yukon—as Tom cried with glee: "Not a single hill between here and Dawson. We can sail right to our gold mine."

Then the boy suddenly shouted: "Pop! Rough ice ahead!" and Buck called back: "I see it. I know how to get past." He swung his pole out, but this time the load was so heavy and the speed so great that the end of the pole caught in a huge block of ice, then wedged itself in a crevice.

When the pole began to bend in an alarming arc, Tom shouted: "Pop! Let go!"

Too late. The pole snapped, the near end dangling uselessly from Buck's hands, the other, jagged and torn, springing forward like an arrow shot from some giant bow. It hit Buck in the middle of his chest, not like a sliver of steel but like the shattered end of a lance, tearing a hole big and crude and brutal.

When Buck saw the blood spurt out, he looked helplessly at his son, and Tom saw his father's wind-hardened face grow ashen. His hands left the pole and reached up, and he clutched at the wound. He looked once more at his son as a pulsating flow of blood gushed from his mouth; then he collapsed as the sled, sail aloft, sped serenely down the lake.

Will Kirby was policing the seven thousand boats being built along Lake Lindeman and the waterway leading to Lake Bennett when he heard that yet another prospector had been killed coming down from Chilkoot Pass, and with a sense of irritation with Americans who barged into dangers they did not comprehend, he hurried up to where reports said the accident had occurred. He was shaken to find that the dead man was Buchanan Venn, who had proved himself so reliable on the pass, and when he came upon the woman Missy and her son and found them shivering beside the lake, bereft and unable to focus upon the manifold problems that now confronted them, he felt great pity for them and did what he could to help.

"We'll look after you. We don't allow women to suffer disadvantage on this trail." Taking Tom aside, he said firmly: "Now we see whether you're going to be a man or not," and he was gratified to watch the boy respond by taking charge of the sled that had killed his father.

Gathering them beside the lake, he said: "It's my job, you know, to see that the dead man's goods are properly handled . . . a legal disposition, that is," and he was startled by the amount of money Buck had carried, and he warned: "Mrs. Venn, I can't just hand this money over to you. Much too dangerous. I'll ask Superintendent Steele to take charge of this till you reach Dawson."

Kirby's statement raised two difficult questions, and Missy took each in turn: "I'm not Mrs. Venn. But half the money Buck carried is mine. And I will not turn my half over to anyone." Kirby nodded, but stood by his first judgment: "We'll wait till Superintendent Steele gets here on his inspection."

The search of Buck's property turned up two items which Missy and Tom would not allow him to keep. The first was an envelope containing the hundred-dollar bill for the Belgian Mare, which, as Missy explained, belonged to her: "We have nothing to do with it except to deliver it."

Sergeant Kirby smiled indulgently: "But, ma'am, don't you see? It's just this kind of money we can't have floating around with a defenseless woman. I must keep it. She'll get it, I assure you."

"But I must deliver it . . . personally. It's an obligation."

"And so you shall." But the envelope with the money he filed in his blouse.

There was no argument about the paper Tom defended: "An engineer drew this for me. It's plans for the boat we'll have to build," and when Kirby handed back the sketch, after surveying it, he said: "That man could draw. Whoever he was, he knew boats."

"If we build like that," Tom asked, "can we sail it to Dawson?"

And now the gravest problem of all arose, one that Will Kirby had had to face several times before: "Sit down, please. I need your full attention." Standing soldierlike and handsome before them in his proper uniform of striped trousers, neat jacket with ornaments and big hat, he was a figure of authority, and both Missy and Tom were prepared to listen to him.

"The question is: 'Do you really want to go on to Dawson?' Now wait, don't answer too fast." And then he outlined the disadvantages of their position: "There's twenty thousand people along these lakes, waiting for the ice to melt. You'll be lost in a stampede. You have no man to help you. Anyone can ride over you. And even if you do get there, you must realize that all the good spots will be taken. And maybe I shouldn't say all the *good* spots, maybe I should say *all* the spots. Your goods will last maybe half a year. Your money will begin to run out. And then what will you do?"

Missy and Tom looked at each other, and she spoke: "The man who gave us that money for the Belgian woman . . . the Klondike Kernel he called himself . . ."

"I've heard of him. Crazy sometimes, but very reliable." He chuckled, then asked: "Did he tell you what I just told you?"

"He did."

"But you came anyway?"

"We did."

"Mrs. Venn . . . Excuse me, the papers say you're Miss Peckham and he's young Mr. Venn. To go to Dawson with a man to protect and guide you is one thing. To go alone is quite another." He felt it necessary to shock these people into considering reality: "Surely, a woman like you . . . you're not planning to enter the cribs, are you?"

Missy did not flinch: "I have not that intention."

"Well, it's my duty to see that Mr. Venn's property is legally handled. I give you and his son the sled, all the gear, the boat-building equipment. The money and the papers other than the boat plans I must hold on to."

To everyone's surprise, even his own, Tom rose and stepped forward: "You can't do that. We saw what happened at Skagway."

Kirby nodded, pleased rather than offended that the boy should take such protective action: "You're right. You're entitled to verification." And he sent Tom scouting around the end of the lake for other members of the North West Mounted Police, and when two young men in uniform reported to the Venn tent, Kirby returned their salute and explained the situation: "From previous experience at Skagway, Miss Peckham and young Mr. Venn refuse to surrender the dead man's goods to our care until an adjudication can be made."

"Oh, but you must!" the younger of the two officers said.

"How can we trust him?" Missy asked. "How can we trust you?"

"Ma'am," the officer said, "if you can't trust Sergeant Kirby, you can't trust anybody," and the other one said: "And if you go to Dawson . . . alone . . . Ma'am, you've got to trust somebody."

The two Mounties watched as Kirby wrote out a receipt, then they signed it and handed it to Missy, but she passed it along to Tom: "He's Buck's son," and one of them asked: "But aren't you his wife?" and she said: "No."

Three days later, as thousands milled about at the lower end of

Lake Lindeman preparing for the dash to Lake Bennett and the building of their boats, Sergeant Kirby brought to the Venn tent a hefty, mustachioed officer who had won the reputation of being the Lion of the Yukon. He was Superintendent Samuel Steele, incorruptible dispenser of frontier justice. Tall, deep-chested and exuding a sense of power, he wore a large black cowboy hat and no visible gun; every movement, every gesture bespoke authority but also compassion. He had jurisdiction over a wild, almost ungovernable domain, with now more than twenty thousand strangers about to descend upon a city which had not even existed three years ago, and all men subject to his orders agreed that he was just.

He allowed a street of prostitutes, where the Belgian Mare ruled. He permitted saloons to run openly and gambling dens too, but the drinks and the wheels had to be honest. Before any bank had opened in his town, he had served as the repository for miners' funds, and no money was lost while in his care. He insisted that Sunday be observed. There was no wild shooting on the streets, as had become so prevalent in American boomtowns, and he outlawed murder. If any man brazenly transgressed his rules, he himself went after him, faced him down, and threw him out of Canada.

It was this man who now stood before Missy Peckham and the boy Tom: "I am most grieved to hear of your tragic loss." Missy said nothing; she was hoarding her strength for the contest ahead. "And I understand your reluctance to have us take charge of your dead husband's money."

"He wasn't my husband," Missy said.

"To us he stood in that regard." As he said this he nodded gravely, for Kirby had informed him as to Missy's stalwart character.

"Now, ma'am, we've decided that the money involved is legally this young man's."

"I agree. It's certainly not mine." But when Superintendent Steele started to smile at this easy concession, Missy stopped him: "But the half that's mine, which I earned as a waitress and aboard the *Alacrity,* that I want."

"And you shall get it," Steele said. "But not here. Not in this jungle where we can't protect you."

"Why not?"

"I'm not thinking about you so much, ma'am, as I am of my men. They can't protect you from here to Dawson. The things you'll be going through . . ." He stopped. "You are determined to go ahead?

We'll help you back over the pass, you know, if you want to return home, like I think you should."

"We're going to Dawson."

"When you reach there, we'll deliver your money, safe and sound."

Missy was close to tears. In the short time since Buck's death, she had made herself into a resolute woman, aware of the dangers that would be facing her and Tom in an unprotected trek to Dawson, but this constant pressure from the struggle up the Chilkoot, from death, and now from these official-looking men was almost too much: "How do we know you're all not another gang of Soapy Smiths?"

It was a frontal attack, and so relevant that Superintendent Steele fell back a step. Yes, how did an unprotected woman know that there was a difference? He gave a strange yet reassuring answer: "Ma'am, I'd like to be in Skagway one week, with three or four men like Sergeant Kirby."

She trembled, put her hand to her upper lip, and looked at the two men, whereupon Kirby told her an amazing fact: "Did you know that on the day of the avalanche, Soapy dispatched four of his men to the scene to see what they could steal of the dead men's belongings? Ugly brutish oaf named Blacktooth Otto led them, and they made off with quite a bit, we're told."

"How could you permit such a thing?" she asked, and Steele reminded her: "That's Alaska, ma'am. Not our territory. That's how they do things over there. In Canada we don't allow it." And Kirby said: "Superintendent Steele and one of his men would handle Soapy in one afternoon. Wouldn't even last till nightfall."

Reassured, she decided she could trust these men, and as they parted, Steele said: "We never lose a customer. We'll see you in Dawson." Then he added: "Sergeant Kirby, see they build themselves a proper boat. And give it a lucky name. We need people like them in Dawson."

They did not see Kirby again until they had painfully moved all their gear across the short distance from Lake Lindeman to the much more important Lake Bennett, which was, in some ways, the water equivalent to the snowy Chilkoot Pass, for here decisions of life and death were made. They concerned boats, because every traveler to Dawson City was required by the Mounties to build or buy a boat capable not only of sailing the five hundred and fifteen miles to Dawson but also sound enough to survive a fearsome canyon and several sets of violent rapids.

The reason they did not see Kirby was that it took him a while to find them. The shores of icebound Lake Bennett housed an exploding tent city of about twenty thousand would-be prospectors, each engaged in building a boat. Trees were felled at a speed which denuded the surrounding hills, and whipsaw pits were dug everywhere. The song of Lake Bennett was the rasping of saws, the hammering of nails, and this music continued around the clock. Men who had never been near water four months ago were now studying how to bend a length of wood to conform to the shape of a boat, and the results were staggering in their ineptitude and variety.

One group of men constructed a scow that could have handled a railroad train. A sole adventurer built himself a snug little boat about eight feet long; the Mounties would not allow it to enter the dangerous passages, so he hired an Indian to help him portage it six miles. Prudent men kept the sails with which they had come down the slopes and across Lake Lindeman, and those who knew something about rapids and rock-strewn gorges built very long, heavy oars which they mounted on the rear of their boats and called sweeps; a man with strong nerves operating a sweep could avoid a lot of trouble.

When Missy and Tom erected their tent on a preferred spot near the edge of the lake with a whipsaw pit already constructed, they were able to do so only because sharp-eyed Missy saw two men about to quit the place and move their finished boat, a twenty-two-footer, to a spot more favorable for quick launching. When she asked them if she could have the spot they were vacating, they said: "Sure. But if you ain't started your boat yet, you're gonna miss the armada."

That afternoon Missy and Tom started the formidable task of building their twenty-three-footer. He visited all the sites within walking distance, asking if anyone had extra planks to sell, or good nails, and in this way he accumulated more boards already sawn than he had expected. He then went into the remaining woods with his ax and felled trees till dusk, and since it was already spring, with the sun heading north, sunset did not come till nearly eight and darkness not till more than an hour later, so he was dog-tired when he quit.

Next morning they were both at work before sunrise, which came at half past four, and this was the way they passed the rest of April. Missy spent the morning cooking for men who paid her well for pancakes, bread and beans and in the afternoon she went into the woods, helping Tom drag home the logs he had felled. When they calculated they had enough to provide the planking needed for their boat, they gritted their teeth and began the cruel work of whipsawing out the boards required.

When they succeeded in maneuvering their first log into position over the pit, they faced the problem of who would work from the top, pulling the saw up, and who down at the bottom, pulling it down. Tom, believing the hardest work to be at the bottom end of the seven-foot whipsaw, volunteered for that spot; he was wrong about the difficulty of the work, for the person topside had to pull upward till his arms ached, but he was right in thinking that the bottom work was much more unpleasant, for down in the pit that sawyer was going to eat a constant supply of sawdust as it fell upon him.

How easy it seemed when one explained the process, how brutally difficult when one had to do it. At the end of the first long day, Missy and Tom had barely squared off the first log, and had done so with such ineptness, the line wandering as if the man who drew it was drunk, that they despaired. But when they faced each other in the tent that night, Missy said grimly: "Dammit, Tom. We learn to cut the boards or we rot here while the others sail on." He did not point out that much of their failure stemmed from the fact that she could not keep the saw in a straight line.

Next day they tackled their work with even more seriousness than they had shown before, and although Missy's line wavered more than it should, they did hack out three rather good boards, and went to bed satisfied that with determination they could master the whipsaw. Tom was so worn-out that he fell asleep before he could brush the sawdust from his hair.

For five dreadful days, as the ice in Lake Bennett prepared to soften, the pair kept to the drudgery of whipsawing. Their hands produced blisters and then callouses. Their back muscles tightened and their eyes grew dull, but on and on they went, stacking up the precious boards upon which their lives would soon depend.

On the day when Missy doubted that she could continue much longer, for she could barely lift her arms to pull the heavy saw, Sergeant Kirby found them after looking into some two thousand tents. "You've done wonders," he said, patting Tom on the shoulder. "I see you have Missy up there where she belongs. Good for you."

The exhausted sawyers were so glad to see Kirby that for the moment they forgot their pains and worked the great saw with a vigor, but he noticed that Missy was operating on courage alone, so he scrambled to the top of the structure, gently lifted her to the ground, and took the top handle. As soon as he did so, Tom could feel the difference. The saw came down with more strength, stayed closer to the line, and was pulled back up with authority. For about two hours the two men ripped down the squared-off log, producing planks at a speed Tom had not felt possible.

At the noon break Missy had soup ready, and Kirby stayed at the pit most of that afternoon. He returned next day to help Tom finish off the planking whose length had been determined by the Kernel's drawing, and that night Kirby stayed for supper.

When the actual building of the boat started, with a heavy keel neatly formed, Kirby appeared frequently to give not only advice but also his valued assistance in shaping the form of the boat. He took his meals there too, providing meat and vegetables from his own sources of supply, and late one afternoon Missy came to Tom with a curious request: "Tom, could you maybe sleep over in the Stantons' tent tonight?" He stood stock-still, hands at his side, his head in a whirl. He was fifteen years old and Missy was twenty-three, and under no conceivable circumstances would he have said that he loved her, but he had admitted to himself many times in recent months that she was the best woman he had ever known. Never did he refer to her as a girl; a girl would be someone his own age and he had met several in school who were attractive, with every promise of becoming more so as the years passed. Missy was a woman; she had been the salvation of the Venns during the years of privation and the agent of his father's rejuvenation. She was a wonderful person, courageous, hardworking, amiable, and on those trips down the mountain on the shovel he had clung to her as if they were one person engaged in a great adventure. Recently, as they worked on the whipsaw, he had known how mortally tired she was, and he had wished that he might have done all the work himself. Indeed, he had pushed up and pulled down with doubled effort to spare her, and he did so almost joyously, for his affection for this strong-minded woman went beyond words. He felt they were a team, not one that conformed to any ordinary description, but a pair of like-minded, strong people. They would cut their planks, and build their boat, and guide it through the canyons and past the rapids, and what happened when they got to Dawson was a problem for another day. Now he was being asked to take his bedroll somewhere else, and he felt displaced.

But when Sergeant Kirby moved into Missy's tent, the building of the boat took a leap ahead, for the Mountie had had numerous experiences with the very rough waters that the stampeders would be facing as soon as they left placid Lake Bennett, and this knowledge caused the first rupture between him and Tom. When he saw that Tom proposed building the boat to the exact specifications laid down in the Klondike Kernel's sketch, he asked: "Are you sure you want it that big? Two people could ride in something a lot smaller."

"That's what he said. Look." There the figures were: "23' long and 5' 6" in the beam" and that's what the boat would be.

"The point is," Kirby said, "there are two places which are extremely dangerous, Miles Canyon and Whitehorse Rapids. A lot of boats are lost there, lives too."

"He said a boat like this would make it," Tom said firmly, not designating who the *he* was.

"I'm sure he said it. But if you had a boat half that size, you could still pack all your gear, and when you came to the bad spots you could hire Indians to help you portage around. You have the money, I know that."

"The boat has to be this long," and it was remarkable to see this city boy, who knew nothing of either wood or shipbuilding, join the timbers to the keel and form them moderately well at the forward post. With help from Kirby and Missy at the difficult joins, and with constant reference to both the sketch the Kernel had provided and the thin metal square his father had bought, Tom built a boat that was better than nine-tenths of those put together by experienced men.

When it was finished, he was disgusted with the number of open chinks he had left where boards did not join accurately, but Kirby laughed: "Tom, all boatbuilders leave chinks. That's why we have caulking."

"What's that?"

"Oakum."

"And what's that?"

"Hemp and tar. You hammer it into the open spots and make the boat watertight. Otherwise you'd sink." And suddenly Tom and Melissa realized that in this leaky craft built by a fifteen-year-old boy they were about to trust their lives on a five-hundred-mile run down extremely dangerous waters.

"Where do you get the tar and the other?"

"You ought to have brought it with you, but you didn't. Your Kernel couldn't think of everything, could he?" But Kirby had an idea: "We'll go to men finishing their boats and see if they'll sell us the caulking they have left over." And when a bizarre collection of substitutes for real caulking was assembled—horsehair, forest moss, strips of linen, burlap—they tamped the mélange into the cracks, then sealed them with another outrageous mixture of wax, bear fat, tar and pitch, and when all was completed, young Tom Venn could send his first letter home to his grandmother:

> *Pop was killed when a spruce pole doubled back and ran him through. He died brave. Missy and I are now in Canada so I think it's all right to give you our address, Dawson City, as I don't think anybody could arrest us here. I have built a boat twenty-three feet long and five and a half feet in the beam and in a test it floated like a duck. As soon as the ice clears the lake we head down the Yukon River, a fine easy trip all the way. I wish Missy had married Pop.*

On Sunday morning, 29 May 1898, the thick ice which had held Lake Bennett in its cold embrace for nearly nine months relaxed its hold and started cascading down the narrow river, which, after ninety miles, tumbled first into a high, rock-walled canyon and then over stupendous rapids before it reached the relative calm of the soon-to-be-clear Yukon. Tom, watching the first open lanes of free water appear like jagged daggers across the surface, shouted: "It's breaking up!" But Missy and Kirby did not hear his cry, because men in all parts of the vast tent city were shouting and firing their guns.

"Lake Bennett is bustin' open!" More than seven thousand home-made boats edged toward the shoreline as if everyone had to be first out of the lake and first to the gold fields of the Klondike. It was an armada such as had never been seen before, with hardly any two of the crazy boats alike, but into the icy waters of the lake they came, pushed and pulled by straining men who wondered why they had built them so big that ordinary men could not launch them. The great scows had to be wedged in; the one-man affairs—those that would be turned back before the canyon—could be carried down on the back of the solitary owner. But all that Sunday and the days that followed, the boats were launched, the sails were set, and the men floated toward their treacherous rendezvous with the rapids.

Each boat that set forth, regardless of size, had to carry a name, a number and, in the files of the Mounties, a list of all passengers, for during the previous year too many had been lost. When the time came to christen the Venn boat, which would be Number 7023, Sergeant Kirby had several appropriate suggestions for a name, but once more Tom interrupted to establish the fact that this was his boat: "It's the *Aurora*. After the northern lights."

It was not launched during the first mad scramble, since, as Kirby pointed out, "you're not rushing to get to the gold fields themselves, let the others break their backs." And then he said a revealing thing: "We can drift down at our own speed."

"Are you coming with us?" Tom asked, part of him hoping that the answer was yes, because he'd heard about the dangers of the canyon and the rapids, part hoping for a no, because he resented Kirby's relationship with Missy.

"I want to be sure you get through the bad parts," Kirby said, and on the second of June he called for help from three other Mounties stationed at Bennett, and with many cries of encouragement, for Tom's boat was heavy, the *Aurora* was launched, the foremast was stepped and guyed, the big sail was made ready, and the long sweep which Kirby would operate from the stern was fitted into its slot.

"Good sailing!" Kirby's fellow officers shouted. "Find yourself a gold mine!"

It was twenty-six miles to the exit from Lake Bennett, and the *Aurora,* despite her ample sail and the professional steering of Kirby, did not reach that spot before a kind of gentle semidarkness settled like a comforting blanket thrown over the water. Eager to get a fair start in the morning, and loath to tempt the turbulent water ahead in the night, Kirby nosed the *Aurora* into the right bank and asked Tom to make fast the line which he threw ashore.

They slept on the boat that night, and early next morning left Lake Bennett for the long run to the perilous segment of their voyage, the three-part terror where careless or boastful men without sure knowledge lost their lives. When the June sun was high, thawing snow on the surrounding mountains, Kirby pulled the *Aurora* into a small stream of melt-water seeping down from the heights, and there he spelled out what lay ahead: "In the space of two and a half miles, so much happens, and so fast, that you can be forgiven if you lose your courage."

"What is it?" Missy asked, for she knew that because she was a woman the decision would be left to her.

"First a canyon, deep and very swift. Water piles up six feet higher in the middle than on the sides. You catch your breath. Then a pair of rocky rapids."

"Then what?"

"Then a peaceful sail downriver to Dawson."

"Have you ever taken a boat through?"

"I have."

"Then let's go!" Tom cried, but Kirby said: "No. You can make this decision only after you've seen for yourself."

"And if we turn coward?" Missy asked, and he whipped about as if he had been struck: "Dammit, ma'am! Some of the bravest men in Canada and America take one look at that canyon and say 'No, thanks.' It's not because they're cowards. It's because they have the good sense to realize they don't know a damn thing about boats." He glared at Tom: "Do you know anything about boats?" And Missy replied: "We don't, but you do."

Subdued by the seriousness of what they were about to encounter, the three people in the *Aurora* moved swiftly downriver toward the entrance to Miles Canyon, first of the tests, but as they neared it, a group of men gathered on the right bank shouted to them: "Better not try the canyon in a boat like that. You'll sink·sure."

Tom, who was steering through the easier water, headed for the shore, and the men, seeing a woman aboard, tried to frighten her: "Ma'am, I sure wouldn't try that canyon in that there boat." Kirby, aware that these men condemned all boats about to enter the canyon, called: "What do you suggest?"

"We're practiced hands. We'll guide you through, safe and sound."

"How much?"

"Only a hundred dollars."

"Too much," Tom cried, and the men yelled back: "Then portage around. Indians'll do it for two hundred."

"Thanks," Kirby shouted. "But we may risk it."

"Ma'am, before you do, please go to the other bank, rest your boat, and climb up that little hill to see what awaits you in the canyon. Then come back and pay us ninety dollars, and we'll see you through, safe and sound, like we say."

Kirby took over the sweep, and when they were well out from shore, he headed directly toward the other bank, as the men had suggested: "I planned to do this anyway. You must see what faces you."

When they were atop the cliff and looking down into the turbulent canyon, even Tom, who had been eager to try it, grew afraid, for below them rushed the icy waters flooding out from the lakes, and as they roared in they turned and twisted and threw white spume.

"Oh!" Missy cried, and when the others looked to where she was pointing, they saw at the exit a series of jagged rocks, barely above the waterline, onto which three or four small craft had foundered. All goods had been lost in the swift current, but it looked as if the passengers had saved themselves by clinging to the rocks.

Suddenly Missy and Tom lost much of their desire to test this canyon, but now a boat much like theirs came down the approach, manned by two bearded prospectors whose faces could not be clearly seen. They might have been in their twenties, but they could also be tested older hands in their forties. The would-be pilots on the bank hailed them, there was the same discussion, and the same rejection of the hundred-dollar offer. The two men would venture into the canyon relying upon their own skills.

They had no rear sweep, but they did appear to be powerful paddlers, and as their craft leaped toward the swirling waters where the canyon narrowed and the rushing water increased its speed, they paddled with fury and dexterity. Tom had never before seen skilled men handle a boat, and he was thrilled when the craft headed directly at a menacing cliff, then swung safely past as the men paddled heroically. In less than a minute and a half the boat shot out the far end, and Tom cheered.

But now the boat must clear the rocks on which former attempts had come to grief, and instinctively Tom shouted: "Watch out!" As if obedient to his warning, the men paddled even faster than before and scraped by the rocks to which the marooned prospectors held. Their heavy boat dipped and darted, more like a bird skimming the calm waters of a lake than a small craft caught in big turbulence. It was a masterful performance, and both Tom and Missy were willing to try duplicating it.

"You ready?" Kirby asked, and Missy asked him: "Can we do as well?" and Kirby said: "That's why I've come along." Then, to Tom: "You're captain. It's your boat."

"Let's go!"

"And if we make it, which I believe we can, do you want to head right into the other rapids?"

"Yes." The boy felt certain that his father, had he lived, would have made the same choices.

So the three climbed down from their perch, returned to the boat, and pushed off as the men on the opposite shore shouted: "Good luck! Hope you make it!"

The passage of the *Aurora* was almost a duplicate of the one made by the two skilled paddlers. Kirby stayed aft to work the sweep, Missy and Tom perched forward with paddles, but they had been in the canyon only a few yards when a rock, not visible before, threatened them from Tom's side, and instinctively he thrust out his paddle and shoved it against the rock. As he did, the paddle bent, and Missy screamed: "Tom!" but he pulled away and no damage was done.

There was another variation. As the *Aurora* shot out of the canyon and neared the rocks on which the castaways were huddled, Sergeant Kirby, in line of duty, headed almost straight for them, cocking his sweep just so, and when he was abreast of the terrified people, but moving so fast that any rescue was impossible, he shouted: "We'll be back to get you. Mounted Police." No words along the Yukon trail could have been more reassuring, and as the *Aurora* sped past, the abandoned men waved and shouted, for now they knew they were to be saved.

When Kirby guided them through the last set of breathtaking rapids, spume high at the prow and wrecked boats leering at them as if to warn: "One false move of that sweep and you join us!" the Mountie headed the tested boat toward a point in the direction of Lake Laberge where he must leave them. As they pulled the nose of the *Aurora* onto dry land, he said approvingly: "Tom, you built yourself a fine boat."

"I was scared," the boy said. "Not in the canyon. You keep to the middle where the water bulges up, you make it. And it's all so swift. All you need there is courage. But in those rapids, there you have to know something. I couldn't have done that."

"Well now," Kirby said. "Maybe you've said the wisest thing on this trip. Courage for the canyon. Knowledge for the rapids." He stopped, winked at this boy who gave such promise of becoming a fine man, and said: "Which is the important factor? What do you think, Missy?"

"I don't think you ever gain real knowledge unless you have courage to begin with."

Tom had other ideas: "Anybody can have courage. Just grit your teeth. But to handle a boat, or a gun, or someone like Soapy Smith . . . that takes knowing."

"Let's not make this too serious," Kirby said. "Lots of men get through that canyon and the rapids."

"And lots don't," Tom said, remembering the wrecks.

The boy hoped that he could retain contact with this excellent man who knew how to meet contingencies. When they crashed through the final rapids with the *Aurora* almost vertical in the air, Kirby had calmly brought her around, then shouted to two Mounties who were checking the numbers of the boats that made it: "Exit from the canyon. Men marooned. Send heavy boat through from the other side." No heroics, no speeches. Find a heavy boat and get started. Tom could visualize how the rescue would be handled, the boat drifting past the rocks, the rope thrown, the kept end led ashore lower down, both ends fastened tight, the people working their way ashore while grasping the rope.

"It would be fun being a pilot through those waters," Tom said, and Kirby replied: "Three years ago not six canoes a year came through. Three years from now there won't be seven."

"Won't the Klondike produce forever?"

"Nothing does."

Tom sensed that Kirby's parting from Missy was going to be a painful affair, so he left the boat and walked along the shore while they said farewell. The sergeant told Missy of his son in Manitoba and of his wife. He reminded her of what an exceptional boy Tom was and he almost commanded her to look out for his welfare. He said that in some ways Dawson City was rougher than Skagway, but that Superintendent Steele could always be counted on. And he challenged her to find sensible employment: "I'll be in Dawson one of these days. I don't want to see you down on your heels in mud."

Then he said that he loved her, and he was heartsick that she had lost Buck Venn, who seemed one of the best men to come over the Chilkoot, and he wished her well. He hoped that her dreams would come true, whatever they were, and he ended with a statement she would cherish: "You're strong. You're like the ravens."

"What does that mean?" she asked, and he said: "They survive. Even in the goddamnedest parts of the arctic, they survive." And he said no more, moving away quickly to avoid the necessity of speaking with Tom again.

At last they could relax. In Chicago they had been afraid of Tom's mother's lawyers, and in Seattle they were always looking over their shoulders lest her detectives track them down. In Skagway they feared Soapy Smith, and on the Chilkoot they had feared everything. Then death came and the horrors of the whipsaw, and then the canyon and the rapids. Now, by damn, they were drifting down the placid ice-free Yukon in just about the best boat on the river, and they took it easy.

Tom found special delight in being alone with Missy, as if the real voyage to the gold fields was back on target, and one afternoon as they drifted past the mouth of the Pelly, a large river coming in from the east, he asked abruptly: "Did you know that Sergeant Kirby has a boy back in Manitoba?" and she replied: "Yes, and a wife too, if that's what's bothering you."

He thought about this for some minutes, then said: "You know, Missy, if you keep going with men who have wives, you're never going to get married."

"Tom, what's getting into you?"

"I was thinking how good it would be for all of us if you could marry Sergeant Kirby." When she made no comment, he added: "Then the three of us could stay together."

Only then did she realize that Tom was disturbed about what they would do when they reached Dawson, and she confessed to him: "Tom, I don't know what we'll do in Dawson. I'm as worried as you are. You remember this. We're a team. We won't be separated."

"We better not be."

"So you look after me, Tom, and I'll look after you."

"Shake hands on that?" They shook hands, and she said: "What's more, we'll seal it with a kiss," and she leaned across the drifting boat and kissed him on the forehead.

In the last warming days of spring, when ice had left the rivers, they passed that series of streams whose waters joined to build the mighty Yukon: the White, the Stewart, the Sixtymile, and when Tom visualized the vast hinterland that had to be drained to form such rivers, he appreciated what an immense land this part of Canada was. America had seemed big when he and Buck and Missy crossed it by train, but it was broken into manageable units by the little towns and big cities along the way. From Dyea, which was nothing, to Dawson City, which hadn't existed at all three years ago, there was nothing, not a town, nor a train, nor even a road.

Some nights they dragged their boat onto the right bank of the Yukon and pitched a tent, especially if they wanted to do some cooking, but on others they simply drifted in the silvery light, for always as they moved farther north the nights became shorter and the twilights so extended that sometimes there seemed to be no night at all, only deepened shadows through which the ever-present ravens flew.

As they lazed along they were sometimes passed by other boats whose passengers, hungry for the Klondike, were rowing through the arctic haze. "Where you from?" a voice would hail, and Tom would shout back: "Chicago," and the voice would respond: "Minnesota," and somehow this simple recitation of names signified a great deal to the travelers.

At last the *Aurora,* showing almost no leakage, turned a bend in the river, and its owners saw ahead on the right the formless outlines of a tent city, much smaller than Dawson had been reported to be, and they were disappointed, but then Tom consulted the sketch the Kernel had provided: "That's got to be Lousetown. And here's the Klondike coming in, and Dawson City will be dead ahead."

And there it was, this fabulous place with more than a thousand boats occupying its riverfront and outlining the site. It was a dream city, composed of nothing, a nightmare city, perhaps, with more than twenty thousand residents now and another five thousand out on the diggings, and both Missy and Tom felt their hearts beat faster as the *Aurora* neared the end of its journey. They were excited not only by the imminence of the decision they would soon have to make but also by the limitless possibilities, and as Tom edged their boat toward the shore and then elbowed his way to a landing spot, Missy suddenly cried: "Tom, we've made it! Tomorrow we'll find Superintendent Steele and be on our way!" She betrayed no doubt as to the success of their adventure.

It was three hectic days before they found Steele's headquarters, and then they learned that he was downriver at Circle, more than two hundred miles away. But a woman at the Mounted Police headquarters assured Missy that yes, the superintendent had alerted her that Miss Peckham would be stopping by, and yes, her money was safe. The superintendent would deliver it as soon as he returned.

In the waiting days Missy and Tom had ample opportunity to explore Dawson, but ten minutes would have sufficed to learn all that was needed. The streets were incredibly muddy, and peopled by men in beards and heavy dark clothing. Material of every description had been utilized in the making of huge white signs proclaiming all the services usually found in an ordinary town plus those unusual additional ones necessary in a mining boomtown. Dawson, it seemed to

Missy, was a place in which thousands of men stood around doing nothing and in which everything was for sale. Six different emporiums announced WE SELL OUTFITS and four others announced that they bought them.

Each night Missy and Tom returned to the riverfront and the tent they had wedged in among a hundred others, and after the third aimless day of wandering these crowded, meaningless streets, they took serious counsel. Missy said: "Tom, you and I will never find a place in the gold fields. That's for men who know what they're doing."

"I'm willing to try."

"No!"

Her curt dismissal annoyed him: "If the men I see are clever enough to find gold, so are you and me."

"Two years ago, yes. But now we'd have to go ten, fifteen miles into the country. Spend a winter there, maybe."

"If I can build a boat, I can build a cabin." The idea of spending a winter helping a woman like Missy was not distressing; it was downright agreeable.

But Missy, haunted by the doleful predictions of the Klondike Kernel, saw that he had been correct. The gold of the Yukon lay in servicing the great mass of men, not in competing with them. Sixteen lucky miners were making money that June on their fantastic finds; six hundred were coining gold from their stores, their rental of horses, their trading in leases, their medical or legal services. She saw also that enterprising women no more skilled or determined than she were doing extremely well with fortunetelling, the running of brothels, the selling of doughnuts and coffee. Three women had banded together to run a laundry, which was stacked with miners' clothing, and one seamstress seemed to be prospering from the sewing of shirts.

"What do we have to offer?" Missy demanded during the long twilight, and Tom replied: "I can build boats."

Unwisely she laughed, and when Tom flushed, she pointed to the riverfront where more than a thousand boats were for sale, their mission accomplished. Realizing the ridiculousness of his proposal, he, too, laughed: "Anyway, I can build cabins."

They talked on, rejecting one impractical alternative after another, but as they spoke, Missy kept looking at their nearby boat, and this gave her a viable idea: "Tom, we have double rations in the *Aurora*. All our food and all of Buck's too," and the more they considered this, the more appealing became the idea of opening a food shop of some kind and selling at profit their excess. The arrival this summer of regular boats up the Yukon from the Bering Sea meant that there would be no starvation in 1898 as there had been in '97, but there would be opportunities for enormous rewards.

Using the sail which Sergeant Kirby had sold them atop the Chilkoot Pass, Tom painted an enormous sign, one which dominated the waterfront: MISSY's GOOD MEALS CHEAP, and the tent restaurant was in business—not along the main street where competition would have been severe, but along the river where thousands of men were almost forced to congregate in the first days of their arrival.

To his own surprise, Tom was not loath to knock apart the *Aurora*, which he had built with such care, and after some of her planks were converted into tables and benches he bought for almost nothing another boat, so poorly built that it practically fell apart.

The two proprietors slaved over their restaurant, Missy doing the cooking, Tom the washing-up and the procurement of additional food from various sources. Mostly they relied upon their own cargo of dried foods so carefully chosen by Buck and the Kernel, and the diet they served was heavy on starches and caribou or moose meat brought in by some hunter.

They learned to equate gold dust, which passed as currency in Dawson, with dollars, and although their banner proclaimed cheap prices, the rates were surprisingly high. Their specialty, a loss leader you might say, was a breakfast of pancakes and syrup, greasy caribou sausage and cups of steaming coffee for thirty-five cents. Hungry men who gorged on this bargain were apt to return for lunch and supper, on which Missy and Tom made a real profit.

They had been in successful operation some six weeks when Superintendent Steele returned, and hearing that they had arrived in Dawson, came looking for them along the riverfront. "Hello," he greeted Tom as he entered the tent. "You remember me? I'm Samuel Steele, and I'm glad to see you prospering."

"Hey! Missy! It's the superintendent!" And when she appeared, obviously involved in heavy work, Steele congratulated her on having, as he said, "found your footing."

He said that he had her money with him and was prepared to turn it over, but he wondered if she might not prefer to deposit it in one of the reliable banks that had opened since he last met with her: "I would advise it, ma'am."

"I think so too," she said, for as a businesswoman she was already beginning to wonder how she and Tom could protect the money they were raking in. "But that special envelope . . . for the woman. I'd want to have that, because it isn't my money."

"I brought it," Steele said, and that afternoon Missy picked her way along Front Street, the main thoroughfare, then ducked off to a more famous street which paralleled it. This was Paradise Alley, where thoughtful men had built some seventy cribs for the prostitutes who were needed in any boomtown. Over the doors of many of the little huts, arranged in neat rows, hung boards proclaiming the names of the occupants:

TIGER FLO
THE MATCHMAKER
BETSY POO

On the largest crib, as befitted the situation:

THE BELGIAN MARE

Knocking sedately on the door beneath this sign, Missy called: "Ma'am, are you in?"

The big woman inside, five feet ten inches tall, a hundred and seventy pounds, was surprised to hear a woman's voice following the customary rapping, and supposing it to be one of the other Belgian girls, she shouted in Flemish: "Come in!" Missy, of course, could not understand the words and waited on the stoop.

When her invitation produced no results, the woman came to her door, and showed surprise at the type of person waiting there. Calling to another crib whose occupant spoke both Flemish and English, she asked: "What does this one want?" and soon half a dozen of the unoccupied girls crowded into the Mare's crib, delighted with the unusual diversion.

"Tell her," Missy said, "that I bring something from the Klondike Kernel."

The interpreter had arrived from Antwerp after the departure of the Kernel on that first boat down the Yukon with news of the strike, so she had not known the man, and at first her explanation made no sense to the Mare, but when Missy repeated the name the big woman's face broke into a beatific smile, and the way she reacted proved she had been unusually fond of the tough Carolinian.

"Ah! The colonel!" she cried in Flemish, and with a military flourish imitating a drum and bugle, she began a vivid march, as if she were one of Wellington's men leaving Brussels for the great battle at Waterloo. Other girls, remembering the Kernel, joined in, and for a few minutes there was jollity and military nonsense and the remembrance of old friends.

"She says," the interpreter explained as the petite march continued, "that Kernel, he was one damn fine man." And another Belgian girl broke in to have the interpreter say: "He was the lucky one. He found the gold. And he was good to us."

The Mare, exhausted from her unusual activity, fell onto the second bed in her crib, and while she regained her breath, Missy said: "Tell her that I liked her dance. She is an artist." And when this was translated, the Mare sat straight up and said with great seriousness: "I was an actress. But the fat, it grew too much. What does this one want?"

Missy wondered if it was prudent for her to display the amount of money the envelope contained, and she decided against it.

Standing so that the other girls could not see, she bent over the Mare, opened the envelope slightly, and allowed her to see the beautiful gold face of the hundred-dollar bill.

Her attempt to protect the Mare was useless, for the latter shouted in French: "Oh my God! Look at what that dear man sends me!" And she ripped the bill from the envelope, showed it to the girls, then paraded it up and down before the other cribs, shouting in Flemish: "Look what that dear man sent me!" and soon almost all the girls were in Paradise Alley, looking at the golden bill. A few customers stuck their heads out, wanting to know what the shouting was about, and after a while the procession halted and the Belgian girls returned to their cribs, while the Mare thanked Missy, calling for the interpreter again: "What business is this one in?" And when she heard that Missy ran the new restaurant down by the river, the Mare went back into the alley and shouted: "This kind lady runs that new restaurant down by the river. Tell the men to eat there."

In this accidental way, Missy and Tom obtained customers they would not otherwise have had, and occasionally one of the girls from Paradise Alley would accompany some customer to the restaurant and share breakfast with him. One morning two girls brought with them a tall, dour miner who had been immured in a lonely cabin atop a hill for most of a year, and they told Missy: "This is one of the loneliest sons-of-bitches in the world. He won't even come to the Alley, but he does bring us fresh meat now and then."

"And what is your name?" Missy asked, and the man grunted through his beard: "John Klope, ma'am."

"From where?"

"Idaho."

Missy laughed, saying: "I didn't know anybody lived in Idaho," and he replied as if she had asked a serious question: "Quite a few do, ma'am."

She noticed that although he seemed to be hungry, he toyed with his pancakes, and on two subsequent visits for breakfast he did the same, until out of curiosity she asked: "Anything wrong with the cakes?" and he said: "They're disgraceful." When she winced, he added apologetically: "No offense to you, ma'am. It's just that you ain't usin' a proper strain of sourdough."

"What does that mean?"

"Ma'am, to make proper flapjacks, you got to have the right starter to begin with."

"I use yeast. Bought it in Seattle."

"You see? You got off on the wrong foot, and can't never recover."

"What do you use?"

"I got my sourdough from an old woman in Fort Yukon. She'd had the same strain for more'n fifty years. I brought it by sled near three hundred and fifty miles, the way we came, in dead of winter. It makes real flapjacks."

"I'd like to taste the difference."

"I'll bring you some of my starter next time I'm in town."

"Where's your claim?"

"El Dorado. On the Bench. Eldorado Crest, Claim Eighty-seven."

"Ooooh, one of those millionaires?"

"No, ma'am. Bench means I'm up on the ridge."

"Nothing?"

"Not yet."

He made the tedious trip to his claim and back, just to bring Missy a batch of his sourdough starter, and when he showed her how to use it in preparing pancakes while conserving the strain by keeping it in a cool jug, she had to agree that his sourdough flapjacks were definitely superior to her ordinary pancakes. They were light, they browned well if a customer wanted them that way, and most did, and they were chewy, blending perfectly with either sorghum or honey. She said: "I'm indebted to you, Mr. Klope, and I hope you strike it rich."

"I will," he said, but an even more important consequence of this second series of visits related to the fine dog he brought with him. Missy paid no attention to the well-formed husky, but Tom recognized immediately that this was a superior animal. He knew little of dogs, really, and nothing about the famous sled dogs of the arctic, but even so, he could see in this dog's bearing, in the intelligence which flowed in his eyes, that he was special.

"Where'd you get him?"

"He pulled our sled . . . down from Fort Yukon." Almost hesitantly he added: "I couldn't let him go. We went through a lot together."

In the weeks that followed, when the miner should have been at his diggings above Eldorado, he lingered in Dawson, appearing each morning at the tent for his sourdough flapjacks.

One morning Superintendent Steele stopped by with some startling news for Missy: "Remember how you suspected my man Kirby because of how Soapy Smith's men behaved at Skagway? And you asked me why I didn't do something about it? And I said I couldn't, because that was America, and America had to clean up its own messes?"

"What happened?"

"Just what I expected to happen. Good men exist everywhere in the world, and when they finally cry 'Enough!'—watch out."

"Was somebody brave enough to cry 'Enough'?"

"Chap named Reid, if I have it right. Engineering fellow. When Soapy's gang stole the entire poke of a quiet fellow heading home out of the mountains, that was bad enough, but when the hoodlums rallied around and made fun of the little man, the poor chap appealed to the conscience of the community."

"And?"

"And Mr. Reid shot Soapy dead."

Missy did not exult, for the dead gambler had on several occasions been good to her and considerate of unfortunates she brought to his attention, but she knew enough of his criminality to realize that sensible people could not allow him to continue unopposed, and she was pleased that he had been stopped: "I should think that Mr. Reid would be a hero in Skagway."

"He's dead too. Soapy got him in the exchange of bullets."

Missy sat down, and as she looked up at Superintendent Steele and saw the quiet determination he represented she realized that her man, Buchanan Venn, had been on his way to becoming such a person. Had the Venns stayed in Skagway, the day would have come when Buck would say "Enough!" and it would have been he who gunned down the petty tyrant.

"Tom, come here," and when the boy stood facing Superintendent Steele, she said: "You hear what he just told me? About Soapy Smith? Sometimes you have to stand up against such men. Remember that."

Steele smiled at Tom, then asked if he could speak alone with his mother, using that word even though he knew it did not apply. He did this because of the nature of what he wanted to say next: "Miss Peckham, it may seem none of my business, but believe me, it is. It's been my business many painful times."

"Do I need a license or something?"

"I want to warn you against the woman you call the Belgian Mare."

"She's been a good friend. Brings me business."

Steele coughed, looked Missy right in the eye, and said: "She's a horrible woman. It's not the German pimp who brings these Belgian girls here. She does. It wasn't the businessmen who built the new cribs. She did. She rents them to her girls, takes a huge slice of their earnings. Please, do not interrupt. These are things you must hear." And he continued with a recital of the Mare's almost criminal behavior: "When a girl is used up, and some last only a short time, she kicks her out. Even at best, they're treated like animals. If she's being kind to you, it's because she knows that lone women sooner or later run out of money. Then you work for her, on her terms."

"Please, Superintendent Steele . . ."

"I tell you only the truth."

"But if she's so terrible, why do you allow her in Dawson?"

"With the services her girls provide, there's no rape in my city."

Aware that he had succeeded only in arousing Missy's indignation, he saluted and left, but he had not been gone long before his place was quietly taken by John Klope, who ordered nothing but who did occupy one of her four stools for nearly an hour, watching her as she worked. She was so busy that she forgot he was there until he suddenly spoke in a loud voice, all in a rush, uttering important words he'd been rehearsing for a week: "You and Tom are people I like. Come out to Eldorado with me and help find the gold that has to be there."

"Now what would the two of us do in a mining camp?" she asked lightly, and he lowered his voice, speaking carefully, as he would to a child: "In the winter we build fires in the earth, to melt the frozen soil. Then we dig in the softened earth. And haul it by ropes to the top, like it was a well and we were drawing water. Because it's so cold, the wet muck freezes immediate, locking in whatever gold we found. Come summer and the thaw, we sluice the muck and find the gold. And then we're rich."

"Have you found any gold yet?"

"No, but I have a feeling I'm getting close."

It was obvious to Klope that his two listeners were still interested in gold and that having come so far, they did not want to return to civilization without having at least tried their hands at the great gamble of mining, so although they said nothing, he pressed his case: "You can go on earning a living here in the tent, but if you come with me, share and share, you might make a fortune." He hesitated: "That's what you came here for, wasn't it? Isn't that why we all came?"

"Where did you come from?" Missy asked as she turned away from her cooking to listen to this strange, compelling man.

"Idaho, like I told you before. All washed up, sort of like you, I guess."

"We were. But now we're safely started. We could have a good life here in Dawson."

For the first time in their acquaintance John Klope smiled: "Ma'am, can't you see? When the gold runs out, Dawson runs out. There's no future here for a tent restaurant. Only future in the Klondike is gold, and when it ends, you end. All of us do."

Missy now left her side of the counter and came to sit on one of the stools: "Just what do you mean, we come and help in your cabin?"

"I need help. I stand very close to gold, of that I'm sure. But when I dig out the softened muck, I need someone to haul it to the top and dump it. In the summer I need someone to help me sluice it. Your son here . . ."

"He's not my son. We . . . It would be too complicated to explain."

"I could use him."

"And me?"

"We'd both need someone to mind the cabin. You know, it's not a shack. It's got real sides and a window."

They did not explore, at this first discussion, the role that Missy as a human being and a woman would play, but on subsequent mornings Klope did quietly intimate that he was not married and that he did not drink. There was nothing about his silent, austere manner which would tempt a woman to move in with him, regardless of the arrangement, and he, realizing this, did not press his case, and things might have ended on that tentative note had not two extraneous incidents muddied the situation of the Venns.

The impact of Klope's suggestion that they move to Eldorado fell most heavily on young Tom, for it caused him to think seriously about his future, and after long speculation and study of Dawson, he drafted a surprisingly mature letter to Mr. Ross back in Seattle:

> *I hope you will remember me. My father, Buck Venn, worked in your office and I think you respected him. He was killed in a freak accident. I hope you also remember my mother, Missy, who worked on your ship the* Alacrity, *but maybe you didn't meet her. I was the newspaper boy who became your helper on the docks. So our whole family was Ross & Raglan, and I hope you remember us well, because we tried to work well.*
>
> *My idea is this. You have a lot of interests here in Dawson City and two of your riverboats come here. Why not let me organize things in Dawson so that you get more business for your boats and sell more of your goods after the boats get here? Everything must be done in three months while the river is open. If you lose time, you lose money.*
>
> *I think you ought to open a serious store here and put me in charge, and your business will double or even double double. I am sixteen years old and understand business like a man. Please let me hear from you.*

He was only fifteen when he wrote, but by the time his letter reached Seattle he would probably be the sixteen he claimed. However, all thoughts of such an opportunity were forgotten when Dawson experienced one of those periodic fires which at one time or another ravaged most boomtowns. This one, unlike the two more famous ones which would gut the heart of the city, merely roamed the tents and shacks along the waterfront, and one of the first it consumed was the

Venn restaurant, whose canvas side walls, heavy with splatter grease, disappeared in minutes, leaving Missy and Tom with only the surplus goods still stacked in the half-demolished *Aurora*.

While the extensive blaze was still ravaging the huts along the riverfront, two men elbowed their way through the crowd explicitly to advise Missy Peckham. The first was Superintendent Steele, who said simply: "Miss Peckham, this is the kind of disaster I warned about. I'm in charge of government emergency funds, which will allow me to ship you and the boy back to Seattle. Frankly, ma'am, I believe that's what you should do."

Even as he spoke, the Belgian Mare came along the waterfront, assessing the damage and consoling those who had lost heavily. Waiting till Superintendent Steele went about other business, she sidled up to Missy and said, with the aid of one of her girls who spoke English: "How sad. If you need help, let me know." Saying no more, she patted Missy on the cheek and wandered on.

The second man to arrive was John Klope, with his dog Breed, and all he said was: "Now you two need me as much as I need you."

That dismal night, when Missy and Tom took shelter in the theater with some fifty other people deprived of their homes, they did not even try to reach any decisions, but in the morning when they returned to where their tent restaurant had been, they saw with sickening clarity that reopening it or anything like it was impossible. They never really said "Klope's offer is all that's left," but each recognized the inevitability, and Tom poked about till he found a handcart which a defeated miner was willing to sell for one dollar.

When Klope saw him pushing it along the waterfront he hurried up, took over, and then helped Missy pack the few things she had saved from the fire. By midafternoon they were on their way to Lousetown, Tom and Klope each pulling a rope tied to the front of the cart, Missy pushing from behind.

From Lousetown they followed the left bank of the Klondike till they came to Bonanza Creek, the tributary on which the squaw man George Carmack had made the first big discovery. Up it they trudged, past claims now famous around the world—*Seven Above, Nine Below*—until they reached the confluence with the Eldorado with its less famous but far richer claims, and after they had passed a score of these immensely productive sites along the stream, they climbed sharply to reach the upper ridge, far above the gold-producing placers, and there, on the high ridge, they came to John Klope's cabin.

It stood on a plot five hundred feet long, paralleling the stream below, by about fifteen hundred feet wide: this gave him about seventeen acres, but the effective portion would be an area close to wherever gold-producing muck was found. "Technically," he explained as they neared the hole which already went deep into the earth, "what we're looking for is bedrock."

"Do we have to blast solid rock?" Tom asked, and Klope said: "No. The gold will be resting on the bedrock—the bottom of some old river."

"How do you know a river used to run down there?"

"How did those fellows down there know the present river had gold? They panned. We dig."

By gold-field standards his cabin was superior, but it was still a miserable affair: nine by twelve feet, four log walls, a solitary window cut into the logs and carefully caulked, a wooden floor, a single bed, stove, pegs jutting from the wall to dry the clothes which seemed always to be soaked, and a change of boots, which also seemed to be permanently wet and mud-caked. It had a chimney which carried away the smoke, but the long exposed run of the piping meant that when the stove was working, the heat inside the cabin was intense, often higher than eighty-five degrees; when the fire was out, the cold could drop to twenty-below.

Because Klope was essentially a neat man who attended to his appearance, he had built an outside stand for washing and shaving and had started his occupancy with a determination to remain clean-shaven, but this resolve had lasted less than a month, for shaving in the Klondike, whether in summer or winter, was a drudgery which he gladly avoided. Now his beard, which he often forgot to trim with his rusty scissors, was long and masked his true age; he could have been either a well-preserved forty or a determined twenty. Actually, he was twenty-eight that year and one of the most dedicated miners on any of the famous streams.

When Missy saw that the cabin had only one bed, she stiffened, but Klope eased the situation by stating: "First thing, we've got to build two more beds," and with Tom's expert help, this was promptly accomplished. However, the supplies they had brought with them could not all fit into the cabin, and this required some ingenuity on Klope's part. He found a solution by bringing the cart flush against one of the windowless walls and erecting over it a kind of sloping roof with two side walls. The front, of course, had to be left open, but none of the gold-field cabins had locked doors, and Klope said: "No danger of anyone stealing things. The Mounties don't permit it."

During the first months of the occupancy, each of the three kept to a separate bed, but as the routine settled into boredom, with Klope down in the hole nine and ten hours a day during the long, cold winter, and Tom topside managing the loads of muck that came up on the windlass, it became obvious that when Klope climbed the ladder at the end of his stint, he was interested in Missy as a woman and not only as the person who prepared his morning flapjacks. So one very cold February night, when the temperature hovered about the minus-thirty mark, Missy, quietly and without a gesture of any kind toward Tom, crept in with Klope, and shortly thereafter, while the men were working the mine, she moved her former bed out into the shed.

So for a third time young Tom was a bystander when this practical-minded woman moved in with a man to whom she was not married. His education in the ways of men and women had not been a conventional one, so he was not troubled by this, and he still felt that Missy was the most nearly perfect woman he had known. As the long months passed, with endless work and little promise of gold at the bottom of the deep mine, it was she who kept the spirits of the place buoyant, the cabin livable and the work moving forward.

In this she was abetted by a new friend whose support she could not have anticipated, the husky Breed. Different from most sled dogs, hence his name and the willingness of Sarqaq to part with him, he had more or less liked his three principal companions, Sarqaq, Klope and Tom Venn, but during the long hours when Klope and Tom were working the mine, he found himself increasingly with Missy. She fed him, summoned him to help her drag logs for the stove, played with him, and spoke to him twenty times to the men's one, so before long he was adjusting his life to hers. Always a dog who appreciated being with humans, he now focused his entire affection on Missy. He became her dog, and once when two miners from the lower claims along Eldorado appeared suddenly to make inquiries about whether Klope could supply them with meat, their moves toward Missy were too abrupt, and within two seconds Breed was at their throats, and only Missy's prompt intervention saved them.

"You ought to keep that one on a chain," one of the men complained as he moved back.

"He's that way only if he thinks we're in trouble," Missy said, hoping that the men would relay that information to the camps below.

"You got any surplus meat?"

"Not right now. But maybe Tom will get some the next few days."

"We'd pay well."

And so Tom and Breed went out on Sundays and after work to scout for deer or bear or caribou, and when they were lucky and had butchered the carcass, Missy peddled the cuts along the river.

She was doing this one wintry morning in 1899 when a Mountie came riding along the river, asking for her whereabouts, and when one of the miners shouted: "Hey, Missy! Someone to see you!" she looked up to see Sergeant Kirby, as neat and trim as ever in his blue uniform.

He led his horse as they climbed the hill to Klope's shaft on the upper ridge, and when he saw the cabin with two beds inside and one stacked beside the cart, he asked no questions: "I came to see Tom Venn, really. Important news for the boy. Startling news, really."

Calling for Breed, she told the dog: "Fetch Tom!" and before long the boy reported.

"Superintendent Steele wants to see you."

"I haven't done anything."

"Yes," Kirby said, with a wide smile, "I rather think you have."

"I couldn't have, Sergeant Kirby. I've been here all the time."

Kirby reached out, grasped the boy by the left arm, and said: "Sit down. The news is very good. In fact, it's spectacular." Then, winking at Missy, he asked: "Did you mail a letter from Dawson City when you arrived?"

"Yes. To my grandmother."

"And maybe one to a Mr. Ross in Seattle?"

"Yes, but I was only asking questions."

"You're going to be amazed, young Mr. Tom, at his reply." And he said that whereas Superintendent Steele would no doubt want to do the explaining, he, Kirby, could reveal that Ross & Raglan had jumped at the ideas proposed by Tom and were sending, on the first R&R steamer to break through the Yukon ice, supplies for a major trade depot at Dawson, along with a Mr. Pincus to run the place, provided Thomas Venn was ready to offer the services he spoke of in his letter of such and such a date.

Before Klope could climb out of the deep shaft—twenty-nine feet straight down, with no timber supports of any kind—Tom and Missy and Sergeant Kirby had agreed that the boy must leave immediately to arrange for space in which to open the R&R branch in Dawson. When Klope was informed of this *fait accompli* arranged in his absence, he behaved in his characteristic way. He scratched his beard, looked at Missy, then Kirby, then the boy, then said quietly: "He's soon to be a man. Anyone would be lucky to hire a fellow as good as this one."

But once he had established that Tom was free to leave if he wished, he sought to forestall action. "Let's all sit down and talk about this," and when the session began he laid out the relevant facts: "Tom, you and Missy have earned part ownership of this claim, and I testify before the Mountie here that when I next get in to Dawson, I'll enter the transfer legally. But only if you stay and help work it."

"It's time for him to go," Missy said with great firmness.

"And you're going with him?" Klope asked.

"I'm staying here."

"Good, because I'm convinced the old river must have run along where we're digging. We're at twenty-nine feet now, another fifteen feet, we've got to strike it."

"Have you shown any color?" Kirby asked, for he had heard predictions like this from a hundred different men in a hundred different locations. The bedrock was always just a little farther down.

"No."

"In all that frozen muck out there, not two cents to the pan when you wash it out this summer?"

"Probably not, but when men started on these creeks, ten cents a pan was enough to make them dream. Then Carmack found four dollars a pan, and the boom was on. Down at that claim you can see from here, eighty dollars a pan, and that far one, they hit a thousand dollars in one pan."

"What he says is true," Kirby affirmed. "Sometimes the midnight bell did toll."

"What I'm shooting for, and it's got to be down there, will be something like five or six thousand dollars a pan. That's what we're hoping for."

His three listeners sat looking at their knuckles, each one afraid to bring him down to reality. Finally Tom said: "I asked Mr. Ross to do something. He's doing it and I got to do my part."

"You understand the gamble?" Klope asked, and when Tom said

he did, the tall, gangling man said with no rancor: "It's your decision, son. I couldn't have asked for a better helper."

While Tom packed, with Missy throwing one useful item after another into his canvas bag, Kirby asked Klope: "Have you any solid reason for believing there's gold down there?"

"The lay of the land."

"But you can't see the lay of the land."

"Every inch I dig deeper tells me something new."

"And you're willing to risk everything . . . on those secrets?"

"I don't have much to risk, Officer."

When the packing was done and Klope had paid Tom for his work in hauling up the muck, the time had come for goodbyes, and the boy went from Breed to Klope to Missy, close to crying as he bade farewell to those with whom he had shared a cabin on an authentic Klondike claim. He sensed that this departure marked a watershed in his life, like climbing the last six feet of Chilkoot Pass and looking down the other side toward Lake Lindeman and the thousands of boats at Bennett.

He said brave words, then knelt and kissed Breed. "Well," he said matter-of-factly when he rose, "I guess we better be going."

He was working in the new Ross & Raglan store on a bright June morning in 1899 when a commotion filled the main street, and he ran out to learn where the new strike had been made. It wasn't the finding of additional gold, it was the arrival of an extraordinary Klondiker come all the way from Edmonton, over the hideous route down the untamed Mackenzie River to a spot far beyond the Arctic Circle and then across hellish, barren heights to the Yukon Territory. When word flashed through Dawson that "a tough little Irishman made it by the Mackenzie route," hardened sourdoughs gathered to see the miracle man who had done what they would never have attempted.

Tom, from the edge of the crowd, saw a medium-sized Irishman in his early thirties, haggard as a hungry ghost but smiling roguishly at the men about him. He had dark, uncut hair which came down about his eyes, heavy clothes tattered from his ordeal north of the Circle, and a positive passion for talking: "Name's Matt Murphy from a town west of Belfast. Five of us from London hurried to Edmonton as soon as we heard of the Klondike find. Set out down the Mackenzie in July 1897, got lost, one man drowned, one starved to death, one died of scurvy. That tall fellow you saw come in with me, he'd had enough. Kited right back to London. Me? I'm here to stay. Determined to find meself a gold mine."

His listeners broke into laughter, not derisively but with a desire to straighten him out: "Every good site taken three years ago."

Tom saw with admiration how the stranger reacted to this shattering news: his shoulders drooped ever so slightly, he took a deep breath, then he asked almost jocularly: "Any place a man can grab a beer?" and when one was provided, the first he had had in two years, he sipped it as if it were nectar, then asked quietly: "Now, if there was to be new sites found, where would they be?" and solemnly the men replied: "There won't be any."

For just a moment Tom wondered if Murphy was going to faint, but then he flashed an irrepressible Irish smile and said softly: "Your news is not comfortin'. I've come so far, so close to starvin' . . ."

The miners, ashamed that they had not acted sooner, led him to a tent restaurant where eggs, bacon and pancakes were available, and Tom, once more at the edge of the crowd, watched as the newcomer ate in a way Tom had never seen before. With infinite care, as if trying to hold back rearing horses, he cut his food into minute portions, eating them one by one like a dainty bluebird. "Ain't you hungry?" asked the miner who was paying the bill, and the Irishman said: "I could eat everything in this tent and in that one over there. I haven't seen food like this in two years."

"Then eat up!" the miner bellowed, but the stranger said: "If I did, I'd drop dead," and he continued placing in his mouth one tiny morsel after another.

In the days that followed, Tom spent a good deal of time with the incredible Irishman, listening to his account of the epic trip north and of the dreadful deaths which had overtaken the gold seekers. "My father died too," he told Murphy. "Pole doubled back on him while we were riding an ice sled with a sail."

The boy was impressed by the self-discipline with which Murphy continued to handle his meals, still eating them piece by piece, but always as they ate, the Irishman asked questions about gold, and Tom could see that he was obsessed by his determination to find himself a site, any kind, at which he could go through the motions of panning or digging. Not wanting to dismay Murphy by reiterating that there were no more sites, Tom threw the burden onto the able shoulders of his friend Sergeant Kirby of the North West Mounted, who had dealt with many latecomers like Murphy.

"Spots to claim? The good ones were nailed down three years ago. Will there be any new ones? Not likely."

When Murphy, gaunt as a bear coming out of hibernation in April, heard this confirmation from an expert, he masked his disappointment, whereupon Kirby made a suggestion: "There's a chap named Klope out on a ridge. Digs day and night. Feels sure he's on to something good. He needs help."

"How do I fit in? Do I buy part of the claim?"

"No, you work for him. He pays you wages, and when he runs out of money, maybe he'll offer you a share of the claim to keep you on the scene."

"You're sayin' he's not finding any gold?"

"Down along the stream you pan the placers and know immediately if you've hit. Up on the benches, you dig, dig, dig and never know anything till you reach bedrock."

Murphy, not yet strong enough to take hard knocks like this, sat down: "You mean . . . I've come all the way from Edmonton . . . You can't know what that's like."

"I think I can," Kirby said. "Half a dozen parties have straggled in. I've had to bury some of them."

"Did any of the Edmonton men find gold?"

"Like you, they never even found a place to dig for it."

For some moments Murphy sat with his face buried in his shockingly thin hands. Then he straightened his shoulders and stood erect: "Where's this Mr. Klope's ridge? By God, I'm the one that came the Edmonton route that's going to make a try, at least."

Kirby drew him a rough map, at the bottom of which he wrote: "John Klope: This man has come from Edmonton. He knows how to work. Will Kirby, North West Mounted Police."

When Murphy climbed the hill above Eldorado and presented his recommendation, Klope said: "We've been at wit's end. I keep digging, but Missy here can't work the windlass and do the cooking both. We need you."

So the Irishman started work for wages, and when Missy saw how emaciated he was, and yet how eager to take over the heavy labors that she had been performing, she felt it her duty to feed him generously, but he would not gorge himself, just carefully ate all those things which would send energy through his body and antiscurvy fluids down his legs. When he found that Klope had a good rifle, he remembered hunting tricks he had learned in Ireland, going far into the country and bringing back quarters of meat when other hunters were getting nothing.

When his strength returned, he proved a diligent laborer, hauling up the muck and getting it ready for the summer washing, so that after the second month Klope raised his pay from one dollar a day, which was standard in the mines that were producing nothing, to a dollar and a quarter, which encouraged Murphy to even greater exertion. But as he worked aboveground while Klope slaved away deep inside the frozen earth, he had an opportunity to spend hours each day with Missy, who became attracted to his witty stories of Ireland, his accounts of horse racing in that country, and especially his explanation of what had gone wrong with the Edmonton gold seekers: "We were like men chasing the northern lights. We could see the golden colors dancing just beyond our reach, but when we struggled to catch them, we found ourselves lost in snow and ice."

When he related his harrowing experiences, she said: "I'm glad you told me this, Murphy. I was beginning to feel sorry for myself on the Chilkoot."

Both Klope and Missy enjoyed the musical manner in which Murphy spoke and they marveled at his use of big words. "You're a poet," Klope said one summer night as the Irishman prepared to take his evening stroll with Breed. He took such a walk fairly regularly, wishing out of delicacy to be away from the cabin part of each night so that Klope and Missy could be alone, but of late in these pleasant ambles, with the twilight lasting for hours, he found himself thinking only of Missy. And one morning, halfway between breakfast and when Klope would be climbing out of his shaft for a bite to eat, while he and Missy were working together at the pile of muck which they would soon be sluicing, he very carefully laid aside his shovel, took Missy's away from her, and kissed her fervently.

She did not respond, nor did she rebuke him. Reaching for his shovel, she handed it to him, then took her own and said: "We're after gold, and don't forget it."

But on subsequent mornings she began placing herself so that Murphy had to pass near her, and they began kissing without the formality of putting aside the shovels, and by autumn, when it was clear that the painfully accumulated muck contained no gold whatever, it was also clear to them that John Klope's would-be mine was a lost hope and that he was lost too. Missy saw him as the big, unresponsive, unimaginative lout he had always been, and Murphy discovered that the poor man had almost no money left to pay anyone to help him dig his unproductive mine.

As the days shortened and Murphy recalled those two tragic winters when he was trapped in the arctic, he began to feel a repetition of that sense of doom, and one morning at breakfast he threw down his fork and said: "I've got to get out of here, Klope. I see no chance of gold on your claim."

"Maybe it's best," Klope replied. "I've little left to pay you with," and then he descended with his hopes into his hole.

Murphy spent that morning packing while Missy worked the lift, but after lunch, when Klope was back at his digging, the two in the cabin drifted almost automatically into a passionate encounter, after which Missy said: "I'm going with you, Matt," and he said: "We'll find something."

They did not tell Klope that night, but he must have suspected something, for instead of staying in the cabin with Missy while Murphy went for a walk, it was he who left, and when he returned, silent and moody as ever, he went right to bed without conversation.

In the morning Missy prepared breakfast, ate none herself, and then informed Klope: "We're going in to Dawson. I pray you'll find your gold, John."

"Leaving?" he asked.

"Yes. It's better."

"Coming back?"

"No. It's worked out, John." He could not tell whether she meant that the mine was finished or her relationship with him. He looked at the Irishman and said: "I could break you in half." Then he shrugged his shoulders: "What would be the use?"

Left alone in the late autumn sunlight, John Klope watched the travelers depart, with Murphy pushing the handcart Tom Venn had bought for the handling of their goods. When the sound of their departure was silenced, he walked purposefully to the hole, adjusted the bucket rope so that he could work the removal of muck by himself, and without any visible sign of emotion climbed down to the thirty-second foot.

Of all the gold seekers who had come up the Yukon River in 1897 on the *Jos. Parker,* not one had found gold. Of those few who had tried the Mackenzie horror, not one had even filed a claim. And of those who scaled the Chilkoot Pass with the Venns and braved the canyons in their wake, not one found gold. But all had participated in the great adventure provided by the dying century, and as Matthew Murphy said on approaching Dawson behind the cart: "I dreamed of digging for gold, and I did."

While John Klope, Matt Murphy and Tom Venn labored in anonymity seeking gold on the Yukon, there was another group of men who attained vast publicity from their participation in the rush. Jack London, the proletarian writer from San Francisco, would find here material for his most notable stories, while the Canadian poet—English born, Scottish reared—Robert W. Service would immortalize the sourdough with poems that may have been no more than jingles but which proved unforgettable:

> *The Northern Lights have seen queer sights,*
> *But the queerest they ever did see*
> *Was that night on the marge of Lake Lebarge*
> *I cremated Sam McGee.*
>
> *Now Sam McGee was from Tennessee . . .*

He misspelled Lake Laberge in order to find an attractive rhyme, but this and his other misconstructions did not matter, for he breathed into his yarns of the Yukon a vitality and charm that will apparently never fade. Two remarkable facts highlight his career: he did not get to the Klondike until 1904, when the great days were long over, and he wrote his most famous poems about it, including those featuring Dan McGrew and Sam McGee, long before he had set foot in Dawson City.

Tex Rickard, famous fight promoter and friend of Jack Dempsey, spent time on the gold fields, as did Addison Mizner, notable wit and Florida real-estate genius, Nellie Bly, the famous New York reporter, and Key Pittman, a future senator from Nevada, notorious and a power in foreign relations.

But early in the existence of the Yukon fields, the flat-bottomed river steamer *Jos. Parker* puffed into Dawson City for an overnight stop, bringing a passenger who epitomized those visitors who stayed only briefly but who nevertheless added to the world's knowledge of the Klondike. He was dressed in Eskimo costume and at age sixty-three was one of the oldest men on the diggings.

His boat laid over in Dawson only one day, but in these twenty-eight hours the little cyclone moved up and down the dusty main street introducing himself to anyone he thought might be an authority: "Hello, friend! I'm Dr. Sheldon Jackson, General Agent for Education for Alaska. I'd like to know what plans you have for schools in your gold camps."

Like a little ferret he pried into the quality of the hotels, the system of paying for purchases in gold dust, and the condition of women, but he spent his major effort in learning about religion in the camps. He was welcomed by ministers as soon as he presented his imposing card:

DR. SHELDON JACKSON
Moderator of the General Assembly
The Presbyterian Churches of America

Knowing clergymen would ask: "Isn't that the highest office in your church?" and he would reply almost apologetically: "Yes. Three of us contended for the post. Our former President, Benjamin Harrison, the millionaire businessman John Wanamaker, and me." Then he would cough modestly: "I won on the first ballot . . . overwhelmingly."

He made a nuisance of himself that day, but next morning when the *Parker* headed down the Yukon, he carried with him knowledge enough to use the rest of his life in his popular lecture: The Gold Fields of the Klondike.

IX

THE GOLDEN BEACHES OF NOME

N O MOVE BY CAPTAIN HEALY AND REVEREND JACKSON TO IM-
prove the quality of life in Alaska elicited the scorn of their enemies like their attempt to import Siberian domesticated reindeer to
feed the starving Eskimos during winter famine. The stubborn do-
gooders were accused of being idiots, thieves and secret agents for the
Russians: "You wait, when the books are inspected you'll find them
two stole four-fifths of the money the government has poured into this
harebrained scheme." And of course Jackson was denounced, with
some justification, for having delivered most of the reindeer that did
reach Alaska to his Presbyterian settlements up and down the coast.

In the spring of 1897 the Army command in Washington dispatched a Lieutenant Loeffler of its Supply Corps to look into these
charges of gross mismanagement: "Tell us whether the idea is practical." In obedience to his orders, the lieutenant visited eight of the
sites where Dr. Jackson had tried to establish his herds, and sent
Washington a just summary of the situation:

> It is prudent for the Army to express interest in this
> experiment because the time could come when our troops
> operating in the arctic would want to rely upon reindeer as a
> major source of food.

*How has the experiment gone? Poorly. Many of the first
imports died either during the sea crossing from Siberia or
shortly thereafter because the Alaskan Eskimos had no
concept of how they should be husbanded. Reindeer which had
been accustomed to the most thoughtful care in Siberia and
treated as if they were valuable cattle on some Iowa farm were
turned loose as if they were wild caribou, with the result that
many reverted to untamed ways and were seen no more, while
others died for lack of attention and their customary food.*

*The result? All the reindeer settled in the Aleutians are now
dead or have disappeared. That experiment was a disaster.
Most of those brought to settlements along the northern
seacoast have fared poorly, so that one must look upon this
adventure as having come to very little. The Army would be ill-
advised to rely for the foreseeable future in any important way
upon domesticated reindeer as a major source of food supply.*

But in fairness, Lieutenant Loeffler did report upon one establishment where the Healy-Jackson reindeer imported from the Cape
Dezhnev region of Siberia had prospered, and he must have liked
what he saw, for he wrote of it with obvious enthusiasm:

*However, I did find one installation where, due to a peculiar set
of circumstances, the reindeer experiment did work. At the
western end of Seward Peninsula, a bleak place which has been
named Port Clarence contains a settlement called Teller
Station, and here a Norwegian named Lars Skjellerup, thirty-
three years old and unmarried, has put together a team of
three helpers who appear to know how to handle reindeer.*

*When Skjellerup came to Alaska he brought with him a short,
tough Laplander named Mikkel Sana, who can think like a
reindeer. Because he anticipates what they're going to do, he
guides them quietly but firmly around to his purposes.*

*The second helper gave me problems. He is Arkikov, no first
name, brought over from Siberia by Captain Michael Healy of
the famed revenue cutter Bear. This Chukchi Eskimo may
know reindeer but I found him surly, not given to following
directions, and difficult to discipline. But when I asked
Skjellerup: "Why do you bother with this man?" he told me:*

"Arkikov is a man, and from time to time in this work you need men."

The third helper was a shy Eskimo lad of nineteen, not tall and with a dark, round face. Skjellerup told me: "Ootenai is special. He has no family, they died during one of the famines, so he appreciates our project as his only chance for a good life. One day he'll be head of this station."

Well, there they are, and should the Army ever be required to work with reindeer in Alaska, I recommend that our officers ignore all other stations and head directly for Teller.

After Loeffler submitted his report in the spring of 1897 he returned to his regular duty in Seattle, where, in the early autumn of that year, he handled the urgent telegram that came from Washington:

DOZEN AMERICAN WHALERS TRAPPED IN ICE POINT BARROW STOP RATIONS SHORT STOP NO MEDICAL STORES STOP EVALUATE RESCUE OPERATIONS AND ADVISE IMMEDIATELY STOP

Since Loeffler had recently been in Point Barrow, he was assigned as second-in-command of the study group, and he spent his first three days along the Seattle waterfront trying to piece together the possible avenues whereby a covey of whalers stuck off Point Barrow could have alerted Washington, D.C., of their plight, and he learned that the owners of some of the stricken vessels had deduced from the nonarrival of their ships that they must be trapped in ice. Canadian officials at Prince Rupert had reached similar conclusions, but most important were appeals for help delivered over the northern snows by dog-team messengers heading south from Barrow.

Loeffler reported to the group: "There is a crisis. The whalers are probably icebound already, and there's no way of breaking them loose till early next summer." Then he added the ominous judgment: "Since they cannot possibly have enough food to last them nine months, a rescue operation is imperative."

The Army officials, with assistance from the Navy and private shippers like Ross & Raglan, began analyzing possible maneuvers, and none was too bizarre to be discarded out of hand. One Army officer said: "I've always heard that Siberia and Alaska are only a few miles apart. Could we telegraph Russia and request them . . . ?"

A Navy man broke in: "Southeast of Barrow that's true. How far apart do you think they are at Barrow?" and a former whaler who knew the northern oceans well broke in: "About five hundred miles." Rescue from Canada was equally impossible—about six hundred miles to the first tiny outpost, which would have no chance of providing enough food or medicine.

The group fell silent, then turned to Loeffler, who said tentatively: "I've looked at every possibility. It's about five hundred miles from any of the nearest mining camps. To cover that distance you'd have to use dogsleds, and where would you get enough food to feed your dogs en route? And what mining camp would have a cache of food big enough for twenty ships?"

"What alternative have you in mind?" the chairman asked, and Loeffler coughed several times before daring to reveal the plan which had been slowly germinating. Then, with the aid of a big map, he said: "Up here at Port Clarence Bay, at the far end of Seward Peninsula, there's a remarkable Norwegian, Lars Skjellerup, supported by a tough, capable team of three. One Siberian, one Laplander, one Eskimo."

The chairman broke in: "What do they have to offer? A superior dog team?" And a longtime sailor pointed out: "By the time we loaded a ship here in Seattle, that place would be iced in," but Loeffler said quietly: "You ask what they have up there?" Pausing dramatically, he said: "Reindeer."

The word brought an explosion from the study group: "We've heard about that fiasco." "How many are still alive? Six or seven?" and "That missionary stopped by Seattle one year and gave us a lecture about how the reindeer was going to solve all Alaska's problems. Whatever happened to the little fraud?" Before Loeffler could explain himself, it was unanimously agreed by the others that the few scattered reindeer at Port Clarence represented no solution whatever.

But then with a patience that won the respect of his superiors, the young lieutenant developed his plan: "Port Clarence has a huge herd of reindeer, actually. Under Skjellerup's professional guidance, the local Eskimos have acquired or bred well over six hundred fine beasts. Some are so domesticated, they serve in harness in place of dogs. And do you appreciate what that means? If we used reindeer, we wouldn't have to carry any food for the animals."

"Why not?"

"Dogs eat meat. Lots of it. Reindeer feed on the moss and lichens as they go along." Allowing time for this important fact to sink in, he added: "And we wouldn't have to carry any food. Because when our reindeer team reached Barrow they'd be slaughtered, and the starving men would be fed."

His arguments were greeted with silence, but now a secretary broke into the meeting with the latest telegram from Washington:

REPORT IMMEDIATELY PLANS TO RESCUE ICEBOUND WHALERS
STOP NATION'S NEWSPAPERS DEMANDING ACTION

Now all the members of the group turned to face Loeffler, who said: "I think the only practical thing to tell them is that I will sail immediately to Alaska with medicines, organize a dog team, and hurry overland to Teller Station, where Skjellerup and his men will start at once for Point Barrow with a herd of four hundred or more reindeer."

"How far would they be traveling?"

"About six hundred miles."

"My God! Siberia's as close as that. Canada too."

"But we have the reindeer, gentlemen, and the men to move them."

With a caution born of long experience in the arctic, one of the shipowners asked: "Is such an operation practical?" and Loeffler replied: "I can't promise that, but what I can promise is this: there's more than three hundred American sailors up there who will die if we don't do something. And this offers our best chance. Let's do it."

So a telegram was dispatched to the White House, with a reply arriving in Seattle that afternoon:

PROCEED WITH REINDEER AND MAY GOD SPEED YOUR EFFORTS
STOP NATION IS WATCHING

It took Lieutenant Loeffler till the middle of January to reach the southern shore of Norton Sound, and when his dogs pulled into the primitive settlement of Stebbins he faced an open crossing of some ninety miles to the north shore, from which Teller Reindeer Station could be approached by land. The prospect of venturing to the other side on ice which might or might not be solidly frozen frightened him so much that he considered making a complete circuit of the eastern end of the sound so as to remain on land. But an old-time Eskimo who ran dogs assured him: "All frozen. No trouble," and when Loeffler still held back, the man said: "I go with you," and in days when the sun barely shone at noon, the two set out, traveling indifferently day or night.

When they reached the northern shore, the old man accepted the payment Loeffler offered him and started his long hike back across the ice, while the young officer speeded his dogs the remaining hundred and twenty miles west to Teller. As he approached where he judged the reindeer station ought to be, for he had previously come to it only from the sea, a sharp-eyed Eskimo outlook spotted him coming and sounded the alarm, so that when his dogs raced joyously into the station, four resolute men, whom he already knew, were waiting to greet him.

The Laplander Mikkel Sana was first to greet him with a vigorous handshake, then the dour Siberian Arkikov, then the dark young Eskimo Ootenai, and finally the tall, thin unbelieving Norwegian, Lars Skjellerup. "How did you come with that dog team?" the latter asked, and Loeffler felt that he ought to deliver the news, as he said, "plain and prompt": "Washington wants you to drive a herd of three to four hundred reindeer to Point Barrow. A score of whalers stranded there. Three hundred sailors starving."

The news was so dramatic that none among the four Teller men knew how to respond, so after a moment of silence, Loeffler said: "Orders. From the President himself. How soon can we leave?"

Once the reality of the situation struck them, the four herders were eager to accept the challenge, for they knew well the scandals that had been circulated throughout Alaska and the United States regarding their deportment and that of other Laplanders and Siberians associated with the reindeer. Skjellerup, as the man in local command, was especially eager in order to demonstrate the capabilities of his reindeer: "How many miles do you guess?"

"Six hundred, maybe," Loeffler said. "Can you do it in sixty days?"

"I think maybe fifty. If we go, we go fast." He consulted with his men, and Arkikov said: "Faster. Lead reindeer Siberian, not your kind." He was referring to the softer Lapland reindeer that Skjellerup had imported by ship from Norway. The Norwegian ignored this implied slur, for he had become accustomed to Arkikov's conviction that only reindeer or herders from his Siberia were of much account.

Loeffler was delighted with Arkikov's estimate that the food and medicine could be delivered in less than fifty days, but his enthusiasm was dashed when Skjellerup said: "We'll depart three days from now."

"Wait a minute! I packed my gear in half an hour for my trip up here. Surely you men . . ."

Quietly Skjellerup reasoned: "You ever try to round up over four hundred reindeer from their comfortable winter quarters . . . which they don't want to leave?" And in the next two days Loeffler learned how much shouting and shoving this entailed, but on Wednesday morning, 19 January 1898, the herd was gathered, the two sleighs were loaded with medicines and food for the trip, and the team was ready for its awesome dash north. Loeffler, watching them depart, called out the message from Washington: "The President says: 'God speed your efforts. The nation is watching.'" And within the half-hour the reindeer, the four leading men, three Eskimo helpers and the sleds were indistinct on the eastern horizon. They would travel almost two hundred miles in that direction before they could turn north for the real drive into Barrow where the starving sailors waited.

It was a heroic run, for the nights were bitter cold, the winds blew more than usual, and on several frightening occasions the deer could find no lichen or moss when they scratched or pawed the snow with their sharp hoofs. Sana warned: "We must find moss. Maybe over there . . . maybe over here? Stop one day," and when this was done the animals did find lichen and the trip could resume.

When long downhill vistas opened, the men urged the reindeer to run free, but always Sana and Arkikov, two of the best herders in the world, watched for shallow crevasses, and when the gallop ended, men and animals started the breath-strangling climb to the crest of the next hill. When they finally made the big turn from their east heading to north-by-northeast, they felt they were at last on the main part of their journey, the long run to Barrow, perched on the edge of the world. Men alone could not have made this punishing run, nor could dogs have traveled as relentlessly as the reindeer, and certainly the dogs could not have fed themselves. Only reindeer could have carried this burden of food over such terrain and across such distances.

When they were approaching the seventieth latitude, far above the Arctic Circle, they were confronted by a spell of weather so cold and blustery that the thermometer dropped to minus-sixty-two. Now came a real test of what the reindeer could do, for when they were turned loose at the end of a twenty-nine-mile run they pawed the frozen snow until food was uncovered, grazed for half an hour, their backs into the wind, then burrowed in the snow until protecting drifts piled up around them.

"We'd better dig in too!" Skjellerup cried as the gale raged, and both Sana and Arkikov drew their sleds into a bulwark position. With the wind howling over them, but deflected by the sleds, the seven men hunkered down, allowing the snow to build drifts over them.

They stayed there for two long days, their bodies warm and dry in the almost perfect gear they wore; even their feet remained comfortable inside their heavy caribou boots, while the porcupine fur around their heads and the mysterious wolverine tips about their faces kept out the cold and ice. Not many could have withstood that assault, but these men had been drilled since childhood in arctic survival, and it was a curious fact, which both the Lapp and the Siberian noticed, that the white man Skjellerup was as gifted in arctic lore as they who had been bred to it. He was an impressive man, and the others treated him not with reverence, for they were his equal, but with respect for his mastery.

When the storm abated they became lighthearted as children, for now Barrow lay only a hundred miles ahead, and with clear weather and adequate food for the deer, it seemed almost as if they could cover that easy distance in a day. It required several, of course, but on 7 March at about ten in the morning they participated in a moment of such beauty that no one who shared it would ever forget. From the north, out of Barrow, came three dog teams drawing empty sleds and traveling at high speed. From the south came hundreds of reindeer, moving at their own steady speed, and for more than half an hour each party could see the other and calculate its mode of travel and its speed.

Skjellerup cried to his men: "They must have become desperate. They were going to try to break through!" and the men in the dog teams cried to one another: "Thank God! Look at those reindeer."

Closer and closer the two running teams moved, until the bearded men could discern each other's faces. Soon there was cheering and embracing and men weeping, and all the while the wonderful, powerful dogs lay panting in the snow and the reindeer pawed through the drifts for lichen.

This twelve-hundred-mile round trip of rescue became significant in Alaska history not because of heroism or reindeer or the fact that the leaders came from four such divergent backgrounds, but rather because of a chance conversation which occurred on the return trip. Skjellerup and the Eskimo boy Ootenai were driving one of the empty sleds while Arkikov and Sana rode in the other, the one drawn by the Siberian deer, and it was Arkikov, of this we can be certain— because years later each man would so testify—who first broached the subject.

"Remember last spring? Me make trip east . . . take deer to miners' Council City . . . meet many men."

"What were they doing?"

"Looking gold."

"Where?"

"To east."

"Did they find any?"

"Not yet. Soon maybe."

"How would they find gold?"

"Along rivers . . . little streams. You dip. You wash. You find."

That was the opening conversation, and on succeeding days as they drifted always southerly south-by-southwest, then due west, these two managed it so they rode together, and repeatedly Arkikov wanted to talk about the gold seekers, those ghost-driven men who prowled creeks, until Sana began to suspect that maybe ordinary men like Arkikov and himself had a chance of finding gold, but suspicious Lapp that he was, he dismissed the idea.

And yet: "What creek do they dig sand from?"

"Any creek. Me hear men say Klondike . . . all creek."

"Do you mean river? Like Yukon, big river?"

"No! Little river . . . maybe jump across." From his conversations with prospectors the Siberian had acquired an accurate sense of what gold seeking consisted of, and he was obviously mesmerized by the possibility of finding gold in some creek along the way home: "When sun higher . . . no snow . . . little streams run water . . . you, me find gold."

"How could we . . . no papers . . . just Lapp, Siberian?"

These were practical matters, and to a methodical Lapp like Sana they were powerful enough to disqualify the whole endeavor, but to a Siberian they were meaningless, a temporary irritation to be sidestepped.

"You, me . . . money . . . we go . . . we find gold . . . sure."

Arkikov gestured so wildly as he talked that in time Skjellerup, riding in the other sled, could not escape noticing it, so when they

stopped to eat he asked: "What's going on? You fighting?" Arkikov
looked at Sana as if to ask: "Shall I tell him?" and when the Lapp
nodded the fateful words were spoken.

"Council City . . . all men look gold . . . little streams . . . maybe
we look too?"

When the big Norwegian stared at his companions as if they were
mad, Arkikov added seductively: "We three . . . find gold . . . buy
many reindeer."

He said this so confidently, his round face smiling in sunlight as if
the gold were already in his hands, that Skjellerup had to be impressed with the possibility of what was being proposed, and found
himself saying: "Well, we do have money enough for a year, even two
years. We need no immigration papers." Then his shrewd practicality
asserted itself: "We were all invited here by the U.S. government. And
we have contracts which allow us to stay."

Before the hasty meal was over he was planning how he and the
other two could leave the station and strike out on a prospecting tour,
and he became so excited by the prospect of huge riches that he told
the others: "Ootenai, you ride with Arkikov. I want to talk with
Sana," and when the switch was made, he asked: "Mikkel, you have
no wife, nor me. Would you be willing to leave the station, the reindeer . . . and go exploring?"

"Yes!" delivered emphatically.

"You're not worried about leaving Lapland?"

"You worried about Norway?"

"Not at all." He considered this for a moment, then added firmly:
"I like Alaska. I liked this run. Maybe you . . . me . . . him . . ." As he
said this he looked toward the other sled, and what he saw outraged
him.

"Stop! Stop!" and when the sleigh was halted he rushed over, bellowing: "What have you done with those traces?" and Arkikov
pointed to his harness, now geared Siberian-style with the traces
coming straight down between the front legs.

"I told you the other way!" His voice rose: "The right way!"

"But these Siberian deer . . . like my way. Stronger now than
when we start." And since there was truth to what he said, Skjellerup
relaxed: "All right. For the rest of the run." But his mind was still on
gold, and once he placed himself in the Siberian's hands, all was lost.

"Mr. Skjellerup! You . . . me . . . him . . . powerful team. We look
all streams. We dig all sand." It was obvious that Arkikov had que-

ried prospectors when he delivered the reindeer to Council City, and most desperately he wanted to be with them searching for something more rewarding than the few dollars he earned tending reindeer.

So on the impulse of the moment, the Norwegian called a halt for the day, to the amazement of Ootenai, who had just that morning been urged to forge ahead so that the journey could be completed within two days. Now Skjellerup was eager only to talk, so while Ootenai tended the deer, he conducted a serious discussion with Sana and Arkikov.

"You say men were looking for gold?"

"Plenty men . . . seven maybe eighteen."

"But were they finding any gold?"

"Not there. But Koyukuk River, yes. Yukon, yes."

"How do they get the right to look?" Sana asked.

Now the Siberian became an expert: "Me ask men . . . 'Me got to ask this man, that man . . . come on his land?' "

"What did they say?"

"They laugh. All free . . . every land free. You find, you keep."

"Could that be true?" It was so alien to what Skjellerup had known in Norway, where land was a jealously protected commodity, that he found it difficult to believe. But in reply, Arkikov ran to a tiny streamlet coming out of rocks and dipped his hand in, washing his palms back and forth as if they contained gravel. "Every stream free . . . to you, to him."

Now Sana spoke in Norwegian: "I heard a Canadian say the same about his country. No one owns the land, millions of acres, so you can mine where you wish. The land doesn't become yours, but the gold does. If Arkikov finds gold tomorrow, it's his. You, me, we can dig anywhere, if what they told me was true."

When he translated this for Arkikov, the three men fell silent, for they were being called upon to make decisions of the gravest import. But there could hardly be three men more eligible to do so. Lars Skjellerup had run his deer to the very top of the world. Mikkel Sana had traveled across Lapland through some of the loneliest terrain on earth. And Arkikov had left his secure homeland in Siberia to trust his luck in Alaska, and had proved his fortitude on this impressive mercy run to Barrow. These were men of resolution, courage and good sense. They were also men jealous of their rights, as the Siberian had just proved in returning to a system of harnessing which he preferred. If one had searched a far territory, he could not have found three men more capable and appropriate than these to go on a prospecting tour. They knew nothing about mining but they knew themselves.

They were unmarried. Skjellerup was the oldest at thirty-four, Sana next at thirty-two, with Arkikov the baby at twenty-eight. In raw intelligence—say in the ability to herd forty reindeer for eight months and wind up with fifty-seven, or to find true north when little was visible—these men were superior. And of great importance, each man had all his teeth and the constitution of a bull. Mining in Alaska was invented for the benefit of such men.

"I think we should make a try," said Skjellerup, and Arkikov, hearing these reassuring words, shouted: "We go many rivers . . . find much gold!" And after that joyous but carefully pondered moment of decision, the three never looked back. In fact, when the delayed trip to the station resumed, Skjellerup looked dispassionately at the flying feet of his marvelous steeds who had performed so well, and thought: Who would believe it? I'm tired of reindeer.

Their successful rescue trip to Barrow occasioned so much favorable publicity that both the Alaska government, such as it was, and the national were prepared to look into further uses of the reindeer, but Skjellerup could express no interest: "It's time I moved on. Young Eskimos like Ootenai are more than capable." When his superiors asked: "What will you do?" he replied: "I'll find something," for he was not ready at this point to reveal that he was about to go prospecting.

Everyone who knew this capable man wanted to employ him, the most unusual proposal being that he become the Presbyterian missionary at Barrow. When he explained "I'm a Lutheran," they said: "Doesn't matter. You're obviously a man of God."

And he was, in his own way. He loved animals, he could work with anyone, and he revered the earth, which seemed to him a special gift from God. But he was also now at the age when he wanted to work at something which produced money: "I've served Norway, Lapland, Siberia and Alaska. Now, by damn, I serve Lars Skjellerup."

In this time of wild movement in Alaska, which had commenced explosively with the discovery of gold along the Yukon, passports and such impedimenta were not in much demand. Of course, both Skjellerup and Sana had documents but they were grossly out of date, and as for Arkikov, he had only his grin. He had been brought to America under unique circumstances and almost any week he could catch a boat back to Siberia, for travel between the two lands was still frequent, convenient and untrammeled.

So on a bright day in late July 1898 the three partners left the station and headed east, taking with them a sled and three Siberian reindeer. Since there was no snow, they allowed one of the deer to pull the empty sled, while their packs were slung across the backs of the other two. They made an interesting study as they set forth on their great adventure, with tall, angular Skjellerup in the rear, tough, lean Sana in the middle and stout, happy Arkikov in front, setting the pace and almost running to get to the first stream.

They were dressed differently too, the Norwegian having adopted the standard dark, heavy clothing of the American prospector, the Lapp retaining his colorful garb, and the Siberian choosing a mixture of the fur clothing used by all the northern peoples. Their gear was modest but extremely practical and almost entirely handmade. Even the hammers had been given their handles by Arkikov and the sieves had been made by Mikkel Sana.

They started their prospecting by moving east, and at one small stream Arkikov panned enthusiastically, failed to notice the minute colors, and shouted to his companions: "No gold this one," so the men moved on. In this casual way they dismissed one of the richest streams in world history, but they should not be ridiculed for having bypassed a fortune, because during this restive summer many others would do the same.

After covering more than a hundred miles eastward, they found themselves in the midst of seventy or eighty other prospectors, and turned back to a spot on the map labeled Cape Nome, which would always be a curious place. There was a Cape Nome, and a Nome River, far apart and in no way connected. Later there would be a Nome City, miles removed from either of the first Nomes. When Skjellerup's team reached the cape, there was of course no town in the vicinity, only a handful of tents, but here they camped, finding nothing. Edging gingerly to the west, they returned to Nome River and again found only disappointment. At this point Arkikov, who fancied himself the expert miner in the trio, insisted that they hurry back to Council City and establish a claim, good or bad, but Skjellerup dissuaded him, and without much hope they and their reindeer wandered on to where the Snake River entered the sea.

It was probably the animals that accounted for the good fortune which was about to overtake them, because on a day in late September three agitated Swedish immigrants, who knew even less about mining than they, came in whispers to consult with Skjellerup in broken English: "You Norwegian? Like they say?" When he replied in good Swedish that he was the man who had made the rescue run to Barrow, they sighed with deep relief and asked: "Can you keep a secret?"

"Always have."

"Are you willing to help us? If we count you in?"

"What's happening?"

Peering about to be sure no one from the tents along the shore was looking, the leader of the Swedes produced in the palm of his left hand a spent cartridge, and when he removed the protective wrapper and tilted the cartridge, a flow of golden dust and small pellets rolled out into the palm of his hand.

"Is that gold?" Skjellerup asked, and the three Swedes nodded.

"Where from?"

"Sssshhhh! We found a creek. It runs with gold. It's unbelievable, really."

"Why do you tell me?"

"We need your help."

"To do what?"

Again the Swedes looked about: "We found the creek, but we don't know what to do next."

It was fortunate that they had come to Skjellerup, for he was the kind of man who knew a little about everything, but not the kind who was arrogant about any of it. He knew, and that was enough.

"I think that within a certain time you have to hold a public meeting, because others have a right to know. Give them a chance to stake their claims. And you have to stake your discovery claim with great accuracy. Then you file some papers. And if you fail in any one of these, you lose everything."

"That's what we feared."

"Who else knows?"

"Nobody, but men have been sneaking around up there. Soon everyone will know."

Lars Skjellerup was one of the ablest men on the gold fields that year, and now he proved it: "I'll help, but I want the right to stake my claim, and tonight."

"That's what we intended," the Swedes said with an honesty that could not be questioned, except that Skjellerup did question it, thinking: That's what they say now, since I've asked. Wonder what they'd have said if I hadn't?

"And for my two partners. We're a team, you know."

"Your name again? Skjellerup? Somebody warned us we can claim only one site each, two for me because I found it. The other claims have to go to somebody. Might as well be to you and your partners."

One of the Swedes asked: "And who are those partners?" When Skjellerup introduced the Lapp and the Siberian, the other Swedes muttered: "Could be trouble. We're all foreigners." It turned out that the leader and one other Swede were naturalized, but that did leave four foreigners among the first six claimants.

"I think the law is clear," Skjellerup assured them. "Anyone in good standing can file a claim. We'll soon find out."

After a few casual inquiries, they learned that a mining district could be declared in a public meeting if six miners were present and if knowledge of the strike was circulated, but none of these six knew the precise procedures and especially not the intricacies of filing a claim. "We must trust one other person," Skjellerup said. "You choose."

By the great good luck that sometimes watches over Swedes and other sensible people, the leader chose an older mining man, down on his luck but a veteran of many honorable battles. Up to now he had always reached the next auriferous area, as a gold field was technically called, six months late. Fate was now about to knock on his door three days early.

John Loden, himself a Swede of some generations back, knew exactly what to do, and advised that it be done with dispatch: "Announce the meeting. Publicize it. Have your claims in order. Then stand back as the stampede begins."

The meeting was held in a tent at the spot where the Snake River emptied into the Bering Sea, and eleven selected men were present, word of promising developments having been quietly circulated. Loden chaired the session and asked repeatedly for assistance from the floor. Two of the prospectors knew more mining law than he, and it was merciful that they were present, because in the wild days to come, their testimony that everything had been done legally was going to be significant.

When the four newcomers heard the seriousness of the seven who were in on the secret, they became wildly excited: "Where is the strike?" and "Are there real colors?"

"In good time, gentlemen, in good time."

When all details were in order, insofar as the members could determine, Loden turned to the major Swede and said: "Tell them!"

"We have struck real colors, an important find, on Anvil Creek."

"Where in hell's that?"

"Up where the big rock hangs over. Looks like an anvil."

One of the listeners yelled, another cheered, and a third shouted: "Jesus Christ, here we go!" The fourth man, more practical than the others, went to the door of the tent and fired his revolver three times in the air to alert everyone in the tents: "Major strike! Anvil Creek!" and some forty wild-eyed miners rushed out into the October night to stake their claims under a harvest moon.

Five, Six and *Seven Above* were staked by the Norwegian Skjellerup, the Lapp Sana and the Siberian Arkikov, and while men along the little stream cheered and fired guns and danced jigs together, Arkikov, in the moonlight, panned the first sand from his claim. It left gold dust at the bottom worth seven dollars. The three partners were going to be very rich.

The situation in the newborn town of Nome was technically much as it had been along the Klondike following that fabulous strike: gold had been found, but so late in the year that no ships could bring stampeders through the icebound Bering Sea. The big push would be delayed ten months; however, miners already in the region were free to rush in and stake claims, and this they did, so that a real town began to develop, with a narrow Front Street running along the bleak waterfront.

In July 1899, when the big ships began crowding in with prospectors, Nome quickly became the largest city in Alaska, with no less than eleven bars, each of which claimed to be "the best saloon in Alaska," so an enterprising newcomer opened a still bigger bar, naming it proudly "Second Best Saloon in Alaska." One of its noisy patrons was a braggart from Nevada called Horseface Kling, who boasted that he "knew more about mining law than any son-of-a-bitch in Alaska," and he was so self-assured that hangers-on began taking him seriously.

"No Russian has the right to come over here and claim on good American mining sites," he bellowed, and as soon as he saw that he was gaining support, he added: "I'm gonna by damn 'propriate *Seven Above* which that Siberian is holdin' illegal." When this appealing battle cry was cheered, he assembled an armed posse, marched to the creek, and took possession.

He apparently did know something about mining procedures, for as soon as he returned to town he gathered his gang about him, appointed a chairman, and convened a general miners' meeting on the spot, which enthusiastically authorized the takeover. "You will all testify," he said at the conclusion of the meeting, "that everything was done legal." And as his men shouted their approval, *Seven Above* was ripped out of Arkikov's hands and deposited in those of Horseface Kling.

The effect on Arkikov was staggering. He had come to Alaska under pressure of performing public service; he had behaved well here; he had participated in the famous mercy run to Barrow; and he had been instrumental in establishing and developing Anvil Creek, and now to have the rewards of his industry torn away was intolerable, and he began to haunt the saloons, asking: "Can do this America?" and people told him: "This ain't America, it's Alaska."

The theft stood, and after days of fruitless appeal, he met with his two former partners, warning them: "Me Russian . . . pretty soon they do same to you Lapp, then you Norwegian," and seeing the reasonableness of his prediction, they began to carry guns and bought him one.

Sure enough, as soon as Horseface Kling had his possession of *Seven Above* digested, he began pestering folks in the Second Best Saloon with complaints against "that damned Lapp, little better than a Russian, who came over here and stole our good claims." This time he was arguing on behalf of his partner, one Happy Magoon, a big man who smiled constantly, and after another miners' meeting, Mikkel Sana was dispossessed of *Six Above,* and it was made pretty clear in the Second Best Saloon that the Norwegian Lars Skjellerup was going to be next.

It soon became apparent that Happy Magoon, now the owner of *Six Above,* was a stupid man not able to think clearly and that Horseface Kling had used him merely as a front for stealing a fine claim. When rumors started to circulate against "that damned Norwegian," Skjellerup and the three Swedes could see that they were going to be next, and that before long Horseface was going to be sole possessor of seven fine claims on Anvil Creek.

How could such flagrant lawlessness be tolerated? Because the United States Congress still refused to give Alaska a sensible government. The region continued to struggle along as the District of Alaska, but what it was a district of, no one could say, and it was still hamstrung by the old Oregon territorial law that had been outmoded at the time of its imposition. Had Congress said: "Let Alaska have the same laws that pertain in northern Maine," it might have made sense, for the two types of land and problems would have been roughly similar, but to equate Alaska with Oregon was preposterous. Oregon was an agricultural state with spacious fields; if there was any flat land in Alaska, it was probably terrorized by grizzly bears. Oregon had been peopled by God-fearing men and women who brought with them a New England Puritan dedication to organized life and work in settlements; Alaska, by drifters like John Klope from a run-down farm in Idaho and rascals like Horseface Kling from temporary mining camps. Oregon, in other words, was a beautifully controlled area which had aspired to be another Connecticut as soon as possible, while Alaska was determined to remain unlike any other American region as long as possible.

But you had to be on the scene to appreciate the real insanity of life in Alaska, and no better laboratory for analysis than Nome could have been found. Since the old Oregon territorial law had not provided for the establishment of new towns like Nome, the burgeoning boomtown could not elect a city government, and since the law did not provide for health services, none could be authorized in Nome; everyone in the town could throw his bathroom slops where he damned well pleased. Craziest of all was the circular insanity which still prevented courts from trying criminals. Oregon law clearly stated that no man could be a juror unless he proved that he had paid his taxes, but since there was no government in Alaska, no taxes were collected. This meant that there could be no trial by jury, which meant that ordinary courts could not exist.

And this preposterous state of affairs meant that criminals like Horseface Kling could commit their thefts with impunity. The famous boast of frontier brawlers in times past, "No court in the land can lay a hand on me," had become a reality in Alaska. The stolen mining claims now belonged to Horseface, and their former owners had no court to which they could appeal.

However, justice of another kind was available, and had an impartial observer familiar with frontiers studied the Anvil Creek dispossessions, he might have warned: "Of all the men in this corner of Alaska to steal from, those three have got to be the most dangerous!" and he would point to the dour, self-reliant Norwegian, the steel-sinewed Lapp and the wildly imaginative Siberian to whom anything was possible. He would point out: "These men have traversed great distances unafraid, slept unprotected in blizzards at sixty-below, and saved Barrow. It seems highly unlikely that they will allow a braggart from Nevada to dispossess them of rights which they gained the hard way." But less sagacious men in the Second Best would point out: "In Nome there is no law."

On 12 July 1899, Horseface Kling was found shot to death at the entrance to his mine *Seven Above,* and shortly thereafter a grinning Happy Magoon was quietly told: "You no longer own *Six Above.*" No one discovered who had done the shooting, and no one really cared, for by this time it was clear that Horseface had intended sweeping up everyone's claim, so his death was not lamented. And when the industrious Lapp, Mikkel Sana, recovered his ownership of *Six Above,* no one protested, for it was now recognized that he had more than earned the right to hold that claim.

However, when the Siberian Arkikov tried to move back onto *Seven Above,* the original protests were revived, and in a raucous miners' meeting it was again decreed that no Russian could hold a claim on Anvil Creek, and he was once more evicted.

This time the rugged fellow was completely distraught, and again he moved from bar to bar trying to elicit sympathy and support, but now a rumor started circulating: "It was the Siberian who murdered Horseface," and the very men who had applauded the death of the usurper resented the fact that a Siberian had slain an American, and he became something of an outcast. His two partners tried to console him with a promise that they would share their profits with him, but this did not pacify him, and he continued to rant about the fact that this should never have happened in America.

But he was at heart an incorruptible optimist, and after several days of venting his resentment, he grabbed his prospecting gear and started up the valley cut by the parent stream, Snake River, testing the gravel in even the tiniest tributary. He found nothing, and as dusk approached on the third day he came back to Nome disconsolate and seething.

What happened next can be appreciated only by another miner, but Arkikov had his prospecting tools—a fifty-cent pan and a sixty-cent shovel—he had plenty of time, and he certainly had a wild lust for gold, so with no further streams to prospect, he looked at the endless stretch of beach before him and he cried with the soul of a true miner: "Whole goddamn ocean . . . me look." And he began to sift the sands of the Bering Sea.

Such things had happened before. Some men, drifting down the Mackenzie from Edmonton, had prospected every creek along the way. Others, near death from starvation, had paused in the mountains to prospect some errant stream. And now the Siberian Arkikov was prepared to prospect the whole Bering Sea. It was irrational, but to him it made sense.

He did not have to move far along the empty beach, for in his second pan, there in the quiet dusk with curlews overhead, he came upon one of the strangest finds in the history of mining. His pan, when washed in seawater, showed colors, and not just flecks, but real, substantial grains of gold.

Unwilling to believe what he saw, he poured the gold into an empty cartridge, then dipped again and once more found colors. Again and again, almost insanely, he ran along the beach, dipping and testing and always finding gold.

July sunset at Nome in those days before time was fiddled with came at about nine-thirty, so all that evening, in the gray-silver haze while the sun toyed with the horizon, this wild Siberian ran along the beaches, dipping and testing, and when night finally fell he had a story to relate that would astound the world.

He whispered it first to his partners, at a table in the Second Best Saloon, for if they had been faithful enough to promise him a share of their wealth, he must reciprocate: "No look round. No speak. Me find something." Quietly he handed the cartridge to Skjellerup, who furtively inspected it, whistled softly, and passed it along to Sana, who did not whistle but who did raise his eyebrows.

"Where?" Skjellerup asked without changing expression.

"The beach."

These two tested miners were the first to hear that the beaches of Nome literally crawled with gold, and like everyone who followed, they disbelieved. Clearly, Arkikov's misfortunes had addled his brain, and yet . . . there was the gold, clean and of a high quality. He had got it somewhere.

They would mollify him, urge him to keep his voice down, and when he was tranquil they would ask: "What stream did you find it in?" But even after they had tried this tactic, they received the same answer.

"You mean the beach? The sea? Waves?"

· "Yes."

"You mean some miner lost his poke on the beach and you found it?"

"No."

"What part of the beach?"

"Whole goddamn beach."

This was so incredible that the two men suggested: "Let's go to our digs and talk this over," and when they did, Skjellerup and Sana found that Arkikov was locked into his story that the common, ordinary beaches of Nome teemed with gold.

"How many spots did you try?"

"Many. Many."

"And all gave colors?"

"Yes."

The two men considered this, and although they were inwardly driven to reject the report as improbable, there in the cartridge rested a substantial amount of gold. Putting half into his hand, Skjellerup held it toward the Siberian and asked: "If the sands are filled with this, why hasn't anybody else found it?" and Arkikov gave the resounding answer that explained the mystery of mining: "Nobody look. Me look. Me find."

It was now midnight, and since the sun would rise at two-thirty, Skjellerup and Sana decided to remain awake and go out in the earliest dawn to test the truth of their partner's implausible yarn. "We mustn't work near each other," Skjellerup warned, "and don't let anyone see us actually panning. Pick up driftwood maybe."

Arkikov said he would not join them. He was tired from his days of prospecting and had to have sleep; besides, he knew the gold was there.

So the Norwegian and the Lapp eased themselves out of their bunks at quarter past two on the morning of 16 July 1899 and strolled casually along the beaches of Nome, stopping idly now and then to salvage driftwood, and at five in the morning Lars Skjellerup sat on a log, covered his face with his hands, and came as near to tears as he ever had: "I am so happy for Arkikov. After what they did to him."

Displaying no emotion, the two stragglers slipped back to their bunks and shook Arkikov: "The beaches are full of gold," and he said sleepily: "Me know. Me find."

That afternoon, following the most careful assessment of how the three partners could best protect their interests in this incredible find, Skjellerup called a miners' meeting at which he spoke with great force:

> "Gentlemen, you know my partner here, Arkikov, who you call 'that damned Siberian.' Well, he's made a discovery that's going to make all of you millionaires. Well, maybe not that much, but damned rich.

> "Now there's no law in Nome, and there's no example that we can apply in handling this stupendous find. The usual claim size just don't pertain. So we'll have to work out special rules, which I believe we can do."

A miner off to the right called impatiently: "What did he find?" and Skjellerup took from his pocket the cartridge, holding it high in his right hand and allowing the golden particles, some of which he himself had picked up that morning, to float down through the afternoon air and into his left palm. Even the men in the farthest corners of the Second Best could see that this was what they had come so far to find, placer gold.

"Where?" voices shouted as men edged toward the door to be the first to claim on the subsidiary sites.

"Like I told you, there's never been a gold field like this one. We need new rules. I'm proposing that each man gets . . . well, let's say ten yards to the side."

This was so preposterously minute in relation to a normal claim—five hundred yards along the stream and across the flow to the top of the first bench—that the men howled.

"All right!" Skjellerup conceded. "This is an organizing meeting and you set the rules. That's proper, so go ahead."

"Like always, five hundred yards along the stream and bench to bench."

"But there are no benches. There is no stream."

"Where in hell is it?"

"Tell them, Arkikov." And the smiling Siberian, all his white teeth showing, uttered the unprecedented words: "Along the beach. Whole goddamn beach. Me find."

Before his last words were pronounced, men were bursting out of the saloon, and within a minute only the three partners and one bartender, the one with a bad leg, were left. The real gold rush at Nome had begun.

The beach strike at Nome was unique in many ways. Because the gold was so readily available, prospectors who had missed earlier rushes now had a second chance; they had only to dig in the sand and take out ten thousand dollars or forty, and if they could devise some ingenious machine for sluicing large quantities of sand with seawater, they were in line to become millionaires. Also, the painful work that John Klope had had to do high on his unproductive ridge above Eldorado—burrowing down forty feet, building fires to thaw the frozen muck and hauling it to the surface—would be avoided at Nome, where a man could go out in the morning, test his luck through an easy day, and complain in the saloons that night: "Today I panned only four hundred dollars."

But there was a similarity between the two historic strikes. As on the Klondike, Arkikov made his discovery so late in the season that even though word did get to Seattle on the last ship south, the Bering Sea froze over before any other ship could come north. This meant that the relatively few men lucky enough to reach Nome before the freeze would have clear pickings from July 1899 through June 1900. But while they sieved, a tremendous backlog of would-be miners would be building up at San Francisco and Seattle, for word had swept the world that "in Nome the beaches are crawlin' with gold," and the handful of miners who went south on that last ship had pouches and bars to prove it. When the ice finally melted in the early summer of 1900, Nome's population was going to skyrocket to more than thirty thousand, and it would still be a city without laws.

The Yukon River presented its own problem, because the *Jos. Parker,* on its last trip upriver before the freeze, carried with it news of the unique find, and even before the boat docked at Dawson, a deckhand was shouting: "Gold found on the beach at Nome!"

The effect was not electric, it was volcanic, because every miner who had missed the big strike on the Klondike knew that he had to get to the next one fast, and within half an hour after that first shout, eager men were crowding the riverfront seeking passage to Nome. As one old miner expressed it to Tom Venn, who was in charge of selling tickets for his R&R's *Jos. Parker*'s homeward run back to St. Michael: "Stands to reason, don't it? It's winter in Nome, just like here, and they cain't no ships get into Nome from Seattle till next June. If'n I kin get there on your boat, I got the field all to meself. This time I stake me a claim." He was distressed when Tom had to tell him: "No bunks left, mister. Last ones sold off fifteen minutes ago."

"What kin I do?" the old man asked, and Tom said: "Sleep on deck," and the miner almost shouted: "Gimme a ticket," and with it clutched in his hand, he ran off to fetch his bedroll for the long trip.

The sleeping bunks had been preempted so quickly because within ten minutes of that first shout of "Gold at Nome," the Belgian Mare had called to her ten girls: "Pack! We're off to Nome!" and she had rushed to Venn's office to grab eleven berths. Like the fabled rats whose departure signaled the sinking of the ship, this departure of the Belgians from their cribs gave notice that Dawson was doomed. For two years it had been a golden city; Nome would be the next thing higher than that.

Tom was preoccupied with trying to calculate how many more deck spaces he could sell on the *Parker* when he received a jolt from his manager, Mr. Pincus, an old R&R hand who had run stores at various locations for the big Seattle firm: "Tom, chance of a lifetime. I'm going to ship everything we have down to Nome. I wish I could get approval from Mr. Ross first, but the motto of our company is 'If it has to be done, do it.' Dawson is finished. Nome will have fifty thousand people this time next year." He smiled at the boy and asked, "How old are you?" and when Tom replied "Seventeen," giving himself the benefit of a year, the manager said: "You're old enough. You've seen what can happen in a gold field. Sail down to St. Michael with the *Parker,* then move your goods over to Nome, build a store, a big one, and give honest service."

"You mean . . . ?"

"I do. Son, it's either you or me, and frankly, it's more difficult to close down a store than to open one. I'm needed here. You're needed there."

As Tom started to tremble, overcome by the gravity of the proposal, the manager called him to his desk: "A wise old man gave me these gold scales, Tom. I've used them on three different fields. There's no rust on them, is there?" When Tom studied the handsome little balances and the set of weights for weighing gold dust, he could see no rust. "I mean moral rust. Tom, I do believe those scales have never weighed a dishonest poke. Keep them polished."

Sailing of the *Parker* was delayed one day so that practically the entire stock of goods from the R&R store in Dawson could be crammed aboard, and while Tom was supervising the placement of the valuable wares for which he was now responsible, he heard such giggling from the cabins booked by the Belgian Mare that he concluded her fare was going to be repaid by the end of this first night in port.

In one important respect the delay was fortunate, for at dawn on the second day, three people of great importance to Tom appeared, two of them seeking passage. They were Missy Peckham, Matthew Murphy and, to Tom's amazement, tall, dour John Klope. Missy and Murphy were the ones who wanted to depart, but they had no money, the gold fields had not been good to them; and since Klope had found no colors deep in his shaft, neither did he.

They had come to throw themselves on the mercy of their common friend Tom Venn, and Klope did the speaking: "Tom, you're like a son to me. I beg you like your father might if he was here today. Take Missy and Matt to Nome. Give them another chance."

"I'd have to charge passage, company rules."

This was a heartbreaking moment, for these three who had striven so valiantly, who had endured between them all the agonies of the gold rush, had nothing to show for their courage and toil. They were broke, dead flat broke, and two of them sought money to escape. For Klope, it seemed there would be no escape; he was locked into his futile shaft forever.

When Tom asked: "Who helps you now?" he said: "Sarqaq. His leg never healed. He can't run dogs no more, but he sells one now and then. We live."

After these diversionary remarks, Tom had to give the waiting trio the bad news: "The boat can take only one more," and without hesitation Matt pushed Missy forward: "She's the one," but then Tom had to say: "Her fare has to be paid . . . by someone." In the discussion that followed, three things were clear: Missy had to get to Nome; Matt would follow later as best he could; and none of the three had the money required for passage.

Klope waited for one of the others to speak, then took Tom aside: "She looked after you . . . when your father died, when you were a kid in Dawson, and at our mine. It's your job to look after her now," and with that, he pushed Tom back to confront the woman with whom his young life had been so closely intertwined.

"Missy," he said in a fumbling manner, "you were better than a mother to me. I'll pay your fare." In silence Missy accepted the ticket, for her hard life on the gold fields had led her to expect no acts of generosity. However, she did look at Tom, wanting to mutter some words of thanks, but when she saw that he was equally embarrassed, she said nothing.

The journey had to be swift, for ice was beginning to form; there could be no more trips this year, and Captain Grimm snorted at the calls for speed: "Two years ago, everybody in a great hurry to get to Dawson. Freeze my boat in the Yukon. This year, everybody in a hurry to get out. Maybe we freeze again."

"Oh my God!" a miner cried. "And miss the claims again?"

"Forced draft, if you'll load the wood promptly at the stops."

Now, since the *Jos. Parker* had become part of a regular shipping line, when Grimm pulled into a wood depot the waiting cords were earmarked for him, as an R&R regular, so it was possible to maintain a forced draft. But even so, it was a touchy race, because as so many riverboat captains had learned in past years, the mouth of the Yukon often froze nearly solid while the upstream parts were still open. This year, however, he slipped through, but as he left the river for the Bering Sea he watched behind him as the great river closed down. His would be the last boat through.

Passengers from the *Parker* were the last people into Nome before the winter freeze clamped fingers of ice over the town. The beaches now contained thirteen miles of canvas tents stretching to the west and another eleven miles reaching eastward toward Cape Nome. At some places the frozen Bering Sea edged to within ten yards of the tents, its icy hummocks towering above them. How will those poor men survive the blizzards? Missy asked herself when she saw the endless string of flimsy white tents, but then she laughed: Wrong question. How will I survive?

After much searching, she found a one-room shack in an alley, but now the question became: How can I pay for it? and the solution arrived in a curious way. For as she looked down at the pathway in front of her shack, she saw that the entire area was encased in a yellow glacier two feet thick composed of frozen urine, and as she stared in disgust at the icy sewage, men from the saloons on Front Street came out to use the alley as a toilet.

She was so enraged by this that she asked the owner of her shack: "Aren't there any public closets in this town?" and he said: "There isn't anything. No closets, no services, no law of any kind," and she asked: "Well, isn't there a doctor?" and he directed her to a tentlike affair in which a young man from Seattle struggled to tend the health problems of Nome.

Blustering into his tent, she asked: "Do you know that the alley in front of my shack is two feet deep in frozen urine?" and he said: "Look at the alley in back of my tent," and when she did she saw a massive pile of human feces.

"Good God, Doctor! This town's in trouble," and he said reassuringly: "Not until the thaw. Then, of course, people will die of dysentery. And we'll be lucky if we escape epidemics of typhoid and diphtheria."

"You need my help, Doctor. I can keep records and keep track of your medicines and help with your women patients." The young man was barely earning enough to support himself, but was persuaded by Missy's strong plea: "Just till my husband gets here. He's in Dawson, but he'll be down one of these days." And in that way she acquired a job that would at least sustain her till Matt arrived.

During her first days at work, she was further shocked to learn that the few wells which had been dug for drinking water had been placed so that anything could flow into them, while the Snake River, from which most of the town's water came, also served as the town's sewer. When Missy protested the situation, the doctor said: "Don't tell me! I saw it three months ago. I can't understand why half the population isn't deathly ill right now. A miracle must be protecting us, but don't drink a drop of water that hasn't been boiled."

With no one responsible for streets, the thoroughfares of Nome were frozen cesspools into the cold morasses of which horses sometimes casually disappeared during a temporary thaw. Theft became common; the Belgian Mare opened her cribs right on the main street; children did not go to school; and there were three saloons for every grocery store. Not far wrong was the newspaper editor who cried: "Nome is a hell on earth."

Missy had been in town only a week when she had an opportunity to witness just how lawless the place had become. Near her shack clustered several canvas tents, each occupied by one man, and following the discovery of gold on the beach, it was likely that in any given tent there would be a small poke filled with the precious metal. Gangs of ruthless thieves had devised a bizarre method of stealing such gold: they scouted saloons until some lone miner rolled home, but since they knew that every miner went armed after the shooting of Horseface Kling, the gang did not attack him till he was in his tent and safely snoring. Then they crept up, slit the canvas near his head, and poked through the hole a long stick with a rag soaked in chloroform tied on the far end. When the miner succumbed to the vapors, the thieves entered casually, spent ten or fifteen minutes methodically taking the place apart, and in this way laid hold of much gold. It was a kind of painless theft, because when the miner woke up, all that was missing was his gold, and when he returned to the beaches he could replace that.

On the night involving Missy, things went wrong as two different gangs worked the tents. In the first one, either the victim had received an inadequate dose of chloroform or the thieves dawdled, because the man awakened, saw through the film over his eyes that two strange men were robbing his poke, and bellowed. This wakened Missy, who ran out in time to see the robbers escape with the gold. Seeing that the victim needed help, Missy ran for the doctor, who easily detected from the smell what had happened. Together they brought the miner back to full consciousness.

While the doctor stayed to care for the man, Missy went to check the other tents. Most of the occupants were still in saloons, but when she came upon a tent with a ripped canvas and peered inside, she saw lying on the cot an inert miner with a big wad of chloroformed rag over his face. Instinctively alarmed, she shouted: "Doctor! Come here!" and when a crowd gathered in the cold November night they found the miner was dead. The fracas in the first tent had frightened the second group of thieves, and they had fled, but when they pulled away the long stick, the heavily dosed rag had fallen off, covering the miner's mouth and nostrils, and asphyxiated him.

When the doctor led Missy back to her shack she bolted the door and propped a chair against the window. "This is a dreadful town," she said as she sat unsteadily on the bed. "You have to protect yourself every minute."

However, after the miner was buried she had a chance to inspect Nome more carefully, and she concluded that two establishments were well run, the Mare's cribs and the Ross & Raglan store, where Tom Venn, only sixteen but more mature than most of his customers, ran a taut shop. He was willing to buy almost anything that destitute miners wanted to sell and to offer it to others at decent prices. She saw Tom at his best one day in mid-November when he came running to her shack pleading for help.

"What's the matter?" Missy asked, and he blurted out: "That idiot who had the little general store before I came down to set up R&R. Can you guess what he did?"

"Steal the funds?"

"Worse. He was stupid." And he led her to an improvised warehouse about which he had just learned. The roof had blown off and a huge stack of canned goods shipped up from Seattle during the summer had been drenched by so many rains that the labels had soaked off.

"Look at them! Five hundred, six hundred cans. All from the same cannery. All alike. And nobody can tell what's in them."

In disgust he applied a mechanical opener at random: "Sweet corn, cherries, plums, sweet potatoes." Missy inspected the four cans, and had to agree that they contained no outer clue which would help identify other like cans in the mess.

"What'll I do?" Tom wailed, but Missy was busy tasting the contents, which, with a smack of her lips, she pronounced delicious. And that's when Tom Venn proved capable of making a practical decision. Taking a huge square of cardboard, he worked in his rude office while Missy and a helper moved the stack of label-less cans to the roadway in front of the store, where they constructed an eye-catching pyramid in front of which Tom placed the sign:

DELICIOUS FOOD
GUARANTEED WHOLESOME
CONTENTS UNKNOWN
5¢ A CAN
TRY YOUR LUCK

Within the hour all the cans were gone and the drifters of Nome were telling one another what a good sport this young fellow who ran the R&R store was.

This imaginative action caught the attention of Lars Skjellerup and the other responsible men who were trying to maintain some kind of order, and despite Tom's youth he was invited to become a member of Skjellerup's informal governing team, as Tom explained in a letter that he dispatched to his superiors in Seattle:

> Under the leadership of men like Skjellerup this town has enormous potential, and although Dawson proves that a gold town can go bust in one year, I find no similarity between the two places. Dawson is landlocked at the far end of the Canadian road, of no interest to anyone but miners. Nome is a seaport at the crossroads between Asia and America and must prosper.
>
> During a clear spell I rode a reindeer sled out to Cape Prince of Wales and could see Siberian Russia only sixty miles away. Boats pass easily between the two coasts and I would expect traffic between them to multiply.
>
> I must warn you about one thing. We are making huge profits, and when forty or fifty steamers lay to off our coast come June, we shall make more. But Nome has no government, none at all, and no system of fire prevention. If one building catches fire, the entire city will go up in flames. Therefore, I shall keep inventory low and remit all money to Seattle as promptly as possible, for one of these days I expect to see my beautiful store in flames.
>
> However, there is hope that we shall soon be allowed to have a government. There's talk that Congress is about to pass a law giving Alaska two judges, and if that happens, one of them is to be stationed here. Then things must improve and I shall expect our young city to forge ahead.

As the last days of 1899 approached, the citizens of Nome, eager for any excuse to hold a celebration, decided to organize a slam-bang affair to welcome the birth of the twentieth century, even though sensible men knew that would not occur until midnight on 31 December, 1900, and during preparations Lars Skjellerup assured Tom: "The days of no law in this city are passing. When the ice breaks next May or June, and the federal judge arrives, things'll begin to hum. No more claim-jumping, no more."

"Can a federal judge do all that?" Tom asked, and Skjellerup had to admit that he did not know, but he did know a man called Professor Hale, a former schoolteacher who would. He was a cadaverous fellow with a huge Adam's apple and a thunderous voice who loved to give his opinion on everything, so on the festive day before Christmas an informal meeting was held in the Second Best Saloon, and Hale demonstrated his wide knowledge.

"In our American system a federal judge is about the finest official we have."

"Better'n the President?" a miner shouted, and Hale snapped: "In some ways, yes. The judge serves for life, and in the long history of our nation, no federal judge has ever been found corrupt. When all else fails, you turn to him for justice."

"You mean, they're responsible only to Washington?" Skjellerup asked, and Hale replied: "They're responsible only to God. Not even the President can touch them." He became almost evangelical: "Gentlemen, I thank you for inviting me here today. A year from now, with a federal judge on the bench, you won't recognize Nome."

Skjellerup and Hale were wrong in jumping to the conclusion that the incoming judge would be from the federal bench but right in assuming that he would arrive with plenipotentiary powers. If he was the proper choice, he could bring Nome quickly into the ranks of civilized society.

"One thing he'll do for sure," Professor Hale told Skjellerup, "he'll restore *Seven Above* to your Siberian friend," and as the old century ended, nearly everyone in Nome, except the chloroform gangs, was prepared to welcome the powerful judge. They were ready, and perhaps even eager, to be regulated in an honest way, for anarchy had sickened them.

Nome had celebrated New Year's Day only three times. In 1897 the entire population, three unsuccessful miners, had gathered in a bitterly cold tent to share a hoarded bottle of beer. As 1898 began, again the whole population, only fourteen and still all men, had celebrated with whiskey and pistol shots, and as 1899 started, with the golden sands about to be discovered, a mixed population of more than four hundred, including the pioneers known by then as the Three Lucky Swedes and Lars Skjellerup's team, had had a high old time with songs in many languages.

But at the end of December this year, the three thousand citizens of Nome, aware that their number must soon explode to more than thirty thousand, brought out caches of whiskey which had been hidden in the big boxes that served as root cellars. Of course, it was impossible to have real cellars; the permafrost would not allow it.

On the last day of what men insisted on calling the dying century, one of Tom Venn's clerks asked: "Everyone says Nome may soon have twenty or thirty thousand more people. How can they know that? If no news can't get in here, how can any get out?"

Tom became defensive: "They don't know for sure, but if you want to know how I made my guess, just listen. When news of gold on the beaches trickled up to Dawson City, our riverboat, the *Parker,* was about to leave with sixteen passengers. Within half an hour we had more than one hundred, and when it sailed, nearly two hundred were aboard, and I do believe it could have picked up another fifty at Circle and fifty more at Fort Yukon, if it could've held them. People slept standing up!"

"What's that mean?" the clerk asked.

"It means you better get that addition finished, because I know in my bones that Seattle and San Francisco are filled right now with people aching to get to Nome."

For a variety of reasons the Nome gold strike was trebly attractive. The gold was on American soil, not Canadian. A miner could get to it on a luxury steamer in no way inferior to those that sailed to Europe. And when he landed, all he had to do, he thought, was to "Sift sand and ship the gold bars home." This was prospecting deluxe. And there was a final attraction: anyone who had missed the earlier strikes in Colorado, Australia and the Yukon could compensate in Nome.

There were drawbacks. Because thick ice captured the Bering Sea early and firmly, ships could operate only from June through September, and even then at grave risk, for the town had no docking facilities and could have none. And the hours of daylight available for gold seeking oscillated radically through the year: four hours in winter, twenty-two in summer; and since these endless winter nights could be formidable, the people of Nome welcomed any diversion, such as the beginning of a new year.

As the sun went down at two in the afternoon on the thirty-first of December, citizens began assembling in saloons, and at the Second Best, Lars Skjellerup assured everyone of three things: "Congress will pass the law giving us a government. We'll get a good judge. And gold on the beaches will never run out, because it goes twenty or thirty feet deep. Any new storm, it uncovers new concentrations."

His listeners spent much of the afternoon arguing as to how the Nome gold got to the beaches, for this had happened nowhere else on earth. One miner who had collected a small fortune said: "The Bering Sea is filled with gold. The tide brings it our way." Another reasoned: "There's this small volcano ten miles out under the waves. It spews gold regular." Others claimed that at some past time a river of lava had run out of a land volcano, now vanished, and had dropped its gold as the rock pulverized in the sea. It was Arkikov's idea, which he had trouble expressing except through wild use of his hands, that the gold was no different from that of the Yukon: "Many years ago . . . little river . . . comes across rocks with gold. Many years . . . gold wash free . . . reaches shore . . . me find . . . me know."

But his broken words failed to convince even his own partners, each of whom had his own bizarre theory. The gold of Nome was regular in every detail except in the way it finally came to rest . . . and its abundance.

When Tom Venn joined the celebration after closing his store for the year, someone shouted: "A drink to the benefactor of Nome," and men cheered.

"What did the young feller do?" asked a miner who had walked overland in November cold from his unrewarding diggings on the Kyokuk River, and another man told the story of the cans of good food which Tom had sold for five cents each: "He'll be the John Wanamaker of Nome."

At a minute to midnight the banker leaped upon the bar and whipped out his watch: "We'll count down to welcome the greatest century Nome will ever have. Forty-five, forty-four, forty-three, forty-two . . ."

When he reached ten, all in the bar were shouting in unison, and as the new year dawned, men started kissing any women in sight and clapping new acquaintances on the back. Tom Venn sought out Missy Peckham and kissed her fervently: "I've wanted to do that since 1893," and Missy said: "High time."

In the three long months following the celebration, Nome went into its yearly hibernation, for life in a frozen mining camp could be unbelievably monotonous. Even Tom Venn, who preferred the town over Dawson, saw that it had disadvantages, which he was willing to discuss with his customers: "It's farther north. Days are shorter. And Dawson never had that bitter wind that whips in from the sea. There's a lot wrong with Nome, but its spirit, that's for me!"

The things Nome did to entertain itself were ingenious, but two diversions were especially regarded. Professor Hale, who had never taught anything beyond grade seven, was prevailed upon to give readings from Shakespeare. Before large audiences of miners who packed one of the halls, he sat in a chair on a platform, clad in a toga-like garment which reached to his toes, and with a tumbler of whiskey at hand to keep his voice lubricated, he read aloud in powerful tones the more popular plays.

He took all parts, all voices, and he had always had such a love for Shakespeare that as the action quickened, or when he came to some part he especially liked, he would rise from his chair, prance about the platform, and shout the words until the smoky hall echoed. When he was required to depict Lady Macbeth or any of the other heroines, he manipulated his toga in such a way that, combined with his high, querulous voice, he became a distraught murderess or a lovesick Juliet. Indeed, it was so much fun to hear Professor Hale that when the cycle of plays ended, the miners insisted that he start repeating them, but this he refused to do. Instead, he advertised a special evening in which he would "deliver in sonorous voice the immortal sonnets of the Bard of Avon."

The hall was filled when he came onto the platform, and those in front could see that in addition to a slim volume of the sonnets, he had brought with him a much larger tumbler than before: "I am not at all certain, ladies and gentlemen, that I can make these sonnets, all to be read in the same voice, as interesting as the plays, but believe me, if I fail, the fault is mine and not Shakespeare's."

He had not reached the great sonnets, those with the singing lines, before he began reading certain ones as if a young girl were uttering them, or an old man, or a warrior, and when he came to the final dozen, with his tumbler near empty and the audience enraptured by his flow of words, he began to let himself go, reading the sonnets as if they were the most powerful and dramatic of the Bard's writings. He was shouting, mouthing, posturing, leaping forward and slinking back, always maintaining the powerful voice which thrilled his listeners. Rarely had the sonnets been accorded such a rousing performance.

The second treasured re-creation was the Eskimo Dance, a bizarre and almost dreamlike affair which had been invented in response to one of Alaska's preeminent features.

For the greater part of its recent history, Alaska has had the problem of men's coming into the district without women, as when the Russian traders came in numbers but without women; or the western explorers probed the seas for years without seeing women of their own kind; or when merchant whalers from New England arrived, always without women; or, more recently, when the gold seekers poured into the area, always forty or fifty men to one woman.

As a consequence, the story of Alaska has had to focus upon the friendships between men, their trustworthiness, their tragedies, their triumphs at the conclusion of incredible heroics. When women did appear in these highly structured affairs they were apt to be prostitutes, or native women already married to some Eskimo, Aleut or Athapascan. In the mining camps, wherever enough men concentrated, the ritual of the evening dance developed, where men hungry for entertainment and any kind of association with women on even bizarre terms would hire a fiddler or two, most often native men who had more or less acquired the skill, and a dance would be announced. Admission: Men $1. Women free.

There might be in the area one white woman who would don her best frock and be expected to dance with each of the men; the rest of the women, perhaps as many as eight or nine, would be natives of any age from thirteen to fifty, and they would come shyly to the dance, often well after the fiddler had started, edging in and standing along the wall, never smiling or giggling or looking directly at any particular white man.

After a period of social thaw, one of the women would step away from the wall and begin a monotonous dancelike motion, mostly up and down but with her shoulders swaying, and when she had done this for a moment or two, some miner would step forward, face her, and without ever touching her, go through his own interpretation of a dance, and so they would move as long as this set of music continued.

Once the ice was broken, and that is not an inappropriate idiom, for the temperature outside might be thirty-below, other women would begin to dance in their own dreamlike way, and other men would join them, never touching, never speaking. Since the women did not remove much of their clothing, they looked like round furry little animals, and some added to that impression by dancing with babies strapped to their backs. It didn't matter, for the lonely miners had come to see women, and many onlookers who constituted most of the paying audience did no dancing themselves. They watched, for they were the kinds of men to whom prostitutes would be unthinkable and actual participation in the dance improbable, or, in extreme cases, absolutely out of the question. They were men desperately wanting to see again what women looked like, and they were content to pay for the privilege.

At about eleven the fiddlers would stop, silence would fill the hall, and one by one the native women would depart, each one receiving a dollar for that night's performance. On most nights no man would have spoken to any woman, or laughed with her, or touched even her arm, and it was customary, when the dance ended, for the women to be escorted home by their men, who had been waiting outside and who now preempted the dollar for family needs.

That was the famous Eskimo Dance, that curious symbol of man's loneliness and hunger for human association, and it came into being almost of necessity, because the men had persisted in coming into the arctic without their women.

At Nome the dance had a peculiarity which occasioned some difficulty for Missy Peckham, for she was an attractive little white woman with whom the miners wanted to dance in the American mode, and they urged her to attend. It was flattering to have young men and some not so young lined up for every dance, but it also had its drawbacks, because during the course of any evening Missy would receive three or four invitations to move into the quarters of this miner or that, so she had constantly to explain that her man Murphy would be arriving from Dawson at any moment.

This caused merriment among her suitors: "How's he gonna come down the Yukon? Swim?" They pointed out that Murphy, if he really existed, which they doubted, "couldn't no way get here before the June thaw, no boats runnin'—so why waste the winter?"

She insisted that he would be arriving anytime now: "He survived the Mackenzie River in Canada, and that's a lot tougher than the Yukon," and like Penelope resisting the suitors who pestered her, Missy never deviated from her conviction that one of these days her Ulysses, through one device or another, would soon be joining her in Nome. But how he would accomplish this she did not know, and if someone had whispered to her what Matt's plan was, she would have thought the scheme plain crazy.

• • •

When the *Jos. Parker,* last ship out of Dawson for Nome, departed with Missy Peckham aboard, it left Matt Murphy stranded ashore, with several unappealing options as to how he might overtake his lady and join her in exploiting the town where "gold nuggets the size of pigeon eggs can be picked up on the beach." He could wait nine months till the Yukon thawed in the spring and catch the first boat down, but by then all the good spots would be taken. Or he could associate himself with some party of men trying to hike down, but as a fiercely independent Irishman, he did not trust group adventures. But doing it alone would necessitate the purchase of a dog team, a sled and enough meat to keep the dogs fit for two months as they tackled the thousand-mile run.

Rejecting all these choices, he settled upon one so bizarre that only a mad Irishman down on his luck could have dared it. Since the Yukon River would soon be frozen almost solid all the way to the Bering Sea, why not use it as a highway and to hell with waiting for it to thaw so that boats could navigate it? The idea was a sound one, but what to use for transportation if walking was out and no money was available for gear?

There was in Dawson a grubby store run by a shopkeeper from San Francisco who had found no gold. He dealt in everything, a kind of minimal hockshop with a worn set of scales for weighing gold dust and, inside his door, hung on pegs on the wall which kept it off the ground, an almost new two-wheel bicycle made by Wm. Read & Sons of Boston. It was the top of their line and had sold in Seattle in 1899 for $105, which included a kit for mending tires, a clever tool for replacing broken spokes and twelve spare wire spokes.

Matt, entering the shop one day to pawn his last possessions for money to keep him alive during the Klondike winter, chanced to see this bicycle, and right then it came to him: "A man could ride a contraption like that right down to Nome." Only a man who had conquered the great Mackenzie River would entertain so daring a scheme for the Yukon.

"What would he use for roads?" the shopkeeper asked, and he was astounded when Matt said: "The Yukon. Frozen all the way," and the pawnbroker said: "The Yukon don't go to Nome," and Matt replied: "But Norton Sound does, and it freezes solid too."

Finally, after pawning his belongings, Matt asked: "How much?" and the dealer said: "That's a special bicycle," and he showed Matt a paper which had come with it and which described the machine as

"Our New Mail Special model used widely by members of the Postal Service. $85."

"Save it for me," Matt said without hesitation, but the dealer said: "It's a hundred and forty-five dollars," and Matt said: "It says here, plain as day, eighty-five," and the pawnbroker said: "That was Boston. This is Dawson."

During the next weeks Matt, captivated by the concept of bicycling to Nome, returned often to the shop to check whether the bicycle had been sold, and he was always relieved to see that it had not. However, two impediments stood in his way. He lacked the money to buy the bicycle, and even had he been able to do so, the machine would have been of little use to him, for he had never sat astride one and had almost no idea of how it worked.

When the great river froze, forming a highway, as he had said, "right down to Nome," he became almost monomaniacal, badgering everyone in Dawson who had a spare dime to give him work. As October, November and December passed he painfully accumulated funds toward the purchase of the bicycle, and on 2 January 1900 he marched into the pawnshop and made a deposit of eighty dollars on the purchase. This done, he begged the owner to let him practice riding the contraption, and when the miners of Dawson saw him trying to pedal along their snow-covered roads, they said: "We better lock him up to save his life," and when they learned that he proposed making it all the way to Nome, they seriously considered keeping him in jail until his madness abated.

But by the middle of February he made his last payment, and with skill painfully acquired, rode out to the middle of the river, where, with the temperature at minus-forty, he waved goodbye to the doubting watchers. At this late point he was struck with an idea that was going to make the long trip a kind of triumph: abruptly he turned and returned to shore, ignoring the jeers: "One taste of that cold, he don't want it! He's brighter'n we thought!"

He had come back to acquire copies of four newspapers then circulating along the Klondike with the latest political news from the United States: Dawson *Daily News,* Dawson *Nugget,* and the two with flaming red headlines, San Francisco *Examiner* and Seattle *Post-Intelligencer.* With these stowed in his gear, he returned to the middle of the river and set forth.

Once his wheels adjusted to the extreme cold, they functioned perfectly, and to the amazement of the onlookers, he quickly disappeared from sight. Like his machine, Matt was undaunted by the cold, which was surprising because he was not dressed as one might have expected—no heavy furs, no goggles, no immense sealskin cap with wolverine edging, no fur-lined mukluks. He wore pretty much what he would have worn on a cold, rainy day in Ireland: heavy boots, gamekeeper leggings, stout fur mittens, three woolen jackets, a scarf about his neck, an ingenious cap made of wool and fur with three big flaps, one for each ear, one to be pulled down to protect the eyes. As he pedaled out of Dawson, old-timers predicted: "Absolutely impossible he can get to Nome. Hell, he won't even get to Eagle," which was a mere ninety-five miles downriver.

Matt covered sixty-three miles that day, sixty-nine the next, and long before even he expected it, he pulled into Fort Yukon, and here his newspapers proved themselves, for the occupants of the rude hotel were so excited by the arrival of news from home that they stayed up all night reading the papers aloud while Matt slept, and in the morning the hotel manager would accept no money from him. Wherever he stopped along the river, and there was a surprising number of solitary cabins—sheds dedicated to mail drops and camps from which woodsmen went out to cut logs in preparation for the summer steamers—he and his bicycle were received with disbelief and his newspapers with joy. And even though this was midwinter, since the Yukon followed a course south of the Arctic Circle, there was a grayish light for five or six hours each day when the temperature rose to a comfortable minus-twenty.

Matt's New Mail Special performed even better than its builders in Boston had predicted, and at the halfway mark he'd had no trouble with his tires except that they froze solid at anything below minus-forty, and only one loosened spoke. During the first days his personal gear, strapped to his back, did cause chafing, but he soon solved that problem by adjusting his pack, and during his long, solitary ride down the Yukon he often amused himself by bellowing old Irish songs. The only thing that held him up was an occasional bout of snow blindness, which he cured with a day's rest in some dark cabin.

He kept going at more than sixty miles a day, and once when he felt he had to make up lost time after an enforced halt because of the blindness, he did seventy-eight. That night he shared a cabin with a toothless old-timer, who asked: "You claim you come all the way from Dawson? How do I know that?" so Matt produced his newspapers with their dates of publication showing, and the old man said: "So you think that git-up'll work on this 'ere river?"

"You don't have to carry food for dogs, or spend an hour cooking it at the end of the day," to which the old man, recalling the hardships he had suffered with his dogs, replied: "Yep, that would be an advantage."

Rider and bike were in such excellent condition that when they reached Kaltag, the village which Father Fyodor Afanasi had served as missionary and in which he had married his Athapascan wife, Matt was emotionally prepared to face the difficult choice laid before him: "You can continue down the Yukon, more than four hundred miles to the Bering Sea, or you can leave the river for a sixty-mile hike across the mountains to Unalakleet."

"How do I get my bicycle across?"

"You carry it."

Matt chose the mountains, and after finding an Indian to lug his gear, he dismantled his bicycle as best he could, lashed it to his back, and climbed the eastern slopes, then scrambled down to the welcome sight of Unalakleet perched on the edge of Norton Sound, which was, as he had anticipated, beautifully frozen all the way to Nome.

Glad to be riding again, he set out blithely on the final dash, a hundred and fifty miles as the crow flies, and on 29 March 1900 at about four in the afternoon he pedaled his way down Front Street in Nome. He was a man who had accomplished one of the remarkable travel adventures of the dying century: Dawson to Nome, solo, depth of winter, thirty-six days.

After turning his bicycle over to admiring bystanders and delivering his four newspapers to the editor of the local paper, he hurried to meet Missy Peckham, who embraced him ardently and informed him: "All the good mining sites are taken, but I'm sure you can get a job somewhere. I did."

During the last week in February, while Matt Murphy and his bicycle were still on the Yukon, the testing time came for men and women living in northern Alaska. Existence was brutal. All through February wind howled in from the Bering Sea, and although little snow fell, it was so whipped about that a ground blizzard obscured buildings just half a block away. Now came the feared whiteout, when earth and horizon and sky blended into one gauzelike whole and trappers went blind if they lacked eye shields. What made this time more difficult were the huge blocks of ice that forced their way upward through the layers of ice already covering the Bering Sea, for they loomed ominously, casting weird shadows when either the midnight moon or the wan noontime sun shone upon them.

"I'll be glad when February goes," Tom Venn said as he watched the sea from his store, but a knowing woman customer warned: "March is the bad month. Watch out for March."

She did not, during that visit, explain this strange statement, and when March did arrive, it brought such fine weather that Tom felt a surge of spring, and he was most pleased when the days began to lengthen and the sea started to look as if would soon relax its icy grip enough to allow ships to arrive. Four days later, when the weather was still perfect, the woman returned: "These are the dangerous days. Husbands start to beat their wives, and men sharing one hut as mining partners begin to quarrel and suddenly shoot each other."

Shortly thereafter, news of two such scandalous affairs reached Tom, and when he asked why they had happened just as winter was relaxing its hold, the same woman customer explained: "That's the reason! In dark January and February, you know you have to remain strong. But in March and April, we have more daylight than dark. Everything seems to be brighter. But the fact is, we face three more long months of winter. March, April, May. The sun shines but the sea remains frozen. We feel life moving but the damned sea stays blocked, and we begin to shout at our friends: 'When will this thing ever end?' Watch out for March!" And Tom found that he was reacting exactly as she had described: he felt winter should be over; ships ought to be coming in with new stores; and there stood the frozen sea, its great hummocks immobile in the ice as if winter would never end.

In his seventeen years he had never experienced a worse month than May when it was spring throughout the world, even in the arctic. Yet still the sea remained locked in the grip of winter. And then, as May ended, the Bering Sea began to break up into monstrous icebergs as big as cathedrals, and despite the fact that navigation was now at its most perilous, for one of these mighty bergs could crush any ordinary vessel, men began to speculate on how soon ships could begin to arrive.

How glorious it was, in an ordinary year, to be in Nome at the beginning of June and watch as the first of that season's vessels hove to in the roadsteads. Men would fire salutes, and study the ships' profiles, and run down to the shore to greet the first arrival of the year. It was the custom for the local news sheet to print in bold letters the name of the first man ashore:

HENRY HARPER, FIRST IN 1899

And each year the cry that greeted every newcomer as he stepped ashore was the same: "You got any Seattle newspapers? You got any magazines?"

This spring of 1900 was to be entirely different, for the desire of many to reach Nome was so great that on 21 May a heavy whaler pushed its snout through the ice, and two days later a legitimate passenger ship arrived, to the astonishment of those who felt that to approach Nome before the first week in June was folly.

But it was what happened next that amazed the citizens, because in swift succession two more passenger ships arrived, then three more, until, amidst the lessening ice, forty-two large ships lay at anchor. Since docking facilities could not exist on this turbulent roadstead, the ships sat about a mile and a half offshore, while improvised barges and lighters ferried back and forth to disgorge more than nineteen thousand newcomers. Nome, in those hectic weeks of thaw, was a more important harbor than Singapore or Hamburg.

And as the stampeders streamed ashore, eying the beaches already crowded with the bizarre machines of prospectors, each hopeful man tried to identify the spot to which he would hurry to pick up his share of the gold. Some had tents, which they erected quickly; others less prudent had to scrounge around for sleeping places; the Belgian Mare rented space, rotating four customers in a bed every twenty-four hours; and Tom Venn had to keep one employee watching the store at night so that men endorsed by the R&R office in Seattle could sleep on the floor.

As more and more ships arrived the chaos in Nome became indescribable, and now the lack of civil government posed a fearful threat, for as health problems mounted, so did crime, and for the same reason. Crime, like disease, can be kept under control in a crowded society only by the exercise of constant policing powers, and if those powers are not allowed to exist, tranquillity cannot exist either.

But one of the big ships arriving on 20 June, with sixteen hundred new miners, brought newspapers confirming the news for which men like Lars Skjellerup and Tom Venn had waited: Congress is about to pass an Alaska Code and the district will receive two additional judges, the more important one to be assigned immediately to Nome.

Sober men cheered the news and even drunks agreed that the time had come to bring order into this vast disorder. Skjellerup sent Sana searching for the Siberian, and when Arkikov stood before him, the Norwegian cried with unwonted enthusiasm: "Arkikov! Your judge, he's coming. *Seven Above* will be yours again," and a broad, robust smile illuminated the irrepressible reindeer herder's face: "Me glad."

In a small town in Iowa in the years prior to the Civil War, a mediocre lawyer developed such vaulting ambitions for his newly born son that he named him John Marshall, after the greatest of the Chief Justices of the United States. The boy could remember that when he was only five his father walked him past the county courthouse and predicted: "Someday you'll be the judge in that building," and during his early years the lad believed that the famous jurist was his grandfather.

John Marshall Grant, alas, had none of the qualities of that noble proponent of justice, for he was essentially a weak human being who developed none of the flinthard character a judge should have. He slouched his way through high school and did poorly in one of Iowa's small colleges. He played no games, avoided books as well, and was notable on campus solely because he became increasingly handsome as the years passed. He was tall, well formed, with even features and a head of wavy hair which photographed so handsomely that people said, when his proud father displayed the cards he carried with him: "Simon, your son looks like a judge!"

At the University of Pennsylvania Law School, one of the best, the future judge did so poorly that in later years his classmates often wondered: "How did John Marshall ever become a judge?" He became one because he looked like one. And as his father had predicted, he was installed in the little Iowa courthouse, dispensing a garbled kind of justice—but his decisions frequently had to be overturned by higher courts because he had failed to understand the simplest common law as applied in courts like his throughout the other forty-four states and in Great Britain.

He was so handsome and so pompous in Fourth of July orations that politicians began thinking of running him for major office, but he was so flabby and lacking in determination that no one knew whether he was Republican or Democrat, and those who knew his pathetic record joked: "Whichever party loses him is to be congratulated." When some Republicans sought a safe candidate who could be elected to Congress, they asked the judge's father what party his son favored, and the old man said proudly: "My son the judge wears no man's collar."

He would probably have bumbled his way to innocuous obscurity, harming few because his worst errors could always be reversed, had he not been invited to address a legal convention in Chicago, where a noted lobbyist heard him speak.

Marvin Hoxey was at age forty-five a man difficult to forget, once he had buttonholed you and stared penetratingly into your eyes. Portly, crop-headed, careless in dress and characterized by a huge unkempt walrus mustache and a perpetual cigar, he derived his considerable power from the fact that he seemed to know everyone of importance west of the Mississippi or in the halls of Congress. Protector of the more powerful interests in the West, he could always find a friend willing to do "a little something for Marvin." He had parlayed his skills into a position of some importance. For his help in gaining South Dakota's admission to the Union in 1889, he had been named National Committeeman for the Republican party in that state, a position from which he orated about "the growing power of the New West."

He thought globally, a man without a college education who could have taught courses on political manipulation. He saw nations as either rising or falling and had an uncanny sense of what actions a rising nation like the United States ought to take next. It then became his job to see to it that only those steps were taken which would serve his clients.

He became interested in Alaska when Malcolm Ross, senior partner of Ross & Raglan in Seattle, employed him to obstruct any national legislation which might give Alaska home rule, for as Ross pointed out: "The destiny of Alaska is to be governed by Seattle. The few people who are up there can rely on us to make the right decisions for them."

At Ross's suggestion he had taken two cruises on R&R ships— one to Sitka, which he found disgracefully Russian, "hardly an American town at all," and one up the great river to Fort Yukon—as a result of which he knew Alaska better than most residents. He saw it for what it was, a vast, untamed area with a shockingly mixed and deficient population: "Not in mental or moral ability, Mr. Ross, but deficient in numbers. I don't think the entire area has as many people, I mean real people, not natives and half-breeds, as my county in South Dakota, and God knows we're thinly staffed." It was his opinion, stated loudly in Seattle and Washington, that "Alaska will never be ready for self-government."

Whenever Hoxey lobbied against legislation for Alaska he repeated the pejorative phrase *half-breed,* spitting it out as if the offspring of a hardworking white prospector and a capable Eskimo woman had to be congenitally inferior to someone purebred like himself with his Scots–English–Irish–German–Scandinavian–Central Asian heritage. He believed, and he worked hard to convince others, that since Alaska would always be inhabited by people of mixed derivation—Eskimo, Aleut, Athapascan, Tlingit, Russian, Portuguese, Chinese and God knows what—it must always be inferior and somehow un-American: "Stands to reason, Senator, a land filled with half-breeds will never be able to govern itself. Keep things as they are and let the good people of Seattle do the thinkin'."

During sessions of Congress, Marvin Hoxey sometimes single-handedly defeated the aspirations of Alaska for self-rule. It was not allowed to become a territory, that honorable preparatory step to statehood, because the firms profiting from conditions as they were could not trust what a self-controlled territorial government might do to diminish their advantages. It was not anything, really. For some years it had been known as a district, but mostly it had been simply Alaska, vast, raw and unorganized, and Marvin Hoxey was engaged to keep it that way.

At the legal convention in Chicago he had already buttonholed several delegates when he learned by telegraph from an aide in Washington that despite all his efforts, a bill was going to be passed giving Alaska a modicum of self-government—about one-fiftieth of what was justified—including two additional judges to be appointed by a superior court in California. There was some talk of choosing them locally, but Hoxey had that killed instantly: "There aren't two half-breeds in all that forlorn region qualified to be judges. I've been there."

He was wandering the halls of the convention, pondering how he could get the right kind of man appointed judge in the Nome district, when he happened to drift into the back of the room where Judge

Grant was orating. His first impression was: I could make a man like that President . . . or an important judge, but it was not until he heard Grant deliver one of his typical sentences in praise of home that he realized that he had come upon something special:

> "The American home is like a fort atop a mighty hill that keeps its powder dry in preparation for the day when assaults from the swamps below, and you can never know when these are going to come, the lawless conditions in our big cities being what they are and fights to resist the agencies of contamination, keeping the flag flying to ensure that it always has a constant supply of gunpowder to do such."

As soon as the judge ended his speech, Marvin Hoxey hurried up, shoved his walrus mustache and cigar close to Grant's face, and said with great feeling: "What a magnificent address! It's of the utmost importance that we talk."

And there, at the rear of a public room in a Chicago hotel, Marvin Hoxey's plan was formally launched. It was magnificently simple: he was going to steal the entire Nome gold field. Yes, with the assistance of Judge John Marshall Grant of Iowa, he would steal the whole damned field. If what the papers said was true, it could amount to fifty million dollars, and if they continued to dredge gold by the bucketful from the beaches, it might run to eighty million.

"Judge Grant, the leaders of this nation are searching for a man just like you to save Alaska. It's a forlorn place that cries aloud for the staunch leadership that only a judge like you can give it."

"I'm flattered that you should think so." He asked for Hoxey's name and address and said that he'd think the matter over.

As the lobbyist bade Judge Grant goodbye, he caught a final glimpse of the handsome, white-haired figure: That's the phrase we'll use to get him the job. *Eminent jurist.* Even better: *Eminent Iowa jurist.*

Defeated in his efforts to kill this legislation favorable to Alaska, he left Chicago for an urgent meeting in Seattle, where he placated his clients, especially Malcolm Ross, whose R&R ships and stores stood to lose some of their freedom under the new rules: "Trust me, we lose a battle but we win the war. Our task is not to fight the new law but to use it to our advantage, and the first thing we have to do is to make sure we get our man into that judgeship governing Nome."

"You have some local man in mind?" Ross asked, and Hoxey said: "Too blatant. Never be blatant, Mr. Ross."

"Who, then?"

"I have in mind an eminent Iowa jurist. Fine-looking man. Knows Western life." This was a cliché of the period, that anyone who had ever been in Denver or Salt Lake automatically understood Alaska.

"Can we get him appointed?"

"That's my job."

And as soon as he returned to Washington, the Eastern one, he launched his campaign. Every Republican leader he had worked with as a national committeeman heard confidential reports on the distinguished Iowa jurist John Marshall Grant, and repetition of that resounding name inspired such confidence that the White House began to receive calls supporting Grant for the appointment "to this here new judgeship in Alaska." By simply stating that his new friend was an eminent jurist, Hoxey was making him one.

In late June 1900, John Marshall Grant was assigned to the new court in Nome, and many newspapers applauded a decision free of even a suspicion of political influence, and shortly thereafter he and his mentor Marvin Hoxey sailed on the steamer *Senator* to his new duties.

On the evening prior to arrival at the Nome roadstead, Hoxey laid down the law that Grant was to follow: "John Marshall, if you play your cards right in Nome, you'll attract so much favorable attention you'll become a United States senator. The name of this ship is an omen, Senator Grant, me and my friends will see to that."

"How do you see the situation, Mr. Hoxey?"

"I've been to Alaska, you remember. Know it like the back of my hand."

"And your judgment?"

"Nome is in a terrible mess. The claims are false as hell. Mining law was not followed in making them. They're not in legal form. And they should all be vacated."

The eminent jurist, knowing nothing about mining law and having neglected to bring along any books which would unravel its arcane lore, listened attentively as it was explained according to the doctrine of Marvin Hoxey: "What you must do, Judge, and do it fast, is to declare . . . let's say fifteen of the major claims invalid. Present owners are disqualified, on the best legal grounds. Then appoint me as the impartial receiver, not the owner, you understand. Oh, of course, you know all about that. What you do is appoint me receiver, and I watch over the property, as an agent of the government, till you decide later on after formal court cases who really has title."

Hoxey stressed two facts: "Speed is essential. New broom and all that. And the receiver must be appointed immediately, so as to protect the property." Judge Grant said he understood.

Now Hoxey came to the ticklish part: "One thing I don't like about the Nome situation—and you must remember that I know Alaska like the back of my hand—is that a bunch of aliens and half-breeds have grabbed up the best claims. Can you imagine a Russian citizen owning a gold mine in America? Or a Lapp, God forbid? Who in hell ever heard of Lapland . . . and their people coming over here and taking up our good claims? And Norwegians and Swedes aren't much better. You must remember that I come from South Dakota, some of my best friends are Scandinavians, but they have no right coming over here and taking up our best claims."

"I thought two of them were naturalized citizens?"

"Subterfuge." With that marvelous word, delivered with a sneer, he settled the goose of the Swedes, and neither man seemed to appreciate that they themselves were engaging in the greatest subterfuge of all.

So it was decided that Judge Grant would do three things immediately upon arrival: outlaw all foreigners, vacate the claims, and appoint Hoxey receiver. He would also make a speech affirming American values and reassuring the men that law and order had come, although belatedly, to Nome. Health law enforcement, land-title paperwork, legal collection of taxes and protection of the public weal would all come later, if ever; the important thing was to outlaw foreigners and clarify the ownership of the gold mines.

"I can see it now," Hoxey said as he accompanied Judge Grant to the ship's bar. "That sign over there is prophetic." It was the crest of the ship done in ornate blue and gold hand-carved letters: *Senator.*

In view of the heinous things Judge Grant was about to do, it is proper to ask: How much did he understand of Hoxey's infamous plan? Not much. He never guessed that if he appointed his trusted friend Hoxey to the receivership of the mines, Hoxey would steal every bit of gold being produced and that such theft could quickly run into the millions. Outstanding men in American history had started their careers as small-town judges, but these men had used their time on the bench to hone their perceptions, to differentiate between the motives of good men and evil; each year such judges grew wiser, more judicial, more honest, until in the end they stood forth as some of the finest products of our nation. Judge Grant had had all the opportunities of an Abraham Lincoln or a Thomas Hart Benton, but he had squandered them. He was now prepared to initiate one of the blackest pages of American legal history.

When the *Senator* anchored well out in the roadstead, lighters sped out to start the unloading; the first one to arrive was commandeered by Marvin Hoxey on the grounds, which he announced discreetly, "that Judge Grant must establish his court at the soonest possible, in obedience to personal instructions from the President." So the eminent jurist and his mentor were ferried toward the shore, but the lighter had such a deep draft that it could not nose into the beach. Important passengers and goods had to be transported that remaining distance on the backs of porters, so now six strong Eskimos, three for Judge Grant, three for Hoxey, hoisted the two men high in the air and carried them ashore.

They were a striking pair as they set foot on the golden beaches: Judge Grant, handsome and severe; Marvin Hoxey, pudgy and red-faced, with that immense walrus mustache and the eyes which took in everything. Holding his cigar in his left hand, he waved it, signaling that it would be proper for the citizens of Nome to applaud the arrival of the judge who was bringing order to their community, and one man started a cheer: "Hooray for the judge!" and with that cry ringing in his ears, Judge John Marshall Grant strode sedately to chambers in the Golden Gate Hotel.

He had barely supervised the placing of his luggage when he began issuing the sheaf of orders which Hoxey had recommended and sometimes drafted. After vacating the leases and appointing Hoxey receiver to protect their assets, Judge Grant let it be known that henceforth no Swedes, Norwegians, Lapps or Siberians could hold claims and that the ones they currently did hold illegally must be turned over to the receiver. By nightfall of that first cyclonic day Marvin Hoxey controlled claims *One* through *Eleven Above,* with a combined capacity of producing nearly forty thousand dollars a month.

No sooner had Judge Grant vacated claims *One* through *Eleven Above* on his first day in Nome than he did one other thing that would have equally heavy consequences. Taking from his pocket a memorandum handed him by Malcolm Ross before the *Senator* sailed from Seattle, he read: "When hiring staff in Nome, consult with our R&R man, Tom Venn, who will know the abilities of everyone." Calling for Hoxey, he said: "Can you get this fellow Venn to come to my quarters?" and very soon Tom reported to the Golden Gate Hotel.

"Judge Grant? I'm Tom Venn, Your Honor. Just got a note from Mr. Ross instructing me to find you a secretary. I've brought along the only candidate I think you'd be interested in, sir. She's waiting downstairs."

"I'd like to see her," and in this way Melissa Peckham, twenty-five years old, met Judge Grant.

"What's your name?" When she said "Missy Peckham," he scowled: "Now what kind of name is that?" and when she said: "It's really Melissa," he said: "That's better. A proper girl needs a proper name, especially if she's going to work for me."

Judge Grant hired Missy to begin immediately, and Matt, again on Tom's recommendation, was hired by Hoxey to act as caretaker of the vacated claims. From her experience in Dawson and on the Eldorado ridge, Missy knew a good deal about mining, much more than Judge Grant, and she was so bothered by some of his early decisions that she began taking careful and secret notes of what was transpiring in this ugly business of depriving the discoverers of a field of their just property:

Thursday 25 July. In the first batch of decisions the Siberian Arkikov, no first name, lost his claim to *Seven Above* on Anvil Creek. He is believed to be one of the discoverers.

Friday 26 July. The Norwegian Lars Skjellerup notified that as a foreigner he cannot hold a claim on Anvil Creek, even though he is known to have been the organizer of the mining district.

Working late into the night to record the judgments of each day, Missy frequently heard, through the thin makeshift wall separating the judge's chambers from her desk, Hoxey discussing plans with Judge Grant. She discussed this growing pattern with Murphy, who said without reflection: "I think this man Hoxey, he's mighty near a criminal. Keep an eye on him," and now Missy inscribed in her small book not only what she thought the judge was doing but Murphy's suspicions as well, and the result was a document so devastating that Murphy told her one night: "You better hide that," and she did.

The impact of Judge Grant and Hoxey on Nome was so shocking that some miners who had been deprived of their rights spoke of lynching, but Lars Skjellerup, who had lost more than most, counseled restraint: "Things like this won't be allowed in a free country. There must be something legal we can do to unmask these men."

There was nothing. Clothed in the dignity of a law which local people had not called into being and supported by the might of a great but remote nation, Judge Grant and Hoxey were free to do as they wished, and now that the mines were working smoothly under their receivership, Hoxey was shipping out of Alaska more than two hundred thousand dollars a month.

When Skjellerup questioned this, he was told by Judge Grant: "Mr. Hoxey is the legal receiver. That means he is to manage the mines as he sees fit until such time as the case against you is legally decided. Of course, you and I both understand that Mr. Hoxey is not to keep such money as his mines—"

"They're our mines."

"The court will decide that, later on, but I must advise you that as an alien breaking the law—"

"Judge Grant! The jury is to decide that, not you. You're stealing our property."

"You can go to jail for contempt, I suppose you know that."

"I'm sorry. I mean Hoxey is stealing—"

"Mr. Skellerby, if that's how you pronounce your name, you don't seem to understand what a receivership is. Mr. Hoxey is there to protect you and the public . . . till the trial can take place. Not a penny of that money, I assure you, will ever accrue to him, except for a small managerial fee to which, even you must admit, he's entitled."

"But it goes out of here on every ship. I've watched."

"For safekeeping. Should the trial be decided in your favor," this being said in a tone of voice which guaranteed that it would not, "you would, of course, get back all the money, except for the managerial fee I spoke of."

"Which is how much?"

"Twenty thousand a month. Set by the court." When Skjellerup exploded, Judge Grant justified the fee: "Mr. Hoxey is an important man in the United States. Adviser to presidents. Counselor to great industries. He can't work for shavings."

Skjellerup had heard enough, and even though his strict Norwegian upbringing had indoctrinated in him a grave respect for policemen, ministers, schoolteachers and judges, he was morally infuriated; his Lutheran sense of rectitude was outraged and he said so: "Judge Grant, an evil thing is being done in Nome. In a democracy like the United States, this can't be allowed. I don't know how it will be stopped, but it will be stopped. You cannot steal a man's honest work."

"Mr. Killerbride, or whatever. Do you know what a deportation order is? The judge signs a paper stating that you're a dangerous alien, and out you go, back to Lapland where you belong."

"I'm Norwegian."

"That's almost as bad. Miss Peckham, show this man out." She did, making note of his name, the location of his mine and the threats made against him.

During most of these trying times Hoxey remained invisible, and men like Skjellerup, who now saw pretty clearly what the plot was—Judge Grant to issue improper orders, Hoxey to steal the property thus turned loose—suspected that the South Dakotan was hiding through fear of being shot, but that was not the case. Hoxey was kept indoors writing an unbroken stream of letters to senators, representatives and even the President, pointing out a mistake that had been made in the 1900 Alaska Code and lobbying for an immediate rectification:

> We simply must have a new law which nullifies any mining
> claim filed by an alien illegally, namely, while he was an alien.
> As you are aware, I know Alaska like the back of my hand,
> and few evils hold this area back like having Scandinavians and
> Russians holding title to mines on American soil. I urge you to
> correct this evil.

If passed, Hoxey's proposed bill would legally confirm the dispossession of aliens like Skjellerup and Arkikov and give sanction to his temporary receivership of the Nome holdings. After that, permanent possession would depend upon his ingenuity and Judge Grant's stupidity. With just a little luck and the continuance of Judge Grant's good health until all the claims had been thrown into receivership,

Hoxey would be a millionaire before half a year was out and a multi-millionaire in due course.

But to nail this down, he must convince Congress to pass his bill, and to make this happen, he must bombard Washington with a blizzard of letters. Obviously, he needed secretarial help, and since Judge Grant had little to do except write dispossession orders, Hoxey borrowed Missy, and this gave her an opportunity to obtain proof of the disreputable relationship between the two men, for boastfully Hoxey would say in some letters: "In these matters we can rely on our good friend, the eminent Iowa jurist," or even more damning: "So far Judge Grant has handed down not one decision adverse to our cause, and I think we can depend on him for the same kind of help in the future."

In the meantime, conditions in Nome worsened. The filth grew deeper in the streets. People began to die of strange diseases. There were robberies, and now and then a miner would be found dead near his claim, now occupied by Hoxey's men. Women were assaulted even in the twilight hours, and feared to move about at night.

One evening, though Missy and Murphy were still not sure they could confide in Tom Venn, they invited him to dinner: "We're so pleased to have a little extra these days so we can show our gratitude."

"I was happy . . . no, I was proud to recommend you to the two gentlemen who are doing so much to make Nome better. What do you think of them?"

"They work hard," Missy said evasively. "At least Mr. Hoxey does."

"I thought you were working for the judge."

"I am, but Mr. Hoxey has to write a lot of letters to Washington. To Seattle too, so he borrows me."

Tom knew that he must not ask a secretary to break the confidence under which she worked, so he asked no more about the letters, but she did feel free to make a general observation: "Mr. Hoxey seems to think that Alaska should be governed from Seattle."

"I agree. They have the brains down there . . . the money . . . they know what's best for the nation as a whole. And my company, at least, does a grand job of protecting Alaskan interests."

Murphy changed the subject: "I've been thinking, Tom, that what Nome needs is not Judge Grant and Mr. Hoxey from Seattle, but Superintendent Steele and Officer Kirby from Dawson. Do you realize that those two men could clean this town up in a weekend?"

So the three shifted to that provocative topic, and they agreed that even one man like Steele, fortified by tradition and supported from Ottawa, could hammer Nome into shape. "The cribs would be out of sight," Murphy said. "Those little buildings that project into the main street, they'd be gone by nightfall. The saloons that steal from newcomers, out! One man could clean up this town, if he was the right man."

"That's certain," Tom said. "In Dawson we never worried about our R&R money, and in the good days we had huge amounts. Superintendent Steele wouldn't allow theft. Here? Everyone at the store sleeps with a gun."

"Would you use a gun?" Missy asked, and Tom replied: "I'd avoid it as long as possible. Even if the other man struck me, I'd still try to calm him down, but if it was hopeless—"

"I'll tell you one thing Superintendent Steele would clear up," Murphy broke in. "What I know of Hoxey, he's got the claims in a real mess here. Three hundred men in town at the beginning, each allowed one legal claim, no proxies. But now they say that fifteen hundred claims were filed."

"Impossible!" Venn cried, but Murphy insisted on his story. "Fifteen hundred claim jumpers, and each one entitled to his day in court before Judge Grant."

"This could go on forever," Tom said, and Missy, knowing what she had seen in the two offices, said: "That's what they intend."

This further irritated Murphy, who broke in: "You know how Superintendent Steele handled claim jumpers? I saw him in operation twice. A man near us on Klope's ridge had a perfectly good claim, but like us, no gold. When word circulated that gold was sure to be found on the ridge—it never was—this big, loud fellow from Nevada, I often wanted to punch him, he said he knew more about mining than anyone in Canada, he tried to jump our friend's claim. Superintendent Steele came up to settle the dispute, recognized the claimant, and said: 'Sir, I been watching you for seven months. Even if your claim is valid, we don't want you in Dawson. It's half past two on Tuesday. If you're in town this time Thursday, you go to jail, and if you want to make a move for your gun, just try it.' And he walked away."

But then Murphy told a more representative story of how Steele operated, and how anyone like him could handle the situation in Nome: "On the stream below us, *Eldorado Nine Below,* a man had a placer that wasn't producing, and he dug deep, came up with a winter's load of gold-bearing muck that froze solid beside his cabin. One day when I was there, Superintendent Steele came by with surveying instruments: 'Sam, I got bad news for you. Your line's skewed. That portion over there's open for whoever claims it, and I've heard someone is going to file tomorrow. Wanted to warn you.' And Sam cries: 'Good God, sir, all my muck is on that property. Assayer said maybe thirty thousand.' And Steele said: 'You know the law. Muck goes with the claim.' Sam grew so weak he had to sit down. A winter's work gone. The only strike he'd ever make. And all on somebody else's property: 'My God, sir, what am I goin' to do?' and the superintendent considered for a while and said: 'I'm supposed to have my office open at nine in the morning. Tomorrow I'll open at seven. If you can find a friend you can trust, have him claim on that piece and have him file early, because tomorrow afternoon will be too late.' With that, he stalked off, because he didn't want to know what kind of deal was made."

"What happened?" Tom asked, and Murphy said: "Sam looked around, saw only me, and in despair asked: 'Murphy, can I trust you?' and I said: 'You better,' and early next morning I was in Superintendent Steele's office and he took me to the registry and I claimed on *Eldorado Nine Below, False Portion* and I got it and here's the paper to prove it," and from his pocket he produced a sweat-stained paper which proved that Matthew Murphy, Belfast, Ireland, had a valid claim to *Nine Below, False Portion:* "I came to Canada to get me a mine, and by God's sacred word I did, and here's proof."

"But what about Sam's muck?"

"I sold it to him for one dollar, but I kept the mine. His muck proved out at thirty-three thousand dollars and he gave me five percent. That's what Missy and I lived on when we couldn't get work in Dawson."

"But your claim?" Tom asked. "What about it?"

"It was only a tiny piece of land, covered with Sam's muck. On the stream, nothing. Below, nothing. But I get great spiritual gratification from that certificate."

"Why?"

"Fifteen hundred men left Edmonton to stake a claim—doctors, lawyers, engineers—and I'm the only one who staked his claim, and it was worth thirty-three thousand dollars . . . from seven in the morning one day till four that afternoon."

"Why did Superintendent Steele protect Sam in that way? That illegal way, I might add."

"When he handed me my certificate he said, off to one side: 'Glad it was you, Murphy. Because the other claimant was a real swine.'"

"Like I said," Missy concluded, "one Superintendent Steele could clean up this town."

In early September 1900 it seemed as if all nature had turned against the good people of Nome. Saddled with a corrupt judge, a cunning expropriator and rampant chloroform gangs, they looked with disgust as the wild summer drew to an end, for the experienced ones knew that with the arrival of the ice pack, they would be locked in with these criminals for eight or nine nearly sunless months. Their experience had been that as the sun receded and the roadstead iced in, the worst came out in what was already bad.

Tom Venn, in the cramped office of his R&R store, felt that he would have enough food supplies for the winter if the large steamship *Senator* could break through the ice one last time and discharge the enormous shipment it was supposed to contain. It would require the R&R barges six days just to unload the supplies onto the shore, and then teams of horses would need another six days to haul them into the store and the nearby warehouses.

As one of the principal businessmen in town, and the leader of those who looked to Seattle for guidance in all things, Tom was no longer happy with the judge and the receiver the men in Seattle had sent to Alaska, for he had begun to see almost daily proof of their deceptive behavior. "It isn't that Seattle sent them. Most of the men R&R send us form the backbone of our country," Tom told Matt and Missy. "It's just that in this case Seattle chose poorly."

As the days shortened, Missy, in her work with the two miscreants, had redoubled proof of their iniquities. In recent weeks, as Hoxey took possession of the many mines Judge Grant placed under his protection, there had been so much paperwork that Missy had worked ten hours a day for Hoxey and rarely saw Judge Grant, although her salary was being paid by the government on his behalf. And although she did not yet wish to bring her little notebook to Tom Venn, she said to Matt: "You know, almost everything they do is corrupt. Last week the judge had to settle a simple problem, the transfer of property belonging to the widow of that workman killed when the boom on that cargo ship broke. It was a simple matter, I could have handled it. But no, he had to involve Mr. Hoxey, and by the time they were through with their mumbo jumbo, eighteen hundred dollars of the widow's money had disappeared."

"You know what I think, Missy? Somebody's going to shoot Mr. Hoxey. I see things that would curl your hair."

"Don't you get mixed up with any shootings, Matt!" After months of struggle and deprivation, this hardworking, reliable pair had an income at last, but her work was beginning to sicken Missy: "Matt, what would you say if we quit? Just quit and ask Tom Venn if he would take us on in some capacity?"

"What could we do? We need money."

"I could keep records, honest ones, for Tom, and you could run the warehouse so the freight's not backed up on the beach. And we could sleep at night."

"Do you lie awake?"

"I do."

"Jesus, Missy, a soul should never lie awake for what he done for someone else during the waking hours."

"I'm scared, Matt. When the shooting starts, and it will, you might get hit. Or me."

Her words were so solemn that half an hour after dawn on the tenth of September they were knocking on the door of Tom Venn's office: "Tom, we want a job."

"You have jobs. I went to a lot of trouble getting you those jobs."

"We can't keep them any longer."

"Why not?"

"Tom, do you remember what I said when you left us to go to work on your own for the first time? Up on Klope's ridge?"

Tom breathed deeply, then put his left hand over his mouth, then mumbled: "You told me always to be honest." He walked away from the pair, turned, and said: "When I left Dawson last year to come down here, Mr. Pincus gave me those assayer's scales. Told me to keep them burnished. Warned me they would rust if I ever did anything dishonest for R&R." For some moments he walked back and forth, kicking up dust. Then he stopped abruptly and looked back over his shoulder: "They're not very nice men, are they."

"No, Tom, they are not," Missy said heavily, and no more was said on that subject.

"Well," Tom said brightly as he came forward as if meeting them for the first time, "Suppose I did have a pair of jobs. What could you do for me?"

"I could keep your records," Missy said, and Matt chimed in: "I could take charge of your goods coming in on the barges."

Only Tom himself could assess how much he owed these two fine people, how deep his debt was to Missy, who had saved his family back in '93 and who had taught him on the Chilkoot Pass what courage was. Only he knew the subtle effect Matt Murphy had had with his lyrical Irish ways, his gentler view of life and his indomitable spirit. Tom was beholden to Matt and Missy for the values which would guide him through life, and if they now needed jobs, he had no choice but to provide them, and then figure out how to explain it to his bosses in Seattle.

"You can't leave the judge and Mr. Hoxey in the lurch, you know. You'll have to give notice."

"Of course," Missy said. "Would two weeks be honorable?"

"It would, and because it might look bad if you quit and then I hired you . . . What I mean, it might look as if I'd approached you. It will be better if I tell them myself. Lay my cards on the table."

And that morning, as soon as their offices opened, Tom went to Judge Grant and suggested that Hoxey be called. When the three were together eating doughnuts, Tom said: "Gentlemen, when you came here I recommended two very old friends of mine, Missy Peckham and Matthew Murphy . . ."

Judge Grant leaned forward, made a lascivious gesture with his fingers, and asked: "Are those two . . . ? I mean, is he diddling her?"

"I wouldn't know," Tom said. He turned to Hoxey: "Winter's coming and the *Senator,* your old ship, is arriving with a huge shipment, and I could certainly use their help."

"That is, you want to hire them away from us?" Hoxey asked belligerently.

"Well, yes. I can find you other help."

"The Irishman isn't worth a damn," Hoxey snarled. "Take him, and good riddance. The girl, well, she's something else."

"I thought she worked for you, Judge."

"After-hours she helps me," Hoxey lied.

"You find you can't let her go?" Tom asked, and when Hoxey said: "I'd take it most unkindly, most unkindly. And when I take something unkindly, I usually do something about it. I am very close to your superiors in Seattle, Mr. Venn, and I would take it most unkindly."

So Tom had to report to his old partners that whereas Matt could start working for R&R at the end of two weeks, Missy would have to stay with the judge: "I'm sorry, Missy, but I'm discovering that few people in this world are ever their own bosses. Mr. Hoxey won't let you go."

"If I could stand those rapids at Lake Bennett, I can stand Mr. Hoxey." It was clear that she would be locked into her position during the interminable winter, and now as she worked she took even more careful note of all that he was doing. During the last two weeks when Matt would also be working for him, she queried Matt on every detail of the dealings at the mines. On the night of the thirteenth of September, she said to Matt: "Remember that story you told us about Superintendent Steele protecting the miner who had his pile of muck on the other man's property? And the reason he gave for doing so, even though it was against the law, you might say?"

"Yes. Steele said: 'Because the other claimant was a real swine.'"

"These men we're dealing with are swine."

On the fourteenth the *Senator* arrived in the roadstead off Nome with its huge cargo for R&R and the last batch of miners for the season. When the latter got ashore they would find all claims along the rich creeks taken and every inch of oceanfront bespoken, but ashore they would come, and by the end of the bitter winter, ten months off, they would have found some way to eke out a living. They would have survived, although not as they had envisioned.

They did not get ashore on the fourteenth, because a major storm brewing in the western half of the Bering Sea began to pile so much water against the Nome beaches that any lightering became quite dangerous, if not impossible. A picket boat did make it ashore with a ship's officer and an official from Ross & Raglan, but by the time they intended returning, the seas were so high that no one wanted to leave, they least of all.

They brought word that eight hundred and thirty-one newcomers were hankering to rush ashore and dig their millions: "Some of them asked us to lay over three days so they could sail back to Seattle with their fortunes. One of our sailors made a tidy sum pointing out to them the choice spots along the beach—all of them taken, of course."

The R&R man brought two bits of good news: that Tom's entire shipping list had been forwarded and lay out there in the *Senator* awaiting the barges, and that his salary had been upped by seven dollars a week. As he handed Tom the shipping list the man said: "We're proud of the way you've handled things. Not many take charge as you have. And do you know what attracted major attention? The way you sold those cans without labels for five cents. Our accountant screamed: 'Debit his account thirty cents a can. That's what they cost us.' And do you know what Mr. Ross said? 'Give the young feller a bonus. For the next forty years they'll talk about how generous R&R was with those perfectly good cans.'"

Then the man added: "There's a Mr. Reed, I think maybe he's from an insurance company in Denver. He's very eager to talk with you, Venn," and from the way this news was delivered, it was clear to Tom that the R&R man might think that he was involved in some shady operation, because insurance inspectors did not come all the way from Denver just to say "How's business?"

"Tom, do you know this Mr. Reed?" the R&R man asked. "From Denver . . . in insurance?"

"Never heard of him. I don't carry insurance yet."

"You should. Every young man who expects to get married one of these days should start an insurance plan. This fellow Reed did mention a Mrs. Concannon. Death claim or something. You know anything about a Mrs. Concannon?"

"I'm afraid not." Then, most suspiciously, he did remember: "Oh yes! Her husband was killed when a boom snapped on one of our ships. The *Alacrity,* I think."

"Were we culpable?"

"Oh no! Act of God, as they say."

"Was her claim in any way spurious?"

"No, couldn't have been. He was killed flat out."

"Did you handle the paperwork on her insurance? I mean for R&R?"

"No." Again he had to correct himself, and again he appeared duplicitous: "I serve as sort of mayor or coroner or something in Nome. We have no government, as you probably know. All of us businessmen . . . Well, I did sign the Concannon death certificate."

"No flimflammery? No complications on your part?"

Tom did not like the way this interrogation was going, and said so: "Look, sir. Everything I do for R&R is open and aboveboard. Same in my private life."

"Son, wait a minute! If tomorrow a man came in here, a responsible insurance detective from Denver with good credentials, and he started asking questions about me . . . Wouldn't you wonder what was up?"

"I suppose I would."

"Well, Mr. Reed, an insurance inspector from Denver, was asking questions about you, and you're one of our employees. Naturally I perked up my ears. Son, you are turning pale. Do you want a glass of water?"

Tom fell into the chair and covered his face for some moments, then said: "He wasn't from Denver. He's from Chicago. And he's not an insurance man. He's a private detective hired by my mother . . . that is, my other mother, the one I don't want."

He was trembling so furiously that the R&R man sat down beside him and asked gently: "Do you want to talk about it?" and Tom said: "Only if Missy is here too," and through the storm that was now beginning to lash Nome, he and the man ran to the Murphy shack, where Tom broke the news.

"One of those detectives we were running away from, Missy, he's found us."

"Oh God!" She fell into a chair and remained silent. She had never told either Klope or Murphy of her flight from Chicago to avoid the law, and she had not the heart now to review that painful time.

But Tom did speak. He told of how Missy Peckham had saved his family and of how his mother and her lawyers had harassed them and of how brave Missy had been on the Chilkoot and of his father's death on Lake Lindemann. As the passions of seven years swept over him he did not weep, but he could say no more.

"What in hell!" the man from R&R, father of six, cried. "You got nothing to worry about. Your mother was a bitch, let's use simple words, and Mr. Reed ought to be ashamed of himself. I'd like to punch a man like that in the nose." A little while ago he had been cautioning Tom against behavior that might bring discredit to R&R, and now he was prepared to slug an insurance inspector. Trying to restore some steel to Tom Venn's backbone, he resorted to comforting old sayings: "Let the dead past bury its dead. Tom, I'd defend you through every court in this land. Besides, an honest man never has anything to fear."

On the morning of the fifteenth, in the last week of summer, the people of Nome awoke to find themselves assaulted by one of the greatest storms of the decade, indeed, five or six decades, as a tremendous wind howled out of Siberia. At dawn it measured forty-seven miles an hour; at eight o'clock it stood at fifty-nine on the anemometer; and then it began to gust up into the seventies and eighties.

Great waves pounded the unprotected shore, sucking rail huts and tents into the sea. Relentlessly, the waves ate away the shore until they lashed at houses and shops two hundred yards inland, and water came up to the steps of the new R&R warehouses. By nightfall a quarter of Nome's houses were destroyed, and for three terrible days the storm raged. A minister, gathering his flock, read passages from Revelation proving that God had come to Nome to scourge the Antichrist, and the men with chloroform swabs looked only to their own safety.

Tom Venn spent the three stormbound days with Missy and Matt, talking over strategy for dealing with the detective and whatever problems he would present. They were a mournful crew, and as squalls swept in from the sea, they anticipated the typhoon of troubles which would soon engulf them. But then Murphy, with his healthy peasant doubt, began to bring some sanity into the discussion.

"Wait a minute! What do you really know about this Mr. Reed? You don't even know who he is."

"He asked about me. More than once, I think."

"You don't even know whether he's an insurance man like he said or a detective like you said. Or maybe neither."

"He was looking into things, personal things."

"You don't know whether he's from Denver or Chicago. Or again, maybe neither."

"What are you suggesting?" Missy asked, for in her time with Matt she had learned to trust his common sense.

"That we wait till this damned storm dies down and your Mr. Reed can come ashore and explain himself. In the meantime, it does no good to get ourselves all worked up over things we don't know."

This was such sober counsel that Missy and Tom stopped lacerating themselves, and while the storm increased in its fury, their fears subsided; the apprehensive pair could not escape their sense of doom but they could maneuver it onto a plateau where it could be managed. And in this waiting period while the storm raged, Tom offered various reflections: "I owe so much to you two, I want to see you happy. I want you to work with me at R&R. Judge Grant and Hoxey will have to leave here soon, or as Matt says, someone is likely to shoot them. Then Missy will be free and we can work together. Matt, why don't you marry her?" and Matt revealed to Tom what he had long ago told Missy: "I have a wife in Ireland." He said this so flatly and with such finality that comment was uninvited, and for some time the three sat, listening to the howling of the wind as it rose in fury to match the pounding rain.

"There'll be a lot of houses go down this morning," Tom said, "and when we rebuild, I'd like to see wider streets. Make this city something to be proud of."

Matt said: "Go careful, Tom. Men like you wanted better government and you got Judge Grant."

"I don't think Nome can stay a big city. When the *Senator* sails, if it's ever able to unload, our committee has more than four hundred miners who want to sail with it. But they haven't a dime."

"What will you do?"

"Our committee will give each one a blue ticket. Free fare south. And I'll bet four hundred others will be paying their own fare to sleep on deck, just to get out of here."

"What will they do in Seattle?"

"Some'll mix in, most'll move on. Drift until they find work, and start over again. If a city is big enough, it can absorb men with no money. A small place like Nome can't."

"Nome's pretty big," Missy said. "Biggest city in Alaska."

Tom listened to the storm as it reached its howling peak, and he said: "I had a vision last night, I guess you'd call it that. Couldn't get to sleep worrying about the detective . . ."

"You're not sure he is a detective," Matt said again.

"And I saw Alaska as a huge ship, much bigger than the *Senator* lying out there, and it survived this storm only because it was firmly anchored. This gold rush has to die down, and when it does I think we must do everything possible to strengthen our lifeline to Seattle. As it goes, we go."

But Missy said: "I'm not so sure. Any good that comes to Alaska, will come from Alaska."

On the evening of the seventeenth when the storm began to abate, Tom and Matt walked through the heavy rain to survey the damage, and were aghast at the large number of houses destroyed, the small number of tents left standing. Nome, with no protection of any kind against the Bering Sea, would have been erased from the map had it not been for the persistence of the miners who were prepared to rebuild their city of gold.

"What we must have, sooner or later," Tom said, "is a sea wall to give us protection against such storms."

As they walked in the fading light they were joined by several businessmen, some of whose establishments had been completely washed away. Others found two feet of water in their stores, and only the better of the sixty-odd saloons were in any condition to reopen.

"The rain did some good," one of the men said. "At least the Golden Gate Hotel didn't burn again."

It was when they came to the beach, to any part of its wild twenty-six-mile extent, that they appreciated the tremendous power of this storm, because not a single piece of gold-dredging equipment was visible. The little box sluices and the huge machines that gobbled up the sand and wrestled it for gold were gone, every one of them. The beach had been swept clean, without leaving a vestige of the great gold rush, and when one of the town's clergymen joined the group, he could not refrain from saying: "Look for yourselves, men. It's as if God had grown tired of our excesses and had wiped the slate clean. There's your gold rush."

"No," a miner said. "Out there's your gold rush, the men waiting on that ship to come ashore. Two days from now, the beach'll be covered with men the way a piece of venison gets covered with ants."

"I agree with you, Reverend," another miner said, "but I reach a contrary conclusion. I think God sent the storm, but He did it to rearrange the placer rights. And to move in a fresh cargo of gold. I can hardly wait to get started again." And as he spoke two older men, dragging behind them some monstrous contraption, came down to the beach, picked a spot where gold had once been abundant, and resumed dredging the sand for gold.

But the lasting image as the historic storm of September 1900 subsided was the large steamer *Senator* far offshore riding the turbulent waves and waiting to discharge the next influx of gold seekers. It held also a Mr. Reed, who was more impatient to get ashore than any of the would-be miners.

If he had been visibly restive at sea, he became almost unnoticeable ashore. Registering at the undamaged Golden Gate Hotel as Mr.

Frank Reed, Denver, Colorado, he spent three days familiarizing himself with the lay of Nome, where its original claims had been along the streams and how the men who came swarming back to the beaches like flies established their rights to this stretch of sand or that. He visited the main stores to see what they were selling and tested the beer at several saloons, where he said nothing but did listen. He was appalled, as any sensible man would be, when he saw the way Nome handled its sewage, and he ate only sparingly those first days.

On his fourth day in town he began visiting the so-called leaders, and his questions were so diverse and unrevealing that three older men went to the Golden Gate asking to talk with him, and on the way they encountered Tom Venn and took him along.

"Mr. Reed, your activities have perplexed us."

"You're no more perplexed than I am."

"Who are you?"

The stranger considered this for some moments and his whole inclination was to reveal himself to these honest, worried men, but since long experience had warned him against being premature, he temporized: "Gentlemen, I'm not at liberty to answer your questions yet, but believe me, I come meaning no embarrassment to men like you." He knew they deserved to know more, so taking a document from his inside pocket, he said: "You're Mr. Kennedy. I was told you were a man of honor. I came here to see you." He read off two other names with similar comment, and then he turned to Tom: "I don't believe I know you."

"You didn't come for me?" Tom blurted out in tremendous relief.

"I didn't come for anybody."

"I'm Tom Venn. Ross & Raglan."

"Well, well!" Mr. Reed cried, evidencing a surprise which he could not mask. "I had no idea you'd be so young. You're the man I wanted to see first."

Tom felt his knees shake and his mouth go dry, but he had agreed with Missy that he would brave this thing out: "What did you want to see me about?" and now Mr. Reed simply had to disclose part of his hand: "The Concannon case."

"Oh!" Tom sighed so heavily that if Mr. Reed had come to look into a major bank robbery, he would have had to judge by that sigh that Tom was the thief.

"You signed Mr. Concannon's death certificate, did you not?"

"Yes. We have no coroner, you know."

"I know."

"So they asked some of us . . . I think Mr. Kennedy here signed it too."

"That's right," Mr. Reed said. "His name was on the document. Now let's sit down, gentlemen, and you tell me what you know about the Concannon case."

He was like a ferret, dissecting even the most remote details of what had been a normal accident at sea when ships rolled and booms snapped: "The *Alacrity* was an R&R ship, was it not?"

"A small one," Venn said, "built for the Skagway run but diverted when the great rush to the beaches began."

"Isn't it rather strange that an employee of the company that owns a ship involved in a fatal accident should authenticate the death warrant?"

"At first I didn't even know he died on our *Alacrity*. I was just called in to sign the papers. Somebody had to, or Mrs. Concannon wouldn't get her insurance."

"Yes, the people in Denver explained that."

"Then you're not from the insurance company?"

"No. They alerted the authorities that something odd might have happened in the Concannon case, and it seemed to fit a pattern."

"What fitted a pattern?" an older man asked, and Mr. Reed smiled: "That's a penetrating question, sir, and it deserves an answer. But I can't give you one yet. I will repeat, I'm not here to inquire about any of you. We've had only the finest reports about you men. Now let's break up, and the less you say about this the better. I know you'll want to discuss it among yourselves, but please, please don't talk about it in public." Then, as the men were about to leave, he added: "Anything else you can tell me about the Concannon case, well, I'd appreciate hearing it."

"Mr. Reed," Tom said firmly. "It could not have been murder."

"Of that I'm sure," Mr. Reed said.

On the fifth day after the storm Mr. Reed summoned that first group of leaders to the Golden Gate along with eight or nine others, including all the clergymen in town, and when they were settled he stood before them.

"Gentlemen, you've been very patient and I appreciate it. You have every right to know who I am and what I'm here for. My name is Harold Snyder. I'm a federal marshal from the California District, and I'm here to take action in the fraudulent conversion of property belonging to miners who had perfectly legal claims on Anvil Creek." Before his listeners could even gasp, he rasped out orders like a spitting machine gun: "I want the fullest details of what happened to claims *Five, Six* and *Seven Above.* And I should like to meet tomorrow with Lars Skjellerup, citizen of Norway, and with Mikkel Sana, citizen of Lapland. What nation would that be a part of?"

"Could be Norway, Sweden, Finland, or maybe even a tip of Russia."

"And the Siberian known as Arkikov, no first name." Then followed a barrage of instructions: "Get me a plat of Anvil Creek. All papers relating to titles. A timetable of the various meetings. And a complete list of miners who attended the first two meetings." He ended with a statement which electrified the businessmen: "Before this session convened I stationed three of your members, including one clergyman, to watch every move that Judge Grant and Marvin Hoxey make. These watchers will not allow them to burn any papers." With that, he dismissed the meeting.

The next day the original claimants to *Five, Six* and *Seven Above* arrived, and when the doors were closed he conducted as minute an investigation as possible, using maps, diagrams, calendars for dates and lists of earlier testimony to nail down the frightful miscarriages of justice which officials in San Francisco had begun to suspect.

At the end of two days he had unequivocal evidence against the two thieves which convinced him but which, he was afraid, would not count for much in a court of law, and apparently Judge Grant and Hoxey knew this, for they continued to operate as usual, with the latter placing aboard the *Senator* a huge shipment of gold to go south to his account.

"The problem," Mr. Snyder warned the committee, "is that what these two rascals have done is almost impossible to prove to a jury. You men know better than anyone else that Judge Grant has been faithless to his oath as a judge, because it was your property he stole. But how do you prove it in court? You know that Hoxey stole your leases, but how are you going to prove it? Juries don't care much for paper rights. However, if we could nail them in the Concannon case . . ."

"What is the Concannon case?"

"We think they bilked a widow of her just insurance. The Denver people smelled a rat, but the rascals covered their tracks. We have nothing to go on, but if we could put a defenseless widow on the stand . . ." He stopped. "Dammit, doesn't anybody know anything about that case?"

It was then that it occurred to Tom Venn that Missy could know something about Concannon. "I can't be sure, Mr. Snyder," Tom said, "but I think Missy Peckham might."

"Bring her here. Now."

So Tom ran first to his store, where he grabbed Matt Murphy: "Go to Judge Grant's—he mustn't see me—and fetch Missy."

"Here?"

"No, the Golden Gate."

When Matt reached Judge Grant's office he was stopped by the three guards watching the place: "You can't go in there."

"Mr. Snyder wants Missy."

"Judge Grant won't let her go."

"I'm going to count three, and then I'm damn well going in and get her."

Missy was delivered, and when she and Tom and Matt sat with Mr. Snyder, the questioning was blunt.

"What do you know about the Concannon case?"

"Not suicide, not murder," Missy said. "Insurance policy. Judge Grant and Mr. Hoxey stole a lot of it."

"How do you know that?"

"I just know."

"Damn it all, everybody says 'I just know' and nobody knows anything that can be used before a jury."

"Well, I do know," Missy said stubbornly.

"How do you know?" Mr. Snyder stormed.

"Because I wrote it all down."

Mr. Snyder, feeling life flow back into the veins of his case, forced himself to ask in a low voice: "You kept notes?"

"Yes."

"Why?"

"Because after one week on the job I knew these two men were up to no good."

"Two men?"

"Yes. I typed all of Mr. Hoxey's letters."

Silence, then very cautiously Mr. Snyder asked: "You took notes on Hoxey's dealings too?"

"I did."

"And where are those notes?"

Now came a very long silence, for Missy was recalling Skagway when Soapy Smith's men dressed like clergymen to defraud, and like mail carriers to steal, and like freight forwarders to gain possession of goods which they never shipped. In those ugly days every man was suspect, and she could even see Blacktooth Otto scurrying like a rat up to the scene of that terrible avalanche to steal the packs of the dead. Like one of Soapy Smith's henchmen, Mr. Snyder could be an imposter brought to Nome by Judge Grant and Hoxey to ferret out and destroy any evidence against them. She would confide nothing further to this unknown man.

"Where are your notes?" Mr. Snyder repeated.

Missy was mute.

"Tell him," Matt said, and his plea was so insistent that she turned in anguish to Tom and blurted out: "It's just like Skagway. How can we know who he really is? How can we trust him? How do we know he isn't working for Hoxey?"

It was a cry that both Tom and Mr. Snyder understood, for when a society allows total chaos, it engenders total suspicion, and the normal processes by which any society is held on a steady keel—trust, dedication, reliability, penalty for wrongdoing—corrode, and things begin to fall apart, for the props are gone.

Patiently, forthright Harold Snyder, no longer a mysterious Mr. Reed, produced his credentials for Missy to finger and digest. He was indeed a federal marshal; he did have orders from the federal court in San Francisco to inquire into the malfeasance of a judge in Nome, and he did have the power to arrest. But still Missy was unconvinced: "Soapy's men had documents. Soapy printed them himself." Looking in turn at each of the three men, she asked: "How can I really know?"

"Missy," Tom said. "Remember what Sergeant Kirby told you when Superintendent Steele wanted to protect your money? 'If you can't trust Superintendent Steele, you can't trust anybody.' Same situation."

She saw that it was, that at some point in any crisis you simply had to trust someone, and she indicated that she would surrender her notebook, and with that, all the fight went out of this sturdy little woman. Too much had hit her in the face in too short a time, and she let her head fall heavily to the table and covered it with her arms.

Matt and Tom left her there, and after a hurried trip to the cabin, returned with the notebook, which Matt placed on the table unopened.

"Is this the famous book, Missy?"

"It is."

"Now let's go over each item carefully."

In the late afternoon Snyder asked: "What does this entry mean?" and she said: "Judge Grant had me claim for seven hours of extra work which I didn't do, but when I was paid he kept the money."

Snyder pushed the book away as if its odor offended him: "Jesus Christ, if a man had his salary, you would not expect him to cheat on his secretary."

But it was when he reached the Hoxey entries that he became really enraged: "I'm an officer of the law and I take it very seriously, but I find myself wishing that I could lock these two in a room with that big Norwegian, that Siberian and that tough little Lapp. I'll bet they could handle this case in fifteen minutes and save the taxpayers a lot of money."

And then, on his second morning with Missy's notebook, he came upon the Concannon case, and he was sickened: "A woman loses her husband in a crazy accident that cannot be explained, and two skunks defraud her of her insurance."

He could read no further. Storming from the hotel, he went to where Judge Grant and Hoxey were skulking and slapped handcuffs on them. "Where are you taking us?" Judge Grant whined, and Snyder said: "Protective custody. So these people here don't lynch you." Two days later, when the *Senator* sailed south, these two were aboard. They had been in Nome less than four months, but in that time they had smeared across the face of blindfolded American justice one of her most disgraceful stains.

The saga of Nome ground to a stumbling halt. The Golden Gate Hotel burned again and was rebuilt. The glacier of frozen urine filled the alleys once more in winter and melted into the sea in summer. The golden beaches continued to throw up gold for another year and then were exhausted, while the placer mines along Anvil Creek continued modestly for several decades.

But there had been stunning if brief glory. In one twelve-month period alone, Nome produced $7,500,000 worth of gold, more than the price paid for all Alaska back in 1867. In all, more than $115,000,000 was taken out when gold was valued at $20 an ounce.

Claims *Five, Six* and *Seven Above,* once more controlled by their rightful owners, produced only modest fortunes because Marvin Hoxey had sequestered the best portion of the gold, and had hidden it so effectively that during his trial in San Francisco and his time in the penitentiary, the government was unable to find his two million in loot. He kept it all.

An outraged judge sentenced him to fifteen years, just punishment for a man who had defrauded so many of so much, but after three months President McKinley pardoned him on the grounds that his health was threatened by imprisonment, and besides, everyone knew he had been, in prior life, an exemplary citizen. He would function another thirty productive years as one of the most effective lobbyists in Washington, continuing to prevent any constructive legislation for Alaska's self-governance. Legislators listened to him, for he continued to boast: "I know Alaska like the back of my hand and, to speak frankly, it's just not ready for self-government."

Judge Grant's case had a surprising conclusion. As Harold Snyder had predicted, despite Missy's notebook, no specific charges could be proved against him, for with an almost animal cunning he had, during his frantic weeks in Nome, conducted his affairs so carefully and with such complete knowledge of what was happening, that he manipulated what evidence that did surface to condemn Hoxey while revealing himself as a forthright Iowa judge striving to do his best. Snyder, listening in court to the evidence, burst into laughter several times: "All of us in Nome thought Judge Grant was the dummy. Used as a cat's paw by clever Marvin Hoxey. No, Grant was the smart one. He maneuvered it so that he went free and Hoxey went to jail." At the end of one court session in which Judge Grant's evidence absolved him and damaged his partner, Marvin came over to Snyder and said: "I was Hoxey, he was foxy."

Declared "Not guilty" by a federal jury, Grant returned to Iowa, where, after a lapse of two years during which he mended his fences, he resumed his position on the bench before which his father had practiced, and there he was known favorably as "the eminent jurist who brought a system of justice to Alaska." Repeatedly, while he was on the bench or delivering orations locally or in Chicago, admiring people would comment: "He looks like a judge," proving that in many circumstances it is more important to look like something than to be something.

Tom Venn prospered, as such dedicated and well-trained young men so often do. He kept his assayer's scales clear of rust, and when the R&R store in Nome was closed because of the catastrophic drop in population—32,000 in 1900, counting drifters; 1,200 three years later, counting almost no working miners—he was promoted to the big store in Juneau, the new capital of Alaska, where he tended to business as before, but also began looking carefully at all his younger female customers for a potential marriage partner.

The biggest change came in the lives of Missy Peckham and Matt Murphy. No, his wife in Ireland did not die so that he could remarry, and since they were Catholic, divorce was not possible, but one July afternoon after the Yukon thawed, a tall stoop-shouldered stranger arrived in Nome, taking a room not in the expensive Golden Gate but in one of the cheaper makeshift places, half wood, half canvas.

He registered, and threw his canvas duffel in a corner without unpacking. Then he started roaming the streets, and after a few inquiries, was directed to a miserable shack, where he knocked on the door and announced himself: "I'm John Klope," and Missy, showing no surprise, quietly said: "Come in, John. Sit down. Can I get you coffee?"

He wanted to know what had happened to them, so Matt recalled his bicycle trip down the Yukon and he and Missy explained how they had fitted in with the famous gold rush: "Got here too late, like always, for the good placers. Didn't even file a claim. Missed the beaches too. That was a madhouse. We found jobs, and I'm sure we did better than most of the people on the beach."

"What kind of job?"

"Missy worked for that corrupt judge, what a mess. I worked for Tom Venn when the store got big."

"Tom Venn! Is he in town?"

"Juneau. Big promotion."

"How is Tom? How'd he do?"

"I just said, big promotion."

"He was a fine boy." He sipped his coffee, then pointed to the mean quarters they shared. "Things not going too well?"

"After the gold stopped," Matt said. "You know how it is."

"How's it with you, John?" Missy asked, for he, too, looked as if he had fallen upon bad times.

"You know how we dug that damned hole?"

"I sure do," Matt almost groaned. "You ever strike anything down there?"

"Lots of rock, no colors."

"I'm sorry," Missy said. "You gave it such an honest try, but your claim was up so high . . . everybody knew the gold was down on the creek where the claims were already taken."

The three oddly matched people, older now and sobered by their experiences, sat quietly cradling their cups, and after a while Klope said: "That must have been a wild storm, the one that blew all the machines off the beach."

"It was."

"We saw pictures. Looked pretty awful."

"Dawson must be a ghost town these days," Matt said.

"You wouldn't recognize it. Not one tent left."

"Remember ours? The grease on the canvas? Those good sourdough flapjacks you taught us how to make?"

As they reminisced about the old days with affectionate nostalgia, Missy said: "You remember the Belgian Mare? Her cribs here burned twice and were blown away once, and we were sorry for her till we found that she had sweet-talked miners into building them for her and she didn't lose a nickel. After each disaster she hiked her prices and made a fortune. One day she just left. Yep, John, she just up and left. Eight girls stranded on the beach without a nickel."

"Where'd she go?"

"Belgium, to buy a farm near Antwerp."

The day was wasting, and it was obvious to Missy that John Klope had something more important to talk about than the storm or the changing fortunes of the Mare. A startling thought exploded in her mind: My God, he's come here to ask me to marry him! And she began to draw back, because in Matt Murphy she had met a man of almost ideal temperament. He was kind, he was witty, he could smell out rascals and identify good people, and she loved sharing life with him, even if he could never seem to find a steady job. But since there was always need for her secretarial skills, she was more than willing to share her income with Matt.

Klope coughed, edged about in his chair, and diddled with his fingers. Finally he said: "Haven't you heard?"

"About what?"

"About me?" When they shook their heads, he said with embarrassment: "I always told you there had to be gold down there."

"But you never found it. You said so."

"Not in the hole the three of us worked. But when I got down to solid rock and threw out my laterals . . ."

"You did that while I was still helping," Matt said.

"Yep, and I found nothing. But I got so mad with all that work, and I was so sure about the ancient river I talked about that I dug me another hole, way down. Didn't you hear?"

"What happened, John?"

"Sarqaq kept with me. Maybe we'd find something. Back down to bedrock, me thawing, him raising the muck, and this time when I sent out my laterals . . ."

He stopped and looked at his two good friends: "First pan from the big crevice, nine hundred dollars . . . in nuggets . . . not flakes."

Yes, before that one lucky lateral was exhausted, John Klope, assisted by the lame Eskimo Sarqaq, took out three hundred and twenty thousand dollars of some of the purest gold produced along the Klondike, His persistence had led him to the deposits laid down by a river that had flowed two hundred thousand years ago.

After Missy and Matt fell silent, emotionally exhausted from exploring all aspects of this tremendous stroke of good fortune, Klope was ready to make the awkward speech which had drawn him from Dawson to Nome on his way back to his farm at Moose Hide, Idaho: "You two and Tom Venn were as much a part of that strike as I was. You kept me goin' in the bad days. Sarqaq, too. All the time I dug out that rich lateral and sent up that muck crawlin' with gold, I thought of you folks."

His voice broke: "You know, a man can't work underground for two years else'n someone believes in him. Here." He thrust into Missy's hand an envelope, and when she opened it two drafts fell out, one to her, one to Matt, drawn upon a Canadian bank. Each check was for twenty thousand dollars. "I'll mail Tom's to him in Juneau," Klope said.

And he did one thing more. As he was about to leave the shack he took from his worn backpack a parcel, which he placed on the rude table: "If you ever open another restaurant, you'll need this." And when Missy removed the wrapper, she realized that Klope was placing in her care one of his prized possessions: the sourdough starter whose recorded history was now nearly a century old.

• • •

Two days later Klope was aboard a ship to Seattle, and as he left he epitomized all the lonely men who had come to Alaska in search of gold. He was one of the few whose dreams had come true, but only at terrible cost. He had braved the Yukon Flats in a blizzard; he had fought his way up the frozen Yukon past Eagle; he had slaved in the shafts atop Eldorado; he had lost Missy, the woman he loved, and Matt Murphy, a partner he had trusted. But he did get his gold.

And it changed him not at all. He did not walk any straighter. He did not suddenly read good books. He made no firm friends to replace the ones he had left behind, and his life had been altered neither negatively nor positively. As an honorable man, he had given twenty thousand dollars to each of the four to whom he knew he was indebted—Missy, Matt, Tom Venn, Sarqaq—but when he returned to Idaho he would do no spectacular thing with what was left. He would not form a bank for assistance to farmers, nor endow chairs at any of the Idaho colleges, nor start a library, nor finance a hospital. He had left Idaho in those first heady days of July 1897, lived through times of cataclysmic changes, and now he was returning home in the sputtering aftermath—the simple inarticulate man he was when he had come to the arctic. There were thousands like him.

Missy Peckham had developed in the Klondike and Nome into a woman of towering strength, beautiful in her integrity, and Tom Venn had grown from a callow youth into an amazingly mature man, but they had achieved this through hardship and failure, not success, and the lessons they acquired would last them through life. John Klope, like so many others, would bring home only gold, which would slowly slip through his fingers, until in old age he would ask: "Where did it go? What did it accomplish?"

The rigs along Bonanza and Eldorado were closed down. The shacks that had protected miners along the Mackenzie during the arctic winters were slowly falling apart, and the marvelous golden beaches of Nome were once again mere sand. When new storms howled in from the Bering Sea they found no tents to destroy, for all was now as it had been before.

No more will be said about gold in this chronicle. Exciting small finds would continue to be made near the new town of Fairbanks, and one of the most rewarding of all operations would be the deep quartz mine across from Juneau, but there would never be another Klondike, another Nome. Through some miracle never to be fully understood, at those favored points gold had somehow risen to the surface and been eroded away, abraded by sand and wind and ice to be deposited arbitrarily in one place and not another.

The metal that drove men mad behaved as crazily as did the men, and in those frenzied years at the close of the century, turned the world's attention to Alaska, but its effect on the area was no more lasting than it had been upon John Klope.

There were, however, three men whose lives were changed by the miraculous gold of Nome. Lars Skjellerup became an American citizen, and one morning, while at the beach watching the arrival of passengers from a ship anchored in the roadstead, he spotted on the near end of the lighter bringing them ashore a wonderfully vivacious young woman, and he was so captivated by her smile, her look of eagerness and her general demeanor, that when sailors manning the lighter shouted to Eskimo porters: "Come! Take the people ashore!" he ran quickly into the surf, offered himself to her, and shivered with a new excitement as she was lifted onto his back.

Step by careful step he carried her to the beach, his mind in a whirl, and after she was some fifteen yards inland she said quietly: "Don't you think you could put me down now?"

Introducing himself somewhat awkwardly, he learned that Miss Armstrong had come from Virginia to teach school in Nome. In the days that followed he haunted the schoolhouse, and when everybody including Miss Armstrong was aware that he was smitten with her, he made the most extraordinary proposal: "I'm taking the job as Presbyterian missionary at Barrow. Would you honor me to come along?" And in this way a young woman who had fled Virginia for the romance of Alaska found herself a missionary's wife in farthest Barrow, where her husband spent most of his time teaching Eskimos how to handle the reindeer replenishment stock he and his wife had driven north.

Mikkel Sana deposited his money in a Juneau bank and returned to Lapland for a bride, but could convince none of those cautious Lapp beauties that he was really a very rich man. He finally persuaded the third daughter of a man who owned three hundred reindeer to take a chance, and what a surprise she encountered when she accompanied Sana to Juneau and found that the bank account really did exist. After she learned English, which she did in six months, she became the town librarian.

In Arkikov's life, a wife did not feature, at least not at first. Having been abused because he was not an American citizen, and having lost *Seven Above,* he was determined to repair this deficiency, and as soon as his claim was returned after Hoxey's arrest, he started naturalization procedures. Of course, since Alaska still had no regular form of civil government, this proved so difficult that twice he almost gave up, but his partner Skjellerup persuaded him to continue, and after Lars became the missionary in Barrow, the letters he sent to Seattle in support of Arkikov's petition were so persuasive that citizenship was granted.

When a revenue cutter officer who came to Nome explained that in America, as opposed to Siberia, it was customary for a man to have first and last names, Arkikov asked: "Me get what name?" and the man said: "Well, some people like the name of their occupation."

"My what?"

"Your job. If you were a baker in the old country, you'd take the name Baker. A goldsmith becomes Goldsmith. What were you in the old country?"

"What country?"

"Siberia."

"Me herd reindeer."

Since it was widely known that this fellow Arkikov now had some sixty thousand dollars in the bank, he had to be treated with respect, and the officer coughed: "We don't hand out many names like Arkikov Reindeer-herder. How about keeping Arkikov as your last name and putting two American names in front?"

"Maybe. What names?"

"Two pairs are very popular. George Washington Arkikov . . ."

"Who is he?"

"Father of this country. Fine general."

"Me like general."

"The other pair is just as good. Abraham Lincoln Arkikov."

"What he did?"

"He freed the slaves."

"What you mean slaves?" And when the man explained what Lincoln had done—Arkikov had never seen an American black—the choice was made: "In Siberia got slaves. Me like Lincoln."

So he became A. L. Arkikov, Nome, Alaska, and in time he took an Eskimo wife, and their three children attended the University of Washington in Seattle, for their father was a rich man.

X

SALMON

East of Juneau, Taku Inlet, a splendid body of water which in Scandinavia would be called a fjord, wound and twisted its way far inland, passing bleak headlands at one time, low hills covered with trees at another. On all sides mountains with snow-covered peaks rose in the background, some soaring to more than seven and eight thousand feet.

A notable feature of Taku was the family of powerful glaciers that pushed their snouts right to the water's edge, where from time to time they calved off huge icebergs which came thundering into the cold waters with echoes reverberating among the hills and mountains. It was a wild, lonely, majestic body of narrow water, and it drained a vast area reaching into Canada almost to the lakes which the Chilkoot miners traversed in 1897 and '98. To travel upstream in the Taku was to probe into the heart of the continent, with the visible glaciers edging down from much more extensive fields inland, where the ice cover had existed for thousands upon thousands of years.

Taku Inlet ran mainly north and south, with the glaciers crawling down to the western shore, but on the eastern bank, directly opposite the snout of a beautiful emerald glacier, a small but lively river with many waterfalls debouched, and nine miles up its course a lake of heavenly grace opened up, not large in comparison with many of

Alaska's lakes, but incomparable with its ring of six or, from some vantage points, seven mountains which formed a near-circle to protect it.

This remote spot, which not many visitors, or natives either, ever saw, had been named by Arkady Voronov, during one of his explorations, Lake Pleiades, as his journal explained:

> On this day we camped opposite the beautiful green glacier which noses into the inlet on the west. A river scintillating in the sunlight attracted my attention, and with two sailors from the *Romanov,* I explored it for a distance of nine miles. It would be quite unnavigable for even a canoe, because it came tumbling down over rocks, even forming at times small waterfalls eight and ten feet high.

> Since it was obvious to us that we were not going to find a better waterway on this course, and since grizzly bears started at us twice, to be deflected by shots over their heads, we had decided to return to our ship with nothing but a fine walk for our labors when one of the sailors, who was breaking the path upstream, shouted back: "Captain Voronov! Hurry! Something remarkable!"

> When we overtook him we saw that his cry was not misleading, for ahead of us, rimmed by six beautiful mountains, lay one of the clearest small lakes I have ever seen. It lay at an elevation, I should guess from the nature of our climb, of about nine hundred feet, not much higher, and it was marred by nothing. Only the bears and whatever fish were in the lake inhabited this magnificent refuge, and we decided on the moment, all three of us, to camp here for the night, for we were loath to depart from such an idyllic place.

> I therefore asked one of the men to volunteer for a hurried trip back to the *Romanov* to fetch tents and to bring with him one or two other sailors who might like to share the experience with us, and the man who stepped forward said: "Captain, with so many bears, I think he should come too," indicating his partner. "And he better bring his gun." I consented, for I realized that I, with my own gun, could protect myself in a settled spot, while they, being on the move, might attract more attention from the bears.

Off they went, and I was left alone in this place of rare beauty. But I did not stay in one place, as planned, because I was lured by the constantly changing attitude of the six mountains which stood guard, and when I had moved some distance to the east, I saw to my surprise that there were not six mountains but seven, and in that moment I determined the name of this lake, Pleiades, because we all know that this little constellation has seven stars, but without a telescope we can see only six. As mythology teaches, the visible six sisters each married gods, but Merope, the hidden seventh, fell in love with a mortal, and thus hides her face in shame.

Lake Pleiades it became, and on three subsequent visits to this eastern area I camped there. It remains the happiest memory of my duty in Alaska, and if, in future generations, some descendant of mine elects to return to these Russian lands, I hope he or she will read these notes and seek out this jewel of a lake.

In September 1900 one hundred million extremely minute eggs of the sockeye salmon were deposited in little streams feeding into that lake. They were delivered by female salmon in lots of four thousand each, and we shall follow the adventures of one such lot, and one salmon within that lot.

The sockeye, one of five distinct types of salmon populating Alaskan waters, had been named by a German naturalist serving Vitus Bering. Using the proper Latin name for salmon plus a native word, he called it *Oncorhynchus nerka,* and the solitary egg of that hundred million whose progress we shall watch will bear that name.

The egg which, when fertilized by milt, or sperm, would become Nerka was placed by its mother in a carefully prepared redd, or nest, in the gravelly bottom of a little stream near the lake and left there without further care for six months. It was abandoned not through the carelessness of its parents but because it was their inescapable nature to die soon after depositing and fertilizing the eggs which perpetuated their kind.

The site chosen for Nerka's redd had to fill several requirements. It had to be close to the lake in which the growing salmon would live for three years. The stream chosen must have a gravel bottom so that the minute eggs could be securely hidden; it must provide a good supply of other gravel which could be thrown over the redd to hide the incubating eggs; and most curious of all, it had to have a constant supply of fresh water welling up from below at an unwavering temperature of about 47° Fahrenheit and with a supersupply of oxygen.

It so happened that the area surrounding Lake Pleiades had varied radically during the past hundred thousand years, for when the Bering land bridge was open, the ocean level had dropped, taking the lake's level down with it, and as the different levels of the lake fluctuated, so did its shoreline. This meant that various benches had been established at various times, and Nerka's mother had chosen a submerged bench which had through the generations accumulated much gravel of a size that salmon preferred.

But how was the constant supply of upwelling water at a reliable temperature delivered? Just as some ancient river had existed where John Klope's present-day Eldorado Creek flowed, but at a much different level, so another subterranean river, emerging from deep in the roots of the surrounding mountains, surged up through the gravels of that sunken bench, providing the rich supply of oxygen and constant temperature that kept both the lake and its salmon vital.

So for six months, his parents long dead, Nerka in his minute egg nestled beneath the gravel while from below flowed this life-giving water. It was one of the most precise operations of nature—perfect flow of water, perfect temperature, perfect hiding place, perfect beginning for one of the most extraordinary life histories in the animal kingdom. And one final attribute of Lake Pleiades could be considered the most remarkable of all, as we shall see six years later: the rocks which lined the lake and the waters which flowed into it from the submerged rivulets carried minute traces—perhaps one in a billion parts—of this mineral and that, with the result that Lake Pleiades had a kind of lacustrine fingerprint which would differentiate it from any other lake or river in the entire world.

Any salmon born, as Nerka would soon be, in Lake Pleiades would bear with him always the unique imprint of his lake. Was this memory carried in his bloodstream, or in his brain, or in his olfactory system, or perhaps in a group of these attributes in conjunction with the phases of the moon or the turning of the earth? No one knew. One could only guess, but that Nerka and Lake Pleiades on the western shore of Alaska were indissolubly linked, no one could deny.

Still only a minute egg, he nestled in the gravel as subterranean waters welled up through the bench to sustain him, and each week he grew closer to birth. In January 1901, deep under the thick ice which pressed down upon the tributary stream, the egg which would become Nerka, along with the other four thousand fertilized eggs of his group, underwent a dramatic change. His egg, a brilliant orange color, showed through the skin an eye with a bright rim and an intensely black center. Unquestionably it was an eye, and it bespoke the emerging life within the egg; the unwavering supply of cold, fresh water welling up through the gravel ensured the continuance and growth of that life. But the natural attrition that decimated these minute creatures was savage. Of Nerka's original four thousand, only six hundred survived the freezing gravel, the diseases and the predation by larger fish.

In late February of that year these six hundred eggs of Nerka's group began to undergo a series of miraculous changes, at the conclusion of which they would become full-fledged salmon. The embryo Nerka slowly absorbed the nutrients from the yolk sac, and as the interchange occurred, he grew and developed swimming motions. Now he obtained the first of a bewildering series of names, each marking a major step in his growth. He was an *alevin.*

When his yolk was completely absorbed, the creature was still not a proper fish, only a minute translucent wand with enormous black eyes and, fastened to his belly, a huge sac of liquid nutrient upon which he must live for the next crucial weeks. He was an ugly, misshapen, squirming thing, and any passing predator could gulp down hundreds of him at a time. But he was a potential fish with a monstrously long head, functioning eyes and a trailing translucent tail. Rapidly in the constantly moving waters of his stream he began to consume plankton, and with the growth which this produced, his protruding sac was gradually resorbed until the swimming thing was transformed into a self-sufficient baby fishling.

At this point Nerka left his natal stream and moved the short distance into the lake, where he was properly called a *fry,* and in this condition he showed every characteristic, except size, of a normal fresh-water fish. He would breathe like one through his gills; he would eat like one; he would learn to swim swiftly to dodge larger predators; and it would seem to any observer that he was well adapted to spend the rest of his life in this lake. It would, in those first years, have been preposterous to think that one day, still to be determined by his rate of growth and maturation, he would be able to convert his entire life processes so radically that he would be completely adapted to salt water; at this stage of his development salt water would have been an inclement milieu.

Ignorant of his strange destiny, Nerka spent 1901 and 1902 adjusting to life within the lake, which presented two contradictory aspects. On the one hand it was a savage home where salmon fry were destroyed at appalling rates. Larger fish hungered for him. Birds sought him out, especially the merganser ducks that abounded on the lake, but also kingfishers and stiltlike birds with long legs and even longer beaks that could dart through the water with incredible accuracy to snap up a tasty meal of salmon. It seemed as if everything in the lake lived on fry, and half of Nerka's fellow survivors vanished into gullets before the end of the first year.

But the lake was also a nurturing mother which provided young fry a multitude of dark places in which to hide during daylight hours and a jungle of underwater grasses in which they could lose themselves if light, dancing off their shimmering skin, betrayed their presence to the larger fish. Nerka learned to move only in the darkest nights and to avoid those places where these fish liked to feed, and since in these two years he was not even three inches long, and most things that swam were larger and more powerful than he, it was only by exercising these precautions that he did survive.

He was now a *fingerling,* a most appropriate name, since he was about the size of a woman's little finger, and as his appetite increased, the comforting lake provided him, in its safer waters, nutritious insect larvae and various kinds of plankton. As he grew older he fed upon the myriad tiny fishes which flashed through the lake, but his main delight was twisting upward, head out of water, to snare some unsuspecting insect. Meanwhile, in the town of Juneau, a scant seventeen miles distant over a glacier-strewn route, impossible to travel on foot, forty miles by an easy water route, creatures of a much different life history were working out their own tangled destinies.

When Tom Venn came down to Juneau to open the Ross & Raglan store in the spring of 1902, he found the thriving little town a joy after the bitter cold and raw lawlessness of Nome. The settlement which many had been proposing as the new capital of Alaska, replacing outmoded Sitka, which lay off to one side at the edge of the Pacific Ocean, was already an attractive place, even though it was cramped into a narrow strip between tall mountains to the northeast and a beautiful sea channel to the southwest.

Wherever Tom looked in Juneau he saw variation, for even nearby Douglas Island, which crowded in from the south, had its own distinctive mountains, while big ships from Seattle berthed a hand's breadth from the main streets. But the majesty of Juneau, which differentiated it from all other Alaskan towns, was the huge, glistening Mendenhall Glacier, which nosed its way to the water's edge west of town. It was a magnificent, living body of ice that snapped and crackled as it ground its way toward the sea, yet so available that children could take their picnics along its edge in summer.

Another glacier, less famous and visible, approached Juneau from the opposite direction, as if it sought to enclose the little town in its embrace, but the encroaching ice did not determine the temperature of Juneau, which was warmed by the great currents sweeping in from Japan. It had a pleasant climate, marked by much rain and fog but punctuated by days of the most enchanting purity when the sun made all components of the varied scene sparkle like jewels.

After he had been in town for only a few days, Tom selected the location for his store, a lot on Franklin Street near the corner of Front. It had the advantage of facing the waterfront, so that he could have easy access to the ships that docked there. But it also had a disadvantage, because a small hut already occupied it, and he would have to buy the shack if he wanted the land. In the long interests of his company, he decided to do so.

When the time came to close the deal, he learned that the land and the building had different owners. The land belonged to a gentleman from Seattle, the building to a local Tlingit who worked along the waterfront. So, after paying for the land, Tom found himself in negotiation with a fine-looking, dark-skinned Indian in his late thirties. An able fellow according to reports along the docks, he bore the unusual name of Sam Bigears, and as soon as Tom saw him he supposed that he was going to have trouble with this taciturn fellow. But that was not the case.

"You want house, I glad to sell."

"Where will you go?"

"I have land, fine spot Taku Inlet. Pleiades River."

"So you're leaving Juneau?"

"No. One day canoe trip, tassall." Tom was to learn that Sam Bigears used this comprehensive word to dismiss a world of worries: "Fish broke the line, got away, tassall," or "Rain seven days, tassall."

Within fifteen minutes Tom and Bigears agreed upon a price for the shack—sixty dollars—and when Venn handed over the check, Bigears chuckled: "Thank you. Maybe house worth nothing. Maybe belong Mr. Harris, along with ground."

"Well, it was your house. You were living in it. And I'd be very happy if you stayed around to help me build the store."

"I like that," and the informal partnership was formed, with Sam Bigears assuming control of materials and the time sheets of the other workmen. He proved himself to be an intelligent, clever craftsman with a positive genius for devising new ways of performing old tasks. Since he was good at woodworking, he took charge of the doors and stairs.

"Where did you learn how to build a stair?" Tom asked one day. "That's not easy."

"Many buildings," Sam said, pointing to Front and Franklin streets where stores and warehouses clustered. "I work with good German carpenter. I like wood, trees, everything."

One morning when Tom reported for work, having had a spacious breakfast in his hotel, he was astounded to find that a gigantic iceberg, much larger than his entire store and three stories high, had been driven into the channel by a westerly storm, and there it rested, right at his worksite, towering over the men hammering nails.

"What do we do about this?" Tom wanted to know, and Bigears replied: "We wait till somebody tow it away," and before noon a surprisingly small boat with a puffing steam engine hurried up, threw a lasso and chain around a projection from the iceberg, and slowly towed it out of the channel. Tom was amazed that such a small boat could dictate to such a monstrous berg, but as Bigears said: "Boat knows what it's doing. Iceberg just drifting, tassall," and that was the difference. Once the berg started slowly moving away from shore, the little boat had no trouble keeping it headed in the right direction, and by midafternoon the berg was gone.

"Where did it come from?" Tom asked, and Bigears said: "Glaciers. Maybe our glacier. You ever see Mendenhall?" When Tom said "No," Sam punched him in the arm: "Sunday we make picnic. I like picnics."

So on Sunday, after Tom had attended the Presbyterian church

and surveyed with satisfaction the progress of his building, he waited
for Bigears to fetch him for the trip to the glacier, and to his surprise
the Tlingit appeared in a two-horse carriage rented from a man for
whom he had worked and driven by an attractive young Indian girl
of about fourteen whom he introduced as his daughter: "This Nancy
Bigears. Her mother see glacier many times, stay home."

"I'm Nancy," she said, extending her hand, and Tom felt both
that she was very young, and that she was quite mature in her solid
posture toward the world, for she looked at him without embarrassment and handled the horses with confidence.

Bowing to the girl, Tom asked: "Why Nancy? Why not a Tlingit
name?" and Sam said: "She got Tlingit name too. But she live with
white people in Juneau. She have name of missionary's wife. Fine
name, tassall."

Nancy was an Indian, no doubt about that, with an even dark skin,
black eyes and hair, and that saucy air of freedom which came from
living in close association with the land. She wore Western clothes, but
with a touch of piping or fur here and there to retain the Indian look,
but the two things which typed her as Tlingit were the handsome
dark braids which hung below her shoulders and the big decorated
boots that covered her feet. They gave her otherwise slender body a
heavy pinned-to-earth look which matched her pragmatic approach.

The ride to the glacier was extremely pleasant, with Bigears explaining where he lived, now that his shack had disappeared, and
Nancy telling of her days in school. She was attending not a mission
school for Indians but the regular white school, and apparently she
was doing well, for she could converse easily on subjects like music
and geography: "I'd like to see Seattle. Girls tell me it's a fine place."

"It is," Tom assured her.

"Did you live in Seattle?" she asked as they approached the turn
to the north which would take them to the glacier.

"Yes."

"You born there?"

"No, Chicago. But I lived in Seattle half a year."

"Many ships? Many people?"

"Just like your friends said."

"I would like to see, but I would never want to leave Alaska." She
turned to face Tom: "Which do you like, Seattle or Juneau?" and he
replied truthfully: "I long to get back to that city. Maybe with R&R,
after my apprenticeship . . ."

"What's that?"

"The years when you learn how to work. When I know all about stores and ships and other parts of Alaska, maybe I'll be allowed to work in Seattle."

"There she is!" Bigears cried as they reached a crest from which the great glacier first became visible, and it was both bigger and more impressive than Tom had imagined from the many photographs he had seen. It was not green-blue, as so many said, but a rather dirty white as centuries of snow, tight-packed, reached the breaking-off point where the crawling glacier died.

He was surprised that Nancy was able to drive the carriage almost to the entrance to a cave in the ice. Here Bigears stayed with the horses while Nancy led Tom inside to a deep cavern. As he stood there, looking about, he saw in the ceiling a spot thinner than the rest where the sun shone through the crystal ice, showing it to be the green-blue he had expected. It was radiant, a glorious touch of nature that not many would ever see, this splendid, vibrating cavern in which sun and ice met.

"My people say the raven was born in this cave," she told Tom, and in his ignorance he asked: "Is the raven something special . . . with you, I mean?" and she said proudly: "I'm a raven," and there deep within the birth-cavern of her totem he learned of how the world was divided between the eagles and the ravens, and he said, reflecting on his study of American history: "I suppose I would be an eagle," and she nodded: "Ravens are more clever. They win the rope games, but eagles are necessary too."

They did not, on Tom's first visit to the glacier, see any icebergs calve; Nancy thought that happened more frequently at other glaciers to the north, but when they left the cave and Tom threw rocks at the snout he could see fragments of ice break away, and he understood the mechanism of how the iceberg which had visited his store had formed and broken away.

Bigears had additional information, gathered by his people over many centuries: "You didn't see no glaciers in Nome, did you? I tell you why. Not so much rain up there in summer, not so much snow in winter. North of Yukon, even north of Kuskokwim, no glaciers. Not enough snow. But down here, much rain, much snow, it fall, it fall, and never melt."

"Where does the ice come from?"

"You pack snow down, this year, next year, many years, it cannot melt. Snow get hard, make ice. Hundred years, thick ice. Thousand years, very thick."

"But how does it crawl along the valleys?"

"Ice comes, it stays, it says like the salmon: 'I got to get to the ocean,' and down it crawls, little bit each year, many years many big icebergs break off, but always crawling to the sea."

"Next year, will that cave still be there?"

"Next week, maybe gone. Always crawling toward the sea."

In the days following the trip to the glacier, Tom was distressed by the fact that Sam Bigears did not report for work, nor was there any word from him, and Tom had to proceed without him. One of the white carpenters, who had come to depend on Bigears for much of the important woodwork, said: "You can't never rely on them Tlingits. Good people for the most part, but when you really need 'em they're never on hand."

"What do you suppose has happened?" Tom asked with real concern, for he missed Bigears, and the carpenter said: "Any one of fifty reasons. His aunt is ill, bad cold, and he feels he must be with her. Pollock have come into the area and he feels he must fish while they're here. Or most likely, he felt that he needed a walk in the woods. He'll probably come sauntering back, Tlingit style, one of these days."

That was a fair prediction, because after two weeks' absence Bigears did come drifting back to resume his carpentering, and when he reported to work as if he had never been absent, he explained to Tom: "I got to get things ready." That was all he volunteered, and when Tom asked: "What things? Where?" he said cryptically: "Store look pretty good. Be finish soon. Then you, me, we go my home."

"But we tore that shack down."

"I mean my real home. Pleiades River."

Tom noticed that he had not brought his daughter back with him, and this vaguely disappointed him, but he supposed that she had been left at the other home, and when the time came, in late August, that the store was, as Bigears had pointed out, in good shape, with only a few refinements left to be finished, Tom judged that he could with safety take a couple days off, so he told Bigears: "We could leave tomorrow, if you can get your canoe ready," and on a bright morning, with the sun rising over the great ice fields back of Juneau, the two set forth for the easy paddle to Taku Inlet.

But anyone in Juneau who took a sunny day for granted was a fool, and they had not progressed far down Gastineau Channel be-

fore rain began to fall. For some hours they traveled through it without complaint, for a Juneau rain was not like that of other places: it
did not fall in big drops, or any drops at all, but came down as a kind
of benevolent mist which permeated everything without getting any
particular item really wet.

The canoe ride was a fresh experience for Tom, a trip of unusual
beauty. Bigears was a strong paddler who kept the canoe thrusting
forward and Tom added youthful vigor from the prow, from where he
studied the changing landscape. Prior to entering the inlet, he saw
about him the hills that protected Juneau on all sides, making its
waterways alluring channels, but when they turned into the inlet the
scene changed dramatically. Now they faced that chain of high peaks
which crowned the Alaska-Canada border, and for the first time Tom
felt as if he were entering one of the fjords he had read about as a
boy. But most of all, he was aware that he was heading into a primitive wilderness, with not a sign of human occupancy anywhere, and
his stroke grew stronger as they glided silently up the inlet.

They had not progressed far when Tom spied a sight so lovely and
balanced that its parts seemed to have been placed where they were
by an artist. From the west came down a small glacier, sparkling blue
in color, in what seemed an attempt to meet a large rock which barely
emerged from the middle of the inlet, while beyond rose the great
mountains of Canada. "This is something!" Tom called back, and
Bigears said: "Low water like now, we see the Walrus, high water no
see." When Tom asked what the Walrus was, Sam pointed to a half-
submerged rock which did indeed resemble a walrus rising from the
sea to catch a breath.

As they passed the face of the glacier Tom cried: "This is a fine
trip, Sam," but to paddle nearly thirty miles, even when the water was
relatively smooth, took time, and when sunset approached, Tom
called back: "Will we get there tonight?" and Bigears replied as he
gave the canoe an extra thrust forward: "Pretty soon dark come, we
see lights," and just as dusk appeared ready to encompass the inlet,
straight ahead on the left bank Tom saw the last rays of sunlight
striking the face of a glacier whose ice glistened like a waterfall of
emeralds, while atop a headland on the right bank glowed the light
coming from the windows of a log cabin.

"Halloo there! Halloo!" Bigears shouted, and on the headland
Tom could see movement, but they were now at the southern end of
the estuary formed by the entry of the Pleiades River, and they had

to do some stiff paddling before they crossed it. As they did, Tom saw an Indian woman and a young girl coming down to the water's edge to greet them.

"This my wife," Bigears said as his powerful hands dragged the canoe well onshore. "You know Nancy."

Mrs. Bigears was shorter than her husband and rounder. She was a taciturn woman who was never surprised at what her enterprising husband did; her task was to supervise whatever house they occupied, and it was clear that she had done a good job at this cabin, for the grounds about it were neat and the interior a model of traditional Tlingit habitation. She spoke no English, but with her right hand indicated that her husband's young guest would occupy a kind of alcove; Nancy, apparently, would have her own corner, while mother and father would take the large spruce-needled bed.

On the iron stove which Sam had purchased some years before in Juneau, various pots were producing an aroma which augured well, but Tom was exhausted from that long day's paddling and fell asleep long before the Bigears family was prepared to eat. They did not waken him.

In the morning, after a huge breakfast of sourdough pancakes and venison sausage, Nancy said: "You must see where we are," and she led him about the wedge of land on which her ancestors had built their refuge from the Russians. "We have this protected hill. Across the inlet we see the green glacier. Down there the bay where the Pleiades River empties. And wherever we look, the mountains that watch over us."

Tom was still admiring the site, so well suited for a cabin, when with a wide sweep of her arm she indicated the spacious land to the east: "In these woods, deer to feed us. In the river, salmon every year. Soon we catch many salmon, dry them on those racks."

As Tom looked toward the drying racks, he saw lying on the ground behind the cabin a large white object stretching a considerable distance, with many chips of some kind scattered about. "What's that?" he asked, and Nancy cried with a mixture of delight and reverence: "That's why my father wanted you to come," and she led him to an extraordinary object—which was to have a permanent influence in his life.

It was the trunk of a large fir tree transported here from a considerable distance. Its bark had been carefully peeled away, exposing the pale-cream wood on which Sam had been working, and when Tom saw the kind of work his carpenter had been doing, he was awed. For this was a Tlingit totem pole in the making, a majestic work of art symbolizing the experiences of its people. In its present position, prostrate on the ground and stretching immoderately, it created a powerful impression, the figures comprising it seeming to flow and crawl and twist in a bewildering confusion.

Tom gasped: "It's so big! Did your father carve it all?"

"He's worked on it for a long time."

"Is it finished?"

"I think so. But it's not cut off at the top, so I don't know."

"What do the figures mean?"

"We better ask Pop." And when she called her father, Sam came out with the tools he had used to carve this masterpiece: an adz, two chisels, a gouge, a mallet, and now a saw for the final act of cutting away the top.

"What does it mean?" Tom asked, and Bigears laid his tools aside, all except the saw, which he kept in his right hand as a wand with which to indicate the twisting figures.

"First the frog who brought us here. Then the face of my grandfather-grandfather who built the fort at Sitka. Then the deer that fed us, the ship that brought the Russians, the trees."

"And the man in the top hat?"

"Governor Baranov."

"Wasn't he your enemy? Didn't he fight you and kill your warriors?"

"Yes, but he won."

"And now he sits at the top of everything?"

"Not quite. Today I finish."

And throughout that entire day Tom Venn sat beside Nancy Bigears as her mother brought food to her husband while he applied his tools vigorously to the wood at the top of the totem. First he sawed off the tip of the fir, leaving two feet of exposed wood. Then, with his rude gouge, he began to hack away the huge chunks that protruded from the top of Baranov's big hat, and his work appeared to be so aimless that Tom asked "What are you doing, Sam?" but received no answer, for it seemed that the carver was working in a kind of trance.

By midafternoon, with a misty rain replacing the morning sunlight, Tom was completely mystified, but now Bigears began working with his adz, using strokes and cuts much less flamboyant than before. Gradually from the top of the fallen tree emerged the shadowy

form of a bird—and no one spoke. Now, with rapid, sure strokes, the
Tlingit artist gave vibrant form to his topmost figure, and in a triumphant conclusion he brought forth the raven, symbol of his tribe and
his people. The Russians in their tall hats had triumphed momentarily, but in conformance with history, atop the Russians stood the
raven. In their quiet way, the Tlingits had also triumphed.

"How are you going to get it upright?" Tom asked, and Bigears,
willing to talk at last, indicated a raised spot from which the totem
would be visible for miles up and down the inlet, and on the river too.

"We dig hole there, you, me, Nancy."

"But how will we drag the totem there?"

"Potlatch."

Tom did not understand either the word or its meaning, but he
accepted the fact that a Tlingit miracle of some kind would move the
totem to the top of the mound and then erect it in an upright position, but what this mysterious potlatch would consist of, he could not
guess.

When the totem was finished, all its rough spots smoothed away,
Bigears mysteriously disappeared in his canoe, and when Tom asked
where he had gone, Nancy said simply: "To tell the others," and for
six days they did not see him.

In the waiting period Nancy suggested that her mother pack a
little bundle of food which she and Tom could take with them on an
excursion to a lake at the head of the river: "It's a beautiful place.
Quiet. All mountains. Nine miles, easy walk."

So off they started on a fine September morning, and as they
hiked along, with Nancy showing the way on a footpath long used by
her people, Tom experienced the quiet charm of this part of Alaska,
so different from the bleak power of the Yukon and the vast emptiness of Nome and the Bering Sea. He liked the trees, the waterfalls,
the ferns lending grace to the scene, and the ever-present rippling of
the little river.

"Any fish in there?" he asked, and Nancy replied: "A few salmon
come all the time. But in September, many, many come."

"Salmon? In this tiny stream?"

"They come to the lake. Soon we'll be there." And at the end of
their climb Tom saw one of the choice spots of southeastern Alaska,
Lake Pleiades, rimmed by its six mountains.

"This was worth the effort," he cried as he looked at the placid
water with the mountains reflected in its surface. Beside its quiet

shore they ate their lunch, and then Tom showed Nancy how he could skip flat stones across the surface of the water, and she said that he must have many skills.

On the way back to the cabin, with a bright sun winking at them as they passed the waterfalls, Nancy was in the lead, some twenty feet ahead, when Tom became aware that someone was coming up behind him, and supposing that it was some Tlingit on his way to the Bigears cabin, he turned to speak, and found himself facing a rather large grizzly bear approaching rapidly.

Since the bear was still some distance away, Tom erroneously supposed that he could escape by running from it, but as he started to dig in his toes and speed to safety he recalled a tale told one wintry night by an old man with half a face: "No man can outrun a grizzly. I tried. It caught me from behind. One sweep of its claw. Look at me."

Driven by an anguished fear, Tom increased his speed, heard the bear gaining, and screamed: "Nancy! Help!"

When she heard his cry she turned and saw with horror that he had no chance of outrunning the bear, for the animal, reveling in the chase, was forging ahead with even greater strides and must soon leap upon Tom from the rear. She was terrified, for she knew that the bear would not stop until it had overpowered its target. With one swipe of a gigantic paw with its swordlike claws, it would rip away Tom's face and perhaps sever his windpipe.

In that instant Nancy Bigears knew what she must do, what her Tlingit ancestors had learned through the centuries when they confronted the grizzly on lands they shared with the fierce creature. "You can do three things," her grandmother had told her. "Run away and be killed. Climb a tree and maybe live. Or stand and talk to the bear, making him think you're bigger than you are."

There were trees at hand, but none close enough to run to, nor fit for climbing if one did reach them. The only hope lay in talking to the bear, and with almost spontaneous bravery Nancy dashed back toward Tom, who was close to being overtaken by the speeding bear, grabbed his hand, and brought him to a stop. Holding him firmly, she turned him to face the bear, who lumbered up, stopped abruptly about ten feet away, and blinked at the object that now blocked its path.

The bear had exceptional powers of smell, and these assured him that what it had been chasing was still at hand, but its eyesight was limited at best and often defective, so it could not determine what it was that stood before it. And then came that low, powerful, unfrightened voice in Tlingit: "Sir Bear, do not be afraid. We are your friends and we mean you no harm."

The bear remained motionless, cocking its ears to hear the reassuring sounds: "Stop where you are, Sir Bear. Go your way and we shall go ours."

Its small brain became confused. In chasing the man, it had been playing a kind of game, no more, and had it overtaken him, as soon it must, it would probably have killed, more in sport than anger. It knew it was not threatened by the man, whom it saw merely as an intruder upon its stream banks, and as long as Tom fled he remained an attractive target to be chased. But now everything was changed, for there was nothing to chase, no slim moving thing to be played with. Instead, there was this big immovable thing, these firm sounds coming from it, this sense of mystery and confusion. In the flash of a moment everything was altered.

Slowly the bear turned around, stared over its shoulder at the strange object in its path, and took a powerful first bound of its retreat. In its ears as it went it could hear those quiet but forceful sounds: "Go your way, Sir Bear. Go to your salmon spot and may the fishing be good."

Only when the huge bear was gone did Nancy relinquish her hold on Tom, for now she knew it was safe for him to relax. Had he run when the bear stood there facing them, or even moved conspicuously, both she and Tom might have been killed; now as she released Tom's hand she could feel him start to sag.

"That was close."

"It was, for both of us."

"I didn't know you could talk to bears."

She stood in the sunlight, her round, placid face smiling as if nothing of moment had happened: "He needed talking to, that one."

"You were very brave, Nancy."

"He wasn't hungry. Just curious. Just playing. He needed to be told."

On Friday the neighboring Indian families began to arrive, coming up Taku Inlet in their painted canoes or drifting down with sails set as the famous Taku Wind blew out of Canada, shoving their boats along. They were dressed not in work clothes but in festive garments, dresses heavy with beads, trousers trimmed in fur. They wore hats that Tom had not seen before, and children were adorned with shells and wore cloaks of decorated deerskin. They were a colorful group, and as each family arrived Nancy and her mother greeted them with the same words, which Nancy interpreted for Tom: "We are honored that you have come. The master will soon be here," whereupon the visitors bowed and moved off to inspect the prostrate totem, which they adjudged to be excellent.

Now there was excitement along the shore, and children ran down to greet Sam Bigears as he paddled his way home, his canoe full of purchases from Juneau. Eagerly the young people helped him unload, handing along from one to the other the parcels which would soon lend dignity to the potlatch. When they came to three small packages of surprising weight they asked impertinently: "What's in here?" and he told them to tear away the wrappers. When they did they found three small cans of white man's paint, and these were taken to where the nearly completed totem lay on the ground.

Its major segments had already been colored in the subdued tones provided by the earth: a soft brown, a glowing blue, a quiet red. What Bigears now proposed was to highlight the pole with small areas of a vivid green, a scintillating carmine and a jet-black. Going directly to the totem without even pausing to greet his guests, he opened the three cans, gave two carvers as gifted as he their own brushes, and explained what he wanted: "Frog got to be green, black spots. Hat black, what else? Faces red, wings of the other bird green, eyes of the beaver red, too."

Deftly the men applied the finishing touches. Purists among them would have preferred that only natural colors be used, as in times past, but even they had to agree that the restrained touches of store-bought paint blended pleasingly with the rest of the design, lending it those accents of brightness which revealed the character of the man who had done the carving.

When the third coat was applied, with the sun beating down to bond it to the wood, the women came to applaud, and all agreed that Bigears had done his work like a carver of the old days. One woman pointed out that the totem in her village was taller, and another was not too pleased with the bright red touches, but in general it was approved: "It will stand properly in this cove, facing the glacier, speaking to all who come up or down the inlet."

Now the potlatch began. Seventeen families had come to participate in Sam Bigears' hospitality, and as the food and the gifts were
presented to the visitors, it was acknowledged that Sam was just as
generous as his forebears had been. Tom Venn was astounded at the
lavishness of the celebration, and thought: This must have cost him a
lot. Sam, as he moved among his guests, gave no indication that he
considered his gifts extravagant, nor did he comment in any way
upon the bountiful piles of food. When Tom, eyes wide, asked: "Do
you hold potlatch often?" Sam evaded a direct answer: "I have luck.
Good job. Good wife. Good daughter."

Tom told him of the adventure with the grizzly, and Sam laughed:
"I wish I know sooner. I put bear on totem. Celebration."

Suddenly Tom wanted to know many things: a celebration of
what? a potlatch in honor of what? these friends assembled on what
principle? the totem representing homage to what power? the force or
spirit which bound these people together stemming from what? And
as these questions pounded through his head, he realized how much
he respected his carpenter and how impossible it was to ask him for
an explanation.

But he could ask about the totem itself, and now as it lay for the
last time on the ground where each part could be inspected at close
hand, he moved along it, asking what role the turtle played, and why
that bird rested the way it did, and why the raven's wings were added
to the post and were not a generic part of it? Sam, obviously proud
of his work and pleased with the way his three store-bought colors
accommodated to the softer earth tones, was happy to speak of the
totem in these hours before it was to be formally erected at the entrance to the cove; it was as if at that moment the totem would become the property of all and no longer his creation.

"No special man, no special bird, no special face. Just how I feel.
Just how the rains fall."

Rain was beginning to fall, so men brought canvases to protect
the still-wet paint, and through that first night of the potlatch one
man played a fiddle, women danced, and Tom Venn complained to
Nancy: "Nobody tells me what it is. A potlatch for what?" and watching the celebration as if from afar, she explained this ancient custom:

> "When all goes well and there is money in the house and
> neighbors think kindly of you, maybe it's proper for you to
> give it all away and start over. Maybe you must prove yourself

again. Maybe you must not rise too high above your neighbors. Look! They dance. They sing. And Sam Bigears grows
bigger in their eyes, for he has made real potlatch.

"The missionaries hated potlatch. Claimed it was the work of
the devil. Too much noise. Not enough praying. Lots of things
happen at potlatch. Good things. Noisy things. Maybe seem
wild. But the celebration . . ."

She nodded her head gently to the screeching of the fiddle and smiled
as she watched her mother dance in a corner as if partnered by a
ghost, dancing to a music which she alone heard.

On the morning of the third day everyone assembled at the totem
to participate in the ritual of its erection. Since the pole was thirty
feet long and ample at the base, this was going to present quite an
engineering problem, but the Tlingits had, through the centuries, perfected a system for getting their massive totems into an upright position, and now came the test.

Bigears and Tom and Nancy had already readied the hole for the
pole, lining it with rocks, so now a trench was dug leading on a gradual slope from the deep bottom of the hole out beside the pole to a
distance of about one-third the length of the totem. When it was
properly graded, the men applied muscle and rope to the task of easing the long pole sideways and down into the sloping trench. The top
end of the totem—that is, the end not in the trench—was propped up
at various points with stout logs, and all was ready, except that at the
last moment men wedged into the waiting hole, along the far face, a
large flat slab against which the bottom of the totem would abut, so
that when the top was raised, this slab would prevent the totem from
gouging out the soft earth as the end of the pole was forced against it.

Now ropes were applied at many points along the top of the pole,
one of the most important being the one which would prevent it from
swinging too far over when it was pulled upright. Other ropes were
attached to keep the totem from weaving from side to side, and men
experienced in raising poles began to shout orders while others
hauled on the ropes. Women, watching in admiration as the handsomely carved totem began to rise majestically in the sunny morning,
its painted surfaces reflecting light, began a chant, whereupon the
men pulled more vigorously, and with those pulling back to prevent
too rapid a rise straining to maintain a balance between speed and
caution, the beautiful totem rose in the air, trembled for a moment as

it approached the perpendicular, then shuddered and quietly slipped down into its hole. Tom Venn, pulling on one of the ropes which prevented sideways motion, felt the great log come to rest.

"Halloo!" the man in charge of the ropes shouted, and everyone let go, and as the ropes fell easily toward the tall pole, men and women alike cheered, for now Sam Bigears' totem stood alone and erect, facing the shore as if to greet all ships that might approach on the inlet.

The potlatch was over. Sam's neighbors carried their gifts to their canoes, each man aware that at some future time he would be expected to repay Sam with a gift of equal value, each woman wondering what gift she could sew or knit that would be as presentable as those Sam's wife had given. Thus the economy of the Tlingits was preserved and enhanced; goods were exchanged; wealth was redistributed; obligations were established which would continue into the indefinite future; and at the entrance to Pleiades River a man, his wife and their daughter preserved a way of life totally alien to the one developing in the town of Juneau, only seventeen miles away as the raven flew.

While Sam Bigears was conducting his potlatch at the mouth of the Pleiades, what was happening in the lake at the head of the river to Nerka and his generation of salmon? By the beginning of 1903, even though he had completed two years, he was still so insignificant that he played no conspicuous role in the lake. Larger fish ate his brothers so incessantly that they were now depleted to a mere eighty. As the devastation continued and even intensified, it began to look as if the sockeye in Lake Pleiades must soon be exhausted, but Nerka, with a powerful urge for self-preservation, kept to the dark places, avoided the predatory larger fish, and continued as little more than a fingerling, unaware that upon the perseverance of other salmon like himself depended the survival of their breed.

In that winter of 1903, while Nerka's generation in Lake Pleiades dropped to two million, and Tom Venn was busy in his new store along Juneau's waterfront, the Ross & Raglan steamer *Queen of the North* docked with a large shipment of goods for the summer trade plus a red-headed gentleman who was about to revolutionize this part of Alaska. He was Malcolm Ross, fifty-one years old and surging with energy. "I'm bursting with plans," he said as he led Tom into the small office from which the Juneau branch of R&R conducted its business. "And I'm warning you, Tom, I want to start now."

Tom had not seen Mr. Ross since that day in 1897 when he began representing R&R along the waterfront, but in the intervening years he had witnessed the tremendous growth of the firm, and he took personal pride in the reports circulating through Alaska that Mr. Ross was a commercial genius.

"What do you have in mind?" Tom asked. "A new store in Skagway?"

"Skagway's finished. The gold rush has ended. That new railway to Whitehorse may be good for a few years. But I can see no future for Skagway."

"Where, then?"

"Here."

Tom was stunned. His store in Juneau was doing well, but it did not warrant any enlargement, and the idea of a duplicate in some other part of town would be precarious at best and more likely a disaster: "Mr. Ross, I know R&R rarely makes mistakes, but a second store here . . . it wouldn't be justified."

"Thank you for an honest opinion, son. But I'm not thinking about another store. I want you to start right now, this morning, to build R&R a major salmon cannery."

"Where?" Tom asked weakly.

"That's for you to find out. Let's start now." When Tom protested that he knew nothing of fishing as an industry, let alone canning, Ross forestalled him: "Neither do I. We start even. But I do know one thing. There's going to be a fortune made on salmon, and we've got to get our share."

Tom had never seen anything like Malcolm Ross; not even Superintendent Steele of the Mounties had displayed the intensity and vigor of this handsome Seattle merchant who knew intuitively that salmon was certain to replace gold as Alaska's contribution to mainland wealth. By eleven that morning Ross had assembled four knowledgeable men, whom he entertained at a lavish lunch so that he and Tom could probe their secrets about salmon fishing.

"What you would need," one of the men said, "that is, if you wanted to do it right . . ."

"I'd do it no other way."

"Well then, get out your pencil. To clean the fish, you need a huge shed. Bigger than anything you see around here. To cook them, you need another shed, not quite as large. To house the Chinese, because they have to be kept separate, they fight with everyone, you need a third shed, a bunkhouse. For the other workers, another dormitory. A mess hall divided one-third for the Chinese, two-thirds for the others. A carpenter's shop for making crates, a welding shop for making the tin cans. A warehouse next to a loading dock built out on pilings so you can tie up at either high or low tide."

"That's a lot of money," one of the other men said, and Ross replied: "I think we can borrow it. But where do we get our fish to put in the cans?"

The first man resumed: "Now we get down to the really expensive part. You would have to have a large ship under your own control, leased perhaps, but better if you owned it."

"We have ships."

"But not like the one out there. You need a ship to bring the Chinese north in the spring, and all the goods you need. And then it collects fish, brings them to the cannery, and at the end of the season hauls away the workers and the canned salmon."

"What do you mean, season?"

"Salmon only run a few months each year. Summer. So you open two months early to get things ready and handle the slow early run. Then work your tail off. Take one month to close. Late fall and all of winter you're shut down."

"Who stays at the cannery during the winter?"

"One watchman."

"All those buildings, all that investment—and one watchman?"

"Mr. Ross, you don't understand. Your cannery will be way out in the country, along some small body of water, nobody around for miles except bears and spruce trees and salmon."

"Where do I find such a place?" Ross asked, and now all the men wanted to talk at once, but the first speaker was not finished, so he silenced the others: "So when you have your big ship to do the big jobs, you must have one or two small ships to move about the waters servicing the thirty-odd boats that do the fishing. You need a lot of boats, Mr. Ross."

"I can believe that. But where?"

Carefully and with mature judgment, these men, well versed in the lore of the sea and its riches, eliminated the unpromising sites: "Most scenic body of water hereabouts is Lynn Canal leading to Skagway, but it has few fish."

"I have no interest in Skagway," Ross said abruptly, "and absolutely none in scenery."

"There's good salmon fishing on Admiralty Island, but the best sites are taken."

"I don't want second-class locations."

"There are some very promising areas on Baranof Island."

"Too far from Juneau. I want my headquarters here."

"With good boats, it doesn't matter much how far away your cannery is. There are some great salmon streams to the south."

"I've fixed my sights here."

"Then there's only one untouched spot—good run of salmon, good anchorage for cannery boats."

"Where?"

"But it has one drawback. The wind that roars out of Canada you won't believe."

"We can build to protect ourselves against wind."

"Not this wind. Eddie, tell him about you and the Taku."

A nearby fisherman, who had been eating prodigiously, laid down his fork and said: "Everybody hereabouts calls it the Taku Wind. It comes down off the mountains in Canada and funnels through Taku Inlet. In fifteen minutes it can beat up from dead calm to fifty miles an hour. Be careful in a Taku Wind."

Ross dismissed the warning: "What kind of salmon run the streams coming into this Taku Inlet?"

"Sockeye, mostly," the men agreed, and with the utterance of this magic word, Ross made up his mind: "We'll find a spot on Taku Inlet where there's protection from the wind," and immediately after lunch he asked Tom to arrange for an exploration of that beautiful body of water.

They found Sam Bigears at work on an addition to the hotel, and he was delighted with the prospect of heading back up the Taku, so one of the small R&R coastal steamers already in Juneau was commandeered, and by noon the expedition was under way.

As soon as the steamer turned the corner into the inlet, Malcolm Ross became aware that he had come upon something special, for the fjord was far more beautiful than he had imagined from the accounts he had heard at lunch. "This is magnificent!" he cried as the shimmering blue face of Walrus Glacier came into view. He was also impressed by the narrow defile between the glacier and Walrus Rock through which the ship nosed its way, and when the inlet broadened out, disclosing exciting new perspectives, his attention focused on the emerald face of Pleiades Glacier, one hundred feet high and gleaming in sunlight: "This is stupendous!"

But then he looked to the east, and behind the headland on which Sam Bigears' cabin stood he saw his first Alaskan totem pole, its varied colors glistening in the sun as if to complement the glacier on the facing shore. "Why would such a pole be erected up there?" Ross wanted to know. "Nothing around but that one cabin."

"That's Bigears' cabin," Tom explained. "He carved the totem. I helped put it in position."

"I suppose the figures mean something. Pagan rites and all that." So Bigears was called to the railing to explain his totem, and he did a much poorer job than his daughter would have done, until finally Ross, somewhat irritated, asked: "Tell me, who's the man in the top hat?" and Bigears said with a big smile: "A white man. Maybe Russian."

"Don't you know?" Ross asked impatiently, and Sam said: "Just a white man. He won."

Ross could make nothing of this, and when he asked about the bird atop the totem, he received another ambiguous answer: "Just a bird. Maybe a raven."

Now Ross became conciliatory: "That's a fine pole. And you have a good location here. Any salmon in the river?"

"Many sockeye," Sam replied, and Ross made careful note of this fact, but his shrewd eye detected a fact of greater significance to a potential salmon cannery: "Bigears, doesn't your headland jutting out and up like that . . . doesn't it protect that little bay from what they call the Taku Wind?"

"Maybe."

"So if I built my cannery on that point to the south, opposite yours, I'd not have to worry too much about the wind, would I?"

"Maybe not."

"Then why did you build your cabin up there where the wind hits?" and Sam replied: "I like wind. It blow too hard, stay inside, build good fire."

After several more twists, the steamer passed close to the sullen snout of Taku Glacier, immensely higher and wider than the earlier ones but lacking the intense blue color, its dirty ice standing in gray-brown pillars. They were, however, massively impressive, as if they were ready to tumble down upon any ship that came too close. As

Ross watched, the captain came down to inform him that ships like this sometimes carried small cannon so that they could fire at glaciers, seeking to precipitate spectacular calving of icebergs, and he said: "I'd bet a big one's about to let loose."

"Have you a cannon?" Ross asked, and he was disappointed when the captain said that only passenger ships carried them. But the captain had another tactic: "We'll go to just the right distance and give our whistle five or six short blasts. Sometimes that'll do the trick," so the ship moved in surprisingly close, and when the blasts reverberated against the face of the glacier, the vibrations did cause a tall pillar of icy snow to break away and thunder down in a monstrous splash. It produced no lasting iceberg, for the snow was not tightly packed, but it did demonstrate how bergs were formed.

Passing the awesome glacier, the steamer ascended two more miles up near the head of the inlet, where a river tumbling out of Canada came into view, and Ross, watching the water churn and boil over huge boulders, asked: "How can a salmon pick its way through that twisted affair?" and Bigears said: "Coming home, they know every bend. Remember from when they came down as smolts," and Ross said: "Encourage them to breed well. They're the ones who'll fill our cans."

The steamer turned around at a point much farther up the inlet than later navigators would be able to go; in their day silt coming out of Canada would accumulate so that big ships would not even be able to reach Taku Glacier, but during the first years of the twentieth century this clogging of the waterway had not yet occurred.

On the trip back down the inlet, Ross stood at the railing, imagining himself a fierce Taku Wind blowing out of Canada, and as the ship neared Sam Bigears' cabin atop the bluff, Ross could feel himself soaring high over the headland and not coming back down till well past the southern side of the Pleiades estuary. Pointing triumphantly at this southern point, so available to shipping yet so well protected, he cried: "We'll build our cannery on that point," but Tom said: "I think we'd better call Sam Bigears over."

"Why?" Ross snapped.

"Because I think he owns both sides of the cove," Tom said.

"Sites are allocated in Washington," Ross said, indicating that he did not want to discuss the matter with Bigears. "I'll get my man in Washington to get working on it right away."

As the steamer departed from Taku Inlet he looked back at the compact, enchanting waterway with its cliffs and mountains and scintillating glaciers, and said to those about him: "It's a proper location for Ross & Raglan. Practically made to order."

To Tom's surprise, Mr. Ross remained in Juneau for two weeks, supervising the purchasing of materials for a major cannery, even though he had as yet no assured location for it, but on the thirteenth day a telegram arrived informing him that he had been granted exclusive rights to the cove at the mouth of the Pleiades River. "Full speed ahead!" Ross cried. "Tom, rush that timber and machinery over to the cove. Start building like a madman, and have things ready to operate by April twenty-fifth."

"Where do I get the boats?"

"That's my responsibility. They'll be here, believe me."

"And what shall we call the place?"

Ross considered this for some moments. For some time now he had feared that the widely known name of Ross & Raglan was being attached to too many ventures; it could engender jealousy. Or a man who was angry at treatment he received aboard an R&R ship might stop trading at an R&R store. Then, too, customers in Alaska might grow resentful of the concentration of power in Seattle. For these and other good reasons he decided firmly against any further use of that designation: "What we need, Thomas, is a name that echoes Alaska. Make local people proud of their affiliation with this new cannery. Let me think about this tonight."

An able man who had honestly striven to outfit thousands for Alaska in the gold-rush years, had provided good shipping and general merchandise needed in the growing communities, and now was planning a first-class cannery operation as opposed to certain fly-by-night enterprises which took money out of Alaska and plowed none back in, Malcolm Ross wanted his salmon venture to be an example of the best that enlightened capitalism could provide, and a name which proclaimed that quality was essential.

At breakfast he informed Tom that he had found the perfect solution: "Totem Cannery. On the labels for our cans, a fine drawing of a totem pole like the one I made when we sailed up Taku Inlet that first day." And from his pocket he produced a lively sketch of Sam Bigears' totem, but with the amusing white man in the top hat eliminated. In his place appeared a brown bear, with the original raven at the top.

Not only would Bigears' land at the mouth of the Pleiades be taken from him, but his totem would also be appropriated, and there would be nothing he could do about either theft. Malcolm Ross in Seattle and his agent in Washington would see to that.

In the days that followed, Tom Venn had ample opportunity to observe just how remarkable his employer was, for two large R&R steamers sailed into Taku Inlet with lumber and hardware for the four main buildings which would have to be in operation by mid-May. Along with these supplies came sixty-five artisans from Seattle, plus tents to house them temporarily and a big portable kitchen. Within a week of landing, this army of men had dug the footings for the principal buildings and had unloaded from a barge the stone and cement that would form the foundations for the large structures whose vertical timbers would soon begin sprouting like a forest of growing stalks after a spring rain.

It was not preposterous for Mr. Ross to expect his buildings to be ready so quickly, for they were essentially barns in which a variety of machinery would be housed; no intricate architectural problems required to be solved. "Get them up fast and strong," he told the men whenever he visited the inlet, and when new ships arrived with the heavy iron retorts in which the stacks of filled cans would be cooked by steam pressure, a place was ready for them, and by the time they were installed, some thirty Indians had been hired to lug in the wood to stoke the fires.

The smaller building, in which wooden crates would be built for shipping the cans to Seattle and then to cities like New York and Atlanta, was erected in four days; *slapped together* would be a more appropriate term, perhaps. But the twin building in which the tin cans would be manufactured from raw stock required more time; it had to be sturdy enough to house the heavy tin-working machinery.

In the meantime, thirty-seven local fishermen had been hired to catch the salmon when the run began, and the two small steamers that would move among them to collect their haul and ferry it to the cannery were brought up from Seattle complete with crews. Along with them came a most useful vessel, a big, tough tug with a pile driver mounted on the stern, and on the deck several hundred long wooden piles which would be driven into the muddy bottom of Taku Inlet to form the wharf at which the large cargo ships would dock when loading the crates of canned salmon.

In early April the scene at Totem Cannery was one of intense activity of the most varied sort. Tom Venn, in charge of keeping the hours and pay scales for everyone working on the project, now had about nine different crews at their tasks twelve and fourteen hours a day. Mr. Ross had given specific orders: "Spend money now and get the work done so that we can make real money in September."

In mid-April he ordered all work on nonessentials to halt so that a long bunkhouse could be whipped into shape at breakneck speed: "Just got word that our people in Seattle have found a gang of Chinese in San Francisco. They hired the lot and are shipping them north sooner than expected. I've been warned that keeping them happy is the secret of any good cannery operation, so we've got to have their sleeping area and mess hall ready in two weeks."

But when Tom tried to decide which carpenters and builders could be taken from which jobs, he found that almost every building was just as essential as the bunkhouse, so he had to scout around for local artisans to fill in. His first thought was to approach his trusted friend Sam Bigears, but Mr. Ross had been told by his Washington lobbyist that "no Eskimo, no Indian is worth a damn. Only white men can do the work needed to build in Alaska," and this prejudice had become ingrained. Tlingit Indians in the Taku vicinity could be employed to dig trenches and unload cargo, but they must not be entrusted to build a bunkhouse, even though Chinese were to occupy it: "I'll have no Indian carpenters, Tom. They can't be trusted."

"Where did you get that idea?"

"Marvin Hoxey told me how they drink, work two days, then disappear."

"Marvin Hoxey! He's never worked with Indians. All he knows are barroom stories."

"He understands Alaska."

Tom Venn, veteran of the Chilkoot Pass, the Yukon River, the frenzy of Dawson and Nome, had become a young man of twenty with the sound character of a man twice his age, and he was not going to have his hard-won wisdom dismissed by a man like Marvin Hoxey: "Mr. Ross, I don't mean to contradict, because you know more about business than anyone I've met. But about Indians like the ones I'd hire for the bunkhouse, you've been given poor advice."

"Hoxey has never let me down. Don't hire Indians for any important work on Totem Cannery."

Tom laughed, and to his own surprise, took Mr. Ross by the arm:

"Who carved that totem pole over there that you admire so much? The Indian I want to hire. And who helped build your Juneau store in what you admitted was record time? That same Indian. Mr. Ross, Sam Bigears—you've met him, on the boat that first day—he's twice as good a carpenter as any of the men you brought up from Seattle."

Malcolm Ross had not become the head of a major Seattle enterprise through ignoring the advice of strong-minded men, for he had always been such a man himself. When his partner Peter Raglan grew afraid of the speed at which the original Ross & Raglan store was expanding under the whiplash of Ross, Malcolm had promptly bought Raglan's interest in the firm. He had taken enormous risks in starting his shipping line, and he was taking greater ones today in trying to open this cannery in such a short time. If a young man who had proved himself as repeatedly as Tom Venn wanted to hire a Tlingit Indian to rush a building to completion, so be it: "If he's as good as you say, get him on the job today. But don't come wailing to me when he shows up drunk tomorrow."

Tom saluted, smiled, and refrained from informing his boss that it was the Seattle carpenters who had smuggled whiskey ashore at the beginning of this hectic job and who mysteriously replenished their stocks whenever an R&R ship entered the inlet. Instead, he suggested that Mr. Ross accompany him in a skiff ride across the cove for an opportunity to see how a Tlingit Indian of noted rank lived.

"I'd like to do just that," Ross said, and he perched in the rear of the skiff as two Indians who worked at unloading cargo took the boat across the cove to the informal landing place which Sam Bigears had scooped out for beaching his canoe and sailboat.

"Hey, Bigears!" Tom shouted as he and Ross climbed ashore. "Boss man to see you."

From the cabin atop the rise Sam appeared, standing for a moment between two doorposts carved and painted in totem style. When he saw Mr. Ross he called: "Welcome. You build pretty fast over there." He led them into his cabin, bare now because so many of its contents had been given away during the potlatch. However, the solidity of the structure was evident, and Ross asked: "Did you build this?" and Bigears said: "Wife and daughter help a lot."

He called for Nancy, whose lovely oval face broke into a smile like her father's. Not deferring in any special way to Mr. Ross, she gave a slight bow and said in lilting English: "Tom is very proud to work for you, Mr. Ross. We're proud to have you in our home. My mother speaks no English, but in Tlingit she says the same."

"I came on business, Mr. Bigears. Tom tells me that you're a fine carpenter."

"I like wood."

"He wants me to hire you to build the big bunkhouse—right now, for the Chinese. They're coming soon."

Sam Bigears said: "Sit down, Mr. Ross," and when the guests were seated, he asked bluntly: "Why you bring in Chinese? Taku Inlet is Indian. Many Indians here work good as Chinese."

"We've hired many of your people."

"But not real work. Not building. Not making boxes. Not making cans."

Ross was never loath to face inescapable unpleasantries: "The fact is, Mr. Bigears, all the canneries have learned to rely on Chinese to do the major jobs—crates, cans, preparing the salmon."

"Why Chinese? Why not Tlingits?"

"Because Chinese work harder than any other men on earth. They learn quickly what has to be done, and they do it. They work like hell, they save their money, and they keep their mouths shut. No cannery could succeed without Chinese."

"Tlingits work like hell too."

Ross was too considerate to say bluntly that yes, on a given day a Tlingit could work as well as a Chinese. He'd been told that by other cannery owners. But he had also been told that after two or three days of intense work, the Indian liked to draw his pay and go fishing—for himself, not for the cannery. Instead, he said: "Will you help Tom build the bunkhouse?" and Sam Bigears replied: "No. You bring in Chinese to take our jobs, so I not work for you. Not here at Pleiades. Not in Juneau no more." With great dignity he led Ross and Venn to the door, and as they left he said quietly: "Many Chinese here, many troubles." And the interview ended.

With what skilled help Tom could find along the waterfront in Juneau, and with a large crew of Tlingits, the shell of the bunkhouse was hastily erected, and as work started on the tiers of wooden bunks in which the imported workmen would sleep during their five-month campaign with the salmon, Venn felt for the first time that this massive project was going to be finished on time. It was the complexity of the action that day which generated this optimism: at the waterfront, the pile driver was hammering home the tall poles on which the floor of the dock would rest, twenty-two feet above the water at low tide; in the cooking shed, the retorts were being installed; in the big gutting shed, tables were being built at which the Chinese would clean the salmon with long, sharp knives; a rude sawmill was cutting Sitka spruce for the boxmakers soon to arrive; and in the tin-can building, intense fires were being prepared for the melting of solder to seal the lids of the cans when the packing was completed. A gigantic operation was drawing to a successful climax; it had been an Alaska-type venture: big, undisciplined on many days, frenzied, exciting. As Tom said to one of the carpenters in the bunkhouse: "You'd never do a job this way in Chicago."

But what sealed this sense of euphoria was the arrival, from the printing house in Seattle, of the first hundred thousand labels to be glued onto the cans before shipping. They were a bright red, the color of a mature sockeye, and the words printed in heavy black read:

PINK ALASKAN SALMON
IT'S GOOD FOR YOU

and beneath that appeared the proud designation:

TOTEM CANNERY
Pleiades Glacier, Alaska

But what caught the eye was a Seattle artist's conception of a totem pole, well drawn and printed in four colors with a blue-green glacier in the background.

It was a striking label, and when Mr. Ross had three samples glued onto the cans of a competing cannery, everyone who saw the result agreed that this was one of the most effective labels so far devised. Indeed, Tom was so pleased with the cans' appearance that he asked to have one, which he took across the cove in hopes that when Sam Bigears saw what a fine product Pleiades Cove was going to produce, his animosity would be relaxed.

"Pretty fine, eh?" Tom said as he handed the can over to his friend. Sam accepted it, studied it for some time, and then handed it back, almost with contempt: "All wrong." When Tom showed that he did not understand what Sam was saying, the latter pointed to the label: "My totem not on same side Taku with glacier. Man missing in totem. Look for yourself, no raven." Tom was about to laugh, when

Bigears voiced the real complaint of his people: "Outside of can bad. Inside even badder."

"What do you mean? Our salmon will be the freshest packed this year."

"I mean inside have Tlingit salmon from Tlingit rivers packed by Chinese, and all money go to Seattle workmen, Seattle ship men, Seattle company." Grabbing the can and holding it in the air, he said with great bitterness: "Tlingit salmon make everybody rich but Tlingits. Seattle get everything, Alaska nothing." Sadly, for he saw with cruel clarity the shape of the future, he handed the can back, and in that gesture cut himself off from his trusted friend. Both he and Tom knew that an unbridgeable alienation had risen between them. Tom henceforth would be of Seattle; Sam, of Alaska.

In mid-May, when resin still seeped from the raw boards in the long bunkhouse, an R&R steamer came into Taku Inlet, eased through the narrows, avoided Walrus Rock, and tied up alongside the newly finished dock. As soon as the gangplank was lashed tight, down streamed forty-eight Chinese who would get the cannery started. They were dressed in loose pajamas, black smocks, cheap rubber-soled shoes and no socks. About a fifth of the number wore pigtails, and these established the character of the group. They were alien, of a different color, unable for the most part to speak English, and with a much different appetite; along with them came the one essential necessary for keeping Chinese workers contented at a cannery: several hundred sacks of rice. And hidden away in various clever places came another essential almost as important: small glass vials not much bigger than a thumb, filled with opium. Since the forty-eight men would have no women with them, no opportunity for ordinary recreation, no respite from twelve- and fourteen-hour days of back-breaking labor, no fraternization with white fellow workers, opium and gambling were about the only relaxation available, and these they would pursue assiduously.

They were a silent, frightening crew as they came ashore, and it fell to Tom to lead them to their quarters. Ill-at-ease and not happy with the prospect of dealing through a long summer with these strange creatures, he walked in silence toward the newly finished bunkhouse, but he was stopped by a tugging at his sleeve and turned to face the one man on whom the success of this operation would come to depend.

He was a thin, frail Chinese who wore his hair in a thick pigtail that reached well down his back. Only slightly older than Tom and markedly shorter, he nevertheless had a commanding presence, and in that first moment of meeting, Venn noticed a peculiarity which he supposed would determine the man's behavior: His yellow face smiles, as if he knows that it will please me, but his eyes do not, because he doesn't give a damn what I think.

"My name Ah Ting. Work Ketchikan two time. Me bossman all Chinese. No trouble."

Although suspicious of the man's motives, Tom was relieved to learn that someone at least spoke English, so he invited Ah Ting to walk with him, and even before they reached the bunkhouse it was clear that Totem Cannery was going to operate as Ah Ting directed, for the other Chinese accepted his leadership. When the line reached the building, the others waited till he allocated the plain board beds and distributed the two skimpy blankets to each man.

"We no eat on ship," he said, and when Tom led the way to the mess hall reserved for the Chinese, Ah Ting quickly designated two cooks, who started at once to prepare the rice. After they had eaten, Ah Ting, and not Venn, divided the men into three groups. One would build crates; one would fabricate tin cans; and the main group, in addition to cleaning the buildings, would prepare the tables at which they would later behead and gut the salmon.

Tom could not guess how many of the forty-eight had worked in canneries before, but he found that he had to give instructions only once, and even though most of the Orientals could not understand his words, they showed an uncanny skill in catching his intention and jumped to do as he indicated. By two in the afternoon the work force was in place, with specialists identifying themselves and taking over the more important jobs, and by three, finished crates and tin cans were appearing.

For example, the making of tin cans to be shipped around the world was a precise task. The long rolls of tin had to be cut in strips for the body of the can, which then had to be rolled around a template and soldered carefully. Disks to close the bottom had to be punched out and then soldered firmly. Finally, disks of a different character were required for the top, and these would be set aside to be soldered in place when the can was filled with raw fish. A small opening had to be left for the suction machine to draw off remaining air and create a vacuum, and then that minute hole had to be soldered. By nightfall it was obvious that cans for Totem salmon were going to be first-class and in good supply.

As the end of May approached, all parts of this huge effort began to mesh: sixty-five white men from Seattle managed the offices, supervised the laborers, and commanded the steamers; the Chinese produced cans and crates for processing the fish; and the thirty natives continued to lift and carry. Now, also, the thirty small boats that would actually do the fishing and the seining—two white men to each boat except for three that were manned by Indians—moved into position, and on a bright morning in June a lookout on one of the large vessels shouted: "Salmon are coming!" and when fishermen rushed to the railing to peer into the dark waters of Taku Inlet, they could see thousands of shadowy forms moving steadfastly up the waterway on their way to distant streams far inside Canada.

But those sailors who looked toward Pleiades Cove could see an impressive group of big sockeye separating from the main flow and heading for that beautiful cold stream down which they had come as smolt three years before.

"They keep comin'!" men shouted from boat to boat, and that year's harvest, the first for Totem Cannery, was under way.

When Nancy Bigears heard the cry she alerted her father, and he went out to inspect the quality of this year's returning salmon, and he was so pleased with what he saw that he sent his daughter back to the house to fetch his dip net, and he was about to cast for his first fishing of the season when a cannery warden with a loud voice shouted from the other side of the cove: "Hey, there! No fishing in this river."

"This my river," Bigears called back, but the warden explained: "This river and the lake too, it's now restricted to Totem Cannery. Orders from Washington."

"This my river. My grandfather-grandfather fished here."

"It's all different now," the warden said as he climbed into a small boat to deliver the new instructions at closer range. When he climbed ashore, Bigears said: "You better pull her higher. She'll drift away," and when the warden looked back he saw that he would have lost his dory had Sam not spoken.

Consulting a paper, the warden said: "You're Sam Bigears, I suppose," and when Sam nodded, the man continued: "Mr. Bigears, the cove has been deeded to us by the officials in Washington. We are to control fishing on this river and adjacent waters. We had to have that reassurance before we could spend so much money on the cannery over there."

"But this my river."

The warden ignored this, and in a tone of conciliation, as if he were granting a generous dispensation to a child, he said: "We've notified Washington that we volunteer to respect your squatter's rights to your home over here plus six acres of land."

"Squatter rights? What that mean?"

"Well, you have no title to your piece of land. It's not yours legally, it's ours. But we're going to let you occupy your cabin during your lifetime."

"It's my river . . . my land."

"No, things have changed, Mr. Bigears. From here on, the government will say who owns what, and it has already said that our cannery has the right to this river. And that naturally gives us the right to the salmon that come into our river." When Bigears looked perplexed, the warden simplified the new instructions: "You and your friends are not to fish in this river any longer. Only those who fish for the cannery. It is closed. The government says so."

He stood at the spot where the river began, wanting to be certain that the Tlingit did not break the new law, and when he saw Bigears put up his pole and trudge back to his house in bewilderment, he said to himself: Now that's a sensible Indian.

When the first big catch was hauled into the gutting shed, with all parts of the cannery functioning as planned, thousands of tall one-pound cans began sliding off the soldering tables and over to the men who pasted on the bright red labels of Totem Cannery. Mr. Ross, hearing that his plant was operating even better than he had hoped, came north, and after a few days' inspection, told Tom: "This place will pay for itself in three years. After that, enormous profits." He felt so gratified with how smoothly things were going that he made several gestures to let the workmen know that they were appreciated: "It's standard R&R procedure. Give everybody who does well an unexpected reward." An extra ration of chicken and beef was issued to Ah Ting for his Chinese, who held in succession a feast, a gambling frolic and an opium session. Tlingit workers were given a small bonus and white workers a large one. Senior staff received chits entitling them to two weeks' extra vacation with pay at the end of the year's campaign, and Tom Venn was told: "A raise for you, Tom, and when you've put everything to bed for the winter, Mrs. Ross and I want you to come down to Seattle for a well-earned rest."

The prospect of visiting the city he admired so much set Tom to dreaming, and he speculated on the possibility that once at head-quarters, he might be given a job there, or perhaps the management of one of the big R&R stores in Seattle. But before such a promotion could come to pass, he must perform the distasteful task which Mr. Ross now threw his way: "Tom, I've generated a grudging respect for that Indian friend of yours. He seems to be a man of character. I want you to row over to his cabin and assure him that whereas he can no longer fish in our river, we're not going to be niggardly with a man who, as you reminded me, helped build our store in Juneau."

"What do you mean, sir?"

"When the catch is in and the end of season in sight, we'll tell the warden to be sure that Bigears—well, see to it, Tom, that he gets a salmon or two. It's only fair."

Mr. Ross directed Tom to make the initial gift of salmon right now, while he, Ross, was still at the cannery, and Tom was given two fat sockeye, brilliant red in their spawning color, to take to the Tlin-git. He did not want this job, for he appreciated the irony of offering Sam Bigears two salmon when his family had for generations held the right to all the fish in the Pleiades; but the order had been given, and as he had done with previous orders, he obeyed it.

He felt uneasy crossing the cove, and acutely distressed when he landed and started up the path to Sam's cabin. Rehearsing possible words he could use to disguise the ugliness of what he must do, he was relieved when Nancy and not her father came to the door. In her cheerful way she said: "Hello, Tom. We've been wondering why we haven't seen you."

"In a new cannery, there's a new job every day."

"I've seen the big ships stopping by to pick up the crates. You send out so many."

"Thirty-two thousand before we close."

"What's in your hand? Looks like a fish."

"It's two fish. Salmon."

"Why?"

"Mr. Ross wants your father to know that even though the river is closed and Indians can't fish here anymore . . ."

"We've heard," she said gravely, and Tom was afraid that she was going to upbraid him, but she did not. She was fifteen now, a bright, knowledgeable young Indian girl who had enjoyed school and whose intuitions about the changing world of which she was a confused part were surprisingly shrewd. And now, even though she saw immediately the sad impropriety of what Tom was saying, she had to laugh, not scornfully, but with compassion for the fool that Tom was making of himself: "Oh, Tom! You didn't come here to tell my father that even though you now own all his fish, you're going to let him have one or two each year? That is, if there's any left after you take what you need?"

Tom was shaken by the adroit way she had phrased her question, and he scarcely knew how to respond. "Well," he fumbled, "that's exactly what Mr. Ross proposes." When she laughed, he added lamely: "But he did express it a little better." Then, with force: "He means well, Nancy, he really does."

Now the girl's face grew as stern as those of her ancestors who had fought the Russians: "Throw your damned fish in the river."

"Nancy!"

"Do you think my father, who owns this river, would allow fish like those in our house? Under such conditions?" When Tom remained at the door with the two salmon in his hands, she reached out, grabbed his package, and smelled it disdainfully. "You must know that these fish are old, spoiled, caught days ago—and now thrown to the Tlingits who watched over them while they were alive in our river."

When Tom tried to protest, she said bitterly: "No Bigears would feed those fish to his dogs," and she ran down to the riverbank, drew back her right arm, and pitched the rancid fish into the stream.

When she returned to the house she washed her hands and offered Tom a cloth to wash his, and then she invited him to sit with her: "What's going to happen, Tom? Each year your cannery will grow bigger. You'll catch more of our salmon. And pretty soon you'll be placing one of those new traps right across our river. And do you know what'll happen then? There won't be any more salmon, and you will have to burn your handsome cannery."

Tom rose and moved uneasily about the room: "What a horrible thing to say! You talk as if we were monsters."

"You are," she said, but then she added quickly: "You're not to blame, I know that. Let's go up to the waterfall and watch the salmon leaping."

"I have to get back. Mr. Ross is handing out final orders before he sails for Seattle." Then, for some reason he could not explain, he said: "He's invited me to spend my vacation there, after the season ends up here."

"And you would be afraid to say no, wouldn't you?" There was such iciness in her voice that Tom said: "I can do as I please," and he took her by the hand, led her from the house, and started up the river to the waterfall where the brown bear had chased them and where the last salmon returning to spawn leaped like ballet dancers up the foaming waters, pirouetting on their tails as they gathered strength for the next leap.

"You see them jump," Tom said. "You can almost touch them. But you can't believe it," and in that moment of confession that Alaska contained mysteries he could not fathom, he became precious to Nancy Bigears, who, in these days of confusion, was meeting only those white men who remained blatantly ignorant of her homeland and all it represented. Tom Venn was the kind of white man who could save Alaska, who could pick a sensible path through the tangle that threatened the land, but whenever he uttered the word *Seattle,* he did so in a way that revealed his longing for that more exciting world.

"If you go to Seattle with Mr. Ross," she predicted, "you'll not come back. I know that."

Tom did not protest with specious assurances: "Maybe it's men like Mr. Ross in Seattle who make the right decisions about Alaska. Look at the miracle he created here. In February he cried 'Let there be a cannery on Taku Inlet,' and in May he had it operating."

"In all the wrong ways," she said with such finality that Tom became irritated. "For a thousand years," he said, "the salmon have been swimming up and down this river, doing no one any good. I guess they had baby salmon and then they died, and next year their babies died, and no one on this earth profited. Well, do you know where the salmon we packed last week are going? Philadelphia and Baltimore and Washington. Salmon that used to swim past your front door are heading for all those places to feed people. This year they're not heading up the Pleiades just to die."

She had nothing to say to this; if he refused to understand the great swing of nature, in which the going and coming of the salmon was as important as the rising and setting of the moon, she could not instruct him. But she understood, and from the destruction she had watched at the mouth of her river—the salmon caught but never canned, the thousands of fish allowed to rot because the gutting shed was swamped—she knew instinctively that conditions could only worsen, and it saddened her that men like Ross and the foremen, and yes, even Tom Venn, refused to see the drift of the future.

"We'd better go back," she said, adding a barb: "Mr. Ross will be wondering what you've been doing with his two salmon."

"You're in an ugly mood, Nancy. Maybe we should go back," but as they started, a pair of sockeye coming home after long travels reached the low waterfall, and with a persistence that had few parallels in nature, they tore into the difficult ascent and almost gleefully leaped and twisted and gained precarious resting places, finally reaching the higher level.

I'm like those salmon, Tom thought. I aspire to higher levels. But it never occurred to him that he could attain those levels in Juneau, or even here along the banks of Taku Inlet.

As they reached the spot where Nancy had spoken to the charging bear, bringing the animal to a halt, they recalled that scene, and both of them began to laugh, and Tom saw her once more as that dauntless fourteen-year-old child who had lectured the bear and perhaps saved both their lives; but now she seemed so much more grown-up and golden and happy in her freedom that he took her in his arms and kissed her.

Now there was no laughter, for she had known that this would happen, and that it was proper for it to happen, but also that it would come to nothing, for they were on different rivers heading in different directions. For a brief spell during the potlatch of the totem raising he had been a Tlingit, appreciative of her people's values, and in the cave at Mendenhall Glacier he had accepted her as a white girl attuned to some new Alaska, but neither moment solidified, and these kisses, which could have been so meaningful, were not a beginning, but a parting.

In near-silence they walked back, feeling none of the elation which should have followed a first kiss, and when they reached the house Nancy called to her father, who had returned with a friend: "Pop! Mr. Ross said we would be allowed to have a salmon now and then. The first two he sent us were rotten, so I threw them in the river."

Sam, ignoring the bitter comment, asked Tom: "Was the season as good as you hoped?" and Tom said: "Better." They left the matter there, but when the two young people walked down to Tom's dory, Nancy said: "I'm sorry."

"About what?"

"I don't know," and she kissed him farewell.

The kiss was viewed by Mr. Ross, who had borrowed a pair of binoculars to see why his manager was so long delayed in delivering two fish across the cove, and when Tom anchored his boat and climbed back to the cannery, he was told that Mr. Ross wanted to see him. The Seattle merchant, disturbed by what he had seen, felt that here was a situation that had to be handled immediately.

"Tom, you have a bright future, a very bright future. But young men like you with everything before you, you sometimes stumble and lose it all."

"I don't know what you mean."

Mr. Ross hated dissembling and was always willing to speak bluntly when affairs of moment were involved: "I mean girls. Indian girls. I borrowed these glasses to see what was keeping you, and I suppose you know what I saw."

"No, I don't."

"I saw you kissing that Bigears girl. I saw . . ."

Tom heard no more of the charge, for he was thinking: I did not kiss her. She kissed me. And what business is it of his, anyway? And then Mr. Ross explained in forceful terms just why a vagrant kiss was his business: "Do you think I could let you keep running the Juneau store if you were married to an Indian girl? Do you think Ross & Raglan would ever bring you to headquarters in Seattle if you had an Indian wife? How could you and your wife meet with the other company officials? Socially, I mean." On and on he went, repeating stories he had heard of the disastrous consequences which followed such marriages: "And in our own experience, Tom, in our various stores, that is, we've seen only tragedy when we hired squaw men. It never works, because you can't mix oil and water."

Tom bristled, and spoke with the same hard sense of integrity that had motivated his employer: "In Dawson and Nome, I saw quite a few squaw men who led better lives than most of us. In fact, the whole Klondike field was discovered by a squaw man."

"On a gold frontier there may be a place for such men, Tom, but we're talking about real society, which is what towns like Juneau will soon have. In real society, squaw men are at a terrible disadvantage." He shook his head in sad recollection, then spoke with extra force:

"And another thing to think about, young man, their half-breed children are doomed from the start."

"I think that settlements like Nome and Juneau will soon be filled with half-breed children," Tom countered. "They'll run those towns."

"Don't you believe it." And Ross was about to cite telling evidence about the total ineptitude of half-breeds he had known in the Northwest when loud shouting was heard from the main shed, and the white foreman bellowed: "Help! The Chinks are running wild."

Tom, who had for some time anticipated such an outbreak, leaped for the wooden causeway leading to the main shed, but Mr. Ross had reacted even more quickly, and as Tom ran toward the sound of rioting, he could see his boss plowing ahead like an enraged bear to join in the fray. As the two white men burst into the brawl, Tom thought: God help the Chinks if Mr. Ross gets really mad.

Inside the cavernous building they met total chaos, with scores of Chinese roaring among the tables where that day's catch of salmon was being gutted, and although at first Tom thought that this was merely one more brawl in which two workmen had fallen into a fist-fight over jealously guarded positions at the worktable, when he ran toward the center of the fighting he saw to his horror that the Chinese were attacking one another with their sharp gutting knives.

"Stop!" he bellowed, but his order had no effect. Mr. Ross, having been involved in riots before, waded into the midst of the fighting, laying about him vigorously and crying: "Get back! Get back!" a command which had no more effect than Tom's.

"Ah Ting!" Tom called, hoping to locate the leader of the Chinese. "Ah Ting! Stop this."

He could not spot the tough little man, nor did he see any evidence that anyone was trying to halt the melee, but then Mr. Ross, infuriated by this frenzied interruption in the canning process, started to grab one Chinese or another, and at first he was unsuccessful.

"Tom! Give me a hand!" And as Venn ran to assist his boss, who had grabbed the pigtail of one of the more vigorous of the fighters, he shouted: "I'm here!" But as he did so, he saw to his horror that Mr. Ross had pinioned the arms of the man he held, rendering him unable to defend himself, and in this exposed position the terrified Chinese could only watch impotently as a fellow worker lunged at him with a long fish knife, jabbing it once into the man's heart and then into his stomach, which he ripped apart with a powerful upward thrust.

As Mr. Ross held the captive in his arms he could feel life seeping out of the tense body, and when the wounded man went limp, both Ross and Tom watched helplessly while three of the dead man's friends leaped upon the assassin, stabbing him many times until he, too, fell dead.

"Ah Ting!" Tom began to shout aimlessly, but the man who had been assigned to prevent just such outbursts could still not be found. But now he was not needed, for the shock of the two slayings caught the Chinese off guard, and they backed away, awaiting the restoration of order. Mr. Ross, still clutching the body of the man whose death he had caused, looked about in bewilderment while Tom continued to call for Ah Ting.

And then Tom saw the aggressive leader. He was pinned against a wall, surrounded by three men, all taller than he, holding their knives against his throat and heart. Some wild dislocation had swept through the cutting shed, something too big to be handled by ordinary procedures, and in its first moments these men, determined to see it to a conclusion, had isolated Ah Ting to prevent him from exercising his authority. Two murders had resulted, and now when Tom ran up to the men, shouting: "Let him go!" they obeyed.

"Big fight, boss," Ah Ting gasped as he shook himself free. "Could not stop."

Mr. Ross lumbered up, his hands red with the blood of the man he had been holding. "Were you in charge here?" he blustered, and Tom interceded: "This is Ah Ting. Leader. Good man. These three held him prisoner."

Mr. Ross's first reaction was to shout "You three are fired!" but before he could utter the words he realized how stupid they would sound, for there was no way of firing unsatisfactory Chinese working at a summer cannery. The men had come from Shanghai to America on a British boat. They had come from San Francisco to Seattle on an American train. And some Ross & Raglan recruiter had placed them aboard an R&R steamer, which had conveyed them to Taku Inlet, where they had been deposited directly from the ship to the cannery. Supposing that Mr. Ross, in his obstinacy, went ahead and fired the three men, where could they go? They were miles from any settled area, and if they did reach some town like Juneau or Sitka, they would be refused entrance, for Chinese were not allowed. They were supposed to arrive by ship in late spring, work all summer at some remote outpost, and leave by ship in early autumn, taking their few dollars with them and surviving in some large, impersonal city till the recruiters summoned them again for the next canning season.

So instead of firing the men responsible for neutralizing Ah Ting, Mr. Ross scowled at them and asked Tom: "What can we do?" and Tom gave the only sensible answer: "Only thing we can do, trust Ah Ting to get the men back to work."

"Do we call the police? There are two men dead over there."

"There are no police," Tom said, and in this statement he described the extraordinary position in which the District of Alaska found itself. There were men in towns like Juneau who were called policemen, but they had no real authority, for there was still no properly organized system of government, and for such improvised officers to venture into an area like Taku Inlet was unthinkable. Each cannery ran its own system of self-protection, which included drastic measures for handling disturbances, including crimes at the plant. Therefore, the murder of the two Chinese workers became Tom Venn's responsibility, and Mr. Ross was most interested to see how the young man proceeded.

He was favorably impressed by the fearlessness with which Tom moved among the agitated workers, directing them back to their tasks and checking to ensure the maintenance of an orderly flow of salmon from the arriving fishing ships. But when the time came for Tom to discipline the men who were seen to have done the stabbing, Mr. Ross was appalled to see that Venn turned the matter over to Ah Ting, and Ross was further dismayed when he watched how the leader of the Chinese handled it. Ah Ting reprimanded the guilty men, did nothing to punish the others who had immobilized him in the fracas, and blandly told the men to pick up their gutting knives and get back to work.

But it was what he did afterward that affected Mr. Ross most profoundly, for Ah Ting directed two men to fetch one of the large barrels used for shipping salted fish to Europe, and when the barrel was in position he himself poured in a three-inch layer of coarse rock salt. Then he leaned deep into the barrel to spread the salt evenly over the bottom, after which he drew himself out, brushed off his hands, and directed his two helpers to bring the first of the slain men. When the corpse lay on the floor before him, Ah Ting helped his men strip away all bits of clothing and then hoist the dead body into the barrel, where it was propped into a sitting position. Now the second corpse was undressed and carefully fitted into the barrel, also in an upright sitting position, facing the first man and adjusting to him.

"What in hell are they doing?" Mr. Ross asked, and Tom explained: "Our contract requires us to ship any dead Chinese back to China for burial in what they call 'the sacred soil of the Celestial Kingdom.'"

"In a barrel?"

"Look!" And as they stared in disbelief, Ah Ting and his helpers packed every cranny in the barrel with rock salt, filling it so to the brim that no sign of the dead men remained visible. Even their nostrils were crammed with salt. And when the heavy lid was nailed tight, the coffin barrel was ready for shipment back to China, where the two slain men would attain whatever immortality this tradition ensured.

Back in the manager's quarters, Mr. Ross was still agitated by what he had seen: "A man murdered while I was holding him. His assailant stabbed half a dozen times. The man supposed to be in charge being held captive. And everything settled by packing the victims in a barrel and salting them down." The more he reflected on this extraordinary behavior, the more distressed he became: "We can't have Chinese in our cannery. You've got to get rid of them, Tom."

"Nobody can run a cannery without them," Venn said, and he reviewed briefly the disastrous experiences of operators who had tried to handle the great crush of salmon with other kinds of workmen: "Indians refuse to work fifteen hours a day. White men are worse. You've seen that our Filipinos cause more trouble than the Chinese and do half the work. Mr. Ross, we're stuck with them, and I don't want today's incident to sour you, especially not in our first year."

"What irritates me—no, it's worse than irritation, it's downright fear—is the way you and I are at the mercy of that Ah Ting. I think he let those men neutralize him. He didn't want to face those knife-wielding wild men."

"But when he was freed, Mr. Ross, he did get the men back to work. I couldn't have done it."

"I will not have a cannery of mine at the mercy of a Chinese scoundrel. We must do something." And as he began to study his Chinese employees, what he saw caused further dismay: "In the whole lot, only three speak any English. They're a tight clan living by their own rules, with their own food, their own customs. And for some reason I can't pinpoint, that Ah Ting unnerves me."

"I've sometimes felt the same way, Mr. Ross."

"What is there about him?"

"He knows he's indispensable. He knows this cannery couldn't handle a single salmon without him. And I think he's clever."

"About what?"

"I'm sure he knew that serious trouble had become inescapable. He suspected there might be knifings and he wanted to be held prisoner while it took its course."

"I want him off our property." When Tom made no reply, Ross continued: "It infuriates me to see him grinning at me, knowing that he's in command, not me."

Tom, aware that there was no chance of dispensing with Ah Ting, neither this year nor next, ignored Ross's unhappiness, and three days later the two men stood together as a crane hoisted the burial barrel off the wharf and onto the deck of an R&R ship loading salmon to ship to a wholesaler in Boston. No Chinese workman bothered to bid the dual coffin farewell as it headed back to China, but as Tom started for his office he caught a glimpse of Ah Ting in the shadows. The wiry fellow was smiling, and Tom entertained a momentary suspicion that Ah Ting was not at all unhappy to have at least one of the men in that barrel disappearing from Totem Cannery.

But preoccupation with the Chinese was abruptly terminated when Mr. Ross learned that the fishermen on whom his cannery relied for its salmon were protesting their meager pay and refusing to take their small boats out unless that scale was increased. The fishermen did not engage in a formal strike; that would be against their principles of freedom and individual responsibility, for as one sailor said: "Strikes are for factory people in Chicago and Pittsburgh. All we demand is fair pay for what we catch." And when Mr. Ross told Tom Venn that additional pay was impossible, and Tom told the fishermen, boats stopped heading up Taku Inlet, and for two desperately long weeks Totem Cannery saw no salmon.

The Chinese workers in the carpentry shop kept building shipping boxes, but the larger number engaged in heading, gutting and cleaning the catch had nothing to do, and in their idleness they started having trouble with the Filipinos, who were also idle. The huge establishment at the mouth of the Pleiades River became such an uneasy place that Tom warned his boss: "If we don't get some salmon in here right quick, there's going to be real trouble."

It was then that young Tom Venn came to appreciate the difficulties of management, for he watched at close hand as Malcolm Ross, a determined and wealthy man of fifty-two who commanded hundreds of men and almost a score of ships, stood helpless before a gang of Chinese and a rabble of fishermen in small boats. He could not command his Chinese to behave if they had no work to do, nor could he halt their wages, and he had to continue feeding them, for they were prisoners at his cannery and could not move elsewhere if they wanted to.

And he was equally ineffective with the fishermen. Fiercely stubborn, they said: "We can live off our savings or what we get peddling fish to housewives in Juneau. Mr. Ross of Seattle can go to hell." Ross, unwilling to grant demands which he felt to be excessive, was powerless to make them fish and incapable of getting his salmon from any other source. Caught in this vise formed by Chinese in one jaw, illiterate white and Indian fishermen in the other, he felt himself so miserably squeezed that he spent one whole week fuming and contriving ways to put himself in a secure position which no Chinese, no fisherman could ever attack: "We must make ourselves self-sufficient, Tom. We must never be forced to sweat out a season like this."

He did not confide to Tom what he was devising, but during the closing days of the second painful week, when the cannery was losing great sums each day, he walked back and forth along the banks of Taku Inlet as if studying its fish-laden waters, and then through the cavernous buildings whose tables and ovens and canning sheds were silent. Only the hammering of the Chinese carpenters as they built boxes that might never be filled broke the solemn quietness, and out of these days of intense study, Malcolm Ross of Seattle constructed his vision and launched his plan to attain it.

"What we shall do before next year," he told Tom almost bitterly, "is surprise these scoundrels. Ross & Raglan will never again be held up by Chinese coolies and hard-drinking fishermen."

"What do you have in mind?"

"To get rid of that grinning Ah Ting. To teach those insolent fishermen a lesson."

"How?"

Ross swung into vigorous action: "Tell the fishermen we'll accept their demands if they double their catch. Tell Ah Ting his sheds must run sixteen hours a day. Send a telegram to get our two biggest boats up here. In the remaining weeks of this season we're going to pack the way Alaska has never seen before."

The fishermen, gloating over the way they had defeated the big man from Seattle, accepted the challenge he issued, and assured of the raise they sought, fished arduously to earn the bonus he promised. And as soon as the handsome loads of sockeye salmon arrived at the cannery dock, Ah Ting's Chinese crew accepted the extra rations Mr. Ross authorized and then worked sixteen productive hours each day, seven days a week.

The gutting tables were never free of fish. The great cooking ovens, made in Germany, received one batch of cans after another. Chinese tinsmiths worked in three shifts to build the great volume of cans required, while skilled men under Ah Ting's direction soldered the lids, and the packing crew stowed them in boxes, forty-eight to a box, and sent them down the slide to the waiting ships.

When the cannery was running at maximum speed, with all parts meshing as Mr. Ross had visualized a year ago, he saw it as an American miracle, an almost flawless operation which provided one of the world's most nutritious foods to eager buyers throughout the world at a price no other form of food could match. Taking one of the cans from the machine which pasted on the bright-red Totem label, he hefted it, tossed it to Tom Venn, and cried: "A pound of matchless salmon. Sixteen cents in stores across America. And next year it's all to be under our control, Tom. No more Chinese. No more men in tiny boats commanding us what to do."

In his euphoria he uttered a phrase which would dominate his actions for the remainder of his life: "It's the job of Seattle businessmen to organize Alaska. And I promise you I'm going to show the way."

"What am I to do?" Tom asked, and he said: "Pay the bills. See that our last ship takes away the Chinese. Close the place down, and after the first of the year, catch one of our ships at Juneau and work with me in Seattle. Because next year we are going to astonish the world." With that, he boarded an R&R ship at the Totem dock, waved farewell to the cannery whose first campaign was coming to an end, and watched approvingly as the ship's captain threaded his way toward the Walrus, out into the channel, and on to his offices in Seattle.

• • •

On 5 January 1904 Tom Venn turned the management of R&R affairs in Juneau over to his assistant and took passage on one of his firm's smaller vessels headed for Seattle, thus fulfilling a desire which had gnawed at him since the day in March 1898 when he and Missy had left that enticing city for the Klondike gold fields. He was so excited about seeing Seattle again that he barely slept the first night out, and when the ship finally entered the quiet waters of Puget Sound he was perched on the railing hoping for a sight of Mount Rainier. When that majestic snow-clad peak appeared, he cried to no one in particular: "Look at that mountain!" Later, when a woman passenger asked: "What's that huge mountain?" he said proudly: "Mount Rainier. It guards Seattle," and the woman told him: "Looks as if an artist painted it," and he nodded.

It was an emotional homecoming for Tom, and as the familiar sights of the city rose from the water, he entertained bold thoughts: If in the next few years I show a profit on the salmon cannery, Mr. Ross will be almost obligated to promote me to the Seattle headquarters permanently. That'll be the day! Whispering to himself, he said: "I'll use the money John Klope gave me to buy a home on one of those hills and watch as our ships sail home from Alaska." As the words formed he could visualize the *Alacrity,* that small white R&R ship on which Missy had worked and on which he, Missy and his father had traveled to great adventure on the Yukon.

How far away those days of high daring seemed, and as he thought of them he resolved to perform as creditably at the cannery as Missy had done in Dawson and Nome: You'll be proud of me, Missy. One of these days you'll be proud of me.

His excitement grew as he left the ship, carrying nothing, and hurried along the dock where he had once sold newspapers. Searching for the familiar sign of the R&R dockside offices, he found that the old building had been replaced by a fine modern one, and when he burst through its doors, three older men inside recognized him: "It's Tom Venn. Loaded with Nome gold." After enthusiastic greetings they told him: "You're to leave your bags aboard ship. We'll send them along."

"Where am I to stay?"

"Mr. Ross left orders for you to go to the main office immediately. He'll give you instructions."

It was ten in the morning when Tom arrived at the building on Cherry Street, its oak door bearing the neatly carved blazon ROSS &

RAGLAN, and as on that first visit nearly seven years ago, he felt a pulse of excitement on entering the waiting room leading to Mr. Ross's office. The same austere lady, Ella Sommers, her hair now streaked with white, guarded the portals, and the same air of busy importance dominated the place, for this was the nerve center from which controlling ganglia spread out to all sections of northwestern America and Alaska.

"I'm Tom Venn, from Juneau. The men at the dock told me that Mr. Ross wanted to see me."

"Indeed he does," Miss Sommers said. "You're to go right in," and she nodded toward the door through which she allowed only a few to pass.

As soon as Tom entered the room he felt once more the spell of the powerful man who sat behind the big blond-oak desk. As before, the red-haired man fitted exactly the setting from which he operated, but this time the office was filled with three smaller tables, on which rested a bewildering array of small wooden models whose interlocking parts moved when Mr. Ross or one of the two men working in the room operated them.

"Tom, these men are from the university. They know salmon. Gentlemen, this is our Mr. Venn from the Totem Cannery, where your machines will be installed, if you ever get them to work." And with these peremptory words the informal session began.

Moving to the largest of the three tables, Mr. Ross explained: "This is Taku Inlet, and this feeder, shown by the blue paper, is our Pleiades River. Our cannery, obviously, is on this point. Professor Starling, show us how it's going to work."

As the first words were spoken, Tom accommodated himself to the diagram; he was in the middle of Taku Inlet, and when the professor said: "Now you must imagine yourself a sockeye swimming upstream to spawn on a warm July day," Tom became a salmon, and from that moment on, he understood viscerally what Starling said.

"This is Taku Inlet as we know it now. The returning salmon, heading for either our Lake Pleiades over here, or to one of the hundred similar lakes upstream in Alaska or over the border in Canada, swim past this point, where your fishermen catch a fair proportion and bring them to the cannery over here."

"The system worked pretty well last summer," Tom said. "And we're enlarging the cannery starting March first."

"It was a respectable catch you canned," the second professor said, a Dr. Whitman, "but it could have been four times that size."

"Impossible!" Tom said without hesitation. "Mr. Ross knows that our boats worked overtime, barring the two weeks they fought about their pay."

Mr. Ross broke in: "These men have a way to help us escape the tyranny of the fishermen and, as they just said, quadruple our catch."

"That would be miraculous," Tom said bluntly, and Ross replied: "It's only miracles that will save our industry, and we have three of them right here in this room. Study closely, Tom."

"What we will do," Professor Starling said, "is throw this weir across a fair portion of the inlet and completely across the entrance to the Pleiades River," and onto the middle portion of the table representing the historic waterway he placed a wooden construction which clearly dominated much of the inlet and all the river. When Tom gasped, protesting that no dam of that magnitude could be built in the deep waters of Taku, Starling laughed: "That's what everybody says. That's what Mr. Ross said in this very room when I put the construction in place for him." The professor looked at Ross, who smiled and nodded.

"What we do," Starling explained, "is float this entire central section out into the channel, anchor it, and then build these wings on the sides as permanent structures fastened to the bottom. And look what we have!"

Tom Venn, still swimming upstream as a salmon, found himself facing an obstruction in his familiar waterway, and when he came to one of its outreaching arms he naturally followed the slant to the left, and this threw him into the heart of the floating trap, which contained a restricted pen large enough to hold five hundred salmon. From it the struggling fish could be easily netted for transfer to the cannery.

"What we have," Starling explained, "is a three-part masterpiece. These long fingers reach out to guide the salmon our way. We call them *jiggers* because they jig the fish along in the direction we want. Then the trap itself, with these narrowing chambers into which the salmon can swim but from which they can't retreat. And finally the big holding pen, where the salmon collect until we process them in the cannery."

When his contraption was fully explained, he stood back admiringly and said: "Consider the virtues. Cheap to build. Cheap to repair. Guaranteed to catch every salmon heading up the Pleiades and a fair share of those heading for Canada." Then came Ross's powerful assessment: "And we can tell the boatmen to go to hell."

Tom, still trapped in the holding pen into which he had swum exactly as Professor Starling had intended, said quietly: "It's catching salmon without having to fish for them," and the three older men applauded, for that was precisely what the weir and its outriding jiggers would make possible.

"We start building this in mid-February," Ross said. "The weir, the holding pen and the western jigger all float. The eastern jigger coming out from our shore, that we'll build permanently."

And then Tom saw the fallacy of the proposed system: "But no salmon can get through to spawn in Lake Pleiades. Three years, four years, you'll wipe out all our sockeyes."

"Aha!" Ross cried. "We've thought of that. Each Saturday afternoon we'll close down the trap, open the jiggers, and let all the salmon swimming upstream Saturday night and all day Sunday get through. Professor Whitman assures us that that will be enough to ensure ample stocks the following years." And Whitman nodded.

"Now for the Chinese!" Ross cried as he moved to the second table, his eyes dancing with excitement. "Look at this, will you?" And on a beautifully constructed model using real tin he demonstrated a clean, simple solution to the problem of making cans: "A large wagon drawn by four horses comes onto the dock here in Seattle, delivering fifty thousand, a hundred thousand of these for shipment to Totem Cannery." And he held in his left hand a small rectangular piece of flattened tin, which Tom could not visualize as a finished can, and said so.

"I couldn't either," Ross said. "When Professor Whitman showed it to me, I laughed. But watch!"

Wedging the piece of tin into position on the complicated machine, he pressed a lever, and slowly a plunger forced its way between what was now revealed as two layers of tin, and when it had made an entrance, another plunger took over, spreading out the welded tin into a perfectly formed can lacking bottom or top. "Every ten seconds," Ross cried triumphantly, "you have a perfect can, ready for the bottom to be soldered on and the insides filled with salmon." Handing the finished can to Tom, he said with great force: "No more Chinese making cans. It will all be done here in Seattle, kept flat to save shipping space, and formed out with one of these machines at the cannery."

"We'll still have to solder the bottoms and the lids," Tom pointed out, and Ross snapped: "You'll teach Filipinos how to do it. I've ordered ten of these machines."

Exulting in his partial victory over Ah Ting and his fractious Chinese, Ross now moved to the final model, by far the most important of the lot: "We don't have this perfected, yet, but Professor Whitman says we're getting close."

"Correction!" Whitman interrupted. "They told me yesterday they've eliminated the problem of adjusting to size."

"They have?"

"Yes. I haven't actually seen the new version, but if what they told me is true . . ."

"Let's go see!" Ross cried impulsively, and before they could protest he grabbed his coat, herded the other three out of his office, down the stairs and onto the street, where he hailed two horse-drawn cabs to take the men to a factory at the southern edge of the business district. Here, in a long, low building, two practical-minded wizards were at work on a machine which, if it ever worked, would revolutionize the salmon industry. Nervous with excitement, Ross led the men into the dark work area of the building and to a long table which contained a bewildering array of wires, moving levers and sharp knives.

"What is it?" Tom asked, and Ross pointed to a hand-lettered sign which some comedian had attached by string to the weird contraption: THE IRON CHINK.

"That's what it is," Ross said. "A machine that does everything a Chinaman does now," and at his signal the two engineers opened a steam valve, whereupon various belts and levers began to operate, and with much creaking, went through a series of motions calculated to cut off the head of a salmon, cut away the tail, and with a special long blade gut it from gullet to anus and whisk out the entrails. Tom, watching the various movements, could visualize how the intricate invention was supposed to work, but he doubted that it would: "Salmon don't all come in the same size."

"That's been our problem," one of the inventors said. "But we think we have it solved," and while the machine was still going through its clanging motions, he fetched from an icebox three salmon, two of about standard size, the third much shorter. Feeding the first of the standards into the machine as would be done at a cannery, he watched with obvious satisfaction as his machine took the fish, lopped off its head and tail, wasting not an ounce of good meat, then turned it on its side and with deft strokes gutted it, swept away the offal, and sent the beautifully cleaned fish on its way.

"That's wonderful!" Tom cried, and as he spoke the second standard salmon came creeping along, and it, too, was handled perfectly. "Great! Great!" Tom shouted above the noise of the belts. "We could sort the fish and send through only those of the same size."

"But wait!" the second inventor shouted, and with an almost paternal affection he introduced into the machine the third, shorter sockeye. A part of the system which Tom had not noticed before came down, sized the fish and adjusted the knives accordingly, so that now the head and tail were cut off quite differently from before, with Tom cheering at the cleverness of the operation.

But when the salmon was turned on its side, the most important of the knives failed to adjust, and in an unguided flash cut the smaller fish to pieces.

"Oh, hell!" the first inventor cried. "Oscar, that damn cam doesn't work."

"It worked last night, didn't it, Professor Whitman?"

"I saw it. Adjusted perfectly."

The disappointed man hammered at the offending cam, fixed it to his satisfaction, then said: "Let's try two more fish," and when the normal-sized one went through, the knives worked perfectly, but when the undersized one came through, the cam once more failed to adjust and once more the big knife shredded the fish.

"What can it be?" the man asked in almost tearful bewilderment, at which the second inventor said with painful honesty: "We thought we could have it ready for the 1904 campaign. I'm sure we can fix it, Mr. Ross, but I can't let you risk it as it stands."

"He's right," the other man said. "I'm positive I can work out a foolproof system, but we don't have it yet," and his partner said ruefully: "You'd better sign up your Chinese for one more year. But by 1905 this little beauty will be doing all your work for you."

"You need any more funds?" Ross asked, and together the two men said: "Yes," and one of them added: "We're very close, Mr. Ross. I have another idea for adjusting to the length of the fish. I preferred it to begin with, but it requires one extra part and I had hoped to keep it simple."

"Keep it simple. Take time and keep it so simple that even a Filipino can fix it," and he snapped at Tom: "Hire the Chinese. One more
time." Then he added gruffly: "But do not hire Ah Ting. Won't have
him on the place." And to his own surprise, Tom said firmly: "We
can't handle the Chinese without him," and that afternoon he arranged for the employment of some ninety Chinese to handle the
increased flow of salmon.

At dusk, exhausted by the long day's work, Tom asked: "Where
am I to stay?" and Ross replied: "I've told the men to deliver your
things to our house. You'll be staying with us," and in the dark, wintry evening the two men rode behind R&R horses to the Ross mansion at the top of a modest rise from which could be seen the grandeur
of the Seattle waterfront with its myriad bays and channels, islands
and promontories. It was a marine wonderland made even more attractive by the height from which Tom saw it; he wanted to express
how much it enchanted him, but prudence told him to remain silent
lest Mr. Ross interpret his enthusiasm as a strategy for angling an
assignment in the city. However, Ross spoke for him: "Isn't this a
grand view of a great city, Tom? I never tire of it," and the two admired it for some moments before turning to face the mansion.

It was a nineteenth-century Gothic castle, not overly pretentious
or grandiose in size but very definitely modeled on some forgotten
Rhine structure, featuring small turrets, battlements and gargoyles.
Had other less flamboyant buildings encroached, it would have
seemed out of place, but since it stood alone among tall pines, it
maintained a quiet grandeur. "Highlands" he had named his castle in
memory of that noble part of Scotland from which his father had
been evicted in the mournful Clearances of 1830, and his neighbors
in Seattle, who knew nothing of the past history of the Rosses, supposed that the name referred only to the height on which the castle
stood and deemed it appropriate.

As with the office building in town, the castle was guarded by two
heavy oak doors, and Tom said approvingly: "You seem to like oak,
Mr. Ross," and the Scotsman replied: "I certainly don't like white
pine."

Mrs. Ross, some years younger than her husband, was a gracious
lady who wore simple clothes and ran the mansion with the help of
only two servants. She exhibited no airs as she moved forward to
greet the young workman who had been invited into her home with
little consultation on her part. Having been informed of his excellent

record on the Klondike, at Nome and now at the cannery, she was surprised at his youthfulness and said so: "How could you have crammed so much into so few years?"

"A lot happens in a gold rush. I was there each time," and she said: "But salmon isn't gold," and he said: "It's Alaska's new gold. And bound to be much more important than the metal kind." She smiled approvingly at the way he expressed himself.

For three happy days Tom Venn stayed at Highlands, working with Mr. Ross on schemes relating to Alaska and pointing out on large maps, often inaccurately drawn, where additional R&R canneries might profitably be placed. At the conclusion of their work, southeastern Alaska, the only part that mattered, was peppered with half a dozen proposed sites, and Ross said, as he looked down at the island world: "Unlimited wealth in those cold waters, Tom. You're to build one new cannery a year as fast as we can get title to the sites. And the man is arriving tomorrow who will make it possible."

He identified the stranger no further, but on Friday noon he and Tom went to the railway station, and were waiting there when the train from Chicago deposited the man on whom R&R would rely for the allocation of vital leases to land for its canneries and, what was much more important, exclusive rights to the salmon-bearing rivers.

Mr. Ross was delighted to see the newcomer descending the steps from the Pullman, but Tom was astounded. It was Marvin Hoxey, forty-nine years old, ten pounds heavier than he had been at Nome, and more ebullient and conniving than ever. On the ride from the station to the R&R offices he expounded grandiloquently on how he had lined up support throughout Congress for the new regulations which Seattle businessmen felt they needed in order to manage affairs in Alaska. And not once in his volcanic explanations of how the new laws would operate did he acknowledge that he had ever seen Tom Venn before, but as they stepped from the carriage to enter the R&R building, Mr. Ross said: "This is Tom Venn, who'll be in charge of our canneries project," and Hoxey said with a kind of noble condescension: "Of course. Mr. Venn and I shared those unpleasant experiences in Nome, dreadful city, frozen tight most of the year."

Later, when Hoxey had moved into the main guest room at Highlands, Tom said tentatively to Mr. Ross: "You know, that man in there . . . he was put in jail, for what he did in Nome," and Ross said with an almost icy formality: "And McKinley pardoned him. Completely. The President knew Hoxey had been torpedoed by jealous political enemies." When Tom started to explain that that wasn't the way it had been, not really, Ross cut him short with a piece of frontier advice long tested in the crucible of practicality: "Tom, many times when you have a job that simply has to be done, the best man to use is a disbarred lawyer. He has to work hard."

During that long weekend Tom paid close attention as Ross, Hoxey and three business leaders of the community laid plans which would bind Alaska and its fisheries indissolubly to Seattle, and in all the projected maneuvering, Malcolm Ross led the way: "What we must do is enact in Washington a law which requires all goods headed for Alaska to pass through Seattle."

"Congress would never pass such a law," one of the other men protested, and Hoxey corrected him: "Congress will pass any law dealing with Alaska that the Western states agree to. Your problem, gentlemen, is to decide what within reason you want."

"We'll begin with the law I just proposed," Ross said, "but we will not present it to Congress in that form."

"What form do you suggest?" the original protester asked with a touch of sarcasm.

"Patriotism, Sam. Our law will forbid ships of any other nation to conduct business directly with Alaska. They must transship all their goods through an American port, which will naturally be Seattle."

"That makes sense," Hoxey cried. "It's reasonable. It's easy to understand. And it is, as Mr. Ross said, patriotic."

"The advantage . . ." Ross began, then stopped to correct himself. "There are really several advantages. Our local stevedores will get paid for unloading the foreign ship and then paid again for loading the goods into our ships. And since cheap competition will be eliminated, our merchants can pretty much establish their own prices. It's expensive to run ships into those cold, island-strewn waters." He paused, looked at each of the men, and asked: "Have you any idea how many ships are lost each year in Alaskan waters?" And when they replied "No," he ticked off the disastrous record, going back to the days when Russia owned the area, losing several ships a year on reefs and hidden rocks: "And the Americans haven't done a lot better. Our company has already lost two."

"Sounds like poor captains and faulty navigation," one of the men suggested, but Ross rejected that charge: "More like sudden storms, wild seas and submerged rocks that haven't been properly charted," and he told them of the ferocious wind that could come roaring out of Canada down Taku Inlet, rattling the roof of the cannery and placing any fishing boat in jeopardy: "Alaska is no place for weaklings. Mining gold was difficult. Mining salmon requires just as much daring. Any profit we make from Alaskan waters, we earn."

"But how can we protect your access to the salmon?" asked a financier whom Ross had approached for funds to cover the rapid development of the canneries he was proposing.

"Tom, fetch that model of Taku Inlet," and when Tom returned from the office with it, Ross said: "Explain to the men how this trap will work." But before Tom could begin, Ross said: "Gentlemen, you are to visualize traps like this in every major salmon stream. Properly administered, they will control the entire production of salmon."

"This isn't a design, or a plan," Tom began. "It shows a real cannery. Totem on Taku Inlet coming out of Canada, where a little river called the Pleiades comes in. Our salmon breed in this little lake up here, and in a hundred others along the Taku River system, most of them in Canada. Up and down Taku Inlet salmon move by the million. So here at this vantage point we float this trap. Costs very little to build, and then we line out these grabbers to steer the fish in. Jiggers we call them, and when they're in place every salmon coming up Taku Inlet becomes a possibility for our cannery here."

It was a beautiful, easy-to-control system as Tom explained it, but one of the more experienced men listening to the details was quick to spot an important problem: "But what about Canada? If the Taku salmon breed mostly in their waters? Won't they raise hell about an efficient trap like this intercepting fish headed for their river system?"

"Tom," Mr. Ross directed, "fetch that big map of the area," and when it was unfolded the men were shown the amazing structure of the area they were discussing: "Here's Juneau, the new capital of Alaska. And a score of miles over here is Canada. You could ride the distance in half a day with a good horse. Except for one thing. Look closely, gentlemen. These mountains along the border are more than eight thousand feet high, rising from sea level in that short distance. And on our side, this entire area is one vast ice field. If you set out on foot to walk from Juneau to Canada, you'd be on a glacier all the way, with crevasses and monstrous uprisings of ice, and it might take you three weeks, if you were lucky enough to get through alive."

While the men studied the forbidding terrain, he dismissed with a wave of his hand all of Canada east of the salmon stations: "Wilderness. Towering mountains. Ice fields. Wild rivers. Inaccessible. Not one settler in a hundred square miles. Not one cannery anywhere and none likely to exist for a hundred years."

Again the men studied the map, that vast expanse of nothingness on the Canadian side, after which Ross summarized: "In building our system of canneries and traps, we can ignore Canada. For our purposes, it doesn't exist." And he turned to more pressing matters: "Hoxey, it's up to you to prevent the government of Alaska, such as it is, from passing any laws that might restrict our access to the salmon. No taxes. No impositions. No inspectors snooping around our canneries. And above all, no legislation governing the operation of traps."

When Hoxey said that that was how he understood his commission, Ross said: "Good. Now execute it," and to the businessmen he said: "Gentlemen, in situations like this one at Taku Inlet—and Alaska has hundreds as good or better—we have a gold mine, a living, swimming gold mine, but we must harvest it with care. Maintain quality. Penetrate new markets. Make salmon the rich man's delight, the poor man's sustenance. Can we do it, Tom?"

"If those two professors can perfect the Iron Chink, the sky's the limit."

"And what is this Iron Chink?" one of the prospective investors asked, and Ross said simply: "A secret which must not go beyond this room. But two men at the university are about to perfect a machine which will make the use of Chinese labor no longer necessary."

"What does it do?"

"An endless supply of salmon moves down the conveyor and automatically the machine cuts off the head and tail, then sizes the salmon and guts it beautifully. Without the help of one damned Chinaman, the fish is prepared for canning, and another comes along in nine seconds."

"Does such a machine exist?"

"Not for this canning season. But sure as the sun rises in the east, by 1905, farewell to those Chinamen and hello to profits you haven't even dreamed about."

But then came a sharp protest from one of the men who had been paying special attention to the Taku model: "Hey, wait a minute! If we throw those weirs clear across the inlet to trap our fish, how are the baby salmon going to get out of the lake when they want to head for the ocean?"

Tom slapped himself on the forehead: "I always forget to explain the most important things. The movable weirs are in position only during the part of the year when we're catching mature salmon coming upstream. When the young ones come down from the lake, they find the inlet open right to the sea."

Hoxey left Seattle on Tuesday morning, a complete strategy for the control of Alaska in his satchel. According to the plan devised principally by Mr. Ross, the fabulous riches of the salmon run could be garnered by his and the other companies without involving more than a handful of Alaskan citizens: "All the lumber for the new canneries is milled here in Seattle and the machinery is assembled here too. Then it sails north in our ships. They're installed by the Seattle workmen who sail with them. The fish are caught in traps built here in the city and placed in position by our men. No more arguments with Tlingit fishermen, or white ones, either. The cans are made here, packed flat, and opened up at the cannery. No more tinsmiths. And best of all, that big bunkhouse filled with Ah Ting and his outfit, it will be filled with machines that'll work faster than that gang ever could and double our working area without adding another building."

He smiled at Hoxey, then said: "And when the cans are sealed and labeled, they come back here in our ships. And we send them throughout America and the rest of the world."

In the two days following Hoxey's departure, Tom drafted plans for the coming season at the R&R headquarters, and whenever he looked at the map in Mr. Ross's office and saw the red stars indicating where future canneries were to be established, he had a sinking feeling which he could share with no one: I'm never to get back to Seattle! I'm to spend my life moving from one Taku Inlet to the next, always building some new plant, and he could visualize the locations: Some remote inlet. No town within fifty miles. No wives. No children. Just traps catching salmon and the Iron Chink processing them.

But then he reflected on the advantages of working with a man like Malcolm Ross, who seemed unquestionably the most effective human being he had ever known: He's not warm and eager like Missy Peckham, who was the most admirable person he had been privileged to watch, but he does have vision and he does get things done. He was content to keep his wagon hitched to Mr. Ross, and as he reviewed the decisions of the past few days, he found that he had no reason to oppose any of Ross's plans for Alaska. Worthy things were to be done and the interests of both R&R and Seattle were to be protected.

It simply did not occur to Tom to question the morality of Seattle's intention to keep Alaska in a kind of serfdom, without political power or the right of any self-determination. He ignored the fact that if the Ross-Hoxey plans were established in law, Alaska would pay some fifty percent more for any goods it imported through Seattle than the similar territory of Hawaii would pay for its freight through San Francisco. Nor did he question the design that would leave Alaska powerless to pass any regional law protecting its salmon, or its trees, or its mines, or even its citizens. He did not at this time know the word *fiefdom,* but the concept would not have worried him: Mr. Ross has a clear vision of how Alaska should be developed, and no one I've met in Juneau has a clue as to what should be done.

No sooner did he reach this conclusion than he felt a twinge of doubt: Maybe Sam Bigears on the other side of the Pleiades, maybe he has a vision of how he and his Tlingits ought to live. And then he thought of Nancy Bigears facing the grizzly bear and talking him down: Maybe she knows, too, and when he visualized Nancy, he experienced a pang of remorse, for she and her father were aspects of Alaska that he could not dismiss.

However, his attention after work was diverted to the study of Mrs. Ross, whose behavior perplexed him. She was, on the one hand, a social leader in Seattle society, the wife of one of the city's richest men and obviously a woman of power. She could be imperious, as a social leader sometimes had to be, and she could look down her nose with the best of them, but even when she was being dictatorial, which she was several times in his presence, she displayed a roguish sense of humor, which bubbled into her eyes and often caused her to laugh quietly—at either herself or at the inadvertent pomposities of her husband.

At the end of his first week sharing the intimacies of the Ross home, Tom blurted out at the dinner table: "You are two of the nicest people I've ever met."

"Why, that's very kind of you, Tom. Surely, though, you've met many kind people in all your travels," and Mrs. Ross turned in her chair to study him.

"Well, I've met lots of nice people. Missy Peckham, who was like a mother to me, was about as good as a person could be. And I knew a goldminer on the Yukon. I'd go anywhere with him. But . . ."

"What are you trying to say?"

"Just that these were good people, maybe the very best, but things never seemed to work out for them."

"How do you mean?" It was obvious that Mrs. Ross was sincerely interested in his perceptions.

"Well, for one thing they never met the right person to marry. And for another, whatever they tried seemed to fail." He hesitated, then came to his significant point: "You're the first people in my life where you're both . . ." He did not know how to finish the contrast between the failures he had known and this pair of well-adjusted, happy people. "I guess what I mean is, I've known some wonderful people, but they were never married to each other." With this confession he looked down at his plate.

Mrs. Ross cherished such moments of honest revelation; her life had been enriched by them and she had no intention of allowing this conversation to end on such a note: "You mean to say, Tom Venn, that you've never before seen a happily married couple?"

"I never have."

"What do you think makes us so different?"

"Well, you both have power, a lot of it, but you don't abuse it."

"That's a wonderful compliment, Tom. I have to work very hard to keep Malcolm here from abusing the power he commands." She winked at her husband. "And he keeps me from being stuffy."

Mr. Ross coughed and said: "There's never been any need for that. Would you like to know why?" and Tom said "Yes," nodding eagerly.

"Well, son," said Mr. Ross, "Mrs. Ross is no ordinary woman. In the early 1860s when Seattle was just beginning, it was filled with adventurous men like my father who had come here after being kicked out of Scotland. Lots of such men and no women. So a far-seeing man named Mercer had this bright idea. He'd go to Washington to seek the government's help in financing a ship, then go to New England, which was suffering heavy losses of men in the Civil War, and invite several hundred young women who might otherwise find no husbands to sail to jobs in Seattle where lonely men abounded. The newspapers of the time gave his expedition such great publicity that when he reached Boston, he found scores of women eager to try their luck out west. A girl named Lydia Dart working in a factory was especially eager to escape from that drudgery.

"Mercer did succeed in convincing hundreds of young women to undertake this adventure, and found much moral support for his plan but had difficulty getting funds for the ship. He finally found a willing financier who agreed to back the venture and provide passage for five hundred passengers at a minimal fee. Well, everything was working fine. Looked like a perfect operation." He stopped, smiled at his wife, and seemed hesitant to continue.

"What happened?" Tom asked.

"Some evil-minded newspaper reporters, they were bastards, really, they started the rumor that Mr. Mercer ran a chain of whore-houses on the West Coast, and that when the girls reached Seattle, he was going to shove them into these brothels. A great scandal exploded. Tears. Recriminations. Fathers and brothers locking young women in their rooms to keep them from sailing. Before Mercer could answer these nasty accusations, more than two-thirds of his potential travelers had changed their minds and refused to reconsider.

"In January 1866 the ship sailed with only a hundred passengers, and of those, fewer than thirty were young unmarried women. Satisfied that Mr. Mercer was honest, they stayed with him, suffered the Victorian scorn of their neighbors, and sailed around the Horn of South America to make their homes in the Northwest. Lydia Dart became their leader. Watched after them. Fended off reporters seeking to create more scandalous stories. And sort of mothered the younger girls when they reached Seattle."

"What happened to them then?"

"They became the soul of the city. These were refined, educated women who had come to the frontier. Many of them became teachers, and within the year they were married to the best young men of Seattle. One, who never married, opened the city's first public school. All of them represented the very best of this city, and four of them are alive today, the grand old ladies of Seattle."

"How was Mrs. Ross connected with them?"

"Aha! The young woman Lydia Dart was the last to marry. She wanted to study the field, and in the end she chose a promising young lawyer named Henderson. And their first child is the gracious lady with whom you're dining tonight."

A huge smile spread across his face as Tom looked at Mrs. Ross and said: "Then you're the daughter of one of those young women?"

"The Mercer Girls they're known as in Seattle history. Yes, I'm the daughter of one of them, and a finer group of women never hit a Western city."

"If you had known Lydia Dart Henderson," Mr. Ross said, "you'd understand why my wife could never be pompous or lacking in a sense of humor. Tell him about the letter she wrote to the Boston newspaper."

Mrs. Ross laughed at the outrageous thing her mother had done, but in relating the incident she obviously took delight in it: "About ten years after the Mercer Girls had descended on Seattle, my mother convened a meeting of them. I remember it well, I was about seven years old, and here came these two dozen women, wives of doctors and lawyers and businessmen, and I listened to their stories. Not a bad marriage in the lot. And that night my mother posted her letter to the newspaper in Boston which had been foremost in creating the scandal about the houses of prostitution."

"What did the letter say?" Tom asked, and Mr. Ross pointed to the wall behind Tom's head where a framed piece of newsprint held a place of honor. Indicating that Tom should take it down, Ross said: "You'll find it amusing. I did when I first saw it."

The editors of this journal have recently received an interesting correspondence from one Lydia Dart, formerly of this city, who ventured out to Seattle in 1866. We thought our readers might find it instructive.

To the Editor:
Last night twenty-five young women who braved public censure to emigrate to Seattle as the Mercer Girls celebrated the tenth anniversary of their adventure. Twenty-four of us are married to the civic leaders of the community and we have nearly ninety children among us. Lizzie Ordway chose not to marry, and she heads the biggest school in the city. All of us own our own homes and all our children of school age are doing quite well. Thirteen of our husbands either are or have been elected officials of our beautiful city.
We invite twenty-five of the young women who refused to come with us in 1866 to meet and send us a letter describing what they have been doing in the meantime.
Lydia Dart Henderson

"That's some letter!" Tom said as he rehung the document, and Mr. Ross said: "My mother-in-law kept writing letters like that till she died. Much of what's good about this city grew out of her Mercer Girls."

"Somebody ought to organize another ship like that for the men in Alaska," Tom suggested. "And they could use a couple of Lydia Darts in Juneau right now." Mrs. Ross smiled and said: "On Friday afternoon, Tom, you'll meet the newest Lydia Dart, except that she's added Ross to her name."

At first Tom failed to catch the significance of what had been said, but when Mr. Ross nodded, it dawned on him that his hosts were speaking of their daughter, whereupon Mrs. Ross said: "She's at school during the week. A convent school, where she's been doing rather well."

"Was the original Lydia Dart a Catholic?"

"As a matter of fact, she was," Mrs. Ross said. "But when her church tried to prevent her from coming to Seattle, she more or less broke away. Then she married this strict Presbyterian from Scotland, and I was raised believing that I was both a papist and a John Knox Presbyterian. Never bothered me a bit, but I've always liked Catholic schools. They teach children something, and our Lydia can profit from their discipline too."

So Tom Venn spent Thursday and Friday in a state of considerable excitement, wondering what Lydia would be like and how he was going to react to the granddaughter of the woman who had written that letter. He feared that he might make a fool of himself, but when he returned from the office late Friday his apprehensions vanished, because Lydia Ross, aged seventeen, was a slender, vivacious girl whose happy life encouraged her to meet everyone with a disarming frankness. Not for her were the torments of adolescence; she supposed that both her famous grandmother and her well-adjusted mother had enjoyed similar girlhoods, and she intended becoming a grown woman much like them. She also adored her father and was at ease with her younger brother, who was developing similar attitudes. When Tom Venn first saw her come swinging in the front door, her blond hair coiled about her head so that her strong neck was revealed, he sensed immediately that she was an extension of the happy family which had so impressed him during his visit.

"Hello!" she said easily as she stretched out her hand. "I'm Lydia.

Father has told me about how good you were in handling the murders at the cannery."

"He told you about that?" Tom asked, showing his surprise that Mr. Ross should have discussed such an unpleasant fact with his daughter.

"He tells us everything," she replied, tossing a strapful of books onto a hall table, where she intended leaving them till Monday morning. "And he told me about your run-in with the grizzly bear."

"It wasn't really a fight. You won't believe this, but an Indian girl told the bear to go back, and it went."

"How big can a grizzly be? Our geography book said they're twice as big as ordinary bears."

"This one was so-so. But a hotel in Juneau has one about ten feet tall. Stuffed, of course."

"He would be quite an attraction if he wasn't."

She was seriously interested in Alaska, emphasizing that she had not yet been allowed to visit there on her father's ships: "What I want to see are the glaciers he tells us about. Are they as big as he says?"

"It seems that everything in Alaska is big. Bigger than you imagine," and he told of the huge iceberg that had floated right to the doorstep of the Ross & Raglan store in Juneau.

"You mean right onto the main street?"

"In the water, of course. But yes, you could reach out and touch it with a pole."

"What happened to it?"

"A fellow with a little tug threw a rope around one part and easily towed it away."

"You mean a tug this little and an iceberg this big?" And the way she moved her hands was so expressive that Tom fell under the spell of her liveliness, her quick reaction to spoken words and her ingratiating smile.

Dinner with the Rosses now became a treasured ritual, and on Saturday night Lydia regaled the table with a burlesque description of how two of the Catholic sisters at her school hoodwinked the young priest who served as principal: "He looked quite simple when they were through with him, so foolish, in fact, that we were sorry for him."

"Did he know what was happening?" Tom asked, and she said: "No. Actually, he never knows what's happening."

Her brother, who was in a public grammar school, asked what

kind of school Tom had attended, and Tom said apologetically: "Just an ordinary school, in Chicago. But I had to drop out."

"Tom has learned in the best school there is," Mr. Ross interrupted. "The kind my father attended. The school of actually doing it." He asked for his son's attention, and said: "The young man sitting across from you, Jake, was practically in charge of our store in Dawson before he was Lydia's age. And a year later he was head of everything in Nome."

"You mean the gold fields?" the boy asked, and when Tom nodded, both the younger Rosses viewed him with more respect.

That weekend was the richest in human experience that Tom Venn had known up to this moment, for he witnessed how a well-organized family interacted, how children were allowed great freedom if they attended to the basic courtesies, and he was especially impressed by the fact that Mrs. Ross, who was obviously proud of her lively daughter, refused Lydia permission to go out on Sunday afternoon until she had finished her weekend homework. Down the books came from the table where Lydia had tossed them, but two hours later she was ready to take a walk over the wooded hills in back of the castle.

It was a walk Tom would never forget. The air was wintry but the sun was warm. Puget Sound glistened at first, then grew somber as a rain squall drifted in from the Strait of Juan de Fuca, and at one point Tom said: "Look down there. It's almost as if the heart of the city lay exposed."

"You use words well," Lydia said, and Tom explained how, in both Dawson and Nome, he had studied books which Missy Peckham had provided.

"Who was she?" Lydia asked, and he replied: "My mother, sort of," and when she asked what that meant, for heaven's sake, he laughed uneasily and explained: "My real mother . . . well, she ran away with another man . . . and my father sort of married Missy. She was a wonderful woman . . . is, I'd better say. She lives in Nome now." He stopped, overcome by the contrast between Missy's chaotic life and the orderliness of the Ross household. He wanted to tell her how this good woman Missy Peckham had been unable to marry his father and was now unable to marry Mr. Murphy, and for much the same reason, but it was too complicated to unravel.

"Father thinks I ought to go on to college," Lydia said, tactfully changing the subject. "Mother has doubts."

"Where would you go?"

"Here in Seattle. The university maybe."

"That would be nice."

"But Grandmother always remembered the Boston area with affection, and she told me before she died . . ."

"I thought she was fed up with Boston."

"No! She wrote that letter to tease them. She loved the place, said it was the lighthouse of America. She wanted me to go back there to school." Then Lydia stopped speaking, for powerful thoughts were coursing through her mind, and after a while she said: "I want to be like my grandmother. I want always to be brave enough to try things. I think I'll need an education to achieve what I want to do."

"And what is that?"

"I don't know. There are so many possibilities, I really can't decide."

Tom had to laugh, because he faced the same quandary: "Just like me. I love the work in Alaska. And I can see unbroken years of it ahead. But I feel more at home in Seattle and I can't see how I'm ever going to find a position here."

"I should think that if you do a good job for Father up in Alaska, it would be only natural for him to bring you down here sooner or later. He has a very high opinion of you, Tom, and so does Mother."

"But he also has a lot of work for me to do in Alaska." He halted that line of talk: "Have you ever met this Marvin Hoxey?"

"He's an awful man. Real slimy. Father knows it, but he says that sometimes you have to use whatever tool's at hand." She kicked at a stone: "Hoxey doesn't fool my father one bit."

They had now swung around to the eastern side of the small hill; Puget Sound was no longer visible, but in its place stood the lakes and waterways which defined this segment of Seattle, and they were as attractive in their more subdued way as the more dramatic sound to the west. "I've always liked this view," Lydia said, "less powerful but safer."

"I don't think of you as someone looking for safety," Tom said, and she corrected him: "I'm not afraid of challenges, but I do appreciate safe havens at the close of day. My grandmother said the same. She told me once: 'I didn't come west for adventure alone. I came to find a good man and build a solid home.' Adventure and a safe haven, that's a good mix."

On Monday morning she told Tom: "Father says you'll be gone

before I come back. It's been real fun talking to you. I can see why Father thinks so much of you, Tom." And off she went, her hair down her back this time, her strapped books bouncing against her right leg.

On Tuesday, Mr. Ross said at dinner: "I want you to supervise delivery and installation of the equipment for making tin cans. Our boat sails Thursday, and after Juneau it will lay over at the cannery. The men from the factory will help you with the machines and the new welding device."

Tom was twenty-one now and amazingly poised for his age, so without embarrassment he suggested: "Couldn't I take Monday's ship north and meet the men at the cannery?"

"Why would you do that?"

"Because I'd very much like to see Lydia again."

A hush fell over the room, broken by Mrs. Ross, who said brightly: "That's a sensible idea, Malcolm. I'm sure Lydia would like to see Tom again." And without further words the decision was reached, with Mr. Ross showing no irritation at having been overruled; he liked Tom Venn and appreciated the young man's forthrightness.

The second weekend was more serious than the first, because all the Rosses, especially Lydia, were aware that Tom had stayed on for the express purpose of exploring further their friendship. She told him frankly, when they were alone, that she had broken two other engagements so that they could spend time together, and when he protested that she should not have done that, she said frankly: "Oh, but I wanted to. So many of the young men I meet are clods."

"They won't be when they're four years older," he said, and she replied: "They're already four years older and they're confirmed clods."

Twice they walked on the hill, seeing Seattle and its environs in its varying moods, and they talked incessantly of school and Mr. Hoxey's political plans and the future of Ross & Raglan, and on Monday morning when Lydia again left for school, she stood in the hallway in the presence of both her father and her mother and kissed Tom goodbye. She did not want there to be any misunderstanding as to how she felt.

When the tin-can machines were installed at Totem Cannery, Tom Venn and Sam Bigears, who had reluctantly agreed to serve as winter watchman over the vacant buildings, began to prepare for the arrival of the Filipino and Chinese workmen. Huge quantities of rice were brought in from Seattle, because both these groups would become difficult if the cannery tried to feed them potatoes, and additional bunks were built for the extra Chinese who would be coming. When Tom paddled across the estuary one day to visit with Sam, whose friendship he wanted to retain, he unwisely told him: "This may be the last year we use Chinese."

Sam, who could never bear a grudge, even though he had been disgusted after Tom's last visit, asked: "Who else you gonna get? Tlingits never work no factory."

Sensing potential trouble, Tom said no more, but on several later occasions Sam wanted to know who would be taking the place of the Chinese: "We don't want no Japanese, no Eskimos brought into our territory. Be damned much better if Chinese and Filipinos both get out."

"Maybe they will, someday," Tom said, but in late April a big Canadian ship, the *Star of Montreal,* hove to off the mouth of the Pleiades River to deposit ninety-three Chinese workers, and as they began to stream down the gangplank, Tom saw what he had expected: Ah Ting was once more in command, his long pigtail trailing, his eyes more challenging than before, if that was possible. This year only one of his co-workers spoke English, and as Tom moved among the gang he suspected that more than half were recent arrivals from China, for they had no concept of what work they would be doing.

"I want two of your best men," Tom told Ah Ting.

"What for?" the leader asked, implying, as usual, that he, Ah Ting, would decide who would work where.

"They're to work a new machine," Tom said, and Ah Ting replied: "I work the new machine," but Tom said firmly: "No, you're needed in here. To keep order."

"That's right," Ah Ting said with no animosity. He was the top man, and it was prudent that he work where he could supervise the largest number of workers. So he designated two good workmen, but when Tom led them away, Ah Ting insisted upon trailing along, for he considered it essential that he know what was going on in every part of the cannery; in fact, he acted as if it were his cannery, an assumption which irritated Tom, as it had Mr. Ross during the rioting last year.

As soon as Ah Ting saw the stacks of flattened cans and the machines which would expand them into usable form, he appreciated the threat this new system posed for his Chinese. Contemptuously he spurned the machines, saying: "No good. No more Chinese working here."

"We'll need two good men on the machines," Tom assured him. "Maybe two more to move the cans around."

Ah Ting would have none of this. Last year he had supervised sixteen of his men in this section; this year there were to be four at most, and he was pretty sure that Mr. Venn would quickly cut that back to three or even two as the men became familiar with the operation of the new system. But what could he do other than sulk? And this he did, with every sign of becoming increasingly difficult as the season progressed.

Faced by this insubordination, Tom was tempted to fire Ah Ting on the spot, but he knew that no replacement could manage the scores of Chinese who would still be required to keep the cutting tables and the cooking ovens functioning. So against his better judgment, Tom bided his time, accepted Ah Ting's protests, and made small concessions on food and bunkhouse space to keep his tenacious manager happy.

And when this was accomplished, more or less successfully, he faced the wrath of the fishermen, for when Professor Starling and his crew came on the scene to erect their trap, and the local men saw the long jiggers stretching nearly across the inlet, they realized that their days of domination were ended, and they began to make trouble. Some of the rougher white men threatened to demolish the weir and cut the jiggers, while others said they would prevent the supply ships from landing at the dock or hauling away the cases of canned salmon. There were other threats too from the Tlingits, but in the end the great trap was built and the jiggers installed, and then the fishermen were both superfluous and powerless to oppose the swift changes that were sweeping their industry.

When the mature salmon began to flood into Taku Inlet, all hands watched carefully to determine whether the trap would collect enough fish to keep the gutting tables filled, and by the end of the first week it was apparent that the weir and its two jiggers were going to succeed even beyond the hopes of the men who had installed it. In fact, when Professor Starling reviewed the operation he spotted a problem which not even he had anticipated: "It's working so well, Mr. Venn, that the holding pen is receiving more fish than it can handle. Your men are not taking the salmon out fast enough."

"We can't handle any more in the gutting shed than we are right now."

"When Dr. Whitman gets his Iron Chink perfected," Starling said, "we can speed up the chain. But what shall we do now?"

Even as he spoke, the efficient jiggers, blocking the movement of the salmon as they fought to reach their natal lakes, kept throwing so many big fish into the trap and from there into the holding area that there was only one solution: "We'll have to let the weaker fish at the bottom die and let their bodies drift downstream with the current."

This was done, and all that summer the trap at the Pleiades caught so many big sockeye that an appalling number of weaker ones were wasted. Now bald eagles from miles around gathered in the skies over Taku Inlet to feast upon the decaying fish, and thousands of fish which could have provided delectable sustenance to hungry people everywhere were allowed to rot and contaminate the lower waters of the Taku.

Even more ominous so far as the future of the industry was concerned, the trap was so effective that knowing fishermen began to wonder whether enough mature salmon were getting past the barrier to ensure perpetuation of the breed. "We do open it up over the weekend," Professor Starling assured the skeptics as he stopped in Juneau on his way back to Seattle, "and if you saw the hordes of fish that get through on those two days . . ."

"A day and a half," someone corrected, and he nodded: "If you saw the hordes of salmon that escape in that period, you'd know their future was secure."

"What about the fish you allow to die in the holding area?" another man asked, and Starling replied: "There's a little wastage in any big operation. Unavoidable, and in the long run it does no substantial damage." And back he sailed to lay plans for six more huge traps to be installed at future Ross & Raglan canneries.

Some concerned men in Juneau took Professor Starling's advice and sailed to the Pleiades River to inspect the operation of the trap, but when their little boat started to dock, Tom Venn appeared on the wharf to warn them that they were approaching private property on which they were not permitted to intrude. "But your Professor Starling invited us to come out and see how the trap works," and Tom said: "He had no authority to do that," but the hardened fishermen of Juneau were not to be so easily turned back.

"We're coming ashore, Venn, and you'll be asking for trouble if you try to stop us."

Such confrontation was avoided, since inspection of the weir and jiggers could be accomplished without trespassing on Totem property. Tom directed the fishermen to take their boat downstream from the trap, from where they could watch the behavior of the salmon, and a stranger to Alaskan fishing would have been astounded at what they saw. The mature salmon swam in from the gyre not in dozens or hundreds but in thousands, three hundred in one solid block, six hundred resting with their noses all pointed against the current. At times the clear water in which the boat rested was solidly packed with salmon, ten or fifteen thousand crowding past, their sleek bodies shining in sunlight a few inches below the surface. It did seem, in such moments of abundance, that the supply was inexhaustible and indestructible.

But when this multitude approached the outreaching jiggers, they faced a situation unlike any they had encountered before. These weirs, these high fences were not like the waterfalls up which their ancestors had leaped for countless generations; these new devices were effective barriers, and after trying to circumvent them, the bewildered fish began taking the course of least resistance. Aimlessly they drifted toward the central trap, and there they slipped into that maze which was so easy to enter, so impossible to escape. Step by step they moved more deeply into the maze, until at last they passed into the relative freedom of the big holding pen.

But now the crowding in the pen became so threatening that the weaker fish began to gasp for water to pass through their gills, and with astonishing rapidity the smaller salmon began to die off, their bodies sinking to the bottom of the pen while Tom Venn's workmen hoisted the survivors onto the track to carry them to the cutting shed, where Ah Ting's men prepared them for the ovens.

The Juneau fishermen who witnessed the magnitude of this revolutionary approach to salmon fishing could see at once that it involved a dreadful wastage which their older process would never have caused. Said one older man: "They have no respect for the salmon. If they keep this up, I don't know what'll happen."

But one of the boats stayed overnight to see what would happen on the weekend, and on Saturday afternoon when the trap was shut down and the jiggers raised, these men watched as the horde of fish came up the Taku, passed the trap, and swam on to their various home lakes along the Taku system. "There's enough fish getting through to populate all Alaska and most of Canada," one of the men said, and thus reassured, they viewed the situation differently.

"It's the modern way," one of the fishermen conceded, and they agreed that despite the regrettable wastage of salmon, enough sockeye probably escaped during the free weekends to maintain the stocks.

In 1904, after the fishermen of Juneau had reached this erroneous conclusion about the safety of the salmon, Nerka, now three years old, had settled into a routine in fresh-water Lake Pleiades that looked as if it would continue throughout his lifetime. But one morning, after a week of agitation, he sprang into unprecedented action, as if a bell had summoned all the sockeye of his generation to the performance of some grand, significant task.

And then, for reasons he could not identify, his nerves jangled as if an electric shock had coursed through his body, leaving him agitated and restless. Driven by impulses he did not understand, he found himself repelled by the once-nurturing fresh water of his natal lake and for some days he thrashed about. Suddenly one night, Nerka, followed by thousands of his generation, began to swim toward the exit of his lake and plunged into the swiftly rushing waters of the Pleiades River. But even as he departed, he had a premonition that he must one day, in years far distant, return to this congenial water in which he had been bred. He was now a *smolt,* on the verge of becoming a mature salmon. His skin had assumed the silvery sheen of an adult, and although he was still but a few inches long, he looked like a salmon.

With powerful strokes of his growing tail he sped down the Pleiades, and when he was confronted by rapids tumbling over exposed rocks he knew instinctively the safest way to descend, but when waterfalls of more ominous height threatened his progress he hesitated, judged alternatives, then sprang into vigorous activity, leaping almost joyously into the spray, thrashing his way down, and landing with a thump at the bottom, where he rested for a moment before resuming his journey.

Did he, through some complex biological mechanism, record

these waterfalls as he descended them, storing knowledge against that fateful day, two years hence, when he would be impelled to climb them in the opposite direction in order to enable some equally determined female sockeye to spawn? His return trip would be one of the most remarkable feats in the animal world.

But now as he approached the lower reaches of the river he faced a major peril, because at a relatively inconsequential waterfall which he could normally have handled with ease, he was either so tired or so careless that he allowed himself to be thrown against a rock protruding from the downward current, so that he landed with an awkward splash at the foot of the falls, where, awaiting just such mishaps, a group of voracious Dolly Vardon trout, each bigger than the salmon smolts, prowled the waters. With swift, darting motions the trout leaped at the stunned smolts, devouring them in startling numbers, and it seemed likely that Nerka, totally disoriented by slamming against the rock, would be an easy prey and disappear before he ever reached the salt water which was luring him.

But he had already proved himself to be a determined fish, and now in an instinctive, brain-clouded way he dodged the first attack of the trout, then dropped into protective weeds from which the larger fish could not dislodge him, and in this quivering manner evaded the hungry attacks of the trout.

Of the four thousand salmon born in Nerka's group in Lake Pleiades in 1901, how many now survived? That is, how many swam down the Pleiades River to fulfill their destiny in the ocean? The constant depletion had been so frightful and so constant that three thousand, nine hundred and sixty-eight had perished, leaving only thirty-two alive and ready for the adventure in the ocean. But upon those pitiful few the great salmon industry of Alaska would be built, and it would be Nerka and the other fighting, cautious, self-protective fish like him who would keep canneries like Totem on Taku Inlet so richly profitable.

At last, one morning Nerka, having fended off long-legged heron and diving mergansers, approached the most critical moment of his life so far: this fresh-water fish was about to plunge himself into the briny waters of the sea, not inch by inch or slowly over a period of weeks, but with one sweep of his tail and the activation of his fins. True, the change from lake water to sea had been in gradations, but even so, the leap from all-fresh to all-sea was momentous. It was as if a human being who had lived in benevolent oxygen were told: "A week from now it's to be only methane gas." No human could survive unless he could make his metabolism and physiological structure take a quantum leap, and that is what Nerka did.

Even so, when he entered the new medium it was an almost lethal shock. For several days he staggered about, recoiling from the salt, and in this comatose condition he faced a terrible danger. An immense flock of voracious white gulls and black ravens hovered low in a sullen sky, eager to dive upon the foundering smolts, catch them in their beaks and carry them aloft for feeding. The devastation wreaked by these screaming scavengers was awesome: thousands of would-be salmon perished in their sharp claws, and those that miraculously survived did so only by pure luck.

Nerka, slow to adjust to the salt water, was especially vulnerable, because from time to time he drifted listlessly on his side, an easy target for the diving birds, but sheer chance, not his own efforts, saved him, and after one near-miss he revived enough to send himself down deep toward the darkness he loved, and there, away from the predators, he worked his gills, forcing the unfamiliar seawater through his system.

Most of that summer Nerka and his fellows lingered in Taku Inlet, gorging themselves on the rich plankton blooms and accommodating to the salt water. They began to grow. Their senses quickened. Surprisingly, they were no longer afraid to battle larger fish. They were now salmon, and gradually they worked their way toward the mouth of the inlet as their appetite made them hunger for the squid, shrimp and small fish that flourished there. And as they matured, they felt an urge to move out into the open ocean to their adventures in its great swirling waters.

Of his thirty-one companions who made it to the mouth of Taku Inlet, about a half perished before they reached the ocean, but Nerka survived, and he swam forward eagerly, scraping past the protruding rock of the Walrus, leaving Taku Inlet, and heading westward to the Pacific.

While Nerka headed toward the Pacific Ocean, Tom Venn was making his first serious mistake in managing Totem Cannery. The Chinese workmen whom Ah Ting had nominated to run the new machines that turned flat slabs of tin into finished cans were not doing a good job. Through either ineptitude or malice they were causing the machines to malfunction, and Tom, convinced that it was a case of sabotage, dismissed them from the section in which they had been working and had the machines moved to the Filipino area, where four young men were instructed how to make cans.

When Ah Ting learned that the tin shop, which used to employ sixteen Chinese, now had jobs for none, he fell into a rage. His customary smile gone, he stormed into Tom's office, demanding that the machines be returned to the Chinese section and that six, not four, of his helpers be assigned to operate them. Such an intrusion into his prerogatives as manager Tom could not allow, and after listening to only the first sentences of Ah Ting's complaint, he said: "I will say who works where. Now get back to the gutting shed." But as Ah Ting retreated, Tom had a premonition that his curt rejection of the man's just complaint might cause trouble, and he started after him to explain more carefully the grounds for his decision. However, he was interrupted by the arrival of one of the Filipinos assigned to the canning operation, so he was unable to placate Ah Ting.

The question was a minor one: "Mr. Venn, how do we get the finished cans to the packing line?" Ah Ting would never have allowed one of his men to ask such a silly question; he would have devised three or four ways to move the cans, tried each, and then reported to Mr. Venn which one was most efficient. But the Filipinos have to learn, Tom told himself, and when the problem was solved in exactly the way Ah Ting would have elected, he returned to his office. He had signed only a few shipping papers when he heard a wild commotion.

Dashing out to the sheds, Tom found that when two of the Filipino workers bringing finished cans to the line trespassed on what had always been Chinese terrain, Ah Ting's men had gone for them with knives.

The Filipinos were an able pair who had often tangled with Chinese in their homeland, where the two races maintained an uneasy truce, and they did not intend to let these Chinese oppress them. Grabbing whatever weaponry lay at hand, including a heavy hammer, the two men held off their attackers, screaming in Tagalog for reinforcements, and in less than a minute some dozen Filipinos had stormed into the building.

This could not be tolerated, for the Chinese considered their work area inviolate, and by the time Tom Venn reached the fray, he found men slamming each other across tables against the walls and slashing perilously close at one another's throats with their knives. Without regard to the danger he was inviting, he grabbed Ah Ting by the arm and shouted: "We've got to stop this!" and in time, due largely to the effectiveness of his Chinese helper, he quieted the screaming and reduced the riot to snarling threats. Fortunately, neither side could understand the vilest charges made by the other, and the Filipinos retreated to their domain, satisfied that they had won a victory.

They had not, because in a carefully controlled meeting between Venn, Ah Ting and the leader of the Filipinos, a sensible man who, like many Manila citizens, spoke both English and Chinese, a truce was worked out whereby the Filipinos would continue to fabricate the cans but leave the transportation of them to the packing line to the Chinese who had been deposed from the tinwork area. In this way, Ah Ting recovered the four jobs he had lost, and when Tom next saw him the big toothy smile had returned.

However, the armistice did not long prevail, because the Filipinos working the two machines jammed first one and then the other, and no one in their section knew how to fix them. When Tom was summoned, he confidently approached the damaged machines but found himself unequal to the task, so with considerable embarrassment he had to call for Ah Ting, the inveterate fixer, to rescue him so that the work of the cannery could proceed.

With an insolent air, as if to tell both Venn and the Filipinos "You can't run anything around here without my help," this master of machines and people went to work, and within two minutes he had identified what needed to be done and within fifteen minutes he had both machines running like new; in fact, he had them working better than they had in their original condition, for he had corrected a design weakness.

Unfortunately, when he finished he said in Chinese, forgetting that the leader of the Filipinos understood that language: "Now maybe even the stupid Filipinos can work the machines without wrecking them."

When the Filipino foreman translated this slur to his companions, four of them leaped at Ah Ting, who defended himself with his tools, but had Tom not jumped forward to assist him, Ah Ting would have crumpled beneath the assault. That evening Tom drafted a letter to Mr. Ross in Seattle:

So I have decided once and for all that we cannot work anymore with these impossible Chinese. I would fire them all

*tomorrow if there was some w ay to operate the cannery
without them. How is that Iron Chink coming along? Can we
rely on it for next year? I certainly hope so.*

When Ross received the query he hurried over to Dr. Whitman's laboratory, whereupon Whitman sent for his colleague Professor Starling, who had installed the very successful trap at the Totem Cannery.
When the three stood before the latest model of their Iron Chink,
Ross asked bluntly: "Can we risk it for next year?" and to his delight,
the two men agreed that the former difficulties had been eliminated.

"This thing works!" Dr. Whitman said in a way that allowed no
doubt, but Ross said: "I'd like to see for myself," so a batch of fish
about the size of salmon was brought in, and when the steam-driven
flywheel had the various leather belts operating the knives, Whitman
began feeding the fish, some long, some short, into the machine, and
unerringly the first knives cut off the heads and tails, while the device
measuring the body of the fish adjusted faultlessly, enabling the third
knife to gut the fish cleanly and send it on its way.

"It's wonderful!" Ross shouted, and after elbowing Whitman
aside, he began feeding the assorted fish into the hopper, and for several minutes the Iron Chink made not a single mistake. "When can
we have this in Alaska?"

Dr. Whitman evaded that question: "I want you to study the way
we have it now. Half as many moving parts. Half as many things to
go wrong. And look how sturdy the parts are that we do use." Grabbing a small hammer, he beat upon the critical joints, demonstrating
how they could withstand the considerable punishment they would
receive when unskilled workmen used them in the field.

"That's good. That's all to the good," Ross said impatiently. "But
how soon can we have them?" And Professor Starling said: "I think
we ought to move this prototype into position right now. See if it
works in Alaska, which I'm sure it will. Make any adjustments by
October first, and we can have your entire cannery using nothing but
these machines by April first next year."

"Agreed!" Ross said. "How many machines do you think we'll
need at Totem?" and Starling, who knew the installation well, said:
"Six will do the job as the plant now stands," and Ross said: "Perfect
this one on the spot, and then build me eight. We're enlarging Totem."

So in July the R&R steamer *Queen of the North* docked in Taku
Inlet with three mysterious long boxes, and when they were hauled to

a new shed which had been hastily built to accommodate the miracle machine, Tom refrained from informing Ah Ting what the equipment was intended to do. But as soon as the parts were unpacked, with boards nailed over the windows to prevent spying, Ah Ting was determined to find ways to penetrate the mystery, and what he saw disturbed him. Furtively inspecting all parts of the new machine, he deduced what its functions must be, and cleverly he identified how it would work. One night, when it was completely assembled, he sneaked into the new shed, and with the aid of matches stolen from the kitchen, he traced each step of the process, figuring out how the moving parts would operate. In the end he had almost as good an understanding of the whole as its inventors.

There in the darkness, his matches gone, he understood the reason for Tom's secrecy: No more Chinese. Tin cans gone to the Filipinos. Pretty soon salmon gone to this damned thing. He reflected on this sad state of affairs for several mournful minutes, then voiced the conclusion which concerned him most directly: "Pretty soon no more Ah Ting."

At nine next morning agitated Chinese stormed into Tom Venn's office, making gestures which he was able to interpret, to the effect that in their shed there was great trouble. Assuming that another Chinese-Filipino brawl had erupted, he grabbed a heavy length of wood much like a baseball bat and hurried to the gutting shed, where no work was being done, and there he learned the cause of the commotion.

Ah Ting was gone. His men were sure that he had not slept in the Chinese bunkhouse last night, and a thorough search of the cannery grounds, a considerable area now, had revealed no trace of him. And the rumor had started that during the night the Filipinos had murdered him.

This accusation Tom refused to accept, and calling for the other Chinese man who understood English, he warned: "Tell your men not to say that. We'll have another riot on our hands. Ah Ting is around here somewhere." He then hurried to the Filipino quarters, where he quickly satisfied himself that there had been no planned attack on Ah Ting. He liked the Filipinos and saw reassuring possibilities for them once the disturbing effect of the Chinese had been removed, and he told their leaders: "No more work today. And do not any of you go near the Chinese sections."

He then turned his attention to Ah Ting, and the more he investigated, the more frustrated he became. The man was not on cannery property, and if he had been murdered, Tom supposed Ah Ting's body could have been weighted and dumped in Taku Inlet, where it would remain hidden forever. By three in the afternoon he ordered everyone back to work, but posted white guards to see that the two Oriental crews remained apart. Ah Ting was gone, and there was no sense speculating any further as to what had happened. Venn himself took charge of the Chinese, and at night, after having tried vainly to settle the endless disputes that erupted within that work force, he sneaked over to the new shed, inspected the miraculous machine housed there, and muttered with grim satisfaction: "We aren't going to get rid of them one day too soon," and he went to bed convinced that 1905 would be a much better year than 1904.

When Ah Ting decoded the mystery of the new machine hidden away in the new building, and realized that it signaled the end of his days at Totem Cannery, he spent about fifteen minutes considering what to do, and his principal decision was one he had never contemplated before: I want to stay here. Upon brief reflection he concluded that he liked Alaska, respected the people like Tom Venn that he had encountered, and had high regard for the few Indians he had known about the cannery. Most significant of all, he loathed the prospect of being sent back to China and his memories of San Francisco were deplorable.

So on the spur of the moment he did what resolute men had often done when faced by a situation they could not tolerate: he decided to strike out on his own and take his chances for a new life that was better than the one he had known in the past or was enjoying now. In addition to his courage, which was of a high order, he had certain self-assurances: Nobody, not even Mr. Venn, knows machines better than I do. No one can work harder. And I doubt if there are many who are willing to take the chances I took in getting out of China or beating off the murderers in San Francisco. If anybody can do it, I can.

He therefore quietly slipped out of the new building by the secret way he had gotten in—by removing a floorboard—left all his petty gear in the bunkhouse, and with only the clothes he wore, walked casually through the darkness to the mouth of the Pleiades River where it widened before joining Taku Inlet. He was clear of the cannery and for the moment safe from detection by anyone outside. Although he was in no degree guilty of any crime, all the Chinese had been warned that Alaska would not allow any Orientals to remain permanently within its borders: "You must all sail back to Seattle in the fall or face arrest."

But with the wisdom he had accumulated during his stay in America, he felt certain that no matter where he settled he could earn a living by fixing things. He estimated his value as a carpenter, a plumber, a builder to be high, and he knew that such people were always welcomed, no matter what the law said. He was, as before, willing to take his chances.

He had heard many times of Juneau, and from what the men who lived there said, he judged it to be an attractive place, precisely the kind of growing community that would provide work for a man of his talents. But how to get there he did not know. On several occasions he had made carefully veiled inquiries, but the white foremen had always said: "We came by boat," and he had no boat. He knew also that Juneau lay on the other side of the two glaciers with which he was familiar; Walrus he had seen three times when the Seattle ship transporting him back and forth had stopped off Walrus Rock to blow its whistle in hopes an iceberg would break off because of the resonance, but this had never happened; and of course he had seen Pleiades Glacier almost daily since his arrival at Totem. They were formidable barriers of ice, and he knew that above them the great ice fields continued for many miles, so he had no desire to trust his luck to such awesome terrain.

Three or four times during his work at Totem he had seen an older Indian workman visit the place, and by chance he had learned that this was the Tlingit with the strange name of Bigears. Because Ah Ting had an insatiable hunger for collecting information that might later be of use, he was able to recall hearing casual remarks which had led him to believe that Bigears was not entirely pleased with having the cannery so close to his home.

And where was that home? Again, by paying the most careful attention, Ah Ting had found out that it occupied that visible headland due north of the smaller point on which the cannery rested, and now in the darkness, when he knew of no friend anywhere that he could trust, he concluded that if he could reach this Bigears, he might find some way to get to Juneau.

Slipping far inland from the Totem dock, he found a spot where the Pleiades River narrowed, and there he waded at first, then swam the short distance to the northern shore. Waiting for an hour in the warm summer night till his clothes dried more or less, he started down the right bank of the river until he came in sight of Bigears' cabin. Seeing a light in the window, he took several deep breaths, committed himself to bold action, and knocked on the door.

Sam Bigears, the man he had seen at the cannery, did not appear, he was in Juneau; but his daughter, Nancy, did, and when she opened the door she betrayed no surprise at seeing a Chinese man standing before her.

"Hello! Trouble at the cannery?"

He understood the question and its implications, and he knew that he gambled his future on what he said next: "I try to get to Juneau."

"Did they send you from the cannery? Why didn't they give you a boat?"

"I run away. No more work cannery." Nancy Bigears, who was also disgusted with the factory across the estuary, understood his plight. "Come in," she said. "Mother, man here to see you." And from a back room Mrs. Bigears walked calmly in, and like her daughter, expressed no surprise at seeing a Chinese facing her.

"His pants are wet," she said in Tlingit. "Ask him if he wants some tea."

And in this way Ah Ting met the Bigears family, with whom he hid for three days until Sam returned from Juneau. When Sam heard the story, which Nancy had developed in detail, he greeted Ah Ting heartily, assured him that there would be a way for him to reach Juneau, and told him further that good workmen were needed on at least a score of building and repair jobs in the youthful capital.

On the second day of Ah Ting's visit with Sam Bigears, the Indian said frankly: "I never like Chinese in Alaska. Good thing they go."

"I work hard," Ah Ting replied.

"That very important in Juneau," Sam said, and that afternoon he took Ah Ting fishing well up the Taku.

It was during their absence that Tom Venn was rowed across the estuary to inquire whether the Bigears family had seen anything of the missing Ah Ting. "He's done nothing wrong," he explained to Nancy, whom he had seen only rarely since their romantic moment. "He's needed at the cannery. He keeps the other Chinks in line."

Without actually lying, Nancy indicated that neither she nor her mother had knowledge of the mysterious fugitive, and as she deflected Venn's inquiries she thought: If Ah Ting wants to escape that prison over there, I'll help him. So she told Tom nothing.

But since he had taken the trouble to cross the estuary, and since he had not seen Nancy for some months, Tom lingered and accepted the tea Mrs. Bigears offered. Still interested in Nancy's future, he asked: "Are you still at school in Juneau?"

"Vacation."

"Are you learning anything?"

"Two good teachers, four pretty bad."

"The good teachers are men, I suppose?"

"All women. The principal is a man, a real dooper."

"And what does that mean?"

"You wouldn't let him shovel snow at your store."

"It's not my store anymore. Mr. Ross says I'm to spend my time opening new canneries."

"All over?"

"As soon as he gets government permission."

"And you'll steal the rivers? Like here?"

"We'll sell a million cans of salmon. Make everyone rich."

She pointed in the general direction of the Totem Cannery: "Nobody here gets rich from that one. You fired all the fishermen. Now I suppose you'll be firing all the Chinese, too."

"Who told you that?"

"People talk. In Juneau they know everything pretty quick. Those two men from the university who came up three weeks ago. They had pictures of a new machine. What will the new machine do?"

"Who told you that?"

"The woman who works in the hotel. She saw the pictures. She knew they were a machine." Nancy, realizing that it would be embarrassing and perhaps even dangerous if Tom Venn was still there when her father brought Ah Ting back, said abruptly: "Well, I suppose you have to get back to work."

"Yes, I'm going." But as he started to walk toward the waiting boatman he felt dissatisfied with the way this visit had gone, so he returned to the house, and when Nancy appeared at the door he asked her to go with him to the totem pole, and in its shadow he said: "What's wrong with you, Nancy? Have I done something to offend you?" And he asked these questions so frankly that she felt ashamed of herself for having treated him so brusquely.

"I thought last time that we agreed we were going separate ways. It's better."

"But that doesn't mean we can't be friends. I admire your father. I admire you."

And now Nancy wanted him to stay, regardless of whether Ah Ting stumbled in or not, and so for several minutes she leaned against the totem as if she were a part of it, and her gently rounded face and dark eyes made her an authentic image of the real Alaska.

"You're going to be a very beautiful woman, Nancy," he said.

"You know many beautiful women last winter in Seattle?"

"I met one. Mr. Ross's wife. She's very special."

"In what way?"

"She's like you. Natural in all she does. Forthright. She laughs like you, too." He did not deem it necessary to reveal that he had also met Mr. Ross's equally attractive daughter.

Now Nancy grew even more eager for him to stay: "What was it like, Seattle?"

"Two big bodies of water meet. Many islands, lakes, little streams. It's a fine city, really."

"Will you be working in Seattle pretty soon?"

"Why do you ask that?" He, too, was leaning against the totem.

"Because your eyes always light up when you say Seattle."

"I have a lot of work to do up here." Since he was looking directly at her as he said this, he could not escape seeing in her eyes a sudden expression of dismay, and when he turned to see what had alarmed her, he found Sam Bigears and Ah Ting heading right for him.

"Hello!" Sam called as if nothing had happened. "You know Ah Ting. I sail him to Juneau tomorrow."

Tom was flabbergasted by at least half a dozen surprises cascading down on him, but he tried to avoid challenging Ah Ting or Sam or Nancy, who had lied to him so outrageously. Swallowing hard, he asked: "What will he do in Juneau?" and Sam said: "You know. Like what I did. Every town needs men to fix things."

"He's very good at that," Tom said weakly. "But I'm sure he knows Chinese can't live in Alaska."

"He won't be Chinese," Sam said. "He'll be workman everybody will need." He looked admiringly at this courageous Oriental, laughed, and said: "I tell him nobody notice if he cut off damned pigtail. But he show me how he tie it in knot under hat."

"Why not cut it?" Nancy asked, relieved that Tom had not made a scene.

"Because it's part of him," Sam said. "Like those bangs are part of you." Reaching out, he rumpled her hair and asked: "Why you not cut your bangs?" and she said: "Because all good Tlingits have bangs. You have them."

Now Tom faced his Chinese foreman and asked: "So you're going to Juneau?" and when Ah Ting nodded, Tom said, with his hand extended: "I wish you luck." Then he added: "And if you don't have luck, come back. We'll always need you at the cannery." But the way Ah Ting looked at him with half-smiling eyes and a sardonic grin twitching at his lips made Venn know that both of them knew the last statement had been hollow.

Impulsively Tom gripped the right hand of this very difficult man: "I do wish you good luck, Ah Ting." And without looking at Nancy, he hurried to his waiting boat.

Sam Bigears not only ferried his Chinese visitor to Juneau in late July 1904, but when they landed, Sam took Ah Ting to three different white men who had construction jobs under way, informing each that "this here Chinaman good worker. Keep cannery Taku Inlet out of trouble." And by the end of the week he had found Ah Ting a place to stay with a widow who took in boarders and who was willing to defer collecting rent until they started collecting wages. She did not have long to wait, for Ah Ting's skills were needed at many sites, and after four weeks on various jobs, workmen started the game that would be carried on in Juneau for as long as he resided there.

Some rowdy fellow would shout: "Goddammit, you know we don't allow Chinks in here," then he would playfully knock off the hat which Ah Ting wore outdoors and in, and down would tumble the coiled pigtail. Then some other man would grab the pigtail, not harmfully, and pretend to haul the Chinese out the door. He never protested. At the end he would recover his hat, show the men how he coiled his pigtail, and sit with them sharing their food. He never drank, but after hours he did enjoy any card game, and since he was brighter and quicker than most of the men he worked with, he usually won. The men liked playing with him, because at tense moments, when big money rested on the turn of a card, he would pray in Chinese and leap with joy if he won. But Ah Ting was a sensible man, and when he realized that he could win pretty much at will, he refrained from doing so. He wanted just enough to stay ahead, never enough to arouse envy.

While Ah Ting was establishing himself in Juneau, the only Chinese who managed to remain in Alaska, Tom Venn was quietly traversing the Pleiades estuary to visit with the Bigears family, and it did not matter much whom he found at home, for he took equal pleasure in talking with them all, even Mrs. Bigears. She was fun because of her propensity for humorous pantomimes of others' follies; she regaled Tom with legends of the Tlingits and accounts of this big man or that pompous woman who had come to grief, and although she spoke words he could not understand, he found that he could understand her imaginative gestures quite easily, and they laughed a good deal.

Her husband preferred talking politics and business, and his observations about the fumbling efforts of the new officials in Juneau were pithy. It was his opinion that Alaska had made an error in moving the capital from Sitka, but when Tom queried him on this, Nancy interrupted: "It's only because the original Bigears lived in Sitka. Juneau is a lot better."

But although Tom told himself that he didn't care which of the Bigears family was there when he called, he was really happiest when it was Nancy. She had matured in so many ways, especially in her ability to fathom the behavior of white men: "They want to steal all Alaska, but they want to be sure they have God's blessing in doing it."

"What do you mean?" Tom asked, and she said: "What the principal says at school meetings, and what the minister says in church, they don't very often agree with what people actually do."

"But what's this about stealing Alaska?" And she pointed out that Marvin Hoxey was back in town, with papers from the government that would give Ross & Raglan control of five more rivers.

As soon as Tom heard this, his interest focused not on the machinations of Hoxey, whom he despised, but on the locations which he proposed obtaining for R&R: "What rivers did he have in mind? Did you hear any specific names?"

"What does it matter? It's stealing, that's all it is."

"But it's very important to me. Because I'm supposed to build the new canneries, and I'd like to know where I'm to be working."

Nancy could not understand how Tom could so loathe a man like Hoxey and at the same time be involved in the evil things he was doing: "I don't like him, Tom, and I'm surprised you let him do business for you."

But Tom was so concerned about his own future assignments, as if one bleak and lonely spot for a cannery was preferable to another, that he requisitioned one of Totem's small boats and had two workmen sail him to Juneau, where he learned what hotel Hoxey was staying in, and there, like some merchant trying to sell the great man a bolt of cloth for a new suit, he applied for an interview.

Hoxey, remembering well this capable young man from Nome and the R&R offices in Seattle, graciously received him, and when Tom wanted to know what sites he had acquired, Hoxey unrolled his maps and indicated the five proposed locations. "I thought there were to be six," Tom said, and Hoxey replied: "There were. But a new firm called George T. Myers beat us to the best one of all in Sitkoh Bay. So we have five." And with a forefinger neatly manicured, he indicated the remote and desolate spots at which huge installations requiring thousands of carpenters would soon be built, and from which millions of cans of salmon would be sent to all parts of the world.

"There's never been anything like it," Hoxey said with unfeigned excitement. "Always before . . . Take the cotton mills in New England—why, you had your factory near some town or even in the middle of it. Out here, look at our five spots! Not a settlement of any kind for fifty, eighty miles. Factories in the wilderness, and the obedient salmon swim right up to them."

Tom asked about rumors that new laws might halt the placement of traps across waterways, or at least cut down the length of the jiggers, but Hoxey reassured him: "It's our job to see that you men doing the work are not hampered."

"No need for such laws," Tom said. "You should see how many salmon go through over the weekends."

"There are always people," Hoxey said expansively, "who want to interrupt the flow of progress." Then he asked: "Will the new machine, what they call the Iron Chink, will it do the job?" And Tom spent the next minutes recounting his adventures with Ah Ting: "If the Iron Chink does nothing else but get rid of the Chinese, it's worth the effort."

When he returned to the cannery he had a fairly good idea of what his life was going to be like for the next years, and although he continued to long for Seattle, life on the frontier was not an unpleasing prospect; the challenges would be great and the rewards commensurate with his efforts. Besides, he found that he liked organizing men and equipment into a major operation in unlikely locations, and the grand openness of Alaska was alluring. But as a normal young man, he began contemplating how he was going to find a wife, and he began asking questions about how the managers of other canneries in southeastern Alaska handled this problem.

One white man who had worked at various sites said: "The manager only has to be at the plant four or five months during the campaign. He's like a sailor. He can have a perfectly good marriage the other seven or eight months." And another man told of two managers he knew who had brought their wives to small private houses attached to the plants: "They brought their kids too, and they had a high old time."

Without revealing any specific plans, Tom said to both men: "I think I'd want my wife to live at the cannery," and the first man issued a caution: "You didn't ask me about that. But I saw a man down near Ketchikan try that once. A disaster. At the end of the campaign she ran off with the engineer in charge of the cooking boilers."

But regardless of how the debate went, during his spare hours Tom traveled more and more frequently across the estuary to visit with the Bigears, and now he had his own skiff, which he operated with such skill that one day Sam said as he greeted him at the Bigears dock: "You handle that like a Tlingit."

"Is that good?"

"Best in Alaska. You ever see one of our great canoes?"

Tom had seen only the smaller ones at the potlatch, but some days later he had an opportunity, for scores of Indians gathered at the Bigears place, and on Saturday afternoon, when the trap was closed down for the weekend, two teams of Tlingits, each with a very long hand-hewn wooden canoe which could hold sixteen men seated on boards slung across the gunwales, held a set of races down Taku Inlet from the mouth of the Pleiades River, around the Walrus, and back to the starting line. As soon as the Chinese workers realized what was going on, they began placing very large bets, some preferring the canoe with a bright-red star on its prow, others backing the one with a carved eagle as figurehead.

Tom was surprised at the appearance of the Indians; they were darker than either Sam Bigears or his daughter, and shorter. But they were quite husky across the chest and their arms were powerful. They dressed almost formally, in heavy shoes, dark woolen trousers that looked rather bulky, and store-bought white shirts buttoned at the neck but without ties. However, when Sam Bigears shot his revolver to start the race, the Tlingits lost all sense of formality, digging their paddles deep in the water and pulling backward with brutal force.

Tom, standing with Nancy, could hardly believe it when Sam came over to say: "See those two men back of eagle canoe? In very small canoe they paddle Seattle to Juneau. Right through high seas, rocks they couldn't see."

When the races ended—the teams having been intermixed after each finish to make the betting more interesting—Tom stayed at the Bigears house, and in the shadow of the totem pole he met with the rowers, only a few of whom spoke English. "They all understand," Sam explained, "just bashful with white man." But as the evening progressed, several of the men became quite voluble, and learning that Tom was associated with the cannery, they wanted to know why Totem had decided to rely upon the trap rather than on fishermen like themselves. And as Tom started to give bland explanations, he found out that eleven of the men had formerly fished for the cannery but had been replaced by the trap.

"You come from Seattle. You take our salmon. You don't leave nothing."

"But all Alaska will profit from the canneries," Tom protested, but when Nancy heard this fatuous claim she burst out laughing, and the men joined.

That evening, inspired by the frivolity of the races and the good humor of the picnic that followed, Tom lingered with the Tlingits, and for the first time since he had arrived in Alaska he caught the full flavor of native life. He liked these men, their frank manners, their obvious love of their land, and he could see the stolid grandeur of their women, those round-faced, black-haired wives who remained observant in the background until some outrageous thing was said. Then they pounced on the man who made the foolish statement and goaded him until sometimes he actually ran off to escape their taunts. To be among a gathering of proud Tlingits was a challenging experience.

When the time came for the visitors who were staying with Bigears to drift off to bed, Tom and Nancy walked down to where his skiff had been dragged ashore, and there they stood for some time in the light of a late-rising moon. On the opposite side of the estuary rose the huge buildings of the cannery, only two lanterns throwing light at entrances. Tom had never before actually studied the immensity of this strange construction in the wilderness, and to see its many buildings now in silhouette, with the moon casting strange shadows from the east, was sobering.

"I never realized what a huge thing we've built," he said. "To be used for just a few months a year."

"Like you said, it's a gold mine, except you mine silver, not gold."

"What do you mean?" And before she could explain, he added: "Oh yes! The silvery sides of the salmon. I never think of them that way. I see only those precious red sides of the sockeye. They're my salmon."

He found no easy way to say goodnight, for having seen the Tlingit women at their best, he appreciated more than ever before the unique qualities of Nancy Bigears. He saw the beauty of her rounded face, the gamin appeal of her black bangs, the lilt in the way she walked. "You are very close to the earth, aren't you?" he asked, and she said: "I am the earth. You saw those men. They're the sea."

Knowing that he must not do this thing, he caught her in his arms and they kissed, then kissed again. Finally she pushed him away: "They told me you were in love with Mr. Ross's daughter."

"Who told you that?"

"Everybody knows everything. They told me that you had paddled over to talk with Mr. Hoxey. To steal more rivers from us." She drew away, leaning against a spruce tree that edged the water. "There's no hope for you and me, Tom. I saw that tonight."

"But I love you more tonight than ever before," he protested, and she said with that frightening clarity which Indian girls like her often commanded: "You saw us for the first time as human beings. It was the others you saw, not me." And then she quietly stepped forward and kissed him gently on the cheek: "I shall always love you, Tom. But we both have many things to do, and they will take us far apart." With that, she went swinging back to her house, where her father and three cronies were singing in the moonlight.

A gyre is a massive body of seawater which retains its own peculiar characteristics and circular motion, even though it is an integral part of the great ocean which surrounds it. The name, pronounced *jire,* comes from the same root as *gyrate* and *gyroscope* and obviously pertains to the circular or spiral motion of the water. How a gyre is able to maintain its identity within the bosom of a tumultuous ocean poses an interesting problem whose unraveling carries one back to the beginnings of the universe. Certainly, in our day, the great Japan Current sweeps its warm waters from Japan across the northern reaches of the Pacific to the coasts of Alaska, Canada and Oregon, modifying those climates and bringing much rain. But this and all other ocean currents have been set in motion by planetary winds created by the differential heating of various latitudinal belts, and this is caused by the earth's spin, which was set in primordial motion when a diffuse nebular cloud coalesced into our solar system. This carries us all the way back to the original Big Bang which started our particular universe on its way.

A gyre, then, is a big whirl which generates at its edges smaller whirls whose motion increases its viscosity, forming a kind of protective barrier about the parent gyre, which can then maintain its integrity eon after eon. One professor of oceanography, name now unknown, striving to help his students grasp this beautiful concept, offered them a jingle:

> Big whirls make little whirls
> That feed on their velocity.
> Little whirls make lesser whirls
> And so on to viscosity.

The Pacific houses many of these self-preserving gyres, one of the most important being the Alaskan, which dominates the area just south of the Aleutian Islands. Reaching more than two thousand fluctuating miles from east to west, four hundred variable miles from north to south, it forms a unique body of water whose temperature and abundant food supply make it irresistible to the salmon bred in Alaska and Canada. This gyre circulates in a vast counterclockwise motion and the sockeye like Nerka who enter it swim with the current in this unvarying counterclockwise direction. Of course, the very fine salmon bred in Japan start from a contrary orientation, so they swim their ordained route clockwise, against the movement of the gyre. In doing so, they repeatedly pass through the larger number of Alaskan salmon, forming for a few hours a huge conglomeration of one of the world's most valuable fish.

For two years, starting in 1904, Nerka, accompanied by the remaining eleven survivors of his group of four thousand sockeye, swam in the Alaskan Gyre, eating and being eaten in the rich food chain of the North Pacific. Mammoth whales would swim past, their cavernous mouths able to sweep in whole schools of salmon. Seals, who had a predilection for salmon, sped through the gyre decimating the ranks. Birds attacked from the sky, and from the deeper waters came big fish like tuna, pollock and swordfish to feed upon the salmon. Each day consisted of a ten-mile swim with the current in an ocean literally teeming with enemies, and in this perpetual struggle the salmon that survived grew strong. Nerka was now about twenty-five inches long, seven pounds in weight, and although he looked almost immature in comparison with the huge king salmon of the Pacific or the even larger members of the salmon family living in the Atlantic, of his type he was becoming a superb specimen.

The reddish color of his flesh stemmed in part from his love for shrimp, which he devoured in huge quantities, although he also fed upon the larger forms of plankton, gradually shifting to squid and small fish. He lived, as one can deduce from these details of his existence, in a mid-range of the ocean hierarchies. Too big to be an automatic prey of the seal and the orca whale, he was at the same time too small to be a major predator. He was a tough, self-reliant master of the deep.

During his three and a half irregular circuits of the Alaskan Gyre, Nerka would cover a total of about ten thousand miles, sometimes swimming largely alone, at other periods finding himself in the midst of an enormous concentration. For example, when he reached the halfway point, where sockeye more mature than he began to break away and head back to their home streams, he was drifting along the lower edges of the Aleutian chain when a massive concentration of salmon composed of all five Alaskan types—king, chum, pink, coho and sockeye—began to form, and it grew until it contained about thirty million fish, swimming in the same counterclockwise direction and feeding upon whatever they encountered.

But now a large collection of seals heading for their breeding grounds in the Arctic Ocean came rampaging through the middle of the aggregation, devouring salmon at a rate that would have exterminated a less numerous fish. Two female seals swimming with amazing speed came right at Nerka, who sensed that he was doomed, but with a sudden twist he dove. The two seals had to swerve to avoid colliding, and he escaped, but from his vantage point below the turmoil he witnessed the devastation the seals wrought. Thousands of mature salmon perished in that ruthless onslaught, but after two days the seals passed beyond the outer fringes and continued on their journey north. But Nerka's group was now down to nine.

Nerka was almost an automatic creature, for he behaved in obedience to impulses programmed into his being half a million years earlier. For example, in these years when he thrived in the Alaskan Gyre he lived as if he belonged there forever, and in his sport with other fish and his adventures with those larger mammals that were trying to eat him he behaved as if he had never known any other type of life. He could not remember ever having lived in fresh water, and were he suddenly to be thrown back into it, he would not have been able to adjust: he was a creature of the gyre as irrevocably as if he had been born within its confines.

But in his second year in the great Alaskan Gyre a genetically driven change occurred in Nerka, compelling him to seek out his natal stream above Lake Pleiades. And now a complex homing mechanism, still not fully understood by scientists, came into play to guide him over thousands of miles to that one stream along the Alaskan coast. Though employing this inherited memory for the first time in his own life, Nerka did so instinctively and expertly, and thus began his journey home.

The clues guiding Nerka were subtle: minute shifts in water temperature triggered his response, or it could have been electromagnetic changes. Certainly, as he approached the coast his sense of smell, among the most sensitive in all the world's animals, detected trace chemical markers similar to those in his own Pleiades. This chemical distinction could have been a difference of less than one part in a billion, but there it was. Its influence persisted and grew, guiding Nerka ever more compellingly to his home waters. It is one of the strangest manifestations of nature, this minute message sent through the waters of the world to guide a wandering salmon back to his natal stream.

The 1905 summer campaign was the last that Tom Venn would spend at the Totem Cannery, since Mr. Ross wanted him to supervise launching the new R&R cannery north of Ketchikan. Tom would have enjoyed making the acquaintance of that distinctive area of Alaska, but the professors who were installing the Iron Chink machines at Totem insisted that a practiced hand like Tom remain there to handle the problems that would inevitably arise when instructing a new work force in such a radical procedure.

For a host of reasons the summer was unforgettable. Tom had spent much of February in Seattle with the Rosses, and had received intimations from both of Lydia's parents and from Lydia herself that as soon as she finished two years of university it might be possible to consider marriage. As if to demonstrate the seriousness of this possibility, in July, after the Iron Chinks were operating at top speed and with an efficiency not even their inventors had envisioned, Mrs. Ross and Lydia sailed to Taku Inlet aboard the Canadian luxury vessel *Montreal Queen,* and Tom had the pleasure of showing them around the cannery.

"I'm really surprised," Mrs. Ross said. "From the tales I'd heard Malcolm and you tell, I'd expected to see hundreds of Chinese, and I find none."

"Well," he reminded her, "didn't you see us studying the Iron Chink that day in your sitting room?"

"That little thing, Tom? It was just a model, trivial, really. I never visualized it as a mechanical monster like this."

He guided Mrs. Ross and Lydia to one side as he explained the workings: "This one machine, and we have these three here, the other two slightly improved on this one . . ." He lost the thread of his reasoning. "Well, as you can see, this Iron Chink as we call it has the capacity to handle a fish a second, but we don't like to run it that fast. At the speed you see, it can take care of more than two thousand salmon an hour."

"Where do you get them all?"

From the window he showed the women the enlarged trap in the center of the inlet with its very long jiggers: "We catch a lot of fish down there. See how the baskets are winched up out of the holding pen . . . And you can't see it, but another winch at the end of our dock lifts them right up to that conveyor over there."

He showed them how, after the salmon were cleaned and slimed by the Iron Chink, the raw flesh, bones and all, was cut by fast-moving machines into appetizing chunks which fitted precisely the famous "tall can" designed for exactly one pound of fish and recognized worldwide.

"You can it raw?" Lydia asked, and he said: "We sure do!" and he showed them how the filled cans passed under a machine which clamped the lid into place.

"That isn't safe," Lydia said. "There's air in there, and bacteria."

"There sure is," Tom agreed. "As a matter of fact, there's even a small hole in the lid, but look what happens next!" And proudly he showed them a standard canning device which his cannery had improved upon: "The filled can with a hole in its lid comes here, and a vacuum expels all the air that Lydia is worried about, and as soon as that happens, this next machine drops down this dab of solder, and whango! the salmon is locked in an airtight can."

He then took them to another building where sixteen massive steam retorts stood in a row, huge ovens, really, into which whole trolley cars loaded with cans of salmon could be wheeled. When the massive iron doors clanged shut, whistling steam under great pressure was let into the ovens, and for a hundred and five minutes the salmon were cooked until even the succulent bones were edible.

"I always ask for the part with the bones," Lydia said as they moved to a third huge building, in which so many unlabeled cans of cooked salmon were stored that the effect was dazzling. At the far end, teams of women, recently employed, applied the distinctive Totem label, now well regarded by better stores throughout the nation, since its cans carried only the superior pink sockeye of Taku Inlet.

Deftly snatching one of the finished cans from the production line, Tom held it before Mrs. Ross and said with pride: "Some woman in Liverpool or Boston is going to appreciate this can when it reaches her kitchen. We do a good job here."

Thousands of wooden boxes, each holding forty-eight cans of Totem salmon, two tiers of twenty-four each to the box, waited to be filled or stood ready for shipment south on an R&R steamer. "How many boxes do you ship a year?" Mrs. Ross asked, and Tom replied: "About forty thousand."

"My goodness, that's a lot of salmon," and Tom assured her: "There's a lot out there."

The Ross women could stay only two days, and then they had to leave by fast boat to catch the *Montreal Queen* as it sailed from Juneau. As they said farewell, they both invited Tom to spend Christmas with them this year, and once more Lydia kissed him warmly as they parted, a fact which would find its way to Nancy Bigears across the estuary.

Some days after they were gone, a most amusing contretemps occurred, for one of the Iron Chinks became temperamental, cutting heads and tails in a way that wasted half the salmon and gutting it so that the backbone was whisked away while the entrails remained attached, partially spilling out of the fish and making a gruesome mess. Despite his normal skill at handling emergencies, Tom was unable to correct the malperformance, and it looked as if he would have to send to Seattle for Dr. Whitman, but one of his workmen suggested that he see if Sam Bigears could do the job: "He's very good with machines." But when Sam sailed over to look at the Iron Chink he said: "Too complicated. But I know man who fix."

"Who?" Tom asked, and he was chagrined when Sam replied: "Ah Ting." However, Sam was so insistent that he took it upon himself to sail to Juneau to fetch the Chinese miracle worker, and Ah Ting saw nothing unpalatable in going back to work on the machine which had displaced him and the other Chinese.

Tom's reception of him at the dock was decidedly cool, which gave Ah Ting no concern. Smiling his buck-toothed smile as always, he lugged his tool kit into the former cutting shed where for two years he had reigned. "Well!" he said as he watched the two functioning Iron Chinks slicing their way through hundreds of salmon. "Good machine I think. Now what's wrong?"

Tom ordered his men to run half a dozen salmon through the malfunctioning machine, and in that first minute Ah Ting spotted the error, but how to correct it he could not determine so quickly. In fact, it took him about two hours to fix what at first had seemed only a simple problem, and as he lay on a piece of bagging under the Iron Chink he called to Tom: "Much better this rod go over here," but Tom shouted: "Don't change anything!" However, Ah Ting had detected a much superior way to relay power to the cutting knives and at the same time protect them from what had disabled the machine. So without seeking further permission, he began hammering and sawing and making such a racket that Tom became distraught, but after some fifteen minutes of this, Ah Ting climbed out from underneath and said, with his usual confident grin: "All right now. You want me fix other two?"

"No!" Tom said, and after paying Ah Ting, he shoved him along to Sam Bigears' waiting skiff. However, some weeks later, one of the other machines broke down in much the same way, and back came Ah Ting to correct the mistake in its design. This time Tom looked the other way when the clever Chinese crawled under the third machine and corrected it too. That night he drafted a letter to Starling and Whitman in Seattle, advising them that he had learned through hard experience that the power transfer under the knives of their Iron Chink could be much improved if they made the changes he outlined in the drawings which accompanied his note.

In late July all kinds of good things seemed to happen, each more pleasing than the preceding. At the government offices in Juneau, where he had gone to consult with officials about extending the jiggers even farther across the inlet, Tom was working over maps when he heard a familiar voice, and when he turned to see who it was, there stood Reverend Lars Skjellerup of the Presbyterian Mission in Barrow, who had come south with his pretty Virginia wife to plead with the government to send schoolteachers, not to the mission, where he and his wife were doing a creditable job with the money he had earned in the gold fields of Nome, but to the Eskimos of the Barrow area in general.

Tom invited the Skjellerups to lunch, where he realized for the first time that one of the greatest joys of a human life is to learn, after a prolonged absence, how people with whom one had shared dangers were doing. Now, as he listened to the adventures of this man he had known so intimately in troubled days, he became almost effusive in his desire to recall old times.

"Lars, you'll never in a hundred years know who sat last year in that very chair you're in. He's advising our firm on land acquisitions."

"Matthew Murphy?"

"No, but I'd sure like to see him. Hold on to your hat. It was Marvin Hoxey."

With a shout that could be heard across the room, Skjellerup jumped up from the chair and cried: "Is he out of jail?" and both he and his wife sat dumfounded as Tom told them how Hoxey had become an even greater force in Washington and the legislative adviser to Ross & Raglan.

He spent three days with the Skjellerups, learning how a man with no religious education could suddenly find himself a missionary in a frozen land, but he was even more impressed by Mrs. Skjellerup, who had reached that distant, frozen mission in such a curious way: "You must have been very brave to go to the end of the earth where one winter night is three months long," and she laughed off the suggestion: "I'd be just as happy in Fiji."

The idea astounded him. He knew nothing of Fiji and he supposed she didn't either, but it was about as far away from Barrow and the arctic ice as one could get: "Do you mean that?"

"Of course I do. And it's the truth. Adventure. Hard work. Seeing good results. That's why we're put on earth."

"Are you religious?" he asked. "I mean, do you believe in God?"

"My wife and I believe in work," answered the man who had driven reindeer to the top of the world, "and I think that God does too."

"Yes," his wife broke in. "I believe in God. I prefer to see Him as an old man with white hair who sits on a throne about six miles higher than the clouds. He sits there with a big book and writes down everything we do, but fortunately for people like me, He has very poor eyesight. You see, He's been writing like that for a good many years."

The Skjellerups were well on their way back to Barrow, where the July midnights were a silvery gray, when Tom started for Taku Inlet, and as he was leaving Juneau's Occidental Hotel, he saw coming up the street from the wharf seven of the most improbable citizens of Alaska. In the forefront, giving orders as usual, came A. L. Arkikov, the Siberian reindeer herder, with his wife and three children, all of them wearing the winter clothing of Siberia. Behind them came two whom Tom had hoped to meet again more than anyone he had ever known, Matthew Murphy and his companion Missy Peckham, and *their* baby daughter.

He saw them before they saw him, and he ran quickly down the hotel steps, dashed into the street, and grasped Arkikov by the waist, dancing him about before any of the newcomers could identify him. Then, as he whirled past, Missy saw him, and she stopped dead in the street, put her hands to her mouth, and fought back tears. Murphy, when he recognized this stranger, joined the dance, and for some minutes, there in front of Juneau's major hotel, the four veterans of the gold fields celebrated in noisy joy.

Insisting that they all accompany him to the dining room, Tom ordered a feast, and once more he posed his riddle: "Who do you think was sitting in that chair you're in, Missy, not too long ago?"

Lowering her gaze, she looked at Tom from beneath her dark eyebrows and asked: "Not that son-of-a-bitch Marvin Hoxey?" and when Tom nodded enthusiastically, as if Hoxey were an old friend, Missy and Matt and Arkikov guffawed. So for the next hour they compared notes on Hoxey and his disciple Judge Grant, and the others became hilarious when they learned that the judge was now a respected member of the Iowa bench. "Hooray for justice!" Matt cried, and the people who had suffered so grievously from the misbehavior of Hoxey and Grant laughed at the pretensions of those two scoundrels, and the bitterness of those frantic days was lost in merriment, after which they filled in the details of the last few years for one another.

Tom learned that Missy, Matt and Arkikov had decided that there was not much future in Nome, now that the seashore provided no more easy gold. "We thought," said Missy, "that the future of Alaska would be decided here in Juneau, and we wanted to be a part of it."

"What part?"

"Who knows? Did you expect to be running a salmon cannery?"

"Never came into my head. But neither did running a restaurant along the banks of the Yukon."

"Weren't they the best pancakes? That John Klope!"

At the mention of their benefactor, Missy and Tom fell silent, and Matt proposed a toast to the man who had finally found his gold mine. And then Missy started to laugh, and she explained to the Arkikovs: "John Klope had this marvelous sourdough, and I would mix up and cook maybe forty, maybe fifty pancakes, stack them outside in twenty-below and allow them to freeze. Anybody came in hungry, he took one of my frozen cakes, thawed it out, and had a good meal."

Then she asked Tom: "What do you suppose we brought to Juneau with us. Yep, that jar of sourdough. You're all invited to come over when we find a house."

"But what are you going to do here in Juneau?" cautious Tom asked, and both she and Arkikov replied: "Something will turn up."

The next visitor to the Juneau area came on a more sober mission. Tom was in his office at the cannery during the final week of the campaign, casting up preliminary estimates of how the season had gone. His carpenters had built about fifty thousand boxes, of which more than forty-four thousand would be filled by the end of the run. At forty-eight #1 cans to the box, that meant that Totem would be shipping out well over two million individual cans. And since each sockeye, by no means the largest of the salmon family, would fill about three and a half cans, Totem had handled over six hundred thousand fish.

"The Iron Chink certainly did the job," Tom said as he pushed back his calculations. "We'll get about four cents a can and the final customer will pay about sixteen cents. Nowhere else can she get a food bargain like that." The industry had recently published a widely circulated brochure which showed that salmon could provide the basic food requirement at twelve cents a pound, chicken at twenty-two cents, steak at thirty-three, and eggs at thirty-six, but as Tom conceded: "That's the cheaper types of salmon. But even at sixteen cents a pound, our choice sockeye will be the housewife's best bargain." He closed his calculations with a guess that for the 1905 campaign, Totem Cannery would show a profit of at least seventy thousand dollars, a stupendous sum for those days.

He was congratulating himself when he saw to his surprise that the *Montreal Queen* was disembarking passengers at the Totem dock, and this was so unusual that he ran from his office to see what was happening. When he reached the dock he saw coming toward him a tall gentleman dressed in the handsome uniform with which Tom had been so familiar during the Klondike days. It was the uniform of the North West Mounted Police and the man wearing it was Sergeant Will Kirby, behind whom trailed a committee of five men in rather formal business suits.

As soon as Tom recognized Kirby, he ran forward to greet him, but to his surprise Will drew back, maintaining his posture of stiff formality: "Mr. Venn, you are the manager of this cannery, are you not?"

Astonished at his friend's rigid decorum, Tom admitted that he was, whereupon one of the other men stepped forward to introduce himself: "I am Sir Thomas Washburn, Canadian government. And these are members of our Fisheries Commission. I presume you've received word from Washington about our visit?"

"I know nothing."

"I'm sure papers are on their way. Captain Kirby will show you our credentials when we're seated. And I assure you, we're here at the invitation of your government." And when the committee was seated in the office, Kirby placed before Tom documents signed by officials in Washington asking all cannery operators in Alaska waters to cooperate with this "commission of experts from our good neighbor Canada."

"The purpose of our visit," Sir Thomas said, "is to ascertain the effect of your new traps on the movement of salmon up and down the various rivers, which, as you know, all start deep in Canada and run only short distances in Alaska. Your Taku River is a prime example of what we mean. May I show you our map?"

When Tom nodded, Sir Thomas asked Kirby to let Mr. Venn see the map which delineated the situation, but as soon as the map was unrolled, one of the committee members laughed: "You've got the Stikine, Kirby," and when Tom looked more closely he saw that the man was right. This map showed the Stikine River, which ran for many miles in Canada before spending less than twenty-five miles in Alaska to join the sea near Wrangell.

"Wait a minute!" Sir Thomas interrupted. "Leave the map, Kirby. It will explain our problems rather nicely, I think." And with his pencil he traced out the far reaches of the Stikine River system, indicating the many lakes it fed and the almost endless tributaries in which salmon bred. "It's a salmon empire, you might say," he concluded as he indicated the extremely brief length of the river in Alaska. "But any dam or dams improperly placed in your small territory forcefully affects all of this." Leaning back as if he had proved his point, he instructed Kirby to lay out the map of the Taku River system, and when this complicated network of rivers, creeks and lakes was displayed, even Tom had to admit that the relative situations were the same: "I see what you mean, Sir Thomas. A great deal in Canada, much less in Alaska." But he added quickly: "However, as you must already know, our trap does not prevent the return of spawning salmon to Canada."

Very dryly Sir Thomas said: "I had rather thought that it did," but Tom pointed out: "To protect you, we keep the trap open, totally free passage, every weekend," and Sir Thomas said: "I'm sure that helps somewhat." He paused just a moment, then added: "Our task is to ascertain whether it helps enough."

Since the canneries had guesthouses in which visitors and company inspectors could be made reasonably comfortable, Tom was quick to extend an invitation to the committee to remain overnight at Totem, but Sir Thomas said: "I'm afraid we shall have to remain three days. We want to see how the weekend opening affects the fish," and he directed Kirby to fetch their bags.

They spent the rest of Friday inspecting the trap itself and comparing the eastern jigger, which was permanently installed by means of pilings driven into the bottom, with the western jigger, which merely floated, and they were amazed that the latter seemed to be as effective as the former. They also checked, with some dismay, the number of salmon that drowned in the holding pen and were not impressed when Tom tried to dismiss the loss as relatively trivial.

When they inquired as to how many salmon Totem Cannery took out of the Taku system each summer, they were not startled by the total, some six hundred thousand, for as one of their experts said: "Quite reasonable, provided enough are allowed to get through the trap to spawn," and then he spotted a problem about which Sam Bigears had often worried: "But the placement of your trap means that even if enough do get through on the weekends to supply the Canadian needs, it looks to me as if your Pleiades River is pretty well cut off from its replenishment," and Tom said with a show of assurance: "I'm sure enough go up that river, too."

On Saturday afternoon the entire commission, including Captain Kirby, was in small boats watching the transit of salmon past the trap and under the jiggers, and so many handsome fish swam past, only a few inches underwater and therefore clearly visible, that Sir Thomas had to admit: "Impressive, truly impressive," and one of his team said: "Problem's simple. Train the salmon to swim upstream only on Sundays," and when the laughter subsided, Tom sought to allay the doubts that had bothered the other team to whom he had explained the system: "You realize, gentlemen, that when the young salmon swim down from your rivers to reach the sea, they encounter no problems. Entirely different season, so the traps aren't operating."

On Sunday morning, after another visit to the trap, the Canadians got down to business, and with their map on Tom's desk they demanded to know: "What will you canners in Alaska be doing to protect our Canadian breeding grounds?" and Tom answered flatly: "The canneries are here, Sir Thomas. In all your area"—he spread his hands over the Canadian part of the map—"you haven't a single cannery. You don't need the salmon. We do."

Sir Thomas did not flinch: "For the present what you say seems to be correct. But we must also consider the future when there will be many Canadians in these parts. Then an assured supply of salmon will be most important, and if you Alaskans prevent or destroy that supply, you will be doing us grave wrong."

Tom would concede nothing: "Throughout Alaska we shut down the traps, as you've seen. I'm positive enough fish get through."

"But the wastage! The dead salmon."

"Not excessive when you consider the numbers."

Sir Thomas was somewhat irritated to be arguing with so young a man, but he had to be impressed favorably by Tom's ability to defend his company's interests, so after stating most emphatically Canada's intention to seek an international agreement protecting her interests in the salmon trade, he listened politely as Tom rebutted his arguments and said that he doubted the United States would ever submit to such an agreement.

Unwilling to prolong the debate when the positions were so contrary, Sir Thomas asked Kirby to pass him another file, and after searching through its papers, he found the document he wanted: "Mr. Venn, do you happen to know a Mr. Marvin Hoxey?"

The surprise on Tom's face proved that he did, and the Canadian continued: "He seems to be our principal stumbling block in Washington. Keeps citing statistics at us demolishing all our claims. We suspect his data are fraudulent. Can you tell us anything about him? Is he really an expert in these matters?"

Without blinking, Tom said: "He certainly is."

"Has he inspected these traps? I mean, your trap in particular?"

"He has."

Sir Thomas said nothing, but he did ask for another paper, which he studied for some moments as if calculating how to use its information. Finally he cleared his throat, leaned forward, and asked in a most conciliatory voice: "Now, is it not true, Mr. Venn, that in the Alaskan city of Nome in the year . . . Let us see, could it have been 1900? Yes, I believe it was. Were you then acquainted with Mr. Hoxey?"

"I was."

"And did you not offer testimony that helped send him to prison?"

Very weakly Tom replied: "I did." But then quickly added: "But you must also know that Mr. Hoxey received a full pardon from the President himself. It was all a political mistake."

"I'm sure it was," Sir Thomas said, and he dropped the matter.

It was not till late Sunday evening that Tom found a chance to talk alone with Captain Kirby, who, after exchanging reminiscences of the old days, asked frankly: "Tom, what kind of man is Hoxey? He's giving us a lot of trouble."

"Confidential?"

"Like in the old days."

"You can use the information, but don't say I told you."

"I think you know you can trust me."

Looking Kirby straight in the eye, Tom said: "If he had shown up when you and I were on the Klondike, after two days you'd have shot him."

No more was said on that subject, but when the conversation returned to the old days, Tom said: "You'd never guess who's in Juneau," and when Kirby said he had no idea, Tom said: "Missy Peckham!" and the two men leaned back and visualized that plucky woman climbing to the top of Chilkoot Pass, where she had first met Kirby. And they spoke of her whizzing down the snowy pass on the shovel, and of building their boat and of the days in the tent at Dawson and on Bonanza Creek.

"She never found any gold, did she?" Kirby asked, expressing regret for Missy's bad luck, and Tom said: "She never did."

"Damn," Kirby said, banging his fist on the table. "That woman has had bad luck all the way."

"Not so bad," and very quietly Tom told of how John Klope had come by Nome one day, bringing great gifts of gold to Missy, to Murphy and to himself.

"Well, I am glad. You say she's in Juneau?"

"Yes. She and Murphy told me they were going to settle there."

"Doing what?"

"They had no idea. But knowing Missy, you can be sure it'll be something lively."

Kirby considered this for a moment, then clapped his hands and asked: "Tom, could you accompany us to Juneau? We have a boat picking us up tomorrow morning." Tom hesitated, but Kirby persisted: "If it's a problem with your boss in Seattle, I'll have Sir Thomas insist that you continue the interviews there. In writing."

In the morning Kirby did deliver a formal request that Thomas Venn, manager-on-site of Totem Cannery, accompany the Canadian Fisheries Commission for further consultations in Juneau, and during the speedy trip to the capital Sir Thomas said: "Mr. Venn, if I were the owner of a cannery, I'd want you for my manager." Then he added: "But you are dreadfully wrong in your interpretation of Canada's interest in this matter. We shall never rest till we arrange an equitable solution to the problem." He did not inquire as to why Kirby had wanted him in Juneau, but when they reached the Occidental Hotel and he saw the delight with which the two younger men greeted the woman staying there with her husband and daughter, he judged that the reasons were substantial.

It was an emotional reunion, one in which Matt Murphy participated as eagerly as the other three. They had known heady days, vast disappointments. Then, in due course, the name of Marvin Hoxey came up, and Matt and Missy revealed the whole sickening story in such lurid detail that Kirby had to ask: "Tom, how can you do business with such a man?" and Tom could only reply: "I don't. The company does."

"And you feel you have to be loyal to the company?"

"I do."

Kirby said nothing, for he felt that he had to be loyal to the Mounted Police, and he knew the pressures that any kind of loyalty can exert. In his case the pressures were legitimate, those of the Canadian government; in Tom's case, illegitimate, as everything associated with Marvin Hoxey had to be. But thoughtful men acknowledged pressure, good or bad, and responded to it in different ways.

But now the conversation turned to the purpose of the Canadian visit, with Missy showing herself to be more than passively interested in the salmon fisheries, and gradually the facts unfolded: "That's part of the reason Matt and I came down here. I don't mean salmon. I mean the rights of native people."

"What do you mean by that?" Kirby asked, and she explained: "Will, wherever we've been, Canada or Alaska, we've seen natives getting the bad deal. You ought to see Nome."

"I can imagine."

"And it seemed to Matt and me, seeing that we came from what you might call native Irish and native American stock . . . well, it seemed to us that we ought to be on the side of the natives. We ought to help them look after themselves better than they're doing now."

Aware that he might be speaking against his own interests, Tom said impulsively: "Isn't that somethin'! When Lars Skjellerup was down here a few weeks ago, he was pleading with the government for native schools. He said almost the same thing you did, Missy."

"What do you mean?" Kirby asked as he turned to face the woman to whom he had once been so deeply attached. Now they met as mature adults, each striving to make his world a more orderly place.

Encouraged by his smile, Missy for the first time voiced in public the principles which would guide the remainder of her life: "I see an

Alaska which is not dominated by rich men in Seattle. I want an Alaska which has self-rule, its own laws, its own freedoms."

Here she became almost vehement: "Do you know that Matt and I can't buy land in Juneau? Why? Because the Alaska government hasn't been allowed to pass land laws, and the United States government won't."

She passed from this grievance, one which infuriated all Alaskans, since it inhibited normal civic growth, to the broader canvas: "We have been looking into the same problems you've come here to study, Kirby." She stopped there, and Kirby asked: "And what have you two concluded?" and she said: "That all the salmon in these waters should be devoted to the welfare of Alaska, not to businessmen in Seattle."

Kirby laughed and pointed to Tom: "She's speaking about you."

"No, I mean it. More than thirty canneries like Tom's operated this summer, I've found, and not one of them leaves a penny behind for us Alaskans." Prior to that statement she had spoken of Alaskans as *they,* as if she wanted to protect *their* rights, but now, subtly, she had herself become an Alaskan, and so she would remain.

At the end of her animated discourse, Kirby asked: "Does this make you and your old friend Tom enemies?" and she said: "If he continues to work for Seattle businessmen, political enemies, yes," and before anyone could respond, Kirby turned to beckon to Sir Thomas Washburn, saying: "Sir Thomas, you ought to listen to this lady," and when the chairman of the commission did, he was astounded at how close her opinions were to his: "Young woman, you've quite a head on your shoulders."

"I fought these battles in Chicago. Among the hopeless, but never without hope."

They spoke for a long time, together, as if the others were not there, and the more they revealed of their aspirations the more clearly Tom Venn saw that they could attain what they wanted only at the expense of his employer, Malcolm Ross. Finally, somewhat provoked, he broke in: "Sir Thomas, with your position and all that, how can you feel the way you do?" and the Canadian gentleman laughed: "My father ran a little store in Saskatchewan. He would have applauded what this young woman is saying, because he used to tell me the same things." And he turned abruptly away from Tom to resume his discussion with Missy.

• • •

Tom had looked forward to spending Christmas with the Rosses, and renewing his friendship with Lydia. But though she greeted him warmly, he soon found that she was deeply involved with a rather polished young man of twenty-two named Horace whom she had met at the university. She seemed not to be actually engaged to him, but she had obligated herself to attend quite a few holiday functions with him. By no means did she cut Tom off, but she was so busy that he often found himself alone with her parents or with other older members of the firm.

From them he learned how profitable the 1905 season had been, how generously the United States Congress had treated the Seattle interests, and how well the plans for the new cannery at Ketchikan were progressing. He learned that he would definitely be in charge of its construction, starting in mid-January, and he surprised them with the information that he was planning to buy a home in Juneau. When they asked why, in voices intended to dissuade him, he said: "I like the town. It has great character and the setting is almost as good as Seattle's. Besides, it's now the capital."

A vice-president of R&R said: "But if you work for us, you have to move around a good deal. We have a lot more canneries in the planning stage, and you're our expert on making them work," and Tom said: "I want the job, but I also want a home," and he reminded them of how the normal cannery year went: "Two months preparation, three months working like a dog, one month to close down, and six months to live. I don't want to spend those six months locked up on some remote spot at the edge of the woods."

"You're right," the vice-president admitted. "And I suppose that pretty soon you'll want to get married. Your wife will probably think the way you do."

The mention of marriage caused an uneasy gap in the conversation, and later that night when the other guests had gone, Mrs. Ross went out of her way to assure Tom that Lydia still thought highly of him and he must excuse her near-rudeness in spending so much time with Horace and so little with him. When she said: "It's to be expected, the excitement of college and all that," he told her: "I understand."

But this winter there were few walks to the hill with Lydia, and practically no extended conversations on even trivial matters, let alone important ones. His disappointment led to two conclusions: I've never met a woman more sensible than Mrs. Ross. If she's a sample of what

Lydia will be at her age . . . mmmmm! and It looks as if Lydia has moved on to a different level. He did not try to pin down what that level might be or what the obvious difference consisted of, but he had a strong feeling that he had lost her, and not even the gay festivities of a Seattle Christmas Eve or the warm celebrations of the day itself modified his conclusions. He was out of place and he knew it.

Cutting short his vacation, he offered the excuse that he had to get back to Juneau to prepare for the move to Ketchikan, and when he departed, the older Rosses noted without surprise that this time their daughter did not kiss him goodbye.

When he returned to Juneau he encountered the contradiction to which Missy had referred in their meeting with Captain Kirby: Alaska had almost unlimited land, but the four southern towns of Juneau, Sitka, Ketchikan and Wrangell existed in such a pinched condition, clinging to a mere foothold on the edge of the ocean, that they gave the impression of meanness and certainly a lack of spaciousness. In fact, usable land was so scarce and precious in Juneau that Tom was unable to find either a house already built or land on which to build, and although he liked the town and considered the mountains which edged it into the sea picturesque, he began to despair of ever finding a place there in which to live.

But since Juneau had a population of only sixteen hundred—many times bigger than either Ketchikan or Wrangell, both of which had far less than a thousand—he was constantly meeting old acquaintances when he was in town, and gradually they found for him a small selection of available houses. They also kept him advised of what was happening in the capital, and when with Missy's help Tom finally decided on a house being vacated by a sea captain, he was ready to make a down payment, but Sam Bigears protested vigorously: "Tom! More better you look back of house?" and when he and Sam explored that area with some care, Tom saw what his friend was warning against, for the land rose precipitously, almost in the form of a cliff. Now, this was common in Juneau, where some of the streets leading in from the sea were not ordinary streets but wooden stairs climbing straight up. Indeed, to live in Juneau one had better have strong legs, because climbing up and down was a part of daily existence.

At first Tom was not worried about the steepness of the rise, but then Sam pointed to the serious problem. Down a ravine, whose end pointed directly at the house Tom was considering buying, loomed a bank of snow so huge that it could be expected at some time or other to launch an avalanche that might bury the house. "Look over there," Sam cautioned. "Used to be house, but last year snow let loose. Poof! No more house. Same happen here, maybe."

Some days after this meeting with Bigears, Nancy appeared in Juneau, eighteen years old and ready to finish her schooling. She was one of the very few Indian children who had progressed so far, and her teachers, one of whom Tom met at the hotel, said that she was a precious find: "Most of the Indians drop out in the seventh or eighth grade, but Nancy has unusual abilities. She can sing with the best and she knows the old Indian dances, but she can also write acceptable papers and she has almost a hunger to know American history and how Alaska came to be what it is." When Tom questioned another teacher, the man said: "I'm the only man in the school, bar the principal, and I don't have much patience with these Indians. I want my kids to study, to make something of themselves, and almost no Indians respond to such discipline, so I pretty much ignore them. But this Nancy Bigears, she's as good as any of the white boys, maybe better. She ought to go to college."

So Tom began to see her again, and on a totally different basis from before. She was now a town girl, dressing and acting like the other students, except that she had a powerful new sense of her capacities. She was studying American history and applying all its lessons to Alaska, and one day as she spoke of the injustices her land suffered, Tom said: "You ought to meet my friend Missy. She's older but her ideas are a lot like yours."

So one January day he invited them both to lunch, and they lingered over their meal so long that darkness descended over the mountains and Gastineau Channel was shrouded before they finished. They spoke of Eskimo and Tlingit tradition, of the difficulties brought by the ways of the white man, of land ownership, and of all the problems that rose to the surface if one lived very long in towns like Nome and Juneau. The two women did most of the talking, and what they said infuriated Tom occasionally, for they made men like him out to be the villains, and this he could not accept.

Once in his anger he voiced for the first time the attitude that he and most white men like him espoused: "Time's wasting. Work's to be done. Maybe the Eskimo up in Barrow can adhere to the old ways. But the Indians elsewhere, all of them, had better enter the twentieth century, and fast."

"And what, pray, do you mean by that?" Missy asked contentiously, and he was not loath to explain: "There aren't many real Americans in Alaska yet, white men and women I mean, but the future of this land, believe me, is to become another Oregon, another Idaho. Indians should receive every consideration and certainly title to their lands, but they have no option but to enter the mainstream, forget their tribal customs, and beat us at our own games." Then, taking Nancy's hands, he said: "And this young lady is the one with the capacity to lead the way for her people."

"I second that!" Missy said enthusiastically, and Tom added: "Mr. Wetherill told me the other day that Nancy was so good in her studies, she should go to college next year. California or Washington, or even back east. Now, what do you think of that?"

He was astonished at what Missy thought: "Tom, that's the wrong answer! Nancy does not need college anymore than I did. Her job is to stay here in Alaska, make a place for herself, show others how to adjust. She could become the greatest woman in Alaska, and don't you and Mr. Wetherill send her off to the States to be ruined."

Tom was prepared to argue that his approach was the one that would save the Indians, but he was prevented from voicing his opinion when Sam Bigears came to the hotel looking for his daughter: "Some people are coming over to Harry's, and they want you to help." Obediently she rose, thanked Tom for the lunch and Missy for her support, and when she was gone, Missy said: "It will always be like that, I'm afraid. There will be a party somewhere, and that comes first."

And then, as they sat in the shadows, for the dining room was not yet open for the evening meal, she said quietly: "I suppose you know, Tom?"

"That you and she are right? I don't know that at all."

"No. That you're in love with her."

Shocked at hearing these words spoken so openly, Tom sat silent, his thoughts in turmoil. A picture of Lydia Ross dismissing him so lightly came to his mind, then Nancy Bigears brimming with excitement here in Juneau, and he recalled the afternoons with her beside the family totem and along the path beside the Pleiades, and the morning she had taken him in her canoe across Taku Inlet to walk upon the emerald ice of Pleiades Glacier, and he realized that Missy was right.

"Seattle is a lost dream, Missy. I flew high and singed my wings."

He smiled ruefully as she listened in silence, unwilling to break the flood of thoughts she knew he needed to express. "I'll stay here and work in one cannery after another, and always in the shadows there will be Nancy Bigears, growing more lovely every year, and finally when the years pass and there is nothing better to do, I'll ask her to marry me."

But then he remembered Mr. Ross's harsh words that day when he had seen them kissing, and he wanted to share them with Missy: "Do you know what Ross told me when he thought I might become involved with Nancy? 'Venn, do you think Ross & Raglan would ever bring you to headquarters in Seattle if you had an Indian wife?' and he scared me away for the moment."

"And then his daughter scared you away from the other direction?"

"How do you know that?"

"Tom, you're like a little boy in grammar school who's kissed a girl for the first time. All the other girls in the room know."

Smiling brightly, as if to change the subject, he asked: "What are you and Matt going to do here in Juneau?" and she said: "We're in no hurry. Irishmen know how to take things as they come." And she started to leave, but as he rose to escort her to the door, she touched his arm and said: "You know you could, Tom."

"Do what?" he asked, and she said: "Marry a wonderful Tlingit girl. You're first-class, she's first-class. Together you could go to the stars." And before he could respond, she was gone.

In succeeding days things began to work out as he had predicted to Missy: Nancy Bigears was always present in the shadows, and almost against his will he began to drift toward her. They met far more often than he intended, and when she directed their conversation into channels which concerned her, like Tlingit rights and the advisability of outlawing alcohol in Alaska, he found that she struck dissonant but powerful chords in his own reflections: rarely did he agree with her, but he had to acknowledge that she did not waste her life on trivialities.

One afternoon he said: "I'd like to go out to the glacier again," and she realized that he was saying this because he wanted to see her once more in the setting where he had first become aware of her, even though she had been only fourteen at the time.

"Are there many states in America," she asked, "where you can leave the capital and ride out to an active glacier?" and he said: "Not many."

It was a beautiful January day and the Japan Current brought enough warm sea air ashore to create a near-summer atmosphere, even though a small family of icebergs huddled in the channel, so they rode with the carriage windows open. At the glacier, whose former cave had been long obliterated by ice crashing down from the face above, they walked for some time along the front, touching the monstrous snout from time to time and even leaning against it when they stopped to talk.

"Missy told me the other day, Nancy, that I was in love with you."

"I've always been in love with you, Tom. You know that. Since that first day in there," and she pointed to where the blue-roofed cave had been.

"Could marriage . . . ?" He could find no words to express the careful definitions he had in mind. But she diverted his reasoning with a question which startled him: "Did the boss's daughter in Seattle let you know she wasn't interested?"

Tom snapped his fingers: "Did Missy tell you to ask that?" and she laughed: "I don't need other people to tell me important things," and from beneath her dark bangs she smiled so provocatively that he burst out laughing.

With Nancy he laughed quite often, and as they walked beside the glacier he thought: What I said was right. We'll drift along and one day I'll say: "What the hell?" and we'll get married. But now she stopped and turned to face him, saying softly: "It wouldn't work. Not in these years, anyway. Maybe later, when we all grow up . . . I mean when Alaska grows up . . ." She said no more, and she resumed walking back to where the horse waited, but he remained motionless, standing close to the glacier, and he felt that like it he was moving slowly, relentlessly in an age of ice.

In due course he overtook her, and as they rode back to Juneau, night came down upon the surrounding mountains and the breath of untimely summer vanished. At the edge of town she pointed to a house lying on its side: "Like Father warned you. Sometimes the snow comes crashing down. As if we had our own little glaciers."

In the morning he told Sam Bigears to stop trying to find him a house in Juneau: "I'll live in Ketchikan while we're building the new cannery. After that . . . ?" And next day he sailed south to his new obligations.

• • •

As Tom Venn headed for his future life in Ketchikan, the salmon Nerka was receiving signals in the far turn of the Alaskan Gyre, warning him that it was time he started for home, and the message was so compelling that even though he was far from Lake Pleiades, he began to swim no longer in aimless circles but with undeviating direction toward his natal water. Sweeping his tail in powerful arcs with a vigor not used before, he shot through the water not at his customary ten miles a day but at a speed four or five times that fast.

In his earlier circuits of the gyre he had always been content to string along with his fellows, male or female, and rarely had he distinguished between the two, but now he took pains to avoid other males, as if he realized that with his new obligations, they had become not only his competitors but also his potential enemies.

From his accidental position in the gyre when these signals arrived he could reasonably have headed for Oregon, or Kamchatka, or the Yukon, but in obedience to the homing device implanted in him years ago, he followed his signal—that wisp of a shadow of a lost echo—and from one of the most isolated parts of the Pacific he launched himself precisely on a course that would lead him to Taku Inlet and Lake Pleiades, where he would undertake the most important assignment of his life.

On the first of May he was still one thousand two hundred and fifty miles from home, but the signals were now so intense that he began swimming at a steady forty-nine miles a day, and as he sped through the gyre he began to feed prodigiously, consuming incredible numbers of fish, three or four times as many as ever before. Indeed, he ate ravenously even when not really hungry, as if he knew that once he left the ocean, he would never again eat as long as he lived.

In early September he entered Taku Inlet, and when he immersed himself in its fresh waters, his body began to undergo one of the most extraordinary transformations in the animal kingdom, an ugly one, as if he sought a frightening appearance to aid him in the battles he would soon be facing. Up to this moment, as he swam easily through the gyre, he had been a handsome fish, quite beautiful when he twisted in the light, but now, in obedience to internal signals, he was transformed into something grotesque. His lower jaw became ridiculously prognathous, its teeth extending so far beyond those in the upper jaw that they looked like a shark's; his snout turned inward, bending down to form a hook; and most disfiguring of all, his back developed a great hump and changed its color to a flaming red. His once svelte and streamlined body thickened, and he became in general a ferocious creature driven by urges he could not hope to understand.

With determination he swam toward his natal lake, but his course brought him to where the trap of Totem Cannery waited with its very long jiggers, making entry to the Pleiades River impossible. Bewildered by the barrier which had not been operating when he left the lake, he stopped, reconnoitered the situation like a general, and watched as thousands of his fellows drifted supinely along the jiggers and into the trap. He felt no compassion for them, but he knew that he must not allow this unusual barrier to stop him from fighting through to his river. Every nerve along his spine, every impulse in his minute brain warned him that he must somehow circumvent the trap, and he could do so only by leaping across the lethal jigger.

Swimming as close to the right bank as he could, he was encouraged by the cold fresh water that came from the Pleiades River carrying a powerful message from the lake, but when he attempted to swim toward the source of the reassuring water, he was once more frustrated by the jigger. Bewildered, he was about to drift toward the fatal center when a sockeye somewhat larger than he came up behind, detected a sagging spot in the jigger, and with a mighty sweep of his tail leaped over it, splashing heavily into the free water beyond.

As if shot from a gun, Nerka sped forward, activated his tail and fins and arched himself high in the air, only to strike the top strand of the jigger, which threw him roughly backward. For some moments he tried to fathom what had caused him to fail when the other fish had succeeded, then, with a greater effort, he tried again, and again he was repulsed by the jigger.

He lay for some minutes resting in the cool water drifting down from the Pleiades, and when he felt his strength returning he started swimming with great sweeps of his tail, and mustering all his strength, he sped like a bullet at the jigger, arched himself higher than before, and landed with a loud splash on the upstream side.

A workman from Totem Cannery, observing the remarkable leaps of these two salmon, called to his mates: "We better add two more strands to the jigger. Those two who got across were beauties."

It was crucial that Nerka survive to complete his mission, for of the four thousand who had been born in his generation, only six still survived, and upon them rested the fate of the Pleiades sockeye.

• • •

Since the new R&R cannery at Ketchikan was being planned for a capacity half again as large as Totem, Tom was kept so busy from the middle of January on, he had little time to think about the mournful way his two conflicting love interests had collapsed. When he reached the site, the four major buildings had already been roughed out; they were enormous, and he gasped when he realized that it was up to him to finish off the eight or ten subsidiary buildings which would be required, and then fill all of them with the needed machinery. So he spent February and March installing crating areas, canning lines and the two great essentials: the Iron Chinks and the huge steam retorts for cooking. He did not like to think what this cannery was going to cost, perhaps four hundred thousand dollars, but he did know that once it started functioning, it would have the ability to pack sixty thousand cases a year, and that was a lot of salmon.

In mid-March, when it became apparent that some of the bunk-houses might not be finished on time, he sent a distress signal to Juneau, and on the next trip south Sam Bigears appeared with four expert helpers. "I still not work in buildings," Sam said, "but I work on them." One of the men, to Tom's surprise, was Ah Ting, and when the local workmen saw him come onto the premises, they complained loudly that no Chinese were allowed in Alaska, but Tom explained that Ah Ting was an exception. They were not happy with the explanation, but when they saw how he could get the temperamental Iron Chinks operating when they could not, they allowed that he served a purpose.

During working hours Sam Bigears often paused to inform his friend Tom of happenings in Juneau, and certain bits of information were both pleasing and amusing: "That crazy Siberian, what's his name, he got one of best houses in town and he and his wife have boardinghouse. He collect rent and she do all the work." He said also that Matt and Missy had yet to find a house they wanted, but that Missy kept sticking her nose into everything: "Call her Lady Governor, she tell everyone what to do."

"Do they get mad at her?" Tom asked, and Sam said: "No. They like what she say. Maybe like her interest," and Tom said: "She was always that way." Sam said that she offered to work at one of the churches, but they wouldn't accept her because no one could be certain whether she was married to Murphy or not: "But her girl go Sunday School that church."

Tom never asked how Nancy was doing, because he could not be sure how much Sam knew about their feelings for each other, and he certainly did not want to say, but whenever Sam spoke of the girl, he listened attentively: "She win big writing contest, which not surprise me. She good at writing, but she also win what they call oratory. That was surprise. She speak 'Tlingit Land Rights' and I think she win because Lady Missy one of judges. She like what Nancy say. Me too."

Thanks to Tom's driving energy, and the hard work of men like Bigears and Ah Ting, Ketchikan Cannery was ready on time, and since the runs of salmon in these southern waters were even more copious than those in Taku Inlet, the big buildings were soon working to capacity and the Juneau men returned home. As Ah Ting left, some of the older workers in the Iron Chink shed told Tom: "It's good to see that one go. No place in Alaska for a Chink," and Tom said: "Aren't you from Seattle?" and they said they were, and Tom surprised himself by saying: "Then it's not your problem, is it?" Ashamed of his curt retort, he returned to the men and said: "You know we couldn't have had this place ready without his help," and the matter was dropped.

His display of temper disturbed him, because on his jobs in Dawson, Nome and Juneau he had been known for his unruffled disposition, and he wondered what had caused him to change. But when he reviewed his recent behavior he came to several conclusions: I've been working at top speed for too long. I need a rest. But then a deeper reason surfaced: Working with Sam Bigears reminded me of what a great girl Nancy is. I want to see her again. And when he announced that he would be sailing back to Juneau with Sam, he accepted the fact that the unintended drift toward Nancy he had spoken of to Missy was under way, and he muttered: "Let it happen."

Before he completed arrangements for other men to run the cannery during his short absence, an R&R supply ship arrived from Seattle, and the captain had a personal message for Tom: "Mrs. Ross is arriving on the next *Montreal Queen,* and her daughter will be with her. They want to spend the day inspecting the new cannery, and when they sail for Taku Inlet, Mr. Ross hopes that you will accompany them. They'll spend a few days there, then catch the *Queen* on its trip back to Seattle."

Wondering what this assignment might imply—there had certainly been no hint of anything like this at Christmas—he felt a surge of excitement on realizing that he was going to see Lydia again, even though she had treated him so badly the last time. He tried to avoid thinking that the visit had any deeper meaning, but he did move about the cannery in a state of euphoria.

One decision was easily made: "Sam, I won't be sailing with you back to Juneau." He said this almost mechanically, as if his decision not to visit Nancy Bigears was a free act without moral or emotional meaning, and that was the case, for it never occurred to him that in turning down Sam in favor of Mrs. Ross, he was also rejecting Nancy in hopes that something better would develop with Lydia.

The citizens of Ketchikan felt a sense of pride when some big passenger steamer sailed in, and since the *Montreal Queen* was the finest, newest ship in the Alaskan service, they lined the dock when the sleek Canadian beauty edged in. As soon as the gangway was dropped into position and secured to the dock, Mrs. Ross appeared at its top, attended by an officer. He was Captain Binneford, a trim, imposing seaman from eastern Canada with years of experience on the Atlantic crossing. Handing her along to Tom Venn, who ran forward to greet her, Captain Binneford said: "Take care of this good lady. We want her safely returned when we stop at Totem Cannery on the return."

As Tom reached to give Mrs. Ross his arm, he saw behind her Lydia, dressed in a white suit with blue nautical trimming. She looked like some carefully chosen young woman posing for an advertisement depicting a European voyage to Paris or Rome: she was an eager traveler prepared to see the sights. "Hello, Tom!" she called out with unladylike vigor, and to her mother's surprise, as well as Tom's, she ran to him as soon as she left the gangway and planted an enthusiastic kiss on his cheek.

They spent that long day seeing what Ketchikan had to offer, and the little town of six hundred went out of its way, with a band concert, a barbecue and a parade back to the ship, which sailed at dusk.

The Rosses had provided a stateroom for Tom, but he had barely entered it when Mrs. Ross asked him to accompany her as she walked the upper deck, and once again he was awed by the easy graciousness of this woman: "It was Lydia's idea, this trip. She knew . . . well, the truth is, I gave her living hell for the way she treated you at Christmas. No, don't speak. These things happen sometimes, Tom, and we're powerless to stop them. But we can correct them. And that's what she wants to do." She chuckled. "I'm not sure she *wanted* to do it, but I made it very clear she had to." They walked some more, and she added: "That's when she suggested this cruise. What a brilliant idea!"

"I respect your daughter enormously, Mrs. Ross. I've never known anyone like her."

"Nor I. She's special, if I say so myself. But then, as you know, so was her grandmother."

"She didn't have to apologize."

"She wanted to, when I pointed out how horrid she'd been."

Later Tom walked the same deck with Lydia, and she too astonished him by the frankness of her comment: "At Christmas, Tom, I thought I was very much in love with Horace. He seemed the proper answer to everything. Now he seems rather fake, and to tell you the truth, I very much wanted to see you again. Because, as Father told me at the time, you're real."

He could not believe what he was hearing, but then she said: "I doubt I'm in love with you, Tom. I doubt I'll be in love with anyone till I'm much older. But the talks I had with you on that hill, they're the best talks I've ever had, and when Horace blathered on about his family and his school and the keen fellows he knew, I couldn't help thinking of you . . . and reality."

They made almost a complete circuit in silence, then Tom said: "I wasn't really hurt at Christmas. I thought that that was the world you were entitled to and I knew I didn't belong."

"Oh, Tom!" She burst into tears and stopped to lean against the railing. Reaching for his hand, she pressed it and said: "Forgive me. It was Christmas and I got caught up in all the celebrations and thought that this was my world." They resumed walking, and after a while she said: "My world is considerably larger than that."

But when they said goodnight, well after one in the morning with the mountains of Alaska looking down on them, she spoke with another burst of frankness: "I don't know what this trip means, Tom. I really don't. Neither of us must take it too seriously, but you must take with great seriousness the fact that I want to keep you as a friend." She laughed nervously, then added: "And so does Father. It looks as if you're to be around for a long time, and I wanted to make peace."

"The pipe is lit."

She kissed him and went to her room.

• • •

When the *Montreal Queen* made her stately way up Taku Inlet, Tom Venn stood at the railing with the Ross women and explained the glaciers on the western shore. The best part of their adventure came when the big ship anchored at the very end of the inlet to disembark passengers for the twenty-minute walk to a hidden lake and the lovely twin glaciers, small and glistening, which fed it.

It was a sturdy walk uphill, but both the Rosses insisted upon taking it, and they were well worn when they reached the beautiful gemlike glaciers, so different from the others. Standing next to them, it was possible to imagine that they really were part of a living field of ice. "They're the daughters of the old woman up there," Lydia said, and they did indeed create that impression.

When they reached the cannery on the return trip down the inlet, Tom learned that Nancy Bigears was home for the school vacation, and when Sam came over to pay his respects, he informed Tom that Nancy still hadn't made up her mind what she was going to do. Mrs. Ross asked what options she had, and Sam said: "Her teachers think maybe college," and this so intrigued Mrs. Ross that she said: "We've always wanted to educate bright young Eskimos."

"We're Tlingits," Sam said, and Mrs. Ross quickly said: "I'm so sorry. Nobody has told me the difference," and Sam said: "No offense. Some my people not much to be proud of."

"But I imagine you're very proud of your daughter."

"I sure am."

"Well, Mr. Bigears, if she's as good as you say, there should certainly be a way for us to get her into college. Could you ask her to come over while we're here?"

So on a bright summer's day, while the cannery was in full swing, Sam Bigears and Nancy came across the estuary to meet two women about whom she already knew a great deal. When they came into the office, Nancy, scowling apprehensively from beneath her sharply edged bangs, looked first at Mrs. Ross, who smiled at her reassuringly as if to make her feel at home, and then at Lydia, whom she was seeing for the first time and whom she knew to be her rival. Mrs. Ross, aware that the setting, with everyone staring at one girl and waiting to hear what she had to say, was too much like a legal procedure, sought to soften it: "Nancy, sit here with me. We've heard such exciting reports about your work in school, we wanted the honor of meeting a girl who could do so well."

Taking the seat indicated, Nancy thought: They keep calling me a girl. I'm older than any of them. But now Lydia, taking the cue from her mother, said: "You know, there's a way you could attend the university," and Mrs. Ross added: "Alaska needs . . . in fact, we all need bright young people who will bring modern ways to everything." Aware that this sounded condescending, she hurried on: "Like Mr. Venn . . . managing this factory." Nancy lost the analogy, for she was looking across the room at Tom, in such a way that Lydia Ross knew instantly that the Indian girl was in love with him.

Tom said: "Mrs. Ross told me it would be a privilege to meet you, and I assured her she wouldn't be disappointed."

Now Nancy was ready to speak: "Are you the wife of the man who owns this cannery?"

"I am."

"Well, you should tell him that he mustn't stop my people from fishing in our Pleiades as we've always done."

Mrs. Ross, surprised by this frontal attack but not unnerved by it, turned to Tom and asked: "Is what she says true?" and Tom had to explain that under the law, when a cannery obtained the right to place its trap at the confluence . . .

"It's wrong, Mrs. Ross, and it ought to be stopped. My family has fished this river for more than fifty years." She continued with such a strong statement about native rights that Mrs. Ross found herself agreeing, but in the end she put a stop to it: "Nancy, we wanted to find out two things. Would you like to attend the university? Have you done well enough in school to succeed if you do go?"

"I don't really know what a university is, Mrs. Ross. But my teachers keep telling me that I could go if I wanted to."

After this frank self-assessment, Mrs. Ross began asking a series of questions calculated to identify the level of the girl's learning, and both she and Lydia were surprised at the mature manner in which Nancy responded. She apparently knew several good works of literature and had a much better than average knowledge of American history. She knew what the Sistine Chapel was and how an opera was structured. But when Mrs. Ross asked about algebra and geometry, Nancy said frankly: "I'm not very good in arithmetic," and Lydia chimed in: "Neither was I," but Mrs. Ross would not allow this easy escape: "If you want to be first-class, Nancy, you really ought to know about proportions and how to solve for simple unknowns," and Nancy replied with disarming frankness: "That's what Miss Foster keeps saying."

Mrs. Ross was disturbed to learn from Nancy and Tom that few Indian children ever persisted past grade six and that Nancy was the first Tlingit girl ever to reach senior year. "She's set a good standard," Mrs. Ross said, and Tom was as pleased as if he had been one of Nancy's teachers.

At this point no one doubted that Nancy could survive in a university, and Lydia said that she was already better educated than many sophomores: "You could have a great time at the university, Nancy," and Mrs. Ross assured both Nancy and her father that a scholarship of some kind would be forthcoming: "It isn't that she needs the university. The university needs her." But it was obvious that Nancy, who would be the first of her kind ever to undertake such a bold adventure, was uncertain about such a move.

"I don't know," she said diffidently, but her father, proud of her deportment this day, said to no one in particular: "If free, she take it," and Mrs. Ross said quickly: "Not exactly free. Could you help her with small funds?" and Sam said: "I do now," and everyone laughed.

At the conclusion of the interview, which had gone better than anyone had expected, the Ross family reached a decision which both surprised and exhilarated Tom Venn. Mrs. Ross announced: "When the *Montreal Queen* stops by on its return trip this evening, I'm sailing to Seattle as planned. But Lydia tells me she wants to stay here a few days and catch our R&R supply boat on Friday." Before anyone could comment, she turned to Sam: "Mr. Bigears, could my daughter stay with your family till the ship comes? She certainly can't stay here with Mr. Venn." She said this disarmingly, with such easy grace that everyone was placed at ease, and Sam asked Lydia: "You ready for real Tlingit potlatch?" and Lydia replied: "I don't know whether you eat it or sleep in it, but I'm ready." So when the Canadian ship arrived, she remained on the dock with Nancy and Tom as her mother boarded.

Mrs. Ross was even more congenial than before as she stopped at the head of the gangway: "Thank you, Mr. Bigears, for watching over my daughter. We'll see you in Seattle in September, Nancy. Tom, you've been a gracious host. And all you good people who work at the cannery, God bless you. We need your help."

The *Montreal Queen,* pride of the Canadian line which sailed out of Seattle to Vancouver and the Alaskan ports, was more than 245 feet long, weighed a majestic 1,497 tons and was legally authorized to carry 203 passengers. But because many tourists wanted transportation to Seattle as the summer season drew to a close, on this trip she carried in hastily erected wooden bunks a total of 309 paying passengers plus a crew of 66. All but two spaces had been filled when the ship left Juneau on its homeward leg, and when it stopped at Totem Cannery to pick up the two Ross women, Mrs. Ross explained that even though Lydia would not be sailing with her, the Rosses would pay for two passages. The purser took the problem to Captain Binneford, who said that in view of Mr. Malcolm Ross's close affiliation with the line, no charge would be made for the unused quarters.

The ship left Totem Cannery in the silvery dusk of a late August day, and because it was somewhat behind schedule, it traveled rather faster than usual in an attempt to make up time and beat the ebbing tide past the rocky portions of the upper inlet. Captain Binneford knew well—for the route had been carefully spelled out by the revenue cutter service years before and partially marked by them—that in passing the Walrus it was obligatory to keep well to the west, that is, to keep the rock safely to port, and this he did, but for some reason never to be known, he cut the margin of safety, and at half after seven on Wednesday night, 22 August 1906, while there was still ample light, this fine ship plowed headlong onto a submerged ledge which reached out from the Walrus. The bow of the ship was punctured, and its forward speed was so great that a gash eighty-two feet long was made down the port side. Almost instantly the *Montreal Queen* was wedged onto the Walrus, its gaping wound exposed as the tide went out.

Mrs. Ross was still unpacking when the speeding ship slammed abruptly onto the ledge, and she was thrown forward, but she was such an agile woman that she protected herself and was not hurt. She was one of the first on deck and the one who best understood what had happened, for she assured her fellow passengers: "My husband runs a shipping company in these waters, and accidents like this do happen. But we have wireless, and other ships will hasten to rescue us." She saw no reason for fear, and said so repeatedly.

However, as she was speaking, Captain Binneford was sending and receiving messages which would exert a powerful effect on the fate of the *Montreal Queen,* for when his company headquarters received news of the grounding, they sent a reply which would become famous in Alaskan history:

IF DAMAGE NOT TOTALLY DISABLING, YOU ARE ORDERED TO
AWAIT ARRIVAL ONTARIO QUEEN SPEEDING TO RESCUE ALL
PASSENGERS. WILL ARRIVE FRIDAY SUNSET.

Had Mrs. Ross been allowed to see this message, she would, as the wife of a shipowner, have understood its implications, for what the parent company was doing was ordering the captain of the stricken ship not to allow any salvage effort by ships of another line or by adventuresome seamen based in Juneau or Ketchikan. Maritime law was such that if a disabled ship allowed any other vessel to aid it, that other craft established a vested interest in the wreck. In this case, easing the *Queen* off the rocks or towing her back to Juneau would be interpreted as providing help, which qualified for a share in the salvage.

If the *Montreal Queen* could hold on till her sister ship, the *Ontario Queen,* arrived from Vancouver, the Canadian company would save considerable money. And when Captain Binneford studied the condition of his ship, he made the gambling decision that it would remain safely wedged where it was throughout Thursday and Friday, by which time the *Ontario Queen* would arrive to carry the passengers on to Seattle. It was a risky decision, but it was not stupid, for it looked to all the officers in charge of the *Queen* that she was so tightly wedged that she must stay safely on the rock indefinitely.

Captain Binneford ordered his staff to so inform the passengers, who that night dined off badly tilted tables and slept in beds that kept rolling them to starboard.

News of the wreck did not filter back to Totem Cannery on Thursday morning until about an hour after word had reached Juneau, so by the time Tom Venn, Sam Bigears and others had launched all the cannery boats to effect a rescue of Mrs. Ross and all who could be crowded into the space available, many small boats from Juneau were already at the scene. Just as Tom and Bigears arrived at the Walrus, a coastal boat of some size which had been unloading at Juneau steamed up, enabling Sam to announce: "We got enough boats here, rescue everybody." It was agreed that they would whisk Mrs. Ross back to Totem, where she could wait for the Friday arrival of the R&R supply ship.

But when the various vessels—from the big one which had just arrived to the smallest boat from Totem—approached the stranded *Montreal Queen* they became enmeshed in that insane law. To protect his company from salvage claims, Captain Binneford refused to allow even one person, passenger or crew, to leave his ship into the care of another vessel, regardless of its size. This meant that the 309 passengers of the *Queen* could line the railing of their badly damaged ship and almost touch hands with their would-be rescuers, but they could not leave the ship to accept help.

Tom and Bigears located Mrs. Ross quickly, where she stood in the midst of many women passengers, assuring them that rescue was imminent; of all the women she showed the least strain. When she saw Bigears, she cried: "Oh, Mr. Bigears! You are a most welcome sight." And she started below to fetch her bags so that she could be one of the first off.

"I'm sorry, madam," a polite Canadian officer apologized as he barred her way. "No one can leave the ship."

"But our cannery boat is alongside. It's our boat. It's our cannery, just a few miles back there."

"I am most sorry, and so is Captain Binneford, but no one can leave the ship. We're responsible for your safety. Your rescue is imminent."

Mrs. Ross, unable to understand the stupidity of such a rule, demanded to see the captain, but the officer told her, reasonably: "Surely you appreciate the strain he's under. He has enough to do to work with the crew." And she was forbidden even to throw her luggage into Tom's boat lest the legal position of the steamship company be compromised.

Tom and Bigears remained at the wreck all that Thursday, trusting that somehow common sense would prevail, but none did, and when a second even larger would-be rescue ship from Juneau arrived on the scene, and men from the various small craft climbed aboard to learn from its captain what the situation was, they were told: "If we were allowed to take off all the passengers, it might cost the Canadian company as much as two thousand dollars."

"Wouldn't the salvage rights to the ship itself also be involved?"

"Never. We're talking about two thousand dollars, at most."

Without hesitation Tom Venn cried: "I'll put up the two thousand," and half a dozen others volunteered to contribute, for as one sailor accustomed to these waters warned: "You can never tell when that Taku Wind will come roaring out of Canada. We better get them off before sunset."

So the captain of the new arrival, the captain of the earlier ship and Tom Venn as representative of the Ross & Raglan line decided to approach Captain Binneford by bullhorn, and Tom served as spokesman in offering to pay all costs involved in disembarking the passengers immediately. Binneford refused even to consider the proposal, because in the meantime he had received a second set of instructions from the home office assuring him that the *Ontario Queen* would arrive at the Walrus two hours earlier than previously estimated. The wireless message had ended:

ALL PASSENGERS WILL BE SAFELY ABOARD ONTARIO BY FOUR FRIDAY AFTERNOON.

Tom, feeling a personal responsibility for Mrs. Ross, remained near the stricken ship, because he still felt that Captain Binneford, whom he had found to be a sensible man during their brief acquaintance on the run from Ketchikan to Totem, would want to ensure his passengers' safety, regardless of instructions which might endanger them, and he wanted to be on hand to protect Mrs. Ross. He therefore sent Sam Bigears back to the cannery in another Totem boat, with instructions to assure Lydia that her mother was going to be all right.

But Sam's craft had barely left the stricken ship when a brisk wind came speeding down the inlet from Canada, and two experienced sailors warned: "If this continues, we could have a full-scale Taku," and because Sam was cautious where gales were concerned, he swung his boat in a full circle and headed back to be ready to disembark passengers if the winds worsened.

In her creaking quarters that Thursday night Mrs. Ross, along with quite a few other passengers, penned notes to relatives. Hers was to Lydia:

This adventure proves one thing to me, and I hope it does to you too, Lydia. No disaster, and the wrecking of this ship is a disaster, justifies you to act stupidly. In fact, at such times you ought to act with superhuman intelligence, and I trust you will always do so.

It is stupid to keep us passengers trapped on this ship, even if there is a modicum of assurance that the other ship will get here in good time. It is stupid to allow a few dollars to obstruct the operation of ordinary intelligence. And it is always very stupid, Lydia, to allow one minor consideration to obscure the right decision regarding a major concern. If we get off this

*pathetic craft alive, which I begin to doubt, I shall want your
father, with the most ardent support from me, to see to it that
Captain Binneford never again sails in Alaskan waters, for his
behavior tonight as the winds begin to rise is indefensible.*

*Yes, the wind has picked up considerably and the boat is
creaking much more loudly than before. I see a dish start to
move across my table as I write, and instead of stopping, it
picks up speed. But I am glad I made this trip with you, Lydia.
I think we both saw young Mr. Venn in new lights, and they
were neither favorable nor unfavorable, just new. That Nancy
Bigears is a gem, lecturing me before I could offer my help. See
that she does well at the university. And take care of yourself.
Make right choices and defend them.*

*I'm far less apprehensive than this letter sounds. I'm sure we'll
be rescued tomorrow.*

When she went to the railing to throw her letter, properly weighted,
down to Tom, an officer tried to prevent her from doing so, again
saying the legal position of the ship would be compromised, but she
pushed him away and said harshly: "For God's sake, young man,
don't be a damned fool."

When Bigears reached the scene he sought Tom's boat, but could
not find it among the scores of little craft eager to rescue the passengers, but later he saw Tom talking with Mrs. Ross, who was leaning
down from the railing. Not wanting to alarm her with the news he
was bringing, he waited till she withdrew, then he climbed into Tom's
boat: "I fear. So do men at cannery."

"What's up?"

"Taku Wind comes. No doubt about it."

"Big enough to push the *Queen* off the rocks?"

"If water rises, maybe."

"Any chance?"

"Maybe yes."

So Tom and Bigears moved among the waiting boats till they reassembled the two captains who had consulted with Captain Binneford earlier that day, and Tom told them: "Sam Bigears here has
lived on Taku Inlet all his life. Knows it better than anyone. And he
says . . . Tell them, Sam."

"Big Taku Wind coming. Maybe before sun rise."

"Sweeping water down with it?"

"For sure."

"And there'll be a pretty high tide too," said Tom.

The two captains needed no more information. Keeping Tom and Bigears with them, they moved close to the *Queen* and shouted: "We want to talk with Captain Binneford."

"He's busy."

One of the captains grew angry: "You tell that stupid bastard he better get unbusy and come talk with us."

"He wants no further interference."

"He's goin' to get it. Because one hell of a big Taku Wind is goin' to blow his ass right off that rock."

When the young officer refused to interrupt Captain Binneford, the captain grew furious, whipped out a revolver, and fired two quick shots over the *Queen.* This brought Captain Binneford on the run: "What's going on, Mr. Proudfit?"

"Trouble," the leader in the rescue boat shouted. "Captain, there's a big wind risin'. You better get everyone off your ship."

"The *Ontario Queen* will be here by four tomorrow afternoon."

"It may find you missing."

Captain Binneford started to leave the railing, but now the second captain shouted at him: "Captain, this man here has lived on Taku Inlet all his life. He knows, and he says there's danger of a real big wind."

In the darkness Captain Binneford, shaken by these words, stared at the man in the boat below as if he were prepared to listen, but at that moment Tom held a lantern to Bigears' face, and when the Canadian skipper saw that Sam was a Tlingit, he turned on his heel and left.

But Sam was correct in his estimate of this wind, because by midnight it had risen so sharply that most of the really small boats, whose skippers knew these waters, had headed for the safety of a protected cove north of Walrus Glacier. Tom and Sam felt they had to stay close to the *Queen* in case the captain came to his senses, but by three in the morning the blasts out of Canada were so powerful that Bigears warned: "If we not go, we sink too," so against his will Tom headed his boat toward a cove south of Walrus Glacier.

As they drew away from the *Queen,* he asked: "What's going to happen?" and Bigears said: "I think she go down," and Tom asked: "Will those two bigger ships be able to rescue them?" and Sam said:

"They got any sense, they leave now," and in the darkness Tom saw with horror that the two larger boats were indeed running for shelter, because their captains knew that a gale strong enough to drive them onto the rocks had to strike the Walrus before long.

In her cabin, with the wind roaring and the ship listing at a more severe angle, Mrs. Ross wrote a final note, which, waterstained, would be delivered to her daughter some weeks later:

> I am sure, Lydia, that your grandmother must have known
> moments like this when all seemed lost. Remember the harsh
> accusations that were made against her and other brave young
> women. They survived and so shall I. But the wind does grow
> stronger and we await the dawn in a kind of dumb terror. It is
> so sad. I can't hold back my tears, because this was all so
> unnecessary. Your father and I would have solved this problem
> in three minutes, and I beg you to develop the same kind of
> character and willingness to assume responsibility, for they are
> great virtues, maybe the greatest. I love you. Tonight my hopes
> must transfer to you.

When dawn broke on Friday morning, with all the rescue ships scattered but watching in horror as the gale increased, raking and churning the water as it swept down the inlet, Tom and Bigears moved out from their sanctuary and, braving the furious chopping swell, tried to approach the foundering *Queen*. But when the light was strong enough for them to see the ship listing perilously to port, the wind became so powerful that Tom cried: "Turn back!" but Bigears shouted: "We got to get Mrs. Ross!" and he kept their small boat plowing through great swells. Then suddenly a combination of intense gusting wind and pounding waves much higher than before rocked the *Montreal Queen* loose and turned her over on her gaping side.

Within minutes the beautiful ship disappeared in the dark waters of the inlet, and because of the tremendous sucking action it generated, not a single passenger of the 309 survived. To prevent a financial loss of two thousand dollars, everyone aboard the *Montreal Queen*, including the crew, perished.

Tom and Bigears stood by the site of the sinking, hoping along with some dozen other small craft to save at least a few of the passengers, but it soon became obvious that there would not be anyone to rescue. Indeed, the capsizing had come with such a sudden rush that there were hardly any stray bits of wreckage to mark where the ship had been. So at about three in the afternoon, just as Tom was about to start back to Totem, Sam Bigears shouted: "Look!" and Tom turned and saw the stately *Ontario Queen,* steaming up an hour early.

At the cannery, Tom was unable to tell the waiting women what had happened. Instead, Bigears climbed onto the dock, walked slowly toward the crowd that had gathered, and embraced Lydia Ross: "Everyone go down. Everyone. Tom has letter."

By the time Tom approached the crowd Lydia had herself under control, but when she saw this gallant fellow whom she had once treated so poorly, she ran to him, collapsing in tears and throwing herself into his arms.

Her father, when he met her on her return to Seattle, suspected rightly that she was being overly emotional when she announced that she was marrying Tom Venn, and he begged her to wait until she saw things more clearly, but she said: "I did see things very clearly during that visit. If Mother had lived, she would have told you that I stayed behind because I did not want Tom to marry that Nancy Bigears, wonderful as you'll find her to be. I wanted him, and I wanted him for the best reason in the world. I love him." Later she added: "I saw him in the storm. He performed the way you would have, Father," and Mr. Ross said: "Most men behave courageously in a storm," but she corrected him: "Captain Binneford didn't."

Her father did prevail upon her not to marry immediately: "I don't give a damn for appearances, as you well know. But there is meaning to that old phrase *a decent interval,*" and she said: "October tenth will be decent. Tom and I have things to do."

Nancy Bigears, now a student at the university, attended the wedding, and although there was uneasiness between her and Lydia, there was none with Tom. She still loved him, and both Lydia and Tom knew this, and in return they loved her, for she was the first of the Tlingit women to test her luck in the white man's world and they wished her well. When she asked where they would be spending their honeymoon, Lydia said: "At Ketchikan Cannery. Tom has work to do," and Nancy kissed them both.

• • •

When Nerka the salmon leaped over Tom Venn's right-hand jigger in order to return to the Pleiades River, he faced the reverse of the problem which had threatened him three years earlier. Now, as a fish acclimated to life in salt water, he must relearn how to live in fresh, and this sharp alteration required two days of slow swimming in the new medium. But gradually he adjusted, and now the excess fat which he had acquired in his hump during his burst of prodigious eating became an asset, keeping him alive and strong enough to ascend the waterfalls of the river, for as we have seen, once he entered fresh water he would never again feed, his entire digestive system having atrophied to the point of nonfunction.

He had nine miles of upstream swimming to negotiate before he reached the lake, and this was a task immeasurably more difficult than swimming down had been, for not only did he have to leap over major obstacles, but he also had to protect himself from the large number of bears that lined the river, knowing that the fat salmon were coming.

At the first rapids he proved his ability, for he swam directly up the middle, breasting the full power of the stream and propelling himself forward with forceful strokes of his tail, but it was when he reached the first waterfall, about eight feet high, that he demonstrated his unusual skill, for after hoarding his strength at the bottom, he suddenly darted at the falling plume of water, lifted himself in the air, and leaped the full eight feet, vibrating his tail furiously. With an effort not often matched in the animal kingdom, he overcame that considerable obstacle.

His outstanding performance came with the third waterfall, not a vertical drop but a long, sliding affair of rapidly rushing, turbulent water some eighteen feet long and with such a sharp drop that it looked as if no fish could master it, and certainly not in a single bound.

Here Nerka used another tactic. He made a furious dash right at the heart of the oncoming flow, and within the waterfall itself he swam and leaped and scrambled until he found a precarious lodging halfway up. There he rested for some moments, gathering energy for the greater trial to come.

Trapped in the middle of the fall, he obviously could not build up forward motion, but rising almost vertically, with his tail thrashing madly, he could resume his attack. Once more he swam, not leaped, right up the heart of the fall, and after a prodigious effort he broke free to reach calm water, in which he rested for a long time.

The most perilous part of his homeward journey, insofar as external agencies were concerned, now loomed, for in his exhausted state he failed to practice the cautions which had kept him alive for six years, and in his drifting he came within range of a group of bears that had gathered at this spot because they had learned, centuries ago, that after the homecoming salmon finished battling that waterfall, they would for some time flop aimlessly about and become easy prey.

One large bear had waded some feet into the river, where it found success in scooping up exhausted salmon and tossing them back onto the bank, where others leaped upon them, tearing their flesh. This bear, spotting Nerka as the most promising salmon of this morning's run, leaned forward like an ardent angler, sent its right paw flashing through the water, caught Nerka full under the belly, and with a mighty swipe tossed him far behind it, like an angler landing a prize trout.

As Nerka flew through the air he was aware of two things: the bear's claws had ripped his right flank, but not fatally, and the direction in which he was flying contained some areas which looked like water. So as soon as he landed with a hard thump on dry land, with two large bears leaping forward to kill him, he gave a series of wild gyrations, summoning all the power his tail, fins and body muscles could provide. As the bears reached out with their powerful claws, he wriggled and flopped like a drunken fly trying to land on unsteady legs, and just as the bears were about to grab him, he leaped at one of the shimmering areas. It was a sluggish arm of the river, and he was saved.

Now, as he neared the lake, the unique signal composed of mineral traces, the position of the sun, perhaps the gyration of the earth and maybe the operation of some peculiar electrical force, became overwhelming. For more than two thousand miles he had attended to this signal, and now it throbbed throughout his aging body: This is Lake Pleiades. This is home.

He reached the lake on 23 September 1906, and when he entered the jewellike body of water with its protecting mountains, he found his way to that small feeder stream with its particular aggregation of gravel in which he had been born six years earlier, and now for the first time in his exciting life he began to look about him not for just another salmon but for a female, and when other males swam by he recognized them as enemies and drove them off. The culminating experience of his life was about to begin, but only he and two others of his original four thousand had made it back to their home waters. All the rest had perished amid the dangers imposed by the incredible cycle of the salmon.

Mysteriously, out of a dark overhang which produced the deep shadows loved by sockeye, she came, a mature female who had shared the dangers he had known, who had in her own way avoided the jiggers reaching out to trap her and who had ascended the waterfalls with her own skills and tricks. She was his equal in every way except for the fierce prognathous lower jaw that he had developed, and she, too, was ready for the final act.

Moving quietly beside him as if to say "I shall look to you for protection," she began waving her tail and fins gently, brushing away silt that had fallen upon the gravel she intended using. In time, employing only these motions, she dug herself a redd, or nest, about six inches deep and twice her length, which was now more than two feet. When the redd was prepared, she tested it again to ensure that the steady stream of life-giving cold water was still welling up from the hidden river, and when she felt its reassuring presence, she was ready.

Now the slow, dreamlike courtship dance began, with Nerka nudging closer and closer, rubbing his fins against hers, swimming a slight distance away, then rushing back. Other males, aware of her presence, hurried up, but whenever one appeared, Nerka drove him off, and the lyrical dance continued.

Then a startling change occurred: both salmon opened their mouths as wide as their jaw sockets would allow, forming large cavernous passageways for the entrance of fresh water. It was as if they wished to purify themselves, to wash away old habits in preparation for what was about to happen, and when this ritual was completed they experienced wild and furious surges of courtship emotions, twisting together, snapping their jaws and quivering their tails. When their marine ballet ended, with their mouths once more agape, the female released some four thousand eggs, and at that precise instant Nerka ejected his milt, or sperm, over the entire area. Fertilization would occur by chance, but the incredible flood of milt made it probable that each egg would receive its sperm and that Nerka and his mate would have done their part in perpetuating their species.

Their destiny having been fulfilled, their mysterious travels were over, and an incredible climax to their lives awaited. Since they had eaten nothing since leaving the ocean, not even a minnow, they were so exhausted by their travel up Taku Inlet, their battle with traps, their swim upstream against waterfalls, that they retained not a shred of vital force. Will power consumed by these tremendous exertions, they began to drift aimlessly, and wayward currents eased them along a nepenthelike course to the spot where the lake emptied into the river.

When they entered the lively swirls of that stream they were momentarily revived, and fluttered their tails in the customary way, but they were so weak that nothing happened, and the current dragged them passively to where the falls and the rapids began.

As they reached the fatal spot at the head of the long falls, where bears waited, Nerka summoned enough energy to swim clear, but his mate, near death, could not, and one of the biggest animals reached in, caught her in its powerful claws, and threw her ashore, where other bears leaped at her. In a brief moment she was gone.

Had Nerka been in possession of his faculties, he would never have allowed the long waterfall to grasp him and smash him willy-nilly down its most precipitous drops and onto its most dangerous rocks, but that is what happened, and the last shuddering drop was so destructive that he felt the final shreds of life being knocked out of him. Vainly he tried to regain control of his destiny, but the relentless water kept knocking him abusively from rock to rock, and the last he saw of the earth and its waters of which he had been such a joyous part was a great spume into which he was sucked against his will and the massive rock which lurked therein. With a sickening smash, he was no more.

He had returned to Lake Pleiades system on 21 September 1906. He had fathered the next generation of sockeye on the twenty-fifth, and now on the last day of the month he was dead. He had lived five years, six months and had discharged all obligations courageously and as nature had programmed.

For three miles his dead body drifted downstream, until waves washed it to sanctuary in a backwater where ravens, familiar with the habits of the river, waited. He reached their domain about four in the afternoon of an increasingly cold day when food was essential, and by nightfall only his bones were left.

Of the one hundred million sockeye born along with Nerka in 1901, only some fifty thousand managed to make it back, and since it is reasonable to assume that these were evenly divided between the sexes, this meant that some twenty-five thousand pairs were available for breeding. Since each female produced about four thousand eggs, a total of exactly one hundred million eggs would be available to ensure a generation born in 1907, and we have seen that this is the precise number required to maintain the lake's normal population. Any diminution in the number of survivors would imperil the chance for continuation.

If the jiggers were raised even higher next year, as planned, the number of breeding salmon able to avoid them would be further diminished, so that year by year the deficiency would worsen.

The greed of Tom Venn and his masters in Seattle had doomed the Lake Pleiades sockeye, one of the noblest members of the animal kingdom, to eventual extinction.

In November when the Thomas Venns, as they were now called, were in the process of closing down Ketchikan Cannery for the winter, after an excellent campaign, an officer from Ross & Raglan headquarters in Seattle stopped by with depressing news: "Mr. Ross asked me to tell you that Nancy Bigears, after only a few weeks at the university, boarded one of our ships and sailed back to Juneau. When asked why she had quit her education, she said: 'Those classes held nothing for me.'"

"What's she doing?" Tom and Lydia wanted to know, and to be sure he gave an accurate answer, the officer took from his pocket a paper which Mr. Ross had given him: "Two weeks after arriving in Juneau, Nancy married a Chinese handyman named Ah Ting."

XI

THE RAILBELT

IN THE SUMMER OF 1919, WHEN MALCOLM ROSS, AGE SIXTY-seven, lay dying, he knew that he was leaving his prominent mercantile establishment, Ross & Raglan, in the most profitable condition it had ever known. In the three areas to which it restricted itself—maritime service to Alaska; warehouses in Anchorage, Juneau and Fairbanks, with retail stores in most of the towns; the catching and canning of salmon—it was preeminent. R&R represented the finest forward-looking leadership in Seattle, and commentators were not far wrong when they said: "R&R is Alaska, and Alaska is R&R," for the relationship was profitable to both partners. R&R received money, a great deal of it, and Alaska received the goods it needed and a reliable transportation service to what was called the Lower Forty-Eight. Since there were no roads from Alaska to either industrial Canada or the United States, and no likelihood of any in the foreseeable future, any goods that Alaska needed had almost inevitably to reach the north in some R&R ship, and any travelers who wanted to leave Alaska for the south had to use that same route.

But Ross had for some time been aware of a potential weakness in his company's benevolent monopoly, and anxious to discuss the situation, he summoned his daughter Lydia to his bedside, asking her to bring along her husband, Tom Venn, who for more than a decade had supervised the company's chain of salmon canneries. When they stood beside him, and saw how frail he had become through over-exertion during the closing months of the recent world war, they were alarmed, but he would allow no sentimentality: "I'm not strong, as you can see, but my mind's as good as ever."

"Take it easy, Father," Lydia said. "The men at the office have things under control."

"I didn't call you here to talk about the office. I'm worried about the insecurity of our shipping lines to Alaska."

"Traffic's impeccable," Tom said, who at an energetic thirty-six had traveled the R&R ships more than any other officer. He knew the shipping line to be in first-class condition.

"For the present, yes. But I'm looking ahead, and I see danger."

"From what?" Lydia asked, and after raising himself on one elbow, her father replied: "Competition. Not from American compa-nies, we have them in line and none of them can touch us. But from Canada, they're able traders. And from Japan, they're very able."

"We have been seeing signs," Venn conceded. "We can hold them off, I'm sure, but what did you have in mind?"

"Cabotage," the sick man said as he fell back. "Do you know what it is?" When the young people shook their heads, he said: "Find out!" and that launched their study of this arcane law of the sea and its coastal waters. The word came from the French *caboter* meaning *to coast along,* and through the centuries it had gained in diplomatic circles a specific application: the right to transport goods between two ports within the same country. As applied by mercantile nations, it meant that a Japanese ship built in Japan, owned in Japan, and manned by Japanese sailors was legally eligible to sail out of Yoko-hama laden with Japanese goods and sail to Seattle, where, if the proper duty was paid, the goods could be unloaded and sold in the United States. The ship could then pick up American goods and carry them back to Japan, or China or Russia.

But when the Japanese ship finished unloading at Seattle, it was forbidden to engage in cabotage, that is, it could not pick up either cargo or passengers in Seattle and carry them to some other Ameri-can port, say San Francisco. And, specifically, it could not deliver American items to Alaska. Any goods or passengers traveling from one American port to another had to be transported in American ships manned by American sailors, and not even the slightest devia-tion was allowed. Businessmen in Seattle revered the principle of cabotage as if it were Scripture, for it ensured them protection from competition from Asian vessels whose poorly paid crews enabled them to move freight at the lowest cost. So the more deeply the two young Venns probed into the intricacies of cabotage, the more clearly they saw that the future of Seattle, and especially the profitability of their family firm, depended upon the retention, strengthening and strict application of cabotage.

When they next gathered at their father's sickbed to discuss the matter, he showed his pleasure at their quick mastery of the situation, but he was distressed at their failure to identify the next step Seattle would have to take to protect itself completely: "Tom, the people of Alaska aren't going to support any strengthening of cabotage. In fact, they're going to fight against it. In Congress."

Venn nodded: "They would get their goods a lot cheaper if ships from Europe and Asia could haul them. Maybe even ships from Canada would be able to undercut us."

"I'm especially afraid of the Canadians. So what you must do when Congress takes up the matter, which the people of Alaska will insist upon, is line up a type of support we've never had before."

"I don't understand. Cabotage is a shipping concern. We're for it. The businessmen of Seattle are for it. West Coast shippers are for it. But who else?"

"That's where statesmanship comes in. Move away from the coasts. Enlist a whole new body of supporters in cities like Pittsburgh, Chicago and St. Louis."

"And how do we do that?"

"Labor. Add one simple provision to the navigation bills and you'll have all labor shouting support for our cabotage bills."

"And what is this magical provision?" Lydia asked, and her father replied: "Require that the American ship, owned by American businessmen and staffed by American officers and seamen, be built entirely in American shipyards by American workers." As he finished his prescription for the ensured growth of Seattle and the R&R shipping lines, he settled back on his pillows and smiled, for he was convinced that if such a bill could be shepherded through Congress, the possibility that Alaska might somehow evade control from Seattle would be eliminated.

But his clever son-in-law spotted the danger in relying upon Congress to pass a law which would aid the few and harm the many. "Alaska will fight like hell to prevent a law like that," he warned the old man, who merely nodded: "Of course they'll protest. They've never understood, up there, that they must rely on us for their well-being. R&R has never taken one nickel out of Alaska that wasn't justified. It'll be the same way with the bill I'm talking about. We'll pass it to protect Alaska from herself."

"How?" Tom asked, and he received a recommendation he did not savor: "We'll do it as we've always done it. The West Coast hasn't enough power in Congress to do it alone, but we do have friends in the other states. We must mobilize those friends, and there's only one man can do that job for us." Tom felt a sinking feeling in his stomach, and he was right to be apprehensive, for Ross said firmly: "Get Marvin Hoxey."

"But he's a crook!" Tom cried, recalling his distaste for this fraudulent operator.

"He still carries weight in Washington. If you want to protect our interests in Alaska, get Hoxey."

This Tom was reluctant to do, but in the anxious days that followed, as the directors of R&R convened to decide whom to select as Malcolm Ross's successor as head of the company, it became clear that Ross was not going to bestow his blessing on Tom Venn unless the latter hired Marvin Hoxey, the proven lobbyist, to maneuver a new maritime bill through Congress. Her father warned Lydia, when she met with him alone: "If Tom doesn't get Hoxey out here right away, I'll tell the board outright that he's not the man to replace me."

"But Hoxey is an evil man, Father. He's shown that again and again."

"He's an able man. He does what he says he'll do, and that's all that counts."

"And you'll block Tom if he refuses?"

"I must think about the safety of my company. I must do what's right."

"You call hiring a crook doing what's right?"

"Under the circumstances, yes."

That night Lydia told her husband: "I think you'd better telephone Hoxey."

"I will not do that."

"But, Tom . . ."

"I will not humiliate myself again in connection with that swindler."

There was a protracted silence, after which Lydia said quietly:

"When Father dies, I'll be the principal stockholder . . . Mother's shares and the ones he'll leave me. So I must act to protect my interests. I'm calling Hoxey." Tom, in disgust, left the room, but as he paced back and forth outside the door he realized that he was forcing a break between himself and his wife, and at a moment when she deserved his fullest support, so he returned to the room, just as Lydia finished putting in the call. Taking the telephone, he said with as much control as possible: "Marvin Hoxey? This is Tom Venn. . . . Yes, we knew each other in Nome during the great days, and during the salmon leases. . . . Yes, I'm married to Lydia Ross. . . . Sorry to tell you that her father is quite ill. . . . Yes, he wants to complete one big job before he dies. . . . He needs you. Right away. . . . Yes, Alaska." A long silence followed, during which the ebullient lobbyist delivered an oration. . . . "Yes, I'll tell her."

When he hung up, he looked sheepishly at Lydia: "The old rascal! He'd already guessed what Seattle would want done on the maritime bill. Had already started visiting congressmen on the assurance we'd call."

"What else did he say? During that one long spell?"

"He said he knew Alaska like the back of his hand and that everything was going to be all right."

Shortly thereafter the wily old campaigner came to Seattle to consult with Malcolm Ross. Sixty-four years old, heavyset, florid of face and clean-shaven, he breezed into the sickroom, cocked his right forefinger as if it were a pistol, and fired an imaginary bullet at Ross: "I want you out of that bed by nightfall. Orders."

"I wish I could obey, Marvin. But the . . ." He tapped his chest and smiled. "Draw up a chair and listen." And as the dying merchant prince lay in bed, he plotted his last great strategy for the enhancement of Seattle.

In these years the state of Washington was represented in the Senate of the United States by a hardworking, amiable Republican named Wesley L. Jones, whose devotion to duty had elevated him to the chairmanship of the important Senate Commerce Committee. Always attentive to the interests of his home state, he had listened when Malcolm Ross consulted with him concerning ways to nail down permanently all traffic heading for Alaska. He agreed early and firmly that nations like Japan and Canada should be eliminated from the profitable trade, and he saw no good reason why the established state of Washington should not take precedence over the unformed territory of Alaska, but he cautioned Ross and his fellow Seattleites: "It's not like the old days, gentlemen. Alaska is beginning to have a voice in our nation's capital. That little son-of-a-bitch Sheldon Jackson, no bigger than a pinpoint, he stirred up a lot of good Christians back there. We can't just run your bill through this time. We'll have to work on it, and work hard."

It was in April of that year that the Seattle men had awakened to the opposition which existed in the industrial states and those along the Mississippi. At the last meeting he chaired before becoming bedridden, Ross had reported: "You'd be astonished at some of the charges they're making against us. They say we're robbers, pirates trying to keep Alaska to ourselves. We've got to come up with some new tactic."

Just who it was who had the clever idea of enlisting labor in the fight to keep Alaska a colony was not recorded; Ross had not been at the meeting when this was first proposed, but as soon as members of his committee brought the suggestion to his bedside, he had grasped its significance: "Ride that one very hard. We're not trying to protect our interests. We're thinking only of the American workingman, the American sailor."

Now, in the closing weeks of his life, he outlined to both Marvin Hoxey and Tom Venn the strategy that would enable Senator Jones to ramrod through a maritime bill in 1920, the one that would remain in force for the rest of the century, binding Alaska in the harshest, most restrictive fetters any American territory would know since the days of King George III's repressive measures which had goaded the Colonies to revolt.

No one in the entire American political establishment was more influential in getting this act passed than Marvin Hoxey. Only three years younger than Malcolm Ross, he had four times the explosive energy and ten times the shameless gall. It took him less than three minutes to perceive the brilliance of enlisting labor in the fight, and before that first meeting ended, he had devised a presentation which would capture the imagination of congressmen in all parts of the nation. It required him to patrol the halls in Washington, while Tom Venn visited those state capitals whose representatives would cast the deciding votes.

Tom did not appreciate the assignment, for it meant that he would have to telephone Washington every night to inform Hoxey as to how things were going, and he might have refused to serve as Hoxey's assistant had not Malcolm Ross taken a sharp turn for the worse. Informed of the situation, Lydia and Tom rushed to his bedside, and when the two stood before him he gave them their last commission: "Any industry of magnitude faces moments of crisis . . . when decisions of life and death are in the process of being made. Choose right, up to the stars. Choose wrong, down to Avernus." He coughed, then flashed that smile which had served him so well at other times when he was striving to convince people: "And the hell of it is, usually we don't recognize that the decision is vital. We make it blind." He coughed again, his shoulders shaking violently; now the smile left his drawn lips and he said softly: "But this time we do know. The prosperity of this part of the nation depends upon getting Senator Jones's bill enacted." He asked Tom to promise that for the next crucial months he would work with full vigor on this campaign: "Let the company guide itself. You get out there and line up the votes." Then he reached for his telephone and called Marvin Hoxey, telling him to catch a night train. But at midafternoon Tom placed another call: "Marvin? Tom Venn. Cancel the trip. Malcolm died forty minutes ago."

The Jones Act of 1920 passed with its three essential provisions in place: no ship of foreign ownership and registry could carry American goods from one American port to another; only ships owned and manned by Americans could do that; the ship itself, even if it was American-owned, had to have been built in the United States by American labor. The future of Seattle was ensured.

The effect of the Jones Act could best be illustrated by what happened to a modest grocery store in Anchorage. Sylvester Rowntree had invested his savings in a new store half again as big as the old one, and by the year 1923 it had again doubled, so that the owner could have profitably ordered, from suppliers across the United States, his goods in cargo lots. But this was not practical, because a custom had evolved whereby goods destined for Alaska had to be handled in curious ways by the railroads and in ways downright insane at the docks in Seattle. Even before Rowntree's cargo was ready for loading onto an R&R vessel he would be forced to pay fifty percent more freightage than if his goods had been destined for some West Coast destination like Portland or Sacramento.

But now provisions of the Jones Act came into play: to use the

Seattle docks for shipment to Alaska cost almost twice what the same dock services cost for a shipment, say, to Japan. And when the R&R ship was loaded, the cost-per-mile of goods to Alaska was much higher than the cost of the same goods being shipped to other American ports by other lines. R&R had a monopoly which exacted a fifty-percent or better surcharge on every item freighted in to Alaska, and the territory had no escape from this imposition, for there were no other avenues by which goods could get in: no highways, no railroads, and as yet no airplanes.

"That damned Jones Act is strangling us," Sylvester Rowntree wailed, and he was right, for the Act exercised its tyranny in the most unexpected ways. The forests of Alaska could have provided wooden boxes for the Alaskan salmon canneries, but the cost of bringing in American sawmill equipment was kept so excessive that it was much cheaper to buy the wood from Oregon than to use trees which stood fifty feet from a cannery, and tariffs kept out non-American.

In the years following passage of the Act, a dozen profitable extractive industries went out of business because of the exorbitant costs imposed by the new rules, and this happened even though scores of Canadian ships stood ready to bring heavy equipment in at reasonable cost and take finished products out at rates that ensured a good profit.

Such discrepancies were explained away by Marvin Hoxey, defending in public the Act which he had engineered, as "inescapable minor dislocations which can be easily corrected." When no attempt was made to rectify them, he told Congress: "These are nothing more than the minor costs which a remote territory like Alaska must expect to bear if it is to enjoy the privileges of life within the American system." In his old age Hoxey had converted himself into a revered oracle, forever prepared to justify the indecencies to which Alaska was subjected.

What infuriated Alaskans like grocer Rowntree was not the pomposity of Hoxey and the self-serving statements of Thomas Venn, president of Ross & Raglan, but the fact that Hawaii, much farther from San Francisco than Alaska was from Seattle, received its goods at substantially cheaper rates. Rowntree's seventeen-year-old son, Oliver, figured: "Pop, if a grocer in Honolulu places a hundred-dollar order at the same time you do with a wholesaler in New York, by the time the two orders reach the West Coast docks, his has a total cost of $126, but yours is $147. Dockage fees being so different, by the time his goods get aboard they cost $137, but yours are $163. And now comes the rotten part. Because R&R rates are the highest in the world, by the time his goods reach Honolulu, they cost $152, while your goods landed in Anchorage cost us $191."

The boy spent the summer of his senior year conducting similar studies regarding various kinds of in and out shipments, and wherever he looked he found this same terrible discrepancy, so that for his graduating paper in English he composed a fiery essay entitled: "The Slavery Continues," in which he drew parallels between the economic servitude under which Alaska now suffered and the governmental chaos of the 1867–97 period. Fortunately for him—as it turned out later—this lament did not appear in the school journal, but Oliver's father was so proud of his son's insight into Alaskan affairs that he had three unsigned copies made, sending one to the territorial governor, one to Alaska's nonvoting delegate to Congress and one to the Anchorage newspaper, which did print it. His arguments played a role in the continuing attack Alaskans made against the cruel provisions of the Jones Act, but nothing was accomplished because in Seattle, Thomas Venn, increasingly active as head of R&R, and, in Washington, the aged warhorse Marvin Hoxey prevented any revision of the Jones Act or even any orderly discussion of its harmful effect upon Alaska.

Young Oliver Rowntree, nursing his outrage, spent the summer brooding about what he could do to retaliate. And that fall, on his way to the University of Washington in Seattle—where he had won a scholarship—he evolved a plan. From then on, as he traveled back and forth on R&R ships, he began slowly and slyly to sabotage them. He stole silverware from the dining rooms and quietly pitched it overboard at night. He jammed pillowcases down toilets. He wrenched fittings off newel posts, messed up documents he came upon, and threw large amounts of salt into any food he could contaminate without being caught. On some trips, if he was lucky, he did up to a hundred dollars' worth of theft and breakage.

Whenever he committed one of his acts of retribution he muttered to himself: "That's for stealing from my father . . . and the others," and twice each year he continued his depredations.

When Tom Venn, from his headquarters in Seattle, studied reports of this sabotage he was at first perplexed, and at dinner one night he told his wife: "Someone is conducting a vicious campaign against us, and we have no way of determining who it is," but when she studied the records she said immediately: "Tom, the worst cases seem to appear in autumn down to Seattle, in spring back to Anchorage."

"And what's the significance of that?"

"Don't you see? Probably some student. Feels a grievance toward our line."

Grasping at this clue, Tom initiated a study of passengers who sailed on the ships that had been attacked, and his staff came up with the names of eighteen young people who had sailed on at least three of the six affected voyages and seven who had been on all of them.

"I want a full report on each of the eighteen, with special details on those seven," Tom ordered, and during the weeks when these were being compiled, Oliver Rowntree was doing some thinking on his own, and he had learned in a math class dealing with the laws of probability that there were many ways by which a shrewd mind could analyze data which seemed at first capricious: Some smart operator could look over the passenger lists and make correlations, and if he was really bright, he could identify four or five likely suspects and then narrow it down intelligently by legwork. Oliver knew that his name would be thrown up by such an approach and what there was in his background which would alert R&R detectives to his being responsible for the sabotage—his essay on the evils of the Jones Act: Damn! Anyone reading that would know it was more than an attack on the Jones Act. It was a blast at Ross & Raglan. And he was glad his father had removed his name from the article.

He was a senior at the university when he completed these deductions: I've been down four trips and back up three. And on each one I've raised hell with something or other. But there must have been others like me who made those same trips. So the problem is: How can I throw the R&R flatfeet off my trail?

For several anxious weeks in 1924 he plotted diversionary actions, and gradually began to see that the best thing he could do would be to enlist into his conspiracy someone who would commit an act of sabotage—the kind he had done—on a northward trip when he was not a passenger, while he followed blamelessly on a later ship. But whom to enlist? Whom to trust with such a delicate mission? Because in the act of explanation he would have to reveal his past culpability, and this would place him in jeopardy.

Looking about the university, he came upon several small groups of students whose homes were in Alaska, and naturally these young people came mostly from Anchorage and Fairbanks; he shied away from the former as being too close to his father's store, and felt no harmony with the latter, but there were four students from Juneau, and he felt both a harmony with them as being more his serious type and an assurance that they, at least one of them, would understand his unusual problem. He therefore started to socialize with them, finding them politically concerned because of the way in which Alaskan politics dominated their hometown, and as the spring term drew to a close he judged it expedient to confide in one of the girls.

She was a beautiful young woman, about nineteen, whose origin was difficult to identify. Her name was one of those alliterative ones popular in the early 1920s, Tammy Ting, which could have made her Chinese, except that she also looked almost completely Indian, so one day after he had spoken to her several times, he asked as they left a student meeting: "Tammy Ting? What kind of name is that?" and she replied with a frank smile: "Tammy Bigears Ting." And she told him about her unusual father—"Only Chinese allowed to remain in Alaska after the big expulsion"—and her equally distinctive Tlingit grandfather—"His family fought the Russians for fifty years and now he fights the government in Washington." And as she spoke young Rowntree was mesmerized.

"Can I trust you, Tammy? I mean, with something big?" He was older than she, a graduating senior while she was only a sophomore who was thrashing around from one course to another, trying to identify subjects that involved her sympathies: "My mom came to Washington, back in the ancient days. Only Alaskan native in the university, but she stayed only a few weeks. When I left Juneau she warned me: 'You come home without a degree, I break both your arms.'"

"What a horrible thing to tell a daughter," Rowntree said, but Tammy corrected him: "The horrible part, she meant it. Still does."

Reassured by such frank comment, Oliver decided he could trust this girl of the new Alaska, and before he finished laying his problem before her, she perceived both his predicament and its solution: "You want me, on a different ship from the one you'll be on, to do everything you'd be doing?" When he nodded, she cried: "Set me loose! I despise Ross & Raglan, the way they punish Alaska," and the plot was hatched.

"Three trademarks," Oliver said, and when he explained about the stolen cutlery, the rip-off of newel posts and the clogging of the toilets, she asked: "But if you always did the same damage, didn't you realize they'd know it was always the same person?" and he said: "I wanted them to know." He hesitated: "But I never wanted them to catch me. I wanted them to know that people in Alaska despised what they were doing with their rotten Jones Act," and she said: "Pop and Mom feel the same way. I'm your girl."

At this point Oliver Rowntree leaves this part of the narrative. He graduated with honors from the University of Washington in 1925, sailed home to Anchorage on an R&R ship which he did not vandalize, so as to confuse anyone tracking his case, lived at home for the summer of 1925, and then left for a good job in Oregon, where he would marry in 1927 without ever returning to Alaska. His father had told him as he sailed: "Don't come back, Oliver. The way those bastards in Seattle and D.C. have things rigged against us, it's impossible to earn a decent living up here in Alaska." And in 1928 the older Rowntree also moved to Oregon, where, having escaped from the economic tyranny under which Alaska lived, he ran a highly profitable grocery store.

The case of Tammy Ting developed quite differently. On the R&R liner *Pride of Seattle,* which carried her north at the end of her sophomore year in 1925, she surreptitiously performed the three acts of sabotage which would earmark the perpetrator as the same one who had been pestering Ross & Raglan for the past four years, plus a couple of inventive and highly costly depredations of her own, but one evening as she was preparing to devastate an expensively carved newel post, a young man came upon her so unexpectedly that she had to dissemble in obvious embarrassment. "I'm sorry I startled you," he apologized, and when he looked more closely he saw that she was strikingly beautiful. "Are you Russian?" he asked, and she said: "Half Tlingit, half Chinese," and as she began to explain how this could be, while they walked in the moonlight with the mountains of Canada on their right, he stopped her abruptly: "Bigears! I've always known about your family. Your mother came to the university, didn't she? Stayed only a couple of weeks. Back at the turn of the century."

"How do you know that?"

"My grandmother provided your mother with the scholarship she used."

Tammy stopped, leaned against the ship's railing, and pointed a delicate finger at her young companion: "Is your name Ross?"

"Malcolm Venn. Named after my grandfather Ross. He founded

this line." After they had discussed for some moments the improbability of such a meeting, young Venn said: "You won't believe this either. But I'm on this ship as a detective. Some damned fool's been committing sabotage on the Alaska run, and Father sent me north to sort of watch things . . . that is, to report anything suspicious." Before she could comment, he added: "We have men like me on all the ships. We'll catch them."

Innocently, Tammy asked: "Why would anyone want to damage an R&R ship?" and he gave her a long lecture about how there were always misguided souls who refused to appreciate the good things that others were doing for them. He explained how the welfare of Alaska depended upon the benevolence of the industrial geniuses in Seattle who looked after the interests of everyone in Alaska. Pleased by having such an attentive and apparently brilliant audience, he progressed to explain how Alaska would never qualify for statehood but how, through the years, it could rely upon Seattle for constructive and parental leadership.

When she had heard enough of this nonsense, she interrupted: "My mother's people, way back, fought against the Russians, then against the United States, and now against you people in Seattle. I think my children and their grandchildren will continue the fight."

"But why?"

"Because we're entitled to be free. We're intelligent enough to run our own state." Flashing fire, she stared at R&R's future owner and asked: "Has your father ever told you how my father, an illiterate immigrant working for sixty dollars a year, solved the mechanical problems in your father's cannery? And then left to start a business of his own? And taught himself to read, and use a slide rule, and acquire lots and lots of land that no one else thought useful? Mr. Ross, if my father was bright enough to do all those things, he's certainly bright enough to run a state government, and I know a hundred others like him . . . in all parts of Alaska."

And as she spoke, young Venn became so enchanted that he dogged her throughout the remainder of the trip, eager to share her vision of an Alaska about which he had never been told. She was flattered by his attention, but on the last night out, when others were celebrating, she detached herself from him, waiting cautiously for an appropriate moment, then tore away an expensive newel post decorating the grand stairway and tossed it into the icy waters of Cook Inlet.

The splash in the dark waters reflected light from one of the ship's portholes, and it had scarcely died when she felt herself caught by strong arms, whipped about, and kissed passionately on the lips. "I've always thought," Malcolm Venn said quietly as they walked the upper deck, "that when my father spoke of those early days at Totem Cannery—the sinking of the *Montreal Queen,* the fight over the salmon in the Pleiades River . . ." He paused, afraid lest he say too much, but then he blurted out: "I'm sure my father was in love with your mother."

"Of course he was," Tammy said. "Everyone knew that. Mother told me: 'Mrs. Ross understood the first moment we saw each other. And she wasn't going to let no goddamned Tlingit marry a boy her daughter might want!'"

Young Malcolm laughed at the idea of anyone's wanting to prevent a marriage with a girl like Tammy Ting, and they kissed again.

In the bitterly cold winter of January 1935 the small towns in the vicinity of Thief River Falls in western Minnesota, close to the Canadian border, were experiencing the full terror of the Great Depression. In Solway, John and Rose Kirsch with their three children were living on one meal a day. In the tiny village of Skime, Tad and Nellie Jackson, also with three children, were close to starving, and in Robbin, right on the border of North Dakota, Harold and Frances Alexander had four children to worry about, with no assured income of any kind. This part of Minnesota was being strangled.

In the crossroads of Viking, a mile or so northwest of Thief River, a tall, gawky farmer named Elmer Flatch left his wife, Hilda, and their daughter, Flossie, in their barren lean-to with its wood-burning stove and led his sixteen-year-old son, LeRoy—pronounced LEE-roy—into the woods north of town with a solemn warning: "Son, we ain't comin' out of these woods withouten we got ourself a deer." Grimly the two Flatches marched into the small forest, well aware that they were hunting out of season: "If a warden tries to stop us, LeRoy, I'm a-gonna let him have it full in the face. Be ready." And with these two determinations—to get a deer and protect themselves in doing so—the two hunters left the dirt road and plunged into the woods.

In the open spaces there had been drifts of snow, some quite deep, but in the scrub forest, last timbered in the early 1920s, the

January snow was sparse, just thick enough to show tracks where animals had crossed it, so during the first hour and a half in the silvery shadows Elmer reminded his son how to identify the various animals that shared the woods with them: "That'n's a hare, you can tell by the big hind marks. Elbow of the leg leaves a dimple. This'n? Maybe a wood mouse. This'n, for sure, a rabbit. That'n a fox, I do believe. Not many foxes in these parts."

As the father probed the secrets of the forest, he felt a sense of well-being, even though he had not eaten a full meal in three days. "Ain't nothin' better in this world, LeRoy, than huntin' on a winter's day. Yonder has got to be some deer." From his earliest days in Minnesota he had been convinced that beyond the next rise there would be deer, and that he could find them. His assurance was justified by his remarkable record in bagging deer where others could not, and on this day, when venison was not sport but almost life-and-death, he tracked with exceptional care.

"Down thataway, not much, LeRoy. Over thisaway, maybe," but as the morning passed without even a track showing where deer had been, the two men—for at sixteen, LeRoy was a responsible partner with a sure manner of handling his gun—began to feel the first signs of panic, not in wild gestures, for the Flatch family never engaged in such display, but in the tenseness which gripped the pits of their stomachs.

"LeRoy, I'm wore out. What do you think?"

"There's got to be deer. Vickaryous got one last month. They told me at the store."

At the mention of his Finnish neighbor, Elmer Flatch stiffened. He did not cotton to the Finns, Norwegians and Swedes who clustered in this part of Minnesota; they were decent enough neighbors but they were not his kind. He stuck with people carrying names that were more American, like Jackson, Alexander and Kirsch. The Flatches, if he understood correctly, came originally from Kentucky, via Indiana and Iowa, "American as far back as you can count." But now he asked his son: "Where did Vickaryous say he got his deer?"

"I didn't see him, but the men in the store said it was at the edge of the clearing."

Admitting a kind of failure, Elmer told LeRoy: "Let's head for that clearing, the big one," and his son said: "That's the one, if I understood right."

At the clearing they encountered nothing, not even tracks, and now the incipient panic intensified, for they simply dared not go home without something to eat: "If'n we see rabbit or a hare, LeRoy, bag it. The women got to have somethin' they can chew on." The boy made no response, but as shadows began to lengthen his fears increased, for he knew what despair there would be in the lean-to if they returned empty-handed. It had been more than a week since anyone in the Flatch family had tasted meat, and even the bag of beans no longer had sufficient contents to stand upright in the corner.

But twilight deepened, with no sign of deer, and what would otherwise have been fifteen minutes of snowy grandeur as night descended upon the Minnesota hills became instead a cause for anxiety. Elmer Flatch, a man whose major pride lay in his ability to go out with his gun and feed his family, faced the disastrous situation of not only failing to find meat but also being unable to buy the poorest canned substitutes at the Viking store.

It was now dark, but Elmer, who like most good hunters kept account of the moon, knew that what he called a "three-quarters waner" would soon begin to show, and he instructed his son: "LeRoy, we're stayin' out till we get us a deer," and the boy nodded, for he was as reluctant as his father to return to the women of his family with no food.

The two men moved cautiously in the dark, with the father reminding his son: "Don't leave my side. I don't want to be shootin' at you in the shadows, thinkin' you're maybe a deer." What he really meant was: "Don't wander over there among the trees and then blaze away at me when I make a sudden noise," but mindful of his son's youth, he refrained from embarrassing him.

They came upon an open glade which ought to have had deer, but none showed, and when they returned to the woods they were in almost total darkness for about half an hour, but then, as they approached another opening, the waning moon rose above the surrounding trees, and a comfortable light suffused the scene, but it disclosed no tracks. At midnight, when the moon was climbing to its apex, the two were still surrounded by empty forest and the father began to grow weak, hunger overcoming him, but he tried to hide his condition from his son, pausing now and then to catch his breath, something he had never had to do before, given his lean frame and his capacity for endurance.

It was nearly two in the morning when the Flatches came upon a moonlit opening across which deer had recently traveled, and at the sight of tracks, Elmer felt a surge of strength, and with masterful commands he vectored LeRoy off to the right, keeping him in sight to prevent a shooting accident, and with great caution moved forward among the trees.

They saw the deer. Among the shadows it saw them and darted away. LeRoy almost wept as the animal's flag twisted and darted to safety, but his father merely bit his lower lip for a moment, then said: "We're on their trail, LeRoy. Over there we catch ourself a deer." And with a fortitude that astonished his son, Elmer Flatch started in pursuit of the deer he knew he must have: "We'll follow it till sunset tomorrow if we have to."

An hour before dawn the two Flatches came upon a solitary doe, handsomely framed in fading light from the declining moon. Mustering all his control, Elmer whispered to his son: "Fire when my right elbow drops. Aim just a little forward in case she leaps ahead." Then he added: "Son, we got to get this one."

Meticulously the two Flatches leveled their guns, protecting them from the moonlight lest a sudden glint startle the doe, and as Elmer signaled with his right elbow, the two fired, dropping her as if she had been struck by lightning. When Elmer saw her fall, he could feel himself falling too, from exhaustion and the sudden relief of having found food, except that as he started to go down, LeRoy caught him: "Sit on the log, Pop. I'll cut her throat." And while Elmer sat in the frozen moonlight, again close to fainting from hunger, LeRoy ran across the opening and began to prepare the deer for carrying.

It was a long walk back to the Flatch lean-to, and the sides of deer were heavy, but the two men walked as if joy were pulling them forward; they seemed to receive strength and sustenance from the mere presence of the bloody meat upon their backs, and as they approached their destination and saw the wisp of morning smoke coming from wood recently thrown upon the fire, LeRoy began to run, shouting: "Mom! Flossie! We got us a deer!"

Unfortunately, his cries alerted the Vickaryous men on the farm nearby, and when the Finns learned that their neighbors had shot a deer, two men and two women came to the Flatch home: "We ain't had food for three days, Mr. Flatch."

The starving settlers studied one another, the four Flatches from back east, the two Vickaryous couples twenty years out of Finland. They were tall and straight, all eight of them, and lean and hardworking. Their clothes were presentable, especially the Finns', and they were at the end of their rope, all of them.

"You got to let us have something, Mr. Flatch," one of the Vickaryous women said, and Hilda Flatch moved forward with a knife: "Of course," and she knelt down to cut off a sizable chunk of venison. As she did, one of the Vickaryous women burst into tears: "God knows we're ashamed to beg. But in this cold . . ."

As the four women were butchering the deer, a guardian angel appeared as if sent by heaven to succor these families. He appeared in a used Ford, badly treated over the past fifteen years, and at first the men in the lean-to thought he might be a game warden. "He don't get this deer," Elmer whispered to the others, and one of the Vickaryous men told his group: "Careful, but don't let him touch that meat. Just don't let him do it."

The visitor was Nils Sjodin, from a government office of some kind in Thief River Falls, and he carried with him a remarkable message and the documents to back it up. Seated in the lean-to, with the eight people clustered about him, he said: "Glad to see you got yourselves a deer. Food's scarce in these parts."

"Who are you?" Hilda Flatch asked, and he replied: "The bringer of good tidings," and with that, he slapped upon the wooden table a pile of papers which he invited everyone to inspect. Since farmers in this part of Minnesota respected education, all in the shack were able to read, even young Flossie Flatch, and in the next moments they received first notice of the revolution that was about to engulf them and their neighbors in this northern part of the United States.

"Yep!" Mr. Sjodin said with the enthusiasm of a Methodist minister or a farm-equipment salesman. "Every word it says here is true. Our government is going to select eight, nine hundred people from areas like this, people really down on their luck through no fault of their own, and we're going to ship you, all expenses paid, to a valley in Alaska . . . cabbages weigh sixty pounds each . . . never saw anything like it."

"To what purpose?" Hilda Flatch asked. All her life she had dealt with flimflam artists and she judged Mr. Sjodin to be the next in that engaging parade.

"To start a new life in a new world. To populate a paradise. To build an area of great importance to the United States—our new frontier, Alaska."

"Isn't it all ice up there?" Elmer asked.

Mr. Sjodin had been waiting for just this question. Producing three new publications, he spread them so that all could see, and for the first time in their lives, the Flatches and the Vickaryouses saw the magical word Matanuska. "Look for yourselves!" Sjodin said with a pride that would have been appropriate had he owned the area he was about to describe: "Matanuska Valley. Set down among great mountains. Girt by glaciers that run mysteriously out of the hills. Fertile land. Crops like you never saw before. Look at this man standing beside those cabbages and turnips. Look at this affidavit, signed by an official of the United States government: 'I, John Dickerson, U.S. Department of Agriculture, do certify that the man standing beside these vegetables is me and that the vegetables are real and not doctored in any way.'" In awe these farmers looked at the produce of this Alaskan valley, then at the crest of glorious snow-capped mountains which enclosed it, then at the sample house erected beside a flowing stream. They were looking at a wonderland, and they knew it.

"What's the catch?" Hilda Flatch asked, and Mr. Sjodin asked everyone to be seated, because he knew that what he was about to say was beyond belief: "Our government, and I work for it, in agriculture, has decided that it must do something to help you farmers who have been so roughly treated by the Depression. And this is what we're going to do."

"Who are you?" Mrs. Flatch asked, and he said: "From a family of farmers just like you. Went to North Dakota State in Fargo. Farmed awhile myself in Minnesota and was tapped by the federals. My present job? To help families like yours move into a new life."

"You don't even know us," Hilda Flatch said, and Mr. Sjodin corrected her politely but sharply: "I've done a great deal of work on the Flatches and the Vickaryouses. I know how much you owe on your farms, what you paid for your machinery, what your credit is at the bank, and your general health records. I know you're honest people. Your neighbors give you good reports, and you're all absolutely dead broke. You know what the grocer in Thief River told me: 'I'd give them Flatches the shirt off my back. Honest as the day is long. But I can't give them no more credit.'" The men in the two families looked at the floor. "So you've been selected. I think all of you can count on that."

"Children too?" Hilda asked, and he said: "Especially the children. We want kids like yours to be the seed of the great new Alaska."

Now that he had their attention, he spelled out the details: "We will carry you to San Francisco on the train, not a penny of expense to you. There we'll place you on a ship to Alaska, not one cent of charge. When you land in Alaska we'll convey you to Matanuska, our charge. There we'll assign you, with you making the choice of location, forty acres. We'll build you a brand-new home and a barn and give you a free supply of seeds and livestock. We'll also build a town center with stores, doctors and a highway to market."

"You mean," Elmer asked, "all this for free?"

"At the beginning, yes. You do not spend a penny. Even the stove comes free. But we do charge against your name three thousand dollars, on which you pay nothing while you're getting started. Beginning in the second year you pay three percent interest on your mortgage. That's ninety dollars a year, and with the way things grow in that valley, you'll be able to pay not only the interest but on the principal too."

As he finished with a grandiloquent gesture, he smiled at the four Finns, as if he wanted particularly to convince them: "The federal government has asked us to specialize getting Swedes, Norwegians and Finns, ages twenty-five to forty, farmers with children. You'd be perfect if you had children."

"We have seven between us," one of the Finnish women said, but before Mr. Sjodin could assure her that this pretty well assured the two families of selection, he was diverted by a soft thud behind him, and he turned to find that Elmer Flatch had fainted.

"He ain't had solid food for four days," Hilda Flatch said. "Flossie, start somethin' cookin'," and she asked Mr. Sjodin for help in lifting her bone-skin husband to a bed.

To the amazement of the two hundred and ninety-nine Minnesota farmers that Mr. Sjodin selected in the winter of 1935 for this bonanza provided by the federal government, he kept every promise he made. A train designated the *Alaska Special* took them in relative comfort to the Southern Pacific Station in San Francisco, and at various stops local citizens, eager to see the New Pilgrims, crowded the railroad stations with canteens of hot coffee, sandwiches and doughnuts. Newspaper reporters flocked to query the travelers and wrote stories that fell into two distinct categories: either the Minnesota people were daring adventurers thrusting forward into unknown frozen frontiers, or they were shameless participants in another of President Roosevelt's socialist schemes destined to destroy the integrity of America. A few penetrating reporters tried to strike a balance between the two extremes, one woman in Montana writing:

> These hardy souls are not plunging blindly into some arctic wasteland where they won't see the sun for six months at a time. This reporter has looked up the climatic conditions at Matanuska and found them to be about the same as northern Maine or southern North Dakota. The valley itself looks a lot like the better parts of Iowa, except that it is surrounded by a chain of beautiful snow-covered peaks. In fact, there is reason to believe that these emigrants are headed for a kind of paradise.
>
> The big question is: Why them and not somebody else? The federal government is handing them all kinds of bonanzas at little or no cost, and the taxpayers of Montana will ultimately have to foot the bill. This reporter could find no justification for heaping this largesse on this particular group of farmers except that they were all from northern states, they were mostly Scandinavian, and they all looked as if they knew how to work. The people of our county who met them at the station wished them well, for they really are launched on a great adventure.

In San Francisco, Mr. Sjodin, as promised, had a ship waiting to carry them north, and even though it proved to be one of the ugliest ships afloat—the old army transport *St. Mihiel,* a slab-sided bucket with deep indentations in the railings fore and aft—it did float, it had abundant food, and each family had a place to sleep. In this first shipment of Matanuska settlers, there were no men without wives and almost no families without children. They were a homogeneous lot, these emigrants from an old world in Minnesota to a new life in Alaska: of similar age and similar background, any fifty of the men chosen at random seemed almost indistinguishable. The majority were of medium height, about a hundred and sixty pounds, cleanshaven and capable-looking. Their greatest similarity was in dress, for unlike the women, who wore varied clothes, these hardworking men all wore dark suits with trousers and jackets made of the same heavy woolen fabric. They wore shirt and tie, the former invariably white, the latter always of some subdued color, but what set them apart from the people they met in San Francisco and the other towns their train had passed were the workingmen's caps they wore, made of some woven fabric with a stiff brim. In appearance these adventurers were the drabbest group of men ever to have attempted settlement in a new locale: they compared in no way with the conquistadors from Spain who braved their way into Mexico and Peru; they wore none of the variegated clothing that characterized Jamestown in Virginia; nor had they the colorful dress of the Dutch who came to New York, or the handsome austerity of the Pilgrims in Massachusetts. They were men from Middle America venturing forth in that period when clothes were at their supreme dullest, and in their banal similarities neither the men nor the women looked as if they were bound for any great exploration.

However, once the *St. Mihiel* was under way, radical differences within the group began to surface. A minority of the passengers proved to be ordinary Americans like the Flatches and their friends, the Alexanders of Robbin, the Kirsches of Solway and the Jacksons of Skime, and almost automatically these families clustered together as if to protect themselves from the overbearing Scandinavians: the Kertullas, the Vasanojas and the Vickaryouses. The Scandinavians were not actually overbearing, they merely seemed that way—keeping to themselves, speaking in their native languages, and conducting themselves with the superior air of men and women many of whom had already taken sea voyages in getting to Minnesota. They moved about the *St. Mihiel* with such confidence that they seemed to own it.

Despite this factionalism, which manifested itself in all aspects of the voyage north, the trivial animosities were forgotten when the ship entered Alaskan waters, for then the great mountains which guarded the western shore of the peninsula shone in splendor, and like Vitus Bering two hundred years earlier and James Cook in the 1770s, these newcomers watched in awe as these majestic mountains and their glaciers came down to the Pacific. As Mr. Jackson said to the American group: "This sure ain't Minnesota," and Mr. Alexander replied: "Hard to believe there's fields you could farm behind them mountains." Elmer Flatch, staring at the great masses of rock, told the Kirsches: "Have we been trapped? There can't be tillable ground in there."

At Anchorage they were surprised when Mr. Sjodin, who despite his own Scandinavian background maintained good relations with both groups, moved them into the cars of a modern train, "as fine," he told them, "as the Union Pacific." They had expected dogsleds, but found themselves in railroad cars much better than the ones in which they had ridden from Minnesota to California. They were further surprised when they saw on the roads paralleling the train tracks a plentiful supply of automobiles that looked the same as the ones they had known in Minnesota. However, young LeRoy Flatch did notice one difference: "Look how the fenders are all rusted. Why?" And Mr. Alexander, who knew automobiles, said: "Salt spray, I'm sure."

They left Anchorage at nine in the morning for the forty-mile run to Matanuska, and during the first three-quarters of the trip they saw nothing that indicated the possibility of farming: uninspiring salt beds lay to the west, forbidding mountains to the east, so that even the hardiest Scandinavians, accustomed to northern terrains, began to despair, while flatlanders like the Flatches and the Jacksons were ready to surrender. "No man can farm that stuff," Mr. Jackson said as he surveyed the western plains, devoid of both trees and grass, and Hilda Flatch agreed, and they were further depressed when the train approached the undisciplined Knik River, a mile wide and apparently six inches deep.

But as their car reached the middle of the bridge, young Flossie Flatch, staring to the east, cried: "Mom, look! Hey, Pop, look!" and the Flatches saw opening before them the kind of prospect European travelers expected when they ventured into the Alps. First there was a nearly circular rim of resplendent mountains, their white caps glistening in the morning sun. Then came the trees, thousands upon thousands of them, hardwood and evergreen alike, a bounty so plentiful it could never be depleted. And then, to delight the farmers, spread the waiting fields and meadows, thousands of acres ready for the plow.

In their varied tongues the Scandinavians shared their assessments of this valley, and all agreed that they had come upon a wonderland as fine as anything in Norway or Sweden, and the magnitude of the components bedazzled them. One of the Vickaryous men, running back to where the Flatches clustered, gripped Elmer by the arm and cried: "With land like this, anything!" And he kissed Hilda Flatch, who was astonished by his familiarity.

For about half an hour the train picked its way slowly along the western edge of the valley, allowing the passengers to see one marvel after another, and what pleased the newcomers especially was the plenitude of little streams cutting their way through the flatlands.

"Everyone can have their farm along a river," Elmer said, but his wife cautioned: "And get flooded out when all that snow melts." Her husband did not hear her, for just then the conductor was shouting: "Get everything ready. Almost there."

"Is there any game out there?" Flatch asked him. "Huntin', I mean?" and the conductor said: "Anyone can't get hisself a moose or a bear in them hills, he ain't no hunter. Even my wife's brother Herman got hisself a moose." So for the remaining moments of the trip to Matanuska, Elmer visualized himself prowling those uplands, so close to the flat fields, on the trail of moose.

When the train finally stopped, at a station called Palmer, it did so in three jolting hiccups, with the cars jamming forward one against the other, followed by a screeching halt. Then onto the wooden platform, much like what would have been found in Minnesota, the immigrants piled out, and one conductor said to another: "Look! They really are different. Most of 'em have cardboard suitcases."

From the train station the families looked across an empty field to where an amazing sight awaited them: Tent City, a collection of some half a hundred white military field tents, each with cots and a black stovepipe protruding from the top. "There it is!" Mr. Sjodin cried enthusiastically. "Your home till your houses are built." When some of the Scandinavians began protesting, Sjodin cried: "Look! They're fine tents. Your sons in the army use them all the time," and the Scandinavians replied: "But not in Alaska," and Sjodin broke into loud laughter: "Go up to Fairbanks! You'll find them in tents right now. Stayed in them all winter."

"Are you living in one of them?" a Swede asked. "I'll bet you have yourself a real house."

"Tent Number Seven, right over there," Sjodin said. "You'll do a lot of business with me in Number Seven."

The Flatches and the Jacksons were assigned a tent in the second row back from the road, Number 19, and since each family had a daughter of an age where she should not be sleeping in the same room with boys, they strung a rope down the middle of the tent and suspended sheets from it. On one side slept the four females, on the other side the five males, and similar arrangements prevailed in all the tents occupied by two families. As the groups were sorted out, Mr. Jackson observed: "Not one case where real Americans are mixed in with the Scandinavians," and this separation would prevail when it came time to draw lots for the land assignments.

This exciting day came relatively late in the settlement at Mata-nuska. The land had to be surveyed, parceled into reasonable hold-ings, and made available by the building of rough roads, but when all was in readiness, Mr. Sjodin and his three superiors announced that the lottery was ready to take place as planned. That afternoon Elmer Flatch went quietly to Tent Number 7 to consult with the man whose performance in getting the Minnesotans to Matanuska had been so exemplary.

"I'd like your advice, Mr. Sjodin."

"That's what I'm here for," and before Elmer could speak further, Sjodin said with great warmth: "Remember that morning I met you. You and your son had just shot a deer. You were sharing it with the Vickaryous family. And now you're all up here in Alaska. Quite won-derful, isn't it?"

"Never figured it would happen," Flatch said, "but now Hilda and me, we got to choose our land. What do you advise?"

With an unusual gift for perceiving personal situations, a skill de-veloped while serving as student manager of the football team at North Dakota State and later as county agricultural agent in Min-nesota, Sjodin recognized that Elmer Flatch probably had desires and plans somewhat different from the other settlers, and he intended to respect them: "Now, before I can advise you, Mr. Flatch, you must share with me your honest statement of what it is you hope to ac-complish here in Alaska."

"Well, like all the others . . . ."

"I don't mean all the others. I mean you."

For almost a full minute Elmer stared at the floor, his tense knuck-les clasped under his chin, wondering if he could level with this Swede. Finally, acknowledging that he must confide in someone, he said slowly: "We won't be movin' never again, Mr. Sjodin. This'n is it."

"Glad to hear you say that. Now tell me the best that you can hope for, and let's see if it's possible."

"I'm fed up to my ass with farmin'. It's a fool's paradise."

"Not to a born farmer—like my father, or me. But for you, maybe yes. Go ahead."

"I'm a hunter. I'm a rifleman. I want me a place near the woods. I want me a runnin' stream. I want to be close to where there's moose and bear and deer. But mostly I do want a runnin' stream."

Before responding to this defensible ambition, Sjodin asked: "But how will you earn a living? A wife and three children?"

"Two."

"How?"

Again Flatch fell silent, then he said tentatively: "I'll work for others."

"What kind of work?"

"Any kind. I can do most any kind of work. Build houses, work on the roads." And then came the most difficult revelation, the one at which Mr. Sjodin might laugh: "Maybe I could sort of guide rich people who want to shoot theirself a moose." Quickly he added: "I can use a gun, you know."

Nils Sjodin leaned back and thought of all the immigrants he had known, those daring men and women who had left Europe to brave the blizzards of the northern United States, and it occurred to him that almost every good one had been driven by some intensely personal image of what he or she could accomplish in a new world. They had not drifted into the snowbanks of the north; they had come impelled by great visions, noble aspirations, and although most of them fell short of their dreams, they would, through the years, be astonished at how many of those dreams had been realized. To Sjodin, Elmer Flatch's dream made sense.

"There's a couple of spots far out I've seen during surveying, I wouldn't mind having one of them for myself. But I have to stay near where the town's going to be. For you, with what you have in mind, perfect."

He borrowed the staff car, a Ford truck, and with Flatch at his side, crossed the Matanuska River, which ran through the heart of the valley before joining the Knik, and after a long ride over almost nonexistent roads, they came to an enclosed valley protected by a magnificent mountain to the south, Pioneer Peak, more than six thousand feet high, with much higher mountains to the west. The kind of stream that Flatch longed for cut through the area: "It's called Dog Creek. Flows out of a beautiful lake up there in the hills, Dog Lake. And up this way, in easy hiking distance, the great Knik Glacier. They tell me it's something to see when the lakes formed by the glacier break through their dam in summer."

"Any sites here?"

"About a dozen. Good ones, that is."

"Any taken?"

"Nobody wants them. Too far out. That's why you can get one without going through the lottery."

As they were strolling about, along the banks of Dog Creek a moose came exploring to see what kind of creature had come into its terrain, this strange shiny object whose sides flashed sun signals. Preoccupied with the truck, it did not see the two men some distance away, so for perhaps six or eight minutes it nosed about, then majestically strolled back toward the hills.

"I'll take this one," Flatch said, indicating the surveyed site at the confluence.

"I don't want you to do that, Mr. Flatch," Sjodin said. "When the creek and the river are both high, you'll have flooding. Look at those twigs in the trees." And after Flatch inspected more closely, he asked: "The water gets that high?" and Sjodin assured him that the records said it did.

So with the Swede's help, Elmer identified a site on the right bank of Dog Creek, facing Pioneer Peak, which seemed about to topple down upon it, with great glaciers, brown bears and wandering moose nearby. It was a spot of supreme natural beauty, one that any hunter would aspire to, and it was far enough from where the new town would be to provide privacy for decades to come. When he and Sjodin marked off the corners with their piles of rocks, Flatch had forty acres of a new life, arranged by the federal government, which would postpone any mortgage reduction for four years and then extend the payments over thirty years at the rate of three percent per annum. It was frontiersmanship on the grand scale, and all it required of the nine hundred and three settlers was hard work, the construction of some kind of economy, and the ability to withstand the Alaskan winter at 61.5° N, about the same latitude as southern Greenland.

As always in a pioneer settlement, the heaviest burden fell upon the women, and when Elmer Flatch eschewed a chance for one of the attractive lots near the center of town—the ones that would be invaluable within a few years—selecting instead the romantic one near the glacier, his wife realized that the task of holding her family together while a cabin was being built and the children established in school would be hers, and like many of the other immigrant women, she was finding the job even more onerous than she had expected. Her husband was a true frontiersman, always ready to cut a new batch of logs or help a distant neighbor who was cutting his. Problems were exacerbated by the fact that those who drew the good sites in town were having their new homes built for them by government carpenters as part of the three-thousand-dollar deal; stubborn out-riders like Elmer Flatch had to build their own.

Marketing posed a special problem for Hilda, because one of those geographical accidents occurred which not even brilliant men can anticipate and over which they have no control. Since the settle-ment was in Matanuska Valley, the newcomers assumed that what-ever town grew up to serve them would be called by that name, but a short distance to the north there already existed the trivial town of Palmer. It had but one asset: the Alaska Railroad had a station there and, as had happened so often before throughout the United States, it was the railroad, not the town fathers, that decided where civiliza-tion would center.

So, despite the fact that a village called Matanuska did take root, Palmer became the local metropolis. But it was far from the Flatch place and it would not be easy to get the doctor or the deliveryman to travel such a distance, especially since no reliable road would reach the Flatches for a long time. But Elmer insisted: "This is where I want to be," and he left it to Hilda to make adjustments. However, when one of the army emergency tents was erected on their plot, with a double lining to ward off the bitter winds sweeping down from the glacier, and she had a wood fire burning in her little iron stove, she found life quite tolerable and worked like a Belgian draft horse help-ing her husband clear the ground and level it for their cabin, which he swore to have under roof by the first heavy snow.

Sometimes at the end of an especially long day, Hilda would sit on a wobbly chair outside the tent, too tired even to worry about sup-per, and at such times she was tempted to complain, but she refrained out of respect for the other members of her family, all of whom de-clared repeatedly that "this is sure a lot better than Thief River Falls." But one day when everything went wrong, she was overcome by a sense of dismay and she couldn't help wondering if the Flatches were ever going to have a family home, and as she perched on her stool she decided that when Elmer and LeRoy returned from whatever they were doing—certainly they weren't doing any work on the house—she would give them an ultimatum: "No more foolin' around. No more helpin' others till we get our own place finished."

But her resolve vanished when at dusk her two men came roaring down from the mountains east of the campsite with astonishing news: "Hey, Mom! We got a moose!"

Knowing that this signified assured food for a long time to come, she cried: "LeRoy, I'm so proud of you."

"You don't know the best, Mom. We got two!"

"Yep," Elmer said as he marched proudly into camp with much the same stride that Roman generals adopted when they came home triumphant from having put down rebels along the borders of the empire. "I got a big one up by the ice. But LeRoy, he got one half again as big. This boy can hunt!"

With this vigorous news, everything stopped, and Hilda assumed command: "Flossie, you run down to the Vasanojas', see if they'll let us borry the horse tomorrow. LeRoy, run to the Kirsches', see if Adolf'll help us butcher tomorrow. I'm goin' in to those people with the six children, ain't been eatin' too well. If they'll help bring down the meat . . . Elmer, how far away are the two animals?"

He told her they were about three miles up toward the glacier, and for just a moment he considered that it might be proper for him to run down to the family with six kids, rather than his wife, but then he rationalized to himself: I been out chasin' moose all day, and she's probably not been doin' nothin' much. Let her go. Off she went to share the good news with her neighbors, and as she hurried westward, following the course of the Knik River, she thought: It's gonna be all right. If Elmer can do his huntin', we're gonna eat and he's gonna be happy.

The women like Hilda who labored so strenuously in building Matanuska, which grew more habitable every week, were aided considerably by an extraordinary old settler in Alaska, a woman of the widest experience who had been assigned by the Alaskan government to represent its interests in the new settlement. She was in her early sixties, white-haired, smallish and with an energy that staggered even proven workers like Hilda Flatch. Her name was Melissa Peckham but she was known as Missy, and in introducing her around the valley, Sjodin told each of the families two relevant facts: "She don't need the job. Made a pile in the gold fields back in the nineties. And she's workin' for nothin', so don't throw your weight around, because she can knock any of you flat, and will."

Missy was one of those women, the immigrant wives discovered, who could face up to any problem without flinching. She controlled a small sum of money provided by the territorial government which she used in dire emergencies and a somewhat larger sum which she provided from her own savings. She took up quarters in Tent Number 7 and made herself an invaluable aide to Mr. Sjodin, but what she did best was ride a horse, which she had bought with her own money, out to the edges of the settlement, where she worked with women like Mrs. Flatch and the mother down the line who had six children. It was also she who organized the Matanuska Lending Library, gathering from all the homes that would participate books no longer in use and placing them in a tent with a fifteen-year-old girl in charge. She helped churches get title to corner lots and then aided them in starting their rude buildings, but the women of Matanuska remarked that she did not attend any of the church services, and a rumor started that Missy had never been married to the Irishman with whom she lived and who helped her in her charities.

Two clergymen were delegated to visit with the Murphys, as they were called, and Missy answered their questions forthrightly: "I escaped Chicago during the bad years. I had no husband, but that's beside the point. On the gold fields at Dawson, I met Matthew there, and his story is twice as interesting as mine. But that's another point. He was married in faraway Ireland. Left his wife. Never went back. We worked together in Nome and Juneau, we have a daughter, and we've been very happy."

The Presbyterian minister was appalled by her story, but the Baptist, a man hardened in the oil fields of Oklahoma, was tantalized by her frequent reference to the dramatic history of Mr. Murphy, and when he made inquiries he learned that this Irishman had not only spent two winters on the Mackenzie River route but had then helped the miner John Klope find one of the great treasures at Dawson, after which he had bicycled—bicycled, mind you—from Dawson to Nome, more than a thousand miles in the dead of winter. The minister, who had been having some trouble with his parishioners who complained that they had to draw water by means of a large wooden crank that pulled a heavy bucket up from a considerable depth, had told them: "All right! Use a shallower well and die of typhoid fever."

Fed up with their self-pity, he went to Missy Peckham and asked: "Would your husband . . . I mean, would Mr. Murphy . . . would he consent to telling our church about the Mackenzie River and the bicycle ride?"

"If you get him started, you'll not stop him," Missy said, and that was how Matthew Murphy of Dawson, Nome and Juneau happened to speak one autumn night at the Matanuska Baptist Church. He said: "We're all immigrants, aren't we?" and when his listeners nodded, a kind of strength came into his voice, nearly seventy years old, and an unaccustomed straightness to his back. He spoke of those exciting days at Edmonton when so many launched forth to conquer the gold fields, and he ticked off the hundreds who failed for one reason or another: "If they went by land, they never made it. If they tried horseback, every horse was dead within five weeks. If they went up the easy rivers, they got lost in swamps. And if they did what we did . . ."

Turning to where the young were sitting, he said: "Often in life you'll be offered a choice of two routes, the right one and the wrong one, and you may not know which is which. If you choose the wrong one, you can spend a couple years thrashin' around in the wilderness while those who choose right quickly get to their target."

A Norwegian man interrupted: "But Mr. Sjodin said that when you reached the Klondike, you found yourself a fortune."

"I found nothin'. Of the hundreds who left Edmonton in search of sure gold, not one of us found a red cent. We all failed."

"But they told us you were rich."

"A man I worked for found it. Years after I left him broke, he come by our place in Nome and gave both Missy and me a lot of money. I think it was because he was always in love with Missy."

This was hardly the way the minister had expected the talk to go. Coughing noisily, he said: "Mr. Murphy, tell us about your bicycle ride."

"Dead of winter, locked up in Dawson, no money. Had to get to the gold fields in Nome, a thousand miles away. Talked a Canadian storekeeper into sellin' me a bicycle cheap, and he said: 'Hell, you can't ride'—if you'll excuse me, sir, but that's what he said. But in less than a week I had the hang of it, and I set out with some tools, spare chain and half a dozen spare spokes, and off I went to the next batch of gold fields—no roads, no trails, just the frozen Yukon River. I made about forty miles a day, one day sixty. A river tight frozen is better'n a highway. Of course, when great blocks of ice heave up at angles, it ain't so much fun. But the fact is, I made that thousand miles startin' on February twenty-second and arrivin' on March twenty-ninth, as this clippin' from a Nome paper proves." And out came a yellow sheet which attested to the fact that Matthew Murphy, who had come to Dawson back in 1899, had traversed the entire distance from Dawson to Nome riding only a bicycle in thirty-six or thirty-seven days: "You figure it out, but remember that the year

1900 which should have been a leap year wasn't. But those of you who live till the year 2000 will have a leap year that time."

The minister feared that the man was wandering, but realized that was not the case when Murphy continued: "Now, don't make too much over this bicycle trip. The next year, 1901, more than two hundred and fifty rode the Yukon. Next year a man named Levie made the thousand miles from Point Barrow to Nome in fifteen days. That's more than twice as fast as I traveled. Can you believe it? A bicycle on ice?"

The Murphys became a center of attraction in Matanuska, for when Missy's story was made known, about her sledding down the Chilkoot and braving the rapids on the Yukon system, the pair were recognized as admirable examples of the Alaskan spirit, but the story persisted that Matt had found himself a gold mine on the Klondike so big and rich that it still paid him dividends.

In 1937, the second year of their occupancy in the cabin, Flossie became the cynosure of the Flatch family. Twelve years old, a handsome child with her father's love of animals, she was sitting at the window one afternoon when she saw a small brown bear come out of the woods leading to the glacier, and when she alerted her family: "Hey, look at the bear!" her brother grabbed his rifle on the solid Minnesota principle that if anything out there was moving, shoot it. This time she stopped him, so instead of receiving a bullet through its forehead, this prowling bear came upon a young girl who moved toward it with two potatoes and a head of cabbage.

The bear stopped, studied her suspiciously, turned and lumbered off, but after some minutes, while she remained stationary, it came back. It could smell her, and the potatoes and the cabbage, and the mix was confusing, so again the bear fled. But it was an inquisitive type, and for the third time approached the place with the tantalizing smells. This time, in the middle of the path it was following, there was a raw potato, which it sniffed several times before chewing it to a tasty pulp.

On subsequent days the bear reappeared, always in late afternoon and always on the alert for this fearless child who approached it with things it liked. One day when she offered a head of cabbage it took it, and before the end of the second week of these visits it was obvious that Flossie had tamed a bear, and when the news circulated through the town, various people came to see the miracle. But it was Mr. Murphy who spoke sense: "Bears can't be trusted. Especially not brown bears."

"I thought it was a grizzly," Flossie said, whereupon Mr. Murphy gave a short lecture on one of the peculiarities of Alaskan life: "If'n a bear up here is found within fifty miles of the ocean, it's called a brown bear. If'n it's more than fifty miles inland, people like to call it a grizzly. Same bear, same habits."

"I want my bear to be a grizzly," Flossie said, and Murphy replied: "Arms of the ocean touch us on all sides, it's got to be a brown." Then, seeing her disappointment, he added: "But there is a way of measurin' that would give you fifty miles to the ocean. So you can call it a grizzly. I'll bet you don't know its Latin name. *Ursus horribilis.* Sounds terrifyin', don't it?" She shook her head negatively: "This grizzly is my friend," and to Murphy's horror, that afternoon when the bear appeared, Flossie walked out to greet it, sat playing with it, and fed it some more cabbage. It seemed much bigger now than when it had first appeared, and had Murphy come upon it of a sudden along a wooded trail he would have been petrified.

As the year progressed, so did the friendship between the girl and her grizzly, but excitement at this development faded when something even more astonishing occurred at the Flatch cabin. Because of Flossie's constant visits with her bear, she began to sense that a much larger animal was in the region, and late one afternoon as her bear vanished up the trail, she saw coming down in the opposite direction an enormous black figure, and at first she suspected that a really huge grizzly was approaching her, but she had enjoyed such success with the first bear that she supposed she could do the same with this one. But when the animal came closer she saw that it was a moose with a body as big as a truck. It was a female, an immense ungainly creature that moved awkwardly but with a compelling majesty that arrested the attention of anything that saw her, animal or human, and Flossie assumed that when her tame bear encountered this massive creature, it would be the bear that stepped aside, not the moose.

On that first meeting the moose came within a few feet of the girl before halting. There was a long inspection by the moose, which had bad eyes, and a wealth of sniffing, then with an inquisitiveness that startled the girl, she came forward to smell more acutely; and once more the wonderful legend that woodsmen believed, and to which Flossie certainly subscribed, came true: "Pop, this moose knew, from one smell, that I wasn't afraid. Maybe she could even smell that I had been playing with the bear, but she came right up to me. I think she knew I was her friend."

Flossie had barely delivered this Matanuska version of the old legend when her father grabbed for his rifle, shouting: "Where is it?" and when Flossie realized that he intended shooting her moose, she screamed: "No!"

Her father was so surprised by this violent reaction that he fell back a step, dropped his hand from the door latch, and said quietly: "But, Flossie, a moose has the kind of meat we can sell. We need . . ."

Again she screamed, the anguished cry of a girl who had grown to love all the animals that shared the edge of the glacier with her. She was one with the bear and knew that with patience she could tame this great moose, ten times her weight and half again as tall at the shoulders. Throwing herself in front of the door, she forbade her father to leave the house with his rifle, and after a tense moment when he considered lifting her aside, he surrendered. Allowing her to take the rifle from him, he grumbled: "When you go to bed hungry, don't blame me," and she replied: "There are others up in the mountains," and he said: "But if'n he walks right up to our cabin, he wants to be shot. He's entitled to it."

"It's a she," Flossie said, and in the days that followed she met with the moose at various locations, and always the huge beast smelled assiduously until she was satisfied that this human being was the one she could trust. On about the seventh visit, Flossie tied a large piece of white ribbon to the hair behind the moose's huge left ear, and she spread word through the school and as much of the town as she could reach that the moose up by the glacier with the white ribbon was tame and belonged to Flossie Flatch.

Unfortunately, the white cloth flopping near her eye irritated the moose so much that by next evening when she came to visit, it had been rubbed off on a spruce branch. However, she approached Flossie with obvious affection and allowed the girl to tie another ribbon far back on her left flank, and this remained in place long enough for the Matanuska people to become familiar with the story of the pet animal.

Mildred the Moose posed certain problems, because when she appeared at the Flatch cabin she expected to be fed, and her appetite was insatiable: carrots, cabbage, lettuce, potatoes, celery, she took all of them in her big mouth, curling her immense upper lip over them and causing them to disappear down her capacious throat as if she were a magician. However, even if the expected meal turned out to be too meager, she did not display bad temper, and her friendly presence around the cabin made the place seem even more a part of Matanuska's natural wonder.

Flossie was distressed, therefore, when at school she heard from the Atkinson children a constant wailing about the hardships in the valley and protests against the federal government for having brought families into this barren wilderness. When Flossie rebuked the four Atkinsons for their lack of an adventurous spirit, they told her harshly that she was stupid to be playing with a bear and moose when the rest of Matanuska was suffering because the government was not living up to its promise of caring for the immigrants.

When Flossie told her parents of this, her father became quite angry: "Them Atkinsons, when they lived in Robbin they didn't have a pot to pee in. Now they're puttin' on airs." Hilda reprimanded him for speaking that way before his children, but he repeated his disgust at people who were offered a new start in life and then complained about little inconveniences.

He had a right to judge, because none of the newcomers had worked harder or longer to establish himself in Matanuska. He had built his own house on land that he had selected for his special purposes and, refusing to farm, he had devised a score of imaginative ways to earn his living. He carpentered for others, helped butcher, plowed fields with either horses or tractors provided by the owners, and drove into Anchorage with other men's cars to pick up important orders of medicine or tools. And he even worked now and then at the graveled Palmer Airstrip, helping to take wheels off airplanes and put on skis for winter travel into camps located in the high mountains. But most of all he hunted, bringing back to his cabin the carcasses of moose and bear and deer which he sold throughout the district.

One night when he returned with a quarter of a moose dragging behind him in the snow, Hilda said: "We're expected at a meeting tonight. Harold Atkinson's makin' a formal protest or somethin'," and when she forced Elmer to accompany her into town, they sat in rigid silence as they listened to the Atkinsons and three or four other couples grumbling about every aspect of life in Matanuska. To hear their litany of disappointments was to realize how differently people could interpret the same conditions. "At every point," Harold Atkinson was lamenting, "we've been defrauded by our government. No roads, no proper school, no agricultural help, no marketing plan for the crops we do grow, and no money in the bank which we can borrow."

Missy and Matt, hearing these picayune complaints, could not restrain themselves, and in the absence of the senior camp officials, who had done a fairly good job so far, even though all schedules did seem to lag, they took the floor, standing together as they had done so often during their Alaskan years. "Everything you say is true, Mr. Atkinson, but none of it has to do with the starting of a new town here in Matanuska. And to tell you the truth, it doesn't have to do with getting your family on a solid footing. I think things are ten times better here than they were in Dawson City in 1898 or Nome in 1900, and that's where Alaska got started."

"This ain't 1898. It's 1937," John Krull shouted from the rear. "And what we got to put up with is a disgrace."

This outraged Matt Murphy, who in his seventieth year saw all situations from a broad perspective. Avoiding any mention of his own heroics in conditions fifty times worse than what the Matanuska settlers were experiencing, he told in lilting voice of the starvation hardships that had driven his people from Ireland during the great famines, and concluded by rebuking the Atkinsons: "You have a right to complain about things promised but not delivered, but to blame the whole operation makes no sense."

He succeeded only in so infuriating the protesters that the meeting broke up in a kind of fracas, and at the close of the next week the Flatches learned that the Atkinsons, Krulls and three other families had left Matanuska, abandoning everything, and were heading back to the Lower Forty-eight. Not long thereafter the settlement was flooded with newspaper clippings mailed by friends who said: "It must be pure hell trying to live in a socialist settlement where everything has gone wrong." One well-intentioned farmer who wrote to the Flatches said: "I suppose we'll be seeing you back here one of these days. When you arrive, look me up. Things are a lot better in Minnesota than when you left and I'll be able to find you a real good farm at a bargain."

What irritated those like the Flatches who stayed in Matanuska, and government people like the Murphys who were doing their best to make the huge experiment work, was the fact that one conservative newspaper after another, across the entire United States, picked

up the complaints of the "go-backs," as they were called, and casti-
gated both the Matanuska people and the Roosevelt administrators
who had devised the program as communists who were introducing
alien procedures into honest American patterns. By 1937 and '38,
recovery from the Great Depression was so solidly under way that
people forgot what conditions had been only a few years before, and
scores of newspapers and magazines used the supposed failure of
Matanuska as proof that socialism never worked.

If there were two human beings in all America less vulnerable to
the charge of socialism than Missy Peckham and Elmer Flatch, they
were not known to the general public. These two had, in the great
tradition of American individualists, pioneered with pennies in their
pockets, triumphed over enormous odds, and accomplished wonders
in their own quiet way. In Matanuska they were doing the same.
Missy, at the apex of her rambunctious life, was helping a new generation of adventurers establish a society in which families would
own their own farms, sell their own produce, and educate their children to do the same. Elmer, having worked in Alaska as few men ever
work anywhere, had watched as his forty governmental acres had
grown to more than three hundred, and although some people had
laughed at him when he had said at the beginning that he wanted to
be a kind of guide to rich men who wanted "to shoot theirself a
moose," by dint of making himself locally famous as the best hunter
in Alaska, he had patiently attracted to himself exactly the type of
big-city hunter who wanted to be shown the tricks that he had mastered. As the hunting season of 1938 approached, he was in such
demand that he suggested to his wife: "Why don't you serve meals to
these hungry coyotes?" and people in places like Los Angeles and
Denver began to talk about Elmer and Hilda Flatch.

And when one of his clients brought with him four clippings
about the communist community sponsored by the government in
Alaska, he felt that he must rise in defense of Matanuska, so with
help from Missy Peckham he drafted a letter, which was mimeographed and mailed to some thirty Lower Forty-eight newspapers.
The opening paragraph set the tone:

*I read in your paper the other day that we people in
Matanuska are all communists, and since I don't know much
about Russia, maybe it's true. But I want to tell you how we
communists up here spend the day. We get up at seven, each*

family on the plot of land it owns privately, and some of us
milk the cows we own and others open the stores they paid for
with their own hard work, and our kids go to the school we
support with taxes, and at the end of the week we gather up
our produce and ship it off to Anchorage to a private
wholesaler who cheats us like hell out of what we think we
ought to get, but when times get tight, we borrow money from
that wholesaler against our next crop.

The next paragraph explained what the Matanuska "communists" did with their spare time, and mention was made of Flossie and her pet animals and Irishman Carmody at the airport who had saved his money to make a down payment on a 1927 plane which he was using as a cargo carrier to serve the gold mines way back in the hills. The mines were owned, Elmer said, by private prospectors, some of whom had been searching fruitlessly for fifty years.

It was the final paragraph that was so widely quoted in the running debate on the practicality of Matanuska; because of that first barrage of adverse comment by men like Harold Atkinson, most readers in the Lower Forty-eight considered the experiment a dismal failure. Of Atkinson and his fellow "go-backs," Elmer and Missy said:

We know that when Columbus set out to discover America and
ran into trouble, many of his crew advised him to turn back.
When settlers headed for Oregon and California hit the great
empty Plains and the hostile Indians, lots of them turned back.
And whenever anything of importance has been tried on this
earth, the fainthearted have turned back. How many
goldminers in 1898 took one look at the Chilkoot Pass and
turned back? Those who persevered found gold and built a new
land. We're building a new land up here, and ten years from
now Matanuska will be a thriving valley filled with big farms
and healthy people and kids who wouldn't want to live
anywhere else. Watch the workers and see. Don't listen to the
"go-backs."

While Elmer was busy drafting his defense of Matanuska, LeRoy was having an exhilarating time in Palmer, where in the last days of his nineteenth year he was being introduced to two of the most exciting experiences a young man could have: girls and airplanes. He first met Lizzie Carmody at a grocery store, where her red hair and Irish smile so captivated him that he furtively followed her home, discovering that she lived in a shack at the edge of the large flattened field which served as Palmer Airstrip. In the days that followed he learned that her father, Jake Carmody, owned one of the planes that serviced the mines tucked away in various canyons of the nearby Talkeetna Mountains. It was a small plane famous in aviation history, a Piper J-3, dubbed the Cub, with wings sprouting from above the pilot's head and in this instance an improvised enclosure for the cabin in which another person could sit. Its insides had been pretty well torn out so as to accommodate the maximum amount of freight for the trips into the mountains.

For some three weeks LeRoy could not decipher whether he hung around the Palmer strip to see Lizzie Carmody or her father's airplane, but toward the end of that period, the latter won out. "What kind of plane is this?" he asked one day as he sidled up to Carmody, and the Irishman said: "A 1927 Survivor," and when LeRoy asked what kind that was, Carmody showed the various dents and tears which symbolized his life as an Alaskan bush pilot: "It's a Piper Cub that's learned to survive. That long scar, landin' in a spruce tree in a fog. This'n, landin' on a riverbank that turned out to be mud when I thought it was gravel. The big tear in the side, a spare dynamo busted loose from in back of my head when I landed too fast on a lake up in the hills." The Cub showed so much damage that LeRoy said: "It looks like flyin' is mostly tryin' to land," and Carmody clapped him on the back: "Son, you just learned all there is to know about aviation. Any damned fool can get a plane up in the air. Trick is to get it down."

"Have you ever been in real danger?" LeRoy asked, and the bush pilot gave no reply; he simply pointed once again to the eight or nine heavy scars, each one of which represented a close brush with death. Awed, LeRoy said: "You must be brave."

"Nope. Just careful." This seemed so contradictory, considering the condition of the Cub, that LeRoy had to ask: "How can you be careful if you've had so many accidents?" and Carmody burst into laughter: "Son, you really cut down to the quick. I am careful. I'm very careful never to crash before seein' a way to walk out alive. Any landin' is the right one if you walk away."

"This plane's a wreck," LeRoy said. "Why don't you fix it up?"

"It still flies. Anyway, I carry mostly freight." He studied his bat-

tered antique and said: "I think I've about had Alaska. I'm plannin'
on buyin' a Cessna four-seater and doin' my flyin' in California, or
some other place Outside."

"Where's Outside?"

Carmody laughed: "You newcomers call down there the Lower
Forty-eight. Us born here call it Outside."

"What will you do with this one? If you do buy a new plane."

"Lookey here," Carmody said, pointing to a bolt. "When I'm
through, I pull that bolt and *whoosh!* the whole thing falls apart."

One day when Carmody was satisfied that LeRoy was a decent
lad with a sincere interest in both Lizzie and airplanes, he asked, as
he was about to climb down after a freight run into the mines: "Son,
you ever been up in an airplane?"

"No, sir."

"Jump in," and in his bare-bones Cub, Carmody took LeRoy on
the kind of flight that can reorder a young man's perceptions. Rising
slowly from the little dirt strip, he flew north along the front of the
snow-covered Talkeetna Mountains, allowing his passenger to peer
into lovely canyons that would normally have been hidden: "You've
never seen Alaska till you see it from the air." Then he cruised over
the gleaming Matanuska Glacier, then westward deep into the glens
of the soaring Chugaches: "You couldn't survive in Alaska without
an airplane. They were made for each other."

As they returned homeward LeRoy shouted: "Over there! That's
our place!" and Carmody dive-bombed the cabin three times before
Hilda appeared at the door, apron over her hands, and looked up to
see her son screaming past, his blond head sticking out from the
plane window.

Elmer's impassioned defense of Matanuska brought a flood of letters from the Lower Forty-eight, sixty percent containing messages
of encouragement, the rest condemning him as a communist. Missy
Peckham, who handled the mail for the Flatches, burned the latter
and paraded the endorsements through the valley, winning applause
for Elmer, but it was short-lived because of a sad affair which reminded the immigrants of the nature of life in any frontier settlement. Matt Murphy, delighted by the attention given him because of
his adventures in old-time Alaska, often spent his days at the Flatch
cabin, helping them build a wing in which hunters could sleep over-

night, or staking out a path to the glacier that overhung the valley. He found special joy in sharing with Flossie her work with animals, and whereas her grizzly resented his presence and sometimes growled at him, Mildred the Moose saw in him one more friend and would sometimes walk considerable distances with him, nudging him along with her nose.

One day she had guided him toward the shore of the Knik River, and he told Flossie: "I think she wants us to go see the George Lakes," and with only this shadowy suggestion the old Irishman organized an expedition to one of the treasures of Alaska.

As the four Flatches and the Murphys crossed the icy Knik with their lunch baskets and climbed its left bank toward the snout of Knik Glacier, Matt utilized the rest periods for a description of what they were going to see: "Way up there a closed-in valley. It ought to flow directly into the Knik, but the wall of the glacier blocks it off, so the backed-up water forms a chain of three beautiful lakes, Upper, Inner and Lower Lake George. And there they stay locked up all through the cold weather, because the frozen glacier serves as a stopper."

At this point the climbers resumed their progress to the prominence from which they would be able to look down upon the marvel that Murphy had promised them, but at the next halt he explained what would be happening one of these days: "When warm weather gets here, the ice in the glacier barrier, it sort of melts. Water in the three lakes, now really one big lake more than a hundred and fifty feet deep, tremendous pressure you can be sure, it begins to seep right through the glacier wall and weaken it. Finally, one day in July the time comes when the pressure from the lake grows so intense, *bang!* the lake breaks through, the walls of the glacier explode, and you have a gorge six hundred feet wide and more than six hundred feet deep."

"Will we see that?" Flossie asked, and he said: "You never know when the break will come. Not many see it. But the gorge stays open about six weeks. The lakes empty. And huge icebergs float down. Government engineers figured the flow. Two million seven hundred thousand gallons a second when the break comes. That's a lot of water."

The Flatches had no concept of what they were to see when they reached the vantage point overlooking where the three lakes had been, but as Murphy led them to the top they could hear the roar of water below them, and he shouted: "I think it broke through!" and finally they saw this miracle of nature, the only instance of its kind in the world, in which an immense lake exploded into the face of a soaring glacier and tore away chunks of ice bigger by far then the *St. Mihiel* on which they had come to Alaska.

Flossie was the first to speak: "Look! That iceberg coming at us is bigger than our house!" then her brother said quietly: "And look at the one behind," but they all fell silent when the rushing lake water cut off a whole side of the glacier, a cathedral of ice that remained upright for a hundred yards, then toppled slowly onto its side as it felt the full force of the flood. It was so immense it did not twist like the others but in supreme majesty made its way down the turbulent chute.

Far down the course of the river the Flatches saw the final grandeur of this extraordinary performance; there, enormous icebergs, having run out of sufficient water to keep them afloat, perched like stranded white seabirds while the more placid water moved quietly past them. It would require weeks of bright summer sun to make them disappear.

"Does this happen every year?" Flossie asked as they were hiking home, and Murphy said: "As far as I know. It's been happenin' every year since I first saw it."

"How long ago was that?" the girl asked, and Matt said: "About a score of years. We came to Matanuska often in the old days. Huntin'. We knew then it was a choice spot. We knew good people would come to it one day." And the old fellow cried: "Now look who's comin' to meet us on this fine day!" And there came Mildred the Moose, stepping carefully along the path to greet the people she had grown to love. She was an admirable creature that sunny afternoon, bigger by far than a deer or a caribou, much heavier than her friend the grizzly, and awkward in the endearing way a thirteen-year-old girl can be when her legs seem so long and uncoordinated.

And then, with the sun on her, she lurched forward as a shot rang out from below. "No!" Flossie screamed as she had that first day when her father had tried to shoot the moose, but as she ran forward, with Mildred still on her feet, there was a second shot, and the huge animal plunged to her knees, tried vainly to crawl forward toward the Flatches, and keeled over. She was still breathing, blood flecks spraying from her nostrils, but before Flossie could cradle her head in her arms, she died.

"You!" Matt Murphy shouted, and with surprising energy he started to run toward the two hunters, men apparently from Anchorage, judging from their expensive guns, but when they became aware that they had shot a tame moose, they scuttled off. Murphy, scandalized at their cruel behavior, chased after them, but he had covered less than a hundred yards when he collapsed, all at once and like the wall of the glacier, and while Flossie, distraught, tended her dead moose, Missy ran forward to care for her man lying on the rocky path.

When the other Flatches reached the fallen man, they saw that he was severely stricken, and Elmer shouted crisp commands: "LeRoy, help your sister. Hilda, find me a couple of poles. Missy, loosen his clothes. Help him to breathe," and with the efficiency he had always shown in moments of crisis, this skilled woodsman set his rescue party in motion, and when his daughter refused to leave her dead friend, this creature from the depths of the forest, he called wisely to his son: "Stay with her as long as she needs," and with the help of the two women, carried the old Irishman to the cabin.

Flossie and LeRoy did not reach the cabin before the old man died, and when the girl realized that not only had she lost her moose but that her much-loved old pioneer was also gone, she gave a mournful cry and fell to her knees, for she sensed in that awful moment that the old days were gone, the days when a girl could tame a moose at the edge of Matanuska, the days when children in church could hear a man explain what it was like to spend two long winters in a narrow lean-to in the heart of the arctic. And there on the floor she began to tremble.

On a scrawled piece of paper Matt Murphy had penciled his will: "Everything to Missy Peckham, but five hundred dollars each to LeRoy and Flossie Flatch, trusted friends of my old age." The Anchorage courts accepted this as a viable document, and just as John Klope's unexpected gift to Missy and Matt that day in Nome in 1902 remade their lives, so now Matt's gift to LeRoy restructured his, because the day after the probate judge awarded him his five hundred dollars, he hurried to Palmer Airstrip, sought out Jake Carmody, pointed to the beat-up Cub, and asked: "How much?" and Jake said: "I really hadn't planned to sell," and LeRoy said: "You told me you were leavin' . . . goin' to buy a new Cessna."

"Three hundred dollars, it's yours," and to the bush pilot's surprise, LeRoy peeled off six fifty-dollar bills, and took possession.

"Flyin' lessons thrown in," Jake said, and that afternoon LeRoy started to learn the intricacies of keeping this old relic aloft. An apt pupil, he took his first solo flight that weekend, and after two more weeks of intensive instruction he felt himself qualified to offer his services to the various mining camps. After one week of such flying with never a mishap, he returned his attention to Lizzie Carmody, who gave many signs of being interested in the young pilot, but when he suggested that he take her up for a spin, Jake roared out of the room where the local pilots waited: "Holy Christ! You're not takin' my daughter up in that crate, are you?" and he forbade Lizzie to go near the perilous junk. Two days later Jake did exactly what he had threatened to do for so long: he took his wife and three children down to Portland, where he bought a new Cessna and entered the local aviation circles.

LeRoy, now the pilot of his own plane and eager to display his talents to someone, asked his mother if she would go up with him, and she said: "I go up with no one," so he propositioned Missy Peckham, who almost leaped at the invitation. Together they flew up the Knik Valley to see from aloft the three George Lakes making their assault on the face of the glacier.

When they returned to a smooth spot near the cabin, LeRoy's parents gave him their only advice about his plane: "Don't go killin' yourself." More specific counsel was provided by an old veteran who flew into the Palmer strip one afternoon after a horrendous flight in the mountains: "Young feller, we welcome recruits like you. But if you want to sit here when you're my age, remember one thing: There is bold pilots like you, and there is old pilots like me. But there ain't never been an old bold pilot." When LeRoy looked perplexed, the man said: "When I was comin' in, real cautious like, for I was still shook up by that fog in the mountains, I seen you actin' up with your plane. Real fancy. And when I landed I asked: 'Who's that young duck with his pinfeathers showin'?' and they told me it was you tryin' out a plane you'd just bought." He stared at LeRoy and wagged his finger: "You're clever, but you ain't clever enough to break the rules."

"What rules?"

"Not many. Five, six? Stay away from whirlin' propellers, they chop you into mincemeat. Never, never climb into your plane without checkin' the gas. An empty tank is remorseless. You'll be flyin' into strange areas without strips, so never, never land straight in. Circle to see whether the ice is frozen or the sand strip along the river is solid. On the way out, check every visible point, you'll need 'em comin' back. Don't hesitate to sleep beside your plane, because tryin' to find your way home at night in a fog ain't really productive. And for Christ's own sweet sake, tie down your cargo. Keep plenty of light rope in your plane and lash down them floatin' objects, or sure as hell they're goin' to smash right into the back of your head at sixty miles an hour." As LeRoy tried to visualize the situations in which these instructions would apply, the old-timer added a special one for Alaska: "And, LeRoy, maybe you wouldn't think of this, but in winter always keep an armful of spruce branches in the rear of your plane, tied down, of course."

It was a magnificent world into which LeRoy Flatch entered with his Cub. It was a sturdy plane, so thoroughly rebuilt after its predictable series of accidents that not much of the original structure remained. Its engine, sixth in the series for this particular craft, was now a 75-hp Lycoming, but it too had been heavily recast after smashups. It gave good mileage to a gallon of aviation fuel, but it had also flown quite a few hours on various hideous mixtures, including one flight on half kerosene, half gasoline, and as the man who was flying it at the time said: "Plus another half alcohol. But the alcohol was in me."

It was a plane that had to be flown by muscle power, for it contained no automatic pilot or the sophisticated instrumentation that would make its successors much easier to operate. It responded slowly to instructions and its various surfaces could be activated only by brute strength, but it had one characteristic which made it revered by its longtime pilots: it could land on almost anything, remain upright, and fly out after repairs had been completed. It was almost an ideal plane for an Alaskan bush pilot, but after LeRoy had flown it several hundred hours he saw that for it to serve him as he intended, it needed two simple modifications, and he spent the remainder of Matt Murphy's bequest to engineer them.

"What I got to have," he explained to Flossie when she flew with him to mining camps far in the hills, "is a pair of pontoons so's I can land on water up in the lake country. A smooth lake is far better than a rough field. And I simply got to have a pair of skis for landin' on the snow in winter."

Reflecting on this, she said: "LeRoy, you'd be takin' your plane apart every four months. Now wheels, now pontoons, now skis," and he said: "It'd be worth it," but when he scouted around for such gear he learned that it was not cheap, and finally he had to approach Flossie: "Only way I can get the plane I need is you lend me the money to buy the other landing gear."

She had the funds to make the loan, Matt Murphy's bequest would take care of that, but she was not satisfied that her brother was really serious about making his living as a pilot until he rushed home one afternoon: "Floss! A man at Palmer is selling his plane, going to Seattle. He has a buyer who doesn't want the extra landing gear. A bargain, a real bargain!"

She accompanied him to the airfield, where she found that what he was saying was true, for an old-timer told her: "Them's the best pontoons around here and the skis are practically new."

"Could my brother get them on and off?"

"I'd teach him in ten minutes."

It was a deal, and with his acquisition of pontoons and skis, LeRoy became a full-fledged bush pilot, able to land on ground, snow or lake, but as Flossie had predicted, switching them was hard work. However, the man who had encouraged Flossie to lend her brother the money now showed him how to approach this difficult task: "You get yourself a long spruce pole, and a short oak stump for your fulcrum. Watch how easy it is to lift the Cub right up in the air!"

When the front end was high off the ground he said: "Now edge this other stump under the middle, and let your pole down bitsy, bitsy, and you have your plane right up in the air where we can work on it." And he showed LeRoy how to switch between wheels, pontoons and skis.

"Of course," the old fellow said, "each year you have to spend four mornings of hard work. Mid-March, off with the skis, on with the wheels. June, put on the pontoons for the lakes. September, you need wheels again, and in early December, back to skis." With this relatively simple shifting back and forth, LeRoy had a most versatile machine, and he used it imaginatively, flying anywhere anytime in almost any weather, promoting new business and earning real income.

At Palmer Airstrip, where he kept his plane when it had wheels, he became acquainted with several young hotshots who performed amazing feats, flying onto glaciers with their skis, landing on remote, uncharted lakes, or carrying immense loads far beyond the stated capacity of their planes, and they were a glamorous lot until the night when they lost their way home and crashed, out of fuel, in a timbered area. If they were picked out of the tree next morning and if their plane could be rebuilt, they were talked about on all the air-fields, while cautious farm boys like himself attracted no attention. But he noticed two important facts: the really great bush pilots, like Bob Reeve and the Wien brothers and Bud Helmericks, took none of these unnecessary chances, and the young bucks who tore the place apart, challenging the far north with their frail planes, invariably wound up dead. Gallant legends, the very heart of the bush pilot's charisma, but very dead.

It had now become standard practice for any Flatch who was at home when LeRoy set out on a flight to tell him: "Don't go killin' yourself," and he did not resent the implication, but even though he was a most careful pilot when he reached his twenties, he did not es-cape the normal adventures that seemed to lie in wait for all bush pilots. On one flight into a high lake in the Talkeetna Mountains north of Palmer where a man from Seattle had a hunting lodge, he was carrying a load of mail and groceries purchased at the local store. He had his pontoons on, and after twenty-two minutes he spot-ted the landmarks leading to the camp. With care he zeroed in, cir-cled the lake to be sure its surface contained no unexpected additions like rafts or loose boats, and made a perfect landing upwind to help him stop his forward progress. Dropping the revolutions on his pro-peller to their lowest practical speed, he steered his Cub deftly up to the floating dock, where the owner of the camp and his wife awaited.

"LeRoy," the Seattle man said, "you make a better landing on this lake than any of the big boys. The minute you get yourself a four-seater, Madge and me are goin' to fly with no one else."

He heard this refrain constantly: "Get yourself a four-seater. You'd have three times the customers." But a used four-seat Waco with pontoons and skis extra would cost not less than forty-five hun-dred dollars plus the Cub, and this he could not afford.

"I pick up the grocery trade," he told the Seattle man. "Or like when you built your new wing."

When he made such deliveries, he tried always to be extra helpful in unloading the gear, doing most of the work himself to let the own-ers know he appreciated their trade, and always if he had time, when he was finished, he asked the wife: "Ma'am, would you like to take a short spin to see the land around here?" and he almost never got a refusal.

Then he would climb into the pilot's seat, instruct the woman as to how she could manage the struts to climb in beside him, and after she was belted in he would take the plane slowly out to the farthest end of the takeoff area and tell her: "Now, ma'am, I don't want you to watch me. I've done this lots of times and it's old hat for me. But you lean way forward, keep your face close to the window, and watch how we use the step."

"The what?" she usually asked.

"The step. The pontoon isn't just straight, you know. Halfway back, it has a step, a break in the smoothness, and unless we can get this plane up on that step, where the adhesion of the water and the friction is less, we won't be able to lift off." When he felt that she understood, more or less, he said: "Watch! Here we go for the good old step."

It was sometimes incredible the amount of lake LeRoy required before his plane went up on the step, and several times the watching wives shouted: "Are we going to make it?" and always he yelled back: "Sooner or later, up we go," and always, when it seemed that the plane was never going to fly, it would mysteriously lift itself onto the step, and then the length of pontoon clinging to the water was diminished by half, and in a few moments, from this more advantageous posture, the plane finally broke completely loose, whizzed along throwing bits of spray, and rose grandly into the air while the passenger clapped and sometimes shouted with triumphant joy. The fact was, LeRoy also wanted to cheer every time this miracle of the seaplane took place; he couldn't believe that it required such a very long takeoff before the pontoons broke loose, and he was cautious about the maneuver because on three occasions, to his great embarrassment, his plane never did get onto the step, and twice he ran right onto the beach at the far end of his attempt. For that reason he added an extra precaution to the ones the old-timer had given him: "When you start to take off from a lake, always study the far shore, because pretty soon you may be on it."

Usually on a sightseeing trip he stayed aloft no more than fifteen minutes, but on this afternoon the lady wanted to investigate the entire area surrounding her family's holdings, so she called to LeRoy: "Give me a real trip. I'll pay for the full hour," and he was happy to comply, for he also enjoyed such exploration. It was a fine sunny day with just a hint of clouds moving in from the distant ocean, and the scores of lakes nestled among the hills glowed like emeralds when the sun struck them. Being careful to maintain his orientation among the mountains which protruded, he spent more than an hour aloft, and this took him well to the north.

"Wonderful!" his passenger shouted. "Let's go home," and when he landed the plane on her lake and ferried her to the dock, she told her waiting husband: "Pay him double. I never realized we lived in such a gorgeous place!"

His unplanned excursion meant that he was delayed about two hours on his return trip south to Matanuska, but this posed no problem, for in late July there would be plenty of daylight—sunrise at 0314 in the morning, sunset not till 2057 at night—but the situation became somewhat more complicated when the dark clouds which had been hovering to the south began to speed in with that astonishing ability to move that made Alaskan weather so unpredictable. A sky could be warm and bright at five, cold and menacing at five-thirty. This evening it was menacing.

It was about eight at night when LeRoy approached the Matanuska area, which meant that he had almost an hour of light left, but this was somewhat irrelevant because he had fuel for not more than forty minutes and the finding of his home lake in light was obligatory. However, by the time he had located Knik Glacier and knew where he was, storm clouds of a rather violent nature rushed in to obscure the area and he knew that any attempt to either find his lake or land upon it was futile. He therefore began casting about for an alternative, and there were a dozen eligible lakes in the area, but now they too were closed down by this rampaging storm.

It'll pass in a hour, he told himself, but that won't do me much good. So he must either speed back northward, hoping to outrun the storm, and land on one of the lakes adjacent to Palmer, where several planes headquartered, or continue south and try landing on some arm of the Knik River or even the bigger Cook Inlet, but to attempt the latter would be risky, for if the storm contained strong winds, it might generate waves too high and powerful for the Cub to negotiate. The situation was becoming ugly.

What to do? He tightened his seat belt, relaxed his hands, shook them twice, then gripped the wheel even more firmly and gave himself time-tested instructions: Now's the time to take a deep breath,

LeRoy. You know you can always land this bird on the ground. Chew up the pontoons, but they can be replaced. You can't.

Looking out, he saw to the right the menacing tops of the Talkeetna Range: Let's get out of here! and he swung sharply to the left, striving to gain as much altitude as he could, but when he did he could see nothing below.

In this extremity he sought no miraculous escape, no sudden revelation of a known lake. He was in dire trouble and he knew it. He would survive only if he flew in a manner to put every chance condition like wind or sudden gusts or choppy water, and only if he flew with but one resolute purpose: Let's get her down. Eight minutes to go.

He would forever remember those eight minutes at the end of which his tank was empty. He flew south till he was certain the Knik River must be under him, within a mile give or take. He descended precisely as he would have done had the terrain been visible, and he trusted the strength of the storm to remain constant. Most of all, he kept control of his plane, adjusting to the wind as if he had wheels and a clear landing strip ahead. When his altimeter showed little free space beneath him, he did not grit his teeth and prepare for some unexpected shock: he continued to breathe evenly, kept his hands at the same pressure as before, and prepared to land in whatever lay below.

Not quite as fatalistic as that: I'll have some visibility. I'll see whether it's water or land, and if it's land, I'll have about two minutes to find water. He did not add that in those minutes it would be vital as to whether he flew north or south at low altitude to find his water.

At the end of the sixth minute he broke through the clouds at an altitude of forty feet and saw below him only land, and extremely rough land at that. To put his plane down in that mix of trees and hills would be insane, but in which direction lay the river? Calmly and for no reason that he could have explained, he estimated that it was behind him, to the north, so in an easy swing he brought the plane about in a 180° turn, dropped even lower, and at the last practical moment saw ahead of him the rippling waters of the river. Breathing just a bit more deeply, he steadied the wheel, judged that he was landing broadside to the wind, which did not seem excessive, and with almost the last cupful of gas he landed the Cub in a faultless approach, and without slowing the engines continued across the river until the front of the pontoons climbed up on grassy bank. Using the luggage ropes he always carried, he tied the plane to a group of trees and set out on foot to find someone to help drag it ashore.

In many ways LeRoy derived his greatest pleasure from his Cub when it wore skis, for then, if a heavy snow had fallen, he would soar over central Alaska with the feeling that he could fly anywhere and land in almost any corner of his majestic world. In the first days of trial and error he learned the limits of altitude to which his little plane could go and the most effective ways of landing on drifted snow. "Hey!" he shouted one morning as he flew into a blazing sunrise with snow covering everything. "This is all mine!" But there was also a financial advantage to flying on skis, as one of his customers explained in a letter to his wife back in Maryland:

> Since I was eager to see the Matanuska experiment, I went to a small airport in the area and asked who their best pilot was and they agreed that a fellow named LeRoy might not be the best but he was certainly the safest, so I engaged him. He had a small rickety-looking plane which he assured me never failed, and after I had inspected the famous valley he asked: "You want to see our glaciers?" and I nodded. But we were still miles from them, flying over snow, when he suddenly shouted: "Lookeeee!" and he dropped the plane in a sickening spiral, whipped open his window, reached for a shotgun from behind his ear, flew the plane with his knees while paying no attention to where we were heading.
>
> "Look at that wolf!" he said, and with great skill he brought our plane about, leveled with the huge beast, and killed him with one shot. Then, swinging the plane about as if it were a leaf, he landed not ten feet from the dead wolf, ordered me out so that he could climb down to retrieve the animal, which he threw into the cabin behind us.
>
> When we resumed flight we had been in the air only a few minutes when he yelled: "Hey! There's his brother," and down we dropped in that sickening spiral. Again he flew the plane with his knees and again he nailed his wolf with one shot. This time when I started to get back into the plane I said: "There's

blood all over my seat," and he became most apologetic,
producing from a little box a clean cloth with which he wiped
my seat clean. I also noticed that he lashed down the two
wolves as carefully as if they were cargoes of gold, and when I
said: "I hope you don't see any more wolves," he explained:
"For flying you I get $40. For each of those wolves, $50
government bounty," and I asked him where he had learned to
shoot so professionally, and he said: "I learned guns in
Minnesota, airplanes in Alaska." I later found that he'd had
two weeks of flying instruction. Believe me, Elinor, flying in
Alaska is a lot different from flying in suburban Baltimore.

It was a few days after this successful wolf hunt that LeRoy stumbled upon the adventure which was to modify his life in ways he could not have anticipated. He was idling at the Palmer Airstrip when a well-dressed, good-looking businessman in his mid-fifties came up: "You LeRoy Flatch?"

"I am."

"The fellow who made that remarkable river landing last summer?"

"Luck and a very strong plane got me down."

"Could I see the plane?"

Bewildered as to why a stranger would want to see an old workhorse like his Cub, LeRoy said: "That one over there . . . on skis. Lot of miles on it. Lot of savvy in it."

The stranger studied the exterior of the plane for some minutes, then asked: "Mind if I take a peek inside?"

"Be my guest," and when the inspection was complete, the man asked: "Son, why don't you get yourself a four-seater?"

"I'm savin' like the devil to get one."

The stranger laughed, extended his hand, and said: "I'm Tom Venn, Ross & Raglan, and my wife and I are building ourselves a hunting lodge up on the flanks of Denali. We need someone to fly in big batches of our gear."

"I'd be interested. How far is it?"

"About eighty miles northwest heading. Could you handle that?"

"I could. But I'd want to top off with some aviation gas when I got there."

"That can be arranged. When could you fly?"

"About ten minutes after you got your stuff here. Will you be flying along?"

"Yes. I want to do some exploring along the way and after we get there."

"You know I'm not allowed to fly into the National Park."

"There's a lot of land outside it," and with that, Venn hurried into the building and phoned the truck waiting at the railroad siding to start bringing out the electrical gear. At half after one the Cub was solidly packed, with all the cargo tightly lashed. Venn, working inside the fuselage and sweating like a deckhand, asked: "Can we throw out these branches?" and LeRoy shouted back: "Not on your life. You remember carefully just where they are. Anytime you fly into mountains you may need them."

The heavily loaded plane, with Venn flying in the right-hand seat, took off neatly from the Palmer Airstrip, rose purposefully to an altitude of four thousand feet and started on a 320° heading. After the routine was set Venn asked: "By the way, have you ever flown in the Denali area?" and LeRoy said: "No, but I've always wanted to," and Venn said with no hint of sarcasm: "Good, we'll explore together."

They had flown about halfway to their destination when LeRoy gasped so audibly, Venn guessed correctly that his pilot had never before seen the extraordinary sight that lay ahead. Rising majestically above a cloud wreath that enclosed its lower elevations, stood that mass of great mountains—Russell, Foraker, Denali, Silverthrone, from southwest to northeast. Except for Russell, these were among the highest mountains in North America, and Denali was the highest.

They formed a stupendous white-crowned barrier across the heart of Alaska, and after gazing at them in awe for some moments, LeRoy told his passenger: "You can come to Alaska forty times and travel around all sides of those mountains and never see Denali," and Venn said: "I know." But there it was, in all its frozen glory, not only the highest peak on the continent but also the farthest north by a large margin. When you paid your respects to Denali, you were knocking on the door of the Arctic Circle, which lay less than two hundred and fifty miles to the north.

For about twenty minutes the great mountain stood in solemn majesty, a peak so grand that only two groups of mountaineers had ever mastered it, the first in 1913 when a Nenana clergyman made it to the top, the second in 1932 when a group of four especially daring men used skis and dog teams, an amazing combination, to master the howling winds and the crevasse-ridden slopes. As the plane approached the outer perimeter of the park, LeRoy explained: "You know, Mr. Venn, the mountain isn't visible from down there," and Venn said: "It rarely is. I was here eight times before I ever saw the darned thing."

So Flatch started to descend, but when he passed through the cloud cover that seemed always to cluster about the mountains as if perversely they refused to let their treasure be seen, he found that the clouds did not end but continued right down to the ground, which in this area was covered with snow of exactly the same coloration. Trying not to alarm his passenger, LeRoy said quietly: "We seem to be caught in a whiteout. Tighten your seat belt."

"Are we going to crash?" Venn asked with that coolness in the face of adversity which had always characterized him.

"Not if I can help it," but when he started to drop cautiously it was clear that neither he nor any other pilot, no matter how skilled, would be able to determine where these snowlike clouds ended and the real snow covering the ground began. There was, in other words, no discernible horizon, and Flatch recalled the shocking number of Alaskan aviators who in such circumstances had flown their planes nose-first into the solid ground, not having a clue as to where they were or in what attitude relative to the earth. Always, of course, in such crashes, the plane exploded, and in only one or two cases could one of the young-bold pilots boast later: "I flew it right into the snow cover and walked away."

In an extremity like this it was essential that the pilot not panic, and Venn, watching LeRoy closely, was pleased to see that he was reacting with admirable calm. Three times Flatch tried to land on the snow, and three times he was thrown into total confusion, for he could not ascertain where clouds ended and snow-covered rock began, so he flew in what he was sure was an upward attitude, and when he had gained some height above what he assumed to be the ground, he told Venn: "We must try to spot something on the ground. Anything. A caribou, a tree, just anything."

So the two men strove to determine where the ground was, and failed. "Mr. Venn, undo your belt, climb back and fetch those spruce branches." After a struggle across the lashed-down luggage, Venn reappeared with a large armful of branches. "Open your window, put your seat belt back on, and when I shout 'Drop,' start throwing out the branches, one at a time. Throw the ones with the most branches first."

For some moments they flew in silence, each man breathing heavily, and then came the command: "Drop!" Out from Venn's window the branches began to fall, but only the first one was required, for when LeRoy saw how quickly it came to rest, that is, how perilously close to the ground he was, he said only one word: "Jesus!" But with the frail bit of directional information provided by the branch, he adjusted in his seat, pulled his plane almost straight up, then circled low until he was lined up with the fallen spruce branch, which stood out on the snow like a great beacon light. Rarely had he been so glad to see something solid.

"Seat belt tight? Good. This could be pretty rough, but we've got to suppose it's level snow," and with no further attention to his passenger, who behaved well, Flatch lowered his flaps, dropped the nose of the Cub, and felt a surge of triumphant joy as the skis struck the smooth snow that stretched in all directions.

When the plane skidded to a safe halt, Tom Venn unfastened his seat belt, leaned back, and asked quietly: "So what do we do now?"

"Send a radio signal to let everyone know we're safe"—which he proceeded to do—"and then wait here till this storm passes."

"All night?"

"Could be," and without further discussion of their plight, the two men settled down for a long wait.

They did have to stay overnight, and early next morning when the skies had cleared, a rescue plane flew over, dipped low to check whether Flatch and his passenger were safe, then flew in large circles while LeRoy revved up his engine, taxied to the end of what looked like a relatively level space, and in one-third of the distance it took the Cub to take off when its pontoons were on water, the skis attained a surprising speed, and the plane was in the air.

Perversely, Denali and its sister mountains stood forth in such clear beauty that Venn suggested: "Let's stay up a while and see this area," and LeRoy said: "I have the fuel. I'd enjoy it," so for about half an hour they surveyed that chain of remarkable glaciers which tumbled southward out of the massif, a sight thrilling and exhilarating to the spirit of anyone who loved nature. When Flatch finally brought his plane to rest on the snow alongside Venn's lodge in the lower hills, the Seattle millionaire congratulated him: "You know how to handle a plane, young man," and when Venn's wife, Lydia Ross Venn, ran out to greet them, a handsome gray-haired woman in her early fifties, he told her: "This is LeRoy Flatch, a most gifted pilot. You and I are going to finance him a four-seater and he'll be flying us in here regularly from now on."

On this first trip LeRoy stayed with the Venns for three days, taking first one, then the other on exploration trips which enabled him to familiarize himself with the great mountains, and when the visit ended, Tom Venn asked: "LeRoy, would you consider flying down to Anchorage to pick up our son and his bride? They're coming here for part of their vacation."

"Glad to, you give me the instructions. But my plane only seats one."

"Rent a four-seater. Try them all out and let me know which one suits this part of Alaska best."

So LeRoy Flatch, in a rented Fairchild with only a few hours on it, reported to the air terminal in Anchorage and paged Mr. and Mrs. Malcolm Venn, and as soon as the young man appeared, LeRoy knew he must be Tom Venn's son, for the resemblance was striking, but he was not at all prepared for Mrs. Venn, who was not a white woman. She was nearly as tall as her husband, extremely slim, with very black hair, and he could not tell whether she was an Eskimo, an Aleut or an Athapascan, three tribes he was still trying to get organized in his mind, and he was too polite to ask. But young Venn solved the problem, for as he tossed their gear into the plane he said: "My wife'll ride shotgun. She wants to see this land. She's half Tlingit and this is all new territory for her."

Since the subject had been broached, LeRoy asked: "And what's the other half?" and Malcolm said: "Chinese. Good mix. Very intelligent, as you'll find out," and by the time the Fairchild reached the Venn lodge at the foot of Denali the three travelers were respectful friends.

"What's that crazy name for your father's place?" LeRoy asked as they unloaded the plane.

"Why didn't you ask him?"

"I thought it might be nosy."

"You asked me."

"But you're not head of the company. He is."

"He named it Venn's Lode."

"Does Lode mean what I think it does?"

"Yes. He said that in the old days men came here probing for gold . . . trying to find their lode. He and Mother are here to find their own lode, happiness. He loves Alaska, you know. Tramped all through it in the old days."

LeRoy Flatch was so busy in the fall of 1939 scrounging around to find a used four-seater that he could afford, even with help from the Venns, that he actually failed to realize that a major war had broken out in Europe. At the reasonable cost of three thousand seven hundred dollars he found a pretty good Waco YKS-7 which had been used in the Juneau district, and with it he discovered Alaska's hunger for aerial transport. American soldiers suddenly appeared asking for transportation to strange places, and gold mines already in being called for new equipment. Road building experienced a spurt, new stores opened everywhere, and wherever commerce or new building flourished, bush-trained aviators like LeRoy were in demand.

"What's going on?" he asked men who lounged about the airstrip, and one night in the winter of 1940 he found out. Friends hauled him off to a meeting at the schoolhouse in Palmer, where a trim young bullet-headed officer from the Army Air Corps gave a clipped lecture that brushed away the cobwebs: "I'm Captain Leonidas Shafter, and I can lick any man who laughs at that first name. My father was West Point and he named me after the Greek hero of Thermopylae. Lost his entire contingent and his head. I propose to do better."

Aided by maps that had been converted by photography into color slides—which, when projected, filled a large section of blank wall behind him—he gave his audience of pilots, bulldozer operators and ordinary workmen fresh understanding of the war in Europe and Alaska's possible relation to it:

"The war over there may have subsided into what they humorously call the Sitzkrieg, with each side trying to outwait the other. But believe me, it's going to explode soon enough, and if past history is any guide, we'll be drawn into it.

"I cannot predict when or how our participation will come, but in one way or another it will have to involve Soviet Russia. The Communists are at present allies of Nazi Germany. This can't last long, but whether it does or not, can't you see how whatever Russia does will involve Alaska? Here at the Diomede Islands, the Soviet Union is a mile and a half from Alaska. All right, they're tiny islands and they don't matter. But across the Bering Sea from Russia to Alaska is trivial for a modern airplane. Contact is almost inescapable, and when that contact comes, your Alaska will be right in the middle of the war."

A flier who had spent time in the Air Corps asked: "Are you speaking of Russia as our enemy or our ally," and Shafter snapped: "I haven't said because I can't guess. The way things stand tonight, she's our enemy. But things won't continue as they are, and then she could become our ally."

"Then how can you make plans?"

"In a case like this you plan for every contingency, and I'm certain that whatever happens, you good people will adjust to it." To emphasize his point, he slapped the area where the Soviet and American frontiers met, and with that, he moved into the heart of his surprising talk:

"Look, please, at this map of North America and the eastern part of Siberia. Let's suppose that the Soviet Union continues to be our enemy. How can they most effectively strike at cities like Seattle, Minneapolis and Chicago? By streaming right across Alaska and Canada, a straight line to their industrial targets. The first battles, the ones that could decide everything, would be fought in places like Nome and Fairbanks and over the airfield on which we're sitting right now.

"But let's suppose that the Soviets turn on Hitler, as they should, and become our allies. How will we help supply them? How will airplanes built in Detroit get to Moscow? I think they'll fly a modified great circle route, across Wisconsin and Minnesota to Winnipeg, then, within six months, maybe over to Edmonton, Dawson, Fairbanks, Nome and into Siberia. Gentlemen, you could very well be using this gravel strip as an emergency landing field for huge bombers."

While the men stared at one another in amazement, he showed a beautifully drawn map of the region between Edmonton and Fairbanks, and said: "Whether the Soviet Union turns out to be enemy or friend, what we ought to do right now is build a highway capable of handling military equipment from here"—and he pointed to Dawson

Creek, northwest of Edmonton—"where the railroad ends, right through this morass to here." And, ignoring the terrible terrain, he marked a sweeping line across Canada and into the heartland of Alaska at Fairbanks. "Don't tell me such a road has been tried before. Don't tell me it would impose all sorts of difficulties. Listen to me when I tell you it must be built."

When a pilot asked "Why?" Shafter grew impatient: "Because the life and death of a great republic is at stake. Two great republics, the United States and Canada. We have got to move war equipment from Detroit and Pittsburgh to the shores of the Bering Sea." And then he said something strange and prophetic, a stray idea that would always be remembered by the men who heard it. "We've got to be prepared to drive off anyone who comes at us from Asia." When this challenge was greeted by silence, he laughed at himself, slapped his right leg, and said jovially: "They tell me the original Americans, Eskimos, everyone up here, they all came across the Bering Sea when it wasn't a sea any longer. Just walked across. Maybe the seas will drop again. Maybe they'll be coming at us across some land bridge. But they'll come, gentlemen, they will come."

In the months that followed, LeRoy Flatch ignored the progress of the war in Europe and the frightening predictions of Captain Shafter, because he now had two planes to look after, the old two-seater Cub and the relatively new four-seater Waco. He kept pontoons on the former and berthed it at a nearby lake, and perfected a speedy way for switching the four-seater first to wheels and then to skis. With this two-pronged attack, which he used creatively, he was able to probe the center of Alaska about as effectively as any bush pilot then operating, for despite his youth, he had acquired a mature appreciation of what his airplanes would do if he kept them in good shape and filled with gas.

In any twelve-month period he would certainly land one of his planes on the following surfaces: wide macadam at an official airport like Anchorage, narrow bumpy macadam at a rural port like Palmer, gravel at one mining camp, loose gravel and dust at the next, grass at some strip beside a hunting lodge, gravel bank beside a river, mud and gravel beside some stream, ice, snow and—very dangerously—ice covered by a thin layer of snow, grass covered with sleet or grass covered with snow, sleet and light rainfall. He would also alight on lakes, rivers, ponds and other bodies of water too limited in length to permit a subsequent takeoff; then he would haul his plane onto dry land, walk out, and get some other daring aviator to fly him back in with a pair of wheels to replace the pontoons and some tools with which to chop down small trees and smooth out a runway:

And sooner or later he would also land in the branches of some tree; then he would scramble down, wait for a replacement wing to be flown in, bolt it carefully to the undamaged stub, and be off again. He was constantly in danger, considering the routes he flew, but with remarkable foresight he saw to it that any of the unavoidable accidents occurred with his old two-seater and not his new four-seat job.

His most enjoyable assignment came whenever he received a telegram asking him to meet one or another of the Venns at the Anchorage airport, for this always meant renewing acquaintance with this exciting family. He liked all of them: the cool, reserved father who ran an empire; the spirited mother who seemed to make many of the decisions; the young man who would one day inherit that empire; and especially the young wife, so pretty and secure in what she wanted to do. "She's certainly not like any of the half-breeds you read about," LeRoy said to his fellow pilots. "Any man would be proud to have such a wife."

"Not me," an old-timer growled. "Half-breeds, native women, sooner or later they all lead a man to hell."

On pickup trips like the ones to Anchorage, LeRoy could never be sure just when the incoming plane would arrive; schedules in Alaska were subject to instant change, sometimes involving whole days. For example, when Bob Reeve flew his crazy planes out to the far end of the Aleutians, you were never certain when he would land on his return trip, because the weather out there was so unpredictable. One Reeve pilot told LeRoy: "I kid you not, we were flying a normal route over Atka when a williwaw come up off the Bering Sea, calm one minute, tempest another, and turned us exactly upside down. Dishes, stewardesses, customers, all up in the air—and me too, if I hadn't been strapped in."

"How long you fly that way?"

"About half a minute. Seemed like two hours, but the next blast of arctic air straightened us out."

"I'd like to fly those islands with you someday."

"Be my guest."

On the long layovers, LeRoy liked to read accounts of the old bush pilots, the ones who had pioneered the routes he covered, and while the best stories dealt with the young men who flew out of the settled places like Sitka and Juneau, the most fascinating, it seemed to him, were about the men who brought aviation to the center of the country—Fairbanks, Eagle, the little settlements along the Yukon like Nulato and Ruby—and especially those intrepid pilots who carried the mail to the really minute villages on the southern and northern flanks of the great, forbidding Brooks Range—Beetles, Wiseman, Anaktuvuk and the camps along the Colville River.

Those guys really had guts, LeRoy thought repeatedly as he read of their exploits, but the tales had a mournful similarity. Harry Kane was about the best of the bush pilots. First man to land at a dozen different sites, field or no field. Loved riverbanks if the sand and gravel were not rippled. But if they were rippled, he landed anyway. Helped three different women have their babies at nine thousand feet. Never took chances. Always a bearcat for safety. You'd fly anywhere with good old Harry Kane, the best of the lot.

And then in the last two pages of the chapter you learned that one night, in a blinding snowstorm, good old Harry, best of the lot . . . kerplooie. Just once, LeRoy reflected, I'd like to read about someone who was the greatest of the bush pilots and who died in bed at the age of seventy-three.

With help from Tom Venn, LeRoy had rearranged the interior of his Waco so that an extra seat was provided back amidst the luggage, which meant that he could now meet the commercial planes flying up from Seattle and carry all four Venns out to their lodge, and once when the Seattle plane was late and he was delayed in reaching Venn's Lode he slept over, and in the morning Tom Venn said: "You know, LeRoy, it's very gloomy to listen to the eight-o'clock news in Alaska."

"Why? Just like the Lower Forty-eight, isn't it?"

"Not at all. Every morning there's this unbroken litany as to where the small planes have crashed the night before. 'Harry Janssen's two-seater, at Lake This-or-That, west of Fairbanks. Twenty-eight hundred feet in snow. Signals indicate survivors.' Or like the one they just broadcast. Some fellow named Livingston. 'Four-seater at a lodge five miles west of Ruby. Snow. No signals. Plane looks to be severely damaged and on side.'"

"Could that be Phil Livingston?" LeRoy asked. "He's one of the best. He doesn't crash in a snowstorm. He doesn't even go out in a snowstorm."

"He seems to have gone yesterday," and when Flatch flew back to Palmer he learned that it was Phil Livingston, one of the best, and he began to listen to the eight-o'clock news with more attention, and the almost daily notice of which airplanes had crashed, where and at what altitudes, with or without visible survivors, brought home to him just how perilous it was to fly small planes in Alaska. "Perilous but inescapable," a veteran said in the pilots' room at Palmer as LeRoy was waiting for a passenger who wanted to explore the wonderful valleys that nestled among the glaciers streaming down from Denali.

But dangerous or not, bush flying in central Alaska was one of the world's most exciting occupations. The weather systems were monumental in extent, whole continents of air rushing madly out of Siberia. The mountains were endless, great armies of peaks many of them not even named, stretching to the horizons. The glaciers were, as one pilot trained in Texas said, "not much like what you see on a flight out of Tulsa." And the diversity of the people who populated the little villages or labored in the mining camps was endless and rewarding.

"Some of the craziest people in civilization," the Texas pilot said, "if you care to call this civilization, are up here in Alaska."

LeRoy met some of them when he was commissioned to fly heavy replacement gear into a hopeless mining camp lost in a back corner of the Talkeetna Mountains north of Matanuska. He had never serviced this outfit before, but with the aid of a penciled map drawn hastily by a fellow pilot who had been there once, he found the place, and when he landed in the snow he saw three typical Alaska mountainmen waiting at the edge of their improvised airstrip: an old-timer from Oregon, a relative newcomer from Oklahoma and a young half-breed fellow with jet-black bangs hanging over his eyes. He had been born, LeRoy learned, in another mining camp well to the north, where his grandfather, a 1902 drifter from New Mexico, had married an Athapascan woman who could neither read nor write. Their son had hooked up with another Athapascan, so that their son, this Nathanael Coop, was really only one-quarter white, three-quarters Indian, but it was customary to call such a person a half-breed. His name was an oddity, for his New Mexico grandfather had arrived in Alaska with a name like Coopersmith or Cooperby, but his son was called by all his friends plain Coop, and it was thus that the name appeared on lists when the various head counts were made. Certainly his grandson was Nate Coop and had never been anything else.

Nate was in his late teens, a silent lad who seemed unrelated to his two older companions; his only friend was a big, surly brown dog named Killer, who had been trained to attack any stranger who trespassed on the mining property. He took an instant dislike to LeRoy, whom he attacked twice before Nate growled "Down!" whereupon he leaped savagely at the snow skis, trying to grasp first one, then the other in his strong jaws before Nate growled a second "Down!" Killer obviously loved his master, for at Nate's command he left the plane but positioned himself so that he could keep a bloodshot eye on both LeRoy and the Cub.

After the cargo was unloaded, LeRoy was informed that on the return trip he was expected to drop Nate off at a parent mine farther into the Talkeetnas: "Nobody told me."

"Nobody needed to. Ten bucks extra, you make the stop."

"I have no idea where it is."

"Nate'll show you," and with the stub of a pencil the Oregon man added a few squirms and squiggles to the map and asked: "Nate, you think you can figure it out?" and the young fellow said: "I guess so." With such preparation LeRoy prepared to fly deep into mountains he had never negotiated before.

"Hop in, Nate. If you know the landmarks, I'm sure we'll make it," and Nate said with no concern: "Never seen 'em from the air, but I guess they can't be much different," and then to LeRoy's astonishment, Killer jumped in too.

"Now wait! I can't have a dog . . ."

"Stays on my lap, no trouble . . ."

Apprehensively, LeRoy allowed the dog to stay even though he could see that the hostility between them had not abated. As the plane climbed up off the snow, he happened to look sideways, and noticed how similar the dog and his master appeared, each with hair in his eyes: Nate and Killer, boy, they're a pair! When the plane achieved altitude, he warned the young miner: "That dog still has it in for me. We could be in trouble if he tried to bite me," but Nate said reassuringly: "He's just protective." But how Killer interpreted this commission, LeRoy could not guess, for although the evil-looking beast did stay on his side of the cockpit, secured in Nate's arms, he also kept his nose so close to LeRoy's right wrist that he could clamp down at the first false move. Killer was not a good passenger, and when the plane flew into rough mountain air which tossed it about, he started to whimper.

With two sharp taps on the dog's forehead, Nate said: "Shut up, Killer," and the complaints stopped.

In this uneasy posture Flatch flew deep into the mountains, his attention diverted by the snarling manner in which Killer maintained watch on him, and after some minutes of purposeful flight he told Nate: "I'm lost. Where's the camp we're looking for?" Nate, no more worried than his pilot about being astray among great mountains in snowy weather, for that was an ordinary Alaskan experience, said blithely: "It's got to be over here somewheres," and, seeking to aid LeRoy, he opened his right-hand-door window to look down as they flew extremely low over a pass. But as he did, Killer saw the kind of chance he often leaped at when on the ground, an opportunity to escape from wherever he was being held, and with a powerful thrust of his legs he turned his back on the pilot he despised, left Nate's arms, uttered a triumphant bark, and jumped right out the open window.

LeRoy, on the left-hand side of the plane, did not see him go but he did hear the bark and Nate's anguished shout "My God! There he goes!" and as the plane twisted in its course, the two occupants watched as big Killer, afloat in the cold air, intuitively spread out his legs to slow his fall and bring it under control.

"He'll be kilt!" Nate screamed. "Do somethin'!" but there was nothing LeRoy could do except circle the plane and watch Killer smash onto the rocks below. However, the dog seemed to have some miraculous guidance system, for, with the bulk of his body parallel to the ground, and the fierce pull of gravity somewhat abated, he drifted and glided toward a snow-filled crevice, a kind of enclosed valley, high in the hills.

When the men saw him land, lie stunned for a moment, then rise and start to snarl, Nate said weakly: "It's a miracle." But now the problem became: "How we gonna get that dog outta there?"

Even a moment's study convinced the two men that landing in that tight valley was an impossibility, for even though the plane did have its skis on, there was not nearly enough space for an approach or takeoff. Killer was marooned high in the Talkeetnas, and for the time being, there was no way to rescue him.

But they stayed over him for some minutes, loath to leave a pet, even an ugly-spirited one, in such a forlorn condition, and during one flyover LeRoy remembered the packet of sandwiches Flossie customarily put in the back of the plane whenever she knew her brother was off on one of his expeditions where food might be scarce, and now he directed Nate: "Find that bundle. Paper tied with string. Break it loose." And on their last flight over the bewildered animal, who had apparently landed uninjured, for he was thrashing about, Nate adroitly dropped the package not far from where the dog stood in the snow, his ugly face turned up toward the plane.

"I told you Killer had the brains of a man," Nate exulted when the dog spotted the descending object, took note of its landing area, and ran to retrieve it. This was an act of such intelligence that LeRoy shouted: "That dog's gonna live!" With Nate's guidance he turned the plane toward the camp.

By that evening all Alaska had been alerted to the drama of the "parachuting" dog, and by the next day several determined outdoorsmen resolved to make a rescue effort, but the valley in which the dog was penned was so inaccessible that he could be kept alive only by food drops delivered from the Cub. Though overland hikes were clearly not feasible, suggestions poured into the camp from all parts of the territory.

The person who became most deeply concerned about Killer's fate was not his owner, Nate, but LeRoy's sister, Flossie, who had lost her tame moose so cruelly but whose considerable affection for animals was undiminished. So it was natural that the next day, when her brother and Nate were going out to feed the prisoner, she asked to go along, and they rigged a seat for her.

Killer had been in his mountain prison for three days when Flossie, on one of the routine flights, saw something that thrilled her: "Nate! Look! He's heading over that hump and down into a better place." And after LeRoy circled several times, they saw that the dog was indeed following the stream that led to the end of the valley, and they watched him cross over the divide and start down another stream that led to a snow-filled surface. Then LeRoy said: "I think I could land in that one."

That night avid listeners heard the heartening news that Killer, the marooned dog, had moved into an area from which it might be possible to rescue him, and newspapermen chartered an airplane at Palmer to interview LeRoy and Nate at the camp.

It was on this hectic night, when the mining camp was full of extra men, that LeRoy became aware that his sister was developing an unusual interest in Nate Coop. Impressed by the young man's de-

votion to his dog and his love for animals in general, and excited by
his manly good looks—raven-dark hair, strong face with sunken
spots beneath his cheekbones, gleaming white teeth when he smiled,
flashing dark eyes—she could not hide her growing preoccupation
with this young fellow who was becoming a hero, and she had even
begun to speculate on what life would be like with such a man. She
confessed to herself that she was seriously attracted to Nate, and
once this was admitted she found herself powerless to hide the fact
from her brother.

"He seems so decent" was all she said, to which LeRoy replied:
"He's a half-breed."

"Aren't we all?" she asked, and there the philosophical part of the
discussion ended, for LeRoy added a practical note: "We better get
you out of here, Floss. We're heading into a mountain blizzard."

He now had an extra reason to speed the rescue, so on the morning of the fourth day they unloaded every bit of gear the Cub could
spare and took off for the mountains. When they found Killer he
was, as they had expected, down at a much lower level where there
were areas of snow extensive enough for a ski plane to land, but the
quality of the snow was dubious. "It doesn't look packed," LeRoy
told the others as he circled not far from where the dog waited, "and
it's certainly not flat."

"You can do it," Flossie said, and it was good that she spoke first,
for Nate was quite sure that the snowbanks were so sloping that the
plane could not land, while LeRoy was uncertain. In the silence that
greeted her enthusiastic endorsement, Flossie said nothing. She was
only sixteen that year, a quiet girl not given to expressing her ideas
boldly in front of strange men, but now when it appeared that they
might turn back, she repeated her verdict: "You can do it, LeRoy.
Over there. You've landed on worse," so in silence the three adventurers approached the more-or-less-level space she had indicated, but
when they saw it close up, even Flossie began to doubt that they
could make it.

But at this moment Killer, aware that something special was
under way, since no food had been dropped, began to leap and bark
in wild excitement, and although they could not hear his cries of encouragement, they knew what he was doing, and Nate said: "Let's go
down." Breathing very deeply to settle his nerves, and adjusting three
or four different times to his pilot's seat, LeRoy asked quietly: "Nate,
you strapped in? Floss, you tied in with those ropes?" Clearing his

throat and swinging his shoulders about to ensure that he would have relatively free movement if required, LeRoy brought his plane in for a mountain landing that would have daunted the average practiced pilot and frightened even the best Alaskan bush pilots.

Over a crest of rocks he brought the Cub down across a heavily rumpled field of snow and onto the fairly flat space where Killer waited. As the plane neared the ground the occupants saw that it was much more tilted to the right than they had anticipated from aloft, and for just a moment LeRoy judged that he ought to abort this dangerous landing, but from the rear Flossie shouted: "It's all right! Better spot on ahead!" and with just a bit more gas her brother kept the plane aloft until he saw the place where he could land.

With a whoosh that terrified Killer waiting below, the plane's two skis reached for the snow while the Cub tilted perilously to the right, as if it were going to tumble down the slope, but then better levels were reached, the plane righted itself, and the skis glided to an easy stop. Before even the doors were opened, Killer was leaping upon the struts and barking his delight at seeing once more a thing he had despised.

Nate, of course, was first out, for the access door was on his side, and when Killer saw him alight the dog leaped into his arms and whimpered the equivalent of sobs of joy, and when LeRoy edged himself out of the plane, the dog ran to him too, licking at him as if past enmities were forgiven. But when Flossie descended, a person Killer had never seen or smelled before, he started at her with a menacing growl. Giving him a solid kick, Nate snapped: "Down, you damned fool. She's the one who rescued you," and to Killer's dismay, his master turned away from him and took Flossie in his arms.

When the two Flatches returned to their cabin at Matanuska, LeRoy convened an emergency session of the family, to whom he reported: "Flossie's been kissin' a half-breed named Nate Coop."

"He the one who owns the dog?" Elmer asked, and LeRoy said: "The same," and the whole weight of the family fell upon silent Flossie. Elmer pointed out that "acrost the states of the two Dakotas and all of Minnesota, no marriage of a white man to no Indian woman, or vicey versey, has ever worked. It's agin the law of nature."

Hilda Flatch, generous in most of her judgments, warned: "You know him for four days! Ridiculous! Besides, Indians drink. They beat their wives and ignore their children."

And LeRoy said, with a perspicacity that surprised everyone: "Why would you bother with a half-breed when you have that perfectly good Vickaryous boy available?"

And suddenly Paulus Vickaryous, scion of the Finnish family about whom the Flacks had always been cool, became a paragon, a young man who knew how to farm and who had acquired land of his own, a responsible fellow who attended the Lutheran church regularly and saved money. He was, according to Flossie's family, about the finest young American or Canadian of this generation, and they began inviting him to dinner.

He was a tall young man with the attractive light-blond hair that nature had given the Finns, whose fair skin could attract even the slightest of the sun's rays that hit their forbidding land. He was well educated, well mannered and as good a farmer as Elmer had said. There was no conceivable reason why a girl like Flossie would not want to marry a man as promising as Paulus, except that she had lost her heart to Nate Coop, his mountains and his dog.

So after young Vickaryous had been rebuffed three or four times in ways so blatant that he could not fail to receive the message, he stopped appearing at the Flatch cabin, and the restrained fury of the Flatch family began to envelop poor Flossie. Day after day she heard stories of how Indian men mistreated their women, and of how no Indian could ever stay sober three weeks in a row, and of how, if you took a hundred miners, Indian or white, ninety-six of them never amounted to a damn. An outsider, listening to the Flatches berating their headstrong daughter, would have concluded that the girl was a delinquent who merited the scorn she was suffering. And certainly the listener would have supposed that young Flossie would never again be allowed to speak with her Indian half-breed.

But in this extremity she found a powerful champion, one prepared to sweep away the cobwebs of the past and misunderstandings of the present. The presumptive widow Melissa Peckham had remained at Matanuska as the representative of the Alaskan territorial government and it was often her counsel that enabled the teetering settlement to find a stable balance. She met with wives unable to accept the interminable winters: "You should have seen the Klondike in February. I made fifty, sixty pancakes at a time. Stacked 'em outside the cabin, dealt 'em off one by one as the hungry men came in. Frozen solid—the pancakes, not the men. Thaw 'em out. Heat 'em up, douse 'em in syrup, and away we go. One stack would last maybe two weeks."

To the husbands defeated by floods and freezes she said: "Now, Mr. Vasanoja, do you think for one minute that life back in Minnesota would be one bit better for you if you returned? For the banker, already there with his millions stolen from the poor, yes, it would be better. And for the sheriff with his big Buick, yes, lots better. But for you, a Finn with no savings? Mr. Vasanoja, did I ever tell you about how my man Murphy rode a bicycle a thousand miles to find his gold mine, and found nothin'?" Missy had in her youth spoken flawless English, but in the gold fields she had on occasion adopted the language of the frontier until she sometimes spoke like the toughest woodsman.

It was this woman, a sixty-six-year-old social worker and mining-camp veteran, who now stepped in to defend Flossie Flatch. Meeting with the girl's distraught family, she glared at them and said: "You remind me of law sessions they used to have in the gold fields before the North West Mounted moved in. Some miner would do somethin' the rest didn't approve of, so they'd hold a court in a saloon, and eight men who'd done a lot worse things would pass judgment on him. Ridiculous." She glared at the older Flatches and said: "You're doin' the same with Flossie. You're really not qualified to judge. This is a new world with new rules."

When she had their attention she said: "Of course he's a half-breed, but so is most of Alaska, one way or another. I've seen a score of good marriages with full-blooded Eskimos and Indians. You, LeRoy, you fly the Venns around, don't you? Surely you've seen that young Venn's wife is a half-breed, haven't you? Chinese and Tlingit. And those very wealthy Lincoln Arkikovs down in Juneau—Siberian and Yup'ik. My daughter married an Arkikov, and I'm damn proud of her family." And then she uttered the simple statement that summarized so much Alaskan life: "You want to be happy up here, you better learn the rules."

"But don't the Indians always drink too much?" Hilda Flatch asked, and Missy snapped: "Sometimes. Alcohol and suicide, the twin curses of the native people. But in good marriages the risk is no greater than with white men and women in general."

"But how would a half-breed like him ever find a steady job?"

Elmer asked, and this infuriated the feisty older woman: "Mr. Flatch, you amaze me. You want guarantees. I don't see you with a steady job. When my husband was alive he used to ask me: 'Why doesn't a reliable man like Elmer Flatch get himself a steady job?' and I said: 'Looks like to me he's makin' a better livin' than you are.'"

Allowing this sharp attack to relax, she asked for a drink—"Anything handy"—and said with a gentleness much removed from her previous arguments: "Now listen to me, you too, Flossie. Years ago, in Chicago, I was a fairly acceptable-looking young woman. Straight teeth, nice hair, a good education. I've never married. Always fell in love with men who already had wives. Great, wonderful men, best in the world, but never free to marry me. So . . . Life comes at you in a thousand different forms, and you better be prepared to accept it when it comes along. Because if you miss it, the years stretch out forever, bleak and lonely and meaningless."

When no one commented, she said with a renewed brightness: "So, you fine Flatches who aren't really as fine as you think you are, nor am I, nor are the Vickaryouses that you've been courtin' . . . It was an accident, a cruel accident perhaps, that this Flossie, who is such a good girl, flew into that mining camp and met Nate Coop. I know nothin' about him except that he took great pains to save his dog. You took your sister there, LeRoy, hotshot pilot, so the blame's on you. Could be the best thing you ever did, because I am going to do everything I can to help your sister marry that boy."

But when she saw the truly tormented faces of all the Flatches but Flossie, she had to try to help them understand the situation: "All right! I agree with you. According to LeRoy, he's an illiterate oaf with hair in his eyes and a grunt for hello. But he's lived in the woods with people who know no better. Marriage in Alaska is often a woman with good sense and an overdose of humanity marryin' a clod like this Nate and civilizin' him. So if your Flossie can tame a moose, she can sure civilize young Mr. Coop."

When Missy finally stomped out of the house, she left expecting that the Flatches would make some kind of conciliatory gesture to their daughter, but what Hilda said was: "If you marry that damned half-breed, your father will throw you out of this house . . . and I'll help." But when Nate flew down to Matanuska in the plane of another bush pilot to present himself to the Flatch family, they had to admit that he seemed like a manly young fellow, with good, though awkward, manners, but he was frighteningly dark-skinned and his features were hopelessly Indian. If Flossie were going to live in the wilderness, he might be acceptable as a son-in-law, but in ordinary town life with other people he was painfully inferior to Paulus Vick-aryous. And he had made the grave error of bringing with him his dog Killer, who showed his growling dislike for all the Flatches, in-cluding Flossie. So when Nate in mumbling fashion asked for Floss-ie's hand, with Killer snarling in the background, all of the Flatches replied with a clear-cut "No!"

Unwilling to accept this as a final answer, Nate remained in the vicin-ity for some days, then vanished. However, he did write to Flossie, but Mrs. Flatch appropriated the letters, and when this was discov-ered by Flossie's asking at the post office if any mail had come in for her, she so informed Missy Peckham, who stormed out to the cabin with some harsh news: "Hilda Flatch, if you prevent United States mail from reachin' its intended owner, you can go to jail. You hand over those letters, right now, to me as an agent of the government. And don't be a damned fool."

When the letters were delivered to Flossie, she carried them home unopened and told her mother: "I'm not mad. You did what you thought was right. But I want to read them here in my own home with you watching," and with a long kitchen knife she opened the letters, one by one, and read them in silence. As she finished each one she handed it over to her mother, sitting on the opposite side of the kitchen table, and that night she wrote to Nate.

As a consequence of this exchange of letters, Nate Coop flew down to Matanuska at the time of year when the three George Lakes could be expected to break through the great glacier wall; Flossie had told him that she wanted to see it actually happen this year and he had come to take her up the Knik River to witness it. He lodged at Missy Peckham's place and came to the Flatch cabin only twice, for when he appeared the second time the older Flatches made it clear that he was not welcome, and he left.

They were shocked, some days later, when Flossie disappeared, and no one could guess where she might have gone; Missy said her lodger had left too, and she supposed they might have flown to Seattle to get married, but when Hilda, who was especially opposed to Coop, ransacked her daughter's mail she found in one of Nate's letters a reference to the dramatic breakup of the lakes, with the comment: "That would be a neat thing to see." Shuddering, she called her son, but he was absent on a trip to Venn's Lode, and by the time he returned it was too dark for him to do anything about finding his sister.

But in the morning he acceded to his mother's wild laments, revved up his Cub, now on wheels, and set out to scout the surrounding countryside, and as he flew up the Knik River toward the glacier he saw, near the promontory from which the shattering collapse of the glacier would best be viewed, a white canvas tent. Dropping low, he buzzed the place, and was relieved but also distressed to see two young people emerge—obviously from sleeping bags, for their hair was disheveled and they wore what could be taken for pajamas or some kind of slapdash substitute. Although he could not identify the pair, he was pretty sure they must be Flossie and Nate, and his uncertainty was removed in a way which infuriated him: the dog Killer burst out of the tent and began yapping at the plane.

Signaling to them by dipping his wings, he made another circuit, now flying so low that he could see their faces, but at this moment his attention was distracted by a gigantic pillar of spume soaring high in the air. The ice plugs which had held the three lakes captive during the past ten months had exploded, and the long-imprisoned waters were now roaring free. LeRoy in his plane, his sister and Nate from in front of their tent, watched in awe as this titanic force broke loose, for as the waters struck the face of the glacier they carved away massive icebergs, which began their tortuous way down the tempestuous river, gouging out smaller icebergs as they ground and jostled and carved their way along. It was the most violent manifestation of nature any of the three had ever seen, and LeRoy circled over the cascading waters and the crumbling icebergs for half an hour, after which he buzzed the tent once more, dipping his wings to the lovers and their excited dog.

When he landed at Palmer he hurried out to the cabin, rushed in, looked at his apprehensive parents, and said: "Well, now they got to get married."

The four Flatches had been so preoccupied with their own affairs, they had remained oblivious to the irresistible manner in which world history had been creeping up on them. In June 1941 the prediction that Air Corps Captain Shafter had made at the Palmer Airstrip in the winter of 1940 came true; Nazi Germany declared total war against Communist Russia, and what Shafter had seen to be an illogical alliance came to an end. This meant, the other pilots at the airstrip pointed out, that "Russia will probably be our ally, if we ever get into this thing." And the more knowing, with whom LeRoy did not associate, began to look more closely at that very narrow stretch of the Bering Sea separating the Soviet Union from Alaska.

At about this time even LeRoy became aware that someone, Canadian or American, he could never tell which, was expressing interest in a chain of would-be airports—skimpy strips in the wilderness, really—linking Edmonton in Canada to Fairbanks in Alaska, and he wondered what was afoot. Once more Leonidas Shafter, a major now, appeared in Palmer with a request, or perhaps it was an order, that all bush pilots in the region meet with him:

> "American participation in the war's inevitable. How we'll enter is anybody's guess. I think Hitler will do something stupid in Europe. The *Lusitania* all over again. But something. Or maybe Russia will begin to fall. When that happens, right here where you are in Alaska becomes of utmost importance.

> "So what we're about to do in anticipation, is rush into being this line of airports, call them emergency landing strips, from Great Falls down here in Montana to Edmonton up here in Canada and over to Fairbanks in Alaska. Then we'll use the little Yukon River strips already existing from Ladd Field in Fairbanks to Nome. To accomplish this we must have the cooperation of you flyboys familiar with the territory."

This time he had with him a map marked Secret, and after asking anyone not a pilot to leave the room, he tacked it onto the wall behind him. It was almost identical to one of those he had displayed on his previous visit, except that this time it had a linked chain of some dozen red stars glued to little-known villages or river crossings in northern Montana, western Canada and eastern Alaska:

> "If you tried to walk the last part of that route, Edmonton to Fairbanks, it'd take about two years, supposing you had a good Indian guide and an airplane to drop supplies. To drive it, maybe fifteen years, granted that the two countries ever woke up to build a road through that wilderness . . . or could do it if they did decide. What we're going to do is build us

eleven emergency fields, right now, and since there are no roads along most of this route, you men are going to fly the equipment in, right now.

"Of course, from the opposite end here in Edmonton, another group of guys just like you will be flying in their share of the cargo. So as of tonight, now, you are all enlisted in one of the damnedest projects Alaska has ever seen. Building airfields where there have never been any. We want you, and we want your planes. An office will be established in Anchorage and I've asked two officers to work out of here, starting right now. Captain Marshal, Army Air Forces. Major Catlett, Army Corps of Engineers. Start signing them up, Officers."

The two officers were delighted to learn that LeRoy Flatch owned, more or less, two airplanes, the two-seater Cub and the four-seater Waco, but they were taken aback when he allowed as how he would lease out the four-seater and keep the two-seater for himself: "It carries more. It can do more things. And when it crashes you walk away from it more often."

So he dropped all other obligations, except for borrowing back his four-seater occasionally for a hurried flight to ferry the Venns into their camp at the base of Denali, and flew one tedious flight after another with huge loads of cargo for the incipient airstrips in the wilderness. The system of linked airfields, primitive and provisional though it was, bore the exalted title the Northwest Staging Route, and since its various components came into service at the most uneven times, with an extremely difficult base operational five months before a much easier one, flights along it were spasmodic, but workhorse pilots like Flatch became accustomed to stops like Watson Lake, Chicken and Tok, with occasional flights to unheard-of places between Fairbanks and Nome. "When we get this damned thing finished," Lieutenant Colonel Shafter told his crews at the various construction bases, "we'll have a first-class route from Detroit to Moscow, because I can tell you the Russians are doing the same on their side of the Bering Sea."

After LeRoy had been serving for six months on the Northwest Route, Colonel Shafter, who seemed able to work twenty-two hours a day when things were going smoothly, thirty-six at times of crisis, and to win a promotion every five months, flew into Palmer Airstrip with surprising news: "Flatch, I've been watching you. They don't come any better. I want you to trade back your four-seater Waco. Give whoever has it your old Cub and become my personal pilot for the whole route, Great Falls to Nome."

"Does this mean I have to join the Air Corps?"

"Not yet. Later on, when we get into this thing, probably."

But his new job did mean that LeRoy had to learn to fly again, for Shafter's job required flying over such vast unexplored areas north of the tree line that the old safeguards of bush-piloting no longer prevailed. "Son," Shafter said in the midst of one dangerous flight, "you got wheels on your crate and skis and you could have pontoons, but none of them is worth a damn if we have to land on tundra down there," and two days later he had a pair of "tundra" tires flown in. They were enormously wide balloonlike affairs inflated only partially, which enabled Flatch to land on humpy or even slightly marshy tundra. But the tires were so huge they altered the flight characteristics of any plane using them, and this required LeRoy to avoid things a prudent pilot would normally do.

A flier familiar with tundra tires instructed him: "Since the tires can't be retracted, no tight turns at low or even moderate speed. The tundras will drag you into a spin. Your maximum altitude will be cut by about two thousand feet. When you land, don't rush things, just sort of skip along. And most important, the wind drag of these monsters cuts your maximum range on a full tank by a large factor."

LeRoy said: "You sound as if using the tundras converts the Waco into a whole new plane," and the pilot said: "You've learned your lesson. Now respect it." But once Flatch adjusted to this plane with its monstrous tires, he gained the ultimate refinement in his career as a bush pilot. Now he really could land almost anywhere.

Confident but never cocky, he flew over the most forbidding terrain, landing occasionally at sites that would have caused the average pilot to shudder, and in the air he exercised stern command, for no matter what some frightened general shouted at him, he would say quietly: "Sit back, sir. I'm gonna land on that stuff right below us, so keep your belt tight." Half a dozen times he terrified Shafter, but after one such flight ended safely, Shafter said: "You did the right thing, son. You bush pilots seem to operate under your own rules of aerodynamics."

As paperwork for the route neared completion, Flatch underwent three emotional experiences. The first came on the Sunday when news of the bombing of Pearl Harbor reached the temporary base at

Chicken at about the same time as a lone American P-40 fighter plane reached that field on a multistop flight from a point near Pittsburgh. The war that Captain Shafter had so clearly foreseen had erupted, and that night, before a startled judge stopping over in Chicken, LeRoy Flatch was sworn into the Air Corps as a second lieutenant, ordinary requirements having been waived.

The second moment he would never forget came in the following January when he received word that his old two-seater Cub had crashed at Fort Nelson, over in Canada. He flew General Shafter there to investigate, and found that a young pilot straight from training camp in California had become engulfed in a whiteout: "General, you couldn't see nothing. Sky, snow, ground all the same. We got two planes down by lighting fires. This boy never knew where he was, but he says calm as you please, I was on the radio: 'Pretty soupy up here . . . everywhere,' and two minutes later he comes roaring down, nose right into the snow, as you see it over there." The plane was a wipeout, its loss more grievous because Flatch was certain that had he been at the controls, it could have been saved.

"You want a photograph of it?" the general asked, and LeRoy said: "No."

"Come on, lad. It was a part of your life. Fifty years from now you'll cherish the memory of this day," and he led LeRoy to the shattered plane, indistinguishable as to make or number, and they were photographed together, the tough young general, the quiet young lieutenant and the 1927 Cub they had both respected.

The third experience was an extraordinary one, for when huge cadres of young Russian pilots began flooding into Ladd Field, Fairbanks, in late 1942 to pick up the American planes they would fly across to Siberia, General Shafter assigned Flatch to special duty at Nome, where a large segment of the historic gold field was converted into the last staging point prior to flight into Siberia. Here LeRoy was to give the daring Russian fliers who would convoy the planes all the way to Moscow, then under dreadful siege, whatever assistance they required, and he was on duty one morning when an unusual Russian pilot came to him, speaking not perfect but very good English: "I am Lieutenant Maxim Voronov. My ancestor Arkady Voronov turned Alaska over to you Americans, 18 and 67. No planes coming, I like to see maybe Sitka. You can take me, yes?"

The idea was so startling that Flatch tried to get in touch with Shafter, but when that proved impossible, he said to the Russian:

"General Shafter told me to do everything within reason to help you. If you make a formal request, we'll go." So Voronov made his request; LeRoy wrote it down; an enlisted man at Nome Base phoned the message over to Fairbanks; and without waiting for a reply, Flatch and Voronov were on their way to the big base at Anchorage, where they obtained a seaplane for the flight to Sitka, which at that time had no landing facilities except in the sound.

It was a bright day, with the sun glistening off the glaciers and the manifold little islands shining in the Pacific like drops of crystal resting on blue satin. Voronov had apparently studied the history of Russian Alaska with some care, for when the seaplane was well aloft he told the pilot from the right front seat, which he occupied: "I would to appreciate much if you show me Kayak Island," and when the plane flew over that strange elongated island on which Vitus Bering's Russians had first landed, LeRoy, sitting in the back seat, saw that Voronov had tears in his eyes. Flatch, never having heard of Kayak Island and seeing it now only as a desolate place which no one would want to bother with, asked what the island signified, but Voronov, studying the terrain with unusual care, indicated that he would explain later.

The visit to Sitka, which LeRoy had seen only twice before when dropping down to pick up military guests for General Shafter, was a powerful experience for both men. Voronov tried to pick out the places where his ancestors had lived: he recognized the Russian church with its onion dome, and he very much wanted to go to the hill on which Baranov's Castle had stood, but during these war years, when an invasion by the Japanese was always a possibility, the mount was restricted to the few military personnel who manned batteries there and in the vicinity.

But Voronov astonished Flatch by knowing in the most intimate detail the conduct of the various battles that had marked the prolonged combat between Russian and Tlingit warriors, and the probable location of the palisades that had once enclosed the town. He knew where the old Tlingit village had been outside the walls and where the lake was from which one of his ancestors had cut ice for sale in San Francisco. He was particularly interested in where the ships had been built for the trade with Hawaii, and he quite startled both Flatch and the pilot of the seaplane by asking whether they could fly down to the famous hot springs south of Sitka.

Permission to do so was difficult to arrange, but an Aleut with a Russian name was designated to take the three travelers, and when the seaplane landed in the bay that fronted the hill from whose side the springs erupted, the pilot remained with the plane while the others climbed up the slope to the springs, where in a rickety house built decades before, they stripped and let themselves down into the hot and sulfurous waters.

As they luxuriated, Flatch thought how strange it was that a great war should have been the instrument which brought this Russian back to the land where his ancestors had served with apparent distinction, but it was the Aleut-Russian guide who was most deeply moved. He spoke no Russian, of course, but he told Voronov of how *his* ancestors had served the Russians in Kodiak Island and then later just north of San Francisco, and Voronov listened attentively, asking many questions as to how the American possessors had treated the Aleuts when they occupied the area. The guide said: "Pretty well. They let us keep our church here. Up till the 1917 revolution, our priest got his salary from Moscow," and Voronov, splashing water on his face, nodded.

When the time came to depart Sitka a local woman who attended the Russian church came to Voronov with a curious reminder of the Russian days: it was an invitation to a dance held annually in Sitka, this one dated 1940, and it had been issued in the name of Prince and Princess Maksutov as if they still occupied the palace: "When we dance, sir, we imagine that the nobility sits on the sidelines as in the old day up in the castle, watching us with approval." She kissed Voronov's hand and said: "We remember your great ancestor well. May you enjoy victory."

When she was gone, Flatch asked: "What great ancestor?" and Voronov explained: "A Voronov who served in that church over there, wonderful man, in touch with God, I think. Served out here on the edge of nowhere and became so holy that they called him back to Moscow to become head of all the churches in Russia."

"Catholic?" LeRoy asked.

"Not Roman, Orthodox. He married an Aleut woman, one of God's great messengers. So I'm part Aleut. That's why the man in the bath . . ." He surprised Flatch by asking: "On the way back to Nome, could we to stop by the Totem Salmon Cannery, on Taku Inlet?"

"You know these waters better than I do," LeRoy said, and Voronov replied: "A son of the great religious leader—I think it was—he discovered that place where the cannery was. Our family has all the records."

So they flew the short detour to Taku Inlet, and up toward the closed end, where the great glaciers came snouting down, Flatch saw the cannery buildings about which he'd previously had no knowledge. "They're immense!" he shouted to the front seat.

"Want me to land?" the pilot asked.

"No need," Voronov said. "But I would like you to fly up that little river. One of my family, Arkady, wrote a poem about it. Pleiades the lake is called at the source."

So the seaplane wound its way inland the short distance to Lake Pleiades, where the three men saw the seven lovely mountains and the cool waters in which salmon bred, and from there they flew along the chain of glaciers back to Anchorage, where Flatch's plane waited for the direct hop to Nome. There American pilots were delivering specially equipped planes for the Moscow front, and Lieutenant Maxim Voronov, twenty-two years old, climbed into one of them, listened to fifteen minutes of instruction, and took off for Siberia. He did not offer any emotional farewells to LeRoy Flatch, merely said: "Thank you," and was off to the wars. In succeeding days some forty of these special planes passed through Nome, and to each of the Russians who took them over, some American said: "Give Hitler hell!" or "Hold fast till we get there," or something like that.

Next morning as LeRoy shaved he reflected on his somewhat perplexing experience with Lieutenant Voronov, and concluded that he had better report it to General Shafter: "He said his name was Lieutenant Maxim Voronov and we had better record his name, for I'm sure he'll be back this way again," but when he did not reappear, LeRoy assumed he had been killed in the air battles over Moscow.

Each male member of the Flatch family had his life seriously disrupted by World War II, and each made a signal contribution to the defense of Alaska, and thereby of the United States itself: LeRoy in the construction of the aviation lifeline which helped save Moscow; brother-in-law Nate Coop as a foot soldier in one of the most confused and demanding battles of the war; and father Elmer in an activity he could never have anticipated. The two young men participated in ways that were extensions of their civilian lives, aviation and outdoor activity, but Elmer was propelled into a life for which he had practically no preparation. He did know how to drive a car, and that was about it.

He was drafted into civilian service by Missy Peckham. As representative of the territorial government she appeared at the cabin one morning with astounding news: "Elmer, the United States has wakened up at last. The dunderheads in Washington see that Alaska's of vital importance. Japanese might land here at any moment and cut our connections with Russia."

"LeRoy's busy building them emergency airfields."

"You're gonna be buildin' a lot more than a bunch of puny airstrips."

"Like what?"

She evaded this direct challenge: "Alaskans always dream of somethin' additional. When I was young we wanted a railroad, Anchorage to Fairbanks. Nothin' but empty land. But in 1923, President Harding himself came here to drive the golden spike. Of course, he died right after. Some blamed poisoned clams he ate here, others claimed his lady friend in California did him in."

"And what do you want us to build now?"

"A highway for automobiles. Right across the worst land in the world. Bindin' us to the Lower Forty-eight."

"And we always decided it was an impossibility. Have a beer?"

As they sat in the Flatch kitchen, with Hilda watching from her corner, Missy unrolled a map provided her by an army detachment based in Anchorage: "We're gonna build a first-class military highway parallelin' the airstrips your son is buildin'," and she revealed the thin red line that would connect Edmonton down in Canada with all the airfields coming into being across the bleakest part of the northwest and into Fairbanks. If building the little airstrips in that wilderness had staggered General Shafter and his airmen, constructing a highway would present difficulties that were unimaginable.

"It can't be done," Elmer said flatly, and Missy replied: "In time of war, it can."

On her map she showed him the results of Allied thinking about the highway that would forever link the United States and Canada, if it could be constructed: "Canadians wanted it to be more or less a coastal road so it could serve their western settled areas, or so they told us at the briefing. The wild men who love the arctic, they wanted to follow that hellish route my man Murphy took in 1897, right up the Mackenzie River damned near to the Arctic Circle, then across mountains and into Fairbanks. The square-headed Americans said: 'We'll take the middle way, the Prairie Route, where the airstrips are already in.' And that's the road you'll be buildin', Elmer."

"Me?"

"You and your truck. Report to Big Delta soonest with a full kit of tools, and start construction from this end."

"I don't know anything about road buildin'!"

"You'll learn." And she was off to enroll the older Vickaryous, Vasanoja and Krull men.

In all, some four hundred Alaskan civilians were conscripted more or less forcibly into the work force that would build over a thousand miles of roadway in Canada, more than two hundred miles in Alaska. They were ordered to complete this gargantuan task in no more than eight months. "We expect to have army trucks filled with battle gear coming over this road by October first," the colonel in charge of Elmer's segment roared whenever anything went wrong. To make this possible, the Americans would provide nearly twelve thousand men in uniform, the Canadians as large a contingent as their population would allow.

The Alcan Highway it was officially dubbed, a roadway that had always been dreamed about by those in the north and one which might have come into being, under normal circumstances, sometime in the early twenty-first century, for the cost was horrendous and the obstacles terrifying. In wartime it would be built, incredible as it seemed, in eight months and twelve days.

When Elmer Flatch reported to army headquarters in Fairbanks he was told to deliver his truck to the central depot and take personal delivery of a huge Caterpillar tractor big enough to knock down trees or haul heavily loaded ten-wheel trucks out of ditches. "I never drove a thing like that," he protested, and the lieutenant in charge of the depot growled: "Start now."

Three of the regiments assigned to duty in the Alaskan sectors were all-black except for white officers, and a big, slope-shouldered black man who had operated dozers in Georgia was in charge of instructing civilians like Flatch in the intricacies of handling the behemoths that would be chopping a roadway through terrain that had hitherto seemed impassable. This huge fellow, Sergeant Hanks, gave concise, sensible instructions in a pronounced Georgia drawl which the Alaskans found difficult to understand: "Learnin' gear shift, chir'n do that. Learnin' stay alive, some you surely fail, we bury you."

Hanks said, with endless repetitions and illustrations, that a driver had to feel in his ass, not his brain, when a slope was too tilted to be negotiated by this dozer: "Not up and down slope, even chir'n handle that."

"What in hell is chir'n," a Minnesota Swede asked, and Hanks explained: "Chir'n. Boys, girls. I got four chir'ns back home. How many you got?"

The perilous slopes that he warned against, the ones that killed careless men by the score, were those which tilted the Cat sideways, especially to the left: "Cat fall right, maybe got a chance. Fall left, crush you ever' time." He repeated that a driver had to feel in his ass, not his brain or with the aid of his eye, when the slope, left or right, was becoming too steep to be negotiated: "You feel that message, back to hell out. And doan' try turnin'. Jes' back out like you back out from a dark room where you hears a ghost."

Under Hanks's repetitious instruction Elmer Flatch, and other ordinary men like him, began to master the intricacies of the great Caterpillars, and after an indoctrination period that seemed perilously brief, they were sent forth to do the job. In early May, Flatch found himself ten miles east of the little town of Tok, where the road from Eagle drops down from Chicken, and he had been on the job only a few hours when a major in the Corps of Engineers started bellowing at him: "You, there. With the coonskin cap. Take your Cat down there and help pull the other Cat back on its tracks." And when Elmer obeyed, he came upon two machines bigger than his own mired in mud as they strove to bring back, upright, a small dozer which had slid down a small slope.

When his Cat was attached by wires to the fallen behemoth, and all three machines pulled in unison, the creature at the bottom of the slope slowly righted itself, whereupon the major screamed: "Hold it! You, there, get the body!" and Elmer remained with his wires taut, as medical corpsmen pried the shattered body of the careless driver free from the seat into which he had been crushed. Watching the gruesome process, Elmer said aloud: "His ass didn't send him the message." Pause. "More likely it arrived but he didn't listen."

The most useful member of the team at Tok was neither wise Sergeant Hanks nor hard-driving Major Carnon, but a short, stubborn Athapascan Indian named Charley. He had a second name, of course, probably something English like Dawkins or Hammond after some early goldminer who had married his great-grandmother up by

Fort Yukon, but no one knew what it was. Charley's job was to grease the Cats and dozers and help install new tracks when the old ones jammed or broke or wore out, but his principal value lay in his eagerness to inform majors and colonels and generals from the Lower Forty-eight when they were about to do something which worked very well down in Oklahoma or Tennessee but which simply did not function up in Alaska. So when he saw well-intentioned Major Carnon preparing to build his road east of Tok the way he had done so often in Arkansas, he felt he must warn the energetic fellow that he was making one big mistake: "Major, sir, down there, maybe okay strip off the topsoil, make solid base. Up here we don't do that."

"Keep those dozers moving forward!" Carnon bellowed, whereupon Charley said quietly, but with some force: "Major, sir, we don't do that up here."

"Keep moving!"

So Charley bided his time, returned to his work area, and resumed threading a new track on a dozer which had shattered its right tread in trying to knock down a nest of trees just a mite too big for it to handle. With a sense of disgust, the knowing Indian watched as Major Carnon stripped away the topsoil until a firm base was reached, and when this desecration continued, he sought out Elmer Flatch, whose dozer he had often serviced: "Flatch, you got to warn the major, we don't do that up here."

Another dozer man, from Utah, hearing the warning, broke in: "You always clear away the soft topsoil till you get a firm base. Then you build. Otherwise you got nothin'."

"Up here we do it different," Charley warned, but still finding no one to listen, he resumed his work, satisfied that after the warm May sun did its work on Major Carnon's roadbed, the know-it-all white men would pay attention.

Charley's message was verified on the twenty-third of May. Early that morning, when Elmer reported to work, he encountered an amazing sight: his monstrous Cat had sunk six feet into the solid earth, leaving only the top of the cab visible. Well, the earth wasn't really all that solid; it had been, three days before when the topsoil was scraped off, laying bare the permafrost, but the sun had melted the frost at an alarming rate, turning what had been almost rigid soil—ideal for serving as a road base—into a quagmire. Not only had Flatch's Cat practically disappeared, but three others had begun to sink into the pit provided by the melting permafrost.

Three days of sheer hell ensued, for as the sun's heat intensified with the coming of summer, the permafrost continued to melt at lower levels, sucking the great machines down and down. Of course, where the topsoil had been allowed to remain in place, protecting the frost from the sun, the whole earth structure had preserved its solid nature, and this was merciful, because a contingent of smaller bull-dozers could move in upon the still-firm ground and haul away at the stranded ones. But the suction of the mud, which seemed bottomless and determined to hold on to anything that fell into its maw, made recovery most difficult.

Cursing, swearing and groaning, the men of the black regiment struggled to rescue their precious Cats, and on some days they suc-ceeded only in surrendering one or two new ones to the tenacious mud. Major Carnon spent three frantic days trying this trick and that to lure his great machines out of their viscous prisons and watching in despair as they sank always deeper into their glutinous graves.

On the third evening, when he seemed powerless to halt the dev-astation, he motioned Charley to sit with him: "I didn't listen, Char-ley. You warned me. What is this stuff?" and the Indian told him about the problems that permafrost presented to builders in Alaska: "Not everywhere. Only in the north. Hundred miles down that way, none," and he pointed to the south.

"Why didn't we build down there?"

"Too close to the ocean. Japanese ships come, shell road, finish." Careful not to gloat over the major's discomfiture, he added: "This middle way definitely best. Use permafrost right, you get damn good road."

"What is the right way?"

Ignoring the question, Charley told of his experiences as a builder's helper in Fairbanks: "Strange city. Permafrost line runs right through middle, I think. Houses here, permafrost plenty. Same street, down here, none. Very important to know, because suppose you got perma-frost under your concrete slab? Heat from human bodies, you don't need no furnace, nothin', just people. It collects in slab, begins to seep down into permafrost, begins to melt, here, there, house winds up on a slant. Sometimes big slant. Sometimes maybe have to leave house."

"How do you avoid it?"

"Like on your road. Leave topsoil in place. Don't move nothin'." Far over to side, dig some more topsoil, pile on top road, high, high. Pack down. You know that thing they call *sheep hooves*?"

"Yes. Lots of little iron knobs, packs earth like sheep walking over it."

"Pack down the extra, tight, tight. You get yourself good road-bed."

As soon as Carnon heard the solution he saw the problem: "How far from the roadbed would we have to go for our topsoil? Too close, the whole area would melt down."

"Ah ha, Major Carnon! You one smart man. Some dig too close, everything melts. I like to go about a hundred yards." He considered this for a while, then asked: "You got lots of wire rope?"

"Never enough. But yes, we got some."

"Tomorrow morning, put your good dozers way off the road. Solid footing maybe. They pull out the stuck ones."

So in the morning three good dozers were placed about fifty yards from the muddy road where the stricken Cats lay buried, and long lines of wire cable were attached to one of the vanished giants. It happened to be Flatch's and he helped supervise the operation, satisfying himself as he stood almost waist-deep in mud that the wires were properly fastened, then moving back as the three pulling dozers began to apply their strength. Slowly, and with vast loud cracking sounds as the Cat broke loose, Elmer's machine began its magical climb out of its prison.

Men cheered as its superstructure became visible, and Major Carnon ran here and there, directing this dozer or that to tighten its pull, and after about an hour of mortal struggle, Flatch's gigantic machine crawled back to life. Caked solidly in mud, it was barely recognizable as a bulldozer, but there it was, ready to be washed down, its vital parts still serviceable.

That night, when all the machines were back in operation, Major Carnon had his scribe draft a report to headquarters in Anchorage requesting that letters of commendation be forwarded to the civilians Elmer Flatch and Charley . . . Here he dispatched a messenger to find out the Indian's name.

It was a summer that those who worked on the Alcan would never forget. One black man with a science degree from Fisk University, who served as a private in the 97th Regiment, wrote to his fiancée in Atlanta:

*Our ship put us down in Skagway after one of the most
magnificent voyages you could imagine. Great mountains
coming down to the sea, glaciers throwing icebergs at us,
beautiful islands left and right. But the best part of all was
getting on a rickety old train at Skagway and riding right
through the biggest mountains you ever saw to a place in
Canada called Whitehorse. Come peace, you and I are going to
take our honeymoon on that railroad. Save your money and I'll
save mine, because there is nothing else like it in the world.*

*That was the end of the good times. From Whitehorse we
moved west to a section of the road you would not believe.
Mosquitoes as big as saucers, swamps without bottom, whole
forests to knock down with bulldozers, then on to the broken
stumps with saws, and to bed in tents, with never a hot meal for
days on end. Can you believe that in such circumstances we
build four miles of road on a good day, two miles even if it's
raining up to your armpits?*

*I miss you. I long for you, but almost no one up here
bellyaches. It's a road that must be built. Someday it could
save the nation.*

Elmer Flatch was one of those many Alaskans who did not bellyache
about the terrible conditions under which the Alcan Highway was
being built, for he better than most appreciated its significance.

At the height of the summer there were seven work groups spotted along the emerging highway at widely separated points, and each had half its force building to the east, half to the west, so that from the air, when work pilots like LeRoy Flatch's successors flew over, the Alcan looked like an endless succession of inchworms, each moving out in studied leaps to meet its neighbor. There were really fourteen separate roads being built that summer.

For Elmer Flatch, forty-five years old and beginning to feel the passing of the years, July and August of 1942 were the closest to hell that he would experience on this earth, for his fifteen- and sixteen-hour days were spent in an exhausting routine: drive through that copse of trees in a straight line, flattening evergreens big enough to produce spars for ships, attach wire ropes to the stumps and yank them out, push in topsoil from the surrounding areas, level the whole, ride back and forth in the interminable dust to compact the surface, fight mosquitoes all day long and especially at night, eat lousy food, and with the help of the able black troops and their efficient white officers finish off four miles before turning in to an exhausted but sometimes sleepless night.

One night as they worked not far from the Canadian border, Major Carnon, the indefatigable, proved that he was very fatigable indeed. As he sat with Elmer and Charley, surveying yet another bulldozer whose careless driver had ignored orders, sinking his machine in dark gumbo from which it might never return, tears came to his eyes and his voice broke. After a while he said: "Forty years from now, if we win this war, this road'll be blacktopped, and people will whisk by here in their Cadillacs. We've been at this damned lake three mud-soaked weeks and we've accomplished damned little. They'll whiz by in three minutes and not even see it. But it had to be done."

Next morning he lost his composure and shouted at another inept driver, who was failing pitifully to take any reasonable part in the rescue operation: "Get down off that dozer. Let a real man handle it," and he pointed to Elmer Flatch: "Show him how it's done."

Elmer knew only how to handle his own big machine; it had an inborn stability created by its sheer mass, and he did not feel at ease aboard a smaller machine which might have better maneuverability but also less reliability. Nevertheless, he climbed aboard the smaller machine, tested the controls, and gradually eased it back until he felt the two wire cables tighten. Waiting for the signal which would send the two other rescue dozers in motion, he adjusted himself to the unfamiliar seat and said: "Ass, send me messages."

The messages did come, warning him that he was placing the smaller bulldozer in a dangerous posture insofar as tension on the cables and torque from the treads was concerned, but it came in a version that Elmer did not immediately comprehend. Ignoring the signals, he applied more pressure, not wanting to lag behind the other two, and when the sunken tractor broke loose, almost springing out of its cavern, the other two drivers, well acquainted with their machines, relaxed tension immediately. Elmer did not. His bulldozer leaped backward, responded unevenly because of torque, and toppled sideways, pinning Elmer beneath it and crushing both his legs.

Major Carnon, seeing him fall under the dozer, was terrified that he might be dead, and it was he who first reached the spot where

Elmer lay trapped, with great courses of pain running up and down his body.

"Get him out of there!" Carnon screamed, but it was obviously impossible to do so while the dozer lay atop him.

"Come around this side," Charley shouted, and when the two other dozers were in position, he and Major Carnon attached the wire cables, but it was Charley who gave the effective orders to the two drivers: "Once you start back, don't stop for nothin'. You got to keep pullin'. You stop, it falls back down on him, he gone."

"Hold everything!" Major Carnon shouted. "You understand what Charley just said?"

"We got it," one of the drivers replied, and there in the bright sunlight for a brief moment the five actors in this dangerous drama froze: Flatch pinned in the mud, Major Carnon trying desperately to save his life, Indian Charley testing the wire cables, and the two dozer men preparing to move their machines slowly, purposefully backward.

"I'm going to count to three, then I'll yell 'Go!' And for Christ sake, pull even. If it twists sideways, it'll grind him to pieces."

Assuming a kneeling position by Flatch's head, so that he could protect him from anything that might slip or bounce off the downed machine, Carnon asked: "You ready, Flatch?" and when Elmer nodded, the major in loud voice gave the preliminary count, then shouted "Go!" The two drivers, obeying hand signals from Charley, eased the toppled bulldozer away, steadily and with no rotating motion. Flatch was saved, but his war was over. The medic who inspected his partially crushed legs said, almost cheerfully: "You were saved by the mud. Hard soil, your legs would've been pulverized." Examining him carefully and probing the tissues, he said: "Marvelous luck. I'm sure they won't have to amputate, soldier."

"I'm not a soldier," Flatch replied, determined not to faint.

Of the fourteen hundred and seven miles of the Alcan Highway, he had been instrumental in building sixty-one. Twenty-two men like him had been killed on the job; seven airplanes had crashed trying to deliver heavy supplies to the various camps; and many black soldiers and white Canadians had suffered severe injuries.

But on 20 October 1942 at a Canadian creek so small it appeared on few maps, Beaver Creek in Yukon Territory, Major Carnon, working south from Alaska, moved forward with his black troops to greet

Canadian workmen moving north. The great road, one of the mar-
vels of modern engineering, had been completed, so that trucks bearing the men and armaments required for the protection of the
continent could take position along the western reaches of Alaska.

Elmer Flatch, hospital-bound, could not be present to witness
this triumph of the human will, but Indian Charley was, standing a
few steps behind Major Carnon as the latter stepped forward to greet
the Canadians. When the brief ceremony ended, Charley whispered
to the major he had served so faithfully: "Up here we do it different.
But we get it done."

On the morning of 3 June 1942, when Elmer and the black troops
had barely begun building the life-saving Alcan, the people of the
United States, and especially those living in Alaska, were shocked by
the news that a daring Japanese task force, containing two aircraft
carriers and hiding behind the storm clouds which clustered permanently in this area of the Aleutians, had crept close to Unalaska, one
of the first big islands off the end of the Alaska peninsula, launched
bombing planes precisely as its predecessor had done six months before at Pearl Harbor, and brazenly bombed Dutch Harbor.

No great damage was done this time, for in the preceding months
America's 11th Army Air Force had secretly constructed undetected
airfields in the Dutch Harbor region, so that when the Japanese
planes from the carriers attacked, our fighters sprang off the unknown fields and drove them off. The enemy landing that had been
planned could not take place, for the Japanese, learning that a frightening number of land-based planes were ready to attack, prudently
withdrew, seeking protective cover under the storm clouds.

But enough damage was done by this attempted invasion to send
a chill through the Alaskan command, because the generals knew
that had the Japanese come in greater force and with more planes,
they might well have established a foothold close to Anchorage from
which they would be able to subdue all of Alaska, and thus place
great pressure upon cities like Seattle, Portland and Vancouver. As
then-Captain Shafter had predicted at his 1940 meetings throughout
the territory, the invasion from Asia was under way.

The response was quick, but during the first three months, not
very effective. Waterfront towns like Sitka constructed shore installations with which to hold off Japanese landing forces. The little air-

fields of the Northwest Staging Route were beefed up, and the big air bases at Fairbanks, Anchorage and Nome were patrolled twenty-four hours a day by dogs, jeeps and combat aircraft. The frontiersmen of Alaska enlisted in a group called the Alaska Scouts, an official branch of the American armed forces, and some of the more daring men, middle-aged or young, were sent on scouting missions involving extreme danger.

On 10 June 1942, a week after the bombing of Dutch Harbor, one of these scouts riding in a small plane radioed appalling news to headquarters in Anchorage: "The big Japanese task force that bombed Dutch Harbor, it sailed west under cover of fog and captured Attu Island. . . . And it looks like they've captured Kiska, too." American territory, a substantial chunk of it and strategically placed, had been occupied by enemy forces, the first time this had happened since the War of 1812, and all America shuddered.

This was the week that young Nate Coop, the half-breed son-in-law that the Flatches had considered illiterate, left Matanuska to volunteer for duty with the Alaska Scouts. The army officers serving as liaison with the scouts quickly determined that Nate was too poorly educated to be of much use in any demanding job, but as they watched how capably he handled himself, they concluded: "He's tough. He seems to have guts. And he knows the land. He might make a good scout." And four nights later a solemn-faced officer, a woodsman from Idaho, sat with the three most promising volunteers and issued their instructions: "We must know what's happening on the islands between here and Attu and Kiska. I can't tell you our plans, and you wouldn't want to know them . . . in case you're captured. But you are entitled to know that we have no intention of allowing the Japs to hold those two islands. And if you're caught, you're free to tell them so."

By this time the three young men could guess what their assignment entailed: "Teschinoff, you know the Aleutians well. We're putting you on Amlia Island. Small boat launched from a destroyer escort. Middle of the night. Food. Radio. Code. Tell us what's happening." When Teschinoff, who was almost pure Aleut except for that Russian great-great-grandfather, saluted, the officer added: "We're sure everyone got off that island, but we need confirmation."

Kretzbikoff, another Aleut, was dispatched to Atka, an important island. And now came Nate's assignment: "We must have information about Lapak. Two of our scout planes reported people there.

They could be very troublesome if they're Japs." He studied the three scouts and thought: My God, they look young. Then he asked: "You understand your missions?" When they nodded, he gave them one further command: "Master your radios. If you don't send us reports in code, you'll be pretty useless." But as they prepared to leave his office, a ramshackle affair that had been used for salting fish, he felt a deep, fatherly affection for these youngsters and gave them a promise: "The army never leaves a scout stranded . . . never."

Nate spent one more week at Dutch Harbor, mastering his radio and poring over two old, conflicting maps of Lapak Island, and in early August he gathered his gear, marched down to the shore where a small boat was ready to ferry him out to a waiting destroyer, and saluted the officers who had come down to see him off and who would be responsible eight days hence for recovering him from Lapak, always supposing that the Japanese, if they were there, didn't get him first. As he stepped into the boat, the officer from Idaho said: "It has about a hundred and thirty square miles. Lots of room to hide, if they are there."

Nate had never before been aboard a ship of any kind, and the severe weather of the Aleutians was hardly the kind one would have chosen for an initiation. Within an hour of leaving Dutch Harbor he was wildly seasick, but so were many of the crew. A sailor who was not gave him good advice as the destroyer dodged westward through heavy fog and heavier seas: "Stretch out when you can. Eat a lot of bread, slowly. Stay away from things like cocoa. And if they serve anything like canned peaches or pears, eat a lot."

When Nate asked, between vomiting spells, how this small warship could stay afloat in such seas, the sailor explained: "This tub can stay upright in anything. No matter how far it heels over, it always comes back. Built that way."

"Where do these waves come from?" Nate asked, and now he had hit upon a subject the sailor enjoyed discussing: "Up there to starboard, the Bering Sea whipped by arctic gales into choppy swells. Down there, to port, the great Pacific Ocean with its endless reach and massive seas. Up above, a constant flow of stupendous clouds roaring in from Asia. Mix that all together, you got yourself one of the hairiest weather cauldrons in the world."

At this point Nate had to hit the railing again, and when he saw those violent seas hammering at the destroyer, he accepted the fact that this was a breeding ground for horrendous weather. But the sailor had good news for him when he returned to lean against the outer wall of the captain's quarters: "You be damned glad, soldier, you're not an aviator. Imagine flying in that stuff?" and he pointed aloft. About an hour later, when Nate heard a plane flying overhead through the incredible storm, the sailor came back: "Let's say a prayer for the bastards involved in that one," and Nate asked: "What do you mean?" and the sailor replied: "I don't know who has it worse, the guys in the plane or the ones in the sea."

"I don't understand," Nate said, and the sailor pointed toward the sound of the plane: "PBY, big flying boat. If it goes out in weather like this, somebody's lost at sea. In these waters you rescue them in fifteen minutes or they're dead." He listened to the droning engines of the big, slow plane and bowed his head.

The destroyer, following a jagged course to confuse any Japanese submarine that might be tailing it, waited for morning light so it could spot the location of Qugang Volcano, the one that guarded Lapak on the north, and when that beautiful cone showed clear, the navigator assured the captain: "Course two hundred ten degrees straight in for the central promontory. Air cover promises no Japanese guns in that region." So into the beautiful land-enclosed Lapak harbor the destroyer came, its guns ready to fire at any prying Japanese aircraft, and when it looked as if all was clear, a rubber boat with oars lashed to the locks was dropped over the side and held fast by a rope extending from the prow. Gingerly, Nate dropped into the rubber craft, adjusted his oars, and set out for shore.

As the destroyer pulled away, vanishing behind the eastern headland for its hurried return to Dutch Harbor, Nate rowed himself toward the central headland, and as he approached it, looking for the deep cove that was supposed to exist on its western face, he was startled to see a middle-aged man striding forward unafraid, attended by what seemed to be either a young boy or a girl in boy's clothing. For one dreadful moment he was afraid he might have to use his revolver if these two were Japanese, but the man shouted in good English: "What in hell is all the secrecy about?"

When Nate got his craft onto the beach, the man and his young companion ran forward to drag it safely inland, and now Nate saw that the helper was a girl. "I'm Ben Krickel," the man said in some irritation. "This is my daughter Sandy, and why in hell didn't that ship, whatever it was . . . ?"

Nate felt it prudent not to reveal that he had come from an American destroyer, but he did ask, "Are you Americans?" and when the man snapped: "We sure as hell are," he confided: "They wanted to know if the island had any people on it."

This infuriated Krickel, who almost roared: "Of course it's inhabited! They know that back in Dutch Harbor— You come from Dutch?"

Nate refused to answer this, so the man continued: "The officials in Dutch know I have the lease on Lapak. Blue fox."

"What?"

"I have the whole island. I grow fox here."

"You mean . . . the little animals?"

"I lease the whole island. Let the fox run wild."

"What do you do with them?"

"Ship them to St. Louis. They've been buying our Aleutian pelts for seventy years."

Nate halted the conversation by asking: "Where's the best place for me to stay?" and Krickel said: "Our cabin. Down where the village used to be. Mind if we ride there with you?" so the rubber boat was refloated, the gear repacked, and the girl placed in the rear as the two men took oars and rowed swiftly down the bay, with the high mountains of Lapak guarding them. As they neared land, Nate informed his passengers: "You know that the Japs bombed Dutch Harbor?" When they expressed shock, he added: "And they captured Attu and Kiska."

"Kiska!" Ben cried. "I had my grays on Kiska. It's less than three hundred miles from here. Much less."

And now for the first time the girl spoke. She was seventeen, with a big placid face that bespoke a native mother and a smile that warmed the island air. She was neither tall nor slim, but she did have a grace in the way she carried her head, cocked to one side as if she were about to laugh, that made her a delightful little elf, even in the rough clothes she wore. It was midsummer, and her man's shirt was carelessly buttoned, revealing a tawny skin that looked as if it was intended to be kissed. "We're glad to have you here," she said from the stern of the boat, and she smiled so engagingly that Nate knew he must clarify the situation right now: "My wife has a smile like yours. But she's from Outside. I'm Athapascan."

The girl laughed and pretended to spit in the bay: "Aleuts, Athapascans not a good mix."

"Are you Aleut?" Nate asked, and her father broke in: "Is she!

Her mother doted on the Russian Orthodox. Named Sandy for Alexandra, last Russian tsarina, the one they murdered in that cellar . . . What date was it, Sandy?"

"Ekaterinburg, 17 July 1918. Every year Mom made me dress in black and she did, too. She used to call me her little tsarina," and Ben added: "Her name was Poletnikova, my wife's, that is."

When they reached the deserted cabin which Ben occupied when trapping his fox on Lapak, Nate explained just enough of his mission to quieten any apprehensions they might have: "The government has removed all Aleuts to the mainland. Camps in the south. We think the Japanese have done the same on Attu and Kiska. Camps somewhere in Japan. I came to see if this island, and maybe Tanaga, is free."

"If they're on Kiska," Krickel said, "they'll be coming here next. Maybe we ought to get out . . . now."

Nate explained that the army men would not be coming back for eight days, at which Sandy chuckled with that freedom that was so appealing: "Our boat wasn't due for eight weeks. If there's war, like you say, they'll probably never come."

Krickel asked: "What if the Japs move east before your boys move west?"

Nate showed them his radio: "To be used only in extreme emergency. They promised they'd come get us . . ." As soon as he said this he stopped; there was no reason why these strangers should know of the two other explorations.

But Sandy caught the slip: "Us?" and he said quietly: "Yes, they meant if there were any people like you on the island."

It was her father who said: "If the Japs are that close, they might fly over at any time. We better hide your boat," and he carried the oars as Nate and Sandy dragged the heavy rubber craft well inland and concealed it behind some trees and under a little nest of branches.

Two days later an airplane, followed by two more, flew low over the island, but they were from the 11th Air Force in Dutch Harbor, so Nate ran out and signaled them with two white handkerchiefs as he had been taught. His message was simple: "No Japanese. No signs of any." He had no prearranged signals for explaining the presence of the two Americans, but when the planes returned to check his message, he wigwagged: "No Japanese. No signs," and then led Krickel and his daughter to where they could be clearly seen. The lead plane dipped its wings alternately and flew back toward Dutch Harbor.

His remaining days on Lapak were some of the best Nate would know during this strange war, for he found Ben Krickel to be a fascinating raconteur about life in the Aleutians, while Sandy was a bright young woman who seemed to know a great deal about life in Alaska: "The churches in Kodiak fight something awful. The Russian Orthodox, that's what I am, thinks it's so high and mighty. The Catholics know they're superior to everyone else. And the Presbyterians are quite impossible. Pop's a Presbyterian."

Nate found his keenest delight in talking with Sandy and walking with her to the old sites on the island. One morning when they returned for lunch her father summoned them both before him in the old cabin: "Nate, you told us honest that you were a married man. Seems mighty young to me, but so be it. You and my daughter, no foolin' around. You hear that, Sandy?" He said that Sandy's mother was dead and that if the war hadn't come, Sandy was to have attended Sheldon Jackson School in Sitka when they returned to Dutch Harbor with their furs: "No foolin', you understand?" They said they did, but that afternoon such matters were forgotten, because when a lone plane flew over the island and they ran out to greet it, they saw that it bore strange markings, which had to signify that it was Japanese.

"My God!" Ben shouted. "They've seen us!"

He was right, for the plane wheeled and came back low, its guns blazing. If there were people on Lapak, they had to be Americans and therefore the pilot's enemies.

He struck no one on that first run, but upon his second try he came perilously close to the cabin, and on his third, lower and slower, he would certainly have wiped them out had not at this moment two American planes sped in from the east. There was a furious air battle, with all advantages to the Americans, for they were higher and they flew in close tandem, one protecting the other. But the Japanese pilot showed skill and courage, and after throwing one of his pursuers off his track, he turned his nose upward, gave his engine an immense burst of gas, and tried to escape to the west, toward Attu.

But the second American plane had not been deceived by his maneuvering, and as he tried to speed past, this plane turned sharply and threw a full blast from his guns right into the fuselage and engine of the Japanese plane. It exploded and pieces fell across Lapak Island, the corpse of the pilot landing somewhere in the high western mountains. In a graceful sweep, the two American planes re-formed, turned west to authenticate the breakup of the enemy plane, then flew a salute to the three American watchers.

His brush with death, the first he had ever had to face as a real possibility, launched a major change in Nate Coop, but even if someone had pointed out what was happening, and especially why, he would not have believed it. The rough treatment he had received from the Matanuska settlers when he sought to marry one of their daughters had scarred him; he had accepted their assessment of half-breeds as worthless and not entitled to the respect accorded white people. In a score of insulting ways it had been hammered into him that he was of a lower category, and he had accepted this judgment. But now to see what a superior young woman Sandy was—wise, informed, neat when she wanted to be, and qualified in every way to take her place in Matanuska society or any other, despite her half-breed status— made him reevaluate himself, and what struck him with great force was that Sandy spoke excellent English while he could barely manage the language, and he swore to himself: If an Aleut can learn, an Athapascan can. And he saw both Sandy and himself as acceptable American citizens, real Alaskans tied to the earth and children of it, and in respecting her he came to respect himself.

On the night before the destroyer returned, Nate borrowed Ben Krickel's lantern and in its flickering light composed a letter to his brother-in-law, LeRoy, in which he spoke of meeting on a remote island a wonderful girl named Sandy Krickel: "She's just the right age for you and you've got to meet her as soon as possible, because you'll never do any better." Then he added a sentence which revealed his resentment of past treatment by the Flatches: "You'll be surprised to hear that she's American-Aleut, like me, and I tell you this even though you gave your sister merry hell for going with me." He ended with a prediction: "When you see her, LeRoy, you'll grab her, and I'll be your best man, and later you'll thank me."

But that was not the end of the letter, because when he showed it to Ben Krickel for his approval, Ben scratched a postscript: "Young man, your brother-in-law is telling the truth. Signed, Her Father."

On the eighth day, as planned, the destroyer returned to Lapak Bay and the fox trappers said farewell to the volcano. The captain, a very junior lieutenant commander, shouted at Nate as he climbed out of his rubber boat: "Who in hell are those two?" and there was great excitement when Nate yelled back: "Ben Krickel and his daughter Sandy. They farm foxes here," and the captain said: "They warned us anything can happen in the Aleutians."

At supper that night the young officers insisted that Miss Krickel dine in their mess, a cubbyhole barely big enough for six places at table, and when Nate looked in from outside and saw how even the captain was paying court to Sandy, he muttered to himself: "That little beauty will be able to handle herself anywhere."

The dreamlike days that Nate spent with the fox farmers were the last easy ones he would know for the next year. As soon as the destroyer landed him back at Dutch Harbor, his superiors interrogated him about the possibility of building an airstrip on Lapak. He told them, in his usual grunting monosyllables: "No chance. Some good ground at beach, but no. Too much hills." However, Ben Krickel was prepared to lecture them rhapsodically on Lapak, but after an hour of listening to his outbursts they reported: "He knows a hell of a lot about foxes, nothing about airstrips. Lapak is out!"

They turned their attention to Adak, midway down the Aleutians and a big inviting island, but they knew little about it. Word was passed: "Anyone here familiar with Adak?" and Krickel volunteered: "I used to raise foxes there," so a scouting team was organized under the direction of a gung-ho Air Corps captain named Tim Ruggles, known to his friends as "a hero waiting to happen," and he chose for his Alaskan guides Krickel and Nate Coop.

Because no one knew if the Japanese had already occupied Adak, the trio underwent intensive training in small arms, machine guns, map work, and the sending of coded messages by radio.

During the training Nate learned of an unusual development in the case of Sandy Krickel: instead of being shipped south to an internment camp, like the other Aleuts, she had, because of her father, been temporarily classified as a Caucasian and given a job typing at headquarters, a low, long wooden building owned by a fishing company. Nate saw her twice and found her to be even more enchanting in her office dress than she had been in men's clothes on the island.

She was therefore in the office when General Shafter and two other generals from the Lower Forty-eight flew out to Dutch Harbor to complete plans for the occupation of Adak. The high brass had come to the Aleutians in General Shafter's plane, which meant that LeRoy Flatch was in the pilot's seat, so that when the generals entered the headquarters building Nate trailed along. While the officers moved into an inner room for their discussions, he was left in the reception area where Sandy was typing, and as he idly watched her from a chair propped against the wall, he thought: She must be the kind of half-Aleut Nate wrote about. If his girl's as lovely as this one, he showed good judgment. And he spent some time analyzing the pretty typist: You can tell she's Oriental. Gosh, you might even take her for a Jap. But she's not too dark and she sure has style. Those teeth and the smile to go with them. Wow!

He became so fascinated by who the girl might be that finally he rose, sidled aimlessly toward her desk, stopped, and said: "Pardon me, ma'am, but could you be one of the Aleuts I've been hearing about?"

Smiling easily and with no sense of embarrassment, she said: "I am. Aleut and Russian and I guess a little English and Scotch."

"You speak . . . I mean, better than I do."

"We go to school." She typed a few words, then smiled again: "What brings you out here to the end. of the world? Secret, I suppose?"

"Yep." He did not know what to say next, but he did not want to leave her desk, and after a silence which was painful for him but not for her, he blurted out: "Were you here when this place was bombed?" and she said: "No." She was about to say that at that time she had been with her father on a remote island, gathering pelts from their blue foxes, and that would have disclosed that she was indeed the girl of Nate's letter, but at this moment Nate's scouting team, led by the feisty captain, tramped into the office on their way to be interrogated by the three generals, and Nate, surprised by the unlikely presence of his brother-in-law, cried: "LeRoy! What you doin' here?" Then he stopped, stared at Sandy, and said: "You've met?" When LeRoy nodded, Nate said: "This is Sandy Krickel. And her dad, he added the stuff to my letter."

"And I meant every word of it," Krickel said as he disappeared into the smaller meeting room, dragging Nate along with him.

Since the generals remained at Dutch Harbor overnight, LeRoy had time to visit with Sandy, who was even more exciting than Nate had said. That evening the two Krickels, Nate and LeRoy borrowed the cabin of a civilian engineer in charge of putting together the gear that would be required for the airstrip, and with food assembled from various sources they prepared themselves a satisfying meal, during which it became obvious that LeRoy was already smitten with this girl of the islands who alternately fended off his unspoken approaches and encouraged them.

In the morning the generals wanted to see Adak from the air, and they insisted that Ben Krickel fly along to point out the features of the island as he remembered them from once having leased part of it for his run of ordinary red foxes. It was a turbulent day, with vast winds sweeping in from Siberia, and it seemed unnecessarily daring for three senior officers to be taking such risks, but LeRoy had learned that General Shafter, at least, was truly afraid of nothing, and he assumed the two other officers were of the same breed.

It was Ben who yelled from a back seat: "Steady her up!" but that was impossible. However, LeRoy found some comfort from the fact that two heavier military planes, bombers no doubt, had joined up and were flying wing positions. But now, when the planes passed in and out of heavy clouds, and then ran into violent rain, he said to no one in particular: "Be safer if they went home."

At Adak they saw very little, for storm clouds hung low over the island, "a foretaste," one of the generals said, "of what our boys will face when they try to land."

"When they land," General Shafter corrected, and the three officers, bouncing about as they tried to peer down through the clouds, laughed. Not Krickel. He called forward: "I'm gonna be sick," and LeRoy called back: "That's your problem. Rule is, you got to clean it up when we land," and Ben proceeded to be very sick.

Disappointed in the flight, one of the generals, who was going to be personally involved in leapfrogging out the Aleutians, suggested: "Could we fly around a bit? Maybe there'll be a break." LeRoy studied his fuel reserve and wished that he could consult with his wingmen, but radio silence had to be observed, so with hand signals he indicated to the man on his left flank that he was going to drop lower and circle, and the other pilot signaled: "Okay."

It was lucky they did, for after a tedious quarter-hour a break did come in the lower clouds, and for about ten minutes they had relatively clear flying over their target, and now Ben Krickel gathered himself together and shouted out the characteristics of one site after another: "Yeah, here's where the flat land begins beachside. Up here, better elevation but not so long. I don't recognize this, must be lost. You can see the rocks over there, stay clear. Yeah, this is Adak, all right. You found the right island, pilot."

The third general, not an airman, wanted especially to see the beach areas, and in the fleeting glimpse he was allowed he saw all he needed: "Another hell spot. Wade ashore and hope the other side didn't get here first." To some senior officers the enemy was invariably *he,* to others *the enemy,* and to this man, a football player at Navy, it was *the other side.*

They remained at Dutch Harbor that night, completing plans, and while they huddled with Krickel over maps, LeRoy and Sandy had a long talk together, and then a longer walk in the August moonlight, at the end of which they knew that they were joyously close to falling in love. He could see that she was as desirable as Nate had indicated in his letter, and she had already been convinced by her Lapak discussions with Nate that LeRoy was a serious young man from a good family and with unusual ability as a pilot. At the conclusion of their walk they embraced, and Sandy was so happy to have found a man she liked and would increasingly respect as she got to know him better, she lingered in his arms and whispered: "You flew in here on a kindly wind," and he whispered back: "In these islands there are no gentle winds. I learned today . . . the hard way."

In the morning, as the visitors were preparing to leave, the army general delivered some bad news: a Seattle review board had reclassified Sandy Krickel as a designated Aleut, so she had to be evacuated with the rest. No appeal. She would be sent to where a large collection of island people had been gathered. "There are four we can choose from," the local commander explained. "All in the southern part of Alaska, what the natives call the Banana Belt. Good climate." And as he rattled off the unfamiliar names, LeRoy stopped him: "Did you say Totem Cannery?" The commander nodded. "On Taku Inlet?"

"I think so."

Turning to Sandy, LeRoy cried: "I know it. Big. Not a bad place. I'll come see you there." But when the plane was about to take off, General Shafter said: "If the girl's leaving, why doesn't she fly to Anchorage with us?" and within a few minutes Sandy collected the few things she had in Dutch Harbor, kissed her father farewell, and headed for what would actually become an American version of a concentration camp.

• • •

During the last week of August 1942 the American high command received so much solid intelligence that the Japanese were about to invade Adak Island and use it as a base for bombing mainland Alaska that they issued peremptory orders: "Grab Adak immediately, rush an airstrip, and we'll bomb them instead."

In less than an hour after the receipt of those instructions Captain Ruggles and his team were rushed aboard a destroyer, which plunged into the heaving waters of the Bering Sea, tossing about, Ben Krickel said, "like a drunken walrus trying to find his way home." Seasick and feeling his way cautiously ashore through knee-deep waves, Nate was afraid even to ask in whispers "What now?" but Ruggles, like an eager Boy Scout, actually shouted: "This way!" and he led them scrambling up a muddy incline to higher ground, where in one blazing instant gunfire erupted from all sides, with tracer bullets etching pathways through the darkness.

They had run into a Japanese team of four equally daring scouts who had been engaged in their own reconnaissance, and an intense, totally confused gunfight ensued, during which the enemy conducted a disciplined retreat to a different beach where a submarine awaited them. Ruggles, now free to probe about the island, rushed everywhere, and shortly after daybreak encoded the message which would authorize a massive invasion fleet to set sail: "No Japanese on Adak. Locations Able, Baker or Roger eligible for bomber strip."

Two days later they stood on an Adak promontory to greet an immense landing force as it streamed ashore with gigantic construction bulldozers that swarmed onto the island like an army of ants, and ten days later, when the first heavy bombers flew in on their way to bomb Attu, the three scouts stood at attention as medals were pinned to their tunics "for heroic actions which speeded the capture of Adak Island."

That night Ruggles and his men hit the hay early, exhausted by the fight and the following days of exertion, but before they fell asleep Ruggles said: "They repeat brave words and hand out medals, but I wonder if they have any idea what it's like to climb up a slippery bank at midnight, not knowing if the Japs are waiting at the top?" and Krickel said: "It ain't difficult. You take three deep breaths, plow ahead like a dummy, and when you see them . . ." He made the rat-tat-tat of a machine gun, after which the captain said: "If I'm ever assigned to hit another beach, I want you men with me," but Krickel cried: "Don't volunteer!"

When the Americans had Adak operating as a powerful forward base, the Alaska Scouts had nothing immediate to do, so Nate Coop was assigned temporarily as driver and helper for a most unusual man—a thin, irascible civilian with the rank of corporal, a heavy black mustache, snow-white hair that stood upright in a butch job, very large glasses and a wry wit. One look at the informal way he dressed or one sound of his rasping, sardonic voice would have assured anyone that "this one was not intended for military duty." A wizard on the typewriter, which he banged with an odd assortment of fingers, he edited the mimeographed newspaper published for the troops, and Nate was responsible for driving him around to the various installations where he picked up news. He was in some ways difficult to work for, but in other ways it was a privilege to be with him, for he could see humor or contradiction or downright insanity in even the direst development.

What interested Nate was that wherever this unusual reporter went, there would be some one or two soldiers or airmen who knew him by reputation, and they would pester him with questions, listening attentively when he deigned to answer, which was not often. From these conversations, Nate concluded that this Corporal Dashiell Hammett had once worked in Hollywood, but since Nate had never even seen a movie, he obviously did not know what the man did.

"Is he an actor?" he asked some airmen as they finished talking with Hammett. "No," they said. "Even worse. He's a writer."

"What did he write?" The airmen thought it strange that a kid Nate's age had never heard of Hammett, so they rattled off the names of some of the films which had given him the reputation of being the hottest writer in town: "Tough ones—*The Glass Key, The Thin Man, The Maltese Falcon* . . ."

"Never saw them." The men were so astonished that they called: "Hey, Mr. Hammett, your driver says he never saw *The Maltese Falcon.*"

The idea that this young fellow who had been so close to him for more than a week had not known who he was or what movies he had made, had not, indeed, ever seen one of them, fascinated Hammett, and during the remainder of Nate's assignment with him he probed the boy's background, and when he saw that Nate was semi-illiterate but also basically intelligent, he took a fatherly interest in him: "What do you mean, you didn't go to school?"

"Back in the woods, the mines . . ."

"You say you've already landed on Lapak and Adak?"

"Yep."

Hammett stepped back, looked at this taut, intense fellow just twenty, and said: "I write 'em, you live 'em." He asked if Nate had a girlfriend, and was surprised when the young man replied: "I got a wife."

Then Hammett became deeply interested in the problems that Nate presented of a half-breed marrying into one of the Matanuska families, and after this had been explored he wanted details about the valley's economic and social life, and when Nate proved ignorant of both, Hammett said: "Jack London would have loved you, Nate."

"Who was Jack London?"

"Never mind."

Hammett accepted Nate as an authentic rough diamond, but when he saw some of Nate's notes, he exploded: "Can you read? I mean big words? Can you write?" He excused Nate from work so that he could study materials the army provided its illiterates, and under Hammett's whiplash Nate began to learn ten new words a day and stand with his hands at his side and speak uninterrupted for five minutes on topics like "How My Uncle Found a Gold Mine." Belatedly, he was getting an education.

When Nate disappeared for two days, Hammett was furious: "Where in hell you been?" But he was mollified when Nate explained: "They're detaching me, Corporal."

"What for?"

"Don't know. But maybe closer to Kiska. Maybe Amchitka."

"Of course it's Amchitka. Everyone knows that. What's that to do with you?"

"Maybe me and Ben Krickel, scout again. Amphib landing."

Hammett was appalled: "Good God, you've scouted two islands. A man's luck runs out." In a low fury he went to complain to the commanding officer, but was sharply rebuked for sticking his nose in where it wasn't wanted.

Nate saw this mercurial corporal only once more; when he was about to be sent off for intensive training regarding Amchitka, Hammett came to him and said gruffly: "You have a real set of balls, Nate. I wouldn't have the guts for one expedition like yours, and you'll be going on your third."

"Guess that's what us scouts are for."

As Nate trained for the new task, he sometimes wondered why, if Dashiell Hammett was as bright as the younger airmen claimed, he was only a corporal, and he never found an answer to his perplexity. But then, in the second week of January 1943 he forgot Hammett, for his old team was reassembled—Captain Ruggles, Ben Krickel, himself—and once more they rowed out in a rubber boat to a waiting destroyer escort, which dodged through Aleutian storms till it reached the long, low, flat island that would provide a splendid airstrip for the bombing of Kiska and Attu, if the Americans were able to occupy the island before the enemy did.

Since Amchitka was only sixty miles east of the major Japanese air base at Kiska, the three scouts had to suppose that the enemy would be boating in his own patrols, and that proved to be the case. For three perilous days and nights Nate and his team moved about the island, hearing the Japanese at times and trying to avoid contact with them. In howling storms, with snow and hail whipping their faces, the Americans protected themselves while they scouted the island's beaches, and one night as they huddled in darkness Captain Ruggles said: "The snow falls in Siberia, but it lands in Amchitka . . . parallel to the ground . . . eighty miles an hour."

They faced the extra danger that came from the Japanese scouting planes which raked the island, bombing any spots where American spies might be hiding, and once when the three had to scramble to escape attack, they rushed shockingly close to a camp occupied by seven Japanese scouts. Gingerly, hearts pounding, the three Americans crept back and escaped detection.

It was difficult warfare, in its way, as difficult as any being conducted throughout the world: heaving seas, whipping blizzards, endless nights, and always great storms lashing at the beaches where any invader would have to land. But resolute men, American and Japanese alike, clung to Amchitka and sent their messages back to their headquarters. Said Ruggles in code: "Jap aircraft overhead constantly. Will pose serious threat to landing craft."

Nate was on lookout when the American armada approached the island, hundreds of ships of all sizes, and he expected Japanese planes to strafe them mercilessly, but now the storms became so violent that no planes could fly, and painfully the great ships moved close to shore. But even though the enemy planes were absent, the landing was hell. The *Worden* sank, drowning fourteen. One group storming ashore spotted the Japanese scouts, took them to be an advance force of a main Japanese army, and destroyed them with flame throwers. Another American team tried four times to make a landing, only to be forced back each time by mountainous waves thundering upon the beach, but as the long day passed into ominous night they kept on trying, and on their fifth attempt, aided by searchlights, they made it.

Next day Pacific Headquarters in Hawaii issued a brief communiqué: "Yesterday our troops made a successful landing on Amchitka," and reporters pointed out: "A prelude to our retaking Attu and Kiska," but no words indicated the hellish conditions the Americans had suffered in gaining this vital foothold in the brutal battle of the Aleutians.

From January till mid-March men like Nate and Ben Krickel worked like draft horses, hauling goods inland from the shore, storing them in piles, and slogging back knee-deep in icy water to break loose more cargo. It was back-breaking work, and usually it had to be done while a Siberian wind formed icicles on eyebrows. And when the gear was finally ashore, the amateur stevedores were transferred hastily to the flat area where the airstrip was emerging from the tundra. But wherever they worked, Nate and Ben lived miserably: food ships failed to arrive, and when they did stagger in they most often had food and clothing that had been destined for the tropics. For days in a row, when he was working at the far end of the airstrip, Nate would have no hot food, and when something was cooked up, it was frequently a type with which he was unfamiliar.

For example, one day Captain Ruggles went to great pains to steal a large bag of whole-wheat flour, the kind that made good, crunchy bread, but when the bakers turned it into loaves, Nate and the other men working with him refused to eat it. One farm boy from Georgia spoke for the group: "Captain Ruggles, we got to be here in Alaska, it's our duty. We got to freeze our ass off, the enemy is just over there. And we got to eat cold food, because there ain't no stoves handy. But by God we don't got to eat dirty bread like that, it's nigger food. We want white bread."

Ruggles tried to explain that whole wheat was twice as nutritious, twice as good for a man who wasn't getting enough roughage, but he was powerless to convince these well-intentioned country boys: "Dirty bread like that, it ain't proper for no white man to eat."

But what caused the most anguish to these men who worked on Amchitka was best expressed by the farm boy from Georgia: "Tears your heart out. You work here at the airstrip, these fine kids climb in their planes, wave goodbye, fly over to Kiska or Attu, hit a storm. Christ, always there's a storm, and they fly right into some damned mountain, maybe three or four of them in one day, and you don't see them kids no more."

The toll was dreadful, for as one frightened airman once added in despair at the end of a letter to his girlfriend which had been otherwise hopeful and of good cheer: "There is nothing in this world like flying in the Aleutians, and we've lost so many of our men I'm scared to death to get into my plane, the chances are so poor."

He wrote one more letter to her, two days later, apologizing for his outburst, and then no more.

It was under such conditions that Nate resumed his study of the textbooks Corporal Hammett had given him, and obedient to Hammett's dictum, he continued to memorize ten new words a day, until his vocabulary became civilized, but he still spoke in fragments, insecure in the substantial knowledge he was acquiring.

He did what he could to protect himself from the blizzards, but he refrained from making friends with the airmen who arrived on Amchitka all bright-eyed and ten days out of training school. He saw that they had special problems which ordinary grunts did not. He told himself: I got to bear this terrible weather. I learn tricks like findin' the buildin's that are mostly underground. Wind can't whip you about. But those in the planes, they got to live in it. Right in the heart of it. And they don't live long.

Of course, he had his own nightmares, for when it was rumored that the next hit would not be nearby Kiska but distant Attu, he knew that the brass would want to put scouts ashore to ascertain just what the situation was. So he went to Captain Ruggles and said: "They call for volunteers this time, I won't go."

"Now wait a minute, Coop. You're the best man we have. You don't know what fear is."

"Yes I do," and to his own amazement and the captain's, his eyes filled with tears, and after a while Ruggles said quietly: "Nate, I'm sure I'll be sent to Attu to see how soon we could have an airstrip after we land. I'd hate to go without you."

"Maybe," Nate mumbled, and when it became obvious that the same three men were going to be ordered to scout Attu, he felt real fear, and he told himself: You can't keep goin' to occupied islands without bein' killed. But he gnawed on his fingernails and kept his apprehensions to himself. One night the orders came: "The PBY is off the southern shore. The pilots say they know a sure place to set you down. Easy paddle in, then you're on your own." Trembling furiously, Nate trailed behind Captain Ruggles and Ben Krickel as they moved in the darkness, but the awkward job of climbing into the PBY so preoccupied him that his nervousness abated, and he spent the flight to Attu concentrating his strength and his courage for the extremely dangerous task ahead.

With great skill the PBY flew a route which evaded Kiska, ducked in and out of storms, and landed in the choppy sea less than a mile from the southern end of Massacre Bay, where the cossack Trofim Zhdanko had landed with his twelve fur traders in 1745. Climbing down into their rubber craft, the three men paddled through the heavy waves, made shore, and hid their boat under a tangle of twigs and low shrubs. Delighted with the ease of their landing, they started inland over the terrain the major landing parties would use in subsequent days, and came at last to a slight rise from which Ben could survey an area he had once known well: "No defense positions here. Our men will get ashore. But up there where the Japs are"—and he pointed to the hills half a mile to the north—"very strong." In the meantime, Captain Ruggles was inspecting with his glasses in the growing light the airstrip which the Japanese were struggling to complete before the expected assault began: "Good! They'll have it in fair shape just as we drive in to take it over."

Scout planes, looking for intruders like these three, flew overhead but saw nothing, and for two days of the most intense concentration the Americans took mental notes of what the conquest of Attu was going to entail, and they were sobered by their conclusions. Ruggles confirmed the plans he had heard at headquarters: "The moment we land at Massacre, we must drive north to Holtz Bay. Hold them off there and clean out the pockets to the east." He asked Ben and Nate to memorize the mountainous lay of the land, and when the second night fell, he and his men crept back to the boat and headed south for their midnight recovery.

When they were safe aboard the PBY, with mugs of hot bouillon to warm their hands, Ruggles poked Nate and said jokingly: "Pretty much like a picnic, wasn't it?" and Nate replied: "Always easy, the Japs stay clear. But when you hit Kiska, leave me out."

• • •

The American reconquest of Attu, which began on 11 May 1943, was one of the significant battles of World War II, for although it involved relatively few troops, it determined whether Japan had any hope of using an Alaskan foothold from which to attack the United States and Canada. The Japanese defenders of Attu were a resolute group of about 2,600 superior soldiers dedicated to the task of retaining this foothold on American territory. Led by officers of great daring and acumen, they had constructed a chain of positions that were the acme of defensive warfare. But there were other holes in the earth, dug almost casually, into which Japanese soldiers would climb knowing that they could never by any conceivable miracle escape. Deep two-man caves flanked the approaches the Americans would probably use, and there was one fiendishly clever line of positions that guaranteed the death of American attackers but also the certain death of the Japanese defenders. To rout heroic Japanese like these was going to be a hellish assignment conducted in arctic storms and Siberian gales.

To accomplish it, 16,000 American GIs plus a few Alaska Scouts and unlimited American air power would apply relentless pressure at merciless cost to both attacker and defender. On the eve of this strange battle, fought at the farthest ends of empire, the character of the entire war in the Pacific hung in the balance: Japan, the bold attacker, was about to become the stubborn defender, while America, the sleepy giant caught off balance, was belatedly gathering its forces for a series of crushing, annihilating blows. As the sun set that evening in a surly glow, no one could predict how the battle for Attu would evolve, but the men engaged on each side were of equal bravery, equal determination, and equally committed to their contrasting ways of life.

At dawn a most fearful armada loomed out of the mists, bearing down upon the northeast corner of Attu, and Nate and Ben, from their landing craft, watched in awe as the huge battleship *Pennsylvania* unlimbered its great guns to pulverize the foreshore where the troops would soon be landing. A hundred and fifty massive shells strafed the shore but killed not a single Japanese, for they had built their revetments so stoutly that only a direct hit would ravage them, and even then the damage would come mostly from flying debris which could be removed later.

The larger portion of the American armada appeared out of the mists enshrouding Massacre Bay, and here the huge ships were able to empty their cargo and their men without serious opposition. But once ashore, as Nate had predicted and as he now saw from his ship, the attackers had to swing sharply uphill toward Holtz Bay, around whose perimeter the Japanese had dug their positions. What had seemed at first an easy landing became a bitter, rainswept, mud-encumbered attack, with hundreds of Americans absorbing sniper bullets which either killed or maimed. Always the Americans died without having seen the enemy.

For nineteen terrible days, usually without respite and often without food, the Americans pressed on, and in this relentless attack Nate Coop and Ben Krickel covered each other, shared foxholes, or ran together to toss activated grenades into the mouths of caves from which sniper fire had come. "It's always the same," Ben said with heavy breathing after attacking a cave, "you throw in your grenade and hear three explosions. The two men inside see it coming, know they're dead, and detonate their own grenades . . . they make the job clean, I guess."

During one hellish period Nate's group cleaned out a whole hill-side of caves, one at a time, most often with that sickening drumbeat of three explosions to each American grenade. In that time no prisoners were taken, little was eaten, and no attacker slept in dry clothes. It was a harrowing, hand-to-shadow battle, no bayonet work, not many mortar shots, just the dull, terrifying work of cleaning out installa-tions that could not be attacked in any other way. No American men ever fought under more difficult conditions than these on Attu, no Japanese ever defended their positions with a greater sense of honor.

At the end of eight days of this cave-by-cave elimination, some fifteen hundred of the enemy were slain, but over four hundred Americans were also dead. Now came the final push when fifteen hundred more Japanese must die, and a hundred and fifty Ameri-cans. On both sides they would perish in chilling rain, blustery storms and mud. None died in a more fiendish way than the brave American officer leading Nate and Ben up a hill, nor the six Japanese respon-sible for his death.

Since Captain Ruggles was an airman, he was supposed to be aloft in some storm-battered plane, but because of his skill in detect-ing where airstrips should be located in the first few hours of a land-ing, he had slipped into a kind of permanent assignment to that most perilous of jobs, for when it was completed he became just one more foot soldier, except that his unusual bravery made him outstanding.

The responsibility Ruggles gave himself seemed routine. The American attackers were strung out along the bottom of a slope which climbed sharply to the north; the Japanese defenders were dug into a line of caves along the crest of the hill. At first glance it might seem that the task facing the Americans was impossible, but Ruggles had long ago devised a solution; it required exquisite timing.

Ruggles, with one or two trusted flank men, would move right up the center of the slope, depending upon a blanket of fire from their team to keep the Japanese away from the mouths of their caves. In the meantime, swift climbers far to the left and right would establish a kind of pincer movement that would carry them to a position well above the line of caves, from where they would creep down upon them from the rear and destroy the enemy with grenades tossed into the mouths.

Such a coordinated maneuver succeeded when all parts functioned perfectly, and Ruggles was one of the best at it: "We finish off that line of caves and then look for some hot chow."

But this time there was to be a subtle difference, because in the middle of the slope, not conspicuous from below, rose a slight but substantial mound, and looking at it, one would have supposed that the Japanese would have placed in it a series of caves pointing downhill to slow any Americans striving to climb up. But this the determined Japanese did not do; instead, they dug six caves on the far side of the mound, pointing *uphill,* and when they were ready, the colonel in charge said solemnly: "The emperor asks for twelve volunteers," and twelve young Japanese, far from home and bitingly hungry from lack of food, stepped forward, saluted, and moved two by two into the doomed caves.

They were doomed because the tactic they were to execute was suicidal from the start: "You will allow the American attackers to pass over your positions. Wait till a sizable number have gone. And then open fire on their backs when they suspect nothing." Many Americans would be killed in this way, but of course the twelve men in the caves would be slaughtered as soon as their positions were identified.

Ruggles, as one might expect, would lead the charge up the front face, with Nate on his left flank, Ben on his right and two skilled teams speeding up the far outside flanks to drop down upon the top caves from the rear, and everything went as planned, except that when Ruggles and his central core sped over the slight rise in the middle of the slope, they were allowed to proceed about twelve yards up the hill. Then from the hidden caves pointing uphill the Japanese fired point-blank into the backs of the attackers, and from habit, most of them aimed at the obvious leader, Captain Ruggles, who fell, cut to pieces by seven fusillades. One hit Ben Krickel in the left shoulder. Three other bursts killed two of Nate's companions, and yet another sped past Nate's ear.

Four Americans survived, including the wounded Krickel and Nate Coop, and for just a moment they were lost in confusion, but then Nate saw what had to be done: "Ben! Back behind the mound!" And he led the remnants of the team to the down side of the mound where they could not be attacked by the men in the caves. There they regrouped, and when they saw their mutilated captain ten yards up the hill, a sullen rage overtook them, so that even Ben Krickel, seriously wounded, insisted upon being part of the next action. Accidently it seemed, Nate assumed charge: "Creep up, belly down, prime grenades, and we'll reach over and slam them in."

They did just this, four determined avengers, closing in upon the caves from the rear, ignoring bullets coming at them from the ridge, and thrusting the deadly grenades into the mouths of the caves, then falling back to hear the three explosions.

That left the two caves on the outer flanks still operating, and Nate shouted: "I have this one! Ben, take over there," but as he cried the words he saw that Ben had fainted, so he pointed to a young lad from Nebraska: "Clean it out!"

But now these men had no more grenades, so two of them tore their shirts into long strips, and a third man doused them with the petrol he carried for such situations, and they were lighted and stuffed boldly into the mouths of the caves, and when four Japanese struggled out, gasping for air, they were brained with rifle butts.

The conquest of this hill represented one of the last orderly assaults by American forces on Attu, and that night, the men assumed that they had conquered the Japanese, but at midnight, with no one on watch, they heard a rustling on the side of a hill where no sensible Japanese would be, and then a patter of feet, and finally the wild shouts of men in a banzai charge, determined to kill or be killed. Now an inferno raged in that stretch of the undefined front. Japanese, maddened in what they knew to be their final moments, rampaged in all directions, grabbing rifles pointed at them, slashing with long knives, setting fire to whatever they could reach.

They were irresistible, overrunning positions that no ordinary human could even attack, let alone subdue. And as they came, they screamed, and it was nearly an hour before Nate and his men established some kind of defensive line. Then amazing things began to happen. One Japanese brandishing only the twig of a tree, not fifteen inches long, came directly at an American soldier armed with a gun, thrust the gun aside, struck the startled American in the face with his twig, screamed and disappeared in the darkness. Two other Japanese, with bayonets tied insecurely to the ends of sticks, rushed right at Ben Krickel, endeavoring to stab him with their flimsy weapons. They struck him, but the bayonets slid to one side, and with his good arm he killed both men with blows to the head.

A fourth Japanese was the craziest of all. Chanting a wild song and brandishing a deadly pistol, he overcame all obstacles and rushed right at Nate Coop, who was powerless to stop him. Thrusting his pistol in Nate's face, he screamed and pulled the trigger. There was a clicking sound; Nate thought he was dead; and then nothing happened. With a sharp thrust of his bayonet, Nate killed the Japanese, and when he studied the man's gun he found that it was a child's toy, filled with paper caps. Wresting the gun from the dead man's fingers, Nate pulled the trigger twice and sent popping echoes through the muddy dawn. The battle for Attu was over.

Now only Kiska remained, not nearly as big as Attu but far more heavily defended: intelligence reports gave twice as many Japanese on Kiska, 5,360, ten times the defensive capability. To subdue the island, more than 35,000 American troops were ferried out the Aleutian chain in by far the biggest, heaviest armada of this front. This time no scouting team was sent in to reconnoiter, for which Nate was grateful; it wasn't necessary; the powerful Japanese installations were visible from the air.

Instead, the 11th Air Force dumped an incredible amount of high explosives on the island, some of the planes flying eastward from the newly activated field on Attu. Also, from a printing press in Anchorage came a hundred thousand leaflets imploring the Japanese to surrender, but these had even less effect than the bombs, which accomplished nothing. Once again, for the last time in the Aleutians, the Japanese were dug in, and digging them out was going to be the brutal climax of this brutal campaign.

Ten weeks after the fall of Attu, the massive assault force was ready, and once again General Shafter flew to the Aleutians with Leroy Flatch as pilot to participate in the final planning. This time when LeRoy asked for his brother-in-law he found Nate morose and edgy: "If the Japs start anything, I'm sure it'll be me and Ben to check them out if his arm's okay."

"Where is Ben?"

"Field hospital. Mendin' his arm." LeRoy was worried by Nate's listlessness, and asked: "Anything wrong?" and Nate snapped: "No! Why?" and LeRoy said: "Well, all these battles . . . and Ben getting wounded," and Nate said: "It's a job."

"Stay with it. Now I got to see Ben," and they found the tired old fox farmer at a dressing station where final touches were being applied to his wound, and he looked much older than his fifty-one years, for, like Nate, he was bone-weary. But he showed surprise as LeRoy assumed an erect military posture, saluted, and said in formal voice: "Mr. Krickel, I've flown all the way to this summer resort to ask for your daughter's hand in marriage."

Years fell from Ben's battle-scarred face and pain from his wounded arm. Staring at young Flatch, he asked in a quiet voice: "Where is Sandy?"

"In Anchorage. With a good job. I used General Shafter's pull and got her sprung from the concentration camp, and we're getting married . . . with your permission." When both Ben and Nate began pummeling him in their joy, he stopped them: "Sandy said she'd never get married without your consent. Said you were her father and mother both." He looked the old islander in the eye: "So have I your permission?" and gravely Ben said: "You have, son. Now let's get stinkin' drunk."

They were not able to do this, because when a messenger came from the meeting of the generals, both Nate and Ben could guess what it meant. Yes, if Ben was up to it, they were to make one last sortie behind enemy lines: "The Japs are behaving strangely. We've got to know how tough those Kiska beaches are going to be. You men have never failed us before." The general in command jabbed at Ben's arm: "Mended well enough for you to make the try?" and both Ben and Nate knew that even a moment's hesitation would excuse him from this perilous assignment, but the fox farmer said: "It's ready," and before dawn these two loyal frontiersmen, these proto-typical Alaskans, were back in their rubber boat heading quietly for the waiting PBY that rose and fell on the dark Aleutian waves. With Captain Ruggles dead, they would be commanded by an enthusiastic young army lieutenant, Gray, who told them as they approached the beach: "You'll get no rank from me. You know far more about this than I do." Then, as if to reassure them, he added: "But when you move out, I'll be there. You can count on it."

As they rowed in darkness toward what might prove to be a blazing confrontation, Gray whispered: "Wow! Landing on a little island occupied by a whole Japanese army!" and Ben, realizing that the young fellow was trying to maintain his courage, said quietly: "Kiska's more'n a hundred square miles. Might be hard to find the Japs even if we wanted to." Then, to ease the tension further, he added: "Were you on Attu, Lieutenant?" and when Gray replied that he had led one of the clean-up assaults on Holtz Bay, Ben said with great warmth: "You got nothin' to prove."

And Ben was right, for in those first perilous moments when the three leaped upon the beach and started running, in those fateful seconds when hidden machine guns might have cut them literally in half, it was Gray who was in the lead, now a man without fear, and kept going until they found themselves well inland. But when they had traversed the beach in miraculous safety, a fearful thing happened. Gray, exulted by the fact that he had done well, turned to ask his adviser: "What do we do now, Ben?" only to see that the fox farmer who had been so composed in the boat stood trembling—not nervously twitching, but shaking as if some fearful blizzard were engulfing him—and it was clear to both Gray and Nate that he was so emotionally exhausted he could no longer function as a member of their team.

For just a moment the young lieutenant was bewildered, for he realized that his group was in a hazardous position with one-third of its component immobilized, but Nate hid Ben behind a rock and said in a consoling whisper: "It's all right. You wait. We'll be back." Then he sought Gray and said: "We split, very quiet, circle out and head for that big thing over there, whatever it is."

With no sense of having had his position of leadership usurped, Gray said: "Solid idea," and he was off like a rabbit.

When the men met at what turned out to be a discarded generator, neither was bold enough to voice what was in his mind, but after poking about, Nate had to speak: "I think nobody's here."

Very quietly, Gray said: "Me too," but then echoes of his training surfaced. "Men," a gruff veteran of the first days of fighting on Guadalcanal had warned when he visited Gray's camp in Texas, "the Jap soldier is the trickiest bastard on earth. He'll fool you in a dozen different ways. Booby traps, sharpshooters tied in trees, buildings left to make you think they're abandoned. You bite on his traps just once, you're dead . . . dead . . . dead."

Ominous and lethal, the silent buildings ahead seemed a perfect example of Japanese perfidy, and Gray's knees grew weak. "You think it's a trap?" he whispered to Nate, who replied: "We better find out," and then Gray resumed command.

"Cover me," and with a bravery few men could have shown, he dashed right at a cluster of buildings that must have been a combined mess hall and laundry, and when he reached it, he jumped in the air, waved his arms, and cried: "It's empty!"

Before Nate could overtake him he began running about, making a disgraceful amount of noise as he sped from one abandoned building to the next, finding each one vacant. Then, remembering that he was in command, but so excited that he could barely issue an order, he cried: "Let's try that one, and if she's empty too, we flash our signal."

So the two men crept toward what must have served as command headquarters, and when in darkness they found it cavernous and empty, Gray grasped Nate by the arm and asked: "Dare we tell them?" and Nate said: "Send the word," and Gray activated his radio and shouted: "They're all gone! There's no one here!"

"Repeat!" came the stern voice from the flotilla commander.

"There are no enemy here. Repeat. Nobody here."

"Verify. Report back in ten minutes. Then return to ship."

It was a strange ten minutes, there in the Aleutian night with the winds whipping in from Siberia and two bewildered Americans trying to figure out how an entire Japanese army could have slipped off this island while American boats patrolled the seas and American planes the skies. "They couldn't all escape," Gray cried petulantly. "But they did," and he ran about, savoring this great discovery, but when Nate Coop returned to the beach to sit with Ben Krickel and saw the pitiful condition he was in, he, too, began to shake. Then Lieutenant Gray ran down shouting: "Ten minutes up! We can verify," Nate said: "Go ahead," but he took no joy in the dramatic news, and during the row back to the PBY he pulled mechanically, not fully aware of where he was.

So a fully equipped American-Canadian army of thirty-five thousand marched ashore against no opposition, but on the first afternoon an American bomber from Amchitka, having failed to get the news, continued his ordained run, saw what he supposed to be Japanese troops operating without cover below, bombed them. Two dead.

The generals, unwilling to believe that the Japanese had been able to evacuate an entire island while bombers were overhead on inspection flights, sent out heavily armed patrols to ensure that no remote pockets of Japanese hidden in caves were waiting to attack. This caution was advisable and it was carried out with proper care, but the men who had come so far to fight were so eager to do so that when one group heard suspicious sounds coming from another group on the other side of a slight rise, gunfire was begun by a nervous American corporal and returned by an equally nervous Canadian sergeant, and in the wild engagement that followed, twenty-five allies were killed by Allied bullets, and more than thirty were wounded.

That was the final battle of the Aleutian campaign. Japan's attempt to conquer America from the north had failed.

No sooner had peace in the Pacific been obtained than a war of equal importance to Alaska erupted. To appreciate its significance, one must follow what was happening to the two young married couples in the Flatch family in the months following the explosions of the two atomic bombs over Japan, and the subsequent collapse of the Japanese war effort.

Nate Coop, strengthened and deepened by his war experiences, now astonished everyone by announcing: "I'm going to take my GI benefits and go to the university in Fairbanks."

When the entire family seemed to ask at once "What for?" he said: "To study wildlife management," and when they chorused: "Where'd you get that crazy idea?" he explained cryptically: "Corporal named Dash Hammett told me: 'When the war's over, get off your ass and learn something.'" He would say no more, but after the first shock, he was supported by his wife, who remembered Missy Peckham's counsel: "If you can tame a moose, you can civilize Nate," and she accompanied him to Fairbanks.

LeRoy Flatch, now a captain in the Air Force, was urged by his superior, General Shafter, to remain in that service, with assured promotions to major and lieutenant colonel: "After that it depends on the impression you make on your superiors, but I have confidence you could be a general one of these days . . . if you get yourself some education." Despite similar recommendations from his fellow officers, LeRoy opted to retire so that he could resume his career as one of the leading bush pilots, and in pursuit of this ambition he decided to apply his bonus money as down payment on a used Gull-wing Stinson four-seater, total cost $10,000, whose former owner had been a mechanical genius. The plane, as he modified it, had both wheels and skis, permanently attached, which meant that Nate could take off, wheels down, fly to some snow-covered field high in the mountains, activate a hydraulic system, and retract the wheels through a slit in the middle of the big wooden skis. On the return home he could take off on skis, punch the hydraulic button, and feel the wheels come down through the slits. Of course, since the system was fixed, he could no longer attach pontoons for the summer lakes. So, to ensure maximum flexibility, he also bought an updated version of his old Waco YKS-7 which had pontoons, but he was shocked by the price increase. He had paid $3,700 for his first Waco, $6,300 for its replacement, which he kept on a lake near his cabin.

But he now had a wife, and the former Sandy Krickel, accustomed to the free and open life of the Aleutians, especially the field trips with her father to isolated islands like Lapak, did not look with favor on being cooped up in a Matanuska cabin with her in-laws.

Matanuska had proved such a signal success, despite the early negative publicity, that it seemed as if half the people who came to Alaska wanted to settle in the valley, which meant that LeRoy and Sandy could find nothing suitable. Sandy suggested acquiring some land up toward the glacier and building their own home, but LeRoy pointed out that with the purchase of two planes he could not swing a house too.

"Why not buy just one plane?" she asked, and he said firmly: "Wheels, skis, pontoons, tundra tires, a guy like me has to have them all," so the possibility of a house vanished.

At this point an old friend, or rather four old friends, helped him make a radical decision, one with which he was going to be quite happy. Tom Venn of Seattle, with his R&R ventures prospering in the peacetime business resurgence, was eager to reestablish himself at Venn's Lode at the side of the great glaciers issuing out of Denali: "I want to spend more time there. So does Lydia. And the young ones,

Malcolm and Tammy, insist. So, LeRoy, I want you to fly the stuff in
and more or less look after the place when we're gone."

"I'm a pilot, not a real estate agent," LeRoy said brusquely, and
Venn said: "So you are. But I think that in the years ahead, bush flying is bound to center on some spot well north of Anchorage. Competition from the big planes will kill you if you stay in Matanuska."

Since Venn had proved many times over that he had an acute
business sense, LeRoy had to listen, and he attended carefully to what
the older man said as they spread before them maps showing central
Alaska: "It's not badly named, this stretch between Anchorage and
Fairbanks. 'The Railbelt,' because the railroad, such as it is, ties it all
together. This is where the vitality of Alaska will focus in the future,
and it's where you've got to focus now." With an imperative finger
Venn stabbed at the Lode: "Our place is over here by the mountains.
Matanuska, your place down here, is too far away for you to service
us properly. Fairbanks is way too far north. But here in the middle is
a delightful little town, Talkeetna, named after the mountains. Within
easy distance to our place. Lots of mines in the area needing flights.
Lots of lakes with one or two cabins along the shore needing groceri-
ies. The railroad runs through, but what keeps it good, the highway
doesn't. Talkeetna stands off to one side. Quiet. Frontier."

"You make some good points," LeRoy said, and the wily businessman concluded: "I've saved the most compelling for last. Move
to Talkeetna and I'll finance your two planes, no interest."

"Talkeetna has just become my headquarters," LeRoy said. Then
he reflected: "You know, Mr. Venn, after you've been an Air Force
captain in charge of big planes, you start to think big and you want
to make something of your life. A wife and all. The best thing I can
visualize, a real good bush pilot, master of this whole frontier," and
he spread his hands over the Railbelt, which would henceforth be his
terrain, its remote fields, its white-outs, its hidden lakes, its storms, its
wonder.

Snapping his fingers, Venn rented a car and together they drove
the eighty drab miles toward the sleepy, false-fronted, wooden-
housed town of Talkeetna, population about one hundred, and during the trip LeRoy was apologetic for the bleakness of the land, but
as they left the main highway for the Talkeetna cutoff they climbed a
short hill, from the top of which there was a superb view of the great
Denali range, high and white and severe, the guardian of the arctic,
and the sight was so majestic, and so rare considering the clouds that

usually prevented any view, that the two men halted the car, parked at one side, and luxuriated in this spectacular revelation of the Alaskan heartland: "Looks like the mountains are sending you an invitation, LeRoy," and the young veteran caught a reinforcing glimpse of what life could be like in this area during his mature years.

But even as they sat there on this day that seemed so perfect, a weather front began to scud in from Siberia at a furious speed, and within minutes the mountains were lost, and LeRoy was reminded that in moving his operations to Talkeetna, he was taking on a whole new set of challenges. He would still have to fly to remote lakes where old men lay dying or young women were preparing to give birth, and he would as always run the risk of being caught in sudden storms, but off to the northwest would rise that tremendous range of snow-capped mountains, and if he were to do a real job of flying, he would have to master them: land on skis at eight thousand feet to deliver and pick up mountain climbers, fly at sixteen thousand feet to scout the flanks of great Denali to locate where the dead bodies lay. It was the kind of flying a bush pilot not only accepted as a challenge but sought.

As the great mountains disappeared, those that would in the years ahead be his white beacons, he said quietly: "I'll do it," and Venn said: "You'll never be sorry," and the switch to Talkeetna with its earthen strip and convenient nearby lakes was done.

Sandy did not find a house they could afford, but with the loan from the Venns she and her husband were able to build one, and when they were ensconced it was she who volunteered to look after Venn's Lode while her husband did his flying. It was also she who purchased what she called "this neat little radio job," on which she could talk to her husband while he was flying out to some remote site or hurrying home ahead of a storm.

The move to Talkeetna was one of the best things LeRoy Flatch ever did, for it introduced him to the heartland of Alaska, the Railbelt that bound the major cities together. As an aviator he had previously been aware of the railroad only as a line of life-saving tracks to be followed when visibility was otherwise nil, but now, with daily trains stopping at Talkeetna, he occasionally had the opportunity to ride north to Fairbanks. Then he appreciated the superlative job his Alaskans had done in building this northernmost railbed. And he was especially pleased with the exceptional beauty that enveloped the land during a few trembling weeks in late August and November.

Then shrub alders turned a flaming gold, blueberry bushes a fiery red, while stately spruce provided a majestic green background against the pristine, icy white of distant Mount Denali. It was Alaska at its best, and LeRoy told his wife: "You can see it only from the train. Looking down from a plane . . . just a blur," and she replied: "From wherever I stand, it looks pretty good."

But later, when they flew to the Lode to dine with the Venns, they learned that others had quite different dreams of what Alaska might become. "There's a lot of loose talk beginning to circulate," Tom Venn said after dinner, "about this crazy idea of statehood for Alaska." He studied the two young people before him and asked: "Do you support such nonsense?"

Since his question practically demanded a negative response, the best Sandy Flatch could do was temporize. Vaguely but not passionately in favor of statehood, she voiced an opinion which would be heard much in forthcoming months: "I wonder if we have a big enough population?"

"We do not!" Venn said firmly. "How about you, LeRoy?"

Since he still owed the Venns for the two planes and his house, and was dependent upon them for much of the business which kept his one-man company afloat, he, too, deemed it wise to be evasive, but in his case he believed rather strongly in the military judgment he now issued: "Alaska's principal value to the United States, perhaps its only value, is to be a military shield in the arctic. With our limited resources we could never defend this territory against Asia. And with Russian communism on the march everywhere, they might be coming at us at any moment."

"You've hit one nail on the head," Venn said enthusiastically, but then he turned to his wife: "Tell them the even bigger idea they missed, Lydia," whereupon she entered the conversation with considerable vigor: "My father saw it in the old days. I see it now. Alaska will never have the people or the power or the finances to operate as a free state, like the others. It must depend on help from the Lower Forty-eight."

"And that means what it's always meant," her husband broke in. "Seattle. We can assemble the money from the other states. And when we have it, we've always known what to do with it."

"The point is," Lydia said persuasively, "my family, for example, we've always tried to do what's right for Alaska. We look after the people up here as if they were members of our own family. We help educate them. We defend their rights in Congress. And we treat their natives far better than they do themselves."

For the better part of two hours the two Venns hammered away at the doctrine that had become almost sacred in Seattle: that statehood for Alaska would be wrong for the people of Alaska, wrong for the nation at large, wrong for the natives, wrong for industry, wrong for the general future of the area, and, although Venn never said so openly, not even at home, terribly wrong for Seattle. The two Flatches, who had entered this chance discussion with no strong convictions, left the Venns' house fairly well convinced that statehood was something to be avoided.

The second Flatch family, fortified by its education at the university, took the other side in this battle. Flossie Coop had only vague and generally unpleasant memories of Minnesota, even though she had been ten during her last year in that state. "It was bitter cold," she told Nate, who had never visited the Outside. "Much worse than Matanuska. And we never had enough food. And Father had to poach to get us a deer now and then. And I left it with no regrets, none at all."

"What's your point?"

"So I was what they call disposed to like Alaska. For me it was freedom and enormous vegetables and a glacier right up the valley and a tame moose. It was excitement, and a new world being born, and great neighbors like Matt Murphy and Missy Peckham, and the feeling that you were taking part in history." She stopped, tears came to her eyes, and she leaned over to kiss her husband: "And what you did in the war."

Suddenly embittered, she rose and stalked about the cabin: "And what my old man did building that road. And the way LeRoy flew his airplanes everywhere in all kinds of weather. People have the nerve to ask me if we're ready for statehood? We were ready the day I stepped off that *St. Mihiel,* and we're a lot readier now."

Nate Coop did not require his wife's surprising histrionics. Alone he had spied out the enemy on Lapak Island. Sometimes alone he had spied on Adak, Amchitka, Attu and Kiska. He rarely spoke of his adventures and never of the death of Captain Ruggles, one of the finest men he had known, but he did feel that from these experiences, and from his years as a miner in the heart of the territory, he knew something about what Alaska was and what its potential could be. He was for statehood. Men like him and his father-in-law working on the Alcan Highway and his brother-in-law flying those planes, they had earned statehood and a whole lot more. He rarely entered into the public discussions that were beginning to spring up across the territory, but if questioned, he left no doubt as to his basic opinion: "I'm for it. We got the brains to run things."

When peace came to Matanuska it modified the life of the elder Flatches very little. They continued to live in their original cabin, and even during the time they had to share it with LeRoy and his wife they felt no inconvenience, mainly because each of them was outdoors a great deal. Because Elmer's broken legs did not heal easily or strongly, the old man could not resume his life as a hunting guide for parties of rich men out of Oregon and California, and he was grateful when young Nate volunteered to replace him. There was trouble when they told Flossie of their plans, for she said: "I want nothing to do with hunters who kill animals," but Nate said: "All you have to do is feed them," and he encouraged her to start a section of the holding in which she kept orphaned animals and those wounded by careless shots.

It was during one of these hunts that Nate first felt emboldened to reveal openly his desire for statehood. He was guiding three well-to-do Seattle sportsmen in the Chugach Mountains; they had wanted to camp out in the old tent-and-blanket style, and rarely had he worked with a team which better exemplified the meaning of sportsmanship, for each man carried his full load of gear, each washed dishes in turn, and each chopped wood. They were a notable group, and on the third night, after the work had been done, one of them, a banker who had helped Tom Venn's Ross & Raglan finance recent expansion in Alaska and who had accepted enthusiastically Venn's interpretation of Alaskan history, said to his companions: "It would be a shame to spoil this wilderness with some expensive nonsense like this statehood folly they're talking about. Keep this as the paradise it is."

"Absolutely!" one of the hunters agreed, while the third, a man connected with the insurance of cargoes bound for Alaska, said: "In a hundred years an area like this would never be able to support itself."

The banker, who had fought in Italy in World War II, said: "The important thing to remember is not dollars and cents. They can be negotiated. It's the military posture of our nation. We need Alaska up here as our forward shield. It should really be under the control of our military."

Each of the three hunters had seen service during the war, but none had served anywhere near Alaska; however, each had strong opinions about the proper defense for the arctic. "The great danger is Soviet Russia. People make a lot of the fact that at the two little Diomede Islands, one American, one Russian, communism is only a mile and a half from our democracy. That's insignificant, good propaganda but not much else. However, from the real Siberia to the real Alaska at one important spot is only sixty miles, and that's a real danger."

The insurance man said: "No way Alaska could defend itself if the Russkies decided to come over," and the banker asked: "What is the population of the place?" and the insurance man replied: "I looked it up. Federal census 1940 showed a total population of seventy-two thousand. Single suburbs of Los Angeles have more than that," and the banker concluded: "Alaska is best seen as a basket case. It'll always need our help, and to give it statehood would be a criminal miscarriage."

Nate, busy stowing gear while this conversation progressed, finally felt obligated to break in: "We defended ourselves pretty well against the Japanese."

"Wait a minute!" the third hunter protested. "I was serving on Guadalcanal, and we were scared out of our minds when the Japanese captured your Aleutian Islands so easily. They had a real pincer movement going, South Pacific, North Pacific."

"We drove them off, didn't we?"

The man from Guadalcanal, thinking that Nate meant the Alaskans alone had defeated the Japanese, said: "You and about fifty thousand mainland troops to help," and Nate laughed: "Me and that fox farmer who scouted the islands didn't have much stateside help."

The phrase *fox farmer* derailed the conversation because the Seattle men had to know what it meant. So Nate spent about half an hour explaining how, on the empty Aleutians, men like Ben Krickel leased entire islands, stocking them with one type of fox, "maybe silver, they bring the most, or blue, they thrive pretty well, or plain red or even a pretty light gray." He told how the Krickels, father and daughter, had harvested the blue foxes of Lapak Island and shipped them off to the dealer in St. Louis, and then he added: "My brother-in-law became an officer in the Air Corps. He married Krickel's daughter."

The insurance man was captivated by this story, and exclaimed with the kind of bubbling enthusiasm which enabled him to get close to people he was trying to sell policies: "I'll be damned! Two marriages in your family, and in each, one person's a standard Minnesotan, the other, half Indian. Isn't that something?"

"I'm half Indian. Sandy Krickel's half Aleut."

"Just by looking, can you tell one from the other?"

For the first time in this conversation Nate broke into a laugh: "Me? I can tell an Aleut from an Indian at a hundred yards. But when I act up, Sandy says she can smell an Indian at a hundred and fifty. Not too much love lost among the various natives."

"But they all have trouble with the white man?" the banker asked, and Nate evaded the question: "You know, there's about half a dozen different kinds of Eskimos, too. And a Yup'ik won't take too kindly to an Inupiat."

"Which is which?" the insurance man asked, and Nate said: "Inupiat is north along the Arctic Ocean, Yup'ik is south along the Bering Sea. I prefer the Yup'iks, but they would both like to beat up on me, if they thought they could get away with it."

"Which they can't?" the insurance man asked, and Nate said: "Three of them coming at me together might."

The banker looked up from the bed he was making: "So with all those differences, you certainly don't want statehood, do you?"

"I do," Nate said firmly, and the banker asked: "With only seventy thousand population," and Nate said: "Like with me barroom-fighting Eskimos, up here one man counts double, or maybe triple."

The person in Matanuska who took the fight for statehood most seriously was Missy Peckham, the feisty seventy-five-year-old who had remained at Matanuska because so many of her friends now lived there. Partly because no one else in the region seemed eligible, the territorial governor had made her the local representative to a Statehood Committee whose job it would be to organize local support for statehood and to represent Alaskan aspirations at meetings in the Lower Forty-eight. For many, such an appointment was a kind of local honor involving no work and not much commitment, but for Missy it became the consuming passion in the remaining years of her life. For she had learned while climbing Chinook Pass or battling for justice at Nome that self-government was not a matter of population size or tax base or conformance to rigid rules, but rather the degree of fire in the human heart. And hers was ablaze, for she had witnessed at close quarters the zeal with which the Matanuska settlers had built a new world for themselves, and she had watched as ardent men constructed their highway through the wilderness. She knew that the people of Alaska were ready for statehood, and that their courage had established their eligibility.

So, taking her assignment seriously, she began to make herself Alaska's civilian authority on one small but important aspect of the problem: the salmon industry. She had never actually worked in a salmon cannery, but her long residence in Juneau had placed her in touch with some dozen operations like Totem Cannery on Taku Inlet, and from her experiences with both the Seattle owners of such places and the men who worked in them, she had a solid founding in the economics of this crucial industry. When she put her data together she was able to present a sickening portrait of an indefensible situation, as she did in her first impassioned presentation at a mass meeting in Anchorage:

> "The facts are these. The canneries have always been owned by rich men in Seattle, only rarely if ever by anyone in Alaska. By remaining in cahoots with powerful interests in Washington, they've always avoided paying taxes to our government in Alaska. They import workers into our areas for the summer months but pay no taxes on their salaries. Oh yes! They do pay five dollars a head, five dollars, to a kind of school tax, but not nearly what they should pay for stealing one of our most valuable natural resources.

> "What burns me up, and ought to burn you up, is the fact that with their fish traps and fish wheels they're destroying our salmon. In the state of Washington and in Canada they don't allow that wanton killing. So their salmon are increasing year by year. Ours are dying. Because the federal authorities have always been under the control of the Seattle interests, never under ours. Because we aren't a state, we have no senators or congressmen to fight for us."

She spoke that first time for about fifteen minutes, making a tremendous impression because of the authority with which she had assembled the facts which condemned the present situation; later, when concerned experts began to feed her even more specifics, her standard salmon speech ran about twenty-five minutes, serving as what one admiring advocate of statehood termed "our barn-burning speech," but at the height of her popularity—a slight, battling woman with a most lively manner of speech—one of the experts warned: "Missy, your talk is all facts and figures. If we send you to the Lower Forty-eight, you'll have to inject more human interest."

Since she had never worked on a salmon boat or in a fishery, she was at a disadvantage, but by accident she received help from a source she could never have anticipated. One evening when she spoke in Anchorage, where the agitation for statehood was growing, she noticed in the audience a handsomely dressed woman in her late forties who leaned forward to follow acutely each of the charges Missy was making. Her presence was perplexing, since Missy could not determine what her race might be: she was certainly not Caucasian, but she was also neither an Eskimo nor an Athapascan: She's probably an Aleut. With those eyes.

At the end of the rally the strange woman did not depart with the others, but stood aside as several men and women surged forward to congratulate Missy on her stirring speech. And when the hall was nearly empty, the woman came forward, smiled warmly, and extended her hand: "We used to meet in Juneau, Mrs. Peckham. I was Tammy Ting, Tammy Venn now."

"You're Ah Ting's little girl? Sam Bigears' granddaughter?"

"I am. Ah Ting and Sam thought very highly of you, Mrs. Peckham."

"Miss." Suddenly, as if caught stealing cookies, she clapped her hand over her mouth and grinned: "Did I say anything awful tonight? About the Venns, I mean?"

And then Tammy said something which would cement the friendship between the two: "Nothing that I don't say. I'm a strong advocate of statehood, Miss Peckham."

Missy stared at her, saw the lovely Chinese-Tlingit shadows which gave her face such a provocative expression, and suddenly leaned upward and kissed her. "I think we better talk," Missy said, and they returned to Tammy's hotel, where they discussed salmon and canneries and Ah Ting's and Sam Bigears' relations to both. "It's always confused me," Tammy said, "but in English my father's name should have been expressed as Ting Ah. He was Mr. Ah, but he always went by Mr. Ting. So did I. I asked him about this one day, and he sneered: 'Mr. Ah this, Mr. Ah that. Sounds if you're sneezing. Mr. Ting, sharp, businesslike.'"

"He was certainly businesslike," Missy said. "Tell me what it was like at the cannery," and the tales which Ah Ting and Sam Bigears had related to their families required hours to unfold. Thereafter, Missy's harangue on salmon took on a most personal touch, with stories of the visit of her old lover Will Kirby to Taku Inlet to try to persuade the Seattle owners to give the salmon a better chance to survive, and the dramatic sinking of the *Montreal Queen*. In fact, Missy's talk became one of the highlights in Alaska's drive toward statehood, for listeners went home and told their neighbors: "You ought to hear the Peckham woman. She knows what for."

The highlight of her personal campaign, insofar as salmon were concerned, came at a big meeting in Seattle, where it was essential to enlist the support of Senators Magnuson and Jackson. She telephoned Tammy Venn as soon as she got off the plane: "Tammy, this is most important. I want to make a good impression and I need your advice." She was astounded when Tammy answered: "You'll have no trouble. I'm going to speak right after you. I'll cover for any mistakes you make."

"You're going to speak in favor of statehood? In Seattle?"

"I certainly am."

"Bless you."

The two women, appearing toward the end of the program—the tough little social worker, the suave Chinese-Tlingit member of Seattle's high society—created a sensation, a powerful opening barrage for the statehood debate. The local papers, of course, featured the fact that Tammy Venn was the daughter-in-law of Thomas Venn, president of Ross & Raglan and an inveterate opponent of statehood for a backward area like Alaska, where so many of the Venn interests centered. Next morning, when reporters reached Venn for his reaction to Tammy's bombshell statement, he said austerely: "My daughter-in-law speaks for herself, but since she left Alaska at a fairly early age, she has not been able to follow recent developments there."

However, when the same reporters tracked down Malcolm Venn, he said: "You mean, my wife came out publicly for statehood?" When they chorused "Yes" he said: "She's as loony as a bedbug. I'll have to speak to her about this." Then he laughed: "Have you ever tried to argue her out of anything?" When asked specifically: "Then you're against statehood for Alaska?" he said seriously: "I sure am. That wonderful area was meant to remain a wilderness. With seventy thousand population, it couldn't run a town council, let alone a state."

Next morning the papers carried Tammy's rebuttal: "I always suspected my husband knew very little about the place where I was born. The 1950 census figures show that we have 128,643 citizens, and I'm sure I'll convince him by the end of this month that we're entitled to statehood." But that weekend the papers displayed a good-natured shot of Tom and Lydia Venn, accompanied by Malcolm, standing off to one side while saucy-looking Tammy posed with a banner that Missy Peckham had given her: STATEHOOD NOW.

The banter in the newspaper produced a most surprising dénouement: a fifty-year-old businessman in a blue-serge suit and highly polished black shoes came to Missy's hotel and introduced himself as Oliver Rowntree, in the freight-forwarding business in San Francisco and here in Seattle on some railroad negotiations important to the entire Pacific Coast. He was obviously surprised to see that it was such an elderly woman who was kicking up this fuss about statehood, but quickly got to his point: "I'm with you a hundred percent, Miss Peckham. I have no position in government and no authority to wield, but I do have a lifetime of information, and it galls me to watch people like Ross & Raglan conspire with the railroads to deny Alaska statehood."

"Why should you be concerned? Other than as a sensible citizen?"

"I was born in Alaska. Anchorage. I watched my father try to operate a grocery story there. One of the best, equal to anything in the Outside, as we called it then."

"Lower Forty-eight now."

"I do a lot of work with Hawaii. Out there they call it the Mainland. And it's my experience with them that has made me so bitter about Alaska. I want to see the people up your way get a fair break, at last."

"You're doing this for your father, aren't you?"

"I suppose I am. I saw the way he had to struggle to earn a buck because his neck was in a noose. Came to Oregon where the laws were sensible, had no trouble at all in building the best grocery north of San Francisco, died a wealthy man with a chain of eight moderate-sized stores, each one a bonanza.

"Now let's get down to facts. I'm discovering that generalized emotion means little in this business. Starving Eskimos are no better now than starving Belgians were in World War One."

The facts he unraveled were so startling that Missy asked him to go over them twice. "Better yet," he said, "I'll send you some reports," but when she received them they produced no substitute for the iron-hard recital he gave during their first meeting.

"It all starts with the Jones Act of 1920. Have you heard of it?"

"Vaguely. I know it's bad news for Alaska. Details? No."

"Well, the father of that shipping man whose photograph was in this morning's paper, old Malcolm Ross, was instrumental in getting it passed. Senator Jones from Washington bird-dogged it through the Senate. What it did, in simple terms, was put Hawaii and Alaska in a straitjacket, but Alaska in far worse shape than Hawaii. It said that the only ships which could carry freight from West Coast ports to either Hawaii or Alaska were ships built in the United States, owned by United States companies, and manned by United States crews. That places Hawaii and Alaska at a considerable disadvantage over ports like Boston or Philadelphia, where European vessels and those under foreign registry can bring in goods from abroad. But Hawaii has it lots better than Alaska, because it has competing lines who work to keep costs down. Alaska has only R&R, and they've continued to strangle people up there the way they strangled my father."

"I can't believe a nation would do this to one of its parts," Missy said, and then Rowntree offered the clincher: "Here's where I came into the picture in a big way. I bring an enormous lot of goods across country by train. Because of tricks the Seattle people slipped into the Jones Act, what costs me one dollar freight to San Francisco for shipment to Hawaii, costs you a dollar ninety-five to get it to Seattle for shipment to Alaska. So if you add up all the disadvantages under which Alaska suffers, it is something like three-to-one against."

"Why does Hawaii get such a favorable break?" Missy asked in disgust, and Rowntree said, only half humorously: "They're smarter. They've learned how to protect themselves in the clinches." And Missy vowed: "We're going to get some brains from Hawaii," and she asked Rowntree's help in drafting and polishing the famous oration which she would deliver more than sixty times in all parts of the Lower Forty-eight, "The Strangling of Alaska."

Her first delivery, at a hall in Seattle, had an unforeseen consequence, for Tammy Venn appeared in the audience with her high-spirited husband in tow, and prior to the meeting, people who knew them joshed Tammy because Malcolm had described her in public as being "as loony as a bedbug." When pressed, he told a listening newsman: "I have apologized most profusely for that statement. It was uncouth and almost indecent. What I should have said was that she's as loony as a pismire." Together they explained in the best of humor that they disagreed on many things: "Tammy's a Democrat, I'm a Republican. She wanted our kids to go to public school, I wanted one of the good private schools back east."

"Who won?"

"Tie. Girl back east. Boy here in Seattle."

"Who's going to win on the statehood issue?"

He replied: "The senators of this great republic have enough sense not to pass that nonsense," and as he spoke she put up behind his head, so the cameras could catch it, the index and little finger of her right hand, making them look like donkey's ears.

After the performance, which Tammy said was delightful and her husband a justification for citizen's arrest because of the way Missy slandered his father, they met with Oliver Rowntree, and at first greeting Oliver and Tammy stared at each other, snapped fingers, and cried: "Hey! I know you!"

"How did that happen?" Malcolm Venn asked as they sat down for drinks, and Tammy began hesitantly: "It's a long story, but do you remember, back in 1925, when you met me on that R&R ship heading for Alaska?" When he looked confused, she said: "Remember? You were working as a private detective. To snare the scoundrel who was sabotaging your father's ships?"

"Of course! We had a damned romantic trip, if I say so myself. But I never did catch the saboteur." Trying to repress a smile, Tammy pointed at herself, and when her husband shouted "You?" loud enough for other tables to hear, she nodded, then appealed to Rowntree to substantiate her story.

"She's telling the truth. For seven passages I was the one who threw the newel posts in the sea and jammed up the toilets," and Tammy broke in: "He met me by accident at the university, told me he had to divert suspicion from himself, and asked me to do what he did when clearly he wasn't present. All the same clues and all that stuff."

"But why?" Venn asked Rowntree, and the latter said simply: "Because you people, with the Jones Act in your pocket, were strangling legitimate business in Alaska. My old man went broke because of your old man. Sabotage was the only revenge I could take."

Malcolm Venn, soon to be president of R&R, stared at this stranger from the past, and broke into a warm smile: "You son-of-a-bitch! I ought to have you arrested."

"Statute of limitations."

"And you helped him?" This to Tammy, who grinned and said: "I sure did. My parents were pretty strong against R&R in those days. Later they relaxed."

They talked a long time about the old days, and Venn said: "My father worked with a real old reprobate named Marvin Hoxey to get the Jones Act passed, for the welfare of Alaska, and now I'll be working with some of the most honest businessmen in the world to combat statehood for Alaska, to protect that marvelous area from her own folly. There's no chance that you three can stampede this thing through, no matter how persuasively you speak, Miss Peckham. The good people of the United States are too clever to fall into your trap."

It seemed that once again the Western states knew what was best for Alaska, for in this early skirmishing, Congress listened to leaders like Thomas Venn and the industrial tycoons of Seattle, Portland and San Francisco, but even more damaging testimony came from Alaska itself, for in one public hearing after another its citizens rose to testify that their area was not ready for statehood, which they opposed for a variety of reasons. In one set of hearings convened by congressmen who flew all the way to Alaska to hear local sentiment, the following types of testimony surfaced:

General Leonidas Shafter, USAF (retired) living on the Kenai peninsula: "You're right, Senator, I did help build the Alaskan airfields and I did serve in the Aleutians during World War Two. From that experience I know the military significance of Alaska. It's the highway through which Russia will one day attack North America, and it must stay under military control. Statehood would be disastrous to the safety of our nation."

Thomas Venn, Seattle industrialist with a home near Denali: "Because of my long association with Alaska and the years I lived and served here in various capacities, I must oppose statehood for this vast, unconnected, unpopulated virgin territory. Present arrangements, tested by time, have proved that they ensure the welfare of the few who live here and spur the development of areas as yet untouched."

Mrs. Henry Watson, housewife, Haines: "I don't know six taxpayers that want statehood. Of course, there are a few Indians and half-breeds who pay no taxes, and they're hot for it."

John Karpinic, grocer, Ketchikan: "Nobody down our way wants to fool around with state government. We got enough trouble with the feds."

Opposed to this barrage in defense of the status quo, a few strong voices spoke up for statehood, and three voices were significant:

John Stamp, editor, Anchorage: "I could give you eighty reasons why statehood for Alaska is overdue, but I cannot improve on the simple words of James Otis on the eve of the American Revolution: 'Taxation without representation is tyranny.' If your hearts do not respond to that embattled cry, you are false to the spirit of the great nation that arose from that cry. Why does Alaska not have the roads that other parts of America have? Because we have no congressmen to fight for them. Why were our railroads not properly subsidized by the federal government? Why do we not have the airfields which we so desperately need? Why do we not have the schools, the hospitals, the public libraries, the great courthouses? Because you have denied us the right to tax the industries which in other parts of the United States help pay for those services. Like the colonists of old, I cry for relief."

Henry Louis Dechamps, professor of geography, University of California at Berkeley, an American citizen but educated at Canada's McGill University: "Gentlemen, in trying to decide what to do about Alaska, I beg you, do not look only at Juneau and Sitka and think you are seeing the heart of Alaska. Don't look only at Anchorage and Fairbanks. Look, I pray you, to the northernmost part of this vast land where it touches the Arctic Ocean, for along those shores and in that icy sea will occur the history that will determine the fate of

North America. We are lagging dreadfully in our knowledge of how to live and operate in the arctic. But I assure you that the Soviet Union is conducting constant exercises there and that her accumulation of knowledge far exceeds ours. We must catch up, for the Arctic Ocean is destined in the future to be not an icebound body of water, but a hidden sea in whose bowels submarines will prowl and other vessels that we cannot today envisage. It will be a highway for airplanes, a settlement for daring men prepared to make strikes against our communications, our forward bases, our shores and our very safety as a nation. Alaska, in the next century, will be one of the premier possessions of the United States. Ignore it and you endanger our nation. Develop it and you have an extra shield. Award it statehood now."

Miss Melissa Peckham, housewife, Juneau (after explaining the monstrosities of the Jones Act and the abuse visited upon Alaska by the railroads and the shore installations at Seattle, she concluded as follows): "I wonder if any single person who has testified before you during these three exciting days has had the wide experience of Alaska that I've had. Because I came young I was able to see the gold fields, the development of the Yukon River, the great salmon industry in the south, the growth of towns and cities, the noble experiment at Matanuska, the coming of the railroads, the building of the Alcan, the rise of aviation. Above all, I've seen the birth of a new people with new aspirations. We're fed up with being a colony. We want our own legislature to pass our own laws. We want to be freed from the condescending control of Seattle. We think we've earned the right to be considered full-fledged citizens with full-fledged rights."

But in the long run the most effective testimony came from people with strange names and even stranger faces who paraded before the microphones with statements so simple, they echoed like gunfire from the walls of the frontier rooms where the meetings were held:

Saul Chythlook, Yup'ik Eskimo cabdriver, Nome: "Demobilized San Francisco after duty on Iwo Jima. Worked awhile in country north of big bridge. Saw many small towns. Not so hot. They all self-governin', why not us?"

Stepan Kossietski, Tlingit teacher, Mount Edgecumbe school, Sitka: "I have my A.B. from the University of Alaska at Fairbanks, my M.A. from the University of California at Berkeley. I must agree with the woman from Shishmaref who testified this morning. Many natives are not ready for statehood. But I imagine that in a state like South Dakota, there are quite a few who are not ready, either. They drink too much. They're lazy. They don't read the newspapers. But let me tell you, the good natives that I know, they're not only ready, they're impatient. Are they capable of running what would be the state of Alaska? Let me tell you they're a lot better prepared than some of the people you send us from the Lower Forty-eight to run it."

Norma Merculieff, Aleut-Russian housewife, Kodiak Island: "My husband fishes for king crab. He and two others own their own boat, a hundred and eighty thousand dollars, all paid, taxes too. You think they don't know how to run a town council? So if they're too dumb, we wives will run the council, let them run the boat. They're buying a new one next year, quarter of a million dollars, they're doing all right."

The antis won, and statehood for Alaska seemed dead, but then various things began to happen, some of nationwide significance, others of arbitrary and even foolish dimension. The citizens of the United States started to think globally, and many who had never before dreamed of Hawaii or Alaska began to realize that the sooner the nation grasped those precious outriders to its maternal bosom, the better. Also, many American men had served in the Pacific and had learned to appreciate both its magnitude and its significance. Those who had hopped islands had discovered how important a nothing island like Wake or Midway could be—sandspits on which the fates of nations were decided, specks invisible from ten miles away on which the airlines of the world would depend—and they were not about to give up substantial islands like Hawaii.

There was always more support for Hawaiian statehood than for Alaskan, and considering their relative populations and wealth, no wonder. But thoughtful men like Professor Dechamps, who had testified before the congressional committee, continued to speak about the significance of the northern lands; the military, too, had new globes now rather than flat maps, and they appreciated the enormous value of a northern defense perimeter. So there was also a growing constituency for Alaska.

But now politics began to assume major significance, and some very curious miscalculations erupted: the greatest experts got things completely backward. They reasoned that because Hawaii was fairly well settled with responsible men and women in charge, it would surely vote Republican if it ever got statehood; while Alaska, being a rambunctious frontier state, would probably vote Democratic. In the long run it turned out the other way, to the astonishment of many people, including the experts.

At this crucial point, the thoughtful military around Eisenhower and the conservatives from Seattle and the West somewhat overshot their hand; they convinced the President that Alaska, at least the ninety percent up north, should be kept in a territorial status under military control. One afternoon, persuaded by their arguments, he gave the Washington press an offhand judgment that while the populated southeast segment of Alaska—Juneau, Sitka, Ketchikan, Wrangell, Petersburg—might have enough people to warrant statehood some time in the distant future, the great empty areas to the north would probably never have enough.

This howling error enabled loyal Alaskans everywhere to rush into print with a startling correction: "President Eisenhower may understand military affairs but he sure doesn't know much about Alaska. The preliminary census for 1960 shows that the southeast which he praises as being crowded with people . . . you take the five towns down there, they have a total population of nineteen thousand, while the Railbelt, that's Fairbanks to Anchorage and down the Kenai Peninsula where our only railroad runs, it's going to show more than fifty-seven thousand. That's exactly three times as much. It's the Railbelt that's ready for statehood, not the general's favorite little burgs down in the forgotten corner."

At this critical moment, when approval for statehood hung in the balance, one of those accidents erupted which sometimes help determine history. The governor of the territory was a gifted former medical student and journalist, Ernest Gruening from Harvard, who in 1928 had written the best book extant on the revolution in Mexico. His perceptive analysis having caught the attention of President Roosevelt, he had been appointed Director of the Division of Territories and Island Possessions, in which capacity he came to know Alaska and respect its potential for greatness. He spoke so often and so loudly in government circles about what Alaska might become that in 1939 he was appointed Territorial Governor, and was later elected to serve as make-believe senator to the United States Congress—allowed on the floor, but not allowed to vote—until such time as statehood was attained and real senators could be elected.

Having learned how much good the proper book at the proper time could achieve, Gruening, always the publicist, had approached a friend, the writer Edna Ferber, with a striking proposal: "Come to Alaska and write a book about us. Do for us what you've just done for Texas." Her immensely popular novel *Giant* had catapulted the foibles and grandeur of the Lone Star State into national prominence, and he supposed that a similar book by the same writer could do the same for Alaska.

Miss Ferber, having weathered the storm of adverse criticism that was rained down upon her by Texas loyalists, rather relished the idea of tackling another contentious problem, so she came to Alaska briefly and hurriedly wrote *Ice Palace,* which gained enormous readership. The consequences were precisely those that this clever man Gruening had anticipated. Of the book he would write later:

> *Ice Palace* made a strong case, in fiction form, for statehood. Some of the literary critics felt it was not up to her best work,

but one of them referred to it quite correctly as "the *Uncle Tom's Cabin* for Alaskan statehood." Thousands who would never have been interested in any of our pro-statehood non-fiction magazine articles, of which I had written several for *Harper's, The Atlantic Monthly* and *The New York Times Magazine,* did read novels.

In the closing weeks of our statehood drive scores of people asked me whether I had read *Ice Palace.* It was called to the attention of many Congressmen. I have no doubt that it changed quite a few votes.

In 1958, when the debate heatened, an elderly gentleman of excellent reputation stepped regally into a Senate hearing room in Washington prepared to testify against statehood for Alaska. He was Thomas Venn, seventy-five years old, here to protect the commercial interests of Seattle. White-haired and puritanically erect in bearing, he created the impression of a man who did not tolerate fools or their foolish opinions, but he was by no means repellent, for he could smile affably when his friends nodded, and he knew that this impression of gentility was heightened by the presence of his wife, Lydia Ross Venn.

As they took their places at one end of the row reserved for testifiers, Mrs. Venn whispered discreetly in her husband's ear, and he looked to the opposite end: "My God! How did she get here?"

It was Missy Peckham of Juneau, whose fiery determination had helped keep the struggle for statehood on the front pages of newspapers. She had a puckish smile and quick wit, and was not at all overawed by either the Senate hearing room or the dignitaries now filing in to conduct the session at which she would testify for the last time regarding the crusade to which she had dedicated her waning years. Now she saw Tom Venn staring at her, and with an innocent smile she nodded as if to welcome him to her party. Stiffly, the color still absent from his face, he bowed. Then he took his seat and listened as his long affiliation with Alaska and Ross & Raglan was explained to the audience. Then, never raising his voice or engaging in polemics, he stated the case of those who opposed statehood, now and in the foreseeable future:

"Gentlemen, no man in this room can speak of Alaska with greater affection than I do. I've known every corner of that vast territory since 1898 when I climbed the dreaded Chilkoot

Pass, and throughout the decades that followed I have always acted to promote the welfare of Alaska. I assure you that in my reasoned judgment Alaska is not ready for statehood, that it would be gross error to give it statehood, and that its future can best be assured by continuing the same benevolent custodianship it has enjoyed in the past.

"The military know how to protect Alaska. The businessmen of the West Coast know how to serve its industrial and banking needs. The sympathetic experts in the Bureau of Indian Affairs know best how to help the native peoples. And the Department of the Interior has proved that it can be relied upon to conserve the national resources. We have in place all the instruments required for a wise and protective system of government, one that has worked admirably in the past and will continue to do so in the future. Like thousands of thoughtful men and women who consider only the welfare of this great territory, I beg you not to encumber Alaska with a form of government it is incapable of handling. I urge you to reject statehood."

As Venn stepped away from the witness chair he had to pass Missy, who had, in a certain sense, reared him, served as his mother, encouraged him in his work, and imparted to him her wonderfully stable set of values. If he had been asked at that moment, he would have said without hesitation: "Miss Peckham taught me most of what I know." As longtime friends they nodded and might even have embraced, for their debts, each to the other, were tremendous. But now she took his place at the table to refute everything he had said:

"Distinguished Senators. [Here she stopped and asked: "Can this gismo be turned up? Can you hear me now? Good!"] Let's settle the biggest problem first. The previous speaker, a distinguished friend of Alaska, has claimed that we do not have a population sufficient to justify statehood. Well, when the fury of the Civil War was about to destroy our nation, President Abraham Lincoln realized that he simply must have two more Senate votes to protect his strategies for winning the war. How did he finagle them? Ignoring every rule for the creation of new states, he wrote his own rules and invited Nevada to become a state. He then bullied her acceptance through the

Congress, and by this headstrong act helped save the Union.
What was the population of Nevada at that historic moment?
It says here: 'Six thousand eight hundred fifty-seven.' Right
now Alaska has thirty-three times that number. And she is
just as badly needed now as Nevada was then.

"Why do you need us? Because we will always be your gateway to Asia, we will always be your outpost on the Arctic.
You need our expertise in living in and conquering the frozen
north. The day will also come when you will need our natural
resources: our vast supplies of wood pulp, our mineral deposits, our fish, and we may even have huge deposits of petroleum. My friend Johnny Kemper, who studied at the Colorado
School of Mines, tells me we may have a large deposit way up
on the Arctic Shelf."

When she left the table she walked purposefully past her onetime
charge, Tom Venn, who whispered: "Thank you for not lambasting
Ross & Raglan," and she whispered back: "We'll take care of you
when we get statehood." They smiled, nodded, and agreed to differ.

In late June 1958 it became apparent that Alaska had a strong chance
of slipping into statehood ahead of Hawaii, the racial mix in the latter territory militating against acceptance. The House had already
approved Alaska by a vote of 210 to 172, with an amazing 51 absten-
tions by congressmen who could not accept the idea that almost-
empty Alaska should have two Senate votes while populous New
York was restricted to the same number. Also, some opposed allowing what someone had termed "a mongrel population trapped in an
icebox" to attain full voting citizenship.

Now only the Senate had to approve, and for a while it seemed
doubtful that it would do so. Some senators tried to limit Alaska to
commonwealth status only: defeated 50 to 29. Others argued persuasively that the military were best fitted to decide Alaska's future: defeated 53 to 31, while a vocal contingent led by Senator Thurmond
supported President Eisenhower's accidental proposal that the entire
northern portion be excluded from statehood, even if the lower districts did attain it: defeated 67 to 16. It seemed to Missy Peckham, as
she listened to the debate, that her enemies could cite fifty arguments
against statehood, while she had only one in support: the time had

come for the Union to embrace without restraint a worthy new member.

On 30 June the deciding vote could no longer be postponed by obstructive amendments, and as the roll call proceeded, striking anomalies became evident. Stalwart Southern conservatives like Harry Byrd of Virginia, James Eastland and John Stennis of Mississippi, Allen Ellender of Louisiana, Herman Talmadge of Georgia and Strom Thurmond of South Carolina, having stated publicly that they were against statehood, now voted against it. But so did conspicuous liberals like Sam Ervin of North Carolina, William Fulbright and John McClellan of Arkansas, and Mike Monroney of Oklahoma.

Two tormented pairs of senators handled their conflicting loyalties in contrasting ways. Warren Magnuson and Henry Jackson of Washington had been pressured heavily by their Seattle business constituents to come out against statehood on the grounds that the state of Washington would lose economic control of the territory. When the vote came, each man had to follow his conscience: "Yes." The two Texas senators, Lyndon Johnson and Ralph Yarborough, were unquestioned liberals who had frequently spoken in favor of statehood, but when the real crunch came they simply could not risk their political careers by voting to admit a huge new state which would relegate Texas to second place. On the day the vote was taken, each man reached the same decision: he dare not vote for Alaska, nor could he in good conscience vote against her; so both were recorded: "Not voting."

The final count: yeas 64, nays 20, 12 not voting. Alaska had become the forty-ninth state, 2.2 times as big as Texas with a total population about the same as Richmond, Virginia. When Tom Venn heard the final count he said: "Alaska has doomed herself to mediocrity," but Missy Peckham, celebrating with friends at an expensive Washington restaurant, rose unsteadily to her feet, raised her glass, and cried: "Now we've got to show 'em!" and she spent the rest of that long night discussing the strange political and social innovations which would make Alaska unique among the states. Her own proposals were startling: "I want a school available to every child in Alaska, no matter what it costs. I want housing for every Eskimo, every Tlingit. We must have control of our salmon and our moose and caribou. We've got to have roads and factories and a dozen settlements like Matanuska." On and on she went, projecting those dreams which she had first voiced during the terrible Panic of 1893 and to which she had devoted her later life.

She became so excited, at age eighty-three, by this vision of an arctic Utopia and by her unaccustomed intake of alcohol, that when her friends helped her to bed, she fell into a deep, contented sleep, from which she did not awaken. When her body was discovered, associates informed Thomas Venn, whom they knew to be her longtime friend, and he hurried to the modest hotel in which she had died, and for perhaps twenty minutes he stood beside her bed, remembering her as she had been in those far-off days when she had brought hope and food to a starving family. At last he bowed down and kissed her pallid forehead, then kissed her again for each of those men whose lives she had illuminated: Buchanan Venn, the betrayed husband in Chicago; Will Kirby, the lonely Canadian policeman; John Klope, the lost soul in the Klondike; Matt Murphy, the indefatigable Irishman.

"I know she would want to be buried in Alaska," Venn said as he left. "Send her to Juneau, and let me have the bill."

XII

THE RIM OF FIRE

IN 1969 THE UNITED STATES GOVERNMENT BEGAN PAYING SERI-
ous attention to the problem of how the ancient land rights of the
Alaskan Natives could be honored and protected, and one honest
principle motivated all decisions. It was best formulated by the senior
senator from North Dakota, who said during debate:

> "Regardless of how we approach this difficult problem of as-
> suring justice to the various Alaskan Native tribes, we must
> do better than we've done with our Indians in the Lower
> Forty-eight. Whatever system we devise must avoid the reser-
> vation which is so destructive of Indian morale. It must assure
> the Native control over his ancestral lands. It must protect
> him against avaricious white men who would deprive him of
> those lands. And, if possible, it must enable him to preserve
> and practice his traditional patterns of life."

In the private debates that followed, two contrasting terms predominated, *reservation* and *mainstream,* the latter used as a verb: "I say the
sooner we mainstream the Indian the better. Cut off all reservation
support. Give him help where needed. But encourage him to enter
the mainstream of our national life and find his own level." In sup-

port of this recommendation, proponents cited horrible statistics stemming from the historic reservation policy:

> "An Indian reservation is a ghetto, and no pious wishes can gloss that over. It destroys initiative, encourages drunkenness, and inhibits the attaining of maturity. To keep our Indians on reservations is to keep them in jail. Of a hundred young Indians who go to college under the most beneficent conditions— scholarships, guidance support, special classes—only three remain to begin their junior year. And why do they fail? Certainly not because they lack inborn intelligence. They fail because the horrible reservation system operates against their continuation, for when they return to it their peers scorn them and their parents whine: 'Why go to college? You'll never get a good job even if you do graduate. The whites won't allow it.'

> "The only solution I can see is to shut down every reservation, throw the Indians into the mainstream, and allow each to sink or swim according to his or her ability. Granted, the first generation may encounter rough times. Those that follow will be ordinary Americans."

Such draconian recommendations were quickly dismissed by those who felt, as congressmen had for the past century, that if only the reservations could be well managed, the present system would function:

> "If you throw the Indian off his reservation, where a benign government endeavors to protect him, to preserve his ancient ways, and to enable him to live a decent life, where will he go? You've seen where he'll go. To the back alleys of Seattle, to the teeming warrens of Minneapolis and to the hopeless dregs of one small town after another. To throw him, as you phrase it, into the mainstream is to invite him to drown."

The debate might have ended there, in the impasse which had persisted for the past century, had not two remarkable witnesses appeared to testify before the Senate. The first was a youngish Jesuit priest who served as principal of a Catholic school on a reservation in Wyoming:

> "It is a bitter joy to see our Native boys and girls in their early teens. America has no young people better than these. The

boys are manly, good at games, spirited and eager to learn. The girls? No more beautiful creatures exist in this country. As you teach them, boys and girls alike, they brim with hope and the promise of becoming adults who can help lead this great nation and improve it as they do.

"That's how they are at age fourteen. At twenty-eight the young women are still hopeful and prepared to work for a decent life, but their husbands have begun to drink, to lie about, and to degenerate. Often they come home drunk and beat their wives, who begin to appear with their eyes blackened and their front teeth knocked out. Then they, too, start drinking and before long all hope is destroyed and they both become prisoners of the reservation.

"At thirty-six they're lost, men and women alike, and they spin out their lives with tangled thread, producing nothing. It breaks the heart to see this remorseless decline, and please allow me to specify exactly what I mean. Four days ago reservation officials came to my office in Wyoming to discuss what to do about the children of John and Mabel Harris. His Indian name was Gray Bird and in normal conditions he would become a chief of some importance in our community.

"But he and his wife have become so addicted to alcohol that they can scarcely function. Their two children, a girl thirteen and a boy eleven, did what they could, with our help, to keep the family together, but it was becoming clear that they would fail, so with anguish I recommended that the children be taken from the Harrises and moved in with a more stable family. Everyone, including the children and the new family, agreed that this was the only solution, but I said: 'A church school can't accept responsibility for taking children away from their parents, even though I personally recommend it,' so the officials accepted the duty and took the children to their new home.

"That night John Harris, wildly drunk, went to the new family's house, shouting and ranting that he wanted his children. But the children themselves, not the foster parents, convinced him that they wanted to remain where they were. So off he stormed, staggered into the path of a reservation garbage truck that was sounding its horn wildly, and was killed.

"His own children, hearing the commotion, ran from the house and reached his mangled body in time to hear the truckdriver telling bystanders: 'He was dead drunk. He was always dead drunk.' And that night—three nights ago today— his wife shot herself. Drunkenness and suicide are the heritage we have given the Indians as a consequence of our laws in contiguous America. Do not reproduce those laws in Alaska."

Indians, too, came before the various committees, pleading with Congress to establish in Alaska some system better than the one operating in states like Montana, Wyoming and the Dakotas: "There must be a better way. It's your responsibility to find it."

The second critical testifier was an Alaskan woman of forty-one who was about as far removed from a Jesuit priest as one could imagine. She was Melody Murphy, granddaughter of that famous Melissa Peckham who had come to the Klondike from Chicago in the 1890s and, via the wild gold fields of Nome at the turn of the century, to the capital at Juneau, where she had proved a thorn in the buttocks of any administration. Fighting always for the rights of the underdog, in 1936, Missy had turned up at the Matanuska settlement, where she had supported whites from Minnesota as vigorously as she had Aleuts from Kodiak. She had died in harness, fighting for statehood and enfranchisement for all Alaskans, and had bequeathed to her granddaughter not only her willingness to combat ignorance or injustice but also her indifference to marriage customs.

In fact, Missy Peckham had lived outside of wedlock with four different men, and by the time her longtime companion Matthew Murphy was finally free to marry her, neither she nor he saw much purpose in his doing so. Her granddaughter Melody, a handsome woman with four radically different strains in her background, had likewise avoided matrimony but not men, and by the time she was thirty she was known favorably as one of the great women of Juneau. Her mother, Melissa's daughter, had been more traditional and at an early age had married the son of a wild Siberian, Abraham Lincoln Arkikov, and his Eskimo wife. So Melody's four grandparents were the American woman Melissa, the Irishman Murphy, the Siberian Arkikov and the Eskimo woman Nellie, and there had not been a weakling in that quartet. And for reasons that she never explained, she early on took the last name of Murphy.

When she sailed into Washington at her own expense, having benefited from the profits of Grandfather Arkikov's uncanny skill in buying up unwanted Juneau real estate on the gut feeling that "Someone's gonna want this later," she spread before Congress her vision of a much different Alaska from the one they had been considering:

> "The informal census last year showed that we now have a population of two hundred ninety-one thousand eight hundred, and I assure you, it will double before the next one comes round. And if we strike oil big, as some are predicting, it could quadruple. We already have the most beautiful state in the Union and the one with the greatest potential for growth. I can see no end to what Alaska might become. But to get it started on the right path, we simply must get our land problems straightened out, and no part of that problem is more complicated than finding a way to assure our Native people their right to the lands they've always occupied."

At this point a senator asked: "Miss Murphy? It is Miss Murphy, isn't it?" and she replied: "It sure is."

"Tell us, Miss Murphy, are you a Native? Do you stand to gain if we allot land to the Natives?"

She laughed, the free and easy chuckle that might have come from any one of her Alaskan ancestors, and she was remarkably attractive as she leaned forward to help the senators: "In the curious mixing way that operates in Alaska, I would be considered half Native. One grandfather was an Irish prospector on the Yukon. He found nothing. The other was a crazy Siberian who sought gold in Nome. He found a beach full of it. One grandmother was of English derivation, the other was Eskimo. Me? I'm Alaskan, and because my Siberian grandfather did find that gold, I can afford to be disinterested where my personal land rights are concerned, but I'm vitally concerned about land rights for others." At this point the chairman had to rebuke the spectators for cheering.

> "Of our total population, thirteen percent can be classified as Native, and they're roughly divided into Indians, Eskimos and Aleuts. But in Alaskan Native life, nothing is ever simple, because the Indians, who should properly be called Athapas-

cans, are divided into various groups, one of the most important being the Tlingits. The Eskimos are also divided, Inupiat and Yup'ik. And even the Aleuts fall into two classes, the original Aleuts from the islands, the self-styled Aleuts from the mainland."

When one of the senators asked: "And what are you?" she said: "My Eskimo grandmother was certainly a Yup'ik. My Siberian grandfather? Now there we have a nice problem. His ancestors way back must have been Athapascan stock. Later on they could have been progenitors of the Inupiat. And if you look far enough back into my English ancestors, God knows what you'll find. I like to think I'm part Pict." Here the audience laughed quietly, but soon broke into guffaws as she concluded:

"Let's say I'm properly mixed. If I was a dog, you'd call me Rover and be damned pleased to have me.

"So Alaska has eight main Native groups—four Indian, two Eskimo, two Aleut—and we live together rather easily. By and large, any solution you come up with must apply equitably to all, and I assure you that the various groups will be prepared to accommodate, even though some of the small particulars might go against their own peculiar traditions. The basic problem? The Natives must have land. Next basic? They must be protected in their ownership until such time, maybe by some year in the next century like 2030, that they can make decisions about their land without these protections."

At the end of her testimony one senator asked the question which perplexed them all: "Miss Murphy, have you testified here today as a Native or as a non-Native?" and she replied: "As I told you, gentlemen, I'm half and half. When I took my oath to tell you the truth I was mindful that Alaska is eighty-seven percent ordinary Caucasian just like you, thirteen percent Native like the pure Eskimos and Athapascans. Your job is to find a solution that will enable both groups to move ahead in security and hope."

The Alaska Native Claims Settlement Act of 1971 (ANCSA) was one of the more intricate and unprecedented bits of legislation to emerge from the American Congress, and its bountiful provisions were due primarily to the fact that the American people suffered from a guilt complex because of the shabby way they had treated their Indians. They were now determined to do better with their Alaskan Natives. It was a collection of laws of which the American people could be proud . . . as those laws were understood in 1971. ANCSA was not a solution for the ages, but it was a generous step forward at that time.

Alaska contained 586,412 square miles—an area 2.19 times larger than Texas—for a total of 375,303,680 acres. Of these the Natives were to be given 44,000,000—12 percent of all Alaska—plus a cash settlement of $962,500,000. So far so good. But to accomplish some of the goals Melody Murphy had espoused, and particularly to prevent extravagant behavior during the euphoria when Natives gained their own land, the vast acreage would not be distributed to them individually but would be delivered into the hands of twelve huge Native corporations located regionally so as to apportion the entire state among them, plus a remarkable thirteenth corporation to include all Alaskan Natives living outside the state and therefore not attached to any specific area of land.

Every Alaskan Native born before 1971 and living anywhere in the world would thus be assigned membership in one of the thirteen huge corporations and receive papers entitling him or her to a proportionate ownership of that particular corporation. For example, Melody Murphy, resident in Juneau, became a shareholder in the powerful Sealaska Corporation, one of the best managed and also favored in the quality of the land it received. Vladimir Afanasi up in remote Desolation Point became part owner of the vast Arctic Slope Regional Corporation with an acreage larger than many states. An interesting provision covered the corporation focusing on the heavily settled Anchorage area, for there most of the best lands had already passed into private ownership; the Native leaders here were allowed by Congress to select comparable government-owned lands in widely scattered parts of the United States, so that an Eskimo living in a village near Anchorage might find himself part owner of a federal building in Boston or an unused warehouse in Honolulu.

Land had been returned to the Natives, but individually they did not receive it, two provisions of the act governing this: no land accruing to the corporation could be sold or mortgaged or alienated prior to 1991, but on the other hand, no taxes could be collected from it by the state. Congress believed that this twenty-year dormant period would provide the Natives with time to master the intricacies of managing their assets in contemporary American society. It was hoped by all and predicted by some that during these two decades the Natives would prosper so outstandingly that at the end of the tutelage period they would not want to sell their shares in their corporation or in any other way dispose of their 44,000,000 acres.

But now, as if to make the chess game more demanding, Congress also encouraged the establishment of some two hundred subsidiary corporations which would control village lands and properties, and this meant that the large majority of Natives belonged to two corporations. For example, up in Desolation Point, Vladimir Afanasi belonged to the enormous Arctic Slope Regional Corporation with its vast holdings, but he also had shares in Desolation Management, the minute corporation which handled business affairs for that village. Early in the new regime it became clear to him that sometimes the interests of the smaller corporation did not coincide with those of the bigger, of which it was a legal part, and he told his friends one day when they were far out on the ice hunting walrus: "It would take an engineer from Massachusetts Tech and a manager from the Harvard School of Business to unravel these complexities." Even though he'd had two years at the University of Alaska at Fairbanks, he felt himself incapable of plotting the course his two corporations should take: "And I wonder if any other Eskimos are clever enough to do so with theirs." The walrus hunters considered this for some time as they watched the icy sea, and one said: "In twenty years our kids can learn, if somebody gives them the right kind of education," to which Vladimir responded: "They'll be the most exciting twenty years in Eskimo history."

When avaricious lawyers and business managers in the Lower Forty-eight learned that the Native tribes of Alaska, often illiterate and uneducated, were going to have nearly a billion dollars, plus all that land, to kick around, they developed a passionate interest in the arctic, and carpetbaggers from places like Boston, Tulsa, Phoenix and Los Angeles began to appear in remote villages, eager to guide the Natives through the intricacies of their new responsibilities, while collecting gigantic fees for doing so.

One fledgling with a bachelor's degree from Dartmouth in 1973 and a first-class law degree from Yale in 1976 had no intention of spending his life in Alaska; indeed, it was doubtful that he had spoken the name outside of grade-school geography, let alone given it serious attention. But when in the summer of 1976 he passed the bar examination with very high marks, his father gave him as a present the choice of a new car or a hunting trip into northern Canada. Jeb Keeler, who had prowled the New Hampshire hills north of Dartmouth in search of white-tailed deer, opted for the Canadian adventure. Heading due north from Dartmouth, he landed on Canada's remote Baffin Island, where he planned to shoot himself a caribou.

, Probing boldly into the tundra north of the Arctic Circle, he accomplished nothing, but one night in July when there was no night he was lounging in the bar of the hunting lodge at Pond Inlet when a big, florid man wearing expensive hunting gear took a seat at his table without asking permission and said: "Son, you look mighty glum."

"I am. Came up here to get me a caribou . . . nothing."

The uninvited visitor slapped the table and said: "Remarkable! I came up here to do the same thing. And I got nothing. Name's Poley Markham, Phoenix, Arizona."

"Somebody around here got a caribou. Look at it hanging over there."

"That's mine," Markham said proudly. "But to bag it, I had to fly over to Brodeur Peninsula."

"Where's that?"

"Smart distance due west." He leaned back, studied his caribou, and said expansively: "That could be one of the most important animals I've ever taken." When Jeb asked what that meant, the Phoenix man called for a round of drinks and launched enthusiastically into a remarkable monologue which had so many unexpected twists that Jeb was enthralled:

"As you've found out, people say that caribou are very common. They're everywhere. But not when you want to shoot one. And they certainly weren't common when I tried to bag one in Alaska. Years ago up on the Yukon River, I determined to get me the Big Eight, and I had seven of their heads on my wall in Phoenix, what hunters call 'the hard ones,' but damned if I could get the eighth, the easiest one of all, the caribou.

"The Alaskan Big Eight? Wonderful mix, a challenge for any serious hunter. The two tremendous bears, polar and Kodiak. I got them early on. Fierce effort in each case, but I did nab them. Then the two big land animals, moose and arctic muskox, difficult but it can be done. Then the two great mountain animals, maybe the most demanding of all, the goat and the Dall sheep. That's six, leaving the most difficult, the walrus, and the easiest, the caribou.

"Well, I flew up to a great site way north of the Arctic Circle, place called Desolation Point where there's a hunter I recommend if you ever head that way. Excellent fellow, Eskimo with a Russian name, Vladimir Afanasi. He had helped me get my polar bear and now he was going to lead me out to the walruses. Four difficult days, but I knocked down a majestic beast, and as we packed the head and tusks for shipping I said offhandedly: 'Now I'll finish off with a caribou and I'll have my Big Eight.'

"You know, I roamed northern Alaska searching for that damned caribou, never saw one. Someone said there were half a million caribou roaming Canada and Alaska, and I never even saw one except from a plane until the other day on Brodeur Peninsula."

Jeb said: "You call them the Alaskan Big Eight, but you shot your caribou in Canada," and Markham said: "It's the animal, not the place where you shoot it. I could well have been in Russian waters when I got my polar bear."

Pleased by the manner in which young Keeler manifested his interest in hunting, Markham asked: "Did you say you just passed your bar exams? From Yale? High marks? Young man, if I were you, you know what I'd do? I'd get on the first plane and fly to Alaska. And since you seem addicted to hunting, when I got there I'd keep right on flying till I got to Desolation Point."

"Look, I'm just starting, and you're talking big bucks."

"I am talking big bucks."

"Nobody earns big money hunting. They spend big money."

"Who's talking about hunting?"

"We are."

"No," Markham said. "We're talking about Alaska, and after you earn your big bucks in Alaska, you spend your vacations collecting your Big Eight," and as he uttered these words Jeb Keeler, twenty-five years old, blond, athletic, unmarried, visualized himself on the ice off Desolation Point hunting either bear or walrus and on the high ridges tracking Dall sheep and the exquisite white mountain goat. But how he would pay for such adventure before his fifties he could not guess.

Then the Phoenix man explained: "Starting in 1967, I served as consultant to an ad hoc Senate committee on Alaskan Native land claims. Got my law degree at Virginia and always had an interest in Indian affairs. Point of my story, in 1971, Congress passed a land settlement act so complicated that no ordinary human being will ever be able to understand it, let alone administer it. On the evening of the day it was signed into law some of us lawyers met for dinner, and the oldest man present raised his glass for a toast: 'To the law enacted today. It'll give us lawyers employment for the rest of the century.' He was right. You ought to go up there and carve yourself a piece of the cake."

"Why aren't you up there?" Keeler asked with the forthrightness that characterized his behavior either on the hunting ground or in class.

"I am. I'm consultant to one of the real big entities facing the Arctic Ocean. I spend three, four weeks trying to sort things out for them. Bond issues and the like. Then three weeks hunting and fishing. Then back home to Phoenix."

"Can they afford to pay you? A bunch of Eskimos?"

"Son, have you heard of Prudhoe Bay? Oil! Those Eskimos are going to have so much money they won't know what to do with it. They'll need men like you and me to guide them."

"Is this for real?"

"I'm doing it. So are several of the team I worked with in Washington. The Native corporations are flowing with money, and smart lawyers like you and me are entitled to our share."

Markham was a big, fleshy man with what looked to be a flabby physique. But he loved the rigors of hunting and surprised the more athletic types when in the field, for he could outlast most of them when tracking an animal he wanted, and now, in pursuit of his hobby, he made a startling proposal: "Keeler, I like you. I can see you understand hunting, and I'd be proud to help you bag your first caribou. I've been working hard in Alaska and I'd enjoy another trip into the field. Want to come along?"

He surprised Jeb by volunteering that he, Markham, would hire a local guide with a float plane and fly north across open sea to Bylot Island, where caribou could be expected at the foot of the glacier. It was a flight of great beauty if you liked desolate places and a feeling

that the world was about to end; as they flew over the main part of
Baffin Island they spotted several great herds of caribou, and Jeb
said: "How can there be so many down there, and so few when I want
to find one?" Markham explained: "That's the lure of hunting. Wait
till you go out for your mountain goat." He turned to study his young
partner, then asked: "You are going to shoot for the Big Eight, aren't
you? Finest challenge in all of hunting, I think."

"How about lions and tigers and elephants?"

"Hell, anybody can tramp through warm jungles on a safe safari.
But you pit yourself against the arctic, against the Alaskan winter to
get your polar bear, that's man stuff."

When they landed, the guide took them to an area where he had
often seen caribou during their yearly migrations: "They swim right
across that channel, or wait till it freezes. Fantastic animals." On the
third day, while the two lawyers were some distance from their tent,
they came upon a fine buck with superior antlers, and Jeb was about
to fire, but Markham restrained him: "Good, but not perfect. Let's
move quietly over there," and when they did, they found just what
this experienced sportsman had wagered: a huge buck stood at the
edge of a small herd, and Markham whispered: "Now!" With a perfect shot, learned at Dartmouth while hunting deer, Keeler dropped
his trophy and tried to look nonchalant while the guide took a Pola-
roid of him posing beside it.

It was that photograph which determined Jeb Keeler's future, for
as he was examining it during the flight back to Pond Inlet, he told
Markham: "I'd like to rack up my Big Eight," and Markham said:
"If you come to Alaska, I'll help you get started. But the rules are a
little tougher now. Guys from the Lower Forty-eight like you and me,
we can't shoot walrus or polar bear or seals any longer. They're protected for the subsistence hunting of the Natives."

"Then why did you tell me about them?" and Markham laid
down the basic law of life in the north: "In Alaska, there are ways to
get around unpleasant rules that hem you in."

"I'd like the challenge," Jeb said, but Markham warned: "The big-
paying jobs with the major corporations have been taken, but you'll
find lots of opportunities with the village corporations. Like that one
at Desolation Point. I'll let Afanasi know that you're coming," and by
the time the plane landed, it was agreed that Keeler would put his
affairs in order, kiss the girls from Wellesley and Smith goodbye, and
head north to start his law practice in Alaska.

But on his return trip to the States, with the caribou head in the belly of the plane, he detoured to New Haven to consult with the man who had steered him through the law school and the bar exams. Professor Katz was one of those Jewish intellectuals who saw law as an interlocking of past human experience and future aspiration, and before Jeb could finish describing the Alaskan Natives' settlement, Katz stopped him: "I followed that through the Congress. Disgraceful to make it so complicated. No way those Natives will be able to manage their corporations and defend them against greedy men from the States."

"Then you agree with Mr. Markham that they need lawyers?"

"Indeed they do! They need guidance, technical support and meticulous advice on how to protect their assets. A bright young fellow like you could provide them with invaluable services."

"You sound as if you'd take the job."

"I would. For a spell, if I were younger. If you went into a New York law firm next fall, what experience would you have? An extension of what we gave you here at Yale. Nothing wrong with that, but it is limiting. However, if you go to Alaska, you'll be thrown into problems that haven't been defined yet. It's a real frontier, an opportunity to beat new paths."

"That man from Phoenix made it sound exciting. You make it sound challenging. I'm going to think this over."

When Professor Katz rose to accompany Jeb to the door he took him by the arm and held him close to his side, as he had done in those final weeks before the exams: "Mr. Keeler, you're a grown man now, but you have the exuberance of youth, and in a frontier society like Alaska's, that could trap you into misbehavior. Laws for the white man are more flexible there, the rules more easily bent. If you do go to work straightening things out, take treble precautions to act honorably. I don't know any other word that applies. I don't mean honestly, because the law covers that. And I don't mean sagaciously, because that implies twisting things to your advantage. I suppose I mean honorably, the way a man of honor would behave."

"I would hope that I've learned that from you, sir, and from my folks."

"You never know whether you've learned it or not till you're tested by reality."

It was under these conditions that Jeb Keeler left the East Coast for Alaska, taking with him his two hunting guns, his outdoor gear and the admonitions of his two advisers. Katz, his Yale mentor, had said: "Act honorably"; Markham, his Phoenix mentor, had said: "You can make a potful of money." He intended to do both and bag the rest of his Alaskan Big Eight in the process. As a start toward his ambitions he already had that fine caribou and a first-class law degree. What he needed now were the seven other animals and an opportunity to put his legal talents to use in some constructive and rewarding way.

When Jeb reached Juneau to establish his lawyer's credentials at the state capital, he found that Poley Markham had eased his way by enrolling him as a member of his firm, which enabled Jeb to skip the local bar exam and get to work within five days of leaving the airport. As Markham had warned, the big jobs were taken, but two of the best-run Native corporations, Sealaska in Juneau and massive Doyon in Fairbanks, found minor assignments for him, and it was while working at these that Jeb learned the basics of serving as a consultant in Alaska.

He had performed well in protecting the corporations' assets in a contract with a Lower Forty-eight construction firm, and was about to submit his bill when Markham flew in from Phoenix to supervise a business deal for his operation on the North Slope. "I'd be interested in checking your papers," Poley said. "We want to keep things consistent." When he saw Jeb's proposed bill he gasped: "You can't submit a bill like that!"

"What's wrong?"

"Everything!" and with a bold pen he struck out Jeb's modest figure, multiplied it by eight, and shoved it back: "Have it retyped," and when the new bill was turned in, it was paid without demur.

As he worked about the state on these minor jobs, Jeb discovered that Markham had served a long apprenticeship in such trivial work before landing his present job with one of the major corporations. He had been everywhere and had apparently offered Eskimo, Athapascan and Tlingit the brotherly kind of help their small corporations needed in the early days. Jeb found that when he mentioned Markham's name in the little villages, Natives invariably smiled, for in his congenial way Poley had given these villagers not only guidance but also a sense of worth. He had convinced them that they could manage their sudden wealth, and one weekend when Jeb had business in Anchorage, he listened attentively as Poley outlined his understanding of the enviable situation in which lawyers from the Lower Forty-eight found themselves:

"Take the average village corporation, and there's more than two hundred of them. There's certain things they have to do, the law demands it. And there's nobody in the village able to do it. They have to incorporate, and you know the paperwork that requires. Then they have to hold elections for officers, with printed ballots and all. But they can't do this before they have a complete enrollment of their members, and to achieve that they must have forms and addresses and letters. When we know who's entitled to the stock, the stock has to be printed and issued and registered, and that requires lawyers.

"Now the fun begins, because the village has to identify the land it's going to select, and that requires surveyors and legal conveyances and filings with the government. Then we have audits for which we have to hire C.P.A.s, the compiling of minutes, the arrangement for public meetings, and most demanding of all, it seems to me, keeping the public and the members informed regarding the operations of the new corporation.

"This is a lawyer's paradise, and not because we made it that way. Congress did. But since it's here and the money is in the bank, we're entitled to drag down our share. What is our share? Well, the government gave the corporations nearly one billion dollars. I'd say we were entitled to twenty percent."

"That would be two hundred million dollars!" Jeb gasped. "Do you mean it?"

"I sure do. If you and I don't take our share, somebody else will."

"You personally? What do you expect, I mean in real terms . . . what's possible?"

"What with one thing and another, I'll draw down not less than ten million."

"Just what do you mean, Poley, 'one thing and another'?"

"Oh, nothing really. Just the way all these deals shake out. But I do have some interesting things on the back burner, north of the Arctic Circle," and Jeb realized that he was never going to obtain a clear picture of how this big, amiable man operated. He was about to conclude that Poley's manipulations tightroped along the edge of legality, when the Phoenix lawyer threw his arm about Jeb's shoulder and said with a laugh: "The rule I follow is the rule you should follow: 'If even eight cents in hard cash is involved, leave a trail of written receipts a yard wide.'"

"I don't intend to steal."

"Nor do I, but three years down the road some bastard will be trying to prove you did."

Upon reflection later Jeb realized that Poley had not said forthrightly, like Professor Katz: "Do nothing dishonorable." What he had said was: "No matter what you do, leave a trail of paper proving that you didn't do it," but his attention was diverted from these moral euphemisms when Poley snapped his fingers and asked suddenly: "Have you flown north to touch base with Afanasi? You haven't? How are you progressing on collecting your Big Eight?"

"Just that caribou you helped me bag."

"Good. We'll fly up to Desolation and try to bag your walrus."

"Didn't you say walrus was illegal for guys like us?"

"Yes and no."

Poley insisted that Jeb clear his desk and accompany him to Barrow, where he introduced him to Harry Rostkowsky and his well-battered one-engine Cessna 185. "Are we going to fly in that?" Jeb asked, and Poley replied: "We always have. And two weeks from now it's going to fly your walrus head out."

When Jeb learned that the distance from Barrow down to Desolation was only forty miles, he hoped that he could avoid flying in Rosty's crate, but when they were aloft, Poley pointed down to the bleak tundra below, with never a tree in sight, just mile upon mile of hummocks, near-swamps and shallow lakes: "No road down there. Probably never will be. Up here you fly or you don't go."

In preparation for landing at Desolation, Rostkowsky flew well out to sea, banked to the left, and as he came in low over the village of some thirty houses, a store and a school that was in the process of being built, Jeb saw to his amazement that despite the thousands of acres of unused land, the settlement was perched at the far southern tip of a spit of land exposed to the sea on one side, a large lagoon on the other. "Snug, eh?" Rostkowsky shouted as he buzzed the place twice to alert the villagers, then dropped skillfully onto the graveled strip and taxied up to where people were beginning to assemble. Before anyone left the plane, he opened his window and tossed out two bags of mail and several parcels; then he unlocked the door and told his passengers: "Yep. With God's help we made it again."

When the citizens of Desolation saw their old friend Poley Markham climbing down, they began moving quietly forward, but no one made any gesture of excited welcome, and Jeb thought: If they treat an old friend with such reserve, how do they greet someone they don't like? But then he looked past Poley to the meager houses of his first Eskimo village and saw, standing off to one side, a short, round man in his mid-forties whose bare head showed that he wore his graying hair in a Julius Caesar cut, short and combed straight forward over his dark brow. Nudging Poley, he asked: "Is that Afanasi?" and Markham said: "Yep. He's not much for show."

When all the villagers had greeted Markham, for he had performed many charitable services for this village, the two men walked over to greet the Eskimo who would be their guide for the walrus hunt, and Poley said: "This is my young friend Jeb Keeler. Lawyer . . ."

"Don't you know anyone who works for a living?" Afanasi asked, and the men laughed.

In the days that followed, Jeb discovered that this quiet, capable Eskimo who owned the only truck in town was distinctive in a score of ways: "You had two years at the university?" Yes. "And you worked in Seattle two years?" Yes. "And you subscribe to *Time* magazine?" Yes, three weeks late. "And you're the head of the local school board?" Yes. And then came the question that perplexed Keeler but not Afanasi: "Yet you prefer to live according to the old traditions of subsistence?"

In uttering this tremendously important word, Jeb Keeler catapulted himself right into the heart of contemporary Alaska, for a great battle had begun, and would continue during the rest of the century, between those Native Alaskans who accepted the inevitability of getting most of their food from store-bought cans but who also wanted to improve their lot by bagging a seal or a caribou now and then in the ancient manner, and those forces of government and modernity which sought to hammer the Native peoples into an urban, money-economy lifestyle. In the halls of Congress the struggle had been described as perpetuation of the reservation versus mainstreaming, and while this disjunction was relevant to the condition of the Indians in the Lower Forty-eight, in Alaska, which had never known formal reservations, it was not: here the struggle manifested itself as a choice between ancient subsistence versus modern urbanization. Afanasi, having experienced the best of both systems, strove to be an eclectic: "I want penicillin and radio, but I also find great spiritual gratification in the subsistence way of life," and Jeb was captivated when he learned what this entailed:

"You're going to hear a lot about subsistence if you work in Alaska, Mr. Keeler, so you better get the definitions lined up. In the Lower Forty-eight, I'm told it means just getting by with the help of government handouts. Subsisting on the poverty level. In Alaska the word has quite a different meaning. It refers to noble patterns of life that go back twenty-nine thousand years, back to when we all lived in Siberia and learned how to survive in the world's most difficult ambiance."

Vladimir's use of this unusual word, and his vocabulary in general, caused Keeler to ask: "Are you an Eskimo? You have such a wide-ranging vocabulary." Afanasi laughed: "I'm about as pure an Eskimo as you'll find these days," which prompted Keeler to ask: "But what about your Russian name?"

"Let's go back five generations, counting me as one. That's not difficult if you're an Eskimo. A Siberian married an Aleut woman, and they had a son who became the well-known Father Fyodor Afanasi, a spiritual light in the north. Rather late he married an Athapascan woman from a mission station where he had worked. His church sent him up here to Christianize the heathen Eskimo, who promptly murdered him. His son, Dmitri, became a missionary himself, as did his son, my father. Me? I had no taste for missionary work. I thought our problem was the challenge of the modern world. But you asked what I was? One-sixteenth Russian without being able to speak a word of that language. Same percentage Aleut and equally illiterate there. One-eighth Athapascan, and not a word of that language. Pure Eskimo, three-fourths, but when I say that twelve of my ancestors were pure Eskimo, only God knows what that really means. Maybe some Boston sailor blood in there, maybe some Norwegian.

"But whatever the truth, I'm an Eskimo committed to a life of subsistence. I want to help my village take a whale or two each year. I want to go after polar bears and walruses when I can. I want two or three caribou when they come stampeding by. And we also live from the ducks, geese, seaweed and salmon. And what's important these days, I want to range pretty far afield to garner what I need to eat. And this puts me in conflict with outside hunters like you. I don't want you flying up here to kill off my game for trophies, taking the head back south and leaving the carcass to rot."

It was as succinct a summary of what subsistence meant to an Eskimo or an Aleut or an Athapascan as Keeler would hear, and in subsequent days when he and Markham went far out among the ice floes to hunt for walrus under Afanasi's direction, his respect for this pattern of life was intensified. One night as they cooked their evening meal in a tent pitched three miles from land, he said: "I've always considered myself a hunter. Rabbits as a kid. A deer in New Hampshire. But you're a real hunter. You hunt or you starve."

"Not really," Afanasi said. "I always have the option of going to Seattle or Anchorage and working in an office. But is that a viable choice for an Eskimo? Someone like me who has known what it means to be out here on the ice? Come back when we're on a whale hunt and see the entire village join in the ceremony of thanks to the whale. Then as we butcher our catch, everyone, even the oldest women, stands by to receive their share of the ocean's gift, whale blubber, the essence of life."

On the fourth day out on the ice, when they had moved to the farthest edge where blue open water showed in the distance, Poley Markham spotted what he believed was a walrus hauling himself onto the ice, and when Afanasi put his Zeiss binoculars on the spot he confirmed the sighting. Then, with a mastery learned from his Eskimo uncles, he directed his team of three into an approach which enabled the youngest member, Jeb Keeler, to put a heavy bullet into the great beast's neck, but just as Jeb fired, both Afanasi and Markham, standing well behind him, fired also, to ensure that a wounded animal was not left to perish in the deep. The three shots were so beautifully synchronized that Jeb was unaware that the other two had fired, and when he ran up to the fallen beast he exulted as if he alone had slain this admirable specimen, but he had scarcely reached the walrus when Afanasi started homeward to inform the villagers that a walrus had been taken.

Jeb and Poley stayed out on the ice that night, protecting their kill, and in the morning they were awakened by a file of villagers, men and women alike, who had come to butcher the catch and haul the fine, nutritious meat homeward. It was a triumphal day, with even the children participating in the rejoicing, and when the meat was distributed several youngsters were on hand to run portions of it to those who were bedridden. In the afternoon a dance was held, with the head of the walrus and his monstrous tusks occupying a place of honor, but now a shadow descended upon the celebration because a young Eskimo sidled up to Keeler and said: "You know, you can't take the head home with you."

"I can't?"

"Against the law. No sport killing of walruses."

This so startled Jeb that he ran over to where Poley Markham was dancing a kind of jig with an elderly Eskimo woman and her husband, the three of them waddling about like ducks on land. "They tell me I can't take the head back to Anchorage."

"That's the law," Markham said, leaving his dance.

"Then why did we fly up here? Just so we could say we'd shot a walrus?"

"We don't have to *obey* the law."

"I don't want to get into trouble. A lawyer at the beginning of his career."

"That's when you have to learn how to handle the stupid laws that legislatures keep passing," Poley said, and when the walrus head mysteriously appeared at Jeb's flat in Anchorage, the young lawyer did not make inquiries as to how it had got there, but hung it in a place of honor.

As Jeb worked with the various village corporations throughout Alaska he observed two facts: wherever financial shenanigans were in progress he discerned the subtle orchestrations of Poley Markham, the Virginia–Phoenix–Los Angeles wizard. Suits against one corporation, legal processes in behalf of another, proxy challenges to protect this large corporation, proxy defenses to subvert the hopes of that small corporation—in all such legal battles Poley was involved, until it appeared that the man had no moral base whatever. His sole function, it seemed to Jeb, was to generate disputes between the Native corporations, then litigate them, and always at such phenomenal fees that it was rumored he was making about a million dollars a year, even though he was in Alaska only three or four months during that time. He was living proof of the prediction that the Native

Claims Settlement Act of 1971 "was going to be a bonanza for the legal profession," especially if, like Poley Markham, the lawyer seemed to have no moral compunctions.

But at the same time, whenever Jeb accepted Poley's help in garnering the next of this Big Eight, he found the man to represent the soul of generosity and sportsmanship. "Why do you waste your valuable time helping me shoot a mountain goat?" Jeb asked one day as they were climbing the high mountains in back of Matanuska Valley.

"I love the high places," Poley replied. "The chase. I got as much fun watching you bag a Dall sheep as I did when I got mine." He would permit no shortcuts in hunting; when you were out with Poley you didn't hire a helicopter, fly into some high point, duck out, and gun down a goat. Not at all. You followed Poley up steep inclines, puffing while he seemed to be tireless, and you staked out the spot where you thought the elusive creatures might pass. You waited, kept downwind of where the goats might be hiding, and you froze, and when you stumbled back without having even seen a goat, you appreciated the great respect Poley had for animals and the thrill of chasing them.

"Of the entire Big Eight," he said one night after they had chased goats unproductively, "I think the greatest excitement came with bagging my mountain goat."

"Even more than the polar bear?" Jeb asked, for although under Poley's guidance he had bagged a big Kodiak, he had not yet managed a polar bear.

"I think so," Poley said. "To get your polar bear you just have to persist. Go out there on the ice floes. And in time you get him. But with a mountain goat you have to climb as high as he does. You have to be as surefooted. And you have to be one degree smarter. That's a tough assignment." He considered this for some time, then added: "I think maybe it's because he's such a handsome animal. Your heart skips a beat when you see a goat in your sights. So beautiful, so small, so high in the mountains." He slapped his leg, pitched more logs in the fire, and said: "Apply the attention test. I watched you when you were in my lodge in Phoenix. All the heads of my Big Eight on the walls. And what did your eyes come back to most often? That splendid white mountain goat. As if it represented the real Alaska."

In three extended expeditions to various mountains in Alaska, Jeb and Poley failed to bring a mountain goat within range, so Keeler's campaign for the Big Eight remained stalled at six: caribou, muskox, Kodiak bear, walrus, Dall sheep and moose, in that order, had been taken, but not the polar bear or the evasive mountain goat. "We'll get them," Poley vowed, and his insistence upon helping kept him constantly close to young Jeb. This, in turn, led him to throw more legal business Jeb's way. For example, when the corporation centering on Kodiak Island staggered into horrendous legal battles over who had a right to sit on the board of directors, Poley was too busy with the oil companies developing the huge reserves at Prudhoe Bay to give the various proxy fights his full attention, so he passed the lucrative Kodiak case on to Jeb, who spent the better part of a year and nearly four hundred thousand dollars' worth of his time unraveling a problem which should never have arisen. At the end of his third year advising the Native corporations in their internecine brawling, he realized that before the age of thirty he was going to be a millionaire.

His real money came when Poley got him involved in the intricate legal battles centering on the great oil field at Prudhoe Bay, for then he flew to that remote location on the northern sea, walked out upon the floes that kept it ice-locked ten months in the year, and watched as men from Oklahoma and Texas kept the drills plunging downward twenty-four hours a day. His first visit to Prudhoe came in January, when there was no daylight and his body gave no advice on when to sleep; it was an eerie experience highlighted by his visit with the team from California which provided the living quarters for the men and the food: "We've learned that to keep workmen from places like Texas up here, we have to provide three luxuries. Good pay, say about two thousand dollars a week. Movies twenty-four hours a day so that they can entertain themselves no matter when they get off work. And the dessert table."

"What's that?" Jeb asked, and the concessionaire from California showed him: "We keep the cafeteria open twenty-four hours, with breakfast constantly and a full dinner served whenever you want. But what makes life tolerable is the dessert table," and he led Jeb to a large area at the end of the chow line. There, on something that resembled in size a big pool table, rested no fewer than sixteen of the most luscious desserts Jeb had ever seen: pies, pecan tartlets, cakes, blancmanges, fruit salads, "and over here what they like best of all." Beside the pool table, in a nest of ice, stood six fifty-quart steel containers, each filled with a different kind of ice cream: vanilla, chocolate, strawberry, butter pecan, cherry with whole cherries and a marvelous concoction called tutti-frutti. And to make the area truly seductive, on two huge plates beside the ice-cream cans rested piles of chocolate-chip or oatmeal cookies.

"Watch!" the concessionaire from California said with a degree of pride. "That big fellow over there, he's already eaten enough dinner for three ordinary men, but now he'll hit the dessert table," and when the Texas oilman did, he took a wedge of pie, a hunk of cake, a huge bowl of tutti-frutti and six chocolate-chip cookies.

"If you keep their bellies satisfied," the California man explained, "they're satisfied. It's the cookies that turned the trick for us. The ice cream they expected. The cookies they appreciated as thoughtful extras." With professional judgment he added: "Men with a sweet tooth always take the chocolate-chips. Those attending to their health choose the oatmeal."

On his second flight in to handle legal problems at Prudhoe Bay, Jeb was accompanied by Poley Markham, and the two lawyers had one of the most terrifying adventures in their lives. It was March, and daylight had returned to the arctic, but as was so often the case with aviation, this proved a hindrance rather than a help, for when the pilot learned from his radio range that he had to be approaching Prudhoe, he began his descent, but the light available was a silvery gray and the wind kicked up enough blowing snow to make the entire visible world one exquisite pastel, with no horizon, no sky, no snow-covered landing field. There was no time, no season, no hour of the day, no discernible anything, just this mysterious, lovely, potentially fatal whiteout.

Unable to detect in what direction—up, down or sideways—the land lay, the pilot was either unable or unwilling to deduce from his flight instruments where he was or in what attitude, so, cutting power drastically, he tried to edge himself down, and he was flying close to the ground when Poley Markham screamed "Bulldozer!" and at the last moment the pilot pulled up in a grinding surge of power, just missing an enormous black dozer parked a hundred yards from the impoverished airfield.

Sick with fear, pilot and passengers circled in a grayness that had no definition, but gradually the omnipresent and inescapable force of gravity began to assert itself, and with the aid of his instruments, the pilot established his position relative to the snow-covered ground that lay somewhere below. Flying far out over the frozen ocean, he zeroed himself on the radio range and told Markham and Keeler:

"Keep watch. The signals are strong and good, thank God," and gingerly the plane felt its way through the deadly grayness, and Jeb thought: I saw a picture like this in a storybook, years ago. The hero was approaching a castle, visor down on his helmet, seeing nothing. And there was a fog, a beautiful gray fog.

Jesus! The snowy field was fifty feet higher in the air than the pilot had anticipated. The plane struck while still in a flying attitude, bounced high in the air, came down again thirty feet before it was supposed to, bounced again, then rolled to a trembling stop. When the ground crew came out in a jeep riding on immense snow tires, the driver yelled up to the pilot: "Land came up at you, eh?" and the pilot said: "It sure did," and the man said encouragingly: "No pain, no strain."

At lunch that day Jeb had a huge plate of tutti-frutti and four big oatmeal cookies.

Jeb earned huge sums from his legal work at Prudhoe, and later, whenever he encountered Poley Markham on the latter's infrequent visits to Alaska, he would say: "We still haven't nailed the mountain goat," and Poley would remind him: "It took me three years to get mine. Don't rush it," and Jeb discovered that he and Poley were quite different in their attitudes. "You like the chase, don't you?" Jeb said. "But I want to round out my Big Eight and get it done with."

Poley said: "You never get it done with. Last month I took a young fellow hunting on Baranof Island, that's where Sitka is, trying to snag a goat, and it was as much fun as when I first went out on my own."

"Poley," Jeb said one day, "I heard some men . . . that is, some local men from Barrow, white men, Eskimos, talking about your work over there. What's up?"

For the first time in their pleasant and rewarding acquaintance-ship Poley became not just evasive, which he always was when he didn't want to answer a direct question, but almost shifty and edgy, as if he were ashamed of what he had been doing: "Oh, they have some big ideas over there. They need counsel." He would say no more, but in the months that followed, Jeb saw less and less of his mentor, and new men from the Lower Forty-eight began appearing in Anchorage and occasionally at Prudhoe Bay. They were a difficult lot to identify or fit into the Alaskan scene. If you saw in the airport at Fairbanks a trio of men who looked like oil-field men from Tulsa in Oklahoma or Odessa in Texas, you could bet that they were either headed for Prudhoe Bay or planning to open a short-order restaurant in Fairbanks for oil-field workers on vacation. But Poley Markham's visitors were a wildly mixed lot: a road builder from Massachusetts, a building contractor from Southern California, an electrical plant manager from St. Louis, and all of them apparently headed north of the Arctic Circle.

Then Markham disappeared for about half a year, and rumors filtered back that he was in Boston arranging bond issues of enormous magnitude: "I got a letter from a friend associated with a small bank in Boston. He said Markham, and he had the full name, was finagling for a bond issue of three hundred million. My man didn't know what for."

And that was the second discovery Jeb Keeler made regarding his friend: Poley was engaged in some very fancy footwork in relation to certain officials in Barrow, and the sums involved were staggering. At first Jeb believed that somehow Poley and his cronies had discovered a new oil field, but his contacts at Prudhoe Bay said: "Impossible. We'd know about it within six hours."

"What is he doing?"

"Who knows?" But then the oilman leveled: "You know, Keeler, this oil field at Prudhoe pumps huge funds into the North Slope. Taxes, salaries. There's a lot of money kicking around up here, and Markham has always been the kind of man who's attracted to money."

"So am I," Jeb said defensively. "So are you, or neither of us would be up here in this godforsaken place."

"Yes," the oil-field manager said reflectively, "but you and I seem to work within defined boundaries. Markham doesn't."

For almost a year Jeb had no opportunity to question Poley, for the latter spent all that time in Los Angeles and New York arranging financing for the huge operations taking place north of the Arctic Circle, but one day while Jeb was unraveling a legal bind at Prudhoe, he received an urgent letter from Markham: "Meet me in Anchorage Friday. I think we may have your mountain goat." Eagerly Jeb flew south on an ARCO plane, to find Poley waiting in a suite at the new Sheraton Hotel: "Man phoned me that a large herd of goats has been seen in the Wrangell Mountains. Let's go." They motored to Matanuska and then in to Palmer, where they both purchased nonresident hunter's licenses at sixty dollars each, with Jeb acquiring for an extra two hundred and fifty the metal tag which he would have to attach to the body of any goat he killed. Then, in a small plane which Markham had used in bringing down his own goat some years before, they flew in to the low hills at the base of the great sixteen-thousand-foot Wrangell range. The pilot, always looking to make a few extra dollars, suggested that he could land the two men well up into the mountains where the goats were likely to be, but Poley would have none of that: "Put us where the law says we're supposed to be," and when they were deposited with their tent and rifles, he led the way up toward the head of the valley where the goats had been reported.

When they reached the closed end of the valley, Jeb looked back and saw one of the loveliest sights of his hunting career: a herd of more than ninety nannies and their kids—not a billy in sight—grazing on rocky slopes interspersed with strips of succulent grass. One view like this, with nannies watching as their kids frolicked in bright sunlight, coats gleaming white, horns a jet-black, and the mountains looming protectively overhead, was worth a lifetime of hunting. "Marvelous," Jeb whispered as they drew closer to the herd, but then his hunting instinct prevailed: "Where are the billies?"

"Hiding by themselves, even higher up," and although he was fifteen years older than Jeb, Markham led the way out of the goat-filled valley and up a steep climb which would place them high on the flanks of Mount Wrangell, a thousand glacier-covered feet above the nannies.

"The trick with billies," Markham explained for the third time, since Jeb had shot nothing on his previous two trips in search of goats, "is to get well above them, because they keep looking for trouble from below, and this way we can get the drop on them."

The tactic did not work, not that day, for the billies, who traveled in twos and threes after the rutting season ended in December, easily detected them and moved well beyond rifle range. Seeing them go, Markham said: "Strange, isn't it? In season they fight one another furiously. Great gouges with those sharp horns, to the death if necessary. But when the passion wanes, old friends. Three weeks fighting and mating, forty-nine weeks traveling about buddy-buddy."

"I wish some of them would buddy-buddy over my way."

"By the way, Jeb, when does your own mating season come on track?"

As they trudged down the valley past the wonderful gathering of snow-white mothers and kids, Jeb said: "I used to invite some pretty fine women up for the weekends at Dartmouth."

"You mean girls?"

"The kind I invited didn't like to be called girls anymore. They made that very clear: 'You're men, not boys. We're women, not girls.'"

"Very tough to live with a girl like that. I've watched."

"They're the only kind fellows like me would want to live with," Jeb said, and Poley laughed: "It ain't never easy, son. Regardless of what the current rules might be, it ain't never easy."

"You divorced?"

"Not on your life! That way lies bankruptcy. My wife lives in Los Angeles, goes to cultural affairs at USC, and this may shock you, but she also takes care of our money."

"They tell me at Prudhoe that you're making a killing on the North Slope."

"Eskimos need guidance. They deserve the best advice they can get, and I provide it."

"Like bond issues and proxy fights and lobbying in Congress?"

"If the United States says 'Stop eating walrus blubber. It's time to move into the modern world,' somebody has to show them how to make the move."

They dropped the subject, and in the two remaining days, during which they never came close to a billy but did remain in contact with the nannies and kids, it was not reopened, leaving Jeb as uninformed as he had been when the hunt started, but as they packed to await the plane that would carry them back to Anchorage, Poley said: "Jeb, you could do me and yourself a big favor. Vladimir Afanasi has asked me to come up to Desolation Point and sort out the problems in his village corporation. I simply haven't the time, but I owe Vlad a lot. Would you go up and see what needs doing?" Jeb said: "I'd like to see that place again. Maybe get me my polar bear. Looks almost impossible to bag a mountain goat."

"One problem, Jeb. I never charge Afanasi for the help I give him. He's sort of the charity that keeps me decent. And I don't want you to charge him, either. But of course, a lawyer can't work for nothing, so I'll pick up your tab," and as the plane flew over the majestic Matanuska Glacier on its way to Anchorage, Markham wrote out a first check for ten thousand dollars.

• • •

In the early years of Alaskan statehood, several contrasting groups of American citizens trekked northward in search of adventure and wealth. With the discovery of oil at Prudhoe Bay in 1968, roustabouts from Oklahoma and Texas flooded in to earn enormous salaries on the edge of the Beaufort Sea, a frozen arm of the Arctic Ocean. Notable were the lawyers and businessmen like Poley Markham and Jeb Keeler, who often spoke of taking up permanent residence but never did. In 1973, when President Nixon authorized the building of a gigantic pipeline from Prudhoe Bay to Valdez, construction workers poured into Fairbanks, from where they worked north and south to construct this miracle of engineering. And now the Flatch family of Matanuska entered the picture.

Son LeRoy, the aviator, was eager to become involved, but just when the oil companies at Prudhoe were sending out urgent calls for local planes to serve as couriers—spare parts needed at once, important visitors to be ferried in from Fairbanks, evacuation of an injured roustabout—LeRoy had the bad luck to crack up his postwar Waco YKS-7, so he could not participate in the bonanza.

When, in a degree of panic, he looked about to see what planes suitable for work in Alaska were available—and he insisted upon one fitted with the revolutionary improvement of permanent snow skis through the middle of which wheels could be let down—the best deal he could find was a new four-seater Cessna-185 at the frightening cost of $48,000, a price far beyond his means. Gathering his family, he said: "I've got to have the Cessna. We're losing a fortune every day." His wife suggested that he try to arrange a loan from a bank, but he feared that this would be impossible, since he had just cracked up his only collateral, and it looked as if the combined savings of the elder Flatches, LeRoy and his wife, Sandy, his sister, Flossie, and her husband, Nate Coop, would fall far short of the down payment.

But now the miracle of Prudhoe Bay intervened, for so many workmen were required at the site that even Elmer Flatch, crippled and in his seventies, was dragooned to serve as a paymaster at the oil rigs, Sandy Flatch was given a job as liaison in Fairbanks, assuring that workmen and their materials moved promptly to Prudhoe, while Flossie and her nature-loving husband received the best jobs of all.

"The head man came to see us particular," Nate explained. "He'd been hunting at our lodge and remembered the way Flossie understood bears and moose, and he offered us a deal in a way you'd never guess. He said: 'Nature freaks are beginning to hammer us over the future of the caribou. They say if we build that pipeline right down the middle of their emigration routes, the caribou will be cut off from their natural habitats. They'll all die.' He wants us to work with the naturalists from the university to see what can be done to help the caribou." They were to start work immediately, and the various Flatches could save practically their entire earnings because food, lodging and transportation to the job would be paid in addition to their wages.

So it became a simple matter for LeRoy to borrow from all of them, fly down to Seattle, pick up his bright new Cessna-185 with permanent skis and retractable wheels, and fly it back to Fairbanks, where he became the busiest courier in the Prudhoe operation. With all maintenance and fuel costs covered by the company, he netted $165,000 the first year.

One night as Hilda Flatch totted up her family's income, which she banked for them, she broke into laughter, and when her husband asked: "What's so funny?" she replied: "Remember how they warned us when we were starving in Minnesota? 'If you go to Alaska, you'll never grow nothin', and the polar bears'll eat you'?"

Salaries like these lured workmen from all over the United States, and Fairbanks was filled with the babble of strange accents as gape-mouthed laborers from Nebraska and Georgia paid $12.50-plus for a breakfast of one cup of coffee, one pancake, one egg and one strip of bacon. Dinner, of course, ran into the high twenties. Not many of these hastily imported workmen would remain in Alaska when the twin Golcondas of the oil field and the pipeline ended, but those who did remain added enormously to the vitality and excitement of Alaskan life. They tended to be outdoorsmen who loved the Alaskan patterns of life and served as the twentieth-century version of the frontiersmen. They were welcome additions.

Oil riggers, bulldozer drivers, welders for the pipeline, lawyers with vivid imaginations—such men continued the tradition of the gold-field immigrant, the daring men who built the first towns and the sailors who served on the *Bear* under Mike Healy, and once more Alaska created the impression that it was a land for men. But there were also women who sought their fortunes in this wild frontier, just as in the old days: nurses, wives, dance-hall girls, fugitives like Missy Peckham, and a few daring souls who simply wanted to see what Alaska was like.

In these years one young woman in particular experienced the lure of Alaska, and her coming north set many wheels in motion.

A flamboyant mayor of New York once opposed censorship by saying "No girl was ever seduced by a book," but in 1983 a young woman in Grand Junction, Colorado, was deceived by a magazine cover. Kendra Scott, twenty-five years old, was teaching her geography class about Eskimos of the Far North, when Miss Deller, the librarian, came to her room with two books Kendra had requested: "I've checked these out in your name. You can keep them till April."

Kendra thanked her, since good material on Eskimos was not easy to come by, and Miss Deller added: "And I've brought you our latest copy of the *National Geographic,* the February issue, but you can have it for only two weeks. We have another request for it."

Since Kendra already knew what was in the two books, she looked first at the magazine, and when she did, she was lost forever. On the cover was one of the most ravishing pictures of childhood she had ever seen. Against the white background of a blizzard in northern Alaska, a little girl—or it might have been a boy, for only the eyes were visible—was walking into the blowing snow, covered from head to toe in the colorful dress of her people: big fur slippers, blue denim trousers double thick, colorful smock edged with fur, bright beaded belt, two caps, one of white wool, the bigger one of heavy quilted corduroy edged in wolverine fur to repel ice and snow, and an enormous brown knitted scarf wrapped around her head three times. Her hands were protected in brightly decorated mittens, and Kendra could only guess that underneath the smock she must have had three or four more layers of clothing.

But what made the child adorable, and Kendra had convinced herself that it had to be a girl, was the resolute manner in which she pressed forward into the storm, her little body fighting the blizzard, her determined eyes, all that could be seen, staring ahead at the goal to be achieved despite the driving snow. It was a glorious portrait of childhood, a depiction of man's will to survive, and Kendra's heart went out to that child battling the elements.

And for a protracted spell she was not in a comfortable elementary school in Grand Junction but on the northern slopes of the arctic, and her class did not consist of middle-class white American children with a few interesting Mexicans thrown in, but a group of Eskimos living in darkness half the year and in bright sunlight nearly twenty-four hours a day the other half. Kendra had been taken prisoner by a little fur-bound child on a magazine cover and she would never again be the same.

For some time she had been aware that she ought to change, that her life was heading into such sterility that unless she made a radical shift, she was destined for a desolate, picayune existence. The responsibility was hers, that she admitted, but her mother, a distraught and frightened woman who lived with Kendra's father in Heber City, Utah, some thirty miles northeast of Provo, was a contributing factor. The Scotts were not Mormons, but they shared the stern discipline which that religion imposed, and when Kendra graduated from high school they enrolled her, without any input from her, at the respectable university in Provo, Brigham Young, where young men were taught to be FBI agents and young women to be God-fearing and obedient wives. At least, that's what Mrs. Scott believed.

"The good part about Brigham Young," Mrs. Scott told her neighbors in Heber City, "is that Grady and I can drive down most weekends to see how Kendra's doing." And this they did, wanting to know what classes she was taking, whether her professors were "decent, God-fearing men," and checking particularly on her roommates, three girls with such disparate backgrounds that the elder Scotts had to be suspicious of at least two of them. One was a Salt Lake City Mormon, so she was all right, but another was from Arizona, where anything could happen, and the third from California, which was even worse.

But Kendra assured her parents that the two outsiders, as Mrs. Scott called them, were more or less respectable and that she, Kendra, would not allow them to corrupt her. This phrase, *corrupt her,* loomed large in the Scott set of values, for Mrs. Scott saw the world as an evil place, more than three-quarters of whose citizens were bent on corrupting her daughter, and she was morbidly suspicious of any men who hove within her daughter's orbit: "I want you to tell me about any man who approaches you, Kendra. You simply must be on your guard against them, and a young girl is not always the best judge of a young man's character."

So during her weekly visits to Brigham Young, Mrs. Scott pumped Kendra for a detailed report on any young man whose name surfaced during her long interrogations of her daughter: "Where's he from?

How old is he? Who are his parents? What business are they in? Why is he studying geology? What do you mean, he spent last summer vacation in Arizona? What was he doing in Arizona?" After eight or ten such grillings Kendra summoned up the nerve to ask her mother: "How were you ever able to find a husband, if you had such endless suspicions?" and Mrs. Scott saw nothing impertinent in the question, for she felt this was a major problem for any young woman: "Your father was raised in a God-fearing family in South Dakota and he was not contaminated by going to any college or university." Kendra thought: Nor was he contaminated by anything else like books or newspapers or talk in a corner saloon. But as soon as she voiced this opinion to herself, she was ashamed of it. Grady Scott was a fine, trustworthy man who ran a good hardware store in Heber City, and if he lacked the courage to stand up against his wife, he had the character to run his business and his life honorably. During these long interrogations of his daughter in the Brigham Young dormitory, he rarely intruded.

In her four years at college, Kendra dated only two men, and they were so similar that they could have been twins: slight of build, washy-blond of hair, hesitant in speech and awkward in movement. The first young man had asked her out three times; the second, seven or eight. But the evenings were so painfully boring and unproductive that Kendra deemed them hardly worth the effort, especially when her mother asked at least fifteen questions about each young man and ended up by actually driving the forty-two miles south to Nephi to investigate the parents of the second young fellow. Mrs. Scott was most favorably impressed with the couple, classifying them as "the best of Mormon society, and that's high praise." She gave Kendra vigorous encouragement to pursue her friendship with the young man, but both he and Kendra were so embarrassed by the entire procedure— and so little interested in each other—that what Mrs. Scott called "Kendra's courtship" ended with neither a bang nor a whimper. In fact, it didn't end at all. It just sort of tailed off like a slow groan.

Kendra graduated at age twenty-one with a B-plus average in education, and her choice of four or five good public schools in which to teach, and now came the first crisis in her life, for one of the schools was in Kamas, Utah, less than twenty-five miles from home, and both the elder Scotts felt that this was where Kendra should teach, at least for the first five or six years of her career, because, as Mrs. Scott pointed out: "You could come home for weekends."

In an act of defiance which startled and alarmed her parents, Kendra accepted, without discussing the matter with them, a job at the school that was farthest from home, in Grand Junction across the state line in Colorado, but even this was within striking distance of Heber City, and during Kendra's first autumn in her new school, Mrs. Scott drove the two hundred and fifty-odd miles on six different weekends to discuss with her daughter the problems she was facing, the women teachers with whom she was associating, and whatever men in either the school or the town she had come to know. It was Mrs. Scott's firm opinion that the men of Colorado were much more dangerous than those in Utah, and she advised her daughter to steer clear of them: "Why you turned down that nice young man from Nephi, I will never know."

"I didn't turn him down, Mother. I never had the opportunity. Nor did I seek it."

Aware that their child was developing headstrong tendencies, the bedside prayers in Grand Junction now began to take subtle shifts: "Almighty God, keep Your daughter Kendra mindful of Your precepts, protect her from arrogant and hasty judgments, and with Your constant supervision, help her to remain pure."

The librarian, Miss Deller, handed Kendra that copy of the *National Geographic* on a Tuesday morning, and during the next three days the little girl heading into the blizzard haunted the younger teacher. She did not turn the magazine over to her students, but kept it on her desk through Wednesday and Thursday, where she stared at it from time to time. On Thursday night she took it home with her, and studied it with great intensity before going to bed. On Friday she rose early, placed the magazine beside her mirror, and compared herself with that extraordinary child. In the glass she saw herself clearly and with neither exaggeration nor denigration; but whenever she compared herself with that child heading into the blizzard, she had to admit with great pain that she came off second best:

I'm intelligent, always got good grades, and I know how to contribute to group projects. I mean, I'm not a dope, nor a recluse, nor anyone sick in the head. And although I'm not a cover girl, I'm not repulsive. Men do stare at me now and then, and I think that if I gave them encouragement . . . Well, that's neither here nor there.

Good complexion, good posture, hair sort of blah but I've got to get rid of those braids, no cavities, thank God, not overweight, no disfiguring blemishes. Not much of a smile, but maybe one could be engineered. And I am liked by my students, I really am, and I think by the other faculty members too.

And then, with the child beside her, she broke into convulsive sobs and uttered words which shocked her as she said them and appalled her when she remembered them later: "I'm such a horseshit fucking failure."

Recoiling as if someone had struck her across the face, she stared at herself in the mirror, clapped her hand across her mouth, and mumbled: "What did I say? What possessed me?" And then, when her passion subsided, she knew exactly what she had said and what had impelled her:

In comparison with that child I'm a shameless coward. Disgustingly, I've allowed my mother to dominate me. I believe in God, but I do not believe that He sits there with a magnifying glass watching everything that an elementary-school teacher in Grand Junction is doing. I've been afraid even to go out in my snowfall, let alone my blizzard.

She grabbed the magazine, brought it to her lips, and kissed the little Eskimo girl in her heavy clothes edged with fur: You've saved my life, little one. You've given me what I never had before. Courage.

Dressing hurriedly, she marched boldly to Terrence's Tresses, the leading hair boutique of the region. Plumping herself grimly in the chair, she said: "Terrence, you've got to cut off these damned braids."

In some shock Terrence said: "But, mam'selle, no one around here has braids as lovely as yours," but she rebuffed him: "My mother uses them to strangle me." Since this obviously baffled Terrence, she added: "Whenever she comes to visit me she insists on plaiting my braids— sitting me on a chair before her . . . to reinforce my captivity."

"But what will Mam'selle do to replace them? What style, I mean?" and she said: "We'll settle that later," and as the scissors snipped away she cried exultantly: "Now I can breathe."

Shorn of her burden, she and Terrence studied a score of photographs showing varied styles, and finally he said: "If I may be so bold, mam'selle, that Dutch-boy bob would be perfect for you, clean and neat like your personality," and she said: "Go for it!" Deftly he applied comb and scissor and spray, producing a result which made Kendra look more sophisticated but at the same time more youthfully adventurous.

"I like it," she said as she hurried off to school, skipped down the hall, and burst into the library: "Miss Deller, I'm going to be very bold—"

"Kendra! I hardly knew you. What a marvelous hairdo! But what about those lovely long braids?"

"Thanks, but my problem is something quite different, and I'm embarrassed, really I am, to bring it up."

"Shoot! I'm a good listener." Miss Deller had short bobbed hair and a brusque manner of speech and movement; she came, Kendra thought someone had said, from Arkansas.

Kendra sat down, took a deep breath, and said: "On the weekends, some weekends, that is, you go over to that lodge in Gunnison, don't you?"

"Several of us do. Special rates to teachers. We come from all around—Salida, Montrose."

"What is it, exactly?"

"A kind of seminar. We invite lecturers from universities. People show slides of Arabia, Uruguay, that sort of thing. Sunday morning most of us go to church, and then we come home, refreshed."

"Do you have to go . . . with a man, that is?"

"Heavens, no. Some do. And sometimes a teacher from here meets a keen guy from Salida, but that happens as the dice happen to roll."

Taking a deep breath, Kendra asked: "Could I go? I mean this weekend?"

"Of course! Some of us wondered about asking you before, but we felt you were rather . . . What shall I say? Aloof, maybe."

"I was." She said thanks so simply and with her head so low that Miss Deller, who was eight years older, left her desk and put her arm about Kendra's shoulder: "What is it, kid?"

"My mother. She comes on so strong, like maybe a neutron bomb, new improved economy-size."

"Yes, some of us have noticed."

"I want to go with you to Gunnison. I'll leave a note on my door that I'm off for the weekend."

"Tell her you've headed to Kansas City with a truckdriver."

"Now wait, she's basically a good woman."

"I'm sure that every neutron bomb is convinced that it's basically good and that whatever it does is for the betterment of mankind. Tell her to go to hell. Don't ask, just tell her you're going. We'll be expecting you."

For just a moment Kendra feared that in asking for help from Miss Deller, she was getting in over her head. What did she know about the librarian? Was she, as her mother would have phrased it, "a nice girl"? And what went on at the lodge in Gunnison? But Miss Deller, as if she knew what Kendra was thinking, squeezed her shoulder and said: "It's never as bad as you think it's going to be, except when it's lots worse. If you ask me, Kendra, you better break loose." Returning to her desk, she snapped her fingers and said: "I do believe you had the right idea. Just leave a note. Do that four or five times and she'll stop coming over."

At the lunch break that Friday, Kendra ran home and typed a neat note, which read:

> *Dear Mother,*
> *I've had to attend a school seminar in Montrose. Sorry.*
> *Very unexpected.*
> *Kendra*

After hurriedly packing two changes of clothes, she gathered up her snow gear and hurried back to school, where she taught with verve about Eskimos.

Four teachers drove the beautiful hundred and thirty miles of mountain road to Gunnison together—Miss Deller, a woman science teacher, an assistant football coach and Kendra—and they were a lively lot. The coach was married, but his wife had been to the Gunnison lodge and had small liking for snow sports or heady discussions, so she stayed home. After an analysis of what was wrong with the administration of the Grand Junction schools and a castigation of western Colorado politics, talk turned to national affairs, and all agreed that President Reagan represented a healthy turn to the right. Said the coach: "High time we got some discipline in this country. He's on the right track."

To Kendra's surprise, the other three were acutely interested in what a Mormon university was like, and since she had enjoyed Brigham Young she gave a good report, but the coach asked: "Do they still discriminate against blacks? You know, you can't have a decent football team these days without them."

"That's all in the past," Kendra assured them. "They didn't discriminate against me, and I'm not a Mormon."

Fifteen minutes after arriving at the lodge, one of those things happened which proved once more how events that could have been set in motion only by chance had the power to alter lives: a young man who taught mathematics in Canon City, a hundred miles to the east, joined the group Kendra was talking with, carrying six mimeographed papers stapled together: "Hiya, Joe! I followed your advice, wrote to the department of education in Alaska, and by return mail got all this."

"What is it?" Joe asked, and the man said: "Information. Application blanks, if you will," and the group showed such interest in his material that he sat down, removed the staple, and passed out pages of his document from Alaska. As various Colorado teachers began reading aloud details from the pages they had received, groans, whistles and cheers filled the coffee shop: "My God! Listen to this! 'Three years experience in a good high school. Recommendations from university school of education. Rural school. You will teach all high school grades and subjects.'" At this reference to a system that had vanished fifty years ago in most of the world, the groans increased, and one man said: "They want a miracle. Four different grades, eight different subjects, and I'll bet it's in one room."

"It is," the reader continued. "Says so right here. 'One general room but not overcrowded,'" and the protesting man groaned, but he was totally silenced by the next line: "'Beginning yearly salary, thirty-six thousand dollars.'"

"What?" The cry came from six different teachers, who started passing the incredible paper from hand to hand. Yes, the figure was accurate, $36,000 for a beginning teacher, with yearly increments thereafter to a level of $73,000 for high school, more for a principal. The Colorado teachers, and this was a superior experienced group, averaged $17,000, and for them to learn that in Alaska mere beginners earned more than twice as much—forget the conditions—was disturbing, and for Kendra Scott, whose salary as a novice was only $11,500, the differential was shocking.

But the single sheet which had wound up in her hands carried a message more profound than the level of salary. It came from an entity she had not heard of, the North Slope Borough School District, and it had been put together by a team of geniuses who had used all the tricks which cruise-ship companies had found useful in luring prospective passengers:

> You will fly to Seattle and board a sleek jet that will whisk you to Anchorage, where a representative of the Alaska education system will direct you to a modern hotel. There you will join fellow beginning teachers for a seminar entitled "Introduction to the North" with colored films. Next morning the same friendly representative will deliver you to the airport, where you will board a smaller jet that will fly you past snow-tipped Denali, on to the northern metropolis Fairbanks and then to Prudhoe Bay, where oil gushes out of the ground, providing Alaska with its millions.

> From Prudhoe you will fly westward over the land of a million lakes, with an arm of the great Arctic Ocean at your right. You will land at Barrow, northernmost point in the United States. There you will spend three days visiting one of the finest high schools in the nation, after which a small, trim plane will fly you south to your school at Desolation Point, site of much Alaska history and an exciting Eskimo village whose citizens will be eager to make you feel at home.

By the time she reached the end of this paragraph, Kendra was so eager to fly off immediately that she quickly scanned the page for a phone number, and on the reverse side she found: Contact collect Vladimir Afanasi, Desolation Point, Alaska, 907-851-3305. The man's name set her guessing as to what history it summarized, and it was easily seen that the first name was Russian, but what the second signified she could not guess: Probably Eskimo, how musical! and she repeated it aloud several times. But it was the next two paragraphs that captured her imagination, and in just the way the insidious drafters had intended:

> You will not be teaching in some frontier shack. Not at all! Desolation Consolidated, one of the most modern and well-

equipped schools in America, provides facilities for both elementary and high school and was built three years ago on a budget of $9,000,000. It sits atop a slight rise overlooking the Chukchi Sea and on a good day from your schoolroom you will see whales playing just offshore.

But the thing that makes teaching at Desolation a rich experience—and don't be scared away by the name, because we love it and so will you—is the children. You'll have in your classes children of the most exciting heritages: Eskimo, Russian, those who sprang from the New England whalers who used to frequent Desolation, and children like yourself who came from missionaries and occasional businessmen who settled here. To see your class in the morning, their faces bright in the arctic light, is to see a cross section of the best that America can provide, but if they are to attain the promise of which they are capable, they will need your help. Would you like to join us in our bright new school?

The invitation was so enticing that it dazzled her. She saw herself walking up the flight of steps leading to the big new school, which must have been built of marble to justify the budget of $9,000,000, and down the splendid corridors to her well-appointed room where some two dozen or more pupils of all colors awaited her, except that they all looked like the little girl on the *National Geographic* cover, with big fur hoods and wide scarves about their faces. Only their eyes peeked out at her, bright and very eager to learn.

When she left her quarters in the lodge to join the others for the Friday evening meal, she looked about for the young man from Canon City, and went up to him with a boldness she had never before displayed: "Are you the man who wrote to Alaska?"

"Yes. Name's Dennis Crider, Canon City. Join us."

She explained that she was with the contingent from Grand Junction: "Kendra Scott, elementary school. May I have this chair?"

"You sure may. You interested in Alaska?"

"I didn't know I was when I came through those doors. But that correspondence you let me read! Wow! Are you thinking of going up there?"

"I'm thinking. That's why I wrote. And from the speed with which they responded, they must be interested too."

"But how did you know whom to write to?" and he replied: "Just

State Education Department, Juneau, Alaska. Didn't even know if I had the right name or address, but they forwarded it to the Eskimo districts."

"Are you considering it seriously?" and her questions became so pointed that both she and Dennis ignored the others at the table as they delved rather deeply into the possibility of chucking their jobs in Colorado and heading for the North Slope of Alaska, wherever that was; they had no map of the region, but deduced from things said that it was near the Arctic Ocean and that beyond it there was nothing but the North Pole.

They spent all Friday evening and most of Saturday analyzing seriously what steps would have to be taken if one were shifting to the far north, and the more they talked, the more practical it became for them to make the move. But Dennis pointed out a condition which had not appeared on Kendra's sheet: "If you are accepted, you should plan to be on the job by the end of the first week in July so as to complete your plans for the winter."

"That poses no problem," Kendra said, but when she finally went to bed, she could not sleep. Ideas and images were thundering about tumultuously in her mind, and some of them were not flattering: What made me use those horrible words? Such words aren't a part of me. Or are they? She speculated on the possibility that she might be two people, the Kendra that her mother had groomed and pruned so carefully, acceptable to the world, and a subterranean Kendra of such tortured ambiguities that she was afraid to dig into them.

After a restless night, Kendra rose for an early breakfast, found Miss Deller sitting alone, and asked: "Could I talk with you?"

"Yes, I noticed that you and Dennis Crider were in pretty deep consultation. Things getting pretty heavy between you two?"

"No, we were talking about Alaska. What I wanted to know, what's the time difference between here and Alaska?" Like many sensible people, Kendra assumed that a librarian knew everything, but the confusion which ensued would have disabused any listener. The two young women spent about ten minutes trying to decide whether Alaska was ahead of or behind Colorado, and then another fifteen minutes arguing heatedly as to what *ahead of* and *behind* meant. They even discussed seriously whether the International Date Line ran east or west of Alaska, and what it meant regardless of where it ran.

They were rescued by a pedantic geography teacher, a man from Montrose, who explained: "Your question about the date line isn't foolish, not at all. Strictly speaking, it ought to cut the Aleutian Islands about in half. Eastern part Monday, western part Tuesday, the same as Siberia. But everybody agreed that it would be better if all of Alaska were on the same day, so the line takes a furious twist, first to the east so that all of Russia can be Tuesday, then an even bigger one to the west so that all of Alaska can be Monday. And then it jogs again to get on track."

"But what about the time difference?" Miss Deller asked, and he replied: "I can't explain anything that complex unless I explain it thoroughly."

"Proceed, Dr. Einstein," and he surprised them by admitting: "I'm not sure I can give you the right answer," and the librarian said with a friendly smile: "But you sound as if you understand everything," and he said: "Trouble is, I know too much, and they've been changing the rules on me."

Asking the waiter to fetch a sheet of paper from the desk, he took out the three colored pens he carried as part of his teacher's equipment, and sketched a surprisingly accurate outline of the Alaskan peninsula: "At the university we had to make reasonable sketches of all the continents, but now I get just a bit hazy," and he drew in eight lines of longitude. "I know there ought to be eight of them from east to west, but how exactly they're numbered, I don't remember. Let's say the date line should run here. That's one-eighty, as you know."

"I didn't know," Miss Deller said, but he assured her that it was. "That makes this one way over here next to Russia one-seventy east, and this one over here at the eastern edge of Alaska, one-thirty west. That is such a very wide span that it ought to have four different time zones. Geographically speaking, it's entitled to them. So Alaska ought to have the same difference in its times as the continental United States does. When it's twelve in New York it's nine in Los Angeles. When it's eight in eastern Alaska it ought to be five at the western tip in Attu."

"Isn't it?"

"No. It's all screwed up. Alaska used to have three different time zones, with the eastern part the same as Seattle, and most of the rest something else and the Aleutians something else again. But I read the other day that they've changed everything around, so now I don't know what the score is. But I suggest we call the telephone company," and when they did, they got hold of a bright girl who said: "I haven't a clue, but I know how to find out," and she called someone in Denver who said: "Anchorage is two hours behind us. Nine o'clock here, seven o'clock in the morning there."

When the geographer sat down, Kendra astonished them by saying: "I'm going to call. He may not be out of bed, but he will be at home."

"Call whom?" Miss Deller asked, and Kendra showed them the memo she had brought with her: Vladimir Afanasi, 907-851-3305. Call collect.

"Are you crazy?" Miss Deller asked, and as Kendra said: "Maybe," the librarian hailed Dennis Crider as he entered the breakfast room: "What have you done to this perfectly normal young woman?" and when he heard Kendra's plan he said flatly: "That's insane. It must be the middle of the night up there."

"It's seven o'clock in the morning, and I'm calling Mr. Afanasi." With that, she went to the pay phone, put in a dime, dialed zero, and said in a controlled voice: "Person-to-person collect to Alaska," and she gave the number. Within less than a minute a deep, husky voice came on the wire: "Hello, this is Vladimir Afanasi."

"I am calling about the teaching job," Kendra said, and for the next five minutes she outlined her credentials, gave a list of people Mr. Afanasi could call if he wanted verification, and then stood with her mouth agape as Afanasi said with the most careful attention to his words: "Before we go any further, I must inform you that I am not empowered to make you a specific offer of any kind. That must be done by our superintendent in Barrow, but since I'm president of the board, I think I can assure you that you sound like just the young woman we're looking for. You've read the details?"

"I've memorized them." At this, Afanasi broke into laughter which concluded with a remarkable statement: "Miss Scott, I think the superintendent will be offering you a job this afternoon."

Clapping her hand over the phone, she turned and said: "My God! He's offering me a job!"

Then came two questions she had not anticipated: "Any conspicuous facial blemishes? Any crippling?"

She appreciated these questions for their frankness: "If I were crippled, not badly, would you hire me?"

"If you could get around, more or less, it wouldn't make a damned bit of difference."

"I want your job, Mr. Afanasi. I'm not crippled. I have no disfigurement. I'm a very ordinary person, in every way I think, and I love children."

"Send me two photographs, and ask two of your professors at BYU—they have one hell of a football team—and your principal and clergyman to rush me references. If all's as you say, I'm sure the superintendent will offer you the job. You know the salary?"

"Thirty-six thousand. It sounds enormous."

"Are you applying because of it?" He did not wait for an answer. "There's a restaurant in Barrow up the line, hamburger with no onion, no cheese, seven dollars eighty-five cents. Enchilada with limited sauce, eighteen-fifty." When she gasped, he said: "But with your experience you'll qualify for forty-four thousand dollars, and that's what I'll be recommending to the superintendent."

She bit her lip lest she say something foolish, then said softly: "Mr. Afanasi, I won't be sending you a recommendation from my pastor. He would get my mother and the whole community lined up against my going."

"You haven't told your mother?"

"No. And I mustn't till it's all settled."

There was such a long silence in the booth, with Kendra's face indicating that no one was speaking, that her friends assumed that Mr. Afanasi had broken off communication, and they were about to console Kendra, when they could hear coming over the phone the conclusion to the interview: "Miss Scott, if you didn't have problems, you wouldn't be interested in this job. Everybody who calls has problems forcing them to drastic behavior. I hope yours are manageable. If they aren't, don't come to the North Slope."

Without hesitation Kendra said: "I told you I was a very ordinary girl and my problems are ordinary."

"I think you're telling me the truth. Now prove it."

And that was how Kendra Scott of Heber City landed a teaching job at Desolation Point, Alaska, at a starting salary of $44,000.

Her flight west from Prudhoe Bay introduced her to the vastness of her new home, for a tourist folder in the pocket before her said: "Believe it not, Alaska has one million islands and three million lakes," and as she looked down she saw the sun reflected from a wilderness mosaic of lakes, thousands of them and some not so small. I guess you have to accept their figures, she thought. Some country!

She landed at Barrow at ten-twenty on a bright July morning, and as soon as she entered the airport to claim her bags she was hailed by a rough voice: "That you, Miss Scott?" and she saw coming toward her an unkempt man in his fifties. Extending his big hand, he said: "I'm Harry Rostkowsky. I fly you down to Desolation." When he saw her three big bags, he said brightly: "You must be expectin' to stay awhile. Last one could take it only three weeks. That's why there's an opening." "But the brochure said there'd be an indoctrination period here at Barrow, three days in the new school," and he laughed: "Normally there is, but they need you in a hurry. Climb in."

The brief flight at low altitude provided Kendra with an excellent introduction to her new home, for she saw below her only the bleak, treeless tundra with its myriad lakes between Barrow and Desolation and the dark, ominous Chukchi Sea beyond. In the entire flight between the two settlements she saw not a sign of human existence, and when Rosty spoke to her through the intercom, she responded: "emptier than I thought," and he pointed with his left hand back toward the east: "And it stays this empty all the way to Greenland."

"When we land at Desolation, will you point out Mr. Afanasi for me?" and he replied: "I won't need to. He *is* Desolation. And they're lucky to have him." Then he added: "He'll be your new boss, and you'll never have a better."

Now came the long swing out over the sea, the swift drop in altitude and the sliding approach to the southern tip of the peninsula nomadic Eskimos had used as their base from time to time during the past fourteen thousand years. "That's my new home!" she called to Rosty and she saluted Desolation Point, now an established settlement. She was astonished how vulnerable to the arctic sea its frail dwellings seemed to be, pinched as they were between the Chukchi on the west and a sprawling lagoon to the east. But she soon forgot their plight, for she was trying to spot the new nine-million-dollar school. She could not locate it among the scatter of small homes, so she supposed it must have been positioned inland to protect it from floods that might sweep in from the sea, but when she scanned the surrounding areas she still could not find it.

After Rostkowsky had buzzed the village twice, the entire population, it seemed, hurried to the landing strip, so that when the Cessna came to a halt, everyone who had business with the new teacher, and that included most of the village, was there to greet her. When she backed out of the plane, stepped gingerly upon the wing, and dropped down to the ground, there were gasps of approval when the villagers saw how young and attractive she was with her pageboy hairdo, her enthusiastic smile and her obvious delight and eagerness to meet the people she would be serving. It was an auspicious beginning, highlighted by a long, low whistle from an Eskimo boy who looked as if he might be a senior in the high school. Others cheered his boldness, and as Kendra was being introduced to members of the school board, one of them whispered to her neighbor: "I think this time we got a good one."

And then, from the back of the crowd, Vladimir Afanasi, bareheaded, gray-haired, clean-shaven and with an Asian face that was almost perfectly round, came forward: "Welcome, Miss Scott. I'm Afanasi. We talked on the phone. Let's go to your quarters," and he led her to what was called the Teacherage, a low, minimal frame building which had two side-by-side front doors. "Mr. Hooker has this side with his wife. They're out fishing. This side is yours, all furniture and bedding are there," and he banged open the door to lead Kendra into a compact apartment—bath, kitchen area, living room—which was smaller than any she had seen in either Utah or Colorado. But it was clean and it did have unobstructed wall space on which she could hang posters or maps or prints. It had the clear making of a comfortable home for a bachelor woman.

When Afanasi said with some pride, for he had ordered the building of this home for teachers: "This could become a comfortable refuge for a young girl," Kendra corrected him: "I call myself a young woman," and he laughed: "Woman it will be. I've found that if people aren't self-proud, they don't amount to much."

When her three bags were delivered and stowed in the middle of the empty room, she made no effort to deal with them; instead she said: "Now, where is the school? I've been dreaming about it ever since that first phone interview."

"That's it, there," Afanasi said, taking her outdoors and pointing to a low, undistinguished one-story wandering building which, although new, already needed some repainting. To Kendra it looked like some nearly abandoned country store in a backwoods Colorado mining town that was down on its luck. Inadvertently she blurted out: "Nine million!" and as soon as she uttered the pejorative words,

Afanasi leaped ahead, turned to obstruct her passage, and thrust his face close to hers: "It's crucial, from the first minute on, that you understand the Alaska to which you've come," and he turned and pointed to each of the compass directions.

"What do you see, Miss Scott? Any trees? Any department stores? Any lumber warehouses? Nothing. The sea, where if we're lucky, we capture a walrus now and then, and maybe a whale. The sky which is dark half the year. And in this direction as far as the mind can reach, the tundra with not even a bush that could be burned." In some agitation he led his new teacher into the bleak schoolhouse, which consisted of two large classrooms separated by a sturdy soundproof wall and a gymnasium much bigger than the rest of the school, a fact upon which she remarked.

"We need the gym. It's the heart of our community," and then he began his instruction. Pointing to a nail which had been hammered into place, he said: "This nail, that strip of wood, that pane of glass, where do you suppose they came from? We didn't go down to the hardware store to buy them, because there is no hardware store. Every item in this building had to be ordered specially from Seattle, had to be ferried up here by barge."

"I didn't know," Kendra said, as if making an apology for her insensitivity. Afanasi bowed, accepting the courtesy, then took her by the arm and explained the real disadvantage of being at the far end of a barge line in the arctic: "You must understand, Miss Scott, that the barge from Seattle comes only once a year, late August usually. So if the builder of this school wants nails, he must anticipate that need almost a year in advance, for if they miss the yearly barge, he must wait a second year. Costs rise under such a remorseless system."

"Couldn't the builder bring the nails in by airplane?"

"Ah, you see the possibilities, and believe me, Miss Scott, that calculation will form a major problem for you. You'll mull that one a hundred times next year."

"I don't understand."

"You can fly in almost anything you need. But your cargo, the keg of nails, for example, must be crated and taken to the Anchorage airport. From there it's flown to Fairbanks. There it transfers to the plane going to Prudhoe, where they're transshipped to Barrow. And from there Rostkowsky, in his little Cessna, flies them over the tundra to here. By barge the keg of nails, maybe thirty dollars. By airplane, maybe four hundred dollars." He stared at her, allowing her time to digest this amazing discrepancy, and when it looked as if she understood, he pointed to various items which made the bleak school a little more congenial: "We flew that in. We flew in the carved backboards for the basketball baskets. We flew in a great many things you'll appreciate, and in the end it cost nine million dollars."

As he spoke she kept nodding her head, and her submission to the reality of Alaska was so genuine that he laughed and led her outside, where he pointed to the sixty concrete pilings on which the building stood: "Why do you suppose we spend two million dollars to build those pillars before we lay a single board?"

"Floodwaters in the spring?"

"Permafrost four seasons of the year," and he explained how, if a heavy structure was built flat on the ground, its accumulating heat would melt the permafrost and allow the building to sink right into the muck, then crack apart when the mud shifted.

He pointed to the Teacherage, in which she would be living: "How much did it cost us to build that for you? Guess."

When she was a child her family had lived in a modest house in Heber City and she remembered what it had cost, for her parents had agonized over what they considered an extravagance: sixteen thousand dollars. "We had a house something like it in Utah," she said quietly. "Sixteen thousand dollars."

"We spent two hundred and ninety thousand . . . so you could be comfortable when the winds howl," and she saw that it had been built on a score of pillars.

"Did you make such decisions? As president of the board, or whatever?"

"The president of the board is in Barrow. But he listens to my recommendations."

"Didn't it cause you some . . . ?" She fumbled for the right word, because even though she had talked with Afanasi for less than ten minutes, she could see that he was a man of strong convictions, one upon whom she must depend in the years ahead.

"You mean, did I wonder if I'd done the right thing? Never. Not even one twinge of remorse. The North Slope is getting millions of unexpected dollars from Prudhoe Bay, and I persuaded our people that the best way to spend this windfall was on education." Leading her back to the Teacherage, he said with quiet pride: "I gave a deposition in the Molly Hootch case."

"The what?"

"A famous case in the Alaskan Supreme Court. Molly Hootch was a little Eskimo girl whose case clarified Alaskan law. Our constitution, which I helped write, said that every Alaskan child had the right to an education in his or her own community. But when I was young, if a child in a Native village wanted a secondary education, he had to leave home for a year at a time and go down to Sitka, and the emotional shock was fearful. The Molly Hootch consent decree changed all that, and now we have good schools all through the bleak regions, some with six students, some with twelve, but all with first-class teachers."

"Is Desolation a Molly Hootch school?"

"We had a school of sorts here before the settlement. Molly Hootch provided us with the money to make it into a secondary school."

"How many students do you have?" and she was amazed by the answer: "In the high school, that's what you'll be teaching, three students, two boys and a girl. In the elementary school, that's where the principal, Kasm Hooker, and his wife . . . You'll like him, he's a teddy bear. He teaches the elementary school because he doesn't want the responsibility of the seniors who might know more than he does."

"How many students do he and his wife have?"

"Grades one through eight, thirteen."

Kendra was so astonished by these figures that she stopped short for a moment, and as Afanasi waited for her to catch up, she exclaimed: "Sixteen students in a nine-million-dollar school?" and he said: "That's Alaska. We put first things first."

But a bigger surprise was in store for her, for when she and Afanasi returned to her apartment he pulled two chairs up to the built-in desk and shuffled through the papers that awaited her there: "Yes, here it is, and we're almost out of time. But make out your order and I'll telephone it down to Seattle tomorrow. Just in time to catch the barge."

Kendra understood not one word he was saying, but when he thrust before her a ninety-six-page catalogue, in fine print, she saw that it referred to groceries and household items like cleaners, toilet paper and toilet articles. "Your supplies for the year. Ross & Raglan in Seattle have a branch that does nothing but ship goods north to people like you and me in the arctic," and in the next two hours Kendra Scott, reared in civilized areas like Utah and Colorado, was inducted into life north of the Arctic Circle, because the time-tested

R&R order forms covered everything that a normal individual or family might need during the next twelve months. In addition to the forms that dated back to the late 1890s, when Buchanan Venn compiled the first version, Kendra had the wise counsel of Vladimir Afanasi, who had helped several young teachers make out their first orders.

The amounts that Afanasi suggested staggered Kendra, who had been used to shopping twice a week for one person: "Miss Scott, I firmly advise you to order four bushels of potatoes."

"Where will I keep them?"

"In the cache," and he rose, opened a door at the rear of the apartment, and showed her a storage room almost bigger than the room she was in: it was lined with shelves and had low platforms onto which barrels and kegs could be placed, and a superrefrigerator for storing meats and frozen goods. It was not until she saw the endless shelving that she appreciated the task in which she was engaged: "I've got to order enough food for an entire year!"

"Not exactly. Like with the nails. You can, when you run out of something, ask R&R to ship it to you airmail. Can of sweet potatoes, two dollars in this order by barge, six dollars by air."

When Kendra finished her list, Afanasi made a hasty calculation of the cost, and the barge bill came to about three thousand dollars. Kendra stared at the total, mouth gaping: "I have no money to pay a bill like that," and Afanasi said: "That's why our school district pays you an advance right now . . . today," and he handed her a check drawn on the bank in Barrow for five thousand dollars.

As he was leaving, he stopped and indicated the apartment next door, the one occupied by the principal, Kasm Hooker: "Many people consider him one of the best teachers on the North Slope, an opinion with which I concur. Early forties, long string bean, married to a woman who adores him, came to us from North Dakota who knows how many years ago. His greatest value, Miss Scott, and never forget this, is what he does with basketball. Help him in that, and you'll make a grand contribution to our school."

"He has a curious first name. Religious?"

"Oh, no. Hooker came from a very limited background. Not literary at all. In his first days in our school he referred to the 'chasm that lies ahead,' but he pronounced it with a soft *ch,* the way you say *church.* After he'd mispronounced it several times, for it was a word he relished—the entire world, in his opinion, faced chasms of the most fearful kind—one of his students came to me and said: 'Mr. Hooker . . . he talks about chasms but he says it wrong,' so I had to come over to his room, he wasn't married then, and I told him outright: 'The word is *chasm,* as if it was spelled *kasm,*' and in his innocence when he met with his elementary classes next day he told them: 'Last night Mr. Afanasi was kind enough to tell me that what I was calling *chasm* is really *kasm,*' and thereafter everyone in town called him Kasm Hooker. You'll hear them cheer him at the basketball games. He's worth every penny of the ninety-four thousand dollars we pay him."

Kendra, amazed at this figure, asked: "And how much does his wife get?" and Afanasi said: "She's had years of experience. Forty-nine thousand dollars." When he was gone, she totted up the salary schedule for her school, and when she saw the total, gasped: "One hundred eighty-eight thousand dollars for sixteen children!" And she was not yet aware of the additional $22,000 paid the part-time Eskimo woman called a "Recognized Expert" who tried to teach the students their Inupiat language, which they ignored in favor of English, or the $43,000 paid the janitor who kept the new building operating. The grand total, which she would learn later, was $253,000, or nearly $16,000 per pupil just in salaries.

That night, the first in her new bed, she awakened at two-forty-five in the morning, sat bolt upright, and hurried to her desk, where the R&R order form lay flat beside its envelope. Grabbing a pen, she added—in the ample space provided for Miscellaneous—shelled pecans, eight pounds; heavy Karo syrup, eight one-quart cans; kumquats, one dozen cans. Then, feeling better, she returned to her bed and a sound sleep, even though it was bright daylight outside.

By the time school opened in the fall, Kendra had ingratiated herself with two-thirds of the families in Desolation, for she proved to them that she was an outgoing enthusiast who liked children and who respected the traditions of the Eskimo. She moved from one small dark house to the next, answering questions about her childhood and what life was like in Colorado; but she also listened as local tales were told about walrus hunts and who in the village was best at tracking the great bowhead whales as they moved north and south with the seasons. However, what assured her acceptance in the community was the speech she gave one night in the gymnasium, to which most of the residents came to see how their new teacher conducted herself.

The announcement billed it as "Right and Wrong," and some attend-
ees were loath to appear because they thought it was going to be a
missionary harangue.

How surprised they were! What Kendra did was stand before
them as an unsophisticated, likable young woman from Utah and
share with them the conceptions and misconceptions she had brought
with her regarding Eskimo life:

> "For some reason I'll never know, the American school sys-
> tem decided years ago that third grade was the ideal year to
> teach our children about the Eskimos. Books are written and
> study kits provided, and one company even sells equipment
> for building an igloo. I taught the Eskimo unit three times and
> I was real big on igloos. I had everyone living in an igloo. So
> when I fly in here in Mr. Rostkowsky's superjet, what do I
> find? Not one damned igloo."

Her use of the near-swear word shocked some, delighted the majority, and on she went irreverently ridiculing her misconceptions about
Eskimo life. In vivid words, gestures and appealing incidents, she
made fun of herself, but when she had the audience laughing with
her, she suddenly became serious:

> "My study books also told me much that was true about you
> people. They told of your love of the sea, of the way in which
> your brave hunters go out to fight the polar bear and catch the
> walrus. They told me of your festivals and of your northern
> lights, which I have never seen. And I hope that in the years
> we shall be together that you will teach me the other truths
> about your way of life, because I want to learn."

She made a special effort to make friends with her principal, and at
first she found the tall, awkward man ill disposed to make friends
with anyone, much less with a brash young teacher who might replace him as the leader of the school. Things remained so tentative
that one day in late August, when she had been rebuffed more than
once, she intercepted him on their common porch and said boldly:
"Mr. Hooker, will you come in for a moment?" and when he was
seated uncomfortably in her bed-sitting room she said: "Mr.
Hooker . . ." and he interrupted: "Call me Kasm." She broke into
laughter and said: "They told me about your name. You handled that
elegantly, I must say," and he smiled thinly.

She said: "I've come a long way to serve in your school and I can't do my job properly without a lot of help and guidance from you." He nodded and said: "You'll have my full cooperation," but she would not accept this weak assurance: "The children tell me that you lost your last teacher because you treated her as if she were a pariah."

"Who said that?"

"Schoolchildren. They said you made her cry."

"She was incompetent and Mr. Afanasi knew it. He was the one who suggested that she'd be better off in the Lower Forty-eight."

"But you could have helped her, Mr. Hooker . . . I mean Kasm."

The tall man sat with his hands gripping his knees in an attitude of jealous self-protection, then grudgingly admitted: "Perhaps under different circumstances . . . ."

"You'll not have that problem with me, Kasm. I like it here. I'm eager to teach, but even more eager to help you and Mr. Afanasi run a good school." Her subtle use of Afanasi's name reminded Mr. Hooker of the fact that she had already built a solid friendship with that powerful citizen, and he began to relent, but just as he was about to say something conciliatory, the most important sound of the year echoed through the village, the belching smokestack of a vessel signaling its approach, and even staid citizens ran about the summer streets, shouting: "Here comes the barge!" And there it was, a huge repository of goods hauled along by an old tugboat.

Its arrival launched two days of celebration, the pouring out of a vast cornucopia when the rewards of previous labors were delivered as if in obedience to some magic command: now came the cases of canned goods, a truck, a boat with an outboard motor, a forklift, stacks of clean lumber, the new hammers, the lengths of bright cloth, the books, the new lanterns with improved wicks for when the electricity failed. And always there were those modern inventions that made life in the dark months more livable: a television set, several tape recorders with two cases of batteries, a dozen basketballs and a shortwave radio. To watch the yearly barge disgorge itself at Desolation Point was to become a part of Eskimo life at a remote outpost, and Kendra was easily caught up in the activities. But she was not prepared for Mr. Hooker's gesture of friendship. When young men in their pickups began to bring from the shore the huge boxes and bundles assigned to her, he stepped forward, stationed himself in her cache, and supervised the orderly storage of her year's food. "We want you to get started right," he said.

The big surprise this year came on the second day toward the end of the unloading, when the supply of new snowmobiles came ashore. In Desolation even children had skidoos, as they were called, and it was not uncommon for a single family to have three of the noisy and dangerous machines. But after some dozen had been brought ashore, several watching boys whistled, for two deckhands came onto the ramp with a radically improved red-and-blue SnowGo-7, with wide treads, a molded plastic windshield and racing-type handlebars, four thousand dollars even.

"Who ordered that?" the boys cried in great excitement, and in response to many such queries, a handsome young fellow, graduated from school two years ago, stepped forward to claim the prize. A woman told Kendra: "Jonathan Borodin. His father and uncle worked at Prudhoe. Earned a fortune." Kendra recognized the name of a family she had not met, the proud Borodins who kept to the old ways, as opposed to Vladimir Afanasi, who accepted many aspects of the new. She wondered how the traditional Borodins had agreed to allow their son a snowmobile; it was a contradiction. But here the wondrous machine was, and as Kendra watched young Borodin push it proudly away she realized that it was going to monopolize both his imagination and his life. Turning to the woman, she asked: "Did he do well in school?" and the answer came: "Very well. He could have made it in college."

"Why would his family waste so much money on a snowmobile? Instead of college?" and the woman replied: "Oh, he went. Last year. To a fine college in Oregon. But after three weeks he got homesick. Missed 'the smokin' and the jokin'' on our village streets at night. So back he came."

Toward evening, after everything was carted away, the citizens of Desolation gathered at the shore to watch the barge weigh anchor and head north to Barrow, where it would unload the remaining cargo. How mournful it was to see the huge craft move off, to be absent for a whole year, the lifeline of the area, the big solid reminder that there was another world down toward Seattle. But especially meaningful was the moment when the barge sounded its foghorn in parting salute, for with this echoing sound the people of Desolation said to one another: "Well, now winter begins."

Kendra spent the rest of August and the first week of September continuing to familiarize herself with the village: the wind-beaten houses, the long, dark runways that served as protective entryways, the pits dug into the permafrost where meats were stored, the lake beyond the southern end of town from which fresh-water ice would be cut and melted later for drinking water—wherever she looked she found evidence that these Eskimos had been wrestling through the centuries with their arctic environment and had found acceptable solutions. So as she sat in the evenings playing Bingo with the women of the village, she studied them with admiration and never a shred of condescension.

They, in return, took it upon themselves to indoctrinate her properly, warning: "You must have someone help you make clothes for winter." As they said this they pointed back over their shoulders toward the Chukchi Sea, whose ice-free waves came to within a few yards of the village: "Come December when the wind howls in off the ice, you got to be warm," but Kendra was astonished at the prices she would have to pay for her gear. "It starts with mukluks," they said. "Keep your feet warm, you win the battle."

She learned that she could go two routes: "You a beginning teacher, not much money, store sells cheap Sorrel Packs, made by machine, rubber, felt insoles and liners, pretty good. You want to be like Eskimo, you get mukluk, oogruk sealskin for soles, caribou for tops coming to the knee, mouton socks, total cost maybe two hundred fifty dollars."

Kendra reflected only a moment: "If I'm in Eskimo land because I wanted to be, let's go whole hog. Real mukluks."

Her parka, the soul of the visible Eskimo costume, presented the same options: "J.C. Penney makes a good commercial one, three hundred dollars, and lots of Eskimos wear them, because real ones too much."

"How much?" and the answer made her head swim: "Skins, sewing, trim to protect face . . ." On and on the list of strange items continued: "Total about eight hundred dollars."

The figure staggered Kendra, who had never been allowed to spend over forty-five dollars for a dress, so after a deep-breathing pause, she asked: "Would I look silly wearing real mukluks and a store-bought parka?" The women consulted among themselves on this significant problem, then gave a unanimous answer: "Yes." Without further hesitation Kendra said almost happily: "Then I'll go for the Eskimo parka."

Not wishing to offend the Eskimo women with a question about money, she waited till she was alone with the Hookers: "How can these poor women afford such prices? And the money they throw around at Bingo?"

Mrs. Hooker broke into laughter: "Miss Scott, these women are loaded! Their husbands make enormous salaries when they work in the oil fields at Prudhoe. And of course, they all get that yearly bonus from the government."

"What bonus?"

"We don't pay taxes in Alaska. The oil money flows so fast, the government pays us. I hear it'll be close to seven hundred dollars this year."

Kasm broke in: "Haven't you noticed that most Eskimo houses this far north have two or three abandoned snowmobiles in the front yard?"

"I was going to ask about that," and Kasm explained: "With the easy money it's cheaper to buy a new one than to have an old one repaired. So they cannibalize them. Steal parts from one machine to repair another."

When the seamstresses decked Kendra in her new winter gear, with the fringe of the hood covering her face and her voluminous clothing masking the outlines of her body, she became one more Eskimo woman, a round, waddling, well-protected bundle, and she began to perspire. But the women assured her: "In December it may not be warm enough," and again they pointed ominously at the sea: "The winds from Siberia. You'll see." And now one of them said solemnly: "Your name now Kunik. Means *snowflake*. She, me, all, we call you Kunik," and as Kunik, the new teacher continued her campaign to understand Eskimo ways and be accepted in the community.

On opening day of her school, Kendra received a series of surprises, some pleasant, some not so. When she came into the cavernous room which could have supported forty high-school students, she found on her desk a bouquet made from seaweed and a kind of heather from the tundra, and never had she received any flowers that carried more emotional impact. Her breath caught as she tried to guess who had made this gesture of friendship, but she could reach no conclusion.

When a ship's bell on the schoolhouse roof rang and the sixteen students filed into the school, thirteen turned left for Mr. Hooker's elementary classes, while only three, a girl and two boys, came toward her section. When these three were seated at the front of the room, the place looked positively vacant, and she realized that it would be her job to fill it with activity and meaning. She was the schoolroom, not the books or the huge structure which had cost half of nine million dollars. Only she could make this inanimate place vital, and she was determined to do so.

These young people, round-faced, dark-haired, black-eyed and obviously eager, were prepared to help her breathe life into this cavern, but although she had come to know each of the three during the summer, she had not then appreciated how Asian they were in appearance when placed in a school situation. They were Eskimos and she was proud to be their teacher.

It was customary in many Eskimo schools for the teacher to address her collected students as "You guys," words which had a fine sense of familiarity, and from the beginning Kendra used the phrase freely. When she wanted to instill a feeling of comradeship she addressed her class as "Hey, you guys, let's get on with the math problems." But when she felt it necessary to establish discipline, she used "Now listen here, you guys, knock off the horseplay," and then they knew she meant business and order was restored.

Intuitively she liked her students, and after the first tentative questions and answers, she concluded that she had three above-average pupils, but before she could begin her serious teaching, there was an interruption which modified the whole day and indeed the entire year.

Vladimir Afanasi came into the room leading by the hand a frightened little Eskimo girl, fourteen years old, and before he had shown the terrified child where to sit, he took Kendra out onto the porch and said: "Her name is Amy Ekseavik, last name in four syllables. Her parents are the pariahs of our village. They fish upriver six months at a time. Live in a hovel down at the far point. Amy's been in school at best seven, eight weeks a year."

"Why is such a thing allowed?" and Afanasi said: "It isn't. I put the Barrow police on them. She must go to school, so her parents have brought her here to live through the winter with Mrs. Pelowook." Coming back into the classroom, he went over to the child and said: "These are your classmates, Amy, and this is your teacher, Miss Scott." With that he kissed the trembling child and indicated to Kendra that she, Kendra, must now take over.

But the teacher did not hear him, for at the moment when Amy first entered her room, Kendra had been struck by an overwhelming sensation: That's the little girl on the magazine cover! and the similar-

ity between the child of six or seven and this maturing girl of fourteen was so striking that Kendra put her left hand to her face and bit
her forefinger. It was a miracle, nothing less, that a replica of the
child whose photograph had lured Kendra to this remote spot should
now be entering her classroom. It was also a command: she had been
called here to serve this child.

"You'll check her out," Afanasi said as he prepared to leave. "She
can read and write some, but it's been a long time since the few weeks
she was in school last year." And with that, he was gone. When Kendra, too startled to react promptly, left her standing there, the girl in
the class rose, went to Amy, and led her to a chair which one of the
boys dragged into the circle; by that thoughtful gesture the strange
child, reared alone at the edge of the world, was made welcome.

On Kendra's third day on the job she happened to find in one of
her desk drawers a pamphlet which stated that the North Slope
school district, of which her school was a part, contained 88,281
square miles with a total population of 7,600. Feeling already a sense
of pride in what she called "my northern turf," she waited till school
ended, then went next door to see if she could borrow Mr. Hooker's
hand-held calculator, and he said almost gruffly: "The school's supposed to supply you with one," and he rummaged about in his desk
until he came up with the fine one which had been intended for her.
When she thanked him, he said: "I probably got some more junk
around here that's yours. I'll sort it out."

The gift of the calculator surprised her, but the more she saw of
this remarkable school, the more impressed she was with its generosity.
Each child was given a free toothbrush, toothpaste, pencils, ballpoint
pen, notebook, all reading material, a breakfast snack, a hot lunch
and full health services. Teachers participated in the bonanza too: fully
paid hospitalization, a life insurance policy of twice the yearly salary,
no rent on housing, heating or electricity, plus the famous Thrift Plan,
which Afanasi explained: "You're invited to deposit six percent of
your salary with us. Twenty-six hundred and forty dollars a year in
your case. We add fifty percent to it, and on the total we pay you eleven
percent each year. We don't want our teachers to go hungry."

To test her calculator, she engaged in the kind of silly game that
academic people find pleasure in pursuing: What state is about the
same size as our school district; and how many of our smaller states
would have to combine to be as big as we are? Using the almanac
supplied by the school, she found to her intense delight that the state

nearest in size was her own: 88,281 square miles for North Slope, 84,916 for good old Utah! and the thought that she was involved in a school district bigger than all of Utah staggered her.

She then proceeded to a second calculation, and found that North Slope was bigger than the ten smallest states combined, starting with Rhode Island and ending with West Virginia, but before gloating she did have the courtesy to question: Yes, but what about the population? and she found that these ten states had a combined population of more than 26,000,000 while North Slope had fewer than 8,000. Only then did she grasp the enormousness of her part of Alaska, and its emptiness.

Chubby-faced Amy Ekseavik, the newcomer, was proving to be a tough little customer; during her first two weeks in school she rebuffed any attempt to break down her reserve, and in her rugged self-determination she repelled students and teacher alike. As an only child living far from the village, she had never had friends, and the concept of being congenial with people or trusting them was alien; she had the gravest suspicions about her fellow students, and since her father and mother had treated her harshly, she could not imagine that Miss Scott was going to be much different, so for some time the atmosphere in the classroom was tense.

At this point Kendra consulted with her principal, and she discovered that where school matters were concerned, Mr. Hooker was a cautious, battle-scarred veteran who approached every problem from the point of view of "How could this hurt me? And if there's potential trouble, how can it be defused?" With that strategy dominating, he was not at all happy to learn that the new teacher was having trouble with her new pupil, because he had reason to believe that Amy Ekseavik was for some reason or other the special concern of Vladimir Afanasi, a member of the North Slope school board, and therefore she was a child to be handled carefully.

"You say she's intractable?" Kendra was often surprised at Mr. Hooker's vocabulary, for although he had acquired an M.A. in education from Greeley, in Colorado, one of the best schools of its kind, he really was a boob, but one with latent possibilities, so she shared her apprehensions with him.

"Amy's like a wild creature, Kasm. I wonder if she was abused at home?"

"Not even a remote possibility. Afanasi doesn't like her parents, but he says they're not brutes. Eskimos never maltreat their children."

"Then you think it's just the result of her being raised alone?"

"Possibly, and it might also be that she finds herself the youngest of your students. Maybe she would be happier, all around, if she dropped back to elementary school. I've been able to thaw out such children."

Automatically, and with force she would not have used had she thought about how it might be taken, Kendra cried: "Oh, no! She's where she should be. Her peers'll help her along, and I certainly aim to make her feel comfortable . . ." Suddenly realizing she was treading in a sensitive area, she backed out, saying "help her learn," at which Principal Hooker smiled with a depth of understanding that surprised Kendra: "You mustn't identify with her too strongly, Miss Scott."

"Please call me Kendra—that is, if you want me to call you Kasm."

"Agreed. So you want to keep her? But is she learning anything?"

"She's very bright, Kasm. She shows a great capacity to learn."

"Then stay with her. Congratulate her when she does something well, and don't be afraid to rebuke her when she stumbles."

So during those haunting autumn days when the sun sank lower and lower in the sky, as if to warn the people of Desolation: "Soon I shall be gone, soon night falls upon you," Kendra worked to break down the reserve of this aloof, almost wild child who had been thrust into her life, and she was fortified in this difficult task by the fact that over her desk at home she had tacked that *National Geographic* cover showing the other Amy as a six-year-old, and the determination of that fur-bound little girl heading into the blizzard consoled her: Any child raised like that would have to be tough at age fourteen. My Amy's just the way she should be now, and it's my job to show her how much better she can be at twenty.

So the difficult educational process that all young animals must undergo if they are to be first-class polar bears or eagles continued, with Kendra applying constant love and pressure and tough little Amy resisting with all her might. The other three students, children of normal upbringing whose individual peculiarities had been knocked into conformity by contact with other children as opinionated as they, progressed rapidly under Kendra's guidance, so that Desolation High was functioning at a rate that had to be classified as far more than satisfactory.

At a church supper that marked in an accidental way the end of autumn and the beginning of the long night of winter, several parents told Kendra: "We hear only good things about you. It was God's will that sent you to us," but the people with whom Amy Ekseavik was boarding said: "She never mentions school. Is she doing all right?" and Kendra said honestly: "She seems to be coming along."

In September, October and early November the citizens of Desolation often referred ominously to "the coming of winter," and Kendra supposed they were referring to the problems of perpetual night, but one day in early November she learned the real meaning. Since the weather had grown cold, down to two degrees below zero with a light snow covering the ground, she had begun to wear her Eskimo garb, and very comfortable it was. But on this morning when she hurried from the Teacherage to the school building, she was struck by a wind of such cruel force that she gasped and puckered her face, and when her students came in swathed in protective clothing, they asked: "How do you like real winter?"

The thermometer stood at minus-forty-two, but the howling wind roaring across the Chukchi from the wastelands of Siberia was so powerful that Barrow radio reported the wind-chill factor as "minus-ninety-one and dropping." It was a cold that Kendra had never imagined, let alone experienced: "Hey, you guys. How long does this continue?" and they reassured her: "Not many days," and they were right, for after three bone-shattering days the wind subsided and she found that minus-twenty-two without a gale was quite bearable.

Now, in the depth of a real arctic winter when people had to draw together for survival, she learned what a superior educator Kasm Hooker was and what a superb citizen Vladimir Afanasi was, for now the gymnasium, which had accounted for more than half what it cost to build the school, became the focal point of the community. There were feasts at Thanksgiving and Christmas to which all the villagers except the parents of Amy Ekseavik brought frozen whale meat, smelts, tom cod and wonderful stews made of duck, goose or caribou. But above all, there were basketball games. Indeed, Kendra sometimes felt that the soul of Desolation Point, at least in winter, resided in the basketball games which attracted almost everyone in the community. But it was basketball as she had never seen it before, because Desolation High had only those two boys, and although they were quite good at dribbling and shooting, they did require at least three other players to make a five-man team.

The problem was resolved in this way: it was agreed by any team which played Desolation that two boys who had graduated earlier would be allowed to play, with Mr. Hooker serving as the fifth member, it being understood that he would not shoot or guard the best player on the opposing team. But whom could Desolation play? Barrow High School had a fully competitive squad of fifteen, but the six other small schools on the North Slope did not. What the school did was a tribute to the imagination of Vladimir Afanasi, who explained the situation to Kendra prior to the first big game: "We have the money, so we pay the travel expenses of other schools to fly up here and play a set of three informal games, sometimes only two. The village goes crazy. Our boys have a great experience. And the players on the visiting teams have an opportunity to see what northern Alaska is like. Everybody profits."

The first team imported under these conditions was from the little Yukon River town of Ruby. Eight players flew in along with the coach and the school principal, and for several days when no sun appeared, Desolation thought only of basketball, and since there was no difference between night and day, the games were scheduled for five in the afternoon, and they were something to behold, for the Desolation team consisted of Kendra's two high-school boys, Jonathan Borodin, the graduate who owned the snowmobile, another boy who had graduated two years earlier, and Mr. Hooker, six feet one inch tall and weighing one hundred and fifty-seven. They appeared in handsome warmup jackets that had cost ninety-seven dollars each and pale blue jerseys proclaiming in bright golden letters NORTHERN LIGHTS. Since three of the players were noticeably short, with Jonathan Borodin of average size and Mr. Hooker reaching toward the stars, they were quite a mixture to look at, but once the whistle sounded and Referee Afanasi tossed up the ball, a game of wild charges and changes ensued.

Kendra was amazed at how skillfully her two students could play, while Borodin was still the star shotmaker he had been when regularly enrolled in school, but at halftime the score was Ruby 28, Desolation 21. Of course, if Mr. Hooker had been allowed to shoot, or had he been permitted to guard the star of the Ruby team, the result would probably have been different. Nevertheless, Kendra was proud of her team and cheered lustily for it.

That night the Desolation team lost 49–39, but the next night the local team, even though it was a hodgepodge, sank shot after shot and won by the comfortable margin of 44–36. Next day, before the chartered plane came to take the Ruby players back to the Yukon, four hundred and forty miles due south, the two teams shared a huge breakfast of scrambled simulated eggs, a sausage made of various meats and muffins provided by Mrs. Hooker. All agreed that the Ruby visit had been a sensational success, and one of the visiting players said in a formal speech of thanks for the hospitality: "I still believe that after we leave, the sun will come up," and one of Kendra's boys, who had starred in the second game, responded: "Come back in June, you'll be right!"

Now Kendra experienced the full wonder of life north of the Arctic Circle in the winter, those seemingly endless weeks of prolonged night, broken by a few hours of silvery haze at noon. Sometimes when the sun nibbled at the edge of clouds hanging over the Yukon River far to the south, Kendra would look out her schoolroom window and see shadowy figures, not distinct enough to be identified, moving slowly through the village, and she would think: I'm caught in a dream world, and none of this is real. But then the twenty-two hours of complete darkness would set in and she would say to herself: This is the real arctic. This is the one I came seeking. Then she would luxuriate in the blackness, as if only she of all the students who had graduated from Brigham Young could have the courage for such an adventure.

She was disposed, therefore, to enjoy the experience at Desolation, and whenever the women of the village arranged a festival of some kind, she helped them decorate the gymnasium and serve the refreshments, until all came to acknowledge her as a member of their community. Reports from her class were reassuring, except that dour Amy Ekseavik, the boarding pupil, volunteered no comment about her whatever.

In late December when Kendra surveyed her larder, she spotted those items which she had added to her order at the last moment, intending them to be a reward for her students, and now she dragged them forth, especially her pecans, Karo and cans of kumquats in heavy syrup. Enlisting the help of two women who had children in school, she made huge stacks of pecan-filled pancakes, links of canned sausage, piles of cookies which she decorated with the colored crystals she had ordered, and gallons of a sweet acid fruit punch made from powdered concentrate.

When all was ready, Kendra invited the entire school plus all the parents and the couple Amy lived with, and no attempt was made to bar curious neighbors who wanted to see what was happening in the school gym. Among those who gate-crashed was Vladimir Afanasi, who complimented Kendra on her gala affair and the friendly way in which she introduced the women of the village to kumquats, but the highlight of the affair for the children was the pecan-filled pancakes, and at the end of the feast even Amy Ekseavik admitted grudgingly: "They were good."

As Kendra watched Mr. Afanasi move off to talk with men of the village, she saw that he had in tow a stranger, and in her first glance at this white man, apparently from the Lower Forty-eight, she was swept by an impression which she would never forget: that he was someone of importance who had been sent to Desolation not by accident but in the completion of some grand design. He was young, medium tall, well groomed and had an engaging smile. He did not look her way, but his blond hair was so outstanding among the Eskimo men with whom he stood, that she could not help glancing at him, and when a break came in the entertainment the students had arranged, she wandered casually over to where Afanasi was speaking, and when he saw her coming he moved toward her as if he had divined her intentions, took her by the hand, and led her directly to the young stranger: "Miss Scott, may I present my counselor-at-law, Jeb Keeler."

"Welcome to our school festival, Mr. Keeler, Counselor . . . ?"

"Dartmouth and Yale Law," Afanasi explained, "and he's invaluable to this community."

"You mean you work here?" she asked, and eager for the opportunity, Afanasi spelled out the unique relationship young Keeler had to the village and its citizens. Kendra was impressed and asked: "Do you have a house here?" and Jeb replied: "I stay with Mr. Afanasi. Most of my work is with him, and it's convenient."

She lingered with the men several minutes more than necessary, then became aware of her intrusion and excused herself awkwardly, revealing the favorable impression the young lawyer had made upon her. But this was not an embarrassment, for she had made the same impression on him. He had once told his mentor, Poley Markham: "I kissed the beauties at Wellesley and Smith goodbye," and he had, but in neither Juneau nor Anchorage, where he continually met people in his legal work, had he met any women who interested him, and now to find in Desolation a young woman as attractive and able as Kendra seemed to be a dividend not to be ignored.

As the gala ended, he maneuvered his way toward where Kendra stood bidding the women of the village goodnight, and as the last of the guests left he asked: "Would you have breakfast with me tomorrow? At Vladimir's, of course, but we cook up some mighty good chow."

"I would like that," she said with a disarming smile. "But you know, Mr. Afanasi is my boss, and I have to be in my classroom at eight."

"I'll pick you up at six."

"But why so early?"

"I have a lot of questions I'd like to ask," and she nodded.

She was up before five the next morning, and was waiting impatiently when at a quarter to six a knock came at her door, with Jeb Keeler standing on the stoop to escort her to Afanasi's for breakfast. As they walked through the dark, her arm linked in his, she sensed that he was just as eager for this conversation as she, and the idea pleased her enormously. It was her first real date between peers, a planned affair with excitement on each side, and she was gratified in some inexplicable way that it was occurring so far north of the Arctic Circle.

After breakfast Afanasi had the good sense to improvise a meeting on village matters, which took him quickly from his house.

"You come here on legal matters?" Kendra asked, and on this invitation Jeb explained his relationship to Poley Markham and the services the two lawyers had provided the Desolation corporation. From there he led her through the intricacies of the Native Claims Settlement Act, on which he had become something of an expert, so that when Afanasi returned, she was able to ask him: "What do you think the result will be in 1991, when you Eskimos gain full title to your lands?"

"You've been talking heady stuff, eh?" He poured himself some coffee and sat with them for the next hour, discussing frankly the perplexing problems his people were facing: "I'm happy about the condition of our local Desolation unit. With sober advice from Poley Markham at the beginning and Jeb here in recent times, we've protected ourselves. Haven't lost money, haven't made a great deal, but have held on to our land constructively. But the big corporations? Ah, now I'm worried. The good ones prosper, the poor ones are in danger of going under. And if they do, when 1991 comes around they'll be eager to sell out to businessmen in Seattle."

"Could that happen?" Kendra asked, and Jeb broke in: "The wolves are gathered at the campfire. Just waiting for 1991 and a chance to grab millions of Alaska's finest acres. Once gone, the Natives will never be able to recover them. A whole way of life shot to hell."

As they discussed this mournful prospect, Jeb's strategy became clear to Kendra, and she respected him for it: "I think that about half the big corporations are doomed. Technically they're in bankruptcy now, or close to it. I judge that those lands are already lost, unless the federal government steps in with some kind of rescue operation. But I do believe that many of the village corporations can be saved and their lands protected far into the future, and that's what I'm trying to accomplish with the ones I work for."

At this point Afanasi became almost poetic in his defense of the Eskimo's traditional relationship to his land: "My land is not this empty tundra, measured in white man's acres. My land is the open ocean, frozen solid in winter, highway for walrus and seal and bowhead whale in spring and summer. Enough safe land for the houses of my village, enough free ocean to ensure the harvest of the sea on which we've always depended." He snapped his fingers: "Come on, Miss Scott, quarter to eight. You ought to be in your classroom!" and he led Kendra and Jeb to the school.

Jeb Keeler's counseling with the corporation leaders required him to remain in Desolation for nine days, and each evening spent with Kendra deepened his interest in her; he found her an intelligent, alert young woman with concerns paralleling his own, and with the shy kind of humor that a man like him appreciated. He wanted a woman to be almost his equal in brain power, but not to be too aggressive about it. He particularly esteemed her maturing attitudes toward the Eskimos, a people he had taken under his protection.

"At first when I looked at their dark, scowling faces I thought: They hate the world, but then I discovered that they were merely marking time till they sized me up. Once I passed muster, they blossomed like peach trees in spring." When he agreed that it took time to interpret the apparent reticence of the Eskimos, she wanted him to meet her four students, so he arranged his duties with Afanasi so that he could spend the afternoon in her class, and there he made a great hit with the three students from Desolation but no impact whatever on Amy Ekseavik, who glared at him as if he were the enemy.

This so challenged him that at the conclusion of his stories about hunting caribou in northern Canada and his skiing days at Dartmouth, he bade the three local students a warm goodbye but asked Amy to stay for further discussion. Dropping her head, she peered at him from behind dark bangs and reluctantly agreed.

"You said nothing in class," he began, "but I could see that you had more questions than any of the others, and I'm sure yours would have been the most interesting. Tell me, what was it you wanted to ask?"

Chin on her chest, hair covering her eyes, she mumbled: "Do all men like you have white hair?"

"It isn't white. It's what we call blond. Sort of like Miss Scott's."

"In magazines I see lots of women with hair like yours. Never no men."

"There are a great many of us around, Amy."

"Why you come here? What for?"

"I bring papers from the government in Juneau, in Washington. You know the big capital in Washington?"

"Sure." The firmness of her response encouraged him to ask her a variety of questions well calculated to test the accumulated intelligence of a girl of fourteen, and both he and Kendra were surprised at the depth and scatter of her learning. Finally he turned to arithmetic, and again she surprised him with her facility: "Amy, you're one of the brightest girls your age I've ever met. You see many things you never talk about, don't you?"

Obviously pleased but also deeply embarrassed at this probing of her secrets, she finally raised her face slightly, looked directly at Jeb, and gave him one of the widest, most encompassing smiles he had ever received. From that moment on, Jeb and Amy were partners, and whereas Kendra had been unable to thaw the self-frozen child, Jeb brought out all the hidden warmth that nestled in this taut bosom, and the more Amy revealed of herself and her extraordinary gifts of perception and understanding, the more Kendra and Jeb realized that they had discovered a burgeoning human being who could achieve almost anything to which she directed her unusual mind.

"We've got to organize it so she can get to college later on," Jeb said, and Kendra agreed: "She's practically ready now. I'm sure the University of Washington will have scholarships for a girl like this."

That evening, Jeb's last in Desolation, they wandered for some time in the darkness, with the thermometer at minus-twenty-nine. The cold,

with almost no humidity, was bracing rather than destructive and they
almost reveled in it. "Not many American lovers wandering about in
minus-twenty-nine," Jeb said, and she drew back: "I didn't know we
were lovers," and he said: "We could be, tonight." And when they
reached the Teacherage he wanted to follow her inside, but she rebuffed
him: "No, Jeb," but then she weakened her answer by reasoning:
"Everyone in the village would know by morning," and he said: "Ah
ha! You wouldn't mind if we were in some neutral place like Anchorage," and her silence betrayed the fact that this was her precise attitude.

She embraced him with ardor and lingered on her doorstep so
that he could respond again and again. He was by all odds the most
desirable young man she had ever met, a lawyer with deep respect for
the law, a friend to the Eskimo and, as he had proved in his adroit
thawing out of Amy Ekseavik, an adult who could project himself
into the world of children. She was in love with Jeb, and under different circumstances, where their privacy would be ensured, she would
have been ready to prove it, but since she shared the Teacherage with
her principal and the prying eyes of the villagers, she had to be con-
strained. "Jeb, you're the most precious thing to enter my life in a
score of years. Please, please let's keep in touch."

"If you feel that way, and me the same, why not let me in?" and
she said, with no great firmness: "Here, it's not possible," and he
asked: "But if you came to Anchorage on a visit? Would it be possible then?" and she said: "Don't rush me," which he interpreted properly as: "Probably."

Her attention was distracted by a chain of events engineered by
Vladimir Afanasi, who seemed determined to prove that Alaska was
both bizarre and unique. On the first of January he learned that payments from the oil fields at Prudhoe Bay were going to be several
times what his board had anticipated, and he announced in public
meeting: "Good! It frees our hands," and that afternoon he called for
Harry Rostkowsky to fly him out to Barrow, where he caught the
Prudhoe Bay plane to Anchorage. There he took a hotel room at the
airport, visiting intensively with the local managers of all the dozen
international airlines that flew over the North Pole to Europe, and in
the end he found that the best price for what he had in mind would be
with Lufthansa, which refused to allow German business to be lost
to some other airline.

With a firm contract for at least as many round-trip tickets as he needed, he hurried back to Desolation, and at a big meeting in the gymnasium revealed his plans: "Citizens of Desolation, by careful supervision and our good luck in having teachers like Kasm Hooker and Kendra Scott, we have in our village one of Alaska's finest Molly Hootch schools." The crowd applauded as Mr. Hooker waved to them: "But it's difficult to sustain morale and learning in the winter months that loom ahead." He stopped here and allowed general discussion of this irrefutable truth: to run a school even this small was most difficult when there was no daylight.

"What you propose doin' about it?" a fisherman asked, and Afanasi evaded giving a direct answer: "I have never wanted to run a parochial school here in Desolation."

"What's *parochial*?" a man asked, and a woman replied: "Catholic," and Afanasi corrected her: "It can mean Catholic, you're right, but in another sense it can also mean *narrow-minded* or *limited*." As he paused to allow this to sink in, Kendra thought: What in the world is he leading up to? and she looked for a clue from her principal, who shrugged his shoulders, for he too had been left in the dark.

"We want our students to understand the world south of the Arctic Circle, don't we? Isn't that why we fly our basketball teams down to places like Juneau and Sitka? Why our dancers and Eskimo Olympians compete in Fairbanks? Well, this time we're going to broaden their horizons in a way not tried before. Ten days from right now, just about all of our students, two of our teachers, three of our board members and three mothers to act as chaperones are going to fly in a chartered plane to Anchorage, board a Lufthansa superjet and fly to Frankfurt, Germany, where we will have classes on the history of Central Europe, after which we'll fly to six other German cities to see what a major European nation is like."

There were gasps, cheers, wild excitement among the schoolchildren, then a sobering question: "Who's gonna pay for this?" and Afanasi's resounding answer: "The school board. Our budget can stand it." Then he recapitulated: "We'll pay like I said. Twelve students. The five real young ones will stay here with Mrs. Hooker. Two teachers. Three board members. Three mothers as chaperones. That's twenty. And if some of the rest of you want to pay your own way, and it'll be a bargain, we can accept five more."

Because the salaries at Prudhoe Bay had been spectacular in recent years, five volunteers shouted their names, with Kendra noting that Jonathan Borodin, the nineteen-year-old with the snowmobile, was among them. Before the meeting ended, all details of the safari to Germany were agreed upon; Kendra and Mr. Hooker compiled lists of vital data for Mr. Afanasi to take to the federal building in Fairbanks in the morning for the issuance of passports, and boys' suits and girls' dresses were hastily refurbished.

In their classes Mr. Hooker and Miss Scott dropped all other studies to conduct crash courses on German geography, history and music. One mother had old copies of the *Geographic* covering Germany and another had recordings of Beethoven's Fifth and selections from *Faust*. Children drew maps of Germany, and little Amy Ekseavik surprised everyone by drawing a fine map of Alaska, in the middle of which, displaying its insignificance in comparison with the North Slope and Yukon Valley, was shown Germany, East and West, drawn to the same scale. Amy would not tell the other students why she had done this, but after school she whispered to Kendra: "I want to go, but it's no big deal."

"There you're wrong, Amy. For two thousand years this part of Europe"—and her right hand almost obliterated Amy's Germany—"has dominated this part of the world. It isn't always bigness that counts." And on a spur-of-the-moment impulse, she grasped Amy by both hands: "You're a young girl, Amy. You could be so very much. Mr. Keeler said, 'You could be anything you wanted to be. Anything.'"

"You're in love with Mr. Keeler, aren't you?"

"I'm in love with Alaska, and all it stands for. I'm thrilled by the wonderful capacity you have stored inside of you. When you go to Germany, Amy, look, and weigh, and listen, and for God's sake, learn something." She released Amy's hands and stepped back. From the door of the schoolroom Amy turned to stare at her teacher, recalling and evaluating all that had been said.

The expedition to Germany was a flawless success. The various planes took off on time. Lufthansa's publicity people peppered European papers with stories and photographs of the Eskimo schoolchildren. Museums, zoos, castles and industrial centers arranged special tours for the visitors, and one financial newspaper carried a long analysis of the financial structure of the North Slope and its petroleum bonanza. The reporter calculated that this commendable school adventure, which was apparently going so well, had cost Desolation Point not less than $127,000, all paid out of oil royalty funds. Afanasi issued a corrective: "Only twenty of our people had their expenses paid by the school board, and this expenditure was roundly approved by the citizens. The other six paid their own fares, because they wanted to share in the experience."

He was right in his numbers. There were twenty official members of the party, plus the five who had volunteered that first night in the gym, plus an unexpected traveler who asked to join the party when it reached Anchorage. Jeb Keeler, lawyer to both the Desolation corporation and the school board, had felt that he ought to come along as a counselor to Afanasi, and he did not deny to himself that the thought of spending time with Kendra in Europe influenced his plans. She was flattered by this proof of his sincere interest, and no two members of the expedition had more joy in the trip through Germany than they. In fact, their pleasure in each other became so obvious that one of the chaperones told the other two: "We've been watching the wrong ones," but everyone approved of the relationship, and speculation rose among the older students as to whether Mr. Keeler slipped in to Miss Scott's bedroom in the various inns at which they stopped.

One of the subjects that Kendra discussed with Keeler would have surprised the students: "Jeb, I know this may infringe on the lawyer-client relationship, but I have to know. The way Afanasi throws money around, this trip for example, is he stealing from the corporation?"

Jeb gasped, then grabbed Kendra by her shoulders: "That's a rotten question. Afanasi's the most honest man I know. He'd cut off his right arm rather than steal a penny." Shaking her, he growled: "And you can testify to the world that I said so."

She was not rebuffed by his spirited defense of his friend: "Then where does he get his money?" and he banged a table with his fist: "Dammit, none of your people from the Lower Forty-eight believe it, but up here Prudhoe Bay money flows like water. Afanasi's school board has money. I have money. My partner Poley Markham has money—all of it legal, all of it verified by receipts. Now accept the facts. Up here money is very common."

The observer who took the keenest interest in the sometimes stormy courtship was Amy Ekseavik, for her attachment to Jeb Keeler had intensified as she watched his courteous behavior in Germany, and she already had a proprietary interest in Miss Scott, because she, Amy, had been the first to detect that her teacher had fallen in love with the nice young lawyer. On several side trips Jeb and Kendra asked Amy to come along, and they were constantly amazed at her mastery of things German. "Amy," Kendra cried one day in the Munich Pinakothek, "you're speaking German as if you'd studied it," and she said: "I have," and she showed them the cheap phrase book which she had practically memorized. That night, after a romantic interlude which moved the lovers much closer to an open avowal of their plans, Kendra said: "If we ever do get married, I want to adopt Amy," and Jeb agreed: "We'll send her to Dartmouth."

The expedition provided two delightful surprises: the American ambassador invited the Eskimos to a formal luncheon in Bonn, and then arranged for a sleigh-ride outing in the nearby countryside, with a halt at a rustic German inn where musicians in costume played old German folksongs and danced with the Eskimos.

As the silvery days of the German winter passed, with the visitors thinking often of the bleak darkness back home, Kendra became aware of something she had not noticed before: Jonathan Borodin was a surprisingly able young man. She had known him only as a rather brash fellow who had no job but did have that very noisy snowmobile whose echoes seemed to disturb her class whenever she was trying to make an important point. During her first six months in the village she had not liked Jonathan, but now as she observed him on the trip, and saw how he cared for the younger children as if he were their uncle, she realized that the boy had possibilities, and she was so disturbed that he was not continuing with his education that during their trip into East Berlin she took a seat beside him in the bus and asked: "Jonathan, why did you drop out of college?" and he replied in surly tones: "I got hungry for village life," and she said without inflecting her words: "Like maybe 'Smokin' and jokin'?" and he replied: "It's our way of life."

She bit her lip, for she knew that if she ridiculed his pathetically limited vision, she would lose him: "But I've been watching you, Jonathan, and you have unusual talents."

"Like what?" he asked, half offensively, half with a desire to hear more.

"You're an excellent manager. Get an education and you could work anywhere, Anchorage, Seattle, maybe a congressman's aide in Washington." When he looked at her in surprise, she said: "I mean it. You have special talents, but if you don't develop them, they'll wither."

He gave an arrogant answer, one that many young Eskimos might have given in these heady days: "I can get a job at Prudhoe Bay anytime I need one. Make four times as much as you do teaching."

She stiffened, for such kind of talk she would not accept: "Who's talking money? I'm talking about the entire future of your life. You drift off to Prudhoe, work there three or four years, waste your salary, and what do you have for the rest of your life? Think about it, Jonathan," and with obvious disgust she rose and stomped off to another seat.

He was a young fellow of some spirit, for later that day, when they were back in West Berlin, he looked for her and asked if he could take the chair next to hers in the restaurant. "Please do," she said, and he astonished her by revealing that he occupied a somewhat special place in Desolation: "My grandfather, you don't know him, but you think Mr. Afanasi is the big man in the village. Corporation, yes. School board, yes. But the real man is my grandfather," and he proceeded to share with her the remarkable gifts his grandfather possessed and the power he exercised over events like the birth of a child or the catching of a whale. Finally, she laid down her knife and fork, stared at him, and asked: "Jonathan, are you telling me that your grandfather is a shaman?" She had heard the word several times since coming to Alaska, so she was well aware of the extraordinary powers shamans had once exercised in those northern parts, but she had never dreamed that a real, live shaman could have existed into the present. Desolation had a Presbyterian minister, eleventh in line since that fateful day when Captain Mike Healy of the *Bear* had put Dr. Sheldon Jackson ashore with timbers to build a Presbyterian mission and staff it with a converted Dmitri Afanasi. Everyone in the village was Presbyterian, always had been, and it was startling to think that a shaman from the ancient days coexisted with the church, conducting a subterranean form of religion to which the villagers surreptitiously adhered. It was heathenish. It was impossible. And it was exciting.

When the group returned to Munich, the German Tourist Board, delighted with the favorable notices the Eskimos were receiving, provided free tickets to the four high-school students, both teachers and the adults in the party to a performance of grand opera in the historic Munich opera house. "I'm sorry it's not for an easy opera like *Carmen*," explained the woman who would accompany the group, "but its effects are magnificent, and I'll explain the action. Wagner's *Die Walküre*. Music you'll never forget."

Amy Ekseavik, of course, procured a copy of the libretto and prepared both her fellow students and her elders for what they were about to see, and with assistance from the guide, the people from Desolation were able to follow the intricate story. Kendra, who had never seen an opera, sat behind the students, with Jeb Keeler on her left and Afanasi on her right, while Jonathan Borodin sat in front of her, but two seats away, so that she could see much of his face, and when the brooding music began and the ancient Norse customs started to unfold, it was clear that the effect upon Borodin was profound. No other student and none of the adults followed the mysterious grandeur of the Wagnerian scene with the intensity that he did, and this prompted Kendra to ask Afanasi during the first intermission: "Is it true that Jonathan Borodin's grandfather is a secret shaman?"

The question had an explosive effect on the wise, cultivated leader of the Desolation community, for he turned abruptly to face Kendra, and asked with force: "Who told you that?" and she pointed to where young Borodin sat alone in a kind of trance, staring at the great curtain which masked the stage.

Afanasi remained silent for some moments, then leaned toward Kendra so that Borodin could not hear what was being said: "We live in a dual world. The Presbyterian minister reminds us of Christian values we've respected for the last hundred years. But the elders remind us of values we followed for the last ten thousand years." He wished to say no more, but when Kendra said nothing, he grasped her by the hand and assured her: "Shaman? In the ugly old sense of that word? No. Magic? Cures? Curses? None of that. But a conservator of valued ancient ways we've followed? Yes."

And there the matter ended, except that during the last two acts of the opera, Kendra saw that Jonathan was transfixed by the majesty on the stage, the dominance of the gods, the wonder of the scenic effects and the power of the singing, the action and the invocations. Like all the Eskimos, including Afanasi, he was seeing an interpretation of northern life that was eerily foreign yet familiar. The guide had apologized when telling the visitors what the opera was going to be, but what she could not have known was that it would be one of the very best to show this group from another northern world.

As they filed out of the grand theater, the most impressive building the Eskimos had ever been in, Kendra found herself walking beside Borodin, and she asked him what he had thought of the opera, and he replied: "They could have been Eskimos. It was like our story," and when little Amy Ekseavik caught up with them, she said: "They lived in a cold land too, didn't they?" and the magic of the performance continued to manifest itself throughout their late supper and the conversation that followed.

On the flight home, Kendra received tardy instruction concerning two verboten subjects of discussion in an Eskimo community, and the repressive warning came from the most worldly of the Desolation community, Vladimir Afanasi. Sitting beside him on a portion of the flight, she congratulated him on how successful the expedition had been, and said: "You did it. When I first heard your proposal to take practically the whole school to Germany, I said to myself: 'What a cockamamie idea!' Two days in Berlin straightened me out," and he replied that it would not have been possible without the help of two teachers like Kasm and Kendra: "People underestimate Mr. Hooker. He's one of those fortunate people in the world who find exactly where they want to be, and it's the place they ought to be. He wouldn't be any good in the high school, where you have to teach specific subjects, because investigators are going to be testing your students. Do you know what he teaches?"

"I've often wondered. When I get his students, they aren't up to speed, as I'm sure you know."

"He teaches the glories of Eskimo life, the walrus hunt, the great whales. He's rather good at simple arithmetic."

"I've noticed that."

"But he despises things like poetry and history and traditional children's stories. Says they're all bunk. What he does stress is the glory of Notre Dame football. And he encourages his students to follow the old Eskimo arts, like carving and basketmaking and skinwork." He reflected on this for some moments, while both he and Kendra studied the tall principal from the rear, then Afanasi said: "In our Molly Hootch schools the curriculum tends to be whatever interests the teacher, and you just pray to God that he or she is interested in something. What, doesn't seem to matter much."

This encouraged Kendra to say: "You know, Mr. Afanasi, we have a near-genius in this little girl Amy Ekseavik."

"You mentioned that before."

"And she told me the other night in Frankfurt that she might have to drop out of school."

"Why? She's doing superbly, what I hear."

Kendra knew that what she was about to say was pejorative, but she had no warning that it was going to be as explosive as it proved: "She told me that her father drinks too much and she might have to go back and help her mother."

She could hear Afanasi suck in his breath and click his teeth: "Miss Scott, there are two aspects of Eskimo life that we do not wish to have ventilated, especially not by strangers who come here from the Lower Forty-eight." His dark face furrowed in anger, he pointed his finger at Kendra and said harshly: "Do not comment on our drunkenness. Do not spread stories about our rate of suicide. These are problems which hide in the Eskimo soul, and we do not appreciate preaching from others. In your case in particular, still a stranger among strangers, I would advise you to keep your mouth shut." Trembling with an old fury, for he had had to give this lecture to many white men and women who moved among the Eskimos, he left his seat and did not resume speaking to Kendra for the rest of the trip, but when they reached Desolation and the father of one of the high-school boys appeared at the plane too drunk to recognize his son, a common occurrence with that man, Afanasi pointed to him and said to Kendra: "It's the canker that gnaws at our soul. But we have to bear it ourselves. You can add nothing, neither condemnation nor hope. So please do what I so rudely suggested. Keep your mouth shut."

Tight-lipped, Kendra started looking more closely at the local situation, and she saw that beneath the good humor of the gymnasium meetings and the lively entertainments to which she invited the parents of her pupils, there was a silent undercurrent composed of the two dark streams that infected Eskimo life: the drunkenness that had been cynically introduced by the Boston whalers like Captain Schransky and his *Erebus,* and the general malaise that had been introduced with the best intentions by the missionaries like Dr. Sheldon Jackson, the bearers of the white man's law like Captain Mike Healy and his *Bear,* and the promulgators of education like Kasm Hooker and Kendra Scott.

Such a wealth of change, all of it defended as superior to the ancient ways of the Eskimo, had been too much to absorb in so few generations, so that this malaise, a sickness of the soul, evolved, with the all too frequent result that those who did not find refuge in drunkenness found release in suicide. Ignorant of the true situation, Kendra had not taken count of the men in Desolation who were drunks, nor had she the information to list the suicides over the past five years, but now that she had been alerted to the two dreadful burdens of the Eskimo, she compiled a sorrowful dossier.

One informant, an elderly woman, unknowingly revealed the cause of Afanasi's harsh reactions: "His grandfather, missionary, he was man come from God, come to help us. He bring many good things. Many times he try to keep alcohol away from the village. But always white men bring it back. Much money. That Afanasi try to help lost ones. Always he say 'turn to God,' but nothing change. And his sons. They lost too. One, Vladimir's father. He always drunk. He should be strong hunter. But he die young. His brother Ivan, uncle to Vladimir, he become very quiet. No more talk. No more fish. No more hunt. Just stop. Then he shoot hisself."

The woman halted her story, studied the young schoolteacher for some moments, and added: "Eskimo sickness jump generations like salmon upstream. First Afanasi noble man, but both his sons destroy selves. Our Afanasi in next generation noble man, but you heard what happen to his son?"

"I didn't," Kendra said, and she gasped when the woman said: "One day, no reason, he shoot hisself." Shaking her head, she concluded: "Maybe someday Vladimir's sister in Seattle have a grandson, maybe noble man too."

That first winter ended with such a savage chain of days in which the thermometer stayed always below thirty and often forty, that Kendra sought to provide respite from the boredom that attacked her students. She told them of the wonders of Salt Lake City and Denver and tried to explain what a rodeo was, and when she learned that one of the Barrow teachers had brought back from a vacation in Honolulu some high-quality movies of the islands, she asked Mr. Hooker if he had funds to invite the teacher down to talk to their students, and he said: "We'll throw it open to the whole community," and it was a festive evening.

But along with the colorful shots of tropical flowers and hula dancers throwing fiery swords from one to the other, the film had an unusual segment which the teacher introduced with special care: "We're now going to witness the dedication of a new high school. See the lovely murals . . . imagine a gymnasium with open sides . . . that's a bell tower. But what I want you to see is this old man—he's coming to bless the building before anyone can enter, reassuring the gods of the islands that all is in order. He's a kahuna . . . he speaks with the gods. He's what we would call a shaman."

The film showed the solemn ceremonies, the mountains behind the new school, the wonderful craggy face of the kahuna as he asked for a blessing: "But I want you to see especially those four men in black looking on . . . Catholic priests. They don't like kahunas but they've invited him to bless their school . . . and can you guess why?" And she stopped the film and said solemnly: "I want you to study these next pictures carefully. Eight months before what you've just seen, an earlier version of the school was finished . . . students about to come to class. And someone warned the Catholic priests: 'You better have the kahuna bless your school because if the gods aren't happy, it might burn down.' The priests said: 'Nonsense!' . . . and look what happened!"

She showed film taken earlier of the huge fire consuming the school, and after several minutes, when the fires abated and the ashes were visible, she said: "The kahuna had warned them and they hadn't listened, so this time when their school was ready, they had him come in. He wears about his neck the leaves of a sacred tree, the maile. He prays to the god of fire: 'Don't burn this school' . . . to the god of winds: 'Don't blow down this school.' And now he blesses even the priests who had fought against him: 'Keep these good men in health and help them to teach.' And now the old man blesses us all: 'Help everyone to learn.' And the school had no more troubles, for the Hawaiian shaman had protected it in the proper way."

The effect of this film on Jonathan Borodin was so disturbing that he could not sleep, and toward two in the morning he came banging on Kendra's door.

"Who's there?" she called.

"Jonathan. I have to speak with you."

"In the morning, Jonathan. I'm sleeping now."

"But I must. I have to see you," so against her better judgment she put on her robe, opened the door gingerly, and admitted the distraught young man.

His problem was unique. Both in Germany and in the film he had seen that sensible men and women revered the ancient ways, and that treasured beings like shamans survived in both cultures. "What's wrong with my grandfather?" he asked, so abruptly and so combatively that she drew back and said quickly: "Nothing at all, Jonathan. I hear he's a fine man. Mr. Afanasi said so."

"Afanasi!" the boy repeated with contempt. "In our little village he opposes everything my grandfather does. But in that big city they respect their shamans. They know they're needed."

Suddenly, without any warning, he fell heavily upon her bed, trembling as if caught by some wracking force, and after several attempts to control himself, he said softly: "I see things that others don't see, Miss Scott. I know when the whales are coming back." When Kendra said nothing, he caught her hand and said quietly but with great force: "That new girl you like so much, Amy, dreadful things are going to happen to her. She'll never go to college the way you want her to. I'm not going either. I'm going to be a shaman."

With that, he rose, bowed toward where she stood, thanked her for her help, and said at the doorway: "You're a fine teacher, Miss Scott, but you won't stay at Desolation very long. You represent the new ways, but with us the old ways never die." Before she could respond he was gone, closing the door silently behind him.

He left a bewildered Kendra, aware that she should never have allowed him entrance to her room. As to his announcement that he intended to follow in his grandfather's steps and become a shaman, she understood the psychological impact the opera in Munich and the kahuna's performance in the film had had, but because her knowledge of Alaskan history was imperfect, she had no basis for judging whether his decision to become a shaman made sense or not. She was distraught and failed to sleep until nearly five in the morning.

She was inclined to report the night's bizarre events to Afanasi, but she judged that this would not be fruitful, for while the Eskimo leader had tried to be impartial in his judgment of shamanism, she had seen that he opposed it in even its mildest and most ineffective survival. What she really wished was that Jeb might have been there, for she knew that his appraisal would have been sober and relevant. In this unsettled frame of mind she prepared to complete her exciting first year of teaching, and sometimes in the late afternoon as spring approached the still-frozen north, she stopped young Borodin as he sped along on his snowmobile and tried to talk with him about returning to the university with the coming of summer.

Cryptically he referred to other interests, saying that he might look for a job at Prudhoe Bay, then adding: "Anyway, whales will be arriving on their way north next week," and with that prediction uttered so carelessly, she was catapulted into the heart of ancient Eskimo experience. For on Thursday the village exploded with excitement when scouts from Afanasi's umiak stationed at the edge of the landfast ice along the inshore lane of open water reported over their portable radio: "Lookout at Point Hope radioed five bowheads heading our way."

Afanasi, who had been waiting many days for just such a report, stopped by the school in his pickup, shouted for Kendra to join him, then waited impatiently while she slipped into her Eskimo gear. "You'll see something now!" he cried exultantly as they went down to the edge of the ice, where a skidoo waited to skim him over the shore ice to the open water of the lane. "I don't like these things," he told Kendra, "but jump on," and over the rumpled ice they sped, picking their way through the hummocks.

When they reached water and the waiting umiak, they were greeted by Afanasi's crew of five tested whale hunters, and Kendra watched with admiration as Afanasi deftly eased himself into position, lest his heavy feet puncture the sealskin bottom.

The whale hunters of Desolation, and any man who took pride in his reputation wanted to be one, used two kinds of craft: the traditional umiak rowed by hand when the bowheads came close to the edge of the landfast ice, and an aluminum skiff with outboard motor when the lane water was wide and the whales stayed far from shore. Afanasi, as the conservator of old ways, abhorred the skiffs as much as he did the noisy skidoos. He was an umiak man.

Moving lazily north up the narrow lane of free water, hemmed in on both sides by thick ice, came four adult whales, two of them more than fifty feet long and weighing fifty tons each according to the rule "One foot, one ton," accompanied by a youthful one not more than twenty feet long, and in stately procession the whales approached the hunters. "Oh!" Kendra gasped as she stood alone at the edge of the ice. "They look like galleons coming back to England after a tussle with the Spanish."

Now Afanasi, as the most practiced and respected hunter, took over, and from the rear of his umiak, not much different from those constructed in Siberia fifteen thousand years earlier, he and his five helpers set forth in freezing seas to harpoon themselves a whale. When the huge lead whale sounded, they knew from long experience that it might stay submerged as long as six or seven minutes, and they assumed that they had missed it. But on came the others, and when they too sounded at irregular intervals, Afanasi's men feared that they might have lost their opportunity. When the second fifty-footer reappeared, it had moved over to the far side of open water, where it slipped by unscathed, but one of the smaller ones, about forty feet long, sounded well south of where Afanasi and his umiak waited, and an Eskimo who had come to stand beside Kendra said: "That one's gonna come up right where Vladimir wants it," and about five minutes later the whale broke through the surface, spouted, and to the disgust of the men in the umiak and those watching from shore, immediately sounded again with its great flukes thrashing, and disappeared before any of Afanasi's men could attack it with any likelihood of success.

"Oh!" the man standing beside Kendra groaned with a pain that was obviously real, and when she looked at him for an explanation, he told her: "The International Whaling Commission, Russia and Canada and them, wanted to halt whaling altogether. But our Alaska Eskimo Whaling Commission said: 'Hey! It's our way of life. Allow us a few each year.'"

"How many did they give you?"

"Desolation? Our quota? Two."

"Per year?"

"Yep, and for the past two years how many do you think we landed? None." He spat, looked out at the open water, so tantalizingly close, so inhospitable, and as he did, the third whale, still far off, broke the surface in a thunderous breach as if to tease Afanasi and his men.

"Has he lost them?" Kendra asked, and the man said: "If anyone can catch us a whale, it's Afanasi. Lifetime he has nine. I have two. Nobody else has more than four. That's why he's headman in our village."

Kendra turned to look at the man: "You mean he's headman because he's brought in more whales than anyone else?"

"Miss Scott, in Desolation it don't count that he went away to college. And it don't count that he has more money and a Ford pickup. What does count is that he can take his umiak, which he mends himself in the summer season when the whales are finished, and go out and catch whales when the rest of us can't. In this village"—and he pointed back over his shoulder—"it's whales that make the difference."

Now the second of the medium-sized whales surfaced unexpectedly at the tail end of the procession, but this time Afanasi was prepared to act. Signaling the two specialists who must kill the whale—the first man holding the harpoon, the second the high-powered rifle—he brought his umiak into exactly the proper position, and in the early years of the century it would have been the gunner who would have fired first. But too many whales were wounded and then lost in that procedure, so now the law prohibited the rifleman from firing until the harpoon had struck.

So, with the frail umiak positioned close to the monstrous whale, the harpooner drew back his right arm, brought it forward with great force, and landed the point of his harpoon just behind the whale's ear. Immediately two bright-red rubber floats four feet in diameter and attached to the harpoon's rope spun into the sea, forming a drag from which the whale would not be able to escape. One second after the point of the harpoon cut its way into the whale's neck, the heavy charge of explosive carried just below the point detonated, destroying much of the whale's muscular system. At that moment the rifleman fired a blast into the base of the whale's neck, and the great sea beast was mortally stricken. Harpoon point, explosive in the body, rubber floats and finally the devastating shot: it was too much for even a forty-ton whale to survive, and its blood quickly reddened the Chukchi Sea.

But now it showed why it was the leviathan of the oceans, for despite its terrible wounds, it continued moving north to rejoin the other members of its pod, and it kept on this course, always lagging farther behind, until it actually passed from the sight of the villagers watching on the edge of the ice. Miles up the coastline, when hunters from another umiak sped out to help finish it off with their explosive harpoon and rifle, the noble beast made one last effort to pull away from the braking bladders, failed, turned on its right side, and perished.

Afanasi, seeing the whale die, slumped on the rear bench of his umiak and felt no sense of triumph; it was the tenth successful whale hunt in his lifetime; he was the undoubted master of this northwestern coast; but he had lost a friend: "Oh, gallant fighter! We honor you!" And he began to sing an old song out of respect to the whale who would bring food to all the citizens of Desolation Point. A thing of mystery had happened, the taking of a whale after two years of failure, and he was awed by the significance.

• • •

Since it required four hours for the men of the two umiaks to raft the dead whale back to Desolation, it was past midnight in a silvery light when the carcass finally approached the ice on which Kendra waited. Two huge block-and-tackle devices, each housing five stout pulleys, had been positioned about fifteen feet apart, with one massive rope roven through the pulleys back and forth. "What are they doing?" Kendra asked, and a man interrupted his work to explain: "When we pull six feet on that end of rope, the block and tackle . . . tremendous leverage . . . what you call mechanical advantage. You'll see the whale move maybe six inches."

She could see nothing on the ice that would serve as an anchor for the inboard end of the device, and certainly no tree or post on shore to which to lash it, but now two teams of men began cutting very deep holes in the ice, about four feet apart, and when everyone was satisfied that the holes were deep enough, a skilled man let himself down into one of the holes and dug an ice tunnel from the bottom of one to the bottom of the other. Then, when another heavy rope was passed down one hole, through the tunnel and up the other, it provided an anchor that could not be dislodged.

The other block was run out to where the whale waited against the edge of the ice, fastened to its great hulk, and activated when Afanasi shouted: "All hands! All hands!" Everyone from Desolation who was on the ice at that moment grabbed the free end of the rope and began straining to pull the whale's block toward the ice-fastened one, and as the man had predicted to Kendra, the mechanical advantage provided by five pairs of pulleys produced such force that slowly, unmistakably the great whale began to worm its way onto the ice and then across it toward safety.

One of Afanasi's team, watching his whale brought home, raised a flag which he traditionally flew at such moments—THANK YOU, JESUS!—and women knelt to pray.

"Come on!" Kasm Hooker shouted to Kendra as she stood watching. "It's your whale too. Lend a hand," and she took her place on one of the ropes, helping to haul the whale the final ten yards onto the landfast ice.

She would always remember the haunting quality of the next few hours—the pale spring light that suffused the arctic night; the excited concentration of almost everyone in Desolation as they pulled together on the huge ropes; an old man, bareheaded, solemnly raising a pennant in the wind to signify the taking of a whale, and the chanting of the old women singing songs inherited from their grandmothers and their grandmothers' grandmothers as the great whale was slowly pulled up onto the shore. Oh, night of triumph! And as Kendra watched the people about her she realized that she had never known them before. She had seen them only as semibewildered Eskimos, whom she had learned to love as they wrestled sometimes unsuccessfully with the white man's ways; now she saw them as masters in their world, finely tuned to their environment and following time-proven ways of survival in the arctic. She was in awe of anyone who could contend on equal terms with the arctic seas. The education of the Eskimo children had begun last September when they appeared before her for their schooling; her education began this May night when silvery light glistened on the ice.

Once the whale was secured, men with long poles tipped with sharp blades stepped forward for the butchering, but they hesitated until Afanasi, their peerless Eskimo, guide and protector of their district, made the first ceremonial cut, and as he drew his flensing knife across the tail and then a fluke he was not a Native who had gone to college and worked successfully in Seattle and run a profitable village corporation; he was an Eskimo, his gray-sandy hair brushed forward till it reached his eyebrows, his hands red with the blood of the whale.

Cheers rose to grace his victory. The other men sped to the butchering. Young people rushed forward to receive their chunks of muktuk, the delicious wedge of chewy outer skin and succulent inner fat. And as full daylight broke over the spot on which Desolation rested, people rejoiced that they had once again proved their ability to take a bowhead whale. Kasm Hooker, thinking it time to take his young teacher back to her quarters, said with some surprise: "Kendra! You're crying!" and she said: "I'm so proud to be a part of this."

But what she enjoyed most, even though it was less spiritually rewarding than the capture of the whale, came much later, in mid-July, when meat from the slaughtered whale was taken from the freezers and the four village umiaks were dragged ashore, tilted on their sides to provide protection against the bitter winds blowing in from the Chukchi, and rested there as gathering spots for the various groups into which the villagers had historically divided themselves. Mr. Hooker was invited as an honored guest into the shadow of Afanasi's umiak, Kendra into the one owned by Jonathan Borodin's family, and she was pleased when Jonathan was called forth to receive a ceremonial cut of meat out of respect for his having predicted when the whales would come past the point. "How did you know?" Kendra asked him when he returned to her side, and he said: "He told me," and for the first time she looked up into the face of an old man who walked with a rude cane fashioned from a length of driftwood which had been washed ashore after some massive storm in Siberia.

The man was Jonathan's grandfather, convinced that his spells had brought the whales to Desolation, and she observed that he looked upon her with disfavor. The young man made no effort to introduce her, and silently the old man withdrew from the festivities.

It was a gala afternoon, an explosion of Eskimo spirits, with their foods, chanting and quiet, sometimes motionless dancing. At the height of the celebration, each umiak sent forward a young woman to participate in the highlight of the day. The men of the village gathered around a huge circular blanket made of several walrus hides stitched together, picked it up and pulled it taut. Then into the middle climbed one of the competing girls, and at a signal, with rhythmic movements which alternately loosened and tightened the blanket, the men all tugged outward, tossing the girl high in the air. The Eskimos had done this on the shore at Desolation for fifteen thousand years, and it still sent chills down the spine to see human beings fly aloft like birds.

But this day was to be special, for when the competition ended, Jonathan Borodin suddenly pushed Kendra Scott forward to the blanket, and a cheer went up urging her to try, and with a courage she did not know she had, she allowed herself to be moved toward the blanket, but she was much relieved when Afanasi came forward to caution the men: "Not too high."

Standing in the middle of the blanket, she felt its instability and wondered how she could maintain her balance, but once the up-and-down motion started she felt herself miraculously kept aloft by the blanket's rhythm. Then suddenly she was fifteen feet in the air, all arms and legs. Her composure gone, she descended in a heap.

"I can do better!" she cried as she sat up, and on the second try she did. Now I'm an Eskimo! she said to herself as she was lifted out of the blanket. I'm part of this sea, of this hunt, of this tundra.

A few days after Desolation's celebration of the whale and while her mind still echoed with reverberations of that awesome capture, Ken-

dra was vouchsafed an ugly glimpse of the flip side of subsistence, for
one of her students dashed into school with exciting news: "Miss
Scott! Hurry to the shore. A new breed just floated in!" And before
she could ask him what he meant he led her to the seashore, where
the obscenity exposed repulsed her so acutely she nearly vomited.

"What is that dreadful thing?"

"The new breed."

"What do you mean?"

"A walrus with no head." And when she studied the sodden mass
she saw that the boy was right. It was the corpse of a walrus, but it
had no head and in its bloated condition it looked as if it had never
had one.

"How did this happen?" she asked, and the boy said: "The law
says that because you're white, you can't kill a walrus. But because
I'm an Eskimo who lives on walrus meat, I can."

"Nobody lived on this walrus."

"Or on any of the other new breeds. Eskimos kill them, like in the
old days. But now they cut off only their heads. For ivory. The rest
can rot."

"How shameful!" and as details of contemporary hunting unfolded, the rotting carcass on the beach became increasingly repulsive. "Does something like this happen very often?" she asked, and he
replied: "All the time." He kicked at the wasted meat of the huge
corpse: "Kill them just for the ivory."

As the months passed, Kendra found along the shores of the peninsula many such bloated remains of animals that had once majestically commanded the ice floes. In ancient days they had fed scores of
people; today they fed no one, and the ugly process was defended by
naive sentimentalists who cried: "The walrus must be preserved for
the Eskimos who use him for subsistence." But the great beasts were
really used to fill curio shops with gimcrackery for tourists from the
Lower Forty-eight.

When Kendra brought this hideous miscarriage of law to Afanasi's attention, she saw again what an excellent man he was, for he
was prepared to admit the anomalies of the situation: "We Eskimos
take refuge in the word *subsistence* in contradictory ways revolving
around the word *ancient*. We want government to respect our ancient
rights to whale and walrus and polar bear. Also our rights to vast
areas of land we hunted over in times past. And we demand special
consideration where land rights are concerned."

"You're a principal champion of such rights," Kendra said admiringly.

"I am. They'll be the salvation of the Eskimo. But I also see the nonsense in the claims. My ancient hunters want to use radios to track whales, and skidoos to rush out to the edge of the whales' lane. And outboard motors when they get there. And explosive harpoons to help kill the whale, and the best block-and-tackle money can buy to haul them onto the landfast ice. And when they feast on their catch, they demand Coke and Pepsi to wash it down."

"But could you return to the true ancient ways, even if you wanted to?"

"No. And if next year NASA devises some trick whereby whales can be spotted by lasers bounced off the moon, we Eskimos will enshrine that device as a time-honored segment of our revered ancient ways." He laughed. "Is it any different in Utah? Didn't your Mormons finally accept blacks as part of the human race only when they needed them for your football team?"

"I'm not a Mormon, and sometimes I suspect you're not an Eskimo."

"Wrong again. I'm the new Eskimo. And with help from teachers like you, there'll soon be thousands like me."

In that trying period when spring had officially arrived but violent storms still gripped the tundra, all the widely scattered schools across the vast North Slope enjoyed a three-day holiday so that their teachers could convene for a Wednesday-to-Sunday professional seminar in Barrow, and Kendra especially looked forward to this opportunity to inspect the famous eighty-four-million-dollar high school in that town. It was arranged for Harry Rostkowsky to fly down to pick up Vladimir Afanasi, Kasm Hooker and Kendra Scott, but when another board member said that she would like to attend the sessions, a curious situation developed: Jonathan Borodin, the would-be shaman, stepped forward with the suggestion that since he was already planning to go to Barrow on his snowmobile, Kendra could ride with him the relatively short and safe distance of forty miles. With the same daring that had prompted her to try the blanket toss, she agreed to the proposal, and when both Afanasi and Hooker warned against it, she replied: "I've always wanted to see the tundra, and Jonathan is an expert with his SnowGo."

"The SnowGo is a great killer of cocky young fellows who think they know how to operate it," Hooker said.

Nevertheless, early on Wednesday morning, when a wondrous light from the returning sun suffused the shoreline of the sea, the two adventurers set forth, with Kendra, her bag and two gallons of spare gasoline stowed behind Jonathan as they set out on a northeast heading for Barrow. Since his machine could do more than forty miles an hour at top speed, he and Kendra figured to be in Barrow well before Rosty left in his plane to pick up the others, and since he could also make well over forty miles to the gallon, they faced no danger of running out of gas in an area so bleak and forlorn that not a single sign of human occupancy would be visible during their entire trip.

Kendra reveled in the journey, and the fact that she was making it with Jonathan posed no problems, for she was six years older than he; a kind of mother-son relationship had developed between them, and he had shared with her many ideas and imaginings that he would never have told anyone else.

However, at the halfway point of their journey she became aware that he had quit the northeast heading which she knew they needed to follow to reach Barrow. He was heading almost due west, right toward the still-frozen Chukchi, and in some perplexity she tapped him on the shoulder: "This isn't the way, Jonathan."

Without turning to answer, he shouted: "You're going to see something, believe me," and after a run along the edge of the ominous sea he stopped at a monument rising from the bleak tundra, and without dismounting, Kendra read the solemn message:

WILL ROGERS AND WILEY POST
AMERICA'S AMBASSADORS OF GOOD WILL
ENDED LIFE'S FLIGHT HERE
AUGUST 15, 1935

"Did they crash here?" she asked in awe, and Jonathan replied: "My grandfather was the one who ran in to Barrow to tell the people."

"Do you know who Will Rogers was?"

"Someone important, I guess. They made a fuss about him."

He was so insolent in his attitude toward the two men that she cried, with an intensity he had not seen her display before: "Dammit, Jonathan, these were fine men. Who accomplished things. As you could if you put your mind to it. Don't you realize the opportunities you're throwing away?"

"Like what?"

"Like almost anything." She spoke as the primordial teachers, the ones forty thousand years ago who had taught the progenitors of the Eskimos how to make better harpoons and use them more productively.

When Jonathan showed his usual indifference to what she was striving to accomplish with him, she lowered her voice and said pleadingly: "When we reach Barrow you'll see Eskimos who lead their people. Study them. Because one day someone like you will have to take their place."

Leaving him sullen and silent by his snowmobile, she went to the shore and gathered a handful of sea-washed rocks, which she arrayed about the base of the monument in homage to a man her father revered as a great American.

The greatest revelation for Kendra on the trip to Barrow stemmed not from the SnowGo ride or the lonely cenotaph by the sea, but from what happened when she reached the famous Barrow High School. From the outside the school looked quite ordinary, about what one would expect in Utah or Colorado in a community that had fallen on hard times; low, rambling, and of no distinguished architecture, it seemed like a makeshift patchwork, and Kendra was disappointed. But when she entered the building and saw the lavishness with which it had been equipped, she was amazed, for she had never before seen anything to compare with such luxury and abundance.

School was not in session, of course, but seniors had been delegated to show the visiting teachers around, and since Kendra was the first to arrive, she fell into the care of the young man who was president of his class. Dressed in a neat woolen business suit, he introduced himself as the son of a Lower Forty-eight electrical engineer who managed the governmental radar installations, and he took her first to a spacious section of the school devoted to electronics: "We have, as you can see, a complete radio and television broadcasting setup, very popular with the students." He then showed her the bank of computers: "Here students learn how to encode and to service computers." The shops where household appliances and automobile engines were torn apart and reassembled were impressive, and the wood shop was better than the average professional carpenter's shop: "There's talk about having the students build a house each year, right in here, and selling it to someone outside. It could be done, you know." The home-economics room was a delight, with every kind of equipment that students might come into contact with if they later on went to Anchorage or Fairbanks to work in the hotels and restaurants.

"Doesn't anyone study books in this school?" Kendra asked, and the president said: "You bet. I do, and so do most of my buddies," and he led her to the academic classrooms, the spacious library and the science laboratories which would have graced the average college, and she said: "Well, the instruments of learning are certainly here, but does anyone learn?"

The young man was a scholar destined to go far; his parents were both university graduates, father from Berkeley, mother from San Diego State, and they had instilled in their three children a love of learning. But their son also had an acute mind where the political realities of any situation were involved, which probably accounted for his having been elected president: "You seem interested, Miss Scott, and you'll appreciate what I have to say. But if you take all the equipment I've shown you and scale it from the most up-to-date to the least, and you come back here next week, you'll find that all the really advanced apparatus, like the television, the radio, the high-powered computers, they're all being used by white kids like me from the Lower Forty-eight whose parents work here for the government, while the older stuff that doesn't cost too much, like for machine overhaul and carpentry, it's all being used by the Eskimos."

Kendra stopped in the hallway, turned to face her guide directly, and said: "What a terrible thing to say," and he replied without blinking: "What a terrible thing to have to say." But there it was: this fantastic school was, at great expense, training white students to take their places at Harvard and Chicago and Louisiana State, and training its Eskimo students, except for the unusual child who broke loose from village constraints, to be waitresses and bellhops and auto repairmen.

She sat on a bench in the hallway outside the library and asked her guide to join her, and this he was eager to do, for he was interested in the problems that concerned her. She mused: "I wonder if it's different anywhere, if you look at things honestly. In Utah and Colorado, there were very few Mexicans or Indians mastering computers. And when I was in Germany, I was told that students were identified at age twelve as to which of three curricula they would follow to determine the rest of their lives. They said it was the same in France and Japan. Very bright guys like you to make decisions. Average guys for drones' work. Below average, laborers to keep the system running." She reflected on this for some moments and said: "I suppose it was the same in ancient Egypt . . . everywhere." Then she touched him on the arm and asked bluntly: "Are you ever ashamed to be in this school?" and he replied with no hesitation or embarrassment: "Not at all. The money keeps pouring out of the ground. I think it's wonderful they had the guts to spend it on something like this."

In the days that followed she saw the young man frequently, and it was at his insistence that they resumed their serious conversation. Then, on Saturday afternoon, he asked: "Could some of us kids talk with you this afternoon?" and she replied: "Yes, if I can bring along an Eskimo boy about your age," and he said: "Delighted."

Seven of them met in the school cafeteria, where the students had prepared light refreshments, and the president asked, before introducing Kendra: "Where's your Eskimo?" She said without emotion: "Tooling around on his snowmobile," and the session began.

Four of the seven local students were white children of specialists imported from the Lower Forty-eight, but the three who showed the keenest interest were Eskimos, two seniors of remarkable perception and a boy in his junior year whose reluctance to speak out did not indicate any lack of sharpness in his ability to follow the discussion. It started with the white students' wanting Kendra's opinion about which colleges to apply to, as if that were the major problem facing them, and they appreciated her knowing response. One girl asked a clever question: "Considering that my hometown is Barrow, Alaska, what first-class university might want someone like me to demonstrate its geographical diversity?" and Kendra said without hesitation: "The top ones. They'll be hungry for someone like you," and the girl asked almost insolently: "F'rinstance?" and Kendra rattled off: "Princeton, Chicago, Stanford, and I hear good reports about Smith," then she added: "You guys are pretty hip. It's a pleasure to meet you." But then she gently led the talk to the situation of the three Eskimos, and only when she had helped the dark-skinned, Asian-looking young people to feel at ease did she unload her blockbuster: "Your president, Paul, when he was showing me around on the first day, pointed out that all the expensive, modern electronics and computer equipment is used almost exclusively by the white students from the Lower Forty-eight, while the less sophisticated stuff like carpentry and auto-repair tools are monopolized by the Eskimos. What about that?"

"It's true," the Eskimo girl said, "but our problems are different from their problems."

"In what way?"

"They'll make their lives in the Lower Forty-eight. We'll make ours in Alaska."

"You don't have to stay in Alaska."

"But we want to," the girl said, and she received surprising support from the reticent boy: "I don't dream of going to Seattle. I don't even dream of going to Anchorage. I dream of working here in Barrow even after the oil money stops flowing."

Moved by compassion for these young people, Kendra said very rapidly: "But don't you understand that to accomplish anything in Barrow, anything important, that is, you'll have to have a college education? Don't you see that all the good jobs, those with good pay, go to educated people from the Lower Forty-eight? Or to the Eskimos who have gotten an education?"

Stubbornly the Eskimo boy replied: "We'll do it the Eskimo way."

"What will you do in Barrow?" she asked almost contentiously, and two years later, when she was a married woman floating around on an ice island five hundred miles north of Barrow, in the heart of the Arctic Ocean, she would remember each word of his amazing answer: "Because the world is going to be interested in the Arctic Ocean, got to be—Russia, Canada, America. And I want to be here at the center."

"What an amazing answer, Ivan. Where did you develop such an insight?" and he said: "You look at a map," and she thought, with tears coming to her eyes: Dear, wonderful boy! But without the education you despise, you'll never make it.

In late May, when the Chukchi Sea remained frozen far out from shore, but with the snow beginning to vanish from the tundra, fearful news crept north from the lonely hut where the parents of Amy Ekseavik lived. A hunter came in to Desolation with a gruesome report: "The old man got hold of some bad rotgut, got blind drunk, tried to murder his wife because she yelled at him, failed, jammed the rifle into the back of his mouth and blew his head off."

Afanasi and Jeb Keeler organized a rescue party and found Amy's mother slightly wounded; a relative from farther south had come to take charge, and both women insisted that Amy leave school to assume responsibility for the hut. When Kendra heard this preposterous suggestion, she exploded: "This girl will not leave my classroom. I forbid it." Afanasi explained that if Amy was needed at home, which she obviously was, she would have to go there, that Eskimo custom demanded this, but Kendra cried: "This child is brilliant. She can accomplish anything. I've written to the people at the University of Washington and they've shown great interest. Might even enroll her at age sixteen if she's as bright as I claim." Her voice broke into a wail: "Mr. Afanasi! Don't sentence Amy to a life of darkness!" Her plea was futile. Amy was needed at home and that took precedence over any other consideration.

On the day this wonderfully gifted child was to go home, Kendra walked with her for two miles across the bitter tundra where no tree sprouted and only the tiniest flowers bloomed. When they parted she embraced the girl, held her to her bosom, and fought to keep back her tears: "Amy, you know that you have a remarkable mind. You've seen in school that you have special gifts. Look, I tell you the truth. You're way ahead of where I was at your age. You can accomplish anything. For God's sake, read the books I've given you. Do something with your life. Do something."

"What?" the girl asked listlessly, and Kendra answered: "We never know, Amy. But if we treasure our life, something turns up. Look at me, Amy. How in hell did I wind up in Desolation? Where will you wind up? Who knows? But keep moving. Oh, Amy . . ." There were a thousand relevant things she wanted to tell this girl in their last moments together, but all she could do was lean down and kiss the round brown face, an act which Amy accepted without emotion.

The next two weeks were bitter cold, more like midwinter than spring, and Kendra was as desolate in spirit as the storm-blown landscape, for she saw that regardless of how ably she and Kasm Hooker managed their school and encouraged their students, the harsh realities of Eskimo life established the limits of what could be accomplished, and one night she invited Afanasi and Keeler to her apartment in the Teacherage to discuss these matters with her and Hooker.

She began by posing a problem which depressed her: "Mr. Afanasi, why are you the only Eskimo in Desolation with a world outlook . . . no, even an Alaskan outlook?"

"I had a good grandfather who taught me what to do, a father and uncle who taught me what not to do."

"How can Kasm and I produce young people with the outlook and the capacities you have?"

"It happens by accident, I think. With Amy Ekseavik, you'd have had a chance. With Jonathan Borodin . . . well, you know, he should be exactly like me. Able to handle himself in the white man's world, a pillar in his Eskimo village. But somehow we missed, and now all he commands is a snowmobile."

"He tells me he may want to become a shaman—in the ancient pattern, but a constructive one."

Afanasi heard this news with great interest: "Now, that's not a crazy idea, not at all. I've thought for some time that perhaps with the pressures of modern life, television, snowmobiles, clatter, that there might be a place for the revival of shamanism as my grandfather knew it." He rose and walked about the apartment, picked at some food, then sat down close to Kendra: "A hundred years ago, when Healy and his *Bear* came here with Sheldon Jackson, the shamans they met were a disreputable lot. Jackson's reports gave the system a bad name, but the shamans my grandfather worked with were a much different sort." He rose and stalked the room again, concluding: "Maybe that Borodin boy, you know he has unlimited talent, you saw that in school, Kasm. I'm going to talk with him."

The conversation never took place, because three days later, in a swale that still contained deep snow, Jonathan Borodin, nineteen years old, got his rifle, his SnowGo-7 and five gallons of spare gas and headed far inland to get himself a couple of caribou, which his grandfather sorely wanted as the best food an Eskimo could eat. Dragging a cargo sled behind him to haul the meat, he rode speedily in an easterly direction toward where lakes and wandering rivers abounded, and in an area which he had often visited before, he shot two big caribou, slaughtered them on the spot, loaded the abundance of fresh meat on the sled and the horns on the back of his snowmobile.

On the way home he met with two disasters: a tremendous storm thundered in from the south, bringing new snow and whipping about the remnants trapped in the swale. When the blizzard struck, he was momentarily frightened, for the hunters of Desolation stood in awe of any storm coming at them from the south. If it were to continue at its present rate, he could be in trouble, but he felt sure that when it abated he could pick his way westward to Desolation. He never con-

sidered abandoning the sled he was dragging and speeding homeward as fast as possible: When I shoot me a caribou I bring it home.

But as he descended a moderate slope, with the bitter wind from
the sea driving hard against his face, he realized that the remainder of
his journey, some thirty-five miles, was going to be rough going: No
worry. I have loads of gas. Then as he climbed the western side of the
slope his motor began to cough, and at the very crest, where the wind
was fiercest, it stopped entirely.

Again he had no immediate fear, for on his varied trips he had
mastered the intricacies of his machine, and he assumed that he
could repair it now. He could not. Some new defect, far more serious
than before, had disabled his SnowGo, and with the gale whipping
about him, he failed in one attempt after another to identify and repair whatever had stalled his engine. As the grayness of late afternoon fused into a whiteout, he realized that he was in peril of freezing.

Only his grandfather was aware that Jonathan did not return that
night, and he felt sure that the boy had taken refuge behind some
hillock, but when noon came and there was still no sign of Jonathan,
the old man began to worry. But he did not alert anyone, because his
mode of life kept him apart from others, so a second night passed
with the boy still missing.

Early next morning the old man, trembling with fear, reported to
the makeshift office from which Afanasi conducted his business, and
there he delivered the appalling news: "Jonathan, he went out, two
days ago, caribou. He not come back."

Afanasi leaped into action, and telephoned Harry Rostkowsky at
the airfield in Barrow to fly south and east of Desolation toward the
lakes to see if he could spot a missing SnowGo with a boy camped
nearby. The area to be searched was due south of Barrow, and Rosty
radioed the airfield three times to report that he had found nothing,
and Barrow reported this by phone to Afanasi, but on a later pass
Rosty saw the stalled machine and an inert body huddled beside it:
"Rostkowsky calling. Barrow. Inform Afanasi Desolation SnowGo
located atop ridge due east. Body nearby probably frozen."

A party of four men and two snowmobiles was organized immediately, with Afanasi riding pillion on one, a highly regarded Eskimo
tracker on the other. Rostkowsky, aloft in his Cessna, spotted them
leaving town and signaled the direction they should take, and after
nearly two hours, for they traveled slowly and cautiously, they came

upon Jonathan Borodin's new SnowGo, his five gallons of spare gas, his two butchered caribou and his frozen corpse.

When Kendra spotted the mournful cortege approaching the village from the east she knew what to expect, for everyone in Desolation had been alerted to the probability of tragedy, but forewarning did not make the death of this excellent young man any easier to take, and she ran to where the corpse lay, still in huddled, frozen posture. "Oh my God!" she cried. "What a terrible waste!" And that was the threnody that sounded throughout Desolation Point.

It was not until the school term ended that Kendra felt the full impact of the tragedies that had darkened the spring months when hope should have been so resurgent, and for two weeks she idled about the lonely school, filing her grocery order for the coming year and purchasing some two thousand dollars' worth of unnecessary specialties to be used for entertaining her students and their parents. But then Afanasi, who seemed to look after everyone in his village, came to her with an order: "It's time to get you out of here. Go to Fairbanks or Juneau or Seattle. We have funds for teachers' travel, and here's a ticket to Anchorage with an extension for wherever within reason you want to go. Utah to see your folks? That would be okay."

"Right now I do not care to see them," she said firmly, but she accepted the tickets, one to Anchorage, one open, and as she flew south with minimum baggage, for her home was now Desolation Point and she was loath to leave it, she looked at herself coldly, as if she had a mirror before her face: I'm twenty-six, I've never been close to marriage, and that article by the woman researcher in Denver made it so clear that with every passing year after twenty-three, an educated woman has less and less chance of ever getting married, but I want to live in Alaska, I love the frontier, I thrill to the challenge of the arctic . . . Oh God, I'm so mixed up.

But of one thing she was certain, and this pertained to the nature of life itself, and as the engines of the jet droned on she continued talking to herself as if she were the subject of an analysis by an outside observer: I love people. Amy Ekseavik is part of my life. Jonathan Borodin—oh God, why didn't I talk to him more? And I do not want to live alone. I cannot face the endless years. The arctic night, I have no problems with it, for it passes, but loneliness of the spirit never passes.

Very slowly and with a recognized confusion she took from the mock-leather portfolio in which she carried her school papers a torn sheet on which was written an address in Anchorage, and at the airport she hurried to a cab, as if she feared she might change her mind, and thrust the paper in the driver's hand: "Can you find this?" and he replied: "I'd be fired if I couldn't. Biggest apartment house in town," and although she was fully aware that she was doing a most dangerous thing, she took the elevator to the fifth floor, knocked on the door, and expected to see Jeb Keeler waiting for her when the door opened. He was, and as she embraced him she whispered: "Without someone to love, I was lost in a blinding snowstorm," and he said he understood.

Later that night as they lay together, she confided: "Amy and Jonathan, they tore at my heart. We come to a place to teach, and the children teach us," and Jeb said: "It's the same with lawyers. We learn much more than we help others."

She stayed with him for five days, and near the end of their time together she said: "Afanasi suspected that I might be coming to see you. I think that's why he gave me the ticket to Anchorage. He says you're a man to be trusted. I asked him if he gave every lawyer that recommendation, and he laughed: 'Not Poley Markham. I love him but I sure don't trust him,'" and Jeb said: "He's wrong there. Poley's different, but I've found him to be completely honest. Never touches a dime that isn't his!"

The conversation then turned to talk of their future, and she said that perhaps at the end of the next school year, if Jeb still wanted to specialize in Alaskan law, particularly north of the Circle, they should consider marriage, with the understanding that Kendra wanted to continue teaching at Desolation, or perhaps move into Barrow. Jeb assured her that with his and Poley's leverage they could get her one of the jobs in Barrow, and she said, as she kissed him goodbye: "Let's think about that. A good teacher with all that expensive equipment ought to be able to turn out some terrific Eskimos."

At the airport, as she waited for her northbound plane, she watched idly the arrival of a Japan Air Lines plane from Tokyo as it discharged those passengers who would be stopping over in Anchorage, and saw five athletic-looking Japanese—three men and two young women—who were also going to have a very deep but much different interest in Alaska.

• • •

They called him *sensei*. Every Japanese addicted to mountain climbing, and they were legion, called him Takabuki-sensei, an honorific which could be translated as something like Revered-and-Beloved-Professor Takabuki. At forty-one his official position was professor of moral philosophy at Waseda University in Tokyo, but arrangements had been made with both the university authorities and the Japanese government for him to be absent on expeditions as often as the funding and a balanced, dependable climbing party could be arranged.

Japan's premier mountaineer, this small, wiry, normally clean-shaven man was familiar to newspaper and magazine readers from his photographs as a heavily bearded figure standing at the windblown, snowy apex of some great mountain. Because Japan lay relatively close to the great mountains of Asia, he had as a young apprentice climbed both Nanga Parbat and K-2, and in later years had led two assaults on Everest, one aborted at 27,000 feet by the death of two members, the other successful when he and two of his team stood on top of the world at 29,028 feet above sea level. The latter had been a classic performance without even one minor accident.

Encouraged by his successes, Japanese supporters had raised funds for him to lead lesser expeditions to Aconcagua in the Argentine, Kilimanjaro in Tanzania, the Matterhorn on the Italian-Swiss border, twice to Mount St. Elias in Alaska and once to Tyree in Antarctica. Even his German competitors agreed that Takabuki-sensei was a complete mountaineer. Said one German periodical specializing in alpinism: "He can do anything he sets his mind to, and he has two salient characteristics. Even in adversity he smiles to keep the spirits of his fellow climbers high, and he brings them back alive. The two deaths that destroyed his 1974 assault on Everest occurred two thousand feet below where he was climbing close to the summit. Two members of his team, unroped, moved carelessly and plunged to their deaths."

But in all his recent triumphs, another challenge gnawed at him, and in time his obsession grew so great that the mountain he had not yet conquered seemed to move about with him wherever he went, filling his mind. It can be done, he assured himself repeatedly. It's not a difficult climb. I could have mastered it when I was a boy. It's no more than a walk, really, but to take that walk requires a mixture of brute strength and infinite delicacy. At this point in his reverie he usually stopped, stood flat-footed, looked off into space, and questioned: If it's so simple, why do so many meet their death on that damned mountain?

He was in this frame of mind on the third of January when he was scheduled to meet with the mountaineering leaders of Japan, especially those industrialists who in the past had financed expeditions. When he and his associate Kenji Oda stood before them he realized that the Japanese New Year celebrations—wildest in the world, with even more alcohol consumed than at Scotland's Hogmanay roistering—had left these gentlemen somewhat hungover and bleary-eyed, but after some friendly joshing as to who had been drunkest—everybody in Japan, it seemed, having been so to some degree or other—they were as ready for business as they were going to be this day.

"How many would be in your team, do you think?"

"Five. Three men, two women."

"Very small in comparison with your Everest teams."

"A totally different climbing method."

"In what way?"

"Fewer camps, much lighter gear."

"But why does Denali fascinate you, Sensei?" Quickly the interrogator added: "Because it does, you know."

Takabuki's face hardened. His hands clenched and he disclosed what tormented him. "Compared to the really great mountains of the world, Everest and Nanga Parbat for height, Matterhorn or the Eiger for rock work, Alaska's Denali is trivial."

"Then why allow it to become an obsession?"

"Because of its challenge. Especially to a Japanese."

"But you just said it was easy."

"It is, except for three facts. It lies close to the Arctic Circle, less than two hundred and fifty miles . . ."

"In kilometers?"

"In Alaska they use miles. Everest is nearly two thousand five hundred miles farther south, and that difference in latitude makes Denali seem quite a few thousand feet higher than it really is."

"Why?" a well-lubricated industrialist asked, and Takabuki said: "At higher latitudes the air is thinner, just as it is at the higher altitudes. Everest, very high and moister. Denali, not so high, but very thin all the way up." Satisfied that he had justified his basic respect for Denali, he moved on to his second point: "It's true that Denali does not present us with much serious rock work, hardly any. And that's where the trouble comes for us Japanese and Germans. Because we're used to steep rock work and very high altitudes, we scamper to the top and yell back jubilantly 'See! It was nothing!' And then on the way down, we grow careless in our euphoria, plunge over the edge or get lost in an avalanche, and no one ever sees us again." He stopped, stared at his questioners, and added: "They don't even find the bodies." Halting again, he said painfully: "Denali is a burial ground for German and Japanese climbers who come down the mountainside rejoicing," and he asked Kenji Oda, who had studied with him at Waseda, to show the committee the map and chart they had drawn up. It displayed the mournful record of the arrogant Germans and the inattentive Japanese.

"Here is a team of four Germans, great climb, record speed I believe. No challenge whatever, they said later. That is, the two who didn't die on the way down." He indicated another group of five Germans: "A masterful team. I climbed with three of them in the Alps. They could go straight up any rocky face. Two more dead." He pointed to the record of a team of seven that had lost two, a team of five that had lost one.

"How could a relatively easy mountain like Denali exact such a heavy toll on experienced climbers?" asked a manufacturer who had climbed with Takabuki-sensei in earlier years, and the dean of mountaineers added his third significant fact about this tall, beautiful and terrible mountain: "Because it lures you, like the sirens of Ulysses, but when you're up there on its peak, triumphant, it's apt to send forth storms of hellish magnitude. Winds of a hundred miles an hour, temperatures of minus-ninety with chill factors to below a hundred and twenty, and when a storm strikes, if you don't burrow into a snow cave like an animal, you perish."

The listeners said nothing, but finally the man who had done some climbing with the sensei pointed out: "But you said the Japanese were careless. If you're hit by a storm like that, it doesn't sound much like carelessness."

And now Takabuki became almost solemn, as if he were the undertaker in some small rural town: "You're right, Okobi-san. Our people dig in, protect themselves from the storm, but when it's over they come romping down the slopes, fail to keep their ropes taut, and over the edge they go."

"How do you know that?" a man asked, and Takabuki replied:

"We don't. We're guessing. All we know are the terrible figures. Show them, Oda-san," and the next doleful summary was displayed. "Look at that record! Eleven Japanese dead, and we've not recovered a single body. They vanished. Into a crevasse here? Over the side there? We don't know. They toiled, they conquered, and they vanished. And Denali refuses to tell us how it conquered them."

At this point he stopped, his hands clenched with suppressed anger, and only Kenji Oda, looking at the man he worshiped, knew what ugly fact Takabuki was going to reveal next: "Gentlemen, we Japanese have performed so poorly on Denali. Going up we're unbeatable, coming down we're . . ." His voice trembled; he mastered it and said bitterly as he pointed at the ridge from which his predecessors had vanished: "Look what they call this place! Come up and look!" and when the men did they saw that American cynics had given the ridge where so many Japanese fell a hideous name. Since most of the committee could read English if not speak it, Takabuki did not translate, but two members asked: "What do the words mean?"

"The Orient Express," he said grimly. "The place where we Japanese roar out of sight," and there the mocking words stood on a map which had become semiofficial.

"It is my job," he said quietly when discussion resumed, "mine and Oda's here, to lead a Japanese expedition which will demonstrate what we can do, how we can discipline ourselves. We've been so careless in the past, so one-man daring and contemptuous of risk, that the people around Denali, the real mountaineers . . . Do you know what they call us when we appear at Talkeetna to climb into the planes that fly us to the mountain? The Kamikaze Crowd. Well, this expedition will not be a banzai charge. Have I your permission? And the necessary budget?"

Before an answer could be given, the chairman brought up a problem which perplexed mountaineers in many nations: "The maps name your mountain McKinley. You climbers call it Denali. I don't understand."

"Very simple," Takabuki said. "It's always been Denali. Real Alaskans and climbers call it nothing else. Honored Indian name, very ancient, meaning the High One."

"Then where does the McKinley come from?"

"In 1896, I believe"—and the sensei looked for confirmation to Oda, who nodded—"the Democratic party nominated for the presidency a minor politician from Kansas, I think it was, man named McKinley. Nobody knew him nationally or thought much of him locally. The party needed some big event to give him prominence, and some politician dreamed up the idea of naming this great mountain after him. Very popular . . . with the Democrats."

The committee members laughed, and one said: "Same sort of thing happens in Japan. Why don't they go back to the real name?" During the discussion which followed, Kenji Oda, who had studied in America, spoke quietly to the chairman: "I could never contradict the sensei in public. Or private either, for that matter, but McKinley was a Republican, their conservative party. Not a particularly bad man. And he came from Ohio, not Kansas."

"Will his name remain on the mountain?"

"Everybody with good sense is trying to remove it."

The season for climbing Denali was rigorously defined: before the first of May the snow, storms and cold were too severe; after the middle of July the heat made the snow so rotten that avalanches came thundering down and bridges over crevasses collapsed. So in early June, Takabuki-sensei and the four members of the expedition took the short flight from Tokyo to Anchorage, where they reported to the shop of furrier Jack Kim, who served as liaison for all Japanese climbers. A Korean with a winning smile and a sharp knowledge of Alaskan business, he knew Takabuki by reputation, and after a brief discussion had the team and their small mountain of equipment packed in a big station wagon headed north for the 133-mile drive to Talkeetna.

At a spot some miles south of the little town, the young man driving swerved to the shoulder of the road, slammed on the brakes, and cried: "There it is!" From the almost level plain rose the three great mountains of the Alaska Range: Foraker to the left, Denali in the center, Silverthrone on the right, with off to one side the remarkable black cube called Mooses Tooth. They formed a majestic march across the blue sky, a line of mountains that would have been commendable in any terrain; here, where the surrounding plain was so low, with an elevation not much above sea level, they soared enormously, white-capped, inviting but filled with subtle menace.

"Each mountain in the world is different," Takabuki-sensei told his team. "And each is precious in its own way."

"What's different here?" one of the women asked, and he said: "The surrounding terrain is so ordinary, so low, and the range of mountains so very high and so close together. They are like conspirators, up where the winds blow, and they are plotting storms. For us."

At Talkeetna, like many Japanese teams before them, they sought out LeRoy Flatch, who now made a business of flying mountain climbers onto the 7,200-foot elevation of the southeast fork of Kahiltna Glacier. With the rear seats of his Cessna-185 removed, he could accommodate, as he said, "three chubby Americans or five trim Japanese." With wheels retracted and skis in place, he had delivered many young Japanese climbers to the starting point of their great adventure, flying back to meet them nineteen or twenty days later when they descended. Of course, if they became cavebound during some monumental snowstorm, he awaited a radio message from the park rangers and came for them after twenty-seven or even thirty days. He was their lifeline for getting on and off the mountain.

When Flatch assured them that he was ready and that weather reports for the next few days looked good, the Takabuki team repaired to the hut provided for visiting climbers, spread each item of their voluminous gear on the deck for a final check, and listened attentively as their sensei reviewed his instructions:

"There is only one purpose for this expedition. To restore the honor of Japan. And there is only one way to accomplish that. To put three men on the top of that mountain and to get five of us back here safely. It is our task to erase the opprobrium of that insolent phrase the Orient Express.

"So, the rules. We'll portage high and sleep low. That means climb diligently all day to get our gear up the mountain, but hurry back down at night so that we acclimatize gradually and in an orderly way. We'll take five days to our camp at eleven thousand feet. Very careful around Windy Corner and up to the last two camps at fifteen thousand and sixteen thousand nine hundred.

"Skis to eleven thousand, crampons the rest of the way. Roped three in my group with me, two in Oda-san's, and no slack. At our last stop we build a solid base which can be extended into a snow cave if a storm comes, and from there the three men ascend to the top, up and back fast in one day while the two women maintain supplies and gear at the camp. Only three thousand feet to cover, and more than a mile, very steep. We'll climb light and hurry back.

"Now"—and here his voice dropped to a whisper—"having attained the summit, the easy part, our real task begins. To get back to this hut, all five of us, in good shape, with no call to the rangers or the air force planes to rescue us, and no disappearances. I want each of you to look at this map."

At this point he spread the offending chart before them, and each of his four climbers read in English the insulting legend the *Orient Express,* and each swore privately that this time there would be no Japanese cascading down those steep slopes to oblivion.

Takabuki's team had been cleverly composed. He, of course, was one of the world's premier climbers, experienced in almost everything that could happen on a mountain. His endurance was extraordinary, a slim man weighing less than a hundred and sixty who could lug up the tallest mountains in the world not only a protective uniform that would stagger most men, but at the same time carry a cleverly packed and disposed backpack weighing just under sixty pounds. Takabuki-sensei was determined to climb Denali, up and down.

Equally determined was Kenji Oda, who had served as base-camp commander in the second Takabuki assault on Everest, the one that succeeded. The third man, Yamada, had not participated in previous expeditions, but was a superb athlete and had a reputation for endurance in various punishing sports. Of the two women, only Sachiko had any experience in mountain climbing; Kimiko, Takabuki's daughter, had begged her father to let her join this expedition, and at the last minute he had consented.

"Women will do the cooking and mind the camp," the sensei had said at the conclusion of his instructions. "Men will set up camp and carry the heavier loads."

The five-man team with all its gear was ferried to the starting station on Kahiltna Glacier in two easy flights in LeRoy Flatch's snow-ski Cessna, and the first afternoon, at 7,200 feet on the face of the snowy glacier, was spent getting the gear in order. When that job was half finished, the sensei said: "Let's run the first load up," so the three

men suited up, put on their skis, hefted the huge loads onto their
backs, and started smartly up the first part of the climb while the two
women finished setting up the camp. In ninety minutes the men were
back, wet with perspiration and ready for a rest. Excellent though
their condition was, the altitude had forced them to breathe heavily
and they were not unhappy to have the women prepare the evening
meal.

Patiently, during the next days they lugged their packs upward,
losing in weight only what they ate, and after the most cautious preparation, as if they were heading for the top of Everest, they reached
the 11,000-foot mark, where they cached the first of their gear, their
skis. Next morning, when they prepared to put on heavy steel crampons, they were reminded of a critical rule of mountain climbing:
"Keep your head clear and your feet warm." If a climber faulted either of those commands, he or she was already in deep trouble, so
Takabuki himself supervised how his team was shod. On bare feet
which had been allowed to breathe during the night, each member
put on a pair of finely woven, extremely expensive socks made of a
silk-polyester-like material, a fabricated stuff that would lead perspiration away from the body. Over them came a second pair of very
thin socks, then a third pair of heavy, loosely knit socks which provided warmth and protection from jarring and jabbing. On top of
this came one of the lightest, most flexible shoelets one could imagine, in part some exotic metal, in part a canvas made from some
newly invented material. This was the secret of the Japanese climber,
this flexible, extremely strong, resilient shoe which gloved the foot
and readied it for the very heavy Koflach plastic boot that was pulled
on over it, forming a massive protection and also a kind of air-
conditioned comfort.

A casual observer, seeing that the foot was now encased in five
different layers of cloth and metal and space-age materials, might
have concluded: "Now you can clamp on the metal crampons," but
that would have been premature, for over the Korean boot was drawn
a heavy, flexible insulated legging which made it impossible for snow
to drift down into the boot or up the pantleg. Only when this was tied
in place was it permissible to attach the crampons by means of heavy
lashings. When this was done, a climber had on nearly four hundred
dollars' worth of footwear so effective that without it there would be
little chance of getting to the top and back down without serious

frostbite, but so heavy that to lift one leg after another, kicking footholds up the steep icy incline, required unusual strength, even without a sixty-pound pack.

Not one person on the Takabuki team would suffer from frostbite that year; not one toe would have to be amputated by the doctors in the hospitals near the foot of Denali.

The climb went well. The three men proceeded boldly along the Orient Express and straight up the last slope to the peak, where amid snow and ice each man photographed the other two. Finally the sensei propped his camera on packed snow at an angle, set the self-timer and shot a picture of all three, with Takabuki proudly raising the banner of the Waseda University Alpine Club atop the world at 20,320 feet.

On the critical descent, things continued to go well, and when they reached the camp at 16,900 feet at about noon, they considered starting down immediately, but Takabuki, not liking the look of the clouds rushing in from the west, said: "I think we'd better get out the two shovels," and by the time the June blizzard struck—for blizzards could hit Denali on any day throughout the year—the five Japanese were snug in their snow cave, where they huddled for three storm-swept days.

There was only one untoward incident. Kimiko stepped outside, intending to move only a few steps to relieve herself, but when her father saw the terrible thing she had done he screamed in a way she had never heard before: "Kimiko! No rope!" And Oda-san reached out and grabbed her by the leg. When they had her safely inside the cave, Takabuki said quietly: "It is just stepping outside, no rope, that kills," and after apologizing for her error, Kimiko said: "I still have to go outside," so she roped up, and Oda-san held the rope around an ice pick jammed into the snow inside the cave, and she was safe.

When the storm abated, they descended to a lower level and started setting up their last major camp, but Takabuki-sensei, mindful of the fact that deadly errors resulted when climbers were tired, personally tested the snow for safety and only then allowed the strong nylon tarp on which the tents would be placed to be laid out. In accordance with Takabuki's ironclad rule "No fire in the big tent"— scores of teams having lost their tents, their provisions and sometimes their lives in fires—the crew erected a simple cook tent nearby, and into it went Kimiko to prepare hot rations. After a few moments

Sachiko went to help, but almost immediately came out, screaming: "She's gone!"

The next twenty seconds were an exercise in iron discipline, for Takabuki moved gently before the exit, arms extended to prevent anyone from running out into what might be mortal danger, for if some terrible mishap had befallen his daughter, the same might engulf anyone who went chasing after her. "By the book," he said quietly, still barring the passage.

Kenji Oda had reacted within seconds, instinctively wrapping a rope about his body, tying knots in strange and powerful ways, reaching for a spare ice pick and handing the far end of the rope to Sachiko and Yamada. Then, moving the sensei aside, he went gingerly outside the tent to see what had happened, certain that behind him Sachiko and Yamada would keep his rope taut, so that he would not drag them to their deaths if he fell into some deep crevasse.

Peering into the cook tent, he at first satisfied himself that Kimiko had not by some freak accident fallen through the heavy nylon flooring. But when he explored the area just to the left of the entrance he gasped and returned to the big tent, ashen-faced: "She's plunged into a crevasse."

No one panicked. The sensei crept into the cook tent, probed with his ice ax, and saw the mysterious hole through which Kimiko had dropped to a depth unknown. Oda, continuing to act swiftly and effectively in unbroken movement, placed the wooden handle of his ice pick at the edge of the hole so that when his rope cut at the edge, the handle would prevent it from digging into the snow and perhaps starting a small avalanche which would engulf the person below. Where Kimiko was, and in what condition, no one could guess.

Without a moment's hesitation Oda eased himself into the opening down which Kimiko had plunged, and deftly lowering himself along his rope by using a figure-eight device to brake his fall, he descended deep into the crevasse.

It was a monstrous, gaping hole, yards wide and with no discernible bottom, but by the grace of the forces which had carved it, the sides were not unbroken smoothness but a series of broken ledges onto which a fallen body might plummet. But Kimiko was not to be seen, and even when Oda switched on his lamp and looked at the terrible icy formations, he saw nothing.

Then he heard a moan, and on a ledge about thirty feet below he saw the outline of Kimiko's body in the dim light, and with rope signals devised decades ago he let the others above know that he had at least seen her. Again without hesitating, he lowered himself deeper and deeper. When he was but a few feet above her he could see that the violent plunge had not only knocked her unconscious but had also wedged her tightly into a constricted area from which she had no way of extricating herself.

"Kimiko!" he called as he drew closer to her, but there was no response. Then, as he waited for the rescue rope to reach him, he considered how he might attach it with maximum effectiveness, but before he started he tied her so securely to himself that if anything happened within the next minutes, she would at least be prevented from falling to her death.

Only then did he grasp the second rope, and with a bewildering series of knots designed for just such emergencies, he tied her into a sling from which she could not fall. But when he tried to pull her loose, he found that she was so firmly wedged into her corner that he could not do so. However, a pull from above, if strong enough, might do the trick, so he signaled for one, and as the three above tugged on the second rope, having secured the first, Oda saw with relief that Kimiko was being eased out of her prison.

As soon as she was freed, he signaled for the hauling to stop, and there in the icy mists of the crevasse, with evening light filtering down, he pinched her face and compressed her shoulders to bring her back to consciousness, but the second part of his therapy was exactly the wrong one, for in her fall she had dislocated her right shoulder, and his pressure was so great that she revived, saw him holding her, and sobbed with pain.

At that moment Alaska had a population 460,837, which meant that perhaps 75,000 young people were of an age at which they might fall in love or consider marriage. Indeed, 6,422 marriages did take place that year, but none was founded upon a troth more extraordinary than the one pledged between Kenji Oda and Kimiko Takabuki as they dangled forty-seven feet inside a crevasse on the frozen slopes of Denali. As she reached over to kiss him, they both saw that had she missed slamming onto the projection which dislocated her shoulder she would not have bounced across the chute and onto some other ledge lower down. She would have plummeted to a depth unfathomed.

This time the Orient Express claimed no Japanese victims.

• • •

When Kendra Scott returned to Desolation Point after her unpremeditated visit to Jeb Keeler's Anchorage apartment, she became vaguely aware that a newcomer had moved into an abandoned shack north of the village, where he was said to be living in squalor with thirteen beautifully trained malamute and husky sled dogs. The rumors were correct. He was one more of that inexhaustible breed of young American men, graduates of good colleges like Colgate, Grinnell and Louisiana State, who had been trained to take over their fathers' businesses, but who quit after five dreary years, leaving both an excellent job and often a wife just as superior, to try their luck racing sled dogs in the wilds of Alaska. You found them on the outskirts of Fairbanks, Talkeetna and Nome, working like slaves unloading barges or other cargo during the summer shipping season to earn the huge salaries that they spent in the winter feeding their fifteen or sixteen dogs. They usually refrained from shaving; sometimes they picked up a little money offering dogsled excursions to tourists; and quite often adventurous girls, from colleges like Mount Holyoke and Bryn Mawr, who also wanted to experience the arctic worked as waitresses and moved in with them for longer or shorter periods.

The dream of each of these men, and they numbered in the scores, was to run the Iditarod, not to win it, for God's sake, just to complete the course which was rightfully considered the world's most demanding organized competition. In the depth of the arctic winter, with blizzards howling out of Siberia and temperatures down to minus-forty, some sixty-odd intrepid dogsled drivers left Anchorage and ran a punishing course to Nome, a distance which was officially stated as 1,049 miles—1,000 miles plus the 49th state—but which actually varied between eleven and twelve hundred miles over incredibly tough terrain. "It's like running from New York City to Sioux Falls, South Dakota, before there were roads," Afanasi told Kendra, "and contrary to what many think, the driver does not usually catch a ride on the rear runners of his sled. He runs behind it four-fifths of the time." Kendra could not understand why any sane person would dump so many thousands of dollars into dog food and pay a $1,200 entry fee to be so abused, especially when first prize was only $50,000, but Afanasi said: "I ran it when I was younger, and the glory of gliding up to that finish line, win or lose, lasts a lifetime."

Of course, the young men from the Lower Forty-eight who came north to compete usually ran the grueling course only once; then they returned home, married, and resumed managerial work in their family business. But behind their desks, as they grew older, hung that framed certificate proving that in 1978 they competed in the Iditarod, and finished—and that separated them from the local athletes who had shot a hole in one at the local course in 1979.

The young man who had moved into the shack at Desolation, wanting to give his dogs the experience of the real arctic, was in many respects a typical example of these intruders—Stanford University graduate, thirty years old, five years of work in the family business, divorced from a socialite wife who, hearing that he had decided to emigrate to the Arctic Circle with thirteen dogs, told her friends that he suffered from a mental disorder—but in certain important respects he was unique. First, he was Rick Venn, scion of the powerful family that controlled the Ross & Raglan interests in Seattle; second, of all the newcomers, he alone had historic ties with Alaska; and third, because he was the grandson of Malcolm Venn and Tammy Ting, he had Tlingit and Chinese blood, which made him part Native. His complexion was so dark and his features so reminiscent of Asia that he could easily pass as another of the half-Russian, half-Native young men of Alaska.

He also differed from the others from the Lower Forty-eight in that whereas he kept his cabin as chaotic as theirs, he did maintain his personal appearance much as he would have in Seattle: he shaved; he cut his hair with his own barber's shears; and he washed a tubful of clothes once a week. But he was like the others in the affection he showed for his dogs and the loving care with which he worked them—in the sand when there was no snow, in the deepest drifts when there was.

Polar was a seven-year-old husky with a strain of wolf from some generations back and, more recently, some malamute. He was not overly big, several of the other dogs in the team being larger, but he was unusually intelligent and the unchallenged leader among them. Perfectly attuned to his master, Polar quickened to Rick's commands. Sled dogs were trained to turn to the right at "gee," to the left at "haw," while half a dozen other calls each carried a particular meaning. But Polar had the remarkable ability to anticipate Rick's intent almost before he shouted a command, and would deftly lead the other dogs in just the right direction.

Though they ran well as a team, it was not uncommon when the dogs were waiting impatiently in their harnesses for two of them to leap at each other, fangs bared, and if someone didn't stop them quickly, the confrontation could rapidly degenerate into a savage, bloody fight. Of course, if Rick was present, he halted the nonsense immediately, but if he wasn't, Polar stepped back, uttered a deep snarl, and the dogs broke off. He also nipped at the heels of any dog he suspected of malingering, and it was always he who leaped forward with greater energy when Rick called for more speed. He was an exceptional dog, and when the snow arrived he found joy in leading his team on ten- and twenty- and even thirty-mile training runs across the tundra to the east.

There being no tourist restaurants in Desolation, no adventurous young waitress from the Lower Forty-eight had moved in with Rick, but when he brought his team into the village for an exhibition on sand, and when the crowd had gathered, he noticed Kendra Scott standing near Vladimir Afanasi. He recognized her as the kind of young woman he would probably enjoy knowing, so after the demonstration he sought out Afanasi and asked who she was.

"Best teacher we've had in a long time. Comes from Utah."

"A Mormon?"

"Maybe so. Maybe that's why she wanted to explore the north."

"Could I meet her?"

"I don't see how you could avoid it."

So one sunny afternoon Afanasi took Kendra out to the tumble-down shack, where she started to laugh as soon as she stepped from Afanasi's truck, for a rather neatly painted signboard proclaimed THE KENSINGTON KENNELS, as if this were an expensive boarding place for pampered dogs. When the owner stuck his head out the door to ascertain the cause of laughter, Kendra saw a good-looking, neat young man, somewhat older than herself, dressed in blue coveralls: "What's going on?"

"I like your sign. You board dogs?"

"Sure do. Thirteen of them," and he pointed to where his huskies and malamutes were tethered, each to his own stake, on a short length of chain which prevented him from molesting the other twelve.

"For the Iditarod?"

"You've heard of it?"

"You must be crazy to attempt a race like that," and he said: "I am," but it was not until he left his shack and came forth to shake hands that she realized how wacky he was, for across the chest of his coveralls was emblazoned the kind of motto that quixotic college students loved: REUNITE GONDWANALAND!

"What's your war cry?" she asked, and he explained that he had been a geology major at Stanford and this had been their rallying cry.

"But where is it?" and he said: "Land mass that broke apart a quarter of a billion years ago. The South Pole was part of it, I believe," and she said: "You can enroll me in your crusade."

In the following days, the more she heard about the rigors of the Iditarod, the more interested she became in the procedures whereby Rick trained his dogs, and when snow came she began to spend her Saturdays and Sundays out at the shack, bringing it into some semblance of respectability, but she avoided any romantic involvement, for she still considered herself in some vague degree engaged to Jeb Keeler. Certainly, when the young lawyer visited Desolation on business with Afanasi he practically lived at Kendra's apartment, staying until three or four in the morning. But when Rick, observing this, asked if she and Keeler were engaged, she said: "It's difficult to make up your mind when you're so far from home."

At least once a week, when the snow was adequate, Rick took her for a long training ride in his sled, and it was a magnificent experience to sit perched there, bundled in blankets, and to head off for a ten-mile run toward the frozen lakes, with Rick running behind and jumping from time to time onto the tail end of the long runners, shouting directions to Polar and encouraging the other dogs occasionally. "I can see why the race fascinates young men," Kendra said one day as they rested at the halfway mark.

"Not men only," Rick said, reminding her that women older than she had won the race in recent years.

"You mean eleven hundred miles? They must be amazons," and he corrected her: "For this race you don't need brawn. You need brains and stamina."

Brains were required because each racer had to arrange with some airplane pilot to drop large caches of dried salmon or other kinds of food along the way for the famished dogs as well as for himself, and the scheduling of these drops required both judgment and money. Many a newcomer spent his entire year's savings, plus money from home, merely to cover expenses for the Iditarod.

"Where'd the name come from?" Kendra asked one day, and Rick said: "Name of an old mining camp. A trail used to run through there, and our race hits it every other year."

For several weeks in the early days of winter Kendra existed in a kind of dream world, fixing up the shack, working with the dogs, reveling in long weekend training trips, and she began to feel that this glorious experience on the endless whitened tundra in gusty blizzards and the wonderful assurance that Rick knew what he was doing would go on endlessly. The possibility of their falling in love had not yet surfaced, for he was still gun-shy from the wreckage of his first marriage and she considered herself more or less bound to Jeb Keeler, but both she and Rick were increasingly aware that after the Iditarod, certain decisions could become inescapable. But for the moment they drifted along.

During one of their casual training trips over the snow to the south she was reminded of how close to disaster the Inupiat Eskimos of the arctic lived, for as they were coasting along quite a few miles distant from Desolation, Rick spotted an old-style earthen dwelling with wooden sidewalls and a heavy sod roof. Without thinking that they might be intruding, he shouted "Gee!" to Polar, who instantly headed the team toward the hut. When the sled drew up before the door, Kendra realized with horror that this was where her prize student, Amy Ekseavik, had been reared and where she now lived, helping her widowed mother, for the girl appeared in the darkened doorway, glared at the dogs from beneath her heavy bangs, and then saw her teacher ensconced in blankets.

It was an icy reunion, for Amy had lost even the slight concession to humanity that she had allowed to develop under Kendra's care. She kept the visitors at arm's length, and when they asked to see her mother she said nothing, but stepped aside.

From the widow, Kendra learned that some kind of fol-de-rol had been exercised whereby the mother was supposed to be teaching her child at home, and this satisfied state law, even though good schools were available at Desolation to the north and Wainwright to the south. But it was obvious that the flame that had finally been ignited in this miraculous child in school the year before had gone out, or was sputtering in such a sickly manner that it must soon be extinguished.

Sick at heart that she had intruded upon Amy and her insoluble problems, Kendra bade the girl an awkward farewell and headed back north, her eyes filled with tears most of the way. When they stopped at one point to rest, she said to Rick: "My heart could break. Really, it's too awful," and she collapsed, sobbing, against his parka.

When he asked what this meant, she told him of Amy's frozen arrival at school last year and her gradual thawing into one of the brightest, most promising girls of her age Kendra had ever seen: "We may have done a dreadful thing, Rick. Stopping there and reminding her of lost worlds." Kendra's fears were justified. Three days later, word trickled in to Desolation that Amy Ekseavik, fifteen years old and with a brilliant future, had left her home-study workbook open on the rough table in the dim light of the sod hut, taken her father's gun, stepped outside, and committed suicide while her mother slept.

The history of Kendra's first year north of the Circle was surprise at local customs, attaining plateaus on which she congratulated herself: Now I understand Alaska, followed by explosions which caused her to confess: I really know nothing. But none of the big revelations were more astonishing to her than the arrival in Desolation of a tall, determined woman who lived with her family in a log cabin some two hundred miles to the east in one of the most forlorn corners of the state, where they ran a hunting lodge from which visitors made spectacular catches of fish and bagged big game.

She was accompanied by her son, and she had a remarkable proposition: "I've been teaching my boy at home—with Calvert study courses mailed from the United States—since he was a child. Although it's a mite early, I think he ought to take the SATs, because I'm convinced he's college material."

Then she introduced her son, Stephen Colquitt, six feet one inch, shy, but with eyes that darted here and there like a hawk's, absorbing everything. "What I came to ask you . . ." she explained nervously to Principal Hooker. "We've heard good reports of Miss Scott here as a teacher who really knows how to teach math. And we wondered if she would tutor Stephen in algebra."

Hooker fumbled: "That would be highly irregular . . . maybe impossible . . . enrolling him in our school when he doesn't live in our district."

"Oh! We didn't mean enroll him in your school. We meant we wanted special outside tutoring," and before the principal could respond, she added: "We'd be prepared to pay—for the outside help, that is."

"I'd not charge anything," Kendra said. "I'd enjoy brushing up on my own algebra."

"And trigonometry," Stephen added, and Kendra said: "We'll have a fling at that too."

The next weeks were so productive that Stephen's triumphant gallop through algebra, geometry and trig drove away somewhat her guilt about Amy's death, and one night Kendra told Afanasi and Hooker: "What this mother accomplished with home-teaching units from Maryland is incredible. When Stephen takes the SATs, stand back, because he's going to bust the system."

Kasm Hooker was impressed by quite a different accomplishment of the young man: "His father played a little basketball in college and they have a regulation basket on flat land beside the river. You wouldn't believe the moves this kid knows."

In the pickup games the village held when no visiting schools were available, it was agreed that Hooker would play Colquitt one-on-one, and in the first game the boy astounded both the principal and the villagers by displaying an ability to tap the ball in on a follow-up without bringing it down to the floor for a wasteful dribble, but what evoked shouts of praise was Steve's adroit use of the double pump, in which he made believe to shoot, thus tricking Hooker into jumping to block his shot, while he, Steve, kept hold of the ball and shot just as Hooker came down and was out of position.

"Where did you learn that?" the winded principal asked during one timeout, and Steve said: "Father has a satellite dish and I used to watch Earl the Pearl."

But it was when Steve's SAT scores came in that everyone realized what Mrs. Colquitt had known all along. "This kid can go to any college," Hooker said, accustomed to scores of less than four hundred, and he forthwith dispatched letters to a variety of schools, attaching a recommendation also from the Fairbanks coach:

> Kasm Hooker of Desolation and I played some good ball at
> Creighton in the days when we had a team, and I assure you
> that this six-foot-one boy of sixteen, who is sure to grow, is
> ready for the big time right now. He's had to train alone, no
> chance to play on a team. Given that chance, he'll be another
> Magic Johnson. Charge me double if I've deceived you.

In the spring Harry Rostkowsky flew in letters from nine leading universities and colleges offering Stephen Colquitt full academic scholarships—Yale, Virginia, Trinity in San Antonio among them—and another six wanted him for basketball. His mother and Kendra sorted out the offers and chose Virginia, which satisfied both Hooker and Steve, since they knew it favorably from the days when Ralph Sampson played there.

On the night they finished completing the entrance forms Kendra could not sleep, for she was trying to fathom how this gaunt woman, living in a remote cabin with not a single advantage except the Calvert correspondence materials and a television saucer, could have produced such a genius: Seems you don't need eighty-four-million-dollar high schools. Then again, maybe they help.

But as she laughed at this conclusion, Kendra suddenly began shivering and a terrible sickness of mind overwhelmed her, and in only her nightgown she ran from her quarters and banged furiously on Kasm Hooker's door. After a long silence, for it was near two in the morning, Mrs. Hooker came to the door and cried: "My God, girl! What is it?"

When Kendra slipped inside, trembling as if assailed by some mysterious fever, it was obvious to the Hookers that she could not control herself: "Kendra, sit down! Throw this robe about you. Now, what in hell goes on?"

It was not until Mrs. Hooker made her some hot chocolate that Kendra regained partial composure: "I was thinking of Stephen and his good luck."

"That's no cause for tears," Kasm said. "Martha and I were rejoicing." Then he added almost sourly: "But that was three hours ago."

"So was I, but in the middle of my congratulations . . . to myself and to him . . . I thought of Amy . . . dead in the mud," and she broke into wracking sobs. The Hookers, used to dealing at least once each term with some catastrophe, let her weep, and after a while she looked up piteously and asked: "Why does a white boy with a determined mother reach the stars, and a girl just as brilliant but with an Eskimo mother fail?" She looked accusingly at the Hookers: "Even you wrote letters to help him. Nobody stepped forward to help her."

"You were magnificent with her, Kendra," Mrs. Hooker said. "Kasm told me."

"It seems so unfair. So awful . . . socially and morally."

Kasm lit a pipe, tapped its stem against his teeth, and said: "Kendra, if you allow school tragedies to affect you so deeply, maybe you ought to consider leaving teaching. I mean it."

"Don't you take them seriously?"

"Seriously? Yes. Tragically? No. Do I allow them to strike at my inner life? I do not." Before Kendra could protest this inhumanity, he sat beside her, and while his wife brought a fresh cup of chocolate he took one of her hands in his and said: "From high school on, I have never been in a school or teaching position but what some kid hasn't done himself or herself in, or died in some terrible accident."

"What did you do?"

"Bury them, comfort the parents, and get on with the job. Because such things cannot be prevented. They can only be adjusted to."

"I refuse to adjust to such unfairness."

"Then, Kendra, what my husband says makes sense. If you allow your students' lives to affect you so deeply, maybe you ought to quit teaching. If you stay on, it'll destroy you."

Kendra reacted to this sage advice, culled from years of school experience, with a renewed attack of shivering so vigorous that Mrs. Hooker sat down and took her other hand: "How old are you, Kendra?"

"Twenty-eight."

"It's very important that you get married. Afanasi told me that his young lawyer, that Keeler fellow, thinks highly of you. And I see the dog man at the north end of the village moseying around. Take one of them while you have the chance. You stay in Alaska as an old-maid schoolteacher worrying about every Eskimo disaster, you'll break your heart."

But Kendra seemed not to hear her: "It all seems so unfair to the young Eskimos."

"Everything is unfair to young people. Years ago when I taught in Colorado it was fast cars and marijuana."

"And a very important point," Mrs. Hooker said. "Eskimos don't like it when good-hearted teachers like you show too much interest in their family troubles. They actually resent it. Death is something that happens, always has, and they don't want you or me snooping around and weeping in public."

Together the Hookers returned Kendra to her room, and in the morning Mrs. Hooker brought her more hot chocolate.

In March all attention in Desolation was centered on Vladimir Afanasi's high-powered shortwave radio, which brought hourly reports from Anchorage on the progress of the Iditarod. In favorable weather, for a change, the sixty-seven teams sped out of Anchorage on a course which this year covered eleven hundred and forty-three miles, with twenty-seven optional stops indicated at which teams could have food, dogs' and drivers', delivered by air. Rick had bought huge amounts of dried salmon for his dogs and Kendra had baked a big batch of rich, chewy high-energy brownies, filled with her pecans, for him. He also favored dried prunes, with pits he could suck on when the flesh was gone. At a designated spot, each team was obliged to rest dogs and drivers for an entire twenty-four hours, and here veterinarians inspected the animals. In recent years two women had won the race—the second, in the astonishing time of eleven days and fifteen hours—and at the camps there was much speculation as to whether a man could reclaim the trophy and the first-prize money of fifty thousand.

Rick, one of the twenty-six novices trying their luck this time, knew he had no chance of winning against the canny experts who had raced many times since the competition started in 1973, but he did confide to Kendra that he hoped "to finish with a 'Single-digit-fifteen,'" that was, within the first nine in not over fifteen days.

During the first week of the race everything seemed to happen. Moose, driven southward by blizzards, strayed onto the marked course, became irritated by the dogs, and leaped among them, thrashing out with their hoofs and killing half a dozen dogs, whose drivers then dropped from the race. A bitterly cold storm blowing straight down from the north, an unusual direction, encouraged seven other mushers to quit, and this same storm prevented nearly a dozen airplanes from delivering dried salmon to supply stations along the route. Thus deprived of fuel, as it were, some competitors were forced to quit the race. At Ruby a Nome musher won two thousand dollars for being in the lead at the halfway mark, but Rick noticed that by now, eighteen racers with teams as good as his had dropped out.

Up in Desolation, Afanasi, Hooker and Kendra maintained a twenty-four-hour watch on the shortwave, Vladimir monitoring it during school hours, the teachers riding herd at night, and they picked up enough fragments of news to know that Rick was still among the active competitors, but where exactly in the standings he stood, they could not determine. Then, on the thirteenth day, as Kendra was teaching algebra to her students, a man in the village who had his own radio burst into her classroom with exciting news:

"When they left Unalakleet, Venn was in third place!" Shortly after, Afanasi ran to the school with confirmation: "My God, no beginner has a right to be in third spot," but Kendra said: "Polar may be the best lead dog in the whole race," and with Mr. Hooker's ardent approval, they dismissed school for the day and accompanied Kasm and Vladimir to the shortwave, where they heard in snatches the account of one of the most dramatic incidents in any Iditarod.

Afanasi explained the situation to Kendra: "You mustn't think of this as an Olympic race with all the runners bunched. In the Iditarod they're scattered out. The Nome man in the lead is ahead by almost half a day. No one will catch him. The sixteenth man may be a day and a half behind. And the last man? Maybe a whole week." Hooker interrupted: "But this time it does seem as if the group behind the leader is bunched," and he was correct.

A woman who had never before placed higher than fourteenth was, surprisingly, in second place, but as she sped her dogs onto the ice of Norton Sound, a moose testing the shoreline nearby panicked, darted in among the dogs, struggled free, and kicked the woman in the stomach and about the legs, wounding her seriously. Rick, well to the south in third place and already safe on the icy stretch leading to the finish at Nome, saw this happening as he came up, and whereas five other racers who also saw it hurried on to claim their spots among the coveted first nine, Rick turned aside, urged Polar to maximum speed, and arrived in time to fend off the enraged moose and place the battered woman on her sled.

With two of her dogs killed, there was no way she could continue as a competitor, but she insisted that she could limp into Nome under her own power, so she thanked Rick for stopping to help, hugged him, and urged him: "Be on your way. You're still in this thing." But he simply could not leave her with the dead dogs still in harness and herself needing attention, so he left the race for about two hours, unharnessed the dead dogs, tended her wounds, and sent her on toward Nome.

He never made up the time lost by this gallant gesture, and as the other racers sped past, he realized that he had lost any chance at third position and probably his place within the first nine. Actually, he finished thirteenth, but when he came to the finish line he was greeted with cheers, the woman having told a reporter stationed along the way what had happened. One drunk came out of his Nome bar to make the most pertinent observation: "I never thought I'd see the day when I'd cheer for any son-of-a-bitch associated with Ross & Raglan, but this one knew what for," and Rick's noble performance became the toast of the town that night.

The winner, a tough veteran from Kotzebue, had finished in fourteen days, nine hours, three minutes and twenty-three seconds, but the race could not be declared over till a week later, when the forty-sixth musher stumbled in to win the honored red lantern, symbolic of the light that used to shine from the caboose of railroad trains to prove that the last boxcar had passed. A college boy from the University of Iowa, he had taken twenty-one days and eighteen hours for this grueling race, and he was almost as proud of his red lantern as the winner was of his fifty grand.

When Rick returned to Desolation with Polar and the twelve other dogs, he was a hero, and many villagers crowded out to Kensington Kennels to pay tribute to the team that had conducted itself so ably and with such honor in the Iditarod. His gallantry had been the subject of articles in the Seattle and New York newspapers, and his picture appeared in *Time* magazine above the caption "Winning Isn't Everything." This spate of publicity brought a long letter from his grandfather, Malcolm Venn, chairman of the board of Ross & Raglan in Seattle. It was the first Rick had heard from his grandfather in more than two years.

He showed the letter to Kendra when she lingered that first evening after the others were gone. She liked the manly phrasing, the obvious pride the older man took in his maverick grandson:

> *When you went north I told you to mimic your great-grandfather. Don't be afraid to try anything, and if you start, finish in style. We followed your progress in the odds and ends of news we got on local television and cheered your prospect of a fifth or even possibly a third, but we were far more proud of your thirteen.*

"I don't get letters like that from my parents," she said without self-pity, and as she looked at him—the certificate proving he had finished thirteenth in the Iditarod hanging just behind him on the wall—she saw him in a much clearer light than ever before: she admired the way he handled his dogs, with love and sternness, instilling in them a fierce and loyal drive to compete; she enjoyed his irreverent humor; and she appreciated the portrait she gleaned from his grand-father's letter of a family that was closely bound together in a long-standing tradition of mutual respect; and above all, she saw him as a stronger, more consolidated man than Jeb Keeler, and something of her thoughts must have shone in her eyes, for as she was about to leave the shack to return to the Teacherage, he reached out for her and said quietly: "Don't you think it's time you stayed here?" and she whispered: "Yes," for she had found a man she could love.

Back in her own quarters the next afternoon, Kendra did what an honorable person would feel compelled to do: she wrote a frank let-ter to Jeb Keeler in Anchorage, thanking him for his valued friend-ship and explaining that she had fallen in love with another man: "It looks as if any chance of our getting married has vanished, and I'm terribly sorry. On your next visit to Desolation let's talk about it, for I yearn to keep you as a friend."

When she had sealed the envelope she said aloud, with the confi-dence that many young women have voiced in such circumstances: "Well, that takes care of that."

Just about this time, in Washington, D.C., things were occurring that would eventually disrupt the lives of quite a few people in the village, the most dramatically affected being Kendra. The sequence of events began when the United States government awoke belatedly to the fact that Soviet Russia, Canada and even Norway were leaping ahead in the acquisition of knowledge about the arctic. In a somewhat fran-tic effort to catch up, a prestigious committee on arctic affairs had been appointed by the President, and it had assembled a consortium of American universities to sponsor and supervise a concentrated research attack on not only how to survive in arctic conditions but also how to utilize the arctic in either peace or war. Once the decision was made and the funds provided, this assembly of very bright men and women concluded that one of the first steps they ought to take was the furtherance of studies begun years ago on T-3, the floating ice island. As soon as that was agreed upon, the scholars in charge began to look about for arctic hands who'd had practical experience on T-3, and this threw them right into the lap of Vladimir Afanasi, who, as a young Eskimo with a university education, had been in charge of maintenance and operations on T-3 for three years.

The telephone call came from the President's scientific adviser in the White House: "This Vladimir Afanasi? The one who served on T-Three? . . . How old are you now, Mr. Afanasi? . . . Can you still operate in real cold weather? . . . Would you be prepared to reactivate T-Three? . . . Right now? . . . Of course, I know that T-Three itself has long since vanished but its successor . . . maybe we'll call it T-Seven. I think that's next in line. . . . You would be prepared? . . . That's very good news, Mr. Afanasi. You cannot imagine how highly you've been praised by the men associated with this project. . . . By the way, you are an American citizen?"

"Is this top secret or anything?"

"Mr. Afanasi! Would I be using an open phone line if it were? We know what the Soviets are doing, they know what we're doing or about to do. Welcome aboard. You'll be hearing from us."

Three days later a committee of three leading arctic specialists— one from Dartmouth, one from Michigan, one from the University in Fairbanks—met in Desolation with Afanasi, and for three hammering days they worked on the reactivation of a research station on what they called T-7. Maps of the arctic were spread everywhere. Old manifests of material required on T-3 were updated, formal agreements were drafted, and at the conclusion of the meetings Afanasi, by far the oldest man present, said: "I want the right to hire my own assistant."

"If he's qualified. If he can be cleared for security."

"He's both. Very knowledgeable in arctic matters. Graduate of Stanford with a fine record. And available, that's important."

"Is he in these parts?"

"He's at the edge of town. I'll take you to meet him." So the four men drove out to the Kensington Kennels, where they were greeted by the agitated yapping of thirteen handsome dogs, whom they stopped momentarily to admire.

They found Rick Venn stretched out on his bed reading one of the great books about Antarctica, Apsley Cherry-Garrard's *The Worst Journey in the World,* and the fact that a man of Venn's age knew this classic endeared him in the hearts of the three scholars. "You informed on Scott's tragedy?" the man from Dartmouth asked, and Rick said: "Only the usual. Amundsen's accounts, some of the recent studies."

"You a Scott man or an Amundsen man?" the scientist from Michigan asked, recalling the bitter animosities that had tormented the two polar explorers, and Rick said: "Strictly Amundsen. He was a professional; Scott, a romantic."

"Let's have nothing more to do with this young fellow," the man from Michigan said. "Rotten to the core."

"Wait," Venn said as he pulled on his trousers. "If I was writing a poem about Antarctica, I'd choose Scott every time."

The man from Michigan laughed: "Not a preferred type, but acceptable. Go ahead."

It was Afanasi who spoke, and Rick was impressed by the way these scholars deferred to the wise old Eskimo: "Rick, we used to have an Arctic Research Lab in Barrow. Run by the Navy. Accomplished lots but the government closed it down. To save nickels and dimes. Russians leaped ahead of us in arctic knowledge, so to catch up we're going to reactivate the research we had been conducting on T-Three."

"I read that it melted away, long since."

"The very words I used when they broached the subject. This is a new island. They're calling it T-Seven this time. They want me to serve as kind of factotum. I want you to come along as my right hand."

"How long? Two years, three years?"

"Who knows?"

Rick Venn was speechless, for this was what young men of ability dreamed about when they were graduate students: to be at the heart of some great enterprise in their field, to be surrounded by the top intellects of the preceding generations, to be applying all that had been learned in the past grueling years and to project learning forward. Those were the hopes of young medical students, geologists, literary critics or geographers. And rarely did an opportunity like T-7 come along.

"I'd be proud to work with you men," he said finally, and the man from Dartmouth asked: "What will you do with your dogs?"

"I'll cry a little and kiss each one goodbye, then pass them along to someone else." He looked out at them: "They carried me to thirteenth place in the Iditarod, you know."

"I heard you could have finished about third," the Michigan man said.

"You read about it? Third place? Who knows?" Suddenly he turned away from the dogs: "Is this in any way secret?"

"No."

"And you are going ahead? This is a job offer?"

Afanasi looked at the other three, and the chairman of this ad hoc committee, the man from Dartmouth, said, extending his hand: "It is."

On the flight back to Barrow in Rostkowsky's Cessna the Dartmouth man said: "Did you notice, neither of them asked about salary," and the Michigan man replied: "This is their world. They love the north and they're a part of it. We're damned lucky to have found them."

That afternoon, over maps left behind by the committee, Rick described his new job to Kendra, who felt a pang of apprehension on learning that the one man she loved was about to leave for an assignment of unlimited duration: "For the past fifty or sixty thousand years, and probably much longer, over here at the northernmost tip of Canada, Ellesmere Island, immense glaciers occasionally calve icebergs that are so monstrous you can't really call them icebergs. They're ice islands, maybe three hundred square miles, a hundred and fifty feet thick."

"That's unbelievable."

"Everybody says that when they first hear about them. Well, they're real, and they circulate clockwise up there in the Arctic Ocean for several years before they drift off into the Atlantic. One of them sank the *Titanic* back in 1912."

He showed her the track of the famous T-3 which had circulated north of Alaska for many years, and she asked: "Why didn't it stay put?" and he said: "Because it's floating in an ocean. Nobody seems to understand that the word *arctic* refers to an ocean; Antarctic, to a continent. But that's what they are." And then he told her the most remarkable fact of all: "The islands are so big and so flat that it's quite easy to level off an airfield right down the middle for as long as you need. You can land something as big as a 747 on an ice island, and the Russians do."

"Do they have certain of these floating islands? And we have others?"

"Not really, not officially. But it works out that way. Or did." And now he came to the critical reasons the Americans had decided to reactivate a research station on an ice island: "Russia is way, way ahead of us in its ability to use the arctic. They've had men on ice islands continuously. We had one spurt, then quit. Fact is, we've pretty well surrendered the arctic to them."

"And the three men who flew in here?" At Desolation Point, even children knew if an important letter arrived. "They're going to start up again?"

"Yes. And they want Vladimir to supervise the day-to-day operations."

"And he wants you to help?"

"He does."

"And you've accepted?"

"I have."

Desperately she wanted to cry "What about us?"—but she intuitively knew that the sure way to lose a strong man like Rick Venn was to lasso him with tears or pin him down with a sense of obligation; he would fight against that and fly off. She also suspected that he was still unprepared to make a lifetime commitment, so she approached her problem obliquely and in a most beguiling way: "What are you going to do about the dogs?"

"I was hoping you'd look after them, and find someone who'll care for them."

"You mean sell them?"

"If you can. If not, give them away. But only to someone who'll run them." He looked at the dogs who had served him so well. "They're champions. They deserve to compete. It's in their blood."

These words had a special meaning for Kendra; she saw Rick as a champion, destined to compete, and the ice island was an appropriate challenge, but this acknowledgment still left her isolated, and she felt like all women who have let one good man go to try for a better, only to lose both in her gamble.

"So I'm supposed to linger here, year after year, looking after your dogs." It wasn't going the way she had intended, but it was to his eyes, not hers, that tears came: "Kiddo! I've found me a real woman! I'll be back."

"And you're sure I'll wait two years, or whatever. You're sure that Jeb won't come knocking and I'll say 'Oh, what the hell?' and marry him?"

"I'm sure," he said simply, and with repeated promises that he would be back to marry her, he closed the shack where they had been so happy, turned over his dogs, and flew with Afanasi to Barrow and then four hundred miles north over the open Arctic Ocean to where a floating ice island, eleven miles long and three wide, awaited their tardy experimentation.

There were experts other than the United States Commission on the Arctic who were interested in the complexities of the North Pacific, and two of the best-informed lived in small Asian villages where they spent their days and many of their nights immersed in studies which would have impact upon Alaska, either immediately or at some time in the distant future, for these two men, better than any Americans, appreciated the fact that Alaska's position, as the keystone of the great arch that encloses the North Pacific, gave her world importance.

The two men, one Japanese, one Russian, did not know each other, nor did they even realize that the other existed, but each kept on the wall of his study a large map showing all the nations bordering the Pacific, from Chile at the southeastern tip through Mexico and the United States on the east, across to Siberia and Japan on the west, and down the southwest to Indonesia, Australia and New Zealand. It was a glorious stretch of terrain made more so by the proliferation of red and black dots which peppered the circumference of this vast ocean: indeed, the map looked as if a hundred bees had stung places like Colombia, Kamchatka and the Philippines, raising ugly red welts. These were the clusters of volcanoes, dead and active, that gripped the Pacific in a rim of fire. These were the soaring, explosive mountains, with lyrical names like El Misto, Cotopaxi, Popocatépetl, Mount Shasta, Fujiyama, Krakatoa, Vulcan and Ruapehu, that bespoke the violent character of these areas.

The black dots, far more numerous, indicated where in historic times huge earthquakes had shaken the land, with heavy black crosses indicating the quakes that had leveled parts of Mexico City in 1985, San Francisco in 1906, Anchorage in 1964, Tokyo in 1923, New Zealand in 1931. The most casual glance at these maps revealed the constant attack of lava and trembling earth along the edges of the Pacific, a record of the tremendous relentless forces of the wandering plates.

Thus, when the Nazca Plate subducted under the continental plate, the edges shattered and parts of Mexico City collapsed in ruins. When the Pacific Plate ground along the North American Plate, San Francisco caught fire, and when the opposite side of the Pacific Plate subducted under the Asian Plate, Tokyo's buildings fell apart. And when, in its northern reaches, the Pacific Plate hammered its way down under the shallow continental Bering Sea, the world's most concentrated chain of volcanoes rose gloriously in the sky, while the earth's most incessant family of earthquakes shook the land and, if they were submarine, sent great tsunamis radiating through the Pacific.

Alaska, occupying the crown of this fiery rim, had a position not only of geographical dominance as the link between Asia and North America, but also of potential economic and military importance, and in these closing years of the century the Japanese expert was concerned primarily with the economic, the Russian with the military.

In a beautiful mountain village some twenty miles west of Tokyo on the minor Tama River, Kenji Oda, the able mountaineer who had rescued Kimiko Takabuki from her fall in the crevasse, pursued his studies. Tamagata, a village of graceful wood and stone houses in the traditional Japanese style, had been chosen by the powerful Oda family as the site of their research operations. The family had many commercial interests, but son Kenji, oldest and ablest of the third generation, had concentrated on the family's wood-pulp holdings, and to perfect himself in this international specialty, he had made himself familiar with the pulp forests of Norway, Finland and Washington State in the United States. While working with paper interests in Washington he had climbed Mount Rainier in the dead of winter with a team of American fanatics.

At thirty-nine he enjoyed his seclusion at Tamagata because it provided a serene environment in which to reflect at a distance on the balancing of these world markets, and also, easy access to the international flights that left Tokyo almost hourly for all parts of the Oda empire: the factories in São Paulo, the newly acquired hotels in Amsterdam and the forest leases in Norway and Finland. But the more he studied the world paper problems and Japan's diminishing access to major forests, the more clearly he saw that the almost endless forests of Alaska had to become a prime target for anyone interested in the making and distribution of paper.

"In many practical ways," he told his study group, "the forests of Alaska are closer to Japan than they are to the major centers in the United States. A manufacturer in the eastern United States can get his wood pulp more easily from the Carolinas, Canada or Finland than from Alaska. Our big Japanese ships can put in to Alaskan ports, load with pulp, and come back across the North Pacific to our paper and rayon plants here in Japan a lot cheaper than the Americans can handle the same wood pulp by truck or train."

A representative of the Oda shipping lines—freight only—pointed out that the maritime distance from Japan to Sitka was rather longer than Kenji had indicated, whereupon the latter chuckled: "You have good eyes. But if we go ahead with this, we're not going to Sitka. I have my eye on a rather substantial island just north of Kodiak, on this side of the bay," and he indicated a densely forested island which could supply the Oda Paper Works for the next fifty years.

"On our mountain-climbing trips to Denali," he explained to the men, "our plane broke out of the clouds right about here, and below I saw this undeveloped island. Since we'd started our descent into Anchorage, we were low enough for me to see that this was prime forest, probably spruce, easy to log, easy to reduce to pulp, easy to ship back to our plants in liquid form."

"Any chance that we can get long-term control? I don't mean outright ownership."

Before replying to this critical question, Oda became reflective, and looking at the big map dominating the wall facing the men, he pointed to Alaska: "Strategically speaking, this area is more a part of Japan than it is of the United States. Every natural resource Alaska has is more valuable to us than it is to America. The oil at Prudhoe Bay ought to be coming straight across the Pacific to us. The lead, the coal and certainly the wood pulp. The Koreans aren't stupid. They're moving in everywhere. China is going to show enormous interest in Alaska; Singapore and Formosa could use Alaska's resources to tremendous benefit."

When the attractive hostesses interrupted the discussion to bring morning tea and rice cookies, Kenji took advantage of the break to suggest that they move into the garden, where the beauties of the Japanese landscape, so manicured compared to the wildness of Alaska, put the men at ease, and there he said as the meeting resumed: "You can understand Alaska best if you view it as a Third World country, an underdeveloped nation whose raw materials are to be sold off to the more developed countries. The United States will never utilize Alaska properly, never has, never will. It's too far away, too cold . . . America has no concept of what it has, and very little interest in finding out. That leaves the marketplace open to us."

"What can we do about it?" one of the men asked, and Kenji replied: "We've already done it. On my last trip back from Denali, I started negotiations to lease that wooded island. Well, not the land, you understand. They'd never allow that. But the right to cut trees, build a chip mill, erect a dock for our ships."

"Any luck?"

"Yes! I'm delighted to inform you that after several months of the most difficult negotiations . . . The Alaskans are far from stupid. I think they see their position just as clearly as we do. They know they're orphans in their own land. They know they have to cooperate with their Asian markets. And they know . . . at least the people I negotiated with knew how intimately they were going to be affiliated with both China and Russia. They can't escape it. So I had no trouble in gaining their attention. I think they'd prefer to trade with Japan, their wood, their oil, their minerals for whatever we can supply in return."

The group, most of whom had motored up to Tamagata before breakfast, relaxed in the sun, munched sembei and drank tea. One of the men, who taught geography as a part-time consultant to a university, said: "I don't want to play the big geopolitician, but that map back there . . . Could we take another look at it?" When they were seated as before, he continued: "We and China enjoy a lucky advantage in our potential dealings with Alaska. But look at how close Alaska is to Soviet Russia! At these two little islands, which don't show on this map, the two superpowers are about a mile and a half apart. If commercial air travel were permitted between the two areas . . . up here where the two big peninsulas jut out, maybe sixty miles apart, you could fly it in maybe ten minutes."

"What's your point?" Oda asked, and the man said: "I think we can predict that Alaska and the Soviet Union will always be suspicious of each other. No trade, no amity possible. Also, what Alaska has, Siberia also has, so they are not natural trading partners. On the other hand, what Alaska has is what we need, what Formosa and Singapore need, not to mention China."

"Your conclusion?"

"Build the pulping plant. Send our tankers to . . . What's the name of the island?"

"Kagak. Old Aleutian word, I believe, meaning something like *rich horizons.*"

"Send our tankers to Kagak. But while we're doing so, let's not overlook the copper mines, the oil which in common sense ought to come our way, and anything else that great empty land will be able to provide in the future."

Now Oda took command: "For some time it has been clear to me that the role of the Third World nations is to provide the technologically and educationally advanced nations with raw materials at a fair price. Allow countries like Japan and Singapore to apply intelligence and mechanical skill to those materials and pay for them by sending back to the Third World countries our finished products, especially those that they will never have the ability to invent or manufacture for themselves."

When several young men well informed on international trade protested that such a simplistic exchange might not be indefinitely possible, Oda pointed to the calculator his financial expert had been using: "Watanabe-san, how many controls on your computer, which as you others can see is about the size of a large playing card?" It took Watanabe more than a minute to summarize the wonderfully intricate capabilities of the thirty-five keys on his hand-held calculator: "Ten keys for the digits and zero. Twenty-five others for various mathematical functions. But many keys can provide up to three different functions. Grand total: thirty-five obvious keys, plus sixty-three hidden variable functions, for ninety-eight options."

Oda smiled and said: "When I bought my progenitor of Watanabe's miracle gadget, it offered me ten numerals and the four arithmetic functions. It was so simple that it could be handled by anyone. But when you add eighty-eight additional function keys, you move it forever beyond the capacity of the untrained, and most Third World citizens will be in that category. They'll have to rely on us to do their thinking, their inventing and their manufacturing."

"Just a minute," one of the team protested. "I visited the University of Alaska at Fairbanks on our last visit. They have scores of students in engineering who can handle bigger computers than Watanabe's."

"Exactly!" Oda agreed. "But when they graduate they'll have to find jobs in what they call the Lower Forty-eight. Their absence will leave Alaska a Third World nation, and let's remember that. Courtesy, assistance, modest stance, listen more than talk, and provide at every turn the help Alaska needs. Because our relationship with that great untapped reservoir can be magnificently helpful, to both of us."

It was on these principles that Kenji Oda and his wife, Kimiko, who knew Alaska from the inside as it were, moved to the island of Kagak north of Kodiak to establish the big United Alaskan Pulp Company. Significant was the fact that the word *Japanese* appeared nowhere in the title or the printed materials of this firm, nor were Japanese workmen involved in building the large and complicated plant which reduced Kagak spruce trees to a liquid pulp for tankering across the Pacific to Japan. And when the plant was ready for operation, no Japanese crews appeared to slash down the trees, and only three Japanese engineers settled in Kagak to supervise the intricate machinery.

Kenji and Kimiko did take residence in a modest house on Kagak Island, and they did rent a modest office in Kodiak, to which highly skilled technicians from Tokyo flew in from time to time to inspect and supervise procedures. After the first few months, at an enterprise which involved some nineteen million dollars, there were only six Japanese on the scene and at least half the ships that ferried the pulp to Japan operated under some flag other than the Rising Sun, for if the great industrialists of Japan were determined to take over the development and utilization of Alaska's raw materials, they did not want to be flagrant about it or generate local animosities.

In such behavior the Odas were exemplary. Kenji performed no act which drew adverse attention to himself, but many which added to his sober reputation in the Kodiak community. Was a string quartet to be invited in from Seattle? He contributed at a level just below the three leading local citizens. Were local literary lights producing a fine outdoor spectacle about Baranov and the Russian settlement of the Aleutians and Kodiak? As a paper expert he contributed all costs for printing the programs. On two occasions he invited leading Kodiak officials to fly with him and Kimiko for a vacation in their wooded village at Tamagata, and on another occasion he underwrote the expenses of two college professors from the University of Alaska at Anchorage to attend an international conference in Chile on the Pacific Rim. As a result of such contributions, he and Kimiko became known as "those fine Japanese who have such a creative interest in Kodiak and Alaska," and someone listening to that assessment would add: "And they both climbed Denali, which is more than we can say for any of the Americans hereabouts." But during his absences from the pulp mill at Kagak, when he was not vacationing at Tamagata or attending conferences in Chile, Oda was quietly probing into the remote areas of Alaska, seeking out sites like Bornite, where copper might be found, or Wainwright, which had rich seams of coal. Once he heard of a distant mountainside in the northwest arctic whose assays looked as if it might contain promising concentrations of zinc, and after shipping to Tokyo samples of ore taken from various spots in the area, he arranged for a ninety-nine-year lease on a vast area. When questioned about this on his next visit to the research headquarters of his family's operations at Tamagata, he said frankly and with as honest an assessment as he could muster: "Japan does not want to 'take over' Alaska, as some critics suggest. All we want is to do with the other raw materials what we're already doing so successfully with wood pulp at Kagak. And let me stress, in case the subject comes up when I'm not available, Alaska profits from our present deal equally with us. It's what you might call the perfect relationship. They sell raw materials they haven't the capital to develop themselves and we get the raw materials which we can process and on which we can earn substantial profits."

"Can we do the same with Alaskan lead and coal and zinc?"

"Better. Their bulk is smaller, potential profits greater."

The wise men of Japan contemplated this for some minutes, for this was the way in which their island empire—no raw materials, excessive manpower, superexcessive brainpower—functioned, but then one older man, who had experienced the great revulsion the world had expressed toward a similar Japan in the 1930s, asked quietly: "But why should the United States allow us to operate in this manner?" and Oda gave the only sensible explanation: "Because they started back in 1867 when they bought Alaska with the idea that the area was worthless, and in the first half century of ownership they totally ignored what they had, unable to perceive it as having any real value. Those injurious misconceptions persist. They contaminate a nation's thought processes. And it will be well into the next century before the leaders of America awaken to what they have in their 'icebox.' In the meantime, Alaska must always be visualized as part of Asia, and that brings it neatly into our orbit."

And on this very day when the Japanese were laying their far-ranging plans to utilize the unattended riches of Alaska, similar industrialists in Korea, Taiwan, Hong Kong and Singapore were reaching the same conclusions and taking comparable steps to bring Alaska into their orbits.

The second Asian intellectual who was contemplating Alaska with assiduous care in these days was a man of sixty-six who lived in a small village south of Irkutsk on the way to Lake Baikal. There he had assembled a treasury of family papers and imperial studies relating to the Russian settlement and occupation of Alaska, and with the encouragement of the Soviet government was making himself into the world's unchallenged authority on the subject.

He was Maxim Voronov, heir of that distinguished family who had provided Russian Alaska with able men and women leaders, including the great churchman Father Vasili Voronov, who took as his wife the Aleutian Cidaq and who left her to become Metropolitan of All the Russias.

Now, in the later years of his life, still slim and erect but with a shock of white hair which he combed back with his fingers, this Voronov had retired to the Irkutsk of his ancestors, where he presided over Russia's outstanding collection of data on her Aleutian discoveries and her governance of Alaska. Since he knew more than any other Russian about these subjects, he certainly knew more than any American, and in the course of painfully analyzing the historical record, spending the years 1947 to 1985 in doing so, he reached certain interesting conclusions which had begun to attract the attention of the Soviet leadership. During the summer of 1986, when the weather in eastern Siberia was almost perfect, a team of three Russian foreign policy experts spent two weeks in protracted discussion with Voronov in which Alaska was kept in constant focus. The three men were all younger than Maxim and they deferred to his age and scholarship, but not to the interpretation of his data.

"What would be your conclusions, Comrade Voronov, as to practical timetables?"

"What I'm about to say should be of crucial importance to your thinking, Comrade Zelnikov."

"That's why we came to see you. Please proceed."

"Barring unforeseen disruptions of the greatest magnitude, I cannot see a propitious moment arising much before the year 2030. That's forty-five years down the road, and of course it could be longer."

"What's your thinking?"

"First, America will probably remain strong till that time. Second, the Soviet Union will not yet have acquired the superiority in either strength or moral leadership to make the move practical. Third, it will take Alaska about that many years to fall so far behind that our move will be both sensible and inviting to her. And fourth, the rest of the world will require about that long to accommodate itself to the practicality and historical justification of our move."

"Will your studies, the basic groundwork, that is, be in better shape in 2030?"

"I won't be here, of course, but whoever follows me will have been able to refine my studies."

"Have you a successor in mind?"

"No."

"You better find one."

"Then you're prepared—that is, Moscow thinks enough of this . . ."

"It's vital. The pot's far on the back of the stove, as they say in America, but it must be kept quietly bubbling. Comrade Petrovsky could be alive in 2030, and if not he, somebody else." Petrovsky smiled and said: "Let's suppose that I am still alive. What sequence of thought should I be pursuing in the interval?"

Patiently, slowly and with great conviction Maxim Voronov spelled out his vision of the future relationship between the Soviet Union and Alaska, and as he spoke his visitors from Moscow realized that through eight generations the Voronovs of Irkutsk had never ceased thinking of the Aleutians and Alaska as an inherent part of the Russian Empire.

"We start with the fact, not the assumption, that Alaska belongs to Russia by the three sacred rights of history: discovery, occupation, established governance. And by the right of geography, because Alaska was as much a part of Asia as it was of North America. And by the fact that Russia gave the area responsible government when we had it and the Americans did not when they took it over. And most persuasively, we have proved that we can develop our Siberia creatively while America lags far behind us in developing her northernmost part of Alaska.

"In their discussions of the future the Americans have invented a highly applicable word, the *scenario,* borrowed from the theater. It means *an orderly scheme governing how things might work out.* What we now require is a Soviet scenario whereby we can regain the Alaska that is rightfully ours and do it with a minimum of international disruption."

"Can there be such a scenario?" Comrade Zelnikov asked, and Voronov assured his listeners that there not only could be, but that there was an actual plan which would bring Alaska back into the Russian orbit.

"We use two great concepts, Russia in the historic past, the Soviet Union in the present, and there is no discontinuity between them. They are one moral entity and neither is in conflict with the other. I shall use the word *Russia* when speaking of the past, the *Soviet Union* when referring to the present or future. Our task is to bring Alaska back into the bosom of timeless Russia, and our Soviet Union is the agency through which we must work. The scenario is simple, the rules governing it implacable.

"First, in the decades ahead we must never disclose our objective, not by word or deed or even the most casual thought. If the United States government learns of our design, they will move to block us. I discuss these plans with no one, which is why I have no indicated successor. You three must keep your own plans just as secret.

"Second, we must never make even the most tentative overt move prematurely. World conditions, not our hopes, will determine when the time is ripe for us to make our intentions and our claims known. Eighty years would not be too long to wait for the propitious moment, because I am positive that it will in due course arrive.

"Third, the significant signal will be the decline of American power and, more important, the gradual wasting away of American will power."

"Can we anticipate such decline? Zelnikov asked, and Voronov replied: "Inescapably. Democracies grow weary. They lose momentum. I can foresee the time will come when they might want to rid themselves of Alaska." He paused: "Just the way we wanted to get rid of it in 1866 and '67." These obiter dicta brought him to his major strategy:

"Now we forget Russia and focus sternly on the Soviet Union. Our argument must invariably be that the men who so cravenly gave away Alaska were not entitled to do so. They did not speak for the Russian people. In no way did they represent the soul of Russia. The sale was corrupt from the moment it was conceived. It had not the slightest validity. It transferred no rights to America and its terms will be reversed by any impartial international court or by the perceived wisdom of the rest of the world. The sale of Alaska was fraudulent, without moral base, and is subject to reversal. Alaska was, is and shall be Russian. The entire logic of world history demands this."

The three visitors, not knowing enough historical detail to judge the merits of Voronov's claim that the transfer had been basically illegal, asked for substantiation, and he cited the three solid bases for the Soviet Union's claim to Alaska:

"I warn you gentlemen and those who follow in your place. Indeed, I've drawn up my most important *aide-memoire* on just this point, and you must keep it on file for your successors and mine. You must base our claim on legal principles, never on force, and I assure you that our legal claim is impeccable. It must prevail in the court of world opinion.

"First, the Russian government as it then existed was incompetent to speak for the Russian people. It was a corrupt tyranny from which the huge bulk of the Russian people were excluded. Since it possessed no authority, its acts were illegal, especially those involving the disposition of territories over which it exercised no moral control. The transfer became illegal at the moment of sale, which was itself totally venal and therefore unenforceable.

"Second, the agent who maneuvered the sale and without whose infamous participation it could not have gone forward was not a Russian; he was not formally authorized to conduct negotiations; and he could not possibly have been construed as acting on behalf of the Russian people. Baron Edouard de Stoeckl, as he liked to style himself, had no right to the title he paraded; he was either a Greek adventurer or an Austrian lackey who interposed himself in the negotiations, God knows how, if you'll forgive an old folk expression, and in much of the affair he acted solely on his own without consultation with St. Petersburg. It was his sale, not Russia's."

At this point Maxim showed the men from Moscow three shelves of books in some seven or eight different languages dealing with Baron

Edouard de Stoeckl and a set of two notebooks in which he, Voronov, had chronicled the life of this shadowy man month by month for a period of nearly four decades. But he had long ago decided that it would not further the Soviet Union's claim to Alaska for him to publish his materials now: "It's all here, gentlemen, in these notebooks. You can publish a devastating biography of De Stoeckl whenever you care to." He laughed nervously: "I'd appreciate it if you'd cite me in one of the footnotes." And now he was ready with one of his most telling points:

> "Third, there is the ugly business of the missing two hundred and fifty thousand dollars. I have facts in this second pair of notebooks, and a miserable set of facts they are. I have traced with infinite detail, accounting for nearly every kopeck, the money that De Stoeckl handled in this malodorous affair, and without the slightest ambiguity or juggling of figures, I have proved that De Stoeckl had in his control not the hundred and fifty thousand dollars which American scholars cite, but nearly twice that much. So what happened to it? American historians have long suspected that Baron de Stoeckl used this money to buy votes in the American House of Representatives, but they've never been able to prove it. I have. With the greatest care and discretion I've bought family records, old accounts, newspaper suspicions and hard proof. American documents, English, German consular reports—and they're a clever lot, those Germans—and this row of Russian sources. Taken together, they prove without question that De Stoeckl corrupted the American Congress to an unbelievable degree."

Here he stopped dramatically, smiled at each of his visitors, and hammered home his major point:

> "Do you understand what this means? That the sale was corrupted from the moment of its completion in Congress. The American government in its wisdom did not want Alaska. It knew those remote areas were no part of its territory. The vote was consistently against either purchasing our land or paying for it when it was purchased. But De Stoeckl, this evil adventurer from nowhere, he forced America to take it, and he accomplished this coercion by paying United States congressmen to vote against the national interest. America's ac-

quisition of Alaska was totally corrupt and must be rescinded."

In the discussion that followed, Voronov proposed that some Soviet scholar, not himself "because that might attract unwanted attention to what I'm doing," be authorized to publish a small hard-hitting volume which might be titled *What Happened to the Quarter Million?* It would reveal the surprising data accumulated here in Irkutsk, name the congressmen who accepted the bribes, and establish in world circles the solid footing upon which the Soviet Union's later claim for Alaska would be based. But Comrade Zelnikov had for some time been developing his own scenario for the ultimate recapture of Alaska, and he counseled patience: "I assure you it would look suspicious if Soviet scholars reopened this subject now. I agree with you, Voronov, it would awaken world scholarship to the facts, and it would build a solid foundation for our later claims, but I fear we would lose far more in the long run than we would gain in the short. Keep your notebooks for 2030, when we'll use them and everything else with devastating effect."

Maxim Voronov came from a family of fighters and he was not prepared to accept a reversal so easily: "Could we encourage foreign scholars to do our work for us?"

"I don't see how. Anything surreptitious we did would be bound to leak out."

"But scholars in the United States and especially in Canada are already probing into these muddy waters to see if they can locate carp hiding at the bottom," and here he showed the men half a dozen remarkable publications, barely known in the West, in which Canadians and Americans dredged up some of the easier facts that he had been uncovering since the end of World War II. Any one of these writers stood on an elevated platform of learning from which he or she could take off and reach the higher levels already occupied by Voronov, but the four plotters could devise no strategy whereby the Soviet Union could encourage or underwrite the necessary studies. "It would be too risky," Zelnikov warned, at which Voronov snorted: "Russians can't do it, and Canadians and Americans can't be pushed. So the truth can only be very slowly revealed. And may be lost if too much time passes."

"Not with your notebooks in existence," Zelnikov said. "And I want to take photocopies back to Moscow with me. We'll start shooting them as soon as we can get an army photography team in here."

"We have good copy machines right here," Voronov said, and Zelnikov smiled: "Would you trust your notebooks to just anybody? The CIA probably runs your machines."

So the time bomb on Alaska began ticking in both Irkutsk, where the individual tiles of the groundwork were being assiduously pieced together by Voronov, and in Moscow, where clever operatives like Zelnikov and Petrovsky were contemplating the geopolitical moves that would be necessary if Alaska were to be successfully reclaimed. All who worked on this sensitive project kept in mind Maxim Voronov's closing statement at the Irkutsk meeting: "The time for our action will never be ripe unless the whole world sees great changes. But century by century such changes do occur, and we should be prepared when the next one arrives." Neither he nor Zelnikov believed that the United States would willingly or even unwillingly surrender its grasp on Alaska. "Those people labored too hard to extend their territory from their foothold on the Atlantic to the Pacific to relinquish anything," Voronov predicted, but Zelnikov corrected him: "They won't do the surrendering. World opinion, world conditions will dictate it, and they'll be powerless to resist."

There was a third expert, not in Asia, who kept his eye trained on Alaska. He was an Italian-born volcanologist who had spent his early days on a farm in the shadow of Mount Vesuvius, and since he was a precocious child, by the age of fourteen he had become something of an expert on volcanoes and earthquakes. At fifteen he enrolled at the University of Bologna, where he excelled in science, and at twenty at the California Institute of Technology, where he earned a doctorate in seismology, his American citizenship and an appointment to a federal seismological station in the Los Angeles region. There he mastered the intricacies of earthquake measurement, assessment and prediction, knowledge in the first two fields being far more sophisticated than in the latter.

Giovanni Spada, forty-one, found himself in the small Alaskan city of Palmer, where the Flatches had done their marketing and where LeRoy had flown his first planes. There, on a quiet street lined with trees, he supervised operations in an inconspicuous white building of the Tsunami Research Center. On behalf of the governments of the United States, Canada, Japan and the Soviet Union, Spada surveyed the behavior of the volcanoes, earthquakes and devastating tsunamis that originated along the northern apex of the Rim of Fire. It was his responsibility, among other tasks, to alert the northern Pacific areas from Japan to Hawaii to Mexico and all points north when the volatile arc of the Aleutians generated a tsunami that might sweep with mounting force across the ocean toward a distant shore.

In the summer of 1986, wishing to impress upon a new group of associates assigned to the Tsunami Center the power of earthquakes to generate huge marine disturbances, he flew his team down to Lituya Bay, some four hundred and fifty miles to the southeast. There he led them to a spot high in the surrounding mountains where they could see the beautiful bay below: "Observe that it's a long, thin bay with steep sides and a narrow opening to the Pacific."

When his younger colleagues had familiarized themselves with the terrain, he told a story which astounded them: "On 9 July 1958 an earthquake registering a massive eight on the Richter scale struck about a hundred miles north of here in the Yakutat area. The jolt was so strong that about forty million cubic yards of rock and earth were dislodged from that little mountain over there at the head of the bay and plunged all at once into the bay. The resulting splash created the greatest wave the world has seen in recorded history, and you can see for yourselves the magnitude of devastation it produced."

As they looked down they slowly began to see that this wave, penned in as it was into the narrow bay, had risen tremendously high, uprooting every tree it encountered, and Spada suggested: "Will someone who's had surveying experience calculate how high on the flanks of the mountainside the wave rose?" and a young man from the Colorado School of Mines laid out with his thumb and forefinger strata from sea level to the line of denudation, and after a while said in an awed voice: "My God, that's more than a thousand feet high!" and Spada said quietly: "Actually, that wave rose one thousand seven hundred and forty feet. That's the kind of tsunami a submarine earthquake can generate in a closed area."

At Palmer, with his battery of delicate seismographs probing the earth's crust, and with instantaneous connections to similar watch stations in Canada, California, Japan, Kamchatka and the Aleutians, Spada monitored the restless plates which ground together deep below the surface of the ocean, now advancing, now submerging, now fracturing and often slipping and sliding one against the other to produce the submarine earthquakes which gave birth to the devastating tsunamis. He was especially responsible for any tsunamis originating in the Aleutians, for they had proved their capacity to overwhelm cities, towns and villages along the coast thousands of miles away, and when the stylus on his seismographs shuddered, indicating that something had slipped somewhere, he alerted some sixty stations throughout the Pacific that a tsunami might be on its way.

But Spada also monitored those earthquakes which were not submarine, or those which transmitted their power directly to inland locations. Thus, in 1964 he had caught the first tremors of that violent quake which struck Anchorage, dropping sections of the city forty feet, raising others, and creating havoc across a wide area. More than a hundred and thirty lives were lost in that quake which first registered on the Richter scale as 8.6 but which was later calculated to have been 9.2, the greatest ever recorded in North America. It was about ten times greater than the quake which had destroyed San Francisco in 1906.

Spada maintained a master map, one that showed in extended detail the supposed structure of the Aleutian chain, and whenever an earthquake struck in that region he filled in with red crayon that portion of the Aleutian arc. To his assistants he said, when his map was completed: "Gradually, since 1850, we've noted the areas where the plates have shifted," and he pointed to nine different arcs which filled in spaces on his map. "At each of these sites an earthquake has eventuated. The plates have readjusted." He allowed his assistants time to digest the data, then added: "So in these three gaps . . ." He need say no more.

From Lapak Island to the west where it joined Tanaga and out to Gareloi, there was a neat arc of red dots; a big earthquake at the beginning of the century had resulted from the shift that occurred in the plates there, but east of Lapak to Adak and Great Sitkin the map was cadaverously white, which meant that the great readjustment of the plates had not yet occurred along that gap. A new man aboard asked: "Can we expect a big quake out there one of these days?" and Spada said: "We can." He had been on solitary duty that night of 19 September 1985 when the Nazca Plate slipped violently, subducting under the bordering South American continental plate. His eye caught the vigorous activity of the tracing arm before the audible signals sounded, and he said to himself: That's rather big, and when he consulted his backup seismographs he whistled: Seven-point-eight! That's got to have consequences.

By now his assistants, roused by the electronic signals flashing in their bedrooms, rushed to the Tsunami Center. "Any likelihood of a movement north?" a new man asked, and Spada said: "Seven-point-eight could give us repercussions anywhere."

"Where's the epicenter?" the young man asked, and Spada said: "We can't pinpoint it yet," but now reports from nearly a dozen other monitoring stations allowed him to triangulate the direction and place the locus of the earthquake fairly accurately at a spot well out in the Pacific Ocean and southeast of Mexico. "It's far enough off-shore not to pose any threat to land areas," he said with some confidence, "but the entire Pacific coastline could be vulnerable to a tsunami."

However, within minutes, reports came rushing in of a massive earthquake beneath Mexico City, and Spada was aghast: "To exert so much power so far from the slippage! It must have been much bigger than seven-eight," and after he had assembled reports from around the world, it was he who first calculated that the Nazca shift had produced a quake of 8.1 on the Richter scale, much stronger than at first supposed.

This time a tsunami did not eventuate; only inland Mexico suffered the full force of this titanic disruption, and even before accurate casualty reports from Mexico City trickled in, Spada warned his team: "There will be many dead," and more than ten thousand were. But three days later his attention was diverted by a modest rumbling of Qugang Volcano on Lapak Island, in an area that generated disturbances of one kind or another. He dispatched a plane to inspect the activity, and relaxed when the report arrived: "Six passes, six different elevations. No sign of major activity and no indication that anything major might develop."

Spada occasioned in his superiors both respect and amusement. He had an uncanny sense regarding volcanoes, earthquakes and tsunamis, as if his childhood experiences near Vesuvius had acclimated him to their behavior, and he was invaluable to Russians, Japanese and Canadians alike for the thoroughness of his watch on their frontiers. He insisted upon calling himself a *vulcanologist,* the Italian and perhaps original spelling of the word rather than the more popular *volcanologist.* As a classicist—his father having been a teacher of Latin and Roman mythology—he believed that the older word related the phenomena with which he dealt to a whole nest of primordial causes, while the latter specified too narrowly its emphasis on volcanoes.

In his spare time, when he climbed the Talkeetna Mountains or explored the fascinating Matanuska Glacier with his American wife, they sometimes rested on a knoll and drank iced tea, munched on sandwiches, and contemplated the violence that marked the North Pacific: "Great ice sheets grind down the mountains. The seas freeze over and throw up huge blocks of ice. Volcanoes like Qugang erupt, spewing millions of tons of lava and ash into the air. Earthquakes devastate cities, and deep in the sea tsunamis are unleashed to sweep away towns."

His wife once responded to these reflections with a sober one of her own: "And all the time, at the poles, ice begins to accumulate, until the glaciers spread relentlessly again to engulf all we've done." As she poured more tea she said: "When you live in Alaska, you live with change," and then laughed at her own pomposity: "Wouldn't it be hilarious, twenty thousand years from now, when the Bering land bridge is open again, if we all walked back to Asia?"

And so the speculation continued. In his vacation sessions at Tamagata west of Tokyo, Kenji Oda conjectured on the economic future of Alaska; in his cottage east of Irkutsk, Maxim Voronov tried to predict when his beloved Russia, whether Soviet or not, would be strong enough to win back Alaska; and in his austere white building in Palmer, Giovanni Spada tracked the behavior of volcanoes, earthquakes and tsunamis.

And deep within the heart of the Arctic Ocean on T-7, Rick Venn struggled to help the United States catch up with the experts of other nations in a comprehensive understanding of the arctic seas, and the rifts in the ocean floor from which new worlds were being built, and the wandering terranes which would one day construct a modified Alaska, and the Rim of Fire which dictated life in the Pacific, and the slowly growing ice caps at the poles, south and north, which would one day engulf so much of the world in another age of ice.

"There's so much to learn," he said to Afanasi as they studied the polar stars. "So much to fit together."

Unbeknown to these civilian geniuses in Japan, Siberia and Alaska, there were in the latter jurisdiction three powerful groups whose duty it was to monitor whatever happened in arctic areas. From Elmendorf Air Force Base near Anchorage and Eielson near Fairbanks, two of the most powerful in the world, pilots flew night and day keeping watch on Russian air movements, and from time to time these sentinels sent back coded messages: "Two invaders over Desolation Point," and American fighter planes would scramble aloft to let the Russians know they were under surveillance. Of course, Russian planes kept similar watch from secret bases in Siberia.

And out on distant Lapak Island, where so much history had occurred since the first arrival of men and women twelve thousand years ago, rose a great black windowless building ten stories tall. It contained secret devices understood by only a few hundred experts throughout the United States (plus some twenty clever analysts in Moscow) and served as America's principal intellectual shield against surprise Communist attacks. Had the ancient mummy still occupied her cave on Lapak, she would have enjoyed this great black building and approved the novel use to which her island was being put.

In this quiet, restless manner the perpetual duel of brilliant minds—Japanese, Korean, Chinese, Russian, Canadian and, sometimes most effective of all, American—continued, with all playing the tantalizing game of "What's going to happen next in the arctic?"

It was autumn when LeRoy Flatch experienced a temporary blackout—which frightened him, for his unconsciousness lasted several moments. Fortunately, he was not flying his Cessna, but when he came to he cried aloud: "Jesus! Suppose I'd been trying to land!" And when he discussed the incident with his wife, she said firmly: "LeRoy, time to quit flying," and she started asking around as to who might want to buy their Cessna-185.

LeRoy was sixty-seven years old that year and not in the best of shape. Some old-time bush pilots flew when they were in their eighties, but they were lean and sinewy men who had cared for themselves, if not for the planes which they kept cracking up. Flatch was not of this breed; he liked beer and greasy Mexican food too much to keep his weight down, and his excesses added about fifteen years to his apparent age, so he listened to his wife's advice, even consulting with the prospective buyers for his plane.

But he was delayed in disposing of what his wife called "your death trap" because of two seemingly unrelated events which involved him again in serious charter flying. In early October word flashed through Talkeetna of an extraordinary discovery near an archaeology dig called the Birch Tree Site, where a lone hunter rafting down a river saw protruding from the bank at his eye level the brown water-stained tusk of a mammoth that must have been trapped there twelve or thirteen thousand years ago. The hunter had attended the university in Fairbanks for two years and from a couple of good geology courses had learned to appreciate the significance of such a find. So, marking the area carefully on his map, he scrambled back to his raft and hurried on to Talkeetna, where he contacted the university: "I'm no authority, but I picked about in the mud enough to think that this one still has most of its skin and hair intact."

The response was electrifying, with two different teams of investigators flying in to Talkeetna and wanting to hire bush pilots to take them to the site. In this way, LeRoy Flatch was lured back into flying to take the college professors and their cargo the fifty-eight miles to the riverbank where, with unusual speed to escape the freeze, the scientists uncovered the complete, unmutilated carcass of a mammoth who could be carbon-dated to 12,800 years ± Before the Present Era. Of course, the remains didn't look like an erect, living mammoth, for eons underground had compressed the carcass into a flat, pancake-like mass, drenched in mud, but there was great excitement when even the novices could see that here was a complete animal, entire hide, with vital organs in place, so that investigators could ascertain what it had been feeding on in the hours before its death.

Flatch was quietly pleased when the scientists selected his plane as the one to fly the mammoth out to Talkeetna, and when the precious body was safely stowed, for there were only a few mammoth finds in either Alaska or Siberia in such condition, he muttered to himself as he prepared for takeoff: "Don't black out now." The flight was uneventful; the carcass was delivered to the much larger plane that would fly it on to Fairbanks, and respectful farewells were exchanged between Flatch and the scientists. Back in Talkeetna, he told his wife: "Isn't every day a man delivers a cargo of meat maybe fourteen thousand years old," and she said: "I want you to get rid of that plane before New Year's."

He was not able to do so, because when the newspapers heard of the remarkable discovery, their reporters streamed into Talkeetna asking LeRoy to fly them to the site, so he was kept busy in November taking his ski plane out to Birch Tree, but when in flying three science writers from the Lower Forty-eight he came close to blacking out, he pulled his nerves together and with little safety margin landed at Talkeetna. Turning away from his plane, he walked the short distance to his office, speaking to no one but feeling in his chest a warning that he might faint again. Inside the cramped little office Flatch pulled off his flight cap and hung it on the wall for the last time. LeRoy was one bush pilot who would die in bed.

With Rick Venn absent on T-7, Jeb Keeler had the courtship field to himself whenever he flew in to Desolation on corporation business, and he proved an ardent suitor, bringing Kendra flowers, a cherished rarity in the arctic, and pressing her to marry him. He pointed out what Kendra already knew, that "Rick could be up there three, four years—and what happens to you?"

But attractive though Jeb Keeler was, she still could not erase from her mind the picture of Rick Venn skimming over the drifts on his thousand-mile chase in the Iditarod, and whenever such images appeared, she realized that fundamentally she wanted two things: to spend her creative years in the arctic and to share her life with Rick Venn.

So in the depth of winter she drafted an extraordinary message to T-7 which she sent by open radio from Afanasi's kitchen, for she had reached a point where she did not care who heard it:

> RICK VENN, T-7, ARCTIC OCEAN. I'M GETTING MARRIED IN JUNE AND I HOPE IT'S TO YOU. KENDRA.

The result was electric. Someone in Barrow monitoring radio traffic to T-7 was so delighted with this unusual message that he passed it along to a Seattle newspaper, whose newsmen were alerted by the name Venn, and they put it on the wire, so that people across the nation learned of plucky Kendra Scott's proposal to a very wealthy young man hiding out on an ice island. A wireless message resulted:

> RICK VENN, T-7, ARCTIC OCEAN. IF YOU'RE LUCKY ENOUGH TO FIND A GIRL LIKE HER, BE THERE IN JUNE. I'LL BE YOUR BEST MAN. MALCOLM VENN.

It was a memorable wedding, held in the school gym, with all of Desolation and a good deal of Barrow and Wainwright in attendance. Mrs. Scott, accompanied by her husband, flew in from Heber

City and was astounded to learn who Rick was, and what an admirable young fellow he seemed to be, although as she pointed out to the Eskimo women with whom she sat at the ceremony: "God does not approve of divorce." She told them of several other things about which God had strong opinions, and one old woman whose men had for generations sought the walrus and the whale told the Eskimo woman sitting next to her: "She sounds like a missionary." Malcolm Venn, who in his sixty years of dealing with Alaska in almost every imaginable capacity had never before been north of the Arctic Circle, had gallons of ice cream and several dozen yellow roses flown in and served as his grandson's best man.

Kendra could not depart Desolation without paying her respects to the Eskimo women who had been so considerate of her when she arrived among them as a stranger, so she invited them all to her quarters for a final breakfast, and afterward she walked alone through the village, staring out at the Chukchi Sea and confessing to herself an honest assessment of her three-year stay in Desolation: I've accomplished nothing. None of my students are going on to college. None of them have awakened to the potential of which they're capable. I couldn't make them study. I couldn't make them write papers the way kids do who are going to be productive, who are going to be leaders. I couldn't even make them come to school regularly or stop walking around aimlessly at night. I came, took my salary, and gave nothing in return. Four more years and I'd be a Kasm Hooker, jollying them along, leaving them no better than when I met them.

Tears started in her eyes, and to control them she snapped: "To hell with their learning and ambitions. The two I loved, I couldn't even save their lives," and when she thought of Amy and Jonathan she cried out in despair: "Wasted years. Wasted lives." Had some villager whispered to her at this moment, "But, Kendra! The people of this village, the men who tossed you in the blanket, we'll remember you as long as we live, for your spirit walked with us, and we felt it," she would not have believed her.

As soon as she adjusted to the fact that she was the only woman on the island, Kendra's life on T-7 became as exciting as she had hoped it would be. Afanasi, as manager of the station, assigned her a paid job of supervising the paperwork streaming into and out of the offices, a task which the senior scientists were happy to have her perform. At first she was not happy with the apparent assumption that as a woman, secretarial work was all she was capable of performing, and she complained to Rick: "It's not exactly what a liberated woman has in mind these days." But when she found that monitoring the flow of information placed her in a critical position, because she knew the latest news before anyone else, she conceded: "A job like mine does have certain advantages." And gradually she inserted herself as an aide to anyone who could utilize her, and thus made herself invaluable.

But the more profound reward she garnered from her bold decision to propose to Rick over public radio and her later insistence that she accompany him back to his ice island came from the long, unstructured discussions these great scientists held during the endless hours when the perpetual darkness of November to February made human contacts and the dissection of human problems almost essential. Kendra frequently found herself in conversation with several scientists at a table in the mess, and one of them would casually say something like: "Suppose that the Soviet Union were somehow to gain total control of Norway. She would then dominate exactly fifty percent of the Arctic Ocean," and another would counter: "But if Alaska, Canada and Greenland can maintain a union of mutual interest, they'll control the half that's nearest the North Pole, and that provides its own advantages for domination."

Almost always the debate called for maps, and Kendra kept folded in her pocket a dog-eared copy of the *National Geographic* map which had accompanied the issue containing that compelling portrait of the little Eskimo girl on the cover, so quite often the scientists, although they had government maps of their own, gathered about Kendra, looking at hers. From such discussions she learned that the group of islands named Svalbard, which she had known as Spitsbergen, was vital to any military use of the Arctic Ocean, and everyone predicted that it would be used, because only in the trough off Svalbard were the seas deep enough to allow sophisticated submarine warfare; all other exits were much too shallow. "And," explained a scientist with military training, "Since the Svalbard Trough connects with the Atlantic, that ocean will be twice as important as the Pacific." When the Pacific experts challenged this, he admitted: "I'm speaking of submarine warfare only, as it relates to major shipping lanes. Think of the haven the Arctic Ocean will be if submarines can lurk here, dart out into the Atlantic, and control traffic between North America and Europe!"

This comparison of the two oceans led Kendra to ask: "Why is it that the Pacific is rimmed by active volcanoes and the Atlantic not?" and this led to the suggestion that they invite Giovanni Spada, the volcanologist from Palmer, to fly north to conduct a seminar for them on recent developments in his field.

In these years T-7, in its ordained peregrinations, lay closer to Barrow than to any other American-Canadian point with a usable airfield, so it was a relatively simple matter for an air force plane to ferry Spada and his charts to Barrow and thence to the ice island, where he was greeted warmly by men who had worked with him in the past. His visit was surprisingly rewarding because he had the latest details of the earthquake which had produced the destruction in Mexico City and educated guesses as to when Mount St. Helens might let loose again.

But now discussion focused on copies of the map he had distributed, showing the disposition of volcanoes clustering about the rim of the Pacific, and he warned: "If I'd had space to show each of the volcanoes along our Aleutian arc, there'd be sixty, and more than forty of them have been active since 1760. This chain of fire, guarding the approaches to the Arctic Ocean, is incomparably the most active in the world insofar as island building, submarine earthquakes and volcanic activity are concerned."

"Is Alaska that volatile?" a scientist from Michigan asked, and Spada offered a somber statistic: "Take any time span you wish—a decade, a score of years, a century—and list all the major earthquakes in the world, all the gigantic volcanic eruptions, and four out of the ten top disturbances, earthquake or volcano, occurred in Alaska. This is incomparably the world's most volatile segment. Plate tectonics make it so."

Everyone but Kendra knew this term, and when she asked: "What's that?" Spada gave a brilliant half-hour summary of how in the middle of the Pacific Ocean—"and also in the Atlantic, because in this part of the puzzle we're not unique"—magma flowed up through an extensive fissure. "Believe it or not, this erupted material spreads the ocean floor outward, forming the great plates upon which the surface of the earth rests, including the tallest mountains and the deepest oceans. Accept that and the rest becomes simple."

Using his hands he showed how the Pacific Plate collided with the North American Plate along the line of the Aleutians, with the former subducting under the latter: "And *voilà*! Where this great clashing occurs, volcanoes are born, earthquakes help discharge the tensions."

The scientists at T-7 queried him for several hours on recent refinements of accepted theories, and he flashed about the Pacific, laying out data from New Zealand, South America, the Antarctic, but coming always back to the Aleutians and his specialty, the Tsunami Warning System, which protected the people of Japan, Siberia, Alaska, Canada and the Hawaiian Islands from the disasters that used to strike them without warning when vast submarine earthquakes launched outward in all directions what used to be called tidal waves.

There, in the continuous darkness of winter, with their island moving imperceptibly in clockwise motion as if held in orbit by an invisible thread attached to a nonexistent North Pole, the scientists listened as Spada told of the event which had modified the marine history of the Pacific:

"April Fool's Day 1946. Qugang Volcano, out here on Lapak Island, erupted. No great deal. Ashes from the fiery belch didn't even reach Dutch Harbor, let alone the mainland. But a little while later one hell of a submarine earthquake occurred on the south side of the island. Displaced millions of tons of soft, sliding earth.

"It gave birth to a tsunami of epic dimension. Not a tidal wave rearing its head high in the air, but a lateral displacement of tremendous force headed for the Hawaiian Islands. Three ships that day had it pass right under them and only one even noticed it. 'Sudden rise ocean surface, but less than three feet,' read the log. But five hours later when it hit the town of Hilo on the north coast of the Big Island, at a speed of four hundred eighty miles an hour, it just kept coming and coming and coming. But it did no damage. However, when the runoff back to the ocean came, it sucked cars and houses and nearly two hundred people to their deaths.

"A tsunami from somewhere wiped out the first Russian settlement on Kodiak Island in 1792. And you've heard about

Lituya, where the water level rose more than seventeen hundred feet."

The scientists wanted to know if such things were likely to be repeated, and Spada said: "Absolutely not. The Rim of Fire will act up, of that we can be sure, but the consequences will always be different. If the April '46 earthquake had been pointed two degrees differently, its tsunami would have missed Hawaii by hundreds of miles. And even so, it wasn't of maximum size, only seven-point-four on the Richter."

Here Kendra broke in: "Everybody talks about the Richter scale, but nobody ever says what it is," and Spada offered a succinct description: "It's an imprecise but helpful rule of thumb. It's a measurement taken about sixty miles from the point of origin and is reported on a logarithmic scale, which means that each major division is ten times more powerful than the one before. Thus, a four-point Richter has ten times the magnitude of a three-point, which is so weak that humans might not even feel it, while a nine-point Richter, which tears the place apart and is close to the maximum so far recorded, has a magnitude a million times that of a three."

He told them what they must remember in their studies was that Alaska did have those sixty-odd potentially active volcanoes, and that the word *active* meant that each one was capable of exploding at any moment: "So in this part of the world we must be prepared for anything. I'm uneasy about being away from my warning system even for an instructive meeting like this, because a significant volcanic eruption or major slippage of the ocean floor could happen at any time."

The more the scientists interrogated Spada, the more Kendra saw that their worlds and his interlocked, and that in the Arctic Ocean, while it presented unique features, mainly a permanently frozen body of water, the ever-changing ice followed patterns of its own, just as the edges of plates, where they clashed, established their own bizarre rules. "But nobody's told me yet," Kendra said, "why it's the Pacific that's rimmed with fire and not the Atlantic," and this provoked considerable guesswork, with some reminding her that Mont Pelée and Etna and Vesuvius had not been trivial volcanoes in their day, but the answer that she preferred came from Spada: "I've considered two theories. It could be that the size of the Pacific Plate, its sheer magnitude, releases greater forces when it collides with the various continental plates. But a more likely explanation would be that the Atlantic Ocean does not ride upon its own plate. It's not surrounded by fracture zones."

On this satisfying note she was about to go to bed, but as she left the mess hall alone, Rick being on duty monitoring ocean-current recordings, she saw in the night sky the most tremendous display of the aurora borealis she had witnessed in Alaska. Running back to where the others still debated, she summoned them outside, where in a mild and windless minus-twenty-four degrees, they witnessed what even they admitted was an incomparable show of vast heavenly arcs, undulating waves and shifting colors.

When the others returned to their work or their beds, for clocks were of little significance in January, Kendra remained behind, trying to correlate these towering cathedrals of the northern lights, the eruptions of the Rim of Fire, the altering salinity of the various parts of the ocean, and the relationships between the Soviet Union and Norway, each of whom claimed with historic justification the ultra-crucial Svalbard islands, past which the submarines would have to go in time of trouble.

As she stood there, she became aware that someone had joined her, and she saw that it was Vladimir Afanasi, who said: "It's breathtaking. Maybe twice in a lifetime, spectacles like these."

She led him to a bench, and as they sat there in the arctic night he said: "Kasm told me that you took Amy's death . . ." He faltered.

"Amy and Jonathan . . . it pains me even to say their names. Sometimes I feel that my stay in Desolation was full of heartbreak."

"The heartbreak never ends, Kendra." He fell silent and remained so for some time, but it was obvious he wanted to say much more, and so Kendra began, and with her sympathy for people she touched the precise nerve that was troubling him: "I heard you say once, Mr. Afanasi, that your father and uncle taught you what not to do. But you never explained."

"They were tragic figures who tried to do the impossible. Stand with one leg in the Eskimo world, one in the white man's. Can't be done."

"You do it."

"No, no! I've never really left the Eskimo. At the university I was an Eskimo. That's why I didn't graduate. At work in Seattle, always an Eskimo. Here on the T-Seven, I'm the Eskimo, me and the polar bears."

"What happened with your father and his brother?"

"It really happened with their father, Dmitri Afanasi, my grand-father. Remarkable man. Born and dedicated a Russian Orthodox priest, had no trouble whatever becoming a Presbyterian missionary. But his Athapascan wife was a powerful influence on the boys. She was Russian Orthodox and refused to change. No fuss. No public argument. 'Just leave me alone as I am.' So my father and uncle were Russian and Eskimo, Orthodox and Presbyterian, white man's world, Eskimo's world. And they both died."

"Are you afraid of the word suicide?"

"No. Not afraid. My son committed suicide, just like the others. My father and uncle were murdered by the dreadful changes in their world."

"It seems to skip generations, the impact I mean. Your grand-father had no problems. His two sons did. Your generation had no problems. Your son did."

"It's never that simple, Kendra. My brother, a wonderful lad, committed suicide at nineteen."

"Oh Jesus! What a terrible burden!" She choked, lifted her hands to her lips, then turned to embrace this sterling Eskimo who had brought so much meaning to her life. As new cathedrals were built, great towering edifices constructed of movement and light and heav-enly design, they sat side by side on the bench, speculating on the dark significance of the north.

History often repeats, but rarely does it make a complete closed cir-cle, yet that is what happened to Malcolm Venn when he was called upon to reverse his family's efforts of over half a century ago.

The Ross and Venn families of Seattle were among the most re-spected on the Pacific Coast. Self-educated, principled, concerned always with the advancement of society and generous with their charities, they demanded only one thing: a monopoly on trade with Alaska. Once assured of that, and satisfied that it was protected by legislation in Washington, the Ross & Raglan heirs were about as worthy public citizens as the nation produced.

They had a sense of humor too, so that when Venn, a distinguished-looking man in his late seventies, received the preposterous assign-ment from his fellow industrialists in Seattle, he was more than aware of its sardonic overtones: "Gentlemen, if I accept this job, and make any public statements about it, I'll be the laughingstock of Seattle, and Alaska too!" They agreed, but pointed out: "This is a crisis situation, and no one has the credentials you do for dealing with it." So, reluctantly, he agreed to place his head upon the chopping block.

Accompanied by his lovely wife, Tammy Ting, the outspoken Chinese-Tlingit beauty from Juneau, he arrived by plane in Sitka, rented a suite overlooking the gorgeous bay, and sat for several hours each day glued to his window with a pair of high-powered binoculars pressed against his face. It was July, and he was watching the arrival in Sitka Sound of an unending sequence of the most beautiful cruise ships in the world. Each morning at six, two or three of these graceful floating hotels would put into Sitka, about a thousand excited passengers would stream ashore from each one to see the old Russian town and spend huge amounts of money, then return to their ship for the conclusion of one of the finest tours in the world: the seven- or eight-day cruise of the fjords and glaciers of southeastern Alaska. If one wanted to see happy and contented tourists, one came to Sitka in the summer, for it was the general conclusion that "we got the best bargain available anywhere."

For his first two days in town Venn was content merely to call off the names of the great ships as they arrived: "That's the *Royal Princess,* of the great P & O Line in London. I forget what the initials mean, but it was the famous line that is supposed to have given us the word *posh.* Legend claims that people of standing, on their cruise from London to Bombay, had their tickets stamped POSH, port out, starboard home. That kept them in the shade, escaping the sun. I'm told the handsomest ship of all, inside, is that *Nieuw Amsterdam* of the Dutch line. But the Chalmers told me: 'If you ever take the Alaska cruise, take that one over there.'" And against the dark peaks that rimmed the bay stood the *Royal Viking,* and beyond it the French *Rhapsody,* a more modest ship.

Tammy Venn, recording the names of the vessels as her husband called them off, said: "They're all foreign. Why aren't there any American ships out there?" and Malcolm replied: "That's what we're up here about. They are all foreign. They're all making simply potfuls of money. And not a cent of it is passing through Seattle."

"Where do they come from?"

"Vancouver. Every damned one of them."

Since her husband rarely used even mild profanity, Tammy knew he was angry, but she asked sweetly: "Why don't you do something about it?" and he growled: "I propose to."

When he felt that he had a preliminary grasp of the situation, he visited commercial shops in Sitka and learned that during the summer season—no cruise ship would dare head north in winter—some two hundred and sixteen of the sleek ships put in to Sitka, with an even greater number, two hundred and eighty-three, docking at Juneau, where there were extraordinary tourist attractions like the great ice field in back of town and the glories of Taku Inlet with its own more typical glaciers.

Local experts calculated that, counting the smaller vessels, an average of about one thousand passengers arrived on each ship—"There's never an empty bed on one of the good boats. The crew has rakes to drag in the money"—which meant that more than a quarter of a million well-heeled tourists a year were coming to Alaska, always through Vancouver, never through Seattle. Counting the time most of them spent in Vancouver hotels, restaurants, nightclubs and taxicabs, the amount of money lost by Seattle in this traffic was astronomical.

Seeking to nail down a defensible figure, on his third day in town Malcolm Venn started visiting the lovely ships, all so clean and polished for display in the old Russian capital, and he happened to tour first the exquisite little *Sagafjord,* a jewel of the cruising trade. As onetime head of his own shipping company, Ross & Raglan having exited the field some years back, he was welcomed aboard, and learned to his astonishment that on this superior ship the fare for the Alaska cruise could run as high as $4,890, but when he gasped, the captain personally took him to a fine small cabin at a mere $1,950.

"What's an average?" he asked, and the captain said: "That's easy. We've had a full ship, so you just multiply the figures," but he warned that his figures were not representative of the trade in general: "You want to study one of the really huge ships," and just coming into the harbor was the stately *Rotterdam.* It carried more than a thousand passengers, all berths taken, of course, at what the pursers said was an average rate of $2,195.

Back in his room, Malcolm multiplied the *Rotterdam* figures by the estimated number of Sitka visitors, and got a result of close to $400,000,000. Adding in the money spent ashore at Vancouver, he stared at a total topping half a billion dollars: And every damn cent of it ought to be passing through Seattle!

In succeeding days he learned things about Alaskan cruising which caused him to whistle in admiration at the brilliance of the European operators who had put together this gold mine. "You've seen it yourself, Tammy. Take that splendid English ship, the *Royal Princess.* She's really five separate ships. Officer cadre, exclusively British. Best men afloat. The dining room, exclusively Italian, no other. Deck crew, Pakistani. Everyone belowdecks, Chinese. And the entertainment team, sixteen or eighteen real stars, all American." Tammy nodded to confirm each description, then said: "And the *Nieuw Amsterdam,* the same divisions, with its own variations. Officers all Dutch. Dining room, what? Italian too, or French? Deckhands all Indonesian. Belowdecks, I think Chinese. Singers, band, all that nonsense, Americans."

With each of the great ships it was the same: wonderfully trained European officers ran them, Italians and Frenchmen provided elegant menus, Asians of one kind or another cleaned and maintained the ship, Chinese kept the engines operating, and Americans provided the fun. A whole world of enterprise had been wrested from the Americans and turned over to foreign experts who performed like magicians. Considering everything, the glaciers, fjords, wildlife and frontier towns along the shore, the Alaskan cruise was indeed the best bargain in the world.

Why had the Americans allowed this bonanza to slip through their fingers? In a series of small, intense meetings attended by both Malcolm and Tammy, he opened the first session: "Gentlemen, we face a shipping crisis in Alaska and on the West Coast. Your tremendous Alaskan tourist trade, which I calculate to gross well over half a billion dollars a year, is all passing through Canada, Vancouver in particular, when it ought to be passing through the United States, Seattle to be specific." There was at this point a very slight disturbance; someone in the back of the room was laughing, and not courteously, but Malcolm plowed ahead: "You and I both know the cause of this disaster." He paused dramatically, then blurted out: "The Jones Act."

For just a moment the room was quiet, then the man in the back guffawed and pretty soon the whole room was echoing with laughter to hear the president of Ross & Raglan excoriating the Jones Act, which that company had engineered, protected, and extended through years of political skulduggery and generations of most cruel and unfair pressures on Alaskan economic hopes.

"Jones Act!" somebody from the side repeated, and the crowd really roared. Venn had foreseen the reception he would get in Alaska, had indeed predicted it before he left Seattle, but his colleagues had reasoned: "You're saying it will make it more effective. What have you to lose, personally or for your company? Be a sport."

He proved to be just that. Holding up his hands, he cried: "All right! All right! My grandfather, Malcolm Ross, thought up the Act. My father, Tom Venn, kept it alive. And later I myself lobbied Congress to keep it on the books. I've always supported it, but the time has come . . ."

At this point Tammy Ting, always an irreverent woman, dipped her handkerchief in her glass, wet it with ice water, rose, and wiped off her husband's forehead as the crowd bellowed.

It was just the touch that was needed, for when the raucous laughter subsided, her husband said: "*Mea culpa,* and if you had a gutting knife, I'd slash my wrists. But now we face not a theory but a situation. An act which made sense in 1920 when we had American ships manned by American men makes no sense at all today when we have no American ships. We're saddled with the Jones Act, can't seem to force Congress to rescind or modify it, and what's the result? Do you know there is not an American ship afloat under the proper ownership required by the Jones Act that could bring passengers from Seattle to Alaska? None. We've given away the oceans."

He asked a man who knew more about these problems than himself to explain further: "The world's changed. Have any of you been aboard that perfectly splendid English ship the *Royal Princess*? Where in hell do you suppose she was built? With labor problems what they are in England, incessant strikes and industrial sabotage, you can't build a ship in England anymore. Scotland's worse. The *Royal Princess* was built in Finland, because in the socialist country company schedules are rigorously honored and the craftsmanship is so fine that the next three ships in the British tourist fleet will be built in Finland too."

He said that in common sense the United States should do, if the Jones Act could be revoked, what the English did with the building of their modern fleet: "Go into all the world's markets, find the best builders, the best sailors, the best officers, and invite them to sail the best ships at the cheapest rates from Seattle to Sitka or anywhere else they damned well please to sail."

The audience cheered.

During his last two days in Sitka, Venn employed a secretary, who did a fine job transcribing his notes and putting them into condition worthy of being presented to his peers in Seattle. The two effective paragraphs were:

> I submit these conclusions as the grandson of Malcolm Ross, who engineered the Jones Act, as the son of Tom Venn, who guided it through the Congress, and as myself, for more than sixty years the recipient of advantages from the Act. It was a good Act when passed. It served a worthy purpose, and it created wealth for Seattle. But it has outlived its usefulness. The tenets upon which it was based no longer apply. Today our city loses as much as half a billion dollars a year because the Act prevents normal traffic from using our wonderful port. It must be rescinded and it should be rescinded now. I recommend we mount a massive effort to rescind the Jones Act and I offer my services as spokesman. My family created it. It's my family's job to eliminate the damned thing.

> I would be less than fair, however, if I did not report to you that our Canadian cousins in Vancouver, seeing the opening we have inadvertently left them, have leaped into it with imagination, brains, ample financing to accommodate some of the finest cruise ships in the world. We should encourage American tourists to enjoy these splendid ships, even though we're not getting a penny from them, for as my father always said: "Whatever is good for Alaska is good for Seattle," and this Alaskan cruising is about the best there is. Now we're entitled to get our share, but to do so we must kill the Act my family and I sponsored.

It was what you might call a typical experience in Alaskan aviation. On Thursday afternoon the governor told his assistant in Juneau: "Washington's sending a man up here to talk to Jeb Keeler about that North Slope debt. See if he can be in my office Monday at noon." It took the telephone operator about twenty minutes to track Jeb down, but she finally found him at Desolation Point, where he was in serious conversation with Vladimir Afanasi in an attempt to arrange a walrus hunt far out on the Chukchi Sea as soon as it froze.

"Jeb? This is Herman. Big boss wants to know if you can meet with him and one of the Feds from Washington. Our office. Monday at noon."

"I've told you guys, I'm clean. I mean it."

"That's what the governor told them, and they said you must be the only man in Alaska who is. That's why they want to ask you some questions. Can you make it?"

"Sure. I'll hop out of here Friday. Catch Mark Air to Prudhoe Bay and on in to Anchorage. The 0905 Monday morning will put me in to Juneau in good style." The phone fell silent for a moment, then: "You're leveling with me? They're not coming up here to put me on the griddle for something I've never done?"

"Jeb, you know what I know. They could be lying to us, but I do believe this is aboveboard. They're just trying to find out how the North Slope debt could have ballooned so high so fast."

"I'll be there."

It was dark when Jeb reached Anchorage, but a cab carried him swiftly to his apartment, where he spent some time in the shadows staring at that irritating blank spot reserved for his mountain goat. Pointing his right forefinger at the vacancy, he said: "Starting tomorrow, bub, we bag you."

On Monday morning his alarm sounded at six. Jumping up, he showered, shaved, and ate a frugal breakfast of orange juice, freeze-dried coffee and whole-wheat toast. Sorting through the papers he suspected the Washington investigator might want to see, he made three phone calls to people he was supposed to interview on Tuesday, telling each: "I'm flying down to Juneau on the morning plane. I'll be back on the evening flight, and I'll see you tomorrow as planned. I'm calling just in case." He then called the agent who looked after his airline tickets: "Morning down, evening back. Like always, A down, F back." She said the tickets would be at the airport.

He was always meticulous about his seating on this flight, because even though the skies were almost always either clouded or foggy between Anchorage and Juneau, if there happened to be a clear day, which occurred about once every twenty flights, the scenery inland to the east was spectacular. "Not interesting," he told strangers, "mind-shattering." So invariably he asked for Seat A southbound, Seat F northbound, and on rare occasions he was allowed to see a wonderland.

Then, just before leaving his apartment, he reached for his Gurkha Traveling Kit and checked its contents: shaving gear, pajamas, clean shirt. Through years of bitter experience he had learned never to board an Alaskan airliner without the wherewithal to spend the night in some unpremeditated bed.

At the huge Anchorage airport, where planes from many different nations stopped on their flights between Asia and Europe, some of them heading almost directly over the North Pole to Sweden, he was told: "Takeoff on schedule. Slight chance of fog at Juneau." He dismissed the information, since there was always a likelihood of fog at Juneau. Rumor had it that when there wasn't a fog, they fired off a cannon in celebration, but of course, this disturbance brought in the fog, so that you wound up, even on a good day, with a window of about fifteen minutes in which to land. Flying in to Juneau was not for the fainthearted.

His A seat was useless on this Monday morning, for when he looked out he saw only fog, and not an indifferent gray kind of fog but one so solid that had the window been opened, he might have been able to walk upon it. "Damn," he told the man riding in Seat B. "No fun landing in Juneau in a fog like this!"

"Not to worry," the man said. "We won't even try in this soup."

"That's a hell of a thing to say," Jeb replied, half seriously. "I have a meeting in Juneau. Important one. The Feds may be throwing me in jail."

"You'll sleep in Seattle tonight," the man said.

"You heading for Seattle?"

"I seem to go there twice a month. But not on purpose. I aim for Juneau, but we often miss it."

The man was right, because when the plane approached Juneau it made a valiant effort to land, dropping lower and lower among the mountains as the radar emitted signals which gave precise locations. When Jeb's knuckles were clasped so tight that no blood showed beneath the skin, he heard the pilot put on the gas as the big Boeing 727 wheeled sharply up and to the right. Nobody in the cabin spoke, but when the pilot went back to his starting point to try again, Jeb asked his seatmate: "Are you as scared as I am?" and the man said: "No. If it's too bad, he'll fly up and off. You'll know." And once more the plane came in lower and lower into that nest of mountains which protected Juneau from storms and airplanes. For just one fleeting moment the fog cleared enough for Jeb to see the waves only a few feet below the wing and the tall dark cliffs menacingly close to the wingtips. "Jesus Christ!" he whispered to the man. "We're walking on water!" But again the pilot rejected the idea of landing, and up and around he went.

"Really," Jeb said, striving to control his nerves, "he's not going to try again, is he?" and the man said: "He often makes it on the third try."

But not this time. In the plane came, skimming the water and dodging the mountains, but at the final moment there was no visibility, so as Jeb tried to keep from fainting the plane rose high and safe into the upper air, far above the mountains, and headed for Seattle. There were forty-nine passengers aboard the 727 with important meetings in Juneau, the state capital, but no one complained to the stewardesses: "We should have tried again." None of them wanted to spend Monday night in Seattle, but on the other hand, none of them wanted to test their fate against that fog in Juneau.

Very close to Seattle's Sea-Tac Airport there was a Vance Hotel which provided good rooms at a reasonable rate for airplane passengers hit with an emergency, and there Jeb unpacked, climbed into his pajamas, and watched *Monday Night Football*. At intermission he thought to call the governor's aide: "I'll be there on tomorrow's noon flight," and the official assured him: "No great loss, Jeb. The man from Washington is staying over. As you suspected, FBI, but you're not the subject of the investigation. You're just another source. Like me."

So on Tuesday morning, Keeler and forty-eight other Alaskans trooped over to the airport and boarded the return flight to Juneau. The plane made its scheduled landings in Ketchikan and Sitka without event, but as it approached Juneau, the weather was so bad that after three spine-tingling but fruitless passes, the 727 had to continue on to Anchorage, with Keeler sitting in his precious Seat F looking out into a fog which was, if anything, even thicker than the one the day before.

After two days of travel, and 2,876 miles of useless flight, Jeb was back in his apartment, but a phone call to Juneau assured him that the weather bureau was predicting clear weather for Wednesday: "We all wish you'd give it a try, Jeb. The you-know-who says your information could be vital." So early on Wednesday, with a fresh shirt in his bag, Jeb went out to the airport, saw that whereas there was some fog, it was clearing so fast that the lovely Chugach Mountains were visible. "I'm sure it's going to be a great flight south," the attendant at the counter said as she gave him Seat A. "You know, it does happen!"

Alaska Airlines was a well-run outfit, with cabin personnel who endeavored to put their passengers at ease. This morning an affable steward announced: "Clear weather all the way to Juneau. Glorious flight. Your stewardesses are Bubbles, Ginger and Trixie, and if anyone smokes in a nonsmoking area, the flight engineer will invite you to step outside."

When the plane rose in the air, Jeb gasped, for the great mountain ranges glistened with such majesty that all who looked at them were dumfounded. He had the good fortune this morning to have beside him in Seat B an older woman who taught geography, and even though she leaned across him to glimpse the mountains out of his window, he did not mind, for she knew the mountains by name and could identify the vast glaciers that swept down from them to tumble into the sea.

"That's the Chugach Range. Not excessively high, but look at them! Eight thousand feet right out of the sea." Then she caught her breath, for directly below them lay the pipeline terminus of Valdez with an ice field of enormous dimension behind it. "There must be . . . How many glaciers would you say were down there?"

"Maybe half a dozen."

"Goodness, you have no eyes. There must be twenty," and when he looked more carefully he saw that out of this one field sprouted at least twenty icy rivers winding through the valleys, scouring the sides, grinding the rocky beds, and finally meeting the sea.

"I never realized so many different glaciers could spring from one source," he said, and she explained that it was only this southern part of Alaska that had glaciers: "The far north doesn't get enough rain to make snow. Very little snow up north. But down here the Japan Current. You know what that is?" When he nodded like a bright schoolboy, she said: "Throws a lot of water on these mountains. So high and so cold, it can't melt. So it builds up into glaciers that flow very slowly down to the sea."

He was about to ask her how she knew so much, when she said gently: "Here's one of the parts I love most. I teach my students to revere this part. See that lovely mountain? Nearly eleven thousand feet high? Mount Steller. And that enormous glacier at its feet? Bering Glacier. Do you appreciate the significance of that pairing? Steller and Bering?" When he said "No," she told him briefly of the relationship between these two remarkable men who had discovered Alaska for the Russians: "One German, one Dane. They didn't understand each other, but there they stand, forever locked together in ice."

Jeb was about to respond when she clutched his arm: "Here they come! My God, I've never before seen them so glorious! Oh!" But before she could explain what had justified this outburst, the pilot came on the intercom to announce: "Ladies and gentlemen, only rarely do we see what's out there to our left. Mount St. Elias, eighteen thousand feet, the first view the Russians had of the mainland. Behind it Mount Logan in Canada, nearly twenty thousand feet. Down their sides flow forty or fifty glaciers, including the great Malaspina."

The teacher blew her nose, drew back from leaning across Keeler, and said softly: "Can you imagine? Vitus Bering in a small leaky ship. Seeing that. Wondering what it signified? And Georg Steller beside him whispering: 'It's got to be a continent. It's got to be America.'"

The pilot came back on the intercom: "A day like this should not be wasted. Because the sky is so perfect we're going to take a little detour and swing over to the east so you can see the Fairweather Range, very high and beautiful. And then real low over Glacier Bay—you'll see it as few ever do. Then, over the great Juneau ice field with its score of glaciers, and on to our landing in Juneau, where the tower is reporting clear skies and light winds coming out of the southeast. Enjoy the view, ladies and gentlemen."

The next minutes were magical. The Fairweather Range, which few travelers ever saw, had a plethora of very high snow-clad peaks rising right from the sea, and enclosing one of the glories of North America, the quiet, gentle, mountain-girt Glacier Bay, into whose waters great chunks of ice thundered off the glaciers as they made their imperceptible return to the sea, alerting the bears that prowled the shores. It was a magnificent bay, with a score of arms reaching far inland, and so many glaciers that no one, even in an airplane, could see them all.

"And now comes what might be the best of all," the teacher said. "Look!" And as the 727 made a grand slow turn to the east, Jeb saw the vast Juneau ice field extending far into Canada, with the ominous Devils Paw mountain reaching up as if to catch the plane and drag it to an icy death. From this field came a score of glaciers, including those that crashed down into Taku Inlet on the south. It was a fitting curtain to a drama that could have been equaled nowhere else, for as the teacher said when they came in for their landing: "On a clear day, this ninety minutes from Anchorage to Juneau must be the most spectacular on earth. I'm told the Himalayas can be stupendous, but do they have this mix of ocean, great mountains, wild ice fields and endless glaciers? I doubt it."

"I wish I'd had you for a teacher," Jeb said, and when she turned to thank him for the compliment she snapped her fingers and said: "Didn't I see your picture in the papers? Aren't you the fellow whose girl proposed to the other chap by open radio?" and when Jeb said: "The same," she said: "That girl must've been crazy," and Jeb said: "I thought so."

On this, Jeb's third try, they landed at Juneau in fine style, but by late afternoon when he wanted to fly home to Anchorage, the fog from the Japan Current had swept back in, closing down all airport operations. Relying once more upon the pajamas in his Gurkha bag, Jeb spent the night at the Baranof Hotel in Juneau and flew home the next morning, occupying his precious seat in hopes of seeing the glaciers again, but of course the clouds were impenetrable.

So his brief two-hour meeting with the government investigator in the state capital had consumed four complete days, Monday morning through Thursday afternoon. One never took a trip to Juneau lightly.

In a perverse way, the four-day trip was worth it, because his interrogation was attended not only by the man from the Department of Justice, but by two local FBI agents and an expert from the state government. When he saw the panel lined up across the table he began to perspire, but the man from Washington saw this and became remarkably conciliatory: "Mr. Keeler, we want to quiz you on some ugly matters, but we assure you at the outset that we're not interested in you personally. Your record, at least as uncovered by these FBI men, is impeccable and we congratulate you on it." He reached over and shook Jeb's hand, which was shamefully sweaty.

"Mr. Keeler," began the Alaska official, "what do you know about the North Slope?"

"I've worked in many parts of it—Prudhoe Bay for the oil companies . . . Desolation Point and its local corporation . . . an occasional job for the big Native corporation, but as you know, Poley Markham handles most of their affairs."

"We do know," the man from Washington said, almost ominously. "But have you ever done any legal work—drafting of commercial contracts, for example—for the North Slope Borough?"

"No. Only the big corporation and its little satellites. Never the borough." He was referring to an Alaskan phenomenon, a vast, empty township larger than a state like Minnesota but with a population of less than eight thousand. What it also had was an income of nearly eight hundred million dollars in taxes paid by the oil companies at Prudhoe Bay, or about a hundred thousand dollars in cold cash for every man, woman and child in the borough.

"A sudden influx of money like that tempts people to do crazy things," one of the FBI men said, and from a typed sheet he read off a few of the more malodorous cases in which unexpected wealth had courted local officials into bizarre behavior: "A heated subway to protect utility lines—projected cost, one hundred million; finished cost, three hundred and fifty; real cost, in Oregon let's say, eleven million. New high school—projected cost, twenty-four million—"

Jeb interrupted: "I know about that one. Finished cost, seventy-one million."

"Wrong," said the FBI man. "It's not finished yet. When it is, maybe eighty-four million."

"What would it have cost in the Lower Forty-eight?" Jeb asked, and the man said: "We had some school construction firms fly in from California and they gave us the figure three million, two." But now the Alaska official broke in: "In California, yes. Let them try to build it on the North Slope, with every nail coming in by barge or aircraft."

The FBI man bowed: "The California men said the same thing. So I asked them what the school should have cost in Barrow, and they said: 'It should have been done for about twenty-four, twenty-six million.'"

The man from Washington growled: "That was the original estimate, the one that's exploded to eighty-four." In disgust he indicated that the FBI man should terminate his recitation of horror stories. Instead, he took a piece of blank paper, scribbled on it, and passed it facedown to Jeb: "In addition to their eight hundred million dollars in tax money, which they've spent, how much do you think those dreamers up there have borrowed on the New York and Boston markets, all of it spent, all of it representing outstanding debt?"

Jeb studied the matter, and from what he had heard about the generosity of borough dealings, he concluded that the indebtedness might be as much as half of what the income had been: "Maybe half the eight hundred million. Maybe four hundred million in bonds sold by the Eastern banks."

"Look at the paper," the Washington man said, and when Jeb turned it over he saw the staggering figure: $1,200,000,000.

"My God!" he gasped. "More than a billion dollars! How could a bunch of Eskimos who never went to college . . . ?"

And then the questioning became short and sharp and brutal: "Do you know of any involvement Poley Markham had with North Slope Borough?" He was involved with everything in Alaska. "Did he arrange for these bond issues?" He helped all the corporations with their borrowing. "Did Markham own any of the contracting companies that got the big jobs?" I don't think he ever invested in other people's companies. He was his own man. "In your opinion is Poley Markham a crook?" In my opinion he's one of the most honest men I know. I go hunting with Poley quite often, and a man's character reveals itself on an ice pack or a mountain slope. "What would you say if we told you that Poley Markham has banked more than twenty million dollars from his Alaska fees?" I would believe it. And I'd bet he had signed vouchers for all of it. He told me years ago the money was lying around up here and could be picked up honestly. "Do you think he earned his share honestly?" Yes, sir, as far as I know. I'm positive he did.

The men thanked him for his responses and reiterated that he himself was not under investigation: "We have no solid proof of wrongdoing up there by anyone, and I will confess that we can find nothing on your friend Markham. But when two billion dollars floats around, we have to look for sticky fingers." That night when Jeb reached his apartment in Anchorage, he tracked Poley down at a country club in Arizona: "The Feds are after you real big, Poley."

"They've been questioning me down here. And they're not after me. They're after the whole incredible setup on the North Slope. Eight thousand Eskimos spending about two billion dollars, all told."

For just a moment an image of the Natives at Desolation flashed through Jeb's mind, and he could not visualize these hunters, who lived by the ways of the frozen sea, incurring such debts, but then he remembered Poley: "Are you clean in this debacle?"

"Jeb, every penny I banked came by check . . . legal fees legally documented."

"That's what I told the fellow from Washington."

"A man with red hair and granny half-spectacles?"

"The same."

"He left here unconvinced. I'm sure he left you unconvinced. But he'll find no trail of sleaze with me." There was a moment of silence, and then Poley added: "Of course, I recommended my friends in California and Arizona for the fat contracts. But they paid me nothing, Jeb. No kickbacks, no hunting lodges built for me in the mountains."

"But two billion dollars! Poley, there has to be something not right somewhere."

"Has there been any with you? No. Any with our friend Afanasi? Never. Any with me? Not on your life. I was mixed up in everything, as you know, but you also remember my golden rule: 'If even eight cents of real money is involved, leave a trail of receipts a mile wide.'"

"The Feds told me they'd tracked more than twenty million dollars of those receipts," and Poley laughed: "I'd never do it otherwise," and Jeb said: "That's what I told them."

Because Poley Markham had to fly to the North Slope to give his clients support during the FBI investigation, he stopped over in Anchorage to verify whatever it was that Jeb told the investigators at the interrogation in Juneau, and he arrived at Jeb's apartment just as there was a flurry on Alaska television. Giovanni Spada, at the Palmer Tsunami Center, had issued an alert that out on the Aleutian chain, Qugang Volcano off the north coast of Lapak Island had begun erupting, with huge clouds of lava dust heading eastward toward Anchorage: "However, the distance is so great that we can expect most of the dust to dissipate before it reaches the Anchorage area."

Nevertheless, by late afternoon there was a cloud of ash in the air, and Poley suggested: "Let's get out of here. A guide told me there were some mountain goats in a cove on the Pacific coast just north of the government lands at Glacier Bay." So they packed their gear, rented a four-seater, and flew down to a primeval area which few people ever saw, and there in air so clear that even a raindrop seemed like an intruder, they trekked in to where they saw, in an area far below them this time, a trio of billies with small handsomely formed horns.

Poley slapped his thigh: "At last we've struck it lucky. This time they're below us, not above. If we move down cautiously, you'll get one of those beauties," but when he inspected the steepness of the descent, he altered his plan: "We'd be bound to dislodge rocks and spook them. Better wait here and let them come up to us," and his judgment was sound, for gradually the goats began working their way up the slope, but so very slowly that the two men had about an hour to wait. This they spent in whispered discussion of the crucial problem which governed Alaskan matters at the moment and the much more important one that would come to a head in 1991. Of the first, Poley said: "Isn't it peculiar? The two states that irritate each other the most are the two that are most alike," and when Jeb asked what that meant, he explained: "Alaska and Texas. When we sent out a call for experienced hands to come in and help us with our oil, seemed like two out of three came from Texas, and I do believe that half our new permanent residents are Texans who stayed on."

Jeb reflected on this and said: "You do see a lot of them in Fairbanks," at which Poley added: "And like in Texas, up here you never hear a bad word said about OPEC. We want those Arabs to keep the price of oil as high as possible. They do our work for us."

But both men agreed that with the disastrous drop in oil prices, the glory days of Alaskan development were ending, just as they seemed to be declining in Texas: "We were lucky to get here when we did, Jeb, and I hope you saved your money, because come 1991, there'll be opportunities up here like you never saw before, and the prudent man who has eight or ten million in hard cash is going to be able to buy himself a major portion of this wonderful state. I can hardly wait."

"You mean when the restrictions on the Settlement Act come to an end?"

"I do."

Only a fellow Alaskan could have appreciated the ominous nature of Poley's response. It meant that he had tracked the operations of the thirteen huge Native corporations, the ones that really owned the land, and had concluded that many of them were in such pitiful shape financially that the Natives who owned them would have to sell to white men from Seattle and Los Angeles and Denver who had the money to buy them out and the know-how to make a fortune on the land when properly managed. Obviously this meant that well-intentioned Eskimos like Vladimir Afanasi were in danger of losing the land upon which their forefathers had depended for thousands of years, but when Jeb, who saw in Afanasi the salvation of Alaska, asked about this, Poley said reassuringly: "I think the North Slope corporation is one that can survive. Even with the huge debt and the collapse of oil prices, we built some very solid social and political structures up there, but of the other twelve, I have good reason to believe that at least five are doomed. They're the ones we'll move in on."

And now, on that lonely mountainside overlooking the Pacific, the wedge that would drive between the two friends manifested itself, for Jeb Keeler, despite his disappointment in losing Kendra Scott, had grown honestly to love Alaska and to see it as a unique blending of white newcomers like himself and longtime natives like the Eskimos, the Athapascans and the Tlingits for whom he had worked. He wanted the groups to coexist in harmony, he told Poley, to develop this wonderland mutually, and to trade its natural resources to countries like Japan and China in return for consumer goods. Specifically, he wanted the Natives to retain ownership of their land so that they could, if they wished, continue their subsistence style of life, and when he stated that conclusion he placed himself athwart the ambitions of Poley Markham, who revealed his plans with astonishing clarity.

"I don't see it your way at all, Jeb. The Natives can never govern their own lands, not in the modern world of airplanes, snowmobiles and automobiles, not to mention supermarkets and television sets. Even the six or seven corporations which are viable today could wither by the end of the century. And men like me will be on hand to pick them off."

For some moments Jeb reflected on this gloomy prediction, whose probability of coming true he had to concede, but before he could comment on what he saw as a tragedy, Poley added a revelation which proved what a Machiavellian character he had: "Why do you suppose I've worked so hard with these corporations? Not for the money—that is, after I solidified my nest egg. I wanted to know the capacity of each one, where the good lands were, what the likelihood of collapse was. Because I realized from day one that the crazy organization Congress established in ANCSA could not survive this century. And that meant that the lands would have to come into the hands of people like you and me."

"Not me," Jeb said firmly. "I'll help the Natives petition Congress for an extension past 1991. We won't allow the lands to be alienated from the Eskimos and the Indians."

Poley drew back to study this young man he had befriended in so many ways, had inducted into the fraternity of Lower Forty-eight experts who knew what was happening in Alaska, and he could not believe what Jeb was saying: "Son, if you go that route, you and me is gonna cross swords."

"I've seen it coming, Poley. I want to keep Alaska unique, a modern wonderland. You want to make it one more Southern California."

"Face it, son," and with the use of this word he had used when talking to Jeb years ago in northern Canada, he indicated the distance that had been reestablished between them, "what is Anchorage but San Diego North?"

"Anchorage, I can surrender," Jeb conceded, "but the rest must be protected from men like you, old friend."

Poley laughed: "Impossible. The next census will show Anchorage with more than fifty percent of the population. Then its representatives will storm down to Juneau and begin to pass laws that bring this state into the modern world. Probably move the capital up to Anchorage, where it should have been long ago."

"The more you say, Poley, the more I realize that I'll have to fight almost everything you'll be trying to do."

If the two debaters had had their radio turned on, they would have heard an urgent broadcast by Giovanni Spada sent to all the nations bordering the North Pacific: "This is a tsunami alert. I repeat, a tsunami alert. There has been a massive submarine earthquake off Lapak Island in the Aleutian chain registering eight-point-four on the Richter scale. All coastal areas are advised that a wave . . ."

Instead of hearing the warning which might have influenced their actions on that vulnerable coast, they were preoccupied with the goats that had begun to behave as Poley had predicted, but before the final stages of the hunt started, Poley wanted to assuage the political differences that had erupted between them, and he switched subjects completely: "You know, Jeb, your mountain goat isn't a goat at all. It's an antelope, misnamed."

Surprised, Jeb turned to face his future adversary. "No one ever told me," and for some moments he considered this strange news: "Suppose the goat had been named *snowy antelope* or *arctic antelope*.

It'd be twice as attractive," and Poley growled: "Not for me. I like things simple and honest." Then he became the ruthless director of the hunt, the role for which he was predestined: "Jeb, you've got to nail one as they come up that draw. Once you let them get above us, they're long gone."

So Jeb, having lost half a dozen goats when he followed his own tactics, slipped silently down the protected side of the ridge, taking precautions that he not be seen by the approaching goats, and when he had positioned himself so that he could intercept them as they came up the other side, he realized that he would be allowed only one shot at whichever of the three billies first poked his head above the skyline. Looking back for confirmation from Poley, he was gratified when from a considerable distance above him Markham signaled an "A-okay" with his right thumb and forefinger forming a circle. The stage was set for the best chance Jeb would ever have to bag the last of his Big Eight.

He held his breath, waited for one of the goats to appear, then experienced the great joy of seeing a billy, snowy white and with perfect black-spiked horns, emerge right onto the crest of the ridge and stand there for a moment. "For Christ sake, shoot!" Poley whispered to himself, frightened lest the merest sound alert the goat, and in the next moment he was relieved to hear the report of Jeb's rifle. The goat lurched forward, trembled, and fell backward out of Jeb's sight on the far side of the ridge.

But Poley from his higher vantage could see clearly that the goat had been killed and had plunged rather far down into the cut on the other side. "Jeb!" he shouted. "You got him but he's well down in the gully. Fetch him and I'll start down with the gear." When Jeb descended to where he had last seen the goat, he took his gun with him, but Poley shouted again: "Leave your gun, I'll get it. He's pretty far down the hill," and when Jeb saw where the goat's body had landed, quite far below him, he appreciated the wisdom of Poley's advice and propped his gun against a rock where Poley could easily spot it. Almost as if the two men were attached by invisible bands, they began to descend together, Poley from his outlook spot to where the gun rested, Jeb from his gun down to where the goat's body had lodged.

As they scrambled down in this triumphant tandem, Jeb kept his eyes fixed on the goat, a magnificent specimen he was convinced, but Poley, from his higher vantage, was able to survey the entire setting: the Pacific Ocean near at hand, the two headlands marking the beginning of the little fjord, the steep flanks on which the three billies had been exploring, and the V-shaped head of the bay into which Jeb was descending to claim his prize. It was almost an artist's miniature stage setting for what would be an ideal Alaskan coastal painting.

But Poley also saw a sudden and persistent suction of water from the bay, and he knew instinctively that something ominous and terrible was happening.

"Jeb! Jeb!" he began to scream, but in Jeb's eagerness to get to his goat he had hurried ahead out of earshot. Nevertheless, the older man continued screaming, for now he saw the water sweeping back into the bay, inexorably piling up as if pushed from behind by some malevolent titan.

"Jeb! Come back!"

And now it became obvious that the dark waves, never very high but with tremendous pressure behind them, were not going to stop before they had filled the valley and flooded upward to some incredible spot seven or eight hundred feet above ordinary sea level, and when Jeb finally became aware of his peril, the water was so high, and piling up so rapidly, that he was incapable of doing anything to save himself. He saw the churning water snatch the goat and toss it about, submerging it in foam, and then the relentless waves were upon him, throwing him sideways and engulfing him as they climbed the sides of the valley faster than the goats had done. His last sight was not of his final trophy, which was mangled in the deep, but of Poley Markham scrambling desperately upward to gain the really high ground which even the Lapak Island tsunami could not reach.

As he was about to perish, Jeb saw that Poley was probably going to make it, and he cried: "Go it, Poley. You win!"

For now, it seemed that Alaska would be going the way Poley Markham wanted it, not as Jeb Keeler and Vladimir Afanasi and Kendra Scott in their various ways had visualized it.